THE BLUE DWARF.

A Novel.

By LADY ESTHER HOPE.

ILLUSTRATED PROFUSELY BY EMINENT ARTISTS.

LONDON:

E. HARRISON, EXETER CHANGE, STRAND;

AND ALL BOOKSELLERS AND NEWSVENDORS.

1861.

THE BLUE DWARF.

BY LADY ESTHER HOPE.

BOOK I.—THE FOSTER BROTHERS.

CHAPTER I.

SHADOWS ON THE WALL.

SHADOWS on the wall! pale, flitting shadows, that come one cannot say whence, and go it is vain to say where.

It has been going on for some time.

The house is vast, and full of intricate and winding passages, like many of the antique mansions of the wealthy, more frequent half a century ago than now. It had been built at various periods, some of peace and plenty, others of rapine and plunder. Ample provision had been made for both contingencies. There were splendid halls, banquetting rooms, numerous offices, kitchens where an ox might have been roasted whole, and dark and gloomy passages, trap doors, secret rooms, where the persecuted and the oppressed, as well as the conspirator and the evil doer, might conceal themselves from tyranny as well as from justice.

But we are now in the broad light of human freedom and modern civilisation. We have not reached the days of Victoria, when liberty, save where shackled by a remnant of feudalism, has grown up to be an example to the wide universe; but still we are speaking of a period when, in comparison of other nations and other epochs, our country was free from the necessity of moated castles, dangerous trap doors and secret passages.

But never does the evil which is in the human heart die out. Long after such appliances as belong to another age are rejected by public opinion will they be made instruments of private vengeance, profligacy, and lust of wealth and power.

Who is this comes down those abrupt steps, shading the light from his lanthorn with his hand, his face pale and livid, his ears drinking in every sound, his eyes devouring the space before him, and his figure casting dark shadows on the wall? It is so every night now, in the old hall—and why?

Treading with extreme caution, he stands upon a carpeted passage, along which he glides more like a ghost than a human being, until he reaches a doorway.

Here he sets down his lanthorn and listens at the key-hole.

Not a sound.

The handle is turned, and in stalks the midnight prowler, still with strangely light step—his feet are covered with list shoes—and approaches a bed. It is a splendidly furnished apartment, and the bed is a large antique four-poster.

Its occupant is a handsome youth of about fifteen or sixteen.

The man, be his intentions what they may, looks sternly on for a few minutes, and perceiving that the other slept soundly, took up a bottle from off a small table beside his bed, and hastily concealing it, replaced it by another. He then left the room with equal caution, and was seen no more in that apartment for the night.

Shadows on the wall again! But, heavens! what is it? From beneath the bed crawls forth a being, which on its hands and knees so closely resembles an animal as to be taken for one at a superficial glance. The light in the room from a shaded lamp is so dim, that its real character can scarcely be detected.

With a low chuckle it pushed forth its hand, as it appeared to be, clutched the bottle which had been left by the first intruder, replaced it by another, and then standing upright, walked across the room into the deep shadow at its other extremity.

A faint clink was heard, and then again all was still, and the sleeper was alone.

* * * *

Loud howls the storm on river and plain;

dark race the clouds over the gloomy heavens, while in the far distance rolls the thunder-blast, as a short active figure is seen to push his way through a dense thicket that skirted the lawn in front of the lordly mansion of the Blakesley's, of Blakesley Hall.

The lawn was swiftly crossed, and the figure might have been seen to halt at an angle of the house. Then it stooped, and picked up a handful of gravel, which it cast upward against a window on the first floor.

The window was opened, and a head protruded.

"Is that you, Dick?" said a hushed voice from below.

"All right, Sir Edgar," replied the other, in the same tone.

No answer was given, but the first speaker held out his hand, and something fell out upon the lawn.

It was a ladder of ropes.

The person below at once began his ascent, using great caution; and in a minute more the window was shut, and all still without.

The two persons who met in this mysterious and clandestine way, now stood face to face in a large and handsome bed room, illumined with one candle only.

They were lads about the same age, and not unlike, both in form and figure. They were about fifteen years of age, the one called Sir Edgar being a little slighter than the other, while his hair was darker, and his eyes of a brown tint. It was a fine, open, manly face, beaming with animation and life, though touched with a shade of gloom—perhaps the produce of recent sickness.

The lad addressed as Dick, though so like him as to cause much whispering as to his parentage, had a degree of cunning in his countenance which caused its expression to be far from winning, or even commonly pleasant.

They were foster brothers, and until within twelve months had been brought up together, enjoying the same masters, and receiving one as much care in education as the other.

"Well, Dick," said Sir Edgar, "how much?"

"Twelve pounds," replied the lad Richard.

"That will do," continued the other. "And now, the sooner we start the better."

"But are you sure," continued the other, "that you have everything all right? I have made inquiries, and for you to be received in the royal navy you must have documents to prove your identity."

"I have them all," said Sir Edgar sadly, "my father's certificate of marriage, that of my birth; while as to my personal identity there can be no doubt."

"All right!" said Dick heartily, "that's the identical thing. What say you? shall we start?"

"The sooner the better, never to re-enter this house until I come as master, to avenge my wrongs," said the other solemnly.

As many others have done before him, and will again, Sir Edgar Blakesley was flying from his home, to seek his fortunes at sea, because his mother had chosen to give him a cruel, rapacious, and harsh step-father.

Affecting no disguise, they descended by the

rope ladder, and left it a witness of their flight. Out into the dark night they went, creeping like malefactors.

The lawn was soon gained, and the two lads hurried across it, never so much as looking back until the plantation was reached. They then struck across a beaten path, nor halted until a good three miles of ground intervened between them and the mansion from which they were hurrying.

They were on a high road, at no great distance from which stood a deserted mill house. It was in a little valley surrounded by brush and trees.

It was a crumbling ruin, moss-grown, and almost roofless.

To this, by previous agreement, the lads took their way, as it was settled they were to take the coach which passed on that road a little after daybreak.

Dick appeared to know the place well enough, as did indeed Sir Edgar, the valley since the abandonment of the mill having become a complete rabbit warren. They were then soon within its gloomy precincts, when the lad Dick produced a leaden box and a lanthorn, which he had conveyed thither for the purpose, and looked around, not without a strange sensation of awe.

They had never before been there at night, and it was rumoured that the cause of desertion had been that a barbarous murder had been committed there many years before.

It was a large room, with a vast fireplace; the roof had fallen in in several places, while the wind howled and whistled through the frequent crannies and fissures of the wall, while a low moaning, that sounded like mortal breathing, came distinctly to their ears.

"The place seems haunted," said Sir Edgar, in a low, hushed tone.

"Nonsense," replied Dick, not without a shudder, while he glanced round with a strange scared look.

"Oh, I'm not going to be frightened, Dick," continued the runaway. "A pretty sailor I'd make if I was afraid of ghosts. But as Peter would say, the place is no cannie, and I shan't feel comfortable until I'm well out of it."

Is there then such a thing as second sight? and does the appalled soul on the threshold of the grave see beyond the veil of futurity, into shadow-land?

Dick made no reply, but taking out a case bottle, poured out above a wine glassful into a tin cup, and handed it to Sir Edgar.

"Drink," he said, "that will give you courage."

Sir Edgar took the proffered glass, and drained it off. It was brandy, and appeared to revive him. But still he did not seem talkative. He was thinking of the bold and daring step which had so suddenly deprived him of a home and sent him forth upon the world, an outcast and a wanderer.

Dick looked keenly at him, until the youth sank slowly back in a heavy and death-like slumber.

"At last!" said the other, with a deep sigh; and the entire expression of his face changed as if by magic. A fierce, hungry, ferocious glance took the place of the half respectful look which he had hitherto assumed.

"At last! I've waited long enough," he said, wiping the cold perspiration off his brow. "Does the fool think I am always going to lackey him? My turn now, Sir Edgar Blakesley, baronet."

And with calm deliberation he searched the recumbent body, and took away the pocketbook, the money which he had sold the other's watch for, a cheque which had been his father's last gift, and which not a soul knew of, and then slowly, and with horrid deliberation, took out a clasped knife, opened it, and plunged it up to the haft in the body of his unfortunate foster brother — his half brother even, some said.

Then with a howl like that of a famished wolf, out went this second Cain into the open air, without once looking behind. He dared not.

But a yell so fearful, it seemed to glue him to the ground, made him halt and fancy his wretched victim was up and after him. But no. All is still. No sound is heard but the footsteps of the murderer as he courses down the valley, eager to place hundreds of miles if possible between himself and the scene of this most unparalleled crime.

It was daylight when he halted on the outskirts of a small town, and lay down for rest and shelter in an outhouse. But he could not sleep. There by his couch stood the spectral form which, until death benumbs his faculties, shall haunt him day and night, and for ever deprive him of the power of peaceful sleep.

CHAPTER II.

BOB GRIGGS.

THE streets of Portsmouth presented all that busy appearance which only appertains to sea ports in time of war. The harbour was full of vessels, while the streets presented a singularly animated and lively spectacle. Officers in uniform hurried hither and thither, sailors crowded round every tavern, girls in flaunting dresses displayed their bronzed faces at every corner, while the Jews and other dealers plied their profitable trade.

Round the celebrated George Inn there were congregated a group of officers of all ranks, for several commanders of vessels were seated within, finishing up all their arrangements preparatory to immediate departure.

It was early in the day, and the London coach was expected.

Several of those juvenile sucking Nelsons, as they are often popularly called, were expected down to join their ships.

The London coach was indeed coming down loaded with its valuable freight, among whom might be distinguished numerous youths leaving home for the first time, and looking as if they scarcely knew whether to laugh or cry, as they thought of the home they were leaving, or looked forward to a glorious and brilliant career.

Among the party was one who joined not in the general conversation. He too was a youth, but his smock frock, fiery red hair, and strange uncouth appearance, appeared to stamp him as one who was likely, if he went to sea at all, to find himself located among the more humble herd in the forecastle.

He scarcely made any response to the banter of some of the youngsters, except through his eyes, which glared horridly around when any jest hit him unusually hard.

The coach stopped a few miles out of Portsmouth, and the countryman alighted, paid his fare, and entering an inn sat down in the taproom.

He looked with a careless glance around, and found that it was tenanted by one man only, a sailor of a rather sinister aspect, heightened by the fact of his having only one eye.

"What cheer, my hearty?" said the British tar after a rather long examination; "and where do you hail from?"

"Don't hail from no where," replied the other with a grin, "and I wants some bread and cheese."

"Pull away at the bell," continued the other, "and the bottle-washer will be here in a jiffy."

The lad did as he was directed, and a girl with ruddy face and bare arms entered. The youth ordered bread and cheese and beer, and asked the stranger what he would take.

"You are a Trojan," he cried with sudden animation; "Susan, my love, a stiff nor-wester. Brandy, and none of your half-water grog."

The girl appeared to linger, as if in doubt.

"Do you want the money?" said the lad, with an angry contraction of the eyebrows.

"Well sir,—the brandy's a shilling, and—"

"Bring me change for a guinea," he interrupted, handing her the coin.

The girl hurried from the room, and the one eye of the sailor glistened. He remained silent for some time, apparently revolving in his mind some plan of operations. The drink was brought in, and was duly honoured. The sailor then waited until the lad had eaten his bread and cheese, when he once more opened the conversation.

"Its my turn, now mate," he said; "what say you? let's play for two stiff uns at cards."

"I aint much of a player," replied the lad.

"Its all luck," said the other, producing a greasy pack of cards.

They were shuffled, cut, dealt, and then for some little time there was nothing heard but the mystic slang of the recondite game of all fours. The sailor lost, cursed his ill luck, and played again. They had now begun to play for money.

The lad's eyes glistened, his face was flushed, his finger moved in a nervous and tremulous way, which at once proclaimed the incipient gambler.

The sailor saw this at a glance, and raised the stakes to five shillings.

The countryman—or rather, youth—lost pound after pound; but he made no complaint. Cold sweat stood upon his brow; his lips were livid.

"More brandy!" he suddenly cried out, when the other had won eleven guineas and his own purse showed but one more.

"With pleasure," said the sailor, whose delight was with difficulty kept within ordinary bounds.

"I'll fetch it," replied the lad; "I don't want the girl to see me playing."

In an incredibly short space of time he was again in the room, with two steaming hot glasses of brandy, one of which he eagerly handed to his opponent, and then resumed play. This time the stake was a guinea. To all appearance it was his last.

The lad played with extreme caution this time, for it was a desperate emergency. The sailor appeared more careless of the result, for had he not won everthing hitherto? The game soon came to an end. The youthful countryman lost.

"I'll play no more," he said, throwing down' the cards and the guinea.

"Just as you like," replied the tar, winking with his one eye; "here's better luck next time.'

"Better luck," said the other gravely as he pledged him in return.

The sailor drained off his glass, and wiped the perspiration from his face with his silk bandana. The lad was seized with a violent fit of coughing, and spilt his grog.

"Take it easy, my little hearty You've lost like a brick. Luck's all; and next time you see if you don't make a fortin'. Always pay for larning, you know. How mighty sleepy I am," he said yawning. "Give us your flipper, I'll go to bed.'

Here he stopped suddenly, his under-jaw fell, and he lay back almost as if suddenly stricken with death. Quick as lightning the lad sprang forward, and clutched a canvas bag which he had seen the other put in his pocket, and secreted it about his own person, the man staring at him with open eyes all the time, but whether conscious of what was going on could not be said.

No sooner had the other performed this feat, than he rose, took his bundle, and went forth, quite unobserved by any. He hurried along the room for some little time, until he noticed a barn in the distance. To this he hurried, determined there to remain until nightfall.

He found it open and vacant, and seating himself, counted his money.

There were fourteen guineas and about as many shillings in the canvas bag. He had made a clear profit by the day's transaction. With a satisfied smile he lay down to sleep, and in a few minutes he was in the land of dreams.

When he awoke he was in total darkness. Rising from the ground he felt for his bundle, and sallied forth into the open air. He thoroughly recollected the proper direction to follow, and hastened on his way. He had much to do that night, and Portsmouth was still several miles distant. He had been careful to make himself acquainted with the road, and found no difficulty in following it. For about half-an-hour he did not meet a human being, but at the expiration of that time he heard footsteps in advance, with low murmurings or mutterings. As he proceeded he soon found that the sound emanated from a drunken sailor, who was tottering on towards Portsmouth, pouring forth as he did so a perfect torrent of execrations.

"Not a shot in the locker—cleaned out—done brown, and by a raw-looking youngster. Bob Griggs done by a powder monkey. But I never forgets, and if I don't ring the thief's neck I'm a Dutchman."

The lad was close behind him. The other walked from side to side with an unsteady motion which proved his incapacity for running. The lad therefore made a bold rush past, and darted away with extraordinary speed.

The sailor stood still, petrified with astonishment; he then made a dash forward, and fell sprawling on the ground.

Half-an-hour later the lad entered Portsmouth, and without asking any questions made his way to the quarter inhabited by the Jews. A rather better looking clothes shop attracting his attention, he entered boldly.

"Vat cansh I do for you?" said a little fat flabby man, bowing, with his hands in his pockets.

"I want a midshipman's undress suit, quite new," replied the lad, with a firmness of manner which was not lost on the Hebrew, who produced from a large chest, with professional rapidity, the costume required.

"The price?" said the lad after a critical examination.

"Sh'lp me, Moses, cost me four guineas," began the Jew.

The lad turned away to leave the shop, his lip curled in scorn.

"Vait a bit, ve can pargin," said the Hebrew hurriedly.

"No," said the other resolutely, "ask me fair prices and you shall have them. *The age of the moon is one.*"

The Jew started as if struck by a blow, and then clutched the other's hand eagerly. From that moment there was no haggling. The mysterous words had produced a magical effect. A suit of clothes, shirts, and other linen, a proper chest and all, were provided with scrupulous regard to fair dealing. Is there then, after all, honour among thieves?

"Vy you not shay dat before?" muttered the Jew. "Holy Moses! I might have shaved a brother; but mine young master, how you know de sign—"

"*Profit is loss, and loss is profit,*" replied the lad gravely.

"I peg one ten thousand pardons," said the other with genuine awe, his eyes starting from his head.

He asked no further questions, but waited upon the lad with perfect obsequiousness. When he had completed his toilette, the aspirant to naval honours hailed a fly, and directing it to take the young gentleman to the Blue Posts, the Jew bowed him out with the reverence due to a prince.

"Mine Got!" said the Jew, as soon as he had left the premises, "so young and so vicked. De vorld is coming to an ent."

Meanwhile, the midshipman had driven up to the hotel, and sending in his box, had entered the public room, where he found several juveniles congregated, among whom he recognised one or two of his companions of the stage coach. But who could recognise in the handsome young officer the red-haired country youth of a few hours before.

"Good evening, gentlemen," he said, in extremely courteous tones. "I hope I am not intruding?"

"The more the merrier," said one of the juveniles, who was making a wretched attempt to smoke a bad cigar, and to drink a glass of grog.

"What's your ship?" growled a mate, a rough customer, with a very red face.

"Whichever ship Sir Edmund Crossley thinks proper to appoint me to," said the other.

"Do you know him?" asked several, eagerly. "Have you seen him?"

"Don't know him. Not a bit. But this is dry talk; here — how many are we? eight. Waiter, half a dozen of port, and let it be good."

The hearty response which followed this announcement left the youth in no doubt as to his present popularity; and when the evening was over, and all retired to rest more or less elevated, he was voted by common acclamation a credit to his new profession.

Early next morning he rose, and dressed himself with peculiar care, put a pocket book in his breast, and sallied forth towards the George Inn.

"I want to see Sir Edmund Crossley," he said, addressing a waiter in a very soft and honied tone.

His face was pale, his lips compressed, his whole mien agitated. But still he acted with perfect coolness and precision.

"Can't see him—busy," replied the waiter.

"Take up that," said the youth with severity, handing a card.

The man bowed, and glancing at the piece of pasteboard, hurried away to present it. He returned in a few minutes, during which a number of officers looked with a smile upon the self-possession and importance of the aspirant to naval honours. They had heard the conversation between the lad and the waiter.

Their astonishment was great then when the waiter hurried down, and spoke to the lad in the most respectful manner.

"Sir Edgar Blakesley is requested to walk up."

The lad looked round with a flushed face, and went upstairs.

"That thing a baronet!" cried an old naval officer. "A pretty pass the service has come to, when youngsters are shown up, while we dangle here, at the will and pleasure of our captains."

All present acquiesced as a matter of course. Then, as now, grumbling was the privilege of naval officers.

CHAPTER III.

THE POSTHUMOUS HEIR.

WE must change the scene for a moment, and ere we return to the old mill where lies the victim of a most cruel murder, or explain the result of the interview between the naval officer and the youth who announced himself as Sir Edgar Blakesley, introduce to the notice of our readers another character in our terrible drama.

On the confines of a wooded district in a remote part of England, which shall be nameless, from obvious reasons, there came to dwell, some years before the commencement of our narrative, a lady. She took an old-fashioned house which had not been inhabited for some time, and furnished it with great taste and judgment.

She was accompanied by several male and female servants.

She wore widow's weeds, and it soon became known in the neighbourhood that her husband had been killed by a mysterious fall from his horse, after one year of married life.

The Honourable Dudley Winterton had married for love; and being extremely wealthy, had, in the exuberance of his uxorial fondness, endowed his wife, and any possible children she might have, with the whole of his worldly wealth.

Failing any heirs, the vast estates and personalities went to two cousins in equal shares.

When the Honourable Dudley Winterton died—and his death was almost inexplicable—he was childless, and all his wealth went to his wife, who, distracted and broken-hearted retired with her steward, lady's maid, and other necessary servants, to pass the first year of her widowhood in retirement, away from those scenes which had so painful an interest in connection with her beloved husband.

The rector of a neighbouring village and the doctor were her only visitors.

About four months after her arrival at Fairy Knowe, as we shall call it, the visits of the latter became more frequent; and then it was publicly announced that an heir was expected to the name and possessions of the house of Winterton.

Great were the rejoicings of all the retainers of the family, who begged the widow to return to Dudley House, the chief residence of the Wintertons, that the heir might be born on the estate. The widow, however, feared the emotion of returning suddenly to the scene of her former happiness, and resolved to remain in the lonely house on the borders of the wild plantation until the interesting event was over.

The two cousins, Frederick Winterton and John Winterton, who had already in imagination divided the estate among them, were furious at the announcement, and wrote to protest against any such imposture being practised.

"I almost pitied them," said the indignant widow, to her medical adviser; "but this insolence is beyond what even my meekness can bear. Let them be strictly forbidden the house."

"But, my dear madam, on the contrary, let them come; let all the world come," said the cautious surgeon.

"No. The rectitude of my own heart, and my scorn of all deception be my defence. I will remain as secluded as ever."

"You are wrong; the world is very wicked," said the surgeon.

"The more reason for keeping it at a distance," continued the widow, sadly.

Dr. Gruby went away dissatisfied. He knew human nature, and he knew that the lust of wealth will incite to the most atrocious deeds, and tempt to extremities of calumny, beyond ordinary imagination.

He knew of the cousins. Frederick was a captain in an infantry regiment, at present on sick leave. John was a man about town, who did not carry about with him the fairest of reputations.

Mrs. Winterton so far yielded to the persuasions of her medical adviser as to increase the number of her servants. She added one man in the house, a porter at a small lodge in front of the house, and an additional kitchenmaid. The nurse the doctor agreed to provide himself.

The man servant who was taken into the house was a little, thin, weazened-face man, named Jones. He assisted the steward, waited at table, and did other offices incident to his situation. He came highly recommended from his last place—in London; no great recommendation to those who formed the general household.

He had a cat-like mode of moving about, which startled and worried—it was not natural. Everybody met him when least expected, and he had a strange fancy for examining the uninhabited rooms. He was, however, respectful to all, and seemed anxious to win everybody's good graces, especially Mrs. Hudson's, the housekeeper. In this he thoroughly succeeded.

One evening, shortly before the interesting event was expected, Mrs. Hudson asked Mr. Jones to tea.

Like all housekeepers' rooms, it was snug and cozy in the extreme. A warm fire burnt on the hearth, the kettle hissed, and the toast was done to a turn, when Mr. Jones knocked at the door. On being told to enter, he glided in with a sidelong movement sufficiently explitive of his humility.

"Sit down, Mr. Jones," she said; "I expect Mr. Dickson directly, but he's gone to D——."

"Just so," replied Mr. Jones, taking his seat; "how werry hodd."

"Quite natural," observed Mrs. Hudson, with a smile at the other's dialect; "he's gone to see the doctor."

"Just so. You don't mean to insinivate, Mrs. Hudson, as how missus is poorly?" added Mr. Jones, with his eyes modestly bent on the ground.

"Not exactly," said Mrs. Hudson, casting hers up to the ceiling, "but expected hourly. The doctor's to come to-morrow."

"Just so," cried Mr. Jones, taking a cup of tea. "Poor dear missus, I hopes she will hall right!"

"The Wintertons always are," said the housekeeper, gravely.

"Just so. Vat a hawful haccident as deprived missus of her husband, and made the babe as is not born a horphan!"

"Awful, indeed!" exclaimed Mrs. Hudson. "But, orphan or not, it is a blessing to know that those two scamps in London won't inherit master's estates."

"Just so," replied Mr. Jones, with a smile which looked like a grimace; "but you'll pardon my hignorance ven I axes who is the gents as you 'onors by the name of scamps?"

"Relations of master's—heirs-at-law. One of them's a captain; the other's a loose fish, who lives on his wits."

"Just so. And a werry fine estate for them as indulges in them articles; but it aint given to us all—eh, Mrs. Hudson?"

"And it is to be hoped that such wits never will be. When they were boys, these two boys nearly broke their fathers' hearts, and my master never would have anything to do with them."

"Just so. I hunderstand. It's arful, the vickedness of 'uman natur," said Mr. Jones; and, with a solemn look, he took another slice of bread-and-butter and another cup of tea.

The conversation continued in this strain for some time, until tea was finished, when, Mr. Dickson not returning, Mr. Jones and the house-keeper sat down to a game of cribbage, which continued until about ten, when, the habits of the house being early, they separated, and Mr. Jones ascended to his room at the top of the house. Entering this, he carefully closed the door, and looked out into the darkness of the night.

Not a light of any kind was visible, a half-ruined cottage being the only house within a mile. This kind of hut was situated in the wood, but could only be distinguished from the mansion by ascending to the top storeys.

Mr. Jones waved his candle once or twice in the air. Scarcely had he done so when a light appeared in the distance.

The man then unlocked a box, and produced several pieces of wax candle, which he proceeded to place on a long flat bit of board with a number of nails in it.

He then lit one, concealing his own candle. The light disappeared in the distance, and then reappeared. Jones now lit two additional ones, after a short time three, and then one. He, after this extraordinary pantomime, closed his window, rubbed his hands, and went to bed.

CHAPTER IV.

THE SUN-IN-THE-SANDS.

ERE we record the events which followed the strange proceedings of Mr. Jones, we must introduce an individual who plays a singular part in the extraordinary events which are preparing in the house occupied by Mrs. Winterton.

On the borders of the forest, and up a somewhat dreary cross road, was a small inn, known to the carters, drovers, and others who chiefly frequented it, as "The Sun in the Sands."

It was an ancient hostelry, and probably, before the high road had been diverted to a more level and commodious part, had been for ages the scene of bustle, business, and activity. It bore every mark of former grandeur. There were the ruins of a large and commodious set of stables, vast barns, and the indications even of splendour in the building itself. The modern kitchen was but a corner cut off from the vast room which had formerly answered that purpose.

Everything had gone to decay. Instead of a burly host and hostess, with numerous servants, ostlers, and stablemen, the whole establishment had dwindled down to a woman, a girl, and a boy.

These, however, will be introduced as occasion may require.

It is evening. Not a customer is anywhere within the house; the boy is asleep in the hayloft, the landlady nods in her chair behind the bar; business is at a stand-still. What voices, then, are these which we hear without?

Beneath the dull oil-lamp which hangs over the doorway stand two figures in whispered conversation. As may occur to the quick imagination of the reader, the speakers are of opposite sexes.

One is a young man about five-and-twenty, in the garb of a gentleman; his coat is rich and well cut, his three-cornered hat stands jauntily on his head, and his thick auburn hair falls in profusion on his shoulders. He is tall, slight, and elegantly formed; his face is thin, with a high, broad forehead, a pale, expressive countenance, set off by a small, dark moustache; his eyes are of the same hue, piercing and expressive, with, as he looks down upon the girl at his side, a soft, winning expression in them, which has forced his companion to look down upon the ground.

The girl is scarcely sixteen—a little, well built, and seductive-looking being, all curls, smiles, and ribbons. Her dress is fanciful, and yet neat—something between that of an English waiting-maid and a Welsh shepherdess.

She is about the middle height, with just sufficient *embonpoint* to show that she is fast budding into womanhood. Her hair is golden, falling in wavy curls upon a neck white as alabaster; her eyes of that deep cerulean blue which seems unfathomable; her cheeks are dashed with native roseate blushes—no purchased colour from the nearest *perruquier;* her teeth, regular and pearly, are continually shown as she smiles a laugh; while the contour of her face exhibits all the charms of youth, beauty, and innocence.

And there is a charm in innocence to which that of mere voluptuous beauty is as nothing—a charm, too, which can never be assumed.

"George," she said, as she leaned upon his arm, and bent her looks upon the ground, "you must not urge me. I have spoken frankly and sincerely."

"You do not love me," replied the other, reproachfully.

"Do not love you!" cried the girl, impetuously. "Why force me to repeat that which I have already said so often? I love you, George, with all the sincerity of a pure and virgin heart, which beats for man for the first time; but—"

The girl hesitated.

"But what?" said the young man, trying to catch a glimpse of her face.

"George, I have already told you. My poor mother is alone; I cannot leave her. Besides—"

"Speak on; I love to hear you, though it drives me mad!"

"You have made no secret of your profession, George," she added, sadly.

"Again! By heavens! Lucy, you are not the girl I thought you. True that I am one who on the highway says, 'Stand and deliver!' But who made me what I am? Who drove me to the only course left open to one who cannot beg, and who was never taught to work? Besides, I have told you that, though my necessities forced me to become a highwayman, no sin of blood is on my soul."

"George," said the girl, sadly, "I am a poor and simple child. An accident has given me a little better education than generally belongs to those of my class; but still I am humbly born and humbly bred. Thrown into your society for the last twelvemonths, I have lost my heart to the handsome Captain George. But I have not lost the faculty of reason. You are an outlaw; you have transgressed your country's laws, and at any moment may be called to pay the forfeit. You love me—you wish me to become your wife. Were I once your wife, it would be my duty to yield and obey; but I am not, and it is my solemn resolve never to be so, until you give up a career fraught with such misery to us both. You love me—I will not forget that; then it is my duty to use my power to wean you from proceedings which must end so fatally."

"It may not—it cannot be. Lucy, I have been driven to this trade by crime and injustice in others. I did not choose it; but having become what I am, there is no retreat."

"There is! there is! George, are there not other climes, where we might, in honour, and by hard work, attain a position, which might make us forget the past and make atonement?"

"You drive me mad. Is this the girl, who when I tell a tale of the road listens with such enthusiasm?"

"Ah! George, you have a way of clothing your deeds with such a veil of romance, I cannot but listen; but in my calmer moments I recollect and weep. Once more, never will I be the bride of Captain George, the highwayman—"

"Enough!" said the other pettishly; and, as if convinced that time was alone required to conquer this resolute conduct in so young a girl, "let us speak of Fairy Knowe. You promised to tell me all."

"I did," replied Lucy sadly; "but why wish you to know?"

"From no bad motive," said the other warmly. "Something strange is going on there, and as I am playing hide and seek just now I would fain learn what it means."

Lucy explained the position of Mrs. Winterton as far as it was known in the county.

"But the lights?"

"What lights?"

"Every night as I ride across the forest I see at the upper window of the mansion an array of signal lights, sometimes one, then three, then two. Somebody is playing a treacherous part in that house."

"Poor lady!" said Lucy gently; "she is sorely tried. Her husband killed, and herself pursued by the hate of the heirs she is about to disappoint."

"Say you so?" cried George, striking his forehead; "then I begin to understand. As I live there is an emissary of the cousins in the house."

"Then heaven have mercy on her," responded Lucy.

"Lucy," said the young man, with flashing eyes, "I see it all, as if it were mapped out before me. They would murder or steal away the child."

"The wretches!"

"But it shall not be.'

"How can it be prevented?" cried Lucy.

"I will undertake the task. You accuse me of much that is evil, and I know that my conscience is not quite clear. But here is a deed which may counterbalance many others. I will baulk these hungry wolves."

"But how?" said Lucy, raising her eyes tenderly to his animated countenance.

"I know not. There is no immediate scheme in my head—but do it I will. Let us in to supper, Lucy, and then away. The highwayman will outwit the harpies, and the poor lady shall have one defender at least."

"Spoken like my own brave George. Ah, why not be always thus?" cried the girl passionately.

"Can't afford it," said the other, shaking his head.

Lucy made no reply, but led the way into the house with a deep sigh. Again had she failed in her earnest endeavour to reclaim her lover from his dangerous occupation.

As soon as the evening meal was concluded, Captain George went out into the stable-yard, saddled and bridled his horse with his own hands, and leaping on the gallant steed, rode to the front door, where Lucy stood in in the shadow of the door-way.

"When shall I see you again?" she asked in a low voice.

"I don't know," replied the highwayman gaily. "I may, or I may not, come back to-night. Be not alarmed if a few days elapse ere I return. Farewell."

And away he rode at a sharp trot, until the highway, some three miles distant, was reached. Just before he entered upon the road, he drew rein, and took from his pocket a mask; not one of those short black ones which were usually worn by gentlemen of his profession, but a mask that covered his whole face, and looked by that light like a human face.

It was that of a man between forty and fifty, with red face and whiskers, and a beard to match.

Keeping close to the trees on the right side of the road, Captain George soon reached a small open glade in the forest, into which he turned; and having found a large tree, with which he appeared familiar, he tied his horse in the very thick of some bush, and clambered up into the boughs of the lofty oak.

From its summit he could clearly distinguish the mansion of Mrs. Winterton. But all was now dark and gloomy. Not a single light was to be seen.

Just then the clock of a distant village struck twelve, and as it did so the garret window of the house was suddenly illuminated.

Captain George with a swift and rapid glance took in all the horizon; but for a minute or two he was at fault. Then, to his utter astonishment, he *heard* a casement open almost at his feet.

"The ruined hut," he muttered; "poachers on my manor."

A rapid interchange of signals now took place

between the mansion and the ruins, and then the casements were again closed, and the highwayman remained in his tree as wise as before.

But he was astute and cunning. He determined to lose no opportunity of penetrating this mystery. With this view he descended the tree, and leaving his horse, advanced to the ruins, with which he was perfectly familiar. More than once during his lawless career had they served him as a place of shelter and repose.

CHAPTER V.

AN UNEXPECTED MEETING.

THE ruined hut was divided into several compartments, one of which alone was habitable. This was a large room, which had more the appearance of a kitchen than anything else. There was a large yawning fireplace, a coarse deal table, three chairs, and three very common truckle beds.

Captain George appeared to know the place well. Going round on tiptoe to the back, he crept cautiously across a falling wall, and using the utmost circumspection, gained a ruined chamber, divided from the only habitable one by a thick oaken door, evidently of recent construction. Peering in, he caught sight of three men, two evidently belonging to the upper classes of society, the other, a kind of mixture between a groom and a valet.

The two were conversing without restriction in the presence of their domestic.

The first was a saturnine dark man of about thirty, with an olive complexion, little piercing gray eyes, a hooked nose, a large sensual mouth, the whole set in a frame of dark whiskers and moustaches.

The second was a tall effeminate youth of about eight-and-twenty, florid, thin, with ruddy whiskers, and an affected mode of speech.

"So-ho!" said the first described, Captain Frederick Winterton, "Master Jones is about to communicate with us. The time is coming. And after all, it's a girl."

"It appears to be so," replied Mr. John. "A gurl. Only imagine how pweposterous, for you and I to be put out by a little ugly red faced gurl."

"Preposterous! I should say so," said the captain, twisting his moustaches.

"But now, weally have you made up your mind?" asked the fop.

"I have, and rather than be baulked would I sacrifice mother and child. But that is unnecessary. The child once dead—"

"Weally Frederick, you are vewy coarse in your obsewations; you don't mean to be so vewy vulgar as to kill it?" drawled his cousin.

"I do. It is our only hope. Mrs. Winterton cannot have any more children."

"She might mawy again," said the young man.

"Might she? I think we could contrive to make any man rather afraid of tackling her," said the half-pay captain fiercely.

"Ye-es—that's true, we might. I always said you were doosed clever, Frederick, and now see it. Oh, Lord!"

"What's the matter?" cried the soldier, fiercely.

"Somebody knocking at the dwore," said the fop.

"Open, Sam. Don't be a fool, John."

The groom, a little fellow about five feet high, pock-marked, gray haired, and with every evidence in his countenance of being a fit attendant on the couple who had taken up so strange a residence, went to the door and opened it. A man wrapped in a cloak, and wearing a slouched hat, entered quickly, and closed the door behind him. The two men started to their feet.

"Well, Jones," cried the captain, "how blows the wind? ready?"

"Just so. The juvenile his now four-and-twenty 'ours old," said the traitor.

"Has the doctor left? is the coast clear?" continued the captain.

"Just so; exactly," replied Jones. "I hexpects the nuss will sleep pertickler hard to-night."

"Have you drugged her beer?" said the other, anxiously.

"Just so. But them women is so cussed obstinate. She von't drink her beer till twelve, when she's done her vurk."

"No matter. The night is long. We shall be ready. Have you seen to everything?"

"Just so. There's no mistake in me, sir. I've greased hall the doors, oiled hall the locks, and paid pertickler attention to the winders. Just you knock, sir, and the winders will open of theirselves."

"'Tis well. Your reward shall be commensurate with your services. But in case you should be missed, had you not better return?"

"Just so. It was my intention to have made the same identical obserwation. Missus is werry fidgetty, and might ring for me, which ain't werry likely, you know; but still it might be, which as I am habsent might be unpleasant."

"You are right," said the captain, thoughtfully. "But a word with you. The chamber occupied by Mrs. Winterton is at a considerable distance from those of the domestics?"

"Just so."

"And by this time all of them will be in bed?"

"Just so. The lazy menials will be snoring like pigs."

"That is well. And you are sure of our reaching the dressing-room without interference or possible discovery?"

"Just so," said Jones, with a low bow.

"And now, remember, whatever you do the first to appear when the alarm is given, and describe us as ordinary highwaymen. We must rob the house, and the child must be killed by accident in the scuffle."

"Just so," said Jones, as coolly as if he had been speaking of a litter of kittens.

"Be cautious, cool, and let slip nothing," said the captain, "and our fortunes are made."

"Just so," replied Jones, with a low bow, and an avaricious twinkle of the eye.

"That fellow will be dangerous," said the captain, in a musing tone, when their confederate had closed the door behind him.

"Do you weally think so?" said the fop, who had listened half unconsciously, half in dismay.

"He will want money. Now, I, for one, am not going to be made a milch cow of, and if this fellow goes too far—hem—never mind."

"Now, weally, what do you mean?" stammered John.

They were whispering low now, so that the groom might not overhear them.

Meanwhile, the highwayman, using the same caution as before, had left the house, and knowing the forest well, had hurried round in such a way as to intercept the confidential Mr. Jones, who, elated by the prospect of a rich reward for his crime, was walking along in a musing way, counting, as so many have done before, his chickens before they were hatched.

He would set up a public-house; he would marry Polly Minton; he would abandon his evil ways—he would become a good man and honourable member of society. Just so!

"Stand and deliver!" said a harsh voice close in front of him.

The man looked up with a terrified and trembling glance, and found himself face to face with a highwayman, whose face was of course perfectly unknown to him.

"Just so," cried Jones, incoherently, as he dropped on his knees. "For heaven's sake, Mr. Highwayman, have mercy on a poor horphan father of a family! I've got no money."

"Rise!" said the other, in a stern tone; "rise, Mr. Jones, and believe me the fewer falsehoods you tell, the better we shall understand one another."

"Just so. I declare, your honour, I hasn't a brass farthing."

"Rise, I say, and listen to me. I have overheard every word which has passed between you and your employers, or fellow criminals."

"Just so. O, Lord! O, Lord! I'm a poor unfortunate devil; have mercy on me!"

"The mercy I will show you," said the highwayman, sternly, "will be a rope and a gallows if you do not cease your insensate cries. I mean you no harm; on the contrary, if you listen to me, I am willing to serve you."

"Just so; but in vich vay, most noble sir?" said Jones, rising.

"Look you, my man; you are wholly in my power. I might insist on sharing whatever reward you have been promised by those cold-blooded villains and assassins."

"Just so; but, good Lord, sir!" whimpered Jones.

"Silence! I said, I might; but such is not my intention. Is there much plate in the house?"

"Just so," said Jones, with a wild gasp; "plenty. But why?"

"I ask questions, but do not answer them. Now listen to me, Mr. Jones, I have overheard the whole of your plot. Nothing prevents my revealing it to the lady who is to be so foully wronged. But I am in want of money. Now you have to choose between impunity and the wages of your treachery, or exposure. In the former case, my bargain is that you receive the money, while I content myself with the plate."

"Just so," said Jones, in a hesitating way.

"My proposition upsets some of your little arrangements, I perceive," continued Captain George. "I presume you intended appropriating the plate as well as the money."

"Just so. But, good Mr. Highwayman, I humbly begs your pardon; I am at your orders. Only say the vord, and whatever you says is done."

"You must now admit me to the house, and allow me to act in my own way. No time is to be lost; your friends will be impatient. And then, my good man, I am hungry, and would willingly discuss a cold joint and bottle of wine. Lead the way."

"Just so," replied Mr. Jones, ruefully, as he led the way, revolving in his own mind how he was to be rid of this most unwelcome guest.

Captain George, holding his pistol carelessly in his hand, walked beside the treacherous manservant, indulging all the time in bantering conversation, which scarcely left the other any time for reflection. In this way they soon reached the bottom of the garden. Jones had no intention of entering by the lodge gates, where a small door had been long closed up. Jones, however, produced a key, and the garden was rapidly entered.

"Excuse me, my dear Mr. Jones," said the highwayman, "but I should like to see that key. Who knows? it may be extremely useful to me."

With a groan the other surrendered the key, and led his companion towards the house, which was entered by an open window.

"No treachery!" whispered George, "remember you are in my power."

"Just so," said the other, in a trembling voice. "It's all serene. Take my hand; this way. And now I'll strike a light."

CHAPTER VI.
THE ABDUCTION.

AFTER a few trembling efforts, the discomfited Mr. Jones contrived to strike a light, which enabled Captain George to examine into his exact position. They were in a large, well appointed, and well furnished kitchen. A fire burned still in the grate, while all around were the evidences of plenty, and at the same time of order and good management; everything was scrupulously clean, and in its place.

"I suppose yonder is the larder?" said Captain George, with a grim smile.

"Just so," replied Jones, who was pale as a ghost; "vill yer vorship like to heat?"

"I don't mind," continued the highwayman, gaily; "especially if you know of some good ale—eh, Mr. Jones?"

The other made no reply, but busied himself in supplying the wants of his strange and certainly unwelcome companion. George appeared absorbed in the discussion of a cold fowl and jug of ale, while in reality he was scrutinising the countenance of the treacherous domestic.

"The time is coming," he suddenly exclaimed; "your friends will be waiting."

"Just so," said Jones, with a start. "I will go let them in."

"But you will lead them in some other way," continued Captain George coldly. "I shall lock myself in. When they have taken their departure we can do our business."

And the highwayman laid a brace of pistols on the table in rather an ostentatious manner. Jones shuddered, and after a moment's thought informed his new taskmaster that he should go round and let them in at the hall entrance. George nodded, and the other took his departure. No sooner was his back turned than the other's manner suddenly changed. Rising, and moving on tiptoe, he crept to the kitchen-door and listened to the sound of the other's footsteps as he moved along the old winding passages of that ancient mansion. Suddenly they ceased altogether. With a lightness of foot and a rapidity of action which appertained in all probability to his occupation, the young man left the kitchen, turned the key of the door outside, and put it in his pocket. He then groped along to where he had seen a small back staircase, which he already knew led to the sleeping apartments. He slowly and methodically ascended to the first floor.

To his great delight, he saw the light of a candle beneath the door of a room.

He tried the handle. It yielded, and he found himself in a large apartment, illumined by a lamp.

In the centre was a large bedstead, surrounded according to the poisonous ideas of the day by heavy drapery.

By a table on which shone a lamp, slept a middle-aged woman, the nurse.

A door communicating with an ante-chamber, was open near to her hand.

Not a sound was heard, save the heavy breathing of the nurse.

"Who is that?" said a soft melodious voice from the bed.

Captain George started, as if struck by a sudden blow, and hastily withdrew his mask from his face and concealed it in his pocket.

"A friend," he then replied, without showing himself.

"Merciful heaven!" cried the soft voice again, "who—what can it be?"

"Is it a voice from the dead? or is it Arabella who speaks?" said George.

"Leopold!" cried the other, wildly.

Next instant, the sick woman and the young highwayman were face to face, with clasped hands, and eyes that were rivetted on each other with wild surprise and deep affection.

"But whence came you? what do you here?" said the lady, who was not more than three-and-twenty, and marvellously beautiful.

"That reminds me. Dear Arabella, I have not a moment to lose. Your child?"

"Is here," said the fond mother, turning down the bed-clothes, and showing its tiny face.

"Arabella, I have not one instant to explain. Draw close the curtains. That vile traitor, your servant Jones, has admitted your cousins to the house. They come to murder the babe. They are armed, and they are many. Do not, I implore you, give way to weakness. Drink this," snatching a cordial from the table near them, "and be not alarmed, I am here. This is the bell-rope; if they attempt any violence on you, ring the alarm."

Stunned, horrified, scarcely able to credit her senses, the young woman obeyed the behest of her voluntary assistant, and the curtains were closed.

*   *   *   *   *

Several minutes elapsed, during which the young mother's lips were heard moving as if in muttered prayer. Then a door was heard to open with violence, and peering through the drawn curtains, Mrs. Winterton saw three masked figures enter her room.

The strangely heavy sleep of the nurse now for the first time struck her.

The men advanced to the side of her couch, and one drew aside the curtains. Mrs. Winterton, despite her weakness, sat up in the bed and confronted them.

"The child," said one, in deep, gruff, and commanding voice.

"What child?" she replied, coldly, though the beating of her heart could be heard.

"No folly, woman," cried the man angrily; "give up the wretched little impostor."

"Now I know you," she said sternly, "ye are my manly cousins. Go. Ye are too late. I expected this. The child is gone."

"Gone! woman—fiend—devil," shrieked the first speaker, throwing the clothes off her.

"Cowards! thus to insult a woman," said Mrs. Winterton, her pale face becoming crimson at the cold-blooded insult.

"D——n!" yelled the man, "the brat is gone. Bring in Jones."

The others, who had not spoken, here rushed out and dragged in the servant, pale, reluctant, and trembling.

"Scoundrel," said the first speaker, clutching him by the throat, "what mummery is this? Where is the child? You know."

"Just so," replied the other, with a wild and vacant countenance, and speaking in a way that showed he was completely bewildered. "The highwayman! the highwayman!"

"The highwayman!" faintly ejaculated the sick lady.

"The highwayman, you blatant fool." roared the first masked figure. "Speak, or I'll blow your brains out."

"Just so," said Jones, in a faint tone of voice. "Don't choke me, and I'll confess all."

"Speak, idiot, and quickly; I know not what keeps me from braining you on the spot."

Stammering, stuttering, and in almost incomprehensible language, Jones told the story of his meeting with an ugly middle-aged; man how he threatened him; how he accompanied him to the house; and finally, how he had left him in the kitchen.

"Why didn't you say so at first. Woman, you are in connivance with this vagabond. Your villany deserves condign punishment. But, egad, you look so beautiful—"

A villanous expression of countenance, menacing, full of voluptuous meaning, and insulting threat, so startled Mrs. Winterton, that she pulled the bell rope.

The alarm bell on the summit of the house sounded with terrific violence through the house.

"To the kitchen! to the kitchen!" shouted the first masked figure.

Jones, frantic with terror, took the lead and rolled rather than rushed down stairs, followed by the whole gang. The kitchen was deserted.

"Oh, oh!" cried the leader, "I hear footsteps. Ah! the cry of a child. We have him."

And with wild and savage oaths they sprang into the garden, just in time to see the gate closed behind them and locked.

Away they flew to the front, where their horses were held for them by the servant of the inn, where they found their dogs.

"Jack," said the chief, addressing this individual, "be off home; we want your horse. Here's a guinea to pay for your walk. Mount, you infernal villain."

"Just so. Infernal villain! But I can't ride," muttered Jones.

"You can—you shall. Mount. You must point out the wretch."

Next minute they were galloping along the road Jones holding on in the most desperate manner.

"Heaven preserve my child!" said the lady above in the chamber. "But Leopold, Leopold! what is this I hear of you?"

CHAPTER VII.

THE SUPPER.

HIGH in the heavens rose the silvery moon, as the four confederates dashed furiously along the road. The night had hitherto been cloudy, but as if the chaste luminary wished to assist the villanies of the cousins, up it now rose, shedding its balmy light over forest and road. After riding a short distance, the whole party reined in at a signal from their leader.

"I hear no sound," said the half-pay captain; "the fellow has no horse."

"Just so," murmured Jones, as if hoping to put them off the scent; "he was a foot-pad."

As if to give him the lie, at that very instant, the loud neighing of a horse was heard, and then a clatter of hoofs on the stony road, while in the distance could be seen the shadowy outline of steed and rider, the latter evidently urging his gallant animal to its utmost speed.

It was a splendid coal-black horse, and dashed along the road with the air of one who laughed at pursuit.

"On! on! on!" shouted Frederick, as he struck his spurs into the flanks of his hired hack; "he must be caught at any price."

"Just so," said the miserable Jones, clinging to his horse from mere terror of the captain.

The others, accomplished riders, needed no urging. The exquisite had as much at stake as the captain, while the groom had the promise of what, to him, was a fortune, if their nefarious plans succeeded. Away then all dashed, at full and furious speed, after the fugitive.

A long reach of road is before them. The pursued has disappeared for a moment from the dip of a hill, but the clatter of his horse's hoofs are still heard upon the road, and presently, just as he ceased to gallop, they saw him slowly ascending the opposite eminence.

"Curse him!" said the captain, "he seems pretty confident of his horse."

"Vewy fine animal—aw—vewy," responded his cousin.

"I only wish I had him within pistol-shot," growled the man of war.

"How vewy rough you are—aw—vewy," said the exquisite; "I presume the gentleman would not require any such pwessing arguments."

A hearty curse from the lips of Frederick was drowned in the noise made by the horses resuming a hard gallop. On they again pressed, just as the solitary horseman again put his steed to its speed.

"Is there not a turnpike soon?" asked the captain, with a violent oath.

"Just so," said Jones.

"Then away with you all. We must stop him now."

And regardless of the steep character of the hill they were ascending, he spared neither whip nor spur, until he had urged the weary animal to a hard trot. The summit of the slope was, however, soon reached, and there, safe enough, was the turnpike, already open, and the rider on the coal-black steed conversing quietly with the taker of dues.

Frantic with rage, and fearful that the man might escape, the captain dashed forward just as the gate was closed, and the keeper re-entered his house.

"Gate! you blind idiot; gate! I say. You must have seen me coming!" shouted the infuriated captain.

"I zeed you a-coming," said the man, standing in his own doorway scratching his head.

"Then why in the devil's name don't you open?" shouted the other, clutching his whip.

"Cus he guv I a guinea to keep you a bit. He! he! he!" continued the man, with a stupid laugh.

"I'll trounce you, you loutish booby!" shrieked the captain, who, now reinforced by his companions, raised his whip.

"Avast there!" said the turnpike-man. "He zed as how you was four highwaymen; and I sees you are by your masks. Keep off, or I'll shoot."

And the man levelled a blunderbus.

"You stupid idiot," cried the captain; "it is he is the highwayman. Here, take this," and he threw two guineas at the other's feet; but open quickly, or the vagabond will escape."

"Eh! but it's a wicked world," said the pike-man, opening the gate. "That a highwayman! he looked more like a gentleman—"

The four dashed through without a word—

"A darned deal than any of your lot," added the other with a grin, as he closed the gate, and then retired into private life, to gloat over the unusual good luck which had befallen him that night.

Meanwhile the pursuers, furious at the delay which had taken place, urged their steeds to the utmost, guided only by the sound of the fugitive still galloping along the road.

Suddenly this means of following up the chase ceased, for they could no longer hear the slightest sound. Without a word, Captain Winterton urged forward his horse, and then reined in, as a narrow glade up between the trees was revealed to them.

"He has doubled on us," cried the captain. "It is the greensward that conceals the sound."

And satisfied of the truth of this, he dashed up the green glade, followed by his companions. For some time the open space grew narrower, and narrower, until at length it merged into a narrow lane, which soon brought them within sight of the same highway they had so recently quitted.

There was the rider on the coal-black horse, with his steed's head turned towards them, riding leisurely along the road.

With a wild cry of triumph they flew to his side, and while two caught the reins of his horse, the others drew their pistols menacingly.

"What on earth is the matter?" said the horseman in a languid voice.

" Where is the child ? Give it up—scoundrel, villain, robber—"

" Gentlemen, don't all speak at once," continued the stranger; " it's a very noisy proceeding. What child are you talking about ? give up what ? And why are you using such very ungentlemanly language ? Is it my purse you want ? I opine from your masks that you are gentlemen of the road : if so, I am sorry."

" Jones," said the captain, in a voice of thunder, " is this the man, or not ?"

" Just so. Not the man," replied Jones, whose eyes stood out from his head with astonishment; " fat, red-haired, old, ugly—"

The captain looked puzzled.

" But, sir, have you met no one ? Did not a horseman pass just now, mounted on a steed very much like yours, with a child in his arms ?"

" You are the first persons I have met to-night," said the stranger.

" I really beg your pardon," replied the officer, " but we were in pursuit of a burglar and highwayman, who stole away an infant, and had but just lost his track when we came up with you. Once more, you really must excuse us."

" No apologies, I beg. What say you ? I have my inn close by ; their punch is excellent. Suppose we drown the mistake in a foaming bowl."

" With all my heart," said the captain.

" Vewy good idea," cried the exquisite. " Is it very far ?"

" Oh, no ; close by," said the young and handsome stranger, leading the way.

He followed the high road for a few hundred yards further, and then turning up a cross lane, in a few minutes halted before the door of the Sun in the Sands.

It was four o'clock in the morning.

The stranger struck at the door with his riding whip, with an energy which very soon brought both the ostler and the daughter of the house to open. They made no remark, being in all probability used to this kind of proceeding on the part of their lodger.

" John, let the horses be well rubbed down. Lucy, the cold roast beef, beer, and a flaming bowl of punch. These gentlemen are friends of mine."

Lucy curtsied, smiled, and after lighting a lamp in the parlour, hurried away to obtain the keys and obey their behests. In a very few minutes the board groaned under the weight of a solid joint, a large cheese, flagons of ale, and such other provender as old fashioned Englishmen were wont to afford in days of yore.

The two gentlemen, after a whispered conference took off their masks, and their attendants did the same.

" Come, gentlemen," said the stranger, heartily, " make yourselves at home. You, my men, cut away as if we were not here."

And setting the example, he filled his plate with eatables, though he scarcely touched any. He, however, drank several tankards of ale. When he saw that the appetites of his new acquaintances flagged, he at once summoned Lucy.

" And now, my dear, a glorious bowl of punch —hot water, sugar, lemons ; brandy and rum. I will brew. Come, quick ! we are all impatient for a bumper," he cried.

The ingredients were soon brought, the punch made, and in rapid circulation. The stranger did not seem to flinch. He rattled on about London, high and low life, the army, foreign parts, sang a good song, and kept the whole party in a roar, until they began to give unmistakable signs of being intoxicated.

" Just so," said Jones, leaning his chin on his chest; and next minute he rolled upon the groom, who was snoring on a bench.

" I say—say—Fred," half whimpered the fop, " d'ye know, Fred, I'm doosed afraid I'm ineb-ineb-inebriated !"

" Drunk ! very drunk !" said the captain, looking at him with stern solemnity; " drunk ! beastly drunk !"

And as if disgusted with his cousin, he laid his head on the table, and in five minutes was sound asleep. The exquisite was snoring.

" At last !" cried the young man, rising. " At last !" And the smile on his face faded, his countenance looked wan and pale, and his whole mien exhibited extreme lassitude and weariness.

He now, however, with extreme activity, searched the pockets of the two gentlemen, and after about five minutes left the room.

Ten minutes later the trot of his horse might be heard on the road.

When the adventurers were roused in the morning, they had neither money, jewellery, or watches.

Their fury knew no bounds. They fiercely called the people of the house, who assured them that the young gentleman who had accompanied them was as total a stranger as they were themselves.

This the cousins did not believe ; but what was the use of making any noise about the matter ? Their own conduct during the night would not bear examination. They were compelled then to put up with their losses and return to their own inn.

Next day the rumour flew over the whole county of the outrage on Mrs. Winterton. She however, did not mention the names of the cousins in connection with the matter.

She seemed to expect that the child would be restored. But days, weeks, months passed ; years fell into the abyss of time—and no tidings whatever came of the beautiful baby-girl which had been so mysteriously spirited away.

Rewards were offered—bills printed—appeals to " LEOPOLD ;" but no answer came.

The bereaved mother was at length compelled to give up all hope. She was now a widow indeed—without husband, friend, or child.

And thus passed thirteen years.

CHAPTER VIII.
THE BLUE DWARF.

WHEN the assassin fled from the old mill house, bearing with him the curse of Cain upon his brow, it was no imaginary cry which pursued him as he rushed down the dell.

A rushing sound followed his escape, and something entered the room in which the foul deed had been done.

It was a man with a dark lanthorn, the light of which was now shed upon the insensible body.

And such a man!

About four feet high, with short legs, and arms that reached considerably below the knee, this sudden apparition appeared to have no redeeming point in his deformity. His face was hideous; grizzly hair like that of a negro, surmounted a low narrow forehead; little red circled eyes, themselves rather green than any other colour; a huge mouth, revealing teeth filed to a point and died jet black; a beardless chin—might have all passed still as accidents of nature to be explained by sickness, or premature birth; or some awful terror on his mother's soul.

But his skin was blue.

Blue as indigo, with spots all over his face, neck, and arms, of a blue black.

He was shaggy too, like an ourang-outang.

He wore a fantastic dress like a gnome king in a pantomime, composed of coarse stuff of foreign make.

It was an unearthly howl he gave as he recognised the victim of the other's crime—a howl more suitable to a wild beast than a man. For some time his exclamations were utterly incoherent, and even expressed in some unknown guttural language. At length, however, his feelings found vent in intelligible words.

"Dead! lost! and Goldy Gordon perjured!" he cried, striking his forehead with his hairy horney hands—which were also blue.

Slowly, tenderly, gently, with all the care a mother would have given to a babe, the dwarf raised the boy's body in his arms.

"He lives!" yelled the dwarf, wildly, as a faint pulsation of the heart made his own veins throb.

To draw out the knife gently, to bind the wound with a handkerchief, to again clasp the lad to his breast, and after wrapping him in a tattered cloak, to hurry from the mill house, was the work of an instant.

Away across the rugged crest of the hill, down the steep, across a purling brook, he took his way; nor did he halt until beneath the dark shadow of some lofty trees, he espied a faint glimmering of fire.

Goldy Gordon, the blue dwarf, had, some twelve years ago, suddenly appeared in the county, coming no man knew whence, and living no man knew where. However disposed the misshapen creature may have been to associate with his fellows, he soon saw that his presence excited hatred, terror, and scorn.

The women were peculiarly averse to him; and there was not an ugly child born within twenty miles of a certain spot, but it was always said the mother had been startled by the Blue Dwarf.

The man saw and understood.

After a brief trial, he utterly secluded himself from all society, and never willingly addressed any one of his fellow creatures.

Still, however, he crossed the path of many by day and night, on his rambles; but the instant he saw any one coming he would conceal himself behind a haystack, or lie down in a plantation, or crouch near a hedge, and let whoever it might be pass.

He never spoke to anybody, and never was known to make a purchase.

And yet the voice of public rumour did not accuse him of any illicit mode of procuring food and raiment.

Despite his ugliness, calumny was silent, for it found not the first peg to hang an accusation on. And for every foul libel on our fellow men, we must find some pretence.

No man could say where he lived—nor how. He was an inscrutable mystery.

His origin, race, history, were all secrets which not the most inveterate gossipmonger could fathom.

He never received a letter, and never wrote one.

Such was the strange and wonderful being which now had charge of the youth who had run away from home, and who had been so foully and cruelly stabbed by one in whom he had put all faith and trust.

"Who comes?" said a loud voice.

"Romany," grunted the dwarf.

No reply was made, and the strange being, to whom the lifeless body seemed a mere trifle, hurried on towards the tents.

"Miriam!" he said, in a sharp, commanding voice.

"I am here, my prince," replied a full rich voice.

A large tent was pushed open, and a woman of about forty years of age, dark, handsome, and of tall and commanding mien, stood out in bold relief.

"What is it?"

"A wounded boy. Quick! there is no time to lose. Into the tent," muttered Goldy Gordon.

The woman gazed curiously on the lad, as the dwarf laid him down beside a lovely girl of about twelve, who slept soundly within the tent.

"He is not dead," gasped the dwarf, in an agonised tone.

"No," said the woman, "but he is bad."

And as she spoke she laid bare the wound. As she did so, the girl awoke, and looked round with startled eyes.

It was indeed a lovely vision. Fair as the driven snow or downy breast of swan, with soft blue eyes, rich golden hair that fell in natural ringlets on her shoulders, she had not a trace of the gipsy in her appearance.

Her countenance was marvellous in contour. The outline was perfection, giving promise as she grew older of really magnificent beauty. The face was oval, with a forehead not high enough to be remarkable, but fully developed, and elevated enough to denote the lurking intellect within; her long almond-shaped eyes were veiled by lashes, the colour of which could scarcely be correctly depicted, but which in after years would be perfect auburn; her nose was almost straight, but with just that little rise below the eyes which is supposed to denote energy of character; her upper lip was curt and sharply defined, while her lips were a model; the mouth was small, and the lips being parted in surprise, revealed a double row of teeth, such as no dentist, royal or ducal, was ever able to produce; the chin was small, delicate, and dimpled; while the general expression of the countenance was that of pity, wonder, and inquiry.

"Who is the poor boy?" she said.

"Never mind," growled the Blue Dwarf, "hold the light while mammy probes the wound."

"You monster!" continued the girl. "Now don't scold; I'm going to be a very good girl."

She took the light, and while the woman examined the wound, fixed her eyes with deep attention on his pale and cadaverous countenance.

"Pretty boy!"

"Ough!" said the dwarf, with a grunt.

He made no further remark, his whole soul being to all appearance on the lad.

"Well?" he said in a hushed whisper.

"Death is hovering around. I can hear his sable wings. I can feel his icy breath upon my shoulder. I can see his dull watery eye fixed upon the house-dweller. But is he a friend of yours, Sapathwa?"

"More than my soul! My life-blood—my very being itself!" cried the dwarf, passionately.

"Give me the golden water," said the woman.

The child quickly handed a small flask from a kind of medicine chest, to the gipsy woman, who inundated his face with the liquid, washed his eyes and lips, and then forced a small quantity down the boy's throat; she then pulled the box to her, replaced the flask, and drew forth an ointment, and plastered the yawning wound all over.

Then the body quivered—shook; a heavy breath was drawn, the lips moved, and the eye partly opened.

Quick as thought the dwarf drew forth a powerful lens, opened the eye with his finger, and examined it with intense interest.

"I thought so," he said with a deep sigh.

"What?" cried the gipsy woman.

"Look!" continued the dwarf; "be quick; for should he see, the portrait will fade."

"What portrait?" said the gipsy.

"That of the murderer," gasped the dwarf.

The gipsy snatched the lens, and looked upon the retina.

"Dick!" she said in a low awe-struck tone.

"May I look?" asked the child in a wondering tone.

"Look once and well," whispered the dwarf, "and as you value justice and truth, never forget."

The girl did look, and then laid down the lens.

"What did you see?" said the being whom the gipsy called Sapathwa, and the house-dwellers Goldy Gordon.

"His own likeness."

"No, child; that of one who much resembles him, but that is all. Remember it well."

The girl made no reply, but leaned back in deep and amazed thought.

The gipsy and the dwarf now busied themselves in making up an extempore bed for the youth, which done, they laid him down to rest.

"And now, Miriam," said the dwarf, giving the woman money, "let him want for nothing; wine, food, raiment, medicine let him have; and when I return, let him be well and strong."

"Whither go you?" asked the woman addressed as Miriam.

"Whither goes the storm? whence comes the lightning? I know not. But as well might you ask me, as demand where I am going—where vengeance calls;" said the dwarf, in loud shrill tones.

"Good," said the gipsy, with an approving nod.

The Blue Dwarf stooped down, kissed the boy's forehead, raised his glaring eyes towards the heavens, clenched his fists, and left the hut.

The girl, who had slept some considerable time, now offered to watch, and to moisten the boy's fevered lips. Miriam accepted the offer, and lay down to sleep.

In a few minutes nothing appeared to possess life in that obscure tent, but the fairy form of that lovely child.

And thus strangely was it that our hero and heroine were brought together.

CHAPTER IX.

CONSCIOUSNESS.

WITH no intention of decrying legitimate medicine, there can, however, be no doubt, that the gipsies, in common with many wandering tribes, possessed secrets which would have made the fortune of any regular practitioner who should have been fortunate enough to become possessed of them.

The wound which had been inflicted on the lad left in charge of Miriam, was a fearfully ugly one, and being accompanied with severe fever and delirium, was a considerable time before its bad symptoms were abated. The woman and the girl were, however, unwearied in their attentions, and about three weeks after his arrival in the tents of the Roma or Zincali he opened his eyes to consciousness.

It was about mid-day, and no one was near him but the child.

"Who are you?" he asked, in a faint voice, gazing with wonder at the lovely apparition.

"Lily's my name."

"But what are you? and where am I?" asked the other, pressing his head with his two hands.

"In the tents of the gipsies," replied Lily.

"But how came I here? have I been ill?" cried the lad. "Has anything happened?"

"You were brought here nearly dead," continued the girl;" then she added with a smile, "but are you *rum*[1] or a *cur*?"[2]

"What?" cried the astonished lad.

"You should ask, too, if I am a *mort*[3] or a *rumy*?"[4]

"What gibberish are you talking?"

"Then you're not a *pal*,[5] and don't *patter flash*?"[6]

"Heavens! my good little girl. You seem a quiet little thing. Don't talk in that way."

[1] A good man. [2] A mean man. [3] A bad girl.
[4] A good girl. [5] A brother. [6] Talk cant.

"Well, I won't," she said, laughing, "if you don't like it; but it's very funny."

At this moment the entrance of the tent was moved on one side, and Miriam peeped in.

"How's the *gentry cofe* (gentleman)?" asked Miriam, in a whisper.

"*Bene* (good)," replied Lily.

"Does he want *bub* (drink)?" she continued.

"My good woman," said the youth in a low, hushed, and, from pain, almost whining voice, "do speak so that I may understand you."

"Well, my little kinchin," said the gipsy woman, with a laugh, "so you have recovered your tongue, and soon will your teeth, I warrant."

"I suppose I have been very ill?" cried the lad; but I don't know how."

"So you have no recollection whatever of how you came here?" said Miriam, seating herself at his head, as soon as Lily had given him a cup of invigorating broth, flavoured with varied herbs.

"None whatever!"

"What is your last recollection?" inquired the gipsy.

The boy closed his eyes and shuddered.

"I was in an old mill house," he said, in a voice of low horror.

"Alone?"

"No. What has become of brother Dick?"

"Boy," said Miriam, gravely, "you have terrible revelations to listen to. You know the Blue Dwarf!"

"I do, poor fellow."

"Goldy Gordon knew of your escape from—"

"Don't mention the place !" cried the lad, in an agony of excitement that showed his mind was slightly unhinged.

"As you please. He, for reasons best known to himself, determined to follow and confer with you ere he took his final departure. Just, however, as he reached the mill house, you were stabbed, unto death, the murderer thought, and rifled of every paper and document which could prove your identity,"

"Who by ?" gasped the lad.

"Cannot you guess ? Who was to be benefitted by your death, by the possession of your papers, being already tolerably like you in person ?"

"Dick !" said the lad, with a groan of both surprise and anguish.

"Unfortunately too true."

"My name, my being, my life—he coveted; however, have mercy on him."

"What intend you to do ?" asked Miriam.

"Can I remain here ?" he asked.

"As long as you please, the gipsies' tents are open to you. Your father was our friend."

"Woman, say not that again. I had no father. Let me remain dead to the world. Let me be henceforth John Smith, until the day and hour comes when I shall rise in my might and crush my enemies. But I want health, strength —aye, all will come in good time."

"As you will; but let the gipsy queen name her child. You must be brother and sister, William and Lilian Lennox. Children, you should be friends, for your fates are similar; and who knows ? the outcast and persecuted gipsy may be your friend. Lily, let him sleep now. I go to L——; when he wakes, give him another cup of broth, and to-morrow a chicken shall roast for him at the camp fire."

With these words Miriam took her leave, and the lad, now William Lennox, overwhelmed, astounded, horrified, at what had been communicated to him, turned his face towards the canvas of the tent and affected to sleep.

CHAPTER X.
THE STEP-FATHER.

THE reader must pardon us, if before we plunge headlong into the whirl of terrible, ludicrous, and startling revelations and adventures which befel our hero and heroine in the battle for life, we introduce certain characters, who are necessary to the elucidation of our mysteries.

The branch of the Blakesleys to which belonged the mansion with which our narrative is more particularly connected, had a strange and mysterious character.

It was a tradition of this family that the eldest son never inherited the baronetcy.

Fifty years previous to the occurrences which we have already related, there was a Sir Nathaniel Blakesley, who had two sons.

John Stewart was the name of the elder.

William that of the second.

John Stewart was an officer in the navy, and during his early career as a midshipman had fallen in love with a Dutch girl. Now the pride of the Blakesleys was great, but not to the degree of objecting that one of its sons should fall in love with a beautiful Hollander. Had John Stewart been a profligate, betrayed the seductive Cornelia, and abandoned mother and child to ruin and destitution, not a word would have been said.

But the descendant of some Norman robber, or Danish pirate, married the girl ! an act of profligacy not to be forgiven.

The old baronet endeavoured to cut off the entail, but could not without the consent of his son.

That son, when he found that his marriage had offended his father, threw up his commission in disgust, and entered the Dutch service.

He and his wife started for Java.

From the day of their sailing neither they nor the vessel were ever heard of.

At the death of his father, William, then a youth, inherited the baronetcy, married a pretty girl of no great energy, by whom he had one son—Edgar.

When the boy was twelve years of age, his father died.

After a year's mourning, his mother married James Tyrrel Blakesley, a distant cousin, and, failing Edgar, the heir to the baronetcy and estates.

The disgust of all her friends was shown by their coldness, and by their ceasing to visit.

Now Lady Caroline Blakesley loved her son, as much as any woman of her listless nature could love anything. But she was vain, coquettish, and passionately fond of admiration.

James Tyrrel Blakesley knew this, and played his cards accordingly.

When he, in affected astonishment and admiration, let forth, as if unwittingly, his belief in her being five-and-twenty when she was five-and-thirty, her heart was gone.

Three hundred and sixty-five days after burying one husband, she was united to another.

James Tyrrel Blakesley was no common man. Profoundly cunning, he saw at once into the character of the young baronet. Of noble and genial character, possessed of talents of no common order, he was peculiarly sensitive. His step-father adopted towards him a course of haughty superiority, which to the lad was peculiarly offensive. Mr. James treated him like a child, snubbed him when he spoke, and precluded him from sitting at table when company was present.

The boy began to mope, and to suffer in health.

Then Mr. James Tyrrel Blakesley went to town for a week, and when he returned the illness of the youth appeared to increase.

Then it was that those ghostly shadows on the wall might have been seen flitting about the passages of the old mansion.

But whatever may have been the objects of the step-father, Edgar would not die.

Utterly disgusted with his home, vague terror assailing him, his mother powerless to defend him, he determined to run away to sea.

He had been gone about three weeks, and the most genuine and persevering efforts had been made to discover his retreat—the mother being inconsolable, and the father terrified lest the boy should fall into hands who might advise him to contest his authority.

The will of the deceased Sir William Blakesley contained a secret clause, as yet unopened, of which his solicitors would not violate the seal, until a circumstance should occur which they declined to indicate.

The husband and wife were at breakfast. It was eleven o'clock. A party of men had stayed late with the master of the house the night before, and the champagne corks had flown pretty profusely. Mr. James Tyrrel Blakesley had a headache, and Lady Blakesley was ill-tempered.

"I am quite sure," said the latter pettishly, "that you have not done your best. Poor dear Edgar! why should he run away?"

"I have always told you, madam, that there was a tint of insanity in his nature," replied the gentleman with great acerbity.

"Mr. James, I am surprised at you. There never was any insanity in my family," continued the lady, with a toss of the head.

"There has been always one madman in the Blakesleys' family," growled the husband.

"I wish, sir, you would keep such indecent observations to yourself," cried the lady.

"Madam, I never make indecent observations."

"But you won't tell me about poor Edgar," said the mother, who was leaning back in her chair in exquisite déshabille.

"I have done everything in my power," he replied. "I have put him in the 'Hue and Cry.' I have given information at Bow-street."

"Mr. Dawson!" said a servant entering, "and very anxious to see you, sir.

"Show him up," replied the gentleman, quickly; "the very man I want to see."

"Really," said Lady Blakesley, languidly, "it is too bad, that even at meal times, when Dr. Good says I should be calm and unruffled, I must be bored with business."

"Very agreeable business, Caroline," replied the husband playfully, the subject always did put him in a good humour, "that of receiving money—eh, Caroline?"

"I take no interest in such low subjects," said the lady with an affected yawn.

"Good morning, Dawson! Had breakfast? Yes? Eh! what's the matter, man? Pale, trembling, agitated! Anything wrong?"

"Well! my respects, sir; my respects Mrs. Blakesley," stammered the steward.

"The man's mad," said James Tyrrel, rising.

"No, sir; not mad," said the steward, wiping his pallid brow, on which the perspiration stood in heavy drops.

"Have you got the money and lost it?" began Mr. James, while the lady quietly sipped her chocolate.

"No; but I have here written directions to pay no more money to you, under any circumstances; in fact, to confine myself wholly to the jointure of—of—your wife."

"D——!" cried the husband wildly; "but why don't you say Lady Blakesley?"

"Because the orders emanate from Sir John Stewart Blakesley's ——," began.

"You drivelling idiot!" cried the other furiously, "he has been dead these fifty years."

"But his son is not!"

"His son! in the name of the devil, what is the meaning of all this?" gasped James.

"Speak, Dawson, or I shall faint," said the lady, laying down her spoon.

"I will explain myself," said the steward, seating himself, and producing a packet of papers. "Last night a special messenger from London came down from Messrs. Grant and Melton, the old family solicitors, whom you, sir, have thought proper to dismiss, informing me that they had received instructions from Sir John Stewart Blakesley, son of the late Sir John Stewart Blakesley, born at Batavia in the year 17—, to take possession of the estates. They enclosed copies of affidavits from the Governor of Batavia, the captain and mate of the ship Herr Klaüs, three doctors, an English clergyman, a nurse, with the dying declaration of the then Mrs. Blakesley."

"Well!" gasped James.

"The evidence is undoubted. There is not a shadow of doubt. The late Sir John Stewart Blakesley was a prisoner several years in Borneo, and his son, it appears, was sold there into slavery. He is now forty-seven years of age."

"But this claim," said James, "will not hold water; it is a monstrous fraud."

Dawson shook his head.

"How mean you? are you leagued with these impostors?" cried James.

"Sir, there is no imposture in the case. I am seventy years of age, and can swear both to the handwriting of the late Sir John. Look at the papers for yourself."

"I suppose this infernal letter," taking one up from a packet of unopened epistles, "is something in relation to the matter."

He tore it open with more of the manner of a savage than a man, and uttered a fearful curse as he read it.

"James! James!" said his wife, in genuine surprise and disgust, "how can you?"

"'Sblood, ma'am, if you can look men in the face, I cannot. This is notice of an action for ejectment against us, as the guardians of Sir Edgar Blakesley. It is utter ruin!"

"But, James, there is my jointure."

"D——n your jointure, ma'am! What is a paltry twelve hundred a-year to me? I married you to become master of twelve thousand."

"What!" shrieked the unfortunate woman; "surely you did not marry me for my money?"

The steward shuddered. How could he be master of twelve thousand a year while the young baronet lived?

"In the name of fortune, madam," said the furious and baffled schemer, "what else could have induced me to tie myself to an old woman, when twenty young girls would have jumped at the chance?"

With a faint cry, a pressure of the hand upon her heart, Lady Caroline leaned back in her chair. Dawson rushed to the bell.

"No!" she said, with a cold smile and a scornful coil of the lip. "I am quite well. A little pang, that was all—it is quite over."

"But, Dawson," said James, after some little

reflection, "we must resist this scheme; we must raise money."

"But the worst is yet to come," replied Dawson, looking down on the ground.

"Merciful heaven, what!"

"An application has been made to the Court of Chancery, and pending the trial for ejectment, a receiver has been appointed to the estates."

"He had better not come here ———," cried James with a savage oath.

"He has come, and this morning served notices on all the tenants not to pay one farthing to you or your agents. They will none of them dare disobey the order of the Court of Chancery."

"And, in the name of all the furies, who is this receiver?" continued James Blakesley.

"The wild cripple, known as the Blue Dwarf," replied Dawson.

"Hell and furies! that accursed, damnable, wicked little fiend!" cried James, raising his clenched fists to the ceiling. "I'll wring his hideous neck. I'll——"

"What will you do, eh?" said a harsh and croaking voice at his elbow.

He turned, and there was the Blue Dwarf, seated on a music-stool, his knees drawn up to his chin, his long arms clutching the seat of the stool, and his whole glance expressing that vindictive style of triumph and malice which only a dwarf can exemplify.

By his side were two genteel-looking individuals, whose garb, at a date when one could tell a parson from a waiter, and a gentleman from a gent, sufficiently indicated their belonging to the profession of the law.

"Who the devil is this whelp?" cried Mr. James Tyrrel Blakesley fiercely.

"Ah! ah! ah! whelp! Good!" grinned the Dwarf, showing his filed teeth.

"Mr. James Tyrrel Blakesley," said one of the black-coated individuals with white chokers, "we should advise you to be more circumspect in your language—would'nt you, John!"

"Exactly," observed the individual spoken to as John.

"And pray who the devil are you," yelled, rather than said, Mr. Blakesley.

"Grant and Grogan," said the first speaker mildly. "Is it not so, John?"

"Exactly," replied the other, whose whole mind seemed absorbed in his gloves—tight ones, which he could not get on.

"Well, Grant and Grogan," continued Mr. James Blakesley in a bullying tone, "what do you want here?"

"Simply that we are obeying the instructions of our client, Sir John Stewart Blakesley, baronet, who has obtained an order from the Chancellor to appoint a receiver to the estates. We are here by the directions of our client, to induct Mr. Goldy Gordon in his function."

"Sir John Stewart Blakesley has been dead these fifty years."

"No! only thirty-seven," said the first speaker. "I believe that is it, John?"

"Exactly," replied the other, taking a pinch of snuff.

"And his son is now Sir John in his place," continued the imperturbable lawyer.

"All this will have to be proved in a court of law," began Mr. James Blakesley.

"So it appears," said the lawyer drily "We are here to demand possession."

"Which I refuse."

"Which you refuse. Exactly," pursued the man of writs and briefs. "I expected as much. I only came as a matter of form. Mr. Blakesley, your most obedient."

"Ah!" said the Dwarf with a hideous and ferocious grin. "So, Mister James, you refuse possession, do you? Well, just as you please. Pride will have a fall."

"Leave my house!" shouted James. "Go! or I will send for a constable and have you expelled!"

"Expelled! Who?" cried the Dwarf, sideling to the master of the house. "Constable! What for? *I hav'nt poisoned any body, I hope?*"

James looked at him with a livid countenance, in which rage overcame every other consideration.

"Go!" he yelled.

"Ough!" said the Dwarf, in a tone impossible to be rendered. "I am going—expelled by Mr. James Blakesley. Oh! oh! oh! Ah! ah! ah! Let those laugh who win. How's your friend, Minto Malespina, eh?"

And with a flash of the eyes like covert lightning, the Dwarf put up his long arms into those of the two lawyers, and slowly left the room.

"The hideous monster!" gasped Lady Blakesley.

"Monster!" said James in a low, hushed tone, his eyes wildly rolling, his lips pale, his countenance livid. "Double distilled monster! But worse than that; vile reptile as he is, we are wholly in his power."

"How so?" said his wife.

"Idiot!" cried the considerate husband, "think you I will trust my secret to a woman."

Lady Caroline Blakesley fixed a withering look upon him, and rising, left the room.

"Dawson," said Mr. James Blakesley as soon as they were alone, "ring the bell for lunch. We will talk matters over, with a foaming glass by our sides. I mean to fight to the last gasp."

"Certainly," replied Dawson, who at the same time rang the bell.

Lunch was brought, flanked by several bottles of wine; and then master and servant sat down to confer on the events which had so terribly startled them.

CHAPTER XI.

THE FLIGHT.

On a sunny bank, where the violet grew, beneath a hedge all redolent of May, beside a clear and crystal stream, in which floated past the finny trout, sat, some months after the accident, or attempted assassination, William and Lily Lennox.

The lad had recovered his health, but not his spirits. A fearful cloud of sorrow and despair appeared to have settled on his soul. He had not recovered the awful shock of his attempted murder. With the exception of Lily, he suspected everybody.

He was, indeed, in the very worst mood of mind in which a human being can find himself, that of chronic suspicion, doubt, and dread—the predecessor too often of madness.

No stranger could come near him without exciting in him feelings of alarm.

He knew it, and knew too that it was the result of physical and mental weakness, produced by his severe illness.

Knowing this, he was wont, taking Lily for his guide, to wander in copse, over plain, and through woodland, in search of health, and, what is above all to be coveted in this world, peace of mind.

But it would not come.

There was a dead weight of sorrow and a memory of horrors which he could not eradicate.

His only relief and rest was conversation with Lily.

"And so," he said, "my little pet remembers nothing previous to the gipsy camp?"

"Nothing," she replied, shaking her rich auburn curls.

"And yet you are not a gipsy," he added.

"No; Miriam has always been careful to impress this on my mind—why I know not—that I am not of her race."

The boy looked curiously at Lily.

"Can you read?"

"No."

"Write?"

"No."

"Merciful heavens!" cried William Lennox, "then what do you know?"

"How to knit baskets and patter flash," said the lively girl innocently.

"Of heaven, of a future state, of your soul, of religion—nothing," said the lad in a hushed whisper.

"I don't know what you mean," replied Lily.

William Lennox clasped his hands and looked at his companion with perfect awe. They were lying down on the fragrant bank, just where the shade of the hedge and a tall tree fell. On the other side of the hedge was a field in which some haymakers had been at work.

Suddenly Lily placed her fingers on her lips, and motioned to William to be silent.

The boy distinctly heard two men in conversation on the other side of the hedge, but what they spoke about he could not understand.

"Is it a *gentry cove*[1]?"

"His *benjamin*[2] was spry, and his *blue-billy*[3] first-rate; but he pattered flash like a rum."

"He wasn't a *bit-faker*?"[4]

"No, a regular blood, free of his *horse nails*."[5]

"And he wanted the *titter*[6] as well as the *kinchin*!"[7]

"And said if we'd meet him at the boozing-kens[8] with the *dell*[9] and kinchen co,[10] he'd carry them off to Rum-ville,"[11] continued the first speaker.

"He's! a *don*—and *fly*? won't *fox* us?"

"Oh, no. We're to have ten neds a-piece."

"Then I'm your stallsman."

And as if the matter was decided, the men now moved away, leaving the lad and girl alone.

1. Gentleman. 2. Coat. 3. Handkerchief with diamond spots. 4. Coiner. 5. Money. 6. Girl. 7. Boy. 8. Pot-house. 9. Girl. 10. Boy. 11. London.

"They were talking about us," said William Lennox, in a low voice, his lips quivering, and his eyes emitting a strange light.

Lily explained all they had said.

"I will not be taken," cried William convulsively; "I will fly."

"But where?"

"Anywhere. I will go at once."

"And leave me?" said the child, in a low hushed voice, her eyes cast sadly on the ground.

"Lily," replied William, taking her hand, "I am pursued by enemies. Rather than I would fall into the power of a man I hate, I would perish in the pool at our feet. I must go. There is no hope for me but in flight. If, then, we may not part you must come with me."

"When I am a woman you will marry me?" said Lily, bending down her eyes.

She had not lived among the gipsies without learning the evil ways of life.

"Yes!" cried William, pressing her hand to his heart; "be my future good or ill, be my fate greatness, or do I fall into the depths and dregs of life, you shall be my wife."

"Then will I go with you," she said.

"Come; it is time to go," he replied, rising.

"Now?"

"This minute. I would not return to the camp and be in those men's power for all the treasures of the world."

And thus, hand in hand, like our first parents leaving paradise, penniless, houseless, with sorry raiment, and no food, the two children—they were little more—went out into the wide world in search of safety from what appeared a relentless foe.

Lily, who was far more advanced in experience of life than William, advised that they should beg their way to London, sleeping at tramp lodging-houses and low inns, where the knowledge of slang, and the mystic hieroglyphics of the thieving and begging professions, tolerably well akin one to the other, would ensure them good treatment and cheap entertainment.

"Beg?" said William, in a low voice.

"Would you rather steal?" replied Lily, in a surprised tone.

Those were her only two ideas of gaining a living.

"No!" cried William thoughtfully; "of course not. But who knows? something better may turn up."

In a hurry to escape a neighbourhood so fraught with danger, he pressed on, so that talking became a somewhat difficult task. Their path was for some distance along the banks of a stream; at length, however, they reached a dusty highway. Close to the bridge which spanned the river was a milestone, and on it was written—

LONDON: 204 MILES.

"Two hundred and four miles," said William aloud; "it is a long way."

"How do you know?" asked the girl.

"Can't you read?" cried the amazed youth.

"No; what's that?" continued Lily.

Scarcely able to speak from astonishment, William Lennox, after a moment or two, explained to the girl his meaning. Naturally quick and shrewd, she soon understood what he meant.

"But you will teach me?" she said.

"With pleasure. And now let us start. The sooner we get to London the sooner we shall be safe;" and, taking her hand, he started on his strange journey.

The road was dusty, the day was warm, and evening came. They were tired, thirsty, and hungry; still William would not think of turning back.

"I am very tired," said Lily at last in a faint voice.

"So am I," replied William; "we must rest. In yonder field is a large barn. We must lie down. After a rest we will start again; we may reach a town before the houses all close."

Poor Lily sighed. Well she might, for she was not only tired but faint with hunger, and feverish from thirst. They were ten miles away from the rich flesh-pots of Egypt.

The barn was capacious, and contained piles of clean straw. It was in good preservation, but though far away from any houses, it was unlocked.

The two weary trampers climbed on some straw, and, hand in hand, lay down to sleep, and soon, despite the keen pangs of hunger and thirst, their eyes closed in slumber.

Qui dort dine, says the French philosopher, and, to a certain extent, there is truth in the axiom, for the sufferer from hunger is often, from the very nature of his thoughts, regaled upon luxurious banquets in his sleep, such as never visit his waking hours.

But terrible must be the awakening of the hungry man who has no hope of a meal.

In no civilised country should such a thing be; nor would it if half that is spent to punish crime were laid out to prevent it.

For one man to own millions of acres in the same land where another is consuming by inches from the visits of the gaunt spectre is a greater crime than to steal.

The earth we live on is our own.

There are no helots in civilised societies.

When society does not provide food, it must expect to have it taken.

*   *   *   *   *   *   *

William Lennox had slept some time when he was awoke by a noise close to him, and opening his eyes he found that the barn was tenanted by several besides themselves, while an insiduous odour of stew assailed his nostrils. With a caution, taught him by his misfortunes, he did not move, but listened.

Without moving, too, he could see.

In the centre of the barn was a small fire, over which, supported by an iron tripod, was a large saucepan, which a stern woman, about forty, was stirring with a long ladle. She was stout, her hair was dishevelled, her face exceeding ruddy, and here and there spotted with roseate pimples. An old battered bonnet, with loose ribbons, was upon her head; while her gown, the waist of which was under her armpits, was of a faded green.

To her right was a youth of about nineteen, who over flesh tights had put on a rough sailor's great coat. His hair was cropped short, and a helmet that had seen service in the wars lay at his feet, while he wiped away the perspiration from his brow with a cotton pocket-handkerchief. Little round eyes, a snub nose, and large mouth, made up a countenance more comical than comely.

A fat girl of about nineteen, with low dress, a face that but for dissipation and drink had once been pretty, stood affectedly on one leg practising a position. She was in the costume of a ballet girl, with exceedingly short petticoats and ancle boots, the former being covered with spangles. She had cast a cloak, that served to screen her somewhat light costume, to the ground, in order to stand up on one leg in an attitude which she believed becoming.

"Now, Anastasia, will you leave off? Toast the Yarmouth capons.[1] And you, Lexy, start for the wobble-shop.[2] There's the jug. Don't forget the start naked,[3] and now vamos![4]"

Anastasia with a sigh came to a more natural standing position, and Lexy put on his helmet.

"Twig the titter,[5]" said Lexy with a growl; "it's always me. I shall tip my boom."

And while growling, he however rose and prepared to depart, while Anastatia hung half-a-dozen bloaters in front of the fire on a kind of rack.

William Lennox waited until the men were out of hearing ere he spoke. He was aware that Lily was awake, because she had touched his arm.

"My good woman," he said, rising up into a sitting position, "dont be alarmed."

"Murder!" shouted the fat woman. "Anastasia where's the barking irons?[6]"

Anastasia clasped her hands, and stood on one leg in an attitude,

"It's only a boy and girl," said William; "we were very tired, and lay down to rest."

"Tired and hungry," exclaimed Lily, "with no *brads*[7] for the *suck-cassa*.[8]"

"Let's look at you," said the stout woman, seating herself on a solid stool.

Both came forward and stood in front of the woman.

"Hold up your twopennies," she cried, "and let's see; you're no street pitchers. Where did you learn to patter flash."

"With the gipsies," said Lily.

"Oh! and you say you're hungry."

"Dying with hunger," repeated the girl.

"Then in the name of heaven sit down and eat," said the woman, snatching up a wooden platter, which she loaded with the stew that filled the barn with its fragrant odour. This she placed before Lily.

"Now it's your turn," she continued, addressing William. "Don't say a word; eat. It's ill talking on an empty stomach."

Our hero and heroine did not wait to be asked twice, but, their appetites whetted by exercise and abstinence, eat the worthy woman's provender with a pleasure which neither of them remembered to have experienced before.

"Don't it do you good to see 'em eat?" said the stout woman, as she helped Anastasia.

---

1 Bloaters.   2 Unlicensed beershop.   3 Gin.   4 Go.
5 Girl.   6 Pistols.   7 Money.   8 Public-house.

"Blest if they won't eat it all," cried the ballet girl. "I say, my little mannikeu, did you ever eat before?"

"Why?" said William, with a smile.

"Because, if you did'nt, you're a remarkable good scholard," responded the girl.

William smiled again, but made no reply. He was by far too busy to talk.

"Eh! what's up?" suddenly said a voice. "What cutters are these?"

"None of your cranky nonsense, you regular crib-biter," replied the stout woman. "Let's have the copus, and don't be a jerry-cowan."

The woman, without further words, poured out a glass of beer for both William and Lily, after which she began questioning them as to their history and future prospects, which she did, to the lad's great delight, without any ad-mixture of slang:

"Our history," he replied, "it is unnecessary to enter into. For reasons of our own we have left the gipsy tribe we had taken refuge with—never to return. Our future prospects are bad enough, for we have no money, and no chance of earning any."

"Ahem!" said the stout woman. "What say you to joining us?—Jottley and Co. I'm Jottley, and the Co. is my husband. We're doing the needles and pin, handkerchief, calico, and Cheap John business now, but when our Co. joins us we does the legitimate dramer, and no mistake. She would make a capital Columbine, and, with care and attention, you might rise to be a 'Arle-quin. Eh! what say you?

"My good woman!" cried William Lennox, warmly, "I accept at once. You raise us from misery and wretchedness to the very height of happiness. You put us in the way of getting our living honestly—what more can we ask."

"I say, missus, ain't you bosky?" said the man, sullenly. "Ain't our company too big already?"

"Silence, bufflehead!" replied the woman. "These two 'ull bring more nor ten of you buskers."

The Clown growled, the ballet-girl cast up her eyes, but no further objection was made; for Mistress Jottley plied them both with food and drink, and one hour later the whole party in the barn were fast asleep.

CHAPTER XII.

THE FLOWER-SHOP.

THERE was a neat little shop in the Strand—not the garish Strand of the present day, with its gas and its universal glare of light; but the sober street of the end of the reign of George III., when oil illumined the scene at night, and watch-men did the duty of the new police. This shop was celebrated as furnishing the fashionable supporters of the theatres and other places of amusement with the very best French gloves, the finest scent, and even the most odorous bouquets in all London.

Far and wide had its celebrity spread, until not to glove at Lipscombe's was to be unfashion-able.

How much of this was owing to the attractions of the *belle bouquetiere* we leave to the sagacity of our readers.

In the full flush of womanly loveliness, with a flood of golden hair, with large almond-shaped eyes, a skin that combined the

"Lily that is all in white"

with the hue of the dainty rose with its tender red; a mouth small, pouting, and tipped as with a blush; with an elegant form of middle stature, and one of those inexplicable winning expres-sions which charm we know not why.

Mrs. Lipscombe was the acknowledged *belle* of the neighbourhood, and not a single trades-man within a considerable radius but would gladly have made her the partner of his joys and sorrows for life.

But Mrs. Lipscombe gently refused every offer, however tempting.

And yet there were hangers on enough. There was not a fop or puppy who bought gloves or scent, but thought himself justified in making love to the *belle bouquetiere*.

They were, however, restrained in their expressions of love by the presence of a kind of companion, who never left the premises, under any pretence, when customers were present.

The lovely owner of the shop, though by no means averse to conversation, and well aware of the necessity in her business of yielding in some degree to the whims and oddities of her customers, never listened for one moment to any importunities.

Did any of her patrons so far forget them-selves as to become too familiar in their pro-positions, they were at once handed over to Miss Martha Snelling, a lady so opposite in all things as to resemble vinegar beside honey.

This system induced the treating of Mrs. Lipscombe with an amount of respect which at length grew habitual.

None liked to be handed over to the sour-faced and pock-marked Miss Martha Snelling.

Still many were the efforts made, numerous the attempts to pervert and corrupt the beautiful girl, whose history was veiled in such singular obscurity.

Was she maid, wife, or widow?

To this question none could give a satisfactory answer.

Among the long list of admirers who fluttered in the orbit of Mrs. Lipscombe's attractions, none was more ardent or persevering than Lord Charles Lutterel.

Lutterel was an officer in the Guards, im-mensely rich, a known *roué* who was prepared to make any sacrifice for the satisfaction of his passions, and whose name had been twice prominent in divorce cases, while it was said that his humbler victims could be counted by hundreds.

He was one of the patrons of those lazars of society—of one of those beings for whom we should fancy there could be scarcely forgiveness in the other world, however deep their re-pentance.

A murderer is a venial criminal to the pro-fessional procurer or procuress.

At the time of which we speak the character was a common one.

We need not say it was lucra ive.

Shame and infamy to those who, with rank, wealth, and power at their command, were the supporters of these vile blots on human nature, these gnawing curses on the fabric of civilisation and enlightenment.

We would fain hope that a better state of things is in existence now.

At all events it is something to know that the odious traffickers in flesh and blood in the present day, are not English. They are either Germans or French.

Lord Charles Lutterel, an experienced man about town, and a professional seducer, had for two whole years devoted a large proportion of his time to the lovely and fascinating Mrs. Lipscombe, and, to his great discomfiture, in vain.

So certain of success had he been—unfortunately he was well aware how seldom women refuse to stoop to folly, when the tempter is a lord—that he had boasted of his coming conquest at his club.

Colonel Grimstone, a rival, who had, despite his high position amid the profligate men about town, utterly failed in the same quarter, had piqued his vanity.

"It's no use, Lutterel," he said, "not the slightest. Where I have been defeated, think not to succeed."

And he glanced at his handsome figure in the club mirror.

"I allow your powers of fascination," replied Lord Charles coolly; "but at the same time I venture to bet you a cool thousand I do."

"Honour bright? no boasting?" said the colonel.

"Exactly. It shall be a perfect victory. She shall decide the bet herself, because I will undertake to appear with her publicly as my mistress."

"Done," said the colonel; and amid the laughter of the club this atrocious bet was booked.

This was about a week before we present Mrs. Lipscombe to our readers; and during that period the young nobleman—he was about five-and-thirty—had gone wholly upon another tack.

He was respectful and melancholy. When he came into the shop he sat down upon a seat in a corner, and scarcely ever spoke. His eyes were all the time fixed upon Mrs. Lipscombe, with an expression of the deepest and most profound melancholy.

The young woman, who could not eject so excellent a customer, became first irritated, then sorrowful, then puzzled.

His obstinate addiction to her shop could do her no possible injury, as her character was well known.

She had, moreover, a strict rule.

Her shop was never allowed to be made a lounge until after four, when her casual and lady customers had transacted all business.

Still, the perseverance of this suitor was, to say the least, disagreeable.

CHAPTER XIII.
THE DARK STRANGER.

MRS. LIPSCOMBE and Miss Martha Snelling were behind the counter.

Lord Charles Lutterel was in his arm-chair sucking the end of his gold-topped cane.

Mrs. Lipscombe and Miss Martha Snelling were replacing numerous packets of gloves in their proper receptacles.

Lord Charles Lutterel was in deep thought.

"I cannot, and I will not stand this state of things any longer," said the young nobleman, suddenly rising.

"What do you mean, my lord," replied the *belle bouquetiere.*

"I mean, angel, devil, or whatever you may be, that I love you to distraction," he said, leaning over the counter.

"I thought, my lord, that subject was prohibited," continued Mrs. Lipscombe, coldly.

"Why be so cold? why deprive me of the only topic in which I feel the slightest interest? I love the very air you breathe; why should I not say so? I doat on the rays of light which fall from those lovely orbs of sunshine. For permission to cull sweets from those ruby lips, I would give my soul——"

"Really, my lord, this is going beyond the bounds of that liberty which you gentlemen allow yourselves with us poor waiters on your pleasure. I cannot and I will not listen."

"Cold icicle! lovely statue! will your heart never beat for man?" he continued.

"My heart is dead," she said coldly, but resolutely.

"But have you no ambition, no pride, no desire to shine above your fellows?"

"How so, my lord?"

"To be a queen among women—to ride in splendid carriages—to dress like a princess, to revel in silks, satins, and laces—to be surrounded by luxury, by dozens of servants obedient to your slightest will," cried Lord Charles Lutterel enthusiastically.

"I am too lowly to become Lady Lutterel," she said coldly.

"By heavens!" exclaimed the nobleman, turning crimson, "who asked you to be so?"

"My lord, do you wish to insult me?" she said.

Standing erect, perfectly Juno-like in her beauty, with flashing eye, her whole rich and voluptuous person swelling with indignation, she looked the incarnation of beauty.

Lord Charles Lutterel bowed for once to womanly loveliness.

"Make your own terms," he said hoarsely; "wife, if you will, Satanic demon; but mine you shall be."

"Never!" she said coldly. "Had you made me this offer at first, I might have thought myself honoured, and have thanked you. But as you do so only after an insult which no right-minded woman can bear, I reject your last offer with as much scorn as I do your first."

"Reflect!" he whispered hoarsely.

"I have decided," she replied.

Her heart strangely fluttered, for as she spoke she could see a pair of dark piercing eyes, gazing at her with keen and absorbing curiosity.

They belonged to a man tanned by the sun, but whose form and features were nearly concealed by a slouching hat and loose cloak.

"Beware," said Lord Charles Lutterel, still in his hushed and hoarse voice, "beware how you

anger me, for by my soul I swear that if you will not be mine as my wife, you shall ask for that title on your bended knees.

"My lord, I scorn you. Leave the premises or I will call the watch," she cried aloud.

"Woman," said the young nobleman, his lips livid, his countenance pale, his eyes red with meteoric light, "woman, drive me not to desperation, for I do love you from my soul."

"I reject and repudiate your love."

"By the heavens that made us," he began, and as he did so he clutched her wrist——

"Unhand me, insulting wretch. Let me go," she cried.

"Never!"

"Let go, *my lord*," said a deep hollow voice at his elbow, at the same time clutching his right and disengaged hand.

"Leopold !"

"George !"

The first exclamation was from Lord Charles Lutterel, who loosened his hold on Mrs. Lipscombe; the latter from the *belle bouquetiere*.

"Yes, *my lord*," said the stranger, emphasising his words, "it is the injured being you allude to; but this is no time or place for us. Go ! When the hour comes I will not shun you. The murderer has yet to be tried."

Without a word, furious, with a blanched cheek, the young nobleman went out. He, however, stood a little way off, and peered in.

Mrs. Lipscombe fell upon the stranger's neck, and wept.

Then appearing to remember her position, she took him by the hand and led him into her little parlour, of which she closed the door.

Lord Charles Lutterel stamped his feet with rage, and re-entered the shop.

"Miss Martha," he said in a low tone, "will you be my friend?"

"My lord, really ——"

"There are a hundred guineas in this purse," he whispered. "There will be no limit to my generosity. I know your worth."

"Really, my lord," simpered the damsel, clutching the purse, and secreting it with a rapidity quite edifying, "you are so persuasive."

"Can you come out to-night?"

"Well, I don't know. Yes," she added bending down her eyes.

"Take this card. I will meet you at nine. Watch that man, who has just gone in. He is an escaped felon. But don't say a word."

And Lord Charles Lutterel vanished, leaving the sour-faced damsel utterly bewildered with astonishment at the rapidity of the nobleman's resolves.

She then read the card. Imagine her astonishment when she deciphered the following:—

STUNNING JOE BANKS,
Dyott-street,
Seven Dials.

Ask for Rowley.

"For mercy sake! what can he mean?" she cried aloud. "But I'll go. A hundred pounds is not to be earned every day. And then, who knows?"

CHAPTER XIV.

THE CHASE.

MEANWHILE Mrs. Lipscombe and the stranger had entered the parlour of the little shop in the Strand, and no sooner were they alone than she fell sobbing and laughing into his arms.

"How could you!" she said.

And that was every word of reproach after an absence of thirteen years.

"My beloved, my soul, my Lucy!" he replied, fondly caressing her flood of golden hair. "I was not my own master. There is no time now to relate the fearful and terrible tale I have to tell. I must fly."

"But why? do you know that man?"

"Know him!" gasped Captain George; "know him! Why he is my brother!"

"Gracious heavens!" cried Lucy, turning deadly pale; "you are then——"

"Leopold Lord Lutterel," said the young man, proudly.

"Say not so; do not repeat that," cried Lucy, wildly.

"Why?" asked the highwayman.

"You are not the assassin of Ada Wilmot," she said, closing her eyes.

"I am not," said he in return. "Lucy, my hands are innocent of blood; and it is to avenge that most foul and unnatural crime, and to rescue

my unhappy father, that I have come to England."

"But how came you to be accused?" she said, raising her eyes to his.

She knew that he had spoken the truth, from the very tone of his voice.

"That is my fearful tale. But the proofs of my innocence are not yet found. There is a witness living who can exonerate me. In the meantime I must not allow my unnatural twin-brother to find me. Even now I have loitered too long. Farewell! I will write, and appoint a meeting. Farewell. Hark! they come," he cried, locking the door from the shop. "Is there a back way?"

"Open, in the king's name!" said a hoarse voice.

"There is none. My God! I have ruined you."

"Is there a means of gaining the roof?"

"Yes; be quick. I will detain them."

Captain George passed through the door leading to the upper part of the house.

"Open, or I will break down the door!" repeated the voice.

"A moment, I am dressing," said the pretended Mrs. Lipscombe, in as calm a tone as she could assume.

Then, quick as thought, she let fall her hair in one loose mass over her shoulders, and, as if yielding to violence, opened the door.

Two out of three officers ran quickly up stairs. They were the old Bow-street runners, the fathers of our detectives.

"Now, marm," said the third, "you'll be getting yourself into precious trouble, a 'arboring 'ighwayman."

"I have harboured no highwayman. A gentleman of my acquaintance, no highwayman, was here a moment ago. He has now departed."

"Not by the shop," said the husky voice of Lord Charles Lutterel.

"You there, my lord?" cried Lucy Lipscombe. "You! Heaven! surely you do not know who it is?"

"I do; and since you force me to speak—the impostor who was foisted on my family as a twin, the false Lord Leopold, the noted highwayman, and the murderer of Ada Wilmot."

"My eye!" said the runner, actually taking off his hat, as much to the eminence of the criminal as to the live lord who stood before him. "Your honour's lordship is sure as 'ow he never vamoosed by the shop?"

"Certain. He is in the house," replied Lord Charles.

Lucy clasped her hands in mortal agony, for at that instant a shot was fired, and a heavy rush down stairs proclaimed that the officers were in full chase.

Without a moment's hesitation the runner shouted out to his companions—"Vich side?"

"The left."

Away scudded the runner at full speed, and dashed into the next shop, which was a chemist's, and without a word, simply showing his staff, rushed up stairs.

"A 'ighwayman's got into your 'ouse," said the second officer.

"Bless my soul!" cried the dentist, a respectable looking old gentleman, with spectacles on his nose; "how very absurd!"

The escape, up to the present moment, of Captain George, as we shall call him until his assertion is proved or disproved, had taken place in a very simple manner. He had bounded up the stairs of the house in the Strand with that lightness of foot which was always a distinguishing characteristic of his physical being. He rushed for the garret, which opened on a gutter, beyond which was a parapet; and seeing that the next was open, was in the act of rushing in when the officer fired.

When the smoke cleared away he was nowhere to be seen.

Still they were persuaded that he had entered there, and with this idea in their heads they divided, one keeping watch, the other going down stairs.

"Vell," said the first speaker, Bill Johnson, a noted runner, bobbing his head out of the other window, "he ain't here."

"Ain't he?" replied the second officer. "Now as I seed him go in——"

He did not finish his sentence, for at that moment he caught a glimpse of his ample cloak and slouched hat on the roof of a house a few stories farther on.

Jumping out of window, he ran along the parapet towards the house in question, which, unlike others, was flat-roofed, while a large platform supported a pigeon cot.

"Now then," said the panting officer, "I sees you. Give up."

And he clutched at the cloak, which remained in his hand. But the man was not in it.

"Well, I'm derluded," said the officer; "but come along—he's got into the Rubicund Quadruped."

And followed by his men, the runner descended a kind of winding stair, and in a few minutes they were at the bar.

"Hollo!" said the landlord, rising from his chair, where he was taking his ease, "what's up?"

"A 'ighwayman, Mr. Potter," replied the officer, "'as just got hinside your roof-trap. Didn't you see him come down?"

"I never," cried Mr. Potter. "A gent did just go out, but I thought he came out of the parlour."

"Done, by gum," said Mr. Bill Johnson, after a cursory glance up and down the street, which, as he had but a very indistinct idea of the man's appearance, was rather useless. "But had he a hat on? Here is his own."

"Licked, by Jove," replied Mr. Potter, after glancing at a peg at the foot of the stairs. "Hanged if he didn't nod to me with my own hat. I thought I knowed it."

The company at the bar, who were of the better sort chiefly, laughed outright.

"Well," said Potter, looking very hard at a man who, seated on a stool without the bar, was smoking and drinking very slowly a glass of gin and water, "it's a pretty thing to be robbed and laughed at too. I say, Stone, you wont buy me a new one, will you, eh?"

There was a general titter, for the man was known to be in debt to the house, and to be very backward in his payments.

Well he might be. His whole substance went at that bar, where he spent his rare earnings. When he was prosperous and well off his credit was good, and then it was he acquired a taste for that fearful curse which was utterly destroying him.

He was a devotee of gin.

"Well," said the landlord, restored to good humour by having the laugh turned against one of the customers he did not fear to offend, "well, Johnson, ain't you going to have anything?"

Before the officer could reply, Lord Charles Lutterel entered the house hurriedly.

"Make haste!" he said, "he crossed over towards the river."

"Hain't no use, my lord," replied the experienced runner; "but I'll run 'im to earth. You just give me a hexact description of 'im, and he sleeps hin quod to-morrow."

"That's very like the chap," whispered the landlord, "only that ain't my hat."

"Curse your hat," said the officer; and then stepping up to the nobleman, he said in a low voice, "Hif your 'onour vill just step this way, I'll take down the pertiklers."

And he opened the door of the landlord's private bar-parlour. Lord Charles, anxious to escape the gaze of the astonished customers, gladly entered, and called for a bottle of wine and a pint of brandy.

If Mr. Potter had any previous doubt of his being a lord, he had none now.

CHAPTER XV.

THE GIN DRINKER.

THE conversation at the bar was resumed with renewed vigour, the presence of a lord, though there was the door between them, giving a zest to the talk which is only to be understood by Englishmen.

Jim Stone took a make-believe sip at his glass of gin, as the door closed, and heaved a deep sigh. He, too, had been in at that door, and treated the landlord with many a bottle of guinea port.

He closed his eyes and tried to conjure back the days when he was not a miserable sot—the lowest pitch of human degradation—but only a jolly fellow.

We do not expect—we would scarcely wish—men to be anchorites and not enjoy their wine and cigars as we do our tea and toast; but how sad a truth is it, that the convivialist too often is carried away, and becomes a curse to himself and his friends.

The genial flow of conversation is aided by the sparkling and rosy wine, but it is the use, and not the abuse, then, which is the secret.

I am old now, and in my time have seen every grade of society, have wandered amid outcasts and criminals, but everywhere, high and low, have I traced crime to avarice, drink, or illicit passion.

But why should I moralise? I have a terrible story to tell. Let me accomplish my task.

Jim Stone was sucking away at a pipe guiltless of tobacco, when a nudge on his elbow awoke him to consciousness.   He looked behind him, and there, where none of the others could see him, was a boy, thin, emaciated, pale, ugly as they generally are, dirty and ragged, one of the Arabs of the Strand—the outcasts of society.

He was making signs to Jim Stone to come outside, and when he saw the other understood him, he vanished.

Jim Stone was too astonished to hesitate, and in a few minutes was in the street, where the boy waited for him.

"What is it?" he asked, looking at the other with his bleared and bloodshot eye.

"A cove give un a teriss¹ to fetch you," said the boy.

"Where is he?" said Stone in a trembling voice.

He fancied there was money to be earned.

"Twig the bloke," replied the boy, pointing to a man who stood a little down a street on the opposite side of the way.

Jim Stone hurried along, and was soon by the stranger's side.

"Do you want me, sir?"

"I do. Would you earn a guinea?"

"What!" said the other, literally gasping for breath, and leaning against the wall.

"Two, if you will act with discretion and honesty," said the man.

"So help me heaven!" cried the gin-drinker, "nobody ever suspected my honour. I am poor, wretched; I once was happy and wealthy; but if I have fallen, I have never done a dishonest action."

"I will trust you. I too am an innocent man wrongfully accused. I just left the house where you were. I took away the landlord's hat—here it is. Will you restore it, and obtain mine if possible?"

"I will. It is hung up in place of the other?" said Stone.

"The runners are there?" asked Captain George, fixing his eyes keenly on the other.

"They are closeted with a lord," replied Jim Stone, the gin-drinker.

"Go then—but, mark you, no treachery. I do not know you. If you sell me to the officers, I shall not hesitate to fire."

"You may trust me," said the man very humbly.

Captain George gave him the hat, a low-crowned affair; and Stone, who having no money and no credit, was tolerably sober, went across the street and entered the house boldly. The landlord's back was to him; the door of the bar parlour was open; Mr. Potter was looking on the refreshments, while every eye was directed from the front of the bar to where the lad sat.

Stone put up the landlord's hat, and took down that of the highwayman, and without an eye being cast in his direction, slipped out, and hastily crossed the road.

"I say, Potter," said Bill Johnson, as the landlord came to the bar to assist his maid a moment, "bring in that 'ere 'at—eh!"

"All right," replied Potter, "all right. I wish I had the vagabond here; I'd ——"

¹. Shilling.

He stopped, aghast, and clutched the offending beaver.

"My eyes!" he cried, "here's a go! If this ain't my hat a come back again!"

And he stood holding it up to the view of his astounded customers.

"What's that?" said Johnson, coming out.

"That vagabond's been here, and took his own hat away."

The officer gazed at the hat of the worthy Boniface in mute astonishment. It was a round, black, low-crowned beaver; while that of the highwayman was a brown, slouching, Spanish *sombrero*.

"But it's impossible," he said; "these here gents 'ud have seed him."

"There's been no one in and out but Stone," said one of the drinkers. "He went up the passage."

Mr. Potter turned round with a countenance as black as night.

"It's him," he said, as soon as he was assured the gin-drinker's place was empty. "That pitiful scamp! He shall not come here any more; no, not if I know it."

The officers rushed out into the street; but no one was to be seen.

There were no gas-lamps in those days.

The discomfited runners returned to their entertainer, more than ever determined to capture the audacious highwayman.

Meanwhile Stone had rejoined Captain George, and given him his own hat.

"Follow me," he then said, and darted down a narrow, low, arched alley, which soon brought them out into a darker and gloomier street, one of the many running down towards the river.

"Well now, my man, you have earned your two guineas; there they are. But now, can you point out a place where I can sleep in safety? The officers will join in a general hunt."

"You have trusted me, sir," said the man; "I will trust you. I will take you where they will never find you."

He was about to hurry down the street, when Captain George checked him.

"Hold, my man; I expect your larder is not very well furnished," he said.

"I have not eaten food to-day," replied the other, in a low tone.

"The deuce you have not!" cried the other, in a tone of wonder and astonishment. "What can we get?"

"Mrs. Dubbs sells everything," replied Stone.

"Then, to Mrs. Dubbs let us go."

Stone made no reply, but hastened back for a few yards, when a small shop, half-grocer, half-green—a chandler-shop, in fact—met their view.

It was down two steps, and was illumined only by a tall tallow candle, behind which stood a sharp little woman. There exuded from this cellar-like shop a strange odour.

It was what has been called by the author of "Town Life" the Little Shop. We scarcely know in these days such vile instruments of extortion as existed in the beginning of the century.

We have improved, but we have not yet become perfect.

It was one of those variegated stores where

the counter is covered by greasy oil-cloth, worn to a shred, which supports dabs of butter, bread, coffee, staylaces, treacle-cans, reels of cotton, and most probably hair-oil, tobacco, pipes, sugar—brown and white soap, herrings, and haddocks.

Candles hang overhead, diffusing their vile odour around; while in bins were potatoes, oatmeal, coals, onions, cabbages, turnips, carrots, and greens; near these might be seen piles of salt, rubbing-stones, pipeclay, bath brick, and whiting.

But the contents of the window—who shall say? The catalogue of the ships in Homer is nothing to it.

Black puddings, pigs' feet, sausages, steaks, bull's eyes, peppermint drops, brimstone, coloured sweets, and gingerbread in every possible shape and form, pigs' heads, tripe, balls of worsted, bacon, penny rolls, kites, whips, and tops.

We pause, out of breath.

Into such a place was it that Captain George entered.

"Now then," said the highwayman, taking up a large basket, "this to begin with. Don't look so astonished, my good woman; we're hungry, and have no time to lose."

"Good lord alive!" she said, in a squeaking voice, "you ain't going for to rob me, Jemmy Stone?"

"Be quiet, you fool!" replied the gin-drinker, irately. "This is a gentleman who will pay you handsomely. You put down the things on your slate."

"I can't book," she began.

Stone threw down a guinea, while Captain George selected his provender. A piece of bacon, a dozen eggs, butter, bread, cheese, biscuits,—all passed into his basket.

Mrs. Dubbs wrote them down with stolid equanimity She knew Stone, and allowed him, so astonished was she, to weigh the articles.

Drunkard as he was, he had a character for integrity which probably saved him from starvation.

"Pay," said the Captain, handing his companion another guinea.

"But knives, forks, plates, a frying-pan ——" said Stone, ruefully.

"Ah, ah!" cried the Captain, who began to enter into the fun of the thing; "so we are short of furniture, are we?"

The astonished Mrs. Dubbs would have, like the Brittany peasant girl, sold the hair off her head for money, had she possessed any. She therefore at once produced the articles required.

"A penn'orth o' bee's wax[1] and a penny buster,"[2] said a squeaky voice.

It was the boy who had been sent for Jem Stone.

"Ah! that you, you little thief. Just look after him, Stone, eh!"

"Serve me," said the boy, sullenly. "I ain't a been to no buz-napper's[3] academy. Here's a hog."

"Master Joe the mudlark must wait till his betters are served," continued Mrs. Dubbs.

Captain George here hurriedly paid, and left the shop; Stone carrying the basket, while the highwayman took charge of the utensils.

"I don't like the look of that boy," said the Captain. "See he don't watch us."

"All right," replied Stone.

But as he spoke, the boy strolled slowly up the street, in an opposite direction.

"Follow," said Stone; and next minute he was descending a narrow broken stair to the bed of the river.

"Where are we going?"

Stone turned up a dark archway, which was flooded at high tide; and after fumbling about a few minutes, struck a light. He then illumined a small candle, and raised it aloft.

They were standing on the muddy bed of the river, beneath an archway about twelve feet high, in the centre of which was a large trap with a padlock on it.

An iron ladder was chained to the roof.

Stone ascended the ladder, produced a key, and opening the padlock, pushed up the trap.

"Anything to drink?" he said.

"Yes, a can of beer and a bottle of brandy," replied the captain, looking about him with an air of astonishment, at the same time handing him money.

Stone took it and hurried away. In a few minutes he was back with the materials for enjoyment, and then both ascended.

The trap was let down, and through the means of a small slide again fastened.

An iron bolt was then pushed right across.

"Sir," said Stone, with melancholy pride, "allow me to welcome you to my house."

The captain bowed with a covert smile.

"My own house," continued the other, "in which once I had a dozen clerks and half as many servants; where I rolled in gold; where I was sole and undivided master. The house which I enter by stealth, when I should come to the front door in my carriage."

Meanwhile the adventurer looked around with surprise.

Close to the trap below, on the top of the ladder, was a little keen face, listening attentively.

It was Joe, the mudlark.

CHAPTER XVI.

JOE THE MUDLARK.

ALL people are acquainted with that celebrated and tuneful bird, the lark, known to naturalists as the *alauda*. It is a small and elegant specimen of the feathered creation.

But how many of our readers are acquainted with the species *mudlark*, genus *homo*, thus described by a learned pundit, who is an authority of such subjects?*

"Mudlarks: men and women, who with their clothes tucked above knee, grovel through the mud on the banks of the Thames, when the tide is low, for silver spoons, old bottles, pieces of iron, coal, or any articles of the least value,

1 Cheese. 2 Penny roll. 3 Thieves' school.

* Slang Dictionary. By a London Antiquary.

deposited by the retiring tide either from passing ships or sewers. Occasionally those men who cleanse the sewers, with great boots and sou'wester hats."

Now Joe was one of this singular fraternity. Descended, on the father's side, from a *tosher*, or man who stole copper from ships' bottoms; on the mother's, from a woman of more than suspicious character, the boy had never known what virtue was.

No one had taken him by the hand and taught him to respect society, its laws and customs, while none had ever even mentioned to him a future state.

He lived but to eat, and drink, and sleep, and to him it mattered not how the means were obtained.

With a small, dirty, dogskin cap upon his head, a coarse jacket, trousers much too large, and thick heavy shoes, his squalid and pinched face was not so much caused by any physical suffering as from the strange, restless, weary life he led.

At daybreak he was by the river side, and sometimes his earnings were large.

At night he would run of errands, hang about the Strand, and do any job by which to earn money.

He was not particular, in fact, how he procured the articles he sold to the marine store-keepers.

Joe, the mudlark, was a miser, though what he did with his savings nobody knew.

This was the being who now was in possession of the secret of the Captain's hiding-place.

Meanwhile, the two had ascended to a room on the first floor, where some old boards served for fuel, and were busily engaged in preparing for supper—the eyes of the gin-drinker glistening at the prospect of a meal such as had not been within his reach for many a long day.

They were engaged in discussing their meal, suspending their conversation for some little time, when suddenly they heard an odd grating noise against the house.

The shutters were closed, and without were iron bars.

"It's a ladder," said Stone.

"Tracked!" cried the Captain. "I feared it. That boy has betrayed us."

"Joe, the mudlark," whispered the other; "but it's no use. Out with the light. They cannot enter this house. My father was a banker as well as a merchant, and there is no means of entry."

"But we cannot leave," said Captain George.

"I don't know that, sir," replied the other.

"This here vinder's barr'd," muttered a voice outside; "it's my idear that boy's been and cooper'd us. Just 'old 'im."

"No, I hain't," said the shrill voice of the boy below; "I seed the don[1] and the tape-drinker."[2]

"Then it's all U P—up. The 'ouse is too well barred. We must give it up."

And the man descended the ladder, grumbling

1 Clever fellow. Our readers must excuse a little slang. We cannot make a boy of the class to which Joe, the mudlark, belonged, speak otherwise.
2 Gin-drinker.

and growling all the time, as if he had given up the chase.

"Won't do, old fellow!" said Captain George, going on with his supper; "not to be caught with chaff. But either you or I must go out to-night. These fellows will watch every avenue."

"I will go out, without fear," replied Stone. "I have had too many reasons for hiding not to be like a fox. They may watch for years, they will never get in here, or suspect how I leave it."

"But I want you to bring back some one undiscovered."

"I will do anything you will, sir!" said Stone, humbly.

"I suppose, my man, you have seen better days?" continued the Captain.

"Seen better days!" cried the other, "why, sir, time was when this house ruled the Indian trade. My father was a merchant prince; and I—threw it all away. Pleasure, women, gambling, neglect, ruined the finest business that was ever left to man."

"Could you not retrieve it?" asked Captain George; "you are still young."

"I am six-and-thirty," said the other, in a low tone. "Alas, sir, it is an idle hope. It would take a hundred thousand pounds to pay my debts."

"And suppose," said the highwayman, laying his hand upon the other's arm, "I could point out to you a means of winning such a prize; supposing I were to tell you, that could I find a man faithful and true I would put in his power much vaster wealth."

"Heavens, sir!" said Stone, with blanched cheek and a brow covered with cold perspiration, "do not play with my feelings. Could I restore the ancient name and splendour of my father's house I would be content to die."

"Serve me faithfully," replied Captain George, in an earnest and solemn tone, "and you shall be made acquainted with a secret of such stupendous nature as shall make you believe you are once more perusing your Arabian Nights' Entertainments, and have met with the magic lamp of Aladdin. But I have no time now to tell my story: it is time for action. I can trust you?"

"With your life, sir. There is nothing I would not do for one who has even suggested the promise that I may once more be restored to society."

Captain George drew out a pocket-book, and taking out a small piece of paper he wrote on it—

"*Trust the bearer. He will lead you to me. Be careful and watchful.* GEORGE."

He then addressed it to Lucy.

Stone rose to go, but at that moment a loud stir in the street attracted their attention. Captain George rushed through the window, and peeped through the cracked shutter.

The street was crowded by a mob of soldiers, link boys with lighted torches, and police officers. A magistrate headed the crowd, who was accompanied by a blacksmith.

"This will not do," began Captain George; "they will burst open the door in a moment."

Stone, with a coolness and decision which an hour before no man would have expected of him, raked out the fire, smothered it with old ashes, collected all the fragments of the feast, placed them in the basket, and then bade the highwayman follow him.

He passed through another room, went up three steps into a kind of closet, and then pushed open a thick door, that appeared a portion of the panelling.

A small staircase was revealed to the anxious view of the fugitive.

"This house," said Stone, closing the door behind him, and pushing a whole system of bolts into place, "was built in troublous times. But I used it to conceal my follies from my father."

"They have entered the house," replied Captain George.

"Never mind, sir; they will not find us," replied Stone, halting now in a cellar full of large, gloomy-looking hogsheads.

They were evidently long since abandoned, and were fast going to decay. One in the centre appeared more solid than its fellows. This Stone pushed in a peculiar way; it yielded, and a dark opening was revealed.

It was a dry arch, such as those of the Adelphi; and being always in gloomy darkness, the ingeniously-contrived exit was not likely to be discovered.

The two men hurried away from the house without speaking, until they reached a dark-looking water-side inn.

"It would be madness to return to your house until the officers are thrown wholly off the scent," said Captain George. "I will wait for you here. Be cautious. Most likely they will keep a watch on her house."

"I know their tricks!" replied Stone. "I will be cunning as a fox. You know not, sir, the energy which a faint prospect of deliverance from this galling misery I endure has given me."

With these words they parted; but Captain George did not go directly into the tavern. He hurried away from the river.

About three-quarters of an hour later, Stone entered the parlour of the tavern, alone, with a disappointed look. His eyes rested on its sole occupant, a country-looking farmer, with bushy whiskers, a brown hat, top-boots, and a loose coat with capacious pockets. He was smoking a long pipe, and glancing carelessly at an old newspaper.

Stone sighed, and turned to leave the room.

"He wouldn't trust me!" he thought.

"Stone!" said the unmistakable voice of the captain.

The man looked round, and saw the countryman laughing.

"Is that you, sir?" he said, in an amazed tone.

"Yes. My other costume was too prominent. I have changed it. What news?"

"I can't say," replied Stone, shaking his head. "It looks odd—but you know best, sir. When I came near to the door I saw a man lounging, with a pipe at no great distance, so passed on as if nothing had happened; when, just as I turned round, I saw the door open—the door of the shop I mean—and out tripped a lady, her face and form wholly concealed by a silk calash,

which she wore over her hat. I did not appear to take any notice of her, but followed on the opposite side of the way. Presently she turned up St. Martin's-lane, and in a minute I was beside her. 'Mrs. Lipscombe?' said I. 'What do you want?' says she. 'A note from the captain,' says I. 'Very good,' says she, and she took and turned towards a lamp; she seemed able to read it, for she said, 'Tell Mr. George I can't come now, but send in the morning——'"

"What can this mean?" cried the highwayman wildly.

"With that she tripped away, light as a fawn, and I after her; keeping, however, out of sight. At last her journey came to an end; and where do you think it was?"

"I cannot guess," said the other, wiping his pallid brow.

"The lowest house in St. Giles. Stunning Joe Banks, in Dyott-street—a crib frequented by the roughs, and by gentlemen out for a spree."

"It could never be her. It must be some mistake," cried the unhappy George.

"She came out of that shop; she took the note addressed 'Mrs. Lipscombe,' and she went into the house I spoke of. I returned to the Strand, but the glove shop was evidently watched. Besides, I had no longer any credentials."

"Good heavens!" cried George, "who knows what use may be made of that? But do not look so distressed. It cannot be helped. What say you? will it not be safer to sleep here for once?"

"As you like, sir," said Stone, sadly.

"Then you must go out, change your clothes—there are Jews open until a late hour—and assume for the present the attire of a rich farmer's serving-man. When you come back, ask for Squire Jones."

He then handed the astonished and bewildered Stone five pounds, with which he went out, utterly unable to speak.

The captain rang the bell, and the landlord, a sly-looking thin man, with a Jewish cast of countenance, responded.

"Can I do anything?" he said, glancing into the four corners of the room.

"I expected to meet a friend here," said George; "he has not come. I suppose he wont come until morning. Can I have beds for myself and servant?"

"Very goot peds," said the other; "very goot—three shilling."

The other, with a stare which made no impression on the hardened soul of the inn-keeper, placed the money in his outstretched palm. The other gave a cringing bow, and retired.

Next morning, in his new disguise, Captain George, having ascertained that the coast was clear, boldly entered the flower shop, and addressed Martha, who was behind the counter.

"Well, where's sister?" he said heartily, and with as broad an accent as he could assume. "Tell her I'm here."

The woman looked at him with her cold, glittering eye, and then made answer—

"Mrs. Lipscombe's gone in the country, and I don't expect her back for many days. She's gone with a friend," she added maliciously.

"It is false. I say she is here," cried the highwayman, impetuously.

"She is not here; but here comes Mr. Bill Johnson; perhaps you would like to ask him."

Our friend hastily left the shop, brushing past the unconscious Bow-street runner, leaped his horse, held by Stone, and next instant the two were rattling along at a furious pace, up the Strand, towards Marylebone field.

CHAPTER XVII.

THE ABDUCTION.

IN Dyott-street, St. Giles's, was a low public-house, already alluded to as kept by Joe Banks, to whom the appellation of Stunning was given by his customers, and which has come down to the present day in the form of a popular vulgarism.

Once for all we have strongly to apologise for the use in these pages of any of that slang which is so varied and picturesque in the great city of Cockayne. But it would be as correct to make a Malay pirate speak French, as certain of the wild tribes of London genuine English.

The inn kept by Mr. Joe Banks was known as the resort of the worst characters, though the house was conducted with the strictest decorum. The landlord obtained a wide reputation for acting as a medium betwixt thieves and their victims. Mr. Banks was willing to act in any delicate transaction, where a watch, or snuff-box, or gold chain, was wanted to be restored, provided always that no questions were asked.

Joe Banks enjoyed the supreme confidence of all the house-breakers, lobbymen, and other depredators of the metropolis, because it was confidently asserted that he never had betrayed one of them.

His house, from one of those singular anomalies which we are at a loss to explain, was often frequented by men of a higher class, and it is asserted that the Marquis of Douro, Colonel Chatterley, and men of their stamp, were accustomed to resort to a private room at this house, when too late or too early to gain admittance to the clubs or more aristocratic establishments.

Mr. Joe Banks stood behind his bar, of middle height, stout, and strongly made, with a showy pin in his "stunning neck-tie."

He was standing with his hands in his pockets smoking a pipe, and occasionally directing two crop-headed waiters who served in the bar.

"Well, mum, what is it?" he said, addressing a respectable and well-dressed female who entered, her face concealed by a calash.

"I want Rowley."

"Eh? got a card?"

"Yes."

"Show it."

The woman handed up the card, which the landlord examined keenly.

"All serene! Go up; third floor; knock," he exclaimed. "Here, Suky, show the lady to the green room."

A sandy-haired, stunted wench, about three feet and a half high, appeared, and, without saying a word, led the way upstairs.

The woman followed her, as if glad to escape the scene below, which was redolent of gin, tobacco, and mephitic odours, though conversation was neither loud nor unruly.

Stunning Joe Banks had a character to lose.

"This here's the green room," said the girl, and pulled a bell.

The door opened of itself, and the woman entered. It was neatly furnished, wax candles burned on a table with a green cloth, and a sideboard displayed numerous bottles of wine and liquors. Near the extreme end of the room sat a man, who rising as she entered, made known the person of Lord Charles Lutterel. He was very pale, and his eyes seemed to stand forth from his head.

"Welcome, Miss Martha," he said, with extreme politeness; "pray take a seat."

"Really, my lad, you are too good," replied the treacherous shopwoman, at the same time seating herself with a smirk and a wavy toss of the petticoats, which some women believe to be very genteel.

"Will you take anything?" continued the nobleman.

"Well—really, my lord—I never do; but if you think it won't hurt me," simpered Martha Snelling.

Lord Charles Lutterel placed a tumbler before her, and filled it with port wine.

"Now listen to me," he said, hastily; "there is no time for circumlocution or delay. I love Mrs. Lipscombe."

"Miss Lucy Lipscombe," interrupted Martha,

"She is not a widow," he exclaimed, with a strange glee in his eye.

"Oh, dear, no; only," here she gulped down half the port, "being, you see, my lord, an unprotected female, you see, and wishing to keep off all lovers but one——"

"But one! who do you mean?" gasped Lord Lutterel.

"She's been engaged these fourteen years," said Martha, "to him as came in so sudden to-night."

The young nobleman rose, and clutched his head between his hands.

"Again! By the powers of h—, he shall rue this. Ha! ha! then shall I not only gratify the fierce love I feel for her, but scorch his heart. If you will put her in my power, I will give you five hundred pounds."

"And the business?" asked Martha demurely.

"Shall be yours; I will stop all inquiry," cried Lutterel.

"Then, my lord, you may hand me the money," exclaimed Martha Snelling, in an agony of delight, "for I have the means in my hand."

"Eh! what do you mean?" said the young nobleman, half alarmed about her sanity.

She placed the pencilled note of George in his hand, the one she had received from Stone.

"I trust you, my lord," she said, with a simper.

"The money is yours," exclaimed the other, drawing from his pocket-book a roll of notes. He was a gambler, and always carried large sums. "Now go home. A messenger will come

in an hour. Do you open. She will follow him without hesitation. If all goes well, remember, I am always your friend.

Martha Snelling rose without a blush on her cheek, and after concealing the proceeds of her infamous treachery, tripped lightly down stairs, and turned towards home, with a ready falsehood on her lips to account for her absence.

She found poor Lucy in a sad and thoughtful mood in her little parlour. She seemed to expect every moment a message from the fugitive.

"Come back!" she said quietly; "come back already! Is your mother better?"

"Mother is not very well," replied Martha, taking off her things; "but I couldn't stop, and you so lonely, dear."

"You are very kind, Martha. I am certainly very lonely. The day's excitement has been too much for me."

"But how is it that the officers should be after so nice a gentleman?" asked the hypocrite.

"Martha, that at present is his secret," replied Lucy gently; "but be sure that he is innocent of the crime of which he is accused."

"But, ma'am, why not surrender, then, and prove his innocence?"

"Martha, I am surprised at such a remark from you. In these days, when innocence is so difficult to prove—when a man is tried on Saturday and hanged on Monday," she said with a shudder; "he is better out of the clutches of the law than in them. But he will clear himself; his innocence will be proclaimed in the light of day, and the guilty who have striven against him shall be punished."

"Lawks, miss, who can you mean?" said Martha, holding up her hands.

At this moment there was a knock at the outer door. Martha's face flushed, and to hide her confusion she hurried to the entrance of the shop.

"'Tis from George," mentally ejaculated Lucy Lipscombe.

"Please, miss," said Martha, returning, "a man with a note for you."

Lucy took a candle and went to the door, where stood a tall, shabbily-dressed man, with white hair, and a rather respectable general appearance.

"Mrs. Lipscombe," he said with a stiff bend of his tall body.

"That is my name."

The shabby-genteel man took off his low-crowned beaver, disfigured by rusty crape, and fumbled for some time amid what appeared to be its rather heterogeneous contents. At last he produced a crumpled scrap of paper, which Lucy eagerly received.

"I am ready," she said, in a resolute and earnest tone. "Martha, my hat and cloak. Is it far, my man?"

"Just so," replied the other, bending his body. "Out of town."

The unfortunate and deceived young woman, hastily put on her outer habiliments, and without a moment's hesitation, followed the messenger. She had no doubt or fears, for did not the letter bid her follow the bearer? A sedan chair was in waiting, with two powerful porters. Into this Lucy entered, the door was closed, and the chair hurried away at a rapid pace.

This continued for about an hour, when the men halted, a gate opened, and Lucy was requested to alight. As she did so she looked around, not without a shudder. She was in the front yard of what appeared to be a lonely farm-house, with high walls excluding any glimpse of the surrounding scenery.

At an open door was a sinister-looking old woman, with a light in her hand, who looked at Lucy with a peculiar smile.

"Is the captain here?" said Lucy, in a resolute tone.

"Yes, ma'am, this way," replied the crone.

The young woman began to fear treachery. A dread of something terrible was on her soul, and yet what could she do? Scream. This, in case she was really about to meet "George," was a dangerous act. She had then no choice but to follow her guide. Pursuing a long passage some distance, they came to a staircase, up which the guide led the way. On the first landing were several doors, to one of which the woman pointed.

"He is there," she said, raising her flickering candle.

With a firm and resolute look, but a wildly beating heart, Lucy turned the handle of the door, and entered. She was alone in an ante-chamber. Advancing across this she found another door. It opened to the sound of her footsteps; she was dazzled by a blaze of light; and when her eyes recovered their capacity for distinguishing particular objects, she found herself in a superbly furnished apartment, in presence of a luxurious and copious supper, while face to face with her, with a curl of triumph on his lip, stood Lord Charles Lutterel.

Lucy did not shriek; she gave way to no fainting or hysterical fits, for she knew the awful peril in which she stood.

The reputation of the young nobleman was one of no ordinary character. He was no mere noisy wrencher-off of knockers—no mere lover of a "spree" with "Charlies" and loose women—no mere gambler or roué, but a cold-blooded assassin of women's honour—a slayer of human hearts.

She accordingly looked him full in the face, and walked deliberately up to the table.

"Well, my lord," she said, coldly, "what means this outrage?"

"Outrage, my beloved Lucy! harsh words!" he replied, "but how can you say so, when you came here of your own accord?"

"This quibbling is unworthy of a man," she continued.

"Lucy, pardon me—but any means was good to vanquish a resistance that maddened me. I love you from my soul, and if you but listen to the voice of prudence, there shall be no woman in England who shall not envy you."

"And if I do not listen to the voice of prudence," said Lucy, standing erect with her cloak thrown back, her beautiful face shaded by her hat, and her right hand leaning on the table.

"Lucy!" he replied, with a lurid glare in his eyes; "you are wholly in my power."

"No, my lord. I am in the power of no man; for sooner than be faithless to the man I love, I will die." And she snatched up a strange long-pointed knife from the table, and clutched it with all the energy of her courageous soul.

"Lucy!" cried the young nobleman, turning somewhat pale; "don't be nonsensical. Sit down to supper; we can then talk over matters. I am disposed to try the effects of time upon your wilful soul. But put down that horrid knife."

"My lord, think not I mean to slay myself, unless as a last resource," said Lucy, in cold, earnest tones. "I will act more wisely than that. Come near me, and I will rid the earth of a monster, who lives but to disgrace the name of man, and the order to which he belongs."

The nobleman made a sudden retreat.

"Lucy, you will repent this!" he said, his face livid with rage; and then, with a sudden spring, he dashed through the door, which he fastened behind him.

Lucy drew a long breath. The man was afraid of her. But, then, he was not alone. What was to be done? On examination, the captive found that the apartment assigned her consisted of the room where the supper was laid out and a bedroom. She examined the doors. They fastened only on the outside.

By great exertions she piled up furniture against the first door, and then, without parting with her weapon, she sat down in an arm-chair to think on her dangerous and perilous position.

In the stillness which ensued she distinctly heard muttered voices outside.

CHAPTER XVIII.

AN OLD FRIEND.

MEANWHILE Captain George and his man Stone had reached the outskirts of London and pulled up in a narrow cross-road. The highwayman knew well that for the moment London was too hot to hold him, and had determined to absent himself until the pursuit had slackened somewhat. But he could not remain in this dreadful state of suspense with regard to Lucy.

"Stone!" he said, after considerable reflection, "you and I have met under singular circumstances. I am disposed to assist you in every way in my power. I have most important tasks to fulfil, which require my presence in the north. My London affairs I must trust wholly to you—will you undertake them? The lady who was in the flower shop, and to whom you should have given my note, is dear to me as my life. I know she is in peril, but I know also that she is brave and good. She has, I have every reason to believe, been trapped in some way by the cruel treachery of Lord Charles Lutterel. Now, to find her retreat, you must dog his footsteps, watch him night and day. Should you find her prison, assist her by every means in your power, and communicate with me."

"I will, sir; and rely on it, you will find me do my duty," said Stone, earnestly.

"I believe you. Money you shall not want. I will write you my address in a few days; and now, my man, farewell. We shall meet soon; and be but true to me in the great object of my life, and all my promises shall be fulfilled."

Captain George wrung his hand, and trotted off to conceal the intense emotion which was kindled in his bosom in relation to his beloved Lucy, the loved of fourteen years.

It was long since the highwayman had been that way; it was many days since his eye had lighted on the scenery of the Northern-road, and yet it seemed familiar. In the early hours of that mad career on which he had entered in a moment of frenzy—when it was wild delight to gallop over the fields, and commons, and heaths—when it was glorious fun to cry, "Stand and deliver"—he had become familiar with every inch of the road. He was now wending his way along the same high road, a traveller, big with great resolutions, and intent upon carrying out designs of the most stupendous character.

Walking his horse after a short gallop, Captain George continued his journey in such a way as to give his horse a chance of accomplishing his task without breaking down. Early in the evening, he halted at a roadside inn, of rather a humble character, where once he had been well known.

A jolly, merry widower had been the host when Captain George knew him, and many had been the bowls of punch they had consumed together.

The captain sighed at the thought of all that had been then, as he dismounted in the yard and gave his steed to the ostler, with strict injunctions as to his feed and treatment generally.

He then entered through a well-remembered side-door, and soon found himself in front of the bar. A stout, rubicund, rather masculine dame, with a profusion of curls and ribbons, met his view; and yet over the door he had read John Henshaw.

"Mr. Henshaw in?" he said, in his usual courteous way.

"Yes, sir," replied the other, with a simper; "but my husband is not able to attend to business. I transact everything."

To enter the bar, to put his arm round the waist of the stout party, and imprint a ringing kiss on her lips, was with Captain George the work of an instant.

"Sir, I'd have you know," said the astonished dame, struggling to release herself.

"Well, Suky, is this the way you welcome an old flame?" said the Captain, laughing.

There was something magical in the tones, for the roses doubled on the stout party's cheeks, as she cast back her memory fourteen years, when she was chambermaid in that inn where now she was mistress.

"And so you're married, Suky?" he said, with a half-comical, half-reproachful glance, which spoke volumes.

Suky redoubled her blushes.

"Ah, George! you were a sad fellow in those days. Well, you went away, and never came back—so—so, as Mr. Henshaw—he always was after me, you know—offered marriage, why —"

"You did the very wisest thing you could have done," cried Captain George, gaily; and then he added, in a graver tone, "What changes have taken place since last we met! and I dare say you could tell me of many. What of Mrs. Winterton?"

"Poor, dear lady!" said Suky, seating herself, and handing Captain George to a chair, "she has never been the same woman. She lives at Dudley House in deep retirement; she will see no one; she dispenses her charities far and wide, and is beloved by the poor; but they catch a glimpse of her only at church. She is dying slowly, but surely, of a broken heart."

"And her cousins?" asked the captain.

"Are away in London, dissipating the inheritance, which, I hope, will never be theirs," said the landlady, warmly.

"I hope so," replied Captain George; "but the child must be found."

"Have you any reason to believe it lives?" said the tender-hearted Suky.

"I know nothing, and yet I am not without hope. But see Arabella I must," he added, half-musing, to himself.

"Arabella!" said Sukey, with a look of surprise; "surely, you do not mean Mrs. Winterton?"

"Did I say Arabella? Well, no matter. There was a day when she and I were as intimate as brother and sister; but that is passed. Still, I would see her."

"She refuses everybody. Her chaplain dispenses all her charities."

"I care not. It is an absolute necessity—if I commit a burglary," he added, laughing.

"They say," said Mrs. Henshaw, "that she walks every evening near the Dark Firs alone.

The park is so well guarded, she does not fear intrusion."

"She acts wisely," replied Captain George, thoughtfully. "But come, Suky, a dish of tea, and then I will take a stroll. Am I not to see John?"

"Certainly; he is inside. But the gout so troubles him, he has not moved for years," added Suky.

Captain George smiled, and entered the parlour, where he found his old acquaintance, honest Jack Henshaw, as he was used to be called, not very much improved by thirteen additional years. He was stout, fat, and his eye had that dull and almost fishy look which is so often indicative of declining intellect.

He gazed upon Captain George with a lacklustre expression which pained his old acquaintance.

"Well, Jack," he cried heartily, "how are you?"

"Jack!" said the gouty patient, without moving a muscle; "Jack! I used to be called that ages ago—eh, Suky? Take anything to drink? Hope your honour slept well last night."

"Good gracious! and I expected Henshaw would give me information of Mrs. Winterton," cried George.

"He must be kept very quiet," observed Suky, calmly; while the ailing man gazed at her with an appealing and imploring look.

"What does he want?" said the captain, curiously.

"Drink—the drink which brought him to this state."

"Just another glass," whined the toper.

The captain shook his head; he saw at once that he had fallen upon one of those hapless cases of idiotcy produced by drink, which are so fearful to contemplate.

Suky ordered tea, and waited upon her afflicted helpmate with a gentleness which showed that her heart was still the same as when the captain knew her.

After engaging a bed, and requesting that his horse might be taken great care of, though the saddle was to be put on, he saw to his pistols, wrapped himself in his cloak, and sallied forth into the open air.

CHAPTER XIX.

THE DARK FIRS.

CAPTAIN GEORGE knew the environs of Dudley Park well. He had not forgotten the days when he was an honoured visitor there, and held his head as high as any in the land. He now approached it as an outcast and an outlaw; though hope whispered the flattering tale that better times were coming.

Alas! to some, good times are always coming, but never come. The hope, however, is in itself a blessing of no mean importance.

The hour was eight. It was already dark, and anxious to avoid any unpleasant meeting, the highwayman struck across some fields, which soon brought him to a cross-road that skirted the well-known park. With a rapidity which showed his knowledge of the locality, he stepped slowly and cautiously up to the ring fence.

The dark firs reached to the very outskirts of the park, and their dark and gloomy boughs hung over the road itself.

Captain George stepped over the fence, and was about to follow a path well known to him, when two men sprang from the thicket and caught him by the throat.

"Move, and you are a dead man," said a voice in his ear.

At a distance he could see a tall and stately figure parading slowly through the dark firs.

"I want to see Mrs. Winterton," he said in a loud voice.

The figure stood still a moment, and with a wild cry of anguish came running to the spot.

"That voice! that voice! Oh give me back my child!" she cried.

The keepers, who, under direction of the steward, always watched when Mrs. Winterton took her lonely walk, hesitated.

"Unhand him," said the bereaved mother. "Leopold! Leopold! why have you been away so long?"

"I have been in a far distant land," he replied, "and my first thought on returning was of you. And have you no news of your little girl?"

"Gracious heavens! know you nothing?" cried the lady.

"You are agitated," said George; "will you not be seated? and I will tell you all."

"Come, come!" she replied, taking his hand in hers, "this way."

And she led him towards the skirt of the plantation of the dark firs.

The keepers shook their heads and resumed their watch.

Mrs. Winterton led the captain—let it be recollected that we call him George until his assertions are proved or disproved—to a small summer house on the edge of the plantation, where she pointed to a seat, and then eagerly begged for an explanation.

"My dear Arabella," said the young man, gravely, "I fear me much, my explanations will give you little satisfaction. On that memorable night, when some providential inspiration induced me to follow in the footsteps of those men, I was, on leaving your house, so hotly chased by your cousins and the man Jones, that I, encumbered by the child, had no chance of escape."

The poor woman groaned bitterly.

"Putting my horse, therefore, to the utmost speed, I easily reached a well known glade, where was a gipsy camp. I knew the queen, and to her care I hastily committed the child, saying that I would one day reclaim it. I then crossed some fields, renewed my march. met the ruffians face to face, and succeeded in disarming all suspicion. Then, by the most foul treachery, I was removed from this country, and—but the story would take all night.'

"Leopold, my heart is ready to burst. Let us start at once. The gipsies—the child with the golden hair. I knew it! I knew it! I knew it!"

And she subsided into a kind of fainting fit on the other's shoulder.

Captain George made a motion as if to lay her down.

"Be still," she whispered; "its only joy. My child, my angel, lives, and I shall see her once more."

"Calm yourself, dear Arabella," began the captain.

"I will be calm. One day, I was strolling in the garden, and mechanically directed my steps to where the grated iron gate opened upon the wood, when my eyes fell upon a group that made my heart beat wildly. A tall handsome gipsy woman—very dark—was seated on a bank, watching the gambols of a little girl about three years old. Ye heavens! why did not Nature speak more loudly? She was fair, with golden hair, a lovely countenance, and the most careless eye would have told that she was no gipsy. But how could I think—how could I suppose the truth. You had taken her away, I thought, to some far distant spot. I approached the woman, and gazed long and ardently at the child.

"'Is it yours?' I said.

"'It is,' she replied coldly.

"I made some remark on its beauty, kissed it passionately, and hurried into the house to weep. But, Leopold, tell me is it not possible that it was my child? Something tells me that it was so."

"It is more than probable," replied the captain thoughtfully.

"Then, in the name of heaven, let us start at once, and never rest until we have found these gipsies. I am rich; I will spend money with a lavish hand; but they must be found."

"My dear Arabella," said the other, after a moment's pause, "we must proceed in our task with care and judgment. These gipsies are wanderers, and may have long since departed from their old camp. Thither am I bound; nor will I pause until I find her. But allow me to go alone; I can travel quicker."

"No; a mother cannot sit idle in such a cause. I, too, can travel night and day. I implore you to have mercy on me: we will go together."

"As you will. But it would be unwise to travel in company. Do you start at daybreak to-morrow in your travelling carriage. I will meet you at Weston Cross. I will keep you in sight, and, if need be, protect you. Recollect, Arabella, the fearful ban there is on me."

"I know! I know! But that you are innocent I would declare in any court of justice," she cried warmly.

"I thank you—and now farewell. I require rest; but fear not, at daybreak I shall be up. Weston Cross, remember."

And shaking her hand cordially, Captain George retired unmolested by the keepers.

CHAPTER XX.

THE FAIRY VISION.

IF there is a pure joy on earth, it is to see the glow of health returning to those cheeks we had heard condemned to bloom no more, to feel the life flowing, beating, at the heart which had apparently ceased to flow with life; but, oh, the accumulated and delirious happiness to a mother, when having long mourned a child as dead, she is roused to believe that that child liveth.

Mrs. Winterton—who for thirteen years had walked about in this vale of tears, a shadow of her former self, pale, careworn, and with a complexion of waxen hue—rose on that glorious morn, to her the dawn of a new life, with a flush upon her cheek, and bright sparkle in the eyes, which told of holy joy and happiness unutterable.

To her it was as the resurrection of the dead.

Long before daylight she was dressed, and seated at an open window; and just as dawn broke she could hear the active preparations below made by her astonished servants. Precisely as the first tint of real light was seen in the eastern sky, her maid knocked at the door to say that all was ready.

Ellen Jay was an active woman of thirty, much attached to her mistress, whom she was to accompany on her journey.

Without a moment's hesitation, Mrs. Winterton descended to the hall, at the door of which the carriage stood. It was one of those convenient travelling vehicles which only our ancestors knew how to make, drawn by four prancing horses.

All the servants crowded round their mistress to bid her adieu. They suspected something.

"Thank you," she said warmly, "I hope not to return alone."

A joyous exclamation intimated the satisfaction this gave to all present; and then, in another moment, she was gone. The horses, as if animated by the spirit of the occasion, dashed off at a rattling speed, and in half-an-hour she was ascending the hill towards Weston Cross.

A solitary horseman came leisurely from a cross road, and preceded the carriage. Mrs. Winterton strained her eyes to see if it were the captain. But, as he was wrapped in a cloak and wore a slouched hat, she could not make him out.

And thus it continued for some hours, the horseman always keeping ahead, but never approaching near to the carriage.

About one o'clock they were passing through a large town, and, as they reached the market place, the postilions slackened their speed, until at last they stood quite still. Mrs. Winterton looked up to see what was the cause of the stoppage.

It was occasioned by a large crowd round a booth, or rather show.

It was of considerable dimensions, with a platform in front, on which stood a stout woman with a large speaking-trumpet, a columbine perpetually pirouetting, and a clown who made dismal attempts at jokes.

Down on the ground, however, surrounded by the mob, appeared the principal attraction. A graceful and elegant girl, in a fancy costume, something resembling a Greek maiden, was dancing on stilts; her shoulders flooded by a mass of golden curls, that she tossed saucily as she danced, while a handsome young man in a strange dress, between Hamlet and Macbeth, kept the crowd back.

"Hoo! hoo! hoo!" said the fat woman through her speaking-trumpet, "walk up, walk up, ladies and gentlemen, and see the live lion stuffed with straw, the Hindoo tiger as takes maidens into the woods and eats them, bone and hall; and this evening the performance will be Macbeth, by the whole strength of the company. Macbeth, Mr. William Lennox, the hinfant Roscious; Lady Macbeth, Miss Lillian, from the Theatre Royal Bostong, United States."

And still the fair girl with the golden hair danced towards the edge of the crowd.

And from a window of an inn opposite a man with a fearful countenance applauded vociferously.

It was the Blue Dwarf, dressed this time according to the prevailing fashion, except that his ugly shape made him, in this costume, doubly hideous.

Mrs. Winterton leaned out to see if the postilions were forcing their way.

Her eyes met those of the girl on stilts.

An electric shock seemed to pass through the veins of both, they knew not why, and then both heaved a deep sigh.

The postilions lashed their horses, and the beautiful vision was lost to view. But for hours Mrs. Winterton found herself thinking of the lovely fairy-like face, the soft blue eyes, of that dancer, hopping about upon stilts for the amusement of a crowd of boors.

She asked herself if this child, too, had a fond mother?

That night she put up at a large hotel in a town of some dimensions; and as she entered the door, she saw the horseman pass slowly without looking her way, but she clearly recognised the face and form of Captain George.

Next morning the journey was renewed, and continued for five more days, Captain George keeping his usual distance a-head; and no adventure occurring, they, late in the evening of the sixth day, reached within a short distance of the end of their journey. Mrs. Winterton put up at an hotel of fashionable appearance, and waited with anxiety the arrival of her guide.

About an hour later, with that rapidity of action and aptitude for disguise which characterised the captain, he sent up his name as Major Seaton, and was at once admitted. He was in uniform, and admirably became his character. As long as the servant of the hotel was in the room he bowed ceremoniously, and hoped her health was quite restored, to which the lady returned most gracious answers.

"But now, my dear Leopold," said Mrs. Winterton in a low tone, as soon as they were by themselves, "why these disguises and false names?"

"My dear Arabella, you little know my brother. I have every reason to believe that my father is somewhere confined in this neighbourhood, in which case be sure he will have plenty of spies on the watch. My every movement would be observed, and myself, perhaps, arrested. As soon as I have been instrumental in restoring a daughter to her mother, I then pursue my own way. My heart is pulled two conflicting ways; my filial affection and my love—

"You, too, love," said Arabella, with a sigh for the memory of the departed.

"Yes; and oh, Arabella, one worthy of my affection. But, Heaven guard her! she has, I fear, been abducted by Lord Charles."

"Gracious Heaven! and you have left her to come to me!"

"It was my duty, after letting your heart bleed for thirteen years."

"Generous man! I thank you. But why is the duke's retreat concealed?"

"Because," said the captain in a hushed whisper, "his evidence would exculpate the innocent, and confound the guilty. His brain was, I believe, affected by that most hideous crime—that most foul, unnatural murder; but his was too great a soul to remain unhinged for long. But put on your cloak, and let us depart. The time is come."

Mrs. Winterton, who was dying to say so, but who did not like to appear careless of her friend's sorrows, hastened to prepare for her walk. To prevent any questions or suspicions, they were about to proceed on foot.

CHAPTER XXI.

THE GIPSY TENT.

THERE was a green and grassy glade at no great distance from the town, which, being on the edge of some timber, belonging in part to the Crown, and in part to a nobleman of high rank, was, to a certain extent, no man's property. It was reached by what once had been a lane used between the distant villages, but a road had subsequently been made and the lane abandoned. The hedges were there still, and they had become, from neglect, so much tangled and overgrown as to form a roof overhead. Some wandering poachers or gipsies had probably cut any too intrusive boughs from beneath, so that men could still make their way along its winding course, but no mounted man could any longer use it.

It was about eight or nine in the evening, and a large party of gipsies were congregated on the spot. Several tents stood round the end of this lane, so useful to the rovers, and in the centre was one larger than the others. Several fires were lighted, and cauldrons set over them, but in front of the principal one there were but a few embers. A woman wrapped in a red cloak, and with a hat tied on by means of a handkerchief that passed under her chin, was seated in front of the tent smoking a pipe, and occasionally stopping to rock herself and chaunt some mysterious verses in her own tongue.

They were sad and monotonous, but they were musical.

Presently she burst into a kind of lamentation, all the more plaintive from the extremely real sadness of her tones.

"*Tauno rumy*¹ is gone, and the false house-dweller stole her away! *lana! lana!* Woe is the romee² that trusts a housedweller! *lana! lana!* May the *sturabin*³ of his own people be his resting place! *lana! lana!* The wreath was made and the pitcher moulded that was to make the two one! *lana! lana!* And what shall I say to the dadi⁴ when he comes for the girl? *lana! lana!*"

"The girl was a *mort* (a free woman) and she had a right to go," said a gruff voice near her. "Why bemoan her? She was *snowt fayre*,⁵ but she a never mill'd a ken."⁶

"Who wanted her to?" cried Miriam, fiercely. "She was as my own child."

"Lyp,"⁷ said the man in a low whisper; "somebody walks."

Two tall gipsies glided away from the fires, and hurried down the lane. The gipsy woman began to chaunt louder than ever.

"Who goes there?" said one of the scouts suddenly as they came close upon the intruders. "Speak, or you will taste a crab-shell."

"*Cut bene whyddes*,⁸ or you will catch better than you bring," said a full commanding voice. "Is Miriam here?"

"Is that you, Captain George?" cried the man who had interrupted Miriam.

"I ask questions, my friend," said George good humouredly.

"Advance!" cried the woman Miriam, rising, and speaking in a deep and earnest tone; "advance! and curse the woman in whom you put your trust."

George, without another word, hurried into the tent, accompanied by Mrs. Winterton, who trembled violently. They both entered it, and stood facing Miriam, who in a few weeks had grown old. Her dress was careless, her locks grey, her eye wild and menacing.

"Miriam, in mercy's name, say at once what mean you. This is the mother of the child."

"Speak, my good woman; spare me a moment's suspense. Is she dead?"

"No," said Miriam in a choked voice; "but a few weeks ago, I have not counted the days, she left me."

"Heaven, I thank thee! She still lives!" said the agonised mother. "But left you, why?"

Arabella Winterton never doubted a moment it was of her child.

"Stay!" she cried suddenly, "you are the woman who came with my child, and it played before my house, and I embraced it. Why did you not save a mother's agony then?"

"He told me never to give it up to any save himself," she coldly replied.

"True! true!" said Captain George, "and Miriam could have done no other. But rest you Arabella, and let us hear all."

Miriam bade them be seated on some skins of animals which served as a carpet for the queen of the gipsies, and in a voice of considerable emotion told her story. Mrs. Winterton, fearful of losing a word, never interrupted

¹ The little girl. ² Gipsy woman. ³ Prison. ⁴ Father. ⁵ Comely. ⁶ Robbed a house. ⁷ Lie down. ⁸ Give good word.

her. The narrative lasted some considerable time.

When Miriam had finished, Arabella burst into an hysterical laugh.

"Her hair is in golden curls, and her eyes are blue, and she is as fair as the whitest marble," she gasped.

"That is her," replied the gipsy, wildly.

"And the lad who stole her is tall, pale, melancholy, but handsome," she continued.

"That is his description," cried Miriam.

"Ah! ah! ah!" wildly laughed Arabella, whose nerves wholly gave way. "And we have been coming away from them for five whole days."

"The market place! the market place! the girl on the stilts!" repeated George. "I see it all."

"Come, let us go at once; money will trace them"

"Stay," said the gipsy, "you will find your child. If she is with an itinerant show, I can trace them in less time than you. But before you go, *Captain George*," added she sarcastically, "when is the red hand to be avenged, and the duke released?"

"Miriam!" gasped the other, clutching her arm; "what know you of the red hand? You mean the murder!"

"What knew I of Ada Wilton!" laughed Miriam.

Red is the curse on Seagrave's height,
Till the coward that slew her sinks in night.

"I tell you, that never shall you know rest until that vile deed is avenged."

"And you have known me all along?" asked Captain George.

"All along. I was at your birth, yours and his; and my hand it was that tied the red ribbon that told the elder born. Your birth was in the bonnie highlands."

"Which was the elder born?" asked George, wildly.

"He who proves his innocence of the murder," replied the gipsy.

"Miriam, I have come home through difficulties and dangers of the most fearful nature to do three things—to restore a child to its mother; to avenge Ada Wilmot; and to free my father, or die," said Captain George, firmly.

"Then will the gipsy queen bless you, for she has lived to see a happy day."

"And now, Miriam, will you assist me?" he asked.

"In what way?" she said.

"You knew Lucy Lipscombe?" he began.

"Ask me," shrieked Miriam, "if I knew the boy of my bosom, who died a year ago. What of her?".

"She is my affianced bride," said Captain George, much surprised.

"There is mercy in heaven!" half whispered Miriam. "But where is she?"

"She has been abducted by Lord Charles Lutterel, who made London too hot to hold me. What I ask of you is to go there, find out her place of concealment, and either save her, or give me a double motive for revenge."

Miriam rose, but Mrs. Winterton reminded

her that she had to save her child from the bad boy who had run away with her.

"Be not so hasty," said Captain George. "If the boy came here with the Blue Dwarf, and 'tis he I think for, I should fear nothing. I knew something of this unfortunate cripple, and a nobler being never lived. William Lennox had some reason for running away, if 'tis the same that fled from Blakesley House."

Miriam nodded her head.

"Still pardon a mother's eagerness," cried Arabella. "Recollect, I have longed for this moment for thirteen years."

Miriam opened a black box, fastened with a stout padlock.

"Does know that, lady?" she said, placing in the mother's hand a tiny chemise and cap, yellow from age.

Totally unable to reply, Arabella pressed them to her lips, and had George not have supported her, would have fainted.

"I worked them myself," she cried, weeping tears of joy. "See! here are my initials, and L. W., those of the child."

"What meant you to have called her?" said the amazed gipsy.

"Lilian," replied Arabella. "It was her father's wish if he had a girl."

"The stars then guided me," cried Miriam, "for her name is Lilian."

The astonishment of the mother was unbounded at the apparent coincidence, which was none at all. But Captain George was too politic to say that Arabella had called the child by its name several times in her terror, and that he had informed the gipsy of it.

In a few minutes more the trio were on their way to the town, the gipsy to sleep at some tramp lodging-house, until she could disguise herself a little; the captain to return to his quarter; Mrs. Winterton to the hotel, full of the dear hope of in a few days embracing her dear child.

CHAPTER XXII.

THE YOUNG MIDSHIPMAN.

When Sir Edgar Blakesley found himself in the presence of Sir Edmund Crossley, he lost none of his self-possession, but bowed with deep respect to a fine, middle-aged officer in full uniform, who was seated at a table covered with writing paper, letters, and despatches.

"So!" cried the gallant officer, "you are the son of my old friend Sir Edgar?"

"Yes, Sir Edmund," replied the other.

"And you want to leave home?"

"I am not happy, Sir Edmund. My mother has re-married."

"Old story—not happy—run away to sea. Well, I always said I would be a father to you, and d——e I will, if you'll only let me. I am busy now. Dine with me at four, and I will then make all necessary arrangements. Go to Jacobs, and get your regular uniform. Say you are going to join my ship."

The sailor held out his hand cordially to the youngster, and shook hands, after which he hurried him away.

"Odd, too!" he muttered, when the boy was gone. "What a cold, fishy hand he's got. His father was as warm as a toast. Can't make it out; devilish like him though. Hope he's a chip of the old block; don't seem so, though."

And evidently a little annoyed at the new midshipman, he rang the bell to change the tone of his thoughts; but all he could do, he did not get the lad out of his head.

Meanwhile, Sir Edgar Blakesley went down stairs with a beating heart to order the uniform which was to indicate his official rank. He then determined to amuse himself as best he might until dinner-time.

Sir Edgar had evidently very peculiar tastes for one of his rank in life; for no sooner had he left the sailors than he glided up a narrow street that led away from the port, and having asked for the Seven Stars, entered a public-house of low demeanour, full of sailors and girls of low degree, drinking, fiddling, fighting, and making love.

The young baronet went into the public room, ordered grog and a pipe, and sat down. The next minute he found himself face to face with Bob Griggs.

His annoyance and surprise may be readily conceived; but with a coolness and decision which alone had carried him through the terrible trials of the previous weeks, the lad gazed at him with an air of perfect unconcern. The sailor had fixed his eyes vacantly on him, as if he had some suspicion, some faint remembrance of that countenance. Still, as he glanced at the uniform, at the hair, and compared them with something which appeared to fill his mind, he appeared to reject the supposition as totally improbable.

"Beg pardon, sir," he said, touching his hat; "belong to our ship?"

"Which is that?" replied the younger, with a knowing nod.

"Her Majesty's ship Rainbow, Sir Edmund Crossley," rejoined the tar.

"Then I do. I've joined to day. Wet your whistle?" asked the young baronet.

"Thank'ee, sir; never say no to a glass of grog," continued the sailor.

And then, without further parley, he seated himself in an obscure corner, where he remained, watching the other with glaring eyes. He could not get his countenance out of his head, while his voice appeared strangely to resemble one that was always ringing in his ears.

The midshipman, in the meantime, while appearing simply to be amusing himself with the scene around him, was revolving in his own mind what he should do. It was a terrible blow, at the very outset to have made an enemy on board his own ship. He could clearly see that the man-of-war's man suspected him, though he had no doubt his rank and position in society would save him from any consequences, as no one would believe Bob Griggs against him. But he had views which necessitated his not having allowed the faintest suspicion to exist against him.

It was a delicate and difficult task; but such

things admirably suited the fancy of Sir Edgar Blakesley.

He pushed away his half-finished grog, laid down his pipe, and, saying he was hungry, asked for lunch. In deference to his middy's uniform the attendant showed him up stairs. As he passed Bob Griggs, he made a sign to him to come up.

"Lunch for two," said the young officer, as soon as they were in a private room.

The attendant, with a low bow, left the room. He knew that most young naval gentlemen liked to be treated as if they were already post-captains.

"So," said the middy, with a hearty laugh, "so you knew me directly, did you?"

"Eh, yer honour," cried the astonished sailor —not astonished at the fact, but at the other's cool and collected impudence.

"Like to take your revenge, eh?" continued the midshipman.

Bob Griggs looked wildly at him. The cool collected manner of the other staggered him.

Suppose he had not been drugged, after all, and that he had been deceived.

"My good fellow," said Sir Edgar Blakesley, in a patronising and haughty way, "I played with you only for fun, just to show you how absurd it is to risk your money in that way. Here are half a dozen guineas; that will satisfy you. Will you be my servant on board?"

The sailor could scarcely speak.

"Why, bless yer honour's heart alive, with pleasure," he said, with a humorous sparkle in his eyes. "Only to think. Well, but yer see, yer honour, Bob Griggs had a bit slewed hisself, and blowed if he didn't think as how you'd a cut away with the blunt."

"You were very intoxicated, and the best thing I could have done was to take care of the money. But that is all forgotten now. Tell me all about the ship, its officers, and what I shall have to do."

The sailor, with a grin of pleasure, entered freely on a topic upon which a Jack Tar is always eloquent; and by the time lunch was over, and the midshipman rose to return to his inn, he had a very fair idea of his brother officers, and a vague outline of his own duties.

The two parted to all appearance friends; but Sir Edgar had a vague dread of Bob Griggs, and the latter quietly determined to keep his weather eye open.

It was with a determination to win the good opinion of his superiors and his equals that the midshipman joined his frigate; and with this view he was calmly respectful to his officers, cordial with the young gentlemen, who, from something in his manner, did not attempt to play him any of those tricks which are usual in the navy when a juvenile joins his messmates in the cockpit.

We should rather say *were* usual, as all things are changing under the sun, and we fear that even boys are getting less frolicksome than they used to be in earlier times.

The Rainbow was one of those vessels which were engaged in cruising about the Channel to watch the vast preparations made at Boulogne for the invasion of this country; and for this very reason the daily routine of the ship was monotonous to a degree.

Several times the frigate ran into port, but only to revictual and water.

It almost immediately returned to its post.

The captain of the frigate, though there was something in the manner of his old friend's son which he did not like, treated him with marked kindness. He had regard for his orphan position, abandoned almost as much by his mother as if she had been dead.

He accordingly asked him to dinner oftener than he should have done, and gave him every opportunity of pursuing his studies. He admitted him, too, to a familiarity on the quarter-deck, which was somewhat the envy of his fellows.

One morning they were beside one another on the deck; the day was calm, and the splendid ship lay tossing on the blue waves, in sight of Boulogne. They were so near that not only town and ramparts were visible, but the ships in the harbour and the soldiers' huts on the hills, where the column now stands.

It was a sight of deep interest to all concerned.

Sir Edmund suddenly laid down his glass with a sigh.

"I would give something to know what is going on yonder," he said; "'tis dull work boxing about in the Channel, uncertain if ever we shall have a chance of a prize."

"I beg your pardon, Sir Edmund," said the midshipman, touching his cap.

"What is it," replied the officer, turning round rather sharply.

"I can speak French like a Frenchman—"

"Well, sir, what then?"

"I could pass for a Frenchy ashore there, and perhaps get the information you require," added Sir Edgar.

"Humph, deuced venturesome," muttered the post-captain. "But you are sure you can pass for a Frenchman—or, rather, boy," he added with a smile.

"My nurse was a Frenchwoman, and always said I spoke like a native," continued the middy, who, reckless and audacious, was tired of board-ship, and eager to accomplish some adventure which should give him personal renown.

"Come down below—tell the first lieutenant I want him," said the captain, a bright flush crossing his weather-beaten countenance. The midshipman touched his cap, and followed his superior's instructions. In a few minutes he and Mr. Collins were below in the captain's cabin, several decanters of wine were placed on the table, and at a hint from the captain both helped themselves.

"I have called you, Collins," said the officer, "to submit to your notice a proposition made to me by this youngster, which I do not like adopting, and do not like refusing. The lad, it appears, speaks the French lingo like a Frenchman, and wants to go ashore, look about him, and make a report."

"Indeed, Sir Edmund!" replied the first lieutenant, raising his eyebrows with astonishment; "if the young gentleman's discretion equals his courage it would, perhaps, produce a result equal to your hopes."

"There is the fear of his being taken for a spy——"

"No, Sir Edmund!" put in the middy; "I assure you I speak even the *patois*[1] of this very locality. My nurse was born here."

"Well, sir," said the post-captain, after a moment's hesitation, "I am almost inclined to risk it, if you will be cautious and prudent. Your plan of landing?"

"Well, Sir Edmund!" replied the midshipman, who was very pale; "I would tar my hands and face, put on one of the boy's suits of clothes, and *run away with the dingy!*"

Both the officers laughed; and, after some further conversation, it was agreed that he should have a trial, and it was further settled that every Wednesday, until his re-appearance, the frigate should anchor at night within a mile of a spot indicated, show a triangle of lights, and wait there until just before break of day.

Despite the war, there was so much smuggling done, that it would be, doubtless, easy for him to get off. Several minor details were then agreed on, and then the three separated.

---

[1] Local dialect.

CHAPTER XXIII.

NEW RELATIONS.

SOFT and slowly rolled the waves from Albion's heights towards the hostile shores that night, which was so dark that, at two miles from the cliffs, not even the lofty coast of Boulogne could be distinguished. This admirably served the intended purpose; so that, a little after nightfall, the frigate stood in under easy sail.

All orders were given in a low tone, and passed from mouth to mouth with every precaution. In this way the ship was brought to like magic, and without a word almost being spoken, the first cutter and dingy were lowered, the latter placed in tow, and six stout rowers slowly and cautiously bent to their work.

Presently, the low and regular wash of the surf could be heard quite distinctly enough to cause any further approach on the part of the crew dangerous.

The midshipman passed into the dingy with his bag, shook hands with his fellow youngster, who steered, and then, without a word, the two boats parted. Any sound of voices might have been dangerous.

The middy stood in the stern sheets of the boat, and began sculling himself towards the shore. About a quarter of a mile to the eastward along the cliffs is a gap or opening, guarded by a martello tower, and which is now often the walk of the visitor to Boulogne. The darkness was great, but so near as he was he could easily distinguish this kind of valley.

The lad held his breath. He was not alarmed; he was only anxious. He had not exaggerated his powers of language, he had even concealed them. He knew even enough Hebrew to serve his purpose.

All this will be explained in good time, with the mystery of his signs and passes at Portsmouth.

Presently he was within about a dozen yards of the shore, when directly, he saw distinctly several dark figures advance cautiously in his direction.

"Oh la, les amis," he cried, "je l'echappe belle!"[1]

Next minute he struck the bank, and was surrounded by several men, both soldiers and sailors.

"D'on viens tu?"[2] said one roughly.

"From England," he replied, in a quiet tone.

"In this boat?" cried the same voice, now holding up a lanthorn.

"No, farceur,[3] I was pressed on board an English man-of-war, half starved, fed on mouldy biscuits alive with maggots,[4] and the first chance I had I ran away. I had a tussle for it; but for the dark they would have caught me."

"Poor little fellow?" said one of the sailors, who had hauled up his boat on shore, "how

[1] "Hollo there, friends! I've had a narrow escape."
[2] "Whence come you?" [3] Joker. [4] See "Les Pontons Anglais" for this and other libels on English Navy and prisons.

lucky to have escaped les damnèes Anglais. But never mind, the day is soon coming when we shall have our revenge."

"Does any one know Claude Placquet?" asked the midshipman.

"Ha! ha! my hearty," said a stout burly sailor; "what do you know about Claude Placquet?"

"Well, considering he's my uncle," observed the middy, "I feel some little anxiety to make his acquaintance."

"Diantre, and who the devil are you, then?" continued the other.

"The only son of Laura Placquet that was—now Madame Carabosse," said the lad, boldly.

"Mon Dieu;" cried the sailor, with considerable emotion, "is it possible? Then my sister still lives, and is married."

"Bah—how funny," said the lad, somewhat agitated himself.

"Tudieu, mon garçon, if this be true," cried the fisherman warmly, "there shall be feasting to-night in the Rue de Duras. Come, my lad, with me. But why has your mother stopped so long in England?"

"Ma foi!" said the lad, "she has a good business, and then she got married, and it ain't easy to get away. The Court adores Madame Carabosse, milliner and artiste in bonnets."

The boy lied. Madame Carabosse kept an old clothes shop.

The sailor took the boy by the hand, and led him away, leaving the soldiers in utter wonder at the extraordinary nature of the meeting, to say nothing of a half-guinea which he left them to drink his health with.

Whatever dislike the French may entertain of the English generally, they have a wondrous love for their gold.

The sailor was a man of few words. This sudden meeting with his sister's child under such strangely romantic circumstances had utterly silenced him, so that they scarcely spoke until he reached one of those narrow steep streets leading from the port, which are all steps, and the summits of which are the top of the cliff itself.

Entering the open door of one of the best-looking houses in this singular lane, where the roof of one man's residence was on a level with the floor of the next, the lad followed with a beating heart. He was armed at all points, it is true—for had he have failed in his fearful undertaking, he knew that France was his only refuge.

"Oh he! the house there," said Claude Placquet in a loud voice.

The principal room, that by which they entered from the street, was not of very small dimensions, though a portion of it was encumbered by nets, now less often used than formerly, because of the English cruisers and privateers, who ran up to the very mouth of the port. It had one of those large old-fashioned fire-places which are redolent of hospitality, a tall chest of drawers, a stone or mud floor, a coarse table, a clock, and half a-dozen cane-bottom chairs, and that was all.

"Eh, mon homme," said a stout dark-eyed woman, of about thirty-four or five, in short red petticoats, blue worsted stockings, and with a red handkerchief about her head, "you are back early. I thought you were going to put out with Francois."

"Eh bien! ma fine," replied the husband, with a loud laugh, "one does not pick up a nephew on the beach every day."

"Nephew—what!" cried the woman, eyeing the lad with astonishment. "Why, whose child is it—and what is his name?"

"Don't know," said the man, with a grin.

"Philip Carabosse, at your service," added the lad, with a bow and a smile.

"It seems my sister Laura married in England," continued Claude, "and this youngster is her son; so you see he has got tired of England, and here he is. Where's Pauline?"

"Pauline," cried the mother, never taking her eyes off the lad.

But Pauline must be formally introduced.

CHAPTER XXIV.

PAULINE.

SHE was sixteen.

Age of dreams!—age of bliss!—age when no phantoms of the past ever rise to chase bright visions of the future from the soul!—age of hope!—age of faith, when the horizon appears never dim, and fortune glances at us with one eternal smile.

There are exceptions to all things, and it is sad to know that for some there is no youth—that for some there is no joy—children of the night—of infamy, of crime, and worse—of poverty.

But we speak now of what youth is in its normal state.

Tall, graceful, with jet black hair confined by a tasty silk handkerchief, with eyes of sloe-like hue that read the very soul; with olive cheeks that were rounded in graceful elegance of form, with a rich full mouth, disclosing teeth of pearly whiteness; there was a lurking sarcasm in the expression of her face that spoke volumes to the heart.

It would cost something to win that heart—but once win it!

Pauline had had many suitors—no lovers.

Pauline was ambitious.

But her ambition was thought by her friends only to picture to herself a husband who should command a fishing boat, and be above his fellows a little. She only openly disdained common sailors.

There was a perfect volcano of passion in that girl's heart, veiled by an appearance of the most charming innocence.

She came bounding into the room, her short petticoated dress, showing legs that would have made her fortune on the stage, her eyes flashing, her mien excited—for she had heard all.

"My boy," said the fisherman, "your papers."

Philip Carabosse, as he called himself, smiled and drew forth a coarse pocket-book—the foresight of that boy was infernal—from which he took a letter. This he handed with perfect ease and grace to Claude.

"Pauline, read it aloud——"

The girl took it, glanced with a pleasant smile at Carabosse, and read—

"London. This — Jan —.

"MY DEAR BROTHER CLAUDE,—If this finds you alive and well as I am, I write to say that England is a vile country, all fogs and rain, but one makes money. Some day I hope to run over, and embrace you all. The bearer of this is my son, who is sick of England—he will explain all. You know I was never much of a scholar, so believe me your affectionate sister,

"FEMME CARABOSSE,

"Born LAURA PLACQUET."

"Pauline!" said the fisherman, earnestly; "embrace your cousin."

The girl advanced towards the lad with a smile. His back was now turned to the father and mother. He was pale. Though a man in appearance and in character, he had never approached his lips to those of a woman.

Pauline offered her two cheeks, one after another, with a coquettish blush and toss of the head.

Philip caught her in his arms, and kissed her hurriedly. As he did so, his head fell on her shoulders, so great was his emotion.

"And now tudieu," cried Claude; "let us have the best we have got. Nephew, we are not rich, but we can still entertain you heartily. There shall be an omelette au lard, a fowl, and a bottle of old cogniac, and then never talk of bed, for we will talk."

Philip turned slowly round to thank his uncle. Pauline ran away to hide her confusion as much as to assist her mother. The emotion of the young stranger had communicated itself to her to a certain degree.

It would take too long to describe the attempt made by that worthy family—husband, wife, and only daughter—to welcome the return of a relative of whom they had never heard, but who was the child of a member of the famille often spoken of by all. Philip delighted them by his accounts of England, his covert sneers at our island and its manners, and above all, by sketches of his mother's grandeur, her connections in high life, and other inventions of his fertile imagination.

His description of the worthy father, Carabosse, who had never existed, except in the fancy of himself and mother, was a masterpiece.

They did not retire until one in the morning, when Philip Carabosse was shown the way to a neat little well-furnished chamber at the top of the house. Any one with half an eye could have told it was Pauline's!

The mother and daughter, on this occasion, slept together.

The father cast himself, dressed as he was, on the pile of nets, smoked a pipe, and was soon in a sound and refreshing sleep.

Philip Carabosse—we adopt whatever alias he may select for the nonce—felt no inclination to sleep. He opened his window to inhale the breeze of the night. His head was full of wild and strange fancies. The main task he had imposed upon himself was a dangerous and a risky one; but already it had nearly vanished, even from his recollection.

He was thinking of Pauline.

The awakening of the first dawn of passion, be it for good or ill, is sometimes like the tornado. Love, at times, is a plant of slow and timid growth; at others, it bursts upon the soul and swells in the bosom like a ball of fire.

In his wild schemes of ambition, of aggrandisement, of avarice, he had never hitherto even thought of love.

It came down upon him now like the sweep of the sirocco. He felt the warm cheek of that lovely girl against his lips.

He fell into a deep reverie.

For one moment he asked himself whether he might not have selected the wrong path; whether the joys of home, of domestic affections, might not be preferable to all that could be won by the grasping and craving desires of his soul for power and wealth.

"This girl is very beautiful. Here I am, free from all fear of consequences. For this country I am rich—why not remain—cast off a servitude I hate, and be happy here? But rank, wealth, power, a dazzling position, are mine in England. No—this girl is very beautiful. I may be tempted to stop here longer than I meant; but then ——"

And with a glance of terrible meaning on his countenance he lay down to seek that sleep which was so necessary to his plan. Clearness of head, sharpness of eye, and cool resolution, were positively demanded; and for all these repose was necessary.

But he could not sleep. Dwell as he would on the plans which had brought him to Boulogne-sur-Mer, his ideas floated round the form of the lovely Pauline.

In his enthusiasm he kissed the inanimate pillow on which her head had been cushioned, he had every reason to believe.

At daybreak he fell asleep, nor did any of the family for some time disturb his slumbers.

CHAPTER XXV.

THE CONFESSION.

TRUE and false passion are so much alike that it is difficult at times to distinguish between them. He who wishes to blight, and he who would shield the loved one from the storms of life, may, in the first instance, use the same language, and be inspired by the same eloquence.

How is a young and innocent girl to know—to understand the difference?

Let all young girls who hearken to the soft, insinuating voice of love, remember that their true object in life is to become good wives and happy mothers.

They can then do little wrong.

Next morning, when Philip Carabosse rose, he found that Claude had gone down to the beech to witness the arrival of some fishing-boats which had come in in the night, after crawling about cautiously to avoid the enemy's cruisers; while the good wife had gone down to the market, according to custom, to look after business, though she had no fish to sell.

When Philip Carabosse came out of his room, he could hear the voice of Pauline, as clear as a bell, singing in the room below.

He came slowly and cautiously down until he stood at the door of the room where he had supped last night.

Pauline had her back turned to him; she was spinning, and as the wheel whirled round, she sang in tune to the sound of the little instrument of woman's labours.

Her head was bent over her work, and her lovely figure was shown to perfection.

Philip Carabosse gazed at her with genuine admiration. The first dawn of love, or passion, whatever we call it, is exclusive. To him there was nothing in the room but the girl, and all the outward sounds of the port were lost in the whir-whir of the spinning-wheel.

Philip stepped into the room. Pauline turned round with a calm and smiling face, that quite astonished Philip, who felt that he was blushing, that his heart was fluttering wildly, and that he could not speak.

"Bon jour, mon cousin!" said Pauline, rising, and offering her hand.

Philip took it and blushed up to the eyes.

"How handsome you look, my cousin," he stammered forth.

"Now, no compliments," said Pauline, showing her white teeth, "I hate them; what will you have for breakfast?"

Philip Carabosse pouted.

"There is soup, broiled fish, and—for your sake, a luxury we seldom indulge in—coffee," continued the girl, quietly laying a milk-white cloth on the table.

"Whatever you please," said Philip, who could not take his eyes off her lovely arms, her bright eyes, her magnificent form.

He was rapidly becoming a connoisseur.

But Pauline would not talk until he took his breakfast. She insisted that he wanted it, and at last so completely conquered her admirer, that he sat down and condescended to do honour to the numerous good things before him.

At this moment the stalwart form, the manly face, and open brow of the fisherman passed through the doorway. His greeting with his new-found nephew was hearty in the extreme.

"Well now, my lad, here you are in France. You say," he continued, after some friendly interchange of courtesies, known to the simple-hearted and the brave, "that your mother is well off, but that is neither here nor there. You are now in France; what do you mean to do for a living?"

Pauline looked at him under her eyes.

"My uncle," said Philip Carabosse, with that frankness which no one could assume better than himself, "I have yet to learn experience of the world. I am entirely in your hands."

"Then, my lad, I have no second advice to give. You must be a fisherman like myself, and like my father before me. It is a glorious trade. Plenty of work, it is true; but whew! a wet sheet and a flowing sea, and now and then, who knows, a slap at the English!"

Claude said this with enthusiasm, which the other appeared to join in.

Pauline looked at him under her eyes, but

oh! so keenly, so curiously, he again felt his heart beat with anxiety as well as love.

The girl was evidently watching him with a strained and yet timid glance.

"My uncle, it shall be as you say. I will learn my business, become a good sailor, and then buy a boat. My greatest happiness will be to remain with you and your family," he answered.

"Ah! ah!" said Claude, with a loud laugh, as he gazed at the somewhat blushing pair; "whew! sits the wind already in that quarter. Well, lad, behave yourself well for a year or two, and then, who knows, more extraordinary things have happened than—your *remaining permanently in our family!*"

Philip turned crimson, and Pauline found some special business in the kitchen.

"Harkee!" said the honest fisherman, with a firmness and decision of manner which, for a moment, awed even the insolence and superciliousness of Philip Carabosse; "harkee, my lad! I like your phiz, I like your mother, and for the sake of the blood that is between us, I receive you into my family. I see you are hankering after my daughter. Philip, she is all I have—recollect, I will have her married with a virginal crown on her head*—you understand *suffit!*"

Philip rose, took his hand, and pressed it to his bosom with a candour and frankness which quite won the heart of the worthy fisherman.

"Uncle, if Pauline will honour me so far, she shall be unto me as a sister, until the day comes when I can claim her as a wife."

"*Touche la!* you are an honest fellow!" said Claude, heartily; "but I only ran on to wish you good morning. I have work until evening, when I shall be in to supper. Pauline will show you the town, which you must be curious to see. At seven we sup."

And with one warning look, Claude left the adder he was warming in his bosom, complete master of the situation.

In a few minutes Pauline came tripping in with a straw hat upon her head, a sweet smile on her lips, and a little *cabas*, or woman's bag, in her hand.

"Where are you going?" said Philip, taking up his hat eagerly.

"To see my aunt," replied Pauline, demurely casting down her eyes.

"Where is that?" asked Philip.

"At the other end of the town," replied the little maid.

"Your father said you were to show me the town," replied Philip, "and this is an excellent opportunity."

And without asking her permission, he sallied forth in her company.

They were a charming pair; he in his taut blue jacket, and straw hat, and smart neckcloth; she in her fanciful Boulognese costume: and so the passers-by seemed to think them. For some time not a word was spoken. Philip Carabosse was too busy looking about him at

the novel scene to address many words to his fair companion.

It was a scene worthy of the eye. On all sides vast preparations were making for that memorable invasion which was to annihilate the power of England. On one side the shipwrights were hammering away at the construction of vessels which were to carry the invading force and the material of war. Everywhere might be seen groups of sailors belonging to the vast to-be-created navy, hanging about the corners of streets, or issuing merrily from wine-shops and estaminets; troops of all kinds marched and re-marched, while the wheels of artillery wagons thundered over the pavement, where now ran the humble *fiacres* of the more pacific British invaders, who, in consideration probably of the connection of the name with England, have since the peace made this city their head-quarters.

Still, while taking in every detail as they caught his eye, Philip Carabosse was thinking far more of the fair creature at his side than of the object with which he had ostensibly landed in Boulogne.

How should he commence that attack, which, despite that solemn promise to Claude, he was bent on making. A strange sensation came over him as he moved. It is so glorious to feel the first sensations of love—to look down into the heart of a woman whose good feelings we covet, that it reacts even upon the bad.

They had reached a shady walk, called the Tintilleries, at that time of day abandoned. A wooden seat, shaded by some trees, caught the young sailor's eye. It overlooked a magnificent prospect of part of the town and the open sea.

"Pauline," he said, taking her hand very gravely, after glancing around to make sure that he was not seen, "I want to speak to you."

"*Comment*," replied Pauline, looking up with her great astonished eyes, "then why don't you begin at once?"

"Let us sit down a moment; I have a good deal to say," said Philip Carabosse.

Pauline looked modestly down on the ground, but allowed herself to be led to a seat.

"Pauline," began the youth, in his lowest and most insidious voice, "do you know that I could not sleep last night?"

"*Pas possible*, why not?" cried the girl with a look of *naïve* astonishment.

"Pauline, I was thinking of you," began Philip.

"Now if you are going to make love," said Pauline, gazing now calmly and deliberately into his eyes, "I warn you at once not to begin. I will never marry a mere fisherman."

Philip's face flushed crimson, and then turned pale.

"It's a fact; so, though I like you very well, I won't think of it," said Pauline.

"My dear *cousine*," replied Philip Carabosse in a low hushed voice, "I love you dearly already, and could I but trust you, I would tell you a marvellous secret. But first, what is your wish as to a position in life?"

There was something commanding and at the same time promising in the words of Philip which made Pauline reflect a moment.

* In many parts of France girls who have fallen from virtue's high estate are not allowed to be married in white veils and with a virginal crown. Their shame is made manifest even on their wedding day.

CHAPTER XXVI.

PAULINE'S IDYL.

"You ask me," she said, after a short pause, "what is the position in life at which I aim. Recollect, M. Philip Carabosse, that I have just returned from a first-rate school in Paris, where I was educated as a little lady, and never expected to be compelled to do any work."

"Then why are you back here?"

"*Monsieur le curieux*, my father saw me go with great unwillingness, and at last, despite the kindness of the ladies who would have brought me up, sent for me home. Imagine, my poor boy, a palace all furnished with pictures, carpets, chandeliers, beds with lace and curtains, all the dazzling brightness of a Paris fashionable school—and then the Rue de Duras, Boulogne."

Philip's breath came and went with unusual energy. He began to understand Pauline.

"I came back to my home very sad; but you must know, *petit*, that I love may father and mother, and would not let them know I was dissatisfied, so they think me happy as the day, until such time as—"

"As what?" gasped Philip, eagerly.

"I find my true position," said Pauline.

"Explain yourself," cried the boy, panting with anticipation.

"I was born for luxury; I want a palace, carriages, rich dresses, servants to do my every wish, a rich and handsome lover—my husband, n fact; that is my dream. Imagine, then, even if the prospect of a captain of a fishing smack as a husband is much pleasure to me," said the girl flippantly.

Philip Carabosse only saw in her words proper ambition.

"No, divine and delightful Pauline!" he said, in a low whisper in her ear, "if I could procure you all this, what then would you say?"

Pauline looked at him as if she thought he was taking leave of his senses.

"Bravo! mon petit; you are quite grand."

"Could I trust you?" said Philip sadly.

"Philip," replied Pauline, gravely, "whatever it may be I will never betray your secret. Though I don't think I can marry you, still I think I shall love you."

Philip kissed her unresisting hand.

"My Pauline, take into your hands my life, my existence, my honour. I am the son of your father's sister, but my name is not Carabosse; my father is an English nobleman of rank; my house is a palace, I have horses, carriages, everything your bold and ambitious soul pants for—and if you will you shall share my coming with me."

"But why are you here?" said the half-alarmed Pauline.

"Because I wished to see my mother's relatives, and because I am tired of the monotony of yonder ship, of which I am an officer," he said, hissing the words into her ear, and by that cold gleam in his eyes, evidently prepared for the worst.

"Hush—let me think. Explain yourself. I wish to hear it all," said Pauline, whose flushed cheeks and panting bosom proclaimed the extreme violence of her emotions.

Philip Carabosse, in a brief but lucid manner, explained his story in his own way; told how his mother had been secretly married to his father; how she had kept the secret to the last, though his father had acknowledged him; and then added that he was only waiting his majority to take possession of title and estates.

"And all this is true," said Pauline, whose lips were dry, whose breath was hot, whose eyes flashed with lurid fire.

"On, my soul! by these bright eyes—and if you will, my soul, my darling, my angel, by this first kiss, which seals our love and our compact," whispered Philip.

The girl dazzled, her head in a whirl, her ambition roused, her hopes set on the rack, and really beginning to like the dashing audacious youth, returned the fond pressure of his hand, and permitted him to cull one kiss from her warm and pouting lips.

"But now," she said, first of the two regaining her composure, "how do you mean to act?"

The frigate came surging slowly up in the distance, defiant, but out of gun-shot, the English ensign at the peak.

"On board that ship is a chaplain, and the moment we arrive on board he shall join our hands. As a young married officer is not allowed to live on board, I will get leave of absence, if not to leave altogether; and away, my darling, for liberty and love."

"But in the meantime?" said Pauline.

"I prefer remaining here—some time. Let us learn to know and esteem each other. Besides, I will not ask you to go until I have placed in your hands the proof of what I have said. It is easy, by means of a smuggler, to communicate with England."

Pauline took his hand in hers now. This last stroke of cunning and policy convinced her.

"But should my father suspect your being an English officer?" said Pauline, anxiously.

The girl had no compunction herself. Her soul was of that order that ambition stifled every other consideration—country, parents, her duty to her relatives and to heaven. What mattered anything, so that she was rich and wore diamonds.

"Your father will never suspect anything. I will run out with him once or twice; it will do me good. In the meantime I shall bask in the sunshine of your eyes, my adored, my beloved; and will that not be happiness?"

"How often have you said this before?" whispered the yielding Pauline.

"Never, on my soul," cried Philip, with startling emphasis; "until yesterday, when my lips touched your cheek, I had no idea of love—not the remotest conception of its transports and delights."

"And you will always love me?" continued the syren, herself feeling the tender emotions of the scene.

"As long as life is given me," said Philip Carabosse.

CHAPTER XXVII.

THE DANCING GIRL.

"Hoo, hoo, hoo!" shouts the fat woman through her trumpet, on the same stage already alluded to, but in a very different tone, but to a very similar collection of auditors; "hoo, hoo, hoo! walk up, walk up! only one penny. This, ladies and gentlemen, is the day performance, that of the evening is threepence, and no money returned."

"He! he! he!" said the clown, grinning from ear to ear; "don't you do nothing of the kind—the live lion's a hungry, and might take it into his idears of things to eat you up."

"Silence, fool!" cried Mrs. Jottley, pretending to be angry; "what means this impertinence? Don't listen to him, my friends. He's touched in the brain—from too much standing on his head——"

The clown, who was *not* very quick at repartee, merely turned a sommersault.

And the fairy girl with the golden hair danced still upon the stilts, and the boy with the strange slouched hat and feather, moved round her, keeping the ground clear.

But the girl was pale, and a hectic flush was upon her cheek, and the lad was very sad.

They had found Jottley and Co. very excellent people. They gave them ample accommodation to sleep, plenty of food, but also plenty of hard work; and strange as it may seem, the girl, brought up as a wild and illiterate girl, just on the verge of bursting into womanhood, taught by the lessons of her companion, began to be ashamed of appearing in public in such a manner and in such a garb. Every hour, every minute, every second which he could take from his duties, did William Lennox devote to the lovely girl confided to his protection. He saw that she was a pearl of great price, and his eager and tender eye first that very morning saw that she was ill.

But he, as yet, had had no time to speak to her on the subject. Still he saw her large and lustrous eyes, he heard her hacking and unpleasant cough, and a cold dread, such as one only feels at the approach of illness in one we love, came upon his soul. William Lennox had seen so much misery in his life, that it had appeared to him, nothing worse—nothing more painful could occur to him, than had already fallen to his lot. Deserted by his natural protectors, abandoned, it appeared, by the mother who bore him, injured by the being in whom he had put his utmost trust, his whole soul had become centred upon the gentle and lovely creature that was to him as a pure and dear sister, confided to his noble and manly care.

William Lennox knew and felt the responsibility that rested on him. He knew how much he had taken upon himself when he stole away that child, whom he now saw blighted by the very education he had given her, fading, fading away.

Then came the performances, that moment when the whole thought is to please and satisfy the fickle and discontented public.

Of course the representation of "Macbeth" was a mere travestie—even a caricature—but the gentle Lilian went through her terrible part of *Macbeth* with a sterner reality, which, with her hacking cough, was terribly painful.

William Lennox felt it to his very heart's core.

When the performance was over, he took Lily in his arms and carried her out into the van, which lay behind the booth in which they were performing. There was something in his manner and tone that alarmed even worthy Mrs. Jottley. She followed him.

William, upon whom Lily smiled painfully, was now laid down upon a straw mattrass in the middle of the van. The windows were open, and a refreshing breeze played through the narrow apertures. For a moment Lily did not speak.

"Now, Lily dear, how do you feel?" said William.

"Better, brother dear; but this life will kill me," replied the weeping child.

"But, why?" said the boy, whose heart throbbed fearfully.

"William, I am dying; it is no use my concealing it. You have explained to me the utter weakness of the life I have been leading, and I know that I am doing wrong."

William shuddered, and made no reply for several minutes.

"My dear, my beloved sister," he began, "if I have said or done anything to so change your opinion of life, that it has hurt your feelings, I painfully regret it. But, Lily, dear, have courage. Mrs. Jottley is a good, worthy woman, and if we only represent to her that it is painful to your feelings——"

"Lord love your souls!" cried the person alluded to, coming up the steps with a heavy, but at the same time, hearty step. "Why, you don't think, children, I would do you any harm? You dear little girl, how are you?"

"Better, ma'am," replied Lily, with timid simplicity.

She had power still to feel that despite the roughness of the woman who had taken up the position of mistress with them, she was still in heart kind and good.

"I'm glad to hear it. Now, Mr. Lennox, excuse me, but I only see one remedy for this. Of course, the dear child must not appear tonight?"

"Of course not," cried William Lennox, somewhat eagerly.

"Well then, my dear, it will require a great deal of thinking over. Don't you see, when the public expects 'Macbeth' to be played, they always somehow expects Lady Hamlet—I begs her pardon—Lady Macbeth—to appear. Now, you sees, as well as I, Mr. Lennox, it carn't be done."

"I know it."

"And yet we must play 'Macbeth,'" said Jottley, whose Co. was so very shy of appearing.

"Cannot we change the play?" suggested William, his eye always fixed upon the only treasure he valued in the world.

"My dear Mr. Juvenile Roscius," said Jottley, with a great show of energy, "take my word for it, never disappoint the public. Better play

'Macbeth' with Lady Macbeth left out, than change the piece."

"Don't let me put you out," said Lily, in her angelic voice; "I will play to-night."

"No," replied William, sternly, "it shall not be. I will play Lady Macbeth; she only comes in once, and then she makes but one speech."

"Bravo!" cried Jottley; "spoken like a man. And mind you, the speech is nothing—learn it in five minutes. It begins—but never mind—you know all about it."

And thus it was agreed that poor little Lily should have a holiday, and lay quiet in her strange home while the performance was going on. It was quite clear that the peculiar life she was leading was killing her. At first, it had been amusing, but, by degrees, as the knowledge of a higher and a better state of things dawned upon her, she began to feel that she was falling in the social scale.

Lily was a born angel, as Pauline was a demon.

In life we meet many of both—who shall say which compose the majority?

There was blowing of trumpets, there was beating of drums, there were fifes that blew shrilly in the air, and the crowd in front was in great glee. The crowds were rushing in steaming hordes, eager to see the promised amusement of the evening. Outside a strong pressure prevented any new arrivals from approaching.

Suddenly there was a fearful clamour from

the borders of the mob, attracted by the outside ; more they could not see.

A post-chaise and four had drawn up, and the inmates were begging to be allowed to pass.

But no one gave way. Curiosity is an universal vice.

"Good people," said a soft voice inside the chaise, "I am seeking for my child."

"And have we not all got children?" said a monumental specimen of a rough and curious countrywoman.

"Out of the way—move—start!" roared a fierce voice, as a horseman rode down, and hit right and left with his riding-whip.

A tall, stalwart gipsy arrested his progress.

"Who do you want to see?" he whispered, recognising the speaker.

"Miriam's kinchin co'," replied the rider, evidently not offended.

"Follow me, and bring your folks with you. The girl is ill."

The post-chaise followed the horseman on the edge of the crowd towards the rear of the show, so full of life and light.

They found themselves at the deserted door of the van in which slept so much loveliness, and, besides, so much of the world's most poignant miseries.

Mrs. Winterton, for of course our readers have guessed that it is the sad and bereaved mother who has thus opportunely arrived to the rescue of her (supposed) unfortunate daughter, guided by the gipsy in the throng, was getting out, when one of her companions in the carriage, who had recognised Miriam, sprang before her from the post-chaise.

"Hoo! hoo! hoo!" went the trumpet on the platform outside.

"Now then, ladies and gentlemen!" cried the clown.

And William Lennox in the inside went through as rapidly as he could the "painful, interesting, and distressing tragedy of 'Macbeth' *for this* night only."

Macbeth : MR. WILLIAM LENNOX.
Lady Macbeth : MR. WILLIAM LENNOX.

It was further intimated that the great female tragedian of the booth was unhappily slightly indisposed.

And there she slept—a pinky rose upon her cheeks, her eyes closed, her pale lips parted, her soft bosom heaving quickly under the influence of the cruel fever, and a heavy sigh every now and then exuding from her oppressed and suffering bosom.

And there she slept. Three figures were eagerly devouring her every feature.

"That is the child you brought me," said Miriam, addressing the highwayman, Captain George.

"Bless her curly hair," replied the young man.

"Hush! silence! Let no one speak a word," whispered the agonised mother. "It is! it is! I know it is my child. Twice before have I seen her; twice before have I felt the divine inspiration which told me it was her, my Lilian. How beautiful she sleeps. She must be weary; I will carry her."

The sleeping child turned round, and sighed forth a word.

"William—dear William," she said, and smiled like an angel.

The mother frowned darkly, despite her love. The child was clearly thinking of another than herself.

"Leave her to me, Arabella," said Captain George gently.

He took her in his arms; he lifted her slowly up, and stood erect.

"She weighed less thirteen years ago," he said, with a smile.

"Come! come!" said the mother, in tones of agony. "They may detain her."

Miriam stood still, and watched the scene, without taking any part in it. The sleeping child was placed in the carriage. None noticed that terrible and hectic flush—least of all the mother.

Indeed, when does a mother confess to herself the dreadful truth that her only child is dying!

Away sped the carriage and four. After a brief conversation with Miriam, Captain George followed as an escort.

Miriam remained. Her eyes were dry, but none the less was her deep emotion. Hence she felt for poor William Lennox. The house dwellers, in their hurry, had not taken the least thought of his feelings.

Mrs. Winterton—who could blame her—had clutched her treasure with all the greedy avarice of a mother who had never known her child. It mattered little to her momentarily selfish love, that she broke the heart, or hurt the dignity of any one.

The void of thirteen years had suddenly been filled up, and the voice she had scarcely heard slept in stillness on her bosom.

The array of authority in favour of this poor unfortunate being, her child, was, to her mind, overpowering. The evidence was clear as crystal. A court of law, a jury might have doubted, but a mother, never! The face, the hair, the nose, the eyes, were all signs without denial. Besides, had not the man who had taken, and the woman who had received, acknowledged and pointed out the babe?

Go thy way, glad mother; clasp thy treasure to thy breast, none will blame thee—none will chide, who know thy true and maternally devoted feeling.

But poor, abandoned, and deserted William Lennox.

He came from the booth, still in the gaudy tinsel of his theatrical robes, painted and spangled, but to rush to the van where Lilian sleepeth. Up the steps he bounds, rushes into the interior of the crazy vehicle, and behold, on the rude mattrass sits Miriam, their gipsy mother.

William gazed wildly round, and missed his beloved treasure—his child, but his darling affianced bride.

"Lily!" he said, clutching the old woman's arm.

"Silence! son of the house-dwellers," she replied proudly. "You stole away my child."

"Woman, drive me not mad," he said. "Where is she?"

"Boy! justly I should punish you; but I see your sorrow. Lily is gone from you for ever."

"Dead!"

"No. Boy! speak not thus. Be not mad. She has not left us; but she has been taken away. Her mother has been here."

"Her mother!" repeated William Lennox, wildly.

"Yes. She came; she found her asleep; she saw that she was ill; and, as was her right, she took her away," said the gipsy gravely.

William Lennox fainted.

CHAPTER XXVIII.

A NEW CAREER.

WHEN William Lennox came to himself, it was with a sensation of horror, for at once the reflection dashed upon his mind that Lily was lost to him for ever.

He was in a comfortable bedroom in an inn, and, as he thought, alone. As soon, however, as he moved, he heard footsteps shuffling along the floor, and there, by the side of his bed, stood the Blue Dwarf, in a costume which, though in part that of the day, was still so disposed as to conceal as much as possible the defects of his person.

William Lennox looked at him with mute surprise, not unmixed with terror. His peculiarities of person, eccentric and even hideous though they were, seemed not even to rouse his astonishment. It was his presence that surprised him.

"I won't go back," he said, softly.

"No, no!" replied the Blue Dwarf, in his strange, harsh, guttural tones; "You shall not go back till your return as master. Feel better now?"

"I want to die!" said William Lennox.

"Why, my boy?"

"Where is Lily?" continued the youth.

The misshapen monster—almost of unhuman appearance—looked at him with a glance which would have been grotesque, but for the tears that hung upon his eyelids, manifesting the genuineness of his emotion.

"Mysterious and inexplicable power!" he said, or rather muttered, "which levels all mankind, and which all must feel except myself—from which, by a monstrous calamity, I am debarred —is thy power already on this child! He loves! Oh! why, on that fearful day when I was born, when the foul fiends played around me, why did not the forked lightning in the *blue* heavens slay me—for never have I, never shall I know what it is to be loved?"

"Goldy Gordon!" said William Lennox. ●

"Well, my boy?"

"I love you, and always did love you. Since I remember *you* have been kind to me. You recollect that when my nurse ran shrieking away I laughed at you and pulled your nose, as you took me in your arms. Ever after I would have no nurse but you——"

"Boy!" said the Blue Dwarf, in a choked voice, "I do recollect it. You do not know,

and perhaps may never know, how much of future joy and happiness, of delight and pleasure, may be yours through this. My life is yours, and when the hour comes the reward shall be rich. What *he* did and you did shall never be forgotten—but of this no more. You spoke of Lily."

"Yes; how many days is it since she left?" cried William Lennox.

"Six."

"Merciful heavens!" said William.

"My boy, have faith in me. Does the girl love you?"

"She did—but why, why did she leave me?"

"They took her away in her sleep. And now, boy, hearken to me. If the affection that has arisen between you and this girl be real, it will but be strengthened by time. I have my reasons for all I do. Wait, and as sure as the sun rises in the heavens all shall go well. When you have strength to get up you shall write her a note, which I will see delivered. What do you intend to do?"

"I cannot remain here—I mean I cannot stay with the troop; everything will remind me of her."

"They have left, and return to-morrow on their way to Birmingham; you must then inform them of your determination."

"But what shall I do afterwards?" said William Lennox.

"What say you to returning under your new name to the rank in life you were born to; I could get you a situation as private secretary to a nobleman where your duties would be nominal. You would be the companion of his son."

"Could you do so?" asked the lad.

"I can. Boy, in this world the humble, the lowly, and the deformed, have sometimes privileges which are little understood. I hold in my hands the fate of many families. Speak, then, will you accept?"

"With heartfelt pleasure—my good, my kind Goldy Gordon; do you know that this revival of my prospects makes me feel better already. I should like to get up."

"Take this," said the Dwarf, handing him a potion from a small phial.

The boy drank it with the utmost docility.

"Lie still awhile and you shall get up," continued Sapathwa, by which name we shall ourselves designate him, as did Miriam.

William Lennox obeyed, and closing his eyes, never moved for six hours. When he awoke again, the roses were once more upon his cheeks, and he smilingly told the Blue Dwarf that he was hungry.

He, who having given him a tonic and narcotic of his own invention, was by no means surprised, had prepared a supper, to which William, with all the elasticity of youth, was soon doing ample justice. He then declared he was never better in his life.

He wanted to write the letter to Lily.

"I know! I know!" said the Blue Dwarf, gravely, when he proposed to write. "Do so; but whatever secrets she may know bid her keep them religiously until the day you are of age."

"I will—but why?"

"You know not the terrors by which you are

surrounded," continued the other; "a fortunat circumstance, horrible as it was, has, perhaps, saved you. Meanwhile, until the day which shall give you the rank and title of manhood, you must live in obscurity. Apart from that, write what you please."

He handed a desk to William.

He in a few lines expressed his feelings.

He then handed it to the other to read.

"No!" said Sapathwa with something like a shudder. "Such letters are not for me. Besides, the subject is sacred. Seal it, and I will take charge of it."

William Lennox did so at once, though he did say to himself that had he known his epistle was not to be read he would have been more expressive.

This was the letter:—

"MY BELOVED LILIAN,—I have been very ill. Your abrupt departure nearly killed me; but I have faith in your truth. Keep my secret as you value my life, even from your mother. A dear friend, in whom I have the utmost confidence, says that in *that* case all will be well. Bright and beautiful, I hope that in the new home you have found, surrounded, as I am assured you will be, by care and luxury, you may regain your sunny smile and your angelic beauty. The day I am twenty-one I will claim you.

"Whatever may occur, whatever may be said, I have your vow, and I hold you to it until that hour, the 12th March, 18—. Should you then have changed, you will be free.

"WILLIAM LENNOX."

Poor fellow! he had forgotten she could not read. He had began to teach her printed letters, but that was all.

CHAPTER XXIX.

LIFE AND DEATH.

THE glorious delight with which the mother pressed to her bosom the child which had been so miraculously restored to her, may be conceived but not depicted. Eloquently and well has the picture been drawn of the reprieve from death coming to the dying soul, which never conceives the awful value of life, until it is ebbing; but who with the power of an angel shall tell the joys unutterable which come gushing to the heart of a mother—which come bubbling up to her soul, at the recovery of a long lost child?

It is an awakening from a dream of the most hideous nature; it is a resurrection from the dead.

And what is not the immeasurable value and sweetness of life, and what the terror, mystery, and gloom of the region of death, whence none have ever returned?

Mrs. Winterton held the girl in her arms, still heavily sleeping (the good-natured Mrs. Jottley had slightly drugged her drink), until they reached a large hotel, into the court-yard of which she drove, accompanied only now by Ellen Jay.

Captain George and Miriam had left her, intending to return at a future period.

Ellen Jay had cast a cloak over the spangled dress, so that the child was borne to a chamber without exciting any unusual curiosity. They then, closing the door behind her, undressed and put her to bed; no miser gloating on a treasure could have bent over her so greedily as did that mother.

She kissed eyes, nose, mouth, neck, arms, as they were gradually revealed to her.

"Is she not beautiful—is she not lovely?" said the fond parent.

"Yes, ma'am—but not well——"

"What!" gasped Mrs. Winterton, with an angry contraction of the eyebrows, revealing how terrible could be her passions if roused; "how dare you say such a thing—how dare you dash the cup of joy from my lips when scarcely full? Heavens! this woman whom I have nurtured as a friend must, after all, be a demon."

"Madam," said Ellen Jay, coldly but firmly, "discharge me if you will, treat me as you like, but I repeat, your little daughter is far from well, she is *very* ill."

"Why not say dying?" shrieked Mrs. Winterton.

"Even so, madam, if care be not taken," continued the domestic.

Mrs. Winterton stared wildly at her, and then at the child. Her eyes became fixed upon the girl's face.

"Forgive me, Jay?" she said, in a low, humbled tone; "forgive me; a mother is not willing to recognise such signs. I see that you are right. She is not well; but Jay, do not—do not, in mercy, say she is very ill."

"My dear and honoured madam," cried the faithful attendant, "it was my duty to inform you that your child was ill ere it was too late. It is equally my duty now to nurse and care for her."

"Yes, yes," said Mrs. Winterton, in a tone of forced calmness. "You are quite right, Jay. Begin, then, at once. Let the best doctor in the town be summoned. Go, speak to the landlady; ask her advice. I will guard my newly-found treasure."

Ellen Jay took her mistress's hand, pressed it respectfully, and went out.

Mrs. Winterton, with a blanched cheek, tearless eyes, and a mien as chilled as at any time during her long bereavement, seated herself beside the fatal bed which contained her every hope of happiness in this world, and waited.

The blow had been an awful one. In the very exuberance of her joy she had been struck down. In the midst of a flood of happiness the ebb had set in, not gradually, but as if by the motion of an earthquake.

Her only arm at this fearful juncture was prayer.

Soon the doctor came. He was a man of middle age, and grave exterior, concealing a kindly heart and generous character. His ability was recognised. Many had been his successful tussles with the grim and ghastly enemy of life.

He bowed to the mother, and then looked at the child.

"She sleeps very soundly," he said, "has she taken any narcotic?"

"I do not know," replied the mother.

"Madam," cried the other gravely, "you must have no reserve with me."

"I will have none," she said. "Be seated, I beg."

Dr. Hartley courteously obeyed, taking the child's hand in his, and laying down his gold-headed cane.

Mrs. Winterton briefly explained all, as far as was necessary. Dr. Hartley listened with profound attention, not unmixed with glances of wonder and surprise.

"Humph!" he said. "Strange—very. Great privations, I suppose?"

"No!" gasped the mother. "With the gipsies she appears to have been happy and well treated."

"But perhaps not with the strollers. That stilt-dancing may have been very injurious, if her chest be weak."

The mother groaned in unspeakable agony.

The Doctor reflected profoundly.

"Madam," he said after a short pause, "you have been very confidential with me, which alone could have saved your child. I will be equally frank with you. Pulse, skin, cheek, tongue, all tell me that she will not die now."

"Thank Heaven!" said the mother, with a most hysterical cry of joy.

"But the seeds of that fatal scourge, which still defies science—*but which will not defy it always*—consumption, are in her. She is young, and they may be eradicated. I have yet an hour—very unprofessional, ma'am—I ought to say haven't a minute to spare—and I will remain. I think she is about to awake. We shall then be better able to judge."

"I am in your hands, sir; I am very wealthy—"

"Madam!" said Doctor Hartley, rising.

"You misunderstand me," hastily rejoined the lady. "I repeat I am rich. If you could devote your whole time to this dear child, I would—"

"Pardon me, my dear madam," said the doctor, reseating himself with a smile; "your proposition is not only impossible, but useless. My constant presence would do more harm than good. Once I have mastered the diagnosis of the complaint, my absence will be necessary, to enable me to judge of its gradual development. But hush!"

And the doctor drew back behind the curtains.

"William—dear William," said the soft sweet voice of Lilian, "I am so much better."

Then some strange sensation appeared to come over her—probably that of the soft and, to her, aromatic bed.

She sat slowly up, and took a survey of the room. It was a handsome apartment for an inn, and the bed was very comfortable.

"Am I still dreaming, or where am I?" she muttered.

"My child," replied her mother, coming forward, and by a violent effort controling her wild emotions, her anxious desire to clasp her to her beating heart, "calm yourself; you are with friends"

"But where is William? I want William—I must have William," she said, attempting to leap from the bed.

"Dear child," gasped the agonised and jealous mother, "you are ill. Be still and calm, and your every wish shall be realised."

"Yes, my dear," said the doctor, coming forward, "you are not well; you must be very quiet; you must do as your friends wish, and you will soon be better."

"I don't want to get well; I want William," said the girl, with a wild burst of tears; "he is my only friend."

"Tell her all," groaned Mrs. Winterton.

"You mus'nt say he is your only friend. If he is one of your friends you will see him again. But are not you aware that there is a dearer tie in the world than all others—a mother?"

"I never knew mine. William said he would find her," said Lilian, still sobbing.

"My child—my daughter!" shrieked Mrs. Winterton, and clasped her to her bosom.

Lilian returned her caresses with a half curious, half alarmed, but listless air.

The doctor observed this, and after a few minutes began the history of the parent's sorrowful bereavement. Lilian listened with profound attention. The doctor expatiated with eloquence on Mrs. Winterton's sorrows. Long before he had finished the mother was weeping tears of joy, the child of indignation and grief, as she fondly caressed her newly-found and so much injured parent.

"My mother! my mother!" she cried, in heartfelt accents, "can you forgive me?"

"My angel! my treasure!" responded Mrs. Winterton. "And now," she added, with an arch smile, "let us talk of William."

"No," said the doctor, "not at all. The patient must now think of dinner; after dinner, a quiet chat; and then, in the evening, we shall see—"

Lilian kissed her mother, and lay back with a look of great exhaustion.

"A light repast, mind," said the doctor, taking Mrs. Winterton aside, "and then complete rest until I return."

The anxious mother thanked the doctor heartily, and then, having obeyed his behests, seated herself, to watch for the spring of life in the heart of her child, even as the weary mariner watches at night for the much-desired light-house.

When Dr. Hartley returned his patient was better, but restless and anxious. Her very eyes told the tale of her woe.

"We must make inquiries about this young gentleman to-morrow," he said, with a significant look at the anxious mother, and a sign for her to yield.

"I will do so without fail," replied Mrs. Winterton.

"I am quite happy now," said Lilian, with an angelic smile. "Good night. mother dear."

Mrs. Winterton gazed at her with Madonna-like joy. It was ecstacy that illumined her countenance. She kissed her again and again, ere she tucked up the clothes and finally committed her to rest.

She then followed the doctor to the door.

"What say you?" she said, a wan, earnest, alarmed expression replacing that which hitherto had illumined her countenance.

"Madam, there is great hope: but she must be humoured. This lad must be found. The slightest cross or vexation may act fearfully on her constitution."

"It shall be done," she said, in choked accents.

She returned to the bed.

"And now, madam," said her faithful attendant, "you must take some rest."

"No, Jay, not to-night—another time, but not to-night. It is my first day of life since Lily was born. To-morrow night I will sleep—*with her.*"

The ecstacy with which this was said would have paled the passionate cry of the most ardent lover, whose bride had suddenly become his wife.

Jay yielded, and went to her room.

Next day it was discovered that the troop of strollers had left the town without William Lennox; but of him no one appeared to know anything.

Lilian, though the intelligence was communicated with the greatest circumspection, turned her head to the wall, and refused to be comforted.

She got no worse, but she got no better. Mother and doctor were both alarmed.

They knew not what to do; and Mrs. Winterton began to tremble, and to lose her own health every day, when suddenly Anastasia was announced. The people of the hotel, regardless of appearances, had been requested to watch for the strollers.

"Show her in," said the child, sitting up, in a quick eager way.

No hesitation was shown, and the ballet girl, in a faded costume, entered quickly.

"La! you dear little cherub," she said, with a low curtsey to the doctor and the lady; "so you've found yer friends. Well, that's nice. I wish I'd a been a fondling, that I do."

"Where's William?" asked Lily, anxiously.

"I've come to tell you," replied Anastasia, seating herself beside the bed, and taking the girl's hand under the bed-clothes.

"Quick! quick! or I shall die!"

"He's very well now, dear; but he has been very ill. When he found as how you was gone, he took and fainted, and never came to for six days."

Lily closed her eyes, and the mother and doctor exchanged strange glances.

"Then he comed to. A ugly little chap—the Blue Dwarf, they call him—took him to the Rose and Crown, where he was till this morning."

"Where is he now?" said Lily quietly.

"Gone to London. He's going to be secretary to a great lord—or something of that sort; and he said he should have come hisself, only he had no right to intrude."

"Intrude! My God!" said Lily, holding up her hands.

"But he said as how he should see you again,

when *all was clear,*" and Anastasia squeezed the hand of the young girl.

Lily started as if struck with a blow, and then lay quite quiet.

The other watched with intense anxiety.

"Thank you," she said; "thank you, Anastasia. Mother dear!"

"My darling!" hastily rejoined Mrs. Winterton.

"I want to speak to you."

The others drew back to a distance.

"What is it, angel?"

"Mother dear, are you *very* rich?" she said.

"Yes, child."

"She is very poor, mother. Money might do her good. Tell her to marry Lexy. Say I said so. *It's wicked not to.*"

The mother stood rivetted on the child's face. She dared not ask for an explanation; but kissing her little pallid face, beckoned the wondering Anastasia into another room.

She closed the door, and pulling out a purse, showed it to her.

"This," she said, 'contains fifty guineas. It is yours on one condition imposed on you by my baby-girl."

Anastasia stood still, stunned.

"My offer is sincere. But," continued Mrs. Winterton, with a strangely earnest countenance, "you are to marry Lexy. *It's wicked not to*—those are her words. Strange words for a child, are they not?"

Anastasia blushed crimson, and hung down her head. Mrs. Winterton watched her with breathless interest.

She had seen the painted spectre of Sin walking about in the form of children.

"The little angel," said Anastasia, after a short struggle with herself. "But you sees, ma'am—poor people's children always knows too much. Don't be hard upon me, ma'am—they can't help it. They lives together higgledy-piggledy like. But I and Lexy always 'tended marriage, only we never could afford the dress. But, ma'am, if you are in earnest in your offer, we will be married."

Mrs. Winterton held out the money.

"No!" said Anastasia, shrinking back; "afterwards."

"What mean you?"

"Well, ma'am, I and Lexy likes a drop, and when we gets all that money we should go mad, and I shouldn't be made an honest woman after all; and that's what I wish."

"It shall be as you please. My child's will is law with me. I will see to all the arrangements. But you are sure my angel child is pure and innocent?"

"As I was myself at fourteen," cried the ballet-dancer, with such a genuine outburst of indignation and anger that it went to the mother's heart.

"Bless you," she said, and with intense energy she wrung the other's hand.

Anastasia, soon after an understanding having been come to, retired from that house a proud and happy woman.

Meanwhile, a very different scene had taken place in the bed-room.

No sooner had her mother retired—and, as she

believed, the doctor—than Lilian drew forth William's letter, which Anastasia had delivered in the secret way in which she was enjoined to.

Lilian at once saw that it was a written communication, and a look of intense agony passed over her countenance as she recollected she could not read.

There are children who win the heart even of the most callous, and Lilian was one of these. Doctor Hartley had never been so taken with a girl of her age before. Her history, too, entranced him and he wished to see the whole matter out.

"My dear girl," he said, "can I do anything for you?"

"Can you read?" she said.

"Yes, my darling," he replied, with a smile.

"Can you keep a secret?" she continued; "not my secret, but his."

"A doctor keeps all secrets," he replied gently.

Lilian eagerly handed him the letter, with a roseate blush on her beautiful cheek.

The doctor, not a little surprised himself, read the epistle out slowly and distinctly.

"I thank that God of whom William Lennox first spoke to me," said Lily aloud, kneeling up and clasping her hands; "and as surely as he is true to me, so surely will I be true to him."

"What means this," asked the mother, looking at her child with perfect awe.

She had come up unperceived.

"May I?" said the doctor with a persuasive smile.

"Read it, mother," replied Lilian gently; "but do not ask for an explanation; it is his secret—not mine."

Mrs. Winterton read, and with a deep sigh, handed the letter back to her child.

But from that hour they—at her wish—sewed the letter in a bag, and placed it round her neck. The girl grew better from that hour, and soon was pronounced out of danger.

CHAPTER XXX.

JUST SO.

THERE is a strange freemasonry in crime, and yet I doubt if associates in villany ever really trust one another. They must live in a constant dread of what may be about to happen.

The cousins, Frederick and John Winterton, found that despite the failure of their own scheme of abduction, the heiress they had so much to dread had really disappeared, and their spies left them no doubt of the sincerity of the widow's lamentations. Their amazement and delight accordingly knew no bounds.

It was something almost miraculous.

At all events they determined to take instant advantage of their position, and having got it made public that only a frail and ailing woman stood between them and the estates, they at once proceeded to raise money on *post obits*, bonds, and bills; renewed and re-renewed enormous sums for the gratification of their luxurious habits and utterly profligate style of living.

The inheritance of the Hon. Dudley Winterton was notoriously prodigious, so that there was no difficulty in accomplishing their purpose. Jews and money lenders are brave as patriots, and rush to the breach with more than superhuman valour.

In thirteen years the cousins had raised a hundred thousand pounds, for which, if things lasted much longer, they would have to pay two hundred thousand at the very least.

They were now, however, hard up, and impatient for a replenishment of the common purse.

In their anxiety to come into instant possession of their future inheritance, they had made one or two underhand attacks on the widow. They found her, however, armed at all points, and surrounded both by sincere friends and sturdy retainers.

The game was too dangerous to be played.

There was no resource left but to bleed some anxious money lender, at an usurious rate of interest.

With this view Captain Frederick Winterton, and Mr. John Winterton, had invited one Corkum Needy, junior partner in a great discounting firm, an intimate and a confidant, to breakfast on a certain morning. They had lavished every resource which ingenuity could conceive to produce a "spread" worthy of the important occasion.

The worthy captain, Frederick, now forty-four years of age, was obese, grey, and had his face seamed with wrinkles and furrows, the result not of age, but of dissipation.

Mr. John was the same florid, effeminate being he was thirteen years before, but his countenance was speckled and bloated.

Their breakfast-room was ornamented with portraits of ballet girls and singing women, alongside winners of cups and other horse-racing prizes, riding-whips, and fencing foils.

"Vewy nice spwed," said the Honourable John, eyeing it through a gold rim, guiltless of glass; "pwitty one cwant eat."

"Deuced nice affair," replied Captain Frederick. "I wish he'd come. I'm hungry."

"Pick a bit," continued the dandy, with the native air of the man who, having too much, knows not that he is committing a crime in wasting it.

"You kept it up, but I was floored early," observed the man of warlike weapons; "got to bed at seven; cussed seedy—did three bottles of soda, and here I am as right as a trivet."

"'Pon honour dwon't thwink I can indulge in a morsel; but damme—ah—here he is."

And Mr. Corkum Needy bustled into the room. The friends rushed to meet him with most fraternal ardour, almost wrenching his arms off in their enthusiasm.

Mr. Corkum Needy was a little oily man of about thirty, very florid, with small eyes, a prominent nose, and a bunch of seals as big almost as his own head. He was dressed in the pink of the fashion, as he understood it; that is badly, exaggerately, with flaming colours, and outrageous shapes.

"Glad to see me," he said, chuckling in his greasy, oily, slippery way, "Well, a good many *is.* I'm useful and agreeable, you know. Hope havn't kept you waiting, you know. Fine tuck out to be sure—set a sprat to catch a whale, eh! —not bad."

And the millionaire laughed heartily at his own wit; the friends joined sincerely, for his being in good humour boded them success. Besides, if they once came into possession of their estates, they would be able to return him both his money and his impertinence—with ample interest.

The trio sat down to their morning meal without any further preparation, and for some time eating and drinking was wholly the order of the day, except when every now and then some of the fashionable slip-slop of the time fell from the lips of the cousins, or city slang from that of the other.

Presently, however, the eatables were cleared away, wine left, and several boxes of cigars placed beside them.

"Cards!" said Corkum Needy, with a grin.

"No!" replied Captain Winterton, gravely; "you are very well aware that this is a business meeting."

"Very good," observed Corkum, now assuming a grave and collected expression of countenance, at the same time producing a rather alarming-looking pocket-book from some secret recess about his person. "I have here a memorandum of the present state of our mutual transactions, and really, in the present state of the money market——"

"Now, Corkum," said the captain, coolly, "this won't do. Put up your book for the present and light a cigar. You know we are about to borrow, not to pay."

"Really, you know our account is already——"

"Mr. Corkum Needy," said Captain Winterton, drily, "knows very well that all these devices are useless with us. We have known one another too long for this. You have the thousand in your pocket—the simple question is as to interest."

"Bravo, Fred!" cried Corkum Needy, with a laugh; "there's no doing you. To speak frankly, I have got the money."

"Positively damme!" said John, with his silly laugh.

"But you see, the old people are beginning to count. The widow hangs on——"

"Forty, if she's a day," replied the captain.

"Thirty-six, to a T!" continued the well-informed money-lender; "and our five-and-twenty thousand is as far off as ever."

"Five - and - twenty thousand!" ejaculated John.

"Hold your tongue," said Frederick; "let our friend explain himself."

"Now we have no fear of the ultimate result; the widow cannot live for ever," said Corkum, with a look of deep meaning. "But money is scarce, and we must really have two thousand for this job, and a thousand on every annual renewal."

"Pwepostewous!" cried John.

"Very severe!" put in Frederick, with a knowing look. "And I tell you what, Corkum —it makes my mind up. You shall have no renewal. I won't spend one sixpence of my five

hundred guineas on pleasure. Fork out the bills, and I'll tell you my plan."

Corkum Needy took out the acceptance, which was already prepared; it was duly signed, and the money handed over in notes.

"Now for your plan," said the money-lender, filling a bumper of champagne at a guinea a bottle. "I'm rather curious to know all about it. The sum of seven-and-twenty thousand is rather a serious amount even for our firm."

"Positively," began John, "I dwon't undwestand much about awithmetic, but seven ——"

"Don't waste time," continued Frederick, who had pocketed the whole thousand himself. "Do you know, Corkum, any fellow, deuced hard up, who could play Captain Frederick Winterton for a week or ten days. You twig. I want to go out of town for—say, a month, but I want to be in Pall-mall, very ill, boxed up—plenty of fellows calling, show myself to one or two."

"You want to prove an *alibi*," said Corkum Needy, coolly.

"Exactly. But the fellow must be clever, and with a nightcap on, and his head tied up— talk like me, so that a dozen young fellows may swear to my being in town day by day."

"By the prince's head, then, he must play like you," said Corkum, laughing; "unless you wish to lose a fortune."

"Exactly so."

"I've your man; close fist, your cut of whisker—voice—hard case—plays like a Corinthian. Egad, it's a fine chance."

"Who is it?"

"Jack Tarleton!"

"By the hookey," said Captain Frederick, with a start, "ain't he dead?"

"No; but enjoying the hospitality of the Bench. We must smug him out. How much will you stand?"

"One hundred, free quarters, and all he wins!"

"Egad, Jack will be in high feather. But we must do it brown; if his creditors twig they'll box him for life. I suppose you know he's over head and ears?"

"If all turns well, I won't see Jack suffer," said Frederick.

"Egad, nothing like the present moment. He owes me a thousand. Give me a note you will pay it when you inherit?" said Corkum Needy, with a grin.

"Anything to oblige, my dear Needy."

This bond was just signed, sealed, and committed to the celebrated pocket-book, when a violent uproar was heard upon the stairs, voices shouted; a struggle evidently took place, and in rushed a maniacal-looking individual in a peaked hat, long gown, and grey beard, who was followed by two servants in livery.

"I vash killed, murdered, robb'd—I vash ruined, an' Master Winterton is de tam tief," he cried in a frantic voice.

"Peter Emanuel," shouted Corkum Needy, turning very pale.

"Ah coot Mhister Corkum," said the frantic Jew—"he! he! he! Ishe swhare dish cough vill be de death of me. I am robb'd, you ish robb'd, and every body ish robb'd. De heiresh ish found

better ash never, and ve ish de tam fools. I shall die in she vurkhous."

"Gentlemen," began Corkum in a tone of stern determination——"

"Mine cot! look at de vaste," continued the moral Jew; "look at de flunkey; de vine, dat ish made to varm de hart—de grapes, de sheegars, de blate—and all bought vith my monish."

"And mine, Mr. Peter," said Corkum.

John Winterton sank exhausted in a chair. The domestics began to look very oddly at one another.

"Dere is men hung for lesh," continued the frantic Hebrew. "I telsh you vat, Maister Vinterton—ash de heiresh ish found, I prove you stole her. Look, Mhister Corkum, coot Mhister Corkum—look at de carpets and de mirrors; and shelp me, Moshes, bought vith my monish!"

And he dashed his hat against his hand. Nothing could stop him.

"I peg, I porrow, I sh—; I mean dat I shall shave de monish to lensh to de Crishan—and dish is my reward!"

No martyr at the stake could have assumed a more injured look.

But the acting man, the devising mind of the two cousins, had now had ample time to collect his ideas.

"Silence," roared the Captain; and then turning to the servants, into whose hands he slipped a guinea, "retire. Forbid me to every body· Say I am transacting business on a large scale with my good friends Peter Emanuel and Corkum Needy—go."

"Abrahams and Isaacs; dish ish de Cristian; they rop us and they laugh at our peards. But," he yelled, "I have de law, Mhister Vinterton, and I vill hang——"

"Silence, you bellowing old fool," said the captain, bolting and locking the door; "and when you are quiet explain all; for if what you say be true, a week shall not pass over my head before mother and daughter sleep in the same tomb."

Awful is the curse of avarice—fearful the greed of gold—hideous the lust of lucre.

Nearly every murderous crime is caused by the yellow dross, and in Governments, firms, and individuals, how often is the gold pile wet with sweat and blood of victims of every age, of both sexes—even of helpless infancy.

"My coot Misther Vinterton," began Peter Emanuel, making up one of his two-hundred-per-cent. faces.

"But how is it to be done?" said Corkum Needy, surlily.

"That is my business," replied the captain, glancing with scorn at the trembling John; "let Jack Tarleton be found."

"Eh? Vat ish dat?" said Peter, looking quickly round.

"Nothing," answered the captain, at once understanding the look of Corkum Needy—at least understanding that he was to be silent; the real motive he little suspected. "Suffice it for you, Mr. Peter Emanuel, that I am a man of my word in every particular. In ten days from this, take my promise for it, there shall be no heiress. And now, explain what it is you mean by this story."

Peter Emanuel handed him a country paper, in which was a full account, with transparent initials, of the discovery of Lilian in the booths of the strolling players. Hints were thrown out of an exposure of the foul play which had cast the poor child helpless on a world of sorrow and toil.

"This, I will allow, is serious," said the captain, folding up the paper; "and yet, at a trial, nothing could be proved. The recovery of the heiress would not hold water one moment. But don't look uneasy. I hate law as much as you do."

He here opened the door of his apartment, and stood with extended hand.

"Gentlemen, you are free to go or to stay. There are several bottles of wine cooling. What say you to a quiet chat?"

"I ish not eat, I ish not trink," said the Hebrew, scarcely recovered from his fright, "for all dish day. I take vonsh glass vine."

"I will follow example," added Corkum.

"Bravo," said Captain Winterton; "and we will drink success to our enterprise, of which I should have no doubt if I only could find, as an assistant and coadjutor, our old friend Slimy Jones."

"Just-so," said that worthy, protruding his head through the door.

CHAPTER XXXI.

THE EMPEROR.

OUR readers are respectfully requested to bear in mind that, in leaping from one part of our narrative to another, we are actuated by the stern exigencies of our plot. There is not an incident, however trivial, which will not ultimately be found to bear upon the whole; and so eventful is our strange and wondrous history, that our very discursiveness will ultimately prove to be necessary to the plan which we have laid down.

Philip Carabosse, as he had chosen to denominate himself, lost no time in insinuating himself into the good graces of Pauline, who, vain, ambitious, and burning for distinction, readily fell into his views.

His arrival was, to her ideas, so fortunate an occurrence, that it was not be cast from her with disdain.

His sharp, incisive, and insidious tongue was always pouring flatteries and compliments into her ears; while he lost no opportunity of describing the glories, pleasures, and splendour of the life to be led in England.

Pauline listened with flashing eyes and bated breath.

Claude Placquet had been decorated by the First Consul, now the Emperor Napoleon, for some act of daring in connection with a wreck; and his darling aspiration now was to obtain the command of a *corsaire*—a privateer—in which, axe and pistol in hand, he might scour the Channel, and levy black mail on the hated English.

Hated as much now as then.

Philip Carabosse was to be one of his lieutenants. But besides that, he had to move heaven and earth to raise the necessary means, and to select a suitable port. Not even a cockle-boat could have put to sea from Boulogne-sur-Mer without the consent of the same perfidious Albion.

Still Claude Placquet persevered, and had a small lugger some three parts finished when Philip Carabosse landed. Still he did not neglect his fishing altogether, and the second week after Philip's arrival it was arranged that he should accompany his uncle.

Madame Placquet cordially wished he might never return. She did not like his soft, insidious ways, and with all a woman's quickness, she saw that Pauline already loved him.

She watched them with the eye of a hawk from the sky watching for its prey, and as far as she was concerned, never left them alone. But Claude laughed at her scruples, declared Philip was the very soul of honour, and insisted that they should be left to themselves.

The mother sighed and yielded, for the authority of "the man" is not to be contested.

Not far from the town, on the Capecure side, was a ball-room entirely frequented by the boys and girls of the fishing class. When the wind was contrary, when business was flat, after a return voyage, here came the sturdy young ploughers of the deep, to solace themselves with *choppes* of beer and noggins of gin, to say nothing of the bright eyes of the Boulognese girls.

No hindrance was placed in their way, for, as is generally the case with these clannish populations, the moment a youth selected a sweetheart, he was, in honour bound, to marry; and *ma foi*, if any little irregularity did occur, it was soon solved by the curé, after certain very proper remonstrances.

Imagine a long, low, narrow room, with tables on each side, and coarse straw-bottomed stools, illumined here and there with quinquets, or tin oil lamps; and in the midst some twenty couple of sturdy fishers and girls in their picturesque costume, capering one against the other in admired confusion; and you will have some idea of a Boulognese ball-room.

Philip and Pauline, young lovers as they were, would rather have strolled about the hills and bye-roads leading to the heights, or in any quiet out-of-the-way place; but then it would have been spoken of at home, and mamma Placquet would have prevented their going out alone for the future.

They were then compelled to go, and necessarily to take part in the amusements, which, once there, was not at all unpleasant to Philip, for in the mazes of the dance did he not press Pauline, fond and lovely, in his arms; and did not her eyes sparkle with a glorious, almost unholy fire, as he whispered, in passionate accents, his words of love.

"All my own!" he would murmur in her ear.

"All your own," she would reply; while the flash of her eyes pierced to his very soul.

It was the evening previous to his first voyage to sea with her father, and they had been to the ball-room. They had left early, and had wandered to the picturesque valley, Denacre; there they had seated themselves beneath the leafy trees, which, sighing overhead, kept time to the whispering below.

Not the keenest listener could have caught a word of what was said; it was one confused murmur of whispers and kisses, vows, and professions, that were lost in the stillness of the night.

The hours waned, and at last Pauline started in confusion to her feet.

"It is very late," she cried.

"The ball is not yet over; but we had perhaps better go, though—" began Philip, kissing her rosy arm.

"We must go—mother will be angry," said Pauline tenderly, as she took his arm; "you won't be long at sea. But mind you, dearest, that must be your first and last journey. I cannot lead this life. My mother's eyes are always on me. She seems to read my soul. Oh, Philip! why did I ever see you?"

This was said with wild and passionate earnestness, as if it had been the last wail for her lost purity and virtue and truth.

"Dearest, more dear to me than life itself, it is only since I have known you that I have learned to live. I, too, long for the freedom you pant for. And it shall be ours before many days. My purpose will be served here, and then —never to part again."

"I hope so," said she in tones of melting softness, "for I love you dearly."

And Pauline was sincere—must have been so; or else, how could she thus have made up her mind to abandon country, parents, her own self-respect, for one she had known for so short a time.

Whispering the sweet words of affection, the lovers gained the town, passing the sentries without difficulty, crossed the fortified old city, which kept King Henry—of Blue Beard reputation—so long at bay, and began descending the wide street which leads to the lower town.

They had not gone far, when they noticed a figure pacing up the middle of the deserted street. The sober dwellers were all long since gone to bed.

It was a dark night, and yet there was a pale glimmering of the moon, which enabled them to distinguish the figure of the officer as he approached them.

He was walking in the middle of the road, his arms were folded behind him, and he was evidently in a state of intense mental abstraction. His eyes were fixed on the ground.

On his head was a cocked hat; he wore a grey coat, buttoned at the breast, and high boots reaching to the knee.

A plain sword hung by his side.

His countenance was pale in the extreme, his jaws heavy, and his brow massive.

The lovers endeavoured, by keeping close to the wall, to escape his notice.

"Who goes there?" suddenly struck upon their ear in a rich, musical tone, the officer halting as he spoke.

"Two children of Boulogne, sire," replied Pauline.

Philip quivered from head to foot to find himself in the dread presence of the great king.

"Humph! I know that voice," said the Emperor; "isn't it Pauline Placquet?"

"Yes, sire."

"Daughter of a brave man. He deserved his decoration. Who is this?"

And he pointed to Philip, who stood cap in hand before him, in an attitude of calm, but proud respect.

"A cousin, your majesty, just escaped from England."

"Ah, been a prisoner!" said the Emperor, quickly.

"No, sire."

"What then?"

"I was born in England," said Philip, with as much humility as he could assume.

"Then how claim you to be a Frenchman?"

And as he spoke, the Emperor eyed him keenly.

"Ah!" said the newly made monarch, "born there; then how are you French?"

"My father and mother both are French."

"Umph! why don't they run away?"

"They cannot, Sire; my father is a very fat man," replied Philip demurely.

Napoleon looked at him keenly, and then smiled. He was completely deceived by the assumption of simplicity on the part of the young officer.

"Do you know much about England?" said the Emperor.

"Not much. Sire, except that I hate it. I lived nearly all my time in an obscure country place, or on board ship."

"Very good, *mon fils;* you shall soon see England a province of France. I am going to overthrow her insolent aristocracy ere many days are passed, giving freedom to her oppressed and down-trodden people."

And with this magniloquent expression the scourge of Europe passed on, leaving Philip Carabosse with a deep sense of the importance of this interview, which he determined to report at any risk to his commanding officer.

They were rather coldly received by the good woman, who disliked more and more the frequency of these absences from home; but Philip, announcing that he was fatigued, went up stairs, secured the door, and covered the window by means of a blanket.

He then spent an hour writing, in a close but clear hand, a narrative of his expedition, exaggerating somewhat the precise nature of the information received from the Emperor Napoleon himself. The letter he addressed to Madame Carabosse, with the word "Open" written on the corner.

He then, too feverish to sleep, washed his face and hands, and went out.

He knew where the lugger lay, and he was aware that Claude Placquet liked early rising and punctuality. The fishing-boat was nearly ready, and in half-an-hour they were at sea.

Towards the afternoon, being tolerably successful, they headed towards the port. About two miles to leeward was a large ship under easy sail.

"What is she?" said Philip, with assumed carelessness.

"An English frigate," replied Claude Placquet, savagely.

"She would take a letter for me to my mother," continued the lad.

"A letter!" cried the sailor.

"Yes. I want my mother to hear how happy I am—and to give her consent to my marriage with Pauline."

Claude smiled.

"I am in earnest, uncle. I love Pauline with all my heart."

"Ha! ha! ha!" laughed Claude.

"You may laugh," said Philip, merrily; "but what say you about the letter?"

"Well," said Claude, after a moment's hesitation, "I dare say she would take it. These large vessels never hurt us. I'll run up to her, if you like."

"Mother would be glad to hear from me. I have, as I told you before, written a letter on chance. If it is not too much trouble ——"

"Trouble, my boy! none whatever. I am sure your mother will be glad to hear from her son."

And without further parley the good fisherman shifted his sails, and ran for the frigate, one of the men holding up a piece of dingy cloth, that once might have been white, on the end of an oar, by way of a flag of truce.

When they came within a short distance of the vessel the officers were clearly visible on the quarter deck.

"What do you want?" shouted a boatswain, savagely. He had learnt French in a French prison.

"A lad here wants to send a letter to his mother, in England," replied Claude.

"Letter be ——! Sheer off, you French son of ——."

"Hold on there!" cried the captain, suspecting the truth at once. "Take the poor boy's letter."

"What does he say?" asked Claude, turning round to Philip.

Philip translated the captain's remark, and held up the letter. At a sign from the captain a log line was cast over the fishing smack, and caught by one of the men. To this Philip tied his precious freight, and away it went on board the frigate.

Philip could not help sighing. Had that letter been found upon him by the enemy his life would not have been worth an hour's purchase.

That night he slept easier, for he had committed a great act of treachery.

CHAPTER XXXII.

TOURLOOROU.

SEVERAL months of impunity made Philip bold; and indeed so wrapped was he in the society of Pauline—one of those women who never wearied an admirer—that he could have remained for years in Boulogne. Indeed, he was in no hurry to leave. He had sent one or two elaborate reports, with drawings and plans, under cover to his mother, of sufficient importance to the Government to warrant his remaining in his character of a spy.

But fate decided otherwise.

Pauline's beauty had become more intensely entrancing than ever. Philip openly avowed his passion, and it was clear that she returned it ardently. Philip pressed, the hypocrite, for a speedy marriage; and their character of lovers being recognised, they were allowed to be very much alone together—not a usual custom in France, but among primitive and simple races like the fishermen, often common.

"Mon homme," said Madame Placquet, one day, "I wish you would recall your objection to the speedy marriage of these children."

"Why, my girl," cried the astonished husband, "do you want to lose Pauline?"

"Claude," said the prudent wife, gently laying her hand upon his arm, "you know that I have been a faithful and obedient wife. You must, therefore, promise for once not to be angry at my resisting your authority. I will give you good reason."

"I promise," continued Claude, considerably puzzled at her observations.

"Pauline is a good daughter, but, my husband, I know her character. She loves this new cousin of hers, and, in fact, the sooner they are married the better."

"*Mon Dieu!*" said Claude, turning pale, "you do not mean to say, the *gredin* ——"

"There is no harm done," replied his wife, hastily; "but, cousin or no cousin, the young man is not to be trusted so much with our daughter. You well know she never loved any one before."

"My dear old girl," said Claude, affectionately, "you make me feel myself again. You made my flesh creep; but you are right. They shall be married in a month."

Madame Placquet would gladly have urged a week, a day, but she knew that would irritate her husband, and she abstained. The mother's soul was filled with vague apprehensions of evil.

The lovers heard the announcement with rapture. That of Pauline was genuine; on the part of Philip Carabosse it was assumed.

That evening the wife and husband went out, leaving Philip and Pauline at home. It was about dark, and they sat on a settle, his arm round her waist, her lovely head nestled on his bosom. They did not speak. Their hearts were too full for utterance.

Suddenly, a step was heard on the threshold, and the two rose, as if by some instinct, but Philip kept his arm round her waist.

A young and very handsome soldier, in the uniform of the imperial guard, with the stripes of a sergeant, stood before them. His glance indicated horror, grief, and incredulous astonishment.

"Tourloorou!" said Pauline, coldly.

"Yes," replied the soldier, in a truly agonised tone; "and who is this *particulier?*"*

"My future husband," replied Pauline, in a tone which indicated her desire to end any discussion at once.

"And you dare say this to me ——?" began the infuriated soldier.

"Dare!" interrupted Philip.

"Not a word," cried Pauline. "Let me settle with this *monsieur*. It will not be long."

"Did you not promise to wait for me?" asked the young man.

"I told you, Simon Roger, that when you returned a captain, I might talk to you. But I never promised to wait."

"You implied as much," cried the other, in an agonised tone, "the very night I went away. I flew to join my regiment with ardour and delight. I have gained my first step, and had come to show you what love had enabled me to do. I find you resting in the arms of another. *Mon Dieu!* it is too cruel."

"I never loved you," said Pauline, coldly. "I love now—it is different. I am about to marry at once; my father wishes it."

"And you dare to tell me this," said the young man, who trembled so he could scarcely speak, "whose whole soul pines for love of you. Pauline! Pauline! you cannot have forgotten your old friend, Tourloorou!"

Pauline stamped on the ground with her pretty foot, but made no answer.

"It is too true," he added. "But hearken to me. You are mine. I vow you shall never

marry this *blanc bec*. I suppose he is the English lad I've heard about. Take care. I will watch—I will ferret out something. I dare say, if the truth were known, he's a spy. If so, let him look to it. I give him one week to escape from France."

And with these terrible words on his lips, he went out, leaving the lovers horror-stricken at his denunciation.

"What is to be done?" said Pauline.

"Fly at once," replied Philip. "This man is dangerous. Our marriage here is unnecessary, as we must be married over again. I tell you what, my love—there is no time to lose. The day after to-morrow there will be no moon. We must run away with a boat. Can you get a boy's dress?"

"Easily. Have you money?"

"Plenty. You must, then, contrive to change your dress in the evening, and join me in the port. Let it be the outermost boat. I will cut the cable and let her drift. We shall be picked up before morning; if not we must run for England."

Pauline acquiesced in everything. She was as anxious to be in England as himself. She yearned for the hour when she should be Lady Blakesley.

They went out little the next day; but all the time, they perceived that they were watched by Simon Rogers, surnamed Tourloorou. They began to be alarmed. This close observation interfered materially with their plans. Philip was in a fearful state of mind; but hesitation was useless. He began to feel that the sooner he got off French soil the better for himself. He certainly wished to take his beautiful mistress with him, but that was a secondary consideration now—for was not his neck in jeopardy?

Still he persevered doggedly in his plans; and on the evening decided on, after giving most minute directions to Pauline, strolled slowly down towards the port. It was a very dark night; not a star was visible; a rather mournful sound passed over the surface of the waters, and a white foam crested the tops of the billows. The clouds were rapidly scudding over the face of the sky; the sunset had been of that watery and sickly hue which portends a coming storm, and the moment was not far distant when the winds would be up, maddening the waves.

Philip shuddered at the thought of what he might have to endure that night, but he hesitated not, for was not death behind if the terrible soldier only made a chance guess at the truth? Already he more than suspected him.

He clutched his pistols, one in each pocket, which, beyond money, was his only burden. He knew there would be water and biscuits in the boat.

The sea-fowl were skimming over the surface of the wild and yeasty waves with those foreboding screams which sound dismally upon the ear in the pauses of the rushing blast.

The sentries were in their boxes.

Philip gained the last boat, which he soon found was all ready for an early morning departure. Going on board, he easily found the painter, which he fastened loosely to a pile, he cut the cable.

The tide was running out like a mill-race This was an element of success. A hundred yards would take them clear of the port, out upon the waters of the sea. Philip knew the qualities of these fishing-boats too well to fear anything but a very rough night.

He had made up his mind to run for England, as a week's unimpeded enjoyment of Pauline's company was not to be despised. He then could make up his mind what to do.

He was not quite sure he would not marry her, if he could find a pastor willing so far to forget his office as to unite them.

"Is that you?" he said, in a low whisper, as a slight figure stole up towards him.

"Yes," gasped Pauline. "But be quick; we are followed. Into the boat."

"Move a step, and you are a dead man!" said a well-known and terrible voice.

Philip was on board—Pauline was in the act of climbing, when from behind some piles darted Simon Roger. He clutched Pauline firmly with his left hand, and presented a pistol with his right.

Mechanically Philip aimed a blow at the head of the young soldier; he evaded it, and fired.

"Fly; I will join you, or die," cried Pauline.

There was no time to be lost; sentries were rushing up, and as the sloop glided past, several musket shots were fired. Drums began to beat, and in ten minutes, town, barrack, camp, and the very heights, were in commotion. Lights were seen glistening in all directions, and officers rushed forth half-dressed.

"The English are coming—the English are coming!" was the universal cry. But Simon Roger, bearing the now insensible form of Pauline in his arms, explained that it was the English spy escaping, when alarm changed to indignation.

But Simon Roger had no time for details. He was rushing madly on in search of assistance for Pauline.

"Simon," cried Claude, as the soldier entered the house and laid his burthen down upon her mother's bed, "who have you there?"

The boy's dress for an instant deceived even the mother.

"Pauline!" said the agonised youth.

"In this dress? The hussy!" cried Claude.

"My poor child! Go fetch Doctor Devaux," said the mother. "She is coming to; but still ——"

"How came she in this disguise?" asked Claude, sternly.

"She was escaping with her lover, the English spy," replied the soldier; and he rushed out of the room.

Claude looked wildly round.

"The English spy—Philip Carabosse. My head is in a whirl; what can it mean?"

"Hush," said the mother, bathing her child's hands and forehead with vinegar; "hush! The child has had some terrible shock."

Claude made no reply. In a few minutes Simon returned, dragging in Dr. Devaux by main force.

"There, my good man," said the worthy little doctor, a small, thin, shrivelled fellow, very clever, but notoriously bitter and sarcastic, and very fond of saying disagreeable things, "that'll do. I dare say the patient is in no hurry. Ah, you don't say so! Pauline Placquet—how very strange!"

And he glanced at her male attire.

The mother threw a sheet over the poor girl, who was now sobbing wildly.

Simon Rogers left the room.

"Let us look at your tongue, my dear. Must—hum! hum! hum! Pulse—hum! hum! hum!"

And the doctor pondered gravely.

"Taken suddenly?" he asked.

Claude explained in tones of great bitterness, the attempted elopement with the young Englishman, Philip Carabosse.

"Hum! hum! hum!" said the doctor; "great febrile excitement, nervous, head bad. Put her to bed. Hum, hum, hum, send a sleeping potion, and then, my good woman, we shall see."

"Is she in danger?" cried the mother.

"There always is danger in these cases," replied Doctor Devaux, with a strangely equivocal smile.

"What mean you?" she gasped.

"Well, well, nothing like a mother—there is no immediate hurry; but," and Devaux stood slightly on the defensive as he eyed Claude, "the sooner the baby's clothes are prepared the better."

With a wild cry the mother laid her head on the bed-clothes and wept aloud. Claude Placquet, pale as death, clutched the doctor's arm.

"You are insulting my child," he began.

"Claude Placquet," replied the doctor, "I have done my duty. Your daughter will, probably before new year's day, add an unit to the population."

"Kill me, kill me!" cried Pauline wildly, "for he is lost to me."

Claude rushed towards her with a wild imprecation; but his wife stood in his way.

"She is our only child—the child of our love," she said gently; "don't hurt her."

With a curse, too terrible to be here repeated, the agonised father turned and fled from the house.

"Doctor!" exclaimed the wife in an imploring tone, "you won't speak of this?"

"Hum! hum! hum!" said the doctor, "of course not. But it can't be always concealed."

"Leave that to me," cried the fisherwoman. "Put Pauline on her feet again, and I shall know how to save the honour of my family."

There was an air of gloomy resolution in her manner which appalled the girl.

"Mother!" she said, as soon as they were alone, "he will be sure to marry me. Forgive him, for my sake."

"He had better make haste," said the fisherwoman gravely.

Pauline shuddered. A vague dread of something terrible, of something fearful, filled her mind; but she resolved to conceal her apprehensions. Her determination was come to at once. There were periodical visits of English smugglers to Boulogne. She would go as cabin boy in one of these. With this thought she dried her tears, and pretended to sleep.

Late that night Claude, haggard, pale, and stern, came in. His wife closed the door of the bed-room, and then taking him by the hand, made him sit down by the fire.

There they conversed in whispers for an hour. When they parted—Claude to go to bed, his wife to watch—there was calmness on his countenance, and in her eyes a brightness which indicated a solemn resolution.

CHAPTER XXXIII.

MADAME CARABOSSE.

THE position of Mr. James Tyrrel Blakesley was indeed a critical one. The supposed heir to the title and estates, he had discovered from a letter written by his captain, was on board a frigate, under the protection of a very old friend of his fathers.

He was there all but invulnerable.

His solicitors found on examination that Goldy Gordon, the Blue Dwarf, had, despite his strange and wild exterior, been appointed by the Lord Chancellor receiver on the whole of the Blakesley estates.

What papers were placed before the great judge could not be known; but they were to a certain extent satisfactory there could be no doubt.

The rents were to be paid into court pending a trial, as of course the young heir would contend his right with this new and strange claimant.

There remained but a very small private fortune of James Tyrrel Blakesley's own and his wife's jointure.

His position was desperate. He was overwhelmed with debt, and already his creditors began to be pressing. To keep up the state of Blakesley Hall was impossible. He therefore took the advice of his solicitors and gave up possession.

He determined to conceal himself in London until matters were settled.

What annoyed him most was the fact that he did not see this new claimant face to face. All machinations were vain while he had a shadow to fight with. But as he knew he must meet him some day or other, he waited.

He took quiet apartments in a busy street near the Strand, under an assumed name. The metropolis was too hot to hold him under his real denomination; and being compelled to forego his usual amusements, was reduced to wandering about the streets, or looking in occasionally at the theatre.

In these peregrinations he wore a slouched hat and a great coat—the collar of which was very much above his ears, as he had not the remotest wish to make acquaintance with John Doe or Richard Roe. One evening he was sauntering about with a cigar in his mouth, communing with himself, cursing his bad fortune and bewailing his fate generally, when it struck him that he would call upon his friend Minto Malespina.

This man was an apothecary, an Italian, and said by popular rumour—though nothing had ever been brought home to him—to be a purveyor of poisons to the million. Certainly his obscure and hideous den was visited by a very large number of persons, ostensibly to purchase the means of exterminating vermin, but very much, it is to be feared, for the destruction of human life.

Minto Malespina was a little dark, saturnine man, of about five-and-forty, with short black hair and a pair of spectacles on his nose, rather to conceal the fierce brilliancy of his little black eyes than for any purposes of vision.

Minto was behind his counter when Mr. James Tyrrel Blakesley entered. The man of medicine bowed low. The disguise denoted an important customer.

"What can I do for you, sir?" said Minto.

"Nothing—about what you have done," replied Mr. Blakesley, with a sneer.

"Good gracious, pray walk in!" cried the other, laying down a pestle with which he had been engaged previously; "pray, what do you complain of?"

"Your patient, whom you had booked for the other world, is as well as ever he was in his life," said Blakesley, tartly.

"Then, he never had the potion, or some one about him must have known the antidote," replied Minto Malespina, positively.

"That rascally Blue Dwarf!" cried Blakesley.

"Eh, what!" said the poisoner, turning livid, "do you know that hideous little beast?"

"Know him! He is the bane of my life."

"Good heavens!" cried the poisoner, wiping his brow with a handkerchief, "then we are ruined!"

"How mean you?" gasped Blakesley.

"One month exactly after you bought the first four bottles, he came here; he had one of them, but as I sell a great deal of it, I could not possibly guess it was yours. He bade me analyse it; I dared not refuse. I told him what it was. He then demanded the antidote, and further added that if the case ended fatally, he would give up both myself and my accomplice.

Blakesley groaned.

"'I watch over the patient,' he said, 'with the eye of a panther watching his prey; but should my vigilance fail, beware! I have evidence enough to hang you both.'"

"That is what the scoundrel meant when he mentioned your name."

"Mr. Blakesley," said the man of poison, hurriedly, "I have a great respect for you—I thank you for your custom, but as you have against you one who has the cunning and power of a demon, I must decline any further transactions of this kind."

"Why, you old villain," cried Blakesley, angrily, "I have not come on business at all. I merely called by way of passing the time. I wish you a very good evening."

And evidently very irritated, he went out of the shop, leaving the poisoner in a state of great trepidation. He had not been threatened by the Blue Dwarf for nothing.

Fuming, angry with himself and all the world, James Blakesley determined to hurry to some place of public amusement—some night-house, where he might drown his sorrows in dissipation. With this view he hurried towards the Strand, and was about to turn towards one of the localities indicated, when he stood still, as if petrified.

He rubbed his eyes to try if he were awake, and then, drawing his hat over his eyes more completely, he ventured nearer.

Pale, careworn, evidently recovering from a severe illness, his clothes coarse and worn, himself all covered with dust, was the youth whom he believed to be on board the frigate, under the protection of Sir Edmund Crossley.

He was looking in at a ready-made clothes shop, intending evidently to make a purchase.

He soon seemed to gain courage, and entered the shop, over which, in large letters, was written—

CARABOSSE, *Dealer in Gents' Wearing Apparel.*

Something like a gleam of light flashed upon the mind of Blakesley, and he determined to follow up his vantage ground.

It was in truth William Lennox, who, with the letters given him by the Blue Dwarf, had come up to town. Acting under advice, he had ridden up outside the coach, with the intention of purchasing a suit, fit to wear, when he should call upon the nobleman, whose secretary he was to be.

Accident, or fate, or destiny, had brought him to the shop kept by the woman Carabosse. It chanced that there was a plain gentlemanly suit of clothes in the window, which caught the eye of young Lennox, and as, in his present state, no respectable house would admit him, he determined to make the purchase at once.

With this view he entered.

Behind the counter was a woman, whose countenance he could not see. The shop was so hung with clothes, and so dark, that he failed to recognise her.

He mentioned his wants, and, finding the suit within his means, purchased it, and some linen; a hat, sword, and shoes. Madame Carabosse sold everything, and, in general, good articles for the money.

"Could you accommodate me with a room," said William, in his gentle, mild way, "where I can change my clothes?"

"Certainly," replied the woman, who kept a great handkerchief to her mouth. "Mary, show the gentleman up to the strong room, and give him a light."

Mary, a miniature domestic, about four feet high, and not more than twelve or fourteen years old, came forward, and made signs to him to follow her, which he did, not a little amazed at the oddity of his conductor. Her face was so concealed by dirt, smoke, and grease, as to be utterly undecipherable; but the sparkling of her eyes showed that there really was life and animation in her.

"Look alive," she said, "or missus will be poisoning the black beetles."

William Lennox stared at her as though she had been a mad girl.

"Or cooking the rats; she's always up to mischief—there;" and laying down the candle she ran away.

William Lennox found himself in a tolerably large apartment, with one window, and that barred. But he cared little then for more than a cursory examination, and at once began the office for which he had ascended. Though it was awkward to dress wholly without a glass, he soon had arrayed himself in his new apparel.

He then made a pile of his old garments, intending to leave them as a perquisite to the girl, and approached the door, and placed his hand on the handle.

It was locked.

William Lennox shook it impatiently, but in vain; it would not give way.

"Merciful heaven," he cried, "what den have I fallen into. But nonsense; it must be a mistake."

And he shouted to be let out, thinking the girl had played him a trick.

But no answer came to that and to repeated other summons. William Lennox now seated himself on the only chair in the room, and looked around. It was quite clear that, somehow or other, some of his enemies had tracked him, and induced the women of the shop to betray him.

Then a horrid thought crossed his mind. He thought he had a faint recollection of the voice of the woman who had spoken to him. If he was correct in this surmise, it was an explanation at once of his position; and his fate would indeed be horrible.

He examined the window. It was closely barred. William, in his desperation, searched the room for some weapon. The room, which had been that used by a pawnbroker for his chief valuables, was empty.

William Lennox was not one of those to lie down and bemoan his fate. By a great exertion of strength he broke up the chair, and made a stout weapon out of this. He then seated himself in a corner and waited.

But no one came near him for some hours, and at last, wearied and exhausted, he fell asleep.

When he awoke the first grey tint of dawn was peeping in through the dark window. Over head he heard a strange rumbling noise.

"You awake?" said a voice from the ceiling.

"Yes," replied William. "But who are you?"

"Mary, the girl. What have you done—killed the cat—no, that was care did that, eh?"

"I have done nothing. I have bitter enemies, but that is all. If you will assist me to escape, I will reward you——"

"Hungry?" said Mary, speaking through a hole in the ceiling, which she had made by dint of working hard all night.

"Not very."

"Well, here's a lump of bread and cheese and a bottle of water. They won't come near you: they are going to starve you."

"Who is *they?*"

"Mother Carabosse and the gentleman."

William Lennox groaned. His persecution was endless. What was to be done!

"What do you want?"

"A chisel, a file, a thick cord —"

"Hark!—all right—I'll see to it. Been all night making the hole."

And the voice ceased. William Lennox remained alone in that dark and gloomy room, where light only penetrated as into a prison.

The youth sank back in deep thought. His persecutions had been such that nothing astonished him. But by what unheard of chance had he been led to this den, and from what motive had he been thus arbitrarily confined?

Once or twice he rose and tried the door; it was too massive for him to make the slightest impression on it. He was compelled, therefore,

to trust wholly to the charity of the girl, who had shown him up into the room, and whose odd way of talking did not promise very high intellectual power.

But he began to be thirsty, and it was therefore with inexpressible delight that he again heard the voice of his friend.

"Down there?"

"I'm listening."

"Look out," she said, and through the large hole, her curiosity had induced her to make in the ceiling during the night, he saw a bundle slowly descend.

"It's all right—ain't I had a job to do it. Ain't she cunning as a fox, but ain't I cunninger?"

"Have you brought anything to drink?" gasped William Lennox.

"Milk and water; couldn't do nuffin else. Don't you be in a hurry. I'll draw the bolts, you take off the lock. How long will you be a doing of it?"

"A quarter of an hour."

"That's right—there's no one in the shop—she's behind the counter."

William Lennox eagerly consumed some cold meat and bread which the kindness of the little servant had provided him with, drank some milk and water, and then went to work. He heard the bolts cautiously drawn, and then a step descend the stairs.

With a muttered prayer, William Lennox set to work.

The lock was large and firmly set, but he had a chisel and file. He was thus able, in the time he had said, to draw out the screws and slip the bolt. With a heart beating with terrible emotions, he clutched the chisel by way of arms. His sword was merely ornamental; he began descending the stairs.

In a few minutes he was in the shop. Behind the counter sat Madame Carabosse, musing. Her eyes were fixed as it were on vacancy. Suddenly she caught sight of the slight figure of William Lennox gliding through the shop.

"Stop, you young madman; where are you going? Your father-in-law ——"

A dark figure now filled the doorway. William could have fallen to the earth, but he knew his fate if captured now. With a despairing cry he dashed passed, and ere his father-in-law could clutch him, he was in the open street.

"Stop thief!" cried Mr. James Tyrrel Blakesley.

"Stop thief!" shrieked two or three little urchins who were passing.

It was broad daylight, and by good chance there were few people in the street. Still the cry might swell, and William Lennox, horrified at this new phase, ran as for his life. Suddenly a figure darted out of a doorway, clutched his hand, and whispered "This way."

Next minute he found himself in a maze of courts and—as the French say—impasses, where none could have followed him.

"There, that will do," said Mary, checking his speed. "I can't run no further."

"What, you here, my good girl?" replied William, as soon as he regained his breath.

"Well, I never; you don't suppose I was going to stay and be eat alive by that old miser, Mother Carabosse, eh?"

"But, my good girl," he added, in an odd, puzzled way, "what are you going to do?"

"Won't you want a servant?" said Mary, demurely. "But what's this?"

And she displayed a splendid gold watch and chain hanging from a button of his coat. In rushing past his step-father he had unwillingly caught his watch, and the cry of stop thief was explained.

"This must be taken back," he said, with a sickly sensation at his heart.

"Does he want for to harm you?" replied Mary.

"Yes; he is the enemy of my name, my life, my honour. If he could hang me he would do it with pleasure."

"And they would hang you for that," said the London girl, emphatically.

"Merciful heavens!" cried the unhappy youth, "what is to be done? If I appear in public he will find me out. I must hide until I communicate with Goldy Gordon. He alone can protect me against this man."

"Do you want to hide where he never will find you?" said Mary.

"Anywhere—in the bowels of the earth," replied William.

"You come along with me. I've got a sweetheart, you know. He's a rum 'un, he is, but he's up to everything. You foller me."

William Lennox made not the slightest resistance to her will, and followed her without looking to the right or left, until they reached a narrow street with a glimpse of the river. She then darted under some arches, groped in the dark, and suddenly emerged into the light of day.

"Joe—Joe!" she cried, "you lazy vagabond, where are you?"

The door of a rude kind of tool-house, in a waste place, surrounded by ruined walls, opened, and a strange head protruded.

It was that of Joe, the mudlark, whom, after introducing to our readers under most strange circumstances, we have so long deserted.

CHAPTER XXXIV.

THE SAVOY VAULTS.

WHAT changes has not London seen since Peter, Earl of Savoy and Richmond, built himself a palace on the river-side in the year 1245, and bestowed it on the fraternity of Montjoy (Fratres de Mont Jovis)! How many historical recollections might we not invoke in connection with this building, beginning with its destruction by Jack Cade and Wat Tyler, to when, in 1750, it was still a most respectable and excellent building.

At the time of which we write—it having been once again burnt down—it was abandoned preliminary to its removal. Its massive walls were covered with ivy and moss, and built of brick, stone, and flint, defied even the efforts of the screw-jack, the pickaxe, and the crowbar. The level left twenty feet of the wall below ground, but there were still means of getting at the vaults and subterranean passages.

Joe the mudlark had taken advantage of the fact that the ruins were rarely visited to make them his sanctuary. With a thorough Arab-like independence of character, he preferred this solitude in a great city to any of the cheap lodging-houses. Besides, it cost him nothing; and whatever money Joe, the mudlark, earned he liked to spend upon the refection of the inner man.

There were those who suspected that Joe had other motives for haunting the ruins.

"Hallo!" said Joe, with a start, "I ain't seen

you, Moll, for a blue moon. Whose this gentry cove?"

"A friend of mine," replied Mary.

"Come in," continued Joe, eyeing the lad with something very like suspicion.

They followed him into his hut, which was simply a kind of tool-house, as we have said. The flooring was the earth, the walls mud, and the roof of thatch. Still it was warm and cosy for one whose days and evenings were spent in the mud of the river.

Joe and Mary conversed for some time in their peculiar slang, and then the former, turning to William Lennox, asked him what he could do for him.

"Return this watch to its owner," said William, starting. "I cannot rest until I know that it is safe."

"Well, my buck, I will," replied the boy, not without a look of supreme contempt; "though why you don't stick to the yack I can't see."

"Oh, Joe," cried Mary, with a reproachful look, "I thought you'd promised me."

"All right, old girl; it's only bamboozle," he said, laughing; "but now direct me what I am to do."

He could speak without slang when he liked, as can most persons.

William Lennox, after being assured that the boy could be trusted, gave him strict directions to go to Mother Carabosse, explain that the watch was taken by accident, and that he, William Lennox, wished it returned to its owner, Mr. James Tyrrel Blakesley.

The boy made him repeat the directions minutely a second time, and then promising to follow them in a satisfactory way, after which, receiving some money to procure food, he started on his errand.

Mary and William remained in the ruins of the Savoy. They went out into the open air; and at any other time, the latter, who was sufficiently poetical in taste, would have admired the massive character of the ancient walls which enclosed them on all sides; but now his own uncertain and perilous position occupied him solely.

Besides, he was curious to know the history of Joe the mudlark and his sweetheart.

It was very much like his own. They had no relatives or friends, and had met under arches, in wretched lodging-houses, in all the strange interior and mystic dens in which London abounds, until the girl had been picked up cheap by Madame Carabosse, and Joe, the mudlark, had been patronised by a long-shore man for his activity.

Madame Carabosse—the girl made no secret of the matter—was what is popularly known as a fence, or receiver of stolen goods, and it was part of her policy to keep about her only children who could neither become initiated very far into her malpractices, nor serve any purpose of the officers, who sometimes took a freak in their heads and made a sudden irruption into her establishment.

Mary said Joe had very bad associates, but that, having the intention of marrying her, he had faithfully promised to be honest.

"He won't betray me, then," said William Lennox, gravely.

Mary grew pale, and looked around with an alarmed and startled glance.

"If he did," she cried, with sudden energy, which made her little queer figure look quite handsome, "though I love him, I would never see him again."

"You are a good little girl; and I dare say it's all right," said William, with a smile.

Mary very thoughtfully led the way towards the dark arch by which they had entered, and listened attentively. William Lennox was glad to commune with his own thoughts, and so seated himself on a stone and waited.

What was to be done now, and how could he face the Earl of Crofton, with such a charge hanging over him? That nobleman, to whom he had letters of introduction, led so public a life, that it would be impossible to keep his position secret from James Tyrrel Blakesley.

A sense of gloomy despair rested on his soul, as he reflected on the fearful trials he had already endured, and was about to endure, ere he reached that man's estate when he might be supposed to be able to defend himself.

Suddenly he was caught by the arm by Mary.

"Something wrong," she muttered in his ear; "Joe is running like winkin."

Something dark passed within the dark shadows of the arch, and next minute they were joined by Joe the mudlark.

"What's the matter?" said Mary.

"We must mizzle, the beaks are after us," said Joe, hurriedly; "I have seen the old cove hisself."

And he darted into the open space of the ruins, followed by both.

"You ain't split?" asked Mary, watching him with deep attention.

"Eh, what?" cried the boy, wiping his heated face with a coarse "belcher;" "keep a quiet tongue in your head. It's all on the square; you'll find no cross in me. But come, we must absquatulate."

And he led the way towards another corner of the ruins, where, overgrown by brushwood, was a narrow hole, through which he crawled, followed by his anxious companions. No sooner were they within than they found themselves in complete darkness.

"We'll tip 'em the double," said Joe, "but don't move; I'm a downy cove, as you'll see."

And in another minute he had struck a light, and had illumined a lantern.

They were on the summit of a ruinous staircase leading to subterranean passages and vaults which exist to this day, though built over in such a manner as to preclude their examination by antiquarians.

The approaches to Waterloo Bridge are built on the portion of the foundations of the old Savoy Palace.

Joe the mudlark held the light on high while the others descended, and in a few minutes they found themselves in a perfect labyrinth of passages and vaults.

"No beaks ever com'd here," said Joe, with a laugh; "all this here's my own."

Mary was very pale. A dread was on the

heart of the girl. She did not know what, but she feared something.

Joe, however, hurried forward, and at last passed through a narrow doorway, down another flight of steps, and then into a deeper vault of small dimensions.

"Here's the *crug* and *bub*," he said, laying down a tolerably large parcel ; "let's sit down and enjoy ourselves."

Still Joe did not look Mary full in the face, which she did not like.

They, however, did ample justice to the bread, cheese, cold meat, and spirits, of which Joe had provided an ample supply. The mudlark drunk out of a tin measure. William took a dram, but wished for water.

"There's a well, I know," said Mary, quickly ; "I've lived here for months ; where's the pitcher, Joe ?"

The lad pointed it out, while in the act of loading a short clay pipe with tobacco.

"There's a *doss*," pointing to a pile of straw, "if you like to lie down. Smoke, eh ?"

"No, I thank you," said William, who, however, did not accept the offer of such an unequivocal bed.

Joe took another stiff drain of gin, and coolly lay down on the rejected straw ; and, as if to avoid conversation, shut his eyes.

Still Mary did not come back. She had started without a light, professing to know every inch of the place.

Suddenly the hurried motion of her tripping footsteps were heard.

She appeared at the head of the steps with the pitcher in her hand, and next minute handed it to William, who gladly took a long draught.

Mary went and sat down on the straw and plunged her hand into the only pocket the mudlark possessed.

"Stow that," said Joe, starting to his feet.

"Judas," whispered Mary, handing William a knife, and displaying five bright guineas ; "is this the blood-money ?"

The mudlark looked pale, and glanced at the door, but William, with an open knife, had him by the throat.

"You have betrayed me——"

"They said it was for your good ; by George then it's true ; he said he was your uncle," said Joe, sullenly.

"They are hunting the vaults, sword in hand, to kill him," returned the girl.

"To kill him !" said Joe, opening his eyes to their utmost width ; "the gentry cove said as how he was mad, and wanted locking up."

"Save him, Joe," replied Mary, firmly, "and I will forgive you. If they hurt him, I swear I will *blow the gaff*."

"You wouldn't ?" said Joe, wildly.

"I would——"

"Then come along, and we'll give them the slip. But once out of here, he must shift for himself."

"That will I," said William, "and thank you. The day will come when I shall be rich, and then you shall have no cause to regret."

"Rich, rich !" said Joe, with eyes that appeared to start from his head. "Shouldn't I like to be."

He then crept up the stairs, hiding the glare of the lantern, until they were in a kind of niche, from which he peered about.

Not twenty yards from them, Mr. James Tyrrel Blakesley, sword in hand, was advancing, while a stout ugly fellow followed, holding up a light.

"This way—*vamos !*" whispered Joe.

And he led them down another vista of the passage and vaults until they reached the water's edge. Here he crept into an empty barge, led the way to the hold, and screening his lantern, began conversing in a whisper with Mary.

————

CHAPTER XXXV.

JOE'S PLOT.

THIS is what had passed after Joe the mudlark left the Savoy.

Though in his heart he looked upon the return of the watch as an extremely foolish act, he was too anxious to please Mary not to yield to her under circumstances of this nature.

He therefore presented himself before Mother Carabosse, with a grave and important mien. The receiver knew him well.

On his entering the shop she came from behind a kind of screen.

"Well, my young conveyancer, what's up ?" she said, holding out her hands.

"Tight cocum," replied Joe ; "it ain't nothing of the sort. A gent here just lost a yack and chain."

"Yes—my cockyoly bird," cried the woman, hurriedly ; "what of him ?"

"Nothing," said Joe, "only here's the ticker."

Mr. James Tyrrel Blakesley suddenly appeared from behind the screen, and caught hold of the boy's arm.

"*Chuff it up*," said Joe, with a startled glance. "I brought it back safe enough."

"All very correct, my boy, and I'm going to pay you well for it." replied Blakesley, with a meaning glance at Madame Carabosse.

Joe assumed as dignified appearance as he could.

"You know where that unfortunate boy is," said the stepfather, taking out his pocket-handkerchief.

"Now then," cried Joe, indignantly ; "do you see anything green, eh ?"

"My good boy, I dare say that he has persuaded you that I want to hurt him ; nothing of the kind. I am his best friend. All I want is to see him once more. He is a little queer about the head. Now this watch really belongs to him."

The man was telling the truth.

"Look here !" laying five golden guineas on the counter ; "they are yours if you restore him to his anxious friends."

Joe's eyes glistened with the horrid lust of gold, which damned the soul of Judas Iscariot.

"You von't hurt him," he said, hypocritically.

"Certainly not, my boy."

"And yer von't split on me ?"

"Of course not."

Joe then pocketed the guineas, and informed the unnatural stepfather that the lad he was in search of was in the ruins of the Savoy; but that he must not take him there.

Joe indicated, however, to Mr. James Tyrrel Blakesley that if he would go to a certain house, in a small street leading out of the Strand, a certain Myers would, on hearing the name of Joe, and on receiving a tip, lead him into certain mysterious dens, where, he promised, the lad should be found.

A light in a certain position would guide him to the right spot.

"If all is well I will double the reward," said Blakesley.

Joe's eyes glistened. Whatever may have been his intentions before, he had now made up his mind.

He then departed, and Blakesley at once hurried in the direction indicated by the lad.

Having made a few hasty purchases, Joe began running, as if some one was following him.

Mary at once knew that something was wrong from the manner of Joe, and she watched him keenly. Like all women, she felt warmly for one she had befriended, as they hate one they have injured.

Under pretence of fetching the water she had slipped out, and watched the only other entrance of the vaults, many feet below the level of the approaches to Waterloo Bridge.

She both saw and heard Mr. Blakesley and Myers, the Jew pot-boy, enter the subterranean retreat.

Now she knew that Joe had betrayed the gentle youth.

Hurrying back, she, partly by her own personal influence, partly by using the power which a stupendous secret gave her over him, induced him to forego his intentions.

Joe had no wish to cause the death of the good-looking youth in whom Mary took such a strange and unaccountable interest. At all events he had his five guineas, and that was something.

Determined, if possible, to restore himself to the favour of Mary, he kept them close until the first dawn of daylight enabled him to look around. Then he sprang from his hiding-place, and peered about with the extreme caution and cunning of a London boy of his experienced station and yet tender age.

The coast was clear.

Nothing appeared to show any life, but where, on a hard, a boat waited, watched by one single man.

To make doubly sure, Joe proposed that they should walk along the shore to the hard, thus avoiding the tavern where Myers, the fat Jew, was pot-boy.

William Lennox, considering this a proof of the sincerity of his intentions, willingly acquiesced, and in a very short space of time they had reached the landing known as the Savoy Stairs.

A boisterous boat's crew of sailors came rushing down the steps.

William Lennox and Joe the mudlark stood aside, to make way for them.

Mary slipped out of sight.

"Handspikes and clew garnets !" said a stout man with a very red face. "Here's the very thing we want. Have a row? eh?"

William Lennox touched his hat to the half drunken captain.

"I beg pardon," he said, with that soft urbanity which made him so seductive in character, "do you want a volunteer?"

He saw by the manner of the crew that they were going to press them.

"Bravo, my hearty !" cried the man; "that's jolly. What say you, my queer one?"

Joe attempted to run, but the man in the boat caught him, and, by way of quieting him, knocked him down, and cast him insensible into the bows.

Mary came running forward with a wild and startling shriek.

"Hillo, my wench !" said one of the sailors, laughing, as they rushed into the boat. "Stole your fancy man, have we? Rum couple, both. Well, don't make 'eye-water in the sea.'"

"Give me back my Joe," cried Mary, endeavouring to clutch at the boat's gunwale.

"'But as they fetched a walk one day
They met a pressgang crew;
And Sally she did faint away,
Whilst Ben he was brought to,'"

shouted the comic man of the party.

"He's only a boy," she cried, clasping her hands in wild agony.

But the boat pushed off, William Lennox waved a sad farewell, and Mary fell kneeling on the hard, utterly broken-hearted.

William Lennox now bent down, and tried to revive Joe by means of water; but ere he had effected his purpose he found himself beside a lugger of a very large tonnage, which, the instant they were on deck, hoisted sail, and started down the river.

Joe the mudlark was laid on a pile of canvas in the hold. William Lennox stood waiting the orders of the skipper.

"Now then, my hearty," said the captain, rather good-humouredly, "you can live like a trump, and you'll find it pay you. What can you do?"

"I'm no sailor. I've had a yacht of my own. That is ——" exclaimed William, blushing.

"A yacht, the devil ! But never mind. I want a clerk who can write; and if he could speak French I'd give him good wages."

"I speak French like a native."

"Then, by jingo, Mister What's-your-name, you are now captain's clerk to the Spanking Sally, John Carter master, bound for Boulogne, for a cargo of spurrits."

"France !" said William, with a smile.

At all events he had escaped Mr. James Tyrrel Blakesley. He had forgot the old Spanish proverb about falling out of the frying-pan into the fire.

People should never forget proverbs : they are often very useful things.

To William Lennox of course the name of Boulogne caused no emotion. It would have been different had he known that one whose name he never mentioned had just escaped from there, after leaving desolation, ruin, and despair behind.

He was about to face Claude Placquet, with that face of his, which so closely resembled Philip Carabosse.

CHAPTER XXXVI.

AN AWKWARD PREDICAMENT.

THE delight of William Lennox knew no bounds when he found himself at last free from all danger on the part of James Tyrrell Blakesley. It is true his present position was far from being either what he wished or expected; but, at all events, it was a relief for the moment. As the lugger spun along the waters of the Thames, and finally reached the open sea, a sense of freedom, accompanied by elation of spirits, took possession of his soul, and he felt disposed most friendly towards his fellow-creatures.

Joe the mudlark having recovered from the effects of the knock-down blow administered to him by one of the rough crew of the Spanking Sally had risen with a sullen determination to resist all attempts to make him work.

The immediate application of a rope's-end vigorously over his shoulders, by a ruffianly Dutchman, who served as mate, only made him roar and blubber, but did not conquer his obstinacy.

William Lennox moved slowly in the direction occupied by the boy in the lugger, and, leaning over the bulwarks, appeared absorbed in contemplation of the glorious spectacle of the outspread German Ocean.

Joe sat wiping his eyes with his rough and dirty hands.

"Joe!" said William, gently.

No answer.

"What is the use of crying?" continued William. "I don't like this trip much; but it cannot be helped, so why say more about it? Get up and work like a man, and you'll soon find it easy enough."

William Lennox now stooped down, and, after some difficulty, succeeded in persuading the boy of the wisdom of a conciliatory policy. Joe the mudlark yielded with a bad grace at first, but having offered to learn some work, and been treated with rough good humour, the elasticity of youth prevailed, and from a mudlark, Joe became a sailor and a smuggler.

William, at his own request, was furnished with a blue jacket and canvas trousers, in the place of his fashionable suit, which the smuggler gave him a chest to put away in, and at once assumed the appearance of a very handsome cabin-boy.

In this dress his resemblance to Philip Carabosse was startling.

At dawn the next day they were off Boulogne; a haze concealed all but the heights, giving the scene a singularly wild appearance. As, however, they neared the harbour, the vapour gradually moved away, and William saw the famous land of France for the first time not without emotion.

The smuggler was, it appeared, well known; and as it was understood that for these worthies there never should be any obstruction, the Spanking Sally anchored within the inner harbour without the slightest let or hindrance.

Mister Franks, the skipper, went on shore at once, taking William with him as interpreter and clerk.

William, having learnt French with his wretched foster-brother, could speak it fluently, and was therefore of great use to the smuggler captain.

They took their way to a rude hostelrie, frequented by men of their own class, where Franks found the person he required, and with him, by the medium of his new interpreter, he quickly transacted his business.

"That's first-rate," he cried, clapping his great hand good-humouredly on the shoulder of the lad; "shan't want you no more, so if you like to speer about you can. Don't care much about this, eh?"

And he pointed to the bottle of Hollands and tobacco.

"No!" said William, laughing, and, making a respectful bow, he left the room.

The town was strange to him, that it was with deep interest he strolled about, taking note of all that was novel and picturesque in the costume of the people, shape of the houses, and even the contour of the streets.

So near England as it is, what greater contrast can be found between Boulogne-sur-mer and Folkestone or Dover.

William at last found that sight-seeing was tiring, and looked about for a place where he might seek both repose and refreshment, and quickly discerned a low one-storeyed building, painted red outside, with the old sign of the bush, and the old emphatic inscription:

"*Ici on donne à boire et à manger.*"*

Satisfied with this clear and, at all events, flattering promise, William Lennox went boldly in, sat himself down among conscripts, sailors, and others of the lower classes; and after a glance around to see what others were doing, ordered wine and bread and cheese.

He then had leisure to examine the scene, which, not only in costume, was different from anything in England, but in every phase and incident.

Preachers against intemperance always point to France as an example. Now it is notorious to any one who knows that country, that the amount of squalid misery produced by drink in France is unparalleled in the history of the world, except in Russia.

In the great manufacturing regions of France the father drinks, the mother drinks, the youthful son drinks, and the girl drinks.

The hideous vice which is the consequence we cannot venture to describe. The women scarcely know at any period of life what the sense of shame means.

England is by far the least drunken of manufacturing nations.

In the present instance even William Lennox

* Here you have to eat and to drink.

could notice that those who were drinking wine and cider were merely satisfying the wants of nature, while others, who poured brandy in constant *petits verres* down their throats, were drinking for drinking sake.

The noise was indescribable. Everybody spoke at once, and nobody listened; and as they spoke different *patois*, the effect was ludicrous in the extreme.

At length, however, William felt weary and drowsy, and taking advantage of the fact that he was in an obscure corner, he soon fell asleep, the noise itself, as it often will, acting as a soporific.

There was as it were a roar, then a hum, then a distant faint whisper, and he was sound asleep, dreaming of sweet Lilian.

Suddenly he awoke, and to his horror and astonishment found himself jolting along a rough road, in a tented cart, his hands and feet secured with cords.

It was pitch dark.

"Where am I—what have I done?" he cried aloud.

"Silence," said a grave and terrible voice; "silence, lest I kill you."

There was something so awfully real in the tone of the menace, that William Lennox shuddered with horror at this new and dreadful peril which had fallen on him.

Fortune was resolved, he thought, to try him, until nature succumbed beneath the weight of woe.

On, on they went jolting, jumping through some rutty lanes and roads, for about an hour longer, when the cart suddenly halted, and a bell was heard resounding through the corridor of what appeared a large house.

A large *porte cochere* was opened, and the cart was driven inside. Then the gates closed behind them with a terrible clang, that was ominous of ill.

A powerful pair of arms were passed beneath the tent of the cart, and William was lifted out, placed on his feet, and his bonds cut.

Rubbing his eyes, dazzled by the sudden light of a kind of torch, William Lennox found himself in the presence of a grave, middle-aged man, in the garb of a fisherman, who looked at him more in sorrow than in anger, and of a handsome young soldier, who eyed him with intense and bitter hatred.

"Philip—viper—serpent!" said the fisherman, "what have you to say before I kill you for your sin?"

"Nothing; because as I never saw you before I can only look upon you as robbers or madmen," said the astonished William.

The soldier raised his clenched fist.

"Stop," said the older man. "And you can stand there and say you know us not?"

"As heaven is my judge, I never saw either of you before."

"And Pauline?" cried the man with uplifted hands.

"Don't know any such person."

"Malediction!" said the other, "I suppose you will say you are not Philip Carabosse, son of my sister, Madame Carabosse!"

William Lennox stood with open mouth, with staring eyes, in an attitude of horror.

"I knew the wretch," he began in faltering accents.

"Silence! liar and hypocrite," roared the incensed Claude Placquet; "come to your victim, and then dare to deny—".

And they literally dragged William Lennox to the door of a room, bolted on the outside, opened it and flung him in.

It was a large bed room lighted by a single lamp.

"Pauline," said the fisherman in a voice of thunder, "here is your *amoureux* and *tonnerre d'enfer*," he added; "he swears that he knows you not. If he does not consent to marry you by twelve to-morrow he dies."

And Claude Placquet drew the door after him, bolting and barring it carefully.

A young girl, who was lying dressed upon a bed, sprang up, and with a wild cry advanced to meet him.

"I am not Philip Carabosse," said William in a voice of considerable confusion and distress, not unmingled with alarm.

His mind was absolutely bewildered with the novel and somewhat piquant style of his adventure.

The girl lifted up the lamp and gazed at him for a moment.

"It is not Philip," she said in a tone of blank despair. "Too good, too gentle."

"Will you explain all this," asked William Lennox gently.

"If you please. But do you know Philip Carabosse?—you are very like him."

"I know a wretch—" began William.

"Hush!—that is what I say sometimes. But then he is to be my husband, and he is the father of my unborn child," said the girl, bending down her head.

William Lennox—the soul of honour and truth—uttered an exclamation of horror.

"Poor girl," he added; "I begin to understand their terrible mistake. But we shall easily be able to explain it."

"I don't know," said Pauline. "The honour of our house is at stake, and they have got you here. Philip Carabosse is far away, and they may pretend to believe in your being the man."

"Merciful heaven! But you would undeceive them," cried William.

"I don't know," said Pauline, clutching him by the arm and whispering in his ear, "Do you know if I don't find a husband they will kill my child."

And in her agony she sobbed upon his shoulder.

"Who, they?" said William.

"My father and mother," sobbed Pauline.

"Who was the young soldier?" asked our hero.

"My *fiancée*. Ah, don't speak of him; he is too good. Do you believe that though he knows all he offered to save my honour and my child—but no—never. Philip is my husband!" she cried, with wild and earnest passion.

"My poor girl!" said William Lennox, gently, "I cannot tell what is to be done. If they persist in their belief they will kill me."

"No, no! cannot you pretend to marry me, and then both fly together!" continued the desperate girl.

"It would be a wicked mockery. But tell me all," added Lennox; "and then we may consult."

Pauline, whose dangerous beauty was even greater than ever, took his hand, looked full into his eyes, and appeared to read his soul.

William, whose whole heart was given to Lily, blushed, and held down his head.

"You have loved," said the syren, in her soft, seductive tones; "I know it."

"I love!" replied William, hardly knowing what he said—his voice trembling.

"I knew it," said Pauline, "and so will conceal nothing of my story. You will excuse and forgive me."

She then told him all, except that she exaggerated somewhat her own virtue and the seductive powers of, Philip Carabosse.

William pitied her from his heart; and yet an inward monitor warned him that had he have been less delicate, he might have at once supplanted his foster brother.

But instinct prevailed, and William felt that all was not right in Pauline herself.

CHAPTER XXXVII.

THE FAMILY TRIBUNAL.

TOWARDS dawn the young people, so strangely and peculiarly situated, fell into a doze, she seated on a box, he in an arm-chair.

Nature was utterly exhausted, and demanded a revival of its powers.

A full stream of light was pouring into the room from the barred window, when the unbolting of the door awoke them to consciousness. They started to their feet, each standing near the spot where they had passed the night.

Claude Placquet entered, followed by Simon Roger, surnamed Tourlourou.

They led in the mother, changed from a handsome matron of thirty-five to an old woman.

Her hair was white, her countenance pale and wan, her steps feeble and tottering.

"Look! there he stands. Speak, mother," cried Claude; "tell me, do my eyes deceive me?"

"That is the man," said the woman, slowly and emphatically.

"Mother," cried Pauline passionately, falling on her knees as she spoke, "you are all mistaken. It is a fatal mistake. This is not my husband."

The three took their seats on a bench, and shook their heads.

"Monsieur, whose name I do not know," said William Lennox, with manly firmness, "I beg again most emphatically to declare that you are the victim of a fatal error. I have explained, to your daughter's satisfaction, that the person against whom your animosity is directed is my foster-brother, a person I have every reason to hate. We were brought up together, and our likeness is wonderful."

"But how came you to speak French?" said Claude Placquet.

"My nurse Placquet taught me. She suckled me at her breast."

"Know you that my name is Placquet?" said the fisherman, moodily.

"I knew it not until you spoke."

"Who and what is Madame Carabosse?" asked the judge.

"Dealer in old clothes, and receiver of stolen goods—a wicked woman," said William Lennox firmly.

"Ah," cried Claude, gnashing his teeth, "dare you insult my sister?"

"I speak the truth," said William.

"He speaks the truth," muttered the unhappy mother; "this is not Philip Carabosse. This man is frank and manly; the other was a coward and a knave."

The three spoke for some time in whispers.

At last Claude Placquet turned to the two young people.

"This is heaping hot coals on fire," he said, gravely; "it is not sufficient that our family is dishonoured, but a stranger is admitted into our confidence. It is an unfortunate and fatal mistake. But what is done may not be undone. Young man, everybody in Boulogne will take you for Philip Carabosse; are you willing to save the honour of our only child and daughter, and marry her?"

"Certainly not," said William, firmly; "I am engaged to be married in my own country."

"It is good, young man; we are very sorry for what we are about to do, but it must be. You never leave this room alive except as the husband of our daughter. Under what appears to be an error you have passed a night with our daughter; of this you must not boast. This door will be blocked up; evening and morning will we come outside and ask; when you say yes, a priest shall be sent for, and the ceremony performed. Until then, farewell! and heaven have mercy on your souls?"

The father rose, with a solemn and resolute mien, and moved towards the door.

"Heaven forgive you and us," said the mother, who was partly insane.

She, too, with her eyes on the ground, moved towards the door.

"I forgive you, Pauline, though you have broken my heart," said Simon Roger.

"Inhuman monsters, shrieked Pauline, maddened by terror and despair; "so, to save your so-called honour, you become assassins. Had this man, Simon Roger, have not acted the part of an eavesdropper and a spy, I should long 'ere this have been the wife of one who would have made me happy, rich, and great. Go, Simon Roger, I loathe, I detest you! And you *mon pere*, and you *ma mere*, you leave me here, the affianced wife of one, alone with his deadliest enemy. Think you I can bless you; my murdered child will curse you enough, I need not do so—ah!"

And she fell into wild hysterics. The family council went out, apparently unmoved, leaving

the young people alone, without one scrap of food or one drop of water.

William Lennox laid Pauline on the bed, where she sobbed herself asleep.

Resolved not to die without at least an effort at releasing himself, William Lennox searched the room and examined the window. The bars were only of thick wood, but he had not the smallest knife in his possession; nothing in the shape of a weapon of offence or defence offered itself, after the most diligent search.

"It is of no use, we must die!" sobbed Pauline, waking up and understanding his object at a glance.

"No, they cannot be so cruel," replied William Lennox; "this is only done to terrify us."

"They are implacable," continued Pauline, shaking her head.

"They are surely not monsters in human shape."

"They will starve us to death!" shrieked Pauline. "Oh! save me, save me! for the sake of my innocent child have mercy on me."

"What can I do?"

"It is but to say the word. I swear by all that is sacred that I will never claim you as my husband—that I will go from you next minute," said the unhappy girl.

"I cannot perjure myself, even to save my own life," replied William.

"Cruel, cruel!" said Pauline, and she turned her face to the wall.

William Lennox sat down at a respectful distance, and began to think over the wretched fate which had been his since the death of his father.

The day passed slowly and wearily; the rays of the sun fell obliquely across the floor from several orifices in the wooden shutters, which reached nearly to the roof, and still they came not.

Night fell, the room became dark as pitch, and still they came not.

A horrible sensation of hunger began to affect their brains; thirst also burned their throats. They were almost delirious. Presently Pauline sat up in the bed and began to sing.

William Lennox joined her frantically at the top of his voice.

And still they came not.

They really seemed to have left them to die a horrible and lingering death.

CHAPTER XXXVIII.

THE FALSE FRIEND.

LORD CHARLES LUTTEREL was terribly shaken by his interview with the lovely Lucy Lipscombe, and retired from it with a mingled feeling of desperate rage and wild passion.

In his eyes the energy of Lucy only made her more beautiful, and he resolved in his heart of hearts that if she could not be his, no one else on the face of the wide earth should ever possess her.

There was one person of all others against whom this feeling operated, and that was against him who professed to be his elder brother.

But the man feared that energy which could brave him in his own den, and he resolved to have recourse to stratagem to effect his abominable purpose.

Drugging was no good.

Lucy Lipscombe solemnly declared her intention to starve herself rather than touch one morsel of food or drink, unless one of her attendants had partaken freely of it.

This infamous procedure became, then, impossible of realisation.

Something else, then, must be done.

For some days he reflected, while drowning his disappointment and annoyance in wine, and the society of roués and demireps. It then suddenly struck him that Martha Snelling was the right instrument to use.

This woman, having once launched on the broad path of guilt, he knew would only become more greedy after gold.

Avarice is, of all vices, that which grows quickest on the soul, absorbing every faculty, and drowning honour, sense, and religion.

Lord Charles Lutterell sent for her to meet him at the old place, and he agreeing to pay well, a plan was devised into which Martha Snelling fell with admirable zest. It made her the intimate *confidante* of a lord.

Besides, now that she had injured Lucy, of course, by a natural process in weak and vicious minds, she hated her with all her heart and soul.

Her object was to conduct Lucy to a supposed place of safety, first getting from her by stratagem the knife which Lord Charles Lutterel lived so much in dread of.

The room occupied by Lucy overlooked a kind of orchard. It was on the second storey, and the windows were unbarred. There would have been no difficulty in escaping by means of her sheets or counterpane; but close under the window were two savage mastiffs that were so chained as to render escape impossible.

This was an insuperable difficulty, and as Lucy Lipscombe sat at her window thinking and looking up at the pellucid sky, she tried, in the simplicity of her heart, to devise some means of taming these ferocious beasts.

But no idea came.

One evening—she had been there a week—the air was peculiarly balmy, and she stood leaning her elbow on the window sill, while gazing out on the orchard, from which rose pleasant and agreeable odours.

"How lovely is this earth, and how lovelier still, did not human passions do their best to destroy and mutilate. Ah, me! am I wholly forgotten—"

"Mrs. Lipscombe! Mrs. Lipscombe," said a timid and trembling voice from the orchard.

"Who calls?" cried Lucy in a loud tone.

"Are you alone?"

"Yes," she replied, with a trembling heart.

"'Tis I—Martha," continued the traitress; "I have tracked you day and night, and, thank Heaven, at last I have found you!"

"Thank you—bless you, my good Martha!" said Lucy warmly.

The dogs began to bark furiously.

"It is no use," she added, "those horrid brutes render all escape impossible."

The dogs flew the whole length of their chain at Martha Snelling.

She cast them each a lump of raw flesh, which they instantly began to devour. Scarcely had they finished when they crept into their sheds, and in a few minutes their heavy breathing proclaimed they were in a sound sleep.

"Ah! ah!" laughed Martha, "I had provided for them. Come, mistress, there is no danger now."

With nervous trepidation, but still with remarkable activity, Lucy fastened the sheets to the window, slid down, and in another moment was in the orchard, embracing the female Judas who had betrayed her.

"There is not a moment to lose, the dogs may recover. Come!" said Martha, in a voice of considerable trepidation.

"One moment, young woman," said a sarcastic voice. "Very much obleeged to you for the assistance, but if it's all the same, we'll just secure you."

And a man seized Martha Snelling, and before she could shriek out had successfully gagged her.

"In the name of Heaven," cried Lucy clasping her hands, "what is the meaning of this outrage?"

"My dear lady," said a tall gipsy-looking woman, "when I say I'm a friend of Captain

George I am sure you will put faith in me. This wretched woman is a traitor; it was she who before betrayed you into the hands of Lord Charles Lutterel. Then she had a hundred pounds; she is to have the same for her night's work."

"Martha Snelling betray me!" gasped poor Lucy.

"Come, lady, and you shall see."

They led the bewildered Lucy through the orchard, Stone—for it was he and Miriam were the deliverers—holding Martha Snelling firmly until they reached a gate, through which they passed and closed it behind them.

There stood a post-chaise, the driver being tied neck and heels in a ditch.

This is what had happened:

The night was dark in the extreme beneath the leafy arches of the wood, when two people coming in opposite directions up a narrow lane met in sudden and violent conflict one with the other. Both were nearly cast to the ground by the shock, and when they rose a lanthorn held by one of them, a woman, showed to the eyes of the man a tall and powerful gipsy—to her a somewhat enfeebled man.

"I pray thee be a little more careful for the future," said the woman, still eyeing him with considerable attention.

"Pardon me, good mother, and delay me not, for there are hawks abroad. I would fain be of service to one that is distressed."

"Dost know one Captain George?" said the other with a smile.

"I do, my benefactor and my friend!"

"Then is your name Stone? No cries of wonder. We are here both to save the loved one of his heart. Hast any news?"

"Follow me, and I will show you. I have nearly worn the flesh off my bones," said Stone with a deep sigh, "but I have succeeded. I heard her give a meeting for to-night in this place. In a few minutes they will be here."

"Lead on, then; I follow," replied Miriam.

Stone, who had tracked the footsteps of Lord Charles Lutterel with the patience of a hound, had, by dint of listening, guessing, spying, contrived to find out that Martha Snelling was to meet him at the lonely farm-house where he had for some days suspected that she had been confined.

He had seen Lord Charles Lutterel start in a post-chaise for the scene of action, and had followed in a hackney cab to rather a short distance of the house.

The gipsy and the poor man Stone reached the spot where stood the carriage. Approaching with extreme caution, they distinctly saw that Martha was in the act of leaving.

"You have had one hundred, Martha," he said; "if you succeed, double that sum is yours."

"I will succeed, my lord," she replied.

The strangely-met confederates waited until Martha was quite out of hearing, and then, rushing suddenly out, Miriam knocked the postboy down with one blow of her good oaken cudgel, while Stone presented a pistol to the brow of Lord Charles Lutterel.

"What want you, villain?"

"I wish your lordship just to step inside the carriage, and to move at your peril. This pistol is very tricksy, and might go off," said Stone, with great gravity.

"You know who I am, and still have the audacity to attack me," cried Lord Charles Lutterel, retreating, however, to the carriage.

"I am the friend, I am proud to say, of Captain George," replied Stone.

"You shall swing for this," blustered the nobleman.

"I am afraid your lordship alludes to your own probable fate," said Stone, coldly.

Miriam, meanwhile, had secured the postboy, and now proposed to tie and gag his lordship.

This proposition was speedily carried into effect, despite a furious diatribe from Lord Charles, and then the two confederates hastened after Martha.

When Lucy saw her persecutor tied inside the carriage she knew that she was betrayed, and guessed the abominable purpose for which Martha had been employed to aid in her pretended deliverance.

"Thank you, my friends, thank you," she cried, clasping her hands; "but let us fly from hence. He may have assistance at hand."

Without a word Stone and Miriam made the nobleman descend from his carriage, and then, without ceremony, tied him and his friend Martha Snelling to the same tree, despite their grimaces and struggles. They then loosened the postboy, and, by the due use of a loaded pistol, made him mount his horse and drive them off to town, Stone sitting on the seat, in complete command of the driver.

They soon reached the Strand, where, by calling in a blacksmith, they soon obtained admission, and though the place was in confusion Lucy Lipscombe was not long ere she was enabled to make her new friends comfortable. They could, however, give no certain news of Captain George.

This saddened the heart of poor Lucy, whose sole thought was for her lover.

But days upon days passed, and he came not, until she began to be very weary with hope deferred.

With a view to her own protection, Lucy Lipscombe made a private deposition before a magistrate, who gave a personal warning to Lord Charles Lutterel, and issued a warrant against Martha Snelling. But that worthy female was nowhere to be found.

Miriam departed on her way. She was determined to find Lilian again before she died.

Stone remained as the guardian of Lucy, doing small jobs about the house.

CHAPTER XXXIX.

THE BENGAL TIGER.

Two or three days, or more, perhaps, after the vain search in the tents of the gipsies, made by Captain George and Mrs. Winterton, there arrived at the very inn at which Arabella had put up, a character of extreme eccentricity. He came in a carriage and four horses, with a black valet who spoke very good English, and a considerable amount of luggage.

His appearance was grotesque rather than prepossessing. He wore a very large beard, whiskers, and moustache, of a fiery red hue, a kind of red Greek cap, and the plain clothes of a lawyer or medical man. His language was English, though to his valet he appeared to speak Arabic—always in a quick, imperious, angry way, as if he believed himself to be somebody of great importance.

He ordered the people of the inn about with great coolness, and made what is generally called a great fuss: but as he paid liberally of course all this was put up with.

He gave his name as Colonel Sparkes Bing, from India.

He would associate with no one, and was so sharp and testy that he soon acquired the name of the Bengal Tiger, which kept all strangers from approaching him.

He had a considerable suite of rooms, but was fond of frequenting the coffee-room, where he read the papers, made angry remarks, never answered questions, asked them angrily and impertinently, and made himself, in fact, particularly disagreeable.

He would go out alone at night for long walks, returning at one or two in the morning, to the great delight of the night porter, whom he paid liberally, though at the same time growling like the celebrated bear which had received some injury about his cranium.

He dined alone, attended by his valet, and indulged in luxurious living, rich tobacco, and wines of the finest and most celebrated vintages.

One day, Colonel Sparkes Bing was up stairs having his dinner, when a very plain travelling carriage came up, from which there descended two very plainly-dressed personages, awfully like retainers of the celebrated Mr. Sloman, who, without discharging their vehicle, entered the hotel.

"What can I do for you," said a waiter, stepping forward, and checking their progress.

"Are you the master?" replied one of the seedy individuals in a tone of deep melancholy, which, combined with what appeared to be a perpetual cold, gave him the appearance of a man who spoke from the cavernous depths of his interior.

"No; do you wish to see him?"

"I do," said the seedy individual.

The waiter perceived, with a vague idea, that something was wrong, still knew not how to shirk the matter. He therefore dived into a small sanctum behind the bar, and there held a conference.

"Pray what is it?" said a rather jolly personage, appearing with a very red face.

"Guv'ner?" replied the cavernous voice, taking off his hat, and speaking in even more sepulchral tones than before.

"My name is Mitchem; my time is precious; who and what are you?"

"Biggs and Waters; got a gent here of the name of Colonel Sparkes Bing," said the cavernous voice, with a knowing wink at his companion.

"And if I have, sir, a gentleman of that name honouring my establishment with a visit, pray what may that be to you?" replied Mitcham, with an uneasy sensation of cold water going down his back.

"Oh, nuffin—in course not," said the perpetual cold; "only he's wanted—that's all."

"Wanted?" cried the irate landlord; "I should advise you to be more careful in your speech."

"Wanted," continued the spokesman of the party; "escaped——"

"Hush!" cried the other, now afraid for the respectability of his establishment.

"Escaped *lunatic*," philosophically observed Biggs and Waters; "and we're keepers."

"You don't say so; how very remarkable," cried the landlord; "first-rate fellow."

"First-rate," said the keeper; "by the bye, got a couple of doctors handy? you'll see how glad he'll be to see us and them. Only you send for good ones—*he'll* pay."

The worthy host began to fancy that the two seedy individuals were the lunatics, but wishing to be convinced on the subject, at once expressed his intention to comply with their injunctions, and accordingly sent for two gentlemen who patronised his hotel.

Meanwhile, the keepers went up stairs, and, after some parleying, were admitted. The domestics listened, but not a sound was heard, and when the two "eminent practitioners" came hurrying up to wait upon the illustrious colonel, they found him plying Biggs and Waters with drink. Satisfied that all was right, they entered with the landlord, and bowed with extreme courtesy.

"What can we do for you?" said one of the medical men, a short, stout, puffy party of about fifty, with a rubicund face, gold eye-glass, and a habit of holding up his coat tails, as if he must put his hands somewhere.

"Do," said Colonel Sparks Bing, from India, "be ——"

"Sir," replied the man of physic, urbanely, "very funny, indeed. Humph, a little touched here."

And he tapped his forehead with a knowing glance at the keepers. The landlord went out of the room.

"Exactly," said the spokesman of the two keepers.

Colonel Sparks Bing rolled his eyes with a ferocious glare, and fidgetted in his pockets.

"Will you sign this?" said the keeper, handing over a paper.

"I wo'nt go back to London," cried the colonel calmly, but firmly.

"Any place in this neighbourhood?" continued the seedy one.

"Oh yes, Messrs. Legg and Toucher," said the medical man eagerly, mentioning friends of his.

"That will do," said the chief keeper, and he handed over the paper, Colonel Sparks Bing grinning ferociously all the time.

"But," put in the second medical man, "really, it appears to me quite doubtful, you see—if, really, the gentleman is—you know—touched."

"If you don't sign and leave off your cursed faces," said the colonel, starting up and presenting a pair of miniature pistols, "I'll shoot you both, like two dogs. There!"

The astonished and alarmed medical men signed without the slightest hesitation, and then shuffled from the room so eagerly as to overset the landlord, who was listening outside.

"Well," he said, rubbing his elbow, "what is the matter?"

"Mad as a march hare, stark, staring insane!" said the first medical man.

"Who'd have thought it?" cried the landlord; "what a good customer!"

The medical men shook their heads and followed the host down stairs, the latter to make up his bill, the former to take a good old glass of port in order to revive themselves after their alarm.

In a few minutes the keepers came down stairs, leading Colonel Sparks Bing, from India, who looked uncommonly ferocious.

Behind came his black valet, grinning.

The landlord bowed low.

"I will return and pay. Have the luggage ready," said the keeper.

They then led their passive prisoner to the ricketty post-chaise in which they had come, thrust him in, and drove off to the amazement of a crowd of boys, women, and men, who had collected to witness his departure.

CHAPTER XL.

THE MADHOUSE.

THE establishment of Messrs. Legg and Toucher, proprietors of what, in those days, was an abominable and atrocious violation of all law and justice—a private lunatic asylum—were celebrated over the whole of that part of England.

Men shuddered as they passed those desolate prison walls.

The house was built in a large garden, with all the iron-barred windows towards the inside; and yet shrieks and groans had been distinctly heard in the dead of night and under the noonday sun.

Messrs. Legg and Toucher divided the labours of the institution.

The former attended to the rich, the really insane—the victims of unhappiness or misfortune, who were placed there by their friends, with every intention of treating them with kindness and affection.

Nothing could exceed the tenderness of Mr. Legg.

Mr. Toucher took under his charge those who were placed there by hate, or fear, or jealousy; in fact, of the miserable victims of an abominable law, of the venality of profligate members of the medical profession, and of their own relatives.

Mr. Toucher ruled the inmates of what was called the pauper department with hideous severity.

Not that Toucher was a whit more of a ruffian than Legg, but this was their plan of action, and with the outward world it was perfectly successful.

Legg was tall and aristocratic, with rings, a white neckerchief, and powdered hair. Toucher was short and vulgar, with great fat hands that clutched the whip with evident delight.

The lash was his only mode of government, as the knout rules Russia, and, as we are ashamed to say, the cat rules the English army.

Infamy which nothing but the voice of the people themselves can abolish.

In private life among themselves Legg and Toucher were jolly dogs, who, looking upon money-making as the only business of life, cared not how it was done. They loved not groans, sighs, curses, yells, and piercing shrieks, for their own sake, like the wretched Neapolitan king; but they succumbed to them as matters of necessity.

"Well," said Legg, casting an Indian silk handkerchief over his knees, and sipping his port with great gusto, "how is number seven?"

The poor patients were spoken of according to the number of their cells. Every number concealed a crime.

"Humph!" replied Toucher, trying to look sad and doleful, "bad. He won't live long."

"Have you examined in all its bearings the relative merits of the question of life and death?" asked Legg, cracking a nut.

"Death produces a thousand, and there's an end of it; but life brings two hundred a year," continued Toucher.

"Good! but a cool thousand is a pleasant sum," said Legg.

"Right; but where's our hold on the gentleman? Once number seven dead—he may repudiate.'

"Good! Your remark is wisdom itself, especially as we know our customer. Toucher, I think I must send your poor patient a leetle—just a leetle—of this fine old port," said Legg, with a peculiarly funny expression of countenance.

Toucher laughed.

At this instant the bell of the establishment rang loudly; the great door creaked on its hinges, and a carriage rolled into the yard.

The two owners of the establishment peered out from the blinds. They were as yet undecided as to who was wanted.

First they saw the two keepers descend from the carriage, then the irascible colonel, and finally the black valet.

This fully decided the matter. Mr. Legg knew that he was wanted in the receiving-room.

In another moment he was face to face with the new patient and his attendants.

The keepers respectfully handed in the document which consigned a fellow creature to that abomination of desolation, a private madhouse.

"Good—very good; happy to see you, sir," bowing low to Colonel Sparkes Bing.

"Are you—can't say as much—sorry?" said the Colonel, showing his teeth.

"Mischievous?" cried Legg, stepping back.

"Lor' bless you, sir, no," put in the keeper, in his most mysteriously cavernous tones; "quite harmless—honly hodd. Do you see, his friends want him treated in tip-top style—a nice room, perfect liberty—pay handsome; but mind you, doctor, they—the friends, you know

— come down once a month; if he complains, away he goes."

" Sir, he shall have every attention, medical and otherwise. Mrs. Legg will treat him like her own brother. This establishment is well known."

"Humph! Shew me my room. You black-guards, send up my luggage," roared the colonel, whose eyes rolled with concentrated fury.

"There is one little preliminary proceeding," began Legg.

"Sir," said the keeper, "here's a fifty on account. Sir Richard Bing will call in a day or two, and arrange particulars. The colonel has money; he is allowed wine, but no spirits. His valet will wait on him—knows him well—must sleep in his room—fits, you know."

Legg made a wry face, but looked at the fifty pound note, and led the way to a really comfortable bedroom, where some little time later he was duly ensconced with tea before him, and his own servant in waiting.

But the windows were barred, and the door was locked.

About ten, all was still in the house, and the black servant slept on a sofa, as sound as those children of the sun usually do.

Colonel Sparkes Bing rose, and approached the window, which he opened. The night was balmy, and the air came in refreshingly upon his evidently heated brow.

Not a light was visible in any part of the establishment.

Then

"a shade-like silence grows, stealing
Onwards impalpable as dreams or light;"

and a flood of music came rushing on the night wind. It was a sweet female voice singing to the accompaniment of the harpsichord.

No organ could have been equally thrilling or penetrating; at times rose tones of silvery sweetness, of which no musical instrument could give the remotest idea. From the depths of darkness these superhuman sounds poured forth with such intensity, that they thrilled through every nerve, creating that depression and languor which open irresistibly the floodgates of the human heart. The tones at length resembled a lament of the condemned about to be for ever cast forth—hopeless, yet calm.

Great God! the music ceases, and is succeeded by the most piercing shrieks and yells, cries of agony and pain, and appeals for mercy which appear not to be heard.

The colonel started back as if shot, and flew to the door; it was, of course, fastened, and resisted all his efforts.

With a scared and pallid countenance, the colonel closed the window, and lay down upon his bed.

Next morning he saw Dr. Legg, but made no remark as to the events of the night. He expressed himself satisfied as to the arrangements, and breakfasted with appetite.

He then savagely ordered his black man to follow him into the garden, which was extensive, even though the patients of the urbane doctor were restricted to half of it.

At the end of the pleasure grounds was a

hedge, and under shelter of this Colonel Sparkes Bing sheltered himself against the heat, which was very great.

He had been so curt and snappish to all the patients at breakfast-time, that they gave him a wide berth, and allowed him a seat under a sycamore to himself.

Meanwhile Doctor Toucher, followed by one of the more brutal assistants, had started on his morning visit to his patients—a visit more dreaded by those unhappy wretches than the last dawn to the prisoner lying under sentence of death.

We shall not harrow the minds of our young and virgin-hearted readers by any detail of the horrors of that prison-house. We have, to a certain degree, remedied all this; let, then, the hideous atrocities of the past be buried in oblivion.

We must, however, briefly allude to the doctor's visit to number seven.

The keeper stood outside, with a basket of provisions in his hand, ready to lend assistance should it be required.

The doctor unlocked the door of the cell number seven, and went alone.

It was a small, white-washed room, looking out upon a narrow yard, bounded by a high wall.

It had no furniture save a truckle-bed and a wooden chair.

On the bed sat an old man—a very old man, to all appearance—whose wan look, eyes moving rapidly about, and long grey locks, conveyed the idea of not only incipient madness, but extreme debility.

He was the victim of a crime.

The doctor entered, and the old man never moved.

"Well, number seven," he began, and hesitated.

No answer.

"Number seven, I say," cried Dr. Toucher, raising his lash; "answer me."

"I am the Duke of X——, and should be tried by my peers; you dare not strike me."

"Ha, ha, ha! how funny—still that old idea in your head. But never mind; it does no harm, if it does no good. Here is some port wine—be a good fellow, and take it; it will give you strength."

"What for? To live under the sway of a ruffian like you, inhuman monster. I will not drink. Take it away—it is poison."

The doctor raised the lash.

"Stop," said the old man, mildly, "and listen to me for once. You know that I am rich; I will write you a cheque for a hundred thousand pounds if you will let me go; and, on the honour and word of a gentleman and a peer of England, I will never even remember the past."

The doctor shook his head with a cunning smile.

"Beware," cried the old man, in a more excited tone, "beware lest vengeance come swift and mighty. Heaven is just, and will not let me die ere *mine*, ere *her*, ere *his* wrongs are redressed. Beware lest, by perseverance in this fearful crime, you go headlong to everlasting perdition."

"Silence!" roared the doctor, in a savage and irritated tone; and again he raised his whip.

"Said I not so?" replied the old man, raising his hands aloft in the attitude of a prophet about to curse or bless; "said I not so—vengeance is mine, said the Lord —"

At the same moment the doctor was felled to the ground like an ox, from a blow with the butt-end of a pistol, and immediately gagged and secured.

Colonel Sparkes Bings then leaped forward to catch the old man in his arms. But he had fainted.

"The wine!" said the colonel in a low but determined tone.

The black valet came in dragging the body of the keeper after him.

The colonel snatched the wine from the basket, and poured some down the patient's throat; while it was still gurgling, the black, after fastening the door of the cell, began to work at the iron bars of the windows.

The old man came slowly to; he wept bitterly, and embraced the eccentric colonel mechanically.

He did not know him.

"Speak, my beloved father," whispered the colonel, taking off his disguise of whiskers and wig, and appearing in his genuine capacity of Captain George.

The old man stared, and clung to him still more closely.

But he evidently could not speak.

The surprise had evidently for a time brought on a stroke of paralysis.

Captain George left him with a groan, and proceeded to assist the other at the window.

Black Jack was the most noted house-breaker in England, and the job was soon done.

Then Captain George peered out of window, and gave the cry of the cuckoo.

In a few minutes it was answered.

Captain George then whistled, and in a few minutes two heads peered over the opposite wall. They looked remarkably like our friends Biggs and Waters.

They eyed the situation for a moment in grim silence, and then with the utmost rapidity drew up a ladder, and with extreme dexterity passed it across to the opposite window.

Captain George, boldly, fearlessly, and without a moment's hesitation, took up the old man, and made for the opposite wall, walking up the ladder without touching it, except with his feet.

The slightest false step would have been fatal. But Black Jack walked close behind.

At this moment a volley of execrations and voices, imploring pity, were heard.

"Take us with you," they said piteously.

The fugitives hurried with all their might, and in a few moments were outside. A carriage with four horses stood under the waving branches of a cluster of trees.

A shot at this moment was fired in their direction. Knowing the necessity of quick action, they made for the carriage, and in another moment were carried away as on the wings of the wind.

The alarm bell of the asylum, in the mean time, rang furiously.

"Quick! quick! for your lives!" shouted the highwayman with compressed lips.

That night they slept in safety, at a distance apparently beyond all fear of pursuit. Captain George, in a state of great anxiety, sent for the first medical men in the town. They examined the patient with attention, and at once declared that he had had an attack of paralysis, from which only care, and attention, and time could relieve him.

Captain George wildly struck his head.

He was as far off his purpose as ever.

Still nothing was to be done for the moment. He therefore determined to send for Lucy Lipscombe, if her retreat was discovered, to nurse the old man.

He, moreover, took an old farm-house in a most retired and secluded situation, where he established himself with his man Black Jack, the sham keepers, two well-known highwaymen, having returned to the road.

By splendid promises of a peculiar kind, the ex-housebreaker agreed to devote himself exclusively to the service of the quondam highwayman.

It remained to communicate with Lucy.

For this purpose Captain George resolved once more to brave the perils and dangers of the great metropolis. His power of disguise and of face was, however, so great, that he incurred less danger than most men.

He left the farm-house in the charge of Black Jack, a hired nurse, two labourers, and a servant maid, with orders to hold out, at all hazards, until his return.

CHAPTER XLI.

THE RESCUE.

AGAIN the light streamed in upon the room, again the carol of birds was heard, and the two sufferers, awakening from a restless slumber, saw near the door a loaf of black bread and a pitcher of water.

Ravenously, almost savagely, they rushed at it, and, dividing the food, Pauline took the first drink of water.

Both thought it the most delightful meal they had ever made, for they were indeed hungry.

They now held a conference, but it ended in nothing—for what could these two young people do?

They were going mad, that was quite clear.

About mid-day they heard a dog barking with extreme violence, then a volley of curses and execrations, and then the noise ceased.

The dog appeared silenced.

Then came a heavy blow at their own window, as if with a huge axe.

"William!" shouted a voice from without, "are you alive, my hearty?"

"Yes," replied the young man, with deep and heartfelt exultation.

"Hurra!" said the voice; and two terrible blows were struck at the window-shutter, which was shivered to atoms, the wooden bars crashing at the same time, and admitting a flood of light.

"Bene chuck!" said a thick voice, as somebody leaped into the room.

It was Joe the mudlark.

"Hook it, my gentry coves," he said, in a hurried tone, "the beaks are after us."

Neither replied ; but the way being now quite clear, both William and Pauline, overwhelmed with emotion and filled with buoyant dreams of hope, passed into the open air.

They were welcomed by the worthy skipper, who stared at Pauline.

"What caper's this ?" he said ; "but no time for talking. Follow me."

And he struck across the fields in an opposite direction to Boulogne. The smugglers' knowledge of the country now served them in good stead, for in about an hour they reached a roadside inn where the skipper was known, and where they agreed to halt until their future proceedings were decided on.

William then found that Joe the mudlark had left the lugger secretly, with the intention of deserting, when he happened to be a witness to the capture of his companion. He saw two men carry him into a cart tied hands and feet, and a feeling of compassion came over him.

William had been very kind to him, and the heart of the poor boy was not all bad.

He determined to fathom the mystery, and, to commence, followed the cart. It was no easy task, but Joe was trained to hard work.

Along the highway, across downs, up narrow lanes he took his way, never losing sight of the canvas roof which covered the prisoner. At length he reached the farm-house.

He concealed himself in some bushes, and watched.

A soldier, mounted on a horse, left in a great hurry, and returned in two hours with a woman in the dress of a fisherman.

Two hours later two men left in the cart, and Joe the mudlark followed them.

He had now been absent nearly twenty-four hours from the lugger, and might expect a warm reception. As he walked up to the gangway he saw the skipper and mate in conversation.

He went boldly on board, and touched his apology for a cap.

"You skulking young hound !" said the mate, raising his fist.

"Where's William ?" cried the captain, restraining him.

"Took to quod," replied Joe, "and I'ze been watching for him."

He then told his story. The skipper at once believed him, and the two set out armed, and provided with axes for the place. They reached it about an hour before their successful rescue. They watched until the coast was clear, and then burst open the gate. A huge dog flew at them. With one blow of his heavy axe the sailor killed him.

William Lennox now related to the skipper as much of his own story as was necessary to the understanding of the fatal error.

"Whew !" cried the other, "a pretty kettle of fish, to be sure. Why, they'll make Boulogne too hot to hold us. A spy—they'd hang the lot ! But don't be downhearted, my chickens; we'll double 'em yet. Never say die is my motter, and curse a Frenchman."

Still for some time no plan could be thought of, until Pauline was called into their councils.

"My good friends," she said, "I can see but one means of escape. William must dress as a market girl, and go in to-morrow at daylight with butter. I will answer for it the dress of Cecile will fit him."

The skipper laughed, and said he was quite sure the daughter of the house would lend her traps.

"I could wear his clothes," added Pauline, blushing and smiling, "and with a little paint, and some soot, could look a roughish chap."

This was said, despite her troubles, with so much archness and humour that even William Lennox laughed.

Joe the mudlark listened with profound astonishment. This new lingo was, to him, something astonishing.

Cecile, the daughter of the innkeeper, was summoned and the question put as to their being able to provide William with a female dress. She laughed heartily, and acquiesced. It was then agreed that, at day break next morning, the whole thing should be done, and the wearied and exhausted fugitives then proceeded to take refreshment and rest.

It was scarcely light when William Lennox was summoned to robe himself, for the purpose of passing the fortifications of Boulogne. The thing was rather a delicate operation, and it was absolutely necessary that our hero should have an assistant.

There was no difficulty about the matter, except such as arose from the modesty of William Lennox. But when he found that both Cecile and Pauline treated the matter as a good joke, he at once yielded, though with a tolerably bad grace.

Such a scene of laughing and joking followed as would have kept an audience in a theatre in a state of constant uproar. Of course William was even more awkward than he would have been had he had to dress himself.

At length, however, the delicate affair being arranged, William retired. while Pauline proceeded to array herself — not, as had been settled before, in the garb of a cabin boy, but in that of a sort of agricultural labourer in charge of a cart of butter.

The skipper and Joe the mudlark went forward and took a public wagon. Their being English might militate against the success of the scheme.

About six the cart was brought out, with its rude leather and rope harness, its gay horse collar and tinkling bells. A cargo of butter, vegetables, fruit and eggs was placed in it, and the freight started. Pauline, in her capacity of boy, drove ; while Cecile and William, transformed into a fine-looking peasant girl, sat on a seat behind him. Despite the dangerous character of the adventure they were about to attempt, the whole party appeared disposed for laughter, and a great deal of merry conversation was kept up. Pauline, certainly, was hysterically merry.

William—who felt a kind of protection in his innocence—was full of spirits, to which the frank, open, and light-hearted humour of the girl, whose clothes he wore, not a little tended.

In this way they arrived in sight of Boulogne-sur-Mer.

The regular road passed through one of the gates of the upper town.

To have evaded it would have been to have aroused suspicion.

They drove up, talking even more merrily and loudly than they had at any time during the journey.

Pauline was an admirable make-up, and not a trace of her hair could be seen beneath her *bonnet de nuit.*

A group of soldiers stood idling at the fortified gate. They all ceased speaking as the cart came up. They appeared inclined for a gossip.

"*Bon jour!*" said one of the foremost; "what have you to sell, my pretty ones?"

Cecile, who was nearest to him, turned up her pretty nose.

"Nothing for *piou-piou's*," she said scornfully.

The soldiers laughed. They had experienced her disregard for blue coats and red continuations before.

"Who is the other donzelle—is she as pert?' said a *sous officier.*

"My cousin Fanchette is devoted to the naval service. She has the tooth-ache, and is going to M. Bosco's to have it out—so no more at present. Drive on, Germain."

And the boy whipped the horse amidst considerable laughter. No one, however, placed any hindrance upon their progress.

They were now in the town, making their way through its narrow streets. A few minutes brought them to the other gate, which they had to pass ere they entered the lower or unfortified town.

At the gate stood Tourloorou, in conversation with another sergeant. He was very irritated, and spoke with vehemence.

The cart passed without any hindrance being offered.

"*Mon Dieu!*" suddenly whispered Pauline, "he is following us."

"Drive faster!" replied Cecile in an earnest tone.

Pauline obeyed, and the cart-horse trotted down the steep street.

Tourloorou did not quicken his pace, but slowly followed in their track.

"We must to the market-place, and keep up the deception," said Cecile.

"He knew us," remarked Pauline, in a hoarse tone; "there is instinct in hate."

"We had better leave the cart, take our bundle, and go on board," said William.

"No," observed Cecile, whose heart had been so taken by the handsome youth she had helped to dress, that she felt no inclination to part with him. "I know where to go. We can hide there until night, and then you can go on board the lugger."

There was something so caressing and affectionate in the manner of Cecile that William blushed, and cast down his eyes. The pretty peasant girl took his hand and kissed it.

Pauline tapped her on the knuckles with the whip. She then received the necessary directions, and drove rapidly down a narrow winding street, until she reached an inn—the renowned *Ecu Blanc.*

Into the courtyard of this they drove. It was filled by horses and carts. Cecile leaped down, and put a bag on the horse's head, and tied it to a ring.

She then pointed to a ladder, and bade William go up first. In a few minutes they were all in a loft nearly full of hay and straw, where they might secret themselves without much fear of detection.

They climbed on to the top near the roof, and lay in such a position that, through a loop-hole under the eaves, they could look down into the yard.

Cecile was next to William. Pauline kept apart, wrapped in reflection.

"Why go away at all?" said pretty little Cecile, half amused, half in earnest, in her desire to make love to the boy in girl's clothes. "We could make you very happy at home."

"I dare say I should be very happy," replied William, returning the tender pressure of her hand; "but you forget I am *un Anglais*, and accused of being a spy."

Cecile was silent. There were tears in her eyes.

"You are not in love with Pauline?" she at last whispered in his ear.

"No," replied William, energetically, but in a low tone. "I am afraid, however, I had better go soon, or I should lose my heart to the pretty girl of St. Preese."

Cecile sighed.

"I shall never forget you," she said, with deep emotion. "I am sorry I ever saw you."

And she cried. What could William do? Vision of Lily, hadst thou seen him, you must have pardoned him. He kissed, or tried to kiss away her tears, and still they flowed.

"Hark!" said Pauline, suddenly.

They started from their day-dream, and looked down into the court. There was Tourloorou and the ostler.

"I didn't see anybody," the waiter said, evidently in answer to a question.

"Then, keep watch, while I go round to the market," replied Tourloorou. "There will be a handsome reward, if you catch the English spy."

CHAPTER XLII.

THE TRAP.

LUCY LIPSCOMBE returned to her shop, we have already said, but with no zest or pleasure. One thought filled her soul, that of Captain George, whose fate was so uncertain. She no longer felt any interest in the business, which had fallen off under the management of Martha Snelling. She, however, attended to it as much as possible, the future being uncertain. Stone kept his word to the Captain, and abstained wholly almost from drink, to the great astonishment of his old comrades.

Lord Charles Luterel did not continue his persecution. He had received a warning from a quarter that overwhelmed him with rage and mortification.

But it was not possible for a man like him to give over all hope. The very difficulty of the matter only inflamed him the more.

But Lucy had in Stone a guardian whose fidelity, vigilance, and patience was indomitable. He kept a strict watch on the young nobleman, as far as his duties would allow.

Months passed, and no tidings of Captain George. Poor Lucy began to fear that something was wrong. A dread came over her soul that he had perhaps deceived her; and yet his words had been very solemn. Of his love she had no fear.

It was a fine bright autumn afternoon, and Lucy, who, in addition to Stone, had taken a smart young lady into her employ, came out of her back room just after dinner. She was dressed for a walk, which Stone had persuaded her to take. He always on such occasions accompanied her at a respectful distance. At this moment a footman entered and delivered a letter.

"Mrs. Lucy Lipscombe," said the domestic civilly.

"That is my name," replied the mistress of the house.

The servant without further words handed her a letter.

It was to this effect:—

"*The Countess of Merton is staying at B— hotel, and, being an invalid, would esteem it a favour if Mrs. Lipscombe would call upon her with some choice scents, gloves, and articles of toilette generally."*

Lucy Lipscombe, rather glad of an object in her walk, replied that she would attend the Countess at once. The domestic bowed and was about to retire.

"But perhaps you may want to carry something," he said, turning round.

"You will oblige me," replied Lucy, who at once made up the parcel and gave it him. She then went out, and the liveried servant followed close behind.

At some little distance Stone, who had been lingering about, also followed.

In this way they reached the then fashionable neighbourhood of Soho, and the domestic knocked at a house of highly respectable appearance. The door opened, and Lucy entered, followed by the servant.

At this moment a hackney carriage stopped, and a tall, powerful woman leaped out, and came rushing up to Stone, who, not knowing her, would have advanced on his way.

"Where is Lucy?" said a well known and commanding voice.

"Gracious heaven! is it you, sir?" cried Stone.

"Hush! shake hands like old friends," continued Captain George, who, on his arrival in town, had changed himself into a female, for one day only.

"How are you, my worthy sir?" he continued, in a low shrill voice. "Where's Lucy?"

Stone pointed to the respectable house whose portals had just closed upon her.

"Merciful heavens!" cried the highwayman, turning pale despite his rouge; "that is the most villanous den in London. Here, coachee! take this guinea, and wait at the corner of the street."

And glancing round, he saw, to his great delight, that the street was free.

He gave a resounding knock at the door of "the respectable" mansion. It opened quickly. The livery servant was alone in the hall. He stared at the shabby genteel man, and apparently coarse low woman.

"What is your business, my good people?" he said, preparing to shut the door.

The disguised highwayman brushed past him, and himself shut the door. He then drew forth a pistol.

"Now, you scoundrel, show me at once, without an instant's delay, where the lady is who just came in."

"I dursn't, sir," replied the other, shaking like a leaf.

"If you don't move at once I'll blow your brains out," said George, sternly.

The man looked in his eye, and quailed. He turned, and Captain George saw him raise his hand towards a bell. He understood his intention, and caught his wrist.

"Beware! another such an attempt, and I will keep my word. Go up."

Stone held his arm, while Captain George clutched the pistol.

The servant stopped on the first landing, and pointed to a door.

"Come in, and show us the way," continued the captain, sternly.

The man, in a state of terror and alarm impossible to describe, opened the door.

Meanwhile, Lucy Lipscombe, without the slightest suspicion of evil, had entered the apartment, which was sumptuously, if meretriciously, furnished. Here she was received by a decent looking woman.

"My lady is in the next room," she said, pointing to an open door.

Lucy Lipscombe walked in, and found herself in a splendid bedroom.

The door closed behind her, and from the bed started Lord Charles Lutterel. Lucy dropped her parcel, and, overcome by faintness, fell back against the door.

"At last, my charmer," said the nobleman, leading her to a seat, which, so helpless was she, she allowed him to do.

"Beware, sir!" she faintly replied. "This outrage will be punished."

"My dear girl," said the nobleman, flippantly, "you have come of your own accord to a house of assignation."

"To see a countess. I have her letter," cried the wretched young woman.

"Where?" continued Lord Lutterell.

Lucy opened the piece of paper in her hand. The characters had all vanished; they were written in an ink which faded in an hour after being written.

Lucy stared around her wildly.

"You have come here of your own accord," said Lutterel; "and I swear that here you pass twenty-four hours. I shall prove this; and who, after that, will believe in the virtue of Lucy Lipscombe?"

A terrific crash, and in came the door; while a man and a woman rushed forward. The latter struck the nobleman senseless, while the former raised the fainting form of Lucy in his arms. Without a word of parley, or an observation of any kind, they crossed the drawing-room, and went down into the hall. A number of people stopped the way, the "respectable" landlady, three men, and one or two women.

'Make way," said Captain George, in a terrible tone, as he levelled his brace of pistols.

The motley crew stood aghast, and then rushed wildly down the staircase leading to the kitchen, women and men rolling over one another in their hurry to escape.

Ludicrous as the scene was, neither were disposed to take notice of it, but hurried out to where they had left the hackney coach.

"Drive to the Bull at Kensington," said Captain George, who, on entering the coach, took the half-insensible Lucy in his arms.

Stone very quietly closed the door, and mounted on the box.

The delight of Lucy may be imagined, when, on her recovery, she found herself in the arms of her faithful and devoted George, whom she recognised, despite his disguise. After the first transports of joy had abated, an explanation ensued, and Lucy Lipscombe at once agreed to sell her business and accept the charge of the invalid whose escape from the lunatic asylum had had so fatal an effect upon her system.

Captain George even pressed her to become his wife at once, but this she resolutely declined until the ban was taken off his good name, and he was once more admitted to his true position in society.

Captain George sighed, but made no reply. He knew she was right.

CHAPTER XLIII.

THE ESCAPE.

It was midnight ere the fugitives in the hay-loft dared to move, and then Cecile, after considerable deliberation, proposed to baulk the zealous watchfulness of Simon Roger, by escaping in a different way from what had originally been contemplated. The loft was open at the back on to a narrow lane rather than a street, and had a kind of window with a pulley and cord, which served to draw up the loads from the carts below.

Cecile's idea was, that William Lennox should lower them in this way, and then himself make fast the rope and slide down. After some talk on the subject the plan was agreed on.

It required coolness and courage; for, though the height from the ground was not very great, the slightest accident might prove fatal. It was determined that Pauline should descend first, but she expressed her total inability to hold on by her hands. William Lennox, however, soon obviated this by means of a piece of wood, of which he made a seat like that of a swing; and Pauline, no longer hesitating, was slowly lowered to the ground below.

Cecile followed, though the young man had as much as he could do to prevent her from moving quicker than was pleasant. He succeeded, however, and then making the rope fast, committed himself to it and launched out.

"Stop, or I fire," said a fierce voice above—that of Simon Roger.

The noise of the pulley had betrayed them to their watchful enemy.

William Lennox slid down into the darkness, and without a word in answer to the other's threat, took to his heels, guided by the girls, who knew the way well. None spoke, nor did they halt, until a considerable distance from the inn, when, slackening their speed, they found that for the moment they were not followed. It was impossible, however, to venture on the port, the Spanking Sally being well known, and doubtless carefully guarded.

Cecile suggested that they might find shelter in a small village on the heights called Outreau, and thence communicate with the skipper, and endeavour to arrange their flight satisfactorily.

William Lennox and Pauline allowed themselves to be guided in all things by Cecile, and without giving cause for suspicion by any particular haste, walked rapidly along towards their new destination.

Pauline began to be very low spirited. The terrible events which she had passed through, the fearful escape from death, which she could yet scarcely believe in, made her look back with something like a feeling of regret to the days when she was innocent. And s'e asked herself if, as the wife of an honest man like Simon Roger, she might not have been happier than as the apocryphal lady of the youth who had, to all appearance, deserted her.

William Lennox and Cecile were more elated, and lightened the way by cheerful talk.

At length they reached Outreau, and found that not a house of entertainment was open at that early hour.

They soon, however, found a shed, and there took shelter until daylight.

Cecile then led them to a small inn which they entered boldly, and asked for bread and cheese. All were hungry, and this was a sentiment which none of them could contend against. The cabaret being kept by a widow, and the girls objecting to sit in a public room, which would soon be filled by soldiers, they were accommodated with what is called a *cabinet*, where, having breakfasted, William Lennox procured writing materials.

Without putting name or address he informed the smuggler that he would not attempt to join the lugger until the night of his departure, which was to be indicated by the loosening of the jib at twelve o'clock precisely in the day.

They then determined to depart, and were about to rise for that purpose, when the public room suddenly filled with soldiers, who swarmed at that time all round Boulogne, members of that great army which was to conquer or revolutionize England.

The whole party shrunk back, and pushing a bolt, remained still in deep silence.

The soldiers called for brandy, gin, and other liquors, and then seated themselves as if for a regular jollification. They talked very loud and all at once, so that their discourse could not be very clearly heard. Still the words "*Espion Anglais*" once or twice caught their attention.

Still they spoke not.

Presently a strange noise attracted their notice, and a kind of sliding panel, which served as a communication between the cabinet and the kitchen, gave way. The landlady, alarmed and angry, stood before them.

At a sign from her they passed through the kitchen into her bedroom.

"So!" she said, angrily, "this is the way you impose upon an honest woman? *Tu Dieu!* afraid of the soldiers — eh? Of course you are! Which is the English spy?"

"Madam," replied Pauline gently, "if you will listen to my story you will change your views. I am Pauline Placquet—"

"What?" cried the woman, gazing with no great favour at the girl in boy's clothes; "ain't you ashamed of yourself to be going about this way—you, the daughter of an honest man?"

"Listen, *ma bonne mere!*" said Pauline with that look of injured innocence which she so well knew how to assume. "I will tell you all, and then if you can blame us betray us."

"My daughter is in the bar, so speak," said the widow, glancing curiously at the two girls, one of whom she knew must be the English spy in disguise.

Pauline then, with an elegance, poetry, and power of moving the heart which showed the native talents she possessed, told her story in a whisper to the woman, and in less than half an hour had her weeping and pitying her.

"The *gredin!*" she said, alluding to Philip Carabosse. "And this poor youth was to pay for his wickedness. Don't be alarmed, I have children of my own, and will not betray you. But here you must remain, quiet as lambs."

"I must post this letter to my captain," said William Lennox, shaking the *cabaretiere* warmly by the hand; "how is it to be done?"

"*Pardi!*" laughed the hostess, "any one can feel that is the shake of a man. I will send it by my son."

"But not to the lugger. It must be posted," replied William.

It was then settled that they should remain there until some plan was matured for their escape. William Lennox informed their hostess that he could afford to pay for their accommodation, and would be glad of some dinner as soon as convenient.

The good-natured woman laughed heartily, and went out to follow their behests.

"Will she be true?" said William Lennox.

"I don't know,' said Pauline, shaking her head.

"As steel," cried Cecile. "There was something motherly and true in her eye when she spoke of her children."

The subject was then changed to that of their chances of escape, but not one could as yet see how it was to be done.

In the evening the son of the landlady returned, with the news that a strict watch was being kept by the direct orders of the Emperor, who had expressed his settled determination to hang the English spy.

The landlady communicated this intelligence with a grave face to the startled trio. Even Cecile began to feel uncomfortable. Her part in the affair might be suspected, and punishment would be swift and terrible.

"*Mes enfans*," said the landlady gravely, "you must leave here to-night. You must make the best of your way to Portel, a small fishing village, where your lugger can take you off at any time. I have a cousin, a good sort of woman enough, who will shelter you, if you pay; there you must lie until your skipper chooses to come for you."

"But we don't know the way," said Pauline, embracing her.

"My son will show you," replied the woman, rubbing her eyes.

So again that night they were wanderers and outcasts. Their way took them over a kind of barren down, with no visible path; but the lad appeared to possess all the keenness of an American Indian, and followed the trail in the most unerring manner.

At length they came to a small cluster of houses, all inhabited by fishermen, at the door of one of which the lad knocked, and they were admitted.

A bargain was soon struck, and next day a second letter was despatched to Captain Carter, who, glad to get out of the place under the circumstances, a few nights after took them off without further difficulty.

CHAPTER XLIV.

LILIAN.

AT the time of which we speak a genuine watering place was a very different thing from what it now is. There were no railroads in those days to carry you, as it were, on the wings of the wind, on errands of pleasure or business, and all distant seaports were either patronised by the local gentry or rich strangers.

Mrs. Winterton, in selecting a spot where to take Lilian, selected one where she was likely to meet neither. Her child was not only delicate and in want of nursing, but she had much to learn, and much to unlearn. Still so apt are some natures to acquire knowledge of all kind, that, ere a year passed, few would have been able to recognise in the tall, elegant girl, with classic features and noble brow, the wandering companion of William Lennox and Mrs. Joplins.

Her mother devoted her whole energies to her education, aided by an emigrant French lady of noble birth, whose accomplishments were of the highest order.

The atrocious attempt of the captain had not come off, he having found some difficulty in tracing the residence of the heiress, and then having found her impregnable.

The good genius of William Lennox, the Blue Dwarf, whose whole soul appeared centered in the lad, had met him face to face, and warned him against any violence.

Captain Frederick Winterton had retreated, and by dint of monstrous promises, obtained further time from his creditors.

He pleaded that time was necessary to the carrying out of his infamous plans.

The banker and Jew had both consented to give him a twelvemonth.

Meanwhile Lilian had become a most lovely creature. Her health appeared wholly re-established, and though there was a pensive tone about her, it only added to her beauty.

The small town near which they had hired a mansion, replete with every comfort and convenience, was above the town, and overlooked the sea. The town was much frequented by hardy fishermen and bold smugglers, who in those days did a roaring trade.

Lilian used often to walk into the town with her governess, being fond of seeing the bustle of the locality; but she never did so without the body guard of two stout serving men, ostensibly armed only with cudgels, but in reality well provided with fire-arms.

A huge Newfoundland dog, Bruno, stalks majestically in company.

The town was then small, and though now of considerable importance, was then chiefly composed of houses inhabited by fishermen, with several places for public refreshment. Several cottages, however, dotted the outskirts.

One of these was near a pathway, which served as a short cut towards the town, and Lilian, whose tastes were rather picturesque, was for a long time much struck by its prettiness. It had a small garden shaded by trees at one end, from behind which Lilian would often gaze at the inhabitants.

They were, it was said, two Jersey girls, one of them, though very young, a widow with a child a little more than a month old.

There was a little mound on which Lilian would often seat herself, protected from view by a bush, and gaze at the two sisters, as they were called.

Little did she suspect their connection with her fate. But she was not long to remain in ignorance.

It was a lovely morning when Lilian and Madame de Gaspe passed on their way to the town, and our heroine, pleading fatigue, sat down as usual to admire the neat cottage, the honeysuckle porch, and to watch for the young women to come into the garden.

"How very odd," said Madame de Gaspe, with a smile, "is female curiosity! What possible interest can you feel in these two fish girls?"

"I don't know," said Lilian, in her quiet, pensive way, "but I do feel great and even entrancing interest. Hush! here they come."

Lilian at the same moment gave a little faint cry, and caught Madame de Gaspe wildly by the arm.

Out came the young woman, mother to the child, leaning tenderly on the arm of William Lennox.

"And you will leave me?" said Pauline, looking up into his face with that unmistakeable glance which speaks of strong affection.

"I must," replied William, somewhat coldly. "I have brought you from your incensed parents; I have saved you from all those horrors at Boulogne; I have provided for you amply. An invisible guardian, whose name be ever blessed, has given you the means of living in comfort. What more can I do?"

"Love me—leave me not!" said the girl passionately.

"Pauline," replied William, coldly, "I have already told you—"

"Come away," said Lilian in a hushed whisper, "come away."

"But what is the matter, my child?" replied Madame de Gaspe, who saw that she was fainting. "Water!—water!"

William Lennox, who heard the hushed but painful cry, moved away from Pauline, and looked over the hedge. The blood flew from his heart. He recognised her at once, and understood her fainting. With an inward curse at the fate which had linked him ever so slightly with Pauline, he darted into the house, and came out with a stone bottle of water.

With one bound he was over the hedge, towards which the two girls followed him.

Lilian lay insensible, her head on Madame de Gaspe's knee.

He kneeled and bathed her forehead with his handkerchief.

"Lilian—my life, my soul—speak!" he cried in agonised tones.

Madame de Gaspe, without being astonished at any thing, had by this time found her smelling bottle.

Lilian slowly opened her eyes, but consciousness had not quite returned. She smiled on William, who seized her hand.

Lilian withheld hers, and leaped to her feet, horror and disgust depicted on her pallid countenance.

"Away—touch me not—pollute me not with your hand—I know you not, sir," she said with every evidence of the most unmitigated disgust and contempt.

"Lilian, in the name of Heaven, listen to me. I am unchanged, the same faithful—"

"Ah!" cried Lilian with flashing eyes, "do you dare to talk to me thus, who have seen you but now with one of your weak victims—"

"Oh, Lilian, if you would hear one word - if you would but let me tell you," he began.

"Begone," said the frenzied girl, stamping her little foot.

Alas, poor Lilian. She had set the whole history of her life, her every hope of happiness in the world, upon this one cast; save her tender mother, this was the one bright spot on the dark current of existence, and he had failed her. Could her eyes deceive her? That was impossible. And had she not heard his cold blooded desertion of this girl?

"No one is dismissed unheard," cried William boldly. "I am not—

"Hush, sir; do not insult my ears, but go. All is for ever at an end between us, so help me—"

"Blaspheme not," shrieked William in such a tone that Lilia paused.

"Now, then, young man, you just move on," said one of two burly fellows armed with stout cudgels, who had just come up, while a huge Newfoundland dog planted himself in front of his mistress.

"Lilian, one word."

But she had coldly turned away.

William rushed madly from the spot despite the cries and shrieks of Pauline.

"What does all this mean?" asked Madame de Gaspe in a tone of utter astonishment.

"That man was my affianced husband," said Lilian with a shiver.

"Pity you did not hear him," observed the governor, quietly. "I am certain there is some fatal error here. That youth was truth and ingenuousness itself."

Lilian turned round, her ghastly pallor turning to rosy tints.

"Is it possible?—can you think so?—but you heard all," gasped the poor girl.

"I did; and though I understood it not, rely upon it there is some blunder," continued Madame.

"Merciful Heaven," continued Lilian, "what shall I do?"

"I know not how to advise," said the other gravely. "Your mother, perhaps—"

"My mother must know nothing about it," said Lilian, wildly. "If I have wronged him, I must suffer alone."

Madame de Gaspe shook her head; but seeing the extreme agitation of the other, she made no remark, especially as the dog barked violently.

But, aware that the men were close behind, she hastily followed Lilian, who, in her desire to be home, had quickened her pace.

But nothing seemed to justify the barking of Bruno, except that presently two men, in rough pilot coats aud tarpaulin hats, crossed the pathway in the direction of Pauline's cottage.

Meanwhile, William Lennox, indignant, broken-hearted, hopeless, coals of fire appearing to consume his brain, his eyes scarcely seeing, was rushing madly over hill and dale. He knows not what he seeks, but still goes onward.

At last, a bunch of willows in the distance appears to guide him; and bounding like the thirsty horse which smells the water afar off, the mad and reckless youth stood upon a bank surmounting a deep and gloomy pond.

"This ends all!" he said; and forward he plunged.

But he never touched the water.

A low, dark figure, panting, breathless, rushed from a hedge, and caught him in his long and bony arms.

It was the Blue Dwarf.

"Let me go—I will die!"

"Hush, maniac," said the deformed man, sternly, "and insult not Heaven by your wickedness and folly."

"I have lost Lilian—why should I live?"

"To repent," said the Dwarf, drily.

William ceased struggling, and sat upon the bank.

"William," continued the Dwarf, gently, "I promised your father never to desert you. While you have been pursuing your own course abroad, instead of going to Lord ——, as I wished, I thought I should best please you by watching over Lilian, who has become as dear to me as yourself."

"But she is lost to me for ever."

"Silence! I have never deceived you. Explain to me all that I know not, and I vow to you, by all that is sacred, that if you are, as I believe, free from all blame, you shall hear your pardon from her own lips this very night."

William Lennox kissed the other's hairy hand, and burst into tears.

"I must not present myself at the house until dark night," continued the Dwarf, with a faint smile, "so tell me all."

William Lennox minutely explained all that had happened since he met James Tyrrel Blakesley in London, adding that on the arrival of the Spanking Sally at Y——, he had taken a cottage for Pauline and Cecile, and knowing how to procure funds through his, the Blue Dwarf's, kindness, had amply provided for them.

"Follow me," said the Blue Dwarf, bluntly; and striding away at a rapid pace, he soon brought William to a kind of hut which he had hired on the borders of a waste seldom visited except by sportsmen.

Opening the door of his one room, he displayed to the astonished eyes of William a well-furnished apartment, with books, writing-desk, and a comfortable couch.

The Dwarf, pointing to a bottle and some glasses, seated himself, and wrote, with his long strange-looking fingers, a brief letter.

He then disguised himself as much as possible with a loose cloak and slouched hat, and started away in the direction of Mrs. Winterton's mansion.

CHAPTER XLV.

LOST AGAIN.

MEANWHILE Lilian, despair and doubt filling her heart, had returned home, with much more certainty of his guilt than his innocence. Pretending fatigue, she had retired to her bed-room, and told her maid to call her by no means until tea-time, as she had a severe headache.

Mrs. Winterton had respected her injunctions, which were law to her, and commanded that her orders should in every way be obeyed.

Madame de Gaspe was on thorns. She knew she was doing wrong in concealing anything from an anxious mother, but she was, at the same time, afraid of the nervous irritability of her pupil.

Her day, then, was peculiarly miserable.

Towards evening, she crept up to Lilian's room to beg that she might be relieved from her promise. But Lilian had closed the door, and would not answer her knock.

"You seem uncomfortable," said Mrs. Winterton kindly, as she returned.

"Very hurt and very uncomfortable," replied Madame de Gaspe warmly. "That dear child made me promise to conceal something from you."

"Heavens!—any bad news? Is she ill?" cried Mrs. Winterton.

"No," stammered Madame.

At this moment a servant entered with a letter on a salver.

Mrs. Winterton took it mechanically, and opened it. Her eyes flashed as she did so.

"Madame de Gaspe," she said gently, "you are absolved by me from your promise. The young gentleman is below, and wishes to explain the quarrel."

"Heavens mercy be thanked," cried Madame de Gaspe.

"Explain, or I shall die," said Mrs. Winterton.

Madame de Gaspe, thus adjured, told all she had heard. Mrs. Winterton at once rang the bell, and directed the servant to show the gentleman up.

Next instant the Blue Dwarf and William Lennox were ushered in.

The servant went out.

The Blue Dwarf bowed low.

"Madame," he said, in his soft and silvery tones, "I warned you that I am a hideous monster, but as I hope that Heaven may give me in the next world that happiness denied me in this, I never told a falsehood; and I solemnly vow that your daughter is under an erroneous impression."

"I am not afraid to see you, sir," replied Mrs. Winterton, "my daughter has told me too much of your kindness to her."

The Blue Dwarf threw aside his cloak and hat, and seated himself. Madame de Gaspe with difficulty repressed a shriek.

"In the name of Heaven, madam," said William, humbly, "ere my friend speaks, tell me how she is; fetch her, let her hear all."

"She is lying down with a headache," replied Mrs. Winterton, a little uneasily, "and I would prefer hearing all you have to say before I fetch my poor child."

William Lennox bowed his head to hide her tears.

Oh! mother—fatal error was this—thy motherly precaution; perhaps pride.

Then the Blue Dwarf, briefly, succinctly, told all, and the narrative took hours.

But at every step Goldy Gordon, or Sapathwa, handed his papers.

He even told her his own extraordinary and incredible history, and she believed him.

"My dear son," she said at last, rising with tears in her eyes, "Lilian shall be yours. She shall ask your pardon ere five minutes are over."

William kissed her hand, and fell back on a couch with excess of emotion.

Mrs. Winterton glided from the room.

Three minutes had not elapsed ere she came back with a wild and passionate cry.

"Gone! gone!" she said, with clasped hand.

William leaped to his feet.

"Silence!" cried the Blue Dwarf, with that stupendous will and quickness of decision which always characterised him.

He then rang a terrific peal on the bell, never ceasing until every servant was in the room; in the meanwhile he had resumed his hat and cloak.

"Miss Lilian is missing," he roared, "and somebody must be privy to it. Speak at once whoever knows anything, or, by the heavens above, the person who conceals the fact shall expiate his folly in Bridewell."

A young girl, Lilian's own maid, stepped forward, fell upon her knees, and burst into tears.

"Speak, woman!"

After some little sobbing, the girl explained that, about two hours before, a young French girl had come with a letter, which she said dearly concerned Miss Lilian, and would quite remove any ailment she might suffer from.

Thinking no harm, she had taken up the letter, which Lilian read greedily, and at once taking her hat and cloak, and charging the maid to say not a word, had hurried down and joined the French girl, with whom she had departed from the house.

"Follow!" said William Lennox, and bounding across the room, through the door, and down the stairs, he was in a moment out of sight.

The Blue Dwarf, Mrs. Winterton, and Madame de Gaspe, the two latter scarcely waiting to put on the cloaks offered them by the domestics, rushed from the house in the track of the young man, the armed domestic alone escorting them.

The distance from the mansion to the cottage was very short, and when they reached it, to their horror and astonishment, they found William chafing the inanimate body of Cecile, whose arms were bound, and whose mouth was gagged.

Aided by the Blue Dwarf, she was soon unbound and brought to.

Her terrible story was as follows:—

Immediately after the quarrel between Lilian and William Lennox, two gentlemen—at all events, men of genteel manners, in pilot coats and tarpaulin coats—had hurried in and demanded speech with Pauline. This the latter readily granted, sending her Cecile into the kitchen with the child. After about half an hour, the child being asleep in its cot, Cecile had been summoned, and Pauline, with every mark of contrition and sorrow, informed her that she had been the unwilling cause of a quarrel between a neat young lady, the affianced bride of William, which these gentlemen friends of his overhearing, had declared could never be healed unless she, Pauline, at once sent for the young lady, and explained the truth.

"I have written the letter, dear Cecile," said Pauline, "will you take it?"

Too glad to serve William, whom she loved with a sincere but hopeless passion, Cecile acquiesced, and Pauline came at once.

No sooner did she enter the house than both herself and Lilian were overpowered and gagged—the latter being forced into a carriage, to which Pauline followed, leaving her Cecile to her fate.

This had taken place about two hours before.

"It is your wicked cousins, rely on it," said the Blue Dwarf; "but, William, what a base cocatrice have you nursed in your bosom."

A faint cry came from the kitchen.

Cecile rushed there, and found that Pauline had abandoned her child.

Mrs. Winterton was distracted, Madame de Gaspe bewildered, William Lennox mad.

The Blue Dwarf alone kept his self-possession.

"You must placard the county," he said to the two burly domestics. "I will to London; you, William, must with me. There can a girl be most easily concealed."

"Madame," cried William.

"No; they are too wise for that. It would be too great a risk. Mrs. Winterton do you follow, and at the very foot of the throne detail your grievances. Rely upon it, Madame, Lilian shall be found."

"Bless you, what can I say?" gasped the poor maddened mother.

"Keep your promise to him," replied the Blue Dwarf, "and, on my honour as a man, I will find her or die."

With these words he hurried William Lennox away to an inn, where the magic power of gold not only procured them a carriage and four, but the intelligence that a post-chaise had started some time before with two gentlemen and two ladies. The description further tallied with the abductors and Lilian so exactly, that the Blue Dwarf wrote a few hasty lines to Mrs. Winterton to assure her he was on the right track, and then started on his way.

CHAPTER XLVI.

THE OLD FARM-HOUSE.

WHEN Captain George chose the spot where to conceal his father until such time as calmness and change should produce a radical cure, he selected one of those wild and unfrequented

parts of Cumberland, with not a house in sight but one of those towers formerly so frequent on the border.

The residence was an old farm-house, which, from its peculiar situation, was built to resist the attacks of an ordinary enemy, but the changes in roads and other circumstances had caused it to be abandoned. Captain George obtained it then as a shooting-box at a most remarkably cheap rate.

Being possessed of a mechanical turn of mind, he soon, with the assistance of his followers, made the place tenable, and a wagon-load of furniture placed every necessary at his command.

A medical man of known talent and great reputation rode out once a week to see the old man, whose emaciated appearance began slowly to disappear.

But the arrival of Lucy Lipscombe produced the greatest change; the silvery tones of her voice appeared to go to his heart with a wild sensation of pleasure.

He shrunk from Captain George, who, with a deep sigh, would sally forth with his dog and gun in search of such game as the neighbourhood afforded.

Sometimes he would prolong his journey until evening, and then enjoy the delights, known only to a reflective mind, of the stillness and poetry of night.

In his rambles he often wandered within reach of the tower already spoken of, and would sit down on a fallen tree to admire the various effects of light and shade which it exhibited. The tower was in excellent preservation, with a deep and wide moat, which showed that the bottom of the tower, below the level of the ground had been once used for some purpose, there being several barred windows of narrow dimensions a few feet from the soil.

The gate at the extremity of the bridge was strong, and plated outside with iron.

Captain George lost himself in conjectures as to the uses to which this tower could be put, and why it was in such a state of preservation.

He was soon to find out.

For a time Captain George, secure of impunity in that secluded spot, had gone out with his gun and dog, without the preliminary provision of a licence; but as the regular season was now approaching, he rode into the county town and procured one under the name of Captain Debuish.

He now felt himself at liberty to enter into field sports with zest and regularity; and on the great day so dear to English sportsmen was up with the lark, and being let out by Black Jack, sallied forth to do execution among the birds.

He had been tolerably successful, when his attention was attracted by distant shots, almost like platoon firing, in the direction of the tower. Much annoyed, and desirous of the strictest incognito, he looked round for a spot to conceal gun, game, and dog, and at once lighted on a hollow tree; then drawing his cap over his eyes, he slowly and cautiously made towards the sportsmen.

He soon came in sight, and perceiving that they were approaching him, hid in a copse.

In a few minutes more, he, to his horror, astonishment, and disgust, saw Lord Charles Lutterel, Captain Frederick, and the Honourable John Winterton, with Corkum Needy, approaching in company with a posse of gamekeepers.

He wasted not one moment on thought, but, stooping low, ran at the top of his speed towards the old farm-house. On his way he took up his gun and game-bag, and then resumed his flight.

Big drops of perspiration fell from his agonised brow as he knocked loudly at the door, which, after a keen examination from a side loop-hole, was at once opened by Black Jack.

Captain George passed into the spacious and comfortable kitchen, where breakfast was smoking on the table.

"Out with the fire," said George, huskily; "let not a curl of smoke pass up the chimney; keep snug within doors, for the enemy are on us."

"To whom do you allude?" asked Lucy, quickly.

"You know I have but one enemy," replied Captain George in a husky tone.

"Merciful Heaven!" asked Lucy, "has he tracked us?"

"I hope not; but be it accident or design, he is here," continued Captain George.

The old man, who had been sitting dozing in his arm-chair, here asked in a querulous tone for his breakfast.

Lucy turned to attend him, and the rest sat down at the large kitchen table to satisfy their appetites, after which Captain George and Black

Jack went up to a kind of loft to reconnoitre, as shots were heard close to the house.

The whole party of hunters were within a hundred yards, making straight for the old farmhouse.

In a few minutes more they were knocking at the huge front gate, the top of which was garnished with formidable spikes.

Of course no answer was given. Even the dogs were kept from barking.

"I tell you what it is," said Lord Charles Lutterel, "this is a regular poacher's den. I saw the fellow run for it, and I'm hanged if I don't get a search warrant."

"Break the door down," replied Captain Fred. Winterton.

The keepers hesitated.

"Don't be afraid, we'll hold you harmless," said Lord Charles Lutterel. "It's my opinion the old house ain't been repaired this way for nothing."

At this moment a couple of gun-barrels were protruded from a side wicket.

"The first man, gentle or simple, who touches the door shall die the death of a burglar," said a menacing voice.

The keepers retreated in such a hurry as to overturn one another.

"My good man," said Lord Charles Lutterel, after withdrawing prudently from the range of the guns, "mind what you are at. A poacher has been traced to your door, so you'd better open."

"My master is not at home," said the voice sullenly. "Captain Dubuish, whose hunting-box this is, don't receive strangers."

"Oh!" cried Lord Charles, "if this be Captain Dubuish's hunting-box I really beg his pardon; but have you not hospitality enough to allow us to enter and refresh ourselves with a glass of ale?"

"Well, I'll see," said the other surlily.

There was now a dead silence for some time, after which a blackmoor-looking face peered over the great gate.

"If as how you gemmen choose to come in, housekeeper says ye can have as much yale as ye like."

"All right," said Lord Charles Lutterel, always craving for novelty.

The door was opened, and the keepers being told to wait outside, and breakfast off their own provisions, the four men entered the old farmfarm-house.

The doors went clang behind them with a rather ominous sound, but no one thought anything of it. In a few minutes the cosy, well-furnished, and warm kitchen was reached, on the table of which were flagons of ale, bottles of wine, and every preparation for a sportsman's breakfast.

Two labourers and two women, with the black serving man, received them and took their guns, which they placed in a closet.

They were then ushered to seats, and the serving maid poured out for each a large mug of country ale, which, after their long walk, was most welcome.

The large kitchen was somewhat gloomy, and

the shutters of the outer windows being closed, made it more so.

Somebody was seated in a large arm-chair; but as he looked like an aged serving man, no one took any notice of him.

At this moment a door opened with such a bang as to startle the guests.

Through the open door came Captain George and Lucy.

"Welcome, gentlemen," said the ex-highwayman, whose hand played with the butt of a pistol.

"Trapped, by the Lord!" shouted Lord Lutterel, pale as ashes, and turning round for his gun. The others did so likewise, but the three men, armed with huge cudgels, stood between them and the cupboard.

"What accursed voice was that?" said the old man, rising from his chair.

Lord Charles Lutterel fell back senseless It was the voice of his father, whom he believed safe in a madhouse.

"What means this audacious outrage?" blustered Captain Frederick Winterton.

"The outrage is on your side," said Captain George, while Lucy induced the old man to be seated. "It is useless to refuse; you are my prisoners, and had better submit quietly. Your drink is drugged, and drugged well. Learn another time to force yourself into a man's house against his will."

Before the alarmed men could recover themselves, they were fast bound, and laid aside by side on the table. In a few minutes all slumbered soundly.

The keepers were then told that the gentlemen intended to await the return of Captain Dubuish, and that they might retire until late in the evening, when, perhaps, their services might be required.

When they came at night, with lanthorns, they found the place in utter darkness, and their masters gagged, and almost insensible, on the kitchen table.

The fury of the Wintertons, the indignation of Corkum Needy, and the terror of Lord Charles Lutterel, are things not to be described.

CHAPTER XLVII.

HUNTED AGAIN.

WHEN Captain George found that his retreat had been discovered by his unnatural brother he determined at once on a course of proceeding with his usual decision and rapidity of action.

He stored every article of furniture in the old farm house upon a wagon, and sent it into the nearest town, where it was sold at a heavy pecuniary loss. He then paid the local servants well, and, accompanied only by his father, Lucy, Stone, and Black Jack, started in the public stage towards London.

After, however, travelling some distance, he left the coach, took a cross country chaise, then walked a mile or two, hired another chaise, and finally put up at a princely hotel at York, having first provided Lucy with a lady's maid.

He next day started for London, in a travelling carriage, Black Jack and the lady's maid occupying the rumble, Stone the box.

On the road he took care to occasionally have the words "duke," and "my lord" freely scattered, without mentioning any names.

In this way they drove up to a fashionable hotel, the landlord of which, happening to be in the hall, rushed forward himself, and opened the door of the carriage.

"Welcome, my lord duke," he said.

"Hush!" remarked Captain George, in a hasty whisper, "my father is still very ill. Pray do not call attention to him by mentioning his name. He must be kept very quiet."

"Certainly, my lord," said the landlord, with a low bow.

The party entered the magnificent mansion, and were ushered into a suite of apartments suited to their rank, where dinner was served up. This being done justice to, the old man, Captain George, and Lucy went out for a walk.

They never returned, and the same evening Stone paid all expenses, discharged the lady's maid, took the address of Black Jack, and went away.

When all this came to the ears of Lord Charles Lutterel, as it speedily did, not a further trace could he find of their passage through London.

He came up post haste from the north, having, after some trouble, found their track. He first, however, visited the mad-house, the keekers of which, afraid of losing their pension, had never given him any account of his father's escape.

His rage knew no bounds when he found how he had been tricked.

But he determined to pursue his revenge both against his injured parent, Captain George, and the lovely Lucy.

Captain George had acted with his usual precaution and tact. After walking slowly and deliberately from the hotel, he suddenly dived down a narrow street, made several turns, until at last he reached a small obscure public-house, where he was well known, and where he was at once provided with a private room until the arrival of Stone, who then guided them to his own house, on the banks of the river Thames.

The reader, who has followed us through the whole of this somewhat complicated narrative, remembers the shelter once offered to Captain George by Stone. It is unnecessary, therefore, to enter into minute descriptions of the *locale*.

They entered the house in the old way, by the Thames, Stone having previously furnished the house in a rude kind of manner—comfortably, but with no show of luxury. To disarm suspicion, he had talked of some relatives expected from America, who would probably restore him to his position in society.

As it was known that shortly before his failure certain of his relations had gone to America this statement excited no surprise.

There was something in the nature of Lucy Lipscombe—shall we call it romantic daring, or peculiar ideality?—which made this wild retreat particularly fascinating and agreeable. As long as the man of her heart was not recognised by society for what he really was she preferred living with him in utter obscurity and retirement.

No sooner were they all settled in that strange retreat than Captain George retired to his own private room, after intimating his particular desire to be left undisturbed for some time.

It was impossible for a man of his daring character and energetic nature to be idle. Besides, he had much yet to do ere he could hope to regain his station in society. Besides, he felt anxious to discover details of the progress of Lilian.

<hr/>

CHAPTER XLVIII.

THE ORANGE-CHAMBER.

THE post chaise and four which contained William Lennox and the Blue Dwarf never stopped on its way to London, except to change horses. Its inmates, in their feverish impatience to reach the great metropolis, took their meals in the vehicle.

Everywhere they received intelligence of the post chaise in front, containing an invalid lady, her female attendant, and, as the officials supposed, her two keepers. But with all the superhuman exertions of Sapathwa, with all his lavish expenditure of money, they could not come up with the fugitives.

Within a dozen miles of London they lost all trace of them.

It was now agreed that they should enter London in an humble way, put up at a small hotel, and commence operations by setting a watch upon the Hon. Frederick Winterton and his cousin. The Blue Dwarf, by means of great coats and slouched hats, was always able to hide everything but his stature, and by this means less of curiosity would be aroused.

They drove accordingly up to a first-rate hotel at Richmond, and, after dining, took an humble conveyance to town, which conveyance took them to the Bull and Mouth, in Holborn. Here they gave themselves out as commercial travellers, Sapathwa disguising the strange and inexplicable blue tint of his skin by means of contrivances which often in the course of his wild and melancholy career he had occasion to use.

"William," he said, as soon as they were alone, "I have promised to restore Lily to you, or die in the attempt. My dear boy, I have already morally died many deaths for your sake; but I will, on one condition, seriously carry out my pledged word."

"What is the condition?" said William.

"That you obey me in all things."

"With pleasure."

"First write to Mrs. Winterton to come to town. Lily has been brought here. These cunning criminals are too cowardly to slay, except at the last extremity. 'Tis a glorious truth, that has saved many lives. It is not every tyrant even likes to *see* the bloodshed he orders. Write, then, to Mrs. Winterton, and bid her come."

"It shall be done."

"Then, William, I will write to Lord ——, explaining your position, and why you did not join him before. I will ask him to introduce you into society; to the theatre, the opera; everywhere where you might meet Captain Winterton. Track him and you will soon be on the trail of Pauline."

"You think—"

"I am certain that wretched creature has become his tool, who knows. She is wicked enough for anything."

"Do you think so?"

"Alas! my boy; though my experience of civilised society is small indeed, I have learned enough to give me an insight into the heart of such women as Pauline."

Further conversation passed, and the young man and his strange guardian retired for the night.

Next morning, after writing a letter to Mrs. Winterton, William Lennox received a packet from the Blue Dwarf, directed to the Earl of ——, and about midday entered a hackney-coach and drove to his residence in Park-lane.

William Lennox, despite his humble position, had about him that something—which nobody can define and all talk about—which stamps the gentleman; and when he knocked a sturdy peal at the nobleman's door the hall-porter came rapidly forward

The sight of the hackney-coach, and the plain garb of William Lennox, slightly cooled him.

"Vat is it, young man?" he said.

"Is the Earl in?" replied William, coldly.

"Don't know. Parsons," addressing a footman who was arranging his neck-tie at a large mirror, "Is my lord in?"

"There is no occasion to tell any untruths," said William, quietly; "my lord is in, and you will be pleased to take up this card and packet."

Parsons, a good-natured but foppish youth, in livery, stepped forward and glanced at the card. As he did so, he started, bowed, begged the gentleman would wait in the library one moment, and hurried up-stairs.

William Lennox strode into the library with a beating heart, which was not calmed by the fact that he had to wait twenty minutes, at the expiration of which time he was summoned to see the nobleman.

He found him in a spacious drawing-room, seated in a large arm-chair; a handsome man, between fifty and sixty.

"Pardon me," he said, without rising, "if I have kept you waiting so long, but I have been absorbed in this letter: excuse my rising, our hereditary enemy, the gout, is peculiarly severe upon me just now."

"Really, my lord—" began William.

"Be seated," continued the earl, "and if I do not address you as I should, remember it is at the earnest request of your admirable and devoted guardian."

"You know him, my lord?" cried William.

"I know, love, and esteem him," said the earl; "but now to business. He wishes you nominally to assume the position of my secretary—be it so; but know, Master William Lennox, that with me and mine you will be as the son of the house, for whom we shall kill the fatted calf."

"My lord," cried William, astonished at the tone of the nobleman, "how can I ever repay this kindness?"

The earl smiled paternally, but made no direct reply.

"Would you be kind enough to ring yonder bell?" he said, "you are younger than I am"

Still more amazed at the earl's condescension than ever. William rose and obeyed his injunction."

A liveried servant came in answer to the peal.

"Tell Ladies Florence and Edith I wish to see them," said the earl.

William rose.

"Be seated," continued the earl; "and, Williams, tell Mrs. Browne to come to me."

The domestic bowed and retired. In another moment two lovely girls—nineteen and twenty-one—came bounding into the room, lovely, glorious, splendid specimens of that English beauty which is never seen to more advantage than in the highly cultured aristocracy of this country.

Mind, this beauty is not the attribute of any race. Take any family, give them the same advantages, and after a generation or two the result will be the same.

The result of too high culture, and of never taking in a fresh stock of popular blood, may be seen in the idiotcy and ugliness of the Bourbons.

Oval and fair faces, a bright, sunny complexion, white and almost massive foreheads, pearly teeth, and that tall, stately air, which is so much the result of habit and education,—it was difficult almost to distinguish one from the other, except that the elder girl was a little more womanly than her sister.

"My children," said the Earl, smiling at their sudden start, at discovering a stranger with him, "I have summoned you to introduce you to one about whom there must rest for a time a certain mystery, but whom I wish you to treat as if he were to be, one day, as it were, your elder brother, and the head of this ancient house."

William stared at the speaker in wild bewilderment; while the Ladies Florence and Edith Darville, concealing their amazement, welcomed the young man with an ease and suavity, combined with affectionate gentleness, which forced him to turn away to conceal his tears.

At this moment Mrs. Browne bustled in.

"You sent for me, my lord," she said, curtseying.

"Yes, Browne. Let the orange suite of apartments be placed at the disposition of this young gentleman, just as they were ——" The earl's emotions checked him.

Mrs. Browne stared with open mouth; the two girls held out their hands, and each caught one of his.

'Welcome,' said Lady Edith; "for, indeed, you must be dear to our father."

Florence smiled her welcome, though a little sadly. That suite of rooms had never been opened since their eldest brother had been drowned at Malta.

CHAPTER XLIX.

THE DEBUT.

FROM that hour William Lennox—though to the outward world he was merely a distant relative, acting in the capacity of secretary—was treated by all as the pet of the house. The earl doated on him, the girls made him their intimate confidante and friend. Except those evenings which were devoted to the Blue Dwarf, he never left their side, and attended them on all public occasions, though not formally introduced.

About a month passed in this way, during which Mrs. Winterton came to town, and joined heartily, though utterly hopelessly, in all the researches for her child, but without avail.

Inquiries were made at the lodgings of Captain Frederick Winterton. It was found, on the most undoubted evidence, that he had not left home except for the moors, and then in company with a party of friends whom he never left.

Not the faintest trace of Lily or Pauline, could be found, though the most prodigious rewards were privately offered for any clue.

Things were at this stage, when Lady Florence and Edith asked William Lennox, who was very melancholy and thoughtful, to attend them to the Opera. He would gladly have declined, but the remembrance of their sisterly affection prevailed, and he acquiesced.

"How sad William Lennox appears," said the younger sister Florence, when their maids had finished attiring them.

Edith looked at her half-blushing face, and smiled.

"Ah! Florence, you little think how strange must be the sensations of a youth in a false position, who has daily to bask in the sunshine of your beauty, and yet knows that he may not aspire ——"

"Why not?" said Florence, with a still deeper tint upon her brow.

"His humble birth," began Edith.

"Sister, dear, our father said, 'Treat him as one who may some day be the head of your house,'" replied the lovely girl.

"True; but beware, pretty butterfly," continued her sister, laughing, "how you burn your wings. There is a mystery about him, you allow?"

"Something, whatever it may be, in no way derogatory to him," said Lady Florence.

Lady Edith was about to reply, when they were told the carriage waited, as also Lady Zebulon Finch, a distant relative, who, on such occasions, played the part of duenna.

Both smiled at the gravity with which William handed down the painted dowager, and even kept up the conversation with her until they reached the house and were ushered into their box.

Those who have never seen the great Italian Opera in the full splendour of one of its great nights, when every shadow of darkness is expelled—first by the myriad lights, and then by that galaxy of bright eyes, of snowy shoulders, and incomparable beauty; by that effulgence of diamonds and jewellery, and that ineffable air of refinement and luxury, which is never seen any.. where else in the world—can conceive what her Majesty's Theatre is on a grand occasion.

This was to be the *debut* of a new *danseuse*, about whom the most wonderful stories were afloat.

The Ladies Edith and Florence, with their chaperone, Lady Zebulon Finch, glided unnoticed into their box, the house being just then occupied about itself, while William Lennox, with an opera-glass in his hand, stood at the back as far from notice as possible.

While the sisters were replying to the conversational remarks of Lady Zebulon Finch, he swept the range of boxes.

The fairy-like nature of the spectacle entranced his romantic nature, and the first act was over before he once opened his lips.

"Who, Lady Finch," said Florence, suddenly, without moving her head to the right or left, "is that horrid man who is staring up from the s a re-box?"

William's eyes were levelled at once in that direction.

"Oh!" cried Lady Finch ecstatically—there are old women who adore perversity in man— "that dear horrid wicked Captain Winterton. I do declare he's moving to come up here."

"I hope not," said William, gravely.

"Why, sir?" cried Lady Zebulon, tossing her head.

"Because, madam, a man so deliberately wicked should not be received into respectable society," continued William, gravely.

"La!" said Lady Finch, laughing, "what can a youth like you know about Captain Winterton's wickedness?"

"I know, madam, that which, if told, would have him hurled among the felons in Newgate," replied William, white as a sheet. "If that coward and assassin comes here, I must leave."

"Well, sir—" began Lady Finch.

"My dear Lady Finch," said Edith, interrupting her, "I am sure William knows what he is talking about. Do not, pray, let him come in."

A gentle knock came to the door, and the box keeper showed himself.

"The Honourable Captain Winterton desires to present his respects—"

William hurriedly took out a card, and wrote something in pencil.

"Give that to Captain Winterton," he said haughtily.

The box-keeper closed the door with a wellbred stare, but did not return.

Lady Edith and Florence glanced inquiringly at William, who was pale, agitated, and whose lips quivered.

But he said nothing, even sitting down and leaning his head upon his hands.

Florence gently stooped towards him, while her sister purposely engaged the irate Lady Zebulon Finch.

"What is the matter?" she said in a whisper.

"Nothing I can speak of now," replied William.

Florence quietly fanned herself, and looked round the house. Gladly would she have taken his hand, and win from him the tale of his sorrows. But like hundreds there present, who, bright without, dark within—life outside, death inward—joy on their cheeks, ashes strewn upon their hearts—were still seen smiling, she tried to look careless and unconcerned.

William leaned back in deep thought; nor did the girls, who guessed at some deep sorrow, interrupt him for a long time, until Florence felt compelled to do so by irresistible curiosity.

"William," she said, speaking behind her fan without turning.

"Lady Florence—"

"Did you ever see such a likeness to yourself in your life?" she continued.

William Lennox, livid, ghastly, his eyes glaring for once with absolute ferocity, followed the direction of her eyes, and by a sudden impulse took from Lady Florence her smelling-bottle, and closed his eyes.

"Hush—take no notice—one day you shall know all," he whispered. And the young girl, seeing his terrible suffering, pitied him and looked towards the stage.

Captain Frederick Winterton, with a pale and cadaverous countenance, was pretending to look across the house, but really examining their box.

At this moment, with a clang of the orchestra, up rose the curtain for the ballet, one of those things of music, light, gauze, tinsel, and handsome legs, which are so popular with all civilised nations.

A dance from the *corps de ballet* opened the affair, and then with a leap and a bound a being so airy, vapoury, and lovely as to bring down thunders of applause, came forward to the footlights.

William Lennox gasped for breath, and his eye mechanically was cast up to where sat, in the uniform of a midshipman, Philip Carabosse.

The dancer was Pauline.

Unable any longer to conceal his emotions, William Lennox, while the applause still lasted, glided from the box.

He went into the crush-room and wrote a note in pencil, which he gave a man a crown to deliver, with a written order for another if quickly delivered.

It was in French; translated it ran thus:—

"*He* is here. Captain Frederick is in the opera-box. The new dancer, Signora Petronilla, is Pauline. Opera House, 11 p.m."

It was directed to Mr. Goldy Gordon, Bull-and-Mouth, Holborn.

William Lennox, to all outward appearance cool and collected, returned to the box and sat down. The ballet continued amid tremendous applause.

Lady Florence fanned herself unceasingly. She was evidently much agitated.

"Lady Florence," he whispered very low, pardon me—but the drama of my existence is being played in this house. Every minute my life hangs upon a thread. With your father's consent I will tell you all some day."

"The actors are three," whispered Lady Florence below her fan.

"Three—"

"The captain, the double, and the actress," she continued in a slightly husky tone.

"True ; a triumvirate of evil, whom, with the help of Heaven, I mean to defeat," whispered William.

"Can I help you ?" said Florence, who blushed deeply as she spoke.

"Leave the house at once, and allow me to bid you adieu at the carriage door," replied William Lennox.

Lady Florence looked at her watch, and faintly yawned behind her fan. Lady Edith looked at her with that telegram of the eyes which is so much clearer, even, than that of modern invention.

"Tired, dear ?" said the elder daughter.

"Yes, rather ; if you don't mind I should like to go," replied Florence.

Lady Zebulon Finch rose majestically, and the party swept from the box with all the usual state and dignity, and were handed down by William Lennox, who bowed, ordered the coachman to drive home, and looked about him.

In the shadow of a pillar stood the Blue Dwarf, wrapped in an ample cloak. His face, by some mysterious means, was whitened.

"One moment," he whispered ; "I have received your note—explain rapidly."

William Lennox told him all he knew.

"Wait here," said Sapathwa ; and before William could add anything to his remark the Blue Dwarf had disappeared by the stage entrance.

In ten minutes, just after the first act of the ballet, he returned with a note in his hand, which he opened under a lamp. He then dragged William into a coffee house, re sealed the letter, and bade William order supper and wait his return.

He was some time ere he came, and then he was rubbing his long bony hands together.

Without any demand from William he told him what had happened.

By means of a liberal distribution of the great talisman, gold, he had reached behind the scenes, and stood at the wing just as the Signora Petronilla came off, to give the *corps de ballet* time to perform a scene in the entertainment. Instead of answering any of the compliments made her, she impatiently waved away her admirers, and looked up at the house.

"That must be he ; an officer, too ; how can I communicate with him ?"

This was said aloud, in French.

"Can I assist you, madam ?" said Sapathwa, in the same language, taking off his cap, and standing in deep shadow.

"Could you take a letter ?" rejoined the danseuse, after a cursory view of the Dwarf—taking him to be some underling of the opera.

"With pleasure ; show me the person."

The danseuse stood back, pointed to the young man, and further described his position and dress.

She then bade him follow her to her room, where she wrote, in pencil :—

"Do we meet again ? To-morrow night there is a grand masquerade at the Prince's ; be there ; wear a black domino, Italian mask, and a yellow cockade. I send a ticket.

"You Know Who."

This letter the Dwarf read.

"What do you mean to do ?" said William.

"I have given him his note. He will be there —*so will we.*"

CHAPTER XLVIII.

THE MASKED BALL.

IF anything more than another marks the progress of English civilisation, it is the wondrous and most marvellous change which has taken place in the manners of the court.

Under Queen Victoria the court of England is so far renowned for its purity, that even foreign potentates are compelled, during a residence here, to observe the outward semblance of decency and virtue.

Under the Georges it was so opposite that were we to give the right name to it, we should soil the paper we write upon.

There was one thing characteristic of Carlton House, which has been allowed by all contemporaries, which was the splendour of the arrangements.

On the evening in question the mansion of the prince was lit up with unusual splendour. The stairs were lined by liveried servants, and about eleven o'clock the company began to arrive. It had been agreed that everybody was to be strictly masked up to two o'clock in the morning, when, at the supper being over, and wine having been served freely, less ceremony would be expected.

The prince received his company of course only by a general bow ; and though in most instances he in reality knew who the parties were, he did not appear to do so.

About twelve the crush was very great, and William Lennox and the Blue Dwarf slipped in unobserved. The latter was made up in such a way as to disguise his deformity, except as regards his short stature.

He, however, no sooner was in the ball-room than he glided away into a corner, and seated himself, answering the many appeals made to him only by a grunt.

Meanwhile William Lennox was on the lookout for Pauline, who had omitted the very essential precaution of describing her own dress.

Presently, however, he started as he saw her coming towards him, masked, and leaning on the arm of a tall man in the dress of a Turk, Pauline, in her genuine Boulogne costume, only masked.

What to do he hardly knew, as the real Simon Pure might at any moment come on the ground. He, however, carelessly placed himself in her way, and allowed her to see the yellow bow.

She looked at him with apparent unconcern, and passed him. As she passed him, she put her ungloved hand behind her. True to his part, he pressed it tenderly.

"I wish to sit down," said the danseuse to her

friend; "so shall wait here for you. I will not be presented to the prince until after supper."

"Very well," replied Winterton; "I won't be long."

And he led her to a seat, bowed, and retired in the direction of the prince's party.

Pauline with one bound was beside William Lennox, and hanging on his arm.

"*Mon ange*," she said, with deep and earnest passion in her tones, "do you still love me?"

"As much as ever," replied the young man through the beard of the mask, easily counterfeiting the other's voice.

"Ah—Philip," she cried, "how I have sorrowed for you—how have I suffered—"

"Tell me all," he replied; "I wish to hear your adventures."

She led him to a seat, and told him all up to her arrival at Y——.

"But how came you to leave the protection of this William Lennox, my enemy?"

"I will tell you. A girl he loves, one Lilian, overheard him speaking to me; and taking offence at his supposed intrigue with me, darling, quarrelled with him. Then came a certain Captain Winterton—of course I knew you too well to expect blame for any act which secured me a position—who offered me money, an introduction to the stage and to good society, if I would assist him to get possession of this Lilian, who, it appears, is an impostor—"

"Indeed?" said the supposed Philip Carabosse.

"I agreed. I knew that from your station in society it would be the only way of finding you—"

"And he obtained possession of the girl?" asked Philip Carabosse.

"Yes. I own that her grief was so great I undeceived her relative to her suspicions—"

The pretended Philip was compelled to cough to hide his emotion.

"Besides, I bargained no harm should be done her, and I know he has kept his word. He brought her to London, and in my presence started her off to some place in the North of England—"

"But this Winterton—what is your position with him?" said William.

Pauline's eyes burnt like coals as she looked the other in the face.

"I hate him, but have been forced to give him hope," she replied.

William Lennox stepped away. He had caught sight of the Turk returning.

"Don't leave your seat," said Captain Winterton, coming up; "the prince will be this way directly, and will himself have you down to supper. I must back to him for a minute or two."

And he hurried away just as some one stooped over the arm-chair in which Pauline was reclining.

"Cockatrice! faithless *coquine!*" said a too-well known voice.

Pauline turned slowly round, and found a masked domino behind her with a yellow cockade.

"*Mon Dieu!*" she cried, "Is that you, Philip?"

"Yes, madame; your outraged, incensed,

Philip," he said, "speak madam; explain your connection with this ruined *debauchee*."

Pauline rose and took his arm.

"I will explain everything," she said; "but is this the first time you have seen me to-night?"

"Certainly."

"Then who is yonder mask?" she faltered, pointing to where William Lennox stood, gazing at the pair.

"How should I know?"

"Shall I tell you?"

"Yes."

"Your foster brother—"

The masked young man tottered against a pillar, and groaned audibly.

"Take me away," he said; "give me air. Come, Pauline, let us fly—there is death in this place."

Pauline acquiesced at once; passed to the vestiary, and took a cloak, without caring whose it was. In ten minutes more they were in a carriage, driving to Pauline's own lodgings, which were close to the theatre.

Her lover had fainted. When she reached her house he was carried in, and laid insensible on a sofa.

A few minutes brought him to; when he regained his senses he glared around like a maniac.

"I did not do it," he gasped.

Then his eye fell upon Pauline.

"Girl," he said—they were now face to face, unmasked—"who put that lie in your mouth."

"Philip," she replied, with a cold, sinister smile, "there are no secrets between us. You did not kill him; he lives, and, mark me, is plotting some deadly revenge."

"Merciful Heaven, do you know him?"

"Considering that he saved me from the hands of my infuriated parents, and provided for me and my poor child—"

"Child—what child?"

"Our boy, who is now down at Y——, under his care and protection."

"Will you drive me mad, or will you speak?" said Philip Carabosse.

Pauline sat down, passed her soft white arm caressingly round his neck, and told him her terrible story, to which he listened stunned, horror-struck, trembling.

"Will you stand by me?" he gasped.

"You are mine and I am yours," she said, with savage energy. "Through every trial and every temptation I have been faithful to you—I will be."

Pauline was sincere, for she dearly loved him then.

"This William Lennox must disappear," he whispered in a husky tone; "we cannot live together on the same earth."

"But how is it to be done?" said the girl, coldly.

"That we must think of," he replied; "but what is that?"

A loud knock was heard at the door, and a hasty step came up stairs; then Captain Frederick Winterton rushed into the room.

"What in the name of the foul fiend is the meaning of all this?" he began.

Prowse.

"Captain Winterton, aid Pauline, coldly, "you have a hat on your head. Allow me to present to you Sir Edgar Blakesly, baronet—my destined husband.

"Husband be——' roared Captain Winterton, "I brought you out on condition—"

"That I became your kept mistress? True, I made some such compact. But there is yet time; and he to whom my whole affection is given—the father of my child—claims me."

"You shall repent this," blustered the captain.

"No threats, sir," said Sir Edgar gravely, " or I shall be under the painful necessity of pulling your nose."

"Sir," began the captain, "these are my apartments. I have paid for them."

Pauline rang the bell, and the landlady, who was listening outside, entered abruptly. She curtsied lowly to Pauline.

"How much has this gentleman paid you, Mrs. Jones?" said Pauline, quietly.

Before the landlady could reply, Captain Winterton, with a foul cry on his lips, darted from the house.

"That will do," said Pauline; "remember, I am never at home to that gentleman."

The complaisant lady bowed and retired, after taking an order for a copious supper. Pauline, since her elevation in the world, began to be a connoisseur in gourmandise.

Ballet girls mostly are.

CHAPTER LI.

AN UNEXPECTED FRIEND

AFTER watching the meeting between the two, Philip Carabosse—alias Sir Edgar William Lennox—turned away with bitter scorn.

He fetched the Blue Dwarf, and the two retired together to a neighbouring coffee-house, where Lennox related what little he had learned.

"She is alive, at all events," said Goldy.

The lover made no reply.

William Lennox, though he had reason to believe, from the statement of Pauline, that the life of Lillian had been spared, could in his own mind form no clue to a discovery of her place of concealment; while the Wintertons might have spared her life, doubtless they had so secreted her—perhaps in a madhouse—that she never would be found.

The Blue Dwarf sat still in his corner, in deep thought.

The coffee-house was, as yet, to all appearance empty.

"Oh, Lilian! Lilian!" suddenly cried William, as if with an irrepressible burst of sorrow; "what shall I do without you? To lose you is to die!"

"Hush," said Goldy Gordon soothingly, "this is unmanly. I have told you she shall be found."

A stout man, with a slouched hat and many-caped great coat, here glided into their box from the next one, where he had hitherto been concealed.

"In the name of Heaven, do you speak of Lillian Winterton, the child of Arabella?" he said.

"I do," faltered William Lennox, while Goldy Gordon smiled.

"What of her, young man?" continued the stout man. "I love her as my own child."

"She has once more been stolen from her mother by the cousins," said William.

"Then I believe I know where she is," whispered the stranger; "but tell me all you know, and then I can judge better what to believe—what to think. Tell him to speak, Goldy Gordon."

"Speak openly as to me," said the Blue Dwarf, "this is Captain George."

"The saviour of Lillian," gasped poor William, "indeed, this is a fortunate meeting."

He then told all he knew of the outrage on Lillian, adding Pauline's statement relative to her being somewhere in the north.

"William Lennox," said Captain George, solemnly, "this is providential. When will you be ready to start for the north?"

"At dawn," replied William.

"No," said Goldy Gordon. "I shall not be ready until mid-day."

"Where shall we meet?" added Captain George.

"I will have a post-chaise and four where you please at twelve," said Goldy.

"I will meet you at the tenth milestone on the northern road," replied Captain George.

This preliminary settled, the Captain glided away, as he never stopped long at one place; and in a few minutes the Blue Dwarf and William Lennox called a coach, and returned to the inn where Goldy Gordon slept. William then wrote several letters, after which he laid down. But not to sleep. It was in vain that he wooed the coy deity of slumber, it would not come to him. When he rose he was pale and haggard, while his eyes were heavy and dull.

"This will never do," said the Blue Dwarf, shaking his head.

"I cannot help it," said William Lennox, sadly; "she is all I have in the world."

Goldy Gordon pursued his occupation, that of breakfast, without another word. Presently he rose and prepared to go—as he always did by day—in a close hackney coach, with a slouched hat and ample cloak.

"Will you be long?" said William.

"No, my boy," replied Goldy Gordon, "but we have a long journey before us, and we shall want plenty of money—of gold, my boy, which buys old and young, rich and poor."

"You must be very rich," said William, in a musing tone, "very rich."

"And so I am," replied the Dwarf, returning and laying his long bony finger upon the other's arm, "and what is the use of it to me? Does not the world shun me, scout at me, point at me with the finger of scorn. But then, ah! ah! ah! I have power, and that is something."

"And you have the affection of all who know you," repeated William, in a caressing tone.

"You do, my boy, I believe," said Sapathwa, more gently; "oh, if you knew all!"

"And Lillian worships you—"

"Does she? Well, well, for your two sakes I will think better of the world," cried Goldy Gordon, laughing a laugh so hideous that even William had some difficulty in not being startled.

At this moment a serving girl opened the door, with a fresh supply of tea and muffins; and so fearful was the picture to her that she literally stood still as if turned to stone, dropped her tray, and would have fled, but that her legs refused their office.

"Be not silly, girl," said the Blue Dwarf, coldly, as he caught the terrified creature by the arm. "I am not so bad as I look. Here are two guineas to repair the damage done."

And he went from the room.

"Bless me, sir, I hope he ain't offended," said the girl, putting her apron to her eyes; "but he did give me such a start like. He is such a kind, good gentleman to us all. Pity he is so very —"

"Hush!" cried William, "don't say the word. He is so good, that I can see no fault in him."

"Well, sir, I meant no offence, I'm sure," said the girl, picking up the fragments.

"I have had quite enough breakfast," remarked William, "you can clear away."

And he went to a window looking out into the yard to watch the horses being put to the post-chaise. There he stood nearly half an hour.

Suddenly he felt himself touched on the arm, and turning round saw the pretty servant girl by his side, all blushes and pouts.

"What is it?" said William, a little surprised.

"You are cross with me about that dear, good gentleman," she said. "Now he was not cross, or else he would not have given me two guineas."

"Of course he was not," replied William, mechanically putting his hand to his pocket.

"I don't want any money," said the girl.

"What then?"

"I want you to forgive me," she said, holding up a very pretty and inviting face.

"If you wish it," cried William Lennox, with a deep girlish blush, and he kissed her heartily.

"He! ho! he!" said the Blue Dwarf, coming forward, "don't be alarmed; I've heard it all. Come away, William, all is ready."

The girl had vanished at the first word, utterly unable to speak.

William Lennox followed his guardian, every thought of his heart given to the idea of Lillian.

Away dashed the post-chaise over the somewhat ill-paved streets, at the rapid pace which only four English horses can give to a carriage. William thought they moved with snail-like motion, so impatient was he to be at the end of his journey.

About one o'clock the horses drew up at a signal from a well-dressed stranger, who, tossing a small portmanteau on to the roof, entered the carriage.

It was, of course, Captain George, who had changed his costume to that of a very plain country gentleman.

The ordinary greetings of gentlemen having passed, all seemed inclined to give way to their own reflections, and ere long the motion of the carriage sent them off to sleep.

CHAPTER LII.

THE TOWER.

MEANWHILE far away in the north, as Pauline had said, Lillian was expiating the fact of being a heiress, under the most painful circumstances.

Ready tools are always to be found for money, and Captain Frederick Winterton found no exception to the rule.

He had once owned a very genteel property on the borders, but by means of his extravagance, every atom of his patrimonial acres had been dissipated, except a right of shooting which he reserved as the only means of keeping up his standing with a certain set in London.

He had, too, a shooting-box already alluded to, and here in the tower, which was admirably preserved, dwelt a gamekeeper and his wife; as wicked, cruel, and desperate a couple as ever appeared under the shape and form of humanity.

Brassy Will, as he was called, had been a desperate poacher, and worse; while Sally, his wife, had been, ever since her tenderest years, his companion and accomplice. In conflicts with keepers she had several times fired her gun, and both had been twice tried and acquitted.

The Hon. Captain Frederick Winterton then took them into his employment, fancying that they were very likely to be useful to him.

Brassy Will had a kind of rude and blind devotion to his protector; but that was his only virtue, except his love for the ugliest, most waspish, and ill-natured terrier that ever was bred.

He admired his wife; but that did not prevent his beating her.

She was a tall, dark, powerful raw-boned woman, with coal-black eyes, and an arm of terrific dimensions.

To this couple it was that the brutal captain had confided the tender being, whom William Lennox so much loved.

They made her a drudge—a Cinderella—a perfect slave.

They took a delight in torturing her, body and soul.

"Hoity-toity!" would the woman say; "how fine we are, and what white skin! But we'll teach you better. Poor people has to work, and you're poor now. Ah! ah! ah! so you must work."

At seven o'clock—let us take any ordinary day—the woman would rise from her comfortable bed, and enter the kitchen, the principal room in the house. In the centre of this kitchen was a trap-door, which she raised, and disclosed a flight of dark, damp, and gloomy steps.

Down these she went, and presently there re-appeared Lillian. But, oh, how changed! Pale, thin, cadaverous, and hollow-eyed; forced up by the brutal pushes of that monster in female shape.

Still she complained not, but silently went to do the woman's bidding. She first lit a fire on the huge hearth, which she swept clean. Then she laid the breakfast things, and prepared that meal; all the while receiving the most lavish abuse.

The very dog barked at her, and strove to snap at her as she passed.

Then she cleared away, and made the bed of the two wretches, who soon after breakfast began to drink. Then, if Lillian did not move fast enough, they struck her.

And thus all day until the hour when, sobbing and moaning, she again went down with the vile woman into the dungeon, where the jailor left no light.

It was some days after the departure of the three friends for the north when Brassy Will and his wife, having been out, returned to the house in a state of intoxication.

At the town they had found a letter, asking if the bird were dead yet.

They came back, in the ferocity of their drunken anger, determined to kill the bird.

"Ah!" said the hag, "hast let the fire out, viper? Light it, quick—"

"Don't hit me," replied Lilian, gently, "I am dying fast enough."

"Are you?" shrieked the woman; "not fast enough for me. So understand me, miss."

"I can't die any faster," continued Lillian, looking meekly up to heaven.

"Can't yer?" laughed the man, "then we'll see if we can't help yer."

And observing that the girl was busy making up the fire, they bent their heads together and whispered. A laugh so hideous as to startle even themselves followed the discovery of a plan.

The hearth was vast, with room for three to sit on a stone seat each side.

The woman took up an armful of wood, and flung it on the fire. She then clutched the girl by the hair of her head.

"Ha, ha, ha!" she shouted in drunken glee; "can't you die any faster? We shall see—we shall see! Ha, ha, ha! Your bones shall crackle and go to ashes, and nobody will ever miss you"

"Heaven have mercy on me!" cried Lillian, divining their terrible intention.

"There's no heaven here," said the man, savagely. He didn't half like the job when he looked at her meek face. "Hang it, Sal! finish her off at once."

Lillian, however, saw that the virago was determined to carry out her monstrous plan, and the natural love of life prevailing over every other consideration, she gave three piercing shrieks.

Heavy blows were showered on the door, and the dog barked furiously.

The wretches gazed at one another in utter consternation; then fear overcoming their inebriety, they rushed to the trap, stifling her cries, and carried her below.

"Who knocks at this time of night?" growled Brassey Will, in a surly and defiant tone.

"Open, or we will beat the door down," said an imperious voice.

"Pass your ways; this is no tavern," replied the woman.

"Open, or I fire through the door," repeated the stranger.

"Two can play at that game," said Brassey Will, advancing towards a huge blunderbuss.

"Exactly," said a sarcastic voice from a corner of the room.

The guilty pair looked in the direction of the sound, and saw before them the Blue Dwarf, in all his native hideousness, gazing on them with a strange expression.

"The Lord have mercy upon us!" yelled the two, falling on their knees.

"Oh, Mr. Devil!" began the man.

"Good Mr. Devil!" repeated the woman.

The Blue Dwarf strode across the room, and taking advantage of their abject terror and alarm, opened the front door, when in rushed Captain George and William Lennox.

"Where is the child—where is Lillian?" shrieked the latter, putting a pistol to the other's head.

"Fast bind, fast find," said Goldy Gordon, whipping a cord round the still kneeling ruffian, and tying him up with the dexterity of a hangman.

Captain George secured the woman.

As soon as they recovered sufficiently to be aware that their assailants were human, their fury knew no bounds, and they sullenly refused to answer any questions.

Goldy Gordon took up a red-hot brand with the tongs and approached it to the cheek of the man.

"Where is the girl?" he said with fearful and savage emphasis.

"What girl?" replied the shrinking ruffian.

"The girl you were beating," cried William, who was wild with passion.

"Ha! ha! ha!" laughed the woman; "why can't a man thwack his own wife? I say, Will, this here's something new!"

"Hush!—silence!—ah!" shrieked William, and he flew like a hungry tiger at the trap-door and hauled it up with the strength of a giant.

Then he plunged down the steps.

"Bring a light," he yelled rather than said.

Both Captain George and the Dwarf bounded down with the flickering candle off the table, and beheld a sight of such horror and woe that their very hearts sickened.

Chained by the waist, on a pile of dirty straw, lay Lillian, the shadow of her former self, clasped in the arms of her young lover, the two shedding mingled tears of joy and sorrow.

To dash the chain in two, to rush up stairs after a moment lost in wonder and astonishment, was the work of an instant. Then they bore her up stairs—pity, grief, almost extinguished by the burning desire for revenge.

But the kitchen was empty, and the smouldering cords showed by what desperate means the fugitives had obtained their liberty.

In one of the cupboards there was wine and food in abundance. This the Blue Dwarf administered slowly and methodically to the poor girl.

"Will she die?" said William Lennox, wildly.

"We have saved her before; why not save her again?" replied the Blue Dwarf, laconically.

"Let us take her to her mother," continued William.

"No," said Goldy Gordon; "write to the mother and say we are on her track; but do not let her see her thus."

As soon as Lillian was a little recovered from her excitement, they bore her into the open air, to a carriage which awaited them behind some trees.

They then drove away in the direction of the neighbouring town.

CHAPTER LIII.

MEANWHILE Captain Frederick Winterton and his lisping and inane cousin were in London—not enjoying the fruits of their villany, but scheming and devising to put off the evil day of payment.

Corkum Needy and Peter Emanuel were beginning to be pressing.

The widow was alive, and young, and pretty. She might marry at any time.

The two confederates were at bay. Their spy, Slimy Jones, was always on the watch, and he had brought them the astounding intelligence that Mrs. Winterton was easier in her mind, and more cheerful than she had been for some time.

"I tell you what it is, John," said the captain, as they walked up and down Pall-mall one afternoon; "something must be done."

"Vewy well. What?"

"Damme, sir, you're the most provoking fellow in the world. I want you to say something."

"Haven't an idewa."

"I don't believe you have," said the captain, in a tone of angry sarcasm.

"Well, bullewing won't do anwy good," drawled the Hon. John.

"Corkum Needy is getting very rusty. The effect of the journey north is over. We must do something. Besides, I've only twenty pounds in the world," sighed the captain.

"Haven't a penwy," said John.

"Well, we must raise the wind," continued the captain.

"Do a bill."

"Who will do _our_ bill?" angrily retorted the captain. "Do you understand?'

"No."

"But anybody would do _her_ bill."

"Of course. But I don't see."

"Of course not. Nobody expects you to help a fellow; nobody wants. We owe, in round numbers, thirty thousand pounds!"

"The doose!"

"Or a little over. Now, I know that, since the _accident_ which deprived Mrs. Winterton of a husband and us of a cousin, she has saved out of her income of ten thousand a-year, about a hundred thousand pounds."

"Goodness gwacious!"

"Now, what more natural than that our dear cousin, hearing of our reverses, should wish to aid us."

"Don't see it."

"Bother your interruptions:—And not liking to sell out, should put her name to a number of little bills, falling due on her dividend days."

"Can't say I see. Vewy much like a whale," said John, shaking his head.

"John, I think you're next door to an idiot,' cried the captain, angrily.

"Well, I think I am," responded the Hon. John, looking hard at the captain.

' Don't be ridiculous,'' retorted the captain. "I must speak plain with you. Our position is so desperate that we must either _sell the heiress_—"

"What?" cried John, starting back.

"_Sell the heiress back to her mother_," continued the captain, coolly, "for half the plunder, or raise the wind.

"Ha! ha! Capital," said the Hon. John, laughing. "Sell the heiress! Well, I vote for the first—fifty thousand, by Jove!"

"Let it be so," responded the captain. "Now to find Slimy Jones—he's the man."

This determination being come to, the confederates moved towards the residence of their worthy agent, who was found in his shop, with his better half, weighing ounces of sugar, and pepper, and tea—or articles presumed to be called by these names.

"Wanted, Jones," said the captain, with a mock polite bow to Mrs. Jones, which nearly sent that lady into hysterics, knowing, as she did, the rank of the gentleman.

"Just so," replied Jones, slipping on a seedy black coat and taking his hat.

He then followed them into the street, and received his instructions, to which he listened with up-turned eyes.

"Just so," was his only remark, and then he shuffled off, leaving the cousins to follow.

On reaching the door of Mrs. Winterton's establishment, which the cousins had discovered only by the most persevering search, Jones knocked humbly.

A stout man servant opened the door.

"We don't want any, my good man; go away," and he would have pushed the door to.

"Just so; Mrs. Winterton's daughter—news!" said Jones, quickly.

The man eagerly ushered him in, rang a bell, and sent up a message to the widow.

"Show the man up," said the waiting-maid, after consulting her mistress.

Jones, his hands encased in gloves without fingers, and clutching the rim of his hat with both hands, walked up the heavily-carpeted stairs, and was ushered into the presence of Mrs. Winterton, who stood calm, grave, and nowise excited before him.

"Your business, sir?" she said.

"Just so," replied Jones, glancing round the room to see that they were alone. "I have news of your daughter."

"Indeed!" said Mrs. Winterton.

"Just so. The fact his, Messrs. Frederick and John Winterton have commissioned me to say that they humbly hapologise for what they have done, and will, hon free pardon from you, restore the dear little girl—"

"Ah!" said the widow, slightly animated.

"Just so; they deeply regret that they should have been forced by the hexigencies of their position to do anything wrong, but on condition—"

"On condition!" slowly repeated Mrs. Winterton. "They make conditions, then?"

"Just so. I perceive has I'm speaking to a lady as understands business."

"What are their conditions?" coldly continued the widow.

"Just so. Well, you see, ma'am, as how the turning up of the gal ruins the prospects of my clients," began Jones.

Mrs. Winterton's eyes sparkled.

"Just so. You see, mum, they're terribly hard up, and they thinks as how if you have the girl with half the fortune—ready tin, I mean—about fifty thousand, and let them have the rest, they will recognise Miss Lilian, and have no more bother about it."

"Not a guinea, not a shilling, not a penny," said Mrs. Winterton, in a stern and implacable voice; "not to save them from utter starvation. Go to them and say," taking up a newspaper off the table, and revealing an open parchment, "that there lies my will, devising everything I have in the world to my daughter _and_ William Lennox, or failing them to the charities of London. Go; they are utterly foiled. I defy them."

"Just so," was all that fell from the amazed agent of the cousins.

Mrs. Winterton rang the bell, and the stout servant man answered the summons.

"Show that man down stairs, and if he comes again give him into custody."

"Custody," whined Slimy Jones. "Just so."

And he hastened down stairs with an alacrity which surprised himself.

He hurried along the street to where, at a tavern, the cousins were waiting for him in a private room. They had a bottle of wine before them.

Without speaking a word he sat down and drank off a glass of wine.

"*Custody—just so,*" he muttered.

"Why. what's the matter, you infernal fool?" said the captain, who was, however, very pale.

"Custody—just so," replied Jones.

"If you say that again I'll kick you," said the captain, clutching him by the collar.

"Just so—cust—"

The captain raised his foot.

"Just so—wait a minute," he roared.

A glass or two of wine, however, having brought him to a sense of his situation, he gave an emphatic and clear description of the whole interview.

The cousins wiped the cold dew of perspiration off their foreheads.

"Ruined—cheated—undone," said the captain. "If this gets wind we shall spend the rest of our lives in gaol."

"Better hook it," cried the Hon. John.

"And live on air; no. Better die in the breach," continued the captain, who was a man not easily subdued. "Something must be done. In the first place Jones must go to our place and find if there is any news from the north. The girl must have escaped."

"Just so," said Jones, and departed on his mission.

CHAPTER LIV.

THE MAN IN POSSESSION.

THE residence of the cousins was in a fashionable street, and in the house of a respectable widow. They occupied a suit of rooms furnished in the most splendid manner, regardless of expense, and were waited on by both liveried and female servants.

Slimy Jones knocked here in his usual jaunty way. The door was instantly opened.

To his astonishment all the domestics were in the hall, supporting the weeping, sobbing, half-fainting landlady, while loud cries of rage, despair, and vindictive invective were showered upon somebody.

"The flaunting, cheating vagabonds—"

"Even the furniture not their own."

"Nothing for anybody—"

"Going to jail."

"Hopes they may rot there."

"Ought to be hung—"

"Just so. Who?" put in Slimy Jones.

"Your rascally masters," said a footman.

"Just so. What's the matter?" cried Jones.

"Man in possession—bill of sale," whimpered the landlady, "and, he! he! he! they owe me a year's rent. He! he! he! such nobs, too—not a penny piece."

"Just so," began Jones.

"The wretch is laughing at us!" roared an angry chorus.

"Just so," cried Jones; "hear me—"

"Let's hear him before we duck him," said the housemaid, specially connected with the first floor.

"Just so. I'll see you all paid," began Jones, holding himself erect. "I've gained a few hundreds in the service of my noble masters, who will soon be as rich as the bank, and I'll pay you all myself."

Every body dried their eyes, smiles took the place of tears, and the whole party surrounded Slimy Jones, the men shaking his hands, the women—yes, actually kissing his cadaverous and pimply face.

Oh, gold! what is not thy power?

"Just so," said Jones, disengaging himself, "but let me go up stairs."

All made way, as if he had been the Shah of Persia, or any other Shah, and allowed the great man to march up stairs.

He entered the magnificent apartments with the air of a man who was quite at home, and was met by Peter Emanuel, book in hand, taking an inventory.

"Just so," said Slimy Jones, with extreme gravity, "pray may I be hallowed to ask what is the meaning of hall this here—what's up?'

"Yas, mine goot Mhister Jones," replied the Jew, with a grin. "I beesh taking mine leetle property away."

"Just so," said Jones, gravely, and he rang a bell.

Two men-servants answered the appeal.

"Kick—just so—kick these low people down stairs," pointing to Peter Emanuel and two subordinates.

"Vat ish you say?" cried Peter Emanuel in a towering passion. "Vy don't you kick. I tellsh you vat, Mishter Jones, if you don't leaf de premishes quick—you'll see."

Slimy Jones put his hat upon his head, pulled off his fingerless gloves, searched his pockets, and, after turning out balls of twine, bits of paper, ends of cigars, and other trifling articles, including cheeseparings, he produced a card and a roll of paper.

"Just so," he said, with an air of deep satisfaction, "take this card to John Snaffle, attorney-at-law; bring him along, and a couple of constables—tell him to bring ancuffs with 'em; be quick, you knows what I promised you."

One of the domestics darted off at a rapid pace, while the other remained to support Slimy Jones if necessary.

The Jew meanwhile stood aghast. His dark complexion turned a mixture of creamy white and blue. He tore at his beard with desperate energy, foamed at the mouth, stamped, and finally approached Slimy Jones in a menacing attitude.

"Just so," said Slimy Jones, putting his hands under his coat tails. "Let me—suit my purpose hexactly. Give you in charge for robbery and assault."

"Mine Gott! he ish mad—my goot sir!" screamed Peter Emanuel, "do you see dish?"

And he flourished a piece of parchment under the other's somewhat prominent nose.

"Just so—what is it?

"A bill of sale. Read de back."

"Just so," said Jones, poring over it with intense coolness, "a bill of sale on all and several the goods and chattels of Captain Frederick Winterton and the Honorable John Winterton, dated the 4th of March, 18—."

"Vell," said the Jew.

"Just so," replied Jones with provoking calmness.

"Sho you go, eh?" groaned Peter Emanuel.

"No," roared Slimy Jones, thrusting another parchment under the nose of the Jew, who drew back, turned pale, and then carefully read the back. He was too agonised to read it out.

"The date?" he muttered.

"Just so—a bill of sale on all and several the goods and chattels of Captain Frederick Winterton and the Honorable John Winterton, dated the 1st of January, in the same year—just so!"

The Jew fell back in the arms of his assistants.

"And dish ish de Christian!" he gasped, "de Jew he peg, he porrow, he sht—he I mean shave—and de gentlemen dey rob him. But I have mine refenge. I hang him like one dog. Dish is vurse an highway robbery. Dish is a shvindle."

"Just so," remarked Jones, coolly, "but as it can't be helped. why not settle it?"

"Ah," said Peter Emanuel, faintly, "how? Dey have no monies."

"Just so," coolly continued Jones, "but you have."

"I have no monish," replied the Jew in an humble penitent tone. "I have losht it every penish. You von't take all?—eh? You give me half?"

At this moment the lawyer sent for entered. The police were a myth.

"Well, my dear Mr. Jones," said the man-at-law, "what can I do for you?"

"Just so; let this man thoroughly understand that this bill of sale is quite right."

"My dear sir," replied the attorney with a look of naïve astonishment, "I made it."

"Dat ish enough," cried the furious Jew; "let me see de signatures."

Jones opened the parchment, and showed both the signature and date.

The Jew made a sign to his acolytes to follow him, and advanced to the door.

"Shelp me Moses," he said, in a voice choked by passion; "I goshe to Bow-street."

"Just so; bad way of getting your money."

"If not I take dere bodies; I lock em up—eh?"

"Just so; only, between you and me, I should wait a bit—just two days."

The Jew re-entered the room and sought for further particulars, but Jones declined giving them, telling them at the same time that something fresh was up.

The Jew then retired, after which Slimy Jones, after thanking his friend Snaffles, between whom and himself there appeared a perfect understanding, summoned the astonished landlady, and placed her in sole charge of the property during the absence of the owners.

Jones then took such letters as happened to be on the table, and left the house amid the bows—we had almost said the genufluxions—of the whole party. Just as the door closed, two members of the Hebrew persuasion came rapidly across the streets towards Jones. Their mock jewellery, chains, rings, watches, dirty linen, huge neckerchiefs, and thick-knobbed sticks, proclaimed at once their profession. Evidently the extremely seedy character of the individual caused the mistake which occurred.

"Ish de parties at home?" said one, in a hollow and mysterious voice.

"Just so—what party do you allude to?" replied Jones.

"The captain and the other swell," continued the bailiff's follower.

"Just so—not at home, and not likely to be, I can tell you. Corkum Needy, I suppose—tell your governor as Captain Frederick Winterton has hooked to Russia with a hairess, and as the Honourable John Winterton is gone in a convent."

"Sold, shelp me Methusaler!" said the officer, while Jones walked away triumphant.

His rapid career was, however, suddenly brought to a close by the apparition before him as he turned the corner of the street of two tattered mendicants, one male and the other female, in the last stage, apparently, of human misery. They were country people, and the soles of their shoes had left them by the way. Their faces was pinched, gaunt, and livid.

"Just so," said Slimy Jones, pompously, "nothing to give, my good man."

"Ain't you?" replied the woman, fiercely, "who cares—we vants your masters, Mr. Jones."

"Bill," cried Jones, starting back, "just so. Speak out. Is it bad news!"

"Very; the gal's took, the gaff's blown, and we've been near murdered," said the man.

"Just so. Follow me," replied Jones, eagerly. "My masters just want to see you."

In ten minutes more they were in the public-house, in presence of the cousins.

"Just so," said Jones, checking their questions, "let me fetch 'em some beer and bread first, and then they'll talk like smoke."

He hurried out and, insisting on being the waiter, procured a loaf, some cheese, and half a gallon of beer, at which the two wretches' eyes glistened. They drank, however, first, and then eat with the appetite of wolves rather than human beings.

They then told their story, amid the execrations of the cousins.

"There are a couple of guineas," said the captain, "to-morrow I will give you more. Send me your address. This garb of yours must be changed; go now and rest."

CHAPTER LV.

THE PLOT.

"This is damnable," said the captain, gravely, "she has got us in a trap. These two wretches must be sent abroad at any price, or we are lost. If it costs a thousand pounds—"

"Just so," put in Jones, "but it's my opinion you'll want all the thousands you can get."

"How do you mean, eh?"

"Just so. There's old Emanuel been and taken possession," began Jones.

"But you didn't let him—"

"Just so, I didn't; but he swore awful. It was very hurtful to my feelings as a man," continued Slimy.

"Bother your feelings—go on."

"Just so. Well, I turned him up—but that's nothing, a tempest in a blessed tea-pot," continued the aggravating Jones."

"Will you explain, you vile hound," said the frantic captain, while Honourable John shook as with the palsy.

"Just so—vile hound—that's the thanks get; but never mind, Heaven is just."

"Will you explain?"

"Just so. Corkum Needy's sent Slocum and Stubbles after you both, that's all."

Honourable John laid his head on the table. The captain groaned with anguish.

"It's all up," said John.

"No, by ——," cried the captain, "it is not up. Jones, order a broiled bone and a bowl of punch. Before to-morrow night we shall be better off than ever."

"Just so; what a genius!" said Jones, after obeying their orders.

"Pen, ink, and paper," continued the captain. The obedient Jones fetched them in.

"Hum!" began Frederick, "we'll soap the rascals to a good tune. *Dear Peter*—yes, that will do—*capital spec—going—to—give—*-hem! yes—*give up the security—in exchange—for half the fortune, payable in quarterly bills the day after her dividends are due. Shall pay you in full*—that I will, by heavens—*and want a little more done, at long dates. Write and appoint a meeting. For self and cousin,*

"FREDERICK W."

"That will do for the rascally Hebrew; now for the wily Christian," said the captain. "Let me see—hum! '*Dear Sir,—I am sick and tired of procrastination, so have bargained to give up the heiress and all claim on the estate for fifty thousand pounds, in bills running over five years. The fond mother, estimating her child at a million at least, has consented—so shall give you the short-dated ones, and cash the others at her bankers. Let me know your views.*

"'*Your obedient servant,*

"'F. W.'"

"That will do — trim him up beautifully. Won't he bite?" said the captain.

"But, in the name of Heaven, what does it all mean?" asked the Honourable John.

"You shall know. Post these letters, and then drive dull care away. Drink and be jolly, leave the rest to me. Some way we must disappear, so let us do it jollily."

In the course of the evening, when the Honourable John had drowned his cares in wine, he unfolded his plan. Both heard him with horror depicted in their countenances, and at first refused all connection with the affair. He, however, artfully, and with specious and cunning representations, induced them to change their minds.

"We shall thwing," said John.

Jones grasped his neck grimly.

"It must be done," continued Frederick; "our case is desperate. But no more to-night."

Next evening the two cousins, apparently in high spirits, met Peter Emanuel and Corkum Needy in a quiet City house, celebrated for its wine and punch. At first the money-lenders were very shy; gradually, however, they thawed.

"There must be no nonsense about this," said Corkum Needy, jingling his money.

"Sir, as soon as the girl arrives, I will write, myself, to Mrs. Winterton; you shall post the letter and see her answer."

"Humph!" said Corkum.

However, it was at length agreed that Corkum Needy was to have thirty thousand worth of bills for his claim, Peter Emanuel five for his, while the two agreed jointly to advance ten thousand on the remaining fifteen.

Captain Frederick cried out against it mightily—vowing it was cruel, but the money-lenders were inexorable.

The meeting then broke up.

Four evenings later the same four met again, when Captain Frederick Winterton showed to the money-lender his letter to Mrs. Winterton, and it was with his own hands that Corkum Needy had posted it.

Next evening came a letter with the arms of Mrs. Winterton clearly stamped upon them. The words were very simple :—

"Mrs. Winterton presents her compliments, and will be at No. 4, —— Court, Temple, on Saturday, according to appointment."

Both Peter Emanuel and Corkum Needy examined the letter, the coat of arms, and the cover.

"Dat ish goot!" said the Jew.

"Winterton, your hand," cried Corkum Needy.

"Sir!" said Captain Frederick, in a tone of dignified reproach, "when you are quite satisfied; then I will shake hands. You shall see her come first."

"My dear boy, you don't bear any malice!" cried the money-lender.

"None," said the captain; "but on Saturday, when we dine, we shall be better able to judge how we stand."

CHAPTER LVI.

—— COURT, Temple, is not a pleasant place. Somehow or other few places are, which are in any way connected with law. There is a grave, musty kind of feeling in connection with conveyancing, sueing, entering appearances, and all that, which militates against genial and warm ideas.

Not that lawyers personally are not pleasant fellows, but then that is when they are out of law.

No. 4, —— Court, Temple, was up three flights of stairs, and it had a most business-like appearance. The name of Snaffles stood upon the door in large letters.

The offices next door were to let, and having been newly painted, the door was open.

On the eventful morning of Saturday the two cousins, Corkum Needy, and Peter Emanuel, ascended the stairs.

The latter entered the uninhabited offices, there to watch the course of events; while the cousins went into the lawyer's chambers.

Exactly at twelve a step, that of a woman, was heard to ascend the stairs, and then the money-lenders saw Mrs. Winterton enter the office of Mr. Snaffles.

Both rushed to the door to listen; but there was a baize door inside. They could see nothing. With flushed and excited faces, they returned to their place of observation.

Half an hour passed, and then the door opened, and Mrs. Winterton came out.

The money-lenders listened with intense anxiety.

"No thanks," said Mrs. Winterton, in her grave and solemn tone. "I hope the money may prove the means of restoring you to your position in society. I bear no malice."

And she went down stairs. The money-lenders rushed in, and found Captain Frederick and the Honourable John dancing round the table, and flourishing a whole handful of acceptances.

"Let us look at 'em," said Corkum Needy.

"Boy's play," cried the captain, as if recovering himself. "Now to business."

And he gravely handed chairs all round.

They seated themselves. The lawyer, a grave, grey-haired gentleman—certainly not the Mr. Snaffles of the other transaction—with huge spectacles and frilled shirt, took the chair.

The acceptances were duly examined, and the whole transaction gone into. The arrangement previously entered into was adhered to. The acceptances were endorsed over to the money-lenders, and the balance due to the cousins paid in notes and gold.

It was then arranged that on the following day there should be a further meeting. It being Saturday the moneyed men had mysterious business in the City.

Peter Emanuel went down stairs, followed by Corkum Needy.

They gained Fleet-street, and by one of those accidents which will occur even in fiction—and which occur every day in real life—Mrs. Winterton's carriage was at a jeweller's door.

The two money-lenders looked at one another, and the same impulse came suddenly into both their minds.

Mrs. Winterton was buying a few pretty things to please her Lilian.

"Shuppose we shows 'em?" said Peter Emanuel.

"Right," replied Corkum Needy; "I'm rather shaky about the affair. I'm afraid there's a screw loose."

Both entered the shop, and bowed profoundly to Mrs. Winterton.

The imposing appearance of the great banker and bill-discounter caused the shop-keeper to pause a moment in his description of his wares.

"I believe I have the honour to address Mrs. Winterton," said the banker in a most urbane tone.

"That is my name."

"You have just left Mr. Snaffles?"

"I have."

"Your business was with your cousins?" continued Corkum.

"No," said Mrs. Winterton, with a withering scorn; "my business was with a wretched victim of theirs."

"Mine monish," cried Peter, clutching the counter; "come."

"No," said the banker, livid but calm; "take a hackney coach; go to Bow-street; bring two —six—a dozen officers. Say great forgery on Corkum Needy."

The Jew vanished as the banker displayed his bills to the astonished Mrs. Winterton.

"I never saw them in my life," she said.

"Madame," continued the banker, still coolly, "I have discounted your acceptances for fifty thousand pounds. My name is Corkum Needy, well known in the City. May I ask the favour of an explanation of the scene which passed in that room?"

"Must I?" she said faintly.

"You will have to tell it before a magistrate," continued the banker, urbanely.

Mrs. Winterton seated herself, and explained what had passed.

But we must tell it in our own way.

The letter seen by the money-lender was never posted. A fac-simile of it was substituted by means of that sleight-of-hand which was always supposed to be the origin of the captain's great success at cards.

The letter sent was from a female friend of the captain, who told Mrs. Winterton a most lamentable tale of her desertion by her cousin, after repeated promises of marriage. She declared that he had taken her child from her, and knowing that they had persecuted her girl, she offered to give any information which might implicate the cousins.

Mrs. Winterton accepted her rendezvous at the office of a respectable solicitor, and gave the woman one hundred pounds, with promise of farther support, to start in a respectable business, but declined her information with regard to her child as unnecessary.

She then came away.

By the time Mrs. Winterton had concluded her narrative, Peter Emanuel, haggard, his face the picture of maniacal distress, came in, followed by the officers.

Had he have staked the empire of the world on the hazard of a die and lost, he could not have been more miserable.

"Come," said Corkum Needy, who was very pale, "will you mind waiting, madam?"

"I will wait," replied Mrs. Winterton, in a faint and timid voice.

The banker, who was well known to the officers, now led the way, and in a few minutes they were in —— Court, and bounding up stairs.

The door was open.

"Done, by ——," shrieked the banker.

Except a table, four chairs, and a few old office things, there was nothing in the place. The inner room was empty.

The rage, fury, and despair of the two money-lenders is something indescribable. Still neither forgot the necessary precautions to be taken. Instructions were given to the officers to issue "a hue and cry," and then the two men rushed off to the Bank of England to stop the notes.

Ere the day was out it was found that the two cousins, on pretence of going out to Spain, had changed every note for gold at some fifty different places in the city.

Corkum Needy vowed bitter revenge. The unfortunate Peter, who had before always cheated instead of being cheated, tore his hair and raved like a maniac.

Mrs. Winterton, after waiting a reasonable time, returned home to where Lilian lay, sleeping on a couch, with William Lennox beside her. She was pale and thin, but oh! how happy.

William Lennox beside her—William Lennox faithful. Her mother, to a certain extent, in the possession of their secret: what could she ask more.

"How long you have been away, mamma!" said the pale and emaciated girl.

"Have I?" replied Mrs. Winterton, forcing a smile.

At this moment the doctor entered, and approached his patient.

"Now, good people!" he said, after a quarter of an hour's conversation, "I am going to talk reason. This child is doing well, and I pledge my professional reputation that real change of air would effect a certain cure. We must go to Spain."

Lillian's face flushed, and William Lennox turned pale.

"Oh!" said the doctor, with a comical glance at Mrs. Winterton—he was an old and intimate friend—"Oh! that's the case, is it? Well, my good mamma, I suppose we must marry the young people. Never knew that prescription fail."

Lilian blushed deeply, but William held his breath, and then gasped like a drowning man.

"No, never, until I stand in the light of day," he said.

The doctor stared; Lillian took his hand, and kissed it. Mrs. Winterton looked very grave.

"Heaven knows, and Lillian, that the one dear hope of my life is this little hand;" and as he spoke he took it. "But Lillian knows that I have a duty to perform, for which one thing is required. I must be a man; until twenty-one I am a slave."

"Why not join a regiment? Brave young fellows can always get commissions."

William Lennox looked keenly at Mrs. Winterton. She had seen a life-like twinkle in her daughter's eye, and mother-like—which is saying with deep devotion and love unutterable—she asked no more.

"Come," she said, holding out her hand, "you are my son."

There only remained to obtain the commission.

CHAPTER LVII.

THE CAPTAIN'S STORY.

MEANWHILE Captain George had returned home, and, as he always did, renewed his entreaties that Lucy Lipscombe should become his wife.

"You have not even told me your story," she said, sadly.

"By heavens!" he cried, "if you will have it, you shall. I had not intended until a future day; but as you still suspect me——"

"No," she said, gently, "I do not suspect you; but I wish to know the truth."

"You shall," he said.

And this was the story Captain George told his father, seated in an arm-chair on one side of the hearth, dreamily unconscious, Lucy Lipscombe on a stool, and himself on the rug at her feet.

The room was dimly lighted from the blazing wood fire, which brought out the polish of the old walnut furniture.

CAPTAIN GEORGE'S STORY.

"I can scarcely remember the day when I did not love Ada Wilmot. Lucy, dear, she is a saint in heaven; and in those days I knew you not, so excuse me if I speak the truth.

"In those days we were all very happy; I and my brother Charles were, as you know, twins, and we lived much at home. My father, the duke, had been so disgusted with the college career of our elder brother by his first wife, that he had us educated at home by the joint efforts of a tutor and governess.

"Ada Wilmot was our companion; she was two years younger than us.

"Who and what she was we never knew. We were only aware that our father loved her much and made her a pet. I fancy she was the orphan child of an old companion in arms.

"Well, at twelve years old, it was truly a lovely sight to see little Ada Wilmot with powdered hair turned back, a parasol in her hand, a silk pelisse long enough to shew her beautiful ankles, strutting about the garden with the two young lords, one on each side—one bearing the fan, the other carrying her lap-dog; or, perhaps, seated on a rustic bench, receiving our solemn homage on our knees.

"It was as good as a play.

"But there was to come a change over the spirit of our dream.

"I was nearly nineteen before I began to understand how inexpressibly dear Ada Wilmot was to me. I might, perhaps, have been longer finding it out but that an accident opened my eyes.

"I was hastening down to the shrubbery to join Ada. We were going out duck-shooting on a large lake which bounded our park, and Ada was to steer. I had my gun in my hand, had a shooting jacket on and gaiters. Flushed with health and spirits, I moved along hurriedly—when suddenly I was struck dumb, motionless, dead.

"I had come upon Ada stooping, as my brother clutched her hand, and on his knees poured forth a passionate declaration of love. His hat, his gun were at his feet. Ada was evidently trying to release her hand.

"'My lord, I beg you will say no more, and let me go. I am sorry, very sorry, but it cannot be.'

"'Why not, charming Ada?' urged Lord Charles.

"'Because I do not, cannot love you, except as a very dear brother,' she said.

"Lord Charles Lutterel rose and confronted her with a look which made me shudder.

"'You love my brother,' he said.

"Heavens! I could have fainted, so wild was the sensations that struck me to the heart.

"Ada stood still. Every atom of blood seemed to have left her cheek, and then the rosy hue of health came rushing back.

"'My lord, by what right should I be lectured upon a subject—which—which—'

"'Enough, I see it all,' he said, and stalked away across the lawn.

"Next minute I was at her feet; and so great was her state of excitement, that with little difficulty I won from her the delicious secret that she loved me.

"Excuse me if I say, Lucy, that was the happiest day of my life. I was young, ignorant of all that was evil in the world, and as innocent as the young creature who had plighted her troth to me.

"'But Leopold,' she said, as we walked down towards the lake, 'your brother will hate me.'

"'I cannot help that,' I said, 'we have given him no cause. But not a word of sorrow must darken this bright day—come, my love.'

"And we hurried to the lake, trimmed the sail of our little bark, and without ever thinking of ducks or shooting, spent the hours in repeating the words of our day-dreams over and over again.

"Towards evening we returned home, but my brother had ridden out.

"For days he avoided us, and then when he did meet us out of our father's presence, he was cold, polite—no more.

"Having expressed a wish to join the army, our father bought him a commission in a crack regiment. After that we did not see him for a year. He came for a short stay, stared impudently at Ada, told her she was more beautiful than ever, and turned on his heel.

"His manners were those of a man about town. He was superciliously impertinent both to myself and Ada; whom however, he gazed at, when he thought himself unobserved, with eyes of fire.

"I did not know what to do. I ought to have declared myself to my father, and have obtained his sanction to present her to the world as my future wife.

"I did not do it.

"Ada slept on the same corridor as ourselves, but near to my father's room.

"One night, after twelve, I was roused out of my sleep by wild shrieks and outcries. Throwing on part of my clothes, I darted out into the passage, which was quite dark, and something at the same instant passed me rapidly.

"I did not stop to clutch the person, but hastened to where I saw a light.

"Imagine my dreadful horror and astonishment on beholding Ada's room-door open, and in a chair my father, insensible.

"I rushed wildly to the bed, and there, weltering in her blood, was Ada.

"Her night-dress was open in front, and the handle of a penknife—one I had given her in exchange for a ring—was sticking out from her side.

"She gave me one glance, and, as I thought, fainted.

"She was dead.

"At this moment my father rose to his feet, and advanced towards where I stood, with the bloody penknife in my hand, my limbs trembling, and my eyes filled with horror.

"At this moment my brother entered, followed by two servants.

"'Secure the assassin,' cried my father, wildly.

"'Aye, secure him,' said my brother, 'and take the duke to his chamber.'

"'Secure the assassin!' repeated the duke, tottering towards my brother. Then, with a wild peal of maniacal laughter, he fell down—his reason had left him.

"'Stand back!' I said, in tones of bitter agony; 'a foul murder has been done. But who lays hands on me dies! There has been done, this night, a deed of horror such as the world never saw before. And, as I live, my whole life shall be devoted to its exposure!'

"And with a terrible glance at my brother I went forth. No one dared to stop me—no one believed me guilty.

"I walked out of the ducal mansion. I was mad. I ought to have stopped and stood by my suffering father. But I fled, like a fool and a coward that I was. I grovelled on the earth, when I should have stood erect like a man.

"You must not be angry, Lucy, if I say that I did love that girl with all the deep devotion of a young and ardent mind.

"It is folly to say that men cannot love twice. When the dear and darling object of our first devotion is gone from among us, there is a void in the heart. Nature will have its sway. Some men are different from others. With me the memory of Ada lives as that of a dear sister. I revere and idolise her still. But, the love of the man is yours—

"'I believe it,' interrupted Lucy. 'Think not I am jealous. I admire and esteem you all the more.'

"You are a glorious girl," continued the young man.

He then continued his story.

"I wandered about hill and dale, woods and fields, until hunger drove me to seek food.

"I had very little money about me.

"*I was mad.*

"I robbed. Do not despise me. A jury of my countrymen declared me a murderer and an outlaw. I turned upon society, which scorned me, and became its enemy.

"My history, until I met you, it is useless to tell. I was hunted through the world as an assassin. At length I resolved to leave England, to take foreign service, to win a name of my own, and return only when independent of the world.

"I was told my father was a helpless lunatic.

"I sailed for India. My ill-luck would have it that we were captured by a Barbary corsair, and I was sold into slavery.

"And now, dearest, you know as much of my story as concerns you. The rest I will tell another time."

CHAPTER LVIII.

THE HIDING PLACE.

No sooner had the Jew money-lender left the lawyer's office than all the joviality of the cousins ceased. The aged-looking and respectable lawyer cast off his wig, and displayed the pale and livid countenance of Slimy Jones.

At the same moment a woman rushed from an inner room.

There is a reaction in crime as in everything else. While the pursuit is going on the excitement keeps up the spirits of the schemers; but with success comes fear. No sooner is the deed done than the dread of what may be comes rushing on the soul.

Under the Draco-like laws of England the four knew that they had committed a crime which doomed them all to death.

"Just so," said Slimy Jones; "Jack Ketch and Co. Fine sight!"

"Hush, you fool," cried the woman, who had been employed to play upon the feelings of Mrs. Winterton; "follow me. They may find us out in five minutes."

And without another word they all rushed down stairs.

To enjoy their plunder in England was out of the question. They must hide. No difficult matter, one would think, in London; but still far more difficult than people imagine.

The regular haunts of crime are so well known that it is in vain to trust to their invisibility.

But there are places, not a hundred miles from London-bridge, where fraudulent bankrupts, forgers—aye, even murderers—have concealed themselves for months, until the heat of pursuit was over, when they have fled to foreign countries.

It was night, and in the murky streets of London. The wind whistled round the bleak corners, and the passers hurried by in silence. The heavy tone of numerous clocks tolled solemnly the hour of midnight, when along one of the poorest streets within the city three men, accompanied by a woman, might have been seen making their way towards a house of the most wretched appearance.

It looked like a relic of a chancery suit in difficulties.

It was falling to ruins; straw and rags were thrust into the broken panes, and no smoke ever was seen to rise from its chimneys.

They knocked at the door, broken and shattered as it was. They knocked, it seemed, in a particular way, for it opened quickly.

They entered the passage, and, groping their way, found the bannisters. The woman led the way, which was up stairs, to the second floor.

A faint light glimmered under the door, which the woman unceremoniously opened.

An old man, feeble and ailing, with strange grey eyes, rose from his seat, and looked keenly at the party.

"It's all right, Isaacs," said the woman; "they're just the boys to pay."

"Crib number one," replied the man, whose eyes sparkled as if the gold he was about to earn would go with him beyond the grave.

"Any," continued the woman, "fly coves, with rhino."

"This way," said the old man, with trembling hands.

Taking a small lanthorn, he left the room, and went up stairs, every plank creaking as they trod and menacing to fall in with them. In a few minutes they were in a room more miserable and dilapidated than the rest of the house—so much so that all shuddered.

"Ha! ha!" said the old man, with gleaming eyes; "you don't like it, eh?"

"Poll!" cried Captain Frederick, sternly, "is this your safe retreat?"

"Yes," said the man, "and such a safe one as no man in London can give you. I invented it myself. Just look round! Eh! no constable would guess this."

And he knocked his knuckles against a dilapidated old cupboard-door.

Then, with a peculiarly knowing glance at the whole party, he held out his hand.

"What does the old fool want?" said the captain, in a peevish way; "he is'nt going to put us in that cupboard, is he?"

"I am," grinned the fellow; "ha! ha! ha! Many a good fellow has died game afterwards have hidden in that cupboard. There was bully John Wesket—he died game, he did; went in the cart in a blue and white frock, with a white cockade in his hat. Ah! ah! he eat oranges at his own funeral, he did."

"But what is all this to us? If there is a place of concealment let us see it."

"There was poor Sixteen-string Jack—poor Rann. Many and many a time has he been there, with all the runners in England after him. He died at Tyburn of a hempen fever—most as goes in there does. He wore a pea-green coat, with a big nosegay. It was very touching. I always goes and sees my customers hung."

"Accursed babbler!" roared the captain, "show us down stairs."

The old man held out his hand with a cunning leer.

"What does the lunatic mean?" said the captain, in a towering passion.

"Garnish," said the woman, laughing heartily. "He never opens his crib under ten pounds."

"May I die at Deadly Never Green,* if I do," said the old man.

"Why didn't you say so before?" said the captain, angrily, at the same time searching his pockets for the necessary amount of cash.

The man's eyes glistened with a kind of unearthly joy, as, with trembling fingers that could scarcely clutch the money, he counted the guineas.

---

* Tyburn Gallows, or Tyburn Tree (or Deadly Never Green), was a celebrated gallows or public place of execution for criminals convicted in the county of Middlesex. It existed as early as the reign of Henry IV, and derives its name from Tyburn Brook. It stood on the sight of Connaught-place, though No. 49, Connaught-square is said to be the spot.

"Teyborne, so called of bornes and springs, and tying men up there."—*Minshue's Dictionary,* fol. 1617.

"Tieburne, some will have it so called, from Tie and Burne, because the poor Lollards, for whom this instrument (of cruelty to them, though of justice to malefactors) was first set up, had their necks tied to the beame and their lower parts burnt in the fire. Others will have it called from Twa and Burne—that is, two rivulets, which, it seems, meet near the place."—*Fuller's Worthies (Middlesex.)*

It was a triangle in plan, having three legs to stand on, and appears to have been a permanent erection.

"*Biron.*—Thou mak'st the triumviry, the corner cap of society,
The shape of love's Tyburn, that hangs up simplicity."
        Shakespeare (Love's Labour Lost.)

"There's one with a lame wit, which will not wear a four-corner'd cap. Then let him put on Tyburn, that hath but three corners."—*Pappe with a Hatchet,* 4to., 1589.

"It was made like the shape of Tiborne—three-square."—*Tarlton's Jests,* 4to., 1611.

"I have heard sundry men ofttimes dispute
Of trees that in one yeare will twice beare fruit;
But if a man note Tyburn, 'twill appeare
That that's a tree that bears twelve times a yeare."—*Taylor, the Water Poet (The Praise and Virtue of a Jayle and Jaylers,* 4to., 1623.)

"*Rawbone.*—I do imagine myself apprehended already. Now the constable is carrying me to Newgate—now, now I'm at the Sessions-house, in the dock—now I'm called—'Not guilty, my lord.' The jury has found the indictment *billa vera.* Now, now comes my sentence—now I'm riding in the cart, riding up Holborn in a two-wheeled chariot, with a guard of halbadiers. 'There goes a proper fellow,' says one. 'Good people, pray for me.' Now I'm at the three wooden stilts (Tyburn.) Hey! now I feel my toes hang i' the cart—now 'tis drawn away—now, now, now!—I am gone."—
        Shirley (The Wedding, 4to., 1629.)

But the ruling passion is strong, even in death. Jonathan Wild the Great picked the parson's pocket of a corkscrew at his own execution, and died with it in his hand.

No sooner had the money passed into the clutches of the old man, but he unveiled the secret of his refuge. With a jerk the cupboard door slided downwards, and exhibited what appeared to be the bare wall. This, however, descended in the same way, and disclosed a landing. They then passed into the next house, to all outward appearance as dilapidated as the others in this old and mouldy street, but, in reality, replete with every comfort.

"It's all your own, sir," said the old man, with cringing civility, "until to-morrow evening, at the same time; then I shall come for another ten guineas."

As he spoke, he opened the door of a well-furnished apartment.

"I put the sitting-room at the top of the house. Gentlemen is apt to be noisy. Anything in the world you want you can have, by paying for it."

"I want peace now," said the captain. "Stay, a bottle of brandy."

The old man held out his hand, with the same old glare.

"How much?" asked Captain Frederick, with a contemptuous smile.

"No credit at this establishment, and no change," grinned the old man, actually taking the guinea out of the other's hand.

He then turned away, and left the room.

"Cursed curmudgeon!" said the captain; "why, Poll, is there no better crib than this?"

"It's the best in London; no man ever was took here," replied the woman.

"I don't stop here long," said the officer, sullenly. "That old extortioner —— "

The woman laughed heartily, unable to speak for some minutes.

"What are you laughing at, you fool?" said the captain, angrily.

"Extortioner!" she cried; "that is good. Why, a man with ten thousand pounds in his pocket."

"Hush!" whispered the captain; "not a word. Here comes the old wretch."

There was a strange gleam in the old man's eyes as he set down the bottle.

"Fifty thousand pounds!" he said, holding up his hands in the air. "My conscience! Well, captain, you beat everybody I ever knew. Fifty thousand pounds! Lord, have you got it about you? I should just like to see it. Honest Isaacs is my name—never rob a customer, but never give him change. Have you got a thousand pounds about you—eh?"

"You doting, prating old idiot," cried the infuriated captain, "what are you talking about?"

"Eh!" said the old man, with a look of comic innocence, "Haven't seen the hue and cry—eh?"

All stood aghast at this remark of the keeper of the refuge.

"Just so," whimpered Slimy Jones. "I know'd it."

"What do you mean?" faltered the captain in a milder tone.

"Only a thousand pounds reward for the apprehension of Captain Frederick Winterton, his cousin, a woman, and one Jones," chuckled the old man.

The captain deliberately took a pistol from his pocket.

"Hands off," said Poll. "Isaacs is true as steel."

"Never sold a man in my life—make 'em pay—give no change. What'll you have for breakfast?"

The captain, somewhat reassured by the positive assertions of the woman, gave the necessary orders, and the old man then retired.

Poll—*who had been there before*—now proceeded to light a fire, bringing out glasses and sugar: in fact, made herself quite at home.

"This is not your first visit," said the captain, sarcastically.

"Certainly not," cried the woman, with brutal laugh, "wasn't I here with Jack Rann."

The captain shuddered. He now recollected for the first that the woman he had made use of as an accomplice was the ex-mistress of a man who was hung for forgery.

This did not render his sensations much the merrier.

"I can't stop here," he said, mixing himself a stiff glass of grog.

"Just so," responded Slimy Jones, with a cold shiver through his whole frame. "All be hung."

"Say that again," cried the captain, "and I'll wring your neck!"

"Stop here as long as you like," said the woman; "we're perfectly safe."

"Safe, but its hideous. I tell you what it is, John, we must enlist."

"Not I," said the craven honorable.

"I mean to leave the country before a week is over," said the captain, "stay who will."

"Just so—and leave us to be hung," whimpered Jones.

"This old man has a crib at Portsmouth," said Poll, "where we can hide till a ship sails: where do you want to go to?"

"To Spain," replied the captain; "that's the easiest place. With money one can enjoy one's self everywhere."

"Well, Isaacs' the chap—ship us anywhere," put in Poll.

"*Us?*" said the captain, with a grimace

The girl looked at him keenly for a moment.

"Captain Frederick Winterton," she said quietly, "by using me as an accomplice, you have put fifty thousand pounds in your pocket. We are all liable to be hung—except the king's evidence!"

"All right, Poll," replied the captain, "I was only wondering how you could contrive to go, that's all."

"I go with you. My neck is quite as precious as yours," said Poll. "And besides, captain, I choose to go, for I like you."

———

CHAPTER LIX.

THE MIDNIGHT TRAGEDY.

WITH the interest of the Earl of —— William Lennox found no difficulty in procuring a commission in a regiment then under the orders of the Duke of Wellington—a title then amongst the things to be—in Spain.

It was arranged that they were all to sail in the same transport. Accordingly one afternoon a travelling carriage started from Mrs. Winterton's door, containing herself, Lilian, and William.

Outside rode a lady's maid.

Sweet is the love of woman—so pure, so unselfish, and so fixed on one object. Lilian loved her mother, but the soul's devotion was for him. She looked up to him with a single-mindedness which is the peculiar characteristic of young and innocent girls.

Have you never seen it? If not, you have lost the brightest vision earth with all its wonders and its treasures can show—the glance of a woman's eye that loves you; a look she can never assume; a something that thrills through you, and makes it glorious to live.

Be what we may; succeed as we can in war, diplomacy, or literature; reach to the pinnacle of human glory—and yet is not the proudest moment of our lives that moment when the sweet conviction fell upon our souls that a woman loved us.

Lilian was happy, and the doctor said that with change of air her convalescence was certain.

Their heavy luggage was sent on by wagon. They were in no hurry, and idled along as if time were of no consequence. Lilian had to be petted, so they stopped often for refreshment, or to admire a landscape, or to walk a little.

And then the shades of evening set in. They were now glad to hurry forward, a sudden change having taken place in the weather. The wind howled cheerlessly over moor and hill, so that all were glad to have the windows closed, while the postillions hurried forward as fast as whip and spur would make the horses move.

Suddenly they pulled up, and William noticing the rapid jerk with which they stopped, opened the window, and thrust his head out.

They were on a wide open plain covered with snow. In the distance was a clump of trees.

A loud, fearful, horrid shriek rent the air.

"That ere's a woman being murdered," said one postilion, philosophically.

William Lennox seized his sword, and rushed out. As he did so, three figures were seen flying from the clump of trees.

But no shriek followed; though, as William Lennox neared the place, loud sobs were heard.

The trees surrounded a kind of pool, over which the stars that rose so serenely in the heavens threw a light, like faint moonbeams. The reeds waved in the night air. The moon itself suddenly appeared, and descended brightly on the water.

At first William saw nothing. Then the breeze parting the reeds, he saw the upturned body of a woman, with pallid face upturned towards the heavens.

To rush in and drag her out, was the work of a moment.

"Help!" cried William, wildly.

The post chaise came across the field to where he stood.

The postilion brought a lanthorn, and Mrs. Winterton leaped out; Lilian, much against her inclination, stayed in the carriage

"Merciful heaven!" shrieked Mrs. Winterton, "my cousins."

"What mean you?" whispered William Lennox, with an anxious glance towards Lilian.

"This is their wretched accomplice," replied Mrs. Winterton; "she is not dead. We cannot leave her; she is only insensible."

Without a word, William Lennox fetched a large shawl out of the carriage, wrapped it round the reeking body of the woman, and lifted her into the carriage, with the assistance of the postilion.

They then drove away to the first tavern, where the woman was put to bed. A surgeon was then sent for, who soon restored her to consciousness.

The woman stared wildly around at the group.

"I need not ask who has done this?" said Mrs. Winterton, gravely.

"No," gasped the woman, wildly; "but when I get better ——"

The surgeon looked meaningly at Mrs. Winterton.

"My good woman," said the surgeon, "it is my duty to tell you ——"

"No," yelled the wretched creature, with a look of horror so fearful that they all shuddered, "don't tell me I am dying; I won't die —I can't die. Oh, mother—mother!"

Mrs. Winterton took her hand. That wild appeal to her parent washed away all her guilt; for sacred above all things is that name we seldom revere enough until it exists no more for us.

"Be calm. Everything shall be done for you. Excitement is bad," she said.

"I can't die," said the woman, sobbing.

"It is just possible," remarked the surgeon, very gravely, "that, with care, attention, and nursing, you might recover; but I won't promise. Another such a burst of rage might kill you."

"I will be very quiet, good sir," she said, in a humble and penitent tone.

And still nobody asked her about the murder.

"Are they taken?" she asked in a low plaintive voice.

"Who?" said Mrs. Winterton, now deadly pale and trembling.

"Captain Winterton, John Winterton, and that vile wretch, Slimy Jones."

A thrill of horror went through the whole assembly, but nobody answered.

"Ah!" she said, angrily, "because they are gentlemen they are to be screened. But I say they shall not. Mrs. Winterton, did you love your husband?"

"My God, yes!" shrieked the widow, clasping her hands.

"Would you let his murderers escape?" continued Poll.

Mrs. Winterton closed her eyes. A sense of horror weighed on her soul.

"Be careful what you say," urged William Lennox.

"As I have a guilty soul," said the woman, "I speak the truth. I was a little girl then, that is, I was seventeen; but my heart was bad. I loved Captain Frederick then—you guess the rest—and then he cast me forth on the wide world—with his life in my hands. But I loved him."

"Merciful Heaven! can such men exist?" said the poor widow.

"Your confession must be taken down in writing," remarked the surgeon.

The woman consented, and paper, pens, and ink being procured, she began, a deep, crimson blush overspreading her pale, coarse, but still beautiful face.

"My name," she said, "is Mary Jarvis." As she spoke she avoided the glance of Mrs. Winterton.

"Gracious Goodness! not Mary Jarvis, my school fellow, whose disappearance excited so much surprise?" said Mrs. Winterton, gasping for breath.

"No wonder you did not know me," resumed the guilty woman. "I believe I was beautiful then. Instead, however, of being contented with the station in which I was born, I preferred being the mistress of a gentleman to the wife of a poor man.

"Captain Frederick was on a visit to your husband. He saw me, and paid me all the flattering attentions which an educated and clever man could show to a woman. He flattered me, told me plainly he could not marry me, and seduced by his honied words, I fell.

"Ah, madame, you virtuous women know not what we fallen women suffer. He knew I loved him, and he swore that if ever he succeeded to your property that then he would set public opinions at defiance, and marry me.

"One day—I wonder Heaven did not blot it out of the history of time—I was in Baintree wood with him. There was a pathway through the wood, which your husband, always followed when returning from assize business.

"There was a bank of odorous thyme, on which he sat for some time. When he liked, that man had the seductive cunning of the serpent. I listened to him with charmed ears.

"Suddenly there came the noise of horses coming wildly down the path.

"Captain Frederick rose and took a stout rope out of his pocket.

"'What are you going to do?' I said, half inclined to laugh.

"To make you mistress of ten thousand a-year!" he replied.

"Heaven give me strength!" said Mrs. Winterton, with eyes flooded by tears.

"Oh, madam, forgive me! A wretched girl brought up to mediocre life, to have the promise of ten thousand a-year—it was too much for my poor brain.

"He rose. I watched him as the serpent is said to watch and fascinate its prey. He tied one end of the cord to a tree, about four feet from the ground, and then walked over to another tree and tied it there.

"And still the horseman came galloping on. Next minute he was in sight. We had retired behind a bush.

"It was your husband, madam. The horse itself, I think, tried to check its speed; but in vain Rider and steed fell—the former stunned.

"Captain Frederick Winterton went up to him and deliberately knocked out his brains with a stone.

"My darling husband!' cried Mrs. Winterton; "and your Arabella blamed your imprudence."

"He then removed the rope, and quietly walked away. I, his guilty accomplice, stunned, awed, horrified, fled with him. We went to London, and returned a few days afterwards.

"All the country was ringing with the fatal accident."

She paused for breath, and looked beseechingly at all.

"If I save your life," said the surgeon, gravely, "will you swear to this in a court of law?"

"I will," she fervently replied.

"But explain your present state."

The woman having received a cordial, continued her narrative up to the moment when we left them in the house of refuge.

But as the woman did not know all, we must ourselves give the narrative.

After stopping at Isaac's four days, they managed to procure disguises, with which they left the refuge in the disguise of tramps. The Jew had indicated to them a man who not only would give them shelter, but procure them drafts on Spain for the money, which they had, in a dozen ways, converted in a portable form, never once using their own names.

They started at night, and, avoiding inhabited places, they stopped in barns, in out-houses, slept under haystacks, anywhere where there was little danger of being discovered. At last they neared Portsmouth, and the three men fell back, as if to converse upon some private matter. Poll, whom the captain had artfully irritated, walked on in front.

"I ain't going to take her to Spain," said the captain, in a low tone.

"Weally," cried the Hon. John, "she'll sell us."

"No," said the captain, savagely. "I say, let's get rid of her."

"How?"

"My good fellow, when people are annoying, what do you do?"

"Eh—weally!"

"D—— it!" cried the ruffian; "if you won't understand, knock her on the head."

"That's murder," said John.

"Just so," observed Jones.

"What harsh words you use!" continued the captain; "but as you please. I mean, to put her out of the way."

"We shall be hung," whimpered John.

"We may be hung if we do, but we shall be hung if we don't."

"Why conswult me?" said John, in a low voice; "you never take my advice."

"Because it's never worth taking," sneered the captain.

They were now close to the pond where Poll was found, and taking a pistol from his pocket, the gallant officer in his Majesty's service walked slowly up towards Mary Davis.

"Well, Poll," he said, in a husky tone of voice, "how are you?"

"Ah!" she gasped, turning quickly round, "you are going to kill me."

"Mary!" he cried.

"I know that tone of voice. When you killed your cousin ——"

The assassin flew at her. The poor woman shrieked, and just then the sound of a post-chaise was heard coming up.

He struck her on the head with the butt-end of his pistol, and cast her headlong into the pond. As he struck her she gave a piercing shriek.

This it was brought William Leslie to the rescue.

"I will have no mercy," said Mrs. Winterton, when the woman had finished.

A magistrate was now ushered in, sent for by the surgeon, and the confession was read over, and signed by the woman.

This done, she appeared relieved, and inclined to sleep.

"Mary," said Mrs. Winterton, in a gentle tone.

"Arabella," replied the woman, going back to her schoolgirl days.

"Would you like me to send for your mother?" continued the widow.

The woman opened her large bright eyes, and smiled.

"I am going to my Heavenly Father," she whispered.

She was dead.

CHAPTER LX.

THE REFUGE.

ABOUT four o'clock in the morning after the atrocious murder committed at the pool on the plain, by which name the tragedy was for ever after known, three men with white and haggard faces crept into the streets of Portsmouth, glancing hither and thither as if every shadow were an officer about to apprehend them.

They would not have dared to ask the way, even if there had been any body in the streets, save drunken sailors, who, as the wind howled round the bleak corners of the streets, hurried away to their respective destinations.

The three men were poorly clad, footsore, like men who have walked a long distance quickly. Welcome, therefore, to them was the sight of an ale-house, not yet closed, and from which the noise of mirth and jollity arose.

"Humph, is it safe?" said one, in a harsh husky voice.

"I'm so tired," said a second.

"Just so," repeated a third.

The first speaker drew his cap over his eyes, and with a coarse blustering manner entered the inn, where were assembled none but sailors and women, who were indulging in a noisy dance to the tune of a half-cracked fiddle.

Few looked at the three tramps, who took up their seats in a corner and asked for strong ale, which they drank eagerly, and then assuming a gayer manner, told the waiter to bring them a bone of any thing he had in the house.

A huge cold shoulder of mutton was placed before them, to which all did ample justice, and then loudly called for more drink.

In a dark corner was a man observing them all the time with a strange eye. He was little, short, thin; but there was in his keen grey eye and Jewish cast of countenance something which denoted power, if only the power of cunning.

From the time the three men came in he never took his eyes off them, all the time smoking his pipe and sipping his glass of grog with the most consummate indifference. He looked like one of those individuals who got their living by going about taverns and public-houses with jewellery, false and real, and who sometimes are worth a great deal of money.

The three men devoured their food like persons who had really walked a long way, and in the excitement of refreshment seemed to forget that there was a woman lying with her face stark staring up at the sky, in that marshy pool on the plain.

Having done justice to their food, they called for grog and pipes, which they relished still more than anything else.

"Valk'd a longish vay?" suddenly said a thin cracked voice, which made the three men start and turn pale.

The captain, however, recollected himself and turned his blanched cheek towards the Jew.

"I'm sure our private affairs cannot concern a stranger?" he said.

"Not a bit," continued the other with a peculiar kind of laugh.

"Then why ask us?"

"A little bit of curioshity, to know if you be the gen'lemen," began the Jew, in a whisper, with a cunning and expressive leer, "as my goots friend Isaacs sent me."

"Nykin Nathan," said the captain quickly.

"Esac'ly," said the Jew.

The three men rose, apparently with a sense of relief, and prepared to follow the Hebrew, who put his pipe in his pocket, and led the way through narrow streets and murky lanes, where a stranger would have been utterly lost.

None spoke. The fugitives knew the extremity of their danger. Halters and scaffolds floated before their imaginations with painful vivacity; and when the Jew, who had been on the look out at the only night house on their road, stopped before a gloomy building, and bade them follow him up a dark passage, their relief was great.

He halted at a thick iron-plated door, and knocked in an odd peculiar way, which at once procured admission.

A little stunted Jewess, who had never been pretty, but who now was ugly to a degree scarcely to be described, opened the door.

Not a word was spoken until a kind of parlour, furnished with a considerable degree of comfort, was discovered.

The Jew produced a bottle of brandy, and poured out a glass each. He then sat down, as if with a determination to enter seriously upon business.

CHAPTER LXI.

"£1,000 REWARD."

FAR different was the entry of Mrs. Winterton, Lilian, and their friend William, into Portsmouth. They were very much saddened and shocked by the death of the wretched woman whom Arabella had known in the happy days of her youth, and still more horrified by the cruel revelation she had made as to the death of her husband.

The magistrates had taken the depositions, and the Hue and Cry was full of rewards offered for the apprehension of Captain and John Winterton, with their accomplice, Slimy Jones. Every dead wall in the country was covered by bills headed

"£1,000 REWARD."

The crimes of forgery and murder were fully explained, and even the persons designated.

Everybody shuddered with horror and alarm. No murder had created such a sensation for years. Nobody thought themselves safe; and even in the highest circles people were suspicious of their neighbours.

There was one consideration which made Mrs. Winterton feel all outer things less than she otherwise would have done, and that was the health of her child. Lilian was evidently better. The presence of William Lennox was all in all to her.

They took up their abode at the first hotel in the town, preparatory to selecting the vessel which should take them on their perilous journey, for such at that time was the voyage to Spain.

Besides, they required to travel by easy stages, and they expected a visit from the guardian angel of their fortunes, the Blue Dwarf.

The hotel at which they took up their abode was situated in a lively and pleasant position, so that when Lilian did not feel inclined to go out she could sit at her window and watch the passers by.

William went out continually to make inquiries relative to vessels.

One afternoon Mrs. Winterton and Lilian were seated at their window talking of the past, of the future, of their journey, in low whispers such as a mother and daughter are apt to indulge in—sweetest of all confidences, because unchequered by one selfish or mundane thought—when the mother suddenly ceased speaking.

Three men were passing in the garb of sailors, tanned and tattooed like those who had been long distances, and yet shuffling along as if their feet scarcely belonged to them. Mrs. Winterton turned deadly pale.

"What is the matter, mother?" said Lilian gently.

"Child," replied Arabella, "see where three men walk along in security? They are the murderers—the wretched assassins of my husband, and the poor woman—your relentless persecutors."

And she rose.

"What are you going to do?" said Lilian, who was very pale.

"To have them arrested—"

"No, mother," replied the young girl, "that is not our duty. You have taught me, mother dear, to forgive my enemies. Will you not do the same?"

"Angel!" cried Arabella, returning to her seat; "but I know I am doing wrong."

At this moment a carriage drove up, and the mother and daughter instinctively looking out, saw that it contained the Blue Dwarf and a tall, well-dressed man, to them a total stranger.

The Blue Dwarf, pulling his hat over his eyes and wrapping his cloak around him, alighted from the carriage and rushed upstairs. The ladies greeted him with that flattering eagerness which made him always so happy to see them.

"This is sooner than we expected," they said in one voice.

"Know you not the duty I have come on?" replied the Dwarf, with bitter emphasis.

"No."

"I come for justice. The assassins are still free. The light of Heaven is blasted by the existence of those three wretches, and I will never rest until I bring them to the foot of that gallows tree they have so long merited."

The Blue Dwarf spoke even more harshly than was his wont; his eyes glared, his whole mien was terrible and threatening, and Mrs.

Winterton quailed before him, and looked on the ground.

"Ah," he said, "you know something you will not reveal. Speak, in the name of Heaven!"

"Forgive me, child," cried Mrs. Winterton, in answer to an appealing glance from Lilian. "I must speak. The three wretches passed not ten minutes ago, in the disguise of sailors."

"And you did not denounce them?"

"My Lilian begged their pardon of me," said the poor widow contritely.

"I do not blame her," replied the Blue Dwarf sternly; "but I do blame you. The curse of Heaven will rest upon the land as long as these wretches are at large. Good morning, Lennox. Do you not agree with me?"

The matter was explained. Lennox looked with tender reproach upon Mrs. Winterton, and then frankly confessed that, in his opinion, they were bound to capture the wretched outlaws.

The Blue Dwarf rubbed his hands, and ringing a bell, requested that Mr. Richard Forester might be sent up. The tall gentlemanly-looking man at once appeared.

"This way, Forester. The villains have been seen opposite this very hotel within half an-hour, disguised as sailors. So our work will be easy."

"I don't know," said Forester, in a tone which slightly belied his gentlemanly appearance. "Them coves is very slippery."

"But this lady can give you their description," said the Blue Dwarf.

"Very likely; but if as how they've changed their togs once, they can again," continued the officer.

"Then what is your advice?" said William Lennox, who saw at once that the officer, like most of his class, wished to have his own way.

The Bow-street officer bowed slightly, and then, accepting an offered seat, resumed—

"Them chaps think themselves secure, take my word—uncommon. Now, I purposes as how we takes a walk this evening, and scours the whole of the slums of Portsmouth; only I'm afraid of the crimps."

"Ah!" said William Lennox. "Mrs. Winterton, will you excuse us? I think this matter must be painful to you, and we men will discuss it over a bottle of wine. I've taken your berths."

Mrs. Winterton acquiesced, and retired with Lilian.

As soon as they were gone William Lennox closed the door, after ordering up refreshments, and explained his sudden reason for excluding the ladies.

CHAPTER LXII.

FRANK HALL.

"This morning," he began, "I went out in search of a ship. I saw several, but liked none of them, and was coming along quite downhearted, when I was accosted by a handsome young sailor.

"'What cheer, messmate?' he said. 'You seem down about the gills.'

"I looked up, and saw that I was addressed by an officer, a handsome youth, with a most pleasing expression of countenance.

"'I see you are a brother officer, though of another service, and I thought it odd to see you look so dull,' he continued.

"'I am seeking a berth to Spain for a young lady, an invalid,' I replied, 'and found none suited to her state of health.'

"'Ah,' he said; 'is that all? Well, let's splice the main-brace, and tell me all about it.'

"Won by his manner, I consented; and no sooner had I told my story than he informed me that his father was captain of the frigate which was to convoy the transports, and would, he was quite sure, be glad to give the ladies every accommodation.

"Quick and mercurial in his movements, he took me at once on board. His father was reading the newspaper, and had just perused the narrative of Mrs. Winterton's sufferings, as recorded in an article commenting on the large reward offered. He agreed at once.

"'Certainly, Francis, you rascal,' he said with a hearty shake of the hand for myself. 'But now sheer off, you son of a gun, and attend to your business.'

"I had curiosity enough to inquire what his business was, and I found it was to man the ship, which was short-handed.

"He told me he was coming ashore, to disguise himself as a common sailor, by which means he intended to do the crimps, and get an inkling into the hiding-place of some of the numerous able seamen who were undoubtedly hid somewhere in the neighbourhood.

"Out of gratitude for his services rendered to me," said William Lennox, with an ingenuous blush, "I agreed to make one of the party."

The Blue Dwarf shook his head.

"The very ticket," said the officer. "Them coves is sure to trust to the crimps. Be sure that this very accident will secure the villains."

"Perhaps so," replied Sapathwa, "but it is a very dangerous game."

"I will be careful, my friend," said William Lennox, taking his hand, "but it was not for a soldier to hesitate where a sailor would go. But here comes the identical Frank Hall."

A smart young officer, of stoutish build, was indeed crossing the open space in the front of the hotel, and in a few minutes was announced.

He gave a slight start at the sight of the Blue Dwarf, and bowed gravely to the runner.

William Lennox, however, at once took him into their confidence, and told him they hoped to use the disguise of the night to capture the three ruffians.

"Well," said the young officer, with a slight grimace, "though I don't much like the turning into a thief-taker, I certainly shall assist you here. They are the most unparalleled scoundrels I ever heard of; but what do you propose to do?"

"You and I must track them," replied William.

"That I agree to. You," addressing the officer and the Blue Dwarf, "must keep in our wake as best you can, and have sufficient force, too, to take them. I shall have my own duties to perform."

"Just you, sir, set me on the track, and leave the rest to me," said Mr. Richard Forester, with professional pride.

"Much depends upon yourselves," replied Mr. Frank Hall, rather authoritatively, "and now my dear Mr. Lennox, we must retire."

The Blue Dwarf demurred.

"My dear sir," said the young officer, "we must be ten miles out of Portsmouth in an hour, and the coach is going. We shall re-enter at nightfall, and then you can follow us. Be at the Anchor and Chain, or in view of it, about eight, and if you have eyes you'll see us plain enough."

With these words he hurried his new friend away, and in ten minutes more they were inside the London coach, which they had all to themselves.

"Do you know," said Frank Hall, after a short pause, "that I've seen some one deuced like you?"

William Lennox scarcely repressed a groan.

"Mr. Francis Hall," replied the young man, in a tone of deep emotion, "it is probable on the voyage out that we may have many leisure hours. I will tell you my terrible story. Until then say nothing to remind me of my half—at all events, my foster-brother."

"Well, tell me about the gentleman with the blue face and peculiar hump," said Frank Hall, merrily; "he seems the right sort."

"The best and most faithful of friends," replied William Lennox; "but you shall know all. Let us arrange our plans."

Frank Hall readily acquiesced, and until they reached their destination, a country inn, they spoke only of the adventures of the coming night.

On alighting they engaged a private chamber, and closeting themselves with a box which they had brought with them, in less than an hour were changed into two as thorough-looking young sailors as ever walked before the mast. They then went down, and informing the pretty barmaid that they were bound for a spree, sat down in the public room and took refreshments,

CHAPTER LXIII.

THE CRIMP.

It was about seven in the evening when the two sailors, with bundles on the end of sticks, came in sight of the lights of Portsmouth. They were covered with dust, and their bare feet—they had heroically taken off their bran-new shoes—were one mass of mud.

But the buoyancy of youth was upon them, and they laughed at what many would have thought a terrible hardship. But then Frank Hall had climbed the tarred rigging at fourteen, and William Lennox had been a tumbler.

They walked pretty quick, and presently came up to a couple of stout, middle-aged seamen. Without the slightest hesitation Frank Hall joined them.

"Going into Portsmouth to-night?" he said.

"Yes—why?" replied the other rather sulkily.

"Well, you see," said Frank, hitching up his continuations, "I and my brother here, who's never been to sea afore, we've made up our minds to join ship, but we don't want any of your b—— man-of-war service."

"Right, my little powder-monkey," said the Jack-tar, squirting out a fearful amount of tobacco-juice, "but ater that fine speech."

"Why, you see, we wants to hide till we gets a ship," continued Frank Hall.

"Got any rhino ?" bluntly asked the sailor.

"Well, not a fortin', but a guinea or two," answered the young man.

"Then you'd better find a ship mighty quick. Them —— crimps is worse nor the boatswain with his catenam ninetails. They'll blue your money in a double-shuffle."

"But they'll find us berths."

"Oh, yes; if you'd plenty of money the purser's monkey rascals 'ud keep you out of one long enough; but as you aint, they'll be in a hurry to get rid of you."

"Well, I suppose we must pay 'em," said Frank, in a melancholy tone of voice.

"They'll devilish soon sell you, if you don't ——"

"Perhaps, ater all," put in Frank, "it's better to avoid all imposition, and enter."

"Avast, younker! none of your traverse sailing. I'd say the same, and be too ready to sarve my country; only I don't like every jackanapes of a lord's by-blow, or the son of a cheese-parer; with more money nor brains—I don't want a parcel of beardless boys, as knows no more about the sea nor the tails of my long togs, which I never had, to bully over me. Besides, it's a disgrace to men to be flogged, and I says never, so long as there's a shot in the locker—never."

"Well," said Frank Hall, slightly wincing at the words of the hearty sailor, "I'll take your word for it—and that's a fact."

They had now reached the outskirts of the town, and the sailor, taking the lead, dived into a series of lanes, which would have baffled the penetration of any one who did not know the streets of the sea-port as well as any ship he had ever sailed in.

Presently he halted before a shop, the windows of which were completely screened by a mountain of coarse garments.

"Well, Bully Williams," said the elder sailor, "here we are again, almost aground."

"Ha! ha! ha!" replied a little man, who was standing in the doorway, almost hidden by the huge pilot coats that hung about; "is that you, Fancy Williams? But come in, my men. There's a rare lot of press-gangs about, and the cat goes awful."

The sailors went into a back parlour, where the usual bargain was made. The crimp had a guinea down for each, and then at once agreed to take them to a hiding-place.

These pests, who did more to discourage men from joining the service in time of war, by their lying exaggerations, than all the hired enemies of war in their puling pamphlets, had an interest in all consumed in the dens to which they took their victims, whom they duly provided with ships as soon as their money was exhausted.

The crimp issued from his shop, followed by the four men, keeping close behind him in single file against the wall. As soon as the whole party was at a tolerable distance two figures crept out of a doorway, glided across the street, and followed in their wake.

After about half an hour's walk the crimp halted at the gates of a slaughter-house.

He looked around keenly, and saw nothing. He then darted up between the gates, turned up a narrow and winding lane, and then suddenly halted in total darkness.

"Stand still," he said; and stooping down, rattled a key along an iron grating.

He then rose, and tapped at a shutter.

In a few minutes a light appeared in a kind of area covered by a heavy grating. The light was held by a small girl.

"What do you want ?" she said surlily.

"Bravo, Titsy!" cried the crimp. "That's fine. It's Bully Williams, my tulip, and four fancy men."

"All right!" cried the girl—this time in a jovial voice.

A stout man now stepped forward, and standing on something, drew a large bolt, and pushed up the grating. A ladder now was seen to be the mode of descent, and the sailors went down.

The man remained for a few minutes in conversation with the crimp, and then again made fast everything, and joined his guests.

"We're rather crowded, master," he said, "but the gangs is about tremendous. A convoy sails for Spain soon, and I knows as a good many on em is short of hands."

"That's your sort," replied the elder sailor.

CHAPTER LXIV.

THE ESCAPE.

THE man pushed open a thick door, and the whole party found themselves in a wide long vault, with a row of pillars down the middle. It was evidently the vault of a public-house.

In fact, there had stood overhead, at one time, a tavern both of celebrity and respectability, but which, from a change in the character of the neighbourhood, having become a low beershop, had been hired by crimps, who had turned the former spirit vaults into a place of refuge for deluded seamen.

The locality was so densely filled with tobacco smoke that they could at last scarcely see. After a short time, however, having seated themselves, they found that they were in company with some thirty or forty able and determined seamen, armed with bludgeons, though some displayed the butt ends of pistols.

The four kept together, and found a table in a corner, which was soon covered with mugs of beer, a bottle of brandy, and pipes. All began to smoke—the seamen from pure relish, the others in self-defence.

William Lennox glanced curiously and anxiously around; but though his eye roved over every face and countenance, he could not recognise the three he was in search of.

Frank Hall smoked grimly enough. He felt very much like a mouse caught in a trap. He had not bargained for such a place as this. He had expected to be taken out to some lonely farm-house, from which he might escape.

The stout man was taking his money.

"Do you know of any coasting vessels?" said Frank Hall, carelessly. "My brother here never sailed before, and I think a short voyage will be best."

"Humph!" replied the stout man, fixing a clear grey eye upon them.

"I'd stand a couple each," resumed Frank, rather ostentatiously, showing his tarred hands, hardened, too, by many a pull at the ropes and halyards.

"I'll inquire," said the man.

"And hearkee," continued Frank, in a low tone, "if you could let the youngster have a bed I'll pay extra."

"Want one yourself?" said the man, with a cold gleam in his eyes.

"Oh, no; not I," replied Frank. And then he bent forward—"But the poor boy is quite ready to cry. He's done up. His pipe makes him sick."

"Hollo, mister!" said the man, with a grin, as he turned to William; "This here smoke's too much for you, eh?" What say you to a bedroom?"

William Lennox looked appealingly to Frank.

"Just as you like, Tom," said Frank; only I fancied you'd be screwed."

This was a preconcerted signal, meaning "make the best of your way out."

"Very well," replied the supposed Tom, rising, as if he thought he was being treated like a child. "I dare say you wern't made a salt in a day."

William Lennox followed the man to the end of the cellar, where was another door. On opening it a hogshead was displaced, and they found themselves in a cold, damp, uninhabited cellar. At the end of this was a stone staircase. The man, who was followed by the girl already alluded to, ascended this, and after drawing several bolts, pushed it upwards.

They were in a kind of passage leading towards the front bar, which was deserted, save by one tall man and a short man in an ample cloak.

William Lennox did not even glance at them, but taking a short light, followed the man to the very summit of the house. Every door he noticed was bolted and barred on the outside, like in a prison.

At the top of the house he was shown into a small room, with a low French bedstead.

"Thank you," said William, with a pout, "but my brother is very unkind—I ain't a bit sleepy."

The man grinned, locked the door, and went down.

William Lennox never hesitated a moment, but throwing off jacket, waistcoat, and shirt, unrolled off his body a long and very strong cord. He then again dressed himself, drew a pair of small pistols from his pocket, and stuck them in his belt.

He then went to the window, and found that —probably on account of its great height—it was not barred.

He peered out, and all he could distinguish was a black void. There was neither moon nor

stars twinkling in the heavens. It was, however, no time to hesitate. William Lennox knew, from the look of Frank Hall, that the emergency was desperate.

He attached the cord to the chimney bars, and slowly uncoiled it. Then, with a silent prayer, he committed himself to the rope. By the advice of Frank Hall, he had assumed a pair of coarse gloves.

Cautiously he descended for about two yards, when voices in hot debate warned him to be cautious. A window just below him showed a light, though he could see that a blanket had been hung so as to temper its brilliancy.

Merciful Heaven! how was it that William Lennox did not fall as he heard the following conversation:—

"B—t you!" said an angry voice, "all this wouldn't have happened, if we'd have cut Lilian's throat at first."

"Just so," replied a lachrymose voice.

"I can't twee it," muttered a third.

Slowly, cautiously, William Lennox let himself down a couple of feet, the projection of the window-sill above alone preventing his jerking against the lighted window.

He could now see in through a broken pane, where the three ruffians, disguised as sailors, and dyed so as to be almost unrecognisable, were seated, smoking and drinking at a small round table.

Fascinated by the sight of his enemies, William Lennox lingered a moment too long. The captain was in the act of raising his glass to his lips, when he gave a fearful curse and hurried to the window.

William went down by the run, narrowly escaping breaking his legs as he touched the ground.

The window flew open, a light was held out, and next moment a peal of bells was heard.

William Lennox ran like one behind whom Death was coming hand-over-hand, and suddenly fell into the arms of a tall man.

"Hillo, master," said the man.

"The three are up stairs—second floor."

"What the devil do you mean?" replied the other. "Who do you take me for?"

"I've made a mistake; but do you know the pass-word, Frank Hall?"

"That's it, my hearty."

"At the end of this lane is a grating. That's the entrance; but, let some men follow me. There, no delay," said William Lennox, wildly, "as the three assassins of the woman are hid in that part."

"Perry, take a dozen fellows and follow this youngster," said the gruff tall man.

He then darted up the lane flashing a lanthorn. by which the grating was soon discovered. There were capstans and crowbars in abundance, with which they began to wrench up the bars.

A fearful tumult was heard below, and then all was quiet.

Meanwhile, William Lennox had guided the others round to the front entrance without any noise. It was, however, fast closed.

He listened a moment.

"I'm a Bow-street officer," said a loud voice, "in search for the bodies of three forgers and assassins; beware how you obstruct me in the execution of my duty."

"You're a —— press-gang crew. Put up them barkers—"

At this moment the door flew open. The Blue Dwarf, who had secreted himself at the first alarm, had pushed the bolts. In rushed the press-gang. At this moment the trap-door at the back opened, and a body of sailors came rushing up. They were chiefly wounded men, and were captured without difficulty.

It was evident that the press-gang was gaining the day below, and presently a loud cry of victory resounded and proclaimed the fight was over.

Then two sailors came up, bearing the lifeless body of Frank Hall, who at once suspected, when the alarm was given, had been felled to the ground.

William Lennox knew that he was not dead, and calling to the Blue Dwarf and the officer to follow him, he rushed up stairs. The room occupied by the three assassins was still barred and bolted. William Lennox opened it hurriedly, but a single glance showed him that it was empty.

The rope dangling from the window above showed how the event had taken place.

"Well, never mind," said the officer philosophically; "they can't be far off."

William Lennox shook his head and went down stairs. He felt assured that fear would lend wings sufficient to carry them long before out of reach of all danger.

He slowly descended the stairs, just in time to see Frank Hall drain off a bumper of brandy.

The mortified and defeated sailors were now marched off in company with the crimp, who had been captured returning from the crib, and the Blue Dwarf, the officers, William Lennox, and Frank Hall remained alone.

Regardless of the curses of the owner of the crib, they walked away quietly and adjourned to the hotel.

CHAPTER LXV.

MONEY EASILY WON.

NEXT day Portsmouth was freshly placarded with bills offering the thousand pounds reward for the apprehension of the three assassins, and not only thief-takers, but amateurs were set upon the *qui-vive*.

Not a trace of them could, however, be found.

About midday, those interested in the matter were seated at lunch, when a stranger sent in word he wished to speak with them.

He was ordered to come in.

It was the stout man of the crib.

He glanced strangely at the array of wines and delicacies placed before the four visitors to his house of the previous night.

"I humbly begs your pardings, gentlemen," he said, with a knowing look, "and hopes you'll excuse all errors; but, I've got news of your birds."

"Indeed," replied the runner, coldly.

"Sorry to say, it ain't much," continued the man; "but it'll put you on the track."

"Out with it."

"I'm a poor man," began the beer-shopkeeper.

The officer whispered to the Blue Dwarf, who laid ten sovereigns on the table.

"If the intelligence turns out true, I'll make it a hundred," he said.

"Well, sir, ye see; I didn't go to bed last night; so I wandered down to the port ——"

"To give the alarm to the other crimps," said Frank, quite good-humouredly.

"Well, sir, that's no part of what I've got to say. On the port I met four watermen, and I told 'em what had happened. 'That accounts for the milk in the koker-nut,' says they. 'Three gemmen—when we say gemmen, coves as paid as such—just been rowed out to where a merchant vessel lay to outside, waiting for convoy; and, by gums, them three hadn't been on board a quarter of an hour, when the vessel set sail.'"

"Have you the watermen?" said the officer, with a very blank face.

"Yes, sir," replied the stout man.

"Bring them in."

Four regular watermen soon appeared, who gave the same version as the keeper of the alehouse.

"Where was she bound for?" continued the officer.

"The Sally Jones? For Madrid," said one of the boatmen.

"Thank you," replied William Lennox, handing them each a guinea; "much obliged."

The men withdrew, followed by the stout man, but not before he had received his ample reward.

The officer looked dejected enough.

"You must follow them—hanged or shot, it matters not which," said the Blue Dwarf.

Mr. Richard Forester brightened up, and some further conversation having passed, it was arranged that the officer should seek a passage in a transport, and meet William Lennox at Madrid.

The Blue Dwarf was to remain. The great action between the new claimant to the Blakesley estates and Mr. James Tyrrel Blakesley was coming on.

As receiver of the estates, Sapathwa's presence was absolutely necessary.

With this understanding, two days later, the party destined for Spain sailed in the gallant ship Bucentaur, Captain Sir Harry Hall, with a large convoy, for Spain.

CHAPTER LXVI.

PAULINE AGAIN.

THE young midshipman of the Rainbow, Sir Edgar Blakesley, baronet, had, with great ease, procured leave of absence from his ship, and being in possession of considerable funds, had contrived to obtain sick certificates from some of those loose and disreputable members of the medical profession, happily as rare now as they were then numerous.

His infatuation for Pauline still continued, and there appeared no change in her.

But his funds were at a low ebb, so much so

that Pauline, or the Signora Petronilla, had to supply the necessities of the house.

It was breakfast time. The Signora, in a most elegant dishabille, was seated in a beautiful arm-chair, playing with her spoon and sipping chocolate. Sir Edgar Blakesley was reading the newspaper.

"Philip," said Pauline, in her softest and most caressing manner—she always kept that as a pet name—"will you be kind enough to put down that paper and talk?"

"Certainly, my dear. What about?"

"Business," continued Pauline.

Sir Edgar slightly coloured, but made no verbal reply.

"Money is very scarce, and you know, my love, that for your sake, I am compelled to expend large sums on dress. My salary for the next six months would not pay my jeweller's bill. Now, my dressmaker and all that sort of people are getting pressing. You must visit your banker."

"Certainly," said Sir Edgar, with an uncomfortable grimace, "my banker will let me have whatever I may require, only—"

"What?"

"I am afraid—"

"Afraid, Philip?"

"Of the *other*. Suppose he has betrayed me?"

"Impossible," said Pauline, with a slight curl of the lip; "you have shown yourself everywhere in public; besides, you know he goes by the name of Lennox. For some reason he has yielded the place to you."

Sir Edgar Blakesley shook his head.

"But, Philip," insisted Pauline, "really you must muster up courage to try. We cannot go on without money. I am now at the head of the *corps de ballet* and must keep up an appearance."

"I will go directly," said the young man, coldly.

Pauline's eyes shone like those of a cat.

No farther conversation occurred; and, as soon as the breakfast was ended, Sir Edgar Blakesly, baronet, went out. He was rather proud of his uniform, and wore it constantly.

He walked slowly in the direction of the bank, which was in the city, and when near it—perhaps because he was thirsty, perhaps to give himself courage—he entered a public-house, and called for brandy and water.

He then drew forth a small pocket-book, and proceeded to take from it several papers.

One was a letter from the late Sir William Blakesly to the bankers, commending his son to them in case of his wife marrying again, and requesting them, from moneys in his hand, to let his son have whatever money he required.

The others were a number of blank cheques.

One of these he filled up for a thousand guineas, and put the others in his pocket.

Having drank his brandy he went out, and in a few minutes was at the door of the bank. Mustering up courage, he ascended the steps, and sent his card in to the principal.

On a former occasion he had been received with open arms.

The clerk in this instance returned and said

that the principal was engaged, but that any business Sir Edgar wished to transact could be done through his clerks.

The young man coloured, bit his lip, and presented his cheque.

They had heard of his scandalous life, of his amour with the great ballet dancer of the day. What did he care for that, so they paid him the money? This they soon did in notes.

With a haughty and insolent step Sir Edgar now proceeded to leave the bank. He was already in the street, and about to hail a coach, when he felt a hand placed upon his shoulder, and a low, still voice whisper in his ear,—

"At last we meet, Sir Edgar Blakesley, baronet."

His eyes dizzy, his feet falling under him, the young man turned and confronted the cold, sarcastic countenance of Mr. James Tyrrel Blakesley.

"What do you want?" he faltered, far more dead than alive.

"*Halves!*" said the other, with a sarcastic grin; "but this is not the place to do business in."

The young baronet now remarked that the husband of Lady Blakesly was seedily dressed —had bleared eyes and a cadaverous countenance.

"But what is the matter?" asked the young officer, recovering himself.

"Haven't you heard?" hissed James.

"My mother," said Sir Edgar, with a blush, "never writes to me."

They were now in the parlour of a tavern, and Mr. James at once ordered a copious repast.

"I have been expelled from Blakesly Hall," he said, as soon as the waiter had retired. "It appears that either the late Sir William's elder brother is alive, or has left a son."

"Merciful Heavens!" cried Edgar.

"It is so. But we must fight it out. Why did you not kill *him*?"

"I thought I had," said the young officer, holding down his head.

"Ah!—indeed. But of that another time. Overwhelmed with debt, my wife's jointure is useless. The accursed lawyers and Jews have me in their net. *I am starving!*"

"Impossible!"

"It is true. I was last night in a gambling house," continued James Tyrrel Blakesley.

Sir Edgar Blakesley now understood it all. The pallid face, the shabby clothes, the wretched appearance, were all explained.

"I lost the last penny I had, and have walked about all night. I was hurrying to London Bridge to end my woes, when I met you—my providence!"

And James Tyrrel Blakesley grinned horribly.

The entrance of the waiter stopped conversation for awhile. The wretched gambler ate ravenously. At the end of his repast he pushed it away with an air of satisfaction.

"How much have you there, and what are your resources?" he said, coldly.

"A thousand," replied Sir Edgar, pulling out the bank-notes.

The gambler's fingers trembled as he counted over the money.

'Browse'

" 'And how often," he said, in a faint voice, "can you replenish the coffer?"

"To any amount, if for a good purpose."

"Ah! then by Heavens, we will defend this impudent claim. Listen."

A long conversation ensued, after which a compact was entered into which caused them to separate sworn friends. They then parted. Mr. James Tyrrel Blakesley hurried home to change his dress and generally renovate his appearance, while Sir Edgar Blakesly, aware how impatient Pauline would be, hurried likewise to his, or rather her residence.

He drove up in a hackney coach, and the door once opened, rushed upstairs.

He found Pauline adjusting her dress before pier-glass. She was ready for a drive.

"Victory!" he cried, and, rushing up, kissed her still rosy cheeks.

"Indeed," said Pauline, almost coldly.

Sir Edgar Blakesley drew back.

"Pauline," he replied, "if I hesitated to do what you asked, you know why. But I plucked up courage, and perfect success attended my efforts. I can draw for what I like."

"Indeed," said Pauline, in a most caressing tone; "but before we go out, let us have some sandwiches and wine."

As she spoke, Pauline went to a side-board and placed before Sir Edgar, who had seated himself, his favourite bottle of port, while she took claret. Both filled bumpers, and drank one another's health.

Pauline's eyes flushed with an infernal light.

Sir Edgar filled a second bumper. The first seemed to have added to his thirst.

"One is enough," said Pauline, coldly.

Sir Edgar stared at her with lack lustre eyes.

"Quite enough," continued Pauline, as the young man fell back in his seat, incapable of speech or motion, but in possession fully of the faculties of sight and sense.

With a dexterous jerk, she took out his pocket-book, and concealed it rapidly about her person. She then spoke in a loud voice—

"Come in, Charley."

A youth, not more than twenty-one, tall, fair, and aristocratic-looking, came forth from the bedroom. He looked very foolish and confused. But Pauline ran up to him and kissed him half-a-dozen times, as if she were wildly in love with him.

Sir Edgar gave a low howl of rage.

"Eh—what's that?" said the youth.

"Sir Edgar Blakesly *drunk*," replied Pauline, scornfully, as she cast a shawl over her lovely shoulders.

She then turned her back to the youth, who stood half irresolute, half frightened, and gave the unfortunate Sir Edgar a look which almost brought him to his feet.

But Pauline knew too well the power of the dose to be alarmed. She calmly tucked up her petticoats, so as to display her foot and ankle, took the arm of her new protector, and left the house with the Most Noble the Marquis of A—.

It was an hour before Sir Edgar recovered from a kind of lethargic sleep into which he fell.

He then drank copious draughts from the wine bottle Pauline had used.

This done, he sat down to meditate revenge, and there swept over his soul a dread idea, one so awful and malicious that it consoled him for all. And still he loved Pauline, in his way, more wildly and passionately than ever.

That night, when the amorous marquis drove away from the opera in a close carriage with his new conquest, there was one more passenger behind than he bargained for.

CHAPTER LXVII.

THE GAMBLER'S WIFE.

IN a shabby second-floor, in a very shabby street off the Strand, lay on a bed, apparently of sickness unto death, the Lady Caroline Blakesley, widow of the late Sir William, and wife of James Tyrrel Blakesly.

There was a miserable bed-room, and an equally miserable sitting-room. This latter had a carpet in the middle, which showed only more prominently the dirt of the portions near the wall, a rickety table, two chairs, and a broken-down couch. The windows, which had no blinds, required none, so thick was the coat of dirt they exhibited. On the table was an empty gin bottle, a pack of dirty cards, a candlestick guiltless of any contents, and two broken mugs.

The fire-grate was empty.

A frying-pan and kettle ornamented it, but not a scrap of food or drink could be seen anywhere.

The woman lay groaning and moaning on the bed, almost insensible. Her illness was one commoner than is believed. She was dying of starvation.

Young ladies, who in the bloom of youth and health, affect to have small appetites and scorn to eat wholesome meat, remember you are often laying the seeds of consumption !

It is not quantity that we want, but quality.

To those who have good, hearty appetites, how wearisome is the half-hour before dinner, how trying the hour which politeness compels you sometimes to grant to a defaulter.

Imagine forty-eight hours without food !

There are hundreds daily—nay, perhaps thousands—who endure this agony. Not beggars, not those who besiege the poorhouse gates, but the bashful poor, who cannot find work, and to beg are ashamed.

Therefore is it that there should be zealous visitation of the humbler homes of England; for for every one that expireth from want shall a judgment be recorded.

A mighty and wealthy nation like England should know no poor.

Away with your vast pleasure-grounds and parks, if there be not soil enough to give employment; down with your vast chases and hunting-grounds, and abolish even royal forests, if they are in the way.

Governments seem created to protect the rich only, to secure their property; why not protect the poor against the rich ?

The day will come when the poor will know that, if there is no work for them, they must be kept, and that the land of God's creation is the common property of all.

Legislation will then be too late.

The groans of the woman were faint, but her hearing seemed quick enough; for when somebody lifted the latch and came in the front room, she spoke, very lowly, it is true, but in a querulous tone of voice.

"Who's that?"

"Weel, and it's Mrs. Maconichie," said a dry, harsh Scotch voice—musical or very harsh are the tones of our northern brethren—"come to knaw if you're a going to pay ?"

"My good woman," replied Lady Blakesly, faintly, "you know I have no money."

"Thin, why do you gang aboot taking people's places ?" said the woman, sulkily.

"One must sleep somewhere," sighed Lady Blakesly.

"You'll be going hame," said the woman, more gently.

"What mean you, woman ? I have no home," replied the sufferer, wildly.

"Ah, my puir creature ! I mean our lang hame, which none can deny."

"Do you mean to say I'm dying ?" shrieked Lady Blakesly.

"Weel, I think ye'll hae peace soon."

"Then, I'm murdered," cried the sufferer, "murdered in cold blood; for I am dying of starvation while my husband spends my gold in riot and gambling."

Several rapid steps were now heard on the stairs, and in another instant Mr. James Tyrrel Blakesly rushed into the apartment, his eyes flashing with excitement and pleasure. He was followed by the servant of a hotel.

"Get up, Caroline," he cried; "all is right. I beg your pardon, Mrs. Maconichie," he added, in a more stately tone, "I did not expect to find you here; but so much the better. Here's a twenty-pound note; find a trusty messenger to send for all these."

And in a mysterious kind of way he thrust the money and a bundle of pawn-tickets into her hand.

"Pay yourself, ma'am; and now levant," he added, addressing both waiter and landlady.

"Is that you, James?" whispered the almost inanimate woman.

"Yes, Caroline. But do not be angry. I, too, was starving an hour ago, when a lucky chance brought me a friend. Here, take this glass of wine; it will revive you."

He poured a cordial down her throat, which at once brought her to, and then sitting up in the bed, she made a meal, such as had not passed her lips for many a long day.

Before it was ended, a slight amount of colour had come to her cheeks.

"What has happened?" she said, pointing to a bottle, at some distance, on the table.

It was a bottle of gin—the fearful refuge from despair to which the gambler's wife had flown.

It is too often thus. The votaries of this fearful and accursed vice — hell-born of all others—send not only themselves to perdition, but draw after them a whole hecatomb in their train.

The husband explained as far as he chose, and then went into the next room to change his clothes, the landlady having by this time brought in numerous packets from the pawn-broker's.

He dressed himself with extreme care and attention.

"Where are you going?" said his wife, querulously.

"To the club."

"All night, I suppose; and ruin to-morrow."

"I have an inexhaustible bank. Besides, I shall be cool now that I know I have resources. It has been my very desperation that makes me lose."

Lady Caroline rose, and, taking her own bundles, dressed herself once more in the garb of a lady.

In a few minutes more the two sallied downstairs to have the door opened by Mrs. Maconichie, who could not sufficiently curtsey her admiration of her lodgers.

"You had better leave me some money," said Lady Blakesly, as soon as they were in the street.

Her husband unhesitatingly gave her fifty pounds in small notes.

If the worst came to the worst, it was a last resource.

At the end of the street the two parted.

. . . .

It was much past midnight. A candle burnt low in the bed-chamber of Lady Blakesly, who lay on her bed evidently insensible from drink, while the pious and virtuous Mrs. Maconichie

snored soundly in an arm-chair from the same potent influence.

Suddenly a step was heard on the stairs, the door opened, and a figure stalked in. It was Mr. James Tyrrel Blakesly—pale, haggard, and looking each way for some hidden enemy.

He smiled a grim and ghastly smile as he saw the state of the case.

In another instant he had rifled his wife's pockets of every farthing, and was stealing downstairs like a lurking midnight thief as he was.

———

CHAPTER LXVIII.

THE VILLA.

The private villa of the Marquis of A—— was a model. Not even the eccentric, versatile, and ingenious author of "Monte Christo" could boast anything more lavishly ornate.

It had been erected as a kind of temple of Venus, and the pictures, statues, and ornaments were all, to say the least, characteristic.

They did not alarm the modesty of Pauline, who had overstepped all the bounds of decorum long ago.

All that she cared about was that everything around her betokened wealth.

Supper was served in an apartment furnished in the most exquisite style. Everything that art could create, or the imagination could conceive, was put in practice to sate the wearied eye.

The supper itself was a marvel of *cuisinerie*. No wonder. The cook of the Marquis of A—— received the wages of an ambassador.

Pauline was in the most delightful spirits. She ate and drank of everything, and insisted on waiting on the Marquis in her ballet-girl costume, which, the more to fascinate the youthful nobleman, she had not taken off.

The young man was, indeed, fascinated.

Suddenly a fancy seemed to strike the artful girl.

"I should like to see my own room," she cried.

The Marquis rose.

"Fie!" she said, laughingly. "I also want to see my femme de chambre."

The Marquis laughed and rang. A male servant came.

"Send Rose to your mistress," said the nobleman; and in another moment Pauline glided away to the chamber provided for her.

The Marquis re-seated himself near the table, filled a bumper, pulled out a cigar, and began to luxuriate on his new conquest.

This young nobleman, heir to a splendid estate and to an honourable name, which we shall not even indicate, had come into his fortune at an age when men are rarely able to be trusted with a five-pound note.

Without anybody to guide him he had launched out into the most wild dissipation that can be conceived, to which the more refined vice of the present day is as nothing.

It is not our intention to defile our pages with any of that pruriency which so delights and degrades the French nation, and which surely will degrade them much more.

A nation must fall when its national and popular literature is written by men whose proper vocation would be that of doorkeeper to a house of ill-fame.

But in painting real life it is not possible to make all *couleur de rose*. A voluptuary will always be a disagreeable character to paint.

The marquis sipped his champagne with a kind of half listless, half self-satisfied air for some little time, and then, as if he thought he had waited long enough, rose with something like a yawn to go upstairs.

"No you don't," said a cold, stern, terrible voice.

The marquis, by nature no coward — no Englishman is—but, the slave of his vices and dissipation, quailed as if he had been shot.

Right in his way, cool, collected, a brace of pistols to back his intrusion, was a man of a most singular appearance. He had a scratch wig, a very red moustache, a half-black complexion, and, at the same time, a most angry look.

"Who the devil are you, sir?" faltered the young nobleman, endeavouring to bluster.

"The devil," said a sharp but powerful voice, "is, I should say, so intimate a relative of your own as to be the last person you ought to quote."

"This insolence, sir—"

"Blustering is of no use here," sneered the apparition. "Pray be seated, my lord."

The nobleman looked at the bells which hung around the room.

"It is of no use, my lord," said the apparition, "at the first attempt at alarm I will stab you to the heart, fire a pistol, and leave you to be buried, as the poet says, with a stake in your inside."

"What do you want?" cried the appalled marquis.

"Have you any cards?"

"Plenty."

"Then produce them and we will play."

The marquis thrust his hand in a drawer and pulled forth a dozen new packs.

The apparition opened a couple and began to shuffle.

"What are we going to play for?" said the marquis, rubbing his eyes and pouring out a tumbler of wine.

"Your very good health," replied the stranger, "we will play for the signora!"

"Sir—"

"Exactly—you love her; so do I. You came in just a moment too soon. I had paid for her."

"Paid for her!"

"Sir Edgar Blakesley had sold her to me, and being a man of his word, he was kind enough to inform me of the transfer she had made of herself without his authority. Now, as I dare say she has received consideration from you, I propose to play."

The marquis listened without understanding; he was totally bewildered. He kept on drinking champagne. Presently, in a most unaccountable manner, a bottle of port came near to his hand.

He drained a tumbler, and as he did so, he fell back all but insensible.

"Good night, marquis," said the apparition, rising.

His countenance was terrible to view. Hate, revenge, and every bad passion of the human heart fluttered round his brow. He approached the marquis and bound both hands and feet.

If eyes could have killed, those of the marquis would have done so : they darted, however, harmless fire.

Then the stranger clutched one pistol, putting the other away, and left the room.

The staircase leading to the upper apartments was carpeted so thick that not a sound could be heard. The apparition could hear the whispering of two women; and still he advanced.

"The marquis!" said a hushed voice, and next minute footsteps were heard hurrying down a back stair.

The apparition entered the bed-room, the luxury of which is rather to be conceived than described, and stood at the foot of the bedstead in which lay the lovely but frail Pauline.

"Wretch!" he said.

The girl, in utter amazement, sat up on that downy couch, and saw before her a man of whom she knew nothing. In one hand was a pistol, in the other a bottle.

But the pistol she cared not for—it could only kill.

In large letters on the bottle was written one word of awful import—

VITRIOL.

Pauline fainted outright. She had no need to ask whence the punishment came.

CHAPTER LXIX.

THE DOUBLE CAVE.

AWAY over the stormy seas, guided by the bright lamp of hope and love, sails the Bucentaur, bearing in its mighty flanks the fortunes of William Lennox and of Lilian.

The voyage was most fortunate. Not an adverse wind checked the progress of the convey, which anchored without a single casualty.

We have thus, it is true, lost the opportunity of showing our powers of description, of painting waves mountain high, of strewing our pages with wrecks, ruin and death; but we are all the sooner in Spain.

The first news which greeted the ears of William Lennox was, that the Sally Jones had arrived three days before them, her strange passengers having left her in a small boat before coming to an anchor.

The skipper, after some hesitation, owned that they had paid a thousand pounds for their passage money.

Mr. Richard Forester made a wry face, but it was no use to repine.

The lovers were delighted with Madrid. Gladly would they have remained quiet in their hotel; but the arrival of a lovely English girl was an event which excited so much enthusiasm that both William Lennox and Lilian were compelled to accept innumerable invitations to balls and parties.

Then came the welcome order to join his

regiment, which occupied a small station in the interior distant one hundred miles.

Mrs. Winterton gladly availed herself of the opportunity to take Lilian into one of the interior towns, said to be unusually healthy.

With this view, a whole drove of mules were hired, servants engaged, and an escort of six raw recruits for his regiment, placed under the orders of Ensign William Lennox.

Mr. Richard Forester, transformed into a kind of steward or major-domo, joined the party in the vague idea that somewhere or other his individuals, as he called them, would turn up.

Bright and glorious was the morn, when, amid the acclamations of the few friends who had risen at so early an hour, the cavalcade started. Lilian, in a riding-habit of most approved make, rode a mule, as did her mother. Two half-terrified English girls, and one bold and fearless Spanish girl, who spoke English enough to be interpreter, followed.

Then came sumpter mules, and muleteers, and the six raw-boned, but sturdy Englishmen, who had been sent out from the depôt in England.

William, now in full uniform, mounted a powerful grey charger, the sturdy Richard following on a fat and stalwart pony.

A lad on foot, something between a thief and a gipsey in look, but said to be faithful, led the van as guide.

To avoid certain positions in the possession of the French, they were going to follow a most peculiar and circuitous route.

The first day brought about no events of any consequence. They rode along conversing, halted to lunch under the shade of some cork-trees, and took up their quarter at a large inn, where they found, as usual in Spain, plenty of large vacant apartments, vermin, and bad wine.

Fortunately they were amply provided with provisions.

The whole party were infinitely amused, and when night drew in, William Lennox, who had provided a select library, read some passages about Spanish inns from two of the best novels ever written by human pen, "Don Quixote" and "Gil Blas."

After this all retired to rest, as the march was to be resumed at daybreak.

They were now about to enter upon the exploration of a mountainous district, said, during those troublous times, to be infested by whole gangs of robbers, who preyed equally upon friend and foe.

William Lennox went to the front with three of his recruits, leaving Richard Forester in command of the other three in the rear.

The muleteers, though not much to be counted on, still flourished their old musquetoons, and looked particularly fierce.

In this way they entered a deep and long defile, gloomy from the denseness of the cork and other trees which lined each side of the path. About twelve o'clock they began to ascend a steep and rugged pathway in the hills, while the trees began to be scarce, and the whole aspect of the scene rugged and arid in the extreme.

About one the muleteers began to urge forward their beasts.

"What is the matter?" asked William Lennox, eagerly; "any signs?"

"I fear, signor," said the chief of the muleteers, "that we are about to have a borasco. The sky looks wild and threatening."

William Lennox looked upwards, but saw no signs of a coming tempest.

The guide came hurrying back.

"On—on!" he cried, "or we shall be blown over the rocks by the wind, drowned by the rain, and burnt up by the lightning."

William Lennox at once saw that something terrible was coming, and urged forward the mules by every means in his power. The animals themselves, as if aware of the danger, rose their speed to a trot.

"Where can we find shelter?" asked William Lennox of the guide.

"In the grotto of Alcantara," said the boy, gravely.

Before any one could speak, a fearful flash of lightning, followed by a roar as of artillery, announced the coming storm.

"Yonder is safety," said the boy, pointing to a grove of cork-trees.

No one spoke again. Everybody urged forward his steed with every exertion of whip and spur. William Lennox holding his own bridle in his mouth, dragged forward the mules of Lilian and Mrs. Winterton, one with each hand.

Suddenly the whole party seemed to disappear in a yawning gulf, as the whole force of the storm burst upon the circumambient air.

Wind, rain, lightning, came upon them with a rapidity perfectly terrific, and made everybody thankful for the shelter they had attained to, whatever its character might be.

The guide and muleteers evidently knew the road well, and were amply provided with torches, which being lit, showed that they had entered beneath the vast roof of a cavern fit to have concealed a hundred horsemen.

It was evidently a very usual halt, as on all sides were signs of fires and other marks left by previous travellers.

The guide pointed out several chambers in the rock, one of which was at once appropriated to the ladies, and soon the gloomy expanse was illumined by a fire that made even a cave look cheerful, while desolation and wrath was doing fearful havock outside.

William Lennox and the officer selected a kind of niche a little higher up in the cave, leaving the muleteers and soldiers to bivouac in the larger chamber.

The storm lasting until considerable after sunset, it was determined to pass the night there.

After the evening meal, by general consent, all retired, leaving a sentry at the entrance, who was to be changed every hour.

William Lennox laid himself on a kind of ledge, and wrapping himself in his cloak, wooed slumber in vain for some time. At length his eyes, as if weary of watching the distant form of the sentry walking up and down, closed, and he fell into what appeared to be a sound slumber.

He never thought of inquiring how long he slept, but he was suddenly aroused by a strange and peculiar noise. He opened his eyes, and glancing upwards, saw a stream of light fall upon the roof of the niche from a small aperture above his head.

He distinctly heard voices.

Rising with extreme caution he stood on his feet and peered through a kind of loophole in the solid rock, not wide enough to have admitted his hand.

Three men in Spanish dresses were engaged in the task, as he at first thought, of digging a grave. One held a torch; the second listened with evident dread; the third was engaged in digging, sometimes using a spade, sometimes a maddock.

William Lennox nearly shrieked.

The digger was Captain John Winterton; the listener was the Honourable John; the man with the torch was Slimy Jones.

Holding his breath, William Lennox awoke Richard Forester, and drew him away. In two words he made him aware of his discovery. The officer, enchanted, hastened to peer through the hole, while William Lennox aroused the chief muleteer.

The man sat up.

"Three ruffians we are in search of are in yonder cave," said William, pointing to the light; "how can we get into it?"

"Ah!" replied the muleteer, "I have heard there was a communication. Well, Signor, unless you can get through that hole, you must go twenty-one miles round to the other cave."

Ere the young cornet could give vent to his disappointment, the report of a pistol, and a loud cry from the runner, startled the whole of the inhabitants of the cave—the woman began to shriek, the soldiers ran to arms, and the din was awful.

"Silence!" roared William, fearful for Lillian; "it is a false alarm."

"My jawbone!" cried Richard Forester, in a lachrymose tone; "the villains!"

"There is nothing the matter," said William, advancing to where Mrs. Winterton stood; "sleep in every confidence—we are watching."

The women ceased their wailings, the soldiers returned to their couches, and William Lennox, drawing the runner, who was slightly wounded in the face, on one side, obtained an explanation.

It appeared that while peering at the three ruffians about, as he believed, to bury their treasure, he had, in the intensity of his anxiety to watch every movement, pressed very hard against the opening, and drawing a long breath, quick as lightning, the Honourable John fired, slightly grazing the face of the over-anxious officer.

Of course, on examination, not a trace of the three villains could be found.

And then William Lennox's orders were to join his regiment without delay. Nothing then remained but to continue on their journey, leaving any further meeting with the assassins to the chapter of accidents.

CHAPTER LXX.

A STRANGE MEETING.

WHEN Captain George had finished his narrative of the terrible murder of Ada Wilmot, he was struck by a certain twinkle in the eyes of his father. For a moment he fancied that reason had returned, and he awaited eagerly the first word which should emanate from his lips.

But none came, except a whimpering demand to be put to bed.

This was done by Snow, who came in at the first summons.

"Will his reason never return?" said Captain George, clasping his hands over his aching forehead.

"Be hopeful," replied Lucy.

"Hopeful!" cried the captain, bitterly. "Have I not hoped to be your husband some fourteen years, and am I still to hope on, hope ever—my fate dependent on the frail fabric of an old man's life?"

"George," said Lucy, glowing with blushes, "if that is all that is needed to make you happy, I will delay our union no longer."

"Heaven bless you, my Lucy!" replied the captain, rapturously.

"But the Church must sanctify our union?" continued Lucy, still holding down her charming head.

"It shall. I know an excellent minister, once a curate in our neighbourhood, who has heard my story, as a priest might do, under seal of confession; and this very night —— "

"Not to night," said Lucy, tenderly.

"It must always be at night," replied Captain George, gaily; "and as the song says, I shall take you while you're in the humour."

"As you will; but be careful, for my sake," faltered Lucy.

"That will I," replied the captain, and taking his cloak, slouched hat, and pistols, he passed through the cellars to the entrance leading to the small street in the Strand.

Not at all fearful of being recognised at that late hour, he turned into that crowded thoroughfare, and stepped rapidly forward. There were but few passers by, and yet scarcely had he walked a dozen paces, when there darted from an alley a girl in tatters.

"For the love of mercy, good gentleman, buy a flower, or give me a penny. I am starving," she said.

There was a dim oil lamp close at hand, and as the captain put his hand in his pocket to feel for some coin, he gazed curiously at the beggar.

She was a little, short, stunted girl, but so thin and attenuated as to appear in the last stage of consumption.

"My poor girl," he said, "you should not be out like this at night.

"No home—no bed—no food," she murmured.

"But I will take you where you shall find all," he replied, kindly.

At this moment a jaunty young sailor in "full nauticals" came up, glanced at the two, gave a wild look of surprise, and, rushing forward, caught the beggar in his arms.

"Poll."

"Joe."

Captain George saw at once that the girl had fainted.

"Follow me," he said, darting down a narrow passage, where he saw a well-known light, that of the Coal Hole, shining in the distance.

In another moment they were in a room of the tavern, luckily untenanted, while Captain George, who had snatched up a decanter of brandy, was pouring some of it down her throat —more of it over her face. The instant he saw she was coming to, he went out, and restored the decanter to its astonished owner.

In about ten minutes he returned and found Mary sobbing violently.

"My interesting friend, Joe the Mudlark," said the captain, drily.

The lad blushed.

"That was my name once, but, thanks to Master William Lennox, I'm Joe the sailor boy now."

"I knew all about it," said the captain, holding out his hand. "Now, you see and give Mary some proper nourishment. I have some business, but will return in an hour. I have secured the room, so order what you please."

With these words the captain hurried from the room, leaving the lovers to their explanations.

CHAPTER LXXI.

THE VICAR AND HOUSEKEEPER.

THE Reverend Dionysius Scrimgour was a vicar of St. Asoph's-cum-Vinculum, a church and parish which the learned reader will vainly search for upon the maps, or in any account of the city of London. It is not always wise or discreet to give correct indications of the places you are describing, as in this way the real names of your personages may be too easily discovered.

Be this as it may, the Reverend Dionysius was vicar of a parish which we shall call St. Asoph-cum-Vinculum, and never was vicar less suited to his congregation.

The worthy gentleman had a church and a district, and considerable business in burying his neighbours; but his congregation was a myth. Somehow or other, whether he was too good for his parishioners, or whether the eloquence of Little Bethel prevailed over orthodox preaching, a fact it is that the Reverend Dionysius might generally on Sundays have shut his church up, as far as a congregation was concerned.

Nobody ever came to hear him preach.

The simple fact was, that his temple was set up in one of the lowest and most dreary quarters of the south side of London. The *genus homo* in his district was chiefly composed of those who prefer Hampstead-heath, Battersea-fields, and the Isle of Dogs, to church on a Sunday morning; in fact, it was composed of all the loose Punch and Judy men, dog fanciers and stealers —if there be any distinction between the two— cats' meat men and sausage makers, purveyors of stray kittens to disconsolate virgins of forty, knackers, bone-boilers, tallow chandlers on a grand scale, ivory-blackmen, leather dressers,

and all the other pariah trades to which poor humanity in large towns is liable.

Now, the Reverend Dionysius Scrimgour was a lazy man, who dearly loved to pore over a Greek play, or annotate Herodotus. He could dream over old Homer, or cudgel his brains with his commentators, annotators, and improvers, for whole months—in fact, do anything that was utterly useless and idle.

To read Greek poetry may be a very pleasant and a very proper thing—so is prayer and fasting; but a man should not fast every day—nay, it might disagree with him if he did; neither should a human being, with a head, containing brains, on his shoulders, pass his life in one continuous course of study.

We come into this world to do, not to think; and until we have done something, our advent has been a failure.

The Reverend Dionysius Scrimgour was not of the same opinion. His conception of life was ten hours a day of Greek poetry, flavoured, by way of sauce, with a fair modicum of Latin and a very small dose of Divinity. Preaching he abhorred, and when his parishioners died he generally tried to lump the burials all into one day.

And a better man never lived than the Reverend Dionysius, whose heart was in the right place, but whose head was screwed on a little on one side.

He should certainly have been married and perpetuated the milk of human kindness that was in him; but here his constitutional laziness interfered, and made him the bond and captive slave of a housekeeper.

The church of St. Asoph-cum-Vinculum had a churchyard, in which the mouldering deposits of ages lay quiet, except when the sexton turned them up six times a week to prepare the last earthly tabernacle for some of the *genus homo*, already alluded to. This churchyard abutted on the Thames, which the oldest inhabitant was often heard to declare was one of the many causes of the softness of the river water.

The vicarage was a little old house, dating from the time of that female tyrant whom servile pens are pleased to call the great, just as time-serving writers designate the Nero of modern times the greatest man of his age.

It communicated with the church by means of a low, dark passage, that would have delighted the heart of the great Mrs. Ratcliffe;* but the passage was seldom used.

Looking out on the churchyard was the library of the vicarage, a room in which the reverend gentleman passed the greater part of his time reading, smoking, and slowly imbibing beer or coffee—that slow poison which Voltaire said took sixty years to kill him.

On the night in question, the vicar, a tall, lanky, cadaverous specimen of humanity, was deep in the mysteries of Hecuba, pausing only in his dreary task to re-fill and light his capacious pipe, when, at the dread hour of midnight, when

---

* An illustrated penny edition of her wonderful novel, "The Mysteries of Udolpho," is being published in the "Parlor Journal Novelist." No lover of the mysterious should be without this book.

ghosts are said to walk—a feat as difficult as for fairies to sit, we should say—there came a knocking at the window.

The reverend gentleman gave an impatient pshaw! laid down his book, and proceeded to light his pipe. He then took a deep draught from a tankard of old ale—Heaven preserve the most vigorous intellect from beer and Greek, the grave of so many Germans—and was about to resume his studies, when again the casement was shaken vigorously.

"Go!" said the vicar, who indulged freely in monosyllables.

"Dionysius!" cried a loud voice.

"Ah!"

"Open the window."

"That voice!" said the vicar; and, slowly and methodically, he rose and opened the casement.

"Leopold Lord Lutterell!" he cried.

"Hush! I'm still Captain George," replied the highwayman, leaping in through the window.

"*Sum*, I am," cried the vicar.

"The same old boy," said Captain George, laughing, "and this is the same old ale. Well, order in another quart. I have to tell you much. It is some years, Dion, since we met, and, by heavens! we will have a frolic."

"*Amo*, I love thee, above all men!" said the parson, staring wildly at the speaker; "but what will Mrs. Wilkins say?"

"And who the devil is Mrs. Wilkins?" cried Captain George, laughing.

"*Diabolus—sum*—I mean Mrs. Wilkins is the devil — I mean housekeeper," faltered the student of Greek.

Captain George coolly rang the bell rather in a sharp style.

A good-looking dame of about thirty-five came bustling in.

"Heaven have mercy on us, Dionysius!" she began. "Sir—I beg your pardon; what would you please to want?"

The housekeeper had entered so quickly, that the first half of her sentence had been blurted out before she saw Captain George. It was spoken in a tone of affectionate remonstrance, changed, like magic, to respectful submission.

"A quart of this glorious October," said Captain George, quaffing from the tankard to conceal his laughter, "and the best the larder provides. My old friend Dionysius, here, looks as if he were half-fed."

The housekeeper tried to look dignified, but the keen eye of the captain was fixed upon her in such a way, that she could not speak—so hurried away to obey his orders.

"Dionysius — Dionysius!" said Captain George, gravely; "so Mrs. Wilkins calls us Dionysius."

"*Familiaritas*," began the reverend, in a tone of deprecation.

"Familiarity breedeth contempt," said George.

"Verily, my dear lord ——"

"Captain George."

"*Alias*. So be it. There is no contempt on the part of Mrs. Wilkins. She has been my housekeeper for now twelve years."

"What a devilish pretty girl she must have been then! But never mind, old boy; you know our old school story."

"*Facilis est*—that is, memory faileth one," said the parson.

"Why it was you used to tell it. A Roman Catholic priest was much talked about for the beauty of his servant girls. His bishop felt bound to reprimand him, and bade him have none under fifty."

"Antiquity is to be venerated. *Quod fecit?*" said Dionysius.

"He took two of five-and-twenty."

"*Magnus est veritas*," replied the parson; "but what brings you here, my old friend?"

"I am going to be married," said Captain George, slapping him on the shoulder.

"*Retro Satanas!*" cried the vicar, "after all these years."

"Why, you old sinner, I'm only thirty-five," said Captain George, laughing.

"A man is a 'fool or a physician at forty," drily replied Dionysius.

"Ah!" said Captain George, smiling. "Here is Mrs. Wilkins, shall she be umpire?"

"Nay—" began the parson.

"What is it about?" asked the spruce housekeeper.

"I am going to be married," said the highwayman, with a very sharp glance at the housekeeper; "and my friend here thinks I am too old."

"Law, sir," cried Mrs. Wilkins, holding up her hands, "you're almost too young."

"*Sum*—I am—confounded—"

"Nonsense. Now you are only ten years my senior. How far happier you would be if you were married!" said Captain George, gravely.

Mrs. Wilkins looked down upon the ground, but blushed up to her very eyes.

"*Avaunt—exorso te*," cried Dionysius.

"Only imagine the comfort, the consolation, the respectability of matrimony. Fancy—instead of finding you poring over a musty Greek play; for all the good they do they might as well have been burnt—I should have found you dangling an urchin on your knee, while mammy was—"

"Sir—" said the housekeeper, with a blushing rebuke on her delighted countenance.

"And then fancy, when old age comes, the joy of having near you one who will tend to your every want, minister to your most minute wishes; instead of having a snuffy, grasping, money-grubbing, old hospital nurse, a dying in your bed deserted by all."

"*Diabolus est!*" cried the Reverend Dionysius Scrimgour, not venturing to look at Mrs. Wilkins, whose stomacher rose and fell with unusual rapidity.

"No," said Captain George, who dearly loved a joke, taking his hand and that of Mrs. Wilkins; "I am certain that I stand between two persons who only want a friendly mediator to bring about an understanding."

"He promised me these ten years," sobbed Mrs. Wilkins.

"*Zoe mou!*" (my life) said the student.

"And when I speak about it calls me names," sobbed the housekeeper.

"*Akribe mou psuke!*" (my dear soul) continued the parson

"You hear him," continued Mrs. Wilkins.

"Come, Dion, you were always advised by me: say the word."

"*Hic jacet!*" cried the vicar, falling back into his arm chair, "I yield—I resign—I give up my liberty, *atque caput!*"

"No! no! your head is safe," said Captain George, laughing. "Well, now, Mrs. Wilkins, do not regret my arrival. We'll be married the same evening; and no later than next Monday night."

The unfortunate vicar, who, from sheer inability to defend himself against the eloquence of his friend, and the imploring glances of Mrs. Wilkins, had yielded up his liberty, gave a faint groan."

Mrs. Wilkins, a widower not usually bashful, was radiant.

"And now, my dear madam," said Captain George, "this business having been so satisfactorily settled, will you allow me to request that you will prepare the wedding feast. For reason of state we shall be married at night."

Mrs. Wilkins curtsied and went out.

The bewildered vicar was half-an-hour recovering himself sufficiently to confer with his friend, and then could with difficulty be persuaded to acquiesce in the arrangements.

"Heaven forgive you, for I cannot," he said, as he retired.

But he had agreed to provide a clergyman who would perform his own ceremony without Captain George was doubly provided against accidents.

CHAPTER LXXII.

THE MARRIAGE LICENCE.

It was nearly morning when Captain George rejoined Joe the sailor and his poor little sweetheart Mary. He found her fast asleep on a bench, and the young fellow walking about in his shirt sleeves. His coat was laid over her, his cap served as a pillow.

A long conversation passed between the captain and the youth, which ended in the former writing a note to the skipper of the Spanking Sally, which the ex-mud-lark agreed to deliver.

They then awakened Mary, who was quite a changed being, and the whole party adjourned to the old house on the Thames.

Captain George related his night's adventures with considerable humour, but Lucy did not laugh. There was a sense of coming ill upon her soul, which deprived her of every faculty of being amused.

"Now that it is decided on," she said, "I wish it were well over."

"So do I," replied the captain, passionately; "but come, you have watched all night. Let us seek rest. At midday I must be out in search of the ring and licence."

It was one o'clock ere Captain George this time, by the aid of his faithful man Snow, in the garb of a gentleman's coachman, sallied forth. A pair of very ruddy whiskers shaded the side of his face, while a broad-brimmed hat concealed his forehead and eyes. To avoid the remotest chance of exciting suspicion, he sauntered along, gazing in at the shop windows, and yet glancing round with caution every now and then.

In this way he reached St. Paul's-churchyard, and was at once, upon his entry into Doctors' Commons, assailed by the harpies who hang about its purlieus, like wolves in white aprons. Like most men who visit this locality for the first time, he yielded to the imposition, and asked to be shown to the residence of a proctor.

The man led him to the required locale, and, having been paid, departed, when Captain George at once procured the necessary licence, and left the same place.

As he did so somebody brushed past him, and entered the proctor's office.

Too elated with his prize, and thinking with rapture on the precious treasure which was so soon to be his, Captain George took no notice of this man, whose slouched hat and cloak should have excited his suspicions.

He hurried rapidly to the river and took a boat.

He was so impatient to be with Lucy, that he forgot all his ordinary precautions.

Joe let him in from the river entrance, and after some happy hours spent in the society of Lucy, he started to arrange matters with the Reverend Dionysius Scrimgour.

He was received by the rosy Mrs. Wilkins with the utmost cordiality, which was nowise decreased when he imprinted a kiss upon her ruddy cheeks.

"Law, captain!" she said, "how dare you? but really men now-a-days are so audacious."

"Even the Reverend Dionysius Scrimgour," replied Captain George with a sly smile.

Mrs. Wilkins introduced him to the vicar, whom he found seated in melancholy mood before the fire, his pipe unlighted, his glass untouched, and his book closed before him.

"What cheer, as they say at sea," cried Captain George, with a sly look at Mrs. Wilkins; "this won't do—we must brighten up."

"Amo, amas! Verily," said the vicar, in a most dejected tone, "verily, there is desolation in Israel."

"Why?"

"Veritas est! Why? hast thou not wrought me to do that which is an abomination unto the flesh?" began the vicar.

"Well, I'm sure," said Mrs. Wilkins, with a peculiar toss of the head.

"Now Dionysius, all this is precious nonsense; it's what we must all come to at last."

"Momentum mori! Dust to dust—ashes to ashes," said the vicar.

"And when we have made up our minds to a thing, it is best to plunge head foremost without any hesitation. I am quite sure you and Mrs. Wilkins will make a very happy couple."

"I'm sure I've done my duty by him these ten years," half sobbed Mrs. Wilkins, "even to calling myself a widow for his sake, when I'm plain Jemima Wilkins, spinster—who—"

"Ecce homo! Say no more," said the vicar with something like a faint blush, "it shall be as it was agreed—there is my hand upon it. Jemima, a bowl of punch."

Her eyes brightened up in the most remarkable manner, as she hurried from the room.

"Jemima," cried Captain George, screaming with laughter; "so it is Dionysius and Jemima. Is it, oh?" he added in a much graver tone; "me thought, most reverend vicar of St. Asaph cum-vinculum, that this marriage is a reparation."

"Peccavi! I always intended it," said Dionysius with an ingenuous blush, "but circumstances prevented it."

"Bravo!—an honest confession is good for the soul—and here is Mrs. Wilkins. Now, my dear Jemima, if you will allow me to call you so, this punch must be brewed by your fair hands."

The blushing Jemima acquiesced, and the three passed a pleasant evening together, the vicar gradually as the punch warmed his heart throwing off all ceremony and vowing that it was the happiest day of his life.

Before they parted they agreed that next day the Reverend Dionysius Scrimgour should procure his own marriage license, and provide the clergyman who should perform the ceremony, the vicar not believing himself qualified to do it himself.

And thus they parted.

CHAPTER LXXIII.

THE WEDDING.

Joe the sailor had performed his mission to the skipper of the Spanking Sally, and brought back an answer, which was of a favourable character.

He appointed a meeting in an out of the way publichouse, and there Captain George went in the dusk of the evening accompanied by Snow and the sailor lad, who wished to be married to Mary, a proposition the ex-highwayman had great trouble in dissuading him from.

The publichouse had a garden door running down to the river, which induced Captain George to go by water, and having reached it without adventure or hindrance, he went into the house and was introduced to the skipper.

This worthy received him heartily, and then in his presence, and that of Snow and Joe, he told the story of his thirteen years' absence from England.

But as Captain George shortly after repeated it to Lucy, it will better find a place there.

His hearers listened to him with open mouth, so startling and wondrous were the revelations they heard.

The skipper could scarcely believe his ears.

"Here's my hand, my hearty," he said when Captain George had concluded. "I'm your man—stick to you, main brace and topsail, yardarm and broadside. When do we sail?"

"On Sunday morning."

Minor details were then entered into, such as the arrangement of a cabin for Captain George and Lucy, a small berth for her attendant Mary, and another for Snow and the old man.

The skipper agreed to everything. The voyage contemplated by Captain George promised better than a dozen trips of an ordinary kind, and he was prepared to make any sacrifice.

They then parted, with the understanding that the Spanking Sally was to run up to the church where the marriage was to take place, and there await the wedding party.

As she had nothing contraband on board, and intended obtaining papers for Malta, in the Mediterranean, there could be no manner of difficulty.

Captain George returned to Lucy, from whom he could not bear to be a moment absent.

Every arrangement was now made for the wedding in the most careful manner.

They were to leave in two boats with the tide, and slowly glide down the stream of the Thames; one of these boats containing the old man, George, and Joe was to make for the schooner, while the other was to go straight to the churchyard.

This was to contain Snow and Lucy.

George was to follow as soon as he had put his father on board.

In accordance with these arrangements everything was packed up, and sent on board the schooner in the open light of day.

Then came the eventful Saturday.

All were pale, anxious, and all had wildly palpitating hearts.

Lucy could scarcely speak or walk. A fearful and terrible dread was on her soul.

Not so Captain George. He was anxious, uncomfortable — almost ill-tempered, a common failing with bridegrooms on their wedding day. But no fear of the future added to his causes for anxiety.

Night came.

The two boats were moored below

Armed to the teeth, and as unlike a wedding party as anything could be, the whole of them crept down the iron stairs from the trap-door, and entered the conveyances they had chosen.

It was gloomy, cold, and the waters hissed angrily as the breeze sped over their murky surface.

No lights were visible but those of the bridges, and the houses on the banks of the river.

There was no moon.

The sky shone one canopy of black, except when in the far-off distance a faint blue streak of lightning passed across the horizon.

It was clear they were in for a storm.

No one spoke a word. Lucy, with a cold shudder, wrapped herself in her cloak and sat down beside the man who was, in so few hours, to call her his bride.

Even Captain George was awed by the dismal aspect of nature.

The journey, however, was performed in safety, and after about an hour they came in sight of the schooner, distinguishable by three lamps hanging one over the other.

One boat pulled quickly to the side of the schooner, while Joe took Lucy and Mary ashore. The door of the vicarage was open, and the two females at once entered.

Joe turned towards the banks of the river.

Meanwhile Lucy and Mary had been cordially received by the vicar and the blushing Jemima Wilkins, who presented them to the strange clergyman, a friend of the Reverend Dionysius Scrimgour.

Two young women in humble life were present, to assist at the simple banquet which was to follow the wedding.

The church was very dimly lighted up, so as not to attract attention, and, time pressing, the *cortege* soon entered its precincts, and the whole party congregated round the altar.

Nobody was wanting but Joe and the captain; the latter of whom, however, stood forward.

In about ten minutes the ceremony commenced. At the express wish of Lucy, precedence was given to the marriage of Mrs. Wilkins with the vicar.

She then stood timidly forward herself, gave a wild shriek, and almost fainted.

"Treachery!" she cried. "This is not Captain George, but the base assassin of Ada Wilmot, the Lord Charles Lutterel!"

The confusion may be more readily conceived than described. All crowded round to gaze at the nobleman, who waved his hands for silence.

"I am the brother," he said, "of that apostate knave, who is an outlaw to the laws of his country. But listen, Lucy. He is my prisoner, and in half-an hour will be in the hands of the minions of the law. Take my hand, become my wife on the spot, and you save his life!"

"Merciful heavens!—can a brother be such a monster?" said poor Lucy.

"Decide."

"*Monstrum horrendum!* I mean, my lord, this is very extraordinary," began the Reverend Dionysius Scrimgour; "and—"

"I seek an answer from Lucy only," replied the young nobleman, haughtily.

"Oh, my lord, be merciful!" cried Lucy; "this is terrible. Where is George? let me see him."

"When you are Lady Charles Lutterel," said the other, coldly.

"But, my lord," put in the strange clergyman, "the thing is impossible—the license—"

"Is here!"

"This treachery has been planned, then; this is no accident," exclaimed Lucy.

Lord Charles bowed as he handed the paper to the clergyman.

"Stop!" shouted a well-known voice, as Captain George and Joe rushed wildly into the church, "I am here! Where is the foul traitor?"

Lord Charles Lutterel moved hastily on one side; and, gaining the door, gave a shrill whistle.

"Good by, until better days!" said Captain George, as he snatched up Lucy in his arms, and fled.

When they reached the churchyard they found a body of sailors in a severe hand-to-hand conflict with a party of police officers. In another moment the women were in the boat, and the two men turned to aid their friends. Their arrival turned the scale, and the officers of justice were hurled over the wall of the churchyard.

Not a moment was to be lost. The sailors at once fled to their boats, and made for the schooner, which, with its lights still displayed, was slowly descending with the stream.

The frantic voice of Lord Charles could be heard shouting for boats.

But there was a gentle breeze; and the skipper of the Spanking Sally was a first-rate pilot; so that, ere the officers could procure boats, they were beyond all danger.

This is what had happened:—

Lord Charles Lutterel had recognised his brother in the street, when he was going to obtain the license at Doctors' Commons. Determined to thwart him, he did not at once seek his arrest.

He wished his revenge to be sweeter.

Entering the same proctor's office, and trusting to his likeness to his brother, he said that a slight error had occurred in the license just taken out, so that he wished it changed.

The fee being double, no difficulty was made; so that he easily obtained a license for Lord Charles Lutterel and Lucy Lipscome, spinster.

He then set a watch on the movements of his brother, and easily became aware of his intentions. He procured the assistance of one or two of his myrmidons, and several officers. The former contrived to capture Captain George while returning from the ship; and the whole plot would have succeeded but for the astuteness of Joe the mudlark.

He was in the churchyard, leaning against a tree, when he not only saw the capture of Captain George, but heard the voices of the officers under the churchyard wall.

He slipped into the water, swam for the schooner, and before the men had succeeded in pinioning Captain George, who struggled desperately, a couple of boats' crews were upon them, the captain rescued, and the officer attacked.

"Thank heaven!" cried Lucy, as the schooner spread its light sails, and London vanished in the distance.

"But we forgot one thing!" exclaimed Captain George, wildly.

"What is that?"

"We are not married."

Lucy bowed her head, blushed, and laid her head on his manly shoulder.

As she did so, she showed him the license just peeping from the bottom of her dress.

"Lucy, you are an angel," he said.

He went at once on deck, and persuaded the captain to put in at Dover for an hour or two.

CHAPTER LXXIV.
PAULINE AND PHILIP.

WHEN Pauline came too Sir Edgar Blakesley was standing by the side of her bed, a cold glitter in his eyes, and a bitter smile upon his lips.

In the *negligé* she wore, Pauline knew the power of her beauty, and she availed herself as much as possible of it. Sir Edgar turned away his eyes.

"Cockatrice!" he said.

"Philip, surely you would not hurt your Pauline," she replied in tones which scarcely trembled.

"Vile and cunning dissembler, I will take care that in future you betray me not. It is your fatal and terrible beauty which alone gives you power over your victims. From this night you shall appear so hideous that all will turn from you in horror and disgust—your name shall be a bye-word for ugliness."

"But, Philip, were you not tired of me? Did you not want to get rid of me? Was not the motive of you languor and peevishness," she whispered.

"You know it was not."

"Philip."

"Silence," said Sir Edgar Blakesley, sternly.

But as he did so he turned his head and—was lost.

"Dress yourself," he replied in husky tone.

A thin, almost imperceptible smile passed over her lips as she leaped from the bed, Sir Edgar Blakesley moving towards the door—his bottle of vitriol still in his hand.

Pauline knew that for a moment she was mastered, and made no attempt at resistance. She dressed herself slowly and methodically, as if to gain time.

She could not explain the long absence of her ardent lover, the Marquis of A———.

"Be quicker," said Sir Edgar, who read her thoughts; "he will not come."

"Surely you have not killed him," she cried.

"What if I have?" he coldly replied.

"You could not be such a monster."

"Dress yourself, Pauline, and in a few minutes you shall see him."

With a cold shudder Pauline obeyed, and in a few minutes more they descended the stairs. The *danseuse* shivered as with cold.

The saloon door was reached, and the two entered.

The marquis sat up, battling with the narcotic, but unable to speak or rise to his feet.

"Gracious heaven! what is the matter?" cried Pauline, wildly.

"Nothing, my charmer, except that he has taken a fancy to your port wine," said Sir Edgar Blakesley with bitter sarcasm.

Pauline shuddered and turned away. Her own wickedness recoiled upon her thus terribly.

Sir Edgar led her from the house without meeting a soul. She had luckily taken the precaution to wrap a warm shawl around, and in this way, silent, sullen, each dwelling upon their own dread thoughts, the once happy, fond and passionate pair moved towards London.

A return post chaise at length came up.

"Going hon, yer honour?"

"All right," said Sir Edgar.

The door was opened, and Pauline handed in. She made no resistance. She was, indeed, too anxious to know what her fate was going to be to cause any delay.

There was something in the cold determination of Sir Edgar which alarmed her.

Had he threatened she would not have minded—but he was in deep thought.

And still, in one hand, was the terrible bottle of vitriol, though now held partially unconsciously. The young man had ordered the driver to put them down in the Haymarket, which was soon reached, and the driver paid and discharged.

"Come," said Sir Edgar moodily, as he passed her arm in his.

"Where are you taking me? Tell me, or I will shriek," replied Pauline.

"Shriek!" said the young man, holding up the bottle of vitriol.

Pauline made no reply, but bowed her head, and once more ceased all attempt at resistance.

Something of her old love, too, seemed to come back, as she saw Sir Edgar roused to such absolute determination and resolution.

They moved along several streets, until they entered one of dark and gloomy appearance.

It was quite dark, and the street did not contain a single lamp.

Sir Edgar counted the houses, until he had reached the twelfth on the right hand. He then knocked and rang.

Somebody appeared sitting up, for the door was opened with magic rapidity, and a man, ugly, repulsive, and dirty, with a dirty nightcap on his head, appeared in answer to his summons.

"Is the room ready?" said Sir Edgar.

"All right, yer honour," replied the man.

Sir Edgar bade him precede them with a light, and then closed the door behind them.

"Mind the chain," said the man, with a grin. "It ain't many can open that."

Sir Edgar turned, and, by a secret he had been taught, put up the chain in a way that was to baffle all who were not initiated from opening it.

"Go first," said Sir Edgar, addressing Pauline.

The *danseuse* looked shudderingly around at the bare walls, the ferocious man, the stern face of her former lover, and her heart fell within her. She, however, resolved to put a good face on the matter.

They reached the summit of the house, and a door was opened leading into a room, which had once been an *atelier*.

It was large and airy, and most elegantly furnished. A bright fire burned on the hearth.

The man bowed and left them.

Sir Edgar went to a cupboard, locked up the vitriol, and turned towards Pauline.

"What is the meaning of all this?" she said in a more courageous tone than she had assumed for some time.

"It means, madam, that for the present, that is, as long as my present fancy lasts, it is your prison," said the young baronet, coldly.

"But my theatrical engagement?" replied Pauline, coldly.

"Is cancelled. I sent in your resignation last night," continued the other.

"You forged my name!" exclaimed Pauline, with sparkling eyes.

"No. Did not you one evening, in a paroysmx of love and delirium, when you swore that the very sight of other men was hateful to you, pen a resignation, which I prevented your sending, but kept as a proof of your love and devotion, and now what are you—a shameless wanton?"

"No!" cried Pauline, wildly, "I have never been unfaithful to you."

"If," said Sir Edgar, in a tone of genuine and earnest passion, "I could believe that, I might yet forgive the intention."

Pauline held down her lovely eyes and blushed. She looked too beautiful to be resisted, and Sir Edgar clapsed her once more in his arms.

The syren knew that her reign had began again, and as she had only been induced to leave him, under the impression that he was poor, she felt easily reconciled to the loss of the namby-pamby suitor who had never had anything to recommend him but his title and money.

CHAPTER LXXV.

THE MULETEERS.

Who has not heard and dreamed of Spain, with its lovely scenery, historic recollections, and most sweet girls,

> "I mean such graceful ladies,
> Their very walk would make your bosom swell."

And, after all, what beauty is there so worthy of our regard as that of the fair descendants of

Eve, who nowhere are to be found more lovely than in Spain—famous for oranges and women.

It was a strange choice for Lilian, if indeed she could ever again doubt William Lennox—still, as the poet says :—

An Arab horse, a stately stag, a barb
  New broke, a cameleopard, a gazelle,
No—none of these will do ; and then their garb !
  Their veil and petticoat.—Alas ! to dwell
Upon such things would very near absorb
  A canto—then their feet and ankles—well,
Thank Heaven I've got no metaphor quite ready,
  (And so, my sober muse—come, let's be steady.

Chaste Muse ! well, if you must, you must) the veil
  Thrown back a moment with the glancing hand,
While the o'erpowering eye that turns you pale
  Flashes into the heart :—All sunny land
Of love ! when I forget you, may I fail
  To—say my prayers—but never was there plann'd
A dress through which the eyes give such a volley
  Excepting the Venetian Fazzioli.

The station to which Cornet William Lennox was ordered was a small and picturesque village, called Casela. It was a kind of dependency on the monastery of Santa Rosalie.

It was an outpost on the very verge of the English lines. A French camp, in winter quarters, occupied a position not ten miles from the English entrenchments.

The village of Casela was picturesquely situated in a deep and lovely valley. At the head of the open space between two hills was a large mill, and beside this a neat cottage, in which Mrs. Winterton and her daughter took up their abode with their domestics, and the delighted Mr. Richard Forester as majordomo.

The village was small, and tenanted by an impoverished population, who, however, contrived to earn some money out of the British.

Cornet William Lennox joined his regiment, commanded by Sir John Coyne, a rigid and severe disciplinarian. For some days he was compelled to give his whole time to drill and the practice of his duties; soon, however, he was able to obtain leave of absence.

With what rapturous delight he rode from the entrenchments to the village of Casela, only those of our fair or masculine readers can tell. He had been eight days without paying a visit to his beloved Lillian; he had not even had time to write to her.

Away, then, he scampered at a pace which was perfectly fearful: his servant who rode behind him being scarcely able to keep him in sight.

There is no magnet like love's young dream.

Jack Horne, the domestic, a newly imported cockney, but a very smart fellow, who had only just finished his lessons in equitation, found his seat very uncomfortable. At first everybody finds this to be a fact. The human frame divine is not case-hardened in a day.

The bridge over the mill-stream is reached, and William Lennox alights, leaving his horse in the charge of his domestic, whom he instructs to wait for him at the neighbouring posada.

Jack Horne, nothing loth, especially as the command was backed by a silver token of regard, alighted also, went and fed the horses, and then entering the inn, marched boldly to the kitchen, asked for wine, bread, and cheese,

determined to make up for the scanty supply of refreshments in the trenches.

The kitchen was large, and tenanted only by the daughter of the host and three Spanish muleteers.

Jack Horne called loudly for his refreshments, and being a remarkably good-looking youth, was attended to with rapidity. He drew up to the fire, and began a conversation with Juanita.

It was little Spanish he could speak, but then there was the language of the eyes.

Somehow or other, when she was giving him change, he took hold of her hand. She did not draw it away.

The muleteers, who were three in number, and who had a huge pitcher of wine before them, looked at the happy pair with a scowl, and continued to smoke, speaking all the time in low whispers.

The young people, who were mutually smitten, paid not the slightest attention. The first dawn of the merest scintillation of love is so pleasant that it drives away every other thought and care.

Presently other travellers came in, and Juanita was compelled to leave her new admirer, who, wearied somewhat, and having imbibed no small quantity of wine, found himself drowsy.

He sought a bench, and was soon apparently in a sound sleep.

The three muleteers continued their conversation in low, cautious whispers.

———

CHAPTER LXXVI.

THE BURGLARY.

LILLIAN and her mother had been wondering at the prolonged absence and silence of William Lennox, and Mrs. Winterton began to look with dread upon the pallid cheek of the sensitive girl.

But she said nothing.

It happened strangely enough, that on the evening on which William Lennox at length obtained leave of absence, they were seated in front of their little house under a verandah. Lillian was silent and thoughtful. Her eyes were fixed upon the mill-wheel for ever turning.

"Of what are you thinking so intently, my child ?" said the mother, anxiously.

"That my life is like yonder wheel, always revolving in the same axis. I have one happy day, and three nights of misery," she said, very mournfully.

"My child, do explain yourself more fully !" cried Mrs. Winterton.

"Why does William neglect me thus—why has he neither written nor sent ?" she said, turning away.

"My dear girl," replied her mother, very gravely, "this sensitiveness is wrong. I dare say poor William is miserable enough. You know not the exigencies of the service. He is a novice, and has much to learn—but see where he comes !" she cried, with a joyous laugh. "Ah, foolish one, all smiles and blushes now."

William came suddenly upon them as she spoke, and Lillian, still tender and delicate in frame, and whose heart was fluttering like that of a frightened bird, fell weeping into his arms.

It was very silly, we dare say; but then she really could not help it.

"My angel!" cried the young officer, "if you knew how weary have been the hours since we parted you would not blame me as I see you do."

"It seemed so long, William," she whispered.

"Lilly, child," said Mrs. Winterton. "I was just reasoning with her when you came in sight. But it is no use scolding her. Her old mother is nobody. It must have its sweetheart—it must, since its given up its dolly."

Lillian blushed, and hid her face in her mother's bosom.

"But come to the house," said Mrs. Winterton, with an angelic smile. She cared in the wide world only to see her daughter happy.

And, in most cases, how easy is it to give joy to the young. As easy as it is, unfortunately, to make them miserable.

The three went into the house, where a collation of fruits and wine was placed before him— the simple and wholesome custom of southern countries.

It is a melancholy fact, but one in the utterance of which all our readers will bear us out, that the description of happiness is always stale, flat, and unprofitable. Who would care to read the record of that happy evening, to pore over the intimate communion of those three happy people?

Mrs. Winterton, whose soul knew neither guile nor selfishness, left them often alone, that they might pour forth unrestrained the joy of their hearts.

Happy the mother who can shed such happiness around her—and accursed the land whose morals are so low, that under no pretence are lovers ever left alone—without fatal results.

Such is the morality of the French as painted by themselves.

Mrs. Winterton came fluttering around them like their guardian angel, which, to a certain extent, she was.

In the words of the great Smollett, "he looked and languished; she flushed and faltered; all was doubt and delirum, fondness and flutter."

Suddenly there came a knock to the door, and in a few minutes—rather uncommonly long ones—the English maid came in and said that "Lieutenant" Lennox's servant wanted to see him.

"What can the fellow want?" said William, angry at being disturbed.

"Bring him in," replied Mrs. Winterton.

"Some stupid hint about our being late," pettishly added William.

Now John Horne was decidedly not sober, and yet was in that state of inebriety which makes a man particularly stiff and rather obstinate, to say nothing of amorous. It must be allowed that Mr. Jack, without any regard to his recent vows to Juanita, had not communicated his message to Mary without levying toll on her ruby lips.

He entered the room as erect, however, as a poker, and then stood still, his head at the salute, for a moment.

"What is it, Horne?" said William Lennox, sternly; for he saw he was slightly intoxicated.

Horne stood at ease, with a quick glance at the two ladies.

"Shall we retire?"

"No. Will you speak, numskull?" said Lennox, who had not been ten days in the army for nothing.

"Danger!" said Jack.

And he looked very hard at Lillian. William Lennox leaped to his feet.

"Will you explain yourself?" cried the Cornet, catching him by the collar.

"Three men — Captain — John — Jones!" gasped John Horne.

"Now, let me manage him," said Lillian, from whose lips the roses fled to be replaced by the cold lily. "Sit down, my man, and tell me all about it."

Jack Horne was forced into a seat, where he sat staring at the beautiful vision with open mouth.

"Horne, if you don't put off that fool's look, and speak —!" said the impatient young officer.

"Silence—I command here. Now, Horne, what three men do you allude to?"

"Captain—John—Jones!"

"Oh! the Captain, John, and Jones. What do they want?"

"You?"

"Where are they?" continued Lillian, waving her hand for silence.

"Posada."

"The infamous scoundrels," cried William. "Do you mean, Horne, that they intend mischief to-night?"

"Twelve o'clock—all in bed!" said Jack.

"Then, by heavens, this shall be their last deed of ruffianism!" continued William Lennox. "Return to the inn for my pistols; be quick, and they shall have a reception."

"Mary," said Jack, without moving.

"Clever fellow this!" observed Lillian, laughing; "he has learned our girl's name already."

"Asked her," said Jack.

Mary was sent for, and brought in two pair of horse pistols in their holsters; and Jack's nervousness wearing off, he explained that he had lain down to rest on a bench, and had fallen asleep. Awakened by the narrowness of his couch, he awoke, and catching the sound of English voices, listened.

He then heard the three supposed Spaniards planning, in very good English, an attack on the cottage of Mrs. Winterton. They proposed, evidently for the most diabolical of purposes, to carry off not only Lillian, but Mary the housemaid.

The three ruffians had set up for regular banditti. It appeared, in the course of their conversation, that by means of their mysterious wealth, they had already a small band of vagabonds at their command. These awaited them in a cork wood near at hand.

As soon as William Lennox heard this, he proposed that the women should be sent upstairs, while he and Jack were left to deal with the ruffians. After some discussion, this was agreed on.

Mrs. Winterton, however, suggested a plot.

"Do not imbrue your hands in the blood of my kinsmen," she said.

She then explained that the shutters which were, in general, never closed, were very strong, and would resist any attack. They fastened on the outside by a bar and padlock, being closed from the verandah. The window of the sitting room could be left open, as it often was on warm nights, and a Spanish servant could be placed in ambush.

"The wretches! I'll do it," said Mary.

It was then so settled, that Mary was to hide in a dense thicket near the window, and the moment she saw the ruffians enter the house she was to close the shutters, slip the bar down, and fasten the padlock.

William Lennox was to remain inside, ready to act on a moment's warning. The ladies the young cornet sent up stairs with the two Spanish girls.

Joseph, a man servant, concealed himself in a summer-house with a huge blunderbuss, to support Mary if necesssary. Mr. Richard Forester had gone down carousing to the camp—a severe loss to the garrison!

It was nearly midnight when the house relapsed into perfect stillness. There were still faint lights in the upper rooms. There was a slight glow in the sitting-room as from the remains of a fire.

Just as the bell of the monastery tolled twelve, the three ruffians came gliding up the garden, and halted only when beneath the verandah.

"Careless, as usual," said Captain Frederick.

"Vewy," repeated John.

"Just so!" whispered Slimy Jones.

Then, after listening with breathless attention, the first speaker pushed aside the heavy curtains and peered round the room. It was empty; he could see that by the glowing embers on the hearth.

"A fire looked so English," said Lillian.

One by one they entered, and the curtain fell behind them. Then, with a step as light as that of the burglars themselves, Mary appeared, pushed to the shutters, which grated horribly.

A suppressed malediction burst from within. But Mary was cool and collected, and the bar was down ere they could rush against it.

"Guard the gate, Joseph!" shouted William Lennox, in a voice of thunder, "and if a head appears, shoot them like dogs!"

A rush against the passage door was the reply.

"Be quiet, or I fire!" said William, sternly.

Then curses, revilings, and threats were heard from within, ending in muttered conversation.

The voices appeared new to them, and surely neither Lillian nor Arabella would betray them unto death.

"We demand a parley with the noble lady of the house," said Captain John; "we but sought food and shelter—we are three poor deserters!"

"No parley until daylight," replied Jack Horne, after a whispered order from William.

The ruffians yielded to the force of circumstances, and were silent.

Jack Horne remained sentry at one door, while Joseph kept guard without. William passed the night in delicious contemplation.

And thus the night passed.

CHAPTER LXXVII.

THE GREAT DUKE.

At daybreak John Horne went down to the pond to fetch the horses. It was William's intention to send off his servant for a guard with which to march the prisoners to the camp. Scarcely had John returned, when a bugle sounded, and, casting their eyes down, they beheld a brilliant staff crossing the bridge.

They were evidently coming that way.

William Lennox turned pale. He should have been in the trenches at twelve.

He was absent without leave in front of the enemy: the punishment was death!

Ere he had recovered the shock, the staff were close upon him.

He knew that man who rode at the head must be the great Sir Arthur Wellesley, the future Duke of Wellington.

With compressed lips, palled lips, and a cold perspiration on his brow, William Lennox saluted his own colonel, who rode beside the duke.

"Consider yourself under arrest," said Sir John. "Adjutant, take his sword."

"Colonel, one word," cried the agonised youth.

"Your explanation will be given before the court-martial, which will take place to-morrow."

"But, Sir John!"

"His crime?" said the future duke, quietly.

"Desertion before the enemy!" replied the colonel

"On my honour, as a gentleman and a soldier," cried William Lennox, passionately, "had I not deserted—to which crime I confess, and am ready to die for it—the honour of two English ladies, one my affianced wife, would have been at the mercy of three murderers and assassins."

"Let us listen to his story," said the duke, mildly.

"I pray you first, Sir Arthur, let the ruffians be secured. Yonder domestic and my servant keep watch over them."

The general ordered a corporal's guard to bring forth the prisoners, who, pale, haggard, and with abject terror in their eyes, were led bound into his presence.

At the same moment Mrs. Winterton and Lillian, warned by Mary, came rushing forth; but William Lennox begged them to be silent.

The young officer told his story, which the general commanding in chief listened to with a grave aspect.

"Had I left them, I must have doomed them to a fate worse than death," he said, at last.

"Young lady," said Sir Arthur Wellesley, "is all this true?"

"If he had left us I should have died," replied Lilian, passionately. "These wretches would have murdered us. But had I known, I would have died rather than he should have stayed."

"Let them be strung up to yonder tree," said the future duke; and, ere they could speak, the three prisoners were pinioned, and a rope was round one of their necks.

"Pardon my intrusion," put in William Lennox, respectfully, "but these are the cousins of the lady. Spare her the sight. This is Captain Frederick Winterton; this the Honourable John Winterton; this their satellite, and doer of evil deeds.'

"So ho!" said a jovial voice. "Got 'em at last. Beg pardon, but these are my prisoners —murder and forgery—one thousand pounds reward."

And Mr. Richard Forester stepped forward.

"Are you an officer of the peace?" asked the commander-in-chief, with a grim smile.

"Richard Forester, at your service, my lord," said the officer, bowing.

"Take your prisoners, then. A corporal's guard shall be at your orders. The convent above will supply you with a dungeon. Mr. William Lennox, as soon as you have bade adieu to your friends, you will join your regiment— *under arrest.*

The young officer started, and Lilian would have fallen but for his support.

"Under arrest!" she said, faintly.

"Fear not for me," whispered William Lennox "Something tells me that the general means me kindly; so, come, I will at least breakfast with you, and then go to my much neglected duties."

William Lennox said this so cheerfully that Lillian was almost persuaded. She knew little of military life, and could not persuade herself that any one could be punished for a good action.

CHAPTER LXXVIII.

THE MONK AND THE RUNNER.

IF ever there was a happy man, it was Mr. Richard Forester. After travelling so many miles, and risking the perils of the ocean, it was at all events satisfactory to have succeeded in his endeavours.

And then only to think of the thousand pounds reward.

He slipped once more upon the pony which had brought him to the scene of action, and rode in the rear of the staff, not the least important individual thereof in his own private and particular opinion.

The prisoners sullen and hopeless, though certainly roused to some little courage by their sudden reprieve from death, walked along with their arms tied behind them, silent and moody.

The ride to the monastery was not more than a mile, and the English staff being expected, were received with open arms. The choicest wines in the cellar of the old house had been brought forth, and the breakfast laid out was far more *recherché* than any of the officers had seen for some days.

Mr. Richard Forester entered the court-yard with his prisoners full of importance and fuss. He considered that in his character of a civil officer he should be listened to before anybody.

But the monks, who were busy, turned a deaf ear to all his dumb motions.

At length a minor monk, a sort of doorkeeper, took pity on him, and led the way by many a winding passage, and by many a flight of steps, to the prison of the monastery.

It was a deep dungeon, the abode of rats—slimy, dirty, damp, and horrible to look at.

"Why, this is rank murder!" said the captain.

"Excutiating," said the Honourable John, with unfeigned horror.

"Just so—murder!" repeated Jones.

"I say—*bono Johnny*—you monk fellow," observed Mr. Richard Forester, shaking his head, "this will never do. It is a great deal too horrible."

The monk did not understand the words, but he understood the gestures. With imperturbable gravity he turned round and led the way to the regions above.

Close to the huge kitchen was a small strong room or cell, used as a place of punishment for small offences. It was built of solid stone, and was quite as secure as the dungeon below.

It opened out upon a guard-room of tolerable dimensions, where Mr. Richard Forester announced his intention of taking up his quarters until the hour of marching arrived.

The monk stared at him for a moment, and then went away for a few minutes to return with a huge roast goose, a vast loaf of bread, and a pitcher of wine, that made the Bow-street runner's eyes sparkle with delight.

He had done his duty, and had a perfect right to enjoy himself when the opportunity offered.

A stout oaken table and two benches constituted the whole furniture of the room; but what would they have? The door of the cell was locked, and the key deposited on the table.

Father Francis seated himself opposite the English heretic, and after mumbling a sort of apology for his own conduct, began to carve the goose with an eagerness which showed how genuine a *bon-vivant* he was.

He served the officer amply, and then filled up his bumper with wine.

They drank in silence to one another's better acquaintance, and then set to at the solids. Father Francis was evidently a lover of good living, and did not spare the viands, while Richard Forester, like a true John Bull, supported him energetically.

They eat for some time in silence, until there remained nothing but the carcase of the goose, which both washed down with abundance of the strong, heady wine of the locality, until their eyes assumed the dull, heavy appearance of intoxication, a result oftener caused by over eating even than by over drinking.

Sweets, custards, and dessert of all kinds were greedily devoured, and still the wine drinking did not cease.

"Friend, heretic," said the monk at last, with a knowing look, "must poor prisoners starve?"

"What?" asked Forester with a drunken leer, "what—d'ye say—eh?"

The monk pointed to the door of the cell, and to the remains of the feast.

"The wretches" he observed, "must a—hunger and a thirst—there is ample for all. Why should they not, though sinners, for the little time they have to live, share the joys of this world? Neither to eat nor to drink is to die—"

"Right you are, old boy. I like you—nothing like good cheer—eh—what dost mean?—give the coves some grub—eh?—well, yes if you like—I will stand guard over them—" said Richard Forester, who was very intoxicated.

"I will—verily—Ave Maria—but my legs are stiff—fetch some more provender — *sanctissima*—" babbled the monk, who then disappeared, and soon returned with a fresh supply of wine and eatables.

Richard Forester, with drunken gravity, cocked a pistol, while the custodian of the gates opened the cell door. The prison room was lighted from above, and the three sat upon some straw in sullen silence.

"Here!" said the monk, "see what the mercy of heaven sends you—behold the good things of this earth which are vouchsafed unto you!"

And he placed them on the ground before them.

"How can we eat with our arms tied?" replied Captain Frederick Winterton.

"True — thy arms must be unbound."

"One at a time," urged Richard Forester.

"Good—thou speakest like a book."

The monk stooped to cut the cord, while the Bow-street runner advanced into the cell.

Captain Frederick Winterton rose to his feet

and shook himself. He still kept his sullen aspect when, seeing the utter state of helplessness in which their guardians had placed themselves, he sprang at Forester, clutched his pistol, knocked him down senseless, and ere the monk could cry out had him on the ground with a knife at his throat.

He then cut the cords which bound his two companions, bade them pick up the provender, and follow him.

He carried the knife and pistol, and having closed the cell, kept a-head of his party.

There was but one passage leading from the guard-room, and this they were compelled to follow. They could tell by the odour that it led to the kitchen.

It was a tall arched passage with lofty windows. One of these the captain opened and peered out.

It opened into the garden of the monastery. Not hesitating one moment, the three men rushed forth and concealed themselves in the shadow of a shrubbery. There was no time to be lost; for, no doubt, instant search would be made for them.

The wall was high, but by the assistance of trees easily climbed. In five minutes they were on the opposite side and in a thicket. They did not, however, hesitate one moment, but took to their heels as fast as they possibly could.

Their escape was not discovered until the evening, when patrols were sent to scour the whole country for them.

But they were nowhere to be found.

The despair of William Lennox, when he heard of their escape, may be better imagined than described.

He was under arrest, and could not fly to the protection of Lillian. He, however, at once wrote to the future duke by Jack Horne, begging that he might be released on parole.

The escape of the three assassins made so great a sensation, even with so many startling events occurring around them, that the commander-in-chief heard of it. He now regretted his having allowed the ruffians a reprieve, and gave orders that they should be shot whenever taken.

The brief note from Lieutenant William Lennox found at once careful attention, and leave of absence was granted to him at once on parole.

Away William galloped at the very top of his speed, followed by his attendant, Jack Horne.

It was night when William Lennox started on his journey, and, reckless of all danger, urged his steed to its utmost speed.

Jack Horne was left far behind.

Something he knew not—an inward dread weighed upon the soul of William. The escape of the dastard ruffians seemed so terrible an event that every dread a man could feel was on his soul.

At length the lights of the village came in sight.

The cottage of Mrs. Winterton displayed its usual amount of lights.

With a wild and beating heart William Lennox dismounted and rushed in. His first visit was to the parlour.

His terror may be conceived when he saw Joseph, the Spanish servant, bleeding on the ground, and Mrs. Winterton either insensible or dead.

"Lillian—where is my Lillian?" he cried, in wild and passionate accents.

"Who calls?" faintly muttered Mrs. Winterton.

William Lennox stooped and raised her up. She opened her eyes, and, when she saw who it was, burst into a passionate flood of tears.

"My angel gone at last," she murmured.

Jack here came in; and, by order of his master, went to the kitchen, where he found the two Spanish servants locked in, and silent from pure fear.

They soon, however, found their tongues, but were sternly told to be still and procure restoratives for their mistress, while they themselves saw to the wounded man.

In about a quarter of an hour she was able to explain.

About an hour before they were sitting in conversation—Mrs. Winterton and Lillian—when the three ruffians glided into the room, and, after a determined resistance, wounded Joseph, knocked Mrs. Winterton senseless, and carried off both Lillian and Mary.

"The villains!" cried Jack Horne.

"My dear Mrs. Winterton," said William Lennox, as if inspired by a sudden thought, "I must leave you at once. These wretches will never trust themselves anywhere near the British camp. They will assuredly fly to the French lines, and there I will follow them, and rescue Lillian or die. Surely the French will force the miscreants to give up Lillian."

"And Mary?" said Jack.

A few more words passed, and then, with an earnest promise of a speedy return, the two started on their wild midnight adventure.

CHAPTER LXXIX.

A FEARFUL PLOT.

THE rage and despair which fell upon the soul of Lady Caroline Blakesley, when she found that her husband had robbed her, knew no bounds. She vented her passion at first on the landlady, Mrs. Maconichie.

At length, however, her husband returned.

"Thief!" was her first word of greeting.

He was haggard, downcast, and half-intoxicated. He glared at her with the eyes of a tiger.

"Woman, be careful!" he muttered.

"I will lead this life no longer," she said; "my jointure is my own. I will return to my own friends, who, once I am separated from you, will gladly receive me. Oh, that my son were here to protect me!"

"Sir Edgar Blakesley!" sneered the gambler.

"Yes. He would not allow his mother to be insulted," she retaliated.

"Caroline," suddenly said James Tyrrel Blakesley, changing his manner, "I will end this life. This very day I will remove into decent apartments, and in a few days go in the country. The trial relative to the Blakesley estates comes on soon, and I believe that we shall prove this new claimant to be an impostor. Your son will then be sole heir."

"Ah, James, if I could only believe you !" sighed the easily satisfied woman.

"You shall see. I have come here to dress only. In two hours you shall see me again."

And James Tyrrel Blakesley went out by appointment to meet Sir Edgar, who had indited a penitent letter to his bankers, informing them that he had broken off his connection with Pauline, and was about to return to his naval duties.

A very cheerful reply was sent to him, and a request not to spare his cheques, which they should always be too delighted to honour.

Sir Edgar answered that he certainly should, as he was buying expensive books and pictures against the day when he should be master of Blakesley Hall.

The two men met by appointment in a coffee-house; and, though there was deep mutual distrust, they were very confidential.

"You will have to attend the trial," said Mr. James Tyrrel, after some conversation.

"What trial ?"

"The great ejectment case," replied Mr. James.

"Oh !" said Sir Edgar; "but I suppose it's some madman has set up. The whole family of John Stewart were hung, or burnt, or drowned, were they not ?"

"So we always thought. But should this claimant be really the heir of John Stewart, adieu to all our prospects. I have secured the best legal advice."

"But your solicitors can be also mine."

"No," said James, drily, "I would rather not."

"Very well; just as you like. I will see to that."

"Sir Edgar."

"Mr. James."

"You do not seem very anxious to see your mother," said the other gravely.

Sir Edgar started, turned pale, and made no reply.

"Her evidence will be very important on the trial," continued James.

"Very."

"She will have to prove your identity."

"Of course."

"Sir Edgar Blakesley, do we understand one another?" said Mr. James, "If we succeed, halves."

"Yes," cried the other, "with all my heart. But we must stick together."

"We will. But now, boy, what about your mother ?"

"Your wife !" said Sir Edgar, significantly.

"Sir Edgar," replied the ruffian, "I am sick and tired of her. I have made up my mind to rid myself of an incubus; how, I scarcely yet know, but I cannot endure her bondage."

"You don't mean to kill her ?" said Sir Edgar, with chattering teeth.

"I don't know. You grow suddenly squeamish," sneered Mr. James Tyrrel Blakesley. "But I forget. You never explained your escape from Blakesley Hall. By heavens ! however, there are so many mysteries connected with that affair that I lose myself in conjectures."

"What do you mean ?—the poisoned phials ?" sneered Sir Edgar

"Yes," faltered James, whose face was now livid.

"The Blue Dwarf changed them every night, and has got every one of yours in his possession."

James snatched at a bottle, poured out half a tumbler of brandy, and swallowed it half.

"The Blue Dwarf ——"

"Sapathwa—Goldy Gordon—that infernal, meddling vagabond !" continued Sir Edgar Blakesley.

The husband of Lady Caroline wiped his brow, on which the cold perspiration stood in big drops.

"That hideous monster ! There is about that man some secret which fills my soul with dread. But there is no use in getting up imaginary dangers. What has become of William Lennox ?"

Sir Edgar started.

"I don't know," he said. "The last time I saw him was at the Prince Regent's Ball."

"I do not understand that boy—his silence, his mysterious connection with the Blue Dwarf," replied Mr. James Tyrrel Blakesley. "But we were speaking of your mother. If she appears at the trial things may go badly for us."

"What is to be done ?"

"Will you join with me, heart and soul ?" replied Mr. James.

"I will."

"She must never see the light of day again," savagely observed James. "My plan is this. Write to her, and say you wish to see her. Of course she will come. In the meantime we must find a way to provide for her. As a prisoner she may live harmlessly enough. Is it agreed ?"

"Agreed."

"Now, then, for the cheque !" cried James; "and to-night you must send her such a letter as may induce her to meet you to-morrow."

Sir Edgar Blakesley assented, and a whole plan was concocted by which the wretched wife of James Tyrrel was in future to be sequestered from the world.

They then went out, and sauntered about awhile in conversation.

As they were going up the Haymarket a hackney coach passed them at a slow pace.

From the window peered the wild eyes of the Blue Dwarf.

He drew his cloak around him, alighted, and followed them. The union of these two men appeared to him a matter of dangerous importance.

Meanwhile Mr. James, after changing his cheque, and wishing Sir Edgar good-bye, returned to his home, and, in furtherance of the scheme laid down between himself and the young baronet, removed his wife at once to a respectable hotel.

Lady Caroline was naturally enough elated, and, when her husband went out that night, they parted to all appearance good friends.

Mr. James rubbed his hands. This man had married Lady Caroline solely to obtain command over the Blakesley estates, which, in default of Sir Edgar, he had every reason to believe came to himself.

The trial now made that doubtful, and his wife was, therefore, an incumbrance.

Crime is a leprous disease, which, once it spots the skin, is apt to spread over the whole body; and Mr. James was not the man to hesitate at the perpetration of any sin by which anything was to be got.

About eight in the evening, just as Lady Caroline began to turn over in her mind an excuse for ordering brandy—her late habits made spirits necessary to her—a domestic brought up a letter.

Caroline told him to lay it down, and hesitated. Before she made up her mind he had disappeared.

Carelessly—expecting it was from her husband —she took it up, and glanced at the superscription.

She opened it, read two words, and shrieked.

She then rang the bell violently, and, when the man re-appeared, spoke with flashing eyes and excited mien.

"Quick!—brandy—a sudden shock!" she said.

The man saw that she was ill, and hurried away. In two minutes he returned with a bottle, water, and glasses.

"Go!" said Lady Caroline, faintly.

"Shall I send up a chambermaid?"

"No. I will ring if necessary."

The man bowed and retired, and then Lady Caroline read the letter, first making a stiff glass of brandy and water.

"*My Dear Mother,—I have taken leave of absence, in order to come up and see you. I understand that Mr. James Tyrrel Blakesley treats you shamefully. Being but ill-supplied with money, I am in very humble lodgings; but, as I cannot risk meeting that man, you must come and see me. I have much to tell you that concerns us both.—Yours, &c.,*

"EDGAR BLAKESLEY."

"My son!" she cried, pushing away the glass, "at last, then, I am free—but the postscript."

"I am at No. —, in Holywell-street. Ask for Mr. Edgar, as my rank is not suitable to my hotel. To-morrow evening at seven, as I have business in the day at the Admiralty."

Lady Caroline laid down the letter. Here was an opportunity not to be thrown away. She might now wholly emancipate herself from her husband's authority, or, at all events, to make terms with him.

With this idea in her head Lady Caroline retired to rest, and slept. To her astonishment when she woke at daybreak, her husband was sleeping by her side.

None are so kind as the Judases that mean to betray.

They breakfasted together with mutual kindness of manner that, to any one not in the secret, would have appeared exceedingly affecting.

After breakfast James Tyrrel Blakesley, whose manner was odd and quick, abruptly bade adieu to his wife and went out.

Shall these two, united by vows of everlasting love, ever meet again in this world

The day appeared fearfully long to Lady Caroline, who towards evening dressed herself carefully in a suit of black, very plainly but neatly, without once touching spirits all day.

Was she not going to see her beloved son?

About half-past six a plain carriage drew up to the door, and the elated wife of James Tyrrel Blakesley entered it, and bade the coachman drive to Somerset House. That was near enough.

Having reached her destination she alighted, and, though trembling with anxiety, managed to reach the end of Holywell-street.

The house to which she was directed was about the middle of the street, which, the night being gloomy and foggy, was deserted.

A solitary figure, short, stout, and somewhat grotesque in appearance, strode up and down near the number to which she was directed.

Suddenly the figure stood in her way.

"Lady Blakesley, a word with you," said the well-known voice of the Blue Dwarf.

"Goldy Gordon," cried the lady, with a start, "what is—do not detain me. My son awaits me."

"Oh, I see; that's the game, is it? Madam, say, rather, death awaits you."

"Gracious heaven!"

"Let me not whisper the words so that they may float on the air. Shall I tell you who waits for you in the house of Madame Carabosse?"

"Speak!"

"Your husband and ——"

The Dwarf bent low.

"My God!" shrieked Lady Caroline, and, without another word, she allowed the Blue Dwarf to lead her back to her carriage, into which he also entered.

CHAPTER LXXX.

CALCRAFT JUNIOR.

CORNET William Lennox had no very definite plan when he started on his journey. He had a vague idea of entering the French lines and appealing to the generosity of the French generals at first passed through his mind; but this idea he rejected, except as a last resource.

He resolved to trust to the chapter of accidents.

In conversation, the previous day, he had learned that the principal strength of the English position lay in the fact that there was only one ford in the river which skirted their lines leading to the French camp by a narrow valley. Now, if the ruffianly abductors of Lillian and Mary had in reality moved in the direction of the French forces, they must have crossed this ford.

Thither, then, the officer and his servant directed their steps.

Jack Horne, who was a particularly thoughtful fellow, had borrowed a lantern, and a leather bottle of wine, in case of accidents. He rode behind his master in no agreeable mood He had made up his mind to kill the three ruffians if they only gave him a chance.

The ford was not reached without difficulty.

They had to pass through the English lines, and, to avoid detention, to pass secretly.

At length, however, the spot was reached, and the river crossed.

Their way was quite clear now, as there was but one path up the valley.

The two now rode about in earnest conversation. A ride of about a mile brought them to the verge of a considerable forest, beneath the leafy arches of which they entered by a beaten path.

They considered it must be about two, when, after making their way with extreme caution, both suddenly came to a stand-still.

"Did you see a light?" said William.

"And heard voices," replied Jack Horne.

The two dismounted, and, tying their horses, crept forward on foot, using every device of woodcraft to avoid making the slightest noise.

In a few minutes a ruined farm-house and mill was presented to their view, round which stood a piquet of horses.

What was to be done?

There was no sentry at the door. The whole party were in right good humour, for shouts of laughter, and cries of astonishment, and congratulation sounded high in the night air.

William and Jack crept almost on their hands and feet towards the old farm-house.

The building was in ruins. Every wall was cracked, and apparently ready to fall.

They knelt down by a chink, and peered in.

Yes; there were the three ruffians in conversation with some half dozen soldiers, who were speaking a language which William directly knew to be German.

Wine and tobacco appeared to be in abundance.

But no sign of the girls.

Again the two young men rose, and crept round the building until they came to the window of a small room, inside that in which were the guests.

Loud rose the voices of the revellers, and Cornet William Lennox shuddered when he heard that, as the wine got in their heads, reference was made to the girls. The non-commissioned officer was in warm dispute with Captain Frederick Winterton.

As yet the dispute took the appearance of a friendly discussion.

With a wild and beating heart William Lennox peered into the little room. As he expected, the two girls were there, seated side by side and hand in hand.

The window was neither barred, nor were its shutters closed. But fear kept the young women from attempting escape.

William lowered his voice to the faintest whisper, and said one word:

"Lillian!"

She did not move, but a soft smile illumined her visage.

"Rise gently, and come to the window," he continued.

The discussion was getting hot and furious.

Lillian and Mary, well aware that a false step would be fatal, rose gently, and came to the window.

In another moment they were outside.

An old saw-pit, overgrown with bushes, was close at hand. Into this the whole party glided.

It was time.

The non-commissioned officer had at last insisted on the girls being brought in to join the carouse. Their flight was instantly discovered.

"Disperse!—scour the woods!" roared the officer. "They cannot be far. I will take the road to the ford."

In five minutes all the French soldiers—soldiers of the German frontiers—had mounted and rode off.

The three men remained behind.

William clasped the hand of his servant.

"Come," he said, and clambered out of the pit.

They walked boldly up to the farm-house, and looked in. The three men were sitting round the fire.

"Curses light on these French fiends!" said Captain Frederick Winterton. "But I will see their superiors, and have justice."

"You shall," replied William Lennox, knocking him on the head with a pistol, while his companion did the same for Slimy Jones.

The Honourable John surrendered without a struggle.

Jack Horne cocked his pistol.

"No; it would be dangerous. Accident has placed a better means in our hands—"

And he pointed to a long coil of rope, such as is used in tethering horses.

Jack rubbed his hands, and, catching it up, made, under his master's directions, two nooses.

The cord was then thrown over a beam.

A noose was passed round the neck of Captain Frederick, and, as soon as he came to, his arms were pinioned, and himself hoisted on a rickety old stool. The noose was round his neck, so that the slightest false step was fatal.

Despite a fierce resistance, the same was done for the Honourable John.

In a few minutes the two ruffians, livid, ghastly, their eyes starting in their sockets, stood on the brink of eternity.

"My good young man," said the Honourable John, "how long are you going to carry on this joke? It's all very fine, but do you know that a false step might make it serious?"

"Release us, and meet one as a man, face to face, and pistol to pistol," added Captain Frederick.

"No!" said William Lennox, sternly. "Have no expectation of mercy from me. Murderers, forgers, and assassins, the laws of your country condemn you to death! As deserters to the enemy, again you deserve death. Make your peace with heaven, for, as surely as I live, you die this night."

"Shall I kick them stools away?" cried Jack.

"Oh! no," gasped Honourable John.

"Wretch!" said the captain.

"No!" replied William Lennox; "let them be their own executioners. Pinion that ruffian who is shamming sleep yonder, and then we will go. They cannot stand long in this position. As a just retribution of their crime they shall be their own executioners."

"Mercy!" cried John.

"Mr. William Lennox," said Captain Frederick Winterton, with forced calmness, "this is mean and cowardly. If we have done anything to deserve death, we have a right to trial by a jury of our countrymen. You have no right to commit this cold-blooded and cruel murder. If you are a man, release us, and you shall hear of us no more."

"Come!" said William Lennox, sternly.

Jack Horne, who had pinioned Slimy Jones, too happy at not being included in the execution to make any resistance, at once obeyed his master, and went out with him without once turning his back.

The cousins looked at one another with a wild and fearful glance. Both knew that the slightest false step would be instant death for one or both. Each, therefore, watched the other's feet with intense and absorbing interest.

"Jones," said Captain Frederick, "are you there?"

"Just so."

"Come and cut us down."

"Just so—tied up myself."

"But Jones, good Jones, you can get free," observed the Honourable John.

"Just so," replied Jones; "but wait a bit, until they are out of sight."

"We can wait, good Jones," continued Captain Frederick, with profound respect in his tones, "but not too long."

"Not too long," said John.

"Just so."

It was true. Jack Horne, in his hurry, had tied Slimy Jones so carelessly that he easily slipped his arms out of the cord, and then untied his feet.

He then coolly filled a tumbler of wine, and drank it off with great apparent relish.

The cousins stared at him with awe-struck eyes.

"Make haste!" said the captain.

"Just so."

"Good Jones," whimpered John.

"Just so," continued Jones, taking up his staff and knapsack.

"You are not going?" cried the captain, aghast.

"Just so."

"Where?" yelled John.

"Just so;—to the cave of Alcantara," coolly responded the ruffian. "The money is mine as residuary legatee!"

"Jones," said the captain, as quick as his beating heart and whirling brain would allow him, "I have been a good master to you."

"Just so."

"Always paid you well."

"Just so."

"Now I undertake, if you will free us, to let you have the whole of that money," he began.

"Just so. Bother," said Jones, and he raised his feet to kick away the stools.

Then there rose on the night air a wild cry of anguish, as of two despairing souls, that made even Jones start. But the villain was determined, and, without daring to look in the faces of his late masters, he raised his foot again.

"In the name of heaven, mercy!" cried Captain Frederick Winterton.

"Mercy!" repeated John.

"Just so. Ha, ha, ha! only to fancy," laughed the cold-blooded wretch; "only to fancy Captain Frederick Winterton and the Honourable John begging their lives of me! One—two—three!"

CHAPTER LXXXI.

THE LEAP.

MEANWHILE Cornet William Lennox and Jack Horne had led the young women to where, luckily for them, they had placed their horses in a thicket. Without a moment's hesitation both mounted, and their steeds being first-rate ones, the additional burthen of the girls was not perceptibly felt. Neither spoke. They felt it necessary to listen, as they knew that the French soldiers would soon return upon their footsteps. With a view to be ready for any contingency they walked their horses, and, finding a pathway which turned to the left, they diverged from their route.

This path was rugged and appeared to ascend, so that it was clear they would have to make a long detour.

Suddenly a faint streak of dawn illumined the sky, as they made their exit from the forest, and appeared upon an arid and rocky plain.

The horses as yet gave no sign of fatigue, but this could not last long with their double burthen.

Suddenly Jack Horne struck his spurs into his steed, and darted away at full speed.

William Lennox did the same, casting, however, one look behind.

The French soldiers were galloping after them as hard as their horses could gallop, yelling, shouting, and calling upon them to stop.

They answered by the free administration of whip and spur, though the race was almost hopeless.

William Lennox looked ahead. All he could see was a rocky slope, up which his heavily burthened horse made his way, panting and stumbling.

Suddenly he was about to rein in at the sight of a deep and gloomy chasm, but, on second thoughts, he gave a terrific dig of the spurs to his horse and leaped.

It was a fearful undertaking, and but for the terrible excitement of the moment, he would never have done it. The river, which he had previously crossed that evening, was here confined between lofty rocks, which might often have been leaped by a fresh and powerful horse.

The steed snorted as he took the terrific stride, and next instant was on the opposite side, just as the French soldiers came whooping and yelling up.

The gallant animal fell, however, on his knees, and the two rolled off on the ground just as the infuriated French soldiers fired a volley of carbines.

They fell harmless as far as the young officer and Lillian were concerned, but the noble steed gave one sigh, and rolled into the depths below.

Before the French soldiers could reload the two lovers were concealed behind a rock.

But not a trace could they see of either Jack Horne or Mary.

The small troop of French soldiers, being nowise inclined to risk the terrific leap which had saved William Lennox and Lillian, turned upon their heels, and in a few minutes were out of sight.

"Jack Horne!" shouted William.

"Here you are, sir," responded that individual, who, unnoticed by the soldiers, had ridden up to a much more easy width in the chasm, and there taken a similar leap to his master.

They now re-united the party, and a halt was declared, as all parties were exhausted with fatigue.

Both Lillian and Mary appeared drowsy, and it was determined that they should all rest awhile ere taking their departure for the English camp. In ten minutes more there was dead silence in the little camp. All were asleep, or appeared to be so.

*　　*　　*　　*　　*

We left Messrs. Frederick and John Winterton in rather an unpleasant position, the noose round their necks, and the cold-blooded Slimy Jones about to perform the office of Jack Ketch *alias* Calcraft.

The wretch appeared to enjoy the sufferings of his late masters.

"Is there anything I can do for you?" he said, with a cold hypocritical grin.

"I have said the money is yours if you save us," reiterated Captain Frederick.

"Just so. Is that all you says afore I works you off?" said Jones.

"Do, there's a good Jones, wait just a little bit," whined John; "life's so pleasant."

"Just so, even on the drop," sneered Master Slimy Jones; "but time's a waluable article—so here goes."

The cousins exchanged glances, and both at the same instant set up a series of the most horrible, fearful, and hideous yells that ever were heard from mortal throat.

"Just so. Will you be quiet, eh?" said Slimy Jones, himself alarmed.

And with furious determination he kicked away the stools.

As he did so he was caught by the throat, and then a sword flashed, and the struggling victims were cut down.

"Eh—what's this?" said the non-commissioned officer, who was not in the best humour in the world.

Slimy Jones didn't know the French language, and the two cousins were yet speechless.

They had, however, been cut down so instantaneously that no harm had been done, and in a few minutes the captain was able to give an explanation.

The non-commissioned officer said a few words to his men, who with a grim smile seized Slimy Jones,

That individual began to shriek and yell with abject terror.

A noose was cast round his neck.

"Just so," said Captain Frederick Winterton, with a saturnine grin; "how do you like it?"

With perfect professional rapidity the French soldiers found an old barrel, on which they stood Slimy Jones, so that he just escaped hanging by standing on tiptoe, Captain Frederick and the Honourable John overwhelming him all the time with curses and ridicule.

"Just so," said the unfortunate wretch, "you knew I was only joking. I would'nt have hurt such kind masters for all the world—you know I would'nt. Pray, good gentlemen, save me, and I will show you a treasure—ten thousand guineas all in gold."

"*Guênees!*" said the French subaltern with a start; "what is that he says?"

"Poor wretch," replied Captain Frederick, with a cold-blooded wink at Slimy Jones. "He says he'd give a thousand guineas not to be where he is."

The French soldiers laughed heartily, and John and Frederick thanked their stars that they did not understand English, and that Slimy Jones did not understand French.

The soldiers now prepared to depart with the two Englishmen as prisoners, the unfortunate partner in their crimes filling the air with imprecations, supplications, prayers, and yells. He cursed, he apologised, he cried, he promised, but all in vain. His employers were too glad to get rid of him, while the rude soldiers were infinitely amused at the sight.

There was plenty of straw and wood about the place, so that, just as they left, a French soldier, who was lighting his pipe, cast the piece of burning paper upon some straw.

"Hung, and then roasted," he said, with a brutal laugh.

The cousins actually shuddered. The ferocity of this savage Alsatian was something which horrified even their seared and hardened souls.

Then up rose from the farm-house one wild scream, and all was still. Every part of it was in flames, even to the old and tindery thatch.

The troop disappeared in the forest.

CHAPTER LXXXII.
THE BLUE DWARF.

THE consternation of James Tyrrel Blakesley and Sir Edgar, when Lady Caroline did not come, was as nothing to the state of mind into which they fell when they found that Lady Caroline had left the hotel in a carriage at the time arranged, and had ordered the coachman to drive her to Somerset House.

They rushed to the livery stables whence the carriage had been sent, and it had not returned. They waited about in an agony of mind such as only the guilty can suffer, and still the carriage came not.

At length, about midnight, it reappeared, and they hastily stopped it.

"Where is the lady you drove out?" said James.

"Do'nt know," was the surly reply.

"Nonsense. You drove my wife out, and I must have an account of where you have taken her. I do'nt mind paying you handsomely, mind."

"Just let me drive into the yard; my hoss is done up," said the jarvey.

Prowse

They willingly agreed; and, as soon as the coachman was ready, adjourned to a public-house.

"Well, you see, sir," said the jarvey, in answer to a question from both at once, "it's little I can tell yer. Your very good health, sir. I druv the lady to Somerset House, when she gets out, and walks away. About ten minutes arter she comes back with the ugliest cove as ever I see."

"Ah!" cried James.

"The Dwarf!" said Sir Edgar.

"And the most ugliest I ever seed," continued the cabby; "and then, arter a while, they tells me to drive to Soady's, his hotel, and wait. Well, I waited nigh three hours, when I goes in and axes if the lady and the little gentleman was a coming. Blowed if they hadn't just past into the yard, hired a postchaise, and been gone two hours and a half, and nobody knew'd which way they had gone."

"Done, by all the furies!" cried James.

"Well, if so be as your lady has been and runned away with that 'ere little man, she's a rummy one, that's all I can say," said Jarvey, with a grin.

"There's two guineas for you, so say no more about it," replied James; and the two rose and left the coachee in a very much better humour than that they had found him in.

"Done!—lost!—ruined!" cried James, as soon as they were alone.

"No," said Sir Edgar Blakesley, with a cunning wink of the eye. "My mother is mad. I will stand to the last. Unless this accursed Dwarf produces *him* in court, his evidence will go for nothing. My father's bankers—you—everybody have recognised me. I have every document in my possession to prove my identity."

"Then *he* must be got rid of before *they* meet."

"But how is it to be done?" said the young man with a shudder.

"I don't know; but done it must be," said James.

"Where is he? What has become of him?" cried Sir Edgar.

"I do not know. But we can easily find out. I dread more his silence than his action."

"He moves in first-rate circles. I saw him at the opera in company with ladies of high rank."

"Still that accursed Dwarf," said James; "but 'away with melancholy'—let us go try the hazard of the die!"

"With all my heart! A broiled bone and some ballet girls after. I want excitement."

"Hurra!" cried James.

Terror in these two men produced a state of phrensy in which they sought for some excitement to drown care. They repaired accordingly to a gaming-house in St. James's-street, and were soon absorbed in the mysteries of chicken-hazard and rouge et noir.

It was a splendid house, furnished in most gorgeous style, and supplied with the very best of wines and every luxury that could excite the appetite, while numerous ladies, who, after the theatre and other occupations, were wont to chance their money on the green board, sat around.

These were chiefly old women, the most rampant gamblers in creation.

But there were several young ones, whose mission was of a different kind.

James Tyrrel Blakesley and Sir Edgar played with varied success for some time, rather winning than losing.

Suddenly the latter raised his eyes, and there, his countenance imperturbably sarcastic, stood the Marquis of A—— gazing at him; while, behind the Marquis was a man in great red whiskers and blue spectacles, who was whispering to the marquis over his shoulders.

The marquis nodded.

A cold shiver passed through the bones of Sir Edgar Blakesley—a nameless horror was on his soul.

"Come away," he whispered to James.

"Why?"

"Come away, I say," he repeated in a hoarse whisper, "I will tell you why."

James Tyrrel Blakesley had already invited two young ladies to sup with them, so that he was less disinclined than he otherwise might have been to leave the gambling house. He then rose and, assisting the young ladies to put on their cloaks, was about to leave, when the Marquis of A—— approached and bowed haughtily to the young man.

"This is my card," he said, "I should be obliged for yours."

"Certainly," replied Sir Edgar, his eyes still fixed on the man in the red whiskers and blue spectacles.

He handed the card and, turning away, offered his arm to one of the young ladies.

CHAPTER LXXXIII.

WALKING THE PLANK.

IT was nearly daylight. High was the revelry in the sitting-room of an hotel where James Tyrrel Blakesley and Sir Edgar had ordered supper. Everything which could tempt the appetite was on the table, with flagons of the most delicious and expensive wines.

James Tyrrel Blakesley and Sir Edgar, without being intoxicated, were excited with wine to the last degree. The girls, worthless and heartless, amused them with their false and hollow gaiety. They sang, told stories, and in every way strove to amuse their entertainers.

But James Tyrrel Blakesley was thinking of his wife and the Blue Dwarf.

Sir Edgar was thinking of the stranger and his duel with the Marquis of A——.

Both were dull, morose, and if they did laugh, laughed with a hollowness which was a mockery on mirth.

"I say, James," said Polly Jameson, a blonde syren about nineteen, whose heart was as cold as marble, "are you going to your own funeral to-morrow."

"Why?"

"Because you look like a mute."

All laughed, and Sir Edgar volunteered a song. He told them to fill the glasses with champagne, and would regale them with a Bacchanalian ditty.

His mouth was open to begin, his glass was raised, when he turned pale as ashes, and gazed wildly at the door.

There, in the open doorway, stern, cold, bitter, even awful in his icy demeanour—was Tourloorou.

Quick as lightning Sir Edgar recovered himself. The other was an enemy, a French soldier—a spy.

He rose to approach the bell.

Tourloorou opened his coat and tapped a brace of pistols at his belt.

The girls shrieked.

The young Frenchman bowed low to the ladies. They gazed at him for a moment with astonishment, and then both of them laughed outright.

"What do you want, spy?" said Sir Edgar haughtily, "have you a charmed life that you come here with a rope round your neck."

"Where is my Pauline—my affianced bride?" said the other in a hollow voice.

"I don't know——"

"Liar and scoundrel! Listen! I have come to see her, to offer her one chance of repentance. Her mother is dying."

"Can't help it," said Sir Edgar.

"Listen, I say! I have two pistols. Lead me to her at once, or I will shoot you dead with one and myself with the other."

This was said with such awful gravity that Sir Edgar Blakesley was alarmed.

"Your friends can wait for you," said Tourlooroa.

"I will come," replied the young man.

"*Pardon*," said the young soldier in French to the two girls, and he went out, followed by Sir Edgar Blakesley, leaving the others dumbfounded.

"What beautiful eyes !" said one girl.

"What a brave fellow !" said the other.

"Madman," observed James. "Fill another glass of wine and let us laugh."

He groaned horribly as he said this; but the girls filled their glasses, and the frightful orgy continued.

Meanwhile Tourloorou and Sir Edgar had left the hotel, the former never taking his eye off the other, and his hand off his pistol, until they reached the door of the house inhabited by Pauline.

Sir Edgar opened it with a latch key, and having lighted his candle, went up stairs.

He produced his key.

"What ?" said the young soldier with a sarcastic smile, "a prisoner ?"

"She left me," replied Sir Edgar, with his hand on the lock, "for that silken thing you were speaking to at the gambling house."

The eyes of the young French soldier flashed fire, and he felt for a moment as if he could have fainted.

"But you brought her back ?"

"I did."

"Open !"

"She is in bed," said Sir Edgar Blakesley sarcastically.

"It matters not," replied the young man bending his eyes down and blushing deeply.

Sir Edgar opened the door, and entered the room.

The window was open.

He rushed to the bed.

"Gone, by heavens !" he gasped.

Tourloroou looked at him keenly.

"I swear to you – I left her here yesterday morning in good health and spirits—the traitress."

A grim smile passed over the lips of Toulouroo, as he replied—

"Pauline is French. and French girls are not easily kept in prison," he said.

"Nor Englishmen either ?"

"No—but irritate me not."

"Monsieur Simon Roger," said Sir Edgar, with a sarcastic smile. "You were all deceived. The youth you so narrowly starved to death was my *frere de lait*—foster brother."

"Ah !" replied Toulouroo, who was musing'; "but who lives in the room opposite ?"

"I don't know."

"We must find out."

"Let us knock them up—it is daylight—the servant will be about."

They prepared to descend the stairs.

Meanwhile we return to Pauline.

The room in which Pauline was confined was, as we have said, at the very top of the house. The girl, from the first moment of her arrival, had made no attempt to leave it. She was meek, and apparently reconciled to her fate.

Sir Edgar Blakesley resumed his fetters, and

was most devoted in his attentions; but he was firm and resolute. There was no chance of her obtaining her liberty from him.

She resolved, however, to obtain it in some way, and to be revenged on her lover.

One morning, while dressing, she stood at the window combing her superb tresses, when she was startled by the sound of a human voice close at hand.

Modesty was no part of Pauline's character. Therefore. though half-clad, she moved nearer to the window and looked out.

A young man in a smoking cap, with long greasy hair and a huge meerschaum pipe, was muttering some verses of song.

"*Mon Dieu !*" cried Pauline, throwing up the window of her room, regardless of the disorder of her dress, "is it possible that you are a countryman of mine ?"

"Beautiful and seraphic vision," said the young man, greedily devouring her charms with his eyes, "I have the honour to be a Frenchman, an *emigré*, a victim of the great Corsican ogre."

"Are you willing to serve me ?" continued Pauline, now coquettishly robing herself in a handsome shawl.

"With my life," said the other.

The window of the young man's room was about three yards from that at which Pauline stood. Both rooms were at the back of the house, the windows being at the side. Below was a paved court.

"Generous stranger—I am an unfortunate girl, the victim of a jealous husband, who has confined me here a prisoner. Will you aid my escape ?" said Pauline, in her low, seductive, and winning tones.

"I will. But how can it be done !"

"Could you not convey a plank to your room in the night, and I will walk across ?"

"*Mon Dieu !*" said the young man with a shudder, "you would never dare ?"

"You procure the plank and try me. Hush ! my husband," and Pauline rushed from the window and began to sing.

Sir Edgar came in with a female servant, who carried breakfast, after which the door was closed again and the key placed, as on all occasions, in his pocket.

The breakfast passed off with unusual gaiety.

"Pauline," said Sir Edgar at last, "I have some good news for you."

"Indeed !" cried the girl.

"I have taken a house for you at Brighton—all the world is mad about that new and royal watering place."

"You don't say so ?"

"Then I have secured a lovely little box of a house, beautifully furnished, and if my Pauline will only be reasonable, we can be as happy as ever. My carriage will be here to-night."

"So soon as that," said Pauline, with an imperceptible glance of the eyes towards the window.

Sir Edgar took no notice, and presently rose to go out, after announcing that a milliner would be sent to replenish her wardrobe.

Then they embraced affectionately and parted.

Pauline flew to the window. The young Frenchman was there with a long plank in his hand.

Pauline could scarcely help laughing at him outright.

The other, however, very gravely pushed it forward, and by the exercise of considerable ingenuity, passed it across.

A key was turned in the door of her room.

With one bound, she was upon the plank, the young man was scarcely able to restrain a shriek, and then she was assisted to leap into his room and the plank withdrawn.

The window of Pauline's room remained open.

Pauline had escaped.

The young man with the greasy hair, moustachios, and smoking cap, gallantly received the young lady in his arms, assisted her to descend, and at once removed the plank and closed the window.

"I thank you," she said with her most seductive smile, "Monsieur, *vous etes un galant homme!*"

The Frenchman bowed.

"I am the Vicomte de Chabannes," he said, "very much at your service."

"Monsieur the Viscount," said Pauline, "we must not remain here. If my husband finds me, I am ruined. We must fly at once."

"We fly," said the Viscount, a cold perspiration coming out over his whole body, "and where shall we find the money?"

"You are poor," she replied, in a caressing tone, "my dear Viscount; but *I* am rich—what matters it, if you will defend me against my husband."

The Viscount's face was suffused with burning blushes. It was true he was poor, but he was proud.

"What can I do for madam?" he said, with a low and respectful bow.

"Give me your arm, call a carriage, and drive to a French hotel. I will engage apartments there."

Again the Viscount bowed.

They descended the stairs together, and went out into the street. At the end was a hackney coach stand.

They both entered one, and the Viscount told them to drive to the Hotel de Louis XIV., then much frequented by emigrants, and where Monsieur the Viscount took his dinner—when he had any money.

Pauline was in high spirits, and when they reached the hotel insisted that the Viscount should join her at breakfast.

After some little hesitation he consented.

If the truth be told he was hungry.

After breakfast they issued forth to look for a respectable lodging.

Pauline had determined to use the services of the Viscount, though he was poor, and therefore was most caressing and seductive in her manner.

One lover, more or less, could make little difference to her.

Most ballet girls think three at a time a very fair allowance.

Casting her eyes on every side to see they were not followed, they took their way to some little distance from the hotel, and then began looking about. Pauline soon found a handsome suite of rooms, and paying very freely, had no difficulty in obtaining them at once.

Pauline said her luggage would come in next day, and having ordered dinner, took the Viscount's arm and went out shopping.

Then the Viscount would have taken his departure, but she had business for him in the evening.

They dined together, they supped together, and the Viscount de Chabannes, alas! did not return home.

*   *   *   *

When Tourloorou and Sir Edgar Blakesley knocked at the house next door, a half-sleepy servant girl who had just risen, opened the door and stared at the intruders.

"My dear," said Sir Edgar, slipping a crown into her hand, "I want to ask you a question or two."

"With pleasure, sir," she replied with a deep curtsey, "will you walk in?"

The two men entered the parlour.

"Who occupies the top room at the back next to No. 12?" asked Sir Edgar.

"Oh, such a funny gentleman," giggled the girl, "the Viscount de Chabannes."

"Oh! is he at home?

"Oh, no—he went out yesterday morning—I see'd him and he brought a great long plank. He took it up in his bed-room, and about an hour after, he comes down with the most beautiful woman I ever clapped eyes on, and went out, and what's more, he ain't even been back again."

Sir Edgar with flashing eyes translated the words of the speaker.

Tourloorou understood a few words of English sufficient to know that he spoke the truth.

"Come away," he said, grinding his teeth, "I must kill you all— you first — the Marquis second, and the Viscount third."

And with a haughty statement that the other would hear from him next day, he strode off, leaving the other standing in the street in no very enviable state of mind.

He did not so much care for the loss of Pauline, as he did for the risk her life ran.

Meanwhile Simon Roger passed away the demon of jealousy in his heart. He was one of those men whose passions, once roused with regard to a woman, could never rest until the complete fruition of his hopes. It was no matter to him that the woman was vile, worthless, and had already yielded herself up to several others; he remembered only as she was once—innocent and virtuous.

Had he have been a wise man he would have scorned her and her paramours.

A worthless woman is worse than a serpent —worse than the deadliest viper in the world.

And their sting is more deadly, for it cancers body and soul.

Before twelve o'clock next day, Sir Edgar Blakesley received a letter announcing that his ship, which had been refitting, was ready for sea, and ordering him to join without one moment's delay.

Sir Edgar posted off to his bankers, showed the letter, received a hearty shake of the hand, and in another hour was dashing off to Portsmouth as fast as his horses could take him.

He however first wrote to the theatre to Pauline to say, that the house at Brighton was at her orders, and that if she would behave herself during his absence, she should marry him immediately on his return home.

CHAPTER LXXXIV.

THE BATTLE.

SUDDENLY Cornet William Lennox and his party were awakened by a heavy fire on their left.

They started to their feet, and saw with astonishment that a very large party of French, some double at least the number of the English at that point, had crossed by the ford, and were making in heavy columns for the English lines.

A heavy cannonade had commenced on all hands, and the British forces were forming on the heights.

"By jakes," said Jack Horn, "we're in a pretty pickle."

"Silence," replied the officer. "Mount, Lillian, mount. Mary, you leap up behind her. I must join my regiment without a moment's delay."

Lillian shuddered at the terrible spectacle offered them, but made no reply. Her lover was right, but she was none the less alarmed at the consequences.

The assault was becoming general, and the battle soon raged on all the lines. The noise of the cannonade, of the musketry, the roll of drums, the fifes—the shrill cries of the wounded—made fearful clamour.

Lillian was glad when she saw the tents of the English, and William bade her hurry in that direction.

At that moment his regiment was ordered to charge down hill upon the French.

Several horses were flying about the field; William and Jack caught one each, and ere the trumpet had sounded the charge, he was with his troop, being welcomed by a loud shout.

In another moment the regiment was pouring down the slope of the hill like a whirlwind.

Then all was smoke, confusion, and horror.

William Lennox knew only that he was hand to hand with several of the enemy, and then, as both parties left off firing, he saw that his dragoons were in disorder; while in front of them were two regiments of infantry, supported by cavalry.

Then he saw in the centre of the line a white bare head, and a dozen bayonets and sabres levelled at it.

He knew it was his Colonel, the rigid and stern Sir John Coyne.

With a spring, he dashed forward—just in time.

A gigantic cuirassier had raised his sabre to brain the colonel, when his sword struck up his arm, and then whirled round upon the other's face.

Still, the colonel was evidently severely wounded.

The regiment was forcibly retreating. The numbers against it were overwhelming.

William, with a loud shout to the men to rally, caught the colonel's hand in his, and, fighting with the other, retreated with marvellous coolness and collectedness.

Then came a terrific shout; the regiment which had reformed, charged, and William Lennox fainted.

When he came to, the colonel was seated on a drum, looking at him, and the Commander-in-Chief was gazing with a smile at the group.

"Are you better, Captain Lennox?" said Sir John Coyne, kindly.

"Better," replied William Lennox, wildly, "Captain! Sir John Coyne!"

"Yes, my brave fellow. Sir Arthur, this lad not only saved my life, when assailed by a dozen men, but rallied the regiment, and made them retreat in order, when every other officer was down. There are two vacant captaincies."

"Well, I suppose, had he not come up in time, I must have made him colonel," said the Commander-in-Chief, with a grim smile.

"Gad! he narrowly escaped it."

"But he is under arrest!"

"He's fleshed his maiden sword, Sir Arthur; so no more of that," said the good old soldier, rigid and severe disciplinarian as he was.

The roaring of the cannon had ceased. The French regiments had re-crossed the river, with great loss.

"Were you successful, Captain Lennox?" said the Commander.

"Yes, Sir Arthur," replied the young captain, so unexpectedly promoted.

"I thought so; I fancy I saw the beauties go by. Will you and the ladies dine with me to-day?"

And the great soldier, having seen the attack repelled, rode away to his quarters as if nothing had happened.

"I say, captain," said Sir John Coyne, when they were alone, "you and I are friends, I suppose?"

"Sir John," replied the young soldier, taking his hand with emotion.

"You know I'm rather rough sometimes, but I make good soldiers."

"God bless you!" said William.

"Recollect, I am your friend for life," said his colonel; "but hush! here come my men, and if they see me shaking hands with a deserter, egad! they'll think I should desert myself next."

William smiled, and assisted his commander to mount.

The dinner was for seven, and Mrs. Winterton, despite her nervous excitement, would not refuse the invitation, especially when she heard the news of William's promotion.

They were all, therefore, to their time, and were received by England's greatest soldier with that gentle courtesy which was part of his character.

After dinner, when they retired, the future duke introduced the young captain to his superiors in terms of high praise.

"Sir Arthur," said the blushing youth, "may I be allowed to speak?"

"Yes, sir."

"I have something to say which may change your kind intentions," said William.

"Speak," replied Sir Arthur, kindly.

"It is a short account of who and what I am."

"Go on."

The officers filled their glasses, and gazed curiously at the youthful officer.

Then, in eloquent, brief, and telling language, the young man, forgetting the presence he was in, and only remembering his subject, told his whole story without reservation or hesitation.

The narrative lasted two hours, and not one of the company even yawned.

"Young man," said the great soldier, "your secret is safe with us. What you have said in no way alters my intention. I will make a note of what you have said, and communicate with the Horse Guards. Padré," addressing the superior of the convent, who had been asleep, "let us have coffee."

We need scarcely say that not a word of what William Lennox had said ever passed the threshold of that door. With few exceptions, English officers are gentlemen.

CHAPTER LXXXV.

THE MASKED BALL.

FROM that hour William Lennox became an immense favourite with his colonel, who was not at all ashamed to let everybody know how hasty he had been.

It happened, however, about two months later that, in an affair of outposts, William was wounded severely, though not dangerously, and was invalided to Madrid.

Mrs. Winterton at once determined to return to the capital for two reasons—first the fear of the cousins, who were known to have aided the attack on the English lines, and then from fear of Lillian fretting on the absence of her affianced lover.

She was such a charming little nurse that William Lennox declared he could not do without her.

Gaily then they set out for Madrid despite the young captain's wound, while Jack and Mary rejoiced equally on the rumble.

They had bought an English travelling carriage.

The journey was performed this time without the slightest interruption, and the whole party arrived in Madrid just in time to partake of the festivities, which the inhabitants of that mercurial capital delighted to give to their deliverers, the English; though by this time their gratitude has evaporated much after the fashion of that of all southern countries.

William Lennox, having been examined by the medical staff, was pronounced out of all danger, though ordered to take strict care of himself.

He was not, however, prohibited from taking part in the festivities, but he was strictly prohibited from dancing.

There certainly was a certain amount of discomfort in this, as it was impossible for Lillian to refuse all offers.

William Lennox, however, knowing her simple and guileless nature, cared for this less than most young officers would have done, though still it was a privation.

It was a splendid masked ball at the great theatre of Madrid, and all the English officers, both of army and navy, had been invited. Captain William Lennox, as usual, accompanied Lillian, who was beautifully dressed. The young officer at once took a seat, and gazed at the scene around him with pleasure. It was a grand and magnificent sight.

Lillian was soon taken from him. The English officers in uniform formed a large party of the assemblage, and it would have been ungracious to refuse them.

William leaned back in an arm chair in a secluded corner, listening to the music, watching the dancers, and amusing himself about as much as any other young man in love.

His pale, handsome, and intellectual countenance, drew great attention from the ladies.

Many a pearly row of teeth turned with a smile towards him, and many a dark eye peered with languishing tenderness on his face.

But William Lennox was steeled against all seductions.

At least, so he thought.

About twelve, Lillian had just left him with an apology for the tremendous number of dances she was having, when a woman, in a pink domino, with a mask, and a fringed beard hanging from it, seated herself at the little table he occupied.

"How patient you are," she said, in one of those voices which vibrate to the soul.

"What mean you, madam?" replied William Lennox, with a slight flush on his pallid countenance.

"I mean, to sit here so long—so quiet. You are ill"—she continued, still softly and seductively.

"I am not well, but I am very happy," said William Lennox, with a smile.

"Happy—alone—deserted," continued the lady.

"No, madam; you are very kind," answered William, "I am not deserted. My doctors won't let me dance, but my future bride is here dancing for me."

The lady drew a long breath and looked him keenly in the eyes.

"Your bride—so young, and yet engaged in marriage," she replied, in a somewhat constrained tone.

"Ever since I was sixteen years of age," he said, smiling.

"Then I suppose you will not come to my evenings," she continued pettishly, and yet half inclined to laugh at a man who would not be made love to, because he was engaged to be married.

"Why not," said William flushing a little in the face, and, as it were, fascinated by her lively voice.

She would not have been pleased had she known that he was afraid she might do some injury to Lillian were she to be offended.

With her lovely hands, her matchless arms, white, round, and adorned with countless jewels, she drew forth a card-case, and taking out a pencil prepared to write.

"Your name, Signor ?"

"Captain William Lennox."

"What a shame!" she cried, clasping her hands, "in the land where I should be a queen you would be a general."

William Lennox could not help colouring with pleasure.

"To-morrow night," she said, squeezed his hand, and disappeared.

William Lennox looked quickly at the card, and under a ducal crown read—

Marie Dolores, Duchess of Castella.

He started, for he knew that she was the most beautiful woman in Spain—at the same time report said that she was not only light of character, but a perfect Messalina.

William Lennox shuddered, and yet there came over him—and with what young and innocent heart would it not have been the same—a wild sense of pleasure at the thought of being loved by one so beautiful.

He had intended to tell Lillian, but now he secreted the card in his pocket.

Alas, for poor human nature !

At this moment his ears were assailed in a way that made him almost start to his feet.

"Just so—very likely—beautiful—but I don't see any fun it; do you? Well, just so—slow work this; suppose we adjourn to the supper-room—wine, yes—just so—wine and women, that's my theory—and, just so, plenty of money, that's it—just so."

Yes, it was. William Lennox looked up, and there, in the superb dress of a Spanish hidalgo, with sword, jewels, and magnificent feathers, was Slimy Jones, while, on each side of him, in the garb of fancy theatrical fishermen, were two English sons of the deep, who seemed to be under his convoy.

William Lennox was so astonished he could not speak, and when, in a few minutes, Lillian came up, he looked so pale that the young girl was quite alarmed.

"Where is your mamma ?" he said, hurriedly. "Are you ill ?"

"No; but fetch Mrs. Winterton," he replied.

Lillian turned away to where her mother sat amid a knot of ladies in one of the boxes, and speedily brought her round.

"What is it, William ?" she said.

"That wretch Slimy Jones is here," he answered.

"Let us go away at once," she replied.

And, regardless of the fact that Lillian was engaged half a dozen deep, they all went away.

A long conference was held at the hotel, and then it was determined to put both the Spanish police and Mr Richard Forester on his track.

William then retired to rest, to dream of

Lillian, the cousins, just so—and shall we add of Marie Dolores, Duchess of Castella.

CHAPTER LXXXVI.

THE RECEPTION.

IT had been decided that the next evening should be a quiet one, and hence William was able to get away from his friends by ten o'clock.

It was with a pang that he bade adieu to Lillian, and for a moment he lingered, as if about to say something.

But a wild and frantic desire to see the duchess overcame every other consideration.

He dressed with unusual care, and a little past eleven o'clock, on showing his card, he was ushered into the superb apartments of the duchess, crowded with all the *élite* of the male society of Madrid in brilliant uniforms and civic costumes, and by a certain amount of beautiful and lovely women.

The very particular among the ladies did not visit the duchess.

William Lennox glided behind the brilliant group of his superior officers, wishing to see the duchess, without being seen at first.

In this way he gradually found himself near a group from which he would like to have retreated.

"Ha ! ha ! my Orlando—my knight of the round table," said the voice of Sir John Coyne; "come hither. How goes it? How is it I have not seen you before ?"

"I have not been well, Sir John," replied the young man, bowing profoundly to the commander-in-chief; "and then your time is valuable."

"Captain Lennox," said Sir Arthur kindly, "I am glad to see you about. Your rank is confirmed, and the note made you requested. Come here."

The young man approached, and the great soldier drew him on one side.

"There is a memorandum of a midshipman claiming the same name as yourself—a young gentleman who has made himself rather notorious in reference to a certain actress."

"Sir Arthur," said the young officer trembling, and turning pale, "that is the wretch; but I have letters from England, the tenor of which is that his time is nearly up—the day of retribution is at hand."

"Very glad to hear it," said the future duke. "Always pleased at rascality being exposed. There is my hand, Captain Lennox, and command me whenever I can be of use. I like courage and modesty."

The young officer bent low to hide his blushes and confusion as he took the duke's hand.

When he was once more erect, the duchess was by his side, holding out her hand with an angelic smile.

William Lennox thought that he had never seen anything so beautiful in his life.

The duchess drew him away, amid a murmur of regret from a dozen cavaliers.

"Brave and modest," she said, raising her

seraphic eyes to his, beaming as they were with liquid light and fire.

"D—— the woman," said Sir John Coyne, "she'll bedevil the boy."

"I think not," replied Sir Arthur Wellesley, drily.

People said—but never mind what people said!

The Duchess of Castella was about the middle height, with an olive complexion, golden hair, deep blue eyes, and a mouth whi.h was the magic charm of her countenance.

It was her bust, however, that was the glorious feature of her wondrous beauty. Never, perhaps, had the wildest imagination of poet, painter, or sculptor imagined anything more glowing, lovely, or beautiful.

And she knew it, and wished to let others know it too.

William Lennox trembled as he walked with her upon his arm, but not with fear. She pressed his arm and looked up into his eyes with an expression that, weak as he was, made his eyes swim.

The Duchess said not a word, but gliding through the bowing and admiring crowds, she suddenly passed through a doorway, crossed a conservatory, and reached a small low arch, concealed by tapestry.

William Lennox's heart beat wildly.

The Duchess drew forth a key and opened a door. They were in a boudoir, and in presence of a table loaded with refreshments of the most exquisite kind.

"It was very kind of you to come," said the Duchess, making him take a cozy arm-chair, "unwell as you evidently are. Come, a bumper of this wine, and the pallor of your cheek will pass. You don't want anything to make your eyes sparkle brightly."

This was said with a merry laugh.

William Lennox blushed.

The Duchess looked at him with eyes of fire. His evident innocence and shamefacedness delighted her. It was something new in her strange career.

She poured out a tumbler of wine; she carved some game, cooked by a French cook of celebrity, and placed it before him.

William Lennox hesitated.

"Eat," said the Duchess in a commanding tone.

The young officer bowed his head, and fascinated in a whirl of excitement and timidity—but undoubtedly, for the moment, of tumultuous happiness—he did exactly as he was told, the lovely Duchess waiting on him all the time.

"Now I must leave you," she said, "or my absence will be talked about. Stay here, I say. I will not have you move. Rest; or if you weary, yonder are books. There is something to think of."

And the Duchess caught him in her arms and kissed—yes, it is no use saying what is not true—his lips and disappeared.

William Lennox lay back in his settee in a state of wild confusion, remorse, and intoxicating joy, which many and many have experienced before him.

Stolen sweets are notoriously delightful; but though the outside of the apple is rosy and lovely, the interior is ashes.

Every wrong carries within it its own sting; and none is more powerful than the sting of conscience.

The fairy innocent form of Lillian flashed before him in strange comparison with that lovely beauty whose warm lips he could still feel pressed to his; and the vision did him good, for he rose and went to the door.

It was locked.

Rather philosophically, we must say, he returned to his seat, and refilled his bumper with delicious wine and drained it off.

Then William Lennox fell into a reverie of the most voluptuous character. The wine had driven from his soul the last remnant of remorse. He was intoxicated, it is true, as much by the charms of beauty as those of wine.

But intoxicated he was.

At length he fell asleep, and there he lay in slumber until he was awakened by the impression of two burning lips upon his own, and the fervent caress of two soft and snowy arms.

With rapture he returned the embrace, and sitting up he knew that the ball was over, for the resplendent and lovely duchess, with those cherry lips, sparkling though languishing eyes, was by his side in dishabille, which revealed her charms even more than her ball costume.

"And so you have slept, you naughty man," said the duchess, devouring every feature of his handsome face with her eyes.

"What could I do?" cried William Lennox. "The time would have seemed so long."

"Flatterer!" laughed the Duchess, tapping him on the cheek with her dimpled hand and casting down her eyes.

William Lennox—more timid an hour or two before—put his arm round her yielding waist, and drew her towards himself, until their cheeks first, and then their lips, met.

CHAPTER LXXXVII.

REMORSE.

To say that William Lennox regained his own private apartment at a small hotel sadly and remorsefully, would be exaggerated. There was a certain amount of remorse in his heart, but there was also joy and luxurious triumph.

His love for Lillian, his innocent bride, was calm and sisterly, though sincere and devoted.

But this woman of the world had roused within him the demon of passion.

While the fit lasted he could not be happy; and when we reflect that he had won in an hour what men as handsome as himself had failed to win in years, the favours of the most beautiful woman in all Spain, his delight may to a certain degree be excused.

But the hour of repentance will as surely come as had come the frailness of his hopes.

There is ever a curse hanging over illicit love which falls sooner or later.

It may be slow, it may be long, but it comes as surely as death and the tomb.

William Lennox was neither hardened nor a

hypocrite, and yet he was compelled to conceal from Lillian his visit to the duchess. He felt he could not endure her questions.

And then, for the first time, he felt the time long in the company of Lillian. The *heure du berger*, as the French call it, was for midnight.

William Lennox had promised to sup with the duchess and a few private friends of hers. He felt himself tied to the chariot wheel of the conqueror, and unable to retreat.

The only drawback was the inevitable deceit which he must now and henceforth practice. This at once was a dire punishment, and reacted at once upon the mind of William Lennox. A specimen of his punishment may with propriety find its place here.

"You are not well to-night," said Lillian, gently passing her hands over the rich curls which the duchess had so admired and caressed the night before.

"Much as usual," replied the young officer, averting his eyes.

Lillian sighed. The intuition of women is wonderful. She felt, without having the slightest suspicion that there was anything serious, that something was wrong.

She little suspected that her devoted lover had fallen into the snares of a beautiful but artful woman.

Pity almost she did not, for, with a being of her loving, gentle, and devoted character, to know would have been to save.

Several friends joined them, Mrs. Winterton's drawing room being never empty, and then a drive was proposed.

William Lennox, Lillian, and Mrs. Winterton went out in an open carriage to the fashionable drive, crowded with equipages both native and foreign. William for a moment allowed the depth of his feelings towards Lillian to overcome every consideration, and he was wrapt in conversation with her when a dashing kind of phaeton drove towards them.

A little, thin, ugly man was driving; by his side was a lovely woman.

She bowed low to William, and stared with well bred impertinence at the ladies.

"Who is that?" said Lillian, with much surprise.

"The Duchess of Castella," replied William, carelessly.

He could feign already.

"The Duchess of Castella!" cried Lillian, while Mrs. Winterton bent her eyes inquiringly on him. "Do you know her?"

"I was introduced to her at the masked ball just before Slimy Jones made his appearance and drove everything out of my head," continued William.

Nothing more was said at the time, but Lillian became thoughtful. She was so little vain of her personal beauty that she could understand any one admiring another more than herself.

And then this woman was resplendently lovely.

The conversation turned wholly another way. They spoke of the war, of their prospects in England, of William Lennox's future position —of anything—but the thoughts of all three were, to a certain extent, turned towards the beautiful duchess.

They returned to dinner, and then got up an extempore concert.

At eleven they parted.

"I wish William did not know that woman," said Lillian, quietly.

"Perverse child!—why?"

"She is so very beautiful. He must love her, she is so glorious in her loveliness."

"Not half so beautiful as my child," said the proud mother.

"That is in your eye," smiled Lillian.

"Besides, my dear, you forget one thing."

"What, mother!"

"What is the use of his loving her?"

"I don't understand, mother."

"She is a married woman, and that was her husband who was driving her," said Mrs. Winterton, laughing.

Lillian laughed, too; the laugh of purity and innocence. She was quite satisfied now. At all events, whatever she might think of the duchess, she could not believe it possible her William could lower himself so much.

Lillian's education had unfortunately taught her that the marriage tie is no safeguard with certain parties.

Still, with all a woman's devoted and sublime love, she never doubted William Lennox.

The young officer left her with a desolate and almost broken heart. He was thoroughly ashamed of himself, and yet his infatuation was as great as ever. A hundred times he had been on the eve of confessing all to Lillian, and breaking off the connection.

Alas! the human heart is weak, and the intoxicating cup of the Circe was strong.

He dressed himself slowly, wrapped a cloak around him, and went on foot to the Castella Palace.

The servants bowed to the ground.

They had seen him go in one evening, and not leave until morning.

They were accustomed to treat the last new favourite as lord and master. The Duke of Castella never troubled them; he had his private establishment, and was rarely at home.

William Lennox ascended the marble stairs, and was ushered into the splendid supper room, where the duchess already awaited him. There were three other gentlemen, Spaniards, and three ladies, the intimates of the duchess.

The supper was already laid, and, by its magnificence and luxury, reminded William Lennox of what he had read of the *petite soupers* of the Regency.

The white shoulders, bosoms, and arms of the ladies, displayed to the utmost, increased the illusion. But there was no time for thought. A soft, fair hand took his, and led him to a seat beside herself, and supper commenced.

Everything beyond these four walls was soon forgotten by these weak and foolish people.

Such is life!

Hovels with a man, his wife, and many children devouring mouldy bread and raw vegetables, with scarce a rag to cover their nakedness—with no work; and prisons, stonebreaking and stripes if they take the beasts of the forest or the fowls of the air for nourishment.

Palaces where every luxury which the voluptuous can conceive, and the cunning of sycophants invent, close at hand.

No wonder if the poor murmur and are discontented.

CHAPTER LXXXVIII.

THE LETTER.

THIS state of things had lasted a month, and still William Lennox continued infatuated in the coils of the charmer.

By a strange idiosyncrasy, which we have no time to elaborate, the more he was unfaithful to Lillian the more he clung to her with his ardent soul.

He compared her—pure and virtuous being—with the duchess, whom he never for one moment respected.

He was fascinated, spell-bound, rivetted to her car, by her resplendent beauty, but nothing more.

With Lillian his love was all ethereal.

With Marie Dolores, Duchess of Castella, it was purely passion.

But he was able to conceal this from his beautiful mistress, and well for him was it.

Several splendid balls were given by the duchess, but at these he did not appear.

He would not have hurt the feelings of Lilliao for the world, and if his visits under these circumstances she must have known.

Alas, poor William! butterfly playing round the flame which is to destroy.

One evening—but let us first introduce an episode into our narrative.

* * * * *

It was, in truth, Slimy Jones who had been seen at the masked ball. The very means taken to secure his death had saved him. The thatch was dry and old, and, burning rapidly. a large bunch had fallen on the wide beam above, and burnt the end through in a moment so that Jones escaped with a few burns and half suffocated into the open air.

He at once marched off to the cave of Alcantara, and digging up the treasure, took with him as much as he could conveniently carry, started for Madrid, where he took up his residence in an obscure inn.

His intention was to collect together all the gold and sail for England in a return transport.

The inn he took up his lodgings at was much frequented by English merchant captains, while now and then a naval officer wishing to be more free than at the stricter hotels, dropped in to smoke, drink, and play cards.

The latter appeared the avocation of all the comers to that place, as it is of all idle people.

The Mexicans, the most worthless race on the face of the earth, are notorious gamblers.

A man with a poncho for all his dress will play for it, and sneak home naked.

This passion, once indulged in, sticks to the body like a leprosy.

It is incurable.

Slimy Jones had been always fond of a hand in a quiet way, a rubber at whist or cribbage—nothing more; but now, when he saw gold changing hands with wild rapidity, he could hold out no longer.

He staked, and won and lost doubloons.

In a week he was a confirmed gambler. Using his marvellous cunning he generally won.

But the reckless sailor captain's dial-case.

One evening there sauntered into the place a young officer, in the garb of a naval officer, who, going up to where Slimy Jones sat, shuffling a pack of cards—the inveterate gambler could not rest—addressed him in rather a jovial tone:

"Well old boy," he said, "seem to be in a hurry to play. What say you to a game?"

"Just so, old lad!"

And Slimy Jones sat as if rooted to the spot —his eyes starting from their sockets, his head thrown back, and his whole body in convulsions."

"Eh! just so."

"You seem frightened, old grampus. Seen me before, eh?" continued the young sailor.

"No—yes—oh! ah! just so — somebody very like you," stammered Jones.

"Somebody very like me?" said the other, drily. Well, never mind, you're mistaken in your man. What do you say to a game at ecarté?"

"Just so," replied Jones, recovering himself, and shuffling the cards mechanically.

The young man sat down and began. He laid a note for five guineas on the table. Slimy Jones, after a slight grimace, put down the same in gold.

The young sailor won.

He placed the five guineas on the note, and motioned to Slimy Jones to double his stakes.

"Just so," said the other, with a savage grin —but he did it.

It would be idle to relate by what acts, by what insinuations, by what cunning the young sailor induced the infatuated man to go on; but he did, and by two o'clock in the morning, Slimy Jones, penniless, in debt, having given several I O U's, was swearing, tearing his hair, and cursing his evil fortune.

"Stumped up?" said the sailor, coolly.

"Just so!"

"All right, that's what I wanted."

"Just so; you're very kind," said Slimy Jones, sullenly, drinking raw brandy.

"I am your best friend."

"Just so."

"How?'

"Shall I tell you."

"Yes—just so."

"Now, look here. All your money is in this pocket. On one condition you shall have every farthing of it back."

"Just so—name it," said Slimy Jones, with open eyes.

"You know William Lennox?"

"I do—just so"

"He is a friend of yours?"

"Just so. Hearken, stranger; don't think to pump me until I know what's what."

"William Lennox is my bitterest enemy. The world would be all before me where to choose were he dead."

"Ah, just so."

"Will you join me against him?"

"Just so."

"To begin—where is he?"

"Here, just so."

"Ah! In this town?"

"Just so."

"His residence?"

"Just so; can't say exactly. He's got three; —just so—part the day his own hotel; evening, Miss Lillians; night, the Duchess of Castella. Ah, ah! just so."

"The Duchess of Castella?" said the other, with a dark frown, "that beautiful woman."

"Just so"

"That man crosses my path everywhere. Is she said to be his mistress?"

"Just so. He spends every night there, and leaves in the morning," said the other, drily.

"Curses light on him! That woman had fixed my imagination, and I had made up my mind to win her. But never mind. I told you once, and I tell you again, that every farthing of money I have here is yours if you will aid me."

"Just so—how am I to win it?" said the other greedily.

"I will tell you," replied the other in a low, hushed tone.

CHAPTER LXXXIX.

TREACHERY.

ONE evening William Lennox arrived at the duchess's at about a quarter to twelve, and found that the duchess had gone to the theatre, and was expected back every moment.

He said he would wait.

With this view he entered the privileged boudoir and took up a book, with which to while away the time; he no longer felt that dreamy intoxication which had lulled his senses to sleep on a former occasion.

He was quite calm, and awaited the coming of the duchess without any impatience.

She had been his mistress a month — an age.

Her intimates were becoming alarmed. The duchess had never been so constant in her inconstancy.

The fact was, the fierce and untameable passions of the southern woman had been aroused as they never had before.

She loved William Lennox.

She loved for the first time in her life, this woman, who, *had* she have done like the princess in the Arabian nights—kept a ring from every lover—would have forged a chain of fabulous length.

But William Lennox felt differently. He passionately admired the duchess; he could not resist the fascination of her eyes, the glow of her cheeks, the honey of her lips—but he did not love her.

Men seldom love their mistresses—in general they despise them.

Men love their wives.

A mistress is a toy, a plaything, something to brag of and show—a wife is something to love.

William Lennox loved Lillian with all his heart and soul. His *liason* with the duchess was, call it what you will, a folly, a crime! but it was a thing that could not last.

Suddenly a respectful knock came to the door. A domestic entered, and with a profound bow presented him with a letter on a golden salver.

William Lennox thanked him, and the man retired.

He opened it, read it, and started to his feet.

These were the words he read.

"*Your old friend, the Blue Dwarf, has arrived out. He has news for you. He regrets to have to send for you to the Castella Palace. Come at once to the Golden Lion on the port.*"

William Lennox started up, took his hat and sallied forth. In the hall he met the domestic who had summoned him.

"Tell the duchess" he said, "that I have received a letter from an old friend. I may not have the honour of presenting my respects to-night.

And he hurried down the marble steps of the palace.

At that moment a carriage drove up, and Marie Dolores, Duchess of Castella, put forth her head.

"William," she said, but he heard her not.

His mind was in a whirl. Delight to see the Blue Dwarf was strangely mingled with dread of his strictures on his conduct. But then his eyes were open; he would confess and be absolved.

With this intention he hurried forward, until he found himself entangled in some streets with which he was not familiar. He paused, and looked around him, hoping to meet some one of whom he could ask his way.

He was in a narrow gloomy street. At some distance two men advanced; they were not together, but both wore ample cloaks.

One of them, in a moment, was close to him.

"Sir stranger," he said, "can you show me the way to the pool."

"Certainly, young man," replied the other, releasing his arm from beneath his cloak as if to point the way.

William Lennox started at the voice of the man, who spoke execrable Spanish. But, before he had an instant to reflect, the other rushed at him dagger in hand, and struck at his heart.

He would have succeeded, so astonished and taken aback was William Lennox, had not a light figure darted forward and struck up the dagger.

"Just so—the duchess," said the assassin.

But the second man approached.

"Diego—Paul," shouted the voice of the duchess.

Two tall domestics rushed forward and would have pursued the flying assassins.

"No; assist the cabelleu—bear him to my house," cried Marie Dolores.

The servants, nothing loth to escape an encounter with a couple of armed assassins, raised William Lennox, bleeding and insensible, as much from the suddenness of the blow as anything else, and bore him quickly to the palace of the duchess, who, with a stern and care-looking brow, walked beside him.

She was vowing vengeance against the assassins.

They bore him to her own bed chamber, and her medical attendant being summoned, at once proceeded to examine the patient.

There was no danger, he said.

William Lennox speedily opened his eyes and looked around. His surprise to find himself in the superb chamber of the duchess, with her kneeling at his feet, and a grave surgeon standing at the head of the bed, may be better conceived than described.

"Well, my angel," said the lady, kissing his pale and marble-looking brow, "how do you feel now."

"Better."

"How came it about," she continued.

"I have deadly enemies. This letter," he said, opening one still clutched in his hand, "was, I doubt not, a trap."

"May I read it."

"Yes," replied William Lennox, and then he added, blushing; "no, I would rather you did not."

The duchess turned pale, and pressed her hand upon her heart.

"Why?"

"Because the absurd forgery reflects on you," muttered Lennox.

"Is that all," cried the duchess joyfully.

"What did you think, then?"

"That you were tired of me, child, and had given me a rival," said Marie Dolores, blushing.

"Madam," murmured William, reproachfully.

"You love Lillian," continued the duchess, pouting.

"Ah, madam, you know her not or you would love her too," he added.

"Love her," cried the duchess with sparkling eyes. "Don't speak of her if you would not have me kill you. Give me the letter."

And she snatched it from him and read it.

"May he talk, doctor?" asked the duchess.

"No."

"Then give him his medicine and I will watch him. Go bid the correyider's son come to me at dawn of day. The assassins must be secured," she added. "Can you identify them?"

"One I know, the other I suspect," said William Lennox, with a deep sigh.

"Describe them," continued the duchess, producing pens, ink, and paper.

"Madam; to morrow I will tell you my history, and then you will know why I cannot denounce one of them without being sure. The other is a reptile I would crush like a worm under my feet.

"Rest my darling," replied the duchess; and William Lennox, glad to repose, turned round and composed himself to sleep.

The surgeon had bandaged his wounds.

The dagger had pinned his arm to his side. His wounds were very painful, but not dangerous.

But sleep, alas! it was out of the question.

In the morning his attempted assassination would be the talk of all Madrid, and it would reach the ears of Lillian. She would insist upon seeing him.

Awful were the stings of conscience of that young man as he lay in his bed, wounded, sick at heart, and in great and feverish dread of the morrow.

It was a splendid room, and the bed, in an alcove, was hung with deep and massive curtains, those curses of health and beauty, while the furniture around was of the most costly character. Pictures — representations all of youth and beauty—hung on the walls, and numerous long lamps gave a subdued and dim religious light amid which the form of the duchess flitted like that of the mysterious guardian of the *locale*.

William Lennox slowly turned his head, and with half-closed eyes watched the scene.

He thought of another and a younger form which should have been flitting about his bedside, and who soon, he had hoped, would have a right to do so.

But that could never be.

His sin had found him.

For hours the unfortunate youth lay on that bed in mortal anguish, groaning and sighing in a low tone, and almost inclined to spurn with loathing the gentle hand which bathed his heated brow, and poured a soothing cordial into his mouth.

At length his senses deserted him, and he slept. But for him that night had no morning. He was delirious and in a terrible and dangerous fever.

CHAPTER XC.
THE DUCHESS.

MRS. WINTERTON and Lillian were preparing for a stroll, to visit one or two of the shops especially set up for the benefit of the English; they were dressed, and Lillian had perhaps never looked more lovely.

A becoming dress set off her budding figure, and that graceful form.

A smile was on her face, for these walks took her past the bow window, where of a morning William Lennox sat watching for her approach.

Just as they were about to ring to give their orders for the day, a servant entered with a card which Mrs. Winterton took, read, and turned pale.

"What is it, mamma?"

"The Duchess of Castella wants urgently to see us," replied Mrs. Winterton.

Before she could utter another word, the duchess most simply, elegantly, and becomingly dressed, entered hurriedly. She was a consummate actress.

"I have to apologise," she said, "for this early call, but I have news for you from one in whom you feel a deep interest."

"William," cried Lillian, turning very pale, and pressing her hand on her heart.

"Well, I don't know his Christian name," replied the duchess smiling, "but Captain Lennox met with a slight accident; now don't be alarmed, and I will tell you all about it—"

"Where is he?" gasped Lillian.

"The poor lad is safe in bed at my house," continued the duchess.

Mrs. Winterton started, but Lillian's eyes plainly said—tell us the worst.

"Do you know of any enemy he has in Madrid?" asked Marie Dolores.

"Yes," said Mrs. Winterton.

"Who would be likely to use the name of the Blue Dwarf to entrap him?" continued the duchess.

"The wretch!" cried Lillian.

"There were two of them."

"Oh, madam, tell me all!" again cried Lillian.

"I will, my dear child. This, then, is the fact. Last night Captain Lennox was decoyed by a letter from his hotel, in which letter he was told to meet his friend the Blue Dwarf at some inn on the port. He appears to have gone directly, and on his way was attacked by two ruffians, one of whom raised a dagger to stab him. As luck would have it, I was passing in my carriage, which at that instant turned round. One leap brought me to his side, and I have the proud satisfaction to say that I had the pleasure, under Providence, of saving his life."

"Heaven bless you!" cried Lillian, kissing her hand fervently.

Mrs. Winterton listened gravely. She almost saw through the actress.

"At sight of my armed servants the assassins fled, and when Captain Lennox came to my house, to which I had him carried, he refused to name them. I sent for a surgeon, who pronounced the wound without danger. He is, however, feverish this morning, and does nothing but call for Lillian; so, my dear child, I set one of my maids to make inquiries, and soon found who the beautiful English girl was about whom he is raving so constantly that I thought it best to come at once for you. And now, my dear madam, do you pardon the intrusion?"

"Oh, madam!" said Lillian. "Come, mother."

"My carriage waits," replied the duchess, and in two minutes more they were on their way to the Castella Palace.

"The wound is in the arm," said the duchess as they proceeded, "and therefore utterly without danger; but the excitement, the shock, has been too much for his nerves. He is *very* feverish. There is no danger, you know, but before you go in, he is delirious, and raves most terribly about Lillian—Just so—Sir Edgar."

Lillian clasped her hands and raised her tearful eyes to heaven.

In a few minutes they were at the palace gates, and in two more at the entrance of the room.

The doctor and Jack Horne were holding down the wounded man!

"Charge, yes—there they hang! I can see them grinning at me. It was cruel, yes; I knew it was cruel; but they would have killed her—"

Lillian approached, and gazed wildly at him. The duchess concealed herself behind the drapery, and there concealed her mortal agony. She had only fetched Lillian in desperation.

"Lillian—my wife—my beloved—the bright angel of my existence! they have killed her. Ah! there came a wily serpent in my path, and led me away; but there is vengeance, and I say it. Hush! I will find her or die. Hark! 'tis the signal. I am to leave the miserable home of my fathers. Is that you, Dick? All right! How much for the watch? Ah! 'tis a knife sticking in my throat. I awake. Is this a heavenly angel or a human creature. Her name is Lillian—gone, gone, gone, stolen away over the seas. Ah! is that a viper. Will you let me go?—I will kill her!" and he fell back exhausted.

"Go for Doctor Graham," said Mrs. Winterton, and now Lillian do not be alarmed. All this is mere nonsense. He is not delirious, only excited. "May I be allowed?" said Mrs. Winterton, preparing to take off her hood and cloak.

"Madam," cried the duchess, "you are at home, in your own house—I go to give the necessary orders."

And she glided from the room to give vent to her feelings in her own private boudoir—the scene of her happiest hours, spent with him.

Lillian made no reply to her mother's words, but took off her cloak and seated herself by the side of the exhausted sufferer.

In a quarter of an hour Doctor Graham, the regimental surgeon, bustled in, pronounced the patient very ill—ugly wound—fever—but on his sticks in a month.

"The boy has nine lives; been nearly dead twice before—cure him third—bother." This to the solemn Spanish surgeon, who thereupon retired in high dudgeon. "Old fool—this won't do. Send him a potion—dress his wound by and bye."

And in a similar disjointed way he went on speaking until his visit was concluded, when he shook the two ladies by the hand, and went out, leaving them considerably relieved.

In half an hour a bottle of physic and some pills came with medical directions.

This was followed by the announcement that lunch was laid in the ante-room, for fear the fumes of the viands might annoy the patient. Lillian would have declined.

"My dear girl, if we are to nurse our patient properly we must take care of ourselves. It would be an ill service to render to William if you were ill on his recovery."

Lillian acquiesced with a sad smile. The lunch was most delicious and *recherche*, and was only laid for two, while two attendants stood behind their chairs.

Lillian ate evidently only to please her mother, who declared firmly that if she did not she would send her home, and drank two glasses of wine.

She then went back into the room, and there lay William Lennox in a calm and tranquil sleep.

Lillian seated herself in an arm-chair by his side and mused deeply.

There was something in all this she did not understand, but what it was she could not say.

Presently her mother came in and joined her.

And thus the day passed away.

It was night ere William Lennox awoke, and then the dull glare of his eye proclaimed that reason had not yet regained its throne.

A female domestic, a kind of duenna, had shown the mother and daughter to a bed-room adjoining that occupied by the young dragoon officer; and to this, about eleven, they both went, though gladly would Lillian have watched all night. But this her mother absolutely refused to allow.

The only point on which she yielded was that Lillian was allowed to sleep in her clothes with the door ajar, so that at the least sound she might be at the bedside of the invalid.

Wearied and exhausted by a long day, Lillian slept soundly for several hours.

Then she awoke with a start, and sat up in the bed.

She could distinctly hear voices in the next room.

Gliding noiselessly from the bed she entered the sick chamber, but could see nothing. The room, in deference to the sleeper, was most dimly lighted, and Lillian in deference to her mother, having taken what she considered a night's rest, seated herself in an arm chair.

Scarcely had she done so when a figure stood in the doorway of the chamber.

It was the duchess in her night dress, a most elegant and magnificent *negligée*

Casting a stealthy look around she glided across the room towards the bed, and peered into the sick man s face as he lay breathing heavily.

Lillian sat spell bound, and would have rubbed her eyes if she could have moved.

Then the duchess s ooped, and kissed first the forehead and then the lips of the speaker.

Lillian pressed her hand to her side. She had never felt such exquisite pain.

"Beloved of my soul!" she muttered, "and is this the end? Despised, unloved for the sake of that little girl. I, who had hoped to wean him wholly from her, and to have him all to myself for ever."

And she walked up and down with hasty and impatient strides.

"But who knows? he must stay here a month, and in that time much may be done. I must go. Were I seen here in this dress they would talk finely, these English prudes."

And the duchess glided away, leaving Lillian petrified, astonished, and almost fainting. But she roused herself, raised one of the lamps a little, and took her station by the young soldier's bedside.

There her mother found her a little before breakfast time.

She shook her head, and gently chid her.

"I will never leave him again," said Lillian, in a husky voice.

"Why, child?"

"There are greater dangers than his wounds."

"What mean you?"

Lillian briefly explained. Mrs. Winterton was naturally shocked, but begged Lillian utterly to disguise her feelings, and she would see that William Lennox was removed as soon as possible.

It was then agreed that the two should watch alternately, aided by Jack Horne.

Lillian, with a slight blush, chose the night watch. She wished to prevent the visits of the duchess.

Marie Dolores came once or twice for a ceremonious visit of five minutes, during which Lillian was always busy with her patient.

Those two women began to understand one another.

It was the fifth evening, when a faint voice was heard from the bed.

"Is any one here?"

"It is I—Lillian," said the girl, darting forward.

William Lennox stared at her wildly for a few minutes ere he could speak.

"Lillian! Ah! I remember—a wound—a woman saved me. Where are we?"

"In the palace of Marie Dolores, Duchess of Castella." replied Lillian.

"Ah!" said William Lennox, shutting his eyes.

Lillian gave him a powerful tonic, and in a few minutes he was able to understand pretty well the state of affairs. The conversation between the lovers was tender, affectionate, and without one particle of that acrimony which the existence of the duchess might have infused into their relations.

After a while there was a pause.

"Lillian!"

"Yes, William."

"Do you know what I want?" he said, with one of his old smiles.

"No."

"I'm hungry, and want something to eat."

Lillian clapped her hands, rose, and rang the bell rather sharply.

It was answered by the Duchess of Castella herself.

Lillian, unperceived by Lennox, drew up, cold as a statue in a corner.

"Is anything the matter?" said the duchess.

"No," replied Lillian in a voice thick with emotion, "but he is awake, and asks for something to eat."

The bosom of the superb duchess rose and fell quickly; her madonna like eyes were raised to heaven, and then, without a word, she disappeared.

In a very few minutes an exquisite cold collation was laid before William Lennox, who did ample justice to it. Lillian was delighted.

Why?

It opened a prospect for his removal from the palace of the Duchess of Castella.

CHAPTER XCI.

JEALOUSY.

THE next morning William Lennox was pronounced out of danger; and youth and a good constitution assisting medicine—which it is an evil fashion too much to despise—Mrs. Winterton went out to prepare her own apartments for the invalid.

Jack Horne accompanied her.

When they returned they found that the Duchess had gone out. Doctor Graham, who came in, on being consulted, said that his state would allow removal.

"Let us take him at once," said Lillian.

Mrs. Winterton readily acquiesced, and wrote a hurried note to the duchess.

Mrs. Winterton presents her compliments to the Duchess of Castella. and begs to thank her for her kind and thoughtful hospitality.

A carriage was sent for, and the bewildered William Lennox carried into it without even a question being asked.

He was put to bed at his own hotel, and then Lillian, freed, happy, and much relieved in mind, took upon herself the office of nurse in earnest.

It was the morning of the fourth day, and nothing had been heard of the duchess.

William Lennox was still confined to his room, but he had nearly recovered.

Lillian had quite recovered her roses.

"To-morrow I may go out," said the young dragoon.

"You will have a drive in an open carriage with me, sir," replied Lillian, gravely.

William smiled.

"Why with you?"

"Why with me? Now, I tell you what it is," replied Lillian, with much gravity, "I'm jealous of the duchess —"

"Jealous! Why?"

His heart throbbed a little.

"I don't know. But I am jealous," she added, more seriously.

William Lennox blushed.

"Yes, I am jealous. I don't mean for one moment to say that you, my William, would look at a married woman. But I am sure she loves you!"

"Nonsense!" faltered the cornet of dragoons.

"And so—I don't mean to allow you to keep up the acquaintance."

"I must call and thank her, in pure courtesy."

"We must!"

"Well, we must," said William, laughing at the pertinacity of his future wife.

And so the discussion ended.

Next day an open carriage, with two splendid horses, was at the door, and William Lennox, escorted by Mrs. Winterton and the lovely Lillian, was assisted to his seat, that of honour, at the back.

The equipage drove slowly along. It was impossible to do otherwise. Every instant some one came up to congratulate the young officer on his recovery.

William Lennox saw at once from the quiet smiles of one or two of his intimates that his residence at the palace of the duchess had excited comments.

The duchess was at home, and they were told at once to walk up.

William Lennox was deadly pale. It is impossible to enter the presence of one who, like the duchess, had been his first mistress, without emotion. He leaned heavily on the arm of Lillian.

She felt the pressure, and a pang went to her heart.

The duchess received them in her state room. Two men, one evidently of high rank, were with her.

She advanced with dignity, and congratulated the young officer on his recovery.

"I am not surprised at your being well so soon," she said with a charming smile, "but then I am not surprised—with so sweet a nurse."

Lillian's wrath was disarmed. She took the hand of the duchess, and blushed deeply.

"You have come in lucky time, captain. This is the corrigider and his secretary—they were coming round with me to the hotel to take your depositions—"

This was said in the most natural tone of voice in the world, as if for four whole days she had not moved heaven and earth to procure this excuse for seeing William Lennox.

The young officer bowed low, and in as brief a way as he could gave his evidence.

He described Slimy Jones accurately, but made no allusion, whatever, to the other.

Blood is thicker than water, after all.

It was his brother.

Who would, that had a spark of nature in his soul, accuse a brother—one of the dearest and most engrossing of human ties.

We doubt whether a wife be nearer or dearer than the companion of our boyhood's joys and sorrows.

It may not be so with all, but we have loved a brother beyond all other human beings, and mourned him longer.

It is a tie so holy, mysterious, and near, that even the sacred bond of matrimony cannot equal it.

We had a common mother.

The corrigider took down his evidence, and promised that the assassins should be in custody before night.

He then left.

Luncheon was served, and the duchess was so gentle and motherly—so kind that Lillian's suspicions were allayed, though in her heart she knew that Marie Dalores loved her affianced husband.

But that was of no consequence!

Did he love her?

They drove back to the inn, and William Lennox, under the doctor's orders, lay down.

In the evening Lillian read to him, and at eleven retired to rest.

He no longer required a nurse.

He was, in fact, wonderfully recovered, and the attendance of Jack Horne was all he required.

Next day Lillian and her mother returned to their own residence, where Captain Lennox became again a visitor.

He had made up his mind not to renew his connection with the duchess.

Nothing was heard of the assassins.

William Lennox began to be uneasy. The fellow might be lurking about.

He went to bed with a pistol by his side, which Jack Horne fired off every evening and then re-loaded.

It was about a week after Lillian had ceased to be a nurse, and William Lennox had been about an hour in bed.

His hotel had once been a palace, but in consequence of the presence, during the winter, of so many English, it had been turned into an hotel.

The room occupied by William was on the first floor, and opened into a long dark passage.

In the days of oil lamps they often went out before midnight.

William Lennox, who had been reading, had blown out his lamp, and prepared for slumber, when he heard a step outside his door.

Jack Horne was asleep in an inner room.

William knew the audacity of his enemy, and, arming himself with his pistol, leaped out of bed and opened the bed-room door.

"Who is there?" he said. "Speak, or I fire!"

He could distinctly see something at no great distance, by the pale glimmer of an expiring lamp; but what it was he could not tell.

William Lennox laid his pistol on a chair.

"Ghost or goblin," he said in an excited tone, "come forward, I say!"

Plain prose might blush at what followed;

let us then sing, in the words of the wiliest of English poets :—

The ghost stopp'd, menaced, then retired, until
He reach'd the ancient wall, then stood stone still.

I now put forth one arm—Eternal powers !
  It touch'd no soul, no body, but the wall
On which the moonbeams fell in silvery showers
  Chequered with all the tracery of the hall.
He shudder'd, as, no doubt, the bravest cowers
When he can't tell what 'tis that doth appear.
How odd, a single hobgoblin's non-entity
Should cause more fear than a whole host's identity.

But still the shade remain'd: the blue eyes glared
  And rather variably for strong death;
Yet one thing rather good the grave had spared—
  The ghost had a remarkably sweet breath :

A straggling curl show'd he had been fair-hair'd ;
  A red lip, with two rows of pearl beneath,
Gleam'd forth, as through the casement's icy shroud
The moon peep'd ; just escaped from a grey cloud.

And Juan, puzzled, but still curious, thrust
  His other arm forth—wonder upon wonder—
It press'd upon a hard but glowing bust,
  Which beat as if there was a warm breast under ;
He found, as people on most trials must,
  That he had made at first a silly blunder,
And that, in his confusion, he had caught
Only the wall, instead of what he sought.

The ghost, if ghost it were, seem'd a sweet soul
  As ever lurk'd beneath a holy hood ;
A dimpled chin, a neck of ivory stole
  Forth into something much like flesh and blood.
Back fell the sable frock and dreary cowl,
And they revealed--alas !
  It was Maria Dolores, Duchess of Castella !

CHAPTER CXII.

THE BLUE DWARF AT HOME.

In a superb apartment, furnished in an eastern style of magnificence, with rich divans, massive chandeliers, and hangings of gold and silver, with a carpet, the pile of which was inches long, and every corner of which was filled by nicknacks, objects of *vertu*, screens, fancy chairs, while the walls were covered by a mass of curiosities, sat a man in a variegated eastern costume, smoking the long hookha, which a slave black as ebony was refilling or lighting.

This man kneeled upon the mat which supported the glass portion of the pipe.

At a desk sat a man of about forty, white, with a strange expression of eyes, and yet an unmistakeable English style of face.

He was pale, wan, careworn, but had a high forehead and a handsome face. He seemed resolutely to keep his mouth closed.

He had a pile of letters before him, of which he was making an abstract; or, perhaps, copying them.

Close beside him stood a young girl.

The pen refuses even in the hands of the great masters of poetry and prose to depict some women. Their loveliness is something beyond all powers of the limner's art.

She was fifteen, and yet a woman; fair, with golden curly hair, soft eye lashes that veiled eyes of a blue black that slumbered yet, but would surely one day speak volumes to the heart of man.

Her characteristic at present seemed repose, as she stood with a guitar in her hand playing a few notes idly and without enthusiasm.

Her dress was purely eastern. A small headdress of precious stones covered the summit of her head, a tunic, open in front, revealed partially her snowy bosom, while from the knee down she appeared clothed in loose trousers covered with spangles.

"You are sad, Leila," said the voice of the Blue Dwarf.

She started, blushed, and went on with the play.

"Sad! no. I was only thinking."

"Of what?"

"I don't know," said the young girl, frankly and truly.

Half the time do we know of what we are thinking—especially young girls.

At this moment the secretary laid down his pen and folded his arms.

"Has Francesco finished?" said the Blue Dwarf.

"Yes," replied Leila.

"Read me the reports," continued Sapathwa.

"From Spain?"

"Yes."

The secretary handed a piece of paper with a sickly smile to Leila, and, as he did so, it became evident that he was dumb.

His tongue had been cut out.

Leila took the paper and read out.

"The letters are full of details, but the brief news is this: William Lennox, though evidently deeply attached to Lillian, has had an intrigue with the Duchess of Castella. As yet it is kept secret. Sir Edgar Blakesley and Slimy Jones have attempted the assassination of William. The wound was severe, but he is out of danger. Sir Edgar continues in daily conference with Slimy Jones, though the whole police of Madrid cannot find them."

"Ah!" said the Blue Dwarf, sternly, as he puffed smoke on all sides. "Write," he continued. "But the cousins?"

"Are still within the French lines," said Leila reading, as Francesco wrote.

"Write."

The secretary took up his pen.

"William Lennox must be sent home on sick leave. Mrs. Winterton and Lillian must come home also. Let Slimy Jones be handed over to the Spanish police; but Sir Edgar is not to be touched."

"He has written," said Leila.

"Ring for Matthews," continued Sapathwa.

Leila struck a kind of gong in a peculiar way, and in a few minutes a man entered by a sliding door. He was about forty; thin, with grizzly hair, a keen but submissive cast of countenance, and an expression which was not very easily translated.

He bowed low.

"Matthews, you must prepare. To-morrow you will start for Spain. Your credentials will be ready to-night."

The man bowed again and left the room.

"What of Pauline?" said the Blue Dwarf.

Again the dumb secretary handed a paper to Leila, who read aloud—

"Pauline has taken up her residence in a lovely house at Brighton. She receives letters from Sir Edgar, and visits from Mr. James Tyrrel Blakesley, who acts for the solicitor. Some deep plot is under weigh, but no clue can as yet be obtained. It is believed that the game is to obtain the royal recognition for Sir Edgar Blakesley in such a way that none will dare to attack him."

"Ah!" cried the Blue Dwarf, with a dark and gloomy scowl, "send for Mitchell."

Leila struck the gong once, and a respectable looking butler — a major domo — made his appearance.

"Mitchell," said the Blue Dwarf, "I want you to leave for Brighton at once. I want a house on the Old Steine—to morrow. The next day I shall remove there with all my establishment."

The major domo bowed and left. Everybody was prepared for everything in that extraordinary establishment where the Blue Dwarf reigned supreme as any emperor or king.

"The child and the French?" continued Sapathwa.

"Are safe in London," replied Leila, for whom the dumb secretary wrote answers on the paper before him.

"Good! and now, child, to lunch."

Lunch was soon brought in, and the dumb secretary and the black slave retired, leaving the unfortunate deformed alone with the lovely girl. She waited on him with a deference, humility, and tenderness, which to the other was almost inexplicable.

Who was she? What was her history? No one knew.

Lunch once finished, the Blue Dwarf wrote or dictated several letters, talked awhile with Leila, changed his dress, and went out to visit both his bankers and his solicitors.

Strange as it may appear, not only were the connections and relations of Sapathwa extensive, but all who knew him treated him with the most profound deference and respect.

There was a halo of power round his head, which not all his ugliness, deformity, or diminutive stature could conceal.

CHAPTER XCIII.

THE REGENT.

MEANWHILE we must move to Brighton, where the first gentleman in Europe holds his court in the Pavilion, most ridiculed and absurd of English palaces.

Brighton was not then what it is now. The little obscure fishing village was rapidly progressing towards prosperity. It had been patronised by a prince in hero worship days, and what more was wanted in a land where we so dearly love a lord. Do we not, kind reader?

Brighton, in those days, was not so crowded as it is now. No Sunday and Monday trains then disgorged their thousands of holiday cockneys on the beach and over the breezy downs.

How shocking a change.

There are very worthy people who deplore the change; who are miserable because the toiling masses come between the wine and their nobility, and snuff the same air as themselves. They little reflect that what to them is a pastime and a pleasure is to others a necessary, saved for, toiled for, thought of for weeks beforehand, while working in close shop, warehouse, over the tailer's board, or plying the busy needle.

Better the rich should fly to Rhine or Switzerland than the masses, who are England's bone and sinew—alas! in great towns little of that is left—should be debarred from breathing the invigorating breezes of the salt and briny ocean.

There were wild bulls in England in the reign of Queen Anne; so that, if so short a time makes such vast changes, who knows but all London may one day afford a day at the sea?—or, perhaps, Government—being changed so as to think a little less of inanimate matters, and more of human beings—may—who knows?—give its assistance, and decree a universal sea-side holiday now and then.

But then there were coaches and post-chaises only for the rich, and wagons or the marrow-bone stage for the poor.

And still, all the world was at Brighton; meaning all that brilliant circle of moths and butterflies which circled round the flame of the great Behemoth (!) the Prince Regent.*

The Pavilion was something new, with its

whispered reputation—half seraglio, half hell—with a great voluptuary at its head, and little sultanas and viziers flocking round him.

On an afternoon, several days after the incidents recorded in the last chapter, it was a magnificent day in Brighton. All the world—and we are not sure that his wife was not there also—were abroad; equipages of the most brilliant and splendid character dashed up and down; chariots, barouches, phaetons, post-chaises—and all full of splendidly-dressed, and beautiful women, with cavaliers of every age and rank.

The Steine was crowded to see them pass, few being other than celebrated personages.

The Prince was not among them. He had a cold; or the toothache; or a pain in his toe; in fact, some ailment sufficient to account of his non-appearance. For the nonce no one troubled themselves about the matter, being too much occupied in seeing and being seen.

That night there was to be a crush at the Pavilion, and many who had never been admitted into the sacred presence were to be introduced.

The number of slaves who were at work to prepare for this saturnalia would have shocked the sensitive ears of the ladies to have only mentioned the sum total. They had been working day and night for the occasion, and vast was the amount of mysterious boxes which came down by coach and wagon to various addresses.

Alas! how many among that throng of fair and bright-looking English girls were looking forward to the hope of winning the favour of a jaded and wretched voluptuary.

Such is the influence of a court on a people. Thank heaven we have so good a queen!

Somewhere at the corner of the Steine, somewhere where now stands a penny post pillar, in the place of a rough stone pillar, stood two men in whispered conversation. One was a man of some position in society, as could be seen by his habit of haughty deportment; the other had the suppleness and subserviency of a valet.

Both wore the costume of foreigners—Russians, with huge fur collars, whiskers, and moustachios—while the tall man had spectacles.

"All the same stale lot; nothing fresh, nothing lively!" said the first man, in a tone of dejection and disgust.

"But—"

"I say it is so! and it is no use dinning anything else into my ears."

"But—"

"There goes fat Lady ——, who might be passable if she weighed six stone less; and beautiful if she did not have such an odd affection for her nose that her two eyes must be ever looking that way."

"Oh!"

"And here is Lady B——, making desperate eyes at that pudding-headed Marquis of A——; it's perfectly sickening!"

"But—"

"It's wearisome, tame! I'd rather be asleep, or before a good bottle of brandy. Ah! who have we here?—what is this?"

It was a woman who had by intuition fallen upon one of those marvellous toilettes which

---

* Though we are compelled to alter the dates of certain events, we are only guilty of anachronism. The facts are true.

are now so frequently seen in the Champs Elysees and the Bois de Boulogne, but which at that time was a complete novelty, an invention, a new discovery.

For an hour every woman had been bursting with rage at the exhibition, while in reality admiring the exquisite make up and the marvellous attractiveness of the whole set out.

The glasses levelled by the man at the creature sufficiently betokened the success of the affair.

She sat in an open barouche, leaning gracefully back, with a small, elegant bonnet on the back of the head—small, but oh! how exquisite in shape. Her feet were raised to the opposite seat, while her dress of seven little flounces filled the whole carriage so completely that nothing would be seen of a gentleman who rode beside her save his head.

All this would have been nothing had not her face have been exquisitely beautiful.

"The deuce—who is she, eh?—don't you know?" said the first speaker impatiently.

"*Know—her?—*"

"*No!* then you ought to—what the deuce are you paid for but to know everything? She's a most beautiful creature. She must come to-night."

"But—"

"She must."

The other bowed and shrugged his shoulders behind the other's back, and then summoning a page who stood at some distance, whispered a few words, and the page, taking orders, ran after the carriage.

"Don't know her—eh? some emigrant seems rich—can't help it. I tell you what, Gervaise, that woman has taken my fancy, and by ——, I will have her—how, when, by what means, I don't care, but it must be done—eh?"

"But—'

"I'll knock you down in a minute," said his irate master. "But what have we here, eh? I'm lost in astonishment. Is the world coming to an end that such loveliness should be and I not know it. You blockhead! where have you been?"

"But—"

"If you say that again I'll brain you," whispered the other, "butt you are, and will ever remain. Now hearken, let this vision of heaven, or whatever else it may be, attend also to night."

"Impossible."

"Nothing is impossible."

The man groaned; and, hailing a groom, pointed out the carriage and resumed his attendance on his master.

At this moment a bustling man of middle height, very neatly dressed and very fussy in manner, came up.

"Ah! how d'ye do Sir Gervaise D——?" he said with a sly wink, "purveying, eh?"

"Mr. H——," replied the other, blushing crimson, "what do you mean, sir?"

"Don't you understand, eh?" and he jerked his finger over his shoulder at the palace, "larder pretty full, and no more little pullets, eh?"

"Sir," stammered the person addressed.

"Don't be ashamed—usual consequence of your position—*who's your fat friend?*" in an audible whisper.

Fat friend, stern and indignant, but utterly silent, peering through his spectacles at the carriages.

"Mr. D——, I'd have you know—"

"Now, Sir Gervaise H——, do not attempt the thing, as if we didn't know. *Who the deuce have you got hold of—a Russian boyard fed upon tallow.*"

"Leave us, I pray you," whispered the miserable attendant, "don't you recognise?—"

"The Marquis? Where, I didn't see him. Hardly fair now, Gervaise— *What's new? who'll get the handkerchief to-night?*"

"These impertinent whispers, if meant for me," said the stately personage angrily, "are in very bad taste, and if not, are in some instances very disgraceful to you, Mr. D——."

"As if I didn't know," replied the other, and only took the liberty for your amusement, your—"

"Hush! come with us," continued the personage, instantly mollified, "take Gervaise's arm, and let us adjourn. I am thirsty."

And taking D——'s arm, so that he was safely ensconsed in the middle, the conversation was continued.

D —— had tight hold of an arm of each. "Your silly talk just now," said the haughty personage, "reminded me of a question I have often asked myself, mentally: 'Whether you were the bigger knave or fool?'"

"*Something between the both,*" replied the other, with a bow, which took in both at once.

There was dead silence for some minutes. The more important of the speakers bit his lip, and was silent for some minutes. He was taking his way evidently in the direction of the Pavilion, which he entered, unchallenged and unnoticed. He walked slowly forward to a small doorway, and, pushing it inwards, entered; nor did he speak until he had gained a kind of boudoir, when he threw himself upon a couch, tore off moustache, wig, and spectacles, put on another peruque, and stood revealed George of Wales, Prince Regent of this great kingdom.

How little wisdom does it require to lead the millions by the nose!

"A goblet," he cried; and as the officious Sir Gervaise H—— handed him a full bumper of wine, he drank it off at a draught.

"And now, Sir Gervaise, send these two invitations," cried the Prince.

"*Et tu, Brnte,*" said D——.

"Do be quiet, D——," continued the Prince, peevishly, "and let me despatch business."

"Very *pretty* business," said D——, with a penitent face.

"Rather," said the voluptuary, with a smile. Like most vicious men, he was good humoured when not thwarted.

"Why don't you send?" put in D——, addressing Sir Gervaise H——. "I'm beginning to be interested."

"How so?"

"Surely his Royal Highness has not invited

them both for himself? His stomach is not so very large!" added the wag, demurely.

The Prince bit his lip, and waived Sir Gervaise away.

A gentle scratching was heard at the door; and then a gentleman, in a superb livery and a napkin, entered the room.

"The dinner for two, as ordered by your Royal Highness, is ready," he said.

The Prince laughed.

"I say, D——, I promised Gervaise that he should dine with me *tête a tête* to-day, to prepare for the labours of the evening. We'll have some fun. No hour was agreed on. Just write two lines."

"Very well," said D——.

"H. R. H. the Prince of Wales wishes me to command you to deliver these two letters in person. As soon as you have done so come with your report to dinner, with what appetite you may. Be speedy, circumspect, and observant."

And, having despatched this, the Prince went on his way rejoicing, as if he had done a wonderful and clever thing.

Poor Gervaise. Well, he'll come in for the wine.

CHAPTER XCIV.

SIR GERVAISE.

OF course, as the decorations and arrangements in connection with these festivities came or were to come out of the pockets of the people, the whole affair was got up regardless of expense.

How generous the steward of a prince's party is, who, on the strength of giving his services gratuitously, is not expected to contribute any money; and how magnanimously select vestries have been known to vote the ratepayers' cash into their own ungodly stomachs.*

At an early hour the servants of the palace were busily engaged in superintending the workmen, who were giving the last touch to the ornamentation of the rooms. The chandeliers were lit, the carpets, squared the chairs, settees and Ottomans placed in due order, and then they all retired to give the last finish to their own persons.

It was about eight o'clock, when a gentleman, who seemed to have the private *entrée* of the palace, came bounding furiously into the long entrance hall. He was very pale; his gar-

ments were torn; there were marks of violence about his whole person.

He literally foamed at the mouth.

"I will stand this no longer! Ill paid, insulted, buffeted, fed upon promises. By the bye, I have not dined, and the Prince is waiting for me!"

With these words he darted away, ran up some stairs, nor paused until he reached a door, the outside of which he knew well.

Shouts of laughter resounded from the inside.

Pale with passion, he opened the door without knocking, and then stood like Banquo's ghost among the guests.

There was a momentary cessation, then a fresh and tremendous burst of laughter.

"Goodness gracious, Gervaise! have you seen a ghost?" cried the now half intoxicated Prince.

Sir Gervaise H—— did not answer for a moment. He looked at the remains of the feast, at the rich dessert, at the wines, and then drily replied:

"Only the ghost of a dinner!"

Fresh laughter.

"But why were you so late? We waited as long as we could," continued the Prince, almost convulsed with uproarious laughter.

"Why was I too late, your Royal Highness," said Sir Gervaise, recovering himself; "because, as usual, I have suffered martyrdom in your Highness's cause—that's all!"

"What! did they beat you?" asked the Prince, with mock gravity.

"If your Royal Highness will allow me, I will relate my adventures," said Sir Gervaise H——, drily.

"Sit down, man, quaff a goblet, and let us hear, for it must be very funny."

Sir Gervaise drained two goblets, eat one or two cakes, and then spoke:—

"The first beauty, who is about nineteen, is, it is said, a Lady Edgar Blakesley, wife——"

"Whew!"

"Of a young officer in Spain—a naval officer.

"I soon found she was a Frenchwoman, and had been a *dansuese*, though, it is said, perfectly virtuous," and the cynic grinned; "of course here I had no hesitation. I at once walked up to the door and sent the lady in my card, with *Pavilion* in the corner. I was admitted."

"Egad! you were," said the Prince languidly; "a lady of easy virtue."

"A dragon," repeated the other surlily. "I saw her; she haughtily asked my business, adding that, out of respect to the sovereign whom her husband served, she had received me, or else she should have declined seeing any of the profligate associates of the misled Prince!"

"*Arcades ambo id est*, blackguards all!" shouted D——, who hitherto had been tranquilly sipping his wine.

The Prince laughed.

"I handed her the card of invitation.

"'From whom?' she said.

"'From the Prince,' I replied.

"She smiled, took it, and bowed me out most coolly. Superb creature, but haughty."

---

* Here is an amusing instance. A few gentlemen went down to see a few pauper children at a school, distributed a few penny buns and twopenny beer, after which they dined. The expenditure was as follows:—

Dinner, £9 9s.; lemon, 1s.; ten bottles of Bucellas, £3; two ditto of sherry, 12s.; punch, 12s.; four bottles of Champagne, £2 8s.; soda, 16s.; rose-water, 2s.; ice for wine, 2s.; twelve bottles of Port, £3 12s.; five bottles of Sautern, £2; Noyeau, 18s.; glass, 5s. 6d.; tea and coffee, £1 7s.; three servants' dinners, 7s. 6d.; waiters, 9s. Total, £26 1s. Coach-hire and turnpikes, £8 11s. 6d. Grand total, £34 12s. 6d.

The Prince looked at him with a glitter in his cold gray eye.

"Did you nothing to offend her?"

"I, sir! I should as soon have thought of making love to Semermis."

"I was thinking of Lady Jane ——" said the Prince maliciously.

"I went down stairs, and was in the hall, ready to open the door, when from the library a fierce-looking individual rushed forth.

"'Pimp! pander!' he cried, and administered one or two severe kicks which, not knowing the person of the fellow, and unwilling to dirty my fingers with some low individual, I did not resent, but walked away haughtily from the door."

"And hang a calfskin on these recreant limbs," said D——.

Sir Gervaise H—— continued:

"I went *next door*, to the residence of Leila, said to be a native Indian princess, and here again, in my devotion to your Highness, sent in my card.

"But I had to wait, and a kind of dumb waiter came down and showed me a slip of paper—

"*Send up your message.*"

"I bowed and gave the card. The dumb waiter retired, and then there faced me the most hideous monster I have ever seen; who, with a rattan cane, cudgelled me almost to death.

"'Pimp, pandar, mean and contemptible knave, he said, 'leave the house.'

"I couldn't fight with a monkey—a veritable ourang-outang, and again had scornfully to leave the house, my shoulder aching, my honour, or rather the seat of it, aspersed, and my dress and wig in disorder.

The Prince leaned back, totally unable to conceal his laughter.

"My poor Gervaise, really it is too bad. I really must have those fellows punished."

The other bowed profoundly, and drained a bumper.

*   *   *

The suite of rooms thrown open for the reception of the invited guests had scarcely received the finishing touch when the guests began to arrive. All were not of the aristocratic and fastidious class, who think it proper always, like modern Bombas, to be too late. Many persons who had taken up their residence at Brighton from motives of health had been invited, and they, blazing with finery in their spic and span new toilettes, began to arrive at an early hour.

There was scarcely one who did not repent it, for there was no one whatever to receive them.

The Prince would appear shortly, said the attendants, when the throne room would be thrown open and themselves introduced to his Royal Highness.

There was nothing for them but to walk about the royal halls and admire the fittings up of the most grotesque residence in Europe.

About ten the more fashionable guests began to arrive, and the throne room was thrown open.

The Prince had taken care on this occasion, when he expected to be exposed to the gaze of a host of strangers—to be somewhat more careful of himself than usual. He had allowanced himself after dinner—not a very common occurrence we are sorry to say.

The first gentleman in Europe was most affable, spoke a word to every body, congratulated this person, condoled with that, and did what is so easy to do when you have a pretty stiff handle to your name, made himself universally popular.

He even danced once, which was an excess of politeness on his part; and then the festivities began in earnest.

The Prince now moved from room to room, leaning on the arm of D—— Sir Gervaise H—— had not yet made his appearance. D—— said that after his kicking and beating he was oiling the parts.

There were two rooms devoted to dancing, the rest were left clear for flirting, walking, and cards.

The Prince moved slowly along, and it would have amused a cynic to have observed the conduct of England's nobles and gentry as they hovered round the sun of that small hemisphere. The men bowed and made way, the women either stood so as to compel his notice, or boldly used their eyes, or languished, or held them down prettily, like willing Circassian captives trying to win the favour of a particular buyer.

Mighty indeed is the influence of a court for good or evil.

This is the worst feature of hereditary monarchy, which, if we were not used to it, would appear too absurd to contemplate.

No matter how good one sovereign, and how that sovereign may influence a land for good, a fool, a knave, a vicious and corrupt monarch may follow and undo all.

The Prince, under all his assumed suavity, and beneath all his calm exterior, concealed great uneasiness and impatience.

No one present pleased him. The rooms were crowded with the rank, beauty, and fashion of the day, and at any other time this great connoisseur in female loveliness might have found ample food for admiration.

He was now looking everywhere for those who had not come—a very common failing of human nature.

"I do believe that accursed, Sir Gervaise never took the tickets," said he in a low but irritated tone.

"I think he did."

"Why?"

"He brought back a receipt in full."

"Then why have they not come?"

"Timidity."

"Nonsense."

"Not ready."

"Women always are. They would go to the devil himself for pleasure," said the irritated regent of this great kingdom.

At this moment a servant approached and bowed with profound humility.

"What is it?"

"A lady."

"What lady?"

"A stranger—she has a ticket, your Royal Highness, but will not enter unless her guardian is admitted with her."

"Admit him."

The domestic bowed and left.

"I suppose it's one of them."

"How happy could I be with either," hummed D——, "were t'other dear charmer away."

"Do go and see," said the Prince, who was now as impatient as a school boy.

CHAPTER XCV.
PAULINE.

In one corner of the room, devoted to flirting and promenading, stood two men, with their backs to a fireless fireplace in conversation. They were both handsome men, and wore their bravery well. They were of the Carlton clique, some of the fertile race of toadies, who do so love to hang round a court, especially where pleasure of a certain kind was always to be had.

They were not *bon vivants*.

A *bon vivant* demands a certain amount of knack, a talent of its own. They were simply fast men of their day—not exactly Mohawks. That honourable fraternity had been dispersed, or hung, or shot.

One was Lord Charles Lutterel.

The other was the juvenile Marquis of A——.

"Dooced slow," said the first.

"Very," said the other.

"One knows all these women, or else they are too dooced respectable; we doesn't want to know them. I think Brighton's a mistake. It's very dull."

"Very," said the other with a yawn.

"No cards as yet," continued Lord Charles Lutterel; "there's nobody playing. I suppose we shall have plenty of it by and by;" and as he spoke he glanced at the spot where stood the Prince and his friend.

"Let us join the Prince," said the Marquis.

"No; I hate that D——, he's so impertinent; spares nobody."

"But the Prince is alone, D—— has just left him."

"Depend upon it he'll be back. But never mind, here goes."

And the two noblemen, the cold-blooded Lutterel and the butterfly Marquis, strolled up towards the Prince.

"Ah, Lutterel! ah! how do you do?" he said good-humouredly. None other had ventured to approach him, as they perceived he wished to be alone. "I wanted somebody to support me. A presentation—some wonderful. Here she comes."

At this moment Pauline, in a most tasteful *recherche* dress, such as would not have disgraced a court in the present day, entered, ushered by the master of the ceremonies, while by her side, pale but resolute, walked Mr. James Tyrrel Blakesley.

At this moment one or two courtiers glided behind the Prince, among them were D—— and Sir Gervaise ——.

"Allow me, your Royal Highness," said the master of the ceremonies, "to present to you Lady Edgar Blakesley, and her relative and guardian, Mr. James Tyrrel Blakesley."

"Welcome lady to our court," cried the Prince gallantly, as she curtseyed low; "how is it that we have so long been deprived of your presence?"

"Your Royal Highness," said Pauline, in that rich foreign accent which is one of the charms of that clever actress, Madame Celeste, "I have been a bride but a few months, and my husband is in Spain, ordered away two days after our nuptials."

"D——," whispered the Marquis of A—— to Lord Charles Lutterel, "it's that little demon the Signora."

"You don't say so."

"As sure as I stand here."

"I pity your husband," said the Prince, gallantly; "but allow me to do the honours of this my poor abode. It is your first visit Lady Blakesley, but I hope it will not be your last."

"Your Highness is too good," replied Pauline, in a languishing tone.

Every one bowed as the two passed down the room, the Prince in high spirits and full of life, for who had hitherto resisted him; Pauline's heart swelling with pride and exultation.

"Ah! Marquis, how d'ye do?" she said in a drawling tone to the Marquis of A——, who bowed low to conceal his confusion.

"Do you know the Marquis?" asked the Prince, drily.

"I met him once," said Pauline, laughing; "my husband and the Marquis were both in such a state then—neither of them have any very distinct recollection of the affair. It was quite affecting. They positively couldn't get up. I can't help laughing, your Highness."

"Been drinking?" asked the Prince in a grave whisper, as if he highly disapproved of such conduct.

"Well, I must say, your Highness, that they had," continued Pauline, whose eyes sparkled like diamonds.

The Prince was intoxicated. There was something in Pauline which he had never met in woman before. Round all men and all women there is a kind of insensible cloud—an atmosphere of their own, which is more or less electric; but with some natures it is far more powerful than others; and just as Pauline's veins ran quicker, and with hotter blood then most of her sex, so was the halo around her more full of mesmeric power than is generally found to exist.

His Royal Highness the Prince of Wales just then wished his guests in a very warm place, and in the utter selfishness of his heart would have sent them forth as they were at a moment's notice had etiquette have allowed it.

He, however, determined to have some private conversation with Pauline.

In the throne-room there was a recess containing a velvet couch, to which he conducted the lovely woman, and, praying her to be seated, took a seat at her side.

It was understood that whenever the Prince

Regent was thus publicly and indelicately paying his court to a woman, that none were to approach him.

A whisper went round the whole suite of rooms. Everybody had seen the new arrival. The women were frantic; both the favourite in *esse* and the favourites in *posse*. An utterly unknown creature, without a name, whom nobody knew, who had been seen that day, driving about in the most absurd of dresses, had monopolised his Royal Highness at an hour when it was usual for him to be unusually courteous, to walk round the rooms.

What was to be done?

Just then nothing. But all resolved at once to get up a cabal against the horrible person who dared to monopolise the divine person of the Royal Prince.

"She's dooced handsome," said Lord Charles Lutterel.

"She is," replied the Marquis, doggedly; "and I will be revenged. Lutterel, I owe that woman a deep and lasting grudge. Will you be my friend? I will do the same for you another time."

"Command me," said the supposed heir to the Dukedom of —— failing his childless elder brother.

"She tricked me nicely; and," whispering very low, "I don't think she can produce evidence of her marriage."

"Fair game," said Lord Charles.

"Honour!" said the Marquis.

"Bright!" replied Lord Charles Lutterel, laying his hand upon his heart.

"Let us move apart and watch," said the Marquis.

CHAPTER XCVI.

THE BARGAIN.

MEANWHILE Pauline, scarcely able to conceal her rapturous delight at being selected from a crowd of titled and beautiful women, took her seat with a modest mien, but flushed cheeks and sparkling eyes, beside the Prince.

Her cheeks wanted no rouge as yet. They were of a lovely pink, which no art was ever yet able to imitate—at least no art that was ever known to the public.

Certain women possessed secrets which have never yet been divulged to the world. To them they owed their success in life.

Some day they may find their way in print.

The Prince was a bold wooer. It was habit made him so—for had he not the right to despise and condemn a sex which lay down at his feet, as did the miserable devotees of a hideous superstition beneath the wheels of Jauggernaut.

"Beautiful lady," he said, in an amorous tone, "how cold and insensible a heart must have been that which, having once seen you, would leave you to single blessedness again."

"He could'nt help it," she said, with a sparkle of the eye—like a diamond flash.

"Why, lady?"

"My husband, though heir to a noble title and to immense estates, is but nineteen, and holds but the rank of a midshipman in his Majesty's service."

"That shall be looked to; but still that does not answer my question."

"He was ordered off to Spain at a moment's notice," replied Pauline.

"How sad for him. But, lovely and brightest of thy sex, I will see that his promotion is looked to. He shall rise rapidly—but, fair lady, I shall keep him abroad at some foreign station."

"Until he's got a glass eye and a wooden leg," said Pauline, with a beautiful pout.

The Prince smiled.

"Then he will be an Admiral."

"Oh! I shall so like that," said Pauline, naively.

"Rely upon it. But, pearl of great price, surely in common gratitude you will bestow some little reward on one who is your slave," said the Prince, taking her hand, and giving her one of these looks which made even Pauline blush.

"My Lord—your Royal Highness—I am a poor weak woman, and, above all, my desire is to retain my true position in society."

"But I do not see"—

"Will your Highness allow me to explain myself," she said with her most insinuating smile.

"With pleasure," he replied, squeezing her soft and willing hand.

"My husband, I have told you, is heir to the ancient baronetcy of the Blakesleys, and to the vast estates and rents connected therewith."

"I understand"—

"He will be of age in about eighteen months. Within the last few weeks an opposition, a new claimant, a foster brother it is said, is about to be set up by a powerful and wealthy body of conspirators.

"Indeed!" said the Prince, becoming interested.

"And ere Sir Edward comes of age their batteries will be prepared. I happen to know that they are moving heaven and earth to win your august mother to their side, and they boast I shall never be presented.

"We shall see," said the Prince, turning crimson.

Pauline's eyes flashed.

"Will you be our friend," continued the young and lovely woman in her most fond and caressing tone.

"I will."

"Oh! thank you," cried Pauline, stooping and kissing his hand.

She remained in this position a moment, and then reared her head, her very neck crimson with blushes.

But they understood one another.

"When will you come and see me alone," whispered the enamoured Prince.

"Oh! your Royal Highness."

"Nobody will know you."

"But"—

"I will give you a signet ring which will open all doors."

"What will be said."

"Nobody need know."

"Alas! men are very wicked, and have no mercy on us poor women when we once give our hearts away," sighed Pauline.

"Then you love me a little?"

"How can I help it—you, so good, so kind, so noble," said Pauline, raising her bright eyes swimming in liquid fire to his.

The Prince's very ears tingled with pleasure. He began to believe she really loved him.

"I shall sup alone to-morrow," said the Prince, will you come."

"Pauline bent down her head and sighed.

"You will not be cruel."

"So soon."

"An age."

"Then if I must, I must," she said, placing her hand in his.

The Prince, with a rapturous smile, took off the signet ring.

"Be at the south gate at midnight; show this. You will be at once admitted, and inside the gate will find a person.

"Who will it be?" said Pauline, quickly.

"No one who will know you."

"How shall I know the person."

"The messenger will say *Spain*, and you will reply *Victory*."

Pauline again sighed as if she half repented her surrender even to a Prince.

At this moment an official appeared at a considerable distance, bowing to his Royal Highness in a peculiar way, in which only chamberlains can bow.

Behind him was Sir Gervaise H——, and a little in the back ground Lord Charles Lutterel and the Marquis of A——.

"What can it be? Some very important affair or they would not dare to interrupt me. Will you pardon me one moment most beauteous lady of my soul."

And the Prince, bowing deeply, hurried away towards the group.

"Well, what is it, Skinner?" said he to the man who was bowing and scraping.

"Please your Royal Highness, the Princess of Borneo," he said.

"Shew her in."

"But, your Highness!"

"What?"

"Such a retinue?"

"What of it—shew her in" said the Prince, with a sudden glance at Pauline, "or rather I will go to meet her."

"But they won't let her in."

"Why," continued the Prince, with a dark and impatient frown.

"Because, your Royal Highness, the Princess's retinue is composed of a dumb secretary and a dwarf chamberlain," stammered the official.

"Bid them enter. I will come to meet them," said the Prince. "Marquis."

"Your Royal Highness?"

"Will you attend Lady Edgar until I return?"

"With pleasure."

No sooner had the Prince left Lady Edgar than a bitter smile of scorn had passed over her countenance, to be followed by a glow of triumph.

"I have them both. This night I will write to Sir Edgar. I can make or unmake him. As for this fat and voluptuous Prince I must mind what I am at. He is selfish and not to be trusted. Ah! Marquis, how d'ye do."

And she held out one finger to him.

"His Royal Highness has sent me to bear you company while he goes to receive some Princess or other."

"Thank you."

"Are we friends, Pauline?"

"Oh, yes. Surely you forgive me when I tell you that nothing induced me to follow Sir Edgar but his solemn promise to make me a wife."

"I do forgive you, but"—with a meaning glance.—"I am sorry he found you so soon."

"Just in time my lord; shall we walk," replied Pauline rather coldly.

And, taking his arm, she slowly returned towards the more crowded room.

Few ventured to enter the throne-room but the initiated.

In the outer room they could already make out that something very exciting was going on, and they hurried forward to see what it was. Near the door, within the throne-room, was a dais. This Pauline mounted and saw all that passed.

CHAPTER XCVII.

THE PRINCESS OF BORNEO.

WHEN the Prince hurried towards the door it was in a state of considerable trepidation.

Two women on his hands at once. It was rather an awkward contingency. But George Prince of Wales had got over more difficulties than that, and so have other men.

No sooner, however, had he fixed his eyes on the lovely being who advanced to meet him, then he utterly forgot Lady Edgar as much as if she never had existed.

A very fickle man was George, Prince Regent.

It was Leila, and Leila dressed in one of the most superb evening dresses that could be conceived.

Her hair was dressed in the most fanciful manner, while her low dress revealed a neck and shoulders such as the Prince had never seen before, except in imagination.

By her side, in a fanciful Eastern costume, was the dumb secretary, while on the other, in the dress of a middle-aged chamberlain, making him look unusually hideous, was the Blue Dwarf, who bowed with the most profound respect to the Prince.

The Regent started. Somehow or other he had in some way heard of this hideous monster, but at the moment for the life of him he could not recollect when, where, or how.

"I have to apologise, your Highness," said the young and lovely girl, with a sparkle in her dark and pellucid eye, "for bringing my retinue. But I never go out without them."

All the spectators who could get near stood round in a respectful circle, admiring and wondering.

Pauline leaned heavily on the shoulder of the Marquis of A——.

"What is it?" he said.

"That little wretch, that monster, is the bitterest enemy of my husband; a being with almost miraculous power. He is here for no good. If you are my friend, Marquis, you will assist me to discover."

"With pleasure, Lady Blakesley."

"For heaven's sake do not let him hear my husband's name!" whispered Pauline, in considerable trepidation.

"I will not. What a beautiful girl."

"Rely on it, Marquis, that girl is his best card. He is going to play it for some purpose. I strongly suspect some foul play. Let the Regent be on his guard."

"His Royal Highness knows how to take care of himself," replied the Marquis.

"Do get nearer, and hear what is going on. I will remain here."

The Marquis, nothing loth, moved forward and mingled with the throng. Pauline at once glided away, and, slipping behind the heavy curtains of a window, remained an unseen spectator of all that was going on.

"Most welcome Princess," said the Regent, "I am most happy to see you, or any of your suite. My house has never looked so bright before. Allow me."

And, taking her arm, he with an almost imperceptible sign waved every body away. The courtiers fell back with a significant smile; the ladies retreated with fury in their hearts.

Twice his well-tried friends had been neglected for total strangers.

This would not have mattered so much because it might have been merely an effort of extreme politeness; but these women were so very beautiful.

It cannot be supposed that amid the many women of title and of rank who had been favoured with the Prince one loved him. Not one. He was too utterly selfish, too little full of sentiment, too brutal in his breakings off for that. But they regretted the position of favourite. While it lasted they were overwhelmed with attentions, with notice, with rich presents, that inflamed their vanity.

Half a dozen cabals were instantly formed both against the Princess of Borneo and against Pauline.

They looked for the latter, to see if they could find her, but she was nowhere to be seen.

"Already," said one lady, with a significant smile.

Another full-blown beauty shrugged her snowy shoulders, shown off to the best advantage.

"Princess of Borneo," cried a middle-aged lady, mother of two willing daughters, neither of them without charms, but of the bony order of creation, "I never heard of such a title. Where is Borneo?"

"Don't know," was a general response on all sides. "Can't think."

"Well," said a little miss, who ought to have been at school, well washed, and put to bed, "I know."

And she gave a perfectly infantine giggle.

"Well, Lady Sue," cried all those around her, "where is it?"

"It's a very hot place, every body black, and all cannibals," continued miss.

A general laugh ensued.

"Then she's no princess at all; only a pretence, all a sham—horrid—must be exposed; and such horrors of men. That Blue Humpback has given me the shivers."

"What's all this?—what's going on?" cried a well-known voice. "Something very wicked or else you would not be looking so happy, Lady Sue."

"You naughty creature!" said miss, who was not sixteen, very rosy, pretty, and unmeaning, but who already had her eyes on the prince.

Observe, we give no names. Bad as the crew around the English Louis XV. were, we wish not to impale their names.

But the fourth George is public property, and cannot be too often held up to public odium.

"Am I? Well I suppose I am, and that's why all the ladies like me," continued Lord Charles Lutterel.

All laughed or tittered.

"But what is it all about?"

"About this little chit who calls herself the Princess of Borneo," said Lady Sue.

"She's very beautiful," continued Lord Charles.

"Oh! oh! oh!"

"Almost perfect."

"Oh! oh! oh!"

"And the Prince is smitten as I never saw him smitten before."

"Ah! ah! ah!" on all hands, in a tone of actual despair.

"She'll be the prime favourite, I'm sure."

"Will you hold your tongue?" said Lady Sue, "Will you, you provoking creature?"

"Well, she would be but for one circumstance."

"And pray what is that?"

"That I have taken a fancy to her myself; and, what is more, mean to win her and keep her to myself."

This was said with so much *aplomb* and apparent sincerity that the bevy of court beauties were a little relieved.

Meanwhile the Prince, over whose mind had passed the waters of oblivion, as far as Pauline was concerned, strutted across the royal apartments with this fairy creature on his arm, bewildered, astonished, confounded.

Leila was to him a new style of beauty, as she would have been to any one else.

It would be as difficult to render her characteristics as it would be to tell why a landscape which one moment appears dull and vapid, at others is bright, sunny, and charms us by its loveliness.

She swam in an atmosphere of light—and beauty is light, for it radiates around with even greater brightness than the sun.

"To what country, to what sphere, to what new and unknown world do you belong, bright lady, that you have so long concealed from us your radiance?" began George, Prince of Wales.

"I am the poor daughter of a native prince of one of the most savage countries in the world," said Leila, laughing, "and am only over here for my education."

"And you intend returning to that savage abode, wherever it may be?"

"Borneo," replied Leila.

"Borneo, ah! Borneo—never heard of it."

"Never heard of Borneo?" cried the princess, with a look of well assumed amazement, "why, it is bigger than England."

"I dare say—but, most lovely princess of an unknown clime, never shall it be said that England, having once gazed upon so much beauty shall again lose it. No. I, as Prince Regent of the kingdom, forbid it."

"How will you manage that?" said Leila, who spoke in a tone of the most provoking bantering.

"I will forbid your departure."

"I would go in spite of that," said Leila.

"How?"

"I came in secret, and I will go in secret. It is nearly time. At sixteen I am to be married," she added, archly.

"Married at sixteen!" cried the Prince, flushing to the very roots of his hair. "May I ask what age you are now?"

"Not quite fifteen," said Leila, with an ingenuous blush, and not without considerable surprise.

It never struck her that her extreme youth and innocence was her mightiest charm. To desecrate and destroy the temple of purity and innocence was his chief delight.

We are depicting an evil and abhorrent nature, but we are writing history.

The Prince was silent a moment. He looked around. Not a soul was observing him. All were engaged in conservation—and then it was not etiquette to watch the master of the house.

"Most adorable and lovely princess," he said, in tones husky with excitement and passion, "allow your humble servant to express his admiration of your beauty by placing at your disposal every part of his palace. This, fair lady, is a room which is reserved to my friends and relatives of royal blood. Let me pray you enter."

And the enamoured Prince opened a side door, and, taking Leila's unresisting hand, led her in.

He would have closed the door, but Leila very firmly declined.

"Your Highness, we shall be observed;" she said, with a strangely haughty glance of her eye.

The Prince bowed, and led the way into an apartment which many had entered to their sorrow and shame.

CHAPTER XCVIII.

THE BOUDOIR AND THE KEY.

THIS boudoir was mysteriously lit from the roof—how, it was impossible to say. Its walls were covered with pictures by great masters, though the subjects were not such as would have suited the sacred shrine of a young and pure unmarried girl. There were Venuses, and Cupids and Dianas, and other gods and goddesses, and fauns and satyrs, all very clever and well executed, but still what is usually called rather warm.

There was a couch, several chairs, a table, and in the corner of the room a screen, the end of which reached to the corner of the couch.

The Prince gallantly handed the lady to the seat, and placed himself beside her.

"At length," he cried, in accents which were meant to be most seducing, "I am alone with you, most charming and divine of her sex."

"A mere child," said Leila, bending her eyes to the ground, but at the same instant giving him a glance which went to his very heart.

"Child! you are an angel. Until I saw you, divine princess, I knew not what woman was, what beauty in its highest stage is."

"Prince, I hate flattery."

"Witty as beautiful."

"Still, Prince—"

"I cannot help it. There is something in that wondrous eye of yours which I fain would read. What is your name?"

"Leila."

"Leila. Never shall you leave this country. I tell you, girl, you have so won my heart that I could not live without you—without you, existence would be a dreary blank. I see but you, I know but you!" cried the Prince, passionately.

By the couch was a carpet stool, it might have been by accident it was there, but some said it was always there for occasions like the present, when the Prince wanted to do the dramatic and pathetic.

"Fie! Prince."

"Leila, so great is my passion that for you I would sacrifice a hundred lives. If you are cruel to me—" she's only a girl after all, thought he, "I shall die."

"And your poor subjects?" said Leila, putting her handkerchief to her face, to hide what—well, we only know that her chest heaved in a very suspicious way.

"D—— my subjects!" cried the future monarch energetically; "they care as much for me as I do for them."

"Upon my soul," he said to himself, "the little minx is laughing at me. Never mind, she is a most charming little innocent, and I am resolved to take no offence."

"Dearest lady," he continued, "I will not rise unless I give you hope."

"Of what!" said Leila, in the most naive manner in the world, looking him calmly and composedly in the face.

"Egad!" thought the Royal George, "she's a fool. Ah! lovely Leila, I want you to promise to love me a little bit."

"That'll be charming," said Leila, clapping her hands, "and do you mean to love me?"

"I adore, I worship you!" he replied.

"Do you; and I like you very much. But sit down beside me, and let us talk sense."

The delighted Prince rose, seated himself by her side, and took one of her hands.

"Now, you see," she said, in a delightfully naive way, "it's arranged that we are to love one another."

"Delightful."

"But you see I am engaged to be married, while you are married."

The Prince stared with his eyes wide open.

"Eh?—what?"

"But do you not mean us to be married," said Leila gravely.

"My dear girl," replied the royal Prince, far more amazed than he was angry, "you are doubtless aware, being yourself a Princess, that these matters are not so easily settled as with persons in a lower condition in life. There are a hundred different things to stop one from realising one's most ardent hopes. There is the consent of the crown to begin with. Now my own candid opinion is that a Prince, ruling a great nation, with a hundred temptations thrown daily in his path, should be allowed as many wives as he pleases. My friend the Sultan is better off than I am. But, dearest Leila, I am a slave to laws and social prejudices. What, then, can I do. Leila, I love you."

"Yes, I know, but what's the good," said Leila, pouting.

"Angel of innocence, were it in my power there is no tie too binding for me not to willingly enter into it. But I cannot. And then, lovely one, after all there is no bond like love. The only true marriage is the marriage of the heart. I detest my wife."

"Detest your wife."

"Certainly; but I love you. And now, angel, is it settled—we love one another."

"It's very naughty," said Leila.

"Everything pleasant, egad," cried the Prince, "seems to be so; but, dearest Leila, you will waive this silly prejudice and love me."

"Well," said Leila, "I don't know. I'm afraid I must think it over."

"And when will you give me an answer," continued the Regent, annoyed and yet delighted.

"I don't know. We may never meet again. You must not come to my house, and I cannot come here."

"But you can."

"Yes, and be ruined in name and character. Leila, Princess of Berneo," said the girl, fixing her deep magnetic eyes upon the other, and laying her hand upon his arm, "has nothing but her good name. That once lost, I'm without hope, without a future. What would be said if I were seen coming here?"

"But no one will see you except my most faithful and devoted attendants."

"Who one day would whisper, with a sneer, that Leila, Princess of Borneo, had visited the Prince Regent by stealth. No! no! Not even your worthy friend Sir Gervaise H—— must know of it."

"My lovely girl," said the Prince, "what you desire is extremely difficult."

"I don't want to come at all, Prince, that I tell you candidly. But as you seemed so very much to wish it."

"I do, I do, can I trust you Leila?"

"What with!"

"A key."

"A key! why not?"

"There is a secret entrance to my private chambers, known only to myself; the architect who erected this part of the palace is dead. Now if I give you this you must let me know the day before, or in the course of the evening that you are coming, and, whatever happens, I will be there to meet you."

"I don't promise to come, mind," said Leila, gravely, "I am very capricious. I like you now, but I'm afraid I'm very like you."

"How so?"

"Very apt to forget."

"I don't understand you."

"Don't you know the old English proverb?"

"Which?"

"Out of sight, out of mind."

The Prince laughed.

"You are a little witch—one kiss before I give you the key."

"Oh fie!" said Leila, turning away, "besides there's somebody looking."

The Prince raised his head and caught a faint glimpse of Pauline.

"When will you come?" he continued, drawing forth a golden key.

At this moment the Blue Dwarf peered cautiously from behind the screen, with a strangely awful expression of countenance. On the other side Pauline thrust her head forward and tried to catch what passed.

"To-morrow, perhaps next day, perhaps not at all," said the wayward girl, taking the key.

"No, no," stammered the Prince, "not to-morrow."

"Why?"

"A cabinet-council will be held, and the fellows will all expect to stop to supper."

"Oh, very well. I won't interrupt you; don't be alarmed," said Leila, laughing; "I know what these cabinet councils are."

"Do you?"

"Of course I do. Am I not a princess?"

"Ah! I had forgotten. Do they tease you much?" said the Prince, smiling.

"Well, my secretary of state for home affairs is dumb, while my prime minister is my slave," replied Leila laughing.

"Who is he?" asked the Prince.

"Sapathwa! the dearest, but kindest-hearted old friend I have. He thinks he's ugly, and says so. But no—"

"Is it the Humpback?"

"The Blue Dwarf?" said Leila, gravely.

"The hideous monster!"

"Prince," said Leila, coldly, "don't repeat these words in my presence again. In your eyes he may be that, but I love him, and can see in him nothing but virtues. He is the noblest and best creature that heaven ever made."

"We'll knight him," cried the Prince, laughing.

"He would refuse. He is too wise and too great."

"I must know more of him. And now, my beloved, we must show ourselves or you will have as many enemies as there are women present. Come."

And they went out.

Pauline glided away, while the Blue Dwarf raised his long arms to heaven.

"God bless her!" he said, and wiped away a tear.

CHAPTER XCIX

THE COMPACT.

To say that Pauline was irritated was to say little. She had not the remotest affection or regard for the Prince, whom she looked upon as a mere selfish voluptuary, but never was French woman more keenly alive to the importance of a position.

She had determined, at any cost, to hold a position in society as the genuine Lady Edgar Blakesley.

This prospect could be materially aided by the assistance of the Prince. In these days judges were more easily influenced than now.

We believe that though prejudices may sometimes rise, bear strongly on the decision of one of the supreme lawyers of the nation, private influence is never of the slightest use.

But then favouritism was the order of the day.

Pauline's idea was, favourite once favourite always, and hence her terrible dread of the influence which might be exercised by the beautiful young Princess of Borneo.

As, then, the Prince passed by with Leila on his arm, a dark frown settled on her face, and she felt that there was no punishment too heavy, no revenge too bitter, no torture too terrible to be inflicted on the young girl who had dared to stand in her path.

With one so unscrupulous as Pauline to come to a resolution, and to carry it out was almost the same thing.

"Our Prince is fairly caught, Lady Blakesley," said a voice close to her.

Pauline turned and found herself face to face with Lord Charles Lutterell.

Pauline gave him a haughty stare, which said as plain as words themselves—*I do not know you.*

"Pardon me, madam," he continued, bowing, "my name is Lord Charles Lutterell, and I had a reason for addressing your ladyship."

Pauline bowed and smiled. Had she have been sure of the Prince she would not so much have cared for the Lord.

"May I speak frankly to your ladyship," said he.

"I adore frankness."

"You will not betray me."

"To whom."

"To the Prince."

"Oh! fie, my lord."

"I have taken an enormous fancy to that little girl, the Princess of Borneo. You don't like her, but the result is the same. Will you assist me in getting her out of the Prince's way."

Pauline raised her eyes quickly, and looked him full in the face. He quailed not before her glance.

"You are not deceiving me?"

"Madam, I never was more in earnest in my life. Mark you, madam, what I am about doing is very dangerous. The Prince is very touchy on these points, and resents any interference bitterly. But you would find, if you knew me, that I am very bold."

"I see you are," said Pauline, with an odd glance from her wicked eyes.

"Why so?"

"Or you would'nt tell one woman you loved another," continued Pauline archly.

"You are an angel," said Lord Charles, laughing. "Will you help me?"

"I will."

"This Princess of Borneo shall trouble you no more."

Pauline shuddered.

"What is the matter, lady?"

Pauline pointed sternly to the Blue Dwarf.

"Beware, my lord, that hideous monster is more dangerous than a wild beast, more cunning than a serpent. I saw his eye upon us but just now, as much as to say, 'I know you are plotting.'"

"Who and what is he?"

"I know him only as the bitter and uncompromising enemy of myself and husband," replied Pauline, "and it bodes no good that he is here."

"He came in the train of the Princess."

"Rather she came in his train. There is some trickery under all this, rely upon it. I would give a thousand pounds to know what is his object in being here."

"Is he so terrible?"

"The wretch is always in the way when he is not wanted. Would you believe it, that he is receiver of my husband's estates, and has set up some man of straw as a claimant against Sir Edgar?"

"Humph!—a slippery, dangerous customer. Well, so as I get the girl from him I care not. He can do nothing to me."

"Do not be so sure of that. But when do you intend commencing operations?"

"I don't know. I must trust chiefly to the chapter of accidents."

"Do you know, my lord, that when you addressed yourself to me you did a very clever thing."

"How so?"

"I can assist you at once."

"Speak, don't tantalise me!" cried the young nobleman.

"I don't know what it means; perhaps you do; but his Highness has given the girl a golden key."

The young lord started and turned rather pale, bit his lip and reflected.

"Then it is more serious than I fancied. The deuce! I must be circumspect. Did you catch when the visit was to take place?"

"Not to-morrow night," said the lady, in a sarcastic tone.

"Why not?"

"Because his Royal Highness did me the honour to recollect that he had promised me an interview relative to my lawsuit," continued Pauline.

"Your arm," said the young nobleman, with a smile; "we will manage to circumvent his Highness and the Princess of Borneo, do not fear."

A little later James Tyrrel Blakesley joined Pauline, and escorted her to her carriage, not, however, before an introduction had passed between him and Lord Charles, who was invited to call.

A short time after it was announced that the Princess of Borneo's carriage stopped the way, and that young lady had the honour of being escorted to the end of the corridor by the Prince himself.

The Blue Dwarf then took her hand, and, with a low bow, led her towards her carriage.

As he did so her eyes fell upon the countenance of a youth, not more than nineteen years of age, who was reading her features with the most intense and agonising scrutiny.

When he saw that Leila observed him he bowed an almost imperceptible, humble, apologising kind of bow.

Leila smiled, and then coloured to the eyes. For the first time in her life her little heart felt a strange and not unpleasant flutter.

That night Pauline wrote a long letter to Sir Edgar Blakesley, and sent it off by a special messenger to town.

James Tyrrel Blakesley had all the evening kept out of the way of the Blue Dwarf, of which he had the most wholesome dread.

"Be assured that unless you bend the Prince to your chariot wheels and make him take our part earnestly and seriously, all is lost. He can do everything. Several of the judges are his friends—and you know there are ways and means of managing these things. My own plan would be to get William Lennox out of the way altogether.

"But how?"

"It is dangerous work to kill him, so many friends as he has. But in war time there are ways and means, you know, of getting rid of obstinate people."

"Nothing like death," said Pauline, with a scornful curl of the lip.

"And yet this youth saved your life," replied James Tyrrel Blakesley.

"Ah!" cried the Frenchwoman, with admirable *naivete*, "and so you expect to find gratitude in the world, do you? Leave that to succeed in the end you have laid down—you must be pitiless. Besides, the youth is handsome enough, and choose to slight me formy cousin. I am one of these women who never forgive that kind of thing."

"Well," there is plenty of time. But impress on Sir Edgar the necessity of returning."

"Mark me," said Pauline, firmly; "unless on the very day after his arrival he weds me, I too am his enemy. I will betray everything, and woe unto those who act with him and make themselves my enemies."

"I shall never be one of them," replied James Tyrrel Blakesley, after some reflection. "On the contrary, if Sir Edgar plays the fool, it is my idea that we should make terms with William Lennox."

"Exactly," said Pauline.

CHAPTER C.

DEATH FLAPS HIS WINGS.

NEVER was young man more utterly miserable than Lieutenant William Lennox. His love for Lillian was the thought of his life; while his amour with the Duchess of Castella was a mere episode in his existence, which he would have broken off at once had he possessed the moral courage to do so.

He began to dislike his mistress. Fatal necessity of almost every illicit connection.

He lived in one perpetual agony. The dread of discovery was for ever on his soul. For all the world's wealth he would not have had his dear affianced wife discover his faithlessness, and yet he had not the moral courage to have said the word which would have released him from all his terror.

The excuse he made to himself was that the Duchess loved him more than ever, and who could be cruel to one who made such daily and hourly sacrifices for him.

And then the poor Duchess spoke so tenderly and softly of Lillian, called herself a wicked woman, and expressed such fervent hopes for their happiness when the day should come, that it was really delightful to hear her.

Poor William Lennox.

But what youth of his age would not have been deceived by an astute or clever woman of six or seven and twenty.

And still he never failed in his visits to Lillian—was out with her more every day.

People said, "What an exemplary and happy pair of lovers! And so it was on the side of Lillian, who was truth and purity itself. She was happy because she had nothing to hide.

To live on the edge of a precipice, ever and anon peering over, and feeling the ground slipping beneath your feet; to fancy every knock that comes a denunciation of your crime; to creep about like a burglar in the night; to walk as it were on ice and to expect every moment a heavy hand on the shoulder; to feel the heart ever bounding, fluttering, and palpitating with alternate joy and terror; to be for ever on thorns; to dare never to face boldly the injured one; and to think every look, every word, every act an indistinct allusion to one's guilt; to tremble at one's shadow; to repent every hour, and every hour to sin again—such is a feeble outline of the results of illicit passion.

As the French truly say *Le jeu ne vaut pas la chandelle.**

Lillian saw nothing of all this. It never struck her that there was anything the matter with him beyond the natural results of his illness. She only fretted that William Lennox should be so long getting well.

There was no self about Lillian, and yet though he saw it not, and her mother saw it not, she was far more in want of sympathy and care than he was.

Ah, me! We approach this part of our narrative with a feeling of awe and sorrow.

Poor Lillian! And yet it has been said that the loved of the Lord die young.

It may be so. But we who know and love them also little like to part with them. Yet a a little longer is always our prayer, and there is a want of good people here below.

Lillian was ill. She had no ailment, that was the worst of it. The English doctor shook his head, and knew not what to do. He had not the slightest suspicion what was the matter with her. Nobody had.

Mrs. Winterton, again, with blindness, which in many cases is such a mercy, saw nothing, until Dr. —— one day abruptly told her that Lillian must be looked to.

"What is the matter?" cried the poor mother.

"Don't know," gruffly said D——; "wish I did. Can't make it out. It isn't consumption, it isn't atrophy. I can trace it to no particular disease, and yet she is really ailing. She must have air and exercise. We must rouse her up. Something must be done."

"What?"

"My own candid advice would be marriage and a wedding tour," said the doctor; "anything for a change of life."

"But I have reason to believe that William Lennox will not wed until he is of age," replied Mrs. Winterton, despondingly.

"I'll soon settle that," said the other.

And he put on his hat, and went to William Lennox's hotel.

He was dressing for a rendezvous at a small village some ten miles from Madrid, where he could never be traced; so said the Duchess of Castella.

"Where are you going?" said the doctor, gruffly.

---

* Free translation. It is hardly worth while.

"Out for a ride."

"Well, listen to me first. Are you aware that Lillian is very ill, dangerously ill, almost hopelessly ill!"

"Gracious heavens!" cried William, seating himself, while a cold shiver passed through his whole being; "what is the matter—anything sudden?"

"No. Ever since your accident there has been a mysterious change about her."

"Does her mother know of this?" said William Lennox, who shook as with the palsy.

"Yes."

"And what do you propose doing?" gasped William.

"I have already told Mrs. Winterton," said the doctor, "of the only plan I can think of. She must be married, and have a long wedding tour. Change, bustle, new scenes, and happiness may save her."

William Lennox laid his head upon the table and groaned aloud.

"You agree?" said the doctor.

"Of course I do. Take me to her."

"We must be very cautious. Lillian has not the slightest suspicion. She is an angel, and will do just as she is told. She would not cross the will of those she loves for the riches of the universe."

"She is an angel, and I—" began William.

"Come at once. My carriage is at the door. We will just make a call. The arrangements must be left to Mrs. Winterton, who doubts of your consent, and said you had reason"

"And so I have—many," cried William Lennox, wildly; "but Lillian in danger, Lillian ill—my life is at her service."

And they dashed away to the residence of Mrs. Winterton.

Lillian was in the drawing-room with her mother, and William Lennox was horrified at the ravages of disease in one day. Lillian was certainly dying of rapid consumption.

The agonised mother cast a terrible glance at the doctor, who drew her away into the next room.

The lovers were alone.

"You don't seem well, darling," said William Lennox, whose heart bled within him as much for his own conduct as her illness.

"I am very ill," replied Lillian, "very ill; and were it not for you, my own dear William, and my poor mother, I should not be sorry—for I must be a sad burthen to you."

"My angel!" cried William, mildly, "do you know why I am here?"

"No, dearest."

"Your mother has sent me to ask you to fix the day for our marriage," whispered William Lennox, kneeling at her feet, "and though I am not worthy—"

"Hush," said Lillian, with an angelic smile; "we are all sinners. But do not talk of marriage, my beloved. I shall never marry."

"Lillian—"

"William, I am very sorry for you, but it is drawing nigh, and you must hear it—I am dying. Hush, dearest, repining is as wicked as it is useless. Even since your terrible accident, I have been failing. A strange, heavy, dull pain at my heart has been keeping me down. I feel the sinking more and more every hour."

She was livid. William Lennox was on his knees, with his eyes starting from their sockets.

He tried to persuade himself he was dreaming.

"Lillian! Lillian! we will call in another doctor; we will try change. This is folly; you shall not die; you must live, live for my sake.'

"It is otherwise decreed, my love. I always thought, William, when you saved me from a life of misery and shame, that I was too happy. I was not thankful enough—not grateful enough. But heaven is very good. All I love are near me. Call mamma—"

They came, and the livid face, those awful eyes, and the white lips, on which was a trace of foam, proclaimed that a terrible crisis was at hand.

William mechanically wiped her lips with a white cambric pocket handkerchief, and put it in his pocket.

The doctor took her hand.

He said not a word.

She looked at them with a soft, placid, and gentle smile.

She could no longer speak.

Her aspect was awful, and yet heavenly. A halo of goodness seem to encircle her head, and the rays of her eyes fell like beams of light.

She made a sign.

All understood; and, as people do in a dream, moved without knowing what they were doing

William took one hand, and Mrs. Winterton the other.

Her lips moved.

William bent low, and two or three words flitted from her lips, which froze the very soul of William Lennox, with horror. They were not spoken—they were not whispered, but still he could fancy he heard them.

When he raised her head, livid, ghastly, pale as death itself, the jaw had fallen, and the doctor was closing her eyes.

Mrs. Winterton lay insensible on the floor of the room.

William Lennox gazed speechless with horror at what remained of the beloved of his heart, and then took her in his arms, and carried her to her bedroom.

He then rang the bell. The Spanish and English servants both came, and then he rushed forth. No sooner had he gained the open air, than he became calm, cool, collected.

The thoughtless boy was a man, stern, cold, implacable.

What were these words that Lillian had kept to herself until the very breath of life was exhaling?

They rang in his ears with an excess of horror such or never he had felt before.

He went to his hotel, wrote a letter to the Duchess of Castella, and then returned to the residence of Mrs. Winterton. She was dangerously ill, and perfectly unconscious of what was passing around her.

CHAPTER CI.

THE FUNERAL.

IT would be idle to attempt, as it would be painful, to record all that William Lennox suffered during that night. It was the culminating horror of his life. He never had, and he never did expect to go through again such an agglomeration of suffering.

She lay in the next room, and he wished the door of communication to be left open.

The maid servants wanted to watch too. He gave them money and sent them away.

William Lennox was alone with the dead.

There never was, during the whole of William Lennox's long existence, and there never will be, I believe, a day that he did not and does not call to recollection the ten or twelve hours that he spent beside the body of the girl—his first, his only love.

She lay on a bed, white and spotless as her own pure and undefiled soul, while, in deference to the wish of the people of the house, four large wax tapers burned beside her.

Graham had thrown a cloth over her face, but William Lennox withdrew it, that, as he walked slowly too and fro, he might now and then gaze upon that countenance, so soon to be shut out of his sight for ever.

He drew off his boots, and walked up and

down like some sentry close upon some enemy's lines—slowly, cautiously, stealthily. He trod as if he feared to wake her—her whom he would have awakened at the expense of his own life.

His face was more pallid, more livid, more fixed than that of Lillian.

His lips were compressed, his brow stern, and his whole mien terrible in the last degree.

It was a fearful sight to see this man—for now he was one—bending over the face of the dead, and gazing mournfully, wistfully, and then fiercely at that still and motionless face, as of one who slept.

There was the same angelic expression, and to his jaundiced eyes, in the flicker of the tapers, even a hectic flush upon her cheek.

Once he stooped with a daring hope.

But his lips touched, as it were, a slab of marble.

Again, with a shudder, he rose and resumed his walk.

What his thoughts were, what his self-reproaches, what his resolutions for the future, what his visions of the past, it would be idle to tell.

He wept not. Not a tear fell from his inflamed and blood-shot eyes.

Mechanically he drew his sword, and waved it in occasional circles round his head. He appeared muttering some fearful revenge against somebody.

Not a sound could be heard in that chamber of death—not even his own footsteps—and yet the time passed too quickly. She was his now—only his. He defied the world in arms to take her from him. But the morning would soon come—and then—others (how he shuddered) would claim her as their own.

Dawn came, and William Lennox saw it not. The curtains were too thickly drawn.

At eight a gentle tap came to the door. It was the English maid, with tears in her eyes.

"Please, Mr. William," said the poor girl with tears in her eyes, "there's some young girls down stairs want to see you."

"What about?" asked the young officer.

"The funeral," sobbed the other, covering her eyes with her hands.

Teresa, the Spanish attendant, looked on with a cold sneer on her countenance, which changed to one of sympathy when she caught the eye of the young Englishman.

"Tell them I will come," he said in choked accents. "You, Rose, remain here."

And he followed Teresa down stairs.

A deputation of twelve young and lovely girls stood in the hall! They came to beg that the beautiful little English lady might be buried upon an open bier, to be carried by them to the church.

It flashed at once across William's mind that Mrs. Winterton was a Roman Catholic, though not an avowed one, and not interfering with those around her—and as this would save her from being immured in a hideous coffin, William Lennox bowed acquiescence.

He could not speak.

"At what hour?" they said.

"To-day."

"It is the law," they replied.

"At two," he gasped forth.

Then he went upstairs, re-entered the room, and shut the door.

"How is Mrs. Winterton?" he said, in husky tones.

"Very bad—insensible."

"So much the better. Rose, you loved your young mistress?"

"With all my heart and soul," said Rose, sobbing ready to break her heart.

"Then you will take my hand, and swear by her who lies there in the cold embrace of death to keep my secret.

"Whatever it may I will keep it for her sake who loved you so well," replied the English girl.

"Swear after me."

William Lennox dictated a terrible oath.

"Your mistress died from poison," he hissed in her ear.

Both stood trembling and holding one another's hands for two minutes, the girl shaking as with the ague from terror, the other from passion.

"Impossible," she gasped after a time.

"She was poisoned, and the accomplice of the villains is in this house. Shriek not, move not, or we may all perish ere we find out the guilty. Who the employer was I guess, who the vile instrument was I know."

"In the name of mercy tell me," said the girl, falling on her knees.

"Teresa—"

Rose would have shrieked, but he placed his hand upon her mouth and stopped her.

"Rose, I live but for revenge. Now, if you would serve me, and punish the guilty wretches who have brought yon angel to this fate, you will dissemble, you will smile upon Teresa—but you will watch her. At the first evidence of any intention to attack any one else, have her arrested. But, Rose, I care not for her, but for the vile employers. If we are careful, we shall discover who they are; but if we allow her to suspect us, all is lost."

"I see it all now. This explains why Teresa was so attentive of a night, why she would always send me to bed, while she gave Miss Lillian a lesson in Spanish—the horrid, wicked, wretched creature."

"Leave her punishment to me—it shall be signal," said Lennox, in a husky tone.

"I will."

"Now, go prepare for the fearful scene," he continued.

And he himself moved away to the drawing-room, where the doctor and others were already collected.

An official came to have a paper filled up, but in presence of the grief of Lennox and the report of the doctor, he did not think it necessary to enter the chamber of death.

The doctor reported Mrs. Winterton in a very precarious state. It was doubtful if she would escape brain fever.

*   *   *   *   *

It was a bright sunny day, and the streets of Madrid were crowded, as the mournful procession left the hotel. In front came the priests carrying aloft the crucifix, and boys with censers, while were chaunted in a dull, monotonous tone, and a nasal squeak, which seems the necessary concomitant of the monkish Latin, the service for the dead.

Then came the open bier, borne by the six first girls, the others standing around to relieve them when weary.

William Lennox walked close beside her, his steps guided by a little child not more than ten years old, so utterly blind and helpless was he.

Then came detachments from several English regiments.

Every man, woman and child, Roman Catholic or not, stood still as the mournful procession passed—the males raising their hats.

The church was full, and when the service was over, the body was removed to a chapel, and the whole day passed in extra masses.

When night came the beautiful Lillian was lowered out of sight.

William Lennox stood still until the last moment, when he walked into the open air alone. He did not notice among the crowd the haggard and pallid countenances of Sir Edgar Blakesley and Slimy Jones, disguised both in Spanish costume.

Everbody saw that words of comfort were useless and vain.

"What are you about to do?" said the doctor, clutching his arm.

"Avenge her," replied William.

"Avenge! man, are you sane?" cried the other, holding him still more firmly.

"Doctor, I know what I am about. In a day or two you shall know more. I have my reasons for all I do."

And he walked away.

The doctor stood still, the fearful words still ringing in his ears.

"Merciful father!" he said, "I never should have fancied this; and yet—and yet, there was a vague, dreamy fear on my soul. But what enemies could poor Lillian have? To-morrow night I will examine the body. I will get permission, and if it should be so—"

The worthy man said no more, but his resolve was taken.

CHAPTER CII.

AN AWFUL DISCOVERY.

LIEUTENANT William Lennox walked to his own apartments and shut himself in. The whole of the rest of the day, and far into the night, he wrote. He wished to vindicate his own conduct in case any accident happened, and to explain whatever might appear strange and anomalous.

About eleven he dressed in uniform, with a band of crape on his left arm, and went out in the direction of the palace of the Duchess of Castella. Concealed by a large cloak, there was little fear of his being recognised.

As he went in the domestics moved on one side with an air of profound respect.

"Is the Duchess in?" he said, in a low, deep, and husky voice.

He was at once shown up to a room in which she sat that evening, not the boudoir.

She was very grave, and had evidently been weeping; a white cambric handkerchief lay on her lap.

"I come to thank you, Duchess," said William in choked accents, "for your mark of respect for the dead. I saw you in the church."

She made no reply but took his hand, and for an hour their voices united in words of sorrow, grief, and condolence.

Then William Lennox rose, bowed, and left the room.

The Duchess walked with him to the very top of the great staircase. She then returned into his room, pensive, grave, and solemn. Her face was wan with grief.

"My heavens!" she cried, "how he did love her. What would I not give to be loved thus."

And she retired to her chamber with a slow and melancholy step.

From that day no man could make William Lennox out. He walked about like a man in a dream. To the astonishment and scandal of the whole army, he made his intrigue with the Duchess of Castella public. He was seen with her everywhere. Not joyous, not merry, but grave, sedate, solemn, like a *jealous Spanish* husband.

His superiors were indignant, and Sir John Coyne publicly cut him in the street. This was about a week after the funeral.

William Lennox wrote a respectful letter to his commanding officer, who the next morning sent for him.

What took place between them was not known, but at the end of the interview they shook hands.

The doctor seemed strangely affected by the affair, for he went about with an evident weight on his brow. He appeared absent and thoughtful.

There was, however, one thing certain. The Duchess of Castella was far from happy. She was full of thought, capricious, showed every now and then a strangely quick temper, and to the nervous suspicious fancy of William Lennox, appeared to want to break with him.

But he renewed his assiduity, little suspecting that what made the Duchess unhappy was the deep and settled grief he evidently felt for the departed Lillian.

She knew that his love was buried in the grave.

And thus three weeks sped away, and brought no change.

"Please, sir," said Jack Horne, one morning when bringing in his master's clothes, after a careful brush, "there's been a Spanish chap arter you, sir, twice yesterday, and he's coming again to-day."

"What does he want?"

"Don't know, sir."

"Well, what does he say?"

"Says nothing—only Captain Lennox; and when I offer to take his message, shakes his head and goes away."

"Send him up," replied William Lennox, "if only to get rid of him."

"Well, here he comes—a ragged, peasan rascal," cried John Horne.

"Show him in."

A few minutes later a man, whom William Lennox at once recognised as a cobbler, entered the room, bowing to the ground.

"Is this the most excellent Captain Lennox?" he said.

"My name is Lennox."

"I have a very strange and important communication to make to your honour," and he glanced at Horne.

"Order breakfast," said the young officer, quietly.

"My name is Telesforo." began the other, "and I live in the street of Little Toledo. I am a cobbler by trade, and, though I say it, an honest and industrious man."

William Lennox closed his eyes.

"On my side of the street are little houses, inhabited by such poor people as myself. On the other side are the backs of palaces and old ruined houses. Well, my lord, for about ten days something very remarkable has happened. Every day, and several times a day, little bits of paper, written in pencil, in a strange language, have fallen down in my street, and every one of them is directed to Captain William Lennox."

He slowly, wildly, opened his eyes, and looked the cobbler full in the face.

What did he think?

Nothing.

But he know also that something was coming.

"Where are they?"

The man thrust forth a handful of little scraps.

William Lennox gave a wild, unearthly cry, and, leaping from the bed, rang the bell.

He was fearful to look at; the blood had rushed back from his heart, his face was livid, his teeth chattered.

The cobbler started back amazed.

"Don't be frightened, my good man," he said, in a husky voice; "sit down. God of mercy, what is the meaning of all this? What fearful drama is being enacted? Horne," to his servant who now re-entered the room, "run for Doctor Graham. Have you heard how Mrs. Winterton is this morning?"

"Very weak, sir, and scarcely sensible."

"Go fetch the doctor."

William Lennox was by this time nearly dressed.

"My man," he said, addressing the cobbler, "here is money. You have done me a service which no money can ever repay. Will you be faithful and true?"

"My lord! sir! signor! Don Lennox!" stammered the cobbler, staring at the handful of doubloons which the other had thrust into his hand; "I am your slave for life—command me."

William Lennox made no reply. He shook as with the palsy, and could scarcely dress. A new and fearful light had been thrown upon the tragedy in connection with Lillian. He felt that if somebody did not come with whom he could confer, whose advice he could ask, he should go mad.

By the time he was fully clothed and ready to go forth, the doctor came. He came panting in, considerably alarmed by Jack Horne's description of his master's state of mind.

"Well, Lennox, my boy, what is the matter?" he cried, as he rushed in.

"Leave us," said Lennox, addressing the cobbler. "Jack, give him some breakfast." Then he said in English, "take the strictest care of him."

As soon as they were alone, William Lennox handed the doctor a chair, and taking one himself, came close up to him.

"Dr. Graham," he said, laying his hand upon his arm, and speaking with a solemnity which awed his companion, "on your honour as a man, did you not think there was something very strange about poor Lillian's demise?"

"Well, I did; I couldn't understand it."

"You suspected foul play?"

"The suspicion was so vague, I dared not breathe my thoughts," continued the doctor; "but I acted."

The other fixed his eyes keenly on the doctor.

"In what way?"

"Are you calm? Can you hear a story to freeze your blood?" said the doctor.

"I can bear anything," replied William Lennox, in a husky tone; "as you shall soon see."

"I had vague but strong suspicions, and no sooner was the funeral over then I determined to satisfy myself of the truth of the affair. I knew that it would shock you too much to propose such a thing; but on my own responsibility I determined to have a *post mortem* examination of the body in the vaults of St. Ildefonso."

William Lennox bowed and groaned.

"It was with strange and almost superhuman difficulty I obtained admission for myself and a surgeon's assistant—himself an Englishman and sworn to secrecy—to the vaults. We took with us two lanterns, were well armed, and under my arm was my case of instruments."

"Well?"

"We reached the vaults, we advanced to the spot where the body of Lillian had been deposited. *The bier was empty—the body was gone!*"

"I knew it! I knew it!' shrieked William Lennox, frantically. "She lives! she lives!"

The doctor looked round for some instrument of defence, and, finding none, made preparations for a rapid retreat.

"Doctor," said William Lennox, endeavouring to speak in a calm tone of voice, "do not think my mad. Read these scraps."

And he handed the other the papers picked up by Telesforo the cobbler.

The doctor put on his spectacles and read—

"*Now, I understand it all. I was not poisoned, but drugged. I live, but dare not write the horrors of my captivity. I know not where I am ; but these scraps may fall into the hands of some kind heart, who will take them to the address written below. They will be amply rewarded.*
"LILLIAN.

' Capt. William Lennox,
"—— Dragoons English Hotel, Madrid."

"May heaven in its infinite mercy be thanked," said the doctor. "When I made the awful discovery of the disappearance of the body, I could not but believe that some of our young doctors had taken a freak in their heads to discover the cause of death. My own opinion was that she was consumed by consumption, and that disease of the heart was the immediate cause of death."

"Graham, the poor girl whispered to me—at least her lips made a faint attempt to whisper which none but a lover could have heard—*poison!* at her last gasp."

"But who administered the drug?"

"Teresa—"

"The wretched traitress," cried the doctor.

"Hush! not a word. She has all the fearful cunning of her race. We must use extreme caution. Above all does my vengeance aim at the punishment of the guilty. Teresa shall not escape—still she is but a tool."

"Whom do you suspect?" said the doctor in a low hushed tone.

"My brain seems on fire when I think of it. The officer still believes that Sir Edgar Blakesley and Slimy Jones are in Madrid. If so, it might be them. But why—"

"May not this Sir Edgar Blakesley have fallen in love with her?" asked Dr. Graham, timidly.

"It is possible," said Lieutenant Lennox, with a shudder.

"He is your enemy and may wish to torture you."

"Again I say, it is possible; but," he added in a low hushed whisper, "I suspect another."

"Who, in heaven's name?"

"One I have had my eyes on all along," hissed Lennox in his ear; "the Duchess of Castella."

The doctor remained silent a moment from awe and astonishment.

"Can a woman be so cruel?" said the honest man."

"I suppose I need make no secret of my temporary infatuation," continued William Lennox, bitterly.

"Temporary!" cried Dr. Graham; "why, it is the talk of the whole army."

"Is it?" said William Lennox with a sardonic grin, "it shall be more."

CHAPTER CIII.

THE INTERVIEW WITH THE DUCHESS.

IT was a dark and gloomy street where the cobbler Telesfero lived. As he said, it was formed on one side of lowly houses, on the other of ruined walks and the backs of several vast and gloomy mansions, some untenanted, others the abode of some of these mighty Spanish hedalgo who lived in almost as great seclusion as the inmates of a Turkish harem.

In modern times Spanish chivalry has not fallen so low as the wretched, vile, and hideous leprosy of Islamism among the degraded and vicious Turks, but still it is no more what it was.

These men kept up a relic of their old grandeur, and that is all.

A small, black, and dismal little shop was that from which Telesfero the cobbler had issued to gladden the heart of William Lennox, and to excite hope which he scarcely yet ventured to believe in.

It was low and gloomy, but to William Lennox it seemed a little instalment of paradise.

He took up his position on the board of the shop, and he looked out into the street. Telesfero could give him no idea of the direction in which the scraps of paper came. They had been found in several parts of the street.

The wind was unfortunately high, and on that day no paper fell in the street.

William Lennox strained his eyes to discover any window likely to be that through which the hand of Lillian might expect to be seen.

But in vain.

When evening came he went away, leaving Telesfero, however, on the watch.

He returned to his hotel, dressed himself with more than usual care, and took his way to the residence of the duchess.

She received him even more tenderly than usual. There could be no doubt about her intense and absorbing passion.

"How wild and pale you look," she said, with an inquiring glance.

"I am not well."

"This grief is unmanly. It is right that you should regret her whom you loved even better than you do me; but there is a limit to the sorrow of a man. Women have nothing else to do."

"I do not mourn the death of Lillian," said William Lennox, quietly.

"What, then?"

"Because she is not dead," continued the young man.

"Not dead!" half shrieked the duchess; "surely this is insanity."

"She is not dead!"

"Will you explain yourself?"

"I say that Lillian is not dead!" solemnly replied the young officer.

"William, I beg you will not be so mysterious, but explain," said the duchess, huskily.

"Read," replied Lennox, as he laid the letter before her.

The duchess had been in England, and knew enough of the language to be able both to speak and read it. She took the letter and read it intently.

"Heavens!" she cried, "can this be within the range of possibility? Is this true? Are you sure it is in her handwriting?"

"Yes."

"But how came it to you? I cannot believe it," cried the duchess,

"It is true," said William Lennox, gravely; "and I came here to ask you to assist me in my researches."

"How?"

"You are intimate with the son of the corregidor," continued the young officer.

The bloom on the cheek of the duchess heightened.

"And he has but to set his agents to work for her to be discovered. I want no public scene—let Lillian be restored to me, and I will leave Spain at once. I have leave of absence."

The duchess turned very pale. There was a wicked glare in her eyes.

"You are weary of me, then?" she said.

"No, duchess; but I have duties to perform. Lillian has been affianced to me from childhood."

"And your love for me?"

"Madam, you will forget me. You have already done me too much honour."

"Enough !" said the duchess, coldly; "this night our intimacy ceases. Go to your icy English bride, who, even if not dead, is as cold as a corpse. William, I had loved you as I never loved before. There was something in your young and fresh heart that charmed me beyond measure. I had hoped—but never mind."

"What, madam ?"

"That you would have resigned all for me—have remained in Spain. I have power, I have influence—our government freely rewards those who serve her."

"I am an Englishman, and as soon as I am of age shall have a patrimony greater than that of any Spanish noble," said William Lennox.

The duchess smiled.

"We part friends," observed William Lennox, who was beginning to be a little alarmed.

"Friends, and that is all," said the duchess.

They shook hands, and the Duchess of Castella saw something in William Lennox's eye which made her start.

They parted, however, without another word.

The moment his back was turned the duchess clasped her hands.

"He loves me still, and was becoming accustomed to the idea of her death. But now this discovery has roused up the old feeling. I have played my cards badly, but I have not lost. A youth of his age does not easily give up a woman like me. But how can this discovery have been made ?"

The duchess rang a bell, and a servant appeared.

"Go, send the Englishman to me," said she.

CHAPTER CIV.

A STRANGE ADVENTURE.

WILLIAM LENNOX, though in the deep recesses of his heart he could not but feel some faint glimmer of regret at the prospect of being entirely deprived of the duchess's company, had such strong suspicions in relation to her being the guilty author of Lillian's abduction, that he went away with but an earnest desire of vengeance uppermost.

He could find excuses, it is true, for the duchess in the extreme violence of her passion. But what had she not made him suffer in the meantime ?

It is true that at first he had believed the beloved of his heart to have been poisoned. Now he had every reason to fancy that she was alive, though, if she were in the hands of a remorseless rival, how long would she be safe ?

This was a terrible and fearful consideration.

After a long and painful reverie he hurried to the quarters of the doctor, and they had a long conference, after which William Lennox went to lay down. He was up again by daybreak and going towards the post of observation.

It was a dark and gloomy morning, and there was a head of fog, which, however, would soon be dispersed by the rising sun.

Through this fog William Lennox was hurrying, when he suddenly saw another cloaked figure crossing the road, a figure too that made him raise his outer garment higher and glide up against the shadow of the wall.

The man, whoever he might be, entered a narrow passage, and disappeared; followed, however, by a second party.

William Lennox's heart beat with mingled hope and dread.

He rushed up the passage after them just in time to hear the click of a lock, and to be aware that a heavy door had been shut in his face.

He tried it with his hands. It was by far too much for his strength.

Without losing an instant of time, William Lennox rushed out, and, calling loudly for Telesfero, told him to fetch Dr. Graham and a corporal's guard.

The cobbler, who worshipped his munificent employer, hurried away as fast as his legs could carry him.

William Lennox returned to his post as a sentry.

In a quarter of an hour the doctor came hurrying to join his friend, accompanied by four troopers.

A light was procured, and the door at the end of the dark passage examined.

It was old and rotten.

It yielded to a rush of two powerful men, one of whom was Jack Horne.

"Let one stay as sentry," said William, drawing his sword.

A faint stifled cry from the summit of the house aroused him to a phrenzied state, and away he darted up-stairs, without even the precaution of deadening the sound of his footsteps.

The others followed, but with more leisurely strides.

In a few minutes William Lennox was on the top-landing of the house. An open door was before him. Entering hastily he found himself in an apartment of large dimensions, furnished with much care, but the windows of which were barred.

An old woman was its sole tenant.

At the sight of the young officer, with his drawn sword and haggard face, she fell upon her knees.

"Where is the lady ?" cried the infuriated youth.

"Eh ?"

"I ask you, woman, where is the lady ?"

The aged person looked at him with awe-stricken wonder.

"Speak, or by the heaven above—"

"Don't hurt me, and I will tell all I know," she began.

"Where is the lady ?"

"But, signor, did she not leave the room with you ten minutes since ?"

William Lennox stepped back as if struck to stone.

The others now entered the room.

"Was she taken away by some one resembling me ?" said the young man, in tones of wild and terrible anguish.

"As like you as two peas are like one another," cried the woman; "but now I see he was differently dressed."

"This is too horrible!" cried the other wild. "Oh, my God! what is to be done? Which way did they take her?"

"Down the back stairs; but they had a coach. I heard it rattle away as you came up."

"But who placed the young lady here?" asked Dr. Graham.

"The two gentlemen who were here just now. They told me she was just recovering from madness, and fancied she had been dead. She had very strange notions."

William Lennox stopped to hear no more, but rushed down by the back stairs of the old house, and in this way found himself in another street altogether.

At the very corner, at a considerable distance, a vehicle was turning the corner.

Mad, wild, frantic, but with superhuman strength, William Lennox followed. When he reached the distant corner of the street, no vehicle of any kind was in sight.

At that hour of the morning no one was about, and William Lennox knew not what to do.

Being soon joined by faithful Jack Horne, he hurried on, and finding a guard house at no great distance, asked if a carriage had passed. Yes; a carriage had passed at a great rate, driven by a Spaniard, but with two men inside who were certainly Englishmen.

Without horses it was useless to pursue, and, under the circumstances of the case, William Lennox turned to the quarters of Sir John Coyne, and though they had to raise him from a sound slumber, were very cordially received.

They told their story, while the testy colonel dressed, and then all took their way to the Duke of Wellington.

After a short interview Sir John Coyne came out with a letter in the great soldier's handwriting.

With this they hurried to the head magistrate of the city, who at once gave them a warrant and two alquazils to back it.

With these they hurried to the residence of poor Mrs. Winterton.

The door was opened by the English servant.

"Where is Teresa?" said William Lennox in a low tone.

The girl pointed to the breakfast room.

William Lennox entered quickly, followed by the alquazils.

"Teresa," he said very sternly, "you are a prisoner."

"What for?" replied the girl, with a start and a blush.

"The murder of Lillian Winterton," said the officer, exhibiting his warrant.

A cold smile passed over the girl's face.

"You are mad, drunk, or foolish," she said. "Poor Miss Winterton died a natural death."

"She was poisoned!" cried William.

"Nonsense. Surely, Mr. William, you are only joking."

"You will find it no joke, I can tell you. Give up the name of your wretched employers, and you may yet find forgiveness."

"I know not what you mean—you are talking nonsense, Mr. William," continued Teresa.

The unhappy young man turned away, and the officers took possession of the girl. She went freely enough, and did not appear to be at all concerned.

All saw at once that she was either innocent, or very certain of the weakness of their case.

CHAPTER CV.

THE DISCOVERY OF LILLIAN.

WHAT to do now William Lennox knew not. He knew very well that in the present disturbed state of the country it would be no very easy task to conceal Lillian, so that he might never find her. But he would not for one moment give way to despair.

Dire as had been the difficulties he had had to encounter, he had somehow mastered the worst of them.

He had wept Lillian as dead, and now she lived.

It was not to be supposed that this one ray of sunshine had come from the heavens only to turn more black and threatening.

He took council with Jack Horne, and afterwards with Dr. Graham. Both thought proper to accede to his proposals, and next morning two men, well mounted and well armed, left the town for the country.

They went by the same road the carriage of the ravishers had taken.

All the previous day and up to a late hour at night experienced officers had made inquiries, and had traced the vehicle to a certain village twelve miles from Madrid.

Then all sign of it ceased. It had left a certain inn about mid-day, but had not been noticed at the next.

It must clearly have followed some of the many cross roads with which the country abounded.

The master and servant, who had both divested themselves of military trappings to assume those of a private English gentleman and his servant, were further disguised, the former by bushy whiskers and spectacles, the latter by a very fanciful cut of clothes.

They both wore arms of course; none ever going about in these days without.

William Lennox was cold, stern, and resolved. With him the recovery of Lillian was paramount to everything—even to his revelation to his true position in the social scale.

It was the one idea of his life, the one wish of his soul.

William Lennox loved Lillian with a passionate love, which made her appear the only woman in existence. He cursed his folly at the thought of the duchess, and yet he began to feel a kind of satisfaction in the idea that she was not the author of his misfortune.

The moment he saw Slimy Jones and Blakesley in conjunction, he understood it all. The latter had seen and dared to covet his bride. Disappointed in taking his life—thanks to such happy and providential escapes—he aimed at what was dearer than life.

Could he but find Lillian once more, how he would treasure her, and how he felt that all he suffered was but a fit punishment for his infidelity.

But surely heaven would be good and declare to him his Lillian—to her for ever and ever he would be faithful and true.

The master and the man rode on without halting until they reached the inn to which the carriage had been traced, and as their plan was to make inquiries without exciting suspicion, they dismounted and called for wine; the master in the best room, the man in the kitchen.

"Bad time for business," said William to the little, short, fat, and obsequious individual who waited on him.

"Bad!" replied the innkeeper, with a low bow.

"Don't get a carriage beyond a muleteer once a week, I dare say?"

"Very rare. A carriage was here yesterday, but the gentleman only drank standing and went away."

William Lennox made no further remark, but as soon as he and his servant had taken proper refreshment, left their horses and walked out upon the road.

It was for Spain a tolerable highway, having been repaired by the English sappers and miners.

They had not proceeded very far when they came to a wall. It was a long, low wall, of some antiquity, and seemed to skirt some park-like grounds of considerable extent.

William Lennox walked over to the other side of the road, and looked over the wall.

The roof of a mansion of considerable extent could be seen in the distance.

They walked on, for just at that moment they could hear in the distance the tinkling of bells announcing the advance of mules.

William lit a cigarette and sauntered on, as if he were merely walking about for pleasure.

In a few moments they came in sight of a string of mules, and several muleteers walking beside them.

William Lennox sauntered slowly up to them, and, pointing to the mansion, inquired its name.

"It belongs to the Duke of Castella," said the muleteer.

William Lennox bowed his thanks and continued on his way, still puffing at his cigarette.

"I thought so," said the young officer, gravely.

"What is to be done?" inquired Jack Horne, sadly.

"I don't know," continued William Lennox, nervously; "my mind is in a whirl. This conglomeration of doubts and fears nearly drives me mad. Let us enter the grounds."

They walked to the very end of the wall and turned down a narrow road, until they came to a kind of fence, which was easily forced through. They then found themselves in a thicket, and beyond this was an open glade, and then the walls of a splendid palace built in a Moorish style of architecture.

It seemed wholly silent and abandoned; but William Lennox had no doubt that inside there were eyes it would be dangerous to affront.

He resolved to await the coming of night.

Still he would not leave the park, but kept his eyes fixed on the grand palatial residence, which he doubted not was the prison of his beloved.

Jack Horne was too old a soldier to be caught campaigning without provender.

Towards dark he produced wine and bread.

William Lennox eat mechanically to pass the time. His face was pale, though every now and then a nervous flush overspread his features.

As soon as it was quite dark, they issued from their cover, and began making the circuit of the palace.

Not a light was visible, not a sound could be heard.

"There is some jugglery in this," cried William Lennox, impatiently.

"It's powerful still," said Horne.

The young officer made no reply. He was overwhelmed with impatience and disappointment.

What was to be done?

That Lillian was concealed in this building he had no moral doubt any more than that the duchess was the author of the original crime. That she had found ready instruments in Sir Edward Blakesley and Slimy Jones, he wondered not, though after all her promises to apprehend his attempted assassins it was indeed rather strange.

Suddenly William Lennox started.

A faint ray of light came through a barred window near the ground.

He approached it with extreme caution, and peered through the chinks. He could see nothing, but he could hear voices.

This was indeed horrible torture.

Once more he hurried round to the front door, and tried it.

It was ajar, and yielded to his hand.

All beyond was dark. The hall exhibited not the slightest glimmer.

William Lennox drew his sword and entered boldly, Jack Horne following close behind.

The young officer felt along the wall with his hand, holding his sword right before him.

He soon found a corridor to his left, at the extreme end of which was a very faint glimmer of light.

Trembling with hope, anxiety, and not exempt from fear, William Lennox groped his way onwards.

Suddenly the light faded away, and then reappeared at the end of a long and narrow passage.

It was evidently a lamp carried by a female figure with a large and heavy veil over her head.

If it were Lillian attempting to escape from her horrid captivity?

His heart beat high indeed now as he hurried forward.

Again the light was temporarily obscured; but still William Lennox sped on his way. The lamp became almost instantly visible again, and this time in what appeared to be a lofty hall.

William Lennox rushed forward, and as he did so a door was closed behind him.

He was in utter darkness and alone.

DUCHESS OF CASTELLA.

"Jack Horne, where are you?" he cried in a husky voice.

And echo answered where.

He was alone in some large dark hall, which, however, on feeling cautiously about, he speedily found to be a chapel.

His feelings may be divined. The whole affair was evidently a trap, and he was in the power of his most bitter enemies.

Suddenly a wild strain of music fell upon his ear, and he started with amazement as a bright light fell along another corridor at the extreme end of the chapel.

He rushed forward and saw that this light emanated from an inner room.

It was an antique apartment hung with tapestry, and in one of those huge fireplaces which belong to a past age, when everything was on a large and massive scale, was a fire, which the abandoned character of the place rendered necessary.

By this fire, with her back turned to it, sat a woman in rich black clothes, with a veil over her head.

A deep sigh escaped her as she raised her hands to warm them.

William Lennox dashed hurriedly forward; the woman turned slowly round, the young officer started back, and, overcome by his emotions, fainted.

CHAPTER CVI.

JOHN HIGGINS AT HOME.

A WORTHY old soul was John Higgins, a merry, light-hearted, and jolly fellow too, fond of his pipe and his glass, and a rare judge of good ale.

And who was John Higgins?

Not to know him within the circumference of ten miles, to say no more, was to argue yourself unknown, unthinking, and a nobody.

John Higgins was the locksmith, whitesmith, blacksmith, and gossip of Brighton.

He had done much in his time, and, among other things, he had worked at the pavilion under the personal direction of its inventor.

A loyal man was John Higgins, one of those who never asked whether or not a royal prince was a fool or rogue, but who was satisfied that because he wore a star and garter therefore he was worthy of being worshipped, and bent the knee to. And a very common loyalty is this in old England, as well as other places.

The Americans went mad about the son of a good queen, but would they not have gone twice as far had they received a visit from the emperor of a neighbouring state, who, say what you will, reached his throne knee-deep in the blood of his subjects, slaughtered because they considered an oath should be kept, and that a constitution voted by a free people should have been respected.

Loyalty is a most unreasoning thing.

On this point rarely one man in a thousand can give a reason for the faith that is in him.

John Higgins was a happy man. He had once been plagued with a shrew of a wife—and all the shrews have not been tamed yet—but she had left him for another and a better world.

It is true she had left a representative in the shape of a very sprightly girl of seventeen, who pulled his beard, and led him by the nose as completely as ever Mother Higgins had done herself; but then middle aged widowers rather like the rule of a daughter, however tyrannical she may be.

And Polly Higgins was a tyrant, and no mistake whatever about the matter.

Now let us introduce our readers to the sanctum of the said John.

It was about seven o'clock, and the blacksmith had discharged his assistants, as was usually his practice, at six. John Higgins prided himself on certain little inventions, which he always kept secret, and accordingly only worked at from six until eight.

There he was in his shop, with a blazing fire, his anvil and bellows, and other tools, and looking in his stout apron, and by the ruddy glow of the fire, a very jolly specimen of an Englishman.

Polly was away in the kitchen making ready for supper, which was always on the table at five minutes past eight; the said five minutes being allowed for the blacksmith to wash and otherwise prepare himself for the table.

It was, we have said, seven o'clock, when a knock very sharp and imperious came to the door.

The blacksmith made no reply. It was after business hours, and he was not in the habit of putting himself at all out of the way for anybody.

Rat, tat, tat!

"Go away, good people; it's past business hours—go away."

Bang—bang—bang on the anvil!

Rat, tat, tat! at the door.

"It tell you what it is," said John Higgins, clubbing his long hammer and advancing towards the door. "If I don't stop your knocking, I'm a Dutchman."

And he opened the door quickly, and peered out into the darkness of night.

As he did so a slight elegant figure, that of a woman in a mask and hat and cloak, glided in and stood before the astonished blacksmith.

"Madam," he said.

"Sir," said she.

At the same moment the door was pushed too, bolted, and barred by a very short gentleman, in a cloak and hat also, but not masked, but with a face which the blacksmith in his heart thought would have been considerably improved by concealment.

"Sir," cried John.

"Your humble and obedient servant," said the other.

"What is the meaning of this?"

"Business!"

"Too late."

"Never too late."

"I know best."

"No, you don't," said the girl; "our business is very pressing."

"After hours," said John, more mildly.

He had a great respect and regard for beauty.

"Pay you well—handsomely!" said the Blue Dwarf.

"What is it?" cried John.

The Blue Dwarf looked at the blacksmith, and handed him a key with his left hand, while with his right he presented a pistol.

The blacksmith examined the key with a cool and collected glance, without taking any notice of the cocked pistol.

"This belongs to his Royal Highness the Prince Regent," said John Higgins, quietly.

"How know you?"

"I made it."

"Then you can make another?"

"I, sir."

"Yes."

"But it's treason."

"Hark ye, friend," said the Blue Dwarf, gravely, "it must be done. I have a reason for it, which I cannot explain. Make it and a hundred guineas shall be your reward. Betray me, or even threaten to do so, and I blow your brains out."

"My worthy sir," said John Higgins, coolly, "I won't make the key, and you won't blow my brains out"

"You are a brave fellow," replied Sapathwa, thoughtfully, "I wish I could trust you."

"In what way."

"With my secret."

" Does it relate to this key."

" It does."

" It is the only way then to get me to make it," replied John.

" You will not betray me ?"

" Certainly not."

" Then I will trust you," and seating himself on a stool, Sapathwa put John in possession of sufficient facts in relation to his plans, to convince him of the honourable nature of the task.

" I will make the key," said John Higgins.

CHAPTER CVII.

THE THENDEZ VOUS.

IT was midnight, and the Prince, after supping copiously and taking a great deal more wine than was good for him, a practice which was universal in those days, awaited the arrival of Pauline with some anxiety.

Though utterly incapable of a real honest passion, George Prince of Wales was as impatient for the visit of a new mistress as any school-boy for a holiday.

He had sent his companions away in reality, not sorry to exchange his society for cards, for though his satellites liked to run themselves in his presence at times, his society was not amusing.

When the wine was in him he was not even ordinarily courteous.

He was remorseless in his jokes, especially relative to personal appearance, which scarcely the best natured man in the world can stand.

It was midnight, or a little past, when a lady wrapped in a black cloak, and with a hat and veil, came up towards the southern end of the pavilion. Her step was light and cautious.

At the end of the space in front of the gates was an oil lamp.

Beneath this stood a sentry.

He advanced and bowed low.

The woman held up a ring.

The men made no reply but stood on one-side.

The gate rolled on its hinges.

A second personage advanced towards the lady.

" Spain," he said.

" Victory," replied the lady.

Not another word was spoken.

The lady followed her guide, who entered the palace and led the way until a brilliantly lighted corridor was reached.

The men pointed to a door and turned away.

Pauline, for it was the Frenchwoman, placed her hand upon the door and pushed it open.

She was in a superb room, with a splendid supper laid out.

On a couch lay the Regent fast asleep.

Pauline turned pale even beneath her rouge. However much a woman may despise a man, she does not like to be received at a rendezvous in this way. But, recovering herself at once, she advanced to the table and began with the most consummate coolness to help herself.

She even opened a bottle of champagne, and drank this seductive beverage until her eyes sparkled with redoubled brightness.

And still the Regent slept.

Pauline looked at him, and played with a dessert knife.

" How easy," she muttered, " it would be to rid the English people of *ce monstre, ce cupidon, ce lossale,* who dares to invite a woman to sup with him, and goes to sleep."

Then she laid down the knife and filled her glass again, after draining which she felt still more impatient and vexed.

She took up a cork and mechanically burnt it in one of the wax tapers.

The Regent heaved a deep sigh, and opened his eyes.

Pauline threw the cork in the fireplace, and without pretending to be aware of the other's presence, went on sipping her champagne, only pausing to pick at a bunch of delicious grapes.

" My dear madam," said the Prince rising, " how long have you been here ?"

" Ever so long."

" And why did you not rouse me ?"

" You appeared so comfortable. Besides I was both hungry and thirsty. Subjects may be fond of wine as well as a royal highness."

The Prince laughed and seated himself beside his charmer.

*　　*　　*　　*　　*

It was nearly daybreak when Pauline stepped into a small close carriage, which she had ordered to await her outside, and which admitting her to sleep comfortably, drove away to Lewes, in order to draw off any attempt at following her.

The next night Pauline returned at an earlier hour.

She had received at dinner the Marquis of A——, and Lord Charles Lutterell.

The Prince had momentarily forgotten his engagement with the Princess of Borneo, or perhaps thought that a bird in the hand was worth two in the bush—the pretty Leila having only given a conditional promise.

Not that all was gold that glittered in the case of Pauline.

She loved him excessively with regard to her husband, without whom, she said, her position in society would be nothing.

The Prince promised everything she liked, and then changed the subject.

Pauline was perfectly satisfied. With all her experience of the world there was one item of wisdom had escaped her.

" Put not your faith in princes."

It is seldom that any one has and not been deceived.

It is a way they have got.

As well might a poor mouse believe in the promise of grimalkin with a fierce eye.

And then Pauline had such faith in her beauty, and in the power of her charms.

CHAPTER CVIII.

THE ABDUCTION.

WE have said that Pauline came earlier on this occasion than the previous evening. She also went away sooner. The Prince did not press her to stay late, and the Frenchwoman herself was in a hurry.

As she left the south entrance and leaped into her carriage, the Blue Dwarf glided from, it appeared, the wall of the pavilion, and went home.

He had only a few steps to walk, and in two minutes he was at the door of his own residence.

A sound of mirth and jollity was to be heard in the next house, but to this he paid no attention.

His thoughts were far away.

Never was he thinking for himself; his heart knew no selfishness.

He rang at his door, and was admitted with that rapidity which was characteristic of his household.

He went straight up stairs to the apartments inhabited by Leila, whom he always saw safe ere he retired to rest.

She had promised to wait up for him.

He entered the rooms.

A lamp or two burnt low, which, believing her to have fallen asleep, he himself trimmed.

"Well, Leila, lazy one, where are you?" he said playfully.

No answer

"No nonsense, child. I have much to say," he continued.

At the same moment a slight confusion in the apartment made him bound with horror.

The guitar, usually the solace of Leila's lonely hours, lay broken on the ground.

He rushed from room to room, and in the bedchamber found her servant gagged and bound.

Releasing her, the terrible story was soon told.

They were alone in the front room conversing when two men, masked and cloaked, appeared before them, how or by what means she could not say.

They at once gagged and bound her, and then ere Leila recovered her astonishment, bore her away.

The girl thought by means of the balcony.

The Blue Dwarf examined the window and found that several panes were broken.

A low wail, rather than anything else, burst from his lips.

"Accursed Prince. Will nothing serve thy infamous soul but this poor child. But this is no time for talk. Revenge is all I have to think of."

He struck the gong.

The secretary appeared.

"Arm yourself and two slaves," said the Blue Dwarf, speaking by means of the finger alphabet.

The man bowed and retired.

Sapathwa then summoned his coachman, and in ten minutes a large and capacious carriage was at the door. All entered this and drove across to the pavilion.

The night was dark and gloomy, and not a soul was to be seen in the streets.

CHAPTER CIX.

THE DUNGEON.

BLACK as pitch.

Silence all around.

A thick oppression in the air.

Such were the sensations experienced by the Regent when he awoke to consciousness.

He rubbed his eyes and endeavoured to collect his scattered senses.

Not the faintest glimmering of where he could be, or what could be the matter, crossed his mind.

He was not accustomed to be in the dark.

"Gervaise—Harper—Jones—what the devil is the meaning of all this," he shouted.

No answer.

And his voice sounded hollow and unnatural.

"D——n," shrieked the regent.

Then he threw himself back, and asked if this were death. Pshaw; it was some outrageous trick being played upon him

He sat up, and, as he did so, stretched out his hands.

He felt a cold sweat burst over his whole body as he touched the polished sides of what appeared a large oaken box.

Whatever might be the truth, he was a prisoner under most fearful circumstance.

He was encased in a long, dark box, certainly with a tolerable supply of air, but otherwise a fearful coffin.

The prisoner shook with terror.

He began to scream and bellow like a madman.

Many men would have done far less. His position was ghastly and fearful in the extreme.

And his lips were parched with thirst—his throat was husky and sore.

Again he called, threatened, imprecated, and prayed. In vain. Either he was were none could hear, or they were inexorable.

It was, doubtless, some awful conspiracy of his enemies.

The fearful audacity of the crime alarmed him. They must have, indeed, taken their precautions well, to have dared to venture on this unexampled act of violence.

But who could have devised and executed this plan?

Ah! were they going to let him die of hunger and of thirst? It appeared probable enough.

For once in his life, the prince utterly prostrated with dread, hopeless yet not resigned, endeavoured to shape his mouth into a prayer.

The words expired on his lips.

"Help—murder—d——n—help," he yelled; "who has done this shall die the death of a traitor, be it joke or earnest. And yet, if there be accomplices, I will pardon one, if he will rescue me. Cowards, villains, monsters, will you let me see you—"

But not a whisper, not a sound responded to his words.

A faintness came over him body and soul.

Then suddenly the creak of a door was heard, and a light appeared through numerous small holes in every part of the box—holes bored for air.

"In the name of heaven, whoever you may be, set me at liberty," he said rising.

"Where is Leila, Princess of Borneo?" replied a harsh and hollow voice.

The prince reflected a moment. He did not know those harsh and hollow tones.

"I know nothing of her," he said.

"You do."

"I do not."

The light moved away.

"In the name of mercy," he said in desparing tones, "whoever you may be hearken. I know nothing of Leila, on my honour as a man, on my faith as a gentleman, on the word of a prince. I would give up fifty Leilas to be out of this horrid den. Who are you? what are you? and what is the meaning of this outrage?"

"Leila has disappeared; Leila had the gold key of your private apartments; I am one who love and adore her. Where is she?"

"What can I say? What can I do? I swear that I know nothing," said the unhappy prince.

"Your word is not sufficient, we must have proofs," said the voice.

Prince George groaned in anguish.

"Further research shall be made; and if what you say be true, you shall be released and safely returned to your palace."

"Where am I?"

"That we cannot explain."

"Beware. The arm of a prince is long."

Ha! ha! ha!

"Laugh, wretches."

"Do not threaten, then. Before we leave, have you anything more to say?"

"I'm perishing with thirst."

A sharp click was heard at the end of the box, and then a silver pitcher of wine, and a small white loaf appeared on a platter.

The prince took up the pitcher of wine, the smell of which he knew well, closed his eyes, and drained the contents,

When he laid it down, all was still and darkness.

It appeared certain now that his life was not aimed at. Some misapprehension existed with regard to Leila, which he had no doubt would be cleared up; and though his quarters were fearful, horrible, detestable, yet still if nothing more than a temporary incarceration was to be his fate, why—

And he yawned and fell sound asleep.

Decidedly the Hungarian wine had put him in good humour.

And, despite all that solemn teetotalers may say, wine does gladden the heart of men, and women, too, for that matter, whose eyes are never so bright and sparkling, whose cheeks never burn with so rich a glow, as when in the delightful ball room she sips her champagne.

A good thing is wine, and though excess be wrong, how foolish and even wicked is the outcry against its use.

That it may be, and is abused, is no argument. So is laudanum, so is arsenic, so is water, so is gold, so is talent—everything, and yet all have their use.

Yield not, then, to the silly clamour of men who get up cheap popularity on the strength of crying out against that which is general, useful, and good. Leave such counter blasts to a King James.

As well abolish wit; for have not the wittiest things in the world been said over our wine?

And there we leave the unfortunate Regent at the mercy of an enemy, who was, however, as just as he was implacable.

CHAPTER CX.

THE LOVER.

THE Blue Dwarf was like a madman.

His daring capture of the Regent's person, which in a few hours more would distract the whole empire, was still unknown—thanks to a suspicion which existed that the Prince of Wales had started on some secret expedition, which he wished unknown even to his usual confidants and associates.

That Leila had been abducted there could be no doubt; but by whom was now the terrible question.

The Blue Dwarf began to suspect that he had made a mistake.

What was to be done?

To set the authorities at work would be to set them on the track of his own deed.

It was just about the time that the fashionable promenade began to fill, when Sapathwa, scarcely knowing what he was doing, wrapt his cloak around him and went forth.

He had scarcely touched the pavement, when a young gentleman came bowing up to him.

Sapathwa looked keenly at him.

He was young, handsome, and evidently of some distinction.

"Your business, sir?"

"Private and important," replied the other, quickly.

"Of what nature? I am very busy just now."

"Leila!"

Sapathwa bounded up the stairs, followed by the youth, and in another moment was in the library.

"Well, sir, speak;" said the Blue Dwarf.

"Has not Miss Leila, or whatever her name may be, been abducted from your house?"

"Yes."

"I knew it. Listen, for we have no time to lose. This morning about three, I was coming home from my club, where I go to pass the time and drown reflection, I had to pass this way. There were several persons on the balcony of the next house, and one on yours."

"Ah!" cried Sapathwa, rising.

"Wait, sir; there is much to tell. It struck me as strange, and I resolved to watch. First, though, I walked lower down, rang at my lodgings, and bade my man saddle a horse. Just as I was coming back, a coach with two armed servants moved off from your door at a gallop. I was alone, unarmed, and without a steed. In a short time, however, my horse came, and away I dashed after the carriage, which took an unfrequented road towards the sea. I soon came within sight of it and followed on. The coach never stopped until nearly half-way to London, where it halted at a little village alehouse. Then I recognised a man who descended from the carriage."

"Who was it?"

"Lord Charles Lutterell."

"Damnation!" shrieked the Dwarf, "let us away at once. But stay, young man, I have no right to command your services."

"My name is Wyndham. Earnest Lord Wyndham," said the youth ingeniously.

"I have heard the name; what then?"

"I am a gentleman and a man of honour. I love your ward, command my services."

"I accept them. Young man, I trust everything in your hands. Go to my stable with this order, take a post chaise and four, follow him up, never leave him, and in a few hours I will be with you."

"I go."

"Stay; in London you must meet me at the —— Hotel. I shall be there almost as soon as you."

They rung hands and separated.

*　　*　　*　　*　　*

When George, Prince Regent awoke, it was in his own bed. By his side was a letter.

"*Your Highness will forgive the act of a desperate man. Leila has been abducted by one of your associates for his own purposes. I had made a sad mistake. The accompanying key was found in Leila's room. I return it to your Royal Highness. Never shall a word transpire of this matter if your Royal Highness will drop all allusion to it.*"　　　　　B. D.

The Prince growled to himself, and then thinking better of it, thought he would drop the subject.

It would be a dangerous thing to make public, very derogatory to the dignity of majesty.

When, therefore, his friends rallied him on his absence, he winked his eye and looked mysterious.

————

CHAPTER CXI.

THE ESCAPE.

WE must, however, leave the Blue Dwarf to pursue his search for Leila, now in the hands of a licentious profligate, and once more return to William Lennox, who, on his recovery from his momentary dizziness, found himself on a couch, with the deep eyes of the duchess fixed upon him with indescribable tenderness, mingled with anxiety.

"Where am I? What is the meaning of all this? Where is Lillian?" he said, in tones of reproach and bitterness.

"Poor boy," replied the duchess, "will you still persevere in suspecting me?"

"Madam, forgive me! but appearances are against you. Lillian has been traced here. How could she enter this house without your connivance?"

"Much grief has made you mad, my dear William. I came here in a carriage, but no one else has been here; of that I can assure you."

"But why did you come here, duchess?"

"Can you ask?"

"I do not understand."

"I followed you. I heard of you at the inn, and knowing your wicked suspicions, came here. William, it is true that loving you as I do, considering you the cue of life, I am jealous of this English girl; but I know that you must marry her, and, as the novelist says, I would say to her—'I will tell you where he will be at home, my dear, and in his place; in the quiet circle of domestic happiness, lettered indolence, and elegant enjoyments, of Waverly—Honour. And he will refit the old library in the most exquisite gothic taste, and garnish its shelves with the rarest and most valuable volumes; and he will draw plans and landscapes, and write verses, and rear temples, and dig grottoes. He will stand, in a clear summer night, in the colonnade before the hall, and gaze on the deer as they stray in the moonlight, or lie shadowed by the boughs of the huge old fantastic oaks; and he will repeat verses to his beautiful wife, who will hang upon his arm; and he will be a happy man."

William Lennox sighed.

"And she will be a happy woman," repeated the duchess in a low tone.

"She is not found yet."

"She shall be."

"Ah! duchess, if I could believe—"

"You may."

"My eternal gratitude shall be yours."

"But in the meantime you are mine. Return with me to Madrid—we will search for her together."

"We cannot return to-night."

The duchess looked at him with her great voluptuous eyes, and smiled.

William Lennox held down his eyes.

He knew that Slimy Jones and Sir Edgar had been active agents in the abduction of Lillian, but was it on their own account or that of the duchess? this it was he wanted to discover. He resolved to dissemble.

"I have been travelling all day. I have neither breakfasted, dined, nor supped," he said.

The duchess clapped her hands.

"Nor has poor Jack Horne."

The duchess rose and took his hand.

"This way. Supper is laid out ready, but I hardly hoped you would honour me," said Doleres of Castella.

She opened a door and led him down a well-lighted passage to a room of considerable dimensions, in which was a large fire-place, and, in consideration of the dampness of the old house, a large and not unwelcome fire.

It was the old banqueting room of the baronial residence.

A splendid supper was laid out.

The duchess pointed to a chair.

William Lennox was very pale and wan. The flush of excitement had passed away from his features.

The long and lofty room, its length in part decreased by a heavy black curtain at the end, was illumined, without regard to its size, only where the table stood.

William Lennox was just about to sit down when a loud ringing, whooping, and shouting, was heard without.

The duchess started.

William Lennox looked keenly at her, with an almost imperceptible smile on her lips.

Little did William Lennox know from what awful peril he was saved by this startling interruption.

A servant entered.

" The duke, madam, has arrived with a party of friends. They were passing, after a long day's hunt, and seeing a light in the banqueting room, came to see if there was anything to eat."

" Do they know that I am here?" said the duchess.

" They do."

" What a relief for you, Captain Lennox," exclaimed the duchess, turning to the young man with a sickly smile, " you will have the society of men instead of that of an old woman."

" Madam—"

" Silence. I see it in your eyes. There is no woman in the world save Lillian. I go to order additional supper, and to meet my lord."

And she went out.

" None save Lillian," repeated William Lennox clasping his hands over his head.

A low, faint, almost inaudible sigh responded to his words.

He rushed towards the heavy curtain, drew it one side, and there, pale, haggard, but still how beautiful, stood Lillian.

" My God !" he said, and it was all that he could say.

" Let us escape," she whispered. " Not a word. They will return."

William Lennox drew a pistol, clutched the arm of his betrothed, and glared around. There was a dark and gloomy passage behind them; down this he hurried, almost carrying Lillian.

It soon brought them to the great hall, which was a blaze of light, and where the duchess stood receiving her husband and his guests.

They could see without being seen.

In a few minutes, however, the whole cortege moved away, and the hall was empty.

William Lennox looked around. There was no one in sight. In an instant he was in the hall, and, utterly forgetful of Jack Horne, unfastened the door and sallied into the open air; first, however, appropriating a cloak which hung on a peg in the hall for the purpose of covering Lillian.

The young officer was in too great dread of pursuit—in too great fear of losing his Lillian—his heart was too full to speak or ask for explanations.

He knew only that he clutched Lillian by the hand and would have defied a world in arms at that moment.

But there were difficulties to be contended with which he little expected.

They had scarcely left the house and entered upon the covering of the plantation when Lillian began to lag.

" Oh, William," she said, " I can go no further."

He said not a word, but caught her in his arms. It was useless in her weak state to resist, and for some time the young officer was able to bear his burden along.

At length, however, he stopped, and, setting Lillian down, leaned against a tree. Illness and sorrow had done its work. He was unequal to the task.

" I must rest a minute, my beloved," he said, " and then I shall be strong again."

" No, my dear William," she said, " it must not be. I have over tried you."

" Hush, darling ! yonder is the wall. That we must cross. Then, perhaps, our chief danger may be over. Never again will I trust you in the clutches of the duchess."

" The duchess," whispered Lillian.

" Come," gasped William Lennox, not at all disposed to enter upon this subject at the moment.

They soon reached the wall, and, after considerable difficulty, got over the wall.

" I must lie down," said Lillian.

" Courage."

" Courage I have, but not strength."

William Lennox took her up once more, crossed a meadow, and made in the direction of a dense clump of trees in a deep hollow. It was a grove of cork trees surrounded by low thickets. In the centre was an open space.

William Lennox laid her down in her warm cloak at the foot of a tree, and hastily collected some dry wood, moss, and chips.

He then drew the charge of his pistol, and loaded it with loose powder and moss.

He fired into the pile, and in an instant the inflammable materials were in a blaze.

He then piled fresh fuel on the flames.

No better place for concealment or a camp could have been selected. It was in a deep hollow, wholly concealed from the adjacent road.

William Lennox kneeled at her feet, and gazed in her eyes with deep and dying love—that mighty passion, of which an intrigue like that with the duchess was but an episode.

" And is it really you," he said in a low hushed voice, " you, my only true love, my soul, my angel, alive and safe !"

" It is Lillian," replied the girl, shuddering as she drew up to the fire, " though I never expected to see you again, my own dear William. What I have suffered you cannot conceive."

" Revenge thy sufferings my angel, I will and can. But now, with your lover kneeling at your feet, tell me the story of your persecution. When you have rested sufficiently we will move on to the inn and take my horses out. In an hour we shall be in Madrid."

Lillian began her story, but as it was suddenly and violently interrupted it will be best not to break the thread of the narrative, but rather to introduce the incident here.

The young girl had scarcely entered upon her story when strange sounds were heard in the distance, as of men fighting, holloaing, and scuffling.

Begging Lillian to be still and remain near the fire, William Lennox cocked his pistol and sallied forth into the road.

What he saw will be best explained by relating what had previously occurred.

*   *   *   *   *

No sooner was Jack Horne separated from his master than he found himself exposed to a blaze of light. Two well-dressed servants stood before him, having appeared as if by magic, holding wax-tapers, and begging him to honour their hall with his presence, while his master supped upstairs with the duchess.

"The duchess," stammered Jack Horne.

"Of course. Did not the captain come to sup with the duchess by appointment."

And the Spanish footmen looked so knowing that Jack Horne, who was mild and virtuous did not know what to think.

Not knowing what else to do, Jack Horne then followed them to the servants' hall, and sat down to a plentiful supper, amply washed down by wine.

Now, as Jack understood very little Spanish, and the servants knew no English, there was not much opportunity for conversation, especially as everybody paid diligent attention to the good things before them.

Jack Horne, therefore, cogitated gravely, and as he did so, he began to think that there was something odd about the whole affair.

He could not, however, make it out.

Like many others, the more he could not make it out, the more he drank, until he not only became intoxicated, but suspicious and half inclined to be quarrelsome.

He drew his sword, looked savagely about, and challenged the lot to fight.

The Spaniards armed themselves with whatever was handiest, and stood upon the defensive, while one or two opened a door and fled.

And Jack after them at the very top of his speed.

"Stop, you bloody murdering villains! Stop, you ragged and cowardly regiment!" he yelled as he ran along. "Stop before one British soldier. I'll lather your yellow skins, you shunks and ruffians. Charge! By the poker I'll have you yet! I see you with yer white eyes all of a cock, you scoundrels!"

And Jack Horne plunged headlong into the open air, and for one moment stood staring vacantly around.

Now, if Jack Horne had felt his departure from sobriety in the house, how much more rapidly did the fumes rise when he found himself in the keen, bracing night air, often very sharp in Spain.

Gazing vacantly at the house, the plantations, and the shrubs, he in all probability imagined himself at least a general, about to charge a column of artillery, cavalry, and infantry.

Intoxication produces strange results at times, and certainly this result was one of the most comic and ridiculous which the hallucination could have produced.

Jack Horne looked around, eyed his supposed adversaries with a half comical, half serious glance, and then with a shout rushed at them with the terrific strides of seven leagued boots.

"Charge—to the right, cavalry! to the left wing of the infantry! guns to the front! Cut down that tall ruffian yonder! Hurra! Up Guards and at 'em! See the Frenchmen fly! Yes, my love, the enemy fly. Charge, charge, charge!"

And having by that good fortune which is the proverbial protection of a drunken man, reached the outside of the park, he rushed wildly along a road, cutting and slashing away at every tree and bush.

At last in a desperate charge, when in his own opinion he had slaughtered at least a dozen of the enemy, he made a desperate lunge at a delapidated sign-post, and fell headlong on the bosom of mother earth.

"My goodness," he said, after a few minutes of repose, "what the dickens is the matter—the deuce to pay and no pitch hot."

"Why, you drunken rascal," cried his master, "what is the meaning of all this?"

"Drunk, sir," said poor Horne, seating himself quietly on the ground, "am I drunk? Well, I think I have been. I'm better now."

And he wiped the blood from a gash on his forehead.

"Can you fetch the horses," asked the captain severely.

"Yes, sir, and be glad to do so. Where to?"

"Come and I will show you," replied the officer.

Jack picked up his sword, and in a very sheepish style followed his master, until they came in sight of the fire.

Jack stared.

"Why, your honour, they said you was a supping with the duchess," said the man.

"Silence; mention not her name," replied William Lennox with unusual sternness.

"But, sir, who's yonder," cried Jack Horne, retreating prudently.

"Lillian," replied the young man, clutching his arm. "Go, fetch the horses, and bring them here. We must be in Madrid to-night."

With open mouth, with staring eyes, Jack Horne moved away without daring to add another word.

William Lennox returned to where Lillian awaited him with impatience, and after a brief explanation of the disturbance which had taken place, he begged Lillian to tell her story.

Lillian took his hand in hers.

"This puts me in mind of old times," she said, smiling.

"When?"

"When we were gipsies."

William kissed her hand respectfully, and then she began her story.

It was as follows, as near as after all these years we can recollect.

We shall not attempt to harrow our readers too much, but the story must be told in all its naked horrors.

———

CHAPTER CXII.

LILLIAN'S STORY.

"I HAD felt a strange sensation creeping over me for days before that fatal hour, when all seemed lost unto me, and my eyes appeared to close in eternal night.

"It was an uneasy numbness, which at first did not alarm me, but which, after a time, produced a fearful languor, that made me almost careless whether I lived or died.

"It was only for yourself, William, and for my own dear mother, that I cared to breathe.

"It is terrible to die young, but it is more terrible to live in agony — or more than agony, in torpor, and this it was I felt was coming on me.

"My own secret conviction was, that I was going mad.

"It was only on the very last day of my illness that the fearful conviction forced itself upon me, that I was suffering from slow and yet sure poison.

"What enemy could I have atrocious enough to commit such a crime as this?

"The cousins who had persecuted my mother were far away, and, besides, they could not now benefit by my death.

"Then I resolved to cnovey my suspicions to you, and ask your advice.

"I whispered this to Teresa, and two hours after, she having tried to dissuade me from it, I was too late.

"I closed my eyes with those I loved near me, and I felt that I was dead.

"How long it was ere I came to a faint consciousness of my existence I know not; I dare say I shall discover in time, but it did come on me, slowly, indistinctly, with awful terror.

"At first I thought I was in my coffin about to be buried alive; and this was horrible enough.

"Then I knew that I had been buried alive.

"I opened my eyes and gazed feebly and without terror around.

"I was in a large and luminous cell; I was lying on an open and exposed bier; I was swathed in the terrible clothes of the dead, while all around me, in mockery as it were, blazed wax tapers.

"Alas! they were near their sockets.

"At first I did not feel alarm. In all probability I was exposed in some *chapelle ardente*, until the day of my funeral should come, and soon I should be able to call attention to my position.

"But the lights burnt low, and as they did so, I saw that it was night, and that all life was shut out from me.

"It would be vain to call out and shriek, and yet I felt the time coming when I should do so.

"The lights went out and I was in total darkness.

"I do not think I yet gave way to absolute, to utter terror. I was so weak, so low, so prostrate, that I was capable of no violent emotion.

"But the tears came slowly to my eyes and trickled down my wan and faded cheeks.

"Then I prayed.

"As I did so, I heard the faint motion of a key in a door; it was very far off I thought.

"I tried to call aloud.

"My voice sounded hollow and faint in those low and gloomy vaults, and so great was the exertions, in my sad state, that I fell again, as if death had clutched me with his icy hand.

"I had fainted.

"When I came to, I felt that something was being poured down my throat that both warmed and refreshed me; and, besides, I heard human voices near me.

"Imagine my dismay, my horror! and how near I was again fainting, when I found that it was Slimy Jones and the man who claims to be Sir Edgar Blakesley.

"They were, however, gentle in their manner, and were engaged in releasing my arms, after which they wrapped me in a cloak and bore me from the house of death into the open air.

"This was something. Life is dear at my age, and I felt some relief to be taken from the fearful dangers of the tomb.

"But it was not enough.

"Take me to my mother—to William," I faintly faltered.

"They made no reply, but placed me in a comfortable carriage, which drove off without a word.

"The motion rocked me to sleep, and when I recovered I was in bed, with an aged crone beside me, who either did not or would not understand my Spanish, but who attended to my wants with scrupulous attention.

"I had tonics, and soups, and wines, which soon brought me round.

"I was able to sit up in bed, and soon to dress and examine my room.

"It was large and commodious; but locked, bolted, and barred.

"I was allowed books, pens, ink, and paper.

"I used the latter in the only way that I thought likely to be useful.

"I scrawled note after note, and gave them to the air, in the faint hope that they might reach you."

William Lennox smiled, and kissed her hand.

"Did any of them reach you?" cried Lillian, with sparkling eyes.

"I have a dozen here," said William, laying his hand upon his heart.

"Did they do any good?"

"They enabled me to trace you."

"Merciful heavens be thanked!"

And Lillian proceeded with her story.

"As soon as my strength got round a little, I received a visit which I must relate, as I believe nothing can rouse you more against the detestable young man."

"Tell me all," said William, in a husky tone of voice.

"One morning I had breakfasted, when my ancient guardian entered the room with a smile on her face, which for an instant inspired me with hope.

"I looked at her keenly, and then noticed that she bore on her arm dresses and clothing of better material than usual.

"Hoping this was a signal of some change, I dressed myself carefully, and even put on the ornaments she pressed upon me.

"She then retired; and in half an hour ushered in, to my horror and disgust, this Sir Edgar Blakesley."

William shuddered, but said nothing.

"He was dressed in the uniform of his service, and approached me with the utmost servility, bowing and scraping like an actor at a fair.

"'Peerless beauty,' he began, 'and how does this retired sojourn please you?'

"'Ill,' I said. 'Why am I thus infamously kept from my friends and relatives?'

"'My dear madam,' he exclaimed, 'in the eyes of all the world you are dead. By the vigilance of devoted and earnest friends you have been saved. The chief of these you see before you. Will you not, divine Lillian, reward him for his deeds by living for him alone?'

"'Monster!' I cried, 'take me back to the sepulchre whence you drew me. Death is far preferable than connection with one so vile!'

"He smiled upon me such a bitter and sarcastic smile—it went to my very heart.

"'For whom, madam, would you live?' he said.

" ' For my mother—for my beloved William !'
I eagerly replied.

" ' Poor girl !'

" ' What mean you ? Speak !'

" ' Poor girl—'

" ' Monster ! have you some hideous news, or
do you wilfully torture me ?'

" ' You are forgotten, Lillian. The man of
whom you speak, apostate and impostor, seeks
in the arms of the beauteous Countess of Castella consolation already !' "

Lillian's manner was now excited and enthusiastic.

William turned pale and red, and hissed
something between his teeth.

"Be not angry, my own dear William," she
said tenderly; "I did not for a moment
believe him."

"Go on," gasped William Lennox.

" ' Liar and foul calumniator,' was my reply,
' seek not to sully the honour of one whose
shoes thou art not worthy to tie, who is as much
above thee in rank as he is in honour and
nobility !'

"His eyes flashed livid fire, and for a moment
he seemed as if he could have struck me."

"What ?" shrieked William.

"He did not do it, William. Only you know
that when men's passions are aroused they do
look terrible; he did, and then, walking up and
down the room, was silent for some moments.

" ' Madame,' he said at last, ' you will have
ample leisure to reflect. This room will remain
your prison until you consent to leave it as the
wife of Sir Edgar Blakesley.'

"I smiled.

" ' Beware !' he said, ghastly pale as he spoke.

" Of what ?

" ' Of nothing ;' " and he left the room.

CHAPTER CXIII.

LILLIAN'S STORY.—CONTINUED.

" He came several times again, brought me
books, was very civil and polite, despite the
coldness of my demeanour, until one morning,
when he and Slimy Jones entered with angry
and passionate countenances, threw a cloak over
me, and hurried me down stairs.

" Then it was I began to hope that my
missives had been successful in their operation,
and had reached some friend who was making
an effort in my favour.

"But I was offered no explanations. I was
placed in a carriage and hurried off towards the
country ; my guardians, who were in a sulky
humour, refusing to answer the slightest of my
questions.

"I was much stronger now, or I could not
have borne all this anxiety and suffering."

"You are a heroine and an angel !" said
William enthusiastically.

"Silence, and listen.

"I was brought to yonder castle, which had
evidently been prepared to a certain extent for
my reception, though I could easily see it had
not often been inhabited. I was assigned a
room and treated with the same care and attention as before, but was also still strictly
guarded.

" Last night—that is, some hours ago—I
received a terrible shock, my William.

Lennox's face could not be seen where he sat.

" This man, this Sir Edgar Blakesley, came to
me, and offered to prove your want of fidelity ;
to prove that so soon after your Lillian's supposed death, you were merry and happy in the
society of another.

"Was it not cruel, my William ?"

"It was."

"I was astonished, horrified ! but determined
to stand the ordeal, so I went with him where
he liked to take me.

"In this way I reached the alcove behind
the curtain, which commanded a view of the
banqueting room."

"Ah !" said William.

"I saw you enter. My head grew dizzy, but
I looked again and I saw that you were wan
and pale. You know the rest. And yet, William, I should be glad to know why you were
there !"

"To avenge you. I believed, and still believe,
the duchess to be the guilty author of all."

"My God !"

"I believe these vile and detestable men, on
whom my vengeance shall fall, too, to be mere
instruments."

"But why ?"

"Why ?"

"Tell me, William."

"Because this woman, this Menalina, this
Spanish Cleopatra, has been weak and silly
enough to fancy me as the toy of an idle hour.
You were, therefore, a stumbling-block, and she
would fain have removed you."

"Can such things be ; can such wickedness
exist ?" gasped the unfortunate Lillian.

"Lillian, you are too good, too pure. This
world was never made for you, you know not
its wickedness."

"Alas ! but all this time I have never asked
—cruel, thoughtless girl that I am—for my mother."

"She is ill—she knows, suspects nothing.
Hark, here comes Jack Horne with the horses.
In two hours we shall be near her, and Lillian
shall once more be safe."

The girl shuddered.

"We will leave Spain."

She sighed.

"You will become my honoured wife."

She shook her head.

"Lillian ! are you changed ?" Have you
ceased, then, to love me ?" he gasped.

"No, William, but do you love me; is
your heart mine ? Have not all these trials
weaned you from me ?"

"No; by the heavens above ! my long lost,
deeply-mourned Lillian, you are now more
deeply loved than ever You are the only
being I live for. Talk not such treason to
our love, my angel."

And William Lennox bowed his knee, and
fondly kissed her two extended hands.

And did he not love her better than ever ?

Of course he did.

When a devoted and passionate heart has sinned against the queen of its soul, is not its devotion more wild, more engrossing than ever?

At this moment Jack Horne came up with the horses, and with one which he had borrowed for the occasion.

All mounted quickly, and as they did so a loud stir was heard in the park.

Torches flashed, — voices were heard, — but in low and cautious tones, searching every place where any one could by any possibility have been concealed.

"Follow me," said William, sternly; "we must be cunning as serpents, when courage is overpowered by numbers."

And walking his horse, he prepared to ascend the slope of the dell.

The night was very dark, and they reached the skirt of the cork trees, along which they began to walk, with the most extreme exercise of caution.

No sooner had they reached the highway than they darted their spurs into their horses, and galloped wildly away for Madrid.

CHAPTER CXIV.

THE MIDNIGHT MURDER.

THERE are in the neighbourhood of London one or two places at all events, where, despite bricks and mortar, we may, if we so choose, breathe freely, and fancy ourselves away from all city cares, and know not even the existence of the busy haunts of men.

Hampstead and Highgate are the lungs of London.

There is a lane on the way to the latter which is dear to the recollection of many.

It is narrow, shaded, and umbrageous, and there was a time when we, in the early days of our youth, enjoyed many a happy hour walking up its winding way, with beauty on our arm.

We are told that this spot, rural even now, when rurality is so rare, is doomed.

Persons are wishing it down.

It is said to be a nursery for the social evil.

This may or may not be, but surely it would be as wise to barricade the Haymarket and Regent-street, close all our theatres and ballrooms, and ask passports at Temple-bar of every young female who shall go west, as close up a delightful walk because a parish is too parsimonious to light it properly, or pay for a policeman to scare away the juvenile Lais, Aspasias, and primitive Menelinas who affright the inhabitants of Highgate and Kentish Town.

There is, however, one comfort, though an able and Conservative newspaper may write it down, and though memorials may be issued and signed by parsons and others, it cannot be shut up.

It is a right of way.

No doubt the efforts are well meant, but we are quite sure that all who wish well to the health of London will oppose, by every means in their power, any attempt to deprive the working man of one last remnant of the country which remains to him.

We shall next have Primrose-hill built upon, or Hampstead-heath enclosed, because it is a favorite resort of persons, to use a vulgar phrase, "coaching."

Now, there was a night—a night ever to be remembered by all persons indicated in this true and faithful history, when this lane was the scene of events which bear so much on the course of our narrative that we are compelled to leave Madrid and the sunny sky of Spain to come to our own foggy clime, so dear with all its faults to every true Englishman.

It was a dark and murky night, and very long before Highgate cemetery was thought of, when four men got out of a hackney coach near the foot of this secluded pathway.

They were wrapped in cloaks, and wore slouched hats.

They slunk up the lane as if they were burglars, intent upon some important crack.

They went up the lane half-way, and then turned off into the fields.

There was, at the time of which we speak, a very old and ruined house, of which not the faintest trace now exists, in the very centre of a field.

There was no road or pathway anywhere near it, only the outline of a road, now completely overgrown by grass and weeds.

It was a red brick house, and its very name will never be forgotten.

Why?

It had acquired a name never to be obliterated from the memory of man.

There had been committed a murder there which had made even the myrmidons of the law shudder and draw back in horror.

A child had been slain!

Murder seemed to drip from the very walls!

There was no road leading to the house.

For sixty years grass had grown around it; the ivy had claimed it for its own; it turned round its base, and nearly buried in its upward progress the half shattered casements.

No one inhabited it; it was left there alone in its desolation, casting by its presence an air of gloom round the neighbourhood, and inspiring every one who approached it with dread and horror. It was unlike any other house of the time; it resembled an ancient castle in its interior arrangements, rather than the abode of a family.

It had the reputation of being haunted; and the children who ventured near it in the daytime fled like guilty things when the shades of evening began to fall, and the crescent moon glanced through the shattered wall of the eastern wing.

The very air seemed to hang thick and dank round the ruins, which even the night owl appeared scarcely to approach.

It was in these days when the gloom of political dissensions was brooding over the land— when the head of a perjured king rolled at the feet of an avenging people—in the days of Charles I.—a terrible crime was committed within these walls.

It was a foggy, misty night.

The road, which has since been overgrown with weeds, was scarcely distinguishable in the intense darkness.

The family had retired to rest early; but during the whole night shadows were seen flitting from chamber to chamber.

It was two o'clock, when a low wail resounded through the corridors of the old mansion.

No one heard it from without; but there were those in the building who knew what it was, and whose very hearts trembled at the sound.

It was the last dying wail of an infant.

Its agonies had been witnessed but by two persons: and upon the lips of these two the mutuality of sin had set its irrevocable seal.

The clock struck two.

A chamber-door opened, and a dark figure emerged stealthily, as if weighed down by the burden of a terrible crime.

In his arms, concealed by a dressing-gown, was the corpse of a child—his own child.

Well might he start and tremble as the wind burst open the casement and swept moaning along the passage, mimicking, in its play, the last dying wail of the murdered child.

Murdered in cold blood!

And now the father, stealthily, fearfully, was passing along the corridors, and wonderingly gazed round him for the means of disposing of the corpse.

He slunk down the stairs, and at length stood before the back door of the house; through the window above the moon sent a bright ray for an instant upon the face of the murdered one. The man hastily covered it over, and leant for support against the wall.

Demons seemed to be around him—above him—beneath him, mocking, laughing at his terror.

Cold perspiration stood upon his brow, and ran trickling down his face. The very air seemed thick and dank, and the dead stillness of the night rendered the cold stone passage like the interior of a charnel-house.

At length, rousing himself by a strong effort, he placed the body on the ground, unbarred the door, and lifting his horrid burden again, emerged into the night.

All was as still as death. "Not a mouse stirred." The moon had again disappeared. Heavy clouds—wreathing themselves into fantastic shapes—chased each other sluggishly along the sky.

There was no fear of detection: his only companions were his conscience and the shadow which followed him dimly along the grass.

Arrived at a secluded nook, he laid the child on the sod, and returning to the house brought a spade and began turning up the ground.

The horrid task was soon accomplished, and laying the body in its resting place, the father leaned down by the side of the lone grave and gazed in an agony of tears upon the child who had fallen a victim to his bad passions.

Misguided passions: cowardly dread of discovery!

How the strong man's heart burned with agony at that moment.! How bitter were those tears of blood which fell scalding to the earth. The glimmering of a faint light in the distance warned the murderer of the approach of a traveller.

Hastily covering over the poor little body which lay there so cold and still under the black sky, the father returned to the house.

No vestige of the upturning of the ground was visible on the next morning.

The child was missed, search was made, but the grass gave no sign of having been disturbed. But the murderer had for all this done his work clumsily.

Above the sod, pointing threateningly towards the sky, appeared the child's hand which the father had left in his haste; and which seemed calling upon man or Providence to avenge the dark and terrible crime.

The household gathered tremblingly round the grave, while the old gardener proceeded to raise from its one-night's bed the body of the child.

A strict investigation was made, but the child who had pointed out its own resting-place could make no further sign; and between the murderer and the object of his guilty passion the secret remained undiscovered.

But the house from that moment became an object of terror and aversion to all.

The family left the neighbourhood, but a century was too short a period to blot out the recollection of the crime.

And so, as time wore on, the grass grew round the mansion, the walls cracked and became green and tottering with age; and two hundred years after the murder, the children held it in traditional awe, and whispered strangely about the midnight murder, and the small white hand which, though cold in death, had called upon man to avenge the crime.

It was near this house that four figures were standing at midnight.

Four men in yellow cloaks, whose bright colours contrasted strangely with the green foliage.

A hurried consultation took place, and the four men moved stealthily along towards the dilapidated mansion.

———

CHAPTER CXV.

THE MAD HOUSE.

ABOUT two hundred yards from the old house was another abode, whose barred windows plainly indicated its use.

A lunatic asylum—but not one such as are found generally in modern times.

The barred windows looked out upon a large garden, enclosed by high walls. In this garden were everywhere to be found human bones, lying scattered about under small mounds—the bones of men who had been quietly and mysteriously disposed of, and as quietly and mysteriously buried.

Men and women moved listlessly about the grounds—some of them perfect models of creation. Men with powerful frames and chiselled features : women with lithe and graceful forms ; but their eyes vacant, without a trace of mind or inward feeling.

In a chamber in this building, on a bed, lay a young girl in her night dress.

It was Leila, Princess of Borneo !

She had paced the room the whole night.

Cries of demons had resounded through the building ; shrieks of beings only human in form, but the last trace of whose intellect had departed. Imprecations, loud and unceasing, had proceeded from the rooms round her.

The terror inspired by the sounds around her, the recollections of the past, and the still more awful anticipations of the future, kept her exhausted frame alive, until at length in the small hours of the morning a kind of lull came over the whole house, and a langour stole over her frame.

She undressed herself by the light of the single lamp, which swung dimly in a corner of the room. The window though barred was open, and she could breathe the fresh and balmy air of night.

This enabled her to sustain herself, while she slowly denuded herself of her clothing ; but she had not sufficient strength to remain long standing, and she at length sank exhausted on the bed.

During the whole time she had been undressing she had, unknown to herself, been watched by greedy eyes.

A small grated window commanded a view of the whole apartment from the passage without ; and through this window Dr. Porteus Framppe —the keeper of the madhouse—had peered eagerly, wistfully ; and a grim smile of satisfaction passed over his diabolical countenance as the girl sank undressed upon the bed.

He then opened the door and entered stealthily.

The light of the lamp cast a dim glimmer over the room.

Leila was lying on the edge of the bed, the pink curtains casting a rich glow over her form. The old German leaned against the bed-post and gazed with a kind of dreamy delight upon the scene.

They were, indeed, a contrast.

Dr. Porteus Framppe was dressed in a blue coat with brass buttons, blue pantaloons, white silk stockings, and shoes with steel buckles.

His head, which was high and conical, was surmounted by a whisp of hair—straw coloured, straggling, as though constantly endeavouring to release itself from the skull. His ears were large and red, his mouth like the entrance to a cavern. His eyes were undistinguishable, being concealed by a pair of huge green spectacles which rested on a nose as hooked and pointed as the beak of an eagle.

Leila was a perfect picture of innocent beauty.

She was, as we have said, lying on the edge of the bed. Her golden curls were then thrown back upon the pillow—her bosom, white as the snow, was heaving with the terrible emotions inspired by those dreams which the recollection of the past day forced upon her.

Her whole form seemed instinct with terror ; but there was no pity in the glance which the German doctor cast upon her quivering form as, in the dim light, he gazed passionately upon her.

He approached the bed and knelt beside it.

There was something repelling in his aspect. His age was so unlike the youth of that fair girl —his age, too, was so opposite to the passion which agitated his frame.

* * * *

During these moments the four men in the yellow cloaks were approaching the house.

* * *

Dr. Porteus Framppe approached the bed and laid his hand on her bosom.

Leila moved uneasily in her heavy sleep, and the doctor started like a guilty thing.

He started on his feet, and gazed anxiously round him.

But his purpose blinded him. He stooped down and kissed the sleeping girl passionately on the lips, and took her yielding form in his arms.

Just then a cry arose ; the doors were dashed violently open, and the four men in the yellow cloaks rushed into the house.

Dr. Porteus released the girl from his grasp and left the room.

CHAPTER CVI.

CAPTAIN GEORGE'S STORY.

WE return to our friend, Captain George, to Lucy, and Joe, the mudlark.

Some of our readers may recollect the failure with regard to the marriage of the highwayman.

They were more, fortunate, at Dover ; and this is the story Captain George told in explanation of his journey to Algiers—

" Disgusted with the life which, as a highwayman, I had been leading in England, I determined upon proceeding to India, and enlisting in the service of one of the Indian princes who were in a state of rebellion against British power.

" We sailed from England with a fairwind ; our ship was a fast sailer, and everything and everybody promised a prosperous and quick voyage.

" I was rather a bad sailor, and was lying lazily in my cabin, when a loud crash was heard on deck.

" Of course, I am always glad of excitement. I was on deck in a moment, and it is needless to say that the scene there was sufficient to warm the very coldest blood.

" A Corsair ship was in sight.

" Our decks were cleared.

" Every man stood to his arms.

" The crash I had heard was the first shot, which announced to us the fact that we must surrender at discretion. Our captain was calm and collected.

"'My men,' he said, 'we must stand by the ship. We are well armed. Are we to fight or strike?'

"A loud cheer was the only answer; and so rather hopelessly, as I thought, we prepared to save our lives, if not our liberty.

"It is needless to describe the scene.

"We neared each other. The vessel of the enemy was larger and better manned than we were.

"We closed. Naked men swarmed among our rigging. Yells as of demons rent the air. Our captain was struck down and cast into the sea. Smoke and flames encircled us; and as I endeavoured in vain to lead a band of men on to the deck of our antagonist, I was blinded by a gush of blood over my temples, and I fell senseless on the deck

"When I awoke we were on *terra firma*.

"The room in which I lay was dark—it was underground.

"I woke only into a state of stupor.

"All around was a gloomy darkness; but as I lay there, I fancied an angel was watching over me, and that angel seemed to take the form of my Lucy.

"I closed my eyes, as if drinking in this imaginary happiness, when a sweet voice spoke—

"'Are you better?'

"'Yes, better; but very weak.'

"'You are in safety.'

"'Where am I?'

"'You are in the house of the Dey. You are a slave, but you will be treated as a friend if you are grateful.'

"These words were spoken in a tender voice, and by a voice, too, which seemed to penetrate my very soul.

"I confess I felt anxious.

"'Cannot I have more light? Do raise the curtain,' I said.

"The curtain was raised, and a vision of beauty stood before me.

"A young girl, not more than twenty, stood beside my bed.

"She was robed in the Turkish style—her loose jacket only half concealing her swelling bosom—her muslin trousers and her gold embroidered vest only serving to enrich the luxurious contours of her voluptuous form.

"Her face was not one of classic beauty, but it was one which I shall remember for ever. Her eyes, dark and rich, were filled with liquid light, and seemed to cast their gaze upon me with a languishing and half-amorous sensation. Her arms were folded across her glowing breast: and as she spoke, her coral lips seemed to breathe forth a living music, and impregnate the whole apartment with light.

"She was the impersonation of all that in my youngest days I had pictured as the original of poetry and passion.

"She must have thought I dreamed, for I looked at her as I should have looked upon a vision, and feared to speak, because I dreaded her departure.

"I confess that I felt half overwhelmed—not only by the presence of this lovely vision, but by my strange situation.

"'Am I a slave?' I asked.

"'Yes.'

"'In whose hands?'

"'You are in the Dey's house.'

"'And may I ask who is my protectress?

"'I am the Dey's daughter. *I will* protect you.'

"These words were said with a languid, half happy, half sorrowful smile, and, with a wave of the hand, she left me.

"It is scarcely necessary to describe the mode of my discovery. I was a slave, but I was tended carefully, jealously by the Dey's daughter.

"I recovered.

"But to what was I doomed?

"Better had it been for me to die there in that dark room than to be ranked as a slave—to be placed in chains—to receive every moment an insult, and be classed every moment as a brute beast.

"I was called before the Dey.

"I was called to humiliation, but a humiliation that brought ever afterwards to a kind of short-sighted happiness.

"For twelve years I was in captivity. I was a gardener.

"This fact ed me into temptation. I tended the garden, and there invariably I met some of the Dey's household.

"The Dey's daughter was in love. I will not say I was. But I was weak. I felt annihilated in the presence of so much beauty.

"I was in the garden one evening, when the sun, just dying, was gilding every leaf and flower.

"All things wore a golden hue, and the Dey's daughter, accompanied by her attendants, luxuriated in a bower overgrown by roses and eglantine.

"A dance was arranged, and four girls began arranging themselves for the performance.

"They knew not of the presence of a man. They divested themselves of all unnecessary clothing, and commenced one of those demonstrative dances, which are the very existence of the East.

"Your ears would tingle were I fully to describe the scene which ensued. Aphrodite was incarnated with her attendant nymphs, and I moved, as if impelled by magic, within the circle of these magicians; and as I stood spell-bound at the delightful scene, a hand seized mine; I advanced and saw the princess. She drew me towards her, and I fell half-fainting on her breast.

*　　　*　　　*　　　*

"For twelve years this continued.

"Time passed but slowly. You may think that I was happy because I was luxuriating in the excess of a forbidden love.

"But I was not happy.

"I regretted my absence from England.

"I reproached myself for leaving its shores; and only regretted that a short campaign in India had not proved the termination of an existence of turmoil and excitement.

"I was quite tired of existence.

"Zanoina loved me, she said; but what of that?

"Could she compensate for what I had lost? Could a love, forced as it were on me, recompense me for an unfulfilled mission—a lost existence?

"But there was one thing held out to me which sustained me through all my misfortunes.

"And this was the hope of escape—Zanoina promised me this; but she also *promised* to escape with me.

"It did not seem, however, as if she desired to attempt the enterprise.

"She was very young. Having passed through but sixteen summers she had seen little of life's dangers and life's rebuffs.

"The Dey himself, though cruel to others, was kind and forbearing to her; and yet she felt a kind of tremulous happiness when discharging his injunctions.

"He had destined her for the wife of a wealthy suitor—a Greek merchant who had by fraud and stealthy dealing amassed an inconceivable amount of riches.

"He was an old man, however, was Ximenes, not suited to fill the place of husband to a blooming beauty of sixteen.

"She was scarcely to be blamed, perhaps; though custom would declare her wrong.

"And having given her heart to the stranger, she hardly cared to attempt his escape, lest in that escape she should not be included, and the whole future of her young life be blighted.

"I must confess that during these years my affection for her ripened; and I felt that I should have desired, if possible, to carry her away with me, and give to her that love which she had in her unguarded faith lavished upon me.

"At length when the girl had ripened into the woman — when the bud of fifteen had settled into the rose of seven-and-twenty—when the soft, yielding girl had risen into the rounded form of the woman—when Zanoina, in fact, had some claim upon me, she called me into her boudoir one day and dismissed her attendants.

"'Dearest Henry,' said Zanoina, 'I have at length succeeded. My father has gone into the interior. We have two days for our attempt. I will effect your escape or perish.'

"I kissed her hand. I could not speak.

"I am afraid, however, that I was ungrateful in my heart, for the idea of escape associated itself less in my mind with the thoughts of a future with her than the anticipations of a free life and a return to England and to you.

"'To-night,' said Zanoina, twining her round arms about my neck, and imprinting a kiss upon my forehead, 'to-night you shall be free.'

"Free!

"The very idea of freedom seemed to paralyse my brain.

"My thoughts reverted to home—to my family —to you—and I utterly forgot her presence."

CHAPTER CVII.

THE ESCAPE.

"It was night, and darkness had fallen over the suburbs of the city.

"I was sleeping on a couch outside the bedroom of the Dey; at the end of a corridor which led from the entrance of the state apartments.

"I fell into a slumber, in which visions of a sweet home—of you, Lucy—and a bright future mingled themselves with dreams of bloody fights, of raging tempests—tempests less of God's wrath than of man's passions.

"A storm of terrific vehemence raged without. The lightning rushed in forked flames round the castle, while the thunder pealed in fearful gusts, shaking the very foundations of the building, and bringing to my recollection some of those dreadful tempests which had roused me out of my infant sleep in my native county— Devonshire.

"Just as I was dreaming a delightful dream of youthful pleasures and youthful aspirations, a light hand touched my breast. My Zanoina stood before me.

"She was arrayed in travelling clothes.

"Her very appearance inspired me with hope.

"My Zanoina,' I said, 'why are you here?

"'I love you, as you know, Henry,' she said, 'and I am come to save you.'

"Save me!' I cried, "after twelve years of captivity here. Can I hope for safety?

"'You know that I have promised you safety, and I have come to give it you. Arise, dress yourself quickly, and fly with me.

"To rise from my couch, to dress myself, and to stand ready for flight before the Princess was the work of a moment. Traversing the long corridors of the Dey's mansion, the Princess led me by the hand, until we arrived at the court-yard of the palace."

"Arrangements had been previously made for our flight.

"The shades of evening had fallen over the city.

"The night was dark, very dark.

"We mounted our horses, and, with two attendants, passed silently through the gates. We had not calculated upon pursuit, and in the blindness of our passion we forgot everything else, except the one fact that we were escaping, and together.

"We had scarcely emerged from the vicinity of the palace, when low noises were heard behind us.

"Evidently our enemies were in pursuit.

"To conceal ourselves was our object— but how?

"I had never emerged from the precincts of the mansion in which for twelve years I had been immured, and was scarcely aware whether the house in which I had been confined was situated in the town or in the lonely country district around it.

"Zanoina, however, was better acquainted with the country.

"She accordingly seized the reins of my steed

upon the first intimation of danger, and dragged me as it were into a grove of olive and citron trees, which terminated the last outskirts of the city.

"My heart, as I have said, was in reality at home, but I could scarcely avoid feeling a kind of sympathy, strong sympathy, with the girl who thus hazarded her life to save mine; and as her soft form lay gently pressed to my bosom, I felt as if I could gladly have yielded up my soul to preserve her from the anger of the enraged Dey.

"But it was not to be.

"The sounds approached. The moon even was up, and peering merrily through the trees.

"We had tethered our horses far in the covert, and we ourselves were trembling with anxiety at the very edge, waiting, as it were, for the approach of those who were to annihilate for ever our happiness.

"They came at last.

"The Dey himself came up accompanied by five guards.

"We waited in silence. They approached stealthily, as if they were aware of our whereabouts.

NOTE.—The Illustration for No. 26 was erroneously inserted in No. 25, and *vice versa*. It is of no consequence to the narrative.

" Unfortunately the moon, which had up to this moment hidden herself in her bed curtains, now peeped forth, and disclosed to the enraged Dey a group, the principal figures in which were myself and his daughter.

" He seemed not to recognise Zanoina.

" Surrender, slave !" he cried in a loud voice.

" ' Never !' I shouted, brandishing above my head a pistol which I had plucked from Zanoina's bosom. 'I have for twelve years groaned under your oppression. I am now a free man, and will sell my life dearly. Beware !'

" Beware ! fatal word as it proved.

" ' Of what ?' he said.

" Better had it have been had I at once fled : not that at the moment I cared for life, for life during those twelve years had become a burden, but I feared for that charge which, though I had not assumed, was still under my protection.

" The Dey was not the man to be discouraged by a show of resistance.

" ' My daughter !' he shouted, in phrenzied tones, ' my daughter ! Deliver her to me and your life shall be spared.'

" What could I do ? Zanoina was with me of her own free will. And then she loved me.

" Oh, for the selfishness of human nature !

" In a moment the thought flashed across my mind. Shall I yield her and seek safety in flight ? but one glance at the poor girl decided me.

" ' Zanoina,' I whispered, ' will you return to your father ?

" ' No, beloved, we live or die together.'

" This decided me.

" ' Dey !' I cried, ' we have fled together— together we remain.'

" A sign was made. The attendants fired at me. They did not harm me, but the bullets intended for me hit her.

" She fell dead from her horse into my arms.

" My startled steed flew with the speed of the wind, and soon distanced all pursuit.

" I pressed my terrible burden to my heart.

" I was mad.

" At last the wearied horse stumbled and fell. For a moment I was stunned, but rising, dragged myself into a pile of ruins bearing with me the stiffened corpse of the girl.

" Wearied, exhausted, worn out in mind and body, I slept.

" It was mid-day when I awoke, and after one long, silent prayer, proceeded to bury my unfortunate companion in such a way as to protect her from the wild beasts of those dreary plains.

" I spent an hour in piling stones above her body. At the end of that time she was screened from sight. With difficulty then I tore myself away, and was about to issue forth into the open air, when I saw my pursuers close at hand.

" They had lost sight of me at night, but with the day had found my track.

" I turned and fled. The ruins were of vast extent, and I expected easily to conceal myself.

" But my pursuers were quickly after me.

" They caught sight of me several times.

" Then I stumbled, rolled over, and was lost to all sense."

CHAPTER CVIII.

THE TREASURE.

" WHEN I came to myself I was in darkness— wearied, sore, and utterly incapable of motion.

" I lay still and waited.

" By degrees I got used to the gloom, and found myself in a kind of cave which opened at the bottom of a dry well.

" As soon as I could crawl about I looked upwards, and saw daylight at no great distance.

" The cave was very cold.

" I had my pistols and powder, and around me were quantities of dry wood. I tore a handkerchief into strips, and saturated it with powder and brandy from a flask.

" In another moment I was warming myself by a genial blaze.

" The cavern was cut in the solid rock.

" Imagine my astonishment when, on one side I saw a door which once, ages ago, had been strong, but which now was powerless to defend.

" I seized a brand, and soon forcing the obstacle from my path, entered.

" I stood amazed and astounded.

" A cell of some dimensions was crammed with sacks, eaten away by time, and from whose open mouths poured rivulets of gold, diamond, and other precious stones.

" I had heard that, during the terrible wars of those regions, the defenders of strongholds had, in the provision of defeat, prepared such places of concealment for their ill-gotten wealth, but I had looked on the whole as fables.

" Here was a revelation beyond my wildest dreams.

" My resolution was taken. I would escape, and at any cost I would return and rescue this mass of inert wealth from its hiding place.

" But it was necessary first to reach England.

" I loaded myself with some of the most magnificent diamonds, and took a moderate sum in gold.

" I then returned to my fire.

" I had now the means of prosecuting my inquiries as to the true position of my father, and to lay the train which was to restore me to my true position in society.

" I lost no time. The wall was old, and in a state of partial ruin.

" I clambered up and reached the summit.

" All was still, and at a distance grazing on the plain was my horse.

" With great difficulty I contrived to capture him, and after one glance at the tomb of the unhappy girl, I rode off in the direction of the sea board.

" I travelled chiefly by night, and after several times losing my way, came in sight of the open sea.

" By great good fortune a vessel, which looked

like an English brig, was in sight, stealing cautiously along the land.

"I hastily made a fire, and waved my cap on a stick from the summit of a rock.

"In the distance I could see a crowd of other vessels evidently under convoy.

"A boat put out from the brig, and I ran down to the shore.

"They approached cautiously.

"I shouted aloud in English.

"I was free.

"And now, dearest, pardon me all that happened. But for that unhappy girl we should never have met again. I was to blame, for nothing can excuse infidelity to those we love. But under the circumstances what else could I do?"

"Poor girl," said Lucy, gravely, and then she added with a smile, "and this is why you would not tell me the story until after we were married."

"I did'nt like."

Lucy shook her head.

"And so you are going to venture in search of this wondrous treasure."

"I am, for many reasons," continued the happy husband. "I think it useful that this vast treasure should come into the possession of English holders. Besides, if even I do not obtain my real name and position, I can carve out a new fortune. Thus, I have promised to reinstate Stone in his old position. Besides, there are hundreds I can befriend in England, so say no more about it."

And so it was settled, and the next day the vessel sailed for its destination.

We shall follow the fortunes of the treasure-seekers at a fitting opportunity.*

We return now to other characters in our history, who have been, perhaps, too long neglected in our anxiety to explain the true character of the expedition undertaken by Captain George, when other interests seemed to detain him in England.

CHAPTER CIX.

COMING TO LIFE.

THE first act of Captain William Lennox, on his arrival in Madrid, was to take Lillian to the hotel occupied by her mother, and to send for Dr. Graham.

He learned at once that Mrs. Winterton was recovering.

* In answer to numerous inquiries it is necessary to state that we cannot enter upon the personal history of the Blue Dwarf at present. The mystery in connection with this being *will* be solved. But it is wrapped up so closely with one part of our narrative, that we must fain prorogue any' explanation until the proper time comes.

With regard to the illustration of No. 26 having appeared in No. 25, that is a mere accident, and does not affect the narrative.

The back numbers are always on sale.

She began to be conscious of the fearful misery which was her lot.

Well might she cry with the great poet:—

"From short, as usual, and disturb'd repose
I wake: how happy they who wake no more!
Yet that were vain, if dreams infest the grave.
I wake, emerging from a sea of dreams
Tumultuous; where my wretch'd, desponding thought
From wave to wave of fancied misery
At random drove, her helm of reason lost."

But grief, biting, sore, fearful as it is, will not always kill. Mrs. Winterton regained her senses and gazed wildly around her.

"Give me my clothes" said she to Mary.

The girl looked uncomfortable.

"What is it?"

"But, madam—"

"What?"

"You have no mourning."

"Why was it not procured?"

Mary hung down her head.

"Child," said Mrs. Winterton, "you did not expect me to live; why not say? Wonder, indeed, that I have got over it. Dress me as well as you can."

Mrs. Winterton rose as well as she could, and, aided by the maid, dressed herself.

No sooner was she ready than Dr. Graham was announced.

"My dear madam," said the worthy doctor, in tones of genuine sympathy, "I am delighted to see you up."

"Why, doctor?" she replied in languid and melancholy tones.

"Because your state, madam, began seriously to alarm me," said the doctor.

"What have I to live for?"

"What, madam?" cried Doctor Graham, with a stare of astonishment. "Why, everything to be sure."

Mrs. Winterton stared at him as if she thought that he was mad.

"My dear Mrs. Winterton, your illness was so very sudden that, remaining as you have done six weeks without signs of consciousness, we were not able to undeceive you as to a supposed melancholy event which has recently preyed very heavily on your mind.

"Sir," gasped Mrs. Winterton.

"My dear Mrs. Winterton, do not excite yourself, or I shall tell you nothing."

"Doctor Graham, I am quite calm; do you not see that I am quite calm? Has all this been a horrible dream—a wild phantasm of the brain; and do you mean, do you insinuate, that my Lillian—my own baby girl—lives?"

"I do; now, no fainting. Take this cordial," he continued, pouring out from a small bottle.

The poor speechless mother took it and drained it to the dregs.

Doctor Graham clapped his hands, and, in another moment, mother and child were clasped in each other's arms.

The doctor drew the young officer away and left them alone.

This joy was too unutterable for any one to witness it.

In an hour they were again admitted, and it

being perceived that Mrs. Winterton was quite as calm as could reasonably be expected, a light refection was ordered.

Then Mrs. Winterton asked for an explanation.

"Madam," said the doctor, "your child has gone, during your illness, through terrible trials. Are you prepared to hear them?"

"I am."

"Let me tell them," said William.

"Will it be too much for you?" asked the mother of her daughter, holding her to her bosom.

"No, mother; I will tell all."

And she began.

Mrs. Winterton listened to her with awe, horror, and astonishment. But such was her wrapt eagerness to know all that she never interrupted her until the moment when she described her revivification from the bier in the vault by Slimy Jones and Sir Edgar Blakesley.

"Heaven bless them!" she cried.

"Those who lose know how to find," said William, gravely.

"What!"

"They were but the wicked agents of a wicked woman," continued William.

"What woman!"

"The Duchess of Castella, mother,' interposed Lillian, quietly, "who thought that William loved me too much. But let me continue my story."

She did so, and her mother heard to the end.

"Let us leave this country," cried Mrs. Winterton, wildly.

Lillian looked at William.

"I have my sick leave," he said, "but I must first procure the punishment of the wretches who have caused all this unexampled misery."

"'Vengeance is mine, saith the Lord,'" continued Mrs. Winterton, shaking her head; "let us go and leave them to the reflections of conscience."

"No," said Doctor Graham, "that would be monstrous."

Mrs. Winterton said no more, but taking her daughter by the hand left the room.

The two men began at once drawing up a memorial to the commander-in-chief.

That night the palace of the Duke of Castella was surrounded by a squad of police and other officers.

The duchess was arrested, to the utter astonishment of the whole populace.

CHAPTER CX.

TERRIBLE RETRIBUTION.

NEITHER the English commander-in-chief nor any one else concerned in the tragedy suspected the true cause of the eagerness with which the officers of the terrible Inquisition clutched at the opportunity.

There was a certain officer of high rank in the Holy Office, a man who had gained his position by the outward practice of the most

intense piety, who used this renown, as many have done before him, as a cloak to his debauchery.

Rome, which dares to declare itself the capital of the world, is a sink of abject iniquity.

In no countries is every vice that can disgrace humanity more rife than where Roman Catholicism has full sway.

This officer, Don Tribuera by name, had dared to elevate his eyes to the duchess.

He had once been her father confessor.

Though not particular in her amours she had laughed him to scorn.

Imagine, then, his delight when she was placed in his power.

He had a terrible weapon in his hand.

Without being believers in anything else, both the duke and duchess were notorious scoffers.

This made them heretics.

The duchess was placed in a cell apart, and allowed no communication with any one.

It was a dark and gloomy recess, and admitted no light.

A small lamp from above alone illumined the dreary place.

The beautiful but depraved woman walked up and down with a haughty and defiant manner, as if she cared nothing for her position but the momentary degradation.

She knew not of what she was accused.

She knew that Slimy Jones and his accomplice had sought safety in flight, and therefore feared not their revelations.

She had promised Teresa too stupendous a reward to dread her much.

She forgot Don Tribuera.

It was about dark, when her cell door opened and a jailor entered: he was masked and cowled.

He bore in his hand a platter with white bread on it, and a small bottle of water.

These he placed on the small wooden table of her cell.

He then paused.

"Prepare yourself," he said, in a hollow voice; "this night at twelve the tribunal meets."

"What care I. I am innocent of any crime?" she haughtily replied.

"Woman, beware! Thy sins are manifold, and unless they are repented of, severe will be thy punishment."

"Of what am I accused?"

"First, attempted murder."

"Ah!"

"Then of the abduction of an English girl."

"Go on!"

"All these are as nothing. There is much worse behind," hissed the speaker.

"What?"

"Heresy, and systematic insults of holy church."

The proud and haughty woman shuddered.

"Who are my accusers?" she continued, rousing up her courage.

"The English officer and the commander-in-chief."

"Yes, yes, I know that. But who dares accuse me of heresy?"

"I do," cried the other, removing his mask

and revealing the features of one known in the world as Don Tribuera, in the Inquisition as Father Anselmo.

The duchess turned haughtily away.

The ex-confessor of the duchess was at all and good looking man of a little over thirty ; rather dark and saturnine, and with eyes that burned like coals.

Withal, a most hideous look of the most depraved voluptuary on his countenance.

"Woman," he said, hastily, "you are not in your boudoir now, but in mine."

"Leave me or I will scream."

"Scream, my bird," he continued, with insolent sarcasm, "none will take notice. You little thought the humble confessor was the head of the mighty Inquisition. Tremble ! You are wholly in my power. Woman, in your oratory you drove me forth with contumely, threatened me with stripes ! *with stripes !* do you not recollect. Now, minion, it is my time. Listen to me. Refuse my prayer now, and there is no revenge which shall not be mine. I, too, threaten with stripes now ; do you hear that, my dainty dame, stripes, and on your naked flesh ; stripes inflicted by men, who will not dare raise their eyes to your loveliness ; stripes which will obliterate and destroy it. Then I shall be avenged !"

"Silence, inhuman monster, and go. I fear you not," shrieked the really appalled duchess.

"No ! I am master here, and where once I sued, will have you sue. Listen, madam, I pledge myself that before the night is over you will offer me that which I once humbly asked for."

The duchess turned away to hide her livid pallor.

"Madam, had you hearkened to my humble and devoted love, you had been safe from all your enemies. But you not only repelled, you insulted me. You menaced me with the cudgels of your lowest menials. I will be revenged."

"I defy you," cried the duchess, who appeared losing her head. "I will expose you before the whole tribunal."

"Who will believe a heretic ?"

"They must."

"A wanton and an assassin. Reflect calmly before you drive me to extremities. Have you heard of the tortures of the Inquisition ?"

"All have."

"Can you conceive them ?"

"I can conceive anything of such monsters," she continued.

"This night you shall know them all,' he replied, and without another word left the cell.

CHAPTER CXI.

THE EXAMINATION.

THE Duchess of Castella, as soon as she was alone, endeavoured to collect her thoughts—no easy matter. She now began to view her imprisonment in its true light.

That William Lennox could prove anything against her, she did not for one moment believe.

His accusations must all be founded on surmise.

But hatred is a terrible accuser, and this man both loved and hated her.

Now, in the course of a career neither celebrated by virtue nor morality, the duchess had not been very choice or select in her amours. Not that at any time, perhaps, the good-looking confessor would have been at all unwelcome, but she was engaged at the moment.

She accordingly rejected him, and when he grew angry and threatened, she laughed at him.

When he grinded his teeth, and vowed vengeance, she menaced him with corporal punishment.

And now she was completely in his power.

A half inclination came upon her to feign a consent to his wishes.

But it was humiliating to yield.

And thus, in doubt and perplexity, the hours passed away.

It appeared verging on morning when she was summoned from her cell to attend the dread tribunal, which, under pretence of ruling the State in the name of religion, made itself the vehicle of fraud, vice, and fanaticism.

Two men in masks took her by the arm, and without saying a single word led her away along several long and gloomy passages.

At length they reached a low vaulted archway, with several steps.

Down this they descended. They now found themselves in a large vaulted apartment, at the end of which was a black curtain, which rose as she entered, and disclosed the terrible array of the judges.

They were three, and sat, one above the other two, while in front of them were the secretaries at a table prepared to write.

Behind a crowd of monks the duchess thought she caught a glimpse of Captain William Lennox and Teresa standing apart.

"Prisoner," said a harsh voice which she appeared to know too well, "what is your name ?"

"Maria Celessa Dolores, Duchess of Castella," replied the prisoner.

"Accuser, step forward."

A way was made for him, and William Lennox, pale and agitated, stood forward.

"Do you know this woman ?"

"I do."

"Of what do you accuse her ?"

"I accuse her of employing, first, one Teresa, a servant in the employment of Mrs. Winterton, to give Miss Lillian a drug, which I at first believed to be poison, but which afterwards proved to be a powerful narcotic. Under this influence Lillian was believed to be dead, and was duly buried. Two agents of the duchess then removed her from the church, and after several adventures I found her in the private palace of the duchess at——"

"Come forward, Teresa," said the judge.

She came forward, pale, but evidently resolute.

"What is your name ?"

"Teresa."

"What say you to the accusation ?" continued the judge.

"That it is absurd and ridiculous," said the girl.

"You never administered drugs to the unfortunate English girl?"

"Never."

"You gave her nothing at the instigation of the duchess?"

"Nothing."

"You gave her nothing at any body else's instigation?"

"At nobody's."

"You never administered anything to her?"

"Only her medicine."

"Indeed. You always gave her that?"

"Always."

"Remove her. Now, Maria Dolores, Duchess of Castella, what have you to say to this accusation?"

"That the whole is a perfect absurdity."

"Do you know anything of the accuser?"

"I do."

"What do you know?"

"He was my lover."

A profound sensation was evinced by a kind of murmur in the auditory. The president's eyes flashed fire.

"Young man, is this true?"

"I should not have mentioned it; but as the duchess says so, I own it," said William Lennox, holding down his head, and avoiding the terrible eye of the duchess.

"Then why did you accuse her?"

"My lord, I am the affianced husband of the young lady who has been so terribly tried. In an unfortunate hour, in a moment of infatuation, I contracted with the duchess one of those passing intrigues which never leave anything but remorse behind them. My own belief is that, discovering the falling away of my passion, the duchess, in a moment of frenzy, determined to leave me no hope in any other quarter, by taking away from before my eyes the betrothed of my childhood."

"What say you, duchess?"

The reply was firm, and said in a slightly sarcastic tone, evidently intended for the ear of Father Anselmo only.

"I loved him so deeply that my whole soul was in him. I wished him success and happiness, even in love," she cried.

"What say you, William Lennox?"

"I am sorry to press my belief—it is that of all my friends—the duchess was the instigator of all."

"Know you the punishment."

"I hope you will only detain her until we leave the country."

The masked inquisitors exchanged looks.

"Duchess, do you confess."

"No."

"Then Heaven decide the right! Let the two women be removed to the question chamber." said the president, gravely.

"No!" gasped William Lennox. "Surely in these days there is no torture."

"Silence, young man. You have set the ball rolling, and nothing can stop it."

"But I withdraw the charge, fiends!" shrieked William, in whose bosom the idea of torture had produced a complete revolution.

Two men clutched him, placed something over his mouth, and he fainted. When he came to himself he was alone, but he could hear voices.

He rose and peered through a chink.

The sight which met his eyes was hideous.

CHAPTER CXII.

THE TORTURE CHAMBER.

ALL histories abound in cruelties, especially those histories which treat of priests and kings; but no history tells of cruelty so horrible as that of the lands where the Holy Inquisition flourished.

The power of this tribunal was unlimited.

When a sagacious villain like Don Tribuera had sway, it may reasonably be expected that when women fell into his power he took ample advantage of his privilege.

The torture room——

But why weary our brain for descriptions of such a scene, when every leaf of history affords us one ready to our hand.

Who has not read the narrative in which we are told by a prisoner of what he saw another suffer? Nor was the chamber less calculated to strike terror into his breast than its inmates. It was not the torture-room visited by the unfortunate man when he explored the subterranean passages of the fortress, but another and larger chamber contiguous to the former, yet separated from it by a wall of such thickness, that no sound could penetrate through it. It was square-shaped, with a deep round-arched recess on the right of the entrance, at the further end of which was a small cell, surmounted with a pointed arch. On the side where the examiner sat, the wall was decorated with thumb-screws, gauntlets, bracelets, collars, pincers, saws, chains, and other nameless implements of torture. To the ceiling was affixed a stout pulley with a rope, terminated by an iron hook, and two leathern shoulder-straps. Opposite the doorway stood a brazier, filled with blazing coals, in which a huge pair of pincers were thrust; and beyond it was the wooden frame of the rack, already described, with its ropes and levers in readiness. Reared against the side of the deep, dark recess, previously mentioned, was a ponderous wheel, as broad in the felloe as that of a wagon, and twice the circumference. This antiquated instrument of torture was placed there to strike terror into the breasts of those who beheld it—but it was rarely used. Next to it was a heavy bar of iron employed to break the limbs of the sufferers tied to its spokes.

Who has not read of those hideous experiments upon human life, tried upon the Marchenen de Brenvitheis, who, great as were his crimes, deserved not such treatment?

Who has not read of the press-room at Newgate, and who needs read of all that was to be seen in the brutal cell at Madrid, which had seen such fearful tortures?

The cell was lofty and well supplied with every conceivable instrument the cunning and wickedness of man could devise for the torture of human beings.

The men who accompanied the duchess and her supposed confederate into the cell were four tall and powerful monks, and a man in a tight-fitting dress, all masked.

The judge passed into another cell.

He could see all that passed without being seen.

"Strip them!" he said, in a tone which from the next room sounded hollow and strange.

All started. But no one made the slightest observation.

"Oh, you wretches!" cried Teresa; "you filthy monsters, I'll tear your eyes out!"

"Remember," said the duchess, in a cold dry tone, "that my rank precludes the possibility of such vile conduct."

The men began to tear of their clothes with wondrous dexterity.

Two held each of them, while the executioner, with a pair of scissors, tore their garments to pieces.

It was a brutal—a hideous scene—such as only the perverted imagination, the disappointed vanity of a cowardly churchman, would ever have thought.

Teresa shrieked, struggled, and made the cell resound again with her cries.

The duchess allowed all her charms to be exposed to view with the most superb indifference.

To her such beings were not men.

They were too far beneath her.

Let them boast as they might, no one would believe them.

But she was not at the end of her misery.

They were stripped, and then allowed to wear some prison clothes about their waists.

The executioner took up a scourge.

Teresa yelled, but for some reason or other she did not seem inclined to make any revelation.

She took the flogging, shrieking, crying, supplicating, but yielded not.

The perspiration poured down the bare shoulders of the duchess, but she said not a word.

She was pale, resolute, and clenched her teeth together with savage energy.

Presently a sign came from the inside of the cell.

They ceased.

"Will you confess?" said a voice so hollow that it startled every one.

"No!" replied the duchess.

"The boot!"

Without waiting to clothe the wretched women, now at least on an equality, the monks forced Teresa down upon a seat, and the executioner took up the hideous boot which has so often been used to drag falsehood from an innocent sufferer, who, in the hope of escaping from present misery, has yielded to that which he knew to be false.

The leg of the girl was enclosed in an iron boot right up to the knee. It was a fair knee and leg to look it, even fairer than that of the mistress. But these ruffians cared not. They delighted, like King Bomba of Naples, in the havoc they made.

The executioner raised his hammer, and placed a piece of wood in the shape of a triangle in the top of the boot.

The duchess shuddered.

One blow, she saw, would maim for life.

This terrified her more than the scourging, which could be remedied.

The other would maim for life.

Teresa looked appealingly to her mistress.

"I will confess," said the duchess, holding down her eyes, "but to the chief judge only, in private."

Two cloaks were thrown over them directly, soon obscurity pervaded the cell, the men retired, and the judge coming out, the duchess whispered a word in his ear.

"Certainly, my daughter. The moment an erring child enters the fold, it is entitled to every indulgence. Let them be removed to the apartments above. Let my own surgeon attend them. I will dismiss the tribunal."

William Lennox saw no more. As soon as he was released, he ran home, and hurried their departure.

He began to suspect something very terrible.

Next night they sailed for England, but not before they had heard that the Grand Inquisitor had been found dead in his bed, with a dagger through his heart.

William Lennox shuddered.

Nor did he tell Lillian what had occurred for many a long day, when awful events almost forced him to do so.

END OF BOOK I.

BOOK II.

CHAPTER I.

HUNG IN CHAINS.

THERE is at the extremity of Hampstead Heath, on the way to the ancient village of Highgate, an inn of very old date, known as the Spaniards.

It commands a splendid view.

At the time of which we speak it was much more solitary than it is now.

In those days, or at all events a very short time before, it required an armed body of a dozen sturdy fellows as an escort back to induce men to go and spend an evening with mine host any where, while a night visit to the Spaniards was in winter almost out of the question.

And yet, on such a night, the heath all covered with white and drifting snow, the air bitterly cold, the sky dark and gloomy, and threatening to pour down its wrath with terrible fury on that bleak and deserted region, a man might have been seen advancing in the direction of the Spaniard, from Hampstead, walking as if for a wager, or as if, at all events, he was determined to keep himself warm under the circumstances.

Every now and then he cast a glance to the right or the left.

To the right could just be distinguished by the dull glare of the oil lamps which alone illuminated London in those days, the dim, ghastly outline of the great city.

To the left there was a huge void, black, dark, and terribly gloomy.

The man was tall, and to all appearance stout. He wore a loose cloak, a slouched hat, and was apparently armed only with a heavy stick. He was very well dressed, and strutted like one who was not exactly used to see himself in such good case.

Had there have been a moon, we need not explain that the figure of the man would have cast some kind of shadow on the snow.

As it was he was shadowless.

So are all the Chinese, says a young lady recently imported from that country to Paris. The air she informs us is so bright that shadows will not lie on the ground.

But England is the land of shadows, and hence of beauty.

Now, had the man cast a shadow, it is more than probable that he might have moved a little quicker in consideration of two other shadows rapidly coming up.

They were seedy shadows, men in ragged and ill-fitting garments, something like those worn by tramps on a journey, especially tramps whose stock in trade is a shipwreck, or an escape from a foreign prison.

These men had sticks, and clutched them in their hands nervously.

The man in the cloak had his collar about his ears; and, besides, the snow deadened the sound.

They were close up to him ere they spoke.

"What cheer, messmate?" said one.

"Got such a thing as a shilling about you?" cried the other.

"Just so; no! You infernal vagabonds," cried the man, facing about, and cocking a pistol.

It was very tremulously though.

"I think he said infernal vagabonds?" observed the first speaker.

"Just so."

"He did?"

"Just so."

"You infernal cheating scamp and vagabond! so we've have got you at last," roared the first speaker.

"Just so, Captain Winterton."

"You cowardly tramping vagabond!" added the other.

"Just so, the Honourable John."

"What have you to say why your head should not be knocked off at once, and without further parley?" roared the captain.

"Without further parley!" repeated the Honourable John.

"Just so."

"Here we are escaped with difficulty with our lives, you cheating son of the hulks, while you are warmly dressed and well off."

"Just so."

It was to be remarked that at each outcry they became more noisy, Slimy Jones more tremulous.

"Speak, you vagabond!"

"Just so, my very worthy and approved good masters," began Jones. "If you will hear me, I will prove that after all I am your very best friend."

"It's cold talking here."

"Just so. Close by is an inn. Will you, my masters, join me in a bowl of punch?"

I have an enterprise in hand, which, if you will join me in, we have incalculable wealth before us; your share of *that* money is safe, and you can have it when you please."

"Oh!"

"Ah!"

"We follow your honour. You'll say we're two poor unfortunate prisoners whom you have met by accident on the road, and have offered a meal of victuals to. Make haste, for we're cold, hungry, and starved."

Slimy Jones held himself once more erect. His former masters, whose arrival in England was, to say the least, annoying, could not, however, for the moment be dangerous to him.

They were poor, ragged, and under the ban of the law.

In general, in England poor people are not very dangerous.

They are looked upon somewhat in the light of criminal nuisances.

In the first place, Why are they poor?

In the next place, How dare they be poor?

Why don't you answer, eh! poor wretch starving in a garret.

And you, miserable being, cowering under the Adelphi arches?

But we forget the hunger of the two gentlemen, recently such ornaments in the circle of society in which they lived.

The hospitable Spaniards' Inn is reached : its door, ever open to the wayfarer, except when of a Sunday afternoon the traveller, who has no other day for recreation or enjoyment, would fain wash away the dust from his throat, and may not, because Scribes and Pharisees say it is wicked to eat and drink of a Sunday.

Why not go farther, and forbid the twenty-two shilling port and sherry in private houses between the hours of three and five on the Sabbath ?

They entered the cosy old-fashioned parlour; and Slimy Jones, who was known, went out and told his story to the landlord, who was in raptures with his noble generosity.

It was something out of the common.

He not only sent them in a joint of cold meat, ample supplies of bread, cheese, and beer, but he bought two tolerable coats of the respected host.

Then, ordering his own patriarchal shilling's-worth of brandy and water, he seated himself and entered into conversation.

" Enjoying yourselves—just so. How long have you been in England?" he began.

" Two days."

" Just so. But what brought you out here?"

" Hum—ah ! taking a walk."

" Just so—hard up."

" Hard up, and desperate."

"Just so! Then you are prepared for anything by which you can regain your position in society?"

"Hearken, friend Jones," said Captain Frederick Winterton quietly, "while we were faint and starving, we allowed you to talk in this domineering and impertinent manner. But now just recollect your true position. You have all our money—one-third we are quite willing you shall keep, but if you go on in this way you'll come to grief pretty quickly. So now talk like a sensible man, and as your own is empty, order in three stiff glasses of brandy and water."

"Just so," said Slimy Jones.

The bell was rung, the glasses replenished and the door closed.

"And now, master Jones, what is this cock and bull story of yours?"

"Just so. A lady of rank and title is in search of two men, of gentlemanly appearance, to carry out a scheme of revenge against one who has bitterly injured her. She is very rich, immensely rich—what say you, my masters?"

"Why, my old bully, Jones, what we say is this—yes—and no mistake about it."

"But," began the honourable John.

"No buts. It's all settled. What style of business are we to do."

"Just so—can't say," said Jones, "but time's up."

He looked at his watch and rose.

"Have we far to go?" said the captain, looking wistfully at the fire.

"Just so—no. But we can return and have another glass presently."

The two tramps, who had not been so comfortable for a long time, rose with a sigh, and Jones having paid, followed out into the open air.

He led them back the way they came, and soon turned to the right where some fir trees stand.

These they rapidly skirted and descended into a little hollow, by which they reached a small platform, on which they crouched, smoking their pipes by way of passing the time.

"A pretty rendezvous for a lady to give," said the captain, in a surly tone.

"Just so—very singular—can't be helped—very cold. Just so—her idea, not mine."

"She must have singular motives for secresy," continued the captain.

"Hush," said John.

"What is it?"

"Just so, what is it?"

"It was a strange rumbling noise, just above their heads. They looked up and started to their feet

Above them, on a jibbet, hung a skeleton of a man in chains.

"You scoundrel," said the captain, "what do you mean by this?"

"Just so. Can't help it; her orders very particular," replied Slimy Jones.

"A queer card she must be."

"Don't like it," muttered John.

"Hush! a whistle," said Slimy Jones.

They looked around, and on the level road they saw a carriage, and at no great distance from it, in a hollow, a light.

A second whistle.

"Just so. Now, you keep in the back ground, and when I whistle, follow."

CHAPTER II.

M. DE VERA-CRUZ.

SLIMY JONES walked across the heath in the direction of the light, and there in one of the quarries, whence the neighbours were wont to draw their gravel, stood a figure in a heavy cloak, slouched hat, and mask.

In the hand of this personage was a sword.

"Who comes?" said a melodious voice with a strong foreign accent.

"A friend."

"Of what?"

"The onyx ring."

"Good, advance."

"Just so. I am here," said Jones, staring at the figure.

"Why do you stare?" asked the other, coldly.

"Just so. I expected to meet a lady."

"And you find a man."

"Just so."

"Well, no matter. I am M. de Vera Cruz, her private secretary," the other said.

"Just so."

"Have you done the behest of the onyx ring?" continued the mask.

"I have."

"Where are the men?"

"Yonder."

"Already. Who are they?"

"Just so. My lady knows."

"But I do not."

"Just so. Captain Frederick Winterton and the Hon. John. Very seedy just now; but gentlemen both, and men about town."

"I have heard of them. Let them advance," replied the mysterious stranger.

Slimy Jones turned round and whistled.

The tramps came up, and, despite their costume, the way they bowed showed the society they had been used to.

"Introduce us," said the stranger, haughtily.

Slimy Jones did so in his heavy way.

"Happy to make your acquaintance, Monsieur de Vera Cruz," said Captain Frederick Winterton, lifting his tattered beaver.

"You speak French," rejoined the other.

"And Spanish," responded the captain, with a low bow.

"Gentlemen," continued the other, looking at them through his mask with eyes of fire, "I shall be happy to meet you under pleasanter auspices. *As soon as you have got rid of the dust of travel*, happy to see you at this address. Whether I am there or not, the person who shows you this onyx is the person you desire to see."

And the stranger drew off a glove, and held out a long white hand, on which, by the light of a lantern, glowed a ring.

"You are a long time looking at the ring," said the stranger petulantly.

"I was admiring the hand," replied the captain in a low tone.

"Discretion and silence," said the stranger. "By the way, if my purse——"

"No, Monsieur de Vera Cruz, we have our banker with us," replied the captain.

The stranger bowed, and went away.

"And now Jones," began the captain, " to your lodgings. There we must dress, shave, and prepare for the comedy."

"Just so—my lodgings."

"Our lodgings, rather. To-morrow, when fully equipped, we may seek others. Don't be alarmed about our dress—two officers just escaped from France—all right, eh!"

"Just so. I'm at the Hummums."

"First-rate!—do splendid. By the way, that little affair—pool on the plain, you know?"

Jones shuddered.

"Speak up, man!"

"Just so—aint been heard of in London at all—hushed up."

"All right. Then we'll have a glorious night. What's your little game, Jones—eh?"

"Just so—little game, and so on—retired contractor, and so on."

"And our friend, Forester, eh."

"Just so—taken a contract in Spain; supply the army with boots—cut thief taking."

"Well, move on, and get a hackney."

"Just so—one waiting. Jack Straw and so on," replied Jones.

"That's the ticket. I see it. Tell him to drive like one o'clock. How I do long for a broiled bone and some of Benson's Champagne."

"Just so. Oh, Lord! what a man," and so on, continued Jones.

The others entered the hackney coach, and buried in thought, spoke not a word until they reached the celebrated hotel alluded to.

CHAPTER III.

A NIGHT AT THE HUMMUMS.

IN the hall of this house of entertainment there stood, about eleven o'clock, several of what we should call at the present day heavy swells. They were new fledged men about town; young officers just appointed to crack regiments, whiling away the time previous to their departure for the seat of war; sons of men newly rich, highly desirous of an aristocratic introduction, and, strange to say, all so new to town as to be devoid of that necessary appendage.

They were discussing what to do when the stoppage of a vehicle appeared to announce a new arrival.

All eyes were directed towards the new comers; eye glasses were raised, and everybody was thankful for at least a moment's novel sensation.

Out came Benson and two waiters.

Conceive then the astonishment of landlord, waiters, and "swells," when two ragged dirty tramps, with a coachman's great coat over their red trousers, shoes tied with strings, and battered old hats, entered with as much easy nonchalance as if they had been the First Lords of the Admiralty.

"Beg your pardon," said Benson, barring the way.

"Fetch a constable," said a waiter.

"Brayvo!" cried one or two swells.

"Ah, ah, constable, brayvo," said the first tramp, while the second pulled timidly at his coat tails. "How de do, Benson. Ah! ah!"

"Benson, Sir. Jones, fetch——"

"Very good, indeed," continued the tramp." "And now Mr. Benson, speaking seriously, if you do not know your best customers because they have passed some months in a French prison, and fashion not allowing nakedness, they appear in ratner an outrè style of dress, why we had better go elsewhere."

"Captain Frederick Winterton, as I live," cried the astounded innkeeper.

"The Honourable John," said the head waiter.

"Just so," said Slimy Jones.

"Gentlemen, walk this way," continued Benson, bowing to the ground. "You may recollect that you left several portmanteaus the last time you were here. They may contain some clothes fit for to night."

"Anything for a change," said Captain Frederick, condescendingly; "and now gentlemen," addressing the astounded spectators, "if you are curious to hear something of our adventures and escapes, I dare say Benson will knock us up something in about an hour. It will take us that to wash off Verdun."

All bowed, and the heroes retired.

All at once the company present began to pump the waiters.

"Great cards, sir," said the head; "most wonderfullest in London! See's the very tiptop of all society. Members of every club. Captain's very downy on to the ladies. Great cards, gentlemen—first in London! Played whist once here with an exalted personage and Colonel Thornton for a whole fortnight, and never went to sleep. Cards, sir—knee deep when they gave up!"

The heavy swells listened with admiration, and at twelve o'clock went up.

It would require the combined power of writer and artist to convey anything like an idea of the change which had taken place in the appearance of the tramps.

They had often stayed at the Hummums, and owed a little bill; but they were too good and useful customers to be offended. When in funds they spent like princes, and never went in debt except when out of luck, and then not on a very large scale.

Their trunks had therefore been duly respected, and contained linen and clothes, which by means of a roaring fire were made available.

"You must excuse any deficiencies," said Captain Frederick Winterton, who was better, if not so expensively, dressed than any man present; "to-morrow we shall see what Blum can do."

"Certainly," repeated the Honourable John, once more delighting in an eye-glass.

"Just so," groaned Slimy Jones, who had been cleared of all his loose cash.

The company were now introduced by the oldest among them, Lord Tom Noddy, and to the delight of the cousins was found to be very generally first-rate.

Captain Frederick Winterton had ordered the most *recherché* supper that could be got for money, and that cash.

Benson had outdone himself.

The guests were delighted.

Captain Winterton kept them in roars of laughter, relative to a whole set of fabulous adventures in reference to their escape from Verdun, in which he every now and then appealed without remorse to the Honourable John.

The Honourable John supported him by every choice asseration that came into his head.

Just as the supper ended and the cloth was removed, the story ended, and the captain yawned.

"There," he said, " I declare I'm quite tired. Benson serve more champagne—iced. Port, sherry, and claret for those who like it. What say you, gentlemen, I hav'nt seen a card these— well, since we left England !"

"Hip, hip, hurrah !" cried all present, delighted to be initiated by such old hands.

Strange to say that all present, except Lord Tom Noddy, had escaped the kites, though a better set of pigeons never were congregated together. The truth was, they were all new to town.

Loo—unlimited loo—the most terrible of games, was introduced, and continued until daylight, when the rooks rose; rook the first with above a thousand pounds in his pocket; rook the second with about six hundred; and rook the third with about a hundred.

The pigeons were delighted.

And so were the rooks.

———

CHAPTER IV.

THE INTERVIEW.

NEXT morning the fashionable tailor was summoned at an early hour. This man had made a mint of money out of them by discounting moderate bills, and being their man of straw when they held promissory notes, &c., so that he hailed their return with unfeigned delight.

"Where have you been, captain, all this time ? So delighted."

"Now, Blum, there is no time to lose. We have been regularly in a French prison. Only got to town yesterday. We want two suits by to-night at seven, two by twelve to-morrow."

"They shall be done," replied the tailor, and without a word of unnecessary verbage departed.

At seven the clothes came.

"Now, John," said the captain, "I will go and call upon this Monsieur de Vera Cruz. Do you make up a nice party for to-night. Benson tells me they are going to ask us to supper. Accept in both our names; but mind you we

must lose a little to-night. We have got into a nice covey—sugar them !"

And without allowing the Honourable John to expostulate as to his going also, Captain Frederick Winterton started on his way.

He had hired a chariot, and with this sought the address given him on the card.

It was one of the houses in Portland-place.*

It was a splendid mansion.

At sight of the chariot the door opened like magic, and two tall servants stood in the way.

"Is Monsieur de Vera Cruz at home ?" said the captain.

"He awaits you in the library," replied the menial, ushering him across the hall towards the open portal of a large room.

Monsieur de Vera Cruz rose from a book he was perusing, and advanced with a smile towards the captain.

Both stood for a moment examining the other.

Monsieur de Vera Cruz was elegantly made, with a long oval face, very slight mustaches and whiskers, eye brows indicating great resolution, and a dark, if not swarthy, complexion.

Altogether a very pretty fellow, likely to please that class of ladies who do not go to the other extreme, and admire only the broad shouldered and massive.

Both smiled and both shook hands.

The Monsieur de Vera Cruz bade the other take a chair.

"Do you smoke ?" said the secretary.

"Certainly," replied the captain.

The secretary pointed to a buffet, where stood several boxes of cigars, as well as bottles of wine. The captain took one of each.

Monsieur de Vera Cruz lit a cigarette.

"Now, captain, have you the least idea of what you have to do ?"

"Not the slightest."

"Do you want money ?"

"I do and I do not."

"Explain your riddle."

"If you allude to small sums, I do not. If you allude to large ones, I am extremely anxious to obtain them."

"Then we understand one another perfectly. You shall have each ten thousand pounds if you carry out the plans of my mistress effectually," began the secretary, puffing away at his cigarette.

"Ten thousand ! Now hearken to me, Mr. Secretary : I am the man of action ; my cousin is only a makeweight. Say eighteen thousand for me, and two for him. It is more than he is worth. Besides, he'll lose it all to me in one evening."

"As you will."

"Agreed."

"Now, Captain Frederick Winterton, my mistress has received a deadly insult from a

* Built in 1788, and called after the then Duke of Portland. Although less fashionably inhabited than in these days, it still numbers peers, baronets, judges, and ambassadors among its occupants. One house at the peace was illuminated by M. Otto, the ambassador, with the words "Peace and *Concord*," while the mob, reading "Peace and *Conquered*," broke every window in the house.

man, and she wishes for revenge. Not the ordinary revenge of dagger and cup, but revenge which shall satiate her soul for years: revenge which shall place the victim into a living hell, and hold his being in chains for the rest of his life. This man has dishonoured, betrayed—not in the way your smile conveys—beyond all conception."

"Well, sir?"

"You are to be the instrument."

"I understand. But who are the parties, and what is to be the revenge?"

"The revenge is to be the ruin of a girl he loves, body and soul."

The captain smiled.

"The parties are Captain William Lennox and Lillian, his future bride."

"Hell and d———!" roared the captain, starting to his feet.

The secretary stared.

"Nothing! nothing!" said the captain, reseating himself.

"There is something, and I must know it," said Monsieur de Vera Cruz, with a frown so portentious that even Captain Frederick was alarmed.

"They are my deadly enemies—one keeps me out of sixteen thousand a year, and the other has foiled me in my every attempt to put her out of the way."

"I had heard something of this."

"But how does this interfere?"

"They could——"

And the secretary looked up towards the ceiling, and jerked his thumb upwards.

"Ah!"

"Still there is a way," said the captain, looking keenly at the secretary; "you foreigners are good at disguises. To succeed in this matter, I must be what I am not."

"That might do—shall do," cried the secretary.

"When shall I begin?"

"To-morrow. My mistress and I will lay down our plans."

"I must see her before I stir a step. I declare most solemnly that once in her service I will be faithful and true to the last. But if I am not trusted——. What would Captain William Lennox and Mrs. Winterton pay to know that?"

"What!" said Monsieur de Vera Cruz, as if feeling for a dagger.

"Shall I tell you?"

"Yes!"

"In your ear—"

The captain whispered.

M. de Vera Cruz fell back, with his eyes almost starting from his head.

"You are a clever and a dangerous man. You shall see my mistress."

Monsieur de Vera Cruz rang.

A domestic appeared.

"Show this gentleman up, and let the countess know that he wishes to see her."

And the secretary reseated himself.

The groom of the chamber merely bowed, went up stairs, opened a door leading into a superb suite of apartments, and announced her name.

Captain Frederick Winterton to see the Countess Remona Areghi-Alcanor.

CHAPTER V.

THE COUNTESS ALCANOR.

THERE rose from a couch a somewhat striking person, about nineteen years of age, dark, handsome, with beautiful hair, arched eyebrows, and an odd mincing way. She was superbly dressed, but wore her dress ill.

"What seek you?" she said in Spanish.

"I seek to see the Countess Alcanor."

"Well, and your business?"

"My business is only with the Countess Alcanor. Pray tell her I am here," said the captain, with a look, however, of admiration.

"I tell you, Sir," she began.

Captain Frederick said one word, upon which the lady flew, and in a few minutes another entered.

The countess was tall. Her hair was black as jet, which made her face look pale when not excited; when excited a beautiful expression rose to her cheeks, and her dark eyes seemed to glow and sparkle with some internal fire.

Altogether she was a superb specimen of female humanity.

"So, sir, you must behold the real star ere you pay homage," she said with a smile.

Captain Frederick Winterton knelt, took her hand, and kissed it. As he did so his eyes fell on the onyx ring.

"There is no other," she said.

"Then—"

"When I send my secretary on special errands, I let him wear it in token," continued the countess.

The captain bowed.

"I have undertaken your mission, madam, upon certain conditions," he said.

"But my secretary has not told you one half of my plans," she continued smiling, "so if you will ring yonder bell, we will take coffee. Have you dined."

"I dined early on purpose to be at your service, madam," added the captain.

"You are very gallant," laughed the countess.

Frederick Winterton showed his teeth in his laugh—and they were very good teeth—as he rose to ring the bell.

The countess leaned upon her hand and reflected deeply.

A very peculiar smile lingered over her face as she followed the captain with her eyes; a sneering smile, and not a very promising one for the worthy, who, undoubtedly good looking as he was, was rather in the sear and yellow leaf, not from age but from dissipation.

Have you not seen a cat play with a mouse? Who has not?

Which was the cat, and which was the mouse?

The beautiful countess was about seven or eight and twenty, and even more perfect in her beauty than foreign women of that age are—when generally in hot climates they become slightly *passe*.

Not old and ugly like American women, but a little faded.

The bloom at all events is gone.

The countess had been standing; she now took a *causeuse*, which admitted of a half sitting, half reclining position, showing off, too, her splendid figure to admiration.

The captain took a stool and reclined at her feet—at a respectful distance.

The sham countess entered.

"Coffee," said the lady Alcanor, in a sharp, quick tone of voice.

The girl retired with a very submissive air, which the captain pretended not to see.

"And now, Captain Winterton," continued the countess, drawing forth a packet of cigarette paper, and rolling it up with true professional art, "there are one or two particulars into which my secretary has not fully entered."

"May I smoke," said the captain.

"Certainly; do I not set the example?"

"There are very fine cigars in the library."

"Bah! not half so good as those in yonder cheffonier.

The captain smiled to find the lady armed at all points, rose and fetched the cigars.

"And now, Captain Frederick, you have been told of the cause of my journey to England?"

"I have."

"And the persons my enmity is directed against?"

"I knew them."

"Have you been told why?"

"I have not, but I know."

"You know?"

"I should like to have been there."

"Silence, not a word, but how did you know?" she said with glaring eyes.

"A low drunken fellow, a sort of executioner employed in the Inquisition, boasted in presence of a lot of men of what he had seen," said the captain quietly. "I was in the room in disguise."

The countess rose and stalked across the room pale as death.

"Was any name mentioned?"

"None."

"How did you know?"

"I did not even guess until William Lennox's name was mentioned in connection with it."

"It is well. Captain, keep the secret, and all will be well. Let it be breathed elsewhere, and we are deadly enemies."

"I am discretion itself," continued Frederick Winterton.

The attendant brought coffee, and for a little while there was silence. Then the countess quietly unfolded her plans.

Reckless and profligate as was the adventurer, even he shuddered and hoped that he might never offend the beautiful tigress before him, at whom, however, he gazed also with a kind of savage admiration.

To disguise his fear he discussed her plans, and even made some suggestions.

They were adopted; for, inspired by the infernal genius of the woman, he had improved upon her diabolical invention.

In the first time in her interviews she generously smiled upon her coadjutor.

They understood one another, and that night Captain Frederick Winterton departed, not without substantial rewards in the shape of money, and the promises of many others.

First, however, he had to provide the theatres on which to play his several parts.

There was to be no violence used. The victims were to be entrapped by cunning.

The deeds of the gallant colonel were to be as varied as they were monstrous and wicked.

But we shall not enter into any explanations; the whole of this fiendish and terrible plot will be unwound as we proceed.

There is nothing in the world so terrible as the revenge of a woman. It is horrible, remorseless, without pity or mercy.

Her satellites were utterly unprincipled, and without one regard for God or man.

CHAPTER VI.

JOE SPRIGGINS.

JOYOUSLY they trod the soil of England, for the sea air had done them good, and there appeared no longer any dread of the future.

Their enemies were left behind in a far distant land, and hence were harmless.

We speak of Lillian and William, of John Horne and Mary, and of Mrs. Winterton, once more a joyous and hopeful mother.

Her child was restored unto her, and what other mercy could she ask?

The first blow to the felicity of William Lennox was the discovery that the Blue Dwarf was absent from town. He was not to be found at the address he always left, nor had any tidings been heard of him for some time.

Apprehending some fearful danger, William Lennox persuaded Mrs. Winterton and Lillian to keep as close as possible in humble lodgings, while he, discarding all military appearance, determined to change his name and reside in obscurity.

Mary remained with the Wintertons; Jack Horne, who had leave of absence, followed his master.

The simple fact of the unaccountable disappearance of the Blue Dwarf, *without whose consent he could not marry*, threw such a gloom over the whole atmosphere as to leave William Lennox in constant dread.

Little did William Lennox dream what terrible trials his guardian friend was enduring.

They had all gone to a quiet, respectable inn on their arrival, from which they sallied forth in search of furnished apartments.

The ladies found theirs in a humble street out of Tottenham-court-road,* but William Lennox—he dreaded he knew not what—told John Horne to take two rooms of a lower grade still.

---

* A market road leading to the prebendal manor of Tothill, Totenhall, or Tottenham Court, described in "Doomsday Book," and originally belonging to the Dean and Chapter of St. Paul's, demised to Elizabeth in 1560. Some very curious records exist of this place.

The honest soldier went about, and though loth to degrade his master by too humble a selection, still in obedience to his commands, and aware of the real danger which existed, selected at length two rooms at the back of a house in the classic region of St. Giles.*

They were by no means pleasant rooms, but they certainly were in a locality least likely to be suspected.

The house had abundance of lodgers, but of that anon.

William Lennox first paid a visit to the Horse Guards, and after a brief conference with the secretary, obtained unlimited leave.

Then he bore a letter from the commander-in-chief, which was all influential.

He then visited his dear friends, now Mrs. and Miss Wilton, and spent the evening.

Jack Horne retired to prepare his master's apartments.

It was ten o'clock when William Lennox left his friends to their repose, and sallied forth armed with a big stick and a brace of pocket-pistols towards his new abode.

William Lennox, he knew not why, was sad. Horrible misgivings were on his soul. He had felt such vast elation on his arrival in England, that when his guardian and friend was found to be absent, his spirits fell as much as they had risen.

Such is life until we reach that bourne—

"Where time and pain and chance and death expire!"

He strolled along until he reached the region where the wisdom of his attendant had established his domicile.

After one or two inquiries he seemed approaching the locality, when a sudden and heavy groan attracted his attention.

He looked about, but could see nothing. He listened, and the groan was repeated.

This time he saw that it proceeded from a door-step—that of a dark and gloomy-looking house.

There was not a soul visible in the street.

William Lennox had heard of so many London tricks, that he was cautious for a man of his age.

He peered into the dark and gloomy doorway, and saw a ragged, forlorn, dirty bundle of rags, that appeared to be a boy, groaning as if he were dying.

"Well, what is it, my lad?" said William.

The lips moved, but gave forth no articulate sound.

William Lennox looked warily round, but seeing no one shook the lad by the arm.

"Well, cheer up lad, what is it?"

"Water—bread," muttered the boy.

"Good God—starving!" cried William.

Starving! yes, young man; starving in this great and wealthy city.

* This parish, once famous for its rookery, could once also show its pound, its cage, its round-house, watch-house, whipping-post, and gallows. Vain precautions! Its church was robbed of its communion plate twice.

Look down, ye stars, and tell us what you see of a night in the mighty Babylon! Not all vice, as many would have it, but sheer desperate battling for the breath of life, and not a crust of bread!

Starving! What was that woman doing, we should like to know, who was found dead at the door of Marylebone workhouse on Christmas-day, 1860?

Aged seventy!

She died of cold and want, *outside* a work-house door.†

Why was she not in the inside?

But the boy is still starving on the door-step.

"Can you walk, my lad, eh?" said William Lennox; "I will give you food."

"Can't walk."

"Do you know where Coal-street is?"

The boy nodded.

"Show me the way," said William, lifting up the lad in his arms, as if he had been a feather—he was truly what is called a light weight—and bearing him on before him, they soon under the boy's guidance reached the street.

It was a dismal, narrow lane, rather than a street.

William Lennox had wrapped his cloak round the boy, who apparently revived, was able to stand by the time they reached the door.

"You don't live here?" he muttered.

"I do; but ask no questions."

By this time he had opened the door with his latch key, a privilege obtained by paying his rent a month in advance.

"That you, sir?" said a husky voice.

"All right, Jack," replied the young officer.

He closed the door, and supported his burden up stairs.

"Hallo, sir! what's this?" said Jack.

"A poor, starving lad I picked up," replied the young officer.

"Oh!" said Jack, with a contemptuous glance at the lad.

William Lennox laid the boy in the arm chair meant for himself, and then very peremptorily told Jack to get on with the supper, which he saw was nearly ready. The honest forager had provided tea, beer, brandy, eggs, chops, and kidneys.

"An egg first," said William.

He then took a teaspoonful of brandy and poured it down the boy's throat.

He heaved a heavy sigh, and looked around.

It was a regular London boy of about fourteen; fair, pug nosed, and good looking, though evidently exhausted and weak. The features were not exactly so much pinched as softened by suffering; and the eye, which was sunken, had evidently once sparkled with mirth and jollity.

His dress, though ragged and dirty, was warm, and covered him thoroughly, though evidently not made for him.

William Lennox, he knew not why, thought he had seen better days, and already felt an interest in him.

† *Daily Papers, Jan.* 10.

He gave him an egg and some tea, which the boy eat slowly and without imprudent eagerness.

As he did so, despite the dirt which begrimed his face, his colour came, and produced a remarkable change in his countenance; he appeared quite a good looking lad.

"Can you manage a chop?" said William.

The boy gave a joyous smile, and nodded his head.

"You eat your supper, sir," said Jack Horne in a surly tone, "I can wait upon him."

"All right, Jack," cried William, laughing.

"Don't laugh at me sir; it aint the place of an officer and a gentleman to be waiting on——"

"Joe Spriggins," said the boy, gravely, and at the same time glancing earnestly about the room.

William Lennox seated himself at the table, and began, in deference to the will of his servant—too often our masters—to eat his supper, though all the while his eyes were fixed upon the boy.

"Feel better now, my lad?"

"Yes, sir."

"How did this come about?"

"Long story, sir. Turned out of my crib, cause I could'nt tip the blunt. Must a thieved or begged—tried the last—never got a half-penny."

"Then you've nowhere to go?" said William Lennox, rather ruefully.

Jack Horne made a hideous grimace.

"Oh! never mind that, sir," cried the lad, "as soon as I've done eating I can walk about. I'm used to it—have been for years."

"You shall not go out this night. I'm an old campaigner. You shall have Jack's bed in the next room, and Jack will lie down here. I have long letters to write."

"See you d—— first!" said Jack.

"Sir."

"If this young varmint takes my bed I'll sit up, sir—I know my place," continued the sturdy dragoon.

"Jack Horne," remarked William, drily, "if my orders are disobeyed, I must go out."

Jack made no reply, but took his supper.

"Oh! sir," cried the boy, scarcely able to restrain his tears, "you are too good. I never had a friend afore. I'll do anything—run errands."

"My parquisite."

"Brush your boots."

"The varmint."

"Shew you every crib in London—do anything you like, for you're the first person as has spoke kind to me for years."

"We'll see, my boy," said William, smiling, "and now that you've had enough, go to bed in the next room. Its yours for to-night. In the morning we shall see what has to be done."

The boy rose with a bright colour, took his candle and went into the next room.

Jack Horne, who was very sulky, cleared away the tea things, placed a kettle on the fire, put a bottle of brandy on the table, a glass, sugar, and a spoon, and then taking off his outer clothes lay down upon the bed.

In a few minutes the tired soldier was fast asleep and snoring

William Lennox filled his glass and wrote a long letter to the Blue Dwarf to be forwarded to him through his agents.

In this way an hour or two passed.

Then once more William Lennox heard a groan.

He started. It came from the next room. Afraid the lad was ill, he took a light, shaded it with his hand and went in. The boy had not undressed, but lay on the bed covered by the counterpane.

He was dreaming, for though in a deep sleep he wept, talked, and groaned.

William Lennox loosened his coarse neck tie which was tied tight round his neck and the groaning ceased.

The young officer then slowly left the room, seated himself by the fire and smoked a pipe. For the rest of the night his eyes were fixed intently on the fire, while indistinct mutterings passed his lips.

About eight, the lad still sleeping, Jack Horne rose, and Willian Lennox sent him out to post his letters, and bring in, from a ready made warehouse, a suit of clothes for Joe.

"Without measure," said Jack, drily.

"Jack," replied William, poking the fire and avoiding the look of the sturdy dragoon, "you are more my body guard than my servant. You must watch over me, keep your eye on my enemies. I want a lad to run of little errands, and do odd jobs. This boy will do. Find him a room up stairs."

"Very good," said Jack.

And he went out half pleased, half annoyed.

Then William Lennox knocked at the door of the bedroom.

"Eh—what—fire," said a voice which made William Lennox start.

He seemed to have heard it before.

"Time to get up," cried William.

There was no reply for some minutes, and then the door opened, and Joe Spriggins came out, looking at least a hundred per cent better than on the previous night.

"Aint you been to bed, sir," he said, timidly?

"No," said William.

"Won't you now, sir?"

"No."

"Are you angry?"

"Yes."

"Why?"

"You are not what you seem. You have deceived me," said William, severely.

"Oh, sir—not I, sir, I assure you, sir."

"Tell me your true history and name."

The boy raised his eyes and looked the young officer full in the face.

William Lennox met his look with a peculiar glance the other was not able to endure.

"I will tell you all."

"Sit down," said William Lennox most kindly.

He felt a strange and irresistable impulse towards the youth.

CHAPTER VII.

JOE SPRIGGINS' HISTORY.

"I will tell you my story," said the girl.

"I listen," said William.

"I am the only child of a clergyman. As you have already discovered, I am a girl."

"Just so," said William, almost blushing.

"I was born," continued the girl, "in Arlen Grove, a little village in the beautiful county of Devonshire, of which my father, the Rev. Charles T. Browne, was perpetual curate.

"Being the only child of my father, as I have said, I was allowed unlimited freedom; and in the summer evenings I was always, from childhood, accustomed to stroll along the shady lanes and crested slopes which led up to the hills of Denmare.

"We saw little company—we were anything but wealthy. My father, though the guardian of a large flock, was dependent entirely upon one of those small pittances which the Church of England is not ashamed to bestow upon its ministers.

"There are poorer than the poor. My father, therefore, who idolised me, was very pleased that I should have opportunities of seeing a little society; and I therefore spent sometimes two evenings a week at the house of

Mrs. Goodwin, a widow lady who lived near the vicarage.

"Mrs. Goodwin was a pleasant, kind woman.

"But she let lodgings."

"Just so, as my friend Slimy Jones used to say," remarked William, "a decided objection."

"I thought so, too," continued the girl, "and I have had reason since then to regard it as a fatal circumstance.

"One evening, as usual, I walked up the green path which led to the ivy-mantled porch.

"Mrs. Goodwin came out smiling to meet me.

"'Jessie,' she cried, 'I have at length been successful. I have found a lodger.'

"'Have you?' I immediately answered; 'who is he?'

"'Well,' said Mrs. Goodwin, as we sat down before the blazing fire in her parlour, 'he is a young single man. He says he is an artist, and has come down here to sketch the beauties of Denmare. He is very handsome, and also very agreeable. He is to board with me, so that you will see him presently.'

"I had been little in the society of men, and I may therefore confess to you that my girl's heart fluttered at the idea of being introduced to a handsome stranger; and I was not at all sorry when at length the servant entered, and announced Mr. Alfred Bennett.

"He was a tall, handsome man, apparently about thirty, with light hair, and dark blue eyes.

"He bowed hastily to Mrs. Goodwin.

"He then gazed intently on me, and remarked—

"'I was not aware you had a daughter, Mrs. Goodwin.'

"This is not my daughter, sir," said Mrs. Goodwin, "this is Jessie Browne, the daughter of our clergyman."

"We had a very pleasant evening. Mr. Bennett paid particular attention to me, and I went away with the impression that he was struck with my appearance. Whether I was pleased or not with his attention I know not, for although he was handsome, although he seemed intellectual, and most intimately versed in all the graces of society, there was something in his eye which made me entertain a feeling of fear for him.

"I suppose I was under a kind of fascination.

"I went again and again to Mrs. Goodwin's.

"I had a great taste for drawing, and it was not long ere I accompanied Mr. Bennett on his mountain rambles; upon which my friend, of course, attended us.

"Mr. Bennett paid little regard to Mrs. Goodwin, and appeared to me also to care very little what scenery he sketched, or, in fact, whether he sketched at all.

"This was of course very flattering to me.

"I saw in his distraction nothing but an increasing admiration for myself.

"This idea was confirmed when, after a month's acquaintance, he obtained, through Mrs. Goodwin, an introduction to my father.

"My father did not like his new friend, but as he appeared an excessive admirer of mine, and seemed a gentleman, he received him cordially, and from that evening Alfred Bennett was a constant frequenter of our circle.

"He made no definite proposal to me: but we somehow or another were regarded as lovers, and in the long spring evenings we were always together, either sitting without lights by the embers of a fire, or wandering along the lanes, whose hedges were just budding into beauty.

"My father knew me to be ambitious, and fancied that my liking for Alfred arose from the fact that I detected in his air and manner something above the station he assumed.

"Whether I did so or not I cannot say: but my love for him, if it was love, was throughout tinctured with a kind of dread, which should have forbidden me to dream of happiness.

"Only in his expression of wild, unrestrained passion for me, did he appear at home.

"There was no mention of a future.

"It was all in the present.

"He loved me, he said, and that was all he would admit.

"In my girlhood's dreams I had always had visions of a happy home—humble it is true, but still happy—of a husband who would be the altar of a pure domestic love, of children who would be our pride and our delight.

"But Alfred spoke only of love.

"He seemed to ignore entirely the idea of a home.

"He was passionately fond of me, he declared, but he never spoke of marriage.

"This I did not notice then; but I notice it now."

"Just so," said Lennox, sententiously; and gazing with a puzzled expression at Jessie's face.

"It was a very happy time with me, however," she continued, "and I can even now look back to it with pleasure.

"He was very kind to me; and I, poor fool, felt honoured by the preference of a man so much older than myself.

"At length the wished-for moment arrived.

"It was a lovely evening in May when we ascended one of the upper slopes of Denmare to gaze upon the sunset.

"My companion was peculiarly taciturn that night.

"My heart trembled.

"Not with fear, however.

"I guessed what was coming, and rejoiced.

"The sun went down in gorgeous splendour. The sky seemed like a sea of fire; and as the day-god disappeared he seemed to be engulphed in crimson billows, which broke their silvery spray against rocks of gold.

"'Look, Alfred,' I cried in rapture, 'is it not beautiful that gorgeous sunset, and see how the gray clouds come surging over the blue hills. Have you not your pencil here?'

"'No, love,' he answered, 'but come; I can remember all this. Let us sit down here. I have much to say to you.'

"We sat down on a fallen tree.

"He took my hand—he gazed into my face, and, slipping his arm round my waist, pressed me tightly to his breast.

"'Jessie, my own,' he said, 'you know I love you?'

"My look answered him.

"'Will you be mine?'

"'Yes.'

"'When?'

"'When you please, Alfred.'

"'Then, will you fly with me to-night?'

"I started up, and gazed at him wonderingly.

"'Fly with you, Alfred,' I cried, 'what do you mean?'

"'I mean, love,' he said, drawing me on his knee, and kissing me again and again, 'I mean, love, that you have promised to be mine; and that I am ready to leave this place with you to-night. A post-chaise will be ready for us at ten at the "Grapes Inn," and will take us direct to London.'

"'But, Alfred,' I answered timidly, 'I do not see the necessity for all this. My father will not oppose our marriage, why then cannot we be married here?'

"'Married,' he muttered between his teeth, 'what does the girl mean?'

"'Let me go,' I cried, struggling to disengage myself from him; 'let me go. I thought you were an honourable man.'

"'Come, Jessie, do not be foolish. I have done nothing to offend you—oh!—well—if you will not stop—there sit down by yourself, and listen to me.'

"I did sit by myself.

"How I could sit there I know not; for each moment I felt as if I should have sunk into the earth with shame.

"'Now, Jessie, I will not ask you again if you know I love you. You know I do. My heart—my fortune, for I am rich—my whole future is yours; but I cannot marry you.

"'I am not what I seem.

"'I am not an artist. I am the son of a nobleman, and I am bound down by law to marry another. You, however, will always be to me the true wife of my heart; you will be my beloved, and will be the real partner of my happiness. Do take pity on me. If it were not an impossibility I would offer you marriage; but seeing that I cannot, will you still be mine?'

"I listened to him because my tears choked me; but his last words were quite enough.

"I rose up indignantly.

"'No, Alfred,' I cried, 'my love for you is gone. I regard you as a traitor and a deceiver. No! I will never be yours, even if the separation were to break my heart.'

"He pleaded much; but it was of no avail.

"There, at least, I was firm.

"'Do not utterly despise me,' he said, at parting; "let me see you once again—once more—and I can then leave here comparatively happy.'

"'I will see you once more,' I answered.

"'To-morrow night, then,' he said, 'at the corner of Beech Tree-lane at nine.'

"'I will come.'

"And so we parted.

"Poor fool!

"'Once more,' I said.

"Alas! it takes women two-thirds of their lives to discover that men can admire without respecting them!"

———

CHAPTER VIII.

"ONCE MORE!"

"So I consented to see him once more.

"And at the corner of Beech-Tree-lane on the following night I punctually kept my appointment.

"Alfred was there first.

"As I came up the lane I saw his cloaked figure passing hurriedly—anxiously up and down the opening of the road.

"He seemed greatly delighted when I came up to him.

"'I was almost afraid,' he said, 'that you would play the truant.'

"'I never fail; I always keep my word,' I emphatically answered.

"'No, don't talk like that, Jessie,' he cried, passionately. 'I was mad last night—forgive me. I did not mean what I said—I did it only to try you. I will marry you! You shall—in spite of friends, in spite of everything—be my wife. But it can be done quietly, and at once. A post-chaise awaits us in Arlen Grove; we will fly to Scotland, and be there married. I will send to your father, and he will know of our marriage as soon as it is consummated; but for the sake of my property I must not yet marry you openly.'

"This and much more he said to me, and I began to yield.

"'But, my father,' I said; 'cannot I see him before we go?'

"'NEVERMORE!' whispered a voice near me.

"I started like a guilty thing.

"But it was only fancy.

"It was but the croaking of an old raven, which had perched on the wayside post.

"'There is no time,' said Alfred; 'besides, if you were to return home, your heart would misgive you.'

"My heart misgive me! Heaven help me! could it misgive me more than it did at that very moment?

"'Oh! Alfred,' I cried, in a broken voice, 'how can I trust you, after all you said last night? How can I believe that you will guard me, and protect me as you used to promise that you would, when yesterday you feared to marry me?'

"But I suppose destiny ordained that I should go; for, after a great deal more persuasion, I dried my eyes and went.

"Went!

"Where?

"And so, into the blind darkness of that starless night we plunged.

"Away we sped.

"Away, away, away!

"Away from home, from father, from friends—from everything I held most dear in life.

"And with whom?

"With a man whose very name I knew not.

"We rode on all night; changed horses at the post town in the morning, and, only stopping to make a hasty breakfast, proceeded again on our way.

"I constantly inquired of my companion where we were.

"At each stage I grew more anxious, and uneasy; but he easily quieted my fears.

"He was very kind; and as I had never been more than twenty miles beyond my native village, it was a matter of no difficulty to deceive me.

"At length one night we pulled up with a dash at the entrance of a house.

"It seemed to stand alone.

"Far and near, as I stepped out of the carriage, I could discover no sign of human habitation.

"The bright stars looked down upon an apparently endless plain—broken here and there only by diminutive hedgerows and the silver wanderings of some tiny stream.

"The house itself was surrounded by high walls, and its projecting windows looked dismally down upon a courtyard in front—and behind a large uncultivated garden, whose beds were undistinguishable from the lawn as the lawn was from the paths.

"When we drew up at the door only one light was visible in the house.

"It was in a top attic, where some one appeared to be watching for our approach.

"Before, however, I entered the courtyard, every room in the building seemed to be illuminated, and even that gloomy waste appeared suddenly invested with life and brightness.

"I was received at the door by an elderly lady, who smiled benignly, or rather pityingly, upon me, and led me into the drawing-room, which was lighted up, and apparently ready to receive me.

"My fatigue and fear banished all ideas of politeness, and I said, very abruptly—

"'My bedroom, please, at once.'

"'Poor thing! You must be tired,' said the lady; 'come with me.'

"And I was just going to follow her up to my room, when an arm seized me, and a voice said, reproachfully—

"'Now, then, Jessie, are you not going to say good night to me first?'

"Alfred kissed me fondly—pressed me in his arms, and whispered some words in my ear, which, though imparting to me a kind of happiness, brought with it an extraordinary amount of fear.

"'Good night, dear Alfred,' I said. 'I am *so* tired. We shall be better friends to-morrow.'

"'I hope so,' he said, significantly.

It was not long before I undressed myself, and crept into bed. I had not rested properly for four nights. I had, it is true, rested each night on Alfred's breast, but the rush of the carriage, and the jolting and rumbling of the wheels, prevented my taking any real repose. Sleep now came to me easily. It was a heavy, but a feverish sleep. I tossed and tossed in my bed, and I have no doubt called aloud many times. Terrible visions floated across my brain.

"Visions there were of early childhood—of my first days of love—of Alfred's terrible announcement to me on the slopes of Denmare.

"And there were visions, too, of scenes which I had not witnessed—the anguish of my father—the curse, perhaps, he might hurl after a child who had fled from him who had never restrained or thwarted her in anything.

"Visions of the past, these!

"But there were visions of the future also.

"I had scarcely before thought of the wrong I had done; but I now saw it all in its terrible clearness.

"Conscience—though it may sleep while you are awake—awakes when you sleep: and now, in my dreams I experienced all the tortures which I deserved, but had not before anticipated.

"I saw myself deceived—discarded—ruined.

"I saw myself ruined—body and soul—and yet, as in dreams it always is, I could stir neither hand nor foot.

"When I awoke, a bright spring sun was smiling in through my window on to my little bed.

"I got up, partially dressed myself, and gazed out.

"My eyesight had partially deceived me the night before.

"The house to which I had been conveyed was not in the centre of a barren waste, as I had imagined it to be.

"Within a quarter of a mile the blue smoke of a village curled itself into the morning air.

"I was at least within reach of other human beings.

"I was reflecting upon my condition, and wondering whether Alfred could deceive me after all, when a servant girl entered.

"'Shall I bring you up some breakfast, Miss?' she asked.

"'Yes,' I said, mechanically, 'but stay—where is this house situate? what village is that?'

"The question was asked so suddenly that she had no time to prevaricate.

"'It is Framley, in Surrey, Miss—about nine miles from London.'

"'That will do,' I faintly said, and as she left the room I sank back upon the bed.

"London!

"Nine miles from London!

"I was then deceived!

"Alfred, after all his vows and protestations, had then betrayed me.

"But I would not even then entirely blame him.

"I hoped he would yet prove that this *ruse* was but an anticipated plan."

CHAPTER IX.

THE FALL OF THE IDOL.

"I WENT down into the drawing-room about twelve o'clock. Alfred was there, smoking and gazing indifferently out of the window.

"'Good morrow, my pretty one,' said he.

"I recoiled from him.

"'We are not in Scotland,' I said, 'we are in Framley, near London.'

"'Who told you that?'

"'The servant girl—but no matter, I need

not implicate any one. I should soon—I must, soon have found it out.'

"'You speak truly.' he said quietly and slowly ' you speak truly. You would soon—you must soon have found it out. You understand it now —so all is well.'

"'Understand what, sir ?' I cried, standing before him and gazing at him with all the contempt which an injured woman can concentrate into a look.

"'Don't be foolish, Jessie. You must know what I mean. Come here, sit down beside me, and I will explain to you everything.

"'Thank you, sir,' I said, 'I listen, and can remain here.'

"'Well, then,' he continued, knocking the ashes from his cigar, 'you must have been mad to think that I could marry you.'

"'I must,' I answered quickly, and looking at him contemptuously.

"'I am, as I said, the son of a nobleman. I have a large fortune, but that fortune I should lose if I were to marry any but the one my father has chosen. You will always be the queen of my heart, always be my own Jessie— come, do not look so sad, but say you will consent to be mine.'

"Need I say that I rejected his offer with indignation ?

"Need I tell you that my blood boiled within me when I heard these insults ?

"Need I tell you that I hated and despised him as much as I had formerly loved him ?

"I told him at once, determinedly firmly, that under such circumstances I would never be his : and that even if he offered to marry me, I would never be his.

"I told him I would leave the house at once —that I would return home—that I would not betray him : but that go I must, and that immediately.

"At this he only laughed.

"He had caged me well !

"'You must not talk of returning home,' he said, rising and gazing down triumphantly upon me. 'You seem to forget that you have been for four days absent from home with a single man. What will they say at Arlen Grove? What will your father think? Are you so great a deity that they will believe you pure where they would swear others to be false? Can you expect more pity—more trust— than hundreds of other girls who have placed themselves in even less perilous positions than this ?'

"All this was very crushing; but, girl as I was, I knew how to resent it.

"'Alfred,' I said, 'you have me to a certain extent in your power. You need not insult me. But remember this, that neither as your mistress, nor as your wife, will I ever be yours.'

"And so saying I quickly left the room, and retired to my chamber.

"From that moment I was strictly watched.

"I scarcely saw Alfred for two days; but upon the third day he entered my bed-room, and locking the door, said—

"'Now, Jessie, this must come to an end. Will you, or will you not, consent to my terms ?'

"I answered him not.

"I was sitting by the open window, gazing out at the dusky day-break.

"I had my back towards my tempter, and did not turn when he spoke.

"He placed his hand upon my shoulder and gently shook me.

"'Don't you hear me, Jessie ?'

"I recoiled as if from the touch of a serpent.

"I felt as if all the hate of years had concentrated itself into my heart.

"I gazed now at him with a look which would have daunted a lesser villain than he, while I replied—

"'I hear you, sir; and that fact alone is sufficient to make me desire your absence.'

"'This is all folly,' he said, passionately, 'folly of the direst kind. This must cease. I am not to be trifled with for ever.'

"'What can you do, sir?' I asked, gazing calmly at his face.

"'Why ask so silly à question,' he answered, as petulantly as a child. 'You are here in my power—helplessly, hopelesly in my power. You can by no mortal means escape; and the very best thing you can do for your own sake is to yield at once.'

"Need I tell you I refused; and need I tell you, also, that he took an oath, a solemn and terrible oath, that come what might I should be his ?

"A sudden thought then struck me.

"I might escape.

"But how ?

"My tempter was there.

"He was still pacing the room.

"I at once hit upon a scheme.

"I would deceive him.

"I would pretend to yield, and thus render him less watchful.

"'Will you be kind to me, dear Alfred,' I said, gazing up at him with as much of treacherous affection as I could command.

"'My charmer !' he cried, rushing up to me, and covering me with his loathsome kisses, 'I will be kind to you. How can you ask me such a question? Trust me, and I will be the kindest, the best of men to you.'

"'Then I will be yours.'

"Oh ! how the words seemed to sting me as I uttered them.

"'Now then, dearest, be mine now.'

"I hid my face in his breast for very shame, as I answered,

"'No, not now. I cannot, it is impossible. To-morrow, dearest, I promise.'

"He stayed with me a long time.

"My promise was enough. He thought he had well entrapped me.

"But even for him my plans were too good.

"That very night I fixed upon for my escape.

"I waited till all were asleep.

"Every hour seemed to pass by on leaden wings.

"At last midnight tolled, and, from the intense quiet around, I felt assured that all the household was at rest.

"For hours I had been well engaged in making a rope of my bed clothes.

"I knew the door was kept locked.

" There was, therefore, no chance of egress, except by the window.

" My room was situated in the rear of the premises, and just under my window rose an an outhouse which shelved off towards the road.

" It was a long descent, but I had great hopes of being able to drop into the lane unperceived, under cover of the dark night, and escape into the nearest village before daybreak.

" At length my rope was finished, and fastening it to the bed-post, I flung it out of the window, and saw with delight that it rested upon the wooden outhouse.

" I then breathed a prayer for safety, and committed myself to my frail support.

" I was soon down. How I held on I do not know, but in less than three minutes I was groping my way towards the wall.

" This reached, I was soon over, and on the high road to London and freedom.

" As day began to break I fell in with a caravan going to a neighbouring fair, and as kindness is always found most readily among the poor, I soon obtained a refuge.

" The van was heavy—the horses poor emaciated creatures – and our progress was exceedingly slow.

" The shades of evening had, therefore, again began to fall when we arrived within a mile of the great metropolis, whose buzz I, for the first time, could distinguish in the distance.

" I therefore determined to remain in the van that night, and see whether the following day might not bring about some means of disguising myself.

" I went to rest early that night.

" But I could get no rest; and as I tossed restlessly about, watching the swinging lamp at the end of our ' room,' I espied, hanging against the wall, a kind of semi-nautical costume, of which I resolved to avail myself.

" When all were asleep, therefore, I crept up to the spot, and, detaching the clothes from the wall, carried them to my ' corner,' and began to undress.

" I was not long making the exchange; and placing the little money I had in my trousers pocket, I unbolted the door noiselessly, and slipped out.

" Like a thief I ran—never looking behind me, but ever gazing where the great capital seethed and struggled before me.

" I had not robbed my benefactors, however.

" The clothes I took—and which I now wear —were worth little, while the dresses and underclothes I left behind were really saleable articles.

" I felt little compunction, therefore, at the exchange; and was glad enough when the bright morning sun awoke me from my sleep on one of the stone benches of Waterloo Bridge.

" I was delighted, as I entered London, at the noise, and the whirl, and the busy throngs which pressed, ever and ever, to and fro.

" While I had money I was tolerably comfortable.

" I took a lodging of the meanest kind, and, still maintaining my character of a boy, wandered about the streets in the day, doing nothing, and not liking to seek employment, for dread of discovery.

" At length my money was all gone, and I was forced to attempt some work.

" I wandered about all day the first day I was penniless.

" I was too proud to beg—

" I would not do worse.

" And so at last, on the morning of the third day, I sat down hopelessly on the door-step of a hovel in Houndsditch.

" I was half dozing with fatigue and starvation.

" I had slept in the streets, for, as I could not pay my rent, I was turned out of my lodging.

" I think tears would have relieved me.

" But they would not come.

" My lips and throat were parched ; and my eyes seemed bolting from their sockets.

" I sat there for about an hour, when a hand was placed on my shoulder, and a squeaking voice said—

" ' What's the matter, boy ?'

" Starving !" I said, without looking up.

" ' Come, come, don't say that. There is no occasion to starve in London, where everybody's got money. Come with me.'

" I was benumbed with starvation and cold, and I followed silently—mechanically.

" He was an old Jew.

" Long gray hairs fell over a dirty, greasy, velvet collar.

" Gray, twinkling eyes were shaded by gray bushy eyebrows.

" A hook-nose of portentous dimensions, partially concealed a mouth which was almost engulphed in a sea of ragged beard.

" He hobbled along with an uncertain, shuffling gait, looking round ever and anon to see whether I was following him.

" We stopped presently at the door of a wretched-looking house, at the entrance of which were crowding various beings of both sexes—some asleep, others playing some unmeaning game, and all gazing with a kind of awe at the squalid creature whom I accompanied.

" ' Come in,' he said.

" And so I entered.

" It was wretched enough, in all conscience

" But it was still a home of some sort.

" We passed up a long, creaking staircase, and entered at length a room of considerable dimensions.

" In it were congregated about a dozen boys and girls, all under the age of fifteen; some gambling, some fighting, some cooking indescribable comestibles before a blazing fire.

" All became as still as death as we entered.

" ' Here, my lively covish,' said the old Jew; ' here's a new pal for you. Tip him something for his grinders, and quick.'

" A plate of smoking soup was placed before me.

" It certainly *was* soup—that is all I can say.

" It was rich enough, too; but it must have contained a particle of every imaginable meat in this world.

" However, I was not in a state of mind to be fastidious.

"I fell to, and soon cleared it up, to the evident satisfaction of my new companions, who stood round me with broad grins on their countenances.

"During my meal Moses had slipped out, so that I was now left to the tender mercies of my new tormentors, as they soon proved to be.

"'Can you lift your livelies?' cried out a miserable-looking ruffian about fourteen, squaring up to me.

"'No.'

"'Can you crack a crib?'

"'No.'

"Such were the questions and answers which occupied my first two hours in that horrid den, which I soon found was the abode of thieves, and other characters of the worst description.

"I stayed there—under compulsion—for some time.

"I was fed well, and treated comparatively well; but I was given to understand that if I attempted to escape I should be well thrashed, if not worse.

"How I managed to preserve the secret of my sex in that detestable place, I know not.

"If I had undressed myself I should inevitably have been found out.

"We all slept in one room.

"Boys, girls, men, women, were huddled together in detestable confusion.

"I never once took off my clothes, and scarcely ever slept.

"All the day was passed in listening to the various adventures of the various members of the gang during the preceding day and night.

"These adventures were told for my special edification.

"I was considered as a novice.

"I was to be initiated into the mysteries of thief-craft.

"At length they considered me sufficiently up to my work; and it was suggested I should join an expedition which was about to issue forth against a neighbouring gentleman's house.

"My heart sank at this proposal.

"At first I determined to plead illness—anything to avoid being implicated in the intended burglary.

"But a sudden idea struck me.

"The expedition might afford me an opportunity of escaping; so I fell in with their plans, and pretended to experience a sort of pleasurable anxiety at the prospect of initiation into this new style of life.

"We sallied forth that night at eight.

"Two thieves walked with me, while Moses and three others went on in a cart which was to take us up as soon as we got out into the suburbs.

"I was watched closely.

"There was no chance of escape for me until the affair was over.

"When we had walked a long way my companions told me we were approaching Kingsland; and a whistle brought out Moses and his cart from the recesses of a dark passage.

"We all mounted, and the horse trotted on merrily along the road.

"We came to a dead stop at the corner of a dark lane.

Moses remained in the cart while I and the five others descended and crept along the wall, until we arrived at the front gate, which was of open iron work.

"We all crept over, I being sent over first for fear of my escaping.

"Everything was prepared, and in less than five minutes the bars of the kitchen windows were being filed through.

"After half-an-hour's work we all stood in the kitchen.

"One was left outside to give the alarm in case of danger.

"I had aspired to this post of honour; but they suspected my intention was to bolt, and I was dragged inside with the rest.

"We had a good supper first of all.

"The juvenile thieves and their leader, Fred the Simple One, never thought of the old Jew, whom they left shivering in the cart.

"Three of them then ascended the stairs, and in a short time returned laden with booty.

"We then went out, closed the shutters, and were just moving off, when a window was opened, and a pistol-shot fired.

All was now confusion. The thieves fled precipitately, and I was glad enough to find myself cowering under a hedge to avoid my pursuers, and still more my quasi-friends.

From that time to the moment when you found me cowering on the door-step in St. Giles's, I have been in a state of wretched destitution, begging for my livelihood; sleeping under the Adelphi arches one night, and the next under the arches of the river.

"This, sir, is my story."

Jessie Browne was pretty, and sixteen.

"I will befriend you," said William Lennox.

CHAPTER X.

AN EVENT.

"JACK."

"Sir?"

"Where is the boy to sleep?

"Sir?"

"Is there a bedroom upstairs?"

"Yes, sir."

"Engage it for him."

"Sir?"

"Well—engage it for yourself."

"I should like to have my page sleep near me. You are my factotum. This boy will run of errands for me."

"Sir?"

"Poor fellow! He has seen sorrow. He has gone through all the miseries of London life, and I will be a friend to him."

"Sir?"

"Why do you look so angry, Jack? I have done nothing to offend your strict views of morality?"

"Certainly not, sir. But this——"

"But what?"

"Nothing, sir."

"That's settled, then. You sleep upstairs—the page sleeps in the room next me."

Somehow or another, Jack Horne did not like the arrangement. Evidently he suspected something.

And, somehow or another, also, Jessie Browne didn't run of errands that day.

Jack Horne had to fetch everything.

The supposed Joe and William Lennox sat talking over the fire.

"Taken a mighty fancy to the new page, I should think," muttered Jack, as he laid the cloth for dinner that day.

"What's that?" asked Lennox.

"Said you'd taken a mighty fancy to your page, as he seems to be kept to do nothing, but only to be looked at," repeated Jack, sturdily.

"Insubordination, Jack!" said William.

He didn't feel quite comfortable, however.

Joe Spriggins, too, had a clean face, and looked hard at the fire to avoid blushing.

"Not insubordination, captain," said Jack, brushing away frantically at the table-cloth. "Not insubordination, captain, but still a page is a page, and is kept to work."

"So he shall, Jack, to-morrow; but remember he is tired and fagged out now—he has been dragged through all the miseries of London life, and is little inclined to work."

Jack Horne was silenced.

But he thought the more.

He slept upstairs that night.

The page retired to rest in the room adjoining that of William Lennox.

The night passed.

Jack Horne came down half asleep to light the fire; for, of course, as he grumbled out, "That 'ere page can do nothing."

He entered Lennox's room to rouse him up.

What a sight met his eyes!

He was half asleep it was true, so he might be dreaming.

He rubbed his eyes.

Could it possibly be true.

He looked again. Yes, there was no doubt of it.

William Lennox was lying there fast asleep, but there was another head also on the pillow. Side by side with William lay Jessie Browne— the soi-disant Joe Spriggins.

CHAPTER XI.

THE CHASE.

WE now return to Leila and the Blue Dwarf. It will be remembered that Dr. Porteus Framppe was prevented from carrying out his diabolical designs against the Princess of Borneo by the uproar occasioned by the entrance into the madhouse of the four men in the yellow cloaks.

He rushed down the stairs, leaving the door ajar, and met them as they were forcing their way up the passage, and driving before them all the assembled domestics of the house.

He was immediately seized and overpowered.

Dr. Porteus looked very blue.

"Where is the young lady whom you have confined here?"

"What young lady?" said the doctor, trembling.

"Leila, Princess of Borneo," cried a figure, who, although concealed under a cloak, could be distinguished as the Blue Dwarf.

"I know no such person."

"You do. Do not add lying to your other iniquities: she is concealed in this house at this moment. Give her up to us this moment, or take the consequences."

"She is up stairs," cried the doctor, in an inarticulate voice, as the Blue Dwarf clutched him convulsively by the throat.

Up stairs they rushed, into the room where Leila had lately been lying under the pink curtains.

In the room—in the bed—under the bed they searched, but they found not what they sought.

There was no Leila there.

By some fatal mistake she had either escaped voluntarily, or been carried away by her enemies.

The window was open.

The bars had been removed, and as the Blue Dwarf and his companions gazed out upon the still night, the rumble of carriage wheels could be heard in the distance.

"Great heavens!" cried Lord Ernest, whom we recognise in one of the cloaked figures, "she has been carried off. Let us fly after her."

A tear glistened in the eye of the Blue Dwarf as this speech proceeded from Lord Ernest's lips.

"Let us go," he said.

And leaving Dr. Porteus bound in his own house, they marched off towards the village of Highgate.

They stopped at "The Fox-under-the-Hill."

"Has a post-chaise been hired here?" cried the Blue Dwarf.

The ostler hesitated.

"Plenty of money!" growled the factotum in the cloak—the fourth was deaf and dumb.

"You will be paid for your information," put in the Blue Dwarf.

"They paid well," remarked the ostler.

"We will pay better," said Lord Ernest.

"Well then, sir, if you must know, a post-chaise cleared away about half-an-hour ago from this 'ere yard.

"In it were two gentlemen and a lady.

"The lady was very young, and seemed half insensible.

"She never uttered a word, but lay in their arms, when they brought her in, like a dead thing.

"They represents that they had rescued her from a madhouse, and were carrying her back to her friends, and—"

"Stay," said the Blue Dwarf; "during all this we are wasting time. Which road did they take?"

"The northern road."

"Then bring out another post-chaise with four horses, and we will follow."

In a few minutes the horses were out and put to; in a few minutes more the whole party were in the coach and dashing along the dark and silent road.

The horses were good; the road was even.

On they dashed, therefore, without impediment.

Up hill, down hill, they plunged, through the darkness of that black, black night.

But then not less quickly went the horses of the pursued.

"Where are they going?" asked the Blue Dwarf, by way of initiating a conversation.

"To Scotland, no doubt," suggested Lord Ernest, "to engage in a false marriage."

"But Leila will not consent."

"The Princess is not the only one to be consulted," said Lord Ernest. "Lord Charles is not one to stick at a trifle. Unprincipled villain that he is, he could brave anything to accomplish his desires."

And so, in conversation, the night passed.

Up the eastern hills the sun climbed.

Grey and dismal peeped the morning over the landscape.

And as the Blue Dwarf gazed moodily out of the carriage-window, up one of the hills in the distance could he distinguish a carriage toiling laboriously.

"We shall be successful," cried Sapathwa, "see, there is our quarry!"

"Heaven be praised!" cried Lord Ernest. "Let the postillion change, and the non again to the chase."

They learned at the next inn that a carriage containing two gentlemen and a lady had left about half-an-hour before.

They had, therefore, as yet gained no ground.

"Put on six horses, then," said the Blue Dwarf.

Again up the hills, and down they rushed.

All day they toiled, changing here and there, until in the evening about dusk the form of the pursued carriage was to be seen about a quarter of a mile in advance.

The efforts of the postillion now redoubled.

The party in the pursuing coach were half standing up with excitement.

From one window of the coach peered forth the anxious melancholy eyes of Sapathwa, from the other those of Lord Ernest.

They were now approaching the crest of a lofty hill.

"We shall never be able to descend that hill at this rate," said the *factotum*.

"We must try," replied Lord Ernest, "their chaise is lighter than ours, and they will go on at full speed. Where they go we must follow."

"Right," said the Blue Dwarf, laconically.

They were now at the very topmost verge of the hill.

The postillion pulled in his horses.

"Why do you stop?" shouted Sapathwa, frantically.

"I can't go down that 'ere hill at that rate," said the postillion.

"You must."

"We shall be upset."

"Chance it! A sovereign if you overtake that chaise before they reach the level road."

Not another word was said.

The postillion settled himself in his seat, and eyed "his work" for a moment.

Then with a leap and a plunge the carriage sped onwards, and slid at a terrific speed down the steep incline.

It was not to them that accidents were destined to happen that night.

The four pursuers had by mutual consent inclined towards the centre of the postchaise, so as to preserve the balance as far as possible.

A shout brought the Blue Dwarf to the window.

The carriage came to a dead stop with a jerk which sent them tumbling into a heap.

"What is the matter," cried Sapathwa.

"Look, sir," said the postillion, "see there at the bottom of the hill, they must be all killed."

One glance was sufficient to exhibit the catastrophe that had occurred.

At the very bottom the post-chaise, containing Leila and her two companions, had overturned.

Horses, driver, everything lay there in one tangled mass.

The Blue Dwarf gazed for a moment in silence, and then leaped out into the road, followed by the other three men in the yellow cloaks.

The horses of the shattered vehicle began to kick and plunge to regain their liberty.

"She will be killed," muttered Sapathwa, as they ran hastily up.

Inside the vehicle lay Leila, white as death, and quite insensible.

The driver was dead.

The horses had killed him with their hoofs; and the poor fellow lay right under their feet.

Leila's companions had left the carriage to endeavour to disengage the plunging animals; and now stood menacingly before the four friends.

"You had better go quietly," said the Blue Dwarf, drawing his sword, "we are four to two."

"But we are well armed," returned Lord Charles Lutterell, "and so saying, he drew a pistol and fired in Sapathwa's face.

The Blue Dwarf fell back into the arms of Lord Ernest.

CHAPTER XII.

SLEEPING AND WAKING.

WHEN Dr. Porteus Framppe rushed out of Leila's room on the entrance into the house of the four men in the yellow cloaks, Leila was still buried in profound slumber.

The wanton caresses of the old man had not roused her from her heavy sleep; they had only served just to disturb her slightly; and as she lay in the pink mellow light thrown over her by the rays of the night lamp through the curtains, she presented a picture of infinite beauty.

Her bosom was heaving with intense emotion—her round, white arm was cast child-like above her head—while her short nightdress had just been sufficiently disordered by the embrace of the old doctor to afford a glimpse of an exquisitely formed leg.

" She with her flushed cheek laid on her white arm,
    And raven ringlets gathered in dark crowd
 Above her brow, lay dreaming soft and warm,
    And smiling through her dream, as through a cloud.
 The moon breaks half-unveiled each further charm,
    As slightly stirring in her snowy shroud,
 Her beauties seized the unconscious hour of night
 All bashfully to struggle into light."

Hardly had Dr. Porteus Framppe left the apartment where this image of beauty was sleeping when the bars of the window were wrenched violently open, the sash lifted lightly, and a man entered the room.

A man about thirty, with dark hair and blue eyes!

Leila was dreaming of happy scenes.

Her breathing was soft and childlike, and the parted lips showed the brightness of the pearls beneath.

The stranger gazed for a moment in unfeigned admiration.

He then locked the door, and threw the key out of window.

Taking up some of her clothes, he hastily covered her over, and shook her gently.

"Leila," he cried, "wake—wake, you are in danger!"

She woke up with a start, and shrieked as she saw Lord Charles Lutterell standing over her.

"Keep quiet," he cried; "there are villains in the house who would murder you. Quick! dress yourself and come with me!"

"What am I to do?" said Leila, faintly, while a crimson blush suffused her cheeks.

He understood her at once.

He walked to the window.

"Be quick!" he said; "I will wait here."

Leila dressed as if under the influence of a spell.

But the spell did not last long.

Was not this man her mortal enemy?

Could any fate be worse than being thrown helplessly, hopelessly in his power?

"I will not go," she said firmly.

"Not go!" said he, petulantly. "Do I not tell you that there are men in this house will stick at nothing—lawless ruffians who will show you no respect."

"They will show me quite as much respect as you," replied Leila; "I will trust to them."

There was at this moment a tremendous noise in the passage down stairs.

"Listen," said he, opening the door, "listen; is it to such men as these you would trust yourself?"

This was a false move upon the part of her tormentor.

She recognised the voice of the Blue Dwarf.

"Thank heaven!" she cried, rushing forward; "there is Sapathwa."

"D——n!" muttered Lord Charles between his teeth; "you shall come now whether you like it or not."

And seizing her in his arms he leaped out of the window, and rushing across the dark lawn was met by his associate in crime.

"Where is the carriage?"

"At the corner of the lane."

"Lead the way, then," cried Lord Charles; "I've enough to do to carry my burden."

And so he had.

Leila was struggling violently, and shrieking loudly for help.

"Stay!" cried his companion; "you must stop that noise, or we shall be discovered."

Fastening a handkerchief tightly round her mouth, they again proceeded this time in silence, and were soon in the post-chaise; the rumbling of whose wheels attracted the attention of the Blue Dwarf when they rushed into the room.

From the time she was laid in the carriage to the moment when she lay insensible amid its ruins, she never uttered a word.

All her faculties seem concentrated into one agony of fear, mingled at length with a slight ray of hope, when the rumble of the pursuing carriage was borne along by the wind.

CHAPTER XIII.

A NEW STRATAGEM.

JACK HORNE was amazed.

He had from the first moment suspected that the sex assumed by Joe Spriggins was false.

There could now be no doubt.

The ringlets were no longer confined by her cap.

Her white throat was no longer hidden by the coarse handkerchief, while the soft, round arm which lay outside the coverlet, would in itself have proclaimed her a girl.

"Devilish nice, I daresay," muttered Jack Horne; "but wrong."

He quietly began lighting the fire.

Jack Horne had a heart.

And that heart was in the right place.

"Shall I wake them," he thought, and he advanced towards the bed.

He respected Jessie's feelings, however; he remembered how extremely awkward it would be for her to wake up under such circumstances, and see him in the room.

He adopted, therefore, a better plan.

He quickly did his work; and then leaving the room, knocked loudly at the door.

William Lennox awoke with a start.

He saw that the fire was alight, and that Jack had been there.

He understood at once how matters stood, therefore, and looked as he felt—very sheepish.

"What is the matter?" said Jessie.

"Why, the fact is, Jessie," replied William, "Jack Horne will be in here in a moment; so you had better get up, and get into your page's clothes as soon as possible, for fear he might suspect something."

So saying he kissed her tenderly, and she slipped away to her room.

Jack Horne, who was only waiting for this opportunity, now entered, looking exceedingly serious.

"What's for breakfast," said Lennox, dressing hastily.

He did not feel at all comfortable.

"Same as usual, sir," said Jack. "Is it your intention, sir, to keep that young woman here as a page."

William Lennox knew he had done wrong.

So, as most people, he thought the best way to get out of his scrape was to carry a high head.

"I do Jack. It is my desire that she remain here; and that you do not allow her to perceive you have discovered her secret."

Lennox was angry with himself, so he pretended to be angry with his servant.

How many of us try to steel our own consciences by thinking of the wrong-doing of others.

It is much easier to censure another than it is to correct oneself.

And so, instead of acknowledging his wrong-doing, William Lennox tried to feel indignant at Jack Horne's presumption: and assumed a highly dignified and insulting demeanour.

Jack Horne would not stay in the room during breakfast.

He was annoyed and grieved at his master's conduct; but still more annoyed that he refused to be spoken to on the subject.

So Jessie Browne waited at table; or, rather, breakfasted with Lennox.

So things went on for a few days.

On the evening of the third day Jessie went out to make a purchase—she was still attired in boy's clothes.

She had proceeded only a short way when a gentleman accosted her.

He was a man about the middle height, with a rather effeminate countenance, and appeared exceedingly nervous and anxious to avoid observation.

A cloak concealed his dress, while a slouched hat partially hid his features.

"Joe Spriggins is your name, I believe?" said the stranger.

"Yes, sir," said Jessie.

"You are page to Mr. William Lennox?"

"I do not know by what right you question me," said the girl. "Let me pass."

"Come now, young man, do not be so hasty. I wish to befriend you. Tell me the truth, and I will reward you."

"I do not wish for reward, neither would I accept a reward for betraying my master."

"I do not wish you to betray anything, I only wish you to tell me his name."

"Why not go to the house and inquire, then, if you intend nothing but what is straight-forward."

"You are a sharp lad. Listen to me. Will you accompany me to see a lady who has an interest in your master? She will not detain you, and will give you a substantial evidence of her favour."

"Are you sure she is friendly towards my master?"

"I am sure."

"Will you promise that I shall not be detained?"

"I promise."

"Then I will follow you."

A peculiar smile of satisfaction passed over the stranger's face when Jessie gave her consent.

"Come on quickly, then," he said, "it shall not be our fault if you are delayed."

He led on through various streets until they arrived at Portland-place.

At the door of a house in this street they stopped, and, entering the spacious hall, Jessie was led at once upstairs into a drawing-room furnished with every luxury.

The room was empty when she entered, but in a few minutes an inner door opened, and a lady elegantly dressed came into the apartment. Jessie rose.

"Pray sit down, Miss," said the lady, "all is discovered, so I hope you will tell me the truth."

CHAPTER XIV.

CAPTAIN GEORGE.

As we said, the vessel containing Captain George and his wife sailed for Algeria.

Joe the mudlark and Mary accompanied them.

Before starting Joe had craved a boon of the captain, and obtained it.

Need we say that that boon was permission to marry Mary?

Little occurred on the journey out of the common order; and the ordinary period saw them safely landed at their destination.

In order to ensure the success of his undertaking, great precaution was necessary.

He might be recognised—if so, certain death would be his portion.

His purpose might be discovered—in such case the peril was no less great.

He hired a small house in the suburbs of the city, a short distance from the palace of the Dey, whose daughter had died in effecting his escape.

Here for some time they lived in comfort and happiness—if happy any one can be called who is a prey to a restless thirst after gold.

At length, after the curiosity excited by the appearance and settling "of the strangers" had somewhat abated, Captain George determined to commence operations.

Two swift horses and a large sack were the only equipments necessary; and so one night, when all the city was asleep, Joe the mudlark and his master sallied forth into the open country.

Captain George knew his way but ill.

When flying for his life he had trusted entirely to Zanoina, and his only chance now of discovering the route they then took was by issuing from the city by the same gate, and keeping on that road until they arrived at their destination.

So, as we have said, they sallied forth one night.

The moon was up, sailing midway in the heavens.

The stars were out in myriads.

The road wound along the country, under the clear sky, like a black snake.

The country itself looked like a misty plain, while the sea beyond seemed, as it danced and glistened in the moonlight, like the surface of a broken mirror.

"Beautiful country, sir," said Joe.

"Yes," said Captain George, laconically.

"Deuced sight more comfortable here than in England," continued the mudlark; "'spose I shan't care about going back."

"Wait till you make your fortune," remarked Captain George.

"Why, captain?"

"Because then you'll want to go and spend it in the old country."

"Um!" muttered Joe; "perhaps I should, and then perhaps again I shouldn't, leastwise as I've got Mary with me."

"Perhaps not."

"What, sir?"

"Nothing, Joe."

Joe didn't think his master in a peculiarly bright mood, and so he held his peace, and they proceeded on in silence.

On they went for hours, only pausing here and there to reconnoitre; until at length, when the night was nearly over, Captain George suggested that as they were now far enough away from the city they might safely take some rest and leave the next day clear before them for work.

"We can't be far off the place now, Joe," said Captain George; "we were scarcely as long as this coming here before. Let us look out for a place for a snooze."

On their left was an unbroken plain.

Behind them was the road to Algiers.

Before them the way stretched on interminably in the distance.

To their right appeared a dark mass, which appeared to be the remains of some building.

"We can't sleep out there, that's very certain," said the captain, pointing to the flat country to the left; "let's explore that ruin, and perhaps we may find a shelter."

The ruins appeared to be those of some ancient fortress.

Vast boulders lay scattered about in all imaginable positions.

Fragments of massive walls were still standing, exhibiting here and there the remains of doors and barred windows.

"Let us sleep here," said the captain, laying his head on a heap of stones. "Go, fasten the horses to the wall, and then go to rest."

So saying, he wrapped his cloak around him, and, without any further thought of the mudlark, relapsed almost immediately into a heavy sleep.

There is no accounting for the sudden recurrence of reminiscences.

Years may have gone by, and events followed events in rapid and endless variety.

Memory of the past may almost seem to have vanished.

Our former selves may appear nothing but dreams of other days.

But suddenly, when we are least prepared for it, the recollection of the past will form itself into palpable shape, and come before us in our dreams.

There seems indeed to some persons to be a second life.

All the principal occurrences of their waking existence they go through again in their sleep.

No sooner had Captain George laid his head upon his stony pillow than he was transported back thirteen years.

He was once more a slave—once more tending the garden of the Dey.

Once more delicious music tempted him to venture into the presence of the Dey's daughter in the garden.

Once more he was passionately in love.

Once more long years of anxious, doubtful happiness passed, and once more he was riding at headlong speed for his life, with Zanoina by his side.

Once more he heard the terrible voice of her father, and once more he knelt in agony by the stony grave, amid the ruins where he had deposited all that remained of the loved and the beautiful.

He awoke with a start, and raised himself on his elbow.

A terrible storm was over the land.

The thunder pealed with terrific grandeur—the lightning seemed to illumine the whole universe with its ever-recurring and vivid flashes.

Could it be true?

Was it a terrible vision?

He started, and kneeling down, stared with straining eyes in the darkness until the next flash should reveal the truth.

The lightning flashed—the thunder rolled louder.

Yes! it was true.

He had chosen for his pillow the heap of stones which he had hastily placed over the dead body of Zanoina, and there, under the black sky, lay the white skeleton which the wild beasts had disturbed in its hiding-place.

Captain George knelt for a moment in silence.

He then rose, walked away, and woke Joe.

He wanted a companion now.

The mudlark was in a heavy sleep, which no thunder could disturb.

"Oh!—oh!—oh!—what's the matter?"

"What! are you asleep, boy?" said the captain; "there's a storm."

"Eh! a storm, eh?" answered Joe, rubbing his eyes; "so there is. I'll get up."

CHAPTER XV.

THE FINDING OF THE TREASURE.

WHEN morning broke calmly, beautifully over the warm landscape, no evidences of the past storm were to be discovered.

The discovery of the skeleton of Zanoina was sufficient to prove that they were near the spot where the treasure lay concealed.

Captain George, however, was at a loss to find the entrance to the cave.

He had discovered it simply through an accident, when he had fallen through a hole when escaping from his pursuers.

"I don't know in the least, Joe," he said, "where the entrance is. So we must commence here at this corner of the building, and search every inch of ground carefully."

The whole day they spent in fruitless search, until at length, just as the sun was declining, Joe, who was in advance of his master, suddenly uttered a loud cry and disappeared.

Captain George darted forward.

Beneath his feet was a large fissure, large enough to allow a man's body to pass through, but the blackness and darkness was so intense that he could see nothing.

"Halloa!" he cried, "are you hurt, Joe?"

"Yes—smashed."

"In that case I'll throw you the tinder-box and you can strike a light."

"Every bone in my body is broken, I think," groaned Joe.

"Never mind," said the captain, "you've found the treasure. Strike a light, and I will come down to you."

"Drop it down carefully. I've got it, sir. Now look down."

Peering down the dark pit, Captain George could perceive that the sides were composed of jagged rock, by which he could easily descend.

Passing to Joe, therefore, one of the torches they had brought with them, he prepared to climb down.

The torch, stuck in a fissure of the earth, sent a merry gleam up the shaft, and he was soon enabled to join Joe in the depths of the cavern.

The mudlark was bruised and much shaken by the fall, but not seriously injured.

So they went immediately to their store.

Everything was there as Captain George had described it.

The sacks still yawned with their golden and sparkling treasures.

"My eye!" was the classic expression with which Joe the mudlark gave vent to his astonishment.

It was concise, and not elegant; but it was more expressive than anything that could have been said.

They did nothing that night, but retired to rest early.

The following morning they began to explore the cavern, in order that in future visits they might be able at once to discover the entrance.

This they found was in a deep ravine, just below the road.

Nothing was observable from the highway.

The opening was entirely obscured by thick brushwood, which had evidently not been planted there originally by nature.

Not a vestige of anything like a portal could be seen from without.

"This is first-rate, Joe," said the captain, "we will use this door and stop up the hole up above. If we don't do that we shall find some other adventurer coming tumbling in some fine morning."

"Yes, sir," said Joe, musingly.

He added after a moment—

"But, captain, if no one can see this door from the outside, how shall we be able to find it again?"

Captain George laughed.

"Joe, you're a philosopher; we must set up some sign in the road before we leave."

The sack was soon filled with its precious burden; and after setting up a little wooden cross in the ravine opposite the entrance, and dragging two immense stones over the fissure in the top portion of the cavern, they set off once more for Algiers.

Captain George had got what he required.

He did not wish to carry away the treasure wholesale.

He only wished for specimens wherewith to tempt the cupidity of some Jew dealer.

He did not waste much time at home.

He showed Lucy his treasure. He spoke enthusiastically of the future, and vauntingly of the present; and at break of day set off on his voyage of discovery.

In a wretched street near one of the quays lived an old Jew.

Michael Spavolo was an Italian Jew, and a queer specimen of humanity.

He was very tall, and very thin.

The hot climate had bronzed his complexion, while his skin appeared to have attained the consistency of parchment.

His eyes were as glistening and rapacious as those of a hawk, while a long nose almost met a pointed chin, from which depended a long and grizzled beard.

His shop was the meanest of the mean; but everyone knew that Spavolo, the Jew, was one of the richest men in Algiers.

"Oh! holy Moshish," he cried, holding up his hands; and then tremblingly plunging them into the sack which Captain George brought him, "vat have we here!"

"Precious stones, Michael, precious stones," said Captain George, "with which you can make my fortune and your own."

"Have you any more of dese tings?" continued Michael, eyeing them as if they were so many drops from his own heart.

"Plenty—a hundred thousand more, if you want them; only you must deal fairly with me."

"Now, shentleman, dat is not right. Everyone knows that Michael Spavolo is honest. I will not pargain if I am not believed."

There was something so ludicrous in Michael's assumption of indignation, that Captain George could not resist laughing.

"Well, well, Spavolo," he said, "I don't suspect you. Now, let's to business."

The bargain was soon made—greatly to the satisfaction of Captain George, but still more to that of the old Jew.

It was arranged that the remainder of the treasure should be brought from the country in a cart.

This settled, Michael soon found the cart; and, after bidding adieu to Lucy, the treasure-seeker once more started off, with Joe the mudlark as charioteer.

They took with them provisions for a fortnight.

They were occupied ten days in placing the sacks in the cart, and another in so covering them over that they should be hidden from observation.

Then, bidding adieu to the empty treasure cavern, they once more retraced their steps.

Silence seemed to reign around. Everywhere—everywhere not a vestige of a human being could be seen as they approached the city.

They came to the gates—there was no guard to oppose them.

A strange presentiment of evil came over the captain's mind as he thought of Lucy.

A few minutes' drive sufficed to confirm his anxiety, and at the same time to almost stupify him with terror.

THE PLAGUE WAS IN ALGIERS!

CHAPTER XVI.

THE PLAGUE CITY.

"BRING out your dead! bring out your dead!"

Heavily laden were the carts which were carrying the dead bodies to the pits yawning in every square in the city.

"Bring out your dead! bring out your dead!"

The cry sounded dismally along the silent streets as the horrid equipage passed along the rough roads, and the death-bell pealed at the corner of every turning.

Business was suspended—no one thought of property.

Everywhere could be seen houses with their doors thrown wide open; and now and then a man would emerge stealthily, bearing in his hand some plunder, which there was no one to prevent his carrying off.

Families who had as yet escaped infection

were hurrying off with bundles on their backs, running, they knew not whither, to avoid contact with the plague-stricken citizens.

The treasure was forgotten.

"Drive home," said Captain George.

At length they reached the door of a large house, into which they entered through a court-yard.

Captain George flew rather than walked though this.

The doors were all thrown open.

Not a vestige of human life could be seen.

The cart and the treasure were left to take care of themselves outside.

Joe could not remain outside while Mary was inside, perhaps dying.

In every room they sought, but no one was visible.

Lucy's room was in great disorder, as if some one had lately been there.

"Some villain has been here," said Captain George, in a husky voice; "some one has taken advantage of our absence to enter my house, and rob me of my all."

"Come," he added, after a moment's pause to Joe, who stood bewildered by his side; "come, let us go to the Jew's, get all the money we can, and that will assist us in recovering our lost treasures. I say 'our,' Joe; for you, too, have lost a dear wife by this misfortune."

They left the house, bolting the doors behind them, and once more proceeded to the domicile of the old Jew.

The same dismal appearances presented themselves everywhere.

Scarcely a soul was visible in the streets.

But the old Jew was untouched.

In the midst of all this death and terrible desolation he still expected his visitors, and was standing at his door ready to meet them when they arrived.

His gaunt, grim figure seemed like the figure of an avenging demon.

"Have you succeeded?" he inquired, eagerly gazing scrutinisingly at their gloomy faces.

"Yes."

"Have you got it all?"

"Yes."

"You do not seem much elated by its possession," cried Spavolo, in astonishment.

"No, I am unhappy."

"Unhappy! when you have riches here unnumbered."

"Some villain has entered my house in my absence, and stolen away my wife, and the wife also of my servant here."

"You can avenge the insult."

"I would if I knew upon whom to wreak my vengeance."

"You can discover."

"How?"

"You are rich: anything can be done by money."

"Well, let us empty the cart."

Captain George looked furtively at the street.

"Ah! ah!" grimly laughed Michael, rubbing his hand, "no one to disturb us, they are all dead—all dead!"

The treasure was soon conveyed from the carts into Michael's house, and for several hours the party were occupied in discussing the amount to be paid over to the captain.

At length all was settled.

Captain George could scarcely believe his eyes or his ears!

He was the possessor of a fortune of half a million sterling!

But happiness is seldom unalloyed.

The loss of Lucy was greater than the gain of a fortune.

"Come to me to-morrow," said the Jew. "Meanwhile I will devise a scheme for the discovery of your wife."

"Thank you."

"Nay, no thanks; although I am a Jew, I have a heart."

And the grim spectre laid his hand upon his breast.

Captain George and Joe the mudlark wended their way home silently.

They passed through the silent streets towards a deserted home.

As they neared the door they perceived a figure standing opposite the doorway.

"A living creature in our house," said Joe. "It is a girl; perhaps she has a message from Lucy."

On perceiving them the girl hastened forward.

She was about fifteen, and dressed in the costume of a Grecian maiden.

She was very pretty—not the simple prettiness of an English girl of her age.

The temperature of those climes ripen maidens into women, where here they would scarcely be doffing their child-clothes.

Her figure was rounded and elastic, and she walked up to the captain with a natural grace which he could not, even sorrowful as he was, regard but with admiration.

"Are you the English stranger?" she said, with an arch gravity, and in the Greek language.

"Yes."

"You have lost one dear to you—your wife?" she continued, with real sorrow.

"I have."

"I will find her for you."

A tear glistened in the captain's eyes as he answered—

"Blessings on you; will you enter, and tell me all you know?"

Together they entered the empty and silent house, and sat down in Lucy's boudoir.

"I live in that habitation opposite," said the girl.

"I had an aunt living there, with whom I staid.

"I left my parents dead in Greece. My last friend is now a victim of this terrible plague.

"Your wife has been very kind to me, very kind, and I will never forget her.

"While you were away a black servant was constantly hovering about the house. You came back too soon, and he discontinued his visits.

"You went away a second time.

"Again the black slave came, and used constantly to enter your house and stay some time.

"At length, one morning I happened to be at my window, and I saw him expelled with violence from your door, and pursued with sticks by your servants up the street.

"I learned from your wife that the slave was the bearer of letters from a rich Pasha who lives just beyond the city, proposing to her to elope and become his principal wife.

"For your sake she bore it quietly for some time; but at length the missives became so importunate, and therefore so insulting, that she could not refrain any longer from giving vent to her indignation.

"Then came the plague, with all its manifold horrors.

"Of this day of calamity and terror her enemy availed himself, and when the doors of the city were open, and the panic-stricken citizens took no notice of anything that passed, four slaves rushed into your house and seized your wife, and the wife, too, of your servant, and conveyed them away to his residence.

"To that place I can take you; but you must not be too precipitate.

"All must be done quietly, and not hastily."

Captain George remained in thought for some moments.

"How can *I* obtain access to his house?"

The girl mused for a time.

"Cannot you," said she, "claim protection in his house during the continuance of the plague?

"He will not dare to refuse you as an Englishman.

"He will most probably retire to his country-house many miles off.

"That is smaller than the one near the city; and you will have more opportunities of seeing his household.

"Your servant must, of course, accompany you."

"I will do as you bid me—stay, what is your name?"

"Haidee Kanairos."

"Then, Haidee," said Captain George, "you had better stay here to-night—you can have my wife's room. But how will you manage to enter the Pasha's residence?"

"As one of your servants."

"Good!—but where *are* my servants?"

"Dead!—either murdered or plague-stricken," said Haidee; "the men with the carts cleared the house of the bodies."

"Let us to rest, then," said the captain, "we will start early."

CHAPTER XVII.

THE GARDENS OF THE SILVER FOUNTAIN.

IN the morning the party started.

Haidee had doffed her Greek dress, and attired herself in the plain clothes of a servant.

They soon reached the house.

The whole place seemed enveloped in gloom.

An atmosphere of death pervaded the mansion.

They passed over the dead bodies of three slaves as they entered.

Not a living soul was to be seen.

The plague had done its work there, too, and the Pasha had fled before it.

"We must return to the city," said Captain George, "and procure a vehicle of some kind. Do you know your way, Haidee?"

"Yes; the Pasha has gone to his country residence—the Gardens of the Silver Fountain—which is about thirty miles hence."

The conveyance obtained, they were soon once more on their road, and proceeded with very few stoppages until they reached their destination.

The feelings of the Pasha upon seeing the arrival of Captain George were of the most perplexing character. From the manner of his guest he could discover nothing. He appeared anxious to avoid the plague—that was all. He even went so far as to say that he believed his wife to have perished with the rest of his household during his absence.

This latter statement chased away all fears from the Pasha's mind.

With great apparent cordiality he invited Captain George to remain there with his servants until the plague was over, and assigned him a splendid suite of apartments.

Captain George mixed little with any of the other persons in the building. He remained in his room all day concocting with Joe the mud-lark various dangerous and impossible schemes for the rescue of Lucy and Mary.

Haidee, meanwhile, was busy as a bee.

She soon got on good terms with the female attendants of the harem and at length with the principal wife of the Pasha, who was a young and beautiful woman.

To her she expatiated and enlarged upon the fabulous riches of the English stranger, and by degrees excited her cupidity.

She was indignant at the introduction into the Pasha's household of an English girl, who was to deprive her of her position as chief wife of her husband.

At length Haidee achieved a bold stroke of policy.

By acting as she did she imperilled the very lives of her friends and herself; but she knew that to be successful she must be bold.

After describing the rewards which would be given to her if she aided in Lucy's escape, she confessed that Captain George was the husband of the English lady, and had come for the express purpose of rescuing her.

Aysha easily fell into the plot; and that night saw Captain George in her presence.

The Pasha's wife was a lovely woman; and as she lay on the divan when the captain entered, he paused a moment in silence to regard her.

She was leaning back, with her jewelled arm cast over her head.

Her dress consisted of a crimson jacket, embroidered with silver; heavy shawls were cast about her hips; and her legs were encased in a pair of delicate muslin trousers.

The vest, which was open down to the waist, revealed the whole splendours of her neck and bosom.

Rich dark curls fell from her classic head, and wantoned between globes as pure and as

white as alabaster, and preserving their roundness and shape by their own firmness.

Her hands were white and delicate as those
of a child.

One of these hands Captain George took and
kissed respectfully.

"Lady," he said, "I believe you are going to
befriend us."

"Yes," said the beautiful vision, "I will.
I am not quite disinterested, you know."

"I know that."

"But still I, who am so jealous, can easily
understand how terrible must be your anxiety.
Through that door you will find a passage which
leads to your wife's room. Remain there only
a short time, as you might be discovered."

So saying she pointed to a door at the side of
the chamber, and a slave led the way.

"Stay," said Aysha, just as they were about
to leave the room. "Remember, I cannot take
all the risk; if this is discovered I can make no
effort to save you."

"Thank you, fair lady," said Captain George,
"upon my head be all the consequences of this
night's adventure."

"And on mine," put in Joe, who accompanied
his master.

The expression was heroic enough, but as
unfortunately no one understood English, it
was lost on the assembled company.

In a few minutes they were standing in the
inner room.

Around a bed stood four slaves, who retired upon the entrance of the fifth.

In this bed lay Lucy asleep; her troubles were for a time not troubling her.

Sheer fatigue and exhaustion had thrown her into a heavy slumber, from which she was awakened by feeling her husband kissing and fondling her.

She awoke with a start, and would have shrieked, had not the captain held his hand tightly over her mouth.

"Hold, dearest, do not cry out! It is I—your husband!"

Lucy trembled like a leaf, sat up in bed, and, after gazing a few moments, threw herself on his neck and wept.

A few explanations were entered into.

"I cannot stay long, Lucy," said her husband, "but I will see you often. I must not get Aysha into trouble."

At this moment a slave knocked and entered.

He approached Captain George, and whispered a few words in his ear.

The Pasha was in his wife's apartment, through which they would be obliged to pass in order to retire to their rooms.

"My mistress says that my master will remain with her until the morning. It will not be safe for you to attempt to pass, even when he is asleep. You must, therefore, remain here to-night."

"Very well," said Captain George; "I have no objection. Whisper to your mistress that I will remain."

The slave left the room, and Captain George passed into the next chamber, where he found another re-united couple—Joe and Mary.

Having communicated the intelligence to them, and having told Joe to sleep lightly, and keep his arms near him in case of a surprise, he retired to rest.

CHAPTER XVIII.

THE STUDENT.

IF our hero is not all that our readers could wish him, or even that we could wish him ourselves, let them recollect the age in which he lived, the manners of the times, and the varied fortunes he had passed through.

It should not have been so, especially guarded as he was by an angel of light in the form of a young and lovely girl.

But the best of us are weak, and let us not be too hard on the feelings of any.

But there was one person who could not forgive the delinquencies of William Lennox, and that was William Lennox himself.

However he might be led away by his impulsive and passionate nature, he saw and regretted his failings.

When he returned each time from a visit to poor Lillian, it was with a firm resolve to cast off an ill-fated connection, and once more be what so long he had been.

And then there was the being so gentle, so loving, so potent, so happy: his heart smote him, and he delayed.

One morning, a few days after Jack Horne had made an unpleasant discovery, William Lennox, dissatisfied, annoyed, vexed with himself, rose early, put his head out of window, and lit a cigar.

Next to his window was another, at which, just as he did so, another head appeared, also smoking.

It was the head of a foreigner, a young man, with long silky moustaches, a little peaky beard, rather bushy whiskers, and with a smoking cap on its head.

"*Bonjour, Monsieur*," said the stranger, with a strong German accent, and a guttural pronunciation in the throat not very pleasant.

William Lennox bowed.

"No speake French," said the stranger, in very bad English.

"*Oui*."

"*Bon*—then we shall be friends. I am *etudient* —student in vhat you call bainting—ah me!"

And he sighed deeply.

"Monsieur is not happy," said William Lennox, struck, despite himself, by the melancholy of the other's tone.

"Very unhappy. I have not one single soul to care for or love me," he continued.

"Would Monsier do me the honour to breakfast with me?" said William Lennox, politely.

The student's eyes flashed in such a way that William Lennox half thought that a breakfast must be an object to him.

"In half an hour," he continued, "breakfast will be ready."

"I will come," replied the other, as William Lennox retired to give orders.

Then there flashed in the stranger's eye another expression which might have been compared to the baleful light of a vampire's eyes, and to nothing else.

William Lennox went to the door of the inner room, and opened it.

"A stranger is coming to breakfast with me—a poor Frenchman; but I don't want any one to see you. I will send in breakfast."

"Very well," said a meek voice.

William Lennox then called Jack Horne, who was ready dressed, and ordered him to prepare breakfast for three.

The rigid soldier, who obeyed his master servilely but coldly, and with evident displeasure, hastened to fulfil his commands.

"Don't be angry," said William, in a low whisper.

"Angry!—I, sir?"

"I know you are."

"Why, sir?"

"You know."

"Sir—"

"All will be well one day."

"I hope so."

"Now, outdo yourself, old boy, to-day," continued his master, gently. "A poor Frenchman, who I believe did not dine yesterday, is coming to breakfast. Let him find it substantial."

"Very good, sir," said Jack Horne, in a more cheerful tone.

And he proceeded to hasten his preparations.

In less than an hour the stranger entered.

He wore a student-painter's blouse, loose

trousers, an elegant boot, while a jaunty cap still covered his head.

"You excuse me," he said, raising it for one moment, and then replacing it; "but habit is so strong."

"Certainly," replied William Lennox, with a smile, "this is Liberty Hall."

"*Merci.*"

Jack Horne served with open mouth. He could not make the student out.

He scarcely ate at all.

Then Jack Horne put some things on a tray, and opening the inner door, thrust them in.

"There, Joe," he said, in sulky tones, "there's your breakfast; and—*I wish it may choke you!*"

(The italics represent asides.)

"Thank you kindly," said Joe.

"Welcome—*to go to the very devil!*" continued Jack.

He then closed the door.

"Can I do anything else, sir?" he said, addressing his master, and eyeing the student askance.

"No, Jack. You can go round to Holborn and inquire for Sapathwa."

"That I will, sir, with pleasure."

"Why?"

"Because when he comes—"

"What, sir?"

"All will be right."

"Go, sir!" said William Lennox, with a blush of anger; "go and stay out until one o'clock."

Jack Horne left the room, and no sooner did he gain the passage than he fell on his knees, and—dragoon though he was—prayed fervently, the most abject terror being depicted on his countenance.

"Merciful heaven grant that he may come soon, for my poor master is in mortal peril!"

CHAPTER XIX.

THE STUDENT'S STORY.

"You are not alone?" said the stranger, with a significant smile, and a glance at the door of the inner room.

William Lennox continued to smile by a great effort, and to repress a blush.

"A poor invalid servant of mine."

"You live in strange lodgings for a gentleman with two servants," said the student, gaily.

"True, but I have specific reasons; you see," pointing to the breakfast, "that poverty is not one of them."

"Neither is it the cause of my retreat from better society," said the student, gravely.

William Lennox bowed.

"I see you are discretion itself, but I am not. I burn to know your story; and, to invite confidence, will tell you mine. I cannot keep it in. You behold in me the victim of a fatal passion!"

And he struck his forehead with all the melodramatic force of a Frenchman.

William Lennox looked in the fire.

"I am not a Frenchman by origin; I am of English parents, but born in France. They were worthy and rather wealthy people, who left me at the age of sixteen alone, independent, and a student of art."

"A very happy fellow."

"*Comme ca!*"

"Pardon my interruption."

"No excuses. Ask me as many question as you like. Rich, free, and independent, I made myself look as old as I could, and started on an art tour. My choice was limited, and my steps first led me to Madrid—"

"Ah!"

"There I revelled in the luxurious beauty of Spanish art, studied Murillo, gave my whole thought up to painting, until one day—" (This was said with a deep sigh.)

"One day!"

"I went into a certain church, in a certain chapel of which was a picture I spent hours a day in examining. I stood with folded arms, gazing with rapture on the scene, when suddenly—"

"Suddenly!"

"My arm was touched, and turning round I saw close by me—"

"What?"

"A woman—"

"Ah!"

"But such a glorious being. It would be vain of me to attempt describing her. Never was there loveliness to equal that of the glorious Dolores—"

"Merciful heaven!"

"Duchess of Castella. But you seem to know her," said the student, fixing his eyes with a strange expression on the other's countenance.

"I know her," said William Lennox, coldly; "but go on. You shall hear my story presently."

"'You love painting,' she said.

"'I do,' I stammered.

"'There are better ones in my gallery,' she continued, with a smile; 'and I love to show them. If you like you can come and see them.'

"'What an honour, madam. When?'

"'Now.'

"And she meant it. She took my arm and led me to her carriage.

"Next day all Madrid knew that I was the favoured swain of Maria Dolores, Duchess of Castella.

"This lasted a few months.

"Then she tired of me, and her door was closed in my face.

"I vowed revenge. But she was powerful, and had me ejected ignominiously from the land. Then began for me a life of a terrible nature. I lived but for revenge. For a long time I could not reach Madrid. At last I did in disguise."

"She had another lover, an Englishman."

"I was that man," said William Lennox, in a sombre tone.

"Merciful heaven!" cried the student, starting to his feet.

"Tell your story," replied William, gloomily, "I will then tell mine."

"My rage was unbounded; and still I could not reach her. She was too well guarded.

"Her enemies were many.

"Her guards were many more.

"Then came a terrible episode.

"It was whispered in Madrid that she had been flogged naked in the vaults of the inquisition for the attempted murder of a young English girl.

"She slew the man who ordered the flogging, and disappeared.

"No one knew where.

"But revenge is persevering.

"I found out."

"Where, in heaven's name?" said William Lennox, with a shudder.

"Here."

"Where?"

"Here in England."

"But where?"

"Under a false name in the suite of the Spanish embassy."

"Heavens, what does this forebode!" said William, with fearful coolness.

"Tell me your story first."

William Lennox told him all that was necessary for him to know. It took a long time. He hid nothing.

Had they not been too deeply intent on their conversation, they would have seen the door of the inner room open slightly, and a pale, haggard face appear thereat, with hot, swift breath, and eyes that started from their orbits.

She was receiving her punishment.

The deserted, abandoned child loved the being who had saved her from death.

Like scorpions' stings are the blows which illicit passion rains upon our devoted heads.

No vice has a swifter punishment.

Imagine her sensations.

We quote some of his words—words which made the student stare.

"I never loved any woman, and never shall, save only Lillian.

"I may feel affection, a kindly wish—I may know desire for others, but love is all for her—for her alone.

"Women do not, or will not understand this.

"Personal infidelity is not always infidelity of the heart.

"A sincere and devoted liking for some gentle creature who is all our own, is not love.

"Love stands on a pedestal too lofty and too pure to be reached by two idols.

"Love and passion may be twins, but love is the elder born.

"Passion alone never leads to love.

"Love carries passion in its train.

"The pure heart delights more in a fond glance from the being whom it loves than in all the joys of passion."

"Vous etes philosophiques," said the student, with a sneer.

"Pardon me if I am philosophical," replied William, with a blush. "I will go on with my story."

When he had finished the other mused for a moment.

"We are brothers in misfortune," said the student, "are we to be brothers in revenge?"

"I want no revenge; but her presence in England disturbs me. I should like to get on her track, however, for doubtless she looks upon me as the cause of her bitter humiliation, when heaven knows I would have taken every blow myself. I shuddered and writhed in agony, as I saw the blows fall upon the soft flesh."

"Saw!"

"Yes, saw."

The student turned pale, despite the darkness of his skin, and his eyes glared like two hot coals.

"I no longer wonder that you fear her," said the student.

"I fear for Lillian. I know that her malignity will take her any length. What is to be done?"

"Find her!"

"How?"

"Listen—"

"I do, with all my ears."

"I am known to the secretary of the Spanish embassy, and he informs me that a grand masked ball is to be given by a certain Countess of Alcaner, at which every body connected with the embassy is to be present. I can obtain tickets. In the crowd we——"

"We—"

"Will you not come?"

"Can I?"

"I will obtain tickets."

"Do."

"Then in the crowd we can listen, examine, spy, and doubtless find. Then shall I be revenged."

"How?"

"I will tell publicly the story of her flogging."

"Horrible. But that is your affair. All I ask is to be able to find her track, and guard my Lillian;" cried William Lennox, sternly. "In her cause I would even slay a woman."

"Then all is agreed," said the student, rising. "To-night I will bring the tickets."

And with a courteous and aristocratic bow the student left the room, after agreeing to sup with the young man at eleven o'clock.

William Lennox sat for some time moodily by the fire, his brow contracted, his face pale, reflecting on the terrible character of the enemy he had had to deal with.

Then he started, as a light hand was laid upon his shoulder. He turned quietly round.

It was the page lad, or rather the girl, who stood beside him—pale, but smiling.

"You had forgotten me," she said, quietly.

"For a moment. I had forgotten myself, but I must be moving."

"Going out?"

"I must."

"To see Lillian?" said the girl, bowing her head, and blushing to the very eyes.

William started angrily back, with a frown upon his face.

"I could not help it."

"How so?"

"You talked so loud."

"Well, no harm is done. Sooner or later you must have known it. I am afraid, Jessie, I am a sad rake—and very cruel to you. But be assured, my dear girl, that you shall never be deserted."

The girl wept.

"Deserted! What care I now. I know that you love another, and that I am but a plaything. But it is not for me to reproach you. This is the first time and the last. Will you allow me to prepare supper for your new friend?"

"With pleasure, my good girl."

And William Lennox went out to make his diurnal visit to Lillian.

Such is life.

In a few minutes after Jack Horne came in, and was surprised to find the page weeping.

"What is the matter?" he said, in his gruff way.

"You don't like me, but oh! if you would but listen to me, we might save *him!*"

"Ah!"

"Will you listen to me?"

"Speak."

"Sit down, for the story is long."

Jack sat down.

"But, first, you saw that man?"

"I did."

"Do you know who he was?"

"I do."

"So do I."

"Tell me —"

Joe Spriggins bent his head and whispered in the ear of the bold dragoon.

"The devil."

"Is it not so?"

"Yes, but how did you know?"

"William Lennox was so minute in his description of all his enemies, and he has many."

The two domestics then determined on a plan of action, after which they shook hands.

They were sworn friends.

CHAPTER XX.

THE SUPPER.

Who had seen the smart men of that little room on that memorable evening might have known that a woman's care had presided at the arrangements. Everything was neat, smart, and elegant. The table cloth was as white as milk, the napkins perfect, the whole *ensemble* worthy of a professional waiter.

There were flowers on the side-board.

Master Joe Spriggins, the page, had taken the liberty, under the advice and guidance of Jack Horne, of having a cold collation ordered in from a first-rate tavern.

William Lennox smiled when he saw the array of eatables and drinkables.

He smiled still more at the elaborate way in which Joe Spriggins had made himself up for a boy. It was unique, a perfect gem.

He would have ordered him to his room, but he looked so beseeching that he yielded.

So Joe Spriggins opened the door as the student knocked.

The young gentleman was now perfectly dressed. His blouse had been exchanged for an elegantly-fitting frock-coat, his cap for a fashionable broad brim, while his trousers and boots seemed to have come fresh from a Parisian tailor.

He grinned with extreme delight at the grand preparations made for the feast.

"*Mais!*" he cried, "one would think oneself one of the *petit soupers* of the *Regence*. If you do this for a casual acquaintance, what would you do for a *belle maitresse?*"

William laughed.

"Thank my servants, not me. They are the founders of the feast."

The student sat down.

In an instant a dish of succulent oysters, with butter, radishes, olives, and anchovies, was placed on the table.

"Let us speak French," said William, in that language.

The other bowed.

He knew only a very little of his mother tongue.

"I never asked you your name," said William Lennox.

"John Dalton; but I don't like it. Call me Henriquez."

They commenced their attack on the viands; the attendants pouring out wine, of which William Lennox, a thorough Englishman in this, drank freely, while the foreigner drank sparingly.

The conversation turned on the conferences of the morning.

"When will the ball take place?"

"In two days."

"Have you the tickets?"

"Yes."

"Where is it to be?"

"I don't know."

"May I see?"

The student took out the tickets and handed them to William.

"The Countess of Alcaner requests the honour of Mr. William Lennox's presence at a masked ball at Hexley House, at H—— road, on Friday evening next."

"I know," said William.

"That's lucky," replied Henriquez; "for I have not the slightest idea."

The conversation continued. William became gay and lively, the student sombre and thoughtful. He ate little and drank less, though the wines were delicious.

At last there came the champagne, of which Henriquez freely agreed to take a bumper.

At the same moment a knock came to the door.

"What is it?" said Joe.

"Please, sir, a lady in a carriage as wants to see Captain Lennox," said the boy.

William blushed, apologised to Henriquez, who stared and half frowned, but said nothing.

William Lennox went out.

Henriquez poured out another glass of champagne, and immediately fell back in a state of insensibility.

* * * *

Meanwhile William Lennox rushed down stairs, and on reaching the door looked to the right and left.

No carriage.

All he saw was a little boy standing over the way, making faces at him on the opposite side of the way.

William stood still, petrified with astonishment, and then, reflecting deeply, went once more up the creaking stairs.

He reached his own door, and opened it.

Imagine his amazement when, seated on one side of the fire, was the lovely Duchess of Castella, her hair hanging about her shoulders.

"Great heaven!" he cried.

"This is your friend the student," said Joe Spriggins.

William Lennox sat down and wiped the clammy sweat from his brow.

"Explain," he gasped.

"Knew her at once," said Jack.

"So did I," said Joe.

"Explain," he continued.

"I listened, and heard your two stories. I had a reason which I will explain another time. I knew her, and on the return of Jack Horne I consulted with him. We arranged both to be here to-night, and fully to betray her—to find out, at all events, if our suspicions were true."

"Thank you; go on."

"I got Jack to buy a powerful and sudden narcotic, which I put in her wine, and sent a boy to call you out."

"Ah!"

"I then took off her wig—"

"Go on."

"Her hair fell about her shoulders."

"How long will she sleep?"

"Until she smells this bottle."

"Replace all as you found it. Say not a word. There's not the slightest suspicion. Leave all to me."

Joe with great agility replaced everything as he found it, and then stood away while William Lennox administered the smelling salts.

"Ah! ah!" said the false Henriquez.

He opened his eyes.

"What is the matter, my friend?" replied the other in a quiet voice.

"A sudden pang at my heart. If death be worse, it must be something terrible, indeed."

"But you are better now."

"Much better."

"Will you take anything?"

"Yes."

"Port wine," said William, addressing the page.

Monsieur Henriquez drank it up, and mechanically placed his hand to his head.

"Better—how long did it last?"

"It was but a spasm. Not more than five minutes," replied William.

"Assist me to my room. I will see you in the morning—at all events the morning before the ball."

The student rose with difficulty; and, leaning on the arm of William Lennox, who perhaps, despite all he knew, not forgetting other happy moments when he had gladly supported her in his arms, supported the student tenderly to the door of his room.

He then shook hands and went away.

When he returned to his room he tottered to a chair and drank off a glass of wine.

"Merciful heavens, my friends!" he said, "what is to be done?"

"Expose her openly," replied Joe.

"No. Forewarned is forearmed. I will go to the ball. But perhaps things may not turn out exactly as she expects."

The dragoon exchanged glances with the page, and then proceeded to remove the feast.

"Sup," said William.

Jack looked at the page.

"We are both his friends," said Joe, holding out his hand.

"We are," replied the great awkward big-hearted fellow, ready to cry.

"Sup," continued William, "and then clear away. After that we will hold a council of war."

And a council of war was held, the result of which will appear as we proceed.

CHAPTER XXII.

THE MASKED BALL.

HEXLEY House, not a trace of which now remains, was one of those old-fashioned houses which, when we happen to fall upon them, speak to us of a byegone age—of days when men had large retinues of servants, and burnt whole trunks of trees instead of small nobs of coal—when gentlemen rode out with six horses, outriders and postilions, instead of coming to town in a one-horse brougham—when vast staircases, admitting of a dozen abreast, yawned before you as you entered the portico—houses that had muniment rooms, strong rooms, secret rooms, secret passages, and even dungeons.

It was surrounded by a park full of large and gloomy trees.

The front was reached through a large grating, the spikes of which had once been gilded, but which now were black and mouldy.

The house had been unlet for a year.

It had a gloomy reputation.

People said that a lady had been immured there for twenty years by a jealous husband.

She had died, and it was said that her spirit still walked its gloomy precincts.

Suddenly an agent came down and took the house, regardless of expense.

It was fitted up magnificently.

As all was paid cash, everything was done in princely style.

On the night of the masquerade it was a blaze of light from the roof to the basement.

About eight the carriages began to roll in from London, all full of splendidly-dressed masqueraders.

By ten the rooms were full.

All were masked, or in fancy dress.

No official presentation took place. It was enough to present a card, with the name of the countess signed in the corner.

* * * *

On the morning of the ball it was agreed between Monsieur Henriquez and William Lennox that the latter should wear splendid Moorish costume, with a white bunch of ribbons on the heart.

The student was to wear a simple domino to enable him to slip about unnoticed.

They then parted, William Lennox pleading business, and Henriquez agreeing, they made arrangements to meet in the evening.

* * * * * *

About eight o'clock a brougham set down a Moor magnificently dressed.

Ten minutes after it was followed by one containing a monk disguised as a British sailor.

The ball-room was splendid.

All the British aristocracy of the day seemed to have given themselves a rendezvous at Hexley House.

It was said that the Prince Regent was there in one of his usual *incognito*.

The rooms were flashing with light.

Pillars of variegated stonework rose to the vaulted ceiling of the principal ball-room, from which depended rows of Chinese lanterns, lost almost amid flowers of every hue.

Beauty and manliness were there, arrayed in every imaginable dress.

Here a Turk elbowed a Moorish lady.

Here a Dominican friar hob-nobbed with a Greek dancing girl.

There a nun listened to vows of eternal love from a cavalier, and there a Puritan forgot his principles in the smiles of a gaily dressed lady.

There were two among the motley crowd who afforded a strange contrast, the one to the other.

One was a tall, strongly-built man, dressed in the costume of an Italian brigand.

The other, a pale-looking boy attired in the dress of a page of the times of Charles I.

These two were inseparable, and appeared to be intently watching the movements of some one.

Suddenly, about an hour after the opening of the ball, the page stopped and clutched his companion's arm.

"Jack!" he whispered.

"Well, what now?"

"Stay here for one moment—I see William."

"Be careful," muttered Jack Horne, for it was he.

"I will; but do not hinder my purpose."

And so saying Joe Spriggins darted off.

At the end of the large room was a small opening, through which a view could be commanded of an inner apartment, where two persons were sitting.

The one was a man dressed in the dress of a cavalier.

The other a tall lady, attired after the manner of Mary Queen of Scots.

In one Jessie easily distinguished William Lennox.

In the other was as easily distinguished the Duchess of Castella.

They were engaged in earnest conversation.

William's language was fervent and impassioned, the duchess listened with a kind of listless wantoness. She evidently did not know her companion.

Jessie Brown stood spell-bound.

She forgot everything.

She forgot time, place—all but her jealousy and her aching heart.

She listened to every word, but she could understand little of what they said.

The conversation was carried on in whispers.

The speakers seemed to be engrossed wholly in each other, and saw not the eager, anxious, miserable countenance which watched them.

Jessie was roused by a shake from a heavy hand.

She looked round.

Jack Horne was standing there, gazing with a kind of puzzled expression at the scene.

"Come, Joe," he said, "it's no use stopping there. No use. Come with me, I have work in hand."

Just as he spoke the duchess rose, held out her hand to William Lennox to kiss, and disappeared as if by magic.

"I thought so," said Jack Horne, "come quickly with me."

They emerged from the folds of the curtain which encircled them, and once more passed through the busy throng.

Another room at the other extremity of the room was the scene of the strange conspiracy which they thus unravelled.

They had hardly time to ensconce themselves behind the heavy folds of the hangings when the Duchess of Castella entered.

Behind her was a figure dressed in the character of a mountebank, but in whom one could easily recognise Slimy Jones.

"Just so," said he; "are we alone?"

"Yes," replied the duchess; "but let us be quiet. You have, I suppose, matured your plan?"

"Just so."

"Lillian must be carried off, no matter at what hazard."

"Just so."

"And when can this be done?"

"Just so," said Slimy Jones, abstractedly; "let me see."

And he began ruminating and counting upon his fingers.

"I want it done directly."

"Just so—so shall it be."

"You know my plan," continued the duchess, "she must be carried out far into the country—to some spot where Captain Winterton can visit her. You understand me."

"Just so."

"The foolish man is almost in love with the girl already. She is not very strong-minded, I think, and I fancy our scheme of revenge may soon be accomplished."

"Just so."

"Then, as to William Lennox?"

"Just so—he must be left to me."

"Truly; but have you decided upon the manner in which he is to be disposed of?"

"Just so, all is arranged."

"Then," continued the duchess, in a very low voice. "you remember at ——"

The remainder of the sentence was given in so low a whisper that neither Jack Horne nor Jessie could hear it.

They determined, however, to use the knowledge they did possess to the best advantage.

Little did Jessie Brown know how great a trial was awaiting her.

CHAPTER XXII.

THE RESCUE.

AMONG the amusements at the gardens of the Silver Fountain was a tame dancing bear.

This animal used constantly to perform before the Pasha; and very often was, in the still summer evenings, led out into the gardens for the amusement of the Pasha's wife and her women.

When, on the following morning, the Pasha had left the apartments of his spouse, and she once more considered herself safe from intrusion, she sent for Captain George and Joe the Mudlark.

Captain George kissed her hand when he entered, and said—

"How can I reward you for all your kindness to me—how show sufficient gratitude for all your favour?"

"Alas!" said Aysha, whose beautiful breast was fluttering quickly beneath her pink gauze vest; "alas! as I said to you last night, I am not quite disinterested.

"I have to save your wife from the outrageous and vicious lust of a man, and that man my husband.

"But I have a plan for your escape, which I must unfold to you quickly, as from what I hear from my maidens, the Pasha is becoming enraged at delay.

"Either the life or the virtue of your wife will be sacrificed before long, if she be not rescued in time.

"There is in this palace a tame bear.

"You may smile, but that animal must be the means of your deliverance.

"Saomi, one of my blacks, has my orders to kill the animal to-day.

"Into the skin of the beast either you or your companion must enter, and carry away Lucy as if in play. In the confusion the other lady can escape."

Captain George was puzzled.

The scheme was ingenious, but it was odd. It was out of the way; and, though of an adventurous turn of mind, the captain considered it rather Utopian.

"You don't seem to like my plan," said Aysha, carelessly, and throwing herself full length on the divan, so as fully to display her magnificently developed bust and figure— "well, I can suggest no other."

"Be not offended, madam," cried Captain George, stepping towards her, and pressing her hand to his lips; "be not offended, I was only meditating how it could be managed."

He kissed her hand. Though his wife was in the next room he almost felt inclined to kiss those cherry lips which belonged to that radiant, glowing figure.

"Now then you must be gone," said Aysha.

"And when is the attempt to be made?"

"To-day, at one, a slave will summon you to my private apartments—there, in that room"— she added, pointing to a door to the right, "in that room either you or your servant can dress himself in his strange attire. At five I shall be in the gardens with my women, and among us Lucy and her maid. Adieu."

"Adieu."

And Captain George left the apartment.

Very slowly the day passed.

Every hour seemed to be gifted with leaden wings.

They paced their rooms—the Captain and Joe —and talked confidentially.

An identity of trouble had made them equals.

They recognised no distinction of rank, but spoke as if they were brothers.

"Do you think that we shall succeed?" said Captain George.

"Don't know," cried Joe, "I'll either die or do it to-day."

"Well said."

"Say well done when it's over."

"But where are we to go—we must return to the Plague City."

"Our treasure is there," said Joe; "or else I should not care to return."

"We must depart from this at any rate," said Captain George; "see, here is the slave."

A black slave now entered.

"All is ready," said he; "follow me."

Passing through Aysha's chamber, which was now vacant, they entered the small chamber which she had indicated in the morning.

In this chamber they found three black slaves, and upon the floor lay the skin of a grizzly bear.

"Which of us is to enter this gloomy abode?" said the captain.

"I had better go in," said Joe; "I am used to jumping, and shall make rather a good bear."

"Very well."

Joe rather liked the experiment.

He made the slaves hold the skin up, and crept in.

He was soon sewn up, and began practising.

He jumped well.

Every one laughed.

"That'll do first-rate!" said Captain George.

"All right," cried a sepulchral voice through the bear's snout. "I suppose I mustn't say much. But it's deuced stinking in here!"

"Well, good bye, old fellow," said Captain George, shaking the bear's paw. "We shall meet this evening in the garden. Remember, take the road to the city, and I will follow."

He then left, and returned to his own room.

The evening set in gloriously.

A rich red sun cast a brilliant halo over the beautiful gardens, with their parterres of olive and citron and lemon trees, and their shady walks.

The silvery fountains seemed to throw up volumes of blood-red spray towards a sky which was undimmed with even the shadow of a vapour.

Before the silver fountain was the tent of the Pasha's wife.

She lay there under an awning.

Her dress was of pure white, and her glowing bosom was unprotected from the evening air, save by a gauze chemise, which only served to render more dazzling the heaving globes beneath.

Her turban was spangled with gold, and her long dark locks coiled like serpents round her neck, and between her breasts.

Captain George crept stealthily along the footway; and as he gazed from his place of concealment at this image of loveliness and passion, he could not resist saying aloud—

"Oh! that a man could wish for any but such an angel."

"Just so," said a sepulchral voice near him.

He turned quickly, and saw the dancing bear performing his evolutions.

For half an hour this continued; when all at once, just as the fun was at its highest point, the bear burst from his keeper, and made a dash away among the bevy of damsels round Aysha.

In an instant all was confusion. Aysha, who, knowing how everything had been arranged, did not care to disturb herself, only half raised herself from her divan, and gazed in apparent horror at the scene.

No one interfered with the bear, who immediately selected his prey. Captain George seized Mary in his arms, and Haidee tripped on lightly before them to lead the way.

Night was coming on, so that, upon emerging from the Pasha's gardens, it was resolved only to advance a few miles, and then to take advantage of the first chance of cover for the night.

They came at length to the skirts of what appeared to be a garden; and here, at haphazard, they entered. The pathways were neglected—the fallen leaves, piled here and there in heaps by the wind, were rapidly decomposing, and imparted a heavy sluggish feeling to the air. At intervals the banana tree shook its gigantic leaves, while its clustering fruit, of a dark purple colour, exhaled an aromatic odour extremely pleasing to the sense. Here were thickets of mimosa, with foliage of delicate green; there groves of pomegranate, and orange, and lemon, and citron trees, with date palms of towering stature rearing their long stems and pendulous leaves and masses of golden fruit to meet the sun's rays, which came streaming richly upon them from the desert.

Below the light seemed to render the fine green leaves transparent as it shot through them, and fell in tremulous patterns on the green sward, or went down the slope till it spread over the broad river beyond. There appeared no termination to the gardens, they seemed to be wandering amid an endless succession of vistas, glades, and leafy avenues, winding tracks, bowers, arbours, and leafy arcades, some of which conducted the eye to the glittering surface of the river, others the turquoise vault of heaven, which stretched its indescribable blue from one edge of the horizon to the other.

There were few hopes of a better habitation.

They were thankful for any spot which would shield them from observation, so here they remained for the night, with no other covering but the sky.

Emerging hence in the morning, they discovered they had lost their way. Four roads faced them. To take either was dangerous; but at length they struck into the one which appeared to lead in an opposite direction to that of the Pasha's house.

All day they travelled, and at length, weary and footsore, they arrived on the confines of a village, outside which, under cover of a thicket, they rested and waited till morning. As soon as dawn came they determined to go into the village, and, by dint of large presents, persuade the inhabitants to grant them a guide.

Haidee, ever thoughtful, had brought with her a little provision, and after they had regaled themselves sparingly, they slept soundly under the starlit sky.

CHAPTER XXIII.

THE FLIGHT.

At length dawn came. Dawn is beautiful in all countries, and nothing is more delightful than to witness it, or even at the distance of years to recall its sublimity. I have always, when observing the opening eyelids of the morning, fancied the earth was undergoing a new creation, and issuing forth, radiant in loveliness, from the hands of its Maker. To others, perhaps, this also appears to be the case, in rich and luxuriant regions, where wood groves, meadows, valleys, mountains, and streams suggest ideas of abundance and happiness.

Dawn in the east is peculiarly beautiful, and though with a very different feeling from that

which an artist would have experienced, Captain George watched its approach with eagerness. At length, over the undulating, sandy plain, the faint, pearly light began to flush the sky on the edge of the horizon. Every instant the arch of splendour expanded, and embraced a larger section of the heavens, while streaks of saffron and crimson, shot up rapidly from some fiery centre, and seemed to pierce the firmament like arrows, blotting out the stars with their quivering pulsations, and imparting to the whole face of nature a profusion of gorgeous features, inexpressibly magnificent.

The figures of poetry could never keep pace with the chariot of Eos. Before language could supply epithets to paint one phenomenon a series of new appearances would have succeeded and vanished. The change from saffron to crimson, from crimson to rose colour, from rose colour to purple, from purple to amethyst, and from this again to coerulean blue, chased, and veined, and quivering tremulously with light, was swift as thought. At length the sun itself arose, and the desert lay blushing before it, like an eastern bride.

Captain George and Joe, as we have said, were watching for the dawn.

They were, therefore, the first to rise.

Haidee, Lucy, and Mary were still wrapped in the arms of the night god.

Leaving, therefore, the women under the shadow of the tall trees, Joe the mudlark and his master entered the village, and made their respects to the first camel driver that appeared.

The man eyed them suspiciously. Their dress, their manners, and their language betokened that they did not belong to the country.

Captain George, however, knew the language well: and, saluting the man, explained in a few moments their errand.

"Allah is great," cried the man musing; "if I aid your escape, the Pasha is powerful and will perhaps take signal revenge."

"But I will reward you," said Captain George, "in such a manner that you will be as great as the Pasha, and may have slaves in your house, and many wives, and may say to him when he seeks you, 'Truly I helped the Christian. I am your equal.'"

The man nervously twitched his spear and thought.

What a concentrated agony was then in Captain George's heart as he waited. At that moment the Pasha might be in full pursuit. They had walked from the gardens of the Silver Fountain, and had made but little progress.

"Well," said the man at length, "I will help you. My dromedaries are swift, and we will be in Algiers ere nightfall."

The beasts were accordingly brought round, seven in number, and the party mounted. They presented quite a formidable array. Abd-el-Razer and his son stationed themselves first to lead the way—then the three women and Captain George, and Joe the mudlark in the rear.

They immediately put their dromedaries to their utmost speed, and faint as they were from hunger, passed through town after town, and village after village.

At length towards evening the guide quitted them, and returned to his village. Afterwards, no doubt, he often related to his wife and children how, in former days, when he was a young man, he saved certain unbelievers from the vengeance of a Pasha; and how, although only performing an act of charity enjoined upon all true disciples of El-Islam, he became, through the bounty of a stranger, a man wealthy and respected.

As night came on they began to enter the extensive olive groves which appeared to cover all that portion of the province. They met numerous small parties making the best of their way home, as in those days of pestilence hungry bands were prowling about everywhere, and it was extremely dangerous to be found out after dark.

But their advance was impeded by the extraordinary nature of the ground; sometimes their road lay through dusky woods where they could not see even the heads of their dromedaries. They would then, perhaps, immerge on a narrow causeway running between two deep and broad canals.

Occasionally they had to climb considerable hillocks or mounds, and then crawl over narrow pathways running along the precipitous banks of the water-courses, where the least slip of the foot would have sent them down headlong, camels and all, into unknown depths. Here and there vast volumes of water were heard rushing through sluices, or falling down precipices with a deafening and perplexing noise, mingling with which they thought they could detect the deep howl of the wolf or the long melancholy cry of the jackal.

As the hours wore on they began sadly to fear that they should not reach Algiers before the closing of the gates, and, consequently, have to pass the night in the open country; afraid to kindle a fire, lest they might attract some straggling party of robbers sufficiently audacious to approach the walls of the capital.

It was with extreme pleasure, therefore, that they at length heard the voice of the muezzin calling to evening prayer. As soon as he had concluded, they knew the gates would be closed, so they violently urged forward their jaded animals, whose instinct strongly assisted them, as they appeared to know quite as well as their masters did that they were to rest and get their suppers at Algiers. They fortunately arrived at the very critical moment, for the porters were in the act of closing the city gate, when camel after camel dashed through as if understanding the dilemma.

CHAPTER XXIV.

HOMEWARD BOUND.

DURING the absence of our adventurers at the gardens of the Silver Fountains, the plague had somewhat abated. A few of the shops had opened, and a little life was apparent among the citizens.

It was too late that night for anything but supper and sleep.

The son of Abd-el-Razer, who had remained to take back the dromedaries and the present to his father, stopped that night in the house of Captain George.

On the following morning the mudlark and his master, taking with them a dromedary, went to the house of the old Jew.

They took the beast with them because they knew not in what manner Michael proposed to hand over to him his fortune.

The street in which Michael resided was as still as death.

On the one side the gaunt houses rose apparently empty towards the sky; on the other lay the waters of the harbour, as dark and muddy as a pond. Only a few tenantless craft dotted the lazy pool, and only one ship had ventured into the precincts of the city. That ship was an English man-of-war.

On arriving at the door of the Jew's house Captain George was struck with a dread presentiment of evil. Could Michael have played him false?

He knocked loudly. No answer came.

In his anxiety about his wife he had entrusted the whole of his treasure to an utter stranger, and not even taken a receipt. If Michael denied the affair there was no redress. The story of the treasure was a wild, improbable one; no one would give credence to it.

He knocked again, but still no response.

"Seems to me, sir," said Joe, "that he's been and hooked it."

"It looks like it, certainly," replied Captain George, with a kind of forced gaiety; "we shall have to burst the door."

Joe didn't want much telling in an affair of this kind.

"That won't take a deal of trying," said he.

And suiting the action to the word, he leaned his shoulder against the old ricketty door, which seemed to yield like magic to the pressure. Everything was as still as death. An air, like the air of a charnel house, pervaded the place; and a sickening feeling came over the two adventurers as they came to the miser's door.

The door was ajar.

They pushed it open, and gazed transfixed with horror.

What a sight met that gaze.

On one side was the bed of Michael untenanted, but evidently having been lately occupied. In the centre of the room was a large trunk containing precious stones and jewellery, and gold heaped together in beautiful confusion. The pearl and the amethyst, the ruby, the sapphire, and the emerald, emitted their bright sparkles amid myriads of golden coins. Hanging over this repository of wealth was the gaunt figure of the Jew, nearly naked; his legs, like those of a skeleton, trailing along the floor; his hands thrust in among the jewels; his eyes fixed and glassy.

He was quite dead, and the close air of the chamber showed that he had been so for many days.

"What a terrible death," muttered Captain George, as he flung open the windows to let in a little fresh air. "But what is this?"

A packet lay upon the table, directed—"For the Englishman."

This Captain George opened. It contained, in French and English notes, the whole amount to which Michael had said he was entitled.

"Honest enough," said the Captain.

Joe the mudlark was extremely fidgetty. His master could not make him out.

"Let's go," said Captain George; "our business is done—we cannot help him now. We must leave him to his wealth and the mercy of the Dey, who, perhaps, will give him decent burial for the sake of the treasure he finds."

"Why should the Dey have it?" inquired Joe.

Captain George smiled.

"We have enough, I think, for ourselves. We cannot take more away. What is it you want?"

"Why, sir," said Joe, "I don't see why we should leave this 'ere wealth for the Dey. Why not give it to the men who saved our lives?"

"Well said," replied Captain George: and so it was done.

So, after selecting two or three bracelets for Lucy and Mary, and pocketing some of the largest and most valuable diamonds and emeralds, they departed home.

Abd-el-Raser's son was despatched to his village with his dromedaries, to carry tidings to his father of the wealth he had acquired by saving the life of the stranger.

That evening the "Firebrand," war frigate, sailed from Algiers.

On its deck, as it cleared the port, stood Lucy and Mary and Haidee, with Captain George and the mudlark.

Darkness was just gently coming on. The ship slid quietly out of the port of the silent city. One last gaze was cast by the sailors at the harbour which they were leaving tenantless, and pervaded by the atmosphere of death. Up went the British flag, the sails were unfurled, the wind caught them merrily, three cheers, and then hey for old England!

CHAPTER XXV.

THE MAGIC MIRROR.

WILLIAM LENNOX was greatly disturbed in mind.

His conversation with the duchess was a good piece of acting. She knew him not, but she half suspected his presence. His manner was fervent, impassioned—just such as to lead her to the supposition that he was still her slave.

When she left him abruptly in order to seek an interview with Slimy Jones, he fancied he detected a slight rustling amid the curtains. He leaped forward, dashed them aside, and saw the retreating forms of Joe Spriggins and Jack Horne.

He did not recognise them; but they had been listening evidently. His brain was on fire—his visit to the ball was purposeless. Tired, hot, and wearied, he left the ball-room, and passed into the marble-floored apartment which skirted it, and where no one at the moment was present.

The room contained scarcely any furniture. Massive marble pillars rose to the ceiling—heavy tapestry covered the walls—a couch was distributed here and there, and in the centre of one side of the panelling was a huge mirror. The light—cast over the room by a few dim lanterns—was faint and heavy; and, fancying he saw the reflection of figures, William Lennox approached and looked.

"Great heavens!" he exclaimed, as with clasped hands he surveyed the mirror.

He looked again and again—then gazed round the apartment. Not a soul was visible. But the scene depicted in the mirror was plain enough.

There, kneeling at the feet of one whom William instantly recognised as Lillian, was a man.

He was tall and fine-looking. His eyes gazed fondly, passionately at the beautiful girl who seemed half terrified, half pleased at his addresses.

William Lennox gazed spell-bound.

The figures moved.

Lillian turned her face half-round towards her admirer, and he snatched a passionate kiss, which she did not repulse.

William Lennox rushed forward to dash down the fatal glass, when some one entered the apartment. The figures faded from the mirror, and left it bright and unstained as before.

The person who entered the room was a lady dressed in a Grecian habit.

She started on seeing William. He bowed and passed from the room.

"Oh! William," murmured the lady, as she sank down on the ottoman opposite the mirror; "how can I believe that you love me when all tell me you are false?"

A slight noise disturbed her. She started, and glanced rapidly at the mirror. There her gaze remained. She moved not—spoke not—but sat there transfixed, drinking in with her eyes the terrible confirmation of her doubts.

The mirror was again instinct with life. This time William Lennox was sitting—moodily, dejectedly, in his own room. A door opens. A small fairy-like figure enters. William Lennox looks up—his dejection vanishes—a smile passes over his face, and he folds the girl fondly to his breast.

The girl was Jessie Browne. Lillian saw no more. What she had witnessed was sufficient. She rose from her seat, and the mirror once more became bright and spotless.

During the continuance of this scene a small wicket by the side of the mirror had been partly opened—just sufficient to allow a view of the couch and its occupant.

Two gleaming eyes watched the progress of the terrible plot, and were well satisfied with the result.

"*My poison works,*" said the Duchess of

Castella, as she closed the wicket, and returned to the drawing-room.

William Lennox did not remain long at Hexley House. He felt stunned, dismayed, as it were, by the events which surrounded him. The Duchess of Castella was in London merely for the sake of her revenge. That that revenge was to take its most terrible form—the ruin of the being he loved best in the world—he could no longer doubt. How was it to be prevented? He resolved to return home, avoid every one, and go early to the house of Lillian to ascertain the meaning of the scene which the mirror had accidentally disclosed to him.

Just as he was descending the marble stairs he saw the student a little way in advance.

"She changes her disguises quickly," thought he, and was about to accost her, when another figure darted from behind a pillar, and said:

"To-night! Everything is ready."

This was Slimy Jones.

"Ah! M. Lennox—delighted vary mush to zee you. I vill go home vith you. I am taired—ennuyè."

"So am I," said William, laconically, and took his arm.

CHAPTER XXVI.

BRACKLEY BRIDGE.

ABOUT six miles from London, and about two from Hexley House, was Brackley Common, now built over, and containing a thriving population. Across the centre of this common ran a small stream, over which the highroad was continued by a wooden bridge, almost obscured by a dense cluster of trees.

It was a lonely spot; and had it not been that the party coming from Hexley House was a numerous one, the revellers would scarcely have deemed it prudent to pass its precincts in the small hours of the morning.

Near this cluster of trees—quite hidden from observation by their deep shadows—three horsemen had stood since twelve. Their animals were tethered to the hedgerow, while they, leaning against the tree-trunks, discussed the probable success of their approaching adventure. They were all masked.

"Devilish cold work this," said one.

"Colder without my forethought," said another, at the same time bringing a well-filled flask to his mouth. "But these adventures are always d——d difficult and unremunerative."

"You say rightly, comrade," replied the first speaker; "but just hand us a swig—will you? Don't nab it all yourself."

These remarks were evidently levelled at the third adventurer, who stood leaning against his horse, apparently in a brown study. He now roused up, however.

"What the deuce are you grumbling at, you fellows?" cried he. "You undertook the job of your own free will. Go away if you don't like it."

"Oh! it's all very well talking. You couldn't do without us: but is the tin square?"

"I have told you before it's first-rate," returned their leader. "But hark! some one is coming. Keep quiet."

The sound of a single horse's hoofs were heard clattering along the road from Hexley House. It did not slacken speed as it approached, and the last speaker, advancing out into the highway, cried—

"Small hours."

"And large pay," returned the horseman, coming to a dead standstill, and then turning and joining the group.

"What's up now?" asked Captain Winterton, who was the leader of the party.

"Just so," said Slimy Jones, dismounting, and wiping the sweat off his forehead; "they will be last. It's all right."

"An accident I suppose?"

"Something amiss with the carriage."

"Ah! an accident done on purpose?"

"Just so," said Slimy Jones. "Something like our accidental meeting here."

In whispered conversation the time passed, until at length the carriages began to roll in from Hexley House.

They drove two or three together for the sake of company, as well as of protection, and it was not long before the rumble of the wheels of the last vehicle was heard faintly receding in the distance.

"Now, then," said Slimy Jones, "wait for the next."

Unfortunately for the intended victims, but fortunately for the adventurers, it was a dark night. Otherwise, for that time at least, their efforts would have been unavailing. As it was, however, the clouds were densely packed—not a glimpse of the moon had been seen the whole night. She seemed, indeed, to have retired behind her bed-curtains to veil her face from the sight of the iniquities which were to be perpetrated under her rays.

It was very early in the morning when the long-expected carriage was seen coming swiftly along the road. It soon approached the spot where the four adventurers were standing, and in a moment, as if by magic, the horses were stopped, the postillion dashed from his seat, and the door opened.

Two ladies occupied the vehicle.

"Ladies," said Captain Winterton, "I must beg that you will alight."

"What is it?—what do you want?" said one of them in a voice half choked with terror. "Here, take all our money; but pray do not detain us here."

"We are not robbers, madam," replied the captain; "pray do as I bid you—resistance is useless, as you perceive."

And he pointed significantly, though politely, to the men with him.

The ladies saw it was useless to resist, and descended half-fainting with terror.

A moment sufficed to show Winterton which he sought.

"This is the lady I seek," said he, taking Lillian firmly by the arm, and stepping between her and her companion, he observed, "I will not detain you; you can proceed."

"No, no—I will not leave her; I will not go

to London alone. Lillian! oh, Lillian!" she shrieked, as Slimy Jones seized the young girl in his arms, and bore her into the covert. Captain Winterton placed his hand over her mouth.

"My dear madam," said he with the most provoking coolness, "your object is to save the young lady. To offer resistance here is useless —you had better at once proceed to London, and set the Hue and Cry after us. For the present, good night."

And so saying, he leaped on his horse, galloped off, and was out of sight in a moment.

When William Lennox reached home that night with his companion, he was startled by the receipt of a note which had been left, Jessie said, by a lady dressed in deep mourning.

It ran thus:—

"*Lillian will be carried off to-night. Do not make any inquiries, but wait another letter. If you seek to discover me, I tell no more.*"

The letter bore no date, and was not signed.

CHAPTER XXVII.

A DOUBLE GAME.

When Lillian recovered her senses, which she had utterly lost for a time when seized upon by Slimy Jones, she found herself in a carriage alone. The vehicle was proceeding at a tremendous speed, and she could perceive by the dark figures which flitted constantly past, and the clattering of horses' hoofs, that she was attended by a party of riders.

She had not the least conception where she was going, or for what purpose; neither could she, by any reasoning, succeed in even a random guess at the person who was instrumental in her abduction. She seemed like one in a dream; and as she felt herself plunging along the country roads in the misty morning, attired as she was, in the dress of a Greek dancing girl, she really began to imagine she was but preparing for a recurrence of the terrible events which she had before been compelled to undergo by her enemies.

They travelled all day. Every necessary had been provided for her comfort. There was no need to stop. Provisions of all sorts were contained in the carriage. Of these, though more than once pressed to do so by Slimy Jones she could not partake. Her whole mind was concentrated in one agony of despair and anxiety.

At length, towards evening, they came to a halt. They appeared to be upon the suburbs of some town. They stopped opposite the door of a mansion, and Lillian, more dead than alive, was led through a large hall into a spacious drawing-room. Here she was left to herself for awhile, and then a serving-maid entered.

"Would you like to take anything, Miss?" inquired the girl, blandly.

"No—no—nothing—where am I?"

"In the house of the Marquis of Glencorn."

Lillian shuddered. The name of the Marquis of Glencorn was well known : he bore the reputation of being the seducer of many an innocent and fair girl whom he had captivated by his wealth or stolen away by force.

"Am I to remain here in this room?"

"We expect the marquis every moment," said the servant.

"Then, for heaven's sake, let me not see him ! Is there no room where I can remain quietly for the night, since I am a prisoner here? I cannot—I will not see any one to-night."

She stood there the very picture of agonised beauty, and the girl gazed at her in pity and admiration. Her Greek turban had just allowed her locks to escape—her vest rose and fell with the tumultuous heavings of her bosom—her tall, slender form was shown off to advantage in her elegant kaftan and white and gold trousers.

She suddenly started forward and seized the girl by the hand. A thought seemed to strike her.

"Surely you have no object in keeping me here. Have you?"

The girl did not answer.

"Surely you do not wish to aid in the ruin of one of your sex?"

Still no answer.

"Have you no sister who might some day be placed in a position like this? If you have, have pity on me, and help me to escape from this horrid house."

"I dare not," replied the girl.

"Dare not !—are you compelled to stay here? But come, if pity will not move you, perhaps the offer of reward will. If you aid my escape, I know one who will reward you well."

The girl's eyes glistened—whether satirically or in avarice it was hard to tell. Lillian thought she was succeeding, and proceeded :

"He will reward you handsomely, and you will not then require to be a servant any longer. Say, now, will you help me ?"

"Perhaps," said the servant-maid; "but I cannot to-night. It is early yet to talk of escape. Come, if you want to go to your room I will show you."

Without emerging again into the hall, the girl led the way along an inner passage into a spacious bedroom, well-appointed, and even luxuriantly furnished.

"You will want a change of dress in the morning, Miss," said she. "I will get you one."

"Thank you," said Lillian, and she was left alone.

It was very early; but, tired and excited as she was by the turmoil of the last twenty-four hours, she was glad enough to creep into the bed which, even in that house of terror, seemed to possess infinite temptations.

Sleep, however, was a stranger to her for many an hour; and when the girl entered the room at ten o'clock, to ask her if she would take anything before finally retiring to rest, she was still gazing with clasped hands at the foot of the bed.

Her thoughts were in a state of terrible commotion. She had seen at Hexley House a confirmation of the faithlessness of William Lennox. To whom, then, could she apply for assistance? Not, certainly, to a man who had forsaken her for another. She felt, as it were, alone in the world. William having proved untrue, it mattered not what became of her.

At length, soon after the girl had been dismissed with a hasty "No," sleep fell over her eyelids—she felt drowsy—extinguished the light, and gave herself up to a heavy sleep, not forgetting, even in her haste, to lock the door against intruders.

*   *   *   *   *

It was that evening, about the same hour, that William Lennox received a second missive from his mysterious informant, which ran as follows:—

"*You have acted discreetly. Lillian is on her road to Paris. Follow her. I will be with you.*"

CHAPTER XXVIII.

THIEVES' INN.

PARIS has in it many queer localities, and, we may safely say, none queerer than the neighbourhood of the Rue du Temple.

The place is queer enough now, but at the time of our story it was entirely a different sort of affair.

The walls, perhaps, were less cracked, but they didn't seem a bit cleaner than they are now, even at this distance of time. Its inhabitants were more closely packed—less honest—more mysterious.

The place to which we have to introduce our readers was a *tapis-franc*—a café frequented by all the thieves and bad characters in that portion of the capital. Not that it was by any means a sanctuary where the suspected might consider himself safe from the persecution of the secret police: but it was a resort where the thief and *even the murderer* might enjoy his pipe and his glass without any fear of being questioned.

Madame Lanfan—or Madame *Trop-long* (as she was denominated in the slang of her customers, on account of her gigantic height), had once or twice been accused of harbouring persons accused of theft; but after having received wholesome reprimands and fines, she had become quite the *beau ideal* of a hostess.

On the evening on which we introduce this extraordinary establishment to our readers the Thieves' Inn was rather full. Madame *Trop-long* was doing a thriving business. In one corner of the large room (at the end of which was the bar from which all commodities were served) sat two men and a woman, engaged in earnest conversation. The one was a thickset, burly man, whose face evidently betokened him an Englishman—the other was a small, wiry-looking fellow, a Frenchman; while the female by his side, an old, haggard woman, was also French. Their conversation, which was rapid, and interesting apparently to them, was interrupted only by frequent gestures of impa-

tience from the Frenchman, and constant glances towards the door.

At length the wicket at the end of the dark passage, leading to the tap-room, opened, and a tall, gaunt figure entered. He gazed round eagerly at the motley group, and seemed scanning each of them curiously and impatiently.

"Here *Squelette* (skeleton), here you are," half shrieked the old woman; "come, you are very late."

Squelette, as he was aptly denominated, immediately joined the party, and the rapid dialogue was resumed.

"He comes over to-morrow," said the Englishman. "When do you propose doing this affair?"

"To-morrow night," replied *Squelette*.

"And who assists you?"

"Henri."

"Is he true?"

"Aye, Monsieur, true as steel."

"And you have been told the terms and the extent to which you are to go to. Mind, no murder."

"No, no, all right," muttered *Squelette*. "Ah, ah, ah! you are excessively nice. No murder—only the vaults."

The Englishman looked uneasy. The little Frenchman glanced furtively round. The old woman trembled, and plucked the skeleton by the arm.

"Keep your merriment till another time, *gamin*," she whispered. "Do you wish us to be *escarpé*" (hung), and she made a significant gesture with her hand.

Just as she spoke a movement was visible at the end of the room. One glance sufficed for *Squelette*. Like magic he vanished, and left the Englishman, though not his companions, thunderstruck at his sudden disappearance.

"What is the matter?" asked the Englishman of the French thief.

"Do you not see?—two agents."

At the other extremity of the crowded room were standing two men, dressed something after the fashion of *ouvriers* in their Sunday clothes. They seemed to observe nobody—ordered wine and pipes—sat down—entered into conversation with one another—and appeared quite at their ease.

"Whom are they seeking?" whispered the Englishman.

"*Squelette*," said the woman, in an undertone.

Underneath the large room of the *Tapis-Franc* was a capacious cellar, which, at the time we are writing of, was lighted by an oil lamp, swinging from the ceiling.

This cellar communicated with the room above by a trap-door.

It was through this that *Squelette* had so dexterously vanished upon the appearance in the café of the two agents of the secret police.

In one corner of the cellar was a bed, on which lay a young man, apparently asleep. Standing by his bedside were a little boy about five years of age, and a little fair-haired girl, of between six and seven.

There were only a table and two chairs to

complete the furniture of this luxurious apartment.

The children shrank together, as down the trap came *Squelette*, and through a side-door a fat, squat woman, with a red handkerchief, tied turban fashion round her head.

"Hist, *Trapue*" (dumpy), cried *Squelette*, "the *mouchards* (secret police) are upstairs. Speak low."

"Edouard," said *Trapue*, without answering *Squelette*, and shaking violently the sleeping youth. "Wake *loir* (dormouse), this is not your bed—take the children up and go to your room, and don't make a noise, as the *mouchards* are here."

The young man did not answer, but silently left the cellar with the children.

Trapue listened until their footsteps could no longer be heard, and then, drawing the chair close up to *Squelette*, said—

"How is it going?"

"All right," returned the man; "but I can't make out what the spies want. I have been quiet lately?"

"Yes, but the Passy affair has not yet been expiated."

"Bah! I served a year—that satisfies them. They must be on some new scent."

"Well, well, let us hope so; for if it be as you say, you cannot be nabbed yet. But I have something to tell you."

Trapue, as she said this, rose up, went to the door and listened. She then returned, and said in a low whisper—

"Edouard knows all."

"*Diable!*"

"Who has told him?"

"The children."

"They have been acting the spy—eh?'

"Yes; they heard all our plans last night, and told Edouard. I was at the door to-night and watched him, when, getting up in a chair, he listened at the half open trap-door. He knows all, as I say, and has sworn to betray us."

"What! betray us to the police?"

"Or rather, I should say," added the woman, "to prevent our plan from succeeding by informing the stranger of our plans."

As *Trapue* said this a kind of grim pallor overspread his features. His mouth worked convulsively, and his large goggle eyes appeared ready to start from their sockets. After a moment's hesitation he rose, and feeling under the table, brought forth a long knife.

"What are you going to do?" asked the woman, trembling.

"I am going to stop Edouard's 'peaching."

"He is our son," cried the woman; "do not kill him."

The man turned his great staring eyes upon *La Trapue*, and said quietly—

"When I say I will do a thing, I will do it. Remember it was Edouard who, as a child, obtained for me fifteen years' transportation, from which I escaped only to curse him; it was he who 'peached upon the gang that killed Porsonier at Papy; he is now going to take my life—I will take his."

For a moment the voice of the hideous *La Trapue* softened as she said—

"Spare him this time; he will not, perhaps, 'peach after all."

Squelette only looked at her with a contemptuous sneer, lit a small lamp, and ascended the old stairs towards Edouard's room. *La Trapue* knew that if she opposed him she would share the same fate, so, in an agony of terror, she followed the man who was about to murder his own son.

At the first landing she stopped and sat down on the steps.

Squelette ascended to the next storey, and stealthily opened the door of a room. A light was still burning. In one corner lay the little boy and girl fast asleep, locked in each other's arms. In the other, on a heap of straw, reposed Edouard, also quite still, his long, dark hair hanging over a face not by any means unprepossessing, though ordinary.

Squelette drew out his knife—and, with a horrid leer, entered the room on tiptoe.

CHAPTER XXIX.

THE SECRET POLICE.

THE alarm of *Squelette* and his companions was quite groundless. The police agents were evidently after other prey.

They seemed in an exceeding good humour, joked often with the hostess, and indulged in various glasses.

"You keep house open late to-night, Madame *Trop-long*," said one of the *mouchards*, laughing.

Oh! no Monsieur!" replied Madame Lanfan, with a bland smile. "Not later than usual."

The other spy whispered in the ear of his companion.

He nodded, and, rising, went to the bar and spoke in an undertone to the hostess.

"Right, Monsieur," said she, though not apparently well pleased. "Jacques," she added, beckoning to the *garcon*, "close the house."

"Good evening, Madame," said the police-agents politely, and, bowing, left the house.

They emerged from the door only to station themselves under a dark archway opposite.

Meanwhile the *tapis-franc* was closed. The guests obeyed reluctantly—the place was soon empty, and the Englishman—last to leave—came out alone.

He looked carefully up and down the street, and then crossed over, with the intention of passing through the archway.

Just as he came into its shadow a strong hand tapped him on the shoulder.

"Your name is Robert Fenton."

"Why do you ask?"

"That is your name."

"You have been to see the *Squelette*."

The Englishman did not answer.

"Mind—you are watched. The police have their eye upon *that* man and know *your* errand. It will be better for you to leave it alone."

Fenton was about to reply when the two spies disappeared in the darkness of the night, and left him standing there alone, and considerably crest-fallen.

He might be very courageous on an English highway; but in the French capital, surrounded by a police which acted as it were by irresistible agency, he was helpless as a child.

He thought for a moment, and then turned down one of the dark alleys leading to the *Rue Grevièr*.

Here for the present we must leave him, and carry our readers elsewhere. The terrible mysteries of our tale are but beginning to evolve themselves.

We left Captain George and party safely arrived in England.

We left Lillian in the house of the Marquis of Glencorn.

We left William Lennox repentant, yet still sinning, and we left Leila still in the power of the enemy.

We must now introduce a new and extraordinary phase in our narrative.

It may puzzle many to comprehend how all the separate plots are to be joined together. Let them have patience, and they will find that all will be explained.

CHAPTER XXX.

THE MILLER.

WE left Sapathwa, the Blue Dwarf, fainting in the arms of Lord Ernest Wyndham.

He had been stunned by the shock. The pistol had been fired close to his head, and had for a moment blinded him.

The spot on which they now stood was a narrow highway between two thickets.

Both were dense in the extreme.

Everybody was busily engaged in endeavouring to bring the Blue Dwarf to life.

At length they succeeded.

"Where is my child?—my Leila. Bring her to my arms," he cried.

All looked eagerly around.

Lord Charles Lutterel and the Princess of Borneo had disappeared.

With a wild cry, like that of some savage beast deprived of her young, Sapathwa turned upon them.

"Why did you save me? Why did you leave the tender one in the hands of the spoiler? Why did you not punish the accursed ravisher?"

"My dear sir," said Lord Ernest, gently, "the blow was so sudden."

"Well, let us not waste time in words. Action is the business of men. Postillion, which way did they go?"

"Well, sir, I didn't see them go nowhere," replied the man.

The Blue Dwarf glared around.

The bank was very steep in most parts, but close at hand was a slope, upon which the marks of footsteps were plainly visible.

"This way," he said, casting his yellow cloak from him. "Postillion, go to the first inn and await us there."

Sapathwa and his companions ascended the bank and found themselves at the entrance of a pathway, into what appeared a large wood.

On the soft soil they could easily distinguish the fresh marks of boots.

"We are on their track," said the Blue Dwarf, all his calmness returning.

"Follow."

"Be calm," said Sapathwa. "We must be like the savage Indian, or those more savage races from among whom I came in days of yore, if we would find them. He cannot go far with such a burden. Let me go first. You follow."

And taking the lead like some Indian scout, he slowly and cautiously tracked the heavy footsteps of the ravisher.

They were the more deeply indented in the soil from the nature of his burden.

Suddenly he halted, where a fallen tree had for a moment checked the progress of the fugitive.

They stepped across, and still the same heavily-indented steps were to be seen.

On they went now with the certainty of victory, and still the wood continued, though the path appeared to become wider and wider.

Presently they came to a small clearing, about two miles from the spot where they had crossed the tree.

"Hist!" said the Blue Dwarf.

All halted.

A heavy footstep was distinctly heard crashing through the wood.

They advanced on tip-toe, and just as they were about to turn a corner, heard the following speech:—

"Dashed if I do it any longer. It are mighty foine, I dare say, but odd rot them boots."

Then they saw a rude countryman cast off a heavy log from his shoulder, and proceed to draw from his feet a pair of handsome horseman's boots.

"They hurt I loike the very devil—darn his old skin—Lord have mercy upon us, here's Old Scratch hisself!"

It was the Blue Dwarf, who, swelling with rage at the deception which had been evidently passed upon him, stood before not an inapt representation to the mind of an ignorant country peasant of the great Lucifer.

"Where did you get those boots from?" he said, in his thickest and fiercest tones.

"Thee knows," replied the awe-struck and trembling peasant.

"How should I know?"

"Thee knows everything—don't 'ee?"

"Trifle not with me, but tell me where is the wretch whose boots you wear," continued the Blue Dwarf.

The man looked at the others, and gaining courage when he saw that they were at all events Christian men, became cool and even saucy.

"I should loike to know what's that to thee," he said.

"Man," cried the Blue Dwarf, clutching him by the arm with all but superhuman strength, "I tell you that if you don't tell me the truth, I will crush you like a shell. Show me where that villain is, and there are five guineas."

"Foive guineas. Well, master, if you'll let I rest a bit, I'll tell you.

"Speak."

"Just now loike—a gen'lman, with a young lady, d'ye see in his two arms, met me.

"Says he, to me, says he—'Two guineas for them shoes.'

"'Eh!' says I, a grinning.

"'I mean it,' says he, a sitting down the lady, all dead loike, and a showing me the money.

"'Eh!' says I, and what am I to wear?

"'Moine!' says he.

"And off he pulled his boots, and we changed about.

"'Now,' says he, 'chuck that ere log on your shoulder, and walk as if you were carrying a heavy load, and when next I sees you I guves you two guineas more.'

"'All right,' says I.

"'Where can I rest till the young lady comes to?' says he.

"'Jackson's mill,' says I.

"'Where's that?' says he.

"'Just through them trees and up ta hill,' says I.

"And away he cuts loike fun."

"Lead us there, and you shall be amply rewarded," replied Sapathwa.

The yokel, who never had in the whole course of his life made so much money, hastily drew on the boots again, and though limping fearfully, turned back and led the way towards the mill, where Lord Charles Lutterel had fled with his unfortunate victim.

CHAPTER XXXI.

AUT BLUE DWARF, AUT DIABOLUS.

THE face of the Dwarf was stern and cold. There was nothing naturally cruel in his nature; in fact he would not willingly have hurt the smallest animal that crawls upon the earth; but his passions were roused.

There were two loves in his life.

The first was William Lennox.

The second was Leila, Princess of Borneo.

It had once been the dream of his existence to unite these two, but he had found that the heart of William was irrevocably gone, and had not even introduced him to his beautiful *protegée*.

He was wise.

We have already seen that, however William Lennox might love Lillian, that love did not prevent him from scattering his fancies abroad upon others.

His was a nature which, however strong it might be in endurance, was weak against the temptations of woman.

The sight of the extreme loveliness of Leila would have been to him an exceeding great temptation.

And this Sapathwa knew.

Now, however, his whole soul was alive to but one thing—the fearful outrage on his beloved *protegée*.

He felt that he could kill Lord Charles Lutterel.

In a few minutes a turn in the road brought them in sight of an old mill.

It was picturesquely situated on a small elevation surrounded on all sides by brushwood and trees.

A genteel cottage beside it seemed to betoken the residence of the miller.

It appeared the abode of peace and happiness, and none could ever have suspected that it could be otherwise.

A road wound through the woods in the direction of the spot.

Leaving the limping peasant behind, unable to advance fast in his boots, the rest hurried on. But, whatever their speed, the Blue Dwarf outrun them all.

To avoid terrifying the dwellers in the place, he had borrowed a cloak from one of his followers, and resumed his slouched hat.

Lord Ernest Wyndham kept close beside him.

A small stream, clear, pellucid, so that you could count the pebbles at the bottom crossed by a little bridge, alone separated them from the mill.

At the door of the cottage stood a young, a good-looking woman.

Her countenance was defiant.

"Where is the villain—where is my poor child?" cried Sapathwa.

"Hoity-toity," replied the woman, "who is a villain, and what child are ye talking about?"

"My good woman," said Lord Ernest, pushing the Blue Dwarf on one side, "my name is Lord Ernest Wyndham; my father is, I believe your landlord, and I am sure, therefore, you will not attempt to deceive me. The man who was just here is a villain and a coward. He carried off, under the most foul circumstances, the ward of my friend, who hates and detests him."

"Good Lord!"

"It is perfectly true."

"Beg pardon, my lord; my good man will be very sorry. But he has harnessed both horses, and driven them off towards Braxbury. They've been gone these twenty minutes. He said the young lady was his affianced wife, chased by a lot of ruffians, and that she had been frightened into a fit by a monster."

"A pack of infamous and monstrous falsehoods," said Lord Ernest. "But, my friend, it is not far to our inn. We shall be in Braxbury before them."

The Blue Dwarf was prostrate. He allowed himself to be led like a child.

They hurried across by a path—the young nobleman began, as soon as he saw the mill, to know the country—which led in the direction of the highway, and in twenty minutes were in sight of the inn to which they had sent the post-chaise and horses.

The chaise was being cleaned while the postillions lounged about smoking.

"Put to the horses."

"None ready," cried the host, a burly man of about fifty.

"Nonsense, Gregion. I am up to all these tricks. Quick, put them to, and let us have two of your very best bottles of port."

"Gracious me, my young lord," said the innkeeper, bowing to the ground.

The horses came out with unexampled rapidity, while biscuits and wine were partaken of by the gentlemen.

Mine host saw that they were in no humour for talk, and so left them to themselves.

In ten minutes the post-chaise was ready.

Away they started, and would soon have reached Braxbury, but at a sign from Lord Ernest the postillion pulled up.

"Jackson, I want to speak to you," said Lord Ernest, addressing a jovial-looking fellow in a cart, jogging gaily along.

"And who may thee be, my foine feller?" replied the miller, with a sneer.

"Lord Ernest Wyndham," said the young man, gravely. "No excuse, man. You have been deceived by an infamous scoundrel. You have been a party to the abduction of an innocent girl, but it is not your fault. Where did you leave them?"

"I beg your pardon, humbly, my lord. That chap told I such foine stories I believed 'un. But just now he met a return chay and took it. The young leddy seemed a-coming to, like. He put her in the chay and drove off."

"To Braxbury."

"Well," said the miller, scratching his head,

"I may 'a been mistaken, but I think I heard 'un say Liketon."

"Thank you," said Lord Ernest; "now, postillion, first road to the left."

And away they sped.

"Liketon is on the borders of an extensive wood, and Lutterel's father owns all thereabout," said Lord Ernest Wyndham, gravely. "Liketon Hall is in ruins, but they keep a housekeeper there, and I've no doubt that's the place. Be guided by me, and we'll find her."

"My lord, you have been too kind all through for me not to yield in some things to you. I am in your hands."

CHAPTER XXXII.

LIKETON HALL.

BEFORE the sad calamity, already fully alluded to, had fallen on the family of the Lutterels, it was the habit of the Duke of ——, who was an excessive lover of the chase, to keep up some sort of establishment at all his numerous residences.

Liketon Hall was one of the very oldest of them, and was chiefly in a ruined and dilapidated state.

There were a roof, and walls, and windows, and the old furniture remained, but the staircases were rotten, the furniture crumbling to pieces, while the wind howled through every nook and cranny.

It was approached by a grand avenue of trees, which avenue was only not impassable, because the neighbouring cotters and villagers were careful to collect all superfluous wood for their own purposes.

The post-chaise was driven up to the entrance, and then told to go on to a small road-side tavern, where the horses might at all events feel the shelter of a shed.

The four men crept cautiously up towards the house.

They kept within the shadow of the trees.

None spoke.

All clutched their arms, as they knew not what myrmidons Lord Charles Lutterel might have enlisted in his service on his own territory.

They were soon in sight of the gloomy and crumbling mansion.

The great door was shut, but a small side door was open.

This looked discouraging.

They, however, all entered, trod lightly, and listened.

They could hear nothing.

Then they advanced slowly, until, chancing upon a passage, they saw a glimmer of light. No one spoke, but everybody hurried in the direction it indicated.

They were soon in full view of the kitchen of the old mansion, huge, bare, and comfortless, but with a fire in the vast hearth over which an aged crone crouched.

"Alone, all alone," she muttered "and yet there was a time when Mart'a didn't sit in the

kitchen—ha, ha, ha! those were times! But they'll never come again. Old, old, old! Such is man. When I was young the kitchen never saw me, and now I'm only good enough to take care of an empty house. He, he, he! how the devil must laugh. And where are my masters? I could a rare tale unfold! I knew who killed Ada Wilmot. It wasn't me, and it wasn't Leopold, and it wasn't the duke. He, he, he! my master Charley. And this is my reward!"

The Blue Dwarf put his fingers on his lips and bade them listen.

"And so they banished me here. Poor, dear, Leopold! They tell me he turned highwayman. It must be a long time ago. And they say the duke is not dead. Lord, my memory is not so good as it was. I recollect now. Good little Lord Leopold came to me here once on his black horse—he was a highwayman then, and I hid him where nobody knows, and nobody would ever find but me and the Lutterels. Peggy, Peggy lass, where art thee?"

"Who killed Ada Wilmot?" said a loud and terrible voice in her ear.

She turned and faced the Blue Dwarf, at whom she gazed with almost the vacancy of an idiot.

"The Lord have mercy on my soul!" cried the wretched woman.

"Who killed Ada Wilmot?" repeated Sapathwa in still more sepulchral tones.

"Lord Charles Lutterel—but oh, good Mr. Satan, good Mr. Devil, do give me time to repent."

"Show me the secret chambers where you concealed Captain George," he continued.

The old woman, who entirely forgot that she had been talking aloud, rose trembling in every limb, and, taking up a lamp, proceeded to guide them on their way.

CHAPTER XXXIII.

THE SECRET CHAMBERS.

SOON after Lord Charles Lutterel, by finding a return chaise, was able to get rid of the miller, for Leila began to come to herself.

The young nobleman had come to a supreme resolution. These dangers, chases, difficulties, and wanderings began to sicken him. He had resolved, then, to amend his life.

By way of a commencement he made up his mind to marry.

And to marry, too, the lovely Leila, Princess of Borneo.

"Release me, monster! wretch!" she cried.

"Beloved of my soul! charmer of my existence! hearken to the voice of the man who loves you. You are, doubtless, labouring under a wrong impression. I mean you no harm. It is as my wife—"

"Your wife!"

"Yes, my darling."

"I would rather be your wanton," she said, with flashing eyes.

"Why?"

" Because then there would be hope of release —as your wife I should be your bond slave for ever."

" Oh, Leila, be not so cruel! Perhaps you think I am not in earnest. Believe me, my very soul yearns to call you my own. Consent, and you shall have the most honoured treatment until the hour when I can call you mine. Refuse—"

" What then?"

" Time will show."

" My lord," said Leila more calmly, " I neither consent nor do I refuse. A maiden at my age does not decide so momentous a question rashly. I am a prisoner in a post-chaise. Give me some liberty of action, and then—"

" You shall have it," cried Lord Charles, who, as Leila's beauty seemed to become more visible as she recovered herself, felt all his passion revive.

It was not long before they reached the walls of Liketon Hall. The post-chaise drew up, was paid, and discharged.

The young nobleman entered.

As luck would have it, Peggy, the granddaughter of Martha, a smart and lively girl of twenty, very coquettishly dressed, was passing across the hall with a taper.

" My lord," she cried.

" Hush—silence! Lead the way to my private apartments. Be quick!"

The girl quickly obeyed. Her grandmother little knew that Lord Charles, with the connivance of the avaricious Peggy, who loved dress above all things, had often used the private rooms of late.

They were so built that, in the windings and turnings of that vast edifice, their existence was not even suspected.

At the end of a long, dreary passage two or three smaller ones branched off.

Near one of these was a niche.

In this niche was a statue of some iron ancestor of ancient days.

Lord Charles pressed against an unseen spring, and the statue slowly moved on one side.

Another passage became visible, and then a door, freshly ornamented, gilded all over, a very Louis XIV. style of thing.

This was opened, and a rich suite of apartments were discovered.

Peggy proceeded to light several wax tapers.

Leila could not help looking round with amazement.

She smiled bitterly to think what men will do for their pleasures, who would not stir an inch or spend a shilling to save a starving family from abject want.

Lord Charles Lutterel led the way.

He opened the door of a magnificent apartment, in an alcove of which was a bed.

" Peggy, this is this lady's room until our marriage," he began.

" Which will never be," said Leila, emboldened by the presence of a woman.

" Leila!" cried Lord Charles.

" I love another"—

" Leave us—wait outside," cried the young nobleman, imperiously.

Peggy retired.

" Leila," said Lord Charles, " you have deceived me. Beware."

" I fear you not. It was revolting to my heart even to pretend encouragement. But now listen to me. You may hack me to pieces; you may do all the evil that a wicked man can against a poor defenceless woman: and then I can but die."

" Leila!"

" See!"

And she plucked a tiny dagger from her bosom, and laid it close upon her heart.

" One little thrust, and I am free."

" Leila —— "

" Murder—fire—rape—!" yelled a voice in the next room.

Lord Charles Lutterel turned, closed the door as he passed into the next room, and found himself face to face with Sapathwa, who held in his hand a drawn sword.

" Where is she, wretch?"

" Sir, she is close at hand and safe; but listen before you strike. Allow me to repeat to you what I have just said to her. I ask her hand in marriage."

" Who killed Ada Wilmot?" said Sapathwa, coldly.

Lord Charles Lutterel tottered insensible towards a couch, just as Lord Ernest Wyndham, who had rushed past the dwarf, led Leila forward in triumph, bright, beaming, and beautiful.

Sapathwa drew from his pocket a small case of instruments, and taking forth one, deliberately cut two cross-strokes on the forehead of the recumbent nobleman.

He and his party then went out.

AND HERE ENDETH THE SECOND BOOK OF THE BLUE DWARF.

BOOK III.

THE GREAT RAT-TRAP.

CHAPTER I.

PLOTS AND COUNTER-PLOTS.

WILLIAM LENNOX, who had not the slightest clue whatever to the true position of Lillian, and who began to believe that the anonymous letter writer was, as such writers usually are, an impostor, returned sadly to his lodgings.

He found an urgent letter from Mrs. Winterton.

In the terrible excitement of the hour he had forgotten her.

He drove hurriedly off, and determined to conceal as much as possible from the bereaved mother the true state of things, determined to feign a severe indisposition, and himself inquire after Lillian.

"What is the matter?" said he, however, involuntarily, as he saw the pale white face of Mrs. Winterton.

"Where is my child?"

"Lillian!" cried William.

"Lost—lost! Mrs. Loftus, a mutual friend, sent her a domino and a ticket for a ball—a private affair at the Countess Alcaner's. You were to be there?"

"I was there, but I saw no Lillian."

"I have since seen Mrs. Loftus."

"Well."

"They were set upon by a party of men at Braxley bridge. Lillian taken out, and no more has been heard of her."

"Merciful heavens! what is to be done? Where is Sapathwa, where is the Blue Dwarf?"

"Here!" cried Goldy Gordon, entering with all his old joyousness of manner.

"Lillian is lost again," cried Mrs. Winterton, wildly.

"Oh!"

"Save her! save her!"

"Tell me all," said Sapathwa.

Mrs. Winterton told all she knew.

"My dear madam," replied the dwarf, "you send for a friend, leave all to me, and all shall yet be well. Trust implicitly."

"I will—trust you both."

"Hem!" said Sapathwa.

"Heaven bless you——"

"You shall hear from me every day," continued Sapathwa, shaking her by the hand, "Come, William."

And he led the way to his carriage. As soon as they were both inside, and the blinds down, he spoke.

"And now, sir, tell me what you know—all; how you have sacrificed this poor girl to your disgraceful amours; tell me of your duchess and your page girl. No equivocations, or never shall you see Lillian again."

William Lennox bent down his head and wept.

"And now, sir, when you have done crying perhaps you will speak."

Lennox told all. He concealed nothing.

"William," said the Dwarf, sadly, "I had thought you to be the most perfect of Heaven's creatures; I loved you as my own child; perhaps you may some day know what that feeling is, and perhaps, too, you may understand why I loved you so much; mind, I do not say that I have ceased to love you—but I have ceased to trust you, and never with my consent shall you marry Lillian until you are worthy of her."

"Sapathwa—"

"Such is my decree."

"But——"

"But me no buts—you know what and who you really are. Be worthy of your high rank and station, show yourself all I could wish you, and you shall be restored to the home of your fathers."

"But no one can prevent me."

Sapathwa looked at him with a melancholy smile.

"No more of this. My own opinion is that Lillian is no more in France than I am. That we shall soon be able to discover. The benevolent notes you received are, in my opinion, from the Duchess of Castella."

"Indeed—yes—no doubt. I will return to my lodgings."

"What for?"

"To see this student, and unmask him."

"No," said Sapathwa drily, "it will take you too near Jessie Brown, whom you will see no more."

William Lennox bowed his head.

"And now, my dear boy, to business. Did you ever see a rat-trap?"

"I do not remember."

"Well, you shall see one, and a fine one; and a nice collection of rats you shall find in it before this day month."

William stared.

"Yes, Slimy Jones, Captain Winterton, the Honourable John M. de Vera Cruz, the Student, the Duchess, Pauline, all our enemies shall be there."

"All!"

"All save one—him I leave to the justice of his country," replied Sapathwa, solemnly.

"As you will."

"We must find Captain George. He will be an admirable auxiliary."

"But how to find him?"

"We will do that together—Jack Horne, Captain George, the Mudlark, Stone, yourself, with the Blue Dwarf for a captain. It will go hard, but we'll defeat the whole gang."

William smiled at the strange assortment.

At this moment the carriage stopped, and they got out in front of a splendid mansion, Sapathwa having first arrayed himself in a rich scarlet and ermine cloak, as well as a hat and feathers, which completely screened his hideous ugliness.

The spot was a most retired one, with scarcely another house in sight. It's garden ran down to the Thames. Cremorne Gardens is now not far off where this house once stood.

A hall door was opened, and numerous domestics in rich liveries stood on each side.

Not one had ever seen the face of their master.

But they obeyed him implicitly.

They went up stairs, a large folding-door was thrown open, and the two walking in, the door closed behind them.

Playing chess, at a table near an open window, were Lord Ernest Wyndham and the Princess of Borneo.

"Leila," saith Sapathwa, as both rose respectfully, "this is my dear boy, of whom you have so often heard me speak."

Leila held out her hand, and shook his warmly.

"I have heard my dear father speak of you often. I am delighted to see you."

William Lennox bent low.

"This, William Lennox, is Lord Ernest Wyndham, a dear friend; and, should his friends agree, soon to be a dearer. As you will have daily to be with them, they must know your history, and enter into the conspiracy."

They all sat down, and tenderly, gently, with the slightest possible reference to his errors, the story was told.

When the Blue Dwarf had concluded, they simultaneously held out their hands.

They were his sworn allies.

That night the plan of the campaign was laid down, and the great rat-trap organised.

CHAPTER II.

CAPTAIN JEHOSOPHAT FIREBRACE.

SLIMY JONES, as it is necessary to call him in contradistinction to any other celebrated Jones who may occur in history, of which we can recollect none at this moment save and except Jones Lloyd, though a moneyed man, and in the service of so great a personage as the Countess Alcaner, was not without his weaknesses.

We have all our little weakness.

His was a pipe and a pot.

Now it is a most notorious fact that no man really enjoys a pipe and a pot out of a pot-house.

Slimy Jones was strongly of this opinion, and accordingly, when the duties of the day were over, he would adjourn to the parlour of a very respectable public, and there, while enjoying his cloud, astonish the natives with stories of adventure by flood and field.

He was a popular man. Since he had become possessed of other people's money, Slimy Jones was vastly liberal, would stand treat, go glasses all round, or do any other mad or absurd thing which came into his head.

Regularly at eight o'clock, if he were not otherwise engaged, Slimy Jones—now Edward Tigsby Jones, Esq., late contractor to his Majesty's Forces in Spain—would enter, take his seat by the fire in the arm chair set apart for his use, and at once, after a little preliminary conversation, proceed to the business of the evening.

"Just so," he would say; "that just puts me in mind——"

And away he would launch into some fearful narrative of adventure, in which his own courage, dexterity, and acuteness were always the heroes.

One evening the room was full. Slimy Jones, by dint of sheer impudence, lying, and unblushing exaggeration, had won for himself the respect of the room. An arrant knave and coward, he had been allowed to degenerate into a bully.

Everybody was afraid of him.

In a corner of the room sat a stranger, reading the newspaper.

He was thin, gaunt, and sallow. On his head was a strange peaky hat, with a broad brim. His shirt collar came up to his ears. His hair hung in lanky confusion around his head. The cut of his jib was decidedly nautical, but he was apparently quiet and inoffensive.

He was beneath the notice of John Tysby Jones.

"One day I was before the lines of Torres Vedras, and General Picton, he says to me—'My men want beef to-day, and beef they must have.'

"'There aint none,' says I.

"'Can't help it,' says he.

"'But'——

"'Shoot you, by G——.'

"'Well, General, if'——

"'No ifs for me; won't do, you know.'

"'It shall be done,' says I.

"I was on a high hill, and my eye had caught sight of a whole drove of beeves in the distance, under guard of a batch of French soldiers.

"What does I do but takes but two of my men, creeps into the valley, gives just a view-halloo, away cuts the French as if the devil had been behind, and in half an hour the whole drove was a being cut up right away."

"Thunder bombs and cockle shells," shouted the stranger, coolly; "whin I wur in Texas I had a hoss. I was a crossin' from the United States overland to Peru. Texas is a reg'lar wilderness—half swamp, half prairie, my——! if my hoss did'nt go an' bust. I didn't kyar. I took off the saddle, rode up to a whole bilin' of wild hanimals—hosses, mustangs—and says, I darned if the best beast shan't have the saddle. My! if the hull druv didn't rush at me like mad, and ten minutes after I was a driving away like a streak of lightning on the back of as fine a charger as ever you did see—*and that's a fact !*"

"Sir," began Slimy Jones, who did not know whether to laugh or be angry.

"Sir, to you—"

"Do you mean to say—just so."

"Sir-r—"

"That that story—"

"Sir-r-r—" increasing in emphasis.

"Just so. Is really true ?"

"Sir-r-r-r—as true as yours !"

A roar of laughter greeted this sally.

"Just so. Have you come here to insult me ?" asked the ex-contractor.

"Sir, my name is Captain Jehosaphat Firebrace, of the Kentucky Half-Horse, Half Alligator Mounted Marine Corps. I can fight, kick, gouge, shoot or sword exercise you, whichever you like ; and, what's more, I'm quite ready now, stranger."

"Captain Jehosaphat Firebrace," stammered Slimy Jones, who was rather white than pale, "I've not the most remote intention of insulting you."

"Cannon ball and chain shots, you see, if you have ; say the word—don't be proud, you know— I'm your man. Wake snakes and walk chalks, I'm ready to a minute."

"Just so. I have no doubt, captain, that all you say is perfectly serene and correct, but this is a social and harmonious meeting, and if you like to join us in conversation, or singing, or anything else, we shall feel proud. As for fighting, I expect we had pretty well enough of that you know in furrin' parts—"

"Quakers and mummy pots ! what d'ye call furrin' parts, stranger ; not the best nation in all creation, I guess—eh ?"

"Just so ; and pray, sir, what may that nation happen to be ?"

"Goose and cucumber ! Why, stranger, where a' you sot for all your created life ?— Amerikee ! to be sure ; what other place would you have me say—eh ?"

"Just so ; my memory is so very treacherous. I used to think—"

"Flax and fleas ! what right has you niggers to think ? We don't think—we know. But never mind, the United States holds out the right hand of fellowship to the old country, and though she is pretty considerable savage, still she hopes to see her come up in time to the high standard of American civilisation."

"Just so. You're very kind."

"Soft sawder and human nature ! I expect I am—but don't let me interrupt the harmony of the evening. Pray let's hear you sing, old hoss."

Jones bowed, and, in a melancholy falsetto, sang as follows :—

A man at a tavern made so free,
  With Perkins' best entire,
He fell from his seat, and asleep laid he,
  Before the parlour fire.

The landlord, who wish'd to shut up shop,
  Cried, " Hang this drunken clown !
Whoe'er will turn him out *neck and crop*,
  I'll give him half a-crown."

A wag, who was taking his parting cup,
  Cried, " Done—just give me a sack,
I'll put him in gently, tie him up,
  And take him away on my back."

So said, so done—at a surgeon's door,
  He gives a gentle kick ;
" I've brought you a subject—five pounds—no more,
  Here—give me the cash—be quick !"

The bargain is struck—the money is paid,
  The fellow cries out, " All's right !"
The drunken man on the floor is laid,
  And the surgeon says, " Good night."

But either the jostling had conquer'd the beer,
  Or by time its strength had fled ;
For noises came to the surgeon's ear,
  That a body can't make that's dead.

Enraged at the trick, he followed the man,
  And cried, " How dare you connive
At an action so base ?—but I'll foil your plan ;
  Why, knave ! the fellow's alive !"

" Alive ! you don't say so," he drily said,
  (It seemed not the least to daunt him) :
" He'll keep the better—don't be afraid,
  You can kill him whenever you want him."

Roars of applause greeted this effusion, which was just of the kind to suit the audience. In those days the trade of the body-snatcher was a dangerous one, and many of its professors were not unknown to fame.

"Hooded snakes and mocassins," cried Captain Jehosaphat Firebrace, "that beats our black sheep trade. I'll tell you what, stranger, if you gets my dander up with any more of your all-fired yaun, I'll tell you another."

" Just so."

"When I was in Orleans, an almighty grand place down South, I was considerable hard up. Wull, I expect you don't know, but I du, stranger, that there's a mighty pile a loafers about them diggens ; fellows who do nothing but play kyards and fight like bars—riglar nuisances."

" Just so."

" Well, I got together a tall lot on 'em, may be some six hundred, and we had a meetin'. I made a proposition. It was accepted. Next night every one on 'em came on board my brig, painted black as niggers, with wool on their heads where natur had planted hair."

" Just so."

" Well, sir, I tuk the lot close by Havannah, and sold every mother's son for real genuine niggers from the coast of Africa, nare a one for less nur a thousand dollars. Thin I hooks to a bay close by. Next morning six hundred as respectable white men as you might wish to see demanded their liberty, and who could help 'em ? In course I guv 'em a free passage to the United States, and we divided the plunder. *And that's a fact.* Let's liquor."

Inextinguishable roars of laughter greeted this sally, and Captain Jehosaphat Firebrace having paid his footing, was free of the room.

His advances, however, were particularly directed to Slimy Jones. Whenever the ex-contractor told a story which required considerable faith to believe, the captain told another of even a more Baron Munchausen character.

The evening became excessively jovial, and, before twelve o'clock, Slimy Jones and the Yankee were sworn friends.

Captain Jehosaphat Firebrace, in the enthusiasm of the moment, invited the worthy ex-contractor to dine with him at an early day to meet a few congenial friends.

Slimy Jones accepted, on condition that he was allowed himself to fix the date.

"Creation! of course, hurry no man's cattle. Any day will suit me, stranger; only when you do come, make up your mind to make a night of it. Shan't let you go in a hurry, you know, my friend. It ain't likely. *And that's a fact.*"

"Just so. You're really very kind," said Slimy Jones, in all the effusion of drunken confidence.

And then Captain Jehosaphat Firebrace gave Jones his card, that he might write to him next day.

"CAPTAIN JEHOSAPHAT FIREBRACE,
        "*American Coffee House.*"

The Yankee then called for a nip all round, and retired amidst loud applause.

At the corner of the street a carriage and pair of horses awaited him, which drove him off at a rapid pace towards the West-end of London.

Inside the carriage was the Blue Dwarf.

CHAPTER III.

THE AMERICAN COFFEE-HOUSE.

SLIMY JONES was a good liver. He rejoiced in whatever flattered his palate, while nothing gave him more satisfaction than a supper with jovial companion.

Jones was a pure animal. Intellectual amusement of any kind was far beyond his ken.

He, therefore, the next day determined at

once to ask his new employer for a holiday, and at once avail himself of the American's hospitable invitation.

The Countess of Alcanor had returned to her residence in Portland-place.

The affair of the masked ball had created a fearful amount of excitement.

No one knew exactly what had occurred, but it was generally rumoured that something wrong had taken place.

The countess was on her guard.

Foreigners were at that moment liable to be expelled at a moment's notice under the provisions of the Alien Act.

The countess knew that active, though secret researches, were being made for the young Lillian.

She resolved to proceed with the utmost caution.

She lay on a couch in her boudoir when Slimy Jones was introduced.

" Is that you, Jones?" she said.

" Just so, madam."

" Well."

" Just so. I came for orders. If your ladyship has nothing better for me to do, please grant me a day or two's liberty."

" Why?—amusement?"

" Just so. I met a fellow last night all fun, madam. Never saw him before—invited me to supper."

" Never saw him before, and invited you to supper?" she said, sitting up.

" Just so."

" Take a chair and tell me all about it," exclaimed the Countess Alcanor.

He obeyed.

" Short-sighted fool!" she cried; " do you not see. It is some of our enemies. There is some plot abroad. But do not look so sheepish. I dare say we can turn it to good. Write to the man, and appoint this evening for the supper. I will be there at your first meeting."

" Just so," cried Slimy Jones, with rather a blank expression of countenance.

And obeying a sign of her hand, he went to a desk and wrote a letter.

He then took a hackney-coach and delivered it himself.

The gentleman was out, but expected every minute.

About six in the evening Slimy Jones received a communication at his private residence that Captain Jehosaphat Firebrace would expect him at nine.

The rendezvous was given for the American Coffee-house, but the supper was to take place in a much more retired locality.

The Countess Alcanor smiled upon him grimly.

" I told you so."

" Just so," replied Slimy Jones.

" Now mark me!" she continued, "there is some treachery on foot. I will have my eyes open. You go at the time. I will follow you and see where you go. If, as I suspect, it is a confederacy of our enemies, use this powder—it is a powerful narcotic, and will disable your adversary. Put it in his wine. I will then appear, and woe be it unto him if I am right !"

Slimy Jones knew too well the character of

his mistress to hesitate a moment, though he was now terribly alarmed.

He went up-stairs to dress, and then prepared to fortify himself with a good dose of brandy.

At half-past eight he departed in a hackney-coach without seeing the mistress of the house.

The place where Captain Jehosaphat had given his address was not an hotel known to fame as might for example be the the London Coffee-house in Ludgate-hill, or Peele's* Coffee-house in Fleet-street.

It was a coffee-house frequented by Americans, chiefly captains of vessels, supercargoes, and others.

The room was large and divided into boxes, so that small parties could be accommodated with refreshments, and be private at the same time.

In one of these boxes, about a quarter to nine o'clock, just before the appointment made between Slimy Jones and Captain Jehosaphat Firebrace, a sailor lad sauntered in, and without taking off a smart round hat, sat himself down in a distant box.

The waiter came forward and took an order.

It was for a bottle of wine and a sheet of paper.

Immediately after Captain Jehosaphat Firebrace sauntered into the room, and ordered grog.

He sat drinking it with all the swagger and independence of a South Carolina gentleman.

Presently Slimy Jones made his appearance, casting anxious looks around.

He, however, had no time for reflection.

" Wall, stranger," said the captain, " all serene—ready for feedin', eh ?"

" Just so," replied Slimy Jones.

" Pigs and whistles! then let's go at it. I cud eat a stewed donkey, I guess."

" Just so. Where are we going to sup ?"

" Round the corner," said the Yankee, taking his arm.

At this moment the sailor boy came brushing past them, and slipped something into his hand.

Slimy Jones started.

" A drain of brandy, stranger?" said Captain Jehosaphat Firebrace.

" Just so."

The Yankee went to the waiter.

" I say, brandy cocktails, nigger, and look alive," he said.

The man stared, but said nothing.

" Tiles and muffins ! did you hear ?"

" Yes, sir—coming, sir."

Meanwhile Slimy Jones had read his note.

" *Beware. The American is our greatest enemy. Give him the enclosed drug. At midnight I will be with you.*

" *If he wakes, kill him !*"

" Now, then," said the Yankee.

Slimy Jones took his brandy, but his hand shook so that he spilled half of it.

Captain Jehosaphat Firebrace took no notice, but led the way towards the door.

* Peele's Coffee-house. I have no record of the date of its first establishment. I find it mentioned for the first time in the *Daily Courant* of 1770.—*Peter Cunningham's London.*

The clock struck nine.

A carriage was standing close at hand with the blinds down.

The Yankee called a hackney coach.

Slimy Jones, with something of the sensations of the criminal who hears the toll of the church bell on the morning of his execution, entered.

The hackney coach drove off without any order.

The carriage followed, just a corner of the blind being raised.

The hackney coach passed along several streets, and halted at a low public house.

"Quiet—very," said the Yankee.

"Just so," replied Slimy Jones, trembling as with the ague.

Captain Jehosaphat Firebrace led the way.

It was very strange. This public-house, in a populous and low neighbourhood, had no customers before or behind the bar. There was a handsome barmaid, and a tall powerful man who acted as landlord.

He bowed respectfully to the American, and led the way upstairs to a small but neatly furnished apartment.

Supper was laid for two.

"Now then, landlord, dish up," cried Captain Jehosaphat Firebrace.

In five minutes more a really good and even *recherchée* supper was on the table; wines of all kinds were placed near at hand.

The waiters then retired.

"Fire away, old panther," said the Yankee.

Slimy Jones, not knowing what else to do, at once took to eating.

The American followed his example. He was on this occasion very different from what he had been on the previous evening.

He was evidently slightly intoxicated, which became more manifest as the supper proceeded.

He poured out the wine in tumblers.

"Wall, old hoss," he said at last, "what do you say—let's champagne?"

"Just so. Ain't it mightily expensive?" cried the other.

"Darn the expense; that's my affair, youngster," replied the other, stooping down to pick up the champagne.

Quick as lightning Slimy Jones poured the powder into the full tumbler of port which stood before Captain Jehosaphat Firebrace.

At that moment a slightly rustling behind his back made Slimy Jones, himself already affected by wine, turn round.

The man was half intoxicated with fear.

But he saw nothing.

When he turned back again Captain Jehosaphat Firebrace was setting down his empty glass.

"Corked, by the thirteen stars and stripes!" cried the Yankee. "No more of that ar stuff."

And he poured out the sparkling liquor, which, in moderation, is the nearest approach to nectar known to human nature.

"I say, alligator, did you notice anything?" said the captain, moving rather uneasily on his seat.

"Just so. What?"

"That ar wise. Catapults and cataracts! Was he—he—up? Not just the thing."

And the Yankee nodded forward.

In two minutes more he was either asleep or insensible.

An ignoble grin passed over the countenance of Slimy Jones.

"Ah, ah! my master, just so. I calkerlate that I've nicked yer," he said aloud.

Then an infernal idea seemed to come across his brain.

He filled another tumbler of champagne. He was ghastly pale. His forehead was covered with heavy drops of sweat. He glared round the room with a kind of affrighted and horrified look.

Then he drew forth a dagger from his bosom. His teeth chattered.

He was, however, too inured to crime to feel much compunction.

He was only frightened.

The stillness of the room, the heavy breathing of the sleeper, the quiet of the house, so mysteriously bereft of all custom, alarmed him.

He feared he knew not what.

But the demon of blood was by his side, and he raised his dagger, his eyes glaring dreadfully as he did so.

One blow and the sleeper would, to all appearance, have passed into another world.

"No!" said a hollow voice beside him.

He turned, and as he did so the Blue Dwarf, who had darted forward from a cupboard, clutched his wrist and arrested his murderous intention.

"Mercy!" cried the wretch, in tones of abject supplication.

"No mercy!" replied the supposed American, casting off his wig and revealing the features of William Lennox.

In another moment Slimy Jones was down on the ground, gagged and helpless.

"*Et d'un!*" said Sapathwa, sternly.

* * * * *

About a quarter to twelve o'clock a carriage drove up to the narrow lane leading to the public-house, from which three men descended. They wore huge great coats and slouched hats. They were guided by a sailor boy.

"It can't be here," said one.

"It is," replied the youth; "I was very particular in taking notice."

"But it's shut up."

"*To let!*" said one of the other men.

"I tell you," said the imperious voice of the sailor boy, stamping his foot at the same time, "it is here. There has been some jugglery about it. Knock."

The first speaker bowed respectfully and then knocked.

No answer came.

"Knock again."

"Now then, you noisy people," said an antiquated watchman, coming round the corner, "move on. What are you kicking up this 'ere row for?—a waking up honest people."

"Some friends of mine," replied the sailor boy, "went into this house about three hours since. It was then open and lighted up."

"Ain't been these two years," said the Charlie.

"But—"

"I tell you it ain't. Move on."

"Now look here," said the sailor boy in slightly foreign accents.

"But—"

He showed him a guinea.

"Listen to me, my man. If you are civil we'll give you this," he began.

"Sir—"

"I tell you that at nine o'clock this house was open, a barmaid stood behind the bar, and three persons, one of them a friend of mine, went in; I was to join them at nine o'clock. How is it the house is shut up?"

"Well, sir," said the watchman, scratching his head, "I never know'd it open these two year."

The sailor boy gave him the guinea.

"Go away," he said sternly, "and don't come round this way for an hour."

The watchman took the money.

"A thousand thanks, my good young gentleman," he began, touching his grey locks.

"Hearkee, friend," said the sailor boy, "if you'll keep off all intruders for an hour here's another guinea."

"You trust to me, sir," replied the delighted guardian of the night.

And he went hobbling away.

"Open that door," said the sailor boy to a short, stout, thick-set individual who stood by his side.

The man bowed and at once proceeded to business. He produced a dark lantern, which he laid upon the ground. He then produced his instruments, and in ten minutes the door was opened.

They all entered and immediately closed the door after them.

The bar was empty, but it was clear that some one had been there.

There were traces of liquor on the stairs.

They followed them up.

They entered a room which evidently had been used recently as a place for mirth. There remained, however, nothing but empty bottles.

"I knew it, I knew it!" cried the sailor boy, casting off all disguise, and appearing in the character of the imperious Countess of Alcaner. "there has been some foul treachery here. That villanous traitor has trapped him. My friends, we must unite, or the enemy will destroy us in detail."

"This has been a deep laid conspiracy," said Captain Frederick Winterton.

"Who was this Captain Firebrace?" said the Honourable John.

"William Lennox," replied the Countess Alcanor, with an indefinable look, half of love, half of hate.

The cousins stood still, petrified with horror and astonishment.

They knew themselves to be in the power of this man.

"Let us retire," said the countess, "this matter is assuming proportions which must be seriously considered. It is war to the knife —a battle of extermination!"

Captain Frederick Winterton made no reply, but, in company with John, followed their chief.

CHAPTER IV.

CHARLES WENTWORTH.

THE night was to be a great one at the hotel which the cousins still patronised.

They had found a new pigeon to pluck.

A young man, certainly not of age, had arrived at the hotel in very dashing style; he came in a post-chaise, with several boxes, and gave his name as Charles Wentworth.

His father was High Sheriff of a distant county.

The youth had come up to town to see a little of life, but strictly under the conduct of a tutor.

This tutor was hourly expected.

The cousins lounged into the coffee-room where the little gentleman was reading the paper over a late breakfast and a headache.

"Good morning, sir," said the captain, with a bow half patronising, half respectful.

"Dooced slow morning," replied Master Charles.

"Seedy," said the captain.

"Vewy."

"Up late?"

"Ain't been to bed," said the youth, with a knowing wink.

"Raking already?" said the captain.

"Fust night in town, yer know."

"Where did you go?"

"Don't know. A fellah I never saw before took me to a crib or two—very funny; but you know one feels it afterwards."

The cousins exchanged looks.

"Going to make any stay?" said the captain.

"Depends. Must amuse myself, you know," continued the juvenile.

"Allow me, sir," continued the urbane captain, "to introduce myself. My name is pretty well-known about town."

And he handed his own card and that of the Honourable John.

"Vewy proud, sir; vewy proud, indeed, gentlemen," said the youth, with, however, the most consummate nonchalance.

"Play billiards?" said the captain.

"A little—vewy little."

"Anything to while away the day," continued the other.

"But I expect my tutor—must be at home for him."

"As you like. But I have a few friends coming to-night here. Will you join us? A particularly jovial crew," said Captain Frederick.

"De—lighted!" replied Mr. Charles Wentworth.

"How about the tutor?" observed the Honourable John.

"Knowing old card—up to everything," said the youth, with a most peculiar wink.

The cousins roared with laughter.

"Ah, ah! doing the governor?" they cried.

"Exactly."

And the juvenile again winked at them with such a terrific attempt at manliness, the others were not able to keep their countenances.

But Master Charles Wentworth was by no means offended. On the contrary, he roared with laughter.

"Just the chap after my heart," he said. "Glad to know you." And so they separated, after many a protestation of mental regard and affection.

About an hour later the tutor arrived.

He was a rather good-looking man; his native looks, however, much impaired by a wig, high white neckcloth, and spectacles, which served to tone down the fire of eyes naturally vivid and bright.

The youth and the tutor were on excellent terms. They took a glass or two of wine, and then retired to dress and take a tour in the park. For this purpose they hired an open carriage.

They took nearly an hour dressing, or, rather, as their rooms were adjoining, and communicated with folding doors, in conversing, and then came out, Mr. Charles Wentworth most elegantly and stylishly dressed, the tutor looking, if possible, more awkward than before.

The carriage was in readiness, and away they drove, the youth evidently, despite his affected denial, delighted with all that he saw.

His eyes sparkled with that generous delight which is the peculiar province of youth.

Youth is the season for bright hopes; but though age may strive to blind itself to the fact, the age also for enjoyment is the present.

As we advance in years we regret the past and dread the future.

But though sometimes a strange shade did come over the countenance of the youth, it was rapidly chased away by more sunny and agreeable thoughts.

The park was reached.

It was early, and yet many carriages were out. The lovers of fashionable life were very different to what they are now.

People did not call supper dinner.

There were numerous equipages, and many horsemen dashing past, or walking their horses to converse with noted beauties of the upper world.

With many also of that world, which, though quite as showy and often more elegant, is very much removed in character and position from the aristocratic regions.

Mr. Charles Wentworth looked on in silent ecstacy.

Suddenly the tutor whispered something in the ear of the youth, who looked eagerly round.

"Isn't she beautiful?" said the tutor, with a strange smile.

Charles Wentworth turned pale, and pressed his hand against his heart.

A phaeton was coming up with two splendid horses and a couple of grooms behind, around which a perfect cavalcade of admiring horsemen was congregated.

They pushed, curvetted, trotted, galloped around, to the manifest danger of all around.

But the driver of the phaeton was imperturbable.

It was a woman.

She wore a superb silk dress, with an ermine cloak, a hat and feathers, while the features beneath were heavenly.

Such a smile.

"That woman is a demon," said the tutor.

"Is it possible?" replied Charles Wentworth.

"The face of an angel, the soul of a devil," continued the other.

The phaeton drove by.

"We shall meet her again," said the tutor.

"Did you see how she fixed her eyes on me?" whispered Charles, with a flushed and heated countenance.

"She did."

"With a half-scrutinising, half-languishing air," continued Charles Wentworth.

"We shall pass her again. Look at them with your glass."

A great stir now proclaimed that somebody of consequence was coming.

Charles Wentworth stood up as an open carriage with four horses came slowly up.

"Who is it?"

"The Countess of J——," whispered the tutor.

"The reigning favourite—but tottering. That demon is striving to supplant her."

The countess and the lady of the phaeton were going opposite ways.

They soon met, and the crowd which followed both caused a stoppage.

The two women eyed one another with instinctive hatred. They forced upon their beautiful countenances the utmost hatred and contempt.

The woman of the phaeton whipped up her horses, and contrived to graze the wheel of the open carriage.

The countess turned slowly towards the driver.

"Creature!" she said, aloud.

The woman turned pale as death, and raising her silver-handled whip, struck the countess across the face.

A terrific murmur of indignation, surprise, and admiration followed.

The countess grew black in the face with indignation, and then, seeing that the phaeton wheels were partially locked in hers, gave a signal to the postillion, who darted off at a gallop.

The phaeton was upset, and away flew the lady of the phaeton, head foremost, over the railing, giving the spectators an ample opportunity of observing the shape of her legs, and some of the secrets of her toilet.

Well, perhaps, we may be better understood if we relate an anecdote, as told by a celebrated character.

"'I remember once in my life,' said the doctor, 'I used to flirt with a little actress, who was a great favourite in a provincial town where I lived, and she was invited to a ball there, and confided to me she had no silk stockings to appear in, and without them her presence at the ball was out of the question.'

"'That was a hint to you to buy the stockings,' said Dick.

"'No—you're out,' said Growling. 'She knew I was as poor as herself; but though she could not rely on my purse she had every confidence in my taste and judgment, and consulted me on a plan she formed for going to the ball in proper twig. Now, what do you think it was?'

"'To go in cotton, I suppose,' returned Dick.

"'Out, again, sir—you'd never guess it; and only a woman could have hit on the expedient; it was the fashion in those days for ladies to wear pink stockings, and she proposed *painting her legs!*'

"'Painting her legs!' they all exclaimed.

"'Fact, sir' said the doctor! and she relied on me for telling her if the cheat was successful—'

"'And was it?' asked Durfy.

"'Don't be in a hurry, Tom. I complied on one condition—namely, that I should be the painter.'

"'Oh, you villain!' cried Dick.

"'A capital bargain!' said Tom Durfy.

"'But not a safe covenant,' added the attorney.

"'Don't interrupt me, gentlemen,' said the doctor. 'I got some rose-pink accordingly, and I defy all the hosiers in Nottingham to make a tighter fit than I did on little Jinney; and a prettier pair of stockings I never saw.'

"'And she went to the ball?' said Dick.

"'She did!'

"'And the trick succeeded?' added Durfy.

"'So completely,' said the doctor, 'that several ladies asked her to recommend her dyer to them! So you see what a woman will do to go to a dance. Poor little Jinney!—she was a merry minx. By the by, she boxed my ears that night for a joke I made about the stockings. 'Jinney,' said I, 'for fear your stockings should fall down when you're dancing, hadn't you better let me paint a pair of garters on them?''"

Well, the spectators of the mishap to the lady of the phaeton had good reason to know that she required no such painting.

Before almost she could have touched the ground, the tutor had lifted her up, while Charles Wentworth was in another instant by her side. They had leaped headlong out of the carriage.

"Are you hurt?" said the tutor.

She opened her eyes and they fell upon the handsome and blushing countenance of Charles Wentworth.

"No—not much," she said, rising and repairing hastily the disorder of her dress.

Meanwhile the grooms, who had alighted previous to the accident to go to the horse's head, had succeeded in raising up the light phaeton.

"You had better take our carriage," said the tutor.

The woman stood still as if dizzy, and then gladly availed herself of the offer. Though unhurt, she was stunned and frightened. She was glad, too, to escape from the mob, which became every minute more dense.

Before, however, she accepted the carriage, she drew forth a card case, and handed it to the tutor.

"Most happy to see you and your young friend"—this with a significant glance at the young man—"at any time."

Both bowed and assisted her to rise.

The tutor read the card, ground his teeth, turned very pale, and moved away without a word.

Charles Wentworth took the card, and, having read it, raised his eyes to Heaven.

What was the matter?

"*Lady Edgar Blakesley.*"

But why did the words on a piece of pasteboard so much affect the lad and his tutor.

We shall probably see before long.

CHAPTER V.

THE TWO SERVING MEN.

CAPTAIN FREDERICK WINTERTON and his cousin the Honourable John contrived, on their return to the inn, to discover that the youth had engaged as his servant a man who, though of London origin, had, it was said, lived some time in his service in the country.

The captain was too much a man of the world not to have himself a groom of undoubted effrontery, cunning, and malice.

His name of William Figg—but he was popularly well known as Bill Figg—and his stature was of the smallest. He was full of the low cunning of a youth who had passed through every phase in London life.

He had the servant of Charles Wentworth pointed out to him, and at once proceeded to obey his master's directions.

"Well, tip us your flipper, old file," he said to the other, a great tall fellow, in a plain suit of livery.

"What for?" said the other, with a grin.

"Well, you see, our masters have been and made friends, so must we. Let's have a pot."

"Two if you likes," groaned the other.

Such a vacant grin.

"He's a fool," thought Bill Figg.

They adjourned without further parley to a parlour frequented solely by their own fraternity, and, it being too early for much company, found themselves alone.

The necessary drink being ordered, Bill Figg took an excessive pull, and, stretching out his legs, putting his hands into his trowsers pockets, with his eyes half shut, began the conversation.

"Good master yours?"

"Very."

"Lots of browns?" continued Bill.

"Lots."

"I say—what's your name?—you don't make your jaws ache with long words, I see."

"No."

"Well, you're a rum 'un! What's your name?"

"Jack."

"What else?"

"Hop—"

"No."

"—ton."

"I tell you what, young fellow," said Bill Figg rather irately, "if you're coming any of your nonsense over me, we'd better give up."

"Give us the beer," said Jack.

"Oh! I see," cried the other, laughing, "I had neglected to hand you the pot."

"Drink first, talk afterwards," said Jack.

And at one long draught he emptied the pot.

"Now," he said, putting down the empty pewter, "order in another, and I'm your man."

The astonished Figg did as he was directed, and pursued his researches after truth.

"Know your master long?" said Figg.

"He ain't werry long hisself," grinned Jack; "but I has known him some time. He's as rich as the Lord Mayor, and a honely son. His father is High Sheriff of ——, and a power of things besides."

"Does the guv'ner tip him pretty lobbishly?"

"Oh, he draws for just vot he likes. At Hoxford hi've known him spend three hundred in a week."

"Nice pickings, eh, Mr. Hop——ton?"

"Pretty middling; only, you see, his clothes don't fit this child, so I sells 'em. Wages not partickler—throws a handful of guineas at me, and says, 'Pay yourself, you rascal.'"

"Vich yer does," said Bill Figg, surprised out of his gentility.

"In course," replied Jack, with a wink.

Figg continued some time in this strain, until he had pumped the other as he thought quite dry, when he rose hurriedly, looked at a silver watch, and appeared very much surprised.

"Good gracious me, Mr. Jack. Pleasant company is a dreadful thing. My master is waiting for his hoss—smoke a pipe this evening—introduce you to the finest set of gentlemen as ever you see—gentlemen as is gentlemen."

"I'm really very much obliged."

"Ah, sir, it's a great mistake that all the real gentlemanly feeling in the country, sir, should be in us, while those who play their parts as 'gents' ain't fit to black our boots—fact, sir."

"Wery true and wery melankerly fact," said Jack Hopton, with intense gravity; "but aint your master a waiting for that hoss?"

"True! true!" cried Bill, and he hurried away.

"What a fool that feller is," thought Bill.

But had he seen Jack Hopton when alone, he might have changed his opinion.

No sooner was the other's back turned than Jack slowly raised his right hand to his face, placed his thumb upon his nose, spread out his fingers, and extended them in the direction of the departing William Figg.

"All very fine, Mr. Ferguson," he said, "but before you're a week older I'll teach you to try and pump me, my fine fellow."

And seating himself, he quietly finished the other pot of beer.

CHAPTER VI.

THE NEW FAUBLAS.

CAPTAIN FREDERICK WINTERTON and the Honourable John, after mature reflection, resolved rather to dazzle the imagination of the youthful Charles Wentworth on the first occasion than make a dead set at him at once.

They were knowing men about town, cool, collected, and in their way, long-headed. They never had been known to brusque a denouement.

They played with the pigeon up to the last moment.

On the present occasion they invited a choice few to meet their intended victim, but, without exception, men far less knowing than themselves—fellows who aspired to the character of rooks without the power of carrying out their plans; burglars, who were as often as not caught in their own toils.

They were all told to be cautious and careful, on which condition they were to be admitted to a share of the prospective plunder.

About eight o'clock the youth entered.

Charles Wentworth was dressed in a well-fitting frock, just open enough to show the snowy frills of a cambric shirt. His hair, which was soft, curly, and profuse, was powdered, while his naturally pale cheeks were slightly rouged.

A round but very handsome face, on which a faint moustache alone represented manly vigour, beamed with smiles. But there was no timidity.

There was even a lurking devil in his eye, which indicated far more aptness of character than any of them were inclined to give him credit for.

Captain Frederick Winterton contrived to place him next to him, with his cousin on the other side.

The dinner was excellent, the conversation decorous—for even blacklegs of the educative class can, until flushed with wine and the excitement of play, act at will like gentlemen—and in many instances sparkling. Captain Winterton spoke with animation of London life, others chimed in, and Charles was evidently fascinated and amused.

He listened, however, rather than took part in any of the talk.

The tutor watched him with a countenance half sad, half envious.

But the tutor was busy amusing his end of the table. When wine came in, and voices were raised, and all began to converse in anecdotes, jokes, and repartees, it proved so attractive that Captain Winterton and the Honourable John almost monopolised Charles Wentworth, who would not, all they could do, be induced to drink much wine.

Captain Frederick bit his lip.

"I never did, and I never will," said the youth, with a very strange glance at Captain Frederick.

He started as if he had been struck.

Charles Wentworth looked him full in the eye and smiled.

Captain Frederick blushed up to the very eyes, and next minute cast them down and fixed them upon the white frill front of the other's shirt.

Charles Wentworth nodded.

The eyes of the captain lit up with a most unholy fire.

"Who and what are you?"

"I will tell you," he whispered.

And taking out from his breast coat pocket a pocket-book, he opened it, and showed a stamped sheet of parchment.

Captain Frederick discovered the words—

"*Credit my daughter, Charlotte Wentworth,*

who will be introduced to you as Charles Went-
worth, with any amount she may require.

" EDWARD CHARLES WENTWORTH.

" *To Messrs. Carter, Harvey, & Co.*"

" But, said Captain Frederick, in a low tone,
" what is the meaning of all this ?"

" Fun."

He took her hand as her eyes sparkled with
liquid fire that made the thing the *roué* called
a heart beat wildly in his veins.

" I will tell you all."

" Where ?"

" At my house."

" When ?"

" To-night."

Captain Frederick nearly lost his head.

" Dangerous syren," he said, " what can have
possessed you ?"

" My father never had a son," continued the
supposed Charles Wentworth, with a slight
grimace, " and he hates girls. For this reason
he always brought me up like a boy.—taught
me to ride, shoot, fish, hunt, and conduct myself in all things as a boy. I often, to please
him, dressed as I do now. At last a devouring
desire seized me to know what London life was.
He had talked to me of it until I could no longer
restrain my vagrant fancy."

The captain smiled, still squeezing the unresisting hand.

The speaker started.

Her left hand was caught violently and devoured with kisses.

A dark saturnine smiled played upon the lips
of Charles Wentworth.

" I am my father's pet. I could always do
with him whatever I liked. I begged first,
prayed next, then insisted He yielded, but
insisted on sending my good old tutor with me.
I drove here, he saying that here, above all
places, I should see life and you see "—this
with an angelic smile—" I begin already to see it."

Another squeeze from both sides.

" And how do you like it ?"

Charlotte held down her eyes.

" I never was so fascinated in all my life.
Oh ! I wish I had been a man."

" I don't !"

" Fie, captain ! Why ?"

" Adorable creature ! because there is something about you which has at once fascinated my
very soul."

" Hush ! we are observed."

" Where are you staying ?"

" In Henrietta-street, No. —."

" May I wait on you ?"

" Heyho ! I'm very foolish," she said in reply.

" Beloved Charlotte ! oh let me, unknown to
any one, have the extreme felicity—"

" Not another word, captain ; make the conversation general. On my return home I shall
play music for an hour—the street-door will be
open. You can come and talk nonsense if you
like "

Captain Frederick Winterton was, we have
said, a *roué ;* but never had female fascination
fallen upon him in such a form.

His imagination, fired by the champagne, led
him to believe that she had come there for himself alone.

" Don't say another word," said the *soi-disant*
Charles Wentworth.

" What would you have ?"

" A glass of champagne—no cards to-night.
That is what my soul thirsts for. Oh ! captain,
I have in imagination felt all the joys of the
gambler, have revelled in the luxury of winning,
and the greater luxury of losing. That is my
panacea."

" You shall be my partner. I will teach you
every game," said the captain.

" Every game ?" replied Charles Wentworth,
with an impudent leer.

" Be silent, angel or devil !" said the captain.

" I will. But drink, and give me some champagne. Fill a bumper for yourselves ; and now
I'll propose your jolly good health, and sing a
song."

The fascinated, bewildered, and astonished
captain filled himself a whole bumper, and
striking the table, silence at once ensued.

" Gentlemen," said Charles Wentworth, rising,
" it falls upon me—unaccustomed as I am to
public speaking—to propose a toast, which—
which—which—gentlemen, really—this wine—
well, as I was going to propose a toast, which I
have no doubt will be received with that amount
of applause which it of itself deserves—gentlemen, I propose the health of Captain Frederick
Winterton."

Loud applause followed, after which the young
gentleman, without further preface, sung as
follows :—

" A traveller wended the wilds among,
With a purse of gold and a silver tongue ;
His hat it was broad, and all drab were his clothes,
For he hated high colours—except on his nose,
And he met with a lady, the story goes.
          Heigho ! *yea* thee and *nay* thee.

" The damsel she cast him a merry blink,
And the traveller nothing was loth, I think ;
Her merry black eye beamed her bonnet beneath,
And the quaker he grinned, for he'd very good teeth,
And he asked, ' Art thee going to ride on the heath ?'
          Heigho ! *yea* thee and *nay* thee.

" ' I hope you'll protect me, kind sir,' said the maid,
' As to ride this heath over I'm sadly afraid ;
For robbers they say here in numbers abound,
And I wouldn't " for anything " I should be found,
For, between you and me, I have five hundred pound.'
          Heigho ! *yea* thee and *nay* thee.

" ' If that is thee own, dear,' the quaker he said,
' I ne'er saw a maiden I sooner would wed ;
And I have another five hundred just now,
In the padding that's under my saddle-bow,
And I'll settle it all upon thee, I vow !'
          Heigho ! *yea* thee and *nay* thee.

" The maiden she smil'd, and her rein she drew,
' Your offer I'll take, though I'll not take you ;'
A pistol she held at the quaker's head—
' Now give me your gold, or I'll give you my lead,
'Tis under the saddle I think you said.' "
          Heigho ! *yea* thee and *nay* thee.*

Immediately the applause had subsided
Captain Frederick Winterton rose, and, in terms
of evident sincerity, returned thanks for the
honour that had been done him by his dear
young friend.

Then followed other toasts, but before the
evening became really uproarious, Charles
Wentworth pleaded fatigue and retired.

* By Samuel Lover.

As he did so, he shook hands with Captain Frederick.

"Not yet," he whispered. "In about an hour."

The Honourable John was so maudlin drunk that he rose at the same time as Charles, and, taking his candle, retired also.

Captain Frederick then drew his friends around him, and proposed one more round, after which, he said, having to rise early, he must himself go to rest.

The others, who saw no chance of play, eagerly availed themselves of the opportunity, and retired to a hell in the neighbourhood, there to waste health, strength, and morals in the most desperate of all amusements.

CHAPTER VII.

THE DOUBLE RENDEZVOUS.

As Charles Wentworth went out third, the tutor went down stairs to order a hackney coach, the former took a cloak from the hands of a domestic.

Out from a side door darted the Honourable John, not drunk, not insensible, but flushed and excited.

"Beautiful and lovely stranger!" he whispered, "let me lay my heart and fortune at your feet."

"Hush!"

"Oh, hear me!"

"Not here."

"Say when—where?"

"To-night—my house—in half-an-hour from this."

"Beauteous damsel, where is your house?"

"Henrietta-street, No.——; the door will be ajar. Come up to the first floor."

And wrapping his cloak around him, Charles Wentworth went down stairs.

The Honourable John lost no time in dressing himself in such a way as to fit himself for a visit to a lady's boudoir.

He then locked his door lest his cousin should be tempted to enter his room, bribed the night porter to say nothing of his going out, and slipped forth into the streets.

It was a bright night; the mid hours had long since passed, and it was verging on morning.

Not a soul was about.

The Honourable John, his imagination fired at the idea of the charming stranger, hurried along at a rapid pace.

He soon reached the number indicated by the disguised maiden.

The shutters were all close fastened, and all was still as death and dark as Erebus.

But the door yielding to his hand, a rich perfume pervaded the whole house.

There was a subdued light on the carpeted stairs.

The heart of the Honourable John beat high as he hurriedly entered.

The door closed behind him.

*   *   *   *

Twenty minutes or less later another figure, wrapped in a cloak, and with a military look, pressed against the open door, glided inside, and this time again the door closed.

About five minutes later a fearful concert of execrations, curses, oaths, and supplications might have been heard, and then the clash of steel.

Swords were evidently being used, and even pistols.

Then the door burst open, and a tall figure darted out, rushed across the street, sword in hand, nor did he stop until he found himself at the door of the hotel where they had spent the night.

His cloak was gone, his hair stood on end, his face ran with blood and perspiration, and he panted like a race horse after a five-mile heat.

He leaned against the railings for a moment, and then rang the bell.

The night porter came.

"Bless me, sir!—what's the matter?" cried the astonished domestic.

"I have been set upon by ruffians," replied the captain; "but say nothing. Get my bill—no—never mind. I shall be back on Wednesday—order me a post-chaise—I am called suddenly to Dover on most pressing business."

"No bad news, sir?" said the night porter, who knew the estimation in which the captain was held in the house.

"D——d bad news, my good fellow," cried the captain; "but never mind, I am in a hurry. Tell my cousin to stop here till I come back. Tell him it is family business, but that one will do."

And one hour later the colonel, after writing several letters, dashed away on the road to Dover, determined never again, if he knew it, to set his foot in any such dangerous locality again.

Now what had happened, and what had the captain seen to alarm him so much.

The Honourable John passed up the soft carpet and the perfumed stairs until he reached a drawing-room superbly furnished.

In the room was a young lady, giving the finishing stroke to her toilette.

The enamoured swain recognised at once the likeness of Charles Wentworth.

"Adorable creature," he began.

"Now don't bother," said the young lady, who was finishing off her ringlets before a glass. "I hate such nonsense; talk English, or, at least, sense."

"But my angel—"

"Now see," continued the precocious Miss Charlotte Wentworth, turning round and slapping her dress with a riding-whip, "if that's the way you are going to make love you'll find yourself in *the* wrong box. Can you ride, shoot, leap a five-bar gate, kill a badger, worry a fox, spear a salmon, snare a hare, swim like a duck, jump in head foremost, dive to the bottom up again—eh! can you? *because if you can't I can.* What do you say, old sober sides?

"My dear madam," said the Honorable John *who had seen* the unlimited credit on Messrs. Bevan and Co., "I can't do all these things, but if I ever could aspire to the adorable privilege of calling you mine, I would do anything you like."

"Well, sit down, old buffer," continued the lovely young lady.

The Honourable John stared, but sat down. It was not a trifle should put him out when a fortune was within his grasp.

"So you've fallen in love with me, Mr. John Winterton?" said the fast young lady.

"I did the moment I set eyes on you. There was no disguise for me," he replied.

"And you are willing to serve me really and truly?" she continued.

"I am."

Miss Charlotte Wentworth approached him closely, and looked into his eyes.

"You love me, and are willing to devote yourself to me in real earnest?"

"I am."

"You've been a sad rogue!"

"Miss!"

"Don't interrupt me."

"But allow me one word?"

"Not a syllable. I know your whole history."

"The deuce you do!" he cried, starting back with sudden palor on his cheeks.

"Every item. Now I have a near and dear friend whom you have deeply injured."

"I?"

"Yes. Now listen to me. I have listened to your declarations of love, and I tell you that if you will act honestly and truly by me there is no sacrifice I will not make."

"Speak?"

"Do you know William Lennox?" she began slowly.

The Honourable John turned deadly pale.

"Now, do not be alarmed," she said, quietly, but firmly.

"But, madame—"

"Restore to his arms his beloved Lillian."

"This is a trap, Jezebel!" cried the terrified John rising; "I will not remain here another moment."

And he turned towards the door.

"Stop, as you love your life!" she cried.

John turned, but drew his sword.

"I will not be tricked, I will not be trapped. This is infamous!"

"Sit down, and hear me out," said Charlotte Wentworth, quietly.

"Never, you infernal jade."

The door of an adjacent room opened, and in rushed William Lennox, followed by the Blue Dwarf.

At the same moment Captain Frederick, who had been an amazed listener to the latter part of the conversation, rushed in.

A third occupant of the other room now joined the Blue Dwarf.

The Honourable John received a wound and fell.

Captain Frederick Winterton darted into the passage, and despair in his heart, the heavy perspiration rolling down his cheeks, defended himself with all the energy of a man who knows that on his own arm rests the only hope of life.

William Lennox pressed him hard, all the while, however, calling upon him to surrender and his life should be spared.

"Never!"

"You shall have your life—"

No answer, but making desperate lunges, he contrived to reach the street door.

It was fastened.

With a howl of despair, the captain fought even more desperately than before.

With his left hand he felt for the latch.

By great good fortune, his hand at last alighted on a spring. He slashed away at the face of William Lennox, in defiance of all the rules of fencing, drew open the door, and darted into the street, flying at a pace which made all attempts at overtaking him useless.

He determined at once to desert the whole conspiracy, to leave the Countess Alcanor in the lurch, and content himself with the glorious revenge of the possession of Lillian.

CHAPTER VIII.

THE DOVER ROAD.

THE captain was amply supplied with money, and away sped the postillions along the road with that tremendous energy which could scarcely ever be extracted from them except by money.

The captain felt that the farther from London the safer was his neck.

And still he cried to the postillions—

"Quick! quick! 'tis matter of life and death."

When about ten miles from town his spirits became calmer, and the postillions stopping to change horses, he called for a pint of wine in a huge tumbler.

Then he slept.

Calm and sweet is the sleep of innocence; dark and gloomy are the dreams of even the aged and careworn — but what are those of crime?

The captain had no sooner closed his eyes than uprose before him the hideous phantoms of the past.

Many and many they passed before his eyes— visions of crime we scarcely have alluded to.

But one stuck fast.

It was the murder of the Pool on the Plain.

Red was the horizon, red with a glare of mingled blood and sunshine, while far up in the sky, huge and gigantic, rose the form of a woman, whose skinny fingers, orbitless eyes and long teeth, did not disguise her likeness to the wretched victim of his lust of gold.

Nearer, nearer she crept and smaller she grew, until the trembling caitiff felt the presence of the thing of horror and of blood.

With a wild shriek he woke.

"Merciful heavens!" he gasped, "what hideous nightmare is this? Why do you haunt me, hags? Have I not repented bitterly of *that* crime?"

Wretch! and with what unholy plot in your brain are you rushing down to a spot near Dover to commit a crime greater than all those you have hitherto committed?

A crime fearful in the eyes of heaven and of man.

The morning was now nearly breaking, and, to cool his fevered brow, the captain put his head out of the window.

They were ascending a hill at a slow pace.

Beside the carriage, but apparently inattentive to anything but his own thoughts, was a gentleman on horseback.

He was well wrapped up against the morning air; his collar was up and his hat drawn over his eyes.

Captain Frederick Winterton never felt more anxious to break the spell of silence.

"Fine morning, sir."

The stranger started, and, as if anxious not to imbibe any of the refreshing element, merely bowed, but made no answer.

"Can you inform me, sir, whereabouts we are? I have been to sleep for some time," continued the captain.

"Don't know," said the other, gruffly.

"Thank you."

At this moment a strange sound reached the ears of the captain.

It was the furious clatter of horses' hoofs.

He looked behind and saw another post-chaise at a considerable distance descending a hill.

He turned ghastly pale and trembled violently.

"Now, then, postillions!" he shouted, "is this the way to earn your money? A guinea a mile if you distance yonder carriage."

And like the very roaring blast itself away went the chaise.

The pace was so rapid that it swayed to the right and left as if it would upset.

The horseman did not hurry his pace, but rather reined in and waited.

He rode a magnificent hunter, and his appearance denoted that he was a sportsman.

In a very short time the second post-chaise came up to him and slackened its pace.

"Could you be kind enough, sir, to tell us what sort of person was in the carriage a-head," said a young man.

"Captain Frederick Winterton," replied a grave and earnest voice.

"Captain George, by all that's lucky!"

"William Lennox, my boy, how are you? But if you want to catch him you must make haste. They are going at a rattling pace. I will keep up with you."

And, without further parley, the post-chaise resumed its course.

In twenty minutes they were in sight of the posting-house, and there, in front of the door, they were putting to the horses.

A low chuckle of congratulation from the Blue Dwarf alone proclaimed their anticipated victory.

In another minute they were all on foot, and entering the hotel, Sapathwa wrapped in his huge cloak.

"Where's the gentleman who came by the other chaise," said William Lennox, in a commanding tone.

"Don't know, sir," replied the host, a little man, with small reddish ferret eyes and turned-up nose.

"Don't know, sir," cried William, sharply, "when he has just alighted from yonder vehicle!"

"I repeat my first words, sir."

"But you don't mean to tell me he did not enter your house?"

"Of course he did."

"Well, sir, and what then?"

"He went out again."

"Which way, sir?"

"Can't say, as didn't look; was mounted on my grey cob—perfect gentleman—paid like a prince. Can I do anything for you?"

And the landlord bowed with an obsequiousness which did not conceal a covert sneer.

"Breakfast," replied William Lennox, who then signed to Captain George to follow him.

They went out into the stable-yard, but all their inquiries ended in nothing.

Captain Frederick Winterton had passed away like a dream.

Not a trace could be found of him, and, except the landlord, nobody confessed to having seen him.

"Let us stop here," said Captain George, in a low tone; "discharge the post-chaises and wait. The horse will be known, and I'll warrant it comes back."

Lennox agreed to follow the advice, and in a few minutes more they were in a private room, discussing over tea, coffee, and ham, their schemes for the future.

The postillions were discharged, the landlord informed that they should dine, and then out they went to scour the country.

Looking out of the window Captain George had remarked a very good cross country road behind the house, and it struck him that this road was the one which had been taken by Winterton.

With this belief he sauntered out with William to smoke a cigar, leaving the Blue Dwarf to watch at the inn.

Sapathwa had made up his mind to capture the whole gang, and then to inflict upon them condign punishment.

His brain had been long racked to find how it should be done.

The punishments must be varied indeed.

CHAPTER IX.

LILLIAN.

THE poor girl Lillian, to her great surprise, found herself for some time utterly undisturbed. No rude aggressor entered to disturb her repose. She was a prisoner, it is true, but this quiet caused her to recruit her health, and even to regain some of her pristine beauty.

But she was, beyond all conception, miserable.

William Lennox was no longer a sacred name in her heart.

And then she was, to all appearance, hopelessly separated from her mother.

The girl who was appointed to wait upon her was not unkind, but she was faithful to her employer, whoever he might be.

The view she looked out upon was that of a small but well kept park; and Lillian, whose love of nature could not be subdued even by her suffering, sighed often as she gazed out upon the swelling hills, the ancestral oaks, and shady bowers.

"Why do you sigh, miss?" the girl would say.

"Girl, I am a prisoner, separated from the whole world, without a hope for the future, without an affection to support me save only my mother. Besides, I am fading away. The very sight of the birds make my poor heart ache."

"Can I trust you, miss?"

"In what way?"

"Would you give me your word not to escape?" she said.

"How mean you?"

"I believe I can trust you. There is something about you which tells me you would not betray a poor girl. If you will give me your word not to escape I will accompany you in walks in the park."

"I will promise not to take advantage of your kindness, but I will not promise to seclude myself for ever."

"I don't ask you that; but while out in the park, in my charge, you will not seek to fly."

"I will not."

"Put on your hat, miss, and let us go."

Lillian followed her advice, and hastily assuming a befitting walking dress, followed the girl into the park.

"How comes it," said Lillian gently, "that I find a girl like you in such a position as this? You appear to be a good-hearted girl."

"Ah ! miss, do not ask me," said the girl, blushing crimson. "Did you know all !"

"I did not mean to hurt your feelings," said Lillian.

"Ah ! miss, if you would but hearken to my tale you might understand and excuse me."

"I will hear it, if not with pleasure with interest. The sorrows of my sex are to me sacred things."

"My name is Mary Hadfield.

"If you glance your eye over to the edge of yonder hill you will see a small cottage surrounded by a farm.

"That is my father's residence—a residence which I shall never enter again !"

"Why ?"

"You shall hear.

"My Lord's late steward was one Roland, a man of evil passion, but handsome and polished in his manners.

"He did me the honour to fall in love with me.

"I never suspected, for one moment, but that his intentions were honourable. His position as steward gave him ample opportunities of seeing me.

"One reason, my father was behind-hand with his rent.

"Mr. Roland gave him every opportunity of payment at his own convenience.

"I blessed him in my heart.

"I then became an assistant to the housekeeper, and resided at the hall.

"Mr. Roland began to make such advances as no young woman could pretend to misunderstand.

"But still he promised marriage.

"I indignantly rejected all his persuasions.

"I even threatened to inform my parents of his suggestions.

"The next day the brokers were put into my father's house.

"They were on the verge of ruin.

"Roland then came upon me like a fiend.

"He painted, in the most desperate colours, the fatal end of my allowing my father to go to prison.

"He swore that as soon as he obtained a renewal of his engagement he would marry me.

"I believed him.

"I fell.

"My father became, by some fatal indiscretion, aware after a time to what means he owed his salvation.

"He spurned me from the door.

"My seducer laughed at me when I begged him to fulfil his promise.

"But he lost his situation, and I, desperate, with character gone, was too glad to conceal my shame beneath the roof of my lord."

"But what has become of him ?"

"I cannot understand it."

"Why has he brought me here ?"

"That is a puzzle and a mystery I cannot unravel. A fortnight ago I received orders to prepare apartments for a young lady, whom I was to watch carefully, and permit no intercourse with any one from without. I obeyed; but, since then, I have heard nothing."

"Is it not strange that men should be so cruel ?" said Lillian.

"It is."

"To deprive of liberty and happiness one who never injured anybody."

"But you injure them deeply," said Mary, in sarcastic tones.

"How so ?"

"Do you not refuse to satisfy the cravings of some chartered libertine ?"

Lillian held down her head, sighed deeply, and spoke not a word for some time.

Suddenly Mary clasped her by the wrist.

"Quick ! follow me ; there is not an instant of time to be lost."

"What is it ?"

Mary pointed to a horseman who was galloping down the road.

"Save me !" said Lillian, wildly.

But Mary had relapsed into the cold and stern guardian.

They hurried on to the house, and in a few minutes they had again reached the room they had so recently left.

In two minutes more Lillian found herself face to face with Captain Frederick Winterton.

CHAPTER X.

THE DARK BOUDOIR.

ON the day following the accident to Lady Blakesley, in Hyde Park, Charles Wentworth called, by the advice of his tutor, at her mansion in Curzon-street, Mayfair.

Her ladyship was located there in magnificent style. She had at length for her friend the most infatuated, and, at the same time, the most extravagant of men—the Prince Regent. He was delighted with her vivacity—charmed with her person, and nothing that she required was denied her.

Her rooms were redolent of luxury. Soft springy couches were grouped tastefully in her reception-room—the carpets yielded to the tread—tiny scented fountains cast fragrance into the air, while the heavy curtains gave, as it were, a mellowness to the atmosphere of the apartment.

Pauline received Charles Wentworth coquettishly ; blushed studiedly at a mention of her mishap, and was evidently inclined to be very pleasant.

"You are very kind, sir," said Lady Blakesley, "very kind, indeed, to think of me. I shall always be most happy to see you."

Charles had wonderful command over his countenance ; he was well disguised, and acted his part admirably. He led the conversation into the proper channel, and affected even a few tender caresses, which the lady, with studied archness, repelled.

In the middle of the conversation, however, an unexpected, though not an extraordinary, interruption took place. A carriage drew up to the door ; a loud knock, and the Prince Regent was announced.

Pauline turned slightly pale, and half dragged, half pushed Wentworth in a side door, which was almost in total darkness.

"Do not stir," she whispered, "I will rejoin you directly."

She then took a hasty glance in the mirror, and settled herself calmly on an ottoman, reclining in an easy and voluptuous position, seemingly half-asleep.

The brow of the Prince Regent was rather darkened as he entered the room, and he appeared scarcely in the mood to admire or appreciate anything.

He took a seat by the side of Pauline on the couch.

"Your Royal Highness seems dull to-day," said she, languidly, and twining her arms round his neck.

"You can scarcely doubt, madam," said the Prince, gently putting her away; "you can scarcely doubt that I am vexed, sorely displeased, in fact."

Pauline knew the bent of his remarks, though she affected ignorance.

"What have I done to offend your Royal Highness?—surely nothing?"

"You know Lady Jersey well?" he demanded.

"Your Highness knows her better."

"She is a friend of mine you are aware?"

"Most certainly."

"Why then insult her publicly? It brings discredit on all."

"You would not have me bear her taunts patiently?"

"No; but there are times and seasons for everything. Lady Jersey is indignant. You have injured me materially with her."

Pauline's eyes glittered with cold, triumphant expression.

"That is not a circumstance which will vex me, your Royal Highness. I love you so well I wish for no rival;" and she turned her warm soft arms around his neck: and smiling down upon her brow, the Prince said, laughingly—

"You are a little evil genius, Pauline; I can't resist you."

"Will you be here to-night?"

"Yes, at ten; but I must go now. I came to scold, I have stopped to be duped. Adieu, *au revoir,* my little fairy."

"One moment, your Highness, excuse me;" and she glided into the apartment where, in the dark, Charles Wentworth was still waiting.

Charles could see nothing; but he felt a glowing arm cast round his neck, a pair of sweet lips pressed to his, and a piece of paper was pressed into his hand.

"Go!—immediately."

And Pauline opened a door.

Charles Wentworth, in a few moments, was in the street, and in a few moments more the prince's carriage rolled away from the door.

The words on the paper were—

"*To-morrow at the Star and Garter, Richmond—at six o'clock.*"

CHAPTER XI.

LILLIAN AND THE CAPTAIN.

THE astonishment of the poor girl may be conceived when she found herself face to face with one of those who had so long persecuted her, and who had been so remorseless towards the man to whom her heart still yearned.

He bowed profoundly.

There was a moment's pause, during which they eyed each other with astonishment.

"My dear Miss Lillian," said the captain, "I have with great difficulty traced you hither—who has been the aggressor?"

"Captain Frederick Winterton," said the young girl, proudly preparing herself for the inevitable contest, "there can be no excuse for this intrusion. You have already persecuted me enough."

"My dear girl," said the man of the world with all that fascination of manner for which he was so celebrated, "I have never been your enemy."

"Sir—"

"Pardon me—"

"Sir!"

"Listen to me—if I have assisted to save you from an unprincipled adventurer—"

"Sir, I say—"

"One who, regardless of the treasure which was within his reach, deserted you for an abandoned woman—"

Lillian turned pale, and her heart appeared ready to burst.

It was with the utmost difficulty she could repress her tears.

"William Lennox has all along been systematically deceiving you," continued Captain Frederick Winterton, taking out his snuff-box with the most consummate nonchalance and the utmost unconcern.

"I beg, sir," said Lillian, who, dressed as she left the ball-room, felt utterly miserable under the ardent gaze of the profligate, "that you will cease dwelling on a subject which to me, under the present circumstances, is painful in the extreme."

"My dear girl, that relationship which exists between us is alone a sufficient excuse for my interference. But there is another reason—"

"Will Heaven have no mercy and release me from this man?" gasped Lillian.

"You call in vain."

"Alas!"

"Lillian, I love you—"

"Persecutor, assassin, and murderer," she cried, frantic with terror, "will you cease—"

"Beloved girl—listen to me calmly. I have

nothing but your dearest interests at heart. Consent but to be mine—and I will at once take you to your mother —"

"Take me to my mother first. But no, I will not pollute my soul with even a suggestion of a friend. Death itself, the very grim king of terror shall be my bridegroom, ere I will descend to your loathesome offer. I scorn it, as I spurn you—leave me, sir."

The man's eyes flashed with most unholy fire his lips quivered, and his hands became clenched.

Then he laid his snuff-box down upon the table.

"Girl," he said, "I give you fair warning. I am not a man to be trifled with. Recollect that you are a young, weak, and defenceless girl. Promise on your soul to be my wife, and I will treat you as such — refuse ——"

"And—"

"I shall become a desperate man," he said, looking her full in the face.

Lillian's lips quivered, but she made no reply.

She glanced at the door; it was closed, but it was not bolted.

He smiled bitterly.

"You cannot escape."

"Coward!"

"Lillian, I have warned you. I shall ask you thrice to become my wife."

"And then—"

"Then beware of all that a desperate man may be driven to do. Once more, humbly, and in the tones of a gentleman, I ask you will you be my wife?"

"Never!"

"A second time?"

"Never!"

"A third time?"

"Again I say, never!"

"Then, by the soul of my father, you shall be mine as my mistress!"

And he advanced towards the terrified girl, in a way that left little hope of safety.

A gentle, feeble girl of seventeen.

A powerful man in the very pride of life.

What could be her chance of escape from him?

Suddenly a kind of inspiration seized her—a magical thought.

She snatched up his snuff-box, and cast with steady and deliberate aim the whole contents into his eyes.

"Malediction!" cried the other, for the moment utterly blinded.

On tip-toe Lillian made for the door, snatching up as she did so her cloak and hat.

Under cover of a storm of curses, she was enabled to open the door.

"Stay!" he yelled, "or by the heavens above you shall rue it."

But fear lent Lillian wings, and she fled up a narrow staircase leading to the upper apartments of this vast mansion.

At this moment Mary came hurrying to the rooms with a startled face.

"A number of gentlemen on horseback," she cried, "have tracked you here, and insist upon seeing you."

He did not reply.

"What is the matter, sir?"

"Water—towel!" spluttered the captain.

She handed him a basin and towel.

"Keep them back. Say I will be down directly," said the captain.

In a few minutes she returned to say that they were in the library.

"Mary," said the captain, "that wretched girl, after nearly blinding me, has escaped."

"Escaped!" exclaimed Mary, inwardly gratified, but not daring to show her feelings.

"Set a watch that she does not leave the hall. Bid all the men servants be ready at a moment's notice to eject these intruders."

He then slowly and calmly descended the stairs, with all the cool self-possession which was so characteristic of this unprincipled man.

In a few minutes more he found himself face to face with Captain George, the Blue Dwarf, and William Lennox.

"To what, gentlemen, do I owe the honour of this unexpected visit?" asked Captain Frederick.

William Lennox stepped forward to speak.

"Where is Lillian?" he said, in stern accents.

"How should I know?" asked Captain Frederick Winterton, calmly.

"We have traced her here," continued William Lennox, "and must find her."

"Search the house," replied the captain; "you are quite welcome—that is, if you have a legal warrant."

And Captain Winterton rang a bell.

CHAPTER XII.

THE RENDEZVOUS AT RICHMOND.

THE evening came on hazily—darkly.

Richmond then was not the Richmond of to-day.

It was an old straggling town; the "Star and Garter" stood alone, with its gardens sloping down to the misty river.

Pauline was punctual to her appointment. Charles Wentworth was awaiting her.

They dined together in a private room, drank wine, and got excessively friendly and communicative.

Charles Wentworth pretended at first to be piqued by her conduct towards him on the occasion of the visit of the Prince Regent.

"Pauline, *ma mie*," said he, as she lay in his

arms on the couch, balancing a half empty glass of sparkling champagne—

"Pauline, you are as fickle as you are fair."

"Why so?" answered the temptress, kissing him tenderly. "Why so? I am faithful to all I love."

"Then you do not love me? else the prince himself would not have prevented your remaining with me yesterday."

"Oh! *ma cher*, you are over-jealous. How could I, in one moment, discard one who so enters into all my amusements—who doats on me—who attends so to all my whims? He is quite mad in his excess of passion for me. I was in need even of assistance. I am now in Curzon-street, Mayfair. *Voila tout.*"

"Well, my charmer," said Charles, abstractedly; "I will not press you too much."

"You are abstracted, my own."

Charles had been repeatedly consulting his watch.

"My head burns," he answered; "let us walk in the gardens—we shall be still alone."

And he impressed a passionate kiss on her lips, and, straining her to his breast, rose.

Pauline hesitated.

"Come, my own," said Charles, hurriedly, "I am ill—the room is so excessively hot—come."

Lady Edgar Blakesley no longer hesitated, but throwing a cloak over her bare and beautiful shoulders, descended into the grounds.

They entered an alcove at the very extremity of the gardens close to the river bank, where a swinging oil lamp cast a dim religious light over the scene.

Here the waiters brought them more champagne: and Charles urged his fair companion to drink deeply.

"You wish to make me quite inebriated, my own one," said Pauline, her eyes flashing and her bosom heaving under the excitement produced by the pale and sparkling wine. "My eyes even now are dazzled, and my senses seem leaving me."

"Nonsense, *ma cheré*," said Charles Wentworth—"your love for me cannot be very great if even wine can overcome its fire—the wine is harmless. Come, kiss me, and talk to me, and the fumes will soon disappear from your brain."

Pauline felt bewildered—and she walked up to her companion.

Some vague misgiving came over her mind.

Could this possibly be a plant of the enemy?

Could this one who pretended so much love for her be indeed so deceitful and treacherous as that.

She was unaware of anything that had happened, and therefore could form no definite idea.

She shivered; the wind seemed to strike cold to her naked shoulders, and, drawing her cloak closely and quickly around her, she exclaimed—

"Come, let us go to our room. I feel chilled."

"Very well, love," replied Charles. "Drink, then, one glass more to our fervent and unchanging love. Here's to our next merry meeting."

Pauline drank off her glass of champagne, which, had she had time to notice it, would have betrayed by its dulness the presence of some deleterious compound quite foreign to its nature.

She had scarcely done so when she fell back in a stupor.

Her eyes were left staring open. She could see and hear all that passed, but was herself incapable of speech or motion.

* * * * *

During this scene a boat with muffled oars had been lying off the gardens.

The boat contained four men, who appeared to be most anxiously awaiting a summons.

* * * * *

Charles Wentworth drew close to her—adjusted the shawl over her neck, and said,—

"Pauline, I am a woman. My deceit has been practised in a good cause. You must come with me — there is no use in resisting."

Charles then went into the garden and gave a low whistle.

It was immediately responded to by those in the boat.

The boat containing the four men shot rapidly and noiselessly up to the gardens where they had been wandering.

Three landed.

William Lennox, Jack Horne, and the Blue Dwarf.

Pauline was then immediately seized and carried away by the strong muscular arms of Jack Horne.

"One more rat for the trap," said the Blue Dwarf, as he stepped hastily and cautiously into the boat.

CHAPTER XIII.

THE RESCUE OF LILLIAN.

WHEN Captain Winterton had delivered himself of the extraordinary and cool speech in regard to the legal warrant, he sat down, beckoned his visitors to sake seats, and lighted a cigar.

A man servaut entered the room.

"John," said the captain, quietly extinguishing his fusee, "show these gentlemen over the house."

The man stared.

"You may well stare," he continued, "but my visitors fancy they have traced some run-

away hither. What the marquis will say I am sure I don't know: but pray do as I bid you."

The Blue Dwarf did not utter a word while Captain Frederick was giving these instructions, but a peculiar smile—half amused, half sardonic—played over his lips. He waited quietly until his enemy had completed his speech, and then remarked—

"Not so, Captain Winterton. In my search through this house I prefer that you should accompany me."

The captain, who knew well the import of these words, turned slightly pale. He was evidently well caged. He had hoped, in their absence, to effect his escape from the house, and thus get the start of them. Lillian, beautiful and prized as she was, was forgotten. His impure heart was incapable of love: he had only desired the possession of her person; and now that he himself was in danger, he only thought of his own personal safety.

Now, however, his last chance of escape seemed cut off. He resolved to temporise.

"Considering the nature of the outrage you are committing in this house," said he, "I think it is scarcely fair to expect I should assist you. You can search the house, but I will not be responsible to the marquis for your presence here."

The eyes of the Blue Dwarf gleamed with a savage fire. He advanced towards the captain, and, looking up into his face, said deliberately—

"No shuffling, sir; we are three to one. Your object is to escape. Go on, we follow."

Captain George, however, led the way. The captain went next, and William Lennox and the Blue Dwarf followed, with their swords drawn.

Arrived at the top of the house they found one room locked and barricaded. They cried out and knocked loudly. The voice of Lillian answered—

"I will not open! Never, Captain Winterton, will I resign myself to you alive. The moment you enter beholds me flinging myself from the window into the garden beneath."

"Open, Lillian, my own!" cried William Lennox; "we are friends. I, William, am here, and Sapathwa, and Captain George—open!"

The barricade of furniture was now removed, the door was flung open, and Lillian appeared, still dressed in her Greek dancing dress.

A look of mingled inquiry and love passed between her and William Lennox; then time, and place, and recollections of evil were alike forgotten, and the two hearts were in another moment clasped tightly and beating wildly against each other. The Blue Dwarf gazed at the reunited lovers for a moment with tears in his eyes, but he still murmured—

"Not yet—not yet."

During this scene Captain George had been standing at the head of the stairs, watching narrowly his prisoner. The entrance of Lillian, however—her strange garb, so slightly made, and so unfitting for the occasion—her greeting of William—all combined to divert his attention for a moment, and Captain Winterton, who was watching his opportunity, saw at once a chance of escape.

Making one dash at Captain George, he sent him reeling down the stairs for several steps, and drawing his sword, rushed madly down the staircase into the hall, and out of the house. The post-chaise which had brought the three friends was standing at the door.

"My man," cried Captain Winterton, "these fellows have been trying to murder me. Take me to the next house like the wind, and name your own price."

The man hesitated not; he very rarely got such fares, so, lashing his horses into a gallop, he was soon bearing the captain away like the wind towards the town of Nortonwick.

CHAPTER XIV.

FOR DEAR LIFE.

THE captain then, for the second time, had succeeded in escaping from the grasp of his enemies. It was now not a mere question of a day or an hour, no point of delay, no fear of his victims eluding his grasp.

He was running for dear life.

When he found himself within the post-chaise, rattling along the road to Nortonwick, he relapsed into utter helplessness.

He knew well the nature of his own crimes; he knew, therefore, what would be the nature of his punishment.

The Pool on the Plain came vividly before his mind; the figure of the murdered girl seemed to be following him and pointing him out as he struggled to escape from his determined pursuers.

Even if the murder were undiscovered, was not his life over and over again forfeited? Would the great forgery on Mrs. Winterton be discovered and exposed? The cold perspiration stood upon his brow, and he sat, convulsively clutching the sill of the carriage window, listening intently for any sounds of pursuit, yet not daring to look out.

At length Nortonwick was reached. The horses were dead beat. The man refused to try their pluck again for love or money.

"Come, come," said Captain Winterton, "it is a matter of life and death. I must reach Dover before twelve to-night."

"It is impossible, sir," growled the man, surlily; "the horses are useless."

The captain strode into the house.

"Landlord," he cried, "I am on most urgent business. Have you no horse you can let me have? I will pay handsomely, and some one of your men can accompany me."

"I have only two horses, sir," replied the landlord; "the one is engaged for Mr. Norton, the lawyer, whom you see there," pointing to a snug chimney corner in the bar parlour; "the other is," he continued, with a knowing wink, "the other, I can scarcely let out to a stranger who is going all the way to Dover."

"I don't look much like a thief," said Winterton, angrily. "My name is Forbes—I am a Captain in one of her Majesty's Regiments—I am going over to France by this night's mail—I cannot, therefore, take your horse with me, and I will pay you handsomely."

"Well, well," said mine host, scratching his head dubiously, "I don't know what to say."

And he looked inquiringly at the lawyer.

Meanwhile Captain Winterton strode impatiently to the door, and gazed out into the darkening evening. The sky portended a storm, and very little could be distinguished on the face of the surrounding country; but in the far distance along the road, which wound like a dark serpent along the earth, he could see the flickering of an uncertain light. Now it appeared—then disappeared—and appeared again.

"That is a post-chaise containing my pursuers," muttered he. "H—l and furies! This dilatory old brute will be my ruin. Landlord!" he cried, as he re-entered the inn, "have you decided? It will ruin me and many others if I do not catch the mail to-night. Am I to have the horse?"

"Yes, sir," said mine host, rubbing his hands over the prospect of making some extra money. "Mr. Norton, who has property with him, will be glad of your company to Dover, where he will point out to you a house at which I am known, and where you can, therefore, leave my horse."

"I am sure," said Captain Winterton, laying a peculiar emphasis on his words, "I shall be most happy of Mr. Norton's company, that is to say, provided he be starting immediately."

"The horses are at the door," cried the ostler.

"Thank Heaven!" said Winterton aloud; then remembering himself, he placed five guineas in the host's hand; and, bidding him good night, followed the lawyer into the courtyard, where they mounted, and were soon on their road.

The night, as we have said, was just drawing in. The sky was lowering and heavy; the country was enveloped everywhere in a kind of hazy mantle. Everything was very still, and scarcely a sign of life was visible except the uncertain lights of the distant post-chaise as it rolled on in quick pursuit.

"We have a long journey before us," cried Captain Winterton, by way of initiating a conversation; "how many miles may it be?"

"Twenty."

"Then we can arrive before twelve?"

"Oh, yes, easily. I expect to be comfortably housed and supping at half-past eleven."

The captain laughed a dry, short laugh, as he answered,

"Ah, ah! I've a different treat before me—giving a supper for the fishes instead of fishing for a supper. Ah! ah! ah!"

"Good, good," laughed Mr. Norton. "You are a bad sailor, then?"

"I am—shocking. These are good horses, though, let's try their mettle."

They accordingly urged their horses to a rattling pace, and soon, having left the town behind them, were speeding along the thickly-wooded country. They were at a very lonely portion of the highroad. Captain Winterton had not spoken for some minutes, but had proceeded on in a kind of moody and determined silence. At length, guiding his horse close up to that of the lawyer, and stopping him by seizing the bridle, he said,

"Mr. Norton, I am not a highwayman; I am simply a desperate man! I am flying for my life! I am without funds, you have money in your portmanteau. I must have it!"

The lawyer gazed at him for a moment in mute wonderment. He then said, calmly,

"Sir, I have five hundred pounds in that portmanteau. You surely do not require it all?"

Captain Winterton's mouth watered. Here was a prize, and no mistake.

"Come, sir, deliver up every farthing quickly and I will not harm you. Refuse, and—"

Mr. Norton heard the unmistakable click of a pistol. He did not speak. He saw that he was utterly at the mercy of a desperate man; and so, with a sigh, he delivered over to Captain Winterton his portmanteau, heavy with gold.

"And now," said the captain, as he emptied the money into his pockets, "although I feel no enmity towards you, but rather friendship, I must bind your hands and tie up your horse, otherwise you will rouse the country and materially affect my plans of escape."

So saying, he leapt off his horse, assisted Mr. Norton to alight, tied his hands behind him, and fastened the horse up to the hedge-side. The new increase in his exchequer enlivened him—made him quite jocular. A sudden thought struck him.

"You will possibly remain here some hours," he said, with a grin. "You will be cold, shall I light you a cigar?"

Mr. Norton did not answer.

"Well, if you won't there's no help for it," cried Winterton, leaping again on his horse. "Good night!" and he sped on rapidly towards Dover.

He arrived there about half-past eleven. The mail, he ascertained, started somewhere about one in the morning. He, therefore, had a clear hour and a half before him in which to effect a disguise. After disposing, therefore, of the horse, by giving it in charge of the ostler of the Kings and Key, he proceeded to a barber's shop. From this abode he sallied forth, in about a quarter of an hour, clean shaved, and with long ringlets of red hair descending over his shoulders. This done, he entered the denser portion of the town, and resolved to make himself merry until the packet started. He went in, therefore, to an hotel on the quay, and ordered brandy.

CHAPTER XV.

NEEDS MUST WHEN THE DEVIL DRIVES.

"Come, send round the wine, and leave points of belief,
To simpleton sages and reasoning fools;
  This moment's flower is too fair and brief
To be wither'd and stain'd by the dust of the schools.
  Your glass may be purple, and mine may be blue,
But while they are fill'd from the same bright bowl,
  The fool who would quarrel for difference of hue,
Deserves not the comfort they shed o'er the soul."

SUCH was the burden of a song which some gay reveller was bawling at the top of his voice in the parlour.

Loud shouts of applause followed, and noisy laughter and jesting.

"There can be no harm entering there," muttered Winterton, and, taking up his glass, he entered, and as he did so he uttered a jaunty "Good evening."

The company was of a very mixed character; all were jovial, some were drunk, so that the entrance of Captain Winterton was received with a maudlin cheer.

Seating himself by the young man who had just finished singing, the Captain ventured to inquire of him at what hour the packet for Calais started.

"It starts at one," was the reply; "but you are surely not going over to-night? The sky is as black as ink, and the wind is high enough to blow away a three-decker."

"Needs must when the devil drives," said the captain, gloomily, and relapsed into silence.

"Hulo, Saunders!" said a voice from the end of the room, addressing a burly-looking citizen ensconced in the chimney corner. "Here's news from London—something after our style, neighbour Grabem," he added, poking in the ribs an ill-looking fellow by his side, who was evidently a sheriff's officer. "Now, then, gentlemen all, listen :—

"'CAPTURE OF A NOTORIOUS SWINDLER.—*We learn, by the last mail from London, that the police have at length succeeded in capturing the noted forger, Edward Tigsby Jones, alias Slimy Jones, calling himself late Contractor to his Majesty in Spain. He has been committed to Newgate, there to await his trial.*'"

The feelings of the wretched captain, when he heard of the capture of his confederate, may be better imagined than we can describe them. Nor were they at all relieved when a tall, quiet-looking gentleman in black said—

"Yes, it is a good thing that scoundrel is caught at length; it will not be long before his companions in crime are keeping him company. One, I believe, is at hand already; the other is trying to escape the country."

Captain Winterton sat upon thorns. He fancied the eyes of the quiet gentleman in black were glaring at him, then he thought that all the people in the room were combining to stare him out of countenance. After nervously sipping his brandy and water for some time, he rose and quietly left the room.

The gentleman in black also rose as soon as the captain had disappeared, and making a peculiar sign over his shoulder to Mr. Grabem, followed him.

It wanted now but twenty minutes to the time when the packet left; so, paying his score, Winterton passed rapidly on to the quay and into the boat. As he leaped on deck a figure followed him, and taking him by the hand, said,

"Ah! ah! How do you do?—glad to meet you again. Not much change."

"You have the advantage of me, sir," said the captain.

"No, no, Captain Winterton, that won't do. You don't forget old friends like that. Sad affair about Jones, though, isn't it?"

Winterton was not to be taken off his guard like this.

"You mistake me for some one else. My name is Forbes. The likeness must be striking."

"It is—very," said the other, drily.

The captain turned round sharply and then walked away, after gazing for a moment with a puzzled look at the face of his interrogator.

It was that of the quiet gentleman in black.

CHAPTER XVI.

PAULINE.

THE party on the staircase—William, Captain George, Lillian, and the Blue Dwarf—looked for a moment at each other in amazement. Captain Winterton had taken them by surprise—pursuit for the moment was useless.

"What are we to do?" said William Lennox, in a tone of vexation.

"Let him go," returned the Blue Dwarf, sardonically; "he refuses to be captured by comparative friends, let him now submit to the law."

"What mean you?"

"I mean," replied Sapathwa, "that he will fly to Dover, and from thence endeavour to escape to France. But at Dover is a detective officer who knows him, and will bring him back. Now let us be going from this accursed house."

They were soon in motion, and returned to the hotel from which they had started. Thence they took a post-chaise for London; and, after a journey devoid of all interest, arrived in the metropolis.

Mrs. Winterton was at home, indulging in uncontrollable grief; and when she heard the post-chaise roll up to the door she scarcely dared to hope that it contained her daughter. Her joy was great, therefore, when she saw Lillian enter, and felt her once more clasped to her heart.

"Alas! how soon again am I to lose you?" said the mother, half inquiringly, half despairingly. "You seem to be restored to me again and again only to be as often snatched from my arms."

"Not again, not again," said William Lennox, smiling, "until I take her from you for good."

"And now," said Sapathwa, "there is no time to be lost. We have to visit our prisoners."

After taking a tender adieu of the re-united pair, Sapathwa and Lennox proceeded to the place where Pauline had been placed in confinement.

They found her sitting in her room, silent, moody, revengeful. She was still attired in the light dress she had assumed to captivate the young Charles Wentworth, and her hands were tied together to prevent her doing herself an injury, as was feared from her extreme violence when captured.

She rose as they entered, and gazed haughtily and savagely at them.

"You have caged me at length," she said, impetuously; "you have, therefore, come to insult me?"

"We came not to insult you," answered the Blue Dwarf, taking a seat at one side of the room, "we came here merely to ask you a few questions."

"Which I shall decline to answer," said Pauline.

"Where is your husband?" asked Sapathwa, not noticing her reply.

Pauline did not utter a syllable.

"I repeat, where is your husband?"

"I know not."

"When and from what place did you last hear from him?"

No reply. Sapathwa reiterated his question.

"I decline to tell," said Pauline. "Do with me what you like, I will disclose nothing. I know well your intentions. I know that to place him in your power would be to deprive him of everything he holds dear. Not that I care for him; but I care for those honours and distinctions which you seek to snatch from him. I will tell nothing."

"You positively refuse to say anything?" said William.

"I do refuse!"

"Then," said Lennox solemnly, "you are in league with our enemies, and must be treated as one of them."

CHAPTER XVII.

THE MURDER IN THE CHANNEL.

THE Calais packet started at the appointed hour in spite of the roarings of the wind and the heavings of the sea.

Captain Frederick Winterton had shaken off his newly-formed acquaintance, and mingled with the throng of persons who crowded on the stern to catch a last glimpse of the town of Dover, whose lights were only now and then visible as the vessel heaved and tossed amid the huge waves.

There is nothing so sickening as a sea voyage in a small sailing vessel across the channel, particularly on a dark, cold night, when the rain is descending in a kind of steady drizzling.

The passengers soon dispersed, and sought each his respective berth, leaving Captain Frederick Winterton alone, as he imagined, on deck. He paced up and down with a comparatively light heart. He was leaving England behind him, and he trusted never to see it more.

He had determined to leave all his confederates to manage how they could in London, and to go either to Paris or the German baths to seek a precarious livelihood at the gaming table.

"Cold night, sir," said the man at the wheel; "likely to have a storm, too, I reckon."

"Do you think so," answered Captain Frederick, lighting a "weed," and appearing quite indifferent about the matter.

He would have preferred a white squall out in the deep ocean to a sight of Sapathwa's face at that moment.

"Yes, there will be a storm presently," said a voice behind him in an ironical tone; and turning quickly round he saw behind him the gentleman in black.

"Confound your impudence, who spoke to you?" said the captain, as he strode forward.

His tormentor followed and confronted him as he turned in his walk.

"Captain Winterton," said he, "I want to say a word to you. We are here alone, and no one can therefore hear. Let's sit down and talk like sensible men."

"You are a d——d nuisance to me, I can tell you," said Winterton. "My name is Forbes, but you are a persevering nuisance, so here goes. Will you take a cigar?"

"With pleasure. But you must quietly listen to what I have to say.

"First of all," said the unknown, crossing his legs and seating himself as if for a long chat, "first of all, your name is not Forbes, it is Captain Frederick Winterton. First of all, you are accused of, and can be proved to have committed the murder at the Pool on the Plain; secondly, you forged to a vast extent on Mrs. Winterton, your relative. For both these little transactions you have forfeited your head. You do not answer. Well, according to the old proverb, you know, 'silence gives consent.'"

"I have simply been silent," returned the captain, "because I am devilishly amused. You are a deuced impudent scoundrel, and you interest me rather."

"You are tolerably disguised," continued his tormentor, "but Jonas the Barber did not give you a well-shaped wig. I prefer those with short curls. They look less pretentious. But not to waste time, I will give you my card. My name is Felix Hawk, my profession is that of a detective officer. My business leads me at present on board the Calais packet to seize the person of one Captain Frederick Winterton. Here is my warrant, and here also is my prisoner."

So saying, he laid his arm on that of the captain, and arrested him in the usual form.

The captain laughed a hoarse, forced laugh; and then shaking him off, said—

"A joke—a good joke; but I say, my good fellow, even this may go too far. If you touch me again I shall be under the painful necessity of knocking you down."

"That, sir, would be incurring the unpleasant chance of handcuffing, which I always endeavour to prevent the necessity of. It is my earnest endeavour, on every occasion, to treat my prisoners with becoming courtesy and kindness. If you consent to come with me quietly there need be no disturbance. I will reveal to no one that you have been arrested on a charge of murder, and you can return by the next packet easily. Otherwise, I shall rouse the ship."

These latter words were spoken in a different voice, and with a determined air that showed plainly that the man was in general only acting a part for the sake of his own amusement.

"Well, well," said Captain Winterton; "although I really do not understand what you want, I will come with you; but, for the sake of appearances, do not make any disturbance."

"Quite so; we understand each other. That is all I want. Meanwhile we will dismiss the unpleasant subject."

They talked on for some time upon various subjects, the detective carefully avoiding all mention of the subject of arrest.

The night was very dark; the wind howled dismally through the rigging, and the sails would ever and anon flap angrily and noisily against the mast.

There was, as we have said, nobody on deck,

with the exception of Captain Winterton, the detective, and the man at the wheel.

The two former were pacing up and down, sometimes one preceding the other, sometimes, again, reversing it.

The detective was a short and rather slightly-built man. Captain Winterton was tall and powerful. When standing on the poop, screened from the observation of the helmsman, a thought suddenly struck him.

It was a thought horrible and deadly; but one which produced no fear in the mind of the desperate man.

Suddenly, when Hawk was least expecting it, he seized him fiercely round the waist, and flung him headlong over the bulwarks. His forehead struck against the ship as it was propelled forward, and stunned him. Not a sound escaped his lips. He fell down into the dark sea, was sucked in by the eddies of the vessel, and *the murder was completed.*

Captain Frederick Winterton picked up his cigar, and after a while descended into his berth. He slept well and soundly; and the morrow saw him safely landed on the French coast.

CHAPTER XVIII.

MONSIEUR LE COMTE DE POINCY.

THE most difficult "rat" to catch was the Countess de Castella.

This the Blue Dwarf knew well, and determined, therefore, to be careful. He was fully aware of the truth of the maxim, "The more haste the less speed," and, therefore, went cautiously—systematically to work.

Money, in such schemes as these, is of course the first and most potent agent, and money was forthcoming in abundance. A plan of unusual intricacy was formed, and Sapathwa already regarded his quarry as caged.

*   *   *

The fashionable world was taken agreeably by surprise when it learned that a French nobleman, of great wealth, had just arrived in the metropolis, and was about to inaugurate his entrance into English society by giving a grand *bal masqué.*

Monsieur le Comte de Poincy—such was the name of the new comer—was represented to be possessed of unlimited resources. He was young, handsome, and unmarried—he had numberless servants—his house was elegant, and it was said that his *petits soupers* in Paris had been of the most luxurious kind.

Mothers' hearts fluttered at the chance of fixing upon him one of the unmarriageable tribe which nature had imposed upon them. Fathers shook their heads and said something about young rakes—foreigners, and so on—but they, nevertheless, accepted the invitations.

Wealth is a solace of everything. Crime is gilded by it, and appears under the garb of virgin purity; nothing is wrong so it has a bank to back it; nobody questions a man who can pay his way.

There is a great mistake made by people in regard to poverty and riches.

The fact that a man is rich does not entitle him to be called honest, no matter how honestly he may have acquired his wealth.

A poor man may be honest from the force of innate perceptions of right and wrong—a rich man merely because he has no necessity to act dishonourably.

It is one, indeed, of the great errors of society to mistake plum-pudding for principle.

So the fathers didn't ask anything about his lineage, his birth, or his manners. They merely learned that he was wealthy, that he was a count, and, as I have said, unmarried.

So the count's reception rooms were filled that evening with a brilliant assemblage. The people, however, were wofully deceived.

It was, as we have said, a masked ball, and the host kept a strict incognito. Young ladies had in vain dressed themselves in the most *outré* style—in vain donned the shortest petticoats and the most scanty of bodices; in vain mothers pryed into every young man's face—the host was nowhere. The room was beautifully fitted up; the halls were one blaze of light; the refreshments elegant; the supper *recherché;* the music delicious. No one could possibly utter a word of complaint—everything was done in the most proper and costly fashion. But still those who had come to angle were disappointed, and went away early.

"Will you do me the honour of allowing me your hand for the next dance?" said a fine, manly voice, to a young Italian peasant who tripped by.

"Men do not dance together," answered the masked figure, with a laugh. "Go seek some fair partner, and leave me."

"Nay," retured the other, clutching her by the arm, "I know thee to be a woman; why, therefore, refuse me one dance—just one?"

"Well, if you must. But let us wait till the next waltz."

The first speaker was a tall, finely-made young man, attired in the dress of a French courtier. His mask almost entirely concealed his features, and his hat was slouched slightly over his face. His companion was short, and attired in a fanciful dress with a light body. Any one could have recognised her as a woman by her slender calves, and the queenly splendour of her bosom, which seemed as if it rebelled against the light imprisonment of the corset. Her face also was almost concealed; but there was sufficient room to allow a glimpse of an exquisitely formed mouth ever wreathing into smiles.

They danced one dance, and then retired into a nook secluded from the rest of the ballroom.

"It is very warm," said the girl, fanning herself vigorously.

"Very."

"A beautiful room, though."

"It is so."

"And everything is so well arranged, is it not?"

"It is."

"Ah! now this is too bad. Here you have

enticed me into dancing with you, and now you not only will not talk to me, but you will not even answer me when I speak. You are cruel."

"No; it is you who are cruel."

"I cruel, *c'est drole*!—I cruel; why do you say that? Have I not danced with you?"

"And have you not also made me love you?"

"Love! ah, ah! you are a funny man. Love at first sight. And not even first sight, I may say, since you cannot see my face."

"Nevertheless I do love you. I have seen you before, I think."

"Where?" inquired his companion, eagerly.

"In Paris."

"Really!"

"Yes; at M. Brassier's."

"Truly, I have been there; and your name?"

"Oh! are we not masked? That would be betraying a confidence."

"Yes; but you say you are in love with me."

"Well, then," said he, taking her small white-gloved hand, "I will tell. I am Monsieur le Comte de Poincy. I am the master of this house, and you—"

"I will tell you, but not here. Can we not retire for a few moments?"

"With pleasure. Allow me," and giving his arm to his fair partner, he passed with her out of the ball-room.

Passing through a long corridor he entered a small room, elegantly fitted up, and closing the door, pointed to an ottoman, and seated himself beside her on it.

"So you are the count himself?" said the lady.

"I am, and you—"

"I am the Countess de Castella."

"Are you residing in England permanently?"

"Yes, that is to say, for a while."

"Do you know many English persons? that is to say, have you a large circle of acquaintances?"

"No—not very."

"Do you know Mr. William Lennox?"

The countess trembled.

"Yes—slightly."

The count removed his mask, and disclosed to the astonished gaze of his companion the features of William Lennox himself.

"Coward," cried the countess, rising, "let me go at once."

"Not so," said Lennox, restraining her, "*you* have this time fallen into a trap, do not complain of it. No one knows that you are here. There is no chance of escape."

The lady breathed hard—her bosom rose and fell with tumultuous emotion—and she said, with an assumption of calmness,

"And pray, sir, what is your purpose in thus entrapping me in this cowardly and unmanly manner?"

"The fact is," said the Blue Dwarf, entering by a side door, "the fact is, madam, I have been preparing a great rat trap, into which our enemies are falling, one by one—Slimy Jones, the Honourable John Winterton, the *soi-disant* Lady Edgar Blakesley, and the Countess de Castella have already been captured. It remains only to find Captain Frederick Winterton to complete the number."

"Vile monster!" muttered the countess.

"Most probably you think so," said the Blue Dwarf, rubbing his hands; "but those are greatest monsters who plot murders and seduce the hearts of the young into evil ways. However, I will not reproach you. If you walk this way with me a maid-servant shall attend you, and enable you to change your apparel."

The door opened, the countess passed through, and William Lennox and the Blue Dwarf remained.

The former stood half hesitating, gazing after her retreating figure with a kind of loving pity.

A shade of anger passed over the face of the Blue Dwarf.

"Not till you are worthy shall you wed Lillian," he said, solemnly; "and you are not worthy yet."

CHAPTER XIX.

CAPTAIN GEORGE IN DANGER.

NEAR the mansion into which Lord Charles Lutterell had inveigled Leila, and into which the Blue Dwarf had so unceremoniously broken, was a half-ruined farm which had, for many years, been in disuse.

It stood at the end of a long avenue of dark trees, and was almost entirely shaded from the observation of those who passed on the high road. Its windows, nearly covered with ivy, were some of them bricked up, and some filled up by wooden planks. The front entrance was also barred against all comers, and the only apparent means of ingress and egress was a small door at the rear.

The night after the visit of the Blue Dwarf, William Lennox, and Captain George to the mansion of the Marquis of Glencorn, a light glimmered in one of the back rooms of the ruined farm. A man stood at the door peeping out into the darkness, and evidently impatiently awaiting the arrival of companions.

Presently he was joined by another, then another, and, after a while, a third figure, wrapped well up in a horseman's cloak, entered, and the door was then closed and secured.

"Well, gentlemen," said the last arrival, who was none other than Lord Charles Lutterell, "I am pretty punctual; and now, as we are business men, let us at once to business."

"Just so," said a burly ruffian, who was manipulating a piece of hard tobacco, and cutting it up ready for use.

"Just so," responded the others, and they accordingly sat in anxious expectation of instructions.

"You are aware," said his lordship, "that my brother is really the heir to the property."

"Just so, and that you killed Ada Wilmot."

"Silence, ruffian!" cried Lord Charles; "speak not, but listen. My brother, as I have said, is the real heir: he came back from Algiers with vast wealth, and will be able shortly to prove his innocence, and seize upon the property in right of my father. You understand me?"

"Just so."

"Well, this must not be allowed to happen.

He must, in some mode or another, be put out of the way."

"We are your men, then," said one ruffian. "I and my friend here, Sloping Harry, will do the business for you in a nicker."

"Well said, Flash Charley," replied Harry. "I guarantee, for my part, that Captain George, as the fancy coves call him, won't be able to eat his dinner very spry before a week is over his head."

Lord Charles Lutterell was thinking, and did not appear to notice the fiendish praises of these ruffians—the one of the other. He sat for some minutes wrapped in thought, and then, getting up, paced rapidly up and down the room.

"My brother," he at length said, in a hoarse, thick voice, "is expected in this neighbourhood to-morrow night. There is some treachery in my household, and I think that he is going to visit Liketon Hall in order to get information against me." He paused.

"This must be prevented," he then continued, clenching his hands together, and appearing to address his words rather to himself than to others ; "this must be prevented, no matter at what risk. You are then prepared to undertake it ?"

"We are."

"Then I leave the method to you. Good night. I shall meet you here at twelve to-morrow night ; let me hear that I am heir to Liketon."

So saying, he strode from the house.

The Blue Dwarf had said that he would leave him to the justice of his country : he was determined that the gallows should have good reason to claim him for its own.

CHAPTER XX.

BLOODHOUNDS.

THE words which had been heard let fall by the lips of Martha at Liketon Hall had roused a new idea in the mind of the Blue Dwarf. Though resolved to leave Lord Charles Lutterell to be tried and condemned by a jury of his countrymen, he thought it as well to obtain evidence of his innocence, in order to be on the safe side of his enemies.

Knowing the multifarious schemes in which Sapathwa was engaged, Captain George resolved to take upon himself the risk of a night visit to Liketon Hall, which he trusted so soon to enter as a master, and accordingly proposed and obtained from the Blue Dwarf permission to absent himself for the purpose.

In the conduct of their expeditions Sapathwa was regarded as a chief, and his permission was asked upon all occasions of this nature.

Accordingly on the night named by Lord Charles Luttrell — his loving and amiable brother—he was to be seen dismounting from his horse, fastening it by the bridle to the hedgerow, and breaking through the brushwood into his estate. It was earlier than was expected by the conspirators, and not a soul was stirring in the grounds. All was as still as death ; save where now and then a rabbit would burst from its covert and tear away, frightened, into the denser underwood. He found no impediment to his progress, and soon found himself standing by the back door, where a large mastiff lay crouched, awaiting his approach. The dog uttered a short, sharp bark, and leaped towards him.

"Down, Carlo, down !" he cried, at the same time, however, standing on the defensive. The dog had not seen him for twelve long years, but he recognised his master even after the lapse of years, and was soon licking his hand and otherwise manifesting his affection.

Captain George knocked cautiously and steadily at the door. For some time no one answered, but at length the gate was quietly opened, and old Martha appeared.

"Soul o' me," cried she, "what is the matter now ? Who is it ?"

"Can I speak to you for a moment, Martha ?" he said, in a low voice.

"Who is that who calls me Martha ?" said the old woman. "Ah, me ! its long—a long, long time, since I heard that name pronounced kindly before. Well, well, sir, who art thou—and what dost thee want ?"

"Look at me," cried Captain George.

The old woman raised the lantern, and gazed steadily in his face.

"Body o' me," she cried, putting it down, and rushing forward ; "excuse me, sir, if I am mistaken ; but you are Leopold, are you not—our Leopold ?"

"Yes, Martha, I am Leopold ; but let me come inside, for my enemies, I fear, will be abroad."

He entered the house, old Martha leading the way, with tears of joy in her aged eyes.

What passed inside we will not now inquire. Suffice it to say that they were undisturbed.

Just outside the back door through which Captain George entered the house of his fathers in the surreptitious manner we have just described, was a slight open space ; but round it were dense trees, with scarcely a break between them, excepting the little path which led from the house to the avenue taking you to the ruined farm-house. Amid the trees composing this miniature forest were concealed four men. As we have before remarked, no one was near the Hall at the time of Captain George's first entrance into the grounds ; but during the prolonged colloquy between him and the old servant, they had crept up and surrounded his place of concealment. They knew well that he would not run the risk of departing by the front door for fear of meeting Lord Charles Lutterell. They, therefore, patiently sat down among the brushwood to await, like bloodhounds, their human prey.

Charles Lutterell, however, did not dare to remain at home while it was receiving a visit from his brother whom he had planned to assassinate. He rode away early in the evening ; and went dashing off along the highroad apparently without any specific purpose.

The night was a dark, windy, rainy one.

The mental murderer heeded nothing, however ; but dashed on—over hill, over dale—each moaning of the blast seeming like the last agonised cry of the brother who was being assassinated at his bidding.

CHAPTER XXI.

THE GAMBLING HOUSE IN THE RUE JACOB.

Captain Frederick Winterton was in Paris. The detective officer, having been quietly consigned to his watery grave, no more troubled him. The cool assassination of this fellow-creature was nothing to him but one plunge more in that pool of blood in which he had already dyed his hands.

He took up his residence in the Rue Letallier—a fine open street—started in the name of Edgar Fortescue, Esq., of New York; and having a capital of five hundred pounds to start with, he resolved to make the best of it by a little clever play, and now and then a *fortunate* throw of the dice.

On the morning of the day after his arrival he he ascertained the whereabouts of a first-rate gambling house in the Rue Jacob; and the evening saw him sauntering into the room and gazing round him with an air of insufferable self-sufficiency. He very discreetly did not appear to be eager to engage in play, but after awhile joined others, played carelessly, and purposely lost. He then appeared disgusted and left. The next evening saw him again there—and night after night he played, not now with variable success, but with.

One evening, some weeks after the first visit of Captain Frederick Winterton to the gambling-house he was surprised greatly to hear himself addressed by name.

The individual who addressed him was a quiet-looking Englishman, not unlike the gentleman in black who had met with such foul play on board the Calais packet. He had resolved to ignore entirely for the future his name and relations, and therefore did not appear to notice the half-whispered question which was put to him by the stranger in English.

"Good evening, Captain Winterton," said the quiet individual, in an undertone, "here you are, on foreign ground again. Too hot in England, I reckon?"

Captain Frederick Winterton made no reply. He appeared not to take any notice of the inquiry, and indeed a practised eye might have been deceived by his indifference. The stranger, however, was not to be put off. Like the quiet gentleman in black, he seemed quite to understand the game which the other was playing. He grasped the captain's arm, and again spoke.

"What do you want, sir?" said Winterton, eyeing him haughtily.

"Don't you know me?" inquired the other.

"Not in the slightest," replied the captain; "nor do I understand what you require."

"Probably not, but I assure you I am a friend; and if you will retire with me into a more retired portion of the room, I will convince you."

Captain Winterton eyed him a moment suspiciously.

"You don't even know my name—you assign no reason for this interruption, and yet you wish me to trust you."

"It is you, my dear sir," said the other, "who don't appear to know your own name. But of that anon. I do not wish you to trust me, but simply to go on one side while I prove I am a friend."

"Come on, then; but only for a moment."

They retired for a minute to where a lamp burned in a solitary corner.

The unknown did not speak, but, holding his hand up to the light, displayed, glistening on his finger—the onyx ring. Captain Winterton did not speak for a moment. At length he said—

"Well—well, it's all right, we understand each other; but what's in the wind now?"

"Slimy Jones is captured—the Honourable John Winterton also—the person calling herself Lady Edgar Blakesley—and the Duchess de Castella. They now want you and the false Sir Edgar Blakesley to complete the number of their prisoners."

"And what do you propose for me to do, and why have you thus introduced yourself to me?"

"Why, I must live somehow. I was sent over here to waylay William Lennox, after he had received the benevolent notes of the Duchess. She is caged—I have now no employer—I must have work from some one. If your side doesn't want me, why I must work for the other party. You understand me?"

"I understand that you threaten me," said Winterton, coldly; "but I never fear the threats of a braggart. I do not fear you!"

"In that case, adieu—Au revoir."

And he moved as if to go.

"Stay," said the Captain, "I will see you elsewhere. What is your name?"

"My name, sir, is Richard Fenton. There is my card—good evening."

And the man bowed and left the room.

"Wherever I go these cursed fellows are after me," cried Captain Frederick. "Hey—presto to-morrow for the German baths."

CHAPTER XXII.

THE SKELETON.—THE CUP AND THE LIP.

IT will be remembered that *La Squelette* (the Skeleton) was left just as he was upon the point of murdering his son Edouard.

He entered the room with drawn knife; and, placing the light in a corner which shaded it from view, crept on his hands and knees towards the bed.

Once or twice he paused, as the sleeper appeared to move uneasily in his slumber; but after a few moments he reached the bedside, and raised his weapon to strike.

But it was not to be.

"There's many a slip between the cup and the lip," says the old proverb.

So there is between the throat and the knife.

With a bound which sent the skeleton rolling on the floor, on his back, Edouard sprang up, and in a moment pinned his father to the floor.

"You are my father," he said, in a hoarse, thick tremulous voice, "or I could throttle you. However, I leave this house to-night, for ever. What is more, I will take the children with me: and the plans which you have concocted against the life and freedom of the young Englishman shall be frustrated."

Squelette was a powerful man, but his son had his knee firmly planted upon his chest, so as entirely to prevent his moving; and in a few moments he was bound and helpless. Edouard then roused up the children, made them dress, and descended the stairs.

His mother was standing, pale and trembling, on the landing place, expecting less to see her son than to behold the ghastly form of her husband, with the knife still red with the blood of his offspring.

"Where is your father?" cried *La Trappe.*

"Up stairs, on his back."

"You have killed him, wretch!"

"Not so; he is bound. I am going to leave this house and take the children. I know you wanted to save me, but I can't stop; and as I don't want you to untie his hands until I am gone, please go down first."

The old woman saw it was no use resisting, so muttering some incoherent entreaties, she stumbled down the old stairs, and opened the door leading to the court behind the Thieves' Inn.

Edouard gave the hideous dame a parting

salute. The children slunk up to their brother, and whispered an adieu to the mother, who only inspired them with hatred and dread: and thus this strange family meeting separated.

To find a home that night was impossible.

So the arches of the Place au Temple were tenanted that night by the houseless wanderers.

CHAPTER XXIII.

THIEVES' INN AGAIN.

RICHARD FENTON, the mysterious agent of the onyx ring, knew well that Captain Winterton would not perform his engagement. He was aware of his desperate position; and was inclined to believe that he desired entirely to shake off all his old associations.

His employer, the Duchess of Castella, having fallen into the hands of her enemies, Fenton, like all others of his class, did not care any longer to identify himself with the fallen fortunes of the conspirators.

He had hoped to threaten and bully Captain Winterton out of money; but, upon making his acquaintance, he at once saw that all trial there was hopeless. Having no money wherewith to go over to England, he immediately hit upon a diabolical plan whereby to secure to himself a passage to his native country.

Accordingly, upon leaving the gambling house, he proceeded to his old rendezvous—the *tapis franc*. *Le Squelette* and *La Trapue* were both in the room, and to them he immediately addressed himself.

"Well, Skeleton," said he, "and you, Mistress Dumpy, how are you?"

"Not much the richer for the little job you promised us, but which never came off."

"Not my fault; the young man smelt a rat, and wouldn't come. But I have another job for you."

"Ah! ah! about as good as the last one, I suppose," laughed the Skeleton; "all promise and no pay."

"Now, now, then, don't be absurd and unreasonable," said Fenton, "but listen to me."

"All right."

"One of the enemies of the young man whom we were to cage is over in Paris.

"He is wanted in London; and a large reward will be given for his apprehension.

"I have seen him to-night, and he will try to leave Paris to-morrow night. We must prevent him—you understand."

"Not by any means."

"Why not?"

"Because," returned *La Squelette*, with a sneer, "after we have caught him for you, and you have him safe, who is to guarantee us our reward?"

"Confound your guarantees," said Richard Fenton, angrily, "if the time were longer I would dispense with your services altogether. But as I must use you this time—which shall be the last—know that in the carriage which takes Captain Frederick Winterton from Paris,

will be a thousand pounds in gold. This we will divide."

"That is a bargain," said the Skeleton, with glistening eyes.

"It is. Now, remember, to-morrow night I shall want you at ten o'clock, but I will let you know before then where you are to meet me."

So saying, he abruptly left the room.

That night Richard Fenton had a private interview with the Prefect of Police. What the conversation which passed was it is not now necessary to state. Suffice it to say, that the police at the barriers received before morning secret instructions from the Prefecture.

CHAPTER XXIV.

OFF THE SCENT.

CAPTAIN GEORGE's consultation with old Martha was one of rather long duration; and it was not until the small hours of the morning that he rose from his chair beside the glowing fire, and wrapped himself up, to brave once more the keen blast and the drenching drizzly rain.

"Of course I need not tell you," said Captain George, "that no one must know of my visit here. It would, of course, spoil all my plans."

"Oh! Mister Leopold," cried the old servant, "it would be as much as my life is worth to let them hear that I had been talking to you of old times."

"And yet, Martha," said Leopold, scarcely noticing her remark, "and yet, Martha, it strikes me that my brother knows of my intention to visit Liketon to-night. Just now, as I came here, I passed queer characters on the road."

"Oh! mercy on us," cried the old woman, in great alarm, "pray don't go away till morning, sir."

"It isn't safe for me to stop here. Now, Martha, can I trust you to do something for me? Go up to the first landing; and, out of the window there, turn the light of your lantern upon the bushes. I will watch from behind, for they must not see me."

"Right—right, Master Leopold."

And the old woman ascended the stairs, and did as she had been bidden.

Amid the brushwood could plainly be distinguished the face of a man lying in wait for some one.

"I thought so," muttered Captain George. "Martha, is there no side-door through which I could make my escape? and thus at any rate get a start of my pursuers?"

Martha thought a moment.

"Yes, my lord," said Martha, after a minute's inward inquiry; "if you like to go through the cellar, and along the undergound passage, you can get out into the highroad. It's a dark, lonesome place, though, I can tell ye."

Captain George laughed merrily.

"Ah, well, Martha," said he, "none the worse

for that. I have been too much accustomed to roughing it to mind a little trouble."

In the times of the Revolution the Lutterells had taken the side of the wretched king; and it was found necessary, in order to ensure the safety of the family, to provide secret means of escape in case of an overwhelming attack.

It was at this time that a subterranean corridor had been cut leading from the vaults under Liketon Hall to the main road.

The entrance was covered with dense brushwood, and was perfectly undistinguishable from the highway.

It was to this place that Martha conducted Captain George. The old woman would not herself venture up the passage, but gave him the lantern, in order to enable him to find his way along the dark and rugged path.

He soon emerged upon the road, just where he had left his horse. This he mounted; and, directing the light of his lantern in among the brushwood, he could easily distinguish the heads of the human bloodhounds who were waiting for him. Drawing a pistol from his belt, he fired it straight at one of the ruffians, at the same time calling out at the top of his voice—

"Hillo! my hearties. Better luck next time. Take that from Captain George."

The startled murderers emerged from their covert only in time to see their prey galloping away furiously on the road to London.

———

CHAPTER XXV.

ERNEST AND LEILA.

DURING all the turmoils and embroilments into which our confederacy of friends were thrown by the machinations of their enemies, there was one person who had unswervingly cherished an undivided affection in his heart.

This was Lord Ernest Wyndham.

To Leila he had not actually declared his love; but his manner, his eagerness in assisting to rescue her from the hands of villains, and his whole language and demeanour, plainly evidenced his affection.

The Blue Dwarf had had, as we have said, a desire to see William Lennox united to Leila.

The one he had loved with as great an affection as the other; but of course from the moment he perceived his evident affection for Lillian, that idea had been entirely discarded.

Lord Ernest Wyndham had found considerable favour in the eyes of Sapathwa.

Young, handsome, possessing an excellent disposition, he was in every way worthy of his ward; and even before he knew the exact condition of his feelings, he half desired their union.

One evening Leila was sitting musingly at her window in the house of the Blue Dwarf.

Evening was coming on—a bright evening; and as she gazed out upon the deepening twilight and the golden sunset, a feeling of intense relief after her recent troubles came over her.

Suddenly she was roused by feeling her hand being taken up lightly, and warmly and lovingly pressed.

She turned hastily round, and saw standing by her side Lord Ernest Wyndham.

A mutual glance of trust and happiness passed.

Truly—
        "There's nothing half so sweet in life
        As love's young dream!"

"It is a lovely evening," said Lord Ernest, by way of initiating a conversation.

The weather always catches it: poor unfortunate weather, it is ever being lugged in to commence an awkward conversation.

When a man is going to "pop the question," he always begins by remarking, sagely, "Beautiful day, is it not, Miss So-and-so."

When, again, he meets a man in the street to whom he owes money, and cannot possibly avoid him, he exclaims, inevitably, "Ah! Mr. So-and-so, how are you to-day? Fine day, now, isn't it. Anything new? — fine weather — tremendous hurry—can't stop," and so on.

So Lord Ernest Wyndham said "It is a lovely evening."

"Yes, Ernest. Let us go in the grounds. I feel so happy that I don't want to be caged up to-night."

Lord Ernest seemed abstracted; he did not answer, but fidgetted about until Leila was ready, and then as silently accompanied her.

A few turns in the garden, and then they sat down by the margin of the tiny lakelet where hundreds of golden fish darted hither and thither in their frolicsome play.

"Leila," said Lord Ernest, at length, in a low, tremulous voice, "do you love me?"

Leila turned her large childlike eyes up towards his face, as she answered,

"You know I do."

"But I mean do you love me as I love you? Will you be my wife?"

A look was sufficient, and in a moment she lay blushing, joyous in his arms.

A brief declaration and a brief answer! But how much more satisfactory than all the cold reasoning and follies of wordly conventionality.

"So ho!" cried the Blue Dwarf, when presently he entered the garden, "so ho! young people; this is all very fine. I suppose you never dreamed of asking me."

"I know you only wished me to be happy," murmured the beaming girl, timidly.

"God bless you," said Sapathwa, while tears stood in his eyes, "God bless you. Take her, Lord Ernest, and make her happy."

"When—"

"When our enemies are all punished, and the injured righted."

———

CHAPTER XXVI.

SLIMY JONES IN NEWGATE.

SLIMY JONES, for whom nobody could feel any sympathy, had been delivered over to the authorities, and by them committed to prison.

He was an arrant coward when in a state of helpless danger; and now that the cold walls of a prison environed him so surely—now, that no possible means of escape presented itself, he sank into a condition the most pitiable and the most abject.

No one visited him in his confinement.

He had never made a friend, so he was left alone in his misery.

* * * * * *

One night he was sitting in his cell meditating upon his chances of escape.

The men who were set to watch over him had fallen off into a doze. The lamp burned low, and he sat there with his manacled hands, gazing wistfully at the starlit sky, a glimpse of which could just be caught through the iron-barred window of his cell.

Presently, in the middle of his reflections, the clanking of a chain was heard, the withdrawal of a bolt, and the door of his cell opened.

A tall man entered.

His face was hidden in his cloak, so that not a feature could be distinguished by the prisoner.

The new-comer gazed around him cautiously, then beckoned to some one without.

A young girl entered.

A glance of recognition passed between her and Slimy Jones.

Not a word, however, was said.

The keepers still slept on, and the two proceeded gently, cautiously to remove the fetters from his limbs. In a few moments he was free; and taking up the lamp followed his liberators along the stone corridors, where, strange to say, no obstacle met them in their progress.

The strangers seemed to possess supernatural power, for the gates opened, the porters bowed to them as they passed, and ere more than a few moments had elapsed Slimy Jones was once more breathing the air of freedom.

"I have saved you," said the girl, sweetly and mournfully, as she gazed on his face. "Don't forget me."

"I will not forget you for it," replied Slimy Jones.

"Come, we must be going quickly," said the man in the cloak.

And the three went on rapidly all night. They travelled part of the next day also, until the afternoon, they were proceeding along a rather unfrequented spot, the girl was walking before.

"We must leave England," said the cloaked figure.

"Yes."

"That girl is in our way."

"Yes."

"Now," said the other, "remember that girl saved our lives—saved my life—saved your life. But she is in our way, so I will kill her."

"Very well."

The cloaked figure advanced towards the girl, who, turning suddenly round, and seeing the expression on his face, shrieked, and drew back, at the same time casting a look of appeal at Slimy Jones.

It was of no avail, however; the unknown struck her on the head with a pistol; the blood poured over her face, her neck, and her white bosom, and she fell down upon the green sward and was pushed by the ruffian into a dank and noisome pool.

Then the figure turned round and disclosed to Slimy Jones the face of Captain Frederick Winterton.

Then with a mighty cry of terror Slimy Jones sprang up—awoke—and found that it was a dream!

The cold perspiration stood in great drops upon his brow, his heart trembled and fluttered like that of a frightened child. In those few moments he repented truly—sincerely, of the part he had taken in the murder of Mary Davis.

The next day, in consequence of repairs in the prison, he was removed to the old prison of Rositton Fields, since levelled with the dust.

CHAPTER XXVII.

ON THE HONOUR OF A GENTLEMAN.

THREE figures were standing outside the Cabriolet-with-Five-Wheels.

Strange name, that!

French people delight in strange names; they are a nation possessed of strange ideas, else the descendant of Hermance and the Dutch admiral would not be termed "Emperor of the French," when he is only "Emperor of the French army."

The "Cabriolet-with-Five-Wheels," was a little ale-house situated on the edge of the high-road leading from the Barrier de Montmartre. The innkeeper was a surly, ill-looking fellow; his wife, blear-eyed and wide-mouthed, seemed more like the grinning mask of a pantomimist than a human being. Pierre Dobos was not particular as to his company; though he had a decided preference to the low and the thievish. To respectable people he was gruff and uncouth: to the cut-throat and the cut-purse he was affable as affability itself.

Richard Fenton stood outside the "Cabriolet-with-Five-Wheels," with *Squelette* and a *confrere* of the name of *Gorgeux*, nicknamed *le Bete* (the beast). The Skeleton seemed in no good humour, apparently dissatisfied with himself and others.

"Never knew such an enterprise as this succeed," muttered he, as he filled his pipe, and folded his lanky arms over his breast.

"What do you mean?" inquired Fenton, who knew it was best to humour the man.

"I don't like the co-operation of the police."

"Why not?"

"Because I and the police are, as you know, deadly enemies."

"So much the better. You now do them a service, and they will not forget you."

"Ah! bas! the *mouchards*—they soon forget kindnesses—they never forget injuries. But is the money all right?"

"Damnation! You are a nuisance in everything. If you don't like the job, go, and leave it to me."

"But you promise half?"

"Half—on the honour of a gentleman. But hist!—they come."

Along the road could now be heard the rumbling of carriage wheels.

Two lights could be seen swaying to and fro in the uncertain distance, and presently a post-chaise, drawn by two grey horses, came dashing up, the animals panting and steaming with their tremendous pace. A rope flung dexterously by *Squelette* brought one of the horses to the ground, and the conspirators rushing to the door, opened it, and confronted Captain Frederick Winterton.

"What want you, fellows?" said he. "This a highway robbery, and—"

"Excuse me," replied Richard Fenton, "we are no highwaymen, but emissaries of the law. I arrest you in the name of that law as a forger and a murderer."

"Just so," said a voice behind, which emanated from the little Englishman who had formed one of the coterie at the *tapis franc*.

"Well, gentlemen, when you have done with this little joke, you will allow me to proceed, if you please."

'Joke, sir, or no joke, you go no further this night," said Richard Fenton. "You unfortunately did not keep your promise with me to-night, otherwise you would not now be in this predicament. I knew you would not come, so I awaited you here."

During this conversation the party had been reinforced by the arrival of two men, who, upon hearing the result of the conference, pushed by, and, seizing the captain, said,

"These gentlemen are quite right. We are police-agents; we will enter with you, and return to Paris."

The *mouchards* accordingly entered the post-chaise with Fenton and the Skeleton, while the other Englishman rode outside. The postilion remounted, and the carriage was soon once more speeding along the road. Arrived in Paris, they stopped at the door of the Conciergerie, and the police agents went in with their prisoner. Fenton, seizing the portmanteau, followed, as did also the Skeleton, who received £200 as his share of the spoils. This, Fenton declared "on the honour of a gentleman," was the exact half of £1,000 pounds found on the person of the captain.

*   *   *   *   *

Four days after these events Captain Winterton was in the house of the Blue Dwarf with the Honourable John.

CHAPTER XXVIII.

A LEAP FOR LIFE.

THE prison to which Slimy Jones was committed after his removal from Newgate was an old dilapidated affair. It was a disgrace even to that period, and would not be tolerated in the present. The walls were dingier and darker than ever seemed proper for a prison. The cells were dank, noisome, and pestilential—the walls reeking with damp. The very warders seemed dingy, sleepy, and ancient. It was, in fact, more like the Chateau D'If than any English repository for English criminals.

Slimy Jones was, of course, as yet unconvicted.

He was not, therefore, placed in one of the *solitary* cells where the prisoners had the *company* of numberless vermin of all kinds. He was located in an upper room, looking out upon the prison yard. Underneath his window was the wall covered with sharp spikes; and beneath the wall was a broad deep ditch, nearly always filled with green and noisome water. In this room he was by himself, and was allowed the comfort of a bed and a book or two, until nine at night.

It was the night before his first examination, when, on fumbling about among some rubbish in a dark corner of his room, he discovered an old rope, which had apparently been knotted by some former prisoner for making an escape. The idea had no sooner flashed across his mind, than he determined to act upon it. His window was not barred—no one contemplated the possibility of escape from such a height. The night was calm—the prison was as still as death. Slimy Jones opened the casement, and looked out.

Not a mouse stirred.

From the window could be seen the lights of the city, flashing in myriad sparkles round.

Here lay a dark field—there a stream in the distance—while close at hand rolled the ever-flowing current of the silvery Thames—flashing and reflecting a thousand spangles under the bright moonlight.

The stars were out in countless numbers.

London seemed reigned over by calm beauty.

Life seemed less to rush impetuously forward, than to ripple on gently and quietly towards its end.

A strange presentiment, a terrible foreshadowing of evil, seemed to creep over the wretched prisoner; and as he leaned out of the casement and gazed out upon the scene, he almost appeared to forget his plan of escape.

"D—d fine night!" he muttered, "d—d deal too fine! I'm afraid I shall be seen, and then its old Joe with me at once. I shall be stuck like a pig in a blanket. If that ere moon would be obliging enough to pop in its head for a moment now I should be all right. I feel tarnation queer to-night—can't make myself out. But it's no use giving up—

" 'Here's to the lass with the bonnie blue eyes—
" 'Here's to the lad that a bumper doth prize.'"

And so singing, Slimy Jones began tying his rope to the bedpost, and securing it well, preparatory to his descent.

This done, he looked down; it was a long way, but it seemed to reach the bottom.

"It's all right, I think," he muttered, as he passed out, "at any rate here goes!"

And taking hold of the rope, he swung himself out of the window, and began his perilous descent.

For a few moments all went right, but no longer.

Presently he heard a sharp twanging noise as he went down. Again, and again, repeated;

and in a minute the conviction flashed across him that the rope was giving way.

Slimy Jones had been used to perilous situations.

With the rope round his neck, and a house burning near him, and scorching his very flesh, he had stood for hours in Spain.

He had witnessed a murder unmoved; and thought, undismayed, upon the chances of capture.

He had been in desperate frays—had passed through terrible dangers.

But never in his life had his blood curdled thus!

Never had his heart seemed thus to stand still with fear!

Never had terror so completely paralysed his faculties!

He was about twenty feet from his cell, and beneath him there were still eighty feet to descend.

To reascend was impossible; his only chance was to run down at full speed, and jump directly the rope gave way into the water of the ditch under the prison wall.

He had scarcely time even to think of the best course to adopt when the rope snapped asunder with a loud report.

He jumped instantly.

It was, indeed, a leap for life.

Beneath him were the spikes of the prison wall; and beneath that the deep and noisome ditch.

He leaped with closed eyes.

CHAPTER XXIX.

CAIN.

LORD CHARLES LUTTERELL was like one completely bereft of sense.

He had spent the first few hours of the night dashing—as we have described—along the high road, over hill, over dale, regardless of all obstacles, and urging his steed on at a frantic speed.

The country people round, who could not, in the darkness of the night, recognise his features, imagined him to be either some escaped lunatic, or felon running from justice; and stared wildly after the extraordinary figure as it swept by on its black horse, its cloak flying in the wind, and its whip continually urging its steed to greater exertions.

When, however, the small hours of the morning had arrived, Lord Charles retraced his steps.

He rode on in less frantic haste.

His horse now had breathing time, and trotted calmly through the now sleeping villages.

His lordship felt considerably relieved.

He began to experience a certain buoyancy of spirit.

Had he not murdered his brother?

Was he not now undisputed heir to the property?

He never dreamed of failure.

He never thought, moreover, that when Cain killed Abel, the brand of murder was on his brow.

It was one o'clock when he arrived at Liketon Hall; and (after putting up his horse himself, in order not to allow the domestics to know the hour of arrival) made his way to the ruined farm-house; there he found awaiting him at the door three men.

"Well," he said, in a deep, husky tone, "is it done?"

"No, he has escaped," replied Sloping Harry.

"Escaped?" cried Lord Charles, tottering to a chair, "escaped! There has been some foul play."

"Aye, there has been foul play, you're right. Look at Flash Charley; he's dying right out, and there's no mistake about it."

The man's words were true enough. Captain George's bullet had taken effect in his chest, and the life-blood was oozing fast.

"D—n your wounds," said Lord Charles, taking off his hat and displaying a broad band of ribbon across his forehead as if to hide some scar, "d—n your wounds! You have acted the fool in some way, or this would never have happened."

"No, my lord; we obeyed your orders to the letter."

"Obeyed my orders!—pooh, pooh! However I shan't give you a penny piece till it is done."

"Very well, my Lord; I don't want any," said Sloping Harry.

"What do you mean by that?"

"Why, if you don't pay for killing, there are plenty who will be glad enough to hear all about the intended killing."

"Villain! would you betray me?"

"Yes, if betray is your word; if you don't keep your promise, I *will* betray you."

"There is no need," said a voice behind him, "there is no need for any betrayal on your part of your base employers. You have all betrayed *yourselves* into the hands of justice."

Lord Charles Lutterell turned sharply round, and then fell back in terror.

Before him stood Captain George, and with him six men.

"Come my worthy brother," said Captain George, "it is now my turn to command. It will not be in Fleet-street that *I* shall bawl out to the crowd, 'Behold, there is a murderer! Seize him!' I shall declare it and *prove it* before the world."

CHAPTER XXX.

THE BARMAID OF "THE EMERALD."

Towards evening on a bright spring day, two figures might have been seen wandering listlessly in the direction of the "Emerald Tavern," Shoreditch.

The one was a squalid, tattered-looking object:

An elderly man, with rather scanty iron-grey locks, a greasy, ill-fitting ragged coat, a battered hut, and boots which let the water in at every step.

The other was a young man of some twenty-one years of age, whose worn aspect and cynical expression of countenance betokened a *mind* which ill-assorted with the appearance which the *body* ought to wear.

How often are the mental faculties at deadly war with the physical!

"And so, sir, we are met again," said the younger of the two passengers.

"Yes."

"And in strange circumstances."

"Yes—strange—passing strange."

"Have you any news to tell me?"

"I have."

"You are peculiarly taciturn and undemonstrative to-night."

"I am. The street is not the place to broach family secrets, or to give way to one's feelings."

"Right."

"No doubt about it. Let's adjourn to some neighbouring tavern."

"More in your line, certainly," muttered the young man; and he silently followed his mud-bespattered and time-bedraggled guide in the back parlour of the "Emerald Tavern."

It was a low place.

Everyone, however, was at his ease.

It was one of those places where extempore sing-songs are organised.

One man feels jovial, and proposes a song; whereupon a dozen half-tipsy convivials organise themselves into a committee, and immediately a vocal concert is celebrated, a concert in which "Bluff King Hal," and "Jolly Millers," &c. &c., are constantly recurring.

The room was divided into various compartments.

Men and women were enjoying themselves there indiscriminately; the whole being waited upon by a young lady, whose dress began too late, and ended too soon; and whose large massive limbs and heavily-moulded bust showed plainly that the hard work at the "Emerald Tavern" did not in the slightest degree affect the even tenour of her health.

A little straw hat, adorned with a cockade of blue ribbons, was stuck jauntily on one side of her head.

A bodice of black velvet, very low in front, was compressed tightly round her figure, a single flower peeped from between her breasts, a petticoat of red stuff reached to the ancle, and blue stockings and red boots completed her attire.

Such was the household fairy which waited upon the customers of the "Emerald Tavern."

The young man ordered spirits and water; and the ill-assorted pair sat down to partake of it.

"Yes," said the elder one, mixing his glass, and sipping it with evident relish; "yes, this is certainly a singular meeting."

"Very."

"And pray, may I inquire what motive brings you over to England again at this moment?"

"You may certainly inquire ——"

"Just so, I understand; I may inquire, but you are not bound to tell me."

"Exactly."

The two men sipped their grog for a moment in silence.

Then the younger spoke.

"Come, now, it's time to leave all this fencing and beating about the bush. Tyrrel, let's to the point."

"You are right," replied the other; "let's to business."

"First and foremost, then," continued the young man, "have you anything to disclose to me that's worth hearing?"

"Truly so," said the individual addressed; "the information I am about to give you would be interesting to anyone, but more especially to *Sir Edgar Blakesley, Baronet.*"

The last words were said in a thick dry undertone, and accompanied by a harsh grating laugh.

"A truce to jesting, now," cried the impostor; "let's hear your news."

"Well, then, first and foremost, as you remarked just now, things are coming to a crisis."

"Clever you are, certainly, to be able to inform one of that fact after the brokers have begun dishonouring my bills."

"Well—that monstrous creature—that hideous deformity—Goldie Gordon, or Sapathwa, the Blue Dwarf, as he calls himself, has been caging all the birds, and formed a kind of Happy Family at his house."

"What mean you?"

"Exactly what I say."

"But whom has he caged—are they our friends or our enemies?"

"He has, in the first instance," said James Tyrrel Blakesley, "caught Slimy Jones—he has caught the Honourable John Winterton, Captain Frederick Winterton, the Countess de Castella, and Pauline, otherwise called Lady Edgar Blakesley."

"Pauline! Hell and furies! What mean you?"

"As I remarked upon a previous occasion, I mean exactly what I say."

"Pauline in their clutches," said Sir Edgar; "that is indeed a misfortune. They will torture her—terrify her into saying anything, and doing anything. You came too late with your news; if you had told me all this a week ago I might have prevented a vast amount of annoyances and trouble."

"Just so; but where was I to find you? Can you tell me that?"

"No; no, of course; but is there anything else?"

"Not much; except it be that they are about to seize upon the Blakesley rents and estates, and prove you an impostor before the world; probably your wife being an accomplice—"

"Call not that woman my wife," cried the false Sir Edgar. "She is not my wife."

"Not your wife! It is now my turn to demand explanations."

"We were never married. I promised this, that, and the other; but we never married, and I have married another."

"Young?"

"No."

"Beautiful?"

"No."

"Elegant?"

"No."

"Noble?"

"The daughter of a tallow-chandler."

"Highly educated?"

"No."

"Then what, in the name of conscience and common sense, did you marry her for?"

"You foolish man; in all your requirements you have neglected the most important of all things."

"What is that?"

"She is wealthy."

"Phew—phe—w! What an old duffer I have been,—to be su—re. Money! and has she got much?"

"Enough to protect us against squalls."

"Which are likely soon enough to happen," said James.

"You are right," said a voice near them; but whence and from whom it emanated they could not tell.

They soon after separated, and returned each to his home, after engaging to meet the following night at a pot house in Wapping.

Their proceedings had been well watched. The girl who had been complaining of the heat of the room had purposely drawn near them during their conversation; and when apparently engaged in wafting cool air from the window upon her heated face and bosom, she was in reality eagerly devouring every word they uttered.

A full, true, and particular account was given to various parties interested on the following morning.

CHAPTER XXXI.

A MELEE IN WAPPING.

THE following evening saw our two worthies enter together the public-house in Wapping, where they had agreed to meet.

The night was dark—very dark—entirely unlike the preceding one; or they would have noticed that their entrance had been seen, and that their departure was eagerly awaited by several men, ensconced in the shadows of the houses.

The place was the resort of the low seamen and crimps of the neighbourhood.

Its parlour was dingy and old; heavy smoky beams reached across the ceiling—where blackened walls clearly betokened the lengthened absence of the whitewasher's brush.

The company was very mixed—here a sailor just off a voyage, and browned and tanned by the weather, sat talking drunken sentimentalities to an ugly girl in a dirty blue bonnet.

Nothing so ugly as a seaman's lass !

After a long voyage to the antipodes, for Jack Tar thinks every woman beautiful.

Here and there among the company were dispersed persons of a less reputable character—sharpers—river thieves—watermen of boats plying illicit trades.

There was a mixture, as it were, of all imaginable kinds.

Altogether it was a scene of uproar and confusion.

Sir Edgar laughed heartily. It reminded him forcibly of Portsmouth and Bob Griggs.

"You certainly have a fine repertory of choice localities, Mr. James Tyrrel Blakesley."

"What's your objection ?"

"Oh ! no objection in the world. I only was amused with the readiness with which you select those pleasing little rendezvous."

"Well, Sir Edgar Blakesley, Baronet," pursued Mr. James, satirically, "now you have done with jesting—a practice you now always indulge in during the early portion of the evening, perhaps you will be kind enough to proceed to business. In the first place, I am a poor man."

"So am I."

"I want money."

"Very likely."

"And without it, recollect, I do not intend to budge one inch."

"Well, I must say it is a new thing to hear terms dictated by a man who is in such great want of money."

"It is not every day that a man is entrusted with such a mission. Have you any money ?"

"Yes; but very little."

"However, you have some—that's all right. Secondly, where does this William Lennox live ?"

"With the Blue Dwarf."

"Good; but we cannot touch him there."

"No, certainly not; but my proposal is this—

that you entice him out under some plea of friendship; and then," he added, in a husky voice, and looking round him stealthily, "get rid of him—no matter how : the method I leave to you ; but I must get rid of him."

"It is well : and the reward ?"

"Is sure."

"Let us, then, have some money. How much have you ?"

"Five hundred pounds."

"A mere fleabite."

"My wife is very particular, and watches me like a cat."

"What think you of this ?" said the other, leaning over, and placing a paper in Sir Edgar's hand.

It was simply a signature,

"Yours ever,
SAPATHWA."

"Well, what of it ?"

"It is the Blue Dwarf's signature—the one he uses at his bankers."

"I understand you," said the impostor, quietly ; "have you a blank cheque ?"

"Yes, see here—that I have also ! You see I am never at a loss, except in one thing—I cannot imitate signatures ; you are used to it, and can."

"Give me the cheque," said the other, without noticing his companion's offensive satire ; and, after looking at the signature and the blank document for a moment, he called for pen and ink.

This being brought to him, he again earnestly scanned the writing, and then, taking a piece of tracing paper, first took an impression on that. Having thus got his hand in, he appeared to collect all his energies and wrote, in a bold, firm hand, the name of Sapathwa.

Sir Edgar Blakesley, the pretender, was a skilful forger.

The cheque was unrecognisable as an imitation.

Even the Blue Dwarf himself would scarcely have been able to detect the crime.

The people had begun to drop off. It was getting towards the small hours of the morning, when a noise was heard at the entrance, and a party of five noisy fellows entered the house.

They appeared drunk—in that stage of intemperance which makes men desirous of fraternising with everybody.

"Well met, messmates !" cried one. "Young woman, bring in seven tankards ; I got lots of money ; I'll pay for everything."

This speech was addressed to a young female serving in the parlour tap, in whose négligée attire, pretty face, and massive bust, an observer might easily have recognised the waitress at the "Emerald Tavern."

The girl tripped away, and in a few moments the whole party were seated cosily together discussing seven foaming tankards of stout.

"Well, my hearties," said one of the new comers, in a confidential tone ; "blow me, if I can help laughing. Ah ! ah ! ah ! It is funny."

"What's the matter," said a little fellow by his side, wrapped up in a cloak. "You seemed merry all of a sudden."

"Aye, verily I am. This place puts me in mind of another place—(hiccup)—down at Portsmouth—plenty of money—youngster cleared me out. Couldn't help laughing for the life of me. Gave it to me all back arter, though. Rum cove, that! as ever I see. Should know him again among a thousand."

"Should you, though?" said one of the party, "what is he like?"

"Well, he be rather tall; young, dark, curly hair," said the sailor, "if it weren't impossible, I should say that 'ere was the gentleman himself."

So saying, he drew back, and pointed to the *soi-disant* Sir Edgar Blakesley.

"Ah, ah! a very good joke," said the impostor, "here's your health, my man. Good luck, and better remembrance. I must go now, as I have particular business elsewhere."

"D—n business!" said Bob Griggs, for it was he; "d—n business. We don't often have a spree of this 'ere sort. Come, Sally, fill up the tankard again, and we'll go home with the milk in the morning. Here's a parody to keep us alive—

"'There is not in the wide world a thing half so sweet,
"'As the drop of good beer in this ale-house we meet.'"

"Brayvo! brayvo!" resounded on all sides; when suddenly, apparently to the surprise of the others, Bob Griggs started up, and cried—

"Blow me tight if that ain't the veritable young duffer. How are you, old file?"

And so saying, he extended his hand to the impostor.

"I do not know you," said he; "I don't mind a bit of fun, but I'd have you know that I am a gentleman, and don't care about this impertinence going too far."

"That cock won't fight," said Bob Griggs. "Gentlemen, reveal yourselves."

The supposed drunken party removed their disguises. Sir Edgar saw before him Bob Griggs, the Blue Dwarf, William Lennox, Captain George, and Lord Ernest Windham.

"A trap!" you treacherous hound," shouted he, making an effort to reach Mr. James Tyrrel Blakesley; but as he spoke his jaw fell, his hands dropped by his side, his eyes glazed, and he sat helplessly at their mercy.

"Now, then," said the Blue Dwarf, "bring him along, we have no time to waste."

CHAPTER XXXII.

A NEW HAPPY FAMILY.

"WELL, William," said Sapathwa, the morning after the occurrence last mentioned; "well, William, this strange, eventful history is drawing to a close. It now remains to punish the guilty, to save the innocent, and proclaim to the world our titles and our rights."

"How do you propose to punish the offenders?" said Lennox.

"Unmercifully," answered the Blue Dwarf, solemnly.

"But, my dear Sapathwa, if you deliver them over to justice, they will be disgracing the family of my Lillian."

"Never fear, boy, never fear. They shall be delivered over to justice, and *they will die*, but they will not publicly disgrace us."

"Surely," said Lennox, shuddering, "you will not have them murdered?"

The brow of Sapathwa darkened.

"William, I am not to be dictated to. When you can prove that I ever did a dishonest or cruel action, then you may be excused for suggesting such a word as 'murder' to me."

"Forgive me," said William Lennox. "I should have known you better than to have imagined that you could consent to anything that savoured of injustice. How do you propose to punish them without the aid of the law?"

"Ask no questions," said Sapathwa; "even to you I will not disclose my plans. But I will tell you one thing:

"As the time for reinstating you in your proper position has arrived, I am going to disclose to our prisoners who and what I am; at this very moment I am going to visit them, and prepare them for their to-morrow-evening's amusement."

So saying, the Blue Dwarf, with a grim smile, beckoned William Lennox to follow him out of the room.

The scene into which they now entered was a curious one.

Had the Blue Dwarf and William Lennox had less deep interest in the personages among whom they now entered, they would scarcely have been able to refrain from laughing at the absurdity of their situations.

The prisoners had each of them separate apartments in the Blue Dwarf's mansion, but during the day-time they occupied the same room.

Their captivity was anything but an unpleasant one. Both Pauline and the Duchess de Castella were anything but particular in the choice of their *cheres amies*, and as there was one lady to each gentleman, there was no possibility of jealousy.

Captain Frederick Winterton made use of the opportunity now afforded him of making up his quarrel with Pauline, who, under the circumstances, was not at all loth to receive his attentions.

The Countess of Castella, moreover, had an arduous admirer in the person of the Honourable John, who, whatever might be his lack of energy in worldly matters, had always a good vocabulary of soft nothings for the ladies.

Up to the evening previous to the conversation we have just narrated, the four captives had appeared like a new addition to the happy family. They had amused themselves with making love, and planning methods of escape.

Each one was deceiving the other, imagining all the while that the deceit was undiscoverable.

But on the previous night a new element was introduced into their society.

The false Sir Edgar Blakesley and Mr. James Tyrrel Blakesley had been brought from the tavern at Wapping, and domiciled at Sapathwa's house.

The excitement produced by their appearance at

the breakfast table the next morning was something indescribable, and was only equalled by the awkwardness of all parties during the day.

Under existing circumstances Sir Edgar did not care to confess to Pauline the fact of his marriage, and therefore left her as much as possible with Captain Frederick, in order to avoid questions.

When the Blue Dwarf and William Lennox entered the room, there was considerable commotion among the six prisoners who, now that they had all been secured, expected some decisive step to be taken.

"I have come to inform you," said the Blue Dwarf, bowing, "that to-morrow evening I shall explain to you all the circumstances of my own life, and that of Mr. William Lennox, and likewise the reasons and purposes of your detention here."

"Which," said Captain Frederick, assuming a menacing attitude, "is as unjust as it is illegal."

"Might, sir, is right, in this instance," replied the Blue Dwarf, with a complacent smile. "Good morning, ladies and gentlemen; remember, to-morrow evening at six."

CHAPTER XXXIII.

THE SUSPENDED KNIFE.

SLIMY JONES had escaped by a miracle.

By leaping just before the rope broke, he had cleared the summit of the spiked wall and fallen in the very centre of the dark and noisome ditch beneath. Dragging himself out of the slush and the mud, he stood upon the edge of the water and reflected a moment upon the course which it was best for him to pursue.

He was an utter outcast from society.

He had no friends, no money, and no hope of any. He had learned of the capture of the Wintertons and his other employers, and knew that any communication with them was impossible. Nothing remained for him, therefore, but to turn out on the high road, and to trust to a swift horse and black mask, and an air-trigger for his subsistence and his safety.

As he walked away hastily from the prison, ruminating on the pleasant prospects which the future opened up before him, a dark thought entered into his head—the Blue Dwarf was the author of all his misfortunes. What, then, if he were to rid the world of the hideous monster, and avenge himself that very night?

Slimy Jones was not anything of a philosopher, and really imagined himself an injured person.

He forgot that he himself was the most confounded scoundrel on the face of the earth.

No sooner had the thought flashed across his brain, than it was matured into a plan, and having procured at a cutler's a long and sharp knife, he proceeded towards Sapathwa's house.

It was about twelve o'clock on the night preceding the promised revelations of the Blue Dwarf.

All the household had retired to rest, with the exception of one of the female servants, who had slipped down after she supposed everybody was asleep, to keep an appointment with Dick Trotter, the policeman.

If Master Dick Trotter had been attending properly to his duties, he would have perceived a dark figure slinking along the wall of the back of the house, absolutely passing under his very nose. But Dick was too eagerly engaged with Betsy to notice anything but her rounded form and her bright eyes. He had enough to do to kiss her bright, red lips, and press her to his heart. He had no time to bother himself about the public safety.

So Slimy Jones passed by, slunk into the court-yard, and into the hall.

Murder was abroad—so was law; but, as usual, they did not meet.

"I fancied I heard a noise," said the maid-servant, looking furtively around.

Dick Trotter kissed her long and loudly.

"Law! there it is again," cried he, laughing.

"Go on with your nonsense, do," said Betsy, and pretending to be greatly injured; "I'm sure somebody went by. Oh! if there's a robbery I shall lose my place."

"Which isn't half so much consequence as mine," returned Dick, philosophically. "I run more risk than you do, and yet you see I ain't afeard."

"Very well; if you say so, I suppose it's all right," said the girl;" but still I don't feel quite comfortable like."

However, as she resigned herself once more to Dick's fondlings and caresses, she soon forgot everything else but her own enjoyment, and left Slimy Jones the run of the house.

Not a sound was to be heard in the whole mansion. Everybody appeared buried in profound slumber. Betsy had left a hand-lamp burning in the hall, so the murderer was well provided. Aided by the light of this lamp, he could see his way, and never once stumbled as he ascended the staircase and along the wide corridor which led to the Blue Dwarf's room.

He had been in the house before. He had been there very recently, and therefore knew his way well.

Sapathwa always slept with his chamber-door opened.

Slimy Jones, therefore, could see well from without everything going on in the chamber.

As if to aid him in his nefarious design, the black slave, whose duty it was to watch over Sapathwa, was sound asleep. The lamp by the bedside burned dimly.

Slimy Jones set his light down in the passage and entered on tiptoe.

The Blue Dwarf was buried in profound slumber. His face, calm and smiling, indicated that he was floating brightly through one of those visions of fairy happiness which only come to us in our dreams. His breathing was as soft as that of a child; his extraordinary features appeared to be quieted down into those of an ordinary mortal.

Slimy Jones pulled down the clothes slightly. It was necessary to look for the heart of one so extraordinary as Sapathwa.

Then, with a diabolical grin, he steadied himself with one hand on the bed, and raised the other, brandishing the long, keen blade, which he had procured for the murder, and which descended, with unerring aim and with tremendous force, full upon the heart of the Blue Dwarf !

———

CHAPTER XXXIV.

THE SEA-FIGHT.

WE have now to retrace our steps for a while, and explain the circumstances which led to the second marriage of Richard Carabosse, the false Sir Edgar Blakesley.

It will be remembered that he received a summons to rejoin his ship, and proceeded at once to Portsmouth, in obedience to it. The vessel was to start immediately, to watch the preparations of the enemy at Brest.

The "Leander," the vessel to which he was appointed as lieutenant, was a fine craft—a frigate—and considered a match for anything of the same size and build which the French could possibly bring against her.

It was, therefore, with some degree of gratification that the crew of the "Leander" beheld, one fine, bright morning, a French frigate crowding all sail towards her. No attempt was made to avoid the coming foe. The deck was cleared for action, and Sir Edgar named to command the boarding party.

Nothing, perhaps, is so exciting as a fight out upon the open sea; and between these two vessels the contest was long and furious.

They neared each other. The French commander called three times upon the English captain to surrender.

"Why do you ask so absurd a question?" shouted Captain Leighton through his speaking-trumpet.

"Because our guns are heavier, and our men more numerous than yours."

"That is fortunate for you," replied the English captain, "because there is more chance of an even fight."

A shower of ball was the answer to this insulting speech—the ships, like two wrestlers, closed with each other—the grappling-irons were thrown out, and Sir Edgar, who, upon these occasions was as brave as a lion, made a dash with his boarders, at the deck of the French vessel.

The enemy were numerous—brave—well armed; but the English proved too much for them.

Three times were the boarders driven back—and three times again were they struggling on the enemy's deck.

Just, however, as Sir Edgar had planted himself, after many efforts, firmly on the poop of the French vessel, the grappling-irons were removed—the ship gave a lurch round to the wind—swung out of reach of the "Leander," and before the English captain was aware of the manœuvre, was making with all haste to the French coast.

As soon as possible, the Leander followed in her tack. But the French vessel was the better sailer; and before evening set in, she was riding safely under the protection of her native batteries.

Sir Edgar Blakesley was a prisoner.

Again he set his foot upon the soil where he had first commenced his disgraceful triumphs over the fair sex.

Again he was in the country with whose people he claimed affinity, and which seemed everywhere to teem with fresh danger and misfortunes for him.

———

CHAPTER XXXV.

THAT BLESSED BABY.

DURING the action at sea, Sir Edgar Blakesley had been wounded severely. In the heat and excitement of battle the hurt had passed unnoticed; but now, in the cabin which was assigned to him, in accordance with his supposed rank, he found that his left arm was shattered by a ball in two places.

The surgeon of the French vessel attended him with care; and he was then transferred to land.

The wounded were distributed among the neighbouring villages, Sir Edgar falling to the lot of an old fisherman with an only daughter He was well cared for, and treated with comparative respect.

Pierre Montresolet was a regular specimen of the rough French peasant. His brown and deeply-wrinkled face was expressive of a considerable degree of bluff good-nature; and he declared himself by no means desirous that the war with England should be continued. With him Sir Edgar had often an amusing chat of a morning before he departed to his duties; but it was his daughter who obtained most favour in his eyes.

Marie Montresolet was decidedly a pretty girl.

She knew it, too, and wore her clothes in such a way as to make the most of her charms.

She had one of those *piquante* faces which you meet with scarcely anywhere except in France. Her forehead was rather low; but for this fault she made up by drawing her dark brown ringletted hair back away from her face. Her eyes of dark hazel, were long, almond-shaped, and expressive, her nose slightly *retroussé*, her mouth beautiful, the lips being full, voluptuous, and bright red—her chin small and dimpled.

She wore the usual dress of the neighbourhood, got up, however, with much greater regard for appearance than many of her neighbours. Her neck and shoulders were bare, the virgin whiteness of her dimpled bosom contrasting most beautifully with her red stuff corset which fitted closely to her rounded and elastic figure. Her petticoat of red stuff, also, was ornamented with blue, and reached just to the ankle, displaying a pretty little neat foot in a pretty little neat boot *a la suisse.*

She was no mock-modest damsel, this Marie Montresolet. Sir Edgar Blakesley (as we must for the present continue to denominate him) was confined to his bed by the fever consequent upon his wounds, and Marie tended him every day with the assiduity of a nurse at a hospital. She would even sometimes sit by his bedside and tell him in her pretty *patois* everything in regard to herself, to her father, and to the neighbourhood. She thought of no wrong, poor girl, though the impure mind of Sir Edgar at once, from the first moment he saw her, entertained unholy thoughts towards her.

Even the sick room is not proof against the sinful lusts of man.

As we have so lately seen, a Sister of Charity is not secure against the machinations of the man to whose safety she devotes her time and exposes her life.

One morning, just after he had begun to feel a little stronger, Sir Edgar was gazing out of his room on to the little garden below where he saw Marie Montresolet issue forth with a little baby in her arms. She seemed exceedingly proud of it, kissing it again and again, gazing at it tenderly, and otherwise manifesting an excessive affection.

"The devil!" cried Sir Edgar; "she is married, I suppose: rather dangerous game; I must be on my guard."

Presently Marie came up with a basin of soup for his *dejeuner*.

"Good morning, Monsieur," cried she merrily. "Good morning. How are you? If you get well so rapidly, you will soon be able to come and help me in the garden;" and she laughed gaily.

"That I will, my pretty one," said Sir Edgar, chucking her under her chin, "that I will. But what will *he* say if he catches me chaperoning you about these grounds?"

"*He!*" cried Marie; "whom do you mean, Monsieur?"

"Why your husband, to be sure."

"Husband!" cried the girl, her face assuming a look something between a broad grin and an aspect of utter stupefaction.

"Yes; the father of the little baby I saw you nursing just now. I did not know until I saw it that you were married."

This was too much for the risible faculties of poor Marie. She sat down on the side of the bed and fairly screamed with laughter, nearly upsetting, in her merriment, the basin of hot soup which she had brought up and forgotten till now.

"*Eh! bien;* you are droll, Monsieur," said she; "but you must drink your soup while it is warm."

"Are you not married, then?" asked he, as he took the basin nervously from her hand.

"Married, Monsieur—no, nor going to be, that I know of, unless Pierrot takes pity on me some day."

"Then whose baby is that I saw in your arms just now?" enquired Sir Edgar, determined to solve the enigma.

"Madame Diderot's," said Marie, flouncing out of the room.

"What the deuce is the good of her telling me it's Madame Diderot's," said Sir Edgar; "who the deuce is Madame Diderot? I say, Marie—Marie, I say, come here."

"No, thank you, Monsieur," cried the girl, half laughing, half in a pet; "I don't want to hear this morning anything more about that blessed baby."

CHAPTER XXXVI.

THE OPENING OF AN ADVENTURE.

"Oh! les yeux de ma brunette,
    Toute joliette—toute mignonette,
    Oh! les yeux de ma brunette,
    Me fait nuit et jour rêver d'amour."*

MERRILY sang out Marie Montresolet on the next morning, as she passed Sir Edgar's room.

"Come in, come in," said he; "I am anxious to know all about Madame Diderot."

Marie stood at the door, with pouting lips.

"Monsieur is unkind—he is ridiculing me."

"Ridiculing you! I assure you, my charmer, nothing is farther from my thoughts."

"Really?"

"I swear it. You have excited my curiosity about Madame Diderot; now I want you to gratify it."

This was merely a *ruse*. He in reality felt not the slightest interest in Madame Diderot. He merely desired to obtain an opportunity of having Marie with him as much as possible. The result of his inquiries was as follows:—

Madame Diderot was a widow, young, and wealthy, residing in Paris.

She was the daughter of a tallow-chandler. Her husband had been a mercer, and had amassed a fortune just in time to leave her, at the age of thirty, a nice catch for any good-looking and intrepid adventurer. She had one child, now a twelvemonth old, which she had placed out to nurse, in order to keep herself free from household cares—that, in reality, it might not serve to scare away the gentlemen who might consent to forget the smell of tallow and the recollection of woollen fabrics in the remembrance of a snug income of five thousand a year in English money.

It was a most fortunate thing that Sir Edgar Blakesley saw that baby. That baby saved Marie Montresolet's honour and perhaps her very life. From the moment that Sir Edgar heard of the likely widow, with five thousand a year, his designs against poor Marie's virtue became very weakly defined, and, finding that she would not ever consent to go beyond the bounds of *outre* flirtation, he gave up the game altogether.

He obtained from Marie the address of her employer, and was allowed to proceed to Paris, on his word of honour not to endeavour to escape.

Arrived at the capital, he proceeded to the banker's, and having ensconced himself at a tolerable hotel, waited patiently until the arrival of the answer, before presenting himself before the woman whom he had resolved to captivate.

The answer came in due course.

---

* Oh! the eyes of my brunette, so little and so dainty—Oh! the eyes of my brunette make me dream night and day of love.

Its purport completely stunned Sir Edgar Blakesley.

He knew that his position was critical—he knew that his enemies were outwitting himself safely but surely. But he was scarcely prepared for this blow. His bankers refused to make any more advances, hinted something about forgery, and demanded his instant explanation and presence in London. What was he to do? He was in Paris, without a farthing. In this extremity he wrote to Mr. James Tyrrel Blakesley. How he got it we cannot now explain, but he certainly sent him back *a hundred* pounds.

CHAPTER XXXVII.

MADAME DIDEROT.

A HUNDRED pounds to such a fellow as Sir Edgar Blakesley was mere child's play at ordinary times, but, seeing the dangerous game he had to play, he determined to husband his resources.

The war between France and England, of course, afforded him an excellent excuse for being without money, as he, of course, could complain of vessels being intercepted, remittances lost, &c. &c. He knew nothing whatever of Madame Diderot, except her name; and it required considerable assurance to present himself at her door. As there was a very profitable game to be played, however, he did not long hesitate; and the morning after the receipt of the letter from Mr. James Tyrrel Blakesley saw him entering, with a low bow, the *salon* of the young French widow.

"Good day to you, monsieur," said Madame Diderot, rising.

"Good day, madame," replied Sir Edgar, feeling, for the first time, awkward.

The young widow was decidedly prepossessing, though anything but beautiful. She had black hair, plainly and carefully braided over her forehead; her eyes were large and brown, shaded by long lashes; her nose *retroussé*, her mouth large, but laughing, and displaying an excellent set of pearly teeth. Her figure had a decided inclination towards *embonpoint*. Her bust was large and well-proportioned—her form altogether admirable. Her white jewelled hand was continually playing with a rich fan, each gem on her taper fingers reminding Sir Edgar Blakesley of the riches which enabled her to sport them.

Madame Diderot was evidently amused.

"To what do I owe this unexpected honour?" she inquired.

"To chance, madame."

"Indeed!"

"Yes, I am a stranger—a prisoner of war, madame, and know no one in this city; but I heard your name, was told of your kindness, ventured to hope that I might initiate a friendship. If I have intruded, pray——"

"Not at all, monsieur—not at all. I beg you will be seated. Are you in the navy?"

"Yes, madame. I am a lieutenant in the English navy."

"You are wounded, I perceive."

Sir Edgar's arm was still in a sling.

"Slightly: a shattered arm—nothing more."

"Slight! I call it terrible."

"No, Madame—not terrible. I bless it, since it has procured me the pleasure of making your acquaintance."

Madame Diderot laughed and blushed—oh! so slightly.

"You are a flatterer, monsieur; but indeed you interest me. How can your wound possibly have been the means of discovering to you my name and my address?"

"The story is brief, madame. Do you know the village of Dubari, near Brest?"

Madame Diderot flushed crimson as she answered,

"Yes, I do."

"Well; after the action in which I was wounded and taken prisoner, I was carried on shore, and placed by my captors at the house of one Pierre Montresolet. You know him?"

"Slightly," said Madame Diderot, coldly.

"A good man, and a true," continued Sir Edgar. "He has a very pretty daughter. During my stay there she tended me, and I noticed in her arms a beautiful little angel, whom I at once concluded was her own. I asked her: she laughed at the idea of her being married, and told me that it belonged to a lady—a widow, who was as kind as she was beautiful. I heard your character, I came to Paris, I knew no one, and—*me voila*."

So saying, Sir Edgar bowed low before the lady, who now appeared somewhat mollified.

Madame Diderot did not greatly care about an introduction through the baby; but as the gentleman had called it an angel, and seemed rather proud of children than otherwise, she made the best of a bad bargain, and appeared all smiles and tears.

"Indeed, monsieur, I am really indebted to you for your visit. And my child—is it well?"

"I bring nothing but good news of it. It is beautiful, and, what is a greater blessing, it is healthy," said Sir Edgar.

"Here's a fix," he thought to himself. "I don't know its name—I don't even know whether it is a boy or a girl. I must change the subject."

"Now, madame, I must go. I am intruding, I much fear?"

"Can you imagine, monsieur," said the tallow-chandler's widow, "that I should allow you to go thus? Will you not dine with me? I dine at five, and shall be alone. You will not be plagued by strangers."

"Thank you, madame. I know no one in this city, so I cannot but accept your kindness. But as I have not yet told you my name, I shall, in begging leave to retire for an hour or so, leave you my card."

So saying, he bowed, placed in her hand a card, pressed that hand gently, and left the room.

"*Ma foi*," cried the lady, gazing with extreme pleasure at the superscription. "'Sir Edgar Blakesley, Bart.' An English baronet! Ah! me. Well, who knows? I may yet possess a title, in spite of the unkind prophecies of *La mere Susanne.*"

Then, rising and leaving the apartment, she proceeded to give directions for the preparation of the best and most *recherché* of dinners, the choice of the finest wines, and punctuality. Then she locked herself in her boudoir, to spend the next three hours in preparing her toilet, to catch the English aristocrat, as she believed him to be.

CHAPTER XXXVIII.

A QUIET LITTLE DINNER-PARTY.

SIR EDGAR BLAKESLEY kept his appointment with Madame Diderot most punctually.

At five she dined, and at five precisely the *soi-disant* baronet presented himself at the door of the house.

"You are exactly to your time, monsieur," said the lady, blandly smiling. "I am like your great general, Wellington. Nothing annoys me so much as want of punctuality."

"I am in his Majesty's service, remember," said Sir Edgar, pressing her hand. "It is less my credit than my custom."

"You are modest."

"I assure you, madame, you are mistaken. I am not in the slightest degree afflicted with that bad quality."

This was said in a tone which brought the rosy blood tingling on the lady's face, and neck, and bosom, and caused her to remark,

"You are very droll, monsieur. Do you, then, think it a bad quality to be modest?"

"In a man, I do."

"And you are not modest?"

"Not in the slightest."

"Well, then, lead me to dinner."

The dinner was laid out in excellent style. The meats were delicious: the wines superb.

Madame Diderot allowed her guest to drink very little of the red wines of France, but pressed upon him the most piquant and *recherché* of champagnes.

They soon became exhilirated and confidential—the lady more especially so.

Sir Edgar—cunning rascal that he was—was always on his guard; and the more he perceived that his fair companion's temperature was rising, the more cautious he became himself. He, upon this occasion, adopted a new character.

"And so," said Madame Diderot, as dinner was removed, and a delightful dessert took its place; "and so you are a prisoner?"

She gazed at him, with pity gleaming in her dark, languishing eyes, now glistening unnaturally from the effects of the champagne.

"Yes, alas!" said Sir Edgar, with a heavy sigh. "Yes, alas, I have no one to care for me."

"Do not say that."

"It is so."

"Have you no friends?"

"Yes, that is to say relatives; but they are not always friends."

"You say truly; but one so young should not be so despairing."

"Oh!" said Sir Edgar, enthusiastically, "you know not how I pant for a companion whose soul is congenial to mine."

This remark was accompanied by a look, which was meant plainly to indicate that Madame Diderot was, in his eyes, a congenial spirit.

But he was cautious. He had not yet made sufficient inquiries. He was not quite sure that the lady was possessed of the large fortune which the world gave her credit for being mistress of. So he did not follow up the look. Madame Diderot took it as it was intended, however; and, as she was a woman of the world, resolved to catch him by worldly means.

Two poor fools!

Each was trying to catch the other.

The one wanted wealth—the other a title.

Why could they not at once have told each other their desires, and struck a bargain between them, as between any other two people of business? But no; each imagined he was deceiving his neighbour.

"I pity you very much," said the widow, sighing, as she fanned herself vigorously, displaying, as she did so, her beautifully rounded arms. "I pity you very, very much. But you are young—you are handsome—"

"You flatter me."

"Ha!—*non, c'est vrai.* As I repeat emphatically, you are young, you are handsome, you are lively, good-humoured—there are many women who would die for such a husband."

"But then, I may not be rich."

"What does that matter?"

"It matters everything."

"Ah! *bas!*" said Madame Diderot, contemptuously. "A fig for a rich husband."

"Surely, madame," replied Sir Edgar, in unfeigned astonishment, "surely you are not one of those eccentric personages who believe in love in a cottage? We, in England, have an old motto which says, 'When poverty comes in at the door, love flies out of the window.' Do you not think that is pretty correct?"

"Oh! yes, I do indeed," said the lady, laughing; "but you have mistaken my meaning. What I think is this, that when a lady has a fortune of her own—a large fortune, such as in my case—it is best for the husband to have none."

"Why?" asked Sir Edgar, most intensely amused.

"Because he can be managed more easily."

A laugh followed on both sides. Sir Edgar drew his chair closer to his female companion; and when at night they parted, they did not separate as they met, with a formal bow, but with a long pressure of the hand, and a meeting of warm lips.

CHAPTER XXXIX.

DIAMOND CUT DIAMOND.

ALTHOUGH, however, Sir Edgar Blakesley pressed the hand and the lips of Madame Diderot at parting, he was not betrayed into making any definite proposition to her. He liked her manners, he admired her beauty, but the riches were what he coveted, and these he resolved to ascertain the extent of.

On the following day, therefore, he went early to the office of M. Campan, whose name Madame Diderot had accidentally let fall as that of her man of business. He was too discreet to allow the object of his visit to peep out immediately; and he, therefore, beat carefully about the bush.

"Good morning, Monsieur," he said as he entered the closet of the little man who sat enveloped in dust and paper, busily writing.

"Good morning, Monsieur," said M. Campan, "whom have I the honour of addressing?"

"My name, monsieur, is Sir Edgar Blakesley. I heard your firm mentioned by Madame Diderot; and as I am but newly arrived in Paris, I at once came to you. I want some business transacted—some transfer of money. Can you arrange it for me?"

He then proceeded to detail an imaginary transfer of money, which he desired to be effected; and likewise let fall something about the purchase of property in France. M. Campan expressed himself delighted at having secured so promising a client.

"I am always delighted at being able in any way to assist a friend of Madame Diderot's."

"Is she a personal friend of yours?" inquired Sir Edgar, indifferently.

"Well, I cannot say that; but then she is very wealthy, and allows me the entire control of her affairs."

"The devil she does," thought Sir Edgar, "it's more than I should care to do."

"Is she so very wealthy, then?" he added aloud.

"Yes, very. She banks, you must know, with Baillè Brothers—the best firm in Paris."

"Indeed!"

"She is worth, I should imagine," continued the talkative old man, "she is worth, I should imagine, between four and five thousand a year, reckoning by your English money."

"You astound me," said Sir Edgar, in eager delight.

"Nevertheless, I speak nothing more nor less than the truth."

"She is indeed a lady to be respected," said the impostor, "indeed, one of whose friendship one may be proud."

At this moment a loud knock come to the door, and in a few minutes a servant entered.

"Madame Diderot, monsieur," said the man.

"Ah! indeed, how very funny," murmured Sir Edgar.

He did feel very funny, indeed. He had no time for thought, however, for without further introduction madame entered the room; she bowed most graciously to M. Campan, and rather stiffly to Sir Edgar Blakesley, who fancied he saw in her altered manner the doom of all his monetary hopes.

"Good morning, madame," said the lawyer, "lovely morning, is it not? Your friend here, Sir Edgar Blakesley, has been here to consult me in regard to a little purchase of land which he intends making in Burgundy—"

"Indeed!" said madame, drily.

"Yes, madame," stammered Sir Edgar. "You accidentally let fall the name of your man of business yesterday, and as I know so few people in Paris, I applied to M. Campan. I am indebted to you for the introduction—unconscious though it was."

Madame Diderot's eyes glistened with a strange light, as she remarked, apparently in a careless manner,

"I remember I did yesterday let fall M. Campan's name, and I am glad you have taken advantage of the knowledge."

After delivering herself of this ambiguous speech, the lady turned towards the lawyer, who was completely bewildered by the little game of cross-purposes which he saw being played out before him.

"M. Campan," she said, "I desire to see those documents in reference to the last transfer of stock. Let me have a glance at them, if they are at hand."

"Certainly, madame," replied the little man of business; "certainly. I will procure them in one moment."

"And now, Sir Edgar Blakesley," said Madame Diderot, when M. Campan had left the room, "I have a word to say to you."

"Perhaps, madame," cried he, rising, "perhaps, as you have come to see M. Campan on business, I am intruding?"

"Not in the least, Monsieur," said the lady; "pray be seated. I have much to say."

Sir Edgar sat down like a victim.

"In the first place, you did not come here to make a proposal in regard to the purchase of land."

"Indeed, madame, you err. I have this morning proposed to M. Campan to purchase for me the St. Estarline estate in Burgundy."

"You said you were not rich," continued the lady; "but of that anon. I am willing to believe that you did make the proposal, but that was not your primary object. You came here to discover whether I mis-stated the amount of my finances."

Sir Edgar winced, but tried to look like an injured man.

"Yes, and you have found," pursued Madame Diderot, "that I did not mislead you. We now, I think, understand each other; you wish to marry me for my money—I want to marry you for your title. Is it not so?"

"Well, madame," said Sir Edgar, who saw that dissimulation was useless with such a woman, "you have so excellent a way of putting it that I cannot dissent from anything you say."

"I am the more pleased, upon the whole," said the lady, calmly, tapping the table with her parasol, "because, if you had taken no trouble whatever to ascertain the amount of my wealth, I should have regarded you as an impostor. Now I am satisfied; so, as all is arranged, pray accept a seat in my carriage when I have completed my business with M. Campan."

Sir Edgar pressed her hand, and in a short time after was once more making love to her in her pretty boudoir.

CHAPTER XL.

COMPLICATIONS.

MADAME DIDEROT and Sir Edgar Blakesley were now on most excellently good terms.

They were, in fact, regarded by her acquaintances as being most devotedly fond of one another—a new Abelard and Heloise, in fact. They breakfasted together—dined together—gave *petits soupers*; and only awaited Sir Edgar's release from captivity to settle the happy day.

Prior to his release, however, he received the following pleasing note from London:—

"DEAR SIR EDGAR,—I know you like to hear all the news, so I hasten to recapitulate everything prior to mentioning your humble servant. Slimy Jones is caught—the Honourable John Winterton is in custody of Goldie Gordon—the Duchess of Castella, moreover, and your wife are in danger of being secured also—Captain Frederick Winterton has proved more skittish, and has bolted. They are on the look out for you. Your account, as you know, is stopped at the bank, and there is some talk of a public prosecution for murder and forgery.

"Yours, ever,

"JAMES TYRREL BLAKESLEY."

"P.S.—I have forwarded your letter about the release to the proper quarter; and no doubt in a week or so all will be right. You can thus be enabled to come over to England just in time to be tried."

"Damn that fellow's impudence," muttered Sir Edgar. "The devil of it is, I am obliged to put up with it. Damn him! he knows the secret—so to quarrel with him would be to quarrel with my own life. Ah! well, I am on to a nice game now."

And so saying, he dressed himself, and proceeded to breakfast with Madame Diderot.

"Edgar, *ma cher*," said the lady, as she lounged back on her *fauteuil*, sipping her coffee daintily, "who is Lady Edgar Blakesley?"

"Why, you are, I suppose," said he.

"Not yet, by a long way," replied she; "but listen, I am curious. I read from an English paper :—

"AMUSING SCANDAL IN HIGH LIFE—The frequenters of Hyde Park were yesterday much scandalised by an affair which occurred in the drive. Lady Jersey—the peculiar favourite of a certain high personage, was driving in the Row, as also was Lady Edgar Blakesley, a lady whose pretensions had for some time lain in the same quarter. The former, in passing Lady Edgar's phaeton, made some offensive observation, when the latter rose up and struck Lady Jersey across the face with her whip. Lady Jersey immediately drove on; and the carriage-wheels being locked, Lady Edgar's phaeton was upset, and her ladyship pitched headforemost to the ground. She is, we are happy to say, uninjured. Were these combatants of the stronger sex, we might expect a duel; as it is, we must rest satisfied with rival boxes at the opera."

Sir Edgar sat upon thorns. He fidgetted about—grew pale and red by turns, and altogether was very uncomfortable.

"Who is Lady Edgar Blakesley?" inquired Madame Diderot.

"She is my cousin, I am sorry to say," said he; "but I hope you will not think the worse of me because I have a relation who has a *penchant* for royalty."

"Oh! no; not at all," said madame, sipping her coffee, "only I should have decidedly objected if she had been your wife."

"Ha, ha, ha!" laughed Sir Edgar, "a capital joke that."

"It's a good thing," said the lady, smiling, "a very good thing for you that I have so much confidence in you, or else I might be inclined to make further inquiries about you."

Sir Edgar did not feel quite comfortable; and so, after a grim attempt at laughter, he remarked, at the same time drawing his chair closer up beside Madame Diderot—

"I expect to-morrow to receive my release, and therefore let us name the happy day."

"When you like, monsieur," responded the lady, without the slightest emotion, "to-morrow, or the next day; it is all the same to me."

"Then, let it be to-morrow," said Sir Edgar.

The subject of marriage was scarcely mentioned by this imperturbable pair of lovers. They understood each other too well to speak of love; and when they separated for the night, they simply regarded the day's performance as the conclusion of an excellent piece of business.

CHAPTER XLI.

THE MARRIAGE.

THE intended marriage of Madame Diderot, the wealthy tallow-chandler's daughter, with an English baronet, was already the talk of all Paris.

The circumstances under which the connection had been formed served to cast a kind of halo of romance over an affair which, under another aspect and in other times, would have been very common-place indeed.

Madame Diderot had a large circle of acquaintance; we will not say friends, because nearly all of those that flocked to her house were attached, not by her amiability or her kindness, but by her great wealth.

On the marriage morning, therefore, a large concourse of people were assembled in the drawing room of the bride, at whose house the ceremony was to take place.

We have said that people looked upon the affair as savouring a little of the romantic.

The bridegroom was an English prisoner of war.

He had heard of his intended wife by accident, falling in love with her from description only; and as soon as his wounds would allow him he started of post-haste to Paris to pay his respects to her.

This was quite sufficient.

The men were anxious to see the lady; the women eager to lionise the baronet.

The appearance of the happy pair on that happy day was irreproachable. The baronet was attired in his naval uniform—sufficient in itself to captivate the hearts of half the young girls present, while the bride was perfection itself.

She was, as we have said, a tall and finely-made woman.

When Sir Edgar told Mr. James Tyrrel Blakesley that she was not beautiful, he was right: her charms were of a different character.

She was pre-eminently a handsome woman; although thirty years of age, she looked scarcely more than twenty-five or twenty-six, if regard were had simply to her face.

Her figure was that, however, of a woman of more mature age, but was, nevertheless, magnificently proportioned.

Madame Diderot was proud of her figure, and was in general nothing loth to allow the world to judge whether her admiration was well placed or not. On her wedding morning she looked superb. Her dress, composed of white satin, covered in the richest Brussels lace, was made less in accordance with the prevailing fashion than with the requirements of her figure.

Madame Diderot was possessed of a splendid bust, and she knew it.

Her dress, therefore, was made very low in front, displaying in their full beauty the glowing treasures of her bosom. A costly pearl necklace glistened round her swan-like neck—and depending from it was a ruby heart, which nestled temptingly between her breasts.

Her dark hair hung in rich massive waves, rather than curls, over her alabaster shoulders; while her arms, soft, warm, and white as those of Aphrodite, were almost entirely bare.

She was truly a picture which an artist might have longed to gaze on—it was scarcely true beauty—it was an incarnation of the passions.

"Truly," thought Sir Edgar, as he gazed on the magnificent creature, who sailed majestically into the drawing-room, "truly, were she not rich she might be a fit prize for anybody."

He began to feel a kind of wanton love for the widow.

She had chosen just the kind of adornment to please his coarse voluptuousness.

She received the congratulations of her friends with a kind of amused gratitude—laughed at the jokes made; and did not pretend to any mock sentimentality.

The ceremony was performed in due course—the service read impressively—the responses made earnestly, and Sir Edgar Blakesley, Baronet and Madame Diderot were man and wife.

The company separated—the place resumed its usual quietude; and looked very much like as it did before.

Sir Edgar sat down by his wife on the sofa, and passing his arm round her waist, said,

"Do you know, a very curious thing has happened, my dear?"

"What is that?" inquired the lady, laughing.

"Why, I have fallen in love with you."

Her ladyship smiled blandly, kissed her husband, and from that moment they were an exceedingly cosy couple.

A fortnight more saw them in London.

CHAPTER XLII.

THE BLUE DWARF AND BLACK HARRY.

IN a little street near Wapping lived Mrs. Robert Brandon and an only daughter.

The former was a widow, the relict of a respectable tradesman, who had left her a comfortable competency.

The latter was a tall, finely-made young woman, with rather massive limbs, and a development of the bust unusual in one so young.

Jane Brandon was eighteen; but her form would have passed for that of a woman of five or six and twenty—and that, too, a fine woman. She had an arch, pretty expression about her face which was extremely prepossessing. In fine, among her friends and acquaintances she was a universal favourite, and was, besides, engaged to a "very nice young man."

She was walking one evening, as was her wont, strolling leisurely and gazing anxiously in every shop-window which presented any attraction,

when a light hand touched her on the shoulder. She turned round sharply, and saw standing beside her a very short man, wrapped in a cloak. His face she could not properly distinguish, but it appeared rather dark, and of a most extraordinary character.

"What is it you require, sir?" she said, crossing herself.

"Your name is Jane Brandon?" inquired the unknown.

"It is, sir."

"And you live with your mother in Down-over-street?" inquired the stranger, in the same tone

"I do, sir," said the girl, who was by this time fairly puzzled.

"Do you want to make your fortune?" said her companion.

Jane Brandon laughed outright—a long, loud, merry laugh, as she answered,

"You're making game of me, sir."

"Not at all," replied the imperturbable stranger; "not at all. My question is simple. Do you want to make your fortune, and are you ready to brave danger to achieve it?"

The girl hesitated, blushed, and looked down on the ground.

"I understand and appreciate your fears," said the unknown; "but dread nothing of that kind. Will you lead me to your mother? I will tell her what is wanted, and if you agree I can arrange it all with her."

"Thank you, sir, thank you," said Jane Brandon, puzzled and startled out of her wits. "Mother is not very well off, and anything I can honestly do to help her I always do."

"Then lead me to your mother," said the stranger.

"I will, sir; I think you mean well?"

This last was said in a tone of inquiry.

Her companion did not answer.

Jane continued—

"She is in great distress of mind at present, sir. My uncle has for many weeks been ill, and we fear he is dying. He is sorely afflicted in spirit; and his sickness is nearly exhausting my poor mother, who is very, very fond of him."

"I will comfort her."

"You, sir!" exclaimed the girl, in surprise. "Do you know my mother!"

"No; but I think I know your uncle."

This conversation took place on their road to the widow's house, which was soon reached.

"You had better enter, and prepare her for a visitor," said the unknown.

"Yes, sir," said Jane; "you will excuse me keeping you in the passage one moment."

And she tripped lightly up the stairs.

In the bedroom of her uncle she found her mother, in a state of uncontrollable grief.

On the bed, motionless, but talking wildly, lay the man, every now and then breaking in a low, chuckling laugh.

"Is uncle worse, mother?" inquired the girl.

"Oh! he is dying, my dear girl; and he is talking so terribly that I dare not send for any one. He is murmuring about robberies and murders—now pleading for mercy, now defying the law."

"But it is mere fancy, mother; do not distress yourself. There is a stranger downstairs who wishes to see you.

"I can see no one, my dear. I am too ill—too unhappy."

"But he says he knows uncle."

"Well, I suppose I must see him. What is he like?"

"He is a very short gentleman, very dark, and seems to be hump-backed."

"I do not know him by your description; but let him come up."

Jane Brandon descended the stairs, and bade the stranger come up. He immediately ascended, entered the room, and bowing to Mrs. Brandon, said gently,

"I fear I am very rude—very rude, indeed, to interrupt you at such a moment as this; but my business is very important. Leave me awhile with your brother, and all will go well."

Jane looked at her mother, and after a moment's hesitation they both left the room.

The stranger approached the bed, removed his slouched hat, and disclosed the features of the Blue Dwarf.

Sapathwa sat down by the side of the sufferer, and gazed earnestly in his face.

The man seemed to recognise him, and muttered,

"This is that Blue Devil that always haunts me. Avaunt, demon!"

"I am no demon, Black Harry," said Sapathwa, kindly. "I know you well; but I am not come to torture, or even to blame you."

"Why do you come here, then? I want you not."

"I come," said the Blue Dwarf, "to give you a chance of retrieving yourself."

"Ah! ah! ah!" laughed the man, hoarsely. "Retrieve myself? Why don't you see I am dying?"

"You may, or may not be dying," replied Sapathwa; "at any rate you can do good while you live, and thus wipe off some of your evil deeds."

The man's eyes gleamed with a strange light.

"Give me the chance," he said, doubtingly.

"I will," said Sapathwa. "You have a niece."

"I have. What of her?"

"I require her services."

"What mean you?" said Black Harry, fiercely.

"You misunderstand me," replied the Blue Dwarf, deprecatingly. "You misunderstand me entirely. I want to employ her for a time. I will give her a good salary, and see that no harm comes to her."

"I will trust you," said the man.

"It is your sister who will require persuasion," said Sapathwa, "for I can tell to no one the purpose for which she is to be used. I engage to send her back again to this house in two months as pure and as untainted as she leaves it."

"I will speak to my sister," said Black Harry, "but tell me what became of Miss Winterton—the young lady whom Captain Frederick Winterton carried off. Has she escaped?"

"She has," said Sapathwa, "and he is now in my hands. I will now go, and leave you to persuade Mrs. Brandon. I will return to-morrow at ten."

CHAPTER XLIII.

THE MAIDSERVANT AND THE TWO BARMAIDS.

SIR EDGAR BLAKESLEY and his new wife took up their residence in Mayfair.

Now that he had fairly caught the fair widow, he made no reserve in regard to his poverty; although he considered it prudent to coin a tale as to the reason for it. He was, he said, a twin brother, and was the youngest of the two by half-an-hour. His brother was an unfeeling, hard-hearted wretch, according to Sir Edgar, and would not even allow him a farthing. A trial, he represented, was even then going on, and he received, at intervals, the visits of a little man, whom he presented to his wife as his lawyer.

Lady Blakesley was not particularly anxious to witness any increase in her husband's resources. She was rich, and as long as the wealth came from her side she possessed the power of an autocrat in her own house. She gave him a regular allowance for his own expenses, and never inquired either what he did with his money, or where he spent his time. On the other hand, however, she never permitted him to exceed the stated amount.

When they arrived in London, and entered their house in Mayfair, they had also to set up an establishment; and among those who presented themselves for the situation of lady's-maid was a tall, finely-built girl, of some seventeen or eighteen.

"You are very young?" said Lady Blakesley.

"Eighteen, madame," responded the girl, modestly.

"Yes, very young for the situation of lady's-maid. Have you had any experience?"

"Yes, madame, two years' experience."

"Where?"

"In the house of Mrs. Brandonwood, of Southwood Square."

"Ah! very good. I will apply to her."

"Thank you, madame."

"And what wages do you require?"

The girl held down her head, and blushed.

"Do not blush, my good girl," said the Frenchwoman, kindly. "Do not be afraid to name a high price. If you are worth it I shall have no hesitation in paying it."

"It is not that which makes me hesitate."

"What is it, then?" inquired the lady, curiously.

"I should so like to come here."

"Well, so you shall, if I like your reference."

"You seem so good, so kind, so gentle—so different from my late mistress. I am sure I should be so happy with you."

The compliment went home.

Lady Blakesley smiled blandly.

"What is your name, my pretty girl?" she said, patronisingly.

"Mary Cartwright."

"Very well—call again to-morrow, at ten."

The girl called again, at ten on the following day, and was engaged. Her reference was not applied to.

Shortly afterwards, Jane Brandon left the situation she held in the house of Lady Edgar Blakesley.

She alleged illness; and left after only a week's notice.

Upon issuing from the house she did not proceed home; but went—boxes and all—to a little house in Edward-street, Farrieird-market.

Here she knocked timidly at the door.

A slovenly, ill-looking servant opened it.

"Is Mr. Tyrrel in?" asked the lady's-maid.

"Yes; do you want him?"

"Yes, if you please."

"Walk up, then."

She followed the ill-favoured girl up a staircase which creaked under their feet, as if it would have given way under them; and at the very summit the guide stopped at the door of a little room. Here she knocked.

"Come in," said a gruff voice.

"Here's a girl as want's you," said the female Cerberus.

"Show her in, then, Margaret."

Mary entered.

It was a squalid apartment—the very picture of a drunkard's home. It contained a table, two chairs, and a bedstead, upon which lay a mattress. A few embers glimmered in the grate; and on the table were a pot of beer and some tobacco.

"Whom may I have the pleasure of addressing?" asked the occupant; a pale, cadaverous, elderly man—palsied with the effect of drink and dissipation.

"I come here to meet the Blue Dwarf, sir," said the girl.

"Oh! you are the young lady who was lady's-maid to Sir Edgar Blakesley?"

"Yes, sir."

"Well, you had better stop here—for I expect him every moment."

"My luggage is downstairs, sir—what am I to do with that?"

"Oh! bring it up here—you will have to stop here, I suppose, to-night."

The young girl gazed round the room with a shudder. Her mother's house was not possessed of many luxuries; but, certainly, the present abode offered anything but a comfortable prospect.

"Needs must when the devil drives," thought the girl; and so she allowed her trunk to be removed out of the cab and placed in the squalid room.

Mr. Tyrrel was sitting by the fire drinking gin.

"Take a glass," he said, as Mary took a seat opposite him.

"No, thank you," replied the girl.

"It'll do you good," said he, pouring one out; "besides we must make ourselves comfortable while we are waiting _for him._"

This was said with a sneer, and a leer at the handsome person of the young lady's-maid, who regarded the worn-out _roué_ with the utmost contempt.

"I would offer you beer, only I have drunk it all," he continued. "Here, drink it up."

"I tell you, I will not," said Mary; "I don't want it."

"Come, now, don't be foolish. I am used to all these little dodges, you know. Don't be mock-modest. Give us a kiss, and let's be friends. I rather like the look of you."

"I cannot return the compliment, sir," said Mary; "and if you attempt to come near me, I shall leave the house, and inform the Blue Dwarf of your conduct."

"Well, well, I will leave you alone," muttered the man, sullenly, "only I _do_ think you are damnably crusty."

He then resumed his pipe and his glass, emptying the gin into a half-finished tumbler of porter.

Neither spoke a word. They seemed to have a mutual hatred and fear of each other. At length a loud knock came to the street door, and after a moment Sapathwa entered the room.

"Ah! my good girl," said he, rubbing his hands; "you are punctual, I see. No time is to be lost; you are to enter into your situation immediately."

"May I go to-night, sir?" asked she.

"Why? are you in a hurry to commence trap No. 2!"

"No, sir; but I do not like the appearance of this place; and from what Mr. Tyrrel said, I feared I might be compelled to remain here all night."

"Oh, no; you will be spared that infliction. I have a cab waiting at the door, and we will go to our destination at once."

"Thank heaven," said the girl.

Tyrrel looked blank. He had meditated a dastardly design against her, which was thus defeated.

The Blue Dwarf, accompanied by Mary Cartwright, stopped at the door of a little tavern in the neighbourhood.

Mary remained in the cab, while Sapathwa had a hurried consultation with the landlord.

In a few minutes he emerged, with a peculiar smile upon his countenance, and bade Mary follow him.

The landlord met them, grinning blandly. He had evidently received his proper equivalent for the part he was to enact in the affair.

"This, then, is my new barmaid," he said, rubbing his hands.

"I am afraid," said Mary, laughing, "you will find me a very awkward assistant."

"Ah! but we are bound to overlook all little mistakes; are we not?" he remarked, glancing knowingly at the Blue Dwarf.

"They will be here to-morrow night," said the latter.

"Very well," replied Mary.

"You must not let the cat out of the bag."

"I will be as demure as a saint."

"Ha, ha, ha!" laughed Boniface. "Very good! A pretty saint, by Jove."

"If you are not, all will be lost."

"You can trust me, surely!" said Mary. "I am certain I can pull as long a face as any one this side Bedlam."

"Well, then, good night, my girl," said Sapathwa; "be careful."

"Trust me," exclaimed Mary, with an arch smile. "Good night."

*   *   *   *   *

The following night Mr. James Tyrrel Blakesley, and the false Sir Edgar Blakesley, of Mayfair, spent an hour or so at this house.

It was the "Emerald Tavern."

* * * * *

The following morning the Blue Dwarf again made his appearance at the public-house.

"Good morning, sir," said the landlord; "you are about betimes."

"Yes, truly."

"Come to see how Mary gets on? She's first rate, sir. Don't want to lose her, I can tell you."

"That's just what I have come to speak about," said Sapathwa; "I am going to take her away this morning."

"Hope it's all right, sir?" exclaimed Boniface, demurely. "Everything has been done as arranged, sir. Every respect shown, sir. Treated her as my own daughter, sir."

"I have no fault to find with you," said the Blue Dwarf; "but she has got to take another situation."

The landlord laughed heartily.

"That's what I call swift work," said he. "Miss Cartwright, you're wanted."

The young girl came down in surprise.

"Good morning, sir," she said, in a tone of extreme wonderment, to her employer. "Is anything wrong?"

"No; only I have found you another situation, which you must enter this morning."

"Very, well, sir," said Mary; and she tripped upstairs to dress herself.

In a few minutes she re-appeared—bade adieu to the landlord of the "Emerald," and once more entered a cab with the Blue Dwarf, and her inseparable companion, the clothes-trunk.

The place to which Sapathwa conducted her, on this occasion, was anything but suited to her taste.

It was one of the lowest of those low pot-houses, in the neighbourhood of Wapping, which are frequented by common sailors, as also crimps, and other characters of the vilest sort.

The landlord was a greasy-looking individual. He seemed to have poured innumerable gallons of oil over his conscience, so as to allow anything and everything to slip through easily. Nothing ever stuck half-way.

A glass of grog led the way pretty easily; but a well-filled purse was sure to sink to the bottom.

In a word, Franklin Leatherhead was up to anything and everything.

Mary Cartwright did not at all like the look of the man or the place.

The aspect of the house, and the company with which even at that early hour in the morning it was filled, caused an inward shuddering, which the Blue Dwarf could not fail to notice.

"My poor girl," he said, "I know this will be very unpleasant work for you. But, for Heaven's sake, don't fail me now."

Mary, who could scarcely repress her tears, said firmly,

"I have undertaken the task, sir, and will perform it."

"At all hazards?"

"Yes—at all hazards."

"Then I was not mistaken in you. I knew you would do it if you promised."

"And besides, sir, it is to effect good."

Sapathwa thought a moment.

"Mary," he said, "Go upstairs and take off your things."

Then, turning to the landlord, he added—

"Mr. Leatherhead, I should like to speak a word with you."

"Very busy," grumbled the landlord.

"Yes—but I have paid you well," returned the Blue Dwarf, quietly.

To a man for whom he had more respect than Franklin Leatherhead he could not have said this.

"True — true," grumbled the fellow; "I didn't mean to be rude; only we are very full."

"You forget you have some one to assist you now—the new barmaid."

"Ah, but she's new."

"She has experience."

"How long?"

"One day."

The fellow laughed in spite of his surliness.

"Well, well, sir, you are a funny gentleman. Walk this way, sir; walk this way."

And he led the way into the bar parlour.

Sapathwa took a seat, and, looking Franklin Leatherhead full in the face, said,

"Your house is frequented by bad characters."

Franklin started.

"Well, I am damned if that ain't pretty plump," he cried; "I am hanged if I ever came across such a cool card as you are."

"Very likely not," said the Blue Dwarf, quietly; "but I never assert anything which I do not know to be true. I repeat—your house is frequented by bad characters."

"Don't know as how it isn't," growled Leatherhead. "I don't think it worth while to ask the business of every one who comes here."

"I don't accuse you of anything," said Sapathwa; "I merely say that, owing to the position of the house, you are not favoured with a very select set."

"No, I am not," said the man.

With a person like the Blue Dwarf it was useless, if not impossible, to equivocate.

"The young lady to whom I have introduced you is a particular friend of mine."

"Yes, sir, so you informed me before."

"I repeat it, then; and not for the world would I have her injured. Do you take me?"

"Yes."

"Well, then, among the ruffians who come here she might possibly come to some harm. I leave it in your hands to protect her."

"Is that all?" said the man.

"Yes, and quite enough, I think," exclaimed Sapathwa. "I will take a deadly revenge, mind you, if she be harmed—so look to it."

And so saying, he left the bar and the house.

"Well, I am damned if that ain't about the queerest buffer I ever fell over. I can't make him out, hanged if I can. But, never mind, Franklin, my boy, he's the right sort, and no mistake."

This was said with a tone of self-congratulation, as he chinked the purse which was given him by Sapathwa.

* * * * *

That night the tap-room of the tavern was filled to excess, and among those present were Mr. James Tyrrel Blakesley and Sir Edgar Blakesley.

Mary Cartwright was peculiarly attentive to this pair.

So attentive, indeed, was she, that not a word of their conversation escaped her.

At one o'clock in the morning entered, as we have described, the Blue Dwarf, William Lennox, Bob Griggs, and others; and at two the happy pair were lodged in the mansion of the Blue Dwarf.

*   *   *   *   *

Mary Cartwright remained at the tavern all the next day; and, although not obliged to do so by her engagement, assisted Franklin Leatherhead in the bar.

During the evening, a tall young man entered the house, and asked if a young lady of the name of Cartwright was there.

The stranger was very dark, and spoke with a slightly foreign accent.

"Mary, you're wanted."

Mary came out, and rushed forward, with a wild scream, into the stranger's arms.

———

CHAPTER XLIV.

THE STEEL CORSET.

Slimy Jones started back in horror, when the knife descended upon the body of the Blue Dwarf.

It seemed as if it had been driven against a rock; and, glancing off, lay quivering and deep in the bed.

Sapathwa started up: a grim smile passed over his features, and, leaping out of bed, he seized the man by the wrist.

Slimy Jones could not resist.

He was paralysed by fear

"Ah! murderer!" hissed the Blue Dwarf. "I have you again. See here, how I guard myself against the assaults of cowardly assassins."

His night shirt was cut open by the knife, and displayed a steel corset composed of the most delicate links, and fitting as closely as india-rubber to the body.

This corset he had worn for many years, only taking it off when he entered his bath in the morning.

Slimy Jones felt as helpless as a child in his grasp.

He trembled violently.

"Let me go," he said, in a husky voice. "Give me sufficient money to enable me to leave the country, and I will never molest you again."

"How are you here? You were in gaol?"

"I escaped by leaping over the prison wall."

"And why do you suppose that I shall trust you?"

"I do not suppose it. I only beg for life."

"Wretched, cowardly miscreant!" said the Blue Dwarf, "I should be letting a demon forth upon society if I allowed you to escape. I will not let you go."

Slimy Jones saw that from him he could expect no mercy.

The door was open.

Why not try to run for life?

With a tremendous effort he strove to wrest his arm from the grasp of the Blue Dwarf.

But Sapathwa was possessed of enormous strength.

Like most deformed persons his power seemed supernatural.

He struggled violently, and endeavoured to reach the bed on which the knife still quivered.

Sapathwa suddenly let go; and springing to the door, shouted out—

"Help! help!"

The sound rang dismally through the old house.

"Help! help!"

Slimy Jones saw that his case was a desperate one.

"Help! help!" still cried the Blue Dwarf.

By this time everybody was roused in the house: and steps were heard coming from the distance.

Slimy Jones had, as I have said, been almost paralysed with fear.

He now grasped the knife: but, under present circumstances, he felt that it would be useless against the steel corset of the Blue Dwarf.

Just as the footsteps approached the door, he caught sight of a brace of pistols which lay on the toilet table.

He made a dash for them—clutched them, and stood prepared for the worst.

At this moment William Lennox and Lord Ernest appeared at the door.

The malefactor gazed at them in despair: and he had just given himself up for lost, when he caught sight of a door which was almost concealed in the panelling.

He ran towards it—opened it—fired one of the pistols at the Blue Dwarf—and clutching the other sped away, locking the door after him.

The Blue Dwarf was unhurt.

A grim smile passed over his face.

"He is caged, gentlemen," he said, pointing to the door; "the room into which he has voluntarily thrust himself has no outlet."

At this moment a violent ringing and knocking was heard at the hall door.

"What can that be?" said Sapathwa. "Go," he said, to one of the servants who now came up, "go and see who it is makes this unseemly disturbance at this hour of the morning."

The man went went as bidden: and the hall door was opened.

The Blue Dwarf stood anxiously listening at the head of the stairs.

A well-known voice was heard exclaiming—

"I am very late. Is your master in bed?"

"Yes, sir," said the servant; "he happens to be up; for there has been an attempt at murder in the house."

"Murder!" cried Captain George; for it was he.

"Yes," cried the Blue Dwarf; "murder: come up, and I will tell you all about it."

Captain George ascended the stairs with his four companions, and between them Lord Charles Lutterell.

CHAPTER XLV.

THE STORY OF MARY CARTWRIGHT.
THE NEW VICAR.

THE village of Flowervale, in Northumberland, is an excessively pretty place.

It nestles just below a lofty hill; and is one, perhaps, of the pretty gems of that most beautiful of counties.

Coming along the highroad you just drop upon the parsonage-house; and a few yards beyond the village church, covered with ivy, and dating its birth hundreds of years ago.

Its windows were newly painted at the time of our story, and contrasted strangely with its old dirty walls.

The churchyard was full to overflowing with the stony memories of the dead—some tottering and green with age.

Inside the church had all the evidences of a new vicar.

The Reverend Carleton le Pluche was a young

gentleman of a new school, something similar in character to that school introduced by the celebrated Doctor Pusey.

His advent was looked forward to with great anxiety.

His arrival startled not a few.

Flowervale was originally a place of worship presided over by the ancient spirit of religion.

Its walls were plain white paint, its pews were high and unornamented, its pulpit plain oak, its altar tastefully neat.

But, after the arrival of the vicar, everything was changed.

The plain white painted walls gave place to ornamental panels containing gilded quotations from scripture; the tall pews were pulled down and replaced by others suited to the new fangled notions of the young clergyman; the pulpit was hung with crimson velvet; the communion table was converted into an altar, with the necessary accompaniments of candlesticks, censers, and crosses; the plain glass windows, which some village rustic had expended no end of labour on, were instantly removed as unfit for a place for worship, and replaced by others of stained glass, duly imported from the metropolis.

The parishioners of Flowervale had been used, all their lives, to sing their hymns after their own humble fashion in their own village church.

Now, however, they were deemed unworthy to worship for themselves.

A choir was, therefore, formed among the youths in the neighbourhood, who were duly attired in vestments bearing considerable resemblance to bed-gowns.

The old gravelled walks through the churchyard were replaced by paths formed of tiny pebbles, ornamented with shells; while the old wooden porch gave way before an arch of clean white stone, surmounted by a huge cross, which appeared constantly threatening to topple over upon those who entered into the regenerated churchyard.

Just before the arrival of the Rev. Carleton Le Pluche, Flowervale Church was closed for repairs.

When that reverend gentleman did arrive, he preached for several days in the open air.

He was a man of some twenty five years of age; with fair hair, small grey eyes, round and twinkling, a straight nose, a femininely-small mouth, and large red whiskers.

He dressed rather fast on ordinary days—that is to say, "fast" for a clergyman.

The good people of Flowervale expected something new, and they found it—decidedly. They flocked in great numbers to his first preaching, which took place on a hillside, just beyond the village. The Rev. Carleton le Pluche was decidedly a scholar and a gentleman. He spoke well, epigrammatically, and energetically. His words were very fervid and impassioned, and he roused his audience, which was evidently delighted at his eloquence.

But, then, he did not preach of hope.

He uttered fierce denunciations; and though when he ceased many were in tears, and all impressed, that impression was one of fear, and not of expected mercy.

"What a handsome man!"

"But, then, how unkind."

"He must speak the truth."

"I like our old pastor better."

"He is young, strong, and energetic. He does not fear to speak of things as they are."

"He makes us doubt if things really are so."

Such were the contradictory opinions which, upon that day, were spread over the village in regard to the new vicar, as he wended his way slowly—book in hand, eyes down—back to the Parsonage House.

Arrived there, he retired to his study; and, flinging himself down on a sofa, wiped the thick drops of perspiration from his brow.

"How much longer is this to last?" he muttered, as he pressed his hand to his fevered temples.

He rang the bell.

A man servant appeared.

"John," he said, "give me some brandy."

The man returned in a few moments with a tumbler half full of raw spirit.

The Reverend Carleton le Pluche smiled sadly as he said—

"Ah! John, I see you know my requirements—"

And drained the glass to the dregs.

The servant left the study; and, as if revived, the clergyman rose and rapidly paced the apartment.

He talked uneasily to himself.

"I looked at all the faces—"

"She was not there. I am certain she was not there."

"I should know her among a thousand. Her sweet, girlish face, with her dark, blue eyes, and golden ringlets.

He stopped, and raised his eyes to Heaven, as if striving to recollect a face.

"Yes, I am certain she was not there," he repeated. "Yet, why should she deceive me?"

He gazed out at the window.

Why did he gasp for breath, and clutch the sill of the window?

At what did he stare with such wild eyes and bated breath?

On the opposite side of the way, tripping lightly along, was a pretty girl of some twenty years.

Golden ringlets, confined under a little jaunty hat, fell over her white shoulders, which were slightly bare.

It was midsummer; and only a light lace covering was over her breast.

Her eyes were large, and blue; her nose straight; her mouth small, and red-lipped; while her cheeks were beaming with the ruddy bloom of health.

"'Tis she! 'tis she!" cried the rector, sinking back in his couch.

He rank the bell.

The man servant again appeared.

"You see that young lady," said the rector, rising, and pointing out to him the young girl who had caused his violent emotion.

The man looked, stared, and said,

"Yes, sir."

"Now, John," said his master, "can I depend on you?"

"Yes, sir."

"I mean, can I trust you with a secret?"

"Yes, sir."

"Well then, listen."

"Yes, sir."

"I want to know," said the rector, "where that young lady is going—where she resides—and what is her name?"

"Very well, sir."

"And John—do not let me be disturbed."

The man left the room; and the clergyman sank back, as if exhausted, on the couch.

CHAPTER XLVI.

THE MAN IN THE CLOAK.

DOWN by the edge of the hill, just beyond the village where the new vicar gave his first sermon, was a little valley, called by the inhabitants of the hamlet, Red Vale.

The people, to whom the golden fruits of literature were as yet denied, were highly superstitious; and very few of them cared to trust themselves in the vicinity of the Red valley at night.

Red Vale possessed a bad name throughout the neighbourhood.

It had been the scene of a murder—

A cold-blooded, deliberate murder.

A man had murdered his affianced bride down in that dark valley, after having accomplished her ruin. It was just the spot for such a deed: for the tangled brushwood, and the weird-looking foliage of the trees on its brink, nearly joined a covering about it, so that in the day time scarcely a ray of the bright sun penetrated to the bottom; and at night it was as dark as Erebus.

It was a few nights after the scene in the vicar's study.

The evening had been dark and gloomy.

Not a soul ventured out; for, as night set in, the stars disappeared; the moon also veiled herself from all outward things; and the wind howled dismally round the chimney-pots.

For an hour before midnight, a man, wrapped closely in a cloak, had been pacing hurriedly along the brink of the Red Valley.

He seemed greatly agitated; and ever and anon as the clock struck the quarters, he would stamp his feet violently on the ground, muttering bitterly between his teeth—

"Another chime, and no Lucy yet!"

"Oh! that I were like other men," he exclaimed, "that I might go whither and do whatsoever I listed. Even now I think I will throw off the trammels of this calling, and trust to chance to enable me to carve my way in the world."

The man seemed violently agitated.

He paced impatiently to and fro. His face was pale, and ever and anon convulsed with terrible emotion.

At length a light step was heard tripping along the road.

The man in the cloak stopped, looked out eagerly from his concealment among the brushwood and listened.

"It's she at last." he murmured.

In another moment a girl stood by his side.

It was the one who had so excited the new vicar after the first sermon on the hillside.

"Lucy," he said, "you are late."

"No, not very," replied the girl, in a tremulous voice.

The man gazed at her inquiringly.

The girl stood looking up into his face with a kind of fear.

She was dressed lightly—a little hat was stuck jauntily on her head.

A scarf just apologised for a covering for her shoulders; her dress was very low in front; while a handkerchief concealed—after the usual fashion of the time—her snowy and exquisitely moulded breasts.

"Come," said the man, taking her hand, and leading her down into the bottom of the valley, "come and sit down with me while we talk about the past and the future."

There was something excessively gloomy in his manner as he uttered these words. The girl trembled, but, nevertheless, followed him.

Their progress was slow through the tangled brushwood, and she had need, indeed, of a guide, for the night was as dark as pitch.

Arrived at the bottom of the Red Vale they sat down, and the man, passing his arm round her soft, warm neck, and with the other hand taking her hand, kissed her fondly, and said:—

"At length, Lucy, we are alone, and I can talk to you."

"Yes, at length, Carleton," said Lucy; "but even now I fear I am doing wrong, very wrong."

She said Carleton. Yes it was, indeed, the Reverend Carleton Le Pluche who sat there in the darkness, with the fair girl by his side.

Their conversation was long and animated. Many a time, as he poured hot passionate words into her ear, a tell-tale blush would suffuse her cheek, and even tears start to her dark eyes.

"Oh! Carleton," she murmured, at length, while her face was buried in her hands, and her bosom palpitated with an emotion she could not suppress, "Oh! Carleton, why do you ask of me this sacrifice? Why can you not suggest other means?"

"There are none," returned Le Pluche, gloomily.

"You say you love me."

"I do," he said, fervently; "you know I do passionately, fondly."

"Well, then, if you so love me why not give up this false ambition, and make me your wife?"

"I cannot—I dare not," he answered, in a hoarse, troubled voice.

"Oh! do," pleaded Lucy, holding his hand, and gazing imploringly in his face. Let me entreat you not to ask of me this sacrifice. You can rise to anything in the English Church. Why not be satisfied with this prospect, and leave the Romish Church to find its votaries elsewhere?"

The Reverend Carleton Le Pluche rose from the ground, and paced to and fro in the dark glen.

His face was strangely working. His agitation was terrible. He appeared more like the emissary of an archdemon than the minister of a true religion.

"Lucy," he said, at length, stopping and gazing at her steadfastly, while his voice was thick and husky with emotion—

"Yes, Carleton," she cried, timidly.

"Do you refuse to be mine, on *my* conditions?"

"I do, Carleton," she said, with more resolution than could have been imagined from her previous manner, "I do; not because I fail in my love for you, but out of respect for you and for myself. I will never be yours except as your wife."

"You refuse my conditions," he repeated.

"I do."

"Then, by Heavens!" he cried, clenching his hands tightly together, "you shall be mine on your own conditions."

"My own dear girl," he added, as he fondly clasped her tightly to his breast, "I will marry you; but it must be done so secretly that no one shall know it: and then I can, in spite of my marriage, carry on my ambitious design."

"Dear—dear Carleton."

And thus did that strange minister of the Gospel betroth himself to the simple girl who imagined that she loved him more than all else besides.

CHAPTER XLVII.

WALLS HAVE EARS.

It was quite two in the morning when the Reverend Carleton Le Pluche and Lucy Cartwright came from out the darkness of the Red Valley.

It would have scarcely been discreet to proceed together on that road towards the village, so, with a long and fervid embrace, they parted.

"Go you that way, Lucy," said the clergyman, pointing to the direct pathway to Flowervale, "it will not be well to be seen together tonight. I will go round by a more circuitous route. Good bye, dearest. Remember, tomorrow night."

Lucy embraced him fondly, and was soon tripping away gaily along the road to the hamlet which lay sleeping calmly under the dark sky.

Gaily, did she?

Well, was it not natural?

Was she not young? Was she not pretty? Was she not beloved? Did not the bright dreams of love cast a golden radiance over every thought and action? Was not her lover about to marry her? Was he not about to brave everything for her—risking the chances of advancement, and therefore too, in his view, earthly happiness?

Truly, as we all have said, and all felt one time or another in our lives, love blinds us to the faults and to the strangeness of those we love.

She did not reflect upon the mystery which appeared to enshroud all the words and the actions of the Reverend Carleton Le Pluche. She never once stayed to consider whether the marriage he proposed was right. She never even paused once to inquire whether it would be legal.

The wedding was to take place the following night at the little chapel which lay about five minutes' walk from a neighbouring village. *He himself was to marry them: the bridegroom was to perform the ceremony.* This, he assured her, was quite in accordance with law. Was he not a clergyman? And so she believed him, and trippingly went along the fields to her home.

Meanwhile the one she had left behind was engaged with far less pleasant thoughts.

When Lucy ran lightly along the path the Reverend Carleton Le Pluche stood gazing after her sadly and thoughtfully.

"Poor girl," he muttered, "I love her dearly, but I dare not do as she would have me to do. It would be ruin—utter irredeemable ruin. Poor Lucy! She will be happy enough, though, for she will never know to the contrary."

"You have not only yourself to trust, Mr. Le Pluche," said a deep voice near him.

A tall dark man, in a foreign cloak and hat, issued from among the brushwood.

"Harry Morton!" cried the clergyman, in a husky choking voice.

"Aye, Sir! Harry Morton."

"What do you here? Why do you dog my footsteps?"

"Because in that consists my revenge."

"Revenge belongeth not to man," said the Reverend Carleton Le Pluche, solemnly.

"Talk none of your religious gibberish to me," shouted the other. "I want money, not psalm-singing and sermonising."

Le Pluche was a bad man, but in regard to the strict part of his religious duties he never failed. Whatever crimes he might have committed he was never known to have ever scoffed at religion or allowed others to scoff at religion in his presence. His education had taught him its holy truths; he, in his own person, acted in defiance of moral law—but in his preachings he preached the real doctrine of Christianity. He appeared, indeed, as if in his sermons he was addressing himself less to the congregation than to himself—endeavouring less to blight and scar their prospects of salvation than to point out to himself how little hope of mercy remained for him.

When Harry Morton, therefore, uttered the blasphemous words Le Pluche shuddered, and said to him in a low, clear, ringing voice—

"Morton, remember! whatever you say to me avoid that subject. I will hear anything—listen to anything—but that."

"The hypocritical caitiff," muttered the other. "Then," he added, in a louder voice, "give me some money."

"I have none for you."

"Then you must get some."

"I will not. The time of our compact is up, and I now defy you."

"Ah! ah! ah!" laughed Harry Morton. "Our compact is truly over; but I have come to make a new one. No need of seal, or covenant, or witnesses, in this affair—the absence of others binds us all the stronger."

"What mean you?" exclaimed Carleton Le Pluche, in a low, gasping tone.

He half suspected the import of the man's words, and trembled at the power he had over him.

"I mean," said Harry Morton, deliberately, "that during the pleasant tête-a-tête you have just been having with Miss Lucy Cartwright I have been a very patient listener."

"Villain," cried Le Pluche between his teeth.

"As yet, very probably," said the other; "you always say that. Deuced quiet night though, so I could hear every word—all about the mock marriage, your ambitious views, &c."

"What the devil is that to you?" cried the clergyman, startled out of his propriety.

"A good deal more than you think," said Harry Morton.

"Do you intend to interfere?"

"No."

"Then what, in the name of all that is mortal, do you mean?"

"Why, I mean you to buy my silence."

"You would dare to betray me," muttered Le Pluche.

"Dare! ah! ah! ah!" shouted Harry Morton; "you ask me, the outlaw, if I dare betray you. What do I not dare to do, let me ask you?"

The Reverend Carleton Le Pluche muttered something to himself between his teeth, and moved to go.

Harry Morton seized him by the arm and detained him.

"Come, old fellow," said he, "that won't do; I want some money, so stump up and say no more about it."

"I have none with me."

"Then I will go with you."

"No—no; you cannot. I will not be seen with you in that dress."

Harry Morton was attired, as we have said, in a cloak, beneath which could be distinguished a costume which presented a queer mixture of the fashion of the day and that of a prestor.

"Ah! ah!" laughed the other, "you object to my theatrical costume. It is a portion of the property of my strolling playhouse."

"Still sinking deeper and deeper in the mire."

"Yes," muttered the other, "plunged into it by you. But, come, it waxes late; I want money. Give it to me."

Le Pluche thought a moment.

"I will give you nothing," he at length said. "I defy you."

And he again endeavoured to depart. Harry Morton once more seized his arm.

"Let me go," hoarsely cried the minister.

"Never!" said Morton.

"Then your blood be upon your own head," exclaimed Le Pluche, as he raised his hand to strike.

It was a lovely night.

As we have said, the clouds hung heavily over the landscape.

Lucy had long ago disappeared, so that there was no human being near to tell the tale.

The hand of Le Pluche descended rapidly, heavily—and heavily, too, fell the body of his companion into the Red Valley.

Not a cry escaped his lips: he fell, stunned and senseless, while the murderer rushed at headlong speed away, away from the scene of his crime, to take refuge from his thoughts in the quiet of the Parsonage House.

CHAPTER XLVIII.

THE MOCK MARRIAGE.

THE marriage of the Reverend Carlton Le Pluche with Lucy Cartwright was, as we have said, to take place at a little chapel adjoining a neighbouring hamlet.

It was, also, five miles from Flowervale; and the journey was made in a little cart, drawn by a mule belonging to neighbour Francis, who never suspected that, in the bearded dark-haired man in strange guise, he saw before him the new vicar who had excited so much turmoil in the neighbourhood.

The evening on which the extraordinary ceremony was to take place was calm and lovely.

Nature appeared to have paused in awe in order to witness the desecration of her temples by one of Heaven's own high priests.

Everything around the village reposed in the utmost serenity, and, as the cart wound its way through the green lanes and pastures, the breath of the newly-born Spring fanned the foreheads of the maiden and her betrayer, as if to lure her into his arms.

Of all seasons of the year spring time is the most joyous and exhilarating. It is like the spring time of life, full to overflowing of youth's beauty and glowing promises for the future. Full it is, too, of incentives to contemplation, as, says Lady Stuart Wortley, in her beautiful sonnet—

" Spring's golden sun is, in its evening hour
And tenderness o'er earth's new freshness broods.
That setting sun now bright'ning o'er the roods
Speaks still of change and parting with deep power,
And tunes the proud strain of our feelings lower;
Evening is the autumn of the day, and moods
Of graver vein, while still one thought intrudes;
Comes o'er our minds, when falls its golden shower
Of glittering beams around—and that one thought
Is of the passing of all earthly things.
Oh! this spring evening's sitting sun hath brought
Hints of calm wisdom to my soul, whose wings
At times though folded are full often taught
To soar where brightly play truth's hallowed springs "

They had just come to a turning in the road from which could be commanded a view of the little hamlet to which they were going when, from behind the hedgerow, started the figure of a man.

Both started up and looked at him with amazement.

Lucy, of course, failed to recognise him, while in his tall, powerful form, and strange forester's dress Le Pluche could not fail to recognise Harry Morton, his supposed victim.

"Ah! ah! ah! villain!" cried Morton; "so you thought to murder me, did you? but you see the blow failed.

"The devil, indeed, appears to take care of his own," muttered Le Pluche, gazing at him with blanched cheeks and starting eyeballs, and clutching a pistol convulsively in his hand.

"Well said," observed Morton; "but you can put up that pistol there, if it be not a trouble to you, for I don't feel in a humour to be trifled with."

"Nor I either," cried the clergyman, "so be off with you."

"Who is this man?" inquired Lucy, who stood pale and trembling, and clutching at the arm of her companion.

"A villain of the blackest dye," replied Carleton, "let us go forward."

And so saying he whipped the mule, who started forward at a rapid pace.

Morton, however, was in no mood to be foiled thus, so, leaping over the hedge, he rushed to the mule's head and stopped the cart.

"This child's play won't do for me, Le Pluche," he shouted. "I will spoil your game. Go not with him, lady. He is ——"

He could utter no more—the pistol was discharged full in his face, and he fell with a groan to the ground.

Le Pluche gave a lash to the mule, and they once more resumed their journey unmolested.

The little chapel was tenantless. No one came to the portal to welcome them. The Reverend Carleton Le Pluche seemed quite at home, however, and, opening the door with a key which he drew from his pocket, bade Lucy enter.

"Here at length we are," he said, kindly; "after all our mishaps we are arrived safely."

The chapel was buried in profound gloom.

It was an old and curiously-built place; and the windows were so small that scarcely a ray of light could penetrate into the interior.

Going up to the altar the clergyman lit a small taper, which shed a flickering uncertain light over the scene.

Then taking from his pocket a prayer-book, he proceeded to read aloud the marriage service —adapting it to the occasion—and then placing upon Lucy's finger a gold wedding ring, said,

"And now, Lucy, you are, indeed, my wife, although there are no witnesses."

"Hold, false priest!" cried a voice from behind the altar; "there are witnesses to this marriage." There, bloodstained and pale, Harry Morton stood before them with a man dressed in black, and another in the garb of a priest.

"Lady," he said, "here is a priest of the Roman Catholic Church who will inform you that the ceremony just performed is not binding, even if there were a hundred witnesses present."

"The young man speaks truly," said the priest, solemnly; "but now I will perform the marriage: and that, before two witnesses, will be binding."

"Never!" cried Le Pluche, retreating.

"What!" cried Morton, "you take a girl away from her home—at a time of night which will make her the talk of all Flowervale—and then, because you are called upon to make her an honourable woman, you refuse."

"I do.'

"Villain!" exclaimed the other; "did you not bring her here to marry her?"

"Yes."

"Then why not marry her now?"

"Because you would expose me publicly."

"Not so; we will not utter a word."

"You swear?"

"Then I will marry her."

"Come, then, my son," said the priest; "since you are resolved to act uprightly, I will marry you."

"Stay!" said Morton, advancing, and taking Lucy's hand; "stay; I have a word to say first, and, for my own part, I think we ought not to forget that this lady has also a word to say. This villain has acknowledged his villany; so that it may not be in accordance with her wishes to wed him now."

Lucy thanked him with a look.

"You will not marry him?"

"No," she said, firmly.

"But yet," said Harry Morton, "since there are two priests and two witnesses here why should there not be a wedding, after all? Lady, will you not take me for a husband?"

"You villain! never!" shouted Le Pluche.

"Stay, sir," cried Harry, laughing; "it is not your turn to speak. I don't want to marry you, but Miss Cartwright."

Le Pluche ground his teeth with rage.

"Lucy," pleaded Harry, "is it to be yes or no?"

"You do not wish to insult me, sir," said she, tremblingly.

"No; not for the world," cried he, vehemently. "Have I not saved your honour? and is it likely I desire to insult you?"

"But you are an utter stranger."

"Ah! I forgot!" he said, tearing off his hat and wig and his false moustache; "Do you not recognise me now?"

"Mark Brandon!" cried Lucy, and fell fainting, sobbing, into his arms."

"Can you forgive me," she said, "for forgetting you for such a vile wretch as that."

"Alas! Lucy," murmured Mark; "we all err sometimes. I forgive you, but I ask my reward."

"I will give it to you," said Lucy.

"Come, then," said Mark Brandon to the priest; "you are not here for nothing. Perform the ceremony."

"I forbid the marriage," cried Le Pluche; but no one heeded his words.

In ten minutes Mark Brandon and Lucy Cartwright were man and wife.

CHAPTER XLIX.

A SERPENT ON THE HEARTH.

WHILE the Reverend Carleton Le Pluche retired discomfited from the scene Mark and Lucy Brandon wended their way from the chapel to the village inn, where the former had taken up his abode.

Here they arranged their plans for the future; and it was decided that, for the present, Lucy should remain at her father's house.

Adam Cartwright was a stern man, and who could scarcely have forgiven his daughter's *secret* marriage with any one; but with Mark Brandon, *never*.

From early childhood Lucy and Mark had known and loved each other, and everyone, except Adam himself, saw how their companionship would end.

Mark Brandon won her heart, and told her father.

"There was no objection," said the old man; "none whatever, provided he could support her; but he must first carve his fortune in the world."

"That I will," cried Mark, enthusiastically; and, at the expiration of a month, he had bidden adieu to Lucy, to Adam, and to Flowervale, and, in a short time after, to the shores of England.

He was bound for India: to a merchant in which country he had received a letter of introduction from Adam Cartwright.

Time went on.

Letters of information were regularly received from the young man, all full of hope, and confident as to future success.

About a twelvemonth after his departure Adam Cartwright paid a visit to the metropolis.

To London he took Lucy; and during their sojourn there he became acquainted with a young man, a curate in one of the churches of the capital.

Adam Cartwright was a Dissenter; and the young curate, the Reverend Carlton Le Pluche, found no favour in his eyes.

He was a well-informed man, possessed of considerable conversational powers, and very soon began making himself agreeable to Miss Lucy Cartwright, and gradually was recognised as a regular visitor during the six months in London.

One evening, as the two were sitting in their little drawing-room, Adam Cartwright chanced to remark:—

"What a long time it is, Lucy, since we heard from Mark Brandon."

Lucy blushed deeply—painfully—as if that name recalled to her the fact that she was but ill-repaying his devotion and his love.

"It is a long time—very long," she replied; "but, perhaps, he has been very, very busy."

Le Pluche had often heard Brandon's name mentioned; and knew well who and where he was, and in what relation he stood to Lucy.

"Mr. Cartwright," he said, fidgetting about uneasily in his chair, "I could tell you the reason of his not writing to you if I should not hurt your feelings."

Lucy turned ghastly pale and gazed beseechingly at her father, who said, "Pray, tell me, sir; it will be doing a service both to me and my daughter."

"If he has acted unworthily it will be better to hear it from the lips of a female than from the lips of others."

A sarcastic smile played over the face of the young clergyman as he said—

"Mark Brandon is in prison!"

"Great Heavens!" cried Adam Cartwright, "you are surely misinformed?"

Lucy sat still, very still, gazing with fixed eyes upon the man who was destroying the fabric of her happiness.

"No, sir, I am not misinformed," continued the Reverend Carleton le Pluche; "the firm in whose service he was employed traded under the name of Carleton, Gavin, and Co."

"They do."

"Mr. Carleton is my cousin," said Le Pluche; "it is from him that I gained my information."

"Then I must e'en believe it," murmured Adam, who seemed crushed and overwhelmed by the intelligence; not, however, so crushed and overwhelmed as Lucy, who sat in her chair apparently transfixed with terror.

"I am afraid," said Le Pluche, rising, "I have done wrong: I really wish I had not spoken. Miss Cartwright, pray forgive me."

"Forgive you, sir?" exclaimed Lucy; "I do most heartily. I am glad to hear of his misfortune that I may write to comfort him."

"Never!" cried Adam; "never! If Mark Brandon is a felon my daughter shall never speak or write to him again."

"Father," said Lucy, "you are unjust, unkind. You have never even asked his fault; you do not even know whether he has been committing wrong, or has been wronged by others, and yet you condemn him."

"True, Lucy, true, I was unjust," replied her father; "condemn no one unheard. Mr. Le Pluche, I cannot hear more to-night; let me see you to-morrow; and, in my study, Lucy and I will hear from your lips the story of his trial and condemnation."

The Reverend Carleton Le Pluche then left the house, and left father and daughter alone.

"Oh, father!" cried Lucy, "I cannot, I dare not believe him guilty."

"Time will show," said he, solemnly. "Good night, and may Heaven bless you and comfort you."

CHAPTER L.

THE FATAL ERROR.

THE Reverend Carleton Le Pluche was punctual to his appointment.

Mr. Adam Cartwright and Lucy awaited him in the study, but scarcely greeted him as he entered, so great was their agitation and their fear.

The indignation of the former had, in the first instance, fiercely raged; but was now absorbed in deep grief and sympathy.

"Well, Mr. Le Pluche," said Adam, placing a seat for the young curate, "I must e'en welcome you, though you bring us but sad and sorrowful intelligence."

"Yes, indeed, sir," observed Le Pluche, as he seated himself and clasped his hands over his knees. "Yes, indeed, sir, it is sad and sorrowful. So much so, truly, that I sometimes think that I have been wrong in telling you."

"No—no," cried Cartwright, "I esteem it

only as the action of a friend. Only a friend would perform such an action.''

A spasmodic smile played over the features of Le Pluche as he said,

"You do not flatter me, sir. I am a friend to you and yours, and hope to be still nearer and dearer to you; I will, therefore, at once proceed to my tale.

"Mark Brandon, as you know, sailed for India with a letter of introduction to the firm which I mentioned.

"At first he went on satisfactorily; but becoming enamoured" — here he glanced at Lucy—"of a wealthy young lady, he misappropriated some of his masters' money, and was soon discovered."

"For what purpose did he use the money?" inquired Adam, in a cold, hard voice.

"In making presents to the young lady," continued the Reverend Carleton Le Pluche.

"And how did you learn this?"

"Through my cousin, as I said.''

Adam sat silent for a few minutes. Lucy sat drenched in tears.

At length the father spoke.

"Lucy," he said, calmly, "we have heard of Mark's unworthiness — his disgrace and his punishment. Let his name never more pass our lips. Poor Mark! I had hoped for a better fate for you; but henceforward his name is a thing of the past."

"Stay, father, you are unkind — unjust," cried Lucy. "You have seen no proofs—you have heard of this only from the lips of one person. Not that I desire to place any reflection on the veracity of Mr. Le Pluche, only I think, before we condemn him, we should either have his own word for it or see some documents."

"You are right," said Le Pluche. "You are right Miss Cartwright. I will now deliver to you the letter which he charged my cousin to forward to you."

And he handed to her a letter.

It ran thus :—

"DEAREST LUCY,—Yes, I will call you so once more, although you are, indeed, lost to me for ever—not through any fault of yours, my injured one; but through my own reckless and terrible folly. I came here to carve a fortune for you and me. I have, instead, achieved our mutual ruin. Others will, no doubt, carefully describe to you my crime. I need not, therefore, tell you more than that I am here in prison, convicted of embezzlement. Forgive me, and, if you can, forget me—for I am no longer worthy to be called

"Your own
"MARK BRANDON.''

There was no doubting the writing—the signature was perfect.

Adam Cartwright bowed his face down, and Lucy left the room to seek the solitude of her own chamber.

The Reverend Carleton Le Pluche soon followed her example.

Mark Brandon ultimately came back from India—a ruined man; and sought confidently the object of his early love.

Here he was refused admittance, and, for a long time, no letter was allowed to reach Lucy.

When at length he found means to forward a missive it was one full of promise and passion, which found its way readily to her heart.

She believed his innocence, though no one else did.

But before he had arrived she had committed a deadly sin.

For sin it is to sacrifice a heart—a true, manly heart—at the altar of selfishness and hypocrisy.

The Reverend Carleton Le Pluche declared his attachment, and pressed her hard to accept him.

He had the cunning of a serpent, but he had the cloak of religion to conceal his wiles.

He was successful; and the Reverend Carleton Le Pluche was the accepted suitor (though secret, by *his* wish) of Lucy Cartwright.

CHAPTER LI.

DEATH IN THE HOUSE.

IT was some twelve months after the secret marriage of Lucy and Mark in the little chapel of the hamlet.

Nothing had transpired.

Lucy had certainly been *absent from home* with a female relative; but, otherwise, things had progressed much in the ordinary course.

We turn now to the house of her old father, who was rapidly sinking to his last sleep.

There was no hope.

The curtains were drawn aside to admit to the dying man a last glimpse of the brightness of a summer's day. There was a deathlike stillness in the house : the doctor and the clergyman had left, and Adam Cartwright lay in his last agony, in the presence of his two daughters.

Lucy and Helen Cartwright were twins; but in that one circumstance alone was comprised their similarity the one to the other.

With rich, golden hair, large, deep blue eyes, and a ruby-lipped mouth—whose every movement seemed to breathe happiness and good nature—Lucy presented a most perfect contrast to the black-haired, stern-eyed girl who was her junior by an hour only.

The expression which, at this terrible moment was visible on their countenances was quite sufficient to prove how entirely opposed were their natures.

Lucy was sitting by the pillow of the dying man, holding his hand, wiping his mouth as the foam of agony wreathed over his lips, and stifling within her the convulsive sobs which might, she feared, even then disturb him, who, alas! was too far sunken to notice any outward thing.

Helen sat at the foot, opposite her sister, gazing calmly, coldly, with compressed lips at her father; and ever and anon directing a glance of scorn, not unmixed with envy, at the sister who was immeasurably superior to her in affection and in grace.

Not a word was spoken.

Half an hour passed. The old man was quiet as the grave.

"It is all over," said Helen, rising quietly; "come."

"All over? What, what, do you mean?" cried Lucy, gazing with a kind of puzzled fear at her sister.

"Do you not see, Lucy, that your father is dead?"

Even when we anticipate evil it is none the less terrible when it comes upon us. The shock, though she knew well it must come, arrived *still* too soon for her to be reconciled to it.

Lucy burst into a passionate flood of tears, and threw herself on her father's body.

Helen looked at her with a mixture of annoyance and scorn; then, seizing her tightly by the arm, she half led, half dragged her from the chamber into the drawing-room.

Lucy was overwhelmed, crushed with grief, and replied only with convulsive sobs to the words of consolation which were offered to her by the numerous friends who had flocked in to express their own grief, and their sympathy with hers. Helen, with majestic self-possession, answered all they said. She shed no tear, but she was pale, very pale; and her mouth ever and anon worked convulsively. This, by strangers, was imagined to be an evidence of profound and well-concealed grief. They were wrong. It was no regret for the past that caused her emotion but a terrible anxiety for the future.

Both sisters spent a restless night—that first night with death !

The one, bathed in tears, lay in a restless fever on her bed; the other, oppressed by dark and terrible emotions, fostering blind and torturing fears in her heart, paced the room from evening until the mellow light of morning streamed in upon her sleeping sister.

CHAPTER LII.

THE WILL.

WHEN Lucy awoke in the morning she found Helen already dressed, and sitting gazing anxiously out of the window on the grounds in front of Adam Cartwright's mansion.

Adam was a wealthy man; he had, therefore, no friends, but many parasites; and among those parasites none was so persistent and so rapacious as Helen, his younger daughter.

She was now in a fever of anxiety.

She was in love: if the passion of one so selfish and so cold-hearted can be called love, or believed to be love by any sophistry of the heart.

Ralph Fenwick was a handsome fellow—full of spirits, strong, manly, active, just the sort of man to excite the passions of a woman like Helen Cartwright.

But he was ambitious; full of enthusiastic hopes for the future, and desiring a fortune to work out plans which his head had matured after long years of study.

Helen had promised him this fortune; and she must have it.

It was with terrible anxiety, therefore, that she awaited the hour when the old man's will was to be read.

By her instructions it was to be read that day before assembled friends. Her instructions, we say, for though the younger sister she assumed already the position of mistress of the house in all things except in attention to its master.

* * * * *

The company assembled.

Friends and curiosity-mongers gathered round the deathbed.

There were present Helen and Lucy Cartwright; Mr. Jonathan Stickfast, the lawyer; Mr. Ralph Fenwick, Helen's *inamorato;* the Reverend Carleton Le Pluche, and others.

Mr. Jonathan Stickfast was a peculiar man. He never liked to be hurried.

Instead of opening the will immediately he laid his hand upon it; and gazing at the company with glasses on nose, said—

"This, then, is the will."

"Yes, yes," cried Helen, impatiently.

"Just so. And you wish it read now?"

"I should think you were aware of my wishes, Mr. Stickfast," said Helen, "before you entered the room?"

She acted as spokesman.

"Just so," said Jonathan Stickfast; "then I will read it."

"Yes; pray do so at once."

"Just so," continued the lawyer, "just so. You are not in a hurry I suppose? No; then I'll wipe my spectacles."

After having accomplished this feat he placed his handkerchief carefully in his pocket, and raising the parchment slowly from the table, unfolded it as slowly, and once more gazed at the company.

"Ladies and gentlemen," he said, solemnly, "I am now about to read the will."

"Lord have mercy on me !" cried Helen, "I've no patience with the man."

"But, before doing so, ladies and gentlemen," continued Jonathan Stickfast, "before doing so, ladies and gentlemen, perhaps you will allow me to—to wipe my spectacles."

And he proceeded again, methodically, through the undertaking.

"Really, sir," cried Helen, "if your eyes are so dim, perhaps Mr. Fenwick or Mr. Le Pluche had better read it."

"It is usual in these cases," said Jonathan Stickfast, "for the lawyer to read the will. Therefore, with your permission, ladies and gentlemen, I will proceed to do so."

"This is, &c.," went the will—a most extraordinary will it was.

We will simplify it.

"I, Adam Cartwright, being at the moment of making this my last will and testament in the possession of my full senses, do hereby, in the presence of competent witnesses, will and bequeath to my beloved daughters, Lucy and Helen, the whole of my property, whether in land, in money, or in securities, to be divided equally between them.

"This property, so equally divided, is to be enjoyed by them until such time as they, being married, have children by their husbands.

"Then the daughter who has the first child is to receive five-sixths of the said property, on condition that the child assumes the name of Cartwright."

"Such, gentlemen and ladies, is the last will and testament of Adam Cartwright," said Jonathan Stickfast.

"My kind, kind father !" said Lucy.

"Thank Heaven !" cried a gentleman, rising from his seat. "My name is Brandon; this," pointing to Lucy, "is my wife, and this child," he added, as a servant entered the room, carrying an infant, "this is the heiress."

"But she is a girl."

"No matter; the will is erroneously worded, and merely says 'child.'"

"However, it is of no use; there is a codicil, gentlemen," said old Jonathan. "If you had kept quiet while I blew my nose I could have stayed all this unnecessary agitation."

"A codicil ?" cried Mark.

"Just so."

"Does it set aside this will ?"

"Just so."

"Then, in Heaven's name, read it !" cried Lucy.

"Just so," said Jonathan Stickfast, "I will do so if you will allow me."

The will was dated April —, 17—, the codicil December, in the same year.

It ran thus—

"I, Adam Cartwright, being at this moment in possession of my full senses, do hereby revoke all and every bequest made in my will dated April —, 17—, and dispose of my property as follows :—

"The whole of my property, whether in land, in money, or in securities, I bequeath to my two daughters Lucy and Helen, to be equally divided between them; five-sixths of the said property to be given after marriage to that daughter who shall first have a child, provided that child assume the name of Cartwright, and provided neither of my daughters are married or have issue at the time of my death, in which latter case my property is to fall to that daughter, who, at the period of my death, shall be unmarried, &c. &c. &c."

Witnesses—JONATHAN STICKFAST, Attorney.
The REVEREND CARLETON LE PLUCHE, Vicar of Flowervale.
EBENEZER RUBRIQUET, Attorney and Clerk.

For a moment all was as still as the grave.

A smile of triumph was on the face of Helen Cartwright; a smile of pleasure on the countenance of Ralph Fenwick.

Ralph was an implicit believer in Helen's truth and love.

Not so Mark Brandon.

Casting one look—half of inquiry, half of consolation at Lucy—he said,

"Mr. Jonathan Stickfast, at the present moment, and in the presence of the dead, I shall not say much. I will only give notice that as the husband of Lucy Cartwright—now Brandon —I shall oppose the operation of that codicil, because I believe it to be a forgery."

"Really now—really now," began Jonathan.

"Let us say no more now; let the future decide," said Mark Brandon.

CHAPTER LIII.

UN CHAT POUR UN RAT.

AFTER the funeral was over, and a decent time had elapsed, notice was served on Mr. Jonathan Stickfast, forbidding him to act upon the codicil which had been appended to the will of Mr. Adam Cartwright.

Two days after the serving this notice the Reverend Carleton Le Pluche called at the house where Helen now resided alone, with the exception of her servants, and requested an interview.

A smile of bland self-gratulation was on his lips, as he said, at the same time pressing Miss Cartwright's hand warmly.

"Our plan has succeeded well, Helen, has it not?"

Miss Cartwright started at the tone of his voice, but answered—

"It has succeeded very well; and you shall be rewarded."

"I trust so for your sake and mine," he said, taking a seat. "I wish to speak to you on important business, Helen, so pray grant me a few moment's conversation. I have much to tell you, and much to hear."

Helen sat down mechanically.

"You see, Helen," he said, taking her hand, "you see I am very ambitious—very."

"I know you are."

"And you can satisfy my ambition."

"I, sir? I really do not understand you."

"Not understand me! It is surely very easy of comprehension."

"I cannot see it."

"Well, then, I will explain. I am ambitious, as I have said. I wish for distinction in the Catholic Church : if I had your fortune I could obtain it."

"Ah! I think I see your meaning now," cried Helen.

"It is well."

"Yes. You want distinction ; and, in order to obtain this distinction, you would have money. You shall have it."

"Pardon me, madame," said Le Pluche, "you entirely misunderstand me. I do not want money alone—I want you."

"Me!" exclaimed Helen, turning slightly pale. "You are surely joking?"

"Not joking—not joking by any means. I mean this, that I wish to marry you, because I want your fortune."

Helen trembled.

"Mr. Le Pluche," replied Helen, "I will hear you no longer upon this subject. What you propose can never be. I love another."

"Love—ah! ah! ah!" laughed the Reverend Carleton Le Pluche; "that is excessively good. Love now-a-days is so exceedingly rare that it is fine to discover one who possesses it. But, seriously speaking, I must have you, because it suits my purpose."

"Villain!" cried Helen, frantically, "how dare you address me in this manner?"

"How dare I, ask you? but stay, I will not parley with you at all. I wish to marry you; and that, too, secretly: and if you refuse I will expose all."

"Cold, calculating wretch!" muttered Helen between her teeth.

"Of course I calculate," said he, "of course I do. But we now understand each other. Good morning."

CHAPTER LIV.

THE TRIAL.

IT was a celebrated trial in its time, that of Brandon v. Cartwright.

The very mention of its probability excited considerable interest; and the day which saw it on the list of causes was one of tremendous struggling and confusion in the court.

It was a trial, as it were, between two sisters.

Lucy would willingly have foregone her claim, but Mark would not allow it.

She had been wronged, grievously, treacherously, and he was determined she should be avenged.

So the two sisters appeared in court that day.

The one whose deep mourning seemed to excite sympathy in the minds of all stood beautifully, tearfully, in the witness box; the other, dressed in the height of fashionable black, seemed to gaze around her with a look, whose every glance seemed to say—

"Possession is nine points of the law."

In five minutes the public had formed their decision; and they seldom err, however much juries may blunder and prevaricate.

Witness after witness was called, until at length Mark Brandon himself stood in the witness-box.

"I object to that man's appearing," said the opposing counsel."

"When you are speaking of gentlemen," said his antagonist at the bar, "be pleased to use more gentlemanly language."

"I object to Mark Brandon's appearance as a witness," persisted Serjeant Merryweather.

"And pray, sir, may I ask why?" asked the judge.

"Because, my Lord Judge," replied the lawyer, "because he is a convicted and escaped felon."

There was a tremendous sensation in the court at these words.

Every eye was directed towards the couple.

Lucy stared as if suddenly bereft of sense. Mark Brandon's cheek was blanched, and his eyes were glassy, but he answered—

"That man is a lying scoundrel, my Lord. I was convicted of misappropriating money while in India, but I was released after a few weeks' detention. Serjeant Merryweather, although he is the counsel of a forger, need not, therefore, vent his spleen upon others, nor try to prejudice my case by destroying my character!"

"Mr. Brandon," said the judge, "you may rest assured that any remarks of this kind will not be allowed to prejudice the case, which is less yours than your wife's. However, I shall feel it my duty to order your arrest after the trial if Serjeant Merryweather perseveres in asserting that his statement is correct. It is out of no disrespect to you, but in the performance of my duty."

"My lord," said Mark Brandon, "I blame you not. It is at the door of Mr. Merryweather and his client that this foul injury lies."

"I do persist in my statement," continued the counsel. "I call upon you, my lord, to order his arrest."

The court had, as it were, held its breath suspended during this colloquy.

But when the judge gave the order for the arrest of Mark Brandon, it was impossible to restrain the expression of the feelings of the audience.

A loud and universal hiss arose, which the officers could not, in newspaper phrase, instantly suppress, but were obliged to allow to continue.

The trial then proceeded. Fresh evidence was adduced, and the jury retired.

Mark Brandon sat with Lucy in the witness-box—their hands clasped anxiously together—their hearts beating in tumultuous unison.

The jury at length entered.

Everyone hoped it would be for the plaintiff, but few believed it.

It came soon enough—it was for the defendant, but left room for a new trial in case of further evidence.

A groan of disapprobation followed the declaration of the finding of the jury.

Lucy went home to her solitary abode—Mark Brandon once more to the gloom and misery of a prison.

———

CHAPTER LV.

WATCHING UNDER THE WINDOW.

IN order to prove the innocence of Mark Brandon it was necessary that a communication should be made to his late employers in India, and that an answer should be received.

This involved a delay of many, many months.

Lucy Brandon determined, therefore, to execute a plan for his escape from England. Well knowing his proud spirit she was well aware that it would be useless, and even worse than useless, to allow him to suppose that he was indebted for anything to her sister. She therefore went one day, quietly and alone, to her sister's house, and represented to her her position. She asked for no allowance out of the vast fortune which was by right her own—she asked only for one thousand pounds to enable her to leave England with Mark, and never intrude upon her again.

This was exactly what Helen wanted.

She instantly consented to give Lucy the money—gave it to her, hypocritically kissed her, expressed tearful regrets that they should ever have been bad friends, and wished well for her future.

Lucy received all her good wishes quietly, though, of course, unbelievingly, and immediately started off again to London.

Mark Brandon was confined in the old prison of Rossiton Fields.

The rules were not very strict at any time, and with prisoners such as Brandon they were scarcely enforced at all.

Of course he was only detained on suspicion; and, though not possessing his freedom, he was not treated in the same manner as the other prisoners.

Lucy was his constant attendant at Rossiton Fields; and after a month had gone by, and nothing whatever happened out of the ordinary way, the turnkeys scarcely ever noticed her entrance or departure.

They became used to her, and at length—oh, happy moment for her!—they ceased searching her.

No sooner was this precaution omitted than advantage was taken of the omission.

A file was introduced into Mark's cell, or, rather, barred room, and, bit by bit, a strong long rope.

Every night an attentive ear could have distinguished the regular rasping of the file against the iron bars of the prison window, and the late working, by a flickering light, of a prisoner, in a prison where every candle was extinguished at nine o'clock, m.t.

The wished for time came at last.

Lucy had been duly informed of the proposed attempt; and round the corner of the street waited anxiously, tremblingly, in a fly.

Time went by as quickly as usual to others, but to her its wings seemed clogged with lead.

An hour, which appeared a long, long night, passed, and still no Mark.

Another hour, and still no sign.

Lucy could wait no longer.

Bidding the man await her return she slipped cautiously round the corner of the street, and crossed over into the shadow of the road, where she could command a full view of the prison.

There certainly was Mark's room, but there was no light—no indication of light.

She gasped with fear.

What if she were discovered? Would it not be almost an evidence of her guilt, and would not all future attempt at escape be rendered useless?

In the middle of her anxiety and fear, however, a faint glimmering light could be distinguished at the window of the prisoner's room.

Then she could plainly see him remove the bars, and cast out the rope which she had carried up to him day by day, so patiently and anxiously.

She knelt down and prayed for his safety.

At length he slid out of the window, grasped the rope, and swung himself hastily down.

He had hoped—he had prayed that he might arrive in safety at the bottom.

He found more!

As his feet touched the ground a soft arm encircled his neck, warm lips were pressed to his, and a sweet low voice murmured—

"Thank Heaven, my own Mark, you are again free"

"God bless you, my own wife," said he, as they hurried together away from the prison wall, away, away, to freedom, and, as he thought, to poverty.

CHAPTER LVI.

WAPPING OLD STAIRS.

THE fly, containing Lucy and Mark Brandon their child, and a young servant maid, was, soon rapidly making its way among the vehicles and passengers towards Wapping Old Stairs.

For a week before this event a curious kind of craft had been lying out in the river nearly opposite the stairs.

No one knew, or at least cared to know, its errand.

Some said it was a smuggling vessel; some a revenue ship "in disguise," but no one troubled his head to find out the truth.

Michael Spenaro was an Irishman, who passed himself off as an Italian.

It is a curious national feeling of the Irish that they are ashamed of their own country and their own countrymen.

No one is so great an "anti-repaler" in England as your Cockney Irishman.

No man so inveterately determined to be taken for an Italian or a Spaniard as your brogue-bedevilled bogtrotter.

Michael Spenaro knew well the nature of good "whiskey toddy," and confidentially I may inform my readers that the various little spirit shops round the neighbourhood of Wapping were always supplied with a first-rate article, invariably dating its in-coming from the day after Spenaro's arrival in the river.

Lucy had accidentally become acquainted with this man, who was a sweetheart of one of her father's servants, and used regularly to correspond with her.

Michael's heart was decidedly in its right place, whatever his other failings might be, and whatever his dislike to his native land.

He at once embraced the enterprise and the purse which Lucy offered to him.

"Arrah, madam," said he; "sure and I'll do everything I can for you, for the sake of dear Hannah, jewel. Though I've never seen the master, I'll fight for him like the devil.'

And so they came down to Wapping Old Stairs.

The "Caravella" received them on board.

The night waned and Michael Spenaro set sail.

"Sure and I'll not be after risking being in the neighbourhood long," said he, as he ascended to the deck to give his orders. "Not that I mind much about the little drop of the 'crater' that I brings over from that bastely bogtrotting place they call Ireland, for the use of these poor human beings here in Wapping. But what should I be done to, ochone, if they found me aiding and abetting in the escape of a returned convict?"

This was intended for consolation; though certainly a very curious kind of comfort.

The "Caravella" cleared safely out of the Thames, sailed merrily along the Channel, and they arrived at Calais.

From thence they proceeded to Paris; and thence again they proceeded until they arrived at Genevento, a little village nestling at the foot of the Appenines.

CHAPTER LVII

UNDER THE APPENINES.

GENEVENTO was a town nestling in the very bottom of a deep valley under the Appenines.

It was protected, on one side, by the lofty rocks; and, on the other, gazed out upon the waters of a huge lake, whose untroubled waters smiled under the influence of a sky and sun—the one of undying blue, the other of unfading brilliance.

Up above the town, on the rocky slopes of the mountains, towered an ancient castle, under whose walls was hidden a half-ruined convent, which nestled there as if for protection.

The town itself was straggling and ill-built, but, from a distance, presented a very picturesque appearance.

The streets were irregular, and sometimes very dirty.

Some of the roads skirted the edges of deep precipices, or climbed up the steep hills.

Everywhere you seemed to climb after what you wanted.

You climbed up to the town ; you climbed up its streets ; you climbed up to the houses by long steps like stone ladders ; you climbed up to the fortress and the convent.

Mark Brandon and Lucy, however, did not betake themselves into the town of Genevento proper.

They located themselves in a little house upon the mountain side overlooking the town and the lake, and surrounded by large gardens, and boasting, also, a considerable amount of meadow land.

With the produce of these gardens and grounds, and the various appurtenances of an "English farm," they were enabled to enjoy a very comfortable subsistence.

The thousand pounds which Lucy had extracted from her sister's fear, if not her kindness, enabled them to stock the place well, to dress well ; and, in fact, to be perfectly independent of the world.

Mary—their first and only child—grew apace, every summer ripening her into fresh youth and beauty ; her fair skin, blue eyes, and piquancy, exciting the admiration and wonder of all who saw her toying with her fond parents among the olive trees and citron groves of La Belle Roche, as the little estate was called.

Mary Brandon—or Cartwright, as she was more properly called—was the very image of her mother ; and, as she grew up, attracted the notice and intense admiration of those young men in Genevento who had fortune sufficient to allow them to think of a girl who appeared to them to possess considerable property.

She was not likely to desire a life of single blessedness.

She had a good specimen of married life in that of her father and mother.

Mark and Lucy were uninterruptedly happy.

No allusion was ever made by him to the error she had committed in so easily giving him up for the wily parson Le Pluche ; while she, moreover, scarcely ever alluded to the sad events in India.

These events he thus explained.

When he first went to India he was entrusted with duties which necessitated very little care, and caused him to wear still less responsibility.

But, as the confidence of his employer increased, he had the handling of considerable sums of money, as much as twenty thousand pounds being at his disposal, on some occasions, for weeks together.

The junior partner, Mr. Frederick Blakesley Carleton, was rather a fast youth : addicted to all kinds of pleasures, and very little suited to the routine of a counting-house.

He received his fair proportion of the profits ; but he always lived beyond his means, and was constantly pestering Mark Brandon to lend him money. Certainly he was a partner in the concern ; but, somehow or other, it did not quite coincide with Mark's notions to lend it to him.

"It's all right," Carleton would say, "it's all right, old fellow. It's as much my money as the old buffer's" (meaning by this friendly term his senior partner).

Mark's answer for a long time was invariably—

"As it is as much your money as his, why not ask him to lend you some ?"

"Oh ! he's a queer odd fish," said Frederick, upon one occasion. "Do, there's a good fellow—stump up five hundred. I only want it until Monday (this was Friday) ; if I don't have it I shall be in a devil of a scrape. It's an affair of honour, you know ; and my name will be all over the place."

Well, after considerable parlance, Mark let him have the money.

The time passed on leaden wings and Monday came, but no return. Mark made repeated applications, but all with no effect, until at length, at the end of the quarter, he had to make up the accounts.

One item appeared—

"Lent to Mr. Frederick Blakesley Carleton, on March 15, 17—, £500."

"What is the meaning of this?" said the senior partner, entering his room with a very pale and stern face.

"I am very sorry, sir ; very sorry," replied Mark, "but Mr. Carleton said he was so very hard pressed, and promised so faithfully to return it in a few days, that I could not refuse."

"Come, come," said the old man, "this sort of thing will not do with me. It's of no use trying to deceive me. What have you done with the money ?"

Mark Brandon stared at the man in complete bewilderment.

"I tell you, sir, that I lent it to your junior partner."

"Mr. Carleton knows nothing whatever about it."

"Does he dare deny it?" cried Mark, "I have his I.O.U. in my desk."

The old man was staggered.

"Well, well, if you can show me that, you know," said he, "it's all right"

Mark Brandon opened the desk.

The I.O.U. was not there !

This only served to irritate the senior partner. He offered to pardon Mark if he would confess he had purloined the money. Mark would not sacrifice his honour to his liberty, and went to prison. It was spoken of in tones of deep anger by the judge, and Carleton was regarded as an injured man. He was sentenced to two years' imprisonment, and escaped.

To find the I.O.U. appeared impossible, and, therefore, it was impossible to prove his innocence.

———

CHAPTER LVIII.

THE MURDER ON THE MOUNTAINS.

THE Convent of St. Heloise was more like a castle than the house of a religious order.

Its battlemented walls, its high turrets, its ever-barred portal, and its dark windows, seemed to indicate rather a place of defence against tyranny. It appeared, indeed, like a continuation of the old fortress.

From the town of Genevento to the Castle of St. Angelo ran a winding and rocky path, ever and anon running through a tiny green pasture, and then hanging, as it were, over the edge of a steep and fathomless precipice.

Mark Brandon was a restless man.

He was not one who cared to lead this quiet life.

Not that he was tired of Lucy, not that he longed for the companionship of others, but he was not ready to sacrifice his portion of the world because the other portion was blind and unjust.

He was often, in the summer evenings, to be found wandering along the precipitous path above all alone, and gazing, as it were upon nothingness.

It was a dark night. Rather darker it was than the evenings on which Mark Brandon generally took his solitary rambles.

It was only eight o'clock, and a summer's evening, too; but the sun had sunk behind a bank of clouds, and seemed as if it had set before its time. Lucy was very affectionate to him at parting that night—more so than usual.

"Anyone would think, love," said he, laughing, as he patted her cheek fondly, "anyone would think that I was never to see you again."

"Don't go on the mountain to-night, dearest," said Lucy, "I feel a strange presentiment."

"Nonsense, dearest, nonsense. My head is hot and feverish. I will not be long."

So Mark Brandon went along the rocky path toward the Convent of St. Heloise.

Just as he reached that portion of the road which led from the castle to the convent a monk stood before him.

"Benedicite," said he.

"Benedicite," replied the holy man.

"It is a strange, dark evening," said Mark. "You must be dull, very dull, pent up amid the mountains here, more especially in these gloomy nights."

"No, no, we are not dull," said the monk, with a strange gleam in his eye. "We, too, have our pleasures. Have you lately arrived from England?"

"No; I have been here many years."

"Then you escaped from prison."

"What mean you?" cried Mark, turning deadly pale.

"I know you. You are Mark Brandon the felon. I was the Reverend Carleton Le Pluche. I am Brother Antonio, and shall be Cardinal Antonio."

"Rascal! consummate, base rascal, I will yet publish to the world that history of your forgeries and seductions which I once threatened.

You are too dangerous a man to allow abroad without some one to watch over you."

They had unthinkingly passed the convent. The mountains towered bleakly and blackly before them.

"You still hate me, then?" said Le Pluche.

"I do."

"So do I you. But you are helpless. I have you in my power."

"What mean you?" said Mark.

"This," answered the priest.

The night was dark, the road lonely. They had passed along a winding, unprotected path, which almost overhung the convent.

When the priest uttered this last word he sprang upon his unsuspecting companion, and plunged him headlong over the rocks.

There he lay, a mangled, disfigured corpse.

"Ah! ah! ah!" laughed Le Pluche; "at last, at last. There is now no witness of my crimes. Hey, for the cardinal's hat!"

Then suddenly assuming a look and voice of grave concern he rushed down the path shouting,

"Help! help! help!"

In a few moments the convent gate opened, and some monks and servitas issued forth.

"Alas!" cried Le Pluche, "Mr. Brandon, of Genevento, has fallen over the rocks, and is killed."

Mark was soon conveyed within the holy precincts, and his wife was sent for.

The next night saw him buried in the vaults of the convent.

Lucy and Mary, with black robes over them, knelt by the side of the grave. A voice which the former fancied she recognised read the service, while the abbess honoured the ceremony by her presence.

Why, no one there knew; but certainly she appeared affected in a most extraordinary manner by the sight of the corpse, and was even so overwhelmed that two nuns were obliged to support her, the one on one side, the other on the other.

At a time of less sorrow and less excitement, Lucy might have recognised in the priest the Reverend Carleton Le Pluche, in the abbess her sister Helen.

And so the murder remained for ever undiscovered.

CHAPTER LIX.

THE BIRTH OF LOVE.

ABOUT six months after the melancholy death of Mark Brandon a stranger arrived at Genevento, and made his way straight to the house of the widow and her daughter.

He represented himself as an Englishman, though his swarthy complexion, combined with dark eyes and almost black hair, seemed to indicate a native of another clime.

He entered the house as if entering the house of an old friend.

"Is Mr. Brandon within?" he said to the servant.

"Surely, sir, you have heard?"

"Heard what?"

"Of Mr. Brandon's death."

"Great Heavens!" cried the stranger; "is he dead? I have come all the way from India to see him."

"It is, indeed, too true, sir, said a voice, thick with emotion, as Lucy came out into the hall. "Will you not walk in?'

"Oh! Madam," said the stranger; "his death at any time would be sad, indeed; but how terrible is it now."

"Why so, sir?"

"Because I have come to bring him the proofs of his innocence!"

"Prove his innocence, say you?" exclaimed Lucy. "Are you really serious?"

"Serious, Madam?" said the stranger gravely; "I should scarcely jest upon such a subject."

"How did you become acquainted with my husband, sir," inquired Lucy.

"Well, Madam," said the new-comer, seating himself; "you see I am still very young. I am but twenty-five years of age.

"Mark Brandon left India seventeen years ago; so that when he quitted that country I was but eight.

"I was engaged in the counting-house of Messrs. Carleton and Co. as a kind of errand boy.

"Being the son of a friend, I had the run of the house, and ultimately obtained a clerkship.

"Mr. Brandon used to be very kind to me; and I, who as a boy, disbelieved the fact of his guilt, as a man, was convinced of his innocence.

"Murder will always out.

"Those who do evil invariably make absurd provisions for the future.

"Instead of destroying the I.O.U. he had given to Mark, and afterwards purloined, Frederick Carleton kept it.

"I succeeded ultimately in making an inspection of Mr. Frederick's papers; and in a corner of his desk discovered the I.O.U.

"You may be sure I lost no time in showing it to the senior partner, who immediately recognised it as the writing of Frederick Carleton.

"He was a just man, and very little time was permitted to elapse before Mark Brandon's innocence was proclaimed throughout the colony, and the guilt of Frederick Carleton equally fully established.

"The announcement gave no small degree of pleasure to the residents of the colony, among whom your husband had formed many acquaintances and obtained many friends. It was proclaimed publicly in court, and spread like wildfire among all classes.

"Carleton himself was called upon to take his trial for false imprisonment; but, of course, was *non est* when the day came on.

"I immediately conceived the idea of proceeding to England, whither I knew Mark had sailed, and of proclaiming his innocence, at the same time that I made an anxious search for the treacherous Carleton who, it is believed, is secreted somewhere by his cousin, a reverend humbug, who styles himself the Reverend Carleton Le Pluche.

"Such, madam, is my story. I have arrived too late."

"Not so, my dear, kind sir!" exclaimed Lucy. "If you wish to carry out your work of benevolence you can do much. I have a child."

"Indeed?"

"Yes, a daughter. About her I should like to speak to you."

"Certainly, madam."

Upon a subject such as this Mr. Stanhope Devereux had not the slightest objection to hear her out.

Mrs. Brandon then proceeded to narrate the history of the Reverend Carleton Le Pluche, the scene in the Red Valley, the forged will of her father, and so on.

Mr. Devereux listened with earnest attention.

He smiled as she finished speaking, and said, with an odd expression,

"Introduce me to your daughter, Mrs. Brandon, and I will settle this affair for you. It will, however, be necessary for us all to return to England. Miss Brandon, or rather Miss Cartwright, shall yet be an heiress. But I wish to remain here six months first"

Mrs. Brandon naturally thought this an odd speech; but then the stranger was an odd man.

CHAPTER LX.

EXPLANATIONS.

MR. DEVEREUX might have been an odd man, but he was certainly an attractive, a handsome, and an intellectual one.

He was well read.

This was certainly an attraction.

There is no greater in the minds of women who possess any degree of refinement.

Handsome men and handsome women are very attractive to look at; but, after all, they are the merest butterflies of the hour.

Mary Brandon was fascinated with him at once; and it was not very long ere her mother could see that they were beginning to be more to each other than so short a knowledge might be supposed to warrant.

One evening, in autumn, Mary and Stanhope were walking down by the mountain side.

It was three months only after their first meeting.

"Mary," said he, as they took a seat on one of the iron benches by the road side, "I have much to say to you. May I speak openly?"

"Yes."

"You know my friendship for your father?"

"Yes, sir, and thank you for it."

"Come, now, before we go any farther, don't call me sir, but Stanhope. You know, I suppose, that we are going to England?"

"Yes, Stanhope."

"And the purpose of our visit?"

"Yes."

"You will then be a prize fit for a king."

"Yes, my money, but not myself."

"Well, do not marry one. Who knows you are wealthy?"

"Why, Stanhope?"

"Because he will never make you happy."

"How can I conceal my wealth?"

"Marry before you obtain it."

Mary blushed.

"Well, well," said Stanhope, laughing, "I will speak more explicitly."

"When I first saw you I loved you. I have not known you for a lengthened period; but during that period we have been more together than many others whose courtship has extended over years. I have seen you every day—I have seen you in sorrow and in happiness. I know your worth. *I can offer* you nothing in return but a true and honest heart. Will you be my wife?"

"Yes."

That word was short.

But oh! how significant.

A moment passed, in which Stanhope Devereux gazed fondly, proudly on her face, and she was clasped lovingly to his breast.

For a few minutes neither spoke. Their hearts were too full to permit of their uttering their thoughts; and they sat there gazing at the sunset in silent happiness.

The great sun set in red glory behind the western mountains.

The country lay in hushed beauty.

The gentle air scarcely moved quick enough

to disturb the autumn leaves, which lay in brown eddies round the roots of the scantily planted trees.

The night birds began to swoop over the valley.

But still they sat there, hand in hand.

If ever two hearts were bound together in true unison then these were so bound.

At length they rose up and returned home.

When they arrived at Belle Roche their smiling and happy countenances quickly betrayed their secret.

"You see, Mrs. Brandon, I have now accomplished my object—Mary has consented to become my wife. There is no longer any necessity for us to delay our departure to England.

"Make her happy," was all Mrs. Brandon's answer.

A fortnight saw them in London; and two days after saw him in the private room of the well-known attorney, Mr. F. A. Davit.

*   *   *   *   *   *   *

In the diligence, on their journey to England, was a man who kept his face concealed as much as possible from the gaze of all observers.

When people show an evident desire not to be looked at they are certain to excite a considerably greater amount of curiosity than if they spoke and acted like ordinary mortals.

Nature will not assist us, moreover, on every occasion in keeping up a character. It was, therefore, not to be wondered at that this individual suffered himself to lapse into a sound sleep.

His cloak dropped off—his hat fell back—whether accidentally or not I cannot say.

No matter how the discovery was made, the fact was still the same.

Lucy saw before her the Reverend Carleton Le Pluche.

CHAPTER LXI

"IN THE CLAW OF THE LAWYERS."

A MISERABLE den, designated "A Lawyer's Office," is the scene before us. It should be termed a vault, for there, day after day, were hopes buried, the aims and objects of years of silent struggling and sad suffering for ever consigned to an oblivion which could never be fathomed.

The extravagant furniture consisted of one large desk, which time had long tarnished, two mouldy chairs, supported upon the most lame of understandings, an antique basket, revelling in its tatters, while cobweb curtains hung in uncertain folds down the walls and around the shattered window.

But one object of interest stood in the foreground of this dismal picture. For thirty weary years had this necessary piece of animated furniture occupied the same post in this dreary chamber of dark deeds.

This object was the lawyer's clerk.

Still, in these thirty years, he had never looked more haggard, worn, more miserable or more seedy than on this bitter winter's morning, with fingers chilled by the damp, December air, and face rigid with cold.

This vampire of the law was about four feet six inches in height, broad shoulders, but with a body balanced upon so agile and frail a pair of extremities that his movements w re characterist'c of the wolf, while his head, covered with grizzly grey hair and shaggy brows overshadowing the restless orbs, gave to every gazer the instantaneous idea of the daring and invincible lion.

Still the student of human character—he who has learnt thro' life the invaluable philosophic lesson to trace the actions to their springs, the motives of the heart, would look more than once upon the map-like face of this minion.

Job Watcher (such was the noble bequest of the godfather and godmother of our subject) had a countenance which a chameleon might envy. He never looked twice alike, and never could his features assume the same aspect for two consecutive moments. His eyes would now flash with a scrutinizing and searching gaze, terrible to the beholder, and, ere the gazer could look again, they were kindling with humour, and brilliant with a glee that spread electrically a sympathy between the seen and the seer.

A brow massive and square, a spacious chamber where a brain, uncurbed and restless, created people and plots as wild and fantastic as ever subtle imagination ruled by avarice and unprincipled ambition could conjure from a vitiated talent.

Mr. F. A. Davit was very attentive to his clients; and the consultation between him and his new friend, Mr. Stanhope Devereux, was long and serious.

The attorney said that the case was a good one.

He was very sharp at discovering a good nest, and always knew when, and how far, he might rob it.

He immediate y was aware of the substantiality of the case opened up to him by Stanhope Devereux.

"My dear sir," observed he, as he bowed his new client into the street; "my dear sir, it is a clear case. There is no doubt about our success."

But then Mr. F. A. Davit always said it was a clear case.

Mr. Stanhope Devereux knew that he always said this kind of thing; but he certainly saw the necessity of pretending to believe him in earnest. He pretended so well that Mr. F. A. Davit did think him in earnest, and rubbed his hands as he saw him depart, saying,

"Ah, ah! a likely one that! I think this is a good case."

CHAPTER LXII.

THE SECRET SIGN.

STANHOPE DEVEREUX was confident of success, but he went about the business in a peculiar manner.

Mr. F. A. Davit was also confident of success, but he also went about the business in a peculiar manner.

Stanhope told the lawyer his own name, and the name of his *protège*, but he assumed before the world the cognomen of Captain Jackson; while Mary Cartwright called herself Jane Brandon; and Lucy, with a wig and a widow's cap, passed as her bereaved aunt—Mrs. Plumtree.

Black Harry—Captain Winterton's companion —happened to be the occupier of the house, and passed as her uncle and the brother of Mrs. Plumtree.

It was the first object of the attorney to see the will.

Not that he saw any necessity for it, but Stanhope Devereux had some strange idea about it.

Jonathan Stickfast, the lawyer of the opposite side, was dead, but had bequeathed the business to his son, Timothy, who was as great an oddity as his father.

To this limb of the law did Mr. F. A. Davit betake himself one morning, accompanied by Stanhope Devereux, alias Captain Jackson.

"Good morning, brother," said Timothy Stickfast, "have you come to turn over a troublesome client to me."

"Not so," said F. A. Davit; "I have come to you because I knew you could gratify a peculiar whim of his."

"And pray what is that?" inquired Stickfast, eyeing both curiously.

"Well," said the cautious attorney, "I am not certain whether you will comply with his request."

"Certainly I cannot," said Stickfast, "if I don't know it."

"Well, then, you see he wants to see the late Mr. Cartwright's will."

"What for?" asked the other lawyer, in a suspicious tone.

"Curiosity," said F. A. Davit; "simply curiosity, I assure you."

"I don't keep my chambers open to gratify people's curiosity," growled Stickfast, leaning back, buttoning his coat up to the chin, and thrusting his hands deep into his breeches' pockets."

"When I said curiosity," said F. A. Davit, "I meant anxiety."

"Why the d—l don't you say what you mean, then?" cried Stickfast.

Stanhope thought that he had remained silent quite long enough during this squabble between the lawyers. He, therefore, resolved upon interposing a few words.

"Perhaps, sir," he said, addressing Stickfast, "perhaps, sir, I can explain matters myself better than my solicitor."

"Devilish hard job if you couldn't," growled Timothy.

"Well, then, in the first place my name is Jackson."

"Just so."

"I am a relative of the Cartwright family— distant you know."

"Very much I should think," said Timothy.

"Not so distant as you imagine," said Stanhope. "Well, my object in desiring to look at the codicil is to convince myself by ocular demonstration that my friend and relative really did leave his property in the extraordinary way in which he is said to have left it."

"Do you doubt my word, sir?" cried Timothy, in great wrath.

"Not in the least, sir," replied Stanhope, blandly; "not in the least. But you may easily imagine that one interested in the family as I am should be loth to believe without real proofs in his relative's insanity."

"Insanity!" shouted Timothy Stickfast, "insanity!"

"Yes, sir, insanity," quietly returned Stanhope Devereux.

Timothy Stickfast thought a moment, and then, resuming the seat from which he had leaped in affright, said quietly—

"Come, come, young gentleman, this won't do. There is no holding a commission *de lunatico inquirendo* on a man who has been dead these sixteen years."

"Not at all—not at all! I wish for no such thing. It is, besides, an impossibility. I merely desire to look at it once."

"And you will return it to me safely?"

"Upon my honour," said Stanhope.

"*I* will answer for the safety of the document," said F. A. Davit.

Stickfast slowly unlocked a bureau, drew out the will, and placed it in the hands of Stanhope Devereux.

Before he did so he cast on it a fond glance, as if parting with a dear friend.

Stanhope hastily unfolded it and read it.

"Exactly," he said, when he had perused it, "exactly. 'This, the last will and testament of Adam Cartwright, leaves all the property to his daughters, to be equally divided between them: the whole to go to that daughter who has a child first.'"

"Just so," remarked Timothy Stickfast, "but then there is a codicil on a separate sheet of paper."

"I thought so."

"Yes, that codicil deprives that daughter who has married at the time of his death of all participation in the property."

"Indeed. Let me look at that, also," said Stanhope."

"Certainly," returned Stickfast, "here it is."

Stanhope gazed at it a moment, and then, when no one was noticing him, held it up to the light.

"Ah! I thought so!" cried he, enthusiastically.

"Thought what?" cried Timothy, in great perturbation.

"Nothing," said Stanhope.

"What did you mean by that exclamation?" said F. A. Davit, as they left the house.

"I have found, by accident, that the will is a forgery, and I can prove it!"

CHAPTER LXIII.

THE THWARTED ASSASSIN.

It will be remembered by my readers that the will was made in April, and the codicil was dated December, in the same year.

We allude to this fact again in order that our readers may understand the manner in which the trial was conducted.

Mark Brandon was certainly dead, but his enemies recognise in Stanhope Devereux his ghost, or rather his avenger.

Notice of a new trial was served on Mr. Stick-fast, and public curiosity was on the tenter hooks of expectation.

It was the evening before the trial.

A dark evening was it, and the scene in a gloomy street.

Not that it was in a very bad neighbourhood.

But it was lonely, and dull, and dark looking.

The oil-lamps were few and scant.

The people had all retired, and very few lights appeared in the windows.

It was not, as I have said, a low neighbourhood.

It was not a very respectable one either.

Queer characters could now and then be seen lurking about at the corners of the streets, and peering up at the windows.

About twelve o'clock a man in a cloak slunk round the corner of one of the roads, and after gazing anxiously up and down the pavement, ensconced himself behind one of the stone pillars of the houses.

He seemed intent upon some important business, which, by the glare of his eyes, would appear to be of no good import.

He appeared anxious, and perplexed, and eager: and ever and anon, as the clock of the neighbouring church tolled the quarters, he would stamp his foot savagely and mutter—

"Will he never come?"

At length his wish was gratified.

Round the corner of the opposite street came another figure, which crossed over to where he had ensconced himself.

As he passed by the ambush he was caught by a strong arm, and almost turned round.

"What now? Who are you?" cried he, "who dares assault me thus in the streets of the capital?"

His hand was on his sword, and the very devil in his eye.

"I assault you not," announced the other. "I wish you no harm. I desire simply to speak with you on business."

"Well, then, out with it," replied his companion, "for this is no time, nor have I any inclination to parley with you."

"Your name is Stanhope Devereux?"

"It is."

"You come from India?"

"I do."

"*You* are the principal witness in the case which is to be heard to-morrow. I mean Brandon v. Cartwright."

"I am."

"Have you any personal interest in the matter?"

"None."

"Then why, in Heaven's name, have you anything to do with it?"

"Because I think it is everyone's business to defend the innocent and oppressed against the oppressor."

"Ah! just so—a matter of pure philanthropy. Well, well, that is all very good, and so on, but it has no depth. Now I, young man, have a peculiar interest in this trial; you have none."

"Query," thought Devereux, but he answered not.

"You do not answer. Well, silence intimates acquiescence. *I* will guarantee you the sum of ten thousand pounds if you will leave England to-morrow morning before the trial commences."

"There is no use in wasting any more time," said Stanhope, "I unconditionally refuse."

"Then I can't help you," cried the other, in a hoarse voice, and whistled loudly.

Four men walked immediately from behind the dark corner of the street, and seized upon Stanhope, who stood perfectly still, and apparently petrified with astonishment.

"This is treachery—foul treachery," said he loudly, as a hackney carriage came round the corner of the street, and he was bundled into it.

The man in the cloak entered with him, with two others: the rest mounted the box.

"Well, my fine fellow," said the man in the cloak, "you had better have accepted my offer."

"Why?"

"Because you will now be *put out of the way*, instead of going off quietly."

"You dare not injure me."

"Dare not! Look at me. Do you recognise me?"

"No."

"I am the Reverend Carlton Le Pluche."

"Whither am I bound?"

"To the river."

"And then?"

"Ask not."

"I will not. I will tell you. I am bound to my own house, and you are bound thither with me."

The false priest sprang up.

"My friends," he said, addressing the two others, "what is this farce?"

"Tragedy you intended it to be," said one, "but it is a farce."

At this moment they drew up at the door of a mansion.

The men alighted first, and the Reverend Carlton Le Pluche was placed in the middle. He tried to bolt, but was seized by strong arms, and hurried up stairs, grinding his teeth with rage and terror.

CHAPTER LXIV.

THE TRIAL.

THE trial came on at length which was to decide, at once, the innocence of Mark Brandon and the fortune of Mary Cartwright. Outside the court house was a bustling, shouting crowd. Everybody was anxious to get in, and no one could succeed.

As we have said before, everyone felt an interest in the trial.

No one had any sympathy with the defendants; everyone's wishes was with the plaintiffs. Every-one believed the will to be a forgery.

Every circumstance connected with the case served to render it an object of interest to all.

The fact of the real plaintiff being dead; the fact, also, of a mysterious witness having suddenly turned up from India to prove Brandon's innocence, the beauty of the heiress, the circumstance of the property being seized by the Roman Catholic Church, each and all tended to cast an air of romance over the case which rendered it peculiarly attractive.

The crowd, therefore, inside the court was quite as anxious and bustling as the one which waited and shouted outside.

The counsel engaged for the opposite side was the celebrated Sir Frederick Fulsyman, Bart., who never took anything but a safe case in hand. His manner in court was, in general, very pompous and blustering, and he generally assumed the manner of a judge rather than that of an advocate.

On the side of the plaintiff was engaged a Mr. Edgar Fames.

He was a popular lawyer was this Mr. Fames.

He was a rattling sort of fellow, full of life and humour; carried everything before him; earned no end of money, and spent more.

He gambled like a duke, dressed like a prince, and looked like a butler.

He was an M.P.—member for a popular borough—was a reformer, an anti-everything repealer, and the biggest libertine in London.

However, he was a famous pleader, though no particular lawyer, and so Stanhope Devereux engaged him as his counsel.

Stanhope was the first witness called. He gave his evidence clearly and concisely, and politely refused to be brow-beaten by the lawyers. He observed several times "that he was aware that he was upon his oath," "that he knew the value of telling the truth," and laughed at the mellifluous absurdities of his own counsel and that of the opposite party. A tremendous sensation was created in court when he described the treacherous attempt of assassination made by the Reverend Carleton Le Pluche; but still more when he said himself to the judge,

"My lord, it will be unnecessary to call my witnesses to prove this will a forgery, because I have certain proofs in my possession."

"If you had positive proofs," said the judge, "why did you allow the trial to proceed?"

"I imagined it was necessary, your lordship,"

said Stanhope, "to comply with all the requisitions of the law. However, I need not delay the court any longer. If I am allowed to have the will and codicil in my hands for a few moments I can prove the latter to be a forgery."

"There can be no objection," said the opposing counsel, "there can be no objection to Mr. Devereux looking at the will and codicil, providing he returns the documents in safety."

"I pledge my word," said Stanhope.

The deeds were thereupon handed to him.

Stanhope, first of all, took the will, and, looking at the signature, said:—

"You will observe, my lord, that this will is dated April 17th, 1794."

"It is," replied the defendant's counsel.

"And the codicil," said Stanhope, is dated 17th December, 1794."

"You are correct again, sir," said the counsel.

"Well then, my lord," said Stanhope, triumphantly, "I must also beg you to observe that the paper on which the codicil is written was not made until the year 1795."

A thrill of delight seemed to penetrate the audience as Stanhope Devereux uttered these words.

"I do not understand you," said the judge; "you must explain yourself better than that before your statement can be taken as evidence."

"Observe, then," said Stanhope, holding the document up to the light, "the water-mark on the paper bears the date 1795."

A loud burst of applause resounded through the court—an evidence of popular feeling which the officers could not possibly repress.

"The evidence is undoubted," said the judge, "the jury must find a verdict for the plaintiff."

Of course there were many objections raised on the part of the defendants, which were at once, however, overruled by the judge.

The verdict was given, the case apparently settled, and only the usual formalities to be proceeded with when Lucy Brandon's counsel rose, and said—

"There is one other case, my lord, that has to be proceeded with to-day.

"It will be remembered that one of the witnesses to the forged document was the Reverend Carlton Le Pluche.

"He was the principal deviser and author of the forgery.

"This man, my lord, is a convicted felon, for the result of this day's trial will be to commit him to prison for a capital offence.

"But, before this trial comes on, I wish to make a few remarks on the recent conduct of this person.

"The object which the forger had in view in fabricating this will was to obtain for the Catholic Church the whole of the Cartwright property.

"For seventeen years that church has had possession of this property, while Le Pluche has been in possession of the person of the plaintiff's sister, Helen Cartwright. Immediately on discovery that Lucy Brandon had met with a friend who had undertaken to commence a renewal of the trial, Le Pluche set out for England from the convent of which Helen Cartwright is the lady abbess.

"Le Pluche, as may be imagined from his former proceedings, was not very particular by what means he obtained possession of the property.

"Searching some of the most hideous dens of this metropolis he discovered a band of ruffians who were ready, in consideration for a sum of money, to dispose of Stanhope Devereux by drowning him in the river Thames.

"Mr. Devereux however was, by the aid of an intimate friend, made aware of the existence of the plot before they had time to put it in execution.

"On the night on which the murder was to have been committed Le Pluche laid in ambush for Mr. Devereux, and, with the aid of the ruffians before mentioned, seized him in the public streets of the metropolis and forced him into a hackney carriage, which, instead of taking them to the banks of the river, drew up at the door of Mr. Stanhope Devereux's own house.

"It may be easily understood that the scoundrels that could be bribed by one party could be as easily bribed by the other, and the Reverend Carlton Le Pluche therefore discovered that he had been caught in his own net.

"The vagabond is now in court, and could be produced for examination if your lordship so desires."

I shall not here pause to describe the further examination of Le Pluche, nor will it be necessary to complete the history of Mary Cartwright until the Blue Dwarf has carried out his intention of telling his own story to the occupants of the Great Rat Trap.

It would, indeed, be difficult to discover the events of her future life from those of the great atonement.

The evening at length arrived when the Blue Dwarf was to disclose to his prisoners the secret of his past life, and the mysteries of the birth of William Lennox.

Sapathwa himself sat upon a raised chair at one end of the room, and round him in circle were the happy family, who were thus compelled to listen to a narrative in which they were to play, comparatively, secondary parts. They were indeed a motley crowd, composed truly of patrons of almost all parts of the globe.

In front of the raised seats sat the prisoners, including the Duchess of Castella, Mr. James Tyrrel Blakesley, the false Sir Edgar Blakesley, Captain Frederick Winterton, the Hon. John, Pauline, and Slimy Jones.

Around the Blue Dwarf were grouped Leila, Lord Ernest Wyndham, Lillian, William Lennox, Mrs. Winterton, Captain George, and Lucy.

Joe Spriggins, in consideration for Lillian's feelings, was absent from the assembly.

Before the Blue Dwarf commenced his narrative Captain Frederick Winterton got upon his legs.

"I don't exactly see the reason," he said, "why we should have to suffer this infliction. You have done us sufficient injury already; you have no occasion to insult us."

"I do not desire to insult you" said Sapathwa, "on the contrary, I wish to explain to you the reasons why you are detained here, and why I, upon all occasions, set myself up as the champion of William Lennox's interests."

And so saying he settled himself to his work, and commenced as follows:—

AND HERE ENDETH THE THIRD BOOK OF THE BLUE DWARF.

BOOK IV.

THE BLUE DWARF'S STORY.

CHAPTER I.

CASTLE FERRY.

CASTLE FERRY stood upon a bluff headland on the Cornish coast, overlooking with its time-worn, and blackened walls the unfathomable billows of the sea. The ivy had claimed it for its own, and encircled it everywhere. It climbed round its base and round its battlements, it climbed over the ruins of the left wing; it crept in at the windows of the right wing; and impeded the swing of the massive bell which hung in the topmost turret. The very pillars which supported the tracea over the front portal were covered with gum parasite, which true to its character, was gradually eating away the mortar, and weakening the stonework of the building.

All that was habitable in Castle Ferry was the right wing and the little that still stood of the keep. From the tower at the corner of the wing a view could be commanded of the sea and the country round for many miles. Just below were masses of jagged rocks, which seemed to forbid all approach to the coast, which was ever covered by the white spray ascending from the breakers. The hill on which the castle stood sloped steeply down inland. The bottom was covered with green sward, as soft as velvet, but it suddenly lost this character, as it neared the spot on which the building rose, and broke off into sterile and rugged cliffs, which frowned darkly on and menacingly over the whispering waves, and the village which nestled on the other side. The castle, however, was far from being regarded as an inhospitable spot. Many were the mariners who blessed that light, which, far into the small hours of the night, shone hopefully over the dark waters, and guided the fishing boats to the snug little bay which lay not a quarter of a mile distant. That light was never wanting, but shone forth over the waves as regularly as the lamp of Eddystone Lighthouse.

The inmates of Castle Ferry were four in number; the " master," his son and daughter, and one servant. Jacob Spelthorne was a fine specimen of the old English gentleman, always attired plainly in a black velvet doublet and trunk hose of the same colour, with a black sash supporting his small and elegant sword. This plainness of attire was not wholly the result of simplicity of mind, it resulted also from the slender nature of his pecuniary resources. The years which had blanched these long and waving locks, which descended like snow over the velvet coat, had not rolled too peacefully over his head; scarcely one of them had seen him in the possession of more than was sufficient to procure the bare comforts of life.

Although the castle presented to the unobservant stranger every appearance of being the abode of persons of " high degree," the economy, which was the presiding goddess within, plainly displayed that few of the bountiful dispensations of Providence found their way inside its ruinous and desolate walls. Jacob Spelthorne was the descendant of a long line of honoured ancestors, but, though he could boast of forefathers who had fought at Cressy, and at Agincourt, who had carried the blood-red banner of Richard Cœur de Lion over the plains of Asia, and who had made the Scotch chivalry skip in many a sanguinary fray, those lands, albeit, had been theirs, and should have been had they not fallen into other hands.

In an adjacent county, Devonshire, there lived, in a mansion which looked a most extraordinary home, the fortunate possessors of those broad acres, which were, by right, the property of Jacob Spelthorne. Sir Marmaduke Mounteagle Selfe, of Selpyshe Hall, Devonshire, had, by some quibble of the law, come into possession of the estate, whose former owner had died, as was stated, intestate; and so poor Jacob Spelthorne resided in Castle Ferry, supporting himself and his daughter upon a slight independence, which was his only possession in this sublunary world.

Everything about the place spoke of departed grandeur. The walls were panelled in oak, and hung with rich but faded tapestry. The high-backed chairs of polished wood, with armrests of faded but once costly velvet. Everything of luxury and comfort, which scrupulous care and industry could produce, was there to be found. The wooden floors were scrupulously glazed; the arms over the great fireplace in the entrance hall shone brightly and merrily on t the well-swept floor boardings; the portraits of

the family, which, few and scant, ranged along the gallery, where stood the armour of bygone days, were carefully covered from the dust; and the domestic, old Jabez Fairlight, who moved solitarily about the old hall, appeared himself to be the incarnation of economy and thrift. He seemed to have imbibed from his master some of the family pride, and gazed as complacently at the grand old empty casque of departed warriors when he regularly dusted them on Saturdays as if they had once contained the craniums of memorable ancestors of his own.

Few were there among the inhabitants of the village near who were aware how many shifts the people at the castle were put to. There was much gossip about their seclusion; many surmises in regard to the absence of any servants save old Jabez; and many were the questions put regularly to the old man when he went on foot to the market to purchase comestibles for the family. But Fairlight was impenetrable, and generally put them off by muttering some things mysteriously between his teeth about the eccentricity of his master, and the aversion of his young mistress to society.

But there could be no room for suspecting the real cause of their quiet manner of living, for many were the visits which Ethel Spelthorne made to the poor of the village, with old Jabez, who generally had a basket with some delicacy for the sick, and some provisions of stronger quality for the poor and hungry.

CHAPTER II.

AN ARRIVAL AT THE CASTLE.

On the night on which our story opens the greatest excitement prevailed in Castle Ferry.

I do not intend, by the word excitement, to convey the idea that everybody in the castle was bustling about and making himself busy with anything but what was useful; but every one seemed to be on the tiptoe of expectation: Old Jabez could not rest quietly in the large stone kitchen, and even the huge buckhound, which usually lolled lazily before the fire, appeared restless and uneasy.

The old domestic would ever and anon rise and proceed methodically up the echoing corridors, until he arrived at the outer gate, and there he would stand sentinel for a few moments, the cool air fanning his cheek, and waving to and fro his white and scanty locks. The dog followed him mechanically in all his movements, pacing after him along the passages with the regularity of an automaton.

Evidently Jabez expected some one.

Leaning out of the low window of the apartment, which she and her father used as their sitting-room, was Ethel Spelthorne. She seemed like the centre-piece of a picture. Golden ringlets floated over a neck and bosom which would have been as fair and as pure as alabaster but that a faint rosy tint displayed the presence of life. Eyes of deep blue were guarded by long dark lashes, which drooped over the rosy cheeks. Arms as rounded and as fair as those which encircled Adonis were bare to the shoulder; and the heaving of the bosom beneath the tight corset showed that the clasping of the little hands was indicative of anxiety not unmixed with terror.

"Oh, father!" cried Ethel, "he must be on his way through Penrhyn Wood now. How dark it must be there; and look, how sombre the sky is. There will be a storm!"

Old Spelthorne rose, and putting his arm round the little waist of his pretty daughter, imprinted a kiss on her rosy cheek, and gazed out upon the scene before them.

"My dear one, I fear there will be a storm; but he must be nearly here now."

It was a cloudy night, and the moon, which earlier had occasionally peeped out of her bed-curtains, seemed now, at length, to have fallen asleep, and veiled her head altogether from outward things. The clouds poured across the heavens in a broken mass; and as they rolled onwards from the south-west they appeared like the billows of the deep, heaving and trooping tumultuously towards the shore under the influence of a mighty tempest. Almost everything that had life had ensconced itself within doors to escape the cheerlessness, if not the cold, moist air, without.

The only thing which appeared at all like life was the flag streaming from the keep of Castle Ferry, and the light glimmering in the room where sat the two watchers, whose forms were so hidden in the encroaching night that they were undistinguishable from without.

Presently, amid a hush in the moaning of the wind, a step was heard coming up the court-yard. The old dog set up a howl, partly of warning, partly of delight, and in another moment a well-known voice was heard exclaiming,

"Well, so I was expected, Jabez, even in this storm?"

"Aye, aye, sir," said the old man; "many is the watch I've kept on board 'The Dawn,' and it ain't likely I should cry off at the first sign of foul weather."

While the old man was slowly uttering these words the young man, followed by the great dog, bounded up the stairs, and in a moment was clasped in the arms of the old man and the young girl.

"Well, uncle, here I am, safe again!" cried the new-comer. "Bad news i' faith—no work, no pay; but still there are other things to be done besides being old Fairweather's scribbler. Ah, fair coz! pretty, arch, and loving as ever, I see," he added, as Ethel looked anxiously at him; "and you will find me just as great a scapegrace, though not a whit the less fond of your beaming, sunny, little face."

And imprinting a long kiss on her full, ripe lips, he sat down wearily in a couch by the fire.

"You must be hungry after your journey, Reginald," cried Ethel, "so no explanations until after supper."

And so saying the domestic fairy disappeared to give orders for such a repast as the old castle could afford.

Notwithstanding her injunctions, however, explanations were entered into while supper was being prepared.

"And what reason did old Fairweather give for dismissing you?" asked old Spelthorne, as he sat opposite his nephew by the side of the large wood fire, which blazed and crackled cheerily up the chimney.

"He said that strange events were about to happen, and that he could not trust a Spelthorne with his secrets. Now I never asked his secret, or even before he spoke suspected he was in possession of one; but I suspect now, though I trust my idea is a wrong one."

"What idea have you, then?" asked Spelthorne.

"I suspect," said Reginald, in a low tone, and looking round as if the very walls would betray him, "I suspect that a French invasion is to be attempted. Our king, they say, has rendered himself obnoxious to several of his best friends at the French Court, and that those will now desert him. He is well aware that none of your blood would remain quietly by while such a plan was being concerted and hatched by persons on this very coast; and not doubting that I should eventually discover and betray him, he deemed it prudent to be rid of me. Wherefore I am here."

"But did anything happen to arouse your suspicions? You say you did not suspect until he spoke of a secret?"

"True, uncle; but this speech of his conjured up strange ideas in my brain. I remembered, then, that he was in communication with persons abroad, and that the letters I wrote for him had frequent reference to me, whom he denominated never by any distinct name, but spoke of as one familiar to all. This correspondence would occupy days and even weeks at a time; and, indeed, my worthy patron appeared scarcely to employ his time on anything else."

The entrance of Ethel and Jabez, bearing covers of various kinds, interrupted the disclosures of Reginald Spelthorne, who exclaimed gaily,

"Truly a more sumptuous greeting than ever awaited me at Fairweather's. This be thy reward, fair hostess," and so saying he imprinted a loving kiss upon her lips.

"Nay, nephew!" cried Jacob; "if thou art so fond of courtship thou wilt grow weary of matrimony. But, truly, this is scarcely a beginning to warrant any very bright prospects for you, my children. I am growing old, and I would gladly see you settled ere I die. Have you no knowledge of good elsewhere?"

"Fairweather," cried Reginald, at the same time quaffing a cup of sparkling cyder, "did not forget me when I departed. He gave me this rouleau of cash, and three letters of introduction to friends in London—the one a deacon, the other a lawyer, and the third an antiquary. The latter being more in my way, I think I shall essay for it. Truly, Ethel, this venison pasty is delicious."

"Nay, coz, thou art over anxious for thy

repast. Your hunger seems to overwhelm all other considerations. What, think'st thou, am I to do when you are in London?"

These words, spoken half playfully, half sadly, caused a flush to pass over the young man's handsome face; and taking the girl's lovely head between his hands, he gazed fondly on her, and said,

"Ethel, dearest, I must go to London to win you. You will be always with me even though I am away."

"And you with me," she murmured softly, as she looked fondly at the manly face which beamed down humbly, frankly, lovingly upon her.

Oh! could she have penetrated the future even for a few short months.

———

CHAPTER III.

THE SELFES.—GOING AWAY.

IT was with mingled feelings of pleasure and sadness that Jacob Spelthorne thought of those youthful days which the presence of Reginald and Ethel conjured up before his imagination. He had all his life been an unfortunate man.

His youth had been chequered and fitful; he had early lost his wife, who had left him but one pledge of affection, and died in presenting it to him; and since then his career had been marked—first by a ruinous and unsuccessful lawsuit with his wife's brother, Sir Marmaduke Selfe, and then by long and dreary days of privation. To educate, and properly bring up his only child, Ethel, old Jacob had sacrificed everything—as help came to him from Selfysh Hall—and it was only lately, when the earnings of his nephew Reginald, who was an orphan, were thrown into the scale, that the people at the castle were enabled to maintain the common necessaries of life. Jacob's brother, to whom Selfe Hall and Castle Ferry belonged, died in a state bordering on imbecility, and was induced to make a will bequeathing everything to Sir Marmaduke and his heirs, leaving all Castle Ferry and its waste and barren lands for poor Jacob, whose delicate health prevented his following any avocation. It had been the object of the lawsuit to prove that a subsequent will had been made; but this attempt failed. The will itself was not to be found. Two witnesses were sworn, and deposed to the fact that Fortescue Spelthorne had made a will bequeathing everything but Castle Ferry to Jacob; but the lawyer who drew it up was nowhere to be found, and the cause failed. Jacob had married Fanny Selfe without the consent of her family; and Sir Marmaduke chuckled over his success as a revenge upon her husband. Reginald's father, who was the third brother, died penniless, leaving a holy task to him to provide for his favourite brother, Jacob, if his strength and fortune enabled him to do so. This task he performed first of all from love for his dead father. He had now a more powerful incentive still—he loved Ethel.

Reginald's presence at Castle Ferry inspired everything with life for awhile. The old man was happy in seeing the radiant faces of the lovers, who for a time forgot how little in life they had to anticipate save the strength of their own affection; while even old Jabez Fairlight and the dog were twice as sprightly as was their wont. But all things must have an end. While Reginald tarried at the castle resources were getting low; and at last those loving eyes, which greeted his arrival with smiles, had to watch his departure with tears. The old servant, and Ethel, and the dog accompanied him to the "Dog with Two Heads," where the "Express" to London, in the shape of a lumbering old coach and four, *whirled* him away from them at the rate of some ten miles an hour. Ethel returned with swollen eyes to Castle Ferry, while Reginald gazed from the top of the old coach at the receding turrets of that dwelling which contained all that in life was most dear to him.

"Sad thing, sir," remarked a voice near him, "sad thing to leave friends; but what, with our hard

'Parting is such sweet sorrow,
That I could say good-bye until to-morrow.'

"Cheer up, then, even though thy sorrow is great."

At any other time Reginald would have resented such familiarity, but anything at the present moment was a relief for his thoughts, while the voice and the manner of the speaker struck him as being peculiar and interesting. He was certainly not a common mortal, though his dress was of the most ordinary kind, and his skin not of the cleanest.

"You speak truly, sir; but yet a long parting is even worse than a brief one. It only feeds our grief."

"The best way to calm one's grief is to out with it. Let not concealment, like a worm in a bud, feed—but stay, I cannot say damask—feed on thy pallid cheek."

The manner in which this was said was such as to provoke a laugh even from Reginald in his moodiness.

"You seem to be well versed in the sayings of the Bard of Avon. Truly, sir, you cannot be a follower of Thespis?"

"Such, kind sir, is my vocation. I prithee pardon me if I have been too free. I will make amends, however, upon the first opportunity by drinking your health in a cup of sack. I will reserve myself and ask no more questions. Troublesome times these, sir."

The extraordinary change in tone in which the speech was uttered convinced Reginald that, with all his eccentricities, his newly-formed acquaintance had still much talent for his profession, and he entered with considerable interest into conversation with him. Before they had passed the first stage he had offered to befriend Reginald in London; and when they descended to rest at the "Three Boars" at P——, they were the best friends in the world.

"My name, sir," answered the actor, in reply to Reginald's query, "is Joseph Tanacourt—but call me Joe, sir, plain Joe; 'what's in a name,' &c."

"Well, then, Joe," said Reginald, "since you allow me such freedom of speech I may e'en tell you I have but little knowledge of London."

"Ah!" said his companion, "'tis bad; you are going to put your neck into a noose without being aware whether it will be drawn tight or not. You are brave, sir; very brave."

This was said affirmatively, but still interrogatively.

"Brave," said Reginald; "Well I don't know that I ever thought of that. Bravery is one thing you know, kind sir; but there is another thing, which is still better, and that is an utter ignorance of that thing which men call fear."

"Well said—bravely said," cried the actor; "but you know nothing, you say, of London—nothing whatever."

"Scarcely anything—scarcely anything whatever," returned Reginald.

"Worse than nothing—far worse than nothing," replied Tanacourt. "'A little knowledge is a dangerous thing,' and so on"

"It is; you say truly: but you are well-versed in the geography as well as the manners of the metropolis, I doubt not."

"Well, now," said Joseph, haughtily, and stroking his chin; "well, now, if I say I am not I lie; if I say I am I lie again; it is something between

THE BLUE DWARF.

the two. I am tolerably versed—moderately, and will undertake to see you are well housed, and not robbed. Will that suit you?"

"Right well; and if I can—"

"Say nought about it, sir, as you would not offend me. I will none of it. For what is it? 'Tis trash, 'tis something—nothing: 'twas yours, 'twould be mine, and would be slave to thousands,' to paraphrase my favourite poet. But if you will grant me your esteem—your friendship—then should I be right glad."

"I think thee an honest fellow," said Reginald. "I will be your friend, though my right hand, except in fighting thy battles for thee, will be of little use."

"'Cry not havoc, nor let slip the dogs of war,'" cried Tanacourt, "I like not battles. I am a man of peace, sir; a man of 'the piece:' a piece, in fact, of the mimic world, part and parcel of men's amusement. I'll not fight."

"So I will for thee. But come, the coach again awaits us."

CHAPTER IV.

THE FIRST SCENE IN THE BETRAYAL OF A HEART.

"HUMANUM EST ERRARE"—it is human to err.

A saying, oh! how trite: but oh! how true, and ever applicable!

Reginald and Tavacourt arrived in London.

Both were laden with the necessity of earning a livelihood: but one was laden with the necessity of earning a livelihood for another—of easing another's heart, of easing another's sorrows, and drying another's tears.

The metropolis of the present day, teeming as it does with life, instinct with a thousand ever-repeated pangs, the home of millions scrambling, fighting after money and fame, is, of course, far different from that into which, at the close of the last century, Reginald was ushered by his theatrical friend.

But still it was even then far different from anything which a young man in the heart of a country district had ever seen or hoped to realise.

The noisy, bustling, hurrying throngs which rushed along every street astonished, and bewildered, while they pleased him.

"Truly," he said, "they are as busy as bees!"

"As busy, verily," replied the actor, "but far different, for bees work for others, nor begrudge to others the fruits of their labours, whereas here each works for himself: each rides over the other—each rises on his fellow's ruin."

"You draw a gloomy picture of London life," said Reginald, "you almost make me fear I am not strong minded enough."

"Nay, say unscrupulous," urged Tavacourt.

"Well, well," laughed Reginald, "I will say incapable of battling with the dweller in this vast ant-hill."

"Never fear, never fear," said the player: "'faint heart never won' &c. Keep in the right path, and 'tis hard if there be not a golden stream at the end of it. 'The darkest day has ever brightest morrow.' But see, here is the place where I propose you should stay for the night, and, if you like, for good."

So saying he led the way into a small hostelry in Queen-street, a middling-class locality, frequented much at that period by lawyers' clerks and second-class writers."

"Dame Margaret," said Tanacourt, "behold me!"

The remark was unnecessary, inasmuch as Dame Margaret was already eyeing him with a benevolent expression of countenance; but then Joseph always liked to be "scenic" in the same manner as every pettifogging little aristocrat says "announce me" whereever and whenever there is an occasion.

"What, Joseph!" cried the hostess, coming forward and embracing the actor in a most decidedly affectionate and alarming manner. "Who'd 'a thought o' seeing you?'

"Not you, I reckon," muttered Tanacourt, with, as he would have expressed it, "bated breath;" "not you, I should imagine. But I thought of you. 'Absence makes the heart grow fonder.' I remembered you and your pretty face, and have brought you as pretty a young gentleman as you could well wish for to make love to you."

"Augh! I've no patience with you," said the dame, with assumed indignation. "Young sir," she added to Reginald, "excuse my manner of address, since this rude fellow has not thought proper to inform me of your name. But, young sir, does it please you to stay with me awhile?"

Comparing her words with the merry twinkle in her eye—the dame was only eight-and-twenty—Reginald was at first doubtful what the lady meant, but he at length answered—

"It does so. If you can accommodate me with a lodging I shall be truly grateful."

"That I will, right willingly," replied the dame, laughing at his demure reply, "even though you are introduced to me by such an ugly and disagreeable specimen of humanity as this Joseph Tanacourt."

Joseph laughed benignly, as he answered—

"My dear friend Reginald, pray enter behind the bar, Dame Margaret is pleased to jest."

"Marry come up, then," said the Dame, "I jest not with such as you."

"Nay, not with me, but with my friend."

"Do you bite your thumb at me, sir?"

"No; but I bite my thumb. 'Tis all the same you know. Pray enter, be not bashful: but pave your way as I always do by saluting the fair lady." So saying, he set the example by implanting a hearty smack on the Dame's cheek.

"Manners!" cried she, "the young gentleman first?"

But Reginald was not satisfied with the cheek —he pouted out her full red lips, and implanted a long clinging kiss upon them.

"He's worth twenty of Joseph," said the Dame, as she drew the sack for her customers.

"And now, then, to business," said Tavacourt, as, pulling his chair up to the fire, he lit his pipe, after a long draught of the grateful liquid. "And now, then, to business."

"Certainly, business first, sir," said Reginald

"Say not so—say not so. I will see that you have some little pleasure as long as I am with you," replied Joseph; "but, *imprimis*, have you any money?"

Reginald coloured slightly, and then laughed heartily.

"Truly," said the player, sententiously, "truly it is a home question; but it is an indispensable one. Come, say frankly; for I ask not from curiosity, I assure you, but from friendship and a desire to serve you."

The tone in which this was said was so free from the usual affectation of the actor, and so full of sincerity, that Reginald was touched.

He held out his hand, and grasped that of his newly-found friend, while he replied, in a voice full of emotion,

"I believe you, Tanacourt—I believe you. I will trust you with a secret which my pride would have prevented my revealing to any but one with whom I felt a sympathy. I am very poor."

"An universal failing," remarked Joseph, "which you propose to remedy. How?"

"I am to be the secretary to an antiquary."

"An antiquary! Shells, and fossils, and cobwebs; Roman coins, and Egyptian mummies! Ye Heavens defend us! Young man, you have mistaken your vocation."

"How so?"

"Verily it is so. You are born to be an actor."

Reginald laughed long and loudly.

Tanacourt sat unmoved until he had collected his cachinations, and then observed—

"You are as merry as a grig, sir—as merry as a grig; but, nevertheless, you were intended by Nature to be an actor. 'All the world's a stage, and all the men and women merely players.' The stage is but a wheel within a wheel: like the scene in Hamlet—a play played to players. The mimic is but a copy of another imitator. Then why refuse the stage?"

"I do not refuse it," said Reginald, seriously (for he was struck by his companion's manner and remarks); "I do not refuse it. I leave it to those who require it as a living. Why rob others who stand in need of a profession when I have the means of following another?"

"Well said, young man," cried Tanacourt; "I like you—have at you now! You are a noble fellow; you will one day do great things. But mark me well—"

He made a long pause—gazed earnestly at Reginald, and then continued—

"Work not upon a frozen heart; for if you steel your heart against the world, the world will steel its heart against you. Never betray another, for fear you will one day be betrayed."

These strange words—seemingly so ill-timed —struck a strange chill into Reginald's heart.

It was only momentary, however.

He knew that, as yet, he had never injured a human being.

There was no need, therefore, to take the words of Tanacourt too deeply to heart.

"Gentlemen," cried Dame Margaret, entering at this moment, "I will, if you please, show to you the rooms which I have set apart for you."

"Stand not, then, upon the order of your going, but go at once," said Joseph. "We follow."

The dame led the way up to the second floor.

She had assigned a room in the front of the house to Tanacourt.

This looked out upon the narrow road, and had but little to recommend it but its size.

The chamber she had appropriated to the use of Reginald was a smaller, less ostentatious, but far more comfortable apartment in the rear of the house.

"This, sir," said Dame Margaret, "is not so large as Mr. Joseph's, but then see what a nice prospect it has."

The window looked out upon long gardens, one of which joined the little plot of ground belonging to the "Weeping Swan," as the hotel was called.

In this garden, at the moment at which Reginald first gazed from the window, were walking an old man and a young girl.

The former was tall and fine-looking, erect and noble, with long white locks descending over his ample shoulders.

He wore a long brown coat, a black-mounted sword, and a little fanciful hat.

His legs were encased in knee-breeches, grey silk stockings, and his shoes were fastened with silver buckles.

The young girl by his side was a beautiful creature, with long, dark ringlets, and blue eyes.

She was dressed in a light muslin robe, loose and flowing, a gauze chemisette, only making more temptingly lovely her exquisite and rose-tinted bosom.

Her face was one which one might have gazed on rapturously for ever. Her form was like that of an angel.

Reginald gazed and gazed—wrapt in wonder and admiration.

Her presence seemed to cast a thrill over his heart, which appeared, as it were, to leave his breast and fly to her.

He never moved from the spot, but looked, on and on, until she and her father left the garden and re-entered the house.

He then started from his reverie; and was bewildered to find he was alone.

How long he had been so he could not tell.

A lamp was burning dimly in his room.

While he had been gazing the shades of evening had fallen over the earth; so, locking his door, he never issued forth to bid Dame Margaret or Tanacourt good night; but retired to sleep.

Sleep—ah! no; we will not say sleep.

Sleep never came to his eyelids. He fell now and then into a heavy leaden slumber.

But something appeared to sit upon his heart and weigh over his feelings.

The memory of that dear one he had left

behind him, in the old castle, was altogether obliterated for a time; and the image of one as young, and still more lovely, was imprinted there in her stead.

CHAPTER V.

THE EMPLOYER AND THE LOADSTONE.

When, upon the following morning, Reginald presented himself at the breakfast table, he saw, by the significant glances that passed between Dame Margaret and Joseph Tanacourt, that she had observed his conduct on the night before, and communicated her discovery to the actor.

He longed to learn who and what the maiden was, and yet he scarcely dared to ask.

There is always a modesty about such matters —at least with persons of delicate minds.

No wonder was it, therefore, that he felt very little inclination to broach a subject which might subject him and her also to unseemly jestings and even ridicule.

Dame Margaret extricated him from his difficulty.

"Young sir," cried she gaily, as she poured out a foaming cup of coffee and placed it temptingly before him, "young sir—you appeared quite wrapped in the beauty of that young girl who was with her father in the garden last evening."

"She is very beautiful, truly," said Reginald.

"Aye, and as good as she is beautiful," added Dame Margaret, "she is everything and all to her dear father."

"Who is he, may I ask?" enquired the young man, endeavouring not to appear anxious.

"He is an antiquary," said Dame Margaret

"An antiquary!" cried Reginald.

"Aye—marry—and why not?" asked the hostess, in surprise.

"No reason, fair dame," said Reginald, "but it surprised me for a good reason. I am come to London to become the secretary of an antiquary, and it would be strange indeed if I should find that I had thus accidentally fallen upon my employer."

"It would so," said Joseph Tavacourt, chiming in, "it would so. But there are more things in heaven and earth, Reginald, than we dream of in our philosophy. It may turn out just as you have surmised."

"What is the gentleman's name," asked Reginald.

"I know not," replied the dame, "I am so little inquisitive about the affairs of my neighbours, that I do not even think to learn the name of a customer."

This was a hint.

"A hit—a very palpable hit," said Tanacourt. "This gentleman's name, Dame Margaret, is Reginald Spelthorne, at your service."

"Well, Mr. Reginald," said Dame Margaret, who invariably, in addressing people, used their Christian names, "well, Mr. Reginald, if you particularly desire to learn that gentleman's name, I will ascertain for you."

"No—no," said the young man, vehemently, "not for worlds would I do so."

"Well, we will not press you. Are you going to visit your employer to-day?"

"Yes—you remind me I must go. Tanacourt, you must lead the way; for I know not whither I am bound."

Tanacourt immediately rose, as if bidden by his stage manager, and placing his hat jauntily on the side of his head, said—

"Procrastination is the thief of time, remember. What is the name of the street you desire to find?"

"Rubicon-street."

"Then have you indeed passed the Rubicon," cried, or rather shouted Joseph, "for behold the garden, in which was the fair lady and her father, belongeth to No. 12, Rubicon-street. By my troth, you have both lost and found."

"How so?"

"You have lost your heart, and found your employer."

"You mistake me"—

"Not I."

"But indeed, sir, you do me injustice," urged Reginald.

"Injustice—nay—nay; no injustice, lad. 'Tis the truth; then never be ashamed of it."

"But it is not the truth—indeed—I assure you."

"Why are you so vehement?"

"Because I have left one behind me whom I love, and to whom my troth is plighted."

"Say you so?" said Tanacourt, "then I am not the man to persuade you to forget her, or to jest at your love. Keep well in remembrance my words to you last night, and you will be happy. Here we are, sir, at No. 12, and I suppose I may now leave you. You can find your way back, I apprehend?"

"Yes—many thanks to you—I can find my way back."

It struck him at the moment, could his heart find its way back.

Oh! sunny face—oh! golden curls—oh! trusting heart! Little did you think of the whirlwind of falseness into which you were sending your lover; or what justification he might afterwards be enabled to plead for your falseness!

Reginald was ushered by the servant into a neatly-furnished drawing-room.

Everything around spoke of comfort, and, more than that, it spoke eloquently of a woman's presence.

A woman, too, endowed with great taste.

The various nick-nacks, placed daintily and tastefully around the apartment—the air of regularity pervading it everywhere—the general aspect of the place—all were evidences of a young guardian angel presiding over the antiquary's room.

Yet to Reginald, when he entered it, it seemed cold.

Why?

Because the guardian angel was not there to welcome him.

But he had a welcome he little hoped for— dared not hope for.

The antiquary was not at home, and instead, therefore, of being greeted by an old man—an austere, grave old man, as he expected him to be—he was greeted by the guardian angel herself.

Miriam was certainly a lovely being.

In a room she lost none of the beauties which adorned her in the garden.

Only she looked more majestic, more queenly, more entrancing.

She came forward with a bewitching archness, and, smiling upon him courteously, held out her hand and said,

"Mr. Reginald Spelthorne, I believe."

"Yes, miss," stammered he, over the warm, white, tiny hand.

But he could say no more, utter no further word.

Miriam did not mistake him for a fool because he was at fault—she knew the cause, and appreciated it.

"You are tired, I suppose, sir?"

"No—not at all—that is to say, I have rested all night since my journey."

"Pray be seated, Mr. Spelthorne," said she, casting her magnificent form on a lounge, "my father will not be long. Have you left a pretty place?"

"Yes, very," he said laconically.

"Ah! I have always heard that Cornwall is a beautiful county."

"It is most beautiful; and Castle Ferry, my uncle's residence, is one of the finest specimens of old architecture extant."

"Castle Ferry; quite a romantic name," cried Miriam; "why, do you know, Mr. Spelthorne, I shall make you take me and papa there some day."

Take her!

Oh! heavens!

To take that being of grace, and light, and love, to outshine his sweet betrothed!

Betrothed!

How strangely that word grated against his inward hearing.

Could it be that he regretted the link?

Was it not easily severable?

It was not one of iron—it was one of silk; but there was a heart between, and when the silk snapped, the heart would break too.

"You are thoughtful, Mr. Spelthorne," said Miriam.

"Yes—I was thinking it would not be a very comfortable home to offer you, even for a few days or weeks."

"Oh, comfort! never mind that. Where there is a true heart, there is always comfort enough for me. But here comes my father."

The door in another moment opened, and the antiquary appeared.

"Ah! ah! an't' said he, in a jovial voice, "you have arrived then, Mr. Spelthorne."

"Yes, sir; I arrived yesterday."

"Not too soon, I can tell you," continued the old man, "for I am really overwhelmed with work, and my Miriam here cannot do all I want, though my pet is very useful."

He was quite a different being to the one Reginald had pictured to himself.

He had imagined that he should find a harsh, crabbed old fellow, wedded to his fossils and his antiquities, and caring little for the amenities of every-day life.

He found instead a jovial, merry hearted, genial gentleman—a lovely daughter—a comfortable home—everything he could desire.

Fortune already smiled on him, it seemed to him.

But, then, amid its smiles were frowns.

And among those frowns was the fact that the more he became interested in his new friends the more he forgot the old.

An invisible hand seemed to be blotting out the past, and bidding him to live for the future.

"We shall be very comfortable, I think," said the antiquary, "you will be quite at home here."

"Very comfortable indeed, sir," replied Reginald.

Miriam's eyes were on him; so he could say no more.

CHAPTER VI.

TIT FOR TAT.

LEAVING Reginald Spelthorne to pursue his course in the metropolis, I must now return to Castle Ferry, and its simple inhabitants.

Ethel Spelthorne was at first inconsolable at the loss of her lover.

His return to the castle had been like a flash of light upon her path. It was what she had for months looked forward to with anxious hope, and now he had as suddenly disappeared.

For a time he had gone, he said—her heart seemed to say it was for ever.

Reginald's letters came regularly—he was happy, he assured her; had secured the good favour of the antiquary, and was on the high road to fortune.

But there was something in his epistles which grated strangely upon her heart, and appeared to foretel the coming of an evil day, which was made more certain by the sudden and total cessation of his letters.

About two months after Reginald's departure for London there was a violent storm upon the Cornish coast.

Mariners were lost on that night—struggling for life, helplessly, hopelessly, out on the dark sea.

The light from the topmost turret of the castle shone out with redoubled brilliance; but its rays were lost amid the surging waters, and the beams, which the sailor had so often blessed, shone out that night in vain.

On land the tempest raged with no less violence.

Trees were uprooted, rivers left their beds, and poured in rushing torrents upon the neighbouring hamlets.

Here and there a hayrick caught fire, struck by the vivid and forked lightning, and hissed and seethed in the drenching rain.

In the midst of the tempest a horse came rattling into the court-yard of the castle.

Its rider—hatless, and soaked to the skin, knocked loudly at the door, and when old Jabez Fairlight opened it, demanded shelter from the storm.

"Enter, sir," cried the old domestic, "Castle

Ferry is ever a refuge to the weary stranger. I will lead you to my master, and will then take your horse to the stable. Follow me."

The stranger thereupon dismounted, and followed the old man up the broad staircase to the door of the room where Jacob Spelthorne sat gazing, with Ethel, at the storm which raged without.

"Welcome, sir, welcome," cried Jacob, coming forward, "none more welcome to Castle Ferry than the stranger who is benighted by the way."

"Many thanks for your kindness," returned the stranger, "but I fear I can scarcely enter your room in my present plight; I had better dry myself by your kitchen fire."

"Nay, nay," urged Jacob, slightly flushing—there was no kitchen fire—"nay, nay, I pray you enter. My servant will receive from you your wet clothes and bring others."

Thus solicited, the new comer advanced into the room, and divesting himself of his hat, his cloak, and his leggings, delivered them to Jabez Fairlight.

Thus denuded of his outer man, he appeared a young fellow of some twenty years, with long, black curls, large blue eyes, and a fine, open expression of countenance.

"You are not so very wet, sir, after all," said Ethel, archly, "you would excite our compassion falsely."

"Nay, fair lady, not so," returned the stranger, taking her plump, white hand, within his own, "I had more respect for your presence and your furniture than to enter in such a plight."

"Furniture!" thought she.

It might truly have been taken for satire; but that, like a true bred gentleman, he never once glanced round as he entered the room.

"Jabez," said old Spelthorne, to the domestic, who now entered the room, after having put up the horse, "Jabez, bring up the supper—our guest needs refreshment."

An agonised look at Ethel was the only reply which Jabez vouchsafed.

His young mistress seemed instantly to comprehend his meaning, and followed him from the room.

"Now we are alone," said the stranger, drawing his chair up nearer to the fire, "now we are alone, it is time to give some mutual explanations."

"Just so," said Jacob, "I will begin by saying that my name is plain Jacob Spelthorne, of Castle Ferry, Cornwall, at your service—I and my daughter being the only occupants of this strange, old place, with the exception of that single domestic and my dog."

"You have other occupants though, I reckon," cried the stranger.

"And what are they?"

"They are the recollections of those who have gone before you—what they did—what they thought—what they suffered—how they lived, loved, and died."

Old Jacob sighed and held his peace.

"Perhaps I have touched upon a chord which brings back painful reminiscences," said the stranger, apologetically. "I pray your pardon. My name is John Stuart Blakesley, the son of the baronet of that name."

"I have heard his name mentioned," said Jacob, courteously."

"Indeed—I am bound for India in a few months. I am now wandering about to have a last glimpse, as it were, of my native land."

At this moment Ethel re-entered, with Jabez.

Somehow or another they had contrived to scrape together a supper, which was decidedly not amiss to place before a hungry guest.

"Good cheer—good cheer," cried he, as he placed himself opposite a smoking dish, "this is far better comfort than I expected this cold and dreary night."

The supper was eaten with great relish by the stranger and old Jacob, who, had it not been for Blakesley's arrival, would scarcely have gone so well filled to bed.

By Ethel it was scarcely touched.

She seemed stricken with some strange feeling. An undefined dread of the future was mingled with a kind of blissful sensation, which crept over her whole body, and penetrated the inmost recesses of her heart.

The handsome, vivacious fellow who sat so unexpectedly beside her, offering her a thousand little attentions, and now and then managing to insert in his conversation a well-timed and graceful compliment, had evidently made a slight impression upon her.

"Do you reside near us?" she asked, timidly.

"Not so. I only happen to be wandering here for amusement, prior, as I have been telling your father, to my departure for India."

"Do you go soon?"

"No—not for two months. I am going to spend that time in having a glimpse of the beauties of my native land. I have found one here."

"Nay—you are a flatterer," said Ethel, pleased, yet chiding.

"Truly, he is not;" said Jacob, "for where among England's flowers is there a sweeter than that which blooms—the last blossom of this fallen line."

"Say not so, father," cried she, "while Reginald is left to us."

"Reginald," murmured he, half to himself, half aloud, "Reginald—who knows?"

Ah! who, indeed!

"Is Cornwall a beautiful country?" inquired Blakesley.

"Yes, beautiful!"

"I may as well stay here awhile, then," said the stranger. "Is there a hostelry near, where I can find accommodation?"

"I shall be offended if you go anywhere but the Castle," said Jacob. "While you remain in Cornwall Castle Ferry must be your home."

And so John Stuart Blakesley remained at Castle Ferry.

CHAPTER VII.

SECOND LOVE.

FIRST love is certainly the purest, the holiest of all those phases of that feeling which is composed so strangely of friendship, affection, and desire.

But it rarely lasts—it rarely possesses sufficient strength to overcome absence and the unkindness of friends.

At passing from that one who has first engrossed our love there may be a sickening of the heart, a deadly faintness in every faculty, a cold fear of all that glimmers obscurely in the future.

But absence, which some tell us " makes the heart grow fonder," teaches us also to forget, and the presence of others, and the formation of new ties and new friendships, soon serve to wipe out the recollections of the love of youth.

John Stuart Blakesley, as I have said, remained at Castle Ferry, and was generally, with old Jacob's permission, accompanied in his rambles by Ethel Spelthorne.

He was handsome, young, accomplished.

His education had not served to make him pedantic, but simply to add a polish to his conversation, to form his character, to render him altogether a delightful and an attractive companion.

Whether from the first he wished to be so I cannot say; certain it is, however, that Ethel soon discovered that her heart was receding surely though slowly from its first altar, and placing itself as a victim upon another, to be sacrificed to a good or evil genius, as might be.

She was very happy; only now and then a thought of Reginald would come over her and chill the fervour of her heart for a while.

They were wandering one evening by the ocean, picking their way carefully, thoughtfully along the pebbly beach.

Evening was coming on, the evening of summer—calm, balmy, voluptuous

Everything seemed buried in delicious repose, and invited the wanderers to prolong their walk, or to lie for awhile watching the tide as it slowly receded from the shore—ever and anon returning to inclose the earth in one last embrace as if loth to retreat from it even for a few short hours.

Ethel Spelthorne and young Blakesley sat down by the sea, and watched the approach of sunset.

" Ere twenty more suns have died," said he looking mournfully at his fair companion, " ere twenty more suns have died I shall be treading that vast ocean, and bidding adieu, perhaps for ever, to you and to England."

There was a strange flutter in Ethel's heart as he said these words, which seemed to choke her, and prevent the utterance of the sentence she had framed in answer.

He spoke on.

" I am going away without a blessing. My friends are wholly indifferent to me. I shall not even go home to bid them adieu."

" Not even to your father?" said Ethel.

" No, not even to him," replied Blakesley, with a strange smile; " when he hears that I have gone, he will say, ' Ah! well, it was the best thing he could have done,' and so it will pass off."

" Is there no one in England whom you regret to leave?" said she.

" Ah! there, now, you alter the case," said he, " that is far, far different—there are many—there is one more especially in England whom I fear to leave; but I cannot hope that they regret my leaving the country."

" Why not hope?"

" I dare not."

" Perhaps you have never asked them?'

Was this imagination, or was this an invitation to tell his love?

He could not but take it as such.

Summoning up, therefore, his utmost courage, he said,—

" Miss Spelthorne—or may I say Ethel?—I wish to say something to you before I depart."

Ethel gave no answer, but allowed him to retain the hand he had taken fondly in his.

" Dearest Ethel, I love you. The first moment I saw you I could not but recognise in my heart the presence of a new and holy feeling. Do you love me? Will you be my wife?"

" Yes."

Oh! first love, where is thy strength?

" Oh! Reginald, where is the power of love?"

For some moments neither spoke.

They lay there in each other's arms, silently happy, lovingly gazing in each other's eyes, and then, anon, at the exquisite landscape which surrounded them.

" And will you come with me to India?"

" Yes, love, of course I will."

" And your father?"

" He must come too."

Blakesley smiled.

" I suppose he must," he said. " He would scarcely like to part with his only daughter on so long a voyage."

" No; I fear he will reproach me."

" Reproach you—why?"

" For Reginald's sake."

" He, also, is false."

" I cannot say that," replied Ethel, sadly, " I have no proofs."

' He has ceased writing to you."

" He may be ill."

" Oh, no; he has ceased writing because he has ceased to love you."

John Stuart Blakesley only argued thus, because he desired to persuade Ethel Spelthorne that in renouncing her former lover she had not acted wrongly.

But he was, nevertheless, right.

Reginald Spelthorne had lost his love for Ethel. Like a spontaneous act their mutual love had departed.

He ceased writing because he could not bear to be deceitful.

" Perhaps it is even so," replied Ethel; " will you tell my father of this?"

" Yes, love, if you wish it?" replied Blakesley. " I know it is the custom; but yet our case is so peculiar, that I would almost desire that you would speak to him yourself."

" I will, dearest," said the pretty girl, as she surrendered herself to the fond embrace he offered to her before betaking themselves home.

CHAPTER VIII.

TELLING FATHER.

ETHEL SPELTHORNE can scarcely be blamed for so easily giving up her fealty to Reginald.

Her love for him had been, after all, but a May-day dream.

Bright, sunny, it had little foundation beyond the fact that it had existence in a heart which had never loved before.

She had never been brought much in contact with the world.

She had never seen any young man for whom she could entertain such a feeling as passionate affection besides Reginald Spelthorne, whose visits to Castle Ferry were few and far between.

These visits, however, had ripened a childish liking into a matured love.

Not that she respected or esteemed him so very greatly, but he was a young man, handsome, full of spirits, manly, active, energetic— just the sort of fellow to excite the admiration of a timid, simple girl.

Ethel was pre-eminently simple.

Not simple as many call it.

She was simple because her heart was pure— because she knew little of the world—still less of its evil doings, its rash passions, and ambitions.

When, however, he went away, and after a

time ceased all communication with her, she began to doubt his faith.

Then came John Stuart Blakesley, another handsome, fine fellow, apparently full of heart, and guiltless of any device but that of manfully battling with the world, and making the woman who loved him happy.

So Ethel Spelthorne gave herself up to him, and tried to forget her cousin.

"Father," she said that evening, as the twilight darkened the old chamber.

Blakesley had purposely left them alone.

"Yes, Ethel."

"Are you weary?"

"No, my own."

"I have something very important to tell you."

"Indeed !"

"Yes, something that will perhaps make you sad for a time."

"And yet you tell it to me?"

"Yes, because afterwards it will make you happy."

"Well, well; what is it ?"

"I am in love."

"I know that," laughed old Jacob.

"You know it ?"

"Yes; why, what ails the girl ? Was it not all settled between you and Reginald before he left Castle Ferry for London ?"

"Ethel's eyes glistened rather more brightly than usual, as she answered—

"I do not wish to speak of him, father."

"Not of him ? of whom then ?"

"I have forgotten Reginald."

"Have forgotten him ?"

"Yes, indeed I have."

"Alas ! alas ! child !" said the old man, sorrowfully; "a wayward heart never led its owner to good."

"My heart is not wayward, father," returned Ethel; "it did not know itself then, it does now."

"Well, well, my Ethel," said old Jacob, kindly; "and what do you wish to say ?"

"I wish to be married soon," said she, archly yet meekly.

"Tut ! child, there is no hurry."

"Yes, indeed, father, there is, as he is going away soon."

"He ! who is he ?"

"Mr. Blakesley."

Jacob Spelthorne was silent.

Then, after a moment's thought, he said, as if to himself,

"Ah ! well, it might have been worse. So it is Mr. Blakesley who has made you play false to Reginald, is it ?"

These words were not meant unkindly, but they seemed to send a sting into Ethel's heart.

"Do not speak thus, father," she said; "he is false also to me. Have I your consent ?"

"Yes, love, yes; and where is he going to take you ?"

The words themselves were simple.

The look which accompanied them was agony personified.

"He will take us both."

"Whither ?"

"To India."

A kind of spasmodic smile passed over old Jacob's face.

"To India, child ?" he answered; "why I should never live to get there."

"Oh, yes, father, you will; and you will be so happy—we shall all be happy, out there. You will have no tiresome relations to worry you."

"And when is the ceremony to take place ?" he said, resignedly.

"The day after to-morrow," she answered, blushingly; "if you will permit it."

"The day after to-morrow, child ?" he exclaimed, in astonishment.

"Yes, father."

"Does Mr. Blakesley wish it to be so ?"

"Yes, father."

"But there are no preparations."

"No, John does not wish to have any one here; he desires everything to be as quiet and as little showy as possible."

"Very well, Ethel," said Jacob Spelthorne, parting her hair from off her forehead, and kissing her sadly, yet fondly; "very well, Ethel, you have my consent."

"Thank you, my dearest father," she cried, throwing her arms round his neck, in deep love; "thank you, my dearest father."

"I hope he will be kind to you," he continued.

"I am sure he will," said Ethel, with a bright confident smile.

"Aye, I will answer for that," cried a free manly voice, as John Stuart Blakesley entered the room. "Never fear, Mr. Spelthorne, I will always be kind to her, and if I am not, why you will be there yourself to punish me."

CHAPTER IX.

MARRIAGE.

THERE is nothing very new to describe in a marriage, more especially when it is one so simple and unadorned as that of Ethel Spelthorne and John Stuart Blakesley.

People, in general, make marriage the occasion of a grand parade and display of wealth.

Even those who are by no means well to do in the world scrape together all their savings and their tawdry finery, to give a certain degree of *éclat* to "the wedding."

Now, in my mind, there is something of indecency in such displays.

Certainly there is nothing to be ashamed of in two persons taking vows to live together in that state of life which Heaven has ordained to mortals, and which is positively necessary to the continuance of human society.

But if a newly-wedded pair think it necessary to keep themselves secluded from the world for a month after the performance of the marriage ceremony, then should it be deemed equally necessary that no public display should be made on the very day when a young virgin is about to deliver herself up to the arms of her husband.

No bride feels excessively ashamed of herself on her wedding day.

On the contrary, she generally appears extremely happy.

She may blush a little—she may seem a little *conscious*.

But the difference between before and after is absurd.

Great excitement there was in the hamlet when it was known that there was to be a wedding at the castle.

No one expected anything very grand.

Everybody was aware of the state of affairs at Castle Ferry.

But there was not a man, woman, or child in the whole village who did not love Ethel Spelthorne; and who was not anxious to be in the church to witness the ceremony which was to make her a wife.

John Stuart Blakesley and Ethel, Jacob Spelthorne and old Jabez Fairlight, composed the party which, on that summer's morning, wound down the path towards the village church.

The children of the hamlet strewed flowers in their path.

The bell tolled out a merry peal.

"God bless her !"

" Heaven bless her !"

"She is so good—she will be sure to be happy !"

Such were the exclamations which greeted Ethel as she blushingly tripped up the steps of the church.

John Stuart Blakesley walked erect.

He was proud of his beautiful bride.

Still prouder, however, was he of the good opinions which every one entertained for her.

The church was entered. The ceremony proceeded.

Ethel and John Blakesley were one.

The register was filled up.

The party wound their way from the sacred edifice.

Ethel felt happy.

John felt supremely so.

No thought of anything crossed her mind at that moment.

She only recognised the fact that she deeply, fondly loved—that she was as deeply loved again, and that she had married the husband whom her heart had chosen.

Just as they were leaving the churchyard a little boy, whose observations of the newly-married pair were far from civil, trod accidentally on Ethel's dress and tore it slightly.

She turned round with a smile.

" Fie ! fie !" said the boy's mother, " go this minute and beg the lady's pardon, Reginald."

" Oh, heavens !" cried Ethel, turning ghastly pale.

" What ails you, dearest ?" said John, who had not noticed the mischance, or heard the name.

"Nothing—nothing," said Ethel.

And so it passed with him.

But with her it was far different.

It left a burning, searing impression on her heart.

The boy seemed to have been sent to her by a special Providence.

She went home with a sadder heart and a more chastened soul.

Not that she regretted the step she had taken.

But she felt that the great joy she had experienced was almost an insult to one who, after all, might be true to her, and might mourn her loss in tears of blood when she was far, far away from him—never to return.

She was so sad in the evening, as they sat in the large drawing-room, holding each other's hands, and gazing out upon the landscape, that Blakesley said, while at the same time kissing her fondly,

"Do you regret the step you have taken, my dearest ?"

"Oh! John! how can you ask me such a question ?" she asked reproachfully.

There was no light in the room.

Therefore he could not see the expression of pain which crossed her features as she answered his query.

"Dearest Ethel," he continued, as he folded her fondly, passionately in his arms; "dearest Ethel, you shall never repent this day, upon which you have so unconditionally given yourself up to me."

Ethel's eyes, bright with tears, were turned on his.

And so, in the darkening evening they sat, watching the passing hours.

* * * * *

A month afterwards saw them hastening towards S———, the port at which they embarked for India.

CHAPTER X.

A LONG FAREWELL TO HOME.

HAPPILY, in the moral world as in the material one, the warring elements have their proscribed bounds, and the flood of grief decreaseth when it can swell no higher; but it is only by retrospection we can bring ourselves to believe in this obvious truth.

The young and untried heart hugs itself in the bitterness of its emotions, and takes a pride in believing that its anguish can end but with its existence; and it is not till time hath almost steeped our senses in forgetfulness that we discover the mutability of all human passions.

But Ethel left it not to the slow hand of time to subdue, in some measure, the grief that swelled her heart. Had she given way to selfishness, she would have sought the free indulgence of her sorrow as the only mitigation of it; but she felt also for her father.

He could not bear the idea of parting with his daughter, and he was taking a long, dreary journey entirely upon her account; could she therefore, be so selfish as to add to his uneasiness by a display of her sufferings?

No; she would strive to conceal it from his observation, though to overcome it was impossible. Her feelings must ever remain the same, but she would confine them to her own breast; and she began to converse with, and even strove to amuse, her kind-hearted father.

Ever and anon, indeed, a run of tender recollections of the soft voice, and kind words of Reginald came across her mind, and then the dreariness and desolation succeeded as the delusion vanished, and all was stillness and vacuity.

Even self-reproach shot its piercing sting into her ingenuous heart. Levities on which in her usual gaiety of spirit she had never bestowed a thought, now appeared to her crimes of the deepest dye.

Though summer had fled, and few, even, of autumn's graces remained, yet over the august features of mountain scenery the seasons have little control.

Their charms depend not upon richness of verdure, or luxuriance of foliage, or any of the mere prettiness of nature; but, whether wrapped in snow, or veiled in mist, or glowing in sunshine, their lovely grandeur remains the same, and the same feelings fill and elevate the soul in contemplating these mighty works of an Almighty hand.

"Oh, Nature, all thy seasons please the eye
Of him who sees a Deity in all."

The eye is now weary of watching the thousand varieties of light and shade as they flit over the mountains, or gleam upon the water. While the ear is satisfied with the majestic silence of solitude, or charmed with the wild roarings of Nature, as heard in the hollow murmur of the wind or the hoarse gurgling of innumerable mountain streams.

Others besides Ethel seemed to have taken a fanciful pleasure in combining the ideas of the mental and elemental world; for in the dreary dwellings where they were destined to pass the night, she found inscribed the following lines:—

"The busy winds roar 'mid the waving boughs,
And darkly rolls the heaving surge to land.
Among the flying clouds the moonbeam glows,
With colours foreign to its softness bland.

"Here one dark shadow melts in gloom profound,
The towering Alps, the guardians of the Lake;
There one bright gleam sheds silver light around,
And shows the threatening strife that tempests wake.

"Thus o'er my mind a busy memory plays,
That shakes the feelings to their inmost core;
Thus beams the light of hope's fallacious rays
When simple confidence can trust no more.

"So one dark shadow shrouds each bygone hour,
So one bright gleam the coming tempest shows,
That tells of sorrows which, though past, still lower,
And thus reveals th' approach of future woes."

These reflections were anything but pleasant to a young bride about to embark with her husband on a voyage of many thousand miles.

Ethel, however, had not to reproach herself for having acted with unnecessary unkindness in this marriage.

She had written a long, earnest letter to Reginald.

A letter blurred and blotted with hot, blinding tears.

In it she confessed all.

Now she reproached herself—then she reproached him with neglect.

Now she begged him to forgive her—now she pleaded against forgiveness.

It was a true woman's letter.

A true type of woman's character, full of contradictions and bewilderments.

It mattered not.

It never reached him!

CHAPTER XI.

BEFORE WIND AND TIDE.

So the wind and the tide bore Ethel Spelthorne away from the house of her ancestors.

There is always a certain degree of regret on leaving home—always a sinking of the heart—a depression of the spirits.

Even though we go of our own free will, when we leave behind us nothing but disagreeable recollections, unkind relatives, fostering friends, or rather acquaintances—even then, there is a certain degree of sorrow in quitting the country that gave us birth.

How much more so when we leave behind us those we love!—and at any rate those whom we can scarcely leave without tears.

"You are sad, my Ethel," said her husband, as they stood together on deck gazing out over the water at the receding land.

The day was a glorious one.

The sun shone down upon the waters with unclouded brilliance.

Not a wave broke the surface of the lake-like ocean.

The ship went along lazily—steadily, before a gentle breeze.

Everything was so calm as to bring over you almost a feeling of melancholy.

"I am not sad, dearest," said the young wife.

"You seem so, indeed," returned he, in a gracious tone, "you sometimes make me think that you regret your marriage."

Tears glistened in Ethel's eyes, as she answered,—

"Do not say so, dear husband, it is unkind—cruel of you."

"I am never intentionally cruel."

"No, love. But you must never tell me I regret our marriage, because that is telling me I do not love you."

"Why then, love, do you seem so melancholy—so often melancholy?"

"I do not know," said Ethel, thoughtfully. "Yet it may be a passing remembrance of those I have left behind me makes me sad."

"*You have not left them behind you.*"

"What, dearest?" asked Ethel.

"I did not speak," said Blakesley.

"Not speak? You are joking!" returned Ethel with a slight laugh, though her cheek was deadly pale.

"No, dear. Did you hear anything?"

"Yes—yes," she said, hesitatingly, and with a slight return of colour.

"What was it?"

" I heard some one say, distinctly and clearly, by me, ' You have not left them behind you.' "

Blakesley turned round quickly.

There was no one on deck except the crew.

" It must have been a fancy of yours," said he, sadly, as he kissed her fondly on the forehead.

" Oh no ! not fancy ; I heard the words distinctly—plainly. They seem to ring in my ears even now."

John Blakesley did not answer, but gazed out sadly over the waves.

" Have I done very wrong, think you ?" asked his wife, after a few moments' pause.

" Wrong, dearest ?"

Ethel blushed.

" I know I am doing wrong to you every moment," she continued, " in thinking of the one I have left ; but still a voice within me seems to tell me that I judged of him too hastily."

Blakesley took her hand, sat down by her, and said kindly,

" Ethel, do not even for a moment imagine that I blame you for remembering that there was one who, before me, held possession of your heart. I never shall blame you until that moment when I find that your heart is leaving me."

" That will never be."

" I hope not."

" Do not say hope—say you know it."

" Well, then, I know it never will be."

" Then you are not angry with me for sometimes thinking of Reginald ?"

" No, love, not angry."

" Do you think, then, I acted very wrongly ?"

" In doing what ?"

" In too soon believing him false ?"

Blakesley smiled.

Perhaps he thought—even he—that she had scarcely acted in reference to his falseness, but rather in reference to her own feelings.

" No, dearest, I do not think you acted wrongly," he answered, " you merely abandoned a childish fancy at the first avowal of true love."

Ethel did not answer.

Her heart was too full.

She replied only with a sweet smile of thanks.

Change of air and variety of scene failed not to produce the happiest effects upon Ethel's languid frame and drooping spirits.

Her cheek already glowed with health, and was sometimes dimpled with smiles ; she still wept, indeed, as she thought of the one she had left, but often, while the tear trembled in her eye, its course was arrested by wonder, or admiration, or delight, for every object had its charms for her.

Her cultivated taste and thoughtful mind would descry beauty in the form of a cloud, and grandeur in the form of the wave, and elegance in the sea-gull, as it dipped its tiny bill in the waves of the sea.

These simple pleasures, unknown alike to the sordid mind and vitiated taste, are ever exquisitely enjoyed by

" ——One whose heart the holy forms
Of young imagination have kept pure."

CHAPTER XII.

JUSTIFICATION.

ON the day following that on which Ethel heard the mysterious voice she was descending the cabin stairs alone, when a conversation from within caused her to stand spell-bound opposite the door.

This door was half-opened, and she could not resist the temptation of looking in.

Just as she leaned forward to catch a glimpse of the inmates of the cabin, her husband joined.

He was just in time to prevent her rushing in, but not in time to suppress the passionate exclamation which rushed unbidden to her lips.

" Oh, God !" she cried, " I am, indeed, punished."

" What is the matter, dearest ?" said her husband.

" See—in there—Reginald," and she fell fainting in his arms.

The scene within was one certainly calculated to excite her deepest grief.

Not one, however, that a husband could well appreciate as exciting such strong emotions in his wife.

On a sofa, inside the cabin, sat a lady—a young and beautiful girl.

At her feet sat a young man, his head half in her lap, his eyes gazing fondly and proudly upon her.

The one was Miriam Mildmay, the antiquary's daughter.

The other—Reginald Spelthorne.

The cabin was fitted up for two persons.

They were evidently man and wife.

" Come," said Blakesley, half sternly, to Ethel when she recovered. " Come—this is your justification. You have greatly wounded my self-love ; you will scarcely, therefore, refuse to gratify one wish of mine."

" What is that, dearest ?" asked Ethel, in a low, painful voice.

" I wish you to enter and introduce me as your husband."

" I will," said Ethel, firmly.

She knocked timidly at the door.

She was quite right.

She acted on the instant.

Had she waited for reflection she would not have been able to go through the ordeal.

" Enter," said a woman's voice.

Ethel went in, followed by Blakesley.

" Ah !" said Reginald, rising and endeavouring to appear unconcerned. " An old friend, Miss Spelthorne—this is my wife, Miriam."

" And this," said Ethel, smiling—it was a superb piece of acting—" this is my husband, Mr. John Stuart Blakesley."

It was a strange meeting, that.

Every one felt awkward, and looked foolish ; but they managed to pass a few minutes in ordinary conversation and then parted.

" This is all for the best," said Blakesley.

" Yes," said Ethel, " perhaps so. But I do not mind confessing to you that it was a hard trial."

" I do not doubt you."

"And you forgive me?"

"There is nothing to forgive."

"Good, kind Stuart," said Ethel, "I appreciate your love, and will do my best to deserve it."

Meantime a different scene was being enacted in the cabin.

CHAPTER XIII.

HOW THE LANDLADY SOLD HER LOVE.

It is necessary to retrace my steps for awhile and explain how Reginald Spelthorne and Ethel Blakesley went on board the good ship Termagant bound for India.

The duties imposed upon Reginald Spelthorne by the antiquary were few and light.

Mr. Courtenay, however, liked to have some one near him : not so much to impose upon him certain duties, but that he might be able to consult with him upon the abstruse subject of antiquity.

Reginald was a good scholar : and moreover a good reader.

He therefore got very quickly into the favour of the antiquary; who at last induced him to take up his residence at his home instead of dreaming his life away at Dame Margaret's.

This was a sore trial to the worthy woman.

Reginald hardly admired the task of telling her.

Tanacourt gave him the opportunity.

"Reginald Spelthorne," said he, waving his hand aloft—it was in the little bar parlour over a glass of grog—"Reginald Spelthorne, my boy, I am about to leave you."

"Say not so, good Tanacourt, say not so," cried Reginald.

"Aye—it is even so," said the actor.

"Whither do you go?"

"To Carlisle."

"And why?"

"To explain to the rustic mind the beauties of the Bard of Avon."

"Ah! then we go about the same time?"

"Are you also about to depart, then?"

"Even so; I have been offered a lodging for nothing, and must accept it."

Dame Margaret was sitting knitting by the fire.

This last observation of young Spelthorne made her prick up her ear and listen.

"You're right, my boy—you're right," said Tanacourt, "never throw aside an offer like that —a bed for nothing is half the battle—is it not, my good dame?"

The actor evidently had made a good joke, though no one appreciated it, for he laughed loudly and long.

"I understand thee not," said the dame.

"We are both about to leave thee," continued the actor, "and such is my estimation of thy worth, good dame, that I will e'en pledge a bumper to thy health."

"What is it to be?" asked Dame Margaret bluntly.

"Sack—bright-eyed one—sack," whiffed the actor.

In a few moments Dame Margaret returned with a foaming tankard.

"And now let us pledge one another," said Tanacourt.

"I want none," said the dame.

"And art thou the only one present?" cried the actor. "Dost thou think that because thou art virtuous there shall be no more cakes and ale? Aye—and ginger shall be hot in the mouth too."

"Thou art ever quoting your good-for-nothing poetasters," said the dame; "but I will even pledge you in a glass."

"That is right— that is right, dame," said Tanacourt; and so they sat and quaffed their wine till the small hours of the morning.

Reginald Spelthorne had just entered his couch when a tap was heard at his door.

"Enter," he cried.

He expected to see the actor.

What, then, was his surprise to behold Dame Margaret coming lamp in hand!

"What is it, good dame?" said Reginald.

The dame had tears in her eyes—so the young man felt awkward.

"I wish to speak to you," she said.

"Sit down, then, I prithee," said Spelthorne.

"Are you really about to leave me?" asked Dame Margaret.

"Yes—I am compelled."

"Why compelled? I will give you lodging for nothing."

"But it is my employer who has offered it to me," answered Reginald.

"What, Mr. Courtenay?"

"Yes, the antiquary."

"But are you not near enough to him now? My house overlooks his garden."

Reginald smiled.

"Yes, dame; but you must remember that he likes one to be constantly near him to read to him, and talk to him."

"What, would you have me believe that he is always dreaming and talking about nothing but his blessed fossils and old coins?"

"Tis so, truly."

"Pooh! pooh!" cried the dame energetically, "it is not the old man who wants you—it is that daughter of his, Miss Miriam—the—"

"Nay, nay, speak not ill of her," exclaimed Reginald Spelthorne.

"What! has she bitten thee too? But I can tell thee, Master Reginald, she is engaged to be married to one Major Doble—so she is no fit one for you."

Reginald answered not.

"Indeed, Master Spelthorne, I will make you comfortable here—indeed you shall want for nothing."

Dame Margaret was six and twenty, and pretty. The situation was awkward.

"I am dissatisfied with nothing, Margaret," said Reginald taking her hand. "I only go because my master bids me."

"Must you go?"

"Yes! indeed I must"

This was too much for the good soul. She bent her face down upon the pillow and sobbed aloud.

"Do not weep, dame," said Spelthorne; "you forget. It is but a short distance, not a long journey that I am going."

"And you will come and see me often?"

"Yes."

"And you will not make love to Miriam Courtenay?"

"That I cannot promise."

But as this answer seemed to threaten a fresh efflux of tears, he added—

"You know I make love to every woman I see."

"Except me?" sobbed the poor dame.

"Nay," said Reginald, kissing her, "that is because you will not notice me."

Dame Margaret's eyes brightened.

"Poor boy, she said," smoothing down his hair; "good night—heaven bless you."

And after a further embrace she left the room.

"Strange being," muttered Reginald.

Nevertheless he turned about and went to sleep, while Dame Margaret spent an hour or two in crying her eyes out.

Next morning he and Tanacourt both left the hostelry: after partaking of a tempting little breakfast prepared by the dame's own hands.

She cried a great deal over him when he paid his rent, kissed him when he went away, and begged of him if he ever got into trouble to come to her and she would always give him a home.

Reginald went through the trial manfully, and was that day installed at the Courtenays.

CHAPTER XIV.

SWEET IS A LEGACY.

LIFE at the Courtenays was anything but exciting.

But to Reginald Spelthorne it had a deep interest.

He had began in reality to forget those whom he had left behind: and after awhile, as he found himself insensibly weaned from the object of his early affections, he ceased to write to her from mere shame at the deceit.

So he left off communicating with Ethel, and gave himself up madly, blindly, to his love for Miriam.

Miriam Courtenay was, as I have said, a fine girl.

And yet fine is scarcely the term to apply to her.

People say a girl is fine if she is tall, full-bosomed, and large-limbed.

Miriam was beautiful.

Her eyes were large, her mouth was sweetly pretty and delicate, her form rounded—each limb moulded with due regard to the proportions of the other.

Her voice was fascination itself, and Reginald Spelthorne *was* fascinated.

Miriam was not insensible to his love.

They neither knew that the other was aware of the fact that they were all in all to one another.

But yet there seemed between them a tacit understanding that in some way or another their futures would be connected.

Miriam was engaged to be married to her cousin, Major Doble, a man far too old to be a fit husband for her.

But somehow or another she never seemed to regard it as a possibility that she should be required to yield up her whole future to him.

She and Reginald were always together—for ever reading, for ever studying the same works.

About this time a distant relative of Reginald Spelthorne died, and left to him an estate in the Indian Archipelago.

This, under other circumstances, would have been just what he desired.

He had come to London to seek a fortune for himself and for old Jacob and his daughter.

He now thought of it only as a means of making himself happy with Miriam.

The only drawback to the gift was the fact of its being necessary for him to go himself to India to superintend the estate.

This was one of the stipulations of the legacy.

"So you are going to leave me," said Mr. Courtenay, one evening as they were walking in the garden.

Poor Dame Margaret was looking at them.

She always watched her young protége when he was in that garden, though he never knew it.

"Yes, sir."

"I wonder whether the climate will suit you?"

"I know not."

"You are abstracted."

"Yes, I fear I am very rude, but I feel strangely bewildered at the idea of leaving England."

"You are engaged to some fair lady, I apprehend?" inquired Mr. Courtenay.

"No, indeed."

"Mr. Fairweather gave me to understand you were engaged to Miss Ethel Spelthorne, your cousin," said the antiquary.

"No. I assure you it is a mistake," said Reginald, enthusiastically.

Mr. Courtenay smiled.

He could not account for Reginald's vehemence.

"When do you propose going?"

"To-morrow!"

"Nay; that is very sudden!"

"What matters? I have none who care for me—none who will grieve at my absence."

"Say not so, say not so," said Mr. Courtenay, "I am sure both I and Miriam will be grieved at parting with you!"

"Oh! if I could only think—but excuse me, sir, I am abstracted to-night."

And so saying, he darted out of the garden, upstairs, into his room!

"That is a strange young fellow," mused the antiquary; "a very strange young fellow, in sooth. He must be in love, love plays us many tricks."

Reginald did not make his appearance again that night.

He remained alone up in his chamber.

A thousand bewildering thoughts racked his brain.

He had to depart almost immediateiy.

Miriam, he knew, was engaged to another.

And yet?

Should he go without telling her of his love?

Should he sacrifice his happiness, and, perhaps, her happiness, because he feared to risk a refusal?

No.

He determined to be brave.

But still, every time that he moved toward the door his heart failed him, and he could not venture.

So, at length, with an aching head and a sore heart, he determined to postpone the trial until the morrow.

The morning at length came—bright, glorious, sunny.

Reginald Spelthorne rose, threw up his window, and while the fresh breeze fanned his cheek and his forehead, gathered strength for the ordeal through which he had inevitably to pass.

He framed many speeches, all of which he forgot as soon as made.

We never make love as we intend to do it.

The sentences gush forth spontaneously.

Foolish or sensible, out they come, as if our tongues had got quite beyond our control.

CHAPTER XV.

HOW REGINALD WENT THROUGH THE ORDEAL.

WHEN Reginald entered the breakfast parlour he found that he had to breakfast alone.

Mr. Courtenay was already in his study.

He persuaded himself for five minutes that he was eating and drinking, and then went to his work.

He made his entry, therefore, into the drawing-room, where, according to precedent, he expected to find Miriam at the window doing her sampler work.

Yes, there she was in her white muslin and coral, with her jet black hair and damask cheeks.

He went and sat down by her after saying good morning; and sat for some minutes in perfect silence watching Miriam work the word "Love" in crimson silk.

At length, "Whom do you love best in the world Miriam?" he asked.

"How can you ask? Whom does *everybody* love best? 'her main-sill,' as the Welshman says, of course," exclaimed the merry maiden.

"Humph! well, whom do you love the next best to yourself?"

"Why, let me see," said the girl, pausing thoughtfully with her needle poised in her hand, "I think that next to myself I love Miriam Courtenay best of all the world.

"I thought so—and I can lay my hand upon my heart and say that you don't love Miriam Courtenay a whit better than I do—no, nor yet half so well. I'll throw down my gage on that and fight it out to extremity. Come, what have

you to say to that?" asked the young man, with all the earnestness in his face and manner that his light words wanted, "say—speak—what do you say to that?"

"Why, that you are as foolish as Miriam herself in loving such a little out-of-the-way baggage, that is neither woman nor child, nor good nor bad, nor anything else in particular."

"Well, at any rate, we both agree in loving and worshipping Miriam, however we may differ in our opinion of her; I, for instance, thinking her a beautiful, joyous, delightful girl—so it's settled, isn't it?"

"What is settled?"

"Oh! you know, you tease."

"I know the weather is settled, if you mean that."

"Pooh!"

"I don't know that the naval trouble with France is settled, if you mean that."

"Pooh, pooh!"

"I know that the marriage dower of two thousand pounds is settled upon my cousin Caroline, if you mean that."

"Pooh, pooh, pooh!"

"Well, I shall not try to guess again lest you say pooh, pooh, pooh, pooh, four times."

"Miriam," said the young man earnestly, "I think, without presumption, I may say that I know your disposition towards me. Miriam, I wish that we should pass all our lives together, side by side. I would like to open my heart and bid you look into it and read for yourself; I hate to say I love you—though, if you could look into my heart! Oh that phrase 'I love you,' Miriam, is so fallen, is so prostituted, so degraded from its high meaning. I love you so often means I need your wealth, need your family influence—I desire your delightful beauty. Oh, Miriam, dearest girl, how then shall I express my true, sincere, earnest devotion to you?

"You needn't—I know you like me Reginald," murmured Miriam very low, and then she added lower still, "but I am nothing but a wild girl, and seriously, I fear, it isn't right for me to listen to such words for years to come yet. And I fear father might not like it only that he likes you so very well."

And Miriam bent over her sampler diligently, commencing the next word HOPE in azure silk.

"I know it, Miriam; dear, candid girl, I know it all—all the seeming error. But, Miriam, I am going away to-day,"—she looked up in surprise—"and I may be gone for several years. Before I go I wish to have a fair understanding with yourself and your father, so that I may go away with some feeling of security. I want you both to promise that when I return you will give me your hand."

"You may speak to father, Reginald; but I tell you frankly now what I wish you had heard before. It is this, that I have been promised to my grim cousin, Major Doble, ever since I can remember anything, and till you came I have always, whenever I have anticipated the future at all, looked forward to being his humdrum wife, and live in a grim, three-storey red brick in a row, and opposite another row of stiff prison like red brick houses, each one of which taken singly is more dreary than the rest. I didn't like the

Prospect, Reginald, but I thought it was my fate, and the best father could do for me, and so I thought of no other possibility but the grim red brick house in the City, and Major Doble; besides, father is so good a father, and so fond and indulgent, that it seemed too wicked to think of disappointing his gentle wishes that more take the form of commands; and so, Reginald, although whenever I would think of the grim brick house with tall, dark chambers, and the narrow, stony, distracting street before it, and Major Doble, my heart would sink very heavy, and I would think, young as I was, that there was scarcely any hope for me at all. Yet I would recollect my dear, good father wished it, and I would pluck up my spirits and feel blithe as a bird again. It was all understood at the school where I got finished, as they call it, and father left word that Major Doble should be admitted to visit me, so when I was there he came to visit me frequently, and took me out riding or driving, and to concerts; and the girls used to whisper together, and say that I was engaged."

"Stop! stop! Pardon me, Miriam! pardon me, dear girl! but I am giddy—indeed I am ill, have you yourself promised to marry him?"

"No, surely not, that is the reason why I consider myself in some sort free, but of my duty to my good father. No, he has never even asked me; he considers my father's promise quite sufficient, and our marriage quite a matter of course, and so I used to consider it, too.

"These things are often done, Reginald—these betrothals, I mean. Anyone might suppose the custom obsolete, having died in the dark ages. It is not; it prevails here to a considerable extent. It is done to keep family property together, or family interest closely cemented. And, Reginald, he has never wanted me yet, you see. He considers me a child yet; so I am, compared to him in years, and so I should be in all things a child, but that the shadow of that grim brick house is always falling on my heart."

"And yet, with all this, you are a very, very merry maiden."

"Yes, so I am—I try to be; I keep a din up in my head to prevent me hearing what my heart wants to say. Goodness! I can do nothing for the poor thing, you know; and what's the use of stopping to listen to its cry? That would only encourage it to complain the more. Don't look so sorry, Reginald. It is not all effort—it could not be, you know. I'm naturally of a glad, elastic temper, and, but for this drawback, Heaven knows what I should be—the wildest, maddest, most harum-scarum, most heels-over-head, skip-over-the-moon madcap that ever turned a quiet home topsy-turvy, and drove a quiet family to distraction. And I, who am naturally so wild and thoughtless, must be sobered, and made thoughtful by the prospect of that prison before me."

"Miriam, does this man love you?"

"Reginald, if I say he does not hate me, it is the extent of all favourable things I can say about the state of his mind towards me. No, he does not love me. It is certainly a betrothal of convenience."

"But, my dearest girl, erase all these troubled thoughts about the future, unnatural to your age, and unwholesome to yourself. This whole cloud must be swept away like a cobweb. He doesn't love you—you don't love him. He has never asked you to marry him—you have never promised to do so. It is merely a betrothal of convenience, made by the parents of both, for the purpose of keeping family property together and cementing family interest. Oh! it is all wrong, and there is nothing in it. I will speak to your father; I will enter the lists with this Major Doble as a competitor for your hand in worldly circumstances, in family wealth, and social position. Am I not his junior? Besides, I wear my lady's favour, which he does not. I will go to your father now, and tell him as much. Shall I, Miriam?"

The young lady was busy threading her needle with golden yellow silk, and did not answer.

He repeated the question.

"Yes," murmured Miriam, beginning to embroider the last word of the trio FAITH in sunbeam silk.

Reginald for the first time folded her in his arms.

"My own Miriam."

"Dear Reginald!"

And so their troth was plighted.

"But you are not really going to India to-day?" asked Miriam.

"No, dear—not now."

"Why not now?"

"You have changed all my plans."

"For the worse?"

"No; every one for the better."

"And your grim cousin?"

"He will look grimmer than ever."

"Not so. He can marry Caroline with her two thousand pounds dowry."

"Shall I suggest it to him?" asked Miriam archly.

"No, I think not," said Reginald; "else would he, indeed, be disinclined to make the exchange."

"Caroline is pretty."

"You are prettier."

"Caroline has bright eyes."

"Nay, now," cried her lover; "you are but angling for compliments, and I will not encourage you."

"What think you, then, of this?" said Miriam. "Major Doble is coming here to-day."

"What for?"

"To say he will wait no longer."

"Then I had better make haste."

"Make haste to do what?"

"To ask your father."

"Tell him I will *not* marry Major Doble, even if he does not consent to your taking his place. The major comes here at one. It is now twelve."

No time was to be lost.

He raised her hand to his lips, and darted upstairs to where Mr. Courtenay sat in his study.

"My dear sir," exclaimed Reginald, bursting in very unceremoniously, "I have something of the utmost importance to say to you. You will, therefore, I am sure, excuse my interrupting you."

"Certainly, my boy, certainly. What is it?"

That's exactly what, at that moment, Reginald could not have explained for the life of him.

He stood, therefore, looking very foolish for a moment.

"What is it?" repeated Mr. Courtenay.

"I love your daughter, Miriam, and I came here to ask your consent to our engagement."

"Whew!" exclaimed the antiquary; "that's it—is it?"

"Yes, sir."

"But the girl's engaged."

"I know that, sir."

"Well, then, what's to be done?"

"She does not love him, sir. You could not surely desire her to marry one for whom she has no affection."

"Certainly not, boy—certainly not; but you say 'engagement.' I like not engagements. They only wear out the hearts and destroy the happiness of the young. Why not marry her, and take her with you?"

Reginald could not speak.

He could only take the old man's hand, press it, and thank him with a look.

So it was arranged.

Major Doble received his *congé* rather unceremoniously, and Reginald did *not go* that day, but in the course of a few days was united to Miriam.

The old antiquary declined their offer to take him with them, and thus it was that they were on board the Termagant bound for India.

CHAPTER XVI.

MA-TA-WINA.

NOTHING can exceed the beauty of the forests of the Indian Archipelago.

Tall and elegant trees, with scarce a branch for more than a hundred feet from the ground, form natural avenues o'ercanopied with thick foliage.

Delicate flowers and tender plants gem the margin of tiny torrents.

A blue sky and a pale sun look down upon an ever-lovely landscape.

Nature seems in these climes to have reserved a home for herself.

She may leave other countries to the terrors of an ice-bound winter, or the glare of an unnatural summer; but in these sea-girt islands the temperature seems to adapt itself to the peculiar wants of the goddess.

No more beautiful spot can well be imagined than the hamlet of Bronerai, near the town of Brunei, in Borneo.

It is situated just on the edge of a great jungle on the margin of the river.

Some of the houses were built over the stream, supported on poles.

Others studded the bank; and one wigwam was concealed in the forest under the shade of a lofty tree.

In this wigwam lived Ta-win-tata and his daughter, Ma-ta-wina.

Ta-win-tata was one of the elders of the village, which belonged to the Malay tribe.

He was a man much respected by his people.

Ma-ta-wina was the beauty of the hamlet.

Certainly there was every opportunity for discerning her beauties, for the Malay men wear only a waist-covering, and the women nothing.

Ma-ta-wina was tall and graceful.

Certainly her skin was golden; but that did not render her limbs less round—her form less agile—her bosom less exquisitely moulded—her eyes less languishingly beautiful.

She was a type of natural beauty. She unwillingly followed Nature's laws.

Surely a woman in this condition is infinitely more lovely—more approaching the ideal of beauty than the thing of furbelows and crinoline we see in European society!

All the young men in Bronerai loved Ma-ta-wina—all sought her hand.

But among those who followed her in the forest and sat at her feet by the wigwams, one only found favour in her eyes.

This was La-sa-tawi, the eagle-eyed—a youth tall as the pine and true as the lion.

He was a warrior—the youngest warrior in the tribe.

And at the moment we introduce them to the reader it was their nuptial day.

La-sa-tawi had prepared a little wigwam to be their home just outside the hamlet, and but little removed from the cabin of her father, Ta-win-tata.

The ceremonies of the simple tribe were over, and the newly-married couple were left together in their home.

They sat there in the deepening twilight—twilight is very late in those climes—gazing out of the little cabin window.

Ma-ta-wina sat upon his knee—her head reclining on his shoulder—her eyes fixed on him in all the trust and love of a newly-wedded life; his strong arm enveloping her exquisite form and pressing her fondly to his bosom.

"The shadows creep over the land, Ma-ta-wina," said he; "but the sun still dwells on our cabin."

"Yes," returned the bride, "it tells us of a bright future."

"Ah!" said the young warrior, "the elders have blessed us, and we shall be happy—happy in our own love—happy in the love of our children."

Thus conversing the hours sped on, until it was time for them to retire to rest.

Just as they were about to betake themselves to their primitive couch of skins a cry was heard without.

La-sa-tawi released his bride from his arms and leaped up.

Hardly had he done so when the door was burst violently open, and into the wigwam swarmed the men of a Dyak tribe.

La-sa-tawi was unarmed, but he had just time to seize a small kriss and stab the first comer.

The man fell dead to the ground.

But it was in vain he thus defended himself.

He was overpowered, dragged away, and reserved for the scalping-knife.

One of the other savages seized upon Ma-ta-wina with a ferocious leer, and bound her to one of the beams which supported the roof.

And there they left her alone with the dead, promising to fetch her away to become the bride of one of their chiefs.

CHAPTER XVII.

VENGEANCE!

THE massacre was complete.

Not one of the old people of the village was spared, except one or two of the chiefs who were reserved for the scalping knife.

Many of the young warriors escaped, and, among them, La-sa-tawi, who had contrived to cut his bonds.

These went away towards Brunei to prepare for the work of vengeance.

La-sa-tawi knew well the customs of his enemies, and felt sure that his virgin-bride would remain untouched—unpolluted for at least a month.

During that time he hoped to be able to rally round sufficient warriors to descend upon the Dyak village, and exterminate them utterly.

Vengeance is a terrible feeling, but we all are slaves to it sometimes.

Even the most highly-polished and educated among us are liable to fearful outbursts of hatred.

How much more terrible, then, is the hatred, the thirst of vengeance, which animate a savage.

It was a dark night.

The sky was strangely obscured.

Certainly it was winter; but then winter in those climes means a thermometer at 50 or 60 degrees.

In the centre of a deep jungle blazed a large fire.

Round it sat about a hundred men.

They were holding a council of war.

Ever and anon one of their number would rise and address the others energetically.

Then, when he resumed his seat, there would be a dead silence for a few moments, until another rose to speak.

At length La-sa-tawi, with a solemn air and a sad visage, began to harangue them.

The young warrior had been chosen their chief.

"Men of the Eagle-eye," he said, " listen—

"I was the youngest warrior of a tribe.

" Nevertheless I was a warrior, I found favour in the eyes of a flower which I took to wear next my heart."

Here his voice was tremulous with emotion, but he continued,—

" The dogs of the Ta-win-sin came down upon us in the night.

" They stole from me my flower.

" Shall I leave it to wither in their wigwams?

" No; I will go to them and take from them my flower; and I will leave them to swelter in their gore.

" I am going; will you come with me?"

An universal shout, an universal starting to their feet, displayed their eagerness to follow him.

Then they all sat down again in silence and smoked a pipe, passing it round from one to the other without a word.

This was a bond of fellowship.

It might be their last night together.

Then under the dark night—it was then ten o'clock, they rose; and put out their fires.

This was all the home they had to leave.

Their wives and their mothers had all gone to the silent lake.

" We have no wives to leave," said La-sa-tawi; " we will take to us wives from among the squaws of the dogs of the Ta-win-sin."

They put out their fires, as I have said, arranged their arms and prepared to set out.

The village of the Dyaks lay about five miles beyond, on the other side of the jungle.

The Dyaks, though more ferocious and more implacable than the Malays, had not arrived at so great a degree of civilisation.

That is to say, they had not yet learned the art of killing so well as their enemies.

They still used their poisoned arrows, their sumpitans, and their hatchets.

La-sa-tawi had determined that his scheme of vengeance should succeed.

He had, therefore, gone down himself to the Dutch settlements and purchased muskets.

With these some of his followers were armed, while others had merely the kriss, the bow, and the hatchet.

Along the silent wood the hundred avengers glided.

They reversed their sandals so that the trace left appeared those of a force traversing an opposite direction.

When they had gone half-way they readjusted them so as entirely to mystify a pursuer.

Not a word was spoken.

They went on quietly as the snake for an hour and a half.

Then the smoke of a camp fire was visible in the distance.

La-sa-tawi gave the word to halt, and with one other glided along on his belly to reconnoitre.

By the camp fire sat four men.

A spasm passed over the face of La-sa-tawi as he gazed upon them.

"That," whispered he to his companion, "that is the dog who carried away my flower. Give me your musket."

Sharp sounded the crack of the rifle in the still night, and the man whom La-sa-tawi had pointed out fell dead into the camp fire.

CHAPTER XVIII.

FORTUNE'S FROLICS.

THE ship which contained the two lovers, so strangely severed and so strangely united, sped rapidly on her way, and landed the adventurers just below the point at which Sarawak now stands.

It was a strange thing that they should all have been bound for the same spot.

Reginald Spelthorne's property lay beyond Brunèi, in the Dutch settlement, and thither, also, John Stuart Blakesley and Ethel betook themselves to seek their fortune.

They had various fortunes.

Reginald had come to continue the cultivation of an estate ready to his hand.

Blakesley had to till the ungrateful soil—to dig and dive for wealth in untilled pastures.

Yet with the former nothing prospered, while with the latter everything seemed to lead to golden showers of fortune.

While the estate of Reginald and Miriam Spelthorne was inundated by the overflowings of the river—while their crops were spoiled—their house robbed—their home uncomfortable—a little spot of wild wealth grew up on the opposite side of the town of Brunèi.

A sunny little bungalow, on the edge of the deep jungle, was the house of Ethel and John Blakesley.

Corn fields waved their golden plenty round

their dwelling, and the Malays near them soon became friendly.

With the money he had brought from England he was enabled to buy labour, and among the young men of the tribe in which La-sa-tawi was a warrior, there were many who, in the time of peace, were glad to lay aside the bow and the hatchet to take up the sickle and the plough-handle.

On the night on which the Dyaks descended upon the village—the night of the wedding of La-sa-tawi and Ma-ta-wina—John and Ethel were seated at an open window, gazing on the landscape.

"Certainly, Ethel," said he, "fortune seems to smile on us."

"It does, indeed, my own," replied the young wife; "I wonder how our neighbours thrive?"

"Alas! they thrive but ill, dearest; the fickle goddess seems to have fixed upon them out of revenge for our prosperity. But, great Heavens! what is that?" he added, rising, and pointing anxiously towards the Malay village.

"The hamlet is on fire, love," cried Ethel, "let us go and see of what assistance we can be."

"No, no," said Blakesley, "go not; rather keep inside, closing every point of entrance into this house."

"Why so, my husband?" cried Ethel, in accents of deep alarm.

"Because, my love, the village is in the hands of the Dyaks, who will have no mercy."

No time was lost.

The labourers on the little estate soon succeeded in barricading the doors, and stood prepared to defend the house.

The savages left them until the last.

They evidently anticipated a stout resistance, and when they had massacred the unresisting people of the Malay hamlet, they came with blood-red hands and angry visages towards the little house.

It was midnight.

Not a soul, however, slept.

Even Ethel stood musket in hand at the window, while John Blakesley and Jacob defended another.

There were in all thirty defenders.

The number of the besiegers was three hundred.

In a hand-to-hand fight resistance would have been useless; but, fortunately, the occupants of the bungalow possessed muskets.

The hamlet burned rapidly.

The houses, built only of wood, and full of inflammable materials, flamed away like tinder, and cast lurid reflections along the quiet river, and among the forest glades.

At length all was destroyed.

The sound of the crackling wood ceased.

There were no longer any cries for mercy.

The dead were lying silently under the bright stars.

The flames ceased to cast their vivid reflections over the faces of the massacred.

There was a dead silence.

An awful lull.

"Now it will be our turn," said John Blakesley solemnly.

There was a strange hush over his soul which he could not understand.

He could not recognise in it a presentiment of evil. The evil was present, no warning was, therefore, needed.

He stood with his arm round Ethel's waist, gazing fondly upon her.

"This will be a terrible struggle," he said kindly, "but you must try to bear up for my sake as well as your own."

"I will, dearest."

"You are a brave girl, Ethel," he said fondly, "but see," he added, pointing to the edge of the forest, "here they come like hungry wolves. Give them a good reception there, boys," he shouted to the Malays.

CHAPTER XIX.

THE ATTACK ON THE BUNGALOW.

ON they came, bloodstained—threatening.

Along the edge of the wood they extended in a double line, waving aloft their hatchets, their spears, their bows and their sumpitans.

The first impediment to their progress which they met with at the White Farm, as the bungalow was named, was the wooden paling which had been set up round the plantation to keep away animals who would destroy the crops.

Behind this were stationed twenty Malays with muskets.

The savages came on, yelling, screaming, wildly gesticulating.

They little anticipated the reception they would meet with.

Just as they were within ten yards of the the stockade they halted.

A blaze of fire—a rush of bullets through the air—a loud report, and twenty of their number lay dead.

They stood still, puzzled and bewildered for a moment.

Then they turned and fled with loud cries towards the forest, followed by a desultory fire from the Malays.

"That's right, my boys," cried Blakesley, enthusiastically; "give it to them like that, and they will not care to return again in a hurry."

He mistook their nature, however, entirely.

Half an hour of suspense followed.

"I almost think," said John Stuart Blakesley, "I almost think we are rid of them for the night. Let us go to supper."

Guards were placed at each corner of the building, one man being ensconced in the topmost tower to give warning of any approach of an enemy.

They sat down to their repast.

Ethel could eat little.

Jacob less.

Blakesley none.

He seemed to have given up the functions of a living man, except the faculty of talking.

"Ethel, dearest," he whispered, "I feel a strange sort of presentiment."

"Say not so, my husband," cried she. "It is fear for me that makes you feel thus."

"No, dearest, I am ashamed to say it, but it is fear for myself."

"What mean you?"

"I shall not survive this night."

Ethel trembled violently.

She could not weep—she could only gaze on him with seared eyeballs—wild, haggard with fear.

Just as he spoke a stray shot was fired.

"They are at it again!" cried Blakesley.

And so they were.

Forth from the wood came the yelling savages again.

The Malays fired, but with less effect; and before they had time to reload the hatchets of the besiegers were dashing against the frail wooden paling.

"Leave the stockade, boys!" cried Blakesley. "Come into the house, and fire from the terrace."

Obedient as automata, the Malays ran from the ground and entered the house.

Round the bungalow ran a broad terrace partially protected from without.

On this was now piled the furniture, and behind the furniture kneeled the defenders.

Not one had yet fallen.

Ethel began to hope for the best.

"Everything goes well," she said to her husband; "not one of our men has fallen yet."

"No; but they have destroyed one of our hopes of safety — the stockade," answered Blakesley gloomily.

The paling was too high for the savages to scale; but it was not long before their hatchets had formed a breach wide enough for them to creep through.

The first man who showed himself was shot down—then another—then another.

Then with a savage yell the Dyaks rushed in in a body, shrieking frantically, and wildly discharging their arrows in all directions.

They made a halt beneath the terrace, and while the Malays were reloading poured in a deadly volley of poisoned barbs.

Several Malays fell, and then old Jacob Spelthorne.

Not a moment of preparation. The barbed arrow cloved his skull, and he fell dead at his daughter's feet.

Ethel stooped down with quivering lips and pale cheeks, and kissed him.

Then she rose up again; and with a firm glance at her husband, said, in a low, determined voice,

"I fought for you both. Now, my husband, I will fight for you."

"Brave girl, brave girl," he murmured; "you had better go in."

"Why—why dearest?"

"There is no occasion for you to expose yourself to danger."

"Why do you do so, then?"

"I must; it is my duty."

"Where your duty calls you, it calls me also," returned Ethel.

And so she remained.

The Malays stuck to their posts like brave fellows as they were.

But, then, so also did the savages.

The latter were exasperated by defeat and the number of their dead.

They had advanced three hundred to the attack; they numbered now two hundred and fifty.

They had altered their mode of attack.

They stationed themselves round the house under the terraces, so that it was necessary for the Malays to lean over in order to fire at them, and thus expose their bodies to their arrows.

They appeared, however, not over anxious to act on the offensive.

A lull came suddenly.

Ethel was pleased.

Blakesley, however, dreaded it.

He went down stairs quietly and silently, without trying to have speech with any one.

He came up again haggard and pale.

"What is the matter, dearest?" asked Ethel.

"It is as I feared," answered he, vaguely.

"What is it? What ails you?"

"They are in the house, Ethel; there is no hope left for us."

He thought a moment.

Then a smile passed over his face—a cold grim smile.

"Let us go down stairs," he said; "follow me."

At the bottom of the house was a passage.

On either side of this were rooms used for preserving meat and vegetables, and separated from it by an iron trellis work.

The savages had quietly broken down the door, and were now in the passage, striving to enter this pantry.

"Now, my men," said Blakesley; "you see that open ironwork. Through that you can fire at those dogs of Dyaks, and they cannot touch you."

"How so, master?" asked the Malay gardener who acted as a kind of leader to the other men.

"Why," returned Blakesley; "none of their broad-headed arrows can enter that ironwork, while your bullets can whistle through at leisure. Go, ten of you, to that side into the smaller room; I will take the others into the larger. You, Ethel, remain up stairs. In such a scene of butchery you had best not take part."

Ethel went up, and sat down upon the top landing.

Down below all was in darkness.

The savages had broken open the door; but except the first faint streaks of morning, which contrived to struggle through into the passage, they had no light.

The Malays crept along the ground up to the iron trellis-work, and there stood up.

The savages worked on in silence, cutting away with their hatchets at the wood-work underneath the iron.

There were fifty inside the passage.

There were twenty-five Malays standing by their side.

Each took deliberate aim.

The savages worked on.

Then a blaze and a roar, and twenty-five

Dyaks fell, to join their companions in the hunting grounds of the dead.

Their companions seemed paralysed for a moment.

They stood stock-still, and gave the Malays time to re-load.

When, therefore, they opened the door, and began to crowd fearfully out of the house, they were greeted by a second volley, almost as deadly as before.

Only fifteen out of the fifty rejoined their comrades outside.

Now, then, was the time for victory.

The savages appeared scared.

Some stood in consultation, others turned and fled.

"Let us sally out upon them," cried Blakesley, warming with victory, and eager for the fray.

The door of the room was therefore thrown open, and the twenty-five rushed forth.

A volley of musketry first, and then the bayonet.

The savages made but a feeble resistance.

They were scared, taken aback, discouraged at the reception they met with, and in a few moments gave way, and fled.

They were pursued only as far as the stockade, which the victors stopped to repair.

"They will come no more to night, Ethel," said Blakesley, as he returned to the house.

"You at least are safe over the time of your prophecy," said she, smiling through her tears.

"Yes, dearest; but your poor father—he has fallen a victim to these wretches."

"Yes, poor father; little did he think when he left Castle Ferry to what a fate I was leading him."

"You, Ethel, say rather that I should not have dared to take you from your home to make you suffer such terrible scenes as this."

A watch was placed at each door and on the terrace, and the little household retired to rest.

CHAPTER XX.

THE LOG ON THE RIVER.

THE night passed without any renewal of the attack.

The sleepers slept long and heavily.

Worn out by the fatigues and terrors of the defence, the sun was high in the heavens before they arose and came down to their lonely meal.

No mention was made of the dead; but the breakfast hour passed in comparative silence.

When the farce of a meal had been concluded Blakesley drew his chair closer to that of Ethel, and said:

"Ethel, dearest, do not think me unkind if I for a moment revert to what happened last night."

"You are never unkind, John," replied his wife, forcing a smile.

"I wish to speak of your father, Ethel," said her husband. "We are in peace at present, but probably ere night falls those red devils will be

down on us again. Let us, then, bury your father. It may seem a hurried burial, but it will be better than leaving his body in any way in the power of those wretches."

"Very well, dear," said Ethel.

And so it was done.

Poor old Jacob Spelthorne was borne to his last home under the burning sun of Borneo.

Ethel begged, with tears in her eyes, that a small monument might be raised to his memory.

But Blakesley refused her request, even though she wept.

He had still hanging over him the dread presentiment which had so oppressed him the night before.

"No, no," he said, gloomily; "leave no vestige, leave no mark by which those devils can trace his tomb and desecrate his remains."

But—who will blame her?—Ethel did not obey her husband in this.

When they left the grave there was, at its head, a tiny white stone, which pointed out, though only to her, the last resting-place of the last Spelthorne of Castle Ferry.

The day passed, and no sign of the return of the savages.

Ethel and John were standing on the terrace.

"Oh! what a lovely evening it is!" she cried; "and how calm and still."

"It only precedes a storm."

"You are very gloomy."

"Yes, love. I have still impending over my heart the weight of that dread presentiment."

"Why, John, I have more cause to mourn than you."

"Why so?"

"Have I not lost my father? Have I not seen him murdered before my eyes?"

"It will be a worse, a far worse fate, for me to die under your very eyes, and see you dragged from me by ruthless savages."

"Oh! my dearest husband, do not give way to these terrible forebodings. Perhaps—who knows?—these Dyaks may not return."

He was about to reply when the Malay, who was standing gun in hand near them, touched his arm, and said—

"Master!"

"Yes; what is it?"

"You can see the river plainly from where you stand?"

"Yes."

"Can you see, just beyond that first clump of reeds, a black log in the water?"

"Yes."

"Did you ever see it before?"

"No, no; why do you ask me?"

"Why, sir, if you notice, the river is flowing towards the left."

"Yes."

"And the log is floating towards the right?"

"Yes; what mean you?"

"Why, sir, the log is floating *against the stream. That is not a log, but a man.*"

"Are you sure?" asked Blakesley.

"Yes, sir; and I will shoot him."

The Malay raised his musket, pointed at the log, and, after the lapse of at least two minutes, fired.

The log sprang up out of the water, then tottered, and fell heavily back into the river.

"He came to reconnoitre," said the Malay; "we shall have them here again before midnight."

"I said so," said Blakesley, moodily.

The evening passed.

The sun set in golden splendour; and at ten o'clock the quiet landscape discovered no trace of an enemy.

"I begin to hope," said Ethel, as they sat down to a light supper; "I begin almost to hope that your forebodings are groundless."

"Why, dearest?"

"Because I think that the death of that spy may prevent the coming of the others."

"It may, love," said he.

He thought a moment.

"It is cruel—unkind," he reasoned, "thus openly to give way to my alarms. Even in the very teeth of my understanding I will assume a hopefulness I cannot feel."

"Yes," he added, "yes; perhaps after the lesson they had last night, and the immediate discovery of their ruse to-day, they will, at length, feel inclined to desist."

He knew well, however, that the lesson they had received the night before was only a lesson of hatred.

He was well aware of their character.

"Let us hope so, indeed," said Ethel. "You will go to bed to-night, love; and not sit up in expectation of an attack."

"I know not what to do," he said; "perhaps it will be as well to sit up."

"You need not do so, sir, excuse me," put in the black servant. "I will watch and give you the alarm in case they should come."

"Do you think they will come, Henry?" asked Ethel.

(They had given English names to all the black domestics.)

"Well, madam, I should not like to deceive you," said the man. "I think they will."

"But they will surely not attempt the same kind of thing as before?"

"No, sir; they will try some treacherous mode or another."

"Just as I feared," said Blakesley; "we are less prepared for treachery than for an open attack."

"They can scarcely come upon us unawares," observed Ethel.

The man was silent.

"You do not speak, Henry."

"I can say nothing, madam. We must watch and do our best."

CHAPTER XXI.

THE SECOND ATTACK.

JOHN BLAKESLEY and Ethel retired early to rest.

They both inwardly expected that they should have but a short time of repose, though neither intimated that to the other.

Sleep came sweetly over Ethel's brow; but Blakesley it refused to visit.

He lay there, gazing with his mind's eye over the past and the future; and, as he kissed his wife's brow, and looked fondly at her as she slumbered softly by his side, something told him plainly it was for the last time.

The first two hours passed in perfect quiet; and had Blakesley been in a different condition of mind he would almost have been inclined to think that the savages had determined upon abandoning the attack.

It was about one o'clock in the morning when a feeling of overpowering heat came over him.

Knowing the extraordinary tricks which Nature plays us in those sultry climes, he at first thought nothing of it.

But it became worse and worse.

Then a smell of burning wood could plainly be discerned.

He gently shook Ethel.

"Ethel, dearest," he cried.

No answer.

"Ethel, dearest."

The heat and the fumes of the fire had partially stupefied her.

"Ethel, I say," he cried, shaking her more roughly.

"Yes, John, yes; what is the matter?" she exclaimed, awakening, and half-sitting up in the bed.

"The house is on fire; be quick and dress yourself."

"They have come, then," she said, calmly, as she hurried on her clothes.

"I know not," said he.

"Have you not been down?"

"No."

"Then how know you that the house is on fire?"

"I know it," he answered.

They were now dressed; and, opening the door cautiously, Blakesley listened.

The smoke came thick and fast up the stairs, but the only sound was the crackling of the wood.

The Malays were evidently all asleep.

In another minute the alarm-bell rang clearly and shrilly through the house.

On descending to the terrace they found the Malay who had been keeping watch dead—pierced through the head by an arrow.

The others were now crowding on the first landing, grasping their muskets, and gazing with eager, anxious looks at Blakesley.

"Well, my men," said he, "here they are again."

"Yes, sir, but where are they?"

"That's more than I can tell," returned he, "where is the fire?"

"In the pantry."

"Well, then, undo the fastenings of the tanks, and flood the house," cried Blakesley.

The bungalow had been so constructed that the water was kept in large tanks over the pantries, and in the very centre, furthest from the outer air, and therefore the coolest spot that could be chosen.

Blakesley's orders were no sooner given than obeyed; and in an instant the whole ground-

floor of the house was inundated by a vast stream of water.

This for a moment subdued the fire.

Only for a moment, however.

The fire had evidently been burning for some time; and an immense pile of wood had been collected quietly by the savages round the house.

The bungalow was built entirely of inflammable materials, and was soon wrapped in flames.

The whole bottom portion of the edifice was now, in truth, one mass of burning timber.

Only the iron pilasters which supported the corners of the building prevented its tottering to the ground.

The savages uttered loud yells of joy as the increasing flames sprang up and caught fresh portions of the house.

"We will give them a still warmer reception," said Blakesley, with white and quivering lips.

"Henry," he cried, "how does our powder run?"

"We have plenty, sir."

"Let me have a barrel of it, then."

The man hesitated.

"Why do you not go at once?" asked Blakesley, with some sternness.

"You will endanger your own life, sir, and Mrs. Blakesley's also," replied the servant, "by having a powder barrel in this room."

"Go, Henry, go," said Ethel, "and do as Mr. Blakesley wishes you to do."

The man went, and soon returned with a small barrel of powder.

Blakesley caught it up eagerly, and rushed to a corner of the room where it was less hot than elsewhere.

"Now then, Henry, the pitch."

In a few moments the barrel was well pitched, and some pieces of rope stuck over it, so that it would burn awhile before the powder caught.

This done, Blakesley cautiously approached the terrace, underneath which the fire raged fiercely.

A crowd of savages were collected beneath.

He then let down the barrel carefully, slowly, having first ignited a portion of the rope.

It was not noticed; and when on the ground it began to blaze it was looked upon merely as a portion of the burning timber.

Presently. however, a tremendous explosion, mingled with shrieks and yells of agony, rent the air.

Then a dead hush.

Twenty savages had been blown to pieces.

"Oh, it is horrible!" cried Ethel, covering her face with her hands.

"Oh master, master!" cried a Malay, rushing in, "they are scaling the terrace!"

And even as he spoke, the gaunt figure of a savage appeared above the trellis-work.

He was knocked over.

But then there came another and another, until they swarmed into the room.

The powder had certainly done execution; but it had also blown away a portion of the parapet.

In they came then, yelling, shrieking, and gesticulating.

The Malays threw themselves in front of their master and mistress; but it was of no avail.

Numbers overpowered them.

"Oh, Ethel!" cried Blakesley in agony, "it is as I said. This is our last embrace!"

Even as he spoke, and as he imprinted a passionate kiss on her forehead, one of the Dyaks advanced towards them.

Blakesley stood up to confront him, and placed Ethel behind him for protection.

It was of no avail, however.

Ten swarmed round them.

Some seized her rudely and dragged her away, while others fell on her husband.

He fought to the last gasp, struggling manfully with his enemies, and killing several.

But he at length sank upon his knees, and still fighting was struck down by a blow from a hatchet.

His prophecy was fulfilled.

By sunrise that morning not a soul remained alive at the White Farm.

——

CHAPTER XXII.

THE VIRGIN BRIDE AND WIDOWED WIFE.

ETHEL was spared the horror of witnessing her husband's death.

Before the hatchet of the savage clove his skull, she had been dragged out of the house and hurried into the forest.

The savages were not long completing their task of blood, and soon set out on their return journey.

Out of the three hundred who had advanced first to the attack on the White Farm, one hundred and eighty only went back to the wigwams of the tribe.

Ethel, Ma-ta-wini, and ten other women were led prisoners into the tents.

Before starting on their journey a terrible indignity was put upon Ethel.

It will be remembered that in those climes the women wear no clothes.

The Dyaks saw no reason why she, more than another, should veil her beauties from the sun.

Everything, therefore, was stripped off her, and she entered the Dyak village like Ma-ta-wina, without a vestige of clothing upon her.

"The daughter of the white man is very fair," said Ra-olao, the chief of the tribe, as he gazed wantonly and wonderingly upon her exquisitely moulded limbs and snowy skin; "but the suns of Borneo will soon make her like the daughters of our tribe. Ra-olao will take her into his wigwam when the new moon comes, and she shall be the chief among his wives."

The extreme of horror struck Ethel's heart as she heard these words.

"Oh, Heaven will never allow it!" she cried, in terror.

"Daughter of the white man," said a voice near her, "fear not!"

Ethel turned round and saw, standing by her side, Ma-ta-wina, the virgin bride.

"You also a prisoner?" cried she.

She had known the Malay girl well in the hamlet by the river.

"Yes, I also am here," said the girl; "but fear not. La-sa-tawi has escaped, and will come here with his slaves to rescue us!"

"Oh, Ma-ta-wina!" murmured Ethel, crimsoning with shame, "will they not let me have my clothes? Shall I be obliged to go about like this always?"

Oh, how lovely did the white girl look in this garb of nature! Still more lovely as the blushes chased each other over her neck and bosom.

"Do not think of that," said Ma-ta-wina; "think only of safety."

"But I cannot help thinking of it," cried Ethel, with tears in her eyes. "Women in our country never go about like this even for a moment."

"Do not think of it, dear lady," said Ma-ta-wina, taking her hand, "it will not be for long—ere the month is over La-sa-tawi and his warriors will be here; and when we return to our village I will make you some garments."

By some lucky chance Ethel and Ma-ta-wina were placed in the same hut.

They were left alone, and were seldom obliged to issue forth among the tribe.

Now and then Ethel was dragged out of her cabin, and forced to appear in some solemn conclave of the tribe, the purport of which she could not understand.

It was certainly nothing new for the Dyaks to see a woman in primitive condition. Ethel was forced to appear amongst them, but still they seemed to enjoy her confusion.

Except, therefore, when compelled, she never emerged from the hut.

On the night on which the report of La-sa-tawi's rifle carried the alarm through the Dyak's hamlet, Ethel and Ma-ta-wina were lying in each other's arms in the little cabin.

They formed a curious picture—the dusky form of the Malay girl contrasting strangely with the white limbs of the English captive.

Some unaccountable cause prevented their sleeping, and they lay there talking until nearly midnight.

"Do you really think he will come?" asked Ethel.

They were speaking of La-sa-tawi.

"I am certain he will come," said Ma-ta-wina.

"Every day makes our position more dangerous, because at the expiration of the month, Ra-olao will certainly carry out his intention of including me among his wives, and there can be no doubt but yours will be a similar fate."

"La-sa-tawi is a brave," replied the Indian girl; "he never fails."

"Let us indeed, hope so," said Ethel.

Just as she spoke the sharp crack of the young warrior's musket resounded through the village.

"Did I not say so?" said Mattawini; "that is my husband's signal."

CHAPTER XXIII.

HOW THEY CAME TO THE RESCUE.

THE man at whom the young man had pointed his rifle fell with a great cry into the camp fire.

His three companions fled away towards their wigwams.

In an instant all was confusion.

Every man in the village armed himself and turned out against the foe, but the dark forest around them revealed nothing. Not an enemy was to be seen anywhere, and as they stood in consultation around the camp fire, fear for the first time took possession of their hearts.

That there was an enemy there could be no doubt, but where he was concealed they could not possibly conceive.

While they were deliberating a long line of flame burst forth from the forest, revealing the forms of the hundred avengers standing in a circle round the village.

The Dyaks were huddled in confusion together around the fire, and many fell under the well-directed volleys of the Malays.

To stand there longer was courting death, so with yells and gesticulations they rushed towards the edge of the jungle and precipitated themselves upon their enemies.

The fight was of very short duration.

The Dyaks hacked and mowed at random with their hatchets, and carried fire and threw stray arrows among the foe.

The Malays, on the other hand, scarcely ever missed their aim; the object was not to gain a victory but to exterminate a tribe.

By three in the morning not one man remained alive in the Dyaks' village.

The Malays, then, who had not lost a single man, advanced to the wigwams.

"Now, then, my brothers," said La-sa-tawi; "we will find our women, and among the young squaws of the dead tribes the rest of you must find companions."

At the commencement of the fray Ra-ola had rushed to the cabin where Ethel and Mat-ta-wina were confined, and fastened them in.

He had too great an opinion of his intended English bride to allow her a chance of escape.

After an eager search throughout the village La-sa-tawi at length broke open the door of Ethel's hut, and in a moment was clasped to the breast of his long-lost bride.

The young warrior gazed in admiration and wonder at Ethel Blakesley, whom, in her utter absence of clothing he did not recognise as the lady with whom he had so often spoken at the White Farm.

"Who is that?" he whispered to the Indian girl, as she clung fondly to him.

"The lady of the White Farm," said Ma-ta-wina

"Yes," said Ethel, advancing, "have you heard anything of my husband?"

The young Indian gave no direct answer.

Ethel saw what he meant.

"Alas!" she cried, "he is dead, and you fear to tell me so."

"Lady," said La-sa-tawi, taking her hand and speaking very solemnly and slowly, "do not give way to grief—he is in the happy hunting-ground."

While they had been speaking, Ma-ta-wina had slipped away unperceived.

She now returned with a bundle of something in her arms.

"See," she whispered to Ethel, "here are your clothes; I found them in Ra-olao's hut. I will take my husband away while you dress."

So saying, she slipped out of the cabin, drew La-sa-tawi away, and closed the door.

Ethel seized upon her garments like a vulture upon his prey.

Never had she experienced so exquisite delight in attiring herself, and it was not many moments before she emerged from the hut decorated in splendour—with flounces, ribbons, and a broad straw hat.

If ever Ma-ta-wina felt a slight tinge of contempt for Ethel Blakesley it was at that moment. The distance between them, moreover, was now lengthened. While she had been living with the Indian girl in the log-hut, sleeping with her and wearing no other garment save which nature had given her, Ethel Blakesley had appeared to Ma-ta-wina as a sister—now she was again the lady of the White Farm.

The Malay warriors now set out for home.

In the midst were placed the rescued women, before them walked the captives; in this way they arrived about midday at the ruins of the Malay hamlet.

Ethel's first visit was made to the White Farm. Scarcely one vestige of the house itself remained, but it could easily be seen that the hands of friends had been busy there.

In the garden were three tombs.

The one for Jacob Spelthorne,—the second for John Stuart Blakesley,—the third a high mound, the tomb of the Malay servants.

CHAPTER XXIV.

A BABOON IN LOVE.

ETHEL BLAKESLEY now fixed her residence permanently in the Malay village.

She was treated with great respect and honour by the young warriors, and lived in a small cabin near that which Ma-ta-wina and La-sa-tawi, the newly-married couple, had built for themselves. I have omitted to mention before this that Ethel was in a fair way to become a mother.

This was a source of great anxiety as well as of sorrow to her.

She would sit for hours in her log hut weeping, thinking of the past and of the still more dreary future.

No father would bend in joy over the little one.

No father would call down blessings upon the first-born.

There was a certain pleasure in thinking that she would possess a remembrance of that husband,—but there was a pain in recollecting that it *was* only a remembrance.

About a fortnight after she had become quietly domiciled in the Malay village a circumstance occurred which materially affected *her* future, as well as the future of her child.

She was wandering along by the side of the river, thinking of the past, and wondering for the future.

Evening was coming on,—the evening of the tropics—calm, balmy, voluptuous.

An inexpressible feeling of languor came over her, and she sank down upon the mossy bank and fell asleep.

How long she slept she knew not, but she was awakened by being violently lifted off the ground and borne along at a rapid rate.

When she opened her eyes she saw grinning down upon her the hideous countenance of an oran-utan—the man-monkey of Borneo.

To resist was useless—her cries were lost amid the dark forest: and it was not long before she found herself lodged in a strange sort of domicile in the topmost branches of a tall tree in the very centre of the jungle.

The oran-utan seemed much delighted with his prize.

He danced round her—he fetched her cocoa-nut milk—he presented to her fruits of the most delicate kind.

To keep him in good temper Ethel partook sparingly of the good things offered to her.

When night came, the oran-utan led her into another room, where a bed of skins and switches was ready for her reception.

This he pointed out to her with a variety of gesticulations, but whether he was wishing her to have a good night's rest, or whether he was offering to become the partner of her slumbers she could not tell.

After much gibbering and attitudinising the monkey left her to herself, and, much more secure than when she was a prisoner in the Dyak wigwams, Ethel went to sleep.

The oran-utans of Borneo are the nearest approach to human beings that have yet been discovered.

They walk erect—they eat off tables,—live in wooden houses in the trees,—make themselves knives, and fight the Malays with sticks.

They are far from ferocious, and have often been known to carry off Malay maidens and make them their spouses.

When morning broke Ethel's feelings were far from enviable.

She knew the peculiar tendencies of this portion of the monkey tribe, and dreaded lest she should become the forced partner of some one of these forest lords.

Death she knew was easily procurable, and this she decided was far preferable to a life of shame with a monkey.

Yet she also was aware that in killing herself she was entailing destruction on another.

It was not only her own existence which would be forfeited, but the existence of that dear pledge of affection which her husband had left to her.

In the middle of these gloomy reflections her captor entered her bed-room, and pointed vehemently towards the outer-room.

Fortunately she was dressed or he would probably not have been over particular to waiting until she attired herself.

What he wanted she could not divine, but on entering the other room, she found a breakfast laid out for her consisting of cocoa-milk, fruit, and some bread, evidently stolen from the neighbouring village.

Of this breakfast Ethel partook copiously, the oran-utan sitting at the very other end, and eating with her, evidently greatly amused.

What seemed to interest him most, however, was her dress.

His monkeyship had been used to see the Malay maiden wandering about the woods in the garb of nature, and was therefore in a state of bewilderment in regard to her clothes.

When breakfast was over, he skipped about the room, cleared away the things, and pushed himself upon the branch of the tree opposite, as if to keep watch.

This kind of life lasted for four days.

"Certainly," thought Ethel, who began to be

sick and faint with dread of being utterly lost, "certainly this is worse than death."

She advanced to the door of the monkey's hut, and looked out.

Beneath her were huge branches of trees spreading out on every side, and giving some little hope of escape.

She seized one, and tried to swing herself down.

But the oran-utan instantly divined her intention.

Seizing her round the waist he hurried her back into the room, and with frightful shrieks and gesticulations testifies his extreme annoyance at her conduct.

Even although her heart was so sick and weary, Ethel could not forbear laughing at the terrible display of anger on the part of the monkey, who sat down with an exceedingly grim countenance at his old post before the door.

Hardly had he done so when the report of a musket rang clearly through the forest glades.

The monkey started to his feet, and rushed along the branches to reconnoitre.

Never had the sound of the dread instrument of death appeared so delightful to Ethel Blakesley as now,—not even when the faithful Malays were engaged in defending her husband against his enemies.

Now, then, was the time for action.

Collecting all her strength, Ethel swung herself off the branch and caught hold of the one below, then another and another, until she found herself cut off from the ground by at east forty feet.

The trunk of the tree was smooth and branchless.

How the oran-utan had borne her up in safety she knew not; but she was well aware that now her only chance of deliverance was to trust herself to him.

She could not reascend the tree, and she lay there for some time breathless and in fear.

At length she saw the monkey advancing.

He was bleeding copiously from the shoulder, in his hand was a long thick stick, and he seemed to be in great pain and still greater terror.

He seized her at once, and flew along from branch to branch, over dizzy heights that made Ethel close her eyes in fear.

He reeled every now and then, and was evidently getting weaker and weaker.

Underneath the trees she could distinguish the forms of persons in pursuit; and she fancied that among them she recognised an Englishman, or, at any rate, some European.

As they came on, however, so the monkey rushed away, until at last, by leaping from the large to the small trees, he reached the ground, and rushed to the edge of the river.

Here he layed her on the bank, and, still holding her dress, plunged into the water his wounded shoulder.

Then he gathered some herbs, chewed them, and applied them to the place.

This done, he seemed at a loss.

Ethel could no longer withstand his dumb entreaties, and his agonised face, and tied her pocket handkerchief lightly round her strange companion's shoulder.

At this the oran-utan became frantic with joy, leaping round her and otherwise testifying his gratitude.

Then as the soporific herb he had used acted upon the wound he lay down, and placing his ugly head in Ethel's lap went off to sleep.

In a few minutes the party of hunters came up.

They were preparing to shoot the monkey as he slept, when Ethel warned them off in English and then in Malay.

The former proved a talisman, for in a moment Reginald Spelthorne was at her side.

CHAPTER XXV.

MONSIEUR COLBERT'S MENAGE.

"This is indeed a strange meeting, Ethel," cried Reginald; "where is Blakesley?"

Her eyes filled with tears.

"Forgive me, Ethel, if I have hurt you. I did not know he also had fallen.

"Yes, Reginald, *he* was murdered with the rest."

"And how came you here?"

"*He* brought me," said Ethel, pointing to the oran-utan, and smiling through her tears.

"He seems to have gained your sympathy," cried Reginald; "he wears your favour."

"Poor fellow, —" said Ethel, "yes I bound up a poisoned wound."

"What do you propose doing with him?"

"Oh! I shall take him back to our village if he will come."

Reginald thought a moment.

"Ethel," he at length said, "if I should not offend you, I would ask you a favour.

"You will not offend me."

"Come and live with us?"

A violent spasm came across Ethel's face.

"We have room enough for you," continued he, "and though our house may not be very luxurious, it is at least as good as yours in the Malay village."

Much persuasion was necessary to induce her to come.

But at length her farewell of the Malays was taken, and she took up her abode with Reginald and Miriam in the house of Monsieur Colbert, in the Dutch settlement.

Monsieur Colbert's was a dull, silent-looking house, situated at the top of the town, and sheltered by the ruins of the ramparts.

The two pillars and the arch, forming together the bay of the porch, had, like the house, been constructed of white stone.

Numerous holes, of unequal size, which the variableness of the climate had fantastically wrought in the stone, gave to the crown of the arch and the jambs of the bay, the appearance of the vermiculated stones used in French architecture, and bore some resemblance to the entrance of a gaol.

Above the crown of arch was a long bas-relief of hard stone, on which figures had once been sculptured, representing the four seasons, but now were worn away, and perfectly blackened by time.

This bas-relief was surmounted by a projecting stringcourse, on which many specimens of vegetable life were growing, of the wallflower and convolvolus tribes, and even a small cherry tree, which had attained a tolerable height.

The door of massive oak, almost black, dried and cracked in all directions, and frail in appearance, was, however, well and securely fastened by a set of bolts of very symmetrical patterns.

A small, square grating, well secured by bars, and discoloured by rust, occupied the middle of the house door, and served as a plate for a knocker, which was fastened to it by a ring, and which struck upon the grinning head of a large nail.

The knocker in question, of an oblong shape, belonged to that class which was termed by our ancestors, " Jacquemart," and resembled, in fact, a large note of admiration.

From a careful examination of it an antiquary might have detected some indications of a face, which bore evidence of having formerly been of a grotesque character, but which long usage had worn away.

Through a little grating, those who were pryingly disposed could see at the end of a dark, mildewed looking passage, several broken steps leading into a garden surrounded in a picturesque manner by thick damp walls, from which the moisture exuded fast, whereon small shrubs of sickly appearance grew as they could.

The walls we speak of were those of the ramparts, on which the gardens of several adjoining houses had been formed. The largest room on the basement storey of the house was called a *salle*, or parlour, the entrance to which was under the archway of the carriage entrance.

The French attach great importance to a *salle*: the *salle* answers the purpose of an ante-chamber, a drawing-room cabinet boudoir, and dining-room ; it is the theatre of domestic life, the household fireside. There the hairdresser of the neighbourhood makes his appearance twice a year to cut Monsieur Colbert's hair; there, too, the tenants, the curé, and the miller's man enter on their several errands.

The floor of this room, with its two windows looking out upon the street, was boarded over, the walls were panelled of a grey colour, with antique mouldings, and were wainscoted from the top to the bottom, the ceiling was traversed by beams similarly painted in gray, and the intermediate spaces filled up with white plaster, which had become yellow with age.

An old brass clock, inlaid with arabesque in tortoise shell, ornamented the indifferently carved mantelpiece of white stone, which supported a greenish coloured mirror, the sides of which, bevelled for the purpose of showing its thickness, reflected a stream of light the whole length of a gothic pier glass opposite of Damascene steel.

The two gilt girandoles which decorated each corner of the mantelpiece answered two purposes, for on removing the roses from each, a socket was inserted which allowed the principal branch to be fitted into the pedestal of bluish-looking marble, and the whole together formed a candelabrum for grand receptions.

The seats around the room, of an old-fashioned form, were covered with worsted work depicting some of La Fontaine's fables, but an acquaintance with that writer's works became necessary to enable any one to discover the meaning of the subjects, for their faded colours and the frequency of the repairs rendered the recognition of the figures very difficult.

At the four angles of this *salle* were placed four *enceigneures*.

An old card-table in marqueterie, the top of which was adapted for a chess-board, was placed against the wall between the two windows.

Above this table was suspended an oval-shaped barometer with a black border, ornamented with gilt bows or knots of carved wood, which had been so shamefully treated by the flies that the gilding was merely conjectural.

Hanging against the wall, opposite to the fireplace, were two portraits in crayons, and reputed to be the likenesses of the grandfather and grandmother of Madame Colbert.

The two windows were hung with curtains of rich *gros de Tours*, looped up by silk cords with large tassels.

These luxurious decorations, so little in harmony with Colbert's usual habits, had been included in the purchase of the house as well as the pier glass, the clock, the piece of furniture in needlework, and the rosewood *enceigneures*.

CHAPTER XXVI.

WELCOME LITTLE STRANGER !

THE little stranger whom Ethel had been nourishing in her bosom at length came to light.

Miriam Spelthorne was also confined at the same time—about two days previously to Ethel.

Miriam's baby was a girl, a bright-eyed, sunny-faced cherub, which was, of course, exactly like her father.

Ethel knew that many hours would not elapse before she also brought her baby into the world ; and as if from some innate fear she prayed that hers might be as pretty, as sunny, and as plump.

At length her time came, and the little stranger appeared.

Astonishment at first held the nurse mute.

Then, in spite of everything, she uttered an exclamation of surprise and almost terror.

Ethel's heart immediately misgave her.

" Is my child, then, indeed so terrible ?" she exclaimed, in a faint voice.

" Ah ! *Mon Dieu !*" said the woman, a French nurse; " it isn't a child at all."

" Give it to me," said the doctor, sternly; " and leave the house this instant."

" Stay," said Ethel; ` do not blame her; let her stop, only let me see the child."

" You require sleep, my dear madam," urged the doctor.

"I require my boy."

"Do let me beg of you to be satisfied, when I tell you that he is alive—healthy and strong—and now go to sleep."

But it was of no avail.

Ethel insisted upon seeing the baby.

Ugly or not ugly, she cared not.

She determined to brave the worst.

"Well, then, madam," said the doctor, taking her hand kindly; "let me beg of you not to agitate yourself. The child is certainly a little out of the common order, but it will, neverthe-less, probably be a very good and a very clever man."

The child was then given to her.

At first a slight cry.

Then a long, steadfast look.

And the baby was pressed tightly, fondly to her breast.

It *was* certainly a child out of the common order.

It was broad and very short.

Its arms were long, and its hands bony and skinny.

Its eyes were large and fishy.

Its nose was broad and yet very long, its mouth wide, its lips heavy, while its back was decorated by a hump.

Such was the monster which Ethel Blakesley brought forth into the world.

It seemed possessed, however, of the sweetest of tempers, laughed at everything—was exces-sively lively.

Miriam was told of it.

Who could blame her?

The only answer she made was to say "poor thing," and hug her own beautiful child more tightly to her breast.

Ethel went bravely through her trouble; and in three weeks was sitting in the verandah facing the sea, inhaling the cool air of evening, and tossing her strange child in her lap.

Ugly, contorted as he was, she loved, aye, almost worshipped him.

Something seemed to tell her that whatever he might outwardly appear, her dwarf child would be a noble-hearted, generous man.

Miriam also sat there toying with her lovely girl, but things had gone very differently with her.

She sat there pale, wan, sickly, the hectic flush on her cheek presaging the advent of a terrible and incurable malady.

"How I do envy you!" said she, placing her thin white hand in that of Ethel's, and gazing with a sad smile up into her face.

"Envy me?"

"Yes, indeed."

"And why?" asked Ethel. "How can *I* be enviable."

"In many things."

"Not certainly in *one particular*," answered Ethel, pointing to the baby.

"No; not perhaps in his appearance."

"In what, then?"

"Why, will it not be a pleasure to nurse, to teach, to watch over him, to see him grow up under your hands, because, no matter how strange a child he may be, his ugliness is not revolting?"

"No, poor little thing; but you have an angel to heed."

"Alas! I have it to heed, but I shall not be here to heed it."

"What mean you?" asked Ethel Blakesley, gazing at her in alarm.

"Oh! Ethel!" cried Miriam, bursting into tears, and leaning her head on her friend's shoulder; "I have not told Reginald my fears, but I feel, I know I have not long to live."

"Oh! you give way to fear, to morbid dread, my dear friend."

"No, indeed I do not; indeed no; but will you promise me one thing?"

"I will promise anything but to encourage you in your terror of the future."

"Terror! say you? Ah! as I have no fear, no dread of the future, I am perfectly ready for the hour whensoever it may come. My only anxiety is for him and my poor child."

"And what do you wish me to promise?" asked Ethel, who thought it best to humour her for a time.

"If I die you will be kind to my child."

"Yes, dearest friend, believe me, you can trust me with it as you might trust me with your own. But there is no occasion for such thoughts. There is no fear of anything of the kind. You must be cheerful, take food and rest, and not give way to grief at an unseen future, or to dread of imaginary evil."

"Indeed, Ethel," said Miriam; "I do not give way to anything imaginary. I have been warned of this as plainly as any human being could warn me"

Just at this moment Reginald came in.

His face brightened up as he saw the family gathering under the verandah.

"Well, girl," said he; "here you are, then. I am right glad to see you thus. How fares our angel Miriam? and how, Ethel, goes it with our new specimen?"

"For shame," cried she; "he is as good a specimen any day as his cousin."

"Indeed, I shall disown the relationsh said he; "but how does the air agree you?"

"Oh, very well, indeed," said Ethel.

She answered because Miriam was silent.

"Do you not think the evening lovely?" asked Reginald of his wife.

"It is indeed beautiful," said Miriam.

And so it was. Everything was hushed and still. Not a bird twittered on the branches.

The landscape before them lay green and pleasant, stretching away in varying pictures towards the edge of the boundless sea, whose tiny waves were dyed bright golden by the rays of the descending sun.

Over the tree-tops poured the flood of light which descended on the ocean, and here and there the patches of sunlight fell in glorious beauty on the green forest glades, casting over the foliage a tint akin to that of autumn.

"Oh! how I wish my poor husband was here," murmured Ethel faintly to herself.

Miriam heard her.

"Think not of the past," she said; "re_

member my words, and try and dream only of the future."

"It is getting late for you to be out here," said Reginald, at length; "perhaps we had better go in now."

Miriam rose silently, and, as she entered the house leaning on her husband's arm, she whispered softly to Ethel—

"Ethel, dearest, this is my last evening out here."

CHAPTER XXVII.

POOR MIRIAM.

MIRIAM'S words proved, alas! too true.

That evening under the verandah was the last she ever spent in the open air.

The next morning she woke up with a burning fever—her eyes sparkling with a strange light, her tongue parched, her hands white, hot, and dry.

"Did I not tell you so?" asked she of Ethel, as she sat with Reginald by her bedside.

"But you did not tell me of your thoughts," said her husband, reproachfully.

"I did not wish to make you sad," she said. "I had hoped even then I might be mistaken. Ethel was so hopeful that I at one time was angry with myself for any forebodings.

"Forebodings of what?" cried Reginald, in alarm.

Miriam started.

Even then he knew not the extent of her danger.

"Of my illness," she answered, in a painful whisper.

After a few commonplace remarks he rose and left the room.

"He is gone in anger," said Miriam, with tears in her eyes.

"Not so," said Ethel; "he is only sad. He is gone for advice."

She was right.

In a few short moments he returned, with Doctor Grandpere, the French physician.

"You must cheer up, lady," said the medical man. "The very worst thing that can be in a patient is her making up her mind to be very bad when she is not."

"Then you do not think me very bad?" cried Miriam, smiling.

"Bad?—not at all."

"Did I not say so?" said Ethel, exultingly, taking her hand and kissing her.

The doctor looked pityingly at the patient a moment, and then turned to Ethel.

"You are getting on famously, Mrs. Blakesley."

"I am, indeed."

"All owing to your excessively good spirits, Madame. Nothing else, I assure you."

Ethel laughed.

"We must make Mrs. Spelthorne rouse up her spirits, too, then."

"That we must," said Grandpere; "and if you will allow me to suggest such a thing, I should like you to be the nurse if possible. That is to say, as soon as you get better?"

"Then is this illness likely to be of long duration?" asked Reginald, anxiously.

"No, no! my dear sir," said the doctor, looking for his hat; "but I say in—case—you—know in case—good morning. Mrs. Blakesley, a word with you, if you please?"

Ethel went out with Grandpere into the front room.

"Mrs. Blakesley," he said, "I think I can confide in you?"

"I hope so, indeed, sir."

"Mrs. Spelthorne is in great danger!"

"You do not mean that, I trust, sir?'

"Yes, madame, I do indeed. She is in a raging fever—that is to say in the commencement of one. To-morrow probably she will be delirious. Are you strong enough to undertake the task of nursing her?"

"Oh! yes, I think I am."

"Now, madame, you must understand me: you will have great trouble with her; but should she have lucid intervals never allow her to talk of her danger."

"No, I will not."

"And do not let her husband be with her too much. Now, good morning—I may depend upon you—yes—good morning. I shall be back in four hours."

And the good old fellow departed.

It was certainly rather a brave undertaking in Ethel Blakesley.

She herself was far from strong, and the nursing of another woman under such circumstances was indeed a terrible task. She did not yield, however.

The doctor came in four hours, and pronounced her worse.

By night she was delirious—raving wildly of England, of her home, of her father, of her husband; and, more than all else—about her baby.

It was indeed a terrible trial—a trial which ended too truly as she herself had predicted.

As Byron says of Haidee—

Twelve days and nights she withered thus—at last,
Without a groan, or sigh, or glance to show
A parting pang, the spirit from her passed;
And they who watched her nearest could not know
The very instant till the change that cast
Her sweet face into shadow, dull and slow,
Glazed o'er her eyes—the beautiful, the black—
Oh! to possess such lustre, and then lack.

Thus lived—thus died she: never more on her
Shall sorrow light, or shame. She was not made
Through years or moons the inner weight to bear
Which colder hearts endure till they are laid
By age in earth; her days and pleasures were
Brief, but delightful—such as had not stayed
Long with her destiny; but she sleeps well
By the sea shore, whereon she loved to dwell.

That isle is now all desolate and bare;
Its dwellings down, its tenants passed away.
None but her own and father's grave is there,
And nothing outward tells of human clay:
You could not know where lies a thing so fair
No stone is there to show—no tongue to say
What was; no dirge, except the hollow seas
Mourn o'er the beauty of the Cyclades.

Reginald Spelthorne was inconsolable at her loss.

He had loved her well, honestly, truly—and her death was to him like the stroke of an avenging angel.

"Oh! Ethel," he cried, as they stood together

by her grave, "after all that has passed —after all I made you suffer, can I ask you to befriend my child?"

"Reginald," said she, "I promised *her* that, and to the best of my power I will perform my promise."

It was a long time before that household resumed its wonted habits.

Even Monsieur Colbert himself seemed affected at the loss of the bright spirit who so merrily and so lightly used to flit about the house.

"It seems, indeed, madame," he would say to Ethel Blakesley, "it seems, indeed, madame, as if you came just in time to take her place."

The poor old man did not mean anything by these words, but they were gall and wormwood to her to whom they were addressed.

———

CHAPTER XXVIII.

THE NEW SPECIMEN AND HIS FRIENDS.

IT will be remembered that Ethel brought with her to Monsieur Colbert's the monkey which had so materially affected her baby's appearance by the terrible fright he had given her.

Master Jocko was exceedingly partial to

Ethel; and he soon began to be as partial to her child.

He, too, was a particular admirer of the oran-outan, and nothing was ever so effectual in stopping his crying as a sight of that grinning, unsightly creature.

Certainly when the monkey seized hold of the baby and danced about the room with it, it caused Ethel, from more than one reason, a pang of horror—for it really seemed as if it partook more of its nature than of a human being.

It did not in the least lose its extraordinary appearance, but seemed rather to increase in unsightliness every day.

To the eyes of Ethel this was not perceptible, but there was not a woman, far or near, black or white, who did not pity her for her trouble.

She, however, seemed each day to become more used to it; and loved it with a passionate tenderness, which to some was wholly unaccountable.

And so the dwarf grew and prospered—his great delight being the monkey and the baby Miriam, named tacitly after the loved and lost.

He was a great favourite among the Indians as well as the Dutch population, and as he grew towards three years, and used to toddle out before the house, he became no longer an object of wonder to any one.

It was about three years after Miriam's death that the young child was wandering about behind the house, in the meadow which graced the slope of the hill on which the house of Monsieur Colbert was situated.

It was evening, and the sun was just drooping behind the tall trees of the jungle.

The monkey was with him, so he was considered to be quite safe.

The oran-outan was always thought to be his best body guard.

Their gambols were something extraordinary to witness, and for some time Reginald and Ethel had sat at the window watching them.

Then, as the sun was setting, Reginald seemed to be getting impatient.

"Will you come now, Ethel?" he said to her tenderly.

"And the children?"

"Miriam is in bed."

"But my boy?"

"Why he is safe enough, you see, with Jocko."

"Very well then, dear, I will come."

And so they left the window.

Whither they went we will not now stop to inquire.

That can be told elsewhere.

We must now follow the fortunes of Jocko, and his infant charge.

They went on playing and gamboling in the field until evening came darkly over them.

Then the oran-outan seemed getting restless and uneasy.

He fidgetted about, ceased to play, and seemed rather to stand sentinel over the baby than to join it in its sport.

At length, as if suddenly making up his mind what course to pursue, he seized the child, and

was just about to rush with it towards the house, when, with a cry of pain, he stumbled and fell.

He was up, however, in a moment.

But this time he left the child on the ground, and looked around him for a tree.

This found, he broke off a branch, and in an instant stripped it of its twigs and leaves.

Then again he took the child, and cautiously proceeded towards home.

But again he uttered a cry, and again stumbled; and at the same moment an old Dyak woman clambered over the fence, and came rushing up to him.

Dropping the baby, Jocko stood on the defensive.

The old woman was armed with a club and a bow and arrows.

With the former she strove to disable the oran-outan, whose strength, however, was a great deal too much for her.

It was a curious sight.

The monkey, with his hairy body and fierce, glaring eyes, stood confronting a being who appeared scarcely one degree higher in the animal creation than himself.

The Dyak woman was about five feet six—big and bony.

She was quite naked, and her body, here and there covered with hair and as brown as a berry, gave her the appearance of a female oran-outan.

She wielded her club with all the ferocity of an animal, and strove to get near the child which Jocko protected.

At length, seeing that all attempts at fair play were useless, she seemed resolved to adopt a more treacherous mode of attack.

Drawing back, as if acknowledging herself beaten, she drew an arrow from her quiver, and directed it at the monkey.

Twang went the bow.

A cry of pain escaped Jocko; and after a leap in the air he fell writhing on the ground.

Like a vulture pouncing on its prey, the Dyak woman seized the child and made off with it.

Jocko attempted to rise, but in vain.

The arrow, which had pierced his lungs, was a poisoned one, and he rolled in all the agonies of death upon the green sward.

His piteous cries brought people from the house.

First Reginald and Ethel, and then the servants.

"Where is my child?" cried the distracted mother, as if the monkey was capable of articulation.

The poor creature seemed to understand her well.

With a piteous look he pointed to his own breast, from which the blood was pouring freely, and then to the jungle, where the Dyak woman had disappeared.

"Go get my rifle," said Reginald to one of his men.

"Where are you going, Reginald?" cried Ethel.

"To seek *our* child," replied he; "meanwhile, I fear this poor animal, who has evidently fought for it to the last, is dying."

Poor Jocko! he licked the fair hands which brought him water, gazed smilingly up at her face, and rolled over dead.

The man returned with the gun, and Reginald, after kissing Ethel fondly, and promising a speedy return, leaped over the hedge, and plunged into the jungle.

Why he kissed her, and why he said "our" child, we must explain in the next chapter.

CHAPTER XXIX.

AFTER LONG YEARS.

REGINALD and Ethel, when they left the verandah that evening, entered together the little room which he called his study.

He closed the door; and placing her on a couch, sat beside her, and taking her hand, said—

"Ethel, dearest! do you remember Castle Ferry?"

"Dear old place! Yes, indeed, I shall never forget it."

"And do you recollect how you and I used to sit for hours in that bay window overlooking the sea, and plan bright schemes for our future?"

"Yes, Reginald," replied Ethel with tears in her eyes. "I recollect it all; but of what avail is it now to think of these things?"

"I will tell you," said he. "When I went away to London I went trusting in you and leaving you trusting in me: was it not so?"

"Yes—indeed I trusted you."

"And I you—too well for my peace of mind. There must, however, have been something amiss with our love, for both you and I forgot our vows, and met, as others have met before, but as we never dreamed of meeting—mutually estranged. Strange to say, though regrets may have sometimes mingled in our cup, we have neither of us had *reason* to repent what we did."

"No, that I have not."

"Nor I. Miriam was ever a good, a kind, and a trusting wife to me. But does it not seem now, Ethel, as if Providence was offering us another chance?"

"What mean you?" asked Ethel, blushing, yet scarcely believing her own heart.

"I mean, my dearest Ethel," said Reginald, gently pressing her to him, "that we have mourned three years—truly mourned for those whom we have lost; and that, therefore, it is not sacrilege again to talk of love. Will you be my own, Ethel, even now; will you, after these long years, be my wife?"

Ethel trembled violently.

Reginald proceeded.

"If you do consent to take this step there can be very little chance of our regretting it. We know each other well. We have lived together for years. You have been a wife to me in all but the dearest part of married life. I know I love you; and I think, Ethel, you have some love for me. Say, then, shall it be so?"

"Yes," said Ethel, burying her face in his bosom, and sobbing.

Tears are strange things: they come to us we know not why or whence; and Ethel sobbed, scarcely with any particular reason.

Sir James Brooke, the Rajah of Sarawak, in that very island of Borneo of which we now are writing, has composed, upon the subject of tears, a poem full of delicacy and tenderness, which my readers will, I am convinced, thank me for introducing to them here :—

Ambition's path may vainly cheat,
Ecstatic love be passing sweet:
Gay hope, with her delusive train,
A moment soothe and cheer the brain—
    Yet nothing lasts but tears.

Friends may be cherished, fond, and true,
Affection's ties like morning dew;
And pleasure's cup be quaffed awhile,
With dimpled cheek and wreathed smile—
    Yet nothing lasts but tears.

As pleasure's poisoned cup we drain,
We find the dregs of woe and pain!
Ambition's dream is quenched in blood :
Time's hand will pluck hope's withered bud—
    For nothing lasts but tears.

O'er friends we love—the fond, the brave,
We live to close the yawning grave:
Affection's dew, which gemmed each leaf,
Sinks blighted by the touch of grief—
    For nothing lasts but tears!

And so Ethel Blakesley wept, and Reginald kissed away her tears.

"Surely, Ethel," he said, "it does not make you sad to think of becoming my wife?"

"No, dearest!"

"Then why weep?"

"Because I feel happy; and yet also because your words, and the result of my accepting you for my husband, brings back to me old times, and the promises of the future which were once before held out to us."

"And which even now may be fulfilled," said Reginald.

They sat for a few moments in silence.

At length Ethel started.

"I fancy I heard a cry," she said, rising from her seat.

Reginald listened.

"Yes—it is surely Jocko."

"Great Heavens!" cried Ethel. "I hope nothing has happened to my child."

"*Our* child, now," said Reginald. "Let us go and see. But there is no occasion to fear; Jocko is a good guardian."

What followed we have already explained.

Ethel returned, sick and faint at heart, into the house : looking with dread now into that future which a few moments before had appeared so bright and blissful.

Reginald pursued his way through the jungle.

He first of all had made inquiries at the Malay village, but no one had seen the woman or the baby; and could give him no account of it.

He himself knew not whom he was pursuing.

Jocko, of course, had only been able to point at the jungle; and whether the child had been carried off by man, woman, or monkey, he was entirely ignorant.

Even if he had known it would have been all the same.

He met not a soul in the forest, and returned empty-handed and with a heavy heart to Monsieur Colbert's house, with the sad tidings that, for a time at least, the child was lost.

*   *   *   *   *

After Reginald had concluded his search, and there was no chance of his issuing forth into the jungle again that night, a figure emerged from the hollow trunk of a huge tree near the plantation.

It was the Dyak, with the child in her arms.

She stayed not to look behind or around her, but plunged away hastily through the trees, towards the spot where the old hamlet of the Dyaks had stood before its destruction by the Malays.

CHAPTER XXX.

A FIT OF THE BLUES.

On the day following the abduction of the little child, a regular expedition was organised, and Reginald, with twenty Malays, set out to scour the woods.

For a week they continued their search, proceeding miles into the interior, and examining every nook and cranny in the woods without avail.

At length they desisted from their search, and waited patiently for awhile to see whether the child would turn up.

Ethel was inconsolable at her loss.

But yet she did not believe him irretrievably gone.

There was no one who could—she thought—have any interest in destroying the child, and if he had been stolen merely for the sake of stealing, there was no fear of his not being easily recognised.

So both she and Reginald waited in the full hope of finding him.

About a month after his abduction they were sitting together in their evening apartment when a servant entered.

She seemed flustered and half frightened.

"What is the matter, Yappo?" asked Reginald, somewhat amused by the woman's manner.

"Oh! sir, I think the baby is found."

"My baby found!" cried Ethel, "where is he?"

And leaping up, she prepared to follow the girl.

"My husband is washing it," said the girl in some confusion.

"Washing it! What for?"

"Because it's *turned blue!*"

"*Turned blue!*" cried Reginald. "The woman's mad. Here, let me go. *I* will fetch you the child."

He went, and returned in a few moments with the child in his arms.

"Stay, Ethel," he said kindly, "let me speak to you before you see it."

"What is the matter? Oh! what have they done to my poor child?" she sobbed in terror.

"Ethel, my dearest," said he, "the boy is well, and will probably continue so; but it has fallen, somehow or another, into the hands of our enemy, who have left the marks of their hatred upon him. They have tattooed him, and turned him completely blue."

"Let me see him?" cried Ethel firmly, and extending her arms.

One sight was enough—

Too much, indeed, for her; for with a loud cry she fell fainting to the ground.

And so indeed it was.

The child was completely blue.

He had been carried away by the Dyak woman, and taken to the encampment, where the scanty remnants of the tribe, all old women, still lived.

At first they resolved upon torturing him.

They then thought of killing it by some horrid process, and sending its body to its mother.

But one of their number, a woman younger than the others, who probably had more reasons than one for being annoyed at the entire absence of men from the camp, suggested a still more diabolical revenge.

This was that they should tattoo the child, and rub into his skin an indelible dye.

This accordingly was done.

The poor child was stripped, tattooed from head to foot, and a blue dye rubbed well into his skin—a dye which no soap, no water, no scrubbing, could ever destroy the effects of.

In this state, when the dye was well soaked in, they re-dressed him as he had been brought to them, and took him back to Monsieur Colbert's house.

Here they laid him on the step, and rang the bell, and bolted away back into the forest, their black hearts bursting with delight at the success of their fiendish revenge.

Ethel, when she recovered her senses, was like one bereft of all intellect.

She sat there crushed.

It seemed, indeed, as if some Nemesis were pursuing her, and at every step she took leading her to fresh misery, and heaping fresh sorrow on her head.

"Come, Ethel," said Reginald, though his voice trembled with emotion, and his heart was faint with grief, "come, Ethel, do not give way to idle tears. I will avenge your child, and I will love it the same. Will not you?"

"Love it? Oh! yes—I will love it. But is it not terrible? Oh! my poor, poor child. When will your troubles cease?"

"Don't cry, mamma," said the poor boy, looking up archly into her face.

"Bless you, my child : I cry only for you."

"Do not cry for me—I am not sad. See what they have done. They have made me all blue. Isn't baby pretty?"

"Yes, my love, yes. Oh! Reginald, is it not terrible?"

"Yes, Ethel, it is terrible. But you have gone through still more terrible troubles than this."

"Oh! no—no indeed."

"Not more trouble? Was not the loss of

your father more terrible—was not the loss of your husband more terrible, than the tattooing of this child? After all it is only skin deep; beauty is only skin deep: so is deformity. His mind will probably, and most probably, be the very opposite of his appearance."

"You always plead hopefully."

"Why not? and remember, too, Ethel," he continued, "that you should thank Heaven that you have him restored to you, not regret in what form he comes."

"You speak truly," said Ethel; "but remember that you speak as a man. I am a woman. I should not complain were it not that it appears that special torments are invented and prepared for me."

"What mean you?"

"Why, dearest Reginald, what other woman has ever suffered so much as I did to bring a being of so deformed a shape into the world; and then, when I had given birth to it, to have it seized by savages and tattooed so as to make it utterly at variance with anything human."

"Never mind," Reginald said, laughing; "our baby has only got a fit of the blues. Perhaps he may yet get out of them."

Ethel did not quite see the force of Reginald's philosophy; but of course she was forced to submit to it.

CHAPTER XXXI.

A MARRIAGE IN THE DUTCH SETTLEMENT.

In two weeks after this Ethel and Reginald were married.

There was certainly less romance about the affair than there would have been had they never been before wedded, and if, as they all had thought, Reginald had led his virgin bride to the altar of the little village church in Cornwall.

But still true love presided over their union; and it was with chastened hearts and an honest determination to do their duty, that they stood before the altar of the little Dutch chapel, where they were joined together.

Nearly all the principal people in the town were there.

Monsieur Colbert, Madame Colbert, his two daughters, married and single, and several others, were specially invited; for in a settlement such as that it was next to an impossibility to have a private wedding.

The clergyman, the Rev. Felix von Rotterham, was a talkative old clerical.

It was indeed a farce for him to preach the doctrine of the two hands.

His right hand never performed an action which his left hand was not well aware of, and his neighbour's left hand, and his neighbour's neighbour's—and so on.

He was like the town-crier: nothing was lost that the Rev. Felix von Rotterham was not well acquainted with.

Not a girl tripped but Felix had predicted it.

Not a stray ass was found in the pound but had brayed his intention of straying beforehand into the worthy father's ear.

He was here, there, everywhere—except where he was wanted.

He was a good-natured sort of busybody, was Felix.

But to trust him with a secret would have been like tying a bell to the tail of a mad-dog.

The idea of a secret marriage, or a marriage in a private way in the settlement, was perfectly preposterous.

No sooner would the ceremony have been performed than the Rev. Felix would have tucked up his clerical coat tails and started off against time to tell his gossips.

"What do you think, Mrs. C.," he would have said; "what do you think? Mr. F. has married Mrs. G.! Now do not on any account tell Mrs. A., as she is a busybody, and might spread the report. I tell you this as a secret."

Then visit No. 2.

"What do you think, Mrs. A? Mr. F. has married Mrs. G. Quite on the quiet, you know, and all that. Mrs. C. tried very hard to find out the story, but I was mum. Now do not say anything to her, there's a good soul —it's quite a secret!"

The reverend gentleman was quite in his element upon the present occasion.

His tongue was allowed full swing; and so by the time the day arrived there wasn't a soul in the settlement who did not know that Mr. Reginald Spelthorne was going to marry Mrs. Blakesley, the mother of the Blue Dwarf, as he began to be called in the place.

So, as I have said, the crowd in the church was pretty numerous, and at Monsieur Colbert's house that day there sat down to breakfast twelve persons, and amongst them the Rev. Felix von Rotterham himself.

That was a pleasant little wedding party.

The bride was unaffectedly, honestly, frankly happy.

She took no pains to conceal the fact.

She did not drown her new white cambric pocket-handkerchief with tears.

Nor did she muffle the responses.

Nor did she faint at the door of the vestryroom.

Nor did she sit at the breakfast-table so confused that the eyes of everyone were thereby drawn upon her.

Nor was she afraid to laugh for fear she should be thought too well pleased or too little impressed.

Nor was she morosely silent or affectedly lost to all appetite.

She simply took upon herself the new position she had assumed with an evident honest pleasure.

"Reginald Spelthorne," said Von Rotterham, with his mouth full of cake; "Reginald Spelthorne, you are a happy man."

"I know that."

"Aye! you're a fool if you don't. That wife of yours is a model. There's no nonsense about her. She is a downright, honest, worthy, good woman; aye," and here he gave Reginald a dig in the ribs and a wink of the eye, and added in a lower voice, "a devilish pretty one, too. Why she's almost good enough for a Dutch woman."

"That is indeed a compliment," said Spelthorne, laughing; "a very great one from you. And I assure you I am well satisfied."

"Satisfied!" cried Felix, in indignation, "satisfied! Why, what more do you want? Good, virtuous, young, pretty, plump, bright-eyed—why I envy you, and you are only satisfied. I wish you would take Mrs. Rotterham here in exchange."

"Avaunt, Satan!" cried his wife. "Did'st ever hear such a man, Mr. Spelthorne? Truly, as I have often told him, he's fitter for a public tavern than the pulpit."

The reverend gentleman shook his burly sides with laughter at this sally; but it was truly no joke.

Felix certainly looked more like a nice, well-to-do publican than a parson any day.

"But we'll make the exchange," said he again.

"I must consult Mrs. Rotterham."

"Oh! I am quite willing," said the lady. "If Felix wants to marry again I will get a divorce, and then there is none I should like so well as Mr. Reginald."

"I say—I say, Mrs. Spelthorne"—how strange that name seemed to Ethel—"I say, Mrs. Spelthorne," said Monsieur Colbert, "I give you warning in time. Here is our good parson's wife over this end of the table making love to your husband."

The day passed very pleasantly, and the people insisted upon a dance in the evening, which they accomplished to their heart's content upon the lawn, to the intense amusement of the Malays assembled to look on.

These also received their share of good cheer, and many a young husband went home that night for the first time—rolling drunk.

At ten o'clock the party separated, and Ethel and Reginald were once more left to themselves.

"And now," said Ethel, laughing, "after all this feasting and gaiety, how much better off are we?"

"I know only one difference," said he.

"And what is that?" asked Ethel, smiling gaily.

"Why," returned Reginald, with a merry twinkle in his eye, "only that I am beginning to be of the worthy parson's opinion, that you are a devilish pretty woman."

Ethel blushed, and playfully tapped his cheek; and so ended the wedding day.

CHAPTER XXXII.

THE COLBERTS.

It is necessary, in order that my readers may understand the future pages of this history, that I should give some account of Monsieur Colbert and his family.

Monsieur Colbert was a man about five feet in height, of a squat, square figure, with the calves of his legs about twelve inches in circumference, with large knee pans and broad shoulders.

His face was full, tanned, and marked with the small-pox, his chin was straight, his lips were marked by the absence of any curve in their shape, his teeth were white, his eyes possessed that steady and fascinating expression which is attributed to the basilisk, his forehead strongly marked with transverse lines, was not deficient in developments, pregnant in many; his hair, a mixture of yellow and grey, looked like silver and gold, as certain young persons said who were not aware of the seriousness of a jest made at Monsieur Colbert's expense; his nose, thick at the end, was ornamented with a knob, or skin full of veins, which the common people said, and not without reason, too, was full of humour.

Upon the whole his face indicated a man of the most dangerous cunningness of character, of the most unimpassioned probity of conduct the egotism of one accustomed to concentrate all the feelings of his nature upon the enjoyment which the passion of avarice afforded.

But although his manners were easy and gentle in appearance, Monsieur Colbert was as hard as bronze.

Always dressed in the same style, anyone who saw him to-day saw him the same as he had been for the last thirty years.

His strong shoes were fastened with leathern strings. Whatever the weather might be he invariably wore thick woollen stockings, short knee-breeches (of course snuff-coloured cloth), with silver knee buckles, a yellow and quince-coloured velvet waistcoat, buttoned across his chest, a full-sized dress coat; also, snuff-coloured with long wide skirts, a black neckerchief, and a quaker's hat.

His gloves, as stout and thick as those which gendarmes wear, lasted him twenty months, and, in order to keep them clean, he invariably placed them on the brim of his hat in the same place, in the most methodical manner.

Madame Colbert was a lean, impoverished-looking woman, yellow as a guinea, awkward and listless in all her movements; one of those women, in fact, who seem made to be tyrannised over.

She had large bones, a large nose, a large forehead, large eyes, and at first sight offered a vague resemblance to those spongy fruits which are destitute both of flavour and juice.

Her teeth, of which she had but few, were black, her mouth puckered up in wrinkles, and her chin was long and peaked.

She was an excellent woman.

The Rev. Felix von Rotterham managed to find occasional opportunities of telling her that she was not very wicked after all, and she believed him. An angelic gentleness of manner, like that of an insect tormented by children, singular piety, the most unfaltering evenness of mind, and a good heart, made her universally pitied and respected.

Her husband never gave her more than six francs at a time for her personal expenses.

Although her appearance excited ridicule, this woman, who, by her own fortune, and the fortunes to which she had succeeded, had brought Père Colbert more than fifty thousand francs always felt herself so deeply humiliated by a dependence and subjection against which her gentle disposition precluded her from protesting, that she had never asked for a sous, nor made a remark about the documents which were submitted to her for signature.

This foolish secret pride—this high-minded generosity of sentiment, constantly misunderstood and wounded by Monsieur Colbert, influenced the conduct of this poor woman on all occasions.

She invariably wore a silk dress, of a greenish hue, which she usually made last her a twelvemonth, and wore, also, a large neckerchief, of thick white muslin, and a straw bonnet, and seldom took off her black silk apron.

As she rarely went out, she hardly ever required new shoes.

And so Monsieur Colbert, sometimes seised with a feeling of remorse when he remembered the long period that had elapsed since he had last given his wife her six francs, always stipulated for what he termed pin money for his wife when he sold his year's produce.

The francs or five louis, with which the Dutch purchaser of Colbert's yearly produce presented him, formed the most available source of Madam Colbert's income.

But when she had received her five louis her husband frequently sent to her, as if their purse was in common—" Have you a few sous to lend me?" and the poor woman, delighted at an opportunity of doing something for a man whom her confessor had bade her regard as her lord and master, gave him back, in the course of the winter, sundry crown pieces out of the pin money.

Whenever Monsieur Colbert took out of his pocket the hundred sous pieces which he doled out every month for such trifling expenses as thread, needles, and articles of dress for his daughter, he never omitted, after he had buttoned up his pockets, to say to his wife, " Well, mother, do you want anything?"

Madame Colbert, animated by a feeling of maternal dignity, invariably replied, " I will see about it, M. Colbert."

The Colbert's family also comprised two daughters and a son-in-law.

The unmarried girl was about eighteen years of age, plump, pretty, and *piquante*—all vivacity and agility.

Indeed Eugenie Colbert was the life of the house, and no one could possibly be dull five minutes together if she were in the room.

Annette Michaut, the married daughter, was as pretty as her sister, but not so lively.

Marriage had sobered her a little.

Her husband, Jerome, was a good-natured, pleasant-spoken sort of individual, anything but an intellectual companion, but possessed of sound common sense and business habits, and very fond of his wife and their one child, an infant of some four years old.

The three children, viz., the Blue Dwarf, (as he was called in the neighbourhood), Miriam, and Francois were brought up very much together.

Being all pretty nearly the same age, they were excellent companions, and in trouble and anxiety an immense amount was saved by their exceeding good-fellowship.

So matters went on, and so went on time.

Nothing of any consequence happened in the Blue Dwarf's early life.

He grew up a fine, intelligent boy, exceedingly good-hearted, and ever ready to help anyone out of a scrape.

Passionately fond of his mother, he received from her the utmost of affection.

His extraordinary appearance—his blue skin, and his crooked limbs—were, however, less obnoxious to her than they were to himself.

She only saw in him a noble, true-hearted boy, ever ready to do a good action, and loved him with all the fervour and passion of a mother's first and only love.

He was nervous and timid with strangers, and scarcely ever would make his appearance if casual acquaintances called.

CHAPTER XXXIII.

THE FIRST HEART ACHE.

THE Blue Dwarf was now eighteen—Miriam the same age; and Francois Michaut nineteen.

As a boy of fourteen, Sapathwa, as his friends the Malays called him, had loved Miriam.

She was indeed a being calculated to inspire love.

Like her mother she was tall, graceful, carrying her head upon her shoulders as proudly as a swan.

Her bust was magnificently moulded and richly-developed, her waist small, her limbs long and sweeping.

Her eyes were of that long almond-shape of which poets rave so eloquently.

Her nose straight and thin, her mouth full and beautifully chiselled.

Oh! those pensive eyes, oh, those sunny curls.

Surely women are sent into this world to be our geniuses, either for good or evil.

They lead us by a sigh or by a smile to perform actions which not all the wealth of the world would otherwise induce us to perform.

The magic of a voice, the charm of a word, is more to us than all the riches of earth.

There is nothing so powerful in this universe as the voice of her whom we love; nothing so powerful for evil, nothing so powerful for good.

And Miriam was possessed of a voice of infinite beauty.

Her walk was grace itself, her slightest movement was elegance.

She seemed formed to make or mar the happiness of some one.

Either she could have done.

For to her beauty of form and mind she added indomitable resolution.

Not that she did not possess all a woman's softness—all a woman's kind-heartedness.

But she had an immense gift of firmness, and would never swerve from her purpose if her purpose were good.

To the Blue Dwarf she was a kind of idol.

He would sit for hours with his head in her

lap, gazing up into her face with worlds of tenderness in his large melancholy eyes.

Or he would sit reading to her—unfolding to her the treasures of English literature, and instilling into her heart a perception of all that is great and glorious in nature.

Miriam used to call the poor fellow her brother.

Brother he was in one sense, truly.

But oh! it was not a brotherly tenderness with which he watched her every movement, which made him her constant, unswerving companion, which made him voluntarily her slave.

"Oh! brother, you are so good to me," cried Miriam one day—they were then sixteen—"you would make anyone love you."

Sapathwa looked up at her with his large, melancholy eyes, and sighed.

"Do you love me, then, Miriam?" he asked.

"Yes, brother, you know I do," she answered kindly; and with her small white hands smoothing his blue forehead.

"Brother!" he muttered to himself; "'tis always brother. Miriam," he added aloud, "do me one favour. Do not call me brother."

"Why?" asked she innocently.

"Oh! I do not know," said he confusedly; "I don't like the sound of it. It is quaint—old-fashioned?"

"Very well, dear," she answered, "I will not. What shall I say, then?"

"Call me John," he said, "I always call you Miriam."

"Why I declare," she cried, laughing, "you are more like a lover than a brother. I shall begin to think you have designs against me. Francois will be jealous."

"Francois!" cried Sapathwa, with a darkened brow; "and what of him? Is he more to you than your own flesh and blood?"

"No, no, dear brother," said Miriam, soothingly. "I did but joke. But Francois is my brother, too, you know."

The Blue Dwarf did not answer.

His large eyes were swollen with the tears which tried to burst forth but could not.

The veins in his temples throbbed violently.

He felt as if his grief was blinding him; so, rising, he was about to leave the room, when Miriam, darting after him, and throwing her arms round his neck, cried,

"Dearest John, do not leave me in anger."

"I am not angry, Miriam," he answered, striving to disengage himself from her.

"Why then leave me?"

"Because you want me not."

"I do, indeed—do stay."

"No, I go to send you Francois. I will never trouble you again."

"Oh! John, do not be so cruel," cried Miriam, with tears in her eyes. "If I have offended you I am very, very sorry. Do forgive me."

In an instant the arms of Sapathwa were around her neck—and led back as obedient as a child, he was soon again seated at her feet—again playing with her tiny fingers—again greedily devouring her words—again eagerly scanning her features.

"And do you really love Francois Michaut?" he at length asked.

"Yes, dear John, as I love you—as a brother."

"That is right—but you must not love him better, good sister."

"Why not?"

"Because you are too young," he answered, evasively.

"Yes—indeed."

"And you have never thought of marriage yet, have you?"

"No," said Miriam, laughing merrily, "I have never yet seen anyone I could love well enough to marry."

She did not see the terrible spasm which crossed Sapathwa's face at these words.

"Have you not?" he said, quietly.

"No—I see no one here."

He did not answer; but at length he said—"Dear Miriam, let me go now—my head aches—is on fire."

"Yes, dear John, if you wish to go; but why not go to sleep on my lap?"

"No, sister, no; I must go."

And with a hurried kiss he left her.

He could bear it no longer.

It was all over.

The charm was broken—the die cast—his hopes for ever shattered.

She loved him not.

His heart felt seared—shaken—broken.

Another moment and he would have wept before her. So away he rushed to the silence of his little chamber, locked himself in, and throwing himself on the bed, relieved his aching heart in a passionate flood of tears.

CHAPTER

AN APPEAL TO THE BEST FRIEND.

BUT as time wore on his manner towards Miriam altered.

He was more reserved to her.

Not that he acted slightingly towards her.

He loved her too well—too passionately—to slight her.

But he seemed to stand aloof from her, as it were, and watch her movements, more especially her behaviour towards Francois Michaut.

Miriam herself noticed the change in his manner towards her.

But as many women do in similar cases she knew not the cause.

She loved Sapathwa dearly as a brother, but as a lover she could not perceive the possibility of regarding him.

To her credit be it said that, young as she was, she would at once have altered in her manner towards him had she for a moment imagined it possible that he loved her as a mistress.

But not seeing it in this light, she let him have his full swing of delight and love.

When she was walking in the cool of the evening on the beach, with his arm round her waist—when she sat embroidering at the verandah, with his head in her lap, or with her hand in his while he read, she felt nothing but

pleasure at the scene or the story he read, while his heart was bursting with delight at the mere fact of being near her and of touching her.

But, as I have said, as time wore on his manner towards her altered.

That scene I have described did much to disenchant him; and it was not long before he perceived that to secure to himself any chance of procuring his heart's dearest wish he must pursue a very different course.

This course he had not shaped out in his mind.

His determination arose simply from the fact that, as one plan failed, a different one must have a greater chance of success.

So, instead of being ever at her side—ever attentive to her slightest wish—ever her obedient slave—he became silent and reserved.

He never walked with her unless she asked him, and, even then, only walked distantly at her side, although his heart was bleeding to cast his arm round her fairy waist as heretofore, and talk gaily to her about the scene and her beauty.

He never sat at her feet musing or reading.

He never spent the evening in listening to her music or her words—two things which to him were equivalent.

He walked out moodily by himself, talked little, and devoted his time to reading.

His time was all his own.

The tide of fortune had turned, and Reginald Spelthorne was a wealthy man.

With his marriage to Ethel came a run of luck.

Everything in his hand turned to gold; and by the time that Sapathwa and Miriam were eighteen, he talked of returning to Europe.

Ethel was happy in her husband's love, and in the love of her only child—for, by her second marriage, she had no children.

She could not but perceive Sapathwa's altered manners—his downcast looks—his reserve and his sorrow.

Reginald noticed it too, and questioned him on it.

But it was of no avail.

"John," he said to him, "what has come to you? what makes you so unhappy?"

"Am I unhappy, father?" said he.

Reginald smiled at the quaint answer.

"You are the best judge of that, my boy," he said. "You seem to us unhappy—you make us unhappy by seeming so, and you will tell no one your trouble."

"Indeed, father, I am in no trouble."

"You ought not to be, indeed," said Reginald, "I leave to you a fine inheritance; and although nature may have played you a dirty trick, your wealth—your mind—your knowledge, make up for that—aye, and your good heart, my boy; for we all know you have a good heart, and love you for it."

Sapathwa longed to unburden himself, but to a man—even though that man was almost a father—he could not.

"Thank you, my dear father," he said, "but I do not grieve for my appearance. Nature certainly seems to have avenged herself on me for some crime or another of which I know not my guilt; but I care not."

"What is it, then?"

"You seem determined to persuade me I am in grief," said the Blue Dwarf, smiling.

"No, I do not wish to persuade you," said Reginald, "but I pray you to tell me if it is true."

"Dear father," said Sapathwa, "I am in grief. I cannot now tell you why, but if it becomes much greater I will tell you."

And so, for a time, the matter rested.

But Ethel was not so easily put off.

She, too, had noticed his wan and haggard appearance, and had sorrowed in secret about it.

At length an incident occurred which enabled her to ask him.

Sapathwa had gone out on one of his solitary rambles.

He wandered slowly down by the sea-shore, thinking of Miriam, and wondering whether the pebbles on the beach were as numerous as the tender thoughts—the particles of that boundless sea of love, which was for ever laving his heart.

His mind was assuming a calmness and serenity which it rarely possessed.

But it was only a calm before a tempest.

On turning a point of rock he beheld two persons sitting together on the shore—a man and a woman.

The former was holding his companion's hand in his, and breathing into her ear words which seemed to fall with great sweetness on her soul, if one might judge by the tender downcast look of her eyes and the smile on her half-parted lips.

The Blue Dwarf gazed at them for a moment, as if to make certain that it was, indeed, as he dreaded.

There was no mistaking them.

It was Miriam and Francois.

Sapathwa's heart stood still with the terror of his grief.

Then, with a loud cry of anguish, he rushed away, shouting to himself as he went—

"Lost—lost! Oh, Miriam—Miriam!"

He never stopped once—never looked back to see if he were followed, but rushed wildly towards his home.

Here, as he was making for his own chamber. he was met by his mother.

"Oh, Sapathwa, my dear boy," she cried, detaining him, "tell me, what is the matter?"

"Oh! mother—a great trouble has befallen me."

But his voice was thick, and his frame so shaken with emotion, that he could scarcely render himself intelligible.

"My dear, dear child," she said, "come into my room and tell me all. Surely you can confide in me—your mother."

He allowed himself to be led—obedient as a child—into the room, and sat down by her side, his arm round her waist—his head resting on her bosom.

"What is it, my dear boy?" said Ethel, kissing his throbbing forehead.

"Oh! mother—my heart is breaking," he said, hiding his face in her shoulder, and then, with a gush, came forth the tale of his deep sorrow—the very words seeming to rend his heart as he uttered them.

"Poor child," said Ethel between her tears, "and do you love Miriam so very much."

"Mother—my love for her is an agony—I know no peace—I am devoured by it. She loves me not—oh, heaven—because I am ugly and deformed, she spurns me, and loves him because he is handsome and tall, and has an English tongue, while his heart is black as night and bitter as gall. Oh! mother—I hate him."

"Say not so, John—say not that; hate no one. He does not willingly injure you."

"Oh, yes—he knows it. I speak evil of none without cause, mother," cried the noble fellow; "have I ever wronged another in my life."

"No, indeed—no," said Ethel, proudly.

"Nor will I now. But Francois Michaut is a scoundrel, and I can prove it—and for him, mother, for him Miriam will throw away herself, and this love of mine, which, oh mother, is so great."

He could find no other words—but the look and the tone were sufficient. Ethel could well appreciate his agony.

"But there is still hope, John. Do not give way to despair."

"There is no hope, mother."

"You have never asked her to marry you?"

"No."

"Then why do you give up? Half the battle has yet to be fought," said Ethel, cheeringly.

Sapathwa thought a moment.

"Mother," he said, at length, "you will not let him marry her in a hurry."

"No, I will not."

"Then, I will try even yet, and then, if it is useless, I will let him take her. But by heavens, mother, he must use her well, for not hell itself will be more unrelenting if he use her ill."

His mother shuddered as he said these words.

His look and voice were terrible.

"God bless and prosper you in your attempt, my dear boy," she said; "lie still here on my breast, and try and quiet yourself awhile."

He answered not.

After his tumult of emotion, came the reaction; and so so, with his head on his mother's bosom, dreaming of Miriam, he fell asleep.

CHAPTER XXXV.

HOW FRANCOIS POPPED THE QUESTION.

ON the afternoon of the day on which Sapathwa had seen Miriam and Francois sitting under the rocks, Miriam had gone out alone for a ramble.

A strange sadness came over her.

She had a slight perception of what was the matter with Sapathwa, because, with a kind of jeer, Francois had hinted it to her.

She was afraid to question her heart upon the point—afraid to commune with her own thoughts.

She resolutely placed before her mind the impossibility of such an union.

She imagined to herself his ugliness and deformity, and determinedly kept out of view the beauty of his mind, which made up for everything which nature could possibly have inflicted on him.

This day—the first on which she had ventured to ramble forth alone—she was compelled to think because, besides the heaving sea and the rustling leaves, she had no other companions but her thoughts.

Unfortunately for Sapathwa he was not alone in her mind.

First came a vision of the Blue Dwarf in all his native deformity.

She imagined herself married to him, jeered at by her friends, and giving birth to a race of monsters.

Then she remembered his goodness of heart, his perfect mind—his soul—his tenderness.

After this came a dream of another.

Tall, handsome, vivacious, with every elegance of body and all the graces which which education can bestow, Francois Michaut was certainly just the sort of fellow to catch the fancy of a girl like Miriam.

Of his heart she knew nothing.

Was it because she tried to know nothing of it?

In his boyhood he had exhibited few traits of gentleness or kindness; and even now, in his manhood, he was morose and surly to his parents.

Before strangers, however, he was all smiles and elegant attentions.

With the girls of the settlement he was a most decided favourite, and he was not slow in taking advantage of the circumstance.

So much so, indeed, that it was said by some that when Marie Dufour, the French nurse, drowned herself in the sea off Craggy point, she did so because he had seduced and abandoned her.

Against such tales as these Miriam resolutely closed her ears.

They were idle, wicked scandals, she would always say, which did credit neither to the narrator nor the listener.

So when she suddenly came down upon Francois round the point of rock where Sapathwa saw them, she blushed up, and was all smiles to receive him.

"Ah! *ma petite Miriam*," cried he, "well met. I am so tired—you look so; let us sit down on the beach."

"Very well, Francois."

So they sat down side by side on the pebbly shore.

"Miriam," said Francois; "I am so glad we have met here to-day."

"I hope you are, sir."

"But seriously, can you be serious for a moment?"

"I will try."

"Well, then, Miriam, I have something important to tell you."

"I'm all attention."

"Miriam," said the young man, putting on his most winning smile and beseeching manner; "dearest Miriam, I have longed for this meeting. Since a boy I have loved you. I think I have shown it: and now, as a man, I adore you. Will you be my wife?"

She did not answer.

He proceeded:

"I have said few words; I have spoken abruptly. Do not, therefore, think that my love is so small that it required few words to express it. I cannot say more than that I love you, because language is too common to express *my* feelings."

All this was great nonsense.

But Miriam thought it was true.

"Dear girl, do speak—tell me will you be my wife?"

It was at this moment, just as he spoke these thrilling words, that Sapathwa came upon them, and before she could answer she heard that piercing cry, the cry of a heart's great agony.

She started and looked round, but saw nothing near them.

The rocky point hid him from her view, and she could not see him as he fled along the cliff, telling to the wild sea the tale of his breaking heart.

But the cry did its work well.

"What was that?" she asked, with agitated voice.

"Nothing, dearest, but a bird," said he; "do answer me."

"Oh! I cannot now," said Miriam, in tears; "it is so sudden, let me have time to think of it. I feel startled and frightened."

"Don't be frightened at nothing, Miriam,' said Francois; "it was only a cormorant or a' sea-gull. Let us take a walk."

"Yes, home," said Miriam.

And so they went home.

She refused, notwithstanding all his entreaties, to say yes or no.

She would, she said, take time to consider.

And with this he was obliged to be content.

He took his leave tenderly, kissed her hand, and walked away jauntily.

"Damned nice girl, enough to make any man's bosom swell," cried he to himself, as he swung himself and his cane up the street; "but probably she won't come to the scratch."

Such was the manner in which this Adonis of Borneo thought proper to talk of Miriam's love.

But so it is with half the men and women in the world.

The man thinks he has only to ask and have, while the woman's heart is harassed by a thousand doubts and fears.

One of your devil-may-care fellows pops the question, gets a consent, and goes off thinking,

"Well, I'm deuced glad of that."

While the girl whom he has gained goes home, retires to the solitude of her chamber, and there weeps with joy over the happiness of having obtained the greatest wish of her life—the heart of the man she loves.

CHAPTER XXXVI.

HOW THE BLUE DWARF TOLD HIS LOVE.

On the evening of the same day Miriam sat in the verandah of Monsieur Colbert's house overlooking the sea.

Embroidery was in her hand.

Certainly she was supposed to be at work; but she sat perfectly still, thinking only of what had happened a few hours before; and trying to still her heart sufficiently to allow her to think quietly over her determination.

In the midst of her communings she felt an arm steal gently round her waist, and on looking up saw Sapathwa leaning over her with all his old tenderness of manner and look.

"You are in a brown study, Miriam," said he smilingly.

"Yes," she answered with a light blush; "I was building castles in the air."

"I hope to heaven they may be," thought he, for he guessed of whom she had been thinking.

"Miriam," he said, sitting down by her; "may I talk to you a bit."

"Yes, dear, if you wish to."

"Miriam," he said, taking her hand; "I have a great secret to tell you. I want you to give me your whole heart for a moment while you listen. Don't listen slightingly, because it is in your power, my dear girl, to make or mar my happiness."

"Your happiness," she said, in a low voice.

"Yes, Miriam, my happiness. I love you, Miriam, oh! beyond life itself. I love you as I might love an angel. I have dreamed of nothing since my boyhood but of you and our future. I dared to couple our beings together in my ideas of happiness, and it is only after a great struggle that I have nerved myself for this terrible trial. Oh! yes, Miriam, it is terrible," he said, as he wiped the great drops of sweat from his brow, and his tone fell so low that he could scarcely be heard distinctly; "for it will be as death to me if I find all my hopes are in vain."

Miriam did not answer.

Her heart stood still with fear.

Sapathwa proceeded.

"Miriam, I have come to ask you to tell me honestly, candidly, can you love me? Will you be my wife?"

Miriam sat like stone.

Her tears were dried up.

"Oh! Sapathwa!" she said; "spare me this great trouble."

"You can say yes or no."

"Oh! no, I cannot—my heart is another's."

The Blue Dwarf did not cry out.

A low moaning sigh escaped him, like the flapping of the wings of his heart's spirit as it fled.

"Oh! Miriam, be not cruel. Think, Miriam, you are wrecking the fond hopes of a lifetime. Oh! believe I love you as man never loved before. It is my soul, my existence—my love for you. Oh! Miriam, my heart is in great agony. Do not tell me that you despise my love."

She believed him.

No one could hear him—see him without telling the terrible agony which agitated his heart and frame.

"Oh! Sapathwa!" cried Miriam; "I can love you as a brother, but as a husband never, never."

"Miriam," said he, in accents of exquisite pain; "oh! do not think so lightly of me. Will you not take time? Oh! will you not give me hope? Oh! for Heaven's sake," he cried, sinking on his knees and sobbing in her lap; "for Heaven's sake you will think of it, and give me at least a week of hope and happiness. It is so cruel to strike the blow at once."

"I dare not bid you hope," said Miriam; "it would be more cruel still. Be a man, Sapathwa, try to overcome it."

"Miriam," he said; "you do well to remind me that I am a man, for in your presence I had almost forgotten that there was another existence to hope for."

He could say no more; but sobbed bitterly, every tear coming forth like drops of blood from his heart.

Miriam could not weep.

She was terror-stricken—awe-stricken at the great agony she beheld.

"Oh! Heavens!" he cried, at last, seizing her hand. "Oh! Miriam, is there no hope, none, none at all? Am I then so wretched a creature that nothing in this world could make you love me?"

"Oh! Sapathwa!" said Miriam, at length finding vent for her sorrow in tears; "I cannot, dare not give you hope. There is none, no hope. I love another."

The Blue Dwarf slowly rose from the ground at these words, and left the verandah.

Miriam spoke not, nor tried to detain him.

He passed away from her like a statue—his face haggard, wan, and terribly convulsed with agony.

His mother met him, and saw it all at once.

"My poor boy, you are in sorrow again," she said; "thank Heaven that you have me to comfort you."

"I do, mother, for I am in deep sorrow. She has rejected me."

And, hiding his head in her breast, he sobbed aloud.

"Mother," he said, at length; "mine is love which cannot be rendered despicable by anything. Therefore I will stoop to anything. I have done all *I* can: but will you—before it is too late—before she hands herself over body and soul to that man, try and move her for me? My heart is broken nearly now. I think my soul will die then."

"Poor boy; yes, I will speak to her. But I fear if *you* cannot move her I shall be of little use."

"But you will try, mother, will you not?" cried he, in anguish; "for it is terrible to lose your only hope in life."

Ethel left the room.

Sapathwa paced up and down it, now and then gazing out on the calm landscape over which the shades of evening were gently falling.

No calm, however, came over his soul.

To him love was everything—life, happiness, were concentrated in one idea.

Had Miriam been able to see into his heart she would scarcely have dared to cast away from her a gift which Heaven rarely grants to a woman—a pure, unselfish, manly love, an adoration more fit for an angel than for her.

But she looked at it with a jaundiced eye.

She could not reject the beauty, the fascination, the worldly advantages of Francois Michaut.

He said he adored her; she believed him thoroughly.

He said he he had never loved before; she also believed this.

Here then was a young man, handsome, accomplished, purely loving her; why reject him for a blue hunchback whom all regarded with pity, if not with ridicule.

Ethel came back in the course of an hour, her eyes red with weeping, her face very pale.

"Any hope, mother, any hope?" he cried, seizing her hand.

Ethel shook her head.

"Then God help me, mother," he cried; "for I cannot help myself."

And in an agony of tears he sank down on his knees by the bedside.

CHAPTER XXXVII.

A FATHER'S POWER.

FRANCOIS MICHAUT called next afternoon to see Miriam, and she received his visit with great pleasure.

"It is a lovely day, Miriam," he said. "Will you come out for a stroll?"

"Yes, with pleasure," and so she went with him.

"Well, Miriam," said Francois, "have you thought of what I asked you yesterday?"

"Yes."

"And will you give me my answer to-day?" he continued, pressing her hand.

"I don't know; I am sorely troubled," said she, evasively.

"Troubled—by what?"

"My heart."

"Your heart! what do you mean, my own one?" said Francois, who, in his selfish heart, dreaded something against his own interests.

"You men," said Miriam, "know little of what we women suffer."

"You are for ever speaking against us, Miriam," he answered, "but, come, tell me what great trouble is so oppressing you now?"

"Since you asked me yesterday to be your wife," said the girl, looking on the ground, "I have had another offer of marriage."

"Another offer! From whom?"

"From the Blue Dwarf."

Francois burst into a long, loud laugh.

"You are jesting with me, surely, Miriam. Why what the deuce does he want a wife for?"

"Why do you?"

"To love, honour, and protect."

"And so does he. Any woman who is fortunate enough to marry him would have her fill of love, honour, and protection," said Miriam, warmly.

"And what was your answer?"

"I rejected him."

"Of course."

"No, it was not a matter of course, Francois, for all last night I was in sore trouble; but I have come through it now."

"And you will be my own—my wife?"

"Yes."

And so this treasure of beauty and loveliness cast away her pearls at the feet of swine.

Just as the pair turned the corner of the plantation, Sapathwa and his step-father, who were standing in the verandah caught sight of them.

The Blue Dwarf staggered, and almost fell.

Reginald touched him on the shoulder and said, kindly—

"Come—come, my boy. I know all. Do not give away to idle grief."

"Why, grief is not idle."

"Ah, but it is. Faint heart never won fair lady. My Miriam there may fancy herself in love with Francois Michaut, but she may get over it."

"Ah! never, never! And yet, father——"

He paused and hesitated.

"Yet what, Sapathwa ?"

"Yet he is a villain !"

"Strong words, these, my boy."

"Aye, but I can prove them."

"And how is he a villain ?" asked his step-father, interestedly.

"You know," said the Blue Dwarf, "you know, or rather you remember, the death of Marie Dufour."

"Yes—well."

"That girl was seduced by Francois Michaut," said Sapathwa.

"Are you certain ?"

"She told me so herself."

"Ah ! and you can therefore swear ?"

"Yes, I can."

"And will you ?"

"I will."

"Then Francois Michaut never marries my daughter."

Sapathwa hid his face in his hands a moment, and was lost in thought.

He looked up and was about to speak, when he found he was alone.

Then his generous heart reproached him for what he had done."

Not that he had said aught that was untrue ;

Not that he pitied Francois ;

But he so loved Miriam that it was a terrible struggle to him to do anything that would make her unhappy, even for a moment.

Then a stern sense of duty came over him, and he could but feel that he had acted justly—even placing aside his own interest.

He followed and joined his father.

"Father," he said, "use her gently. Do not break it too roughly to her."

"My boy, I will not be unkind to her—was I ever unkind to you ?"

"No. I only spoke because the remembrance of my heart's great agony makes me anxious to preserve others from like trouble."

That evening Miriam was called into her father's study.

"Miriam," said Reginald, kindly, but firmly, "I must beg you will do one thing to please me."

"What is that, father ?"

She trembled violently, for she almost guessed, from his manner, what was coming.

"When you were a child," said her father, "you were allowed to roam about and choose your own companions. I have been very remiss in allowing your childhood's manners to be still adhered to, while you have grown into a woman. You are now eighteen. It is time now, therefore, to commence an altered line of conduct. Do you understand me, Miriam ?"

"No, father, indeed I do not trouble."

"I will be more explicit, then," said Reginald, sternly. "I do not wish you to wander about alone with the young men of the settlement."

"Nor do I," said Miriam, "except with my brothers Sapathwa and Francois."

"Francois is not your brother."

"Indeed, father," said she meekly, "you made me believe so."

"When you were children you were brought up as brother and sister ; but you are now too old for such things. I wish you to discontinue your intimacy with him."

Miriam flushed up a moment, and then burst into tears.

"Why are you so excited, my child ?" asked Reginald kindly.

"Because you are so cruel, father," answered the girl between her sobs.

"Cruel, Miriam ! it is the first time a child of mine has ever called me cruel. Is Francois so very much to you then ?"

Miriam thought a moment, and then said,—

"Father, Francois Michaut has asked me to be his wife, and I have consented."

"Oh ! Great Heavens, Miriam !" cried Reginald, "why did you let it come to this without letting me know ?"

"Letting you know, father ?—he only asked me yesterday."

"Well then, girl," said Reginald, in a stern and excited tone, "it must be all broken off; you must see him no more."

"See him no more ! Oh, father, it is impossible ! I love him !"

"You love him; so did Marie Dufour, who threw herself over Craggy Point when he had seduced and abandoned her."

"You, too, father—how can you believe so wicked a scandal ?"

"It is no scandal, Miriam ; I know it to be true. I have proofs—positive proofs, girl, that it is a fact.

Miriam looked up half in terror, half in wild amazement.

"Positive proof !" she murmured between her blanched lips.

"Yes, girl, positive proof. I would not run the risk of hazarding my child's happiness for a whim, but Francois Michaut can never be son of mine."

"Oh, father, I shall break my heart !"

And she left the room in tears.

CHAPTER XXXVIII.

"OPENING FIRE ON THE GUV'NOR."

THE most unpleasant thing in courtship is that portion of it which in technical phrase may be denominated "opening fire on the guv'nor."

Popping the question is all very nice and pleasant in its way, because if your suit is successful there are one or two kisses—one or two squeezes of the waist and the hand—one or two pressures to your heart of that form which you are so anxiously striving to be master of altogether.

But when this is all over—when your lady-love has said "yes," and given you leave to ask papa, you begin to feel nervous, because papa isn't a person whom you can come over by a few well-put-in kisses and squeezes.

He wants to know how old you are.

He wants to know how you intend keeping his girl.

He wants to know your antecedents, your present condition, and your prospects for the future.

He very often wants to know whether you are going to take her as a gift, or whether you are going to buy her, or require a small premium to take her off his hands.

These "wants to know," are formidable things sometimes.

And so Francois Michaut felt as on that eventful morning he pulled off his new glove at the door of Mr. Spelthorne's drawing-room, and walked as if he had been on stilts.

"Good morning, Mr. Spelthorne," he said, because that is generally the first observation to be made.

"Ah, good morning, Mr. Michaut," observed Reginald; "pray take a seat."

"Deuced formal, this morning," thought Francois, "the old codger knows, perhaps, what my errand is. However, here goes."

"My dear Mr. Spelthorne," he proceeded, "I have come to see you this morning upon a matter of great importance—yes, sir, a matter affecting my whole future. I have for a long time entertained a desire to unite myself to a young lady in this settlement who combines a natural beauty with grace, intelligence, and worth. Need I say, Mr. Spelthorne, that I mean your daughter?"

"No, you have no need to say it at all," said Mr. Spelthorne gruffly; "for if it's Miriam you want, you can't have her."

"Rather curt party," was Francois' inward exclamation, but he only said,—

"Indeed, sir, you suprise me. We have been brought up together from childhood, and I have always framed an idea in my own mind that I might with justice look forward to the moment when I could ask her to be my wife."

"Indeed, young sir, you have, ever since you were a boy, wished to marry Miriam?"

"Yes, indeed sir."

"And yet while you were meditating this, you inveigled in your snares poor Marie Dufour, and when you had accomplished your vile purpose, abandoned her."

"That is a foul calumny—a despicable invention of some of my enemies."

"You can lie with a good grace, sir," said Reginald, quietly.

"What mean you, sir?" cried Francois with assumed indignation.

"I mean, sir, that when you say that the story of your seduction and abandonment of Marie Dufour is false, you lie; because I have positive proofs of the fact."

Francois turned deadly pale.

"I defy you to produce them."

"Do you? then I will produce them before the whole settlement."

"In the name of Heaven, sir, take care what you do!" cried Michaut, in great terror.

"Oh! innocence is always able to refute calumny," said Reginald quietly. "I will carry out my intention."

"I entreat you, sir," said Francios, "if not for my sake, at any rate for the sake of my family, not to do any such thing."

"I will give you that promise," said Reginald Spelthorne.

"Oh! Heaven bless you!"

"But on one condition."

"And that is?"

"That you renounce for ever all claim to my daughter's hand."

"For ever?"

"Aye, for ever."

"But is that one error so great, so heinous, that nothing can ever atone for it in your eyes?" said Francois.

"Oh, do not talk to me of that one error," cried Reginald indignantly, "remember that is not the first nor last."

"What mean you?"

"I mean that your crime with poor Marie Dufour is not the first nor last, but the only one generally known."

"I know of others."

"Name them?"

"Charlotte Marlun, the daughter of the Italian refugee; Anna Medlow, my English servant——"

"Stay, stay, sir, I am indeed in your power. I will trouble you no more."

"Trouble not Miriam, either," said Reginald, as you love your fair name in the colony. For if I find you once again conversing with her, I will proclaim it in public, and make this place far too hot to hold you."

"Good morning, sir," said Francois, "you may reckon on my discretion."

And so he left the house with very much that kind of feeling with which a dog leaves a place where he has been beaten and slinks off with his tail between his legs.

Revenge, deep, dark, deadly revenge rankled in his heart.

He knew of no one but one who could have told Mr. Spelthorne.

He knew but one against whom his hatred turned fiercely.

Against one only he determined to vent his venom of revenge.

And that one was the Blue Dwarf.

CHAPTER XXXIX.

FACE TO FACE.

IF Francois was anxious for a meeting with Sapathwa, he had not long to wait.

That very evening, as he wandered along the cliff to cool his heated brow, he met the Blue Dwarf.

Sapathwa was walking slowly along with his eyes cast upon the ground, exhibiting, in fact, every sign of dejection.

He started upon seeing Francois, and endeavoured to avoid him.

Francois seized him by the arm, saying—

"Ah! monster, now I have at length a chance of a reckoning."

A strange gleam shot through the eyes of the Blue Dwarf at these words.

"What!" he exclaimed in a low voice, "do you wish to sacrifice an annual victim on this spot?"

A flush of anger, and then a crimson blush, passed over the countenance of Francois Michaut.

He knew well the significance of Sapathwa's words.

They were standing on Craggy Point, where poor Marie Dufour had committed suicide when he abandoned her.

"I want no victim," he said, in a hoarse voice; "I require explanations."

"What if I refuse them?"

"I must have them."

"First of all, what do you want to know?" asked the Blue Dwarf.

"Why you interfered between me and Miriam Spelthorne."

"Because I love her."

"Love her! Ah! ah!" laughed Francois; "a monkey falling in love with a white virgin! Ah! ah! that is excellent. Why the devil himself is not uglier than you are."

That strange gleam again shot over Sapathwa's face, but he spoke calmly.

"I know one thing," he said, "much more ugly than my appearance."

"And that?—"

"Is your heart."

"I don't understand sentimentality," said Francois, contemptuously; "all I know is this, that as you have had influence enough to get me turned away from your stepfather's house, you must use it now to obtain my return."

"Must!"

"Aye, must."

Sapathwa laughed a short, dry laugh.

"Must is a strange term to use to me," he said, smiling.

"Aye, but remember what you once told me."

"What is that?"

"Never harbour revenge."

"I harbour no revenge," said Sapathwa; I simply do not desire to see Miriam united to a seducer—aye, and very nearly a murderer. By the way, Mr. Michaut, be kind enough to take your hand off my arm—you hurt me."

Francois paid no attention to this demand, but continued—

"Remember, then, if you do not as I bid you, I will have my revenge. I am not a fellow to be trifled with."

"Are you deaf?" exclaimed the Blue Dwarf; "I told you to release my arm. I must do it myself."

And, so saying, he twisted his arm away from Francois with such force that the latter fell back some distance.

"I once for all tell you, Francois Michaut," he continued, "that I refuse to aid you in any way—that, on the contrary, I shall endeavour to do my utmost to prevent your marrying Miriam; and, what's more, I do not, after to-day, desire to hold any communication with you."

"Then, by Heavens!" exclaimed Francois, springing towards him, "you shall bear the mark of my anger."

A knife gleamed in his hand.

The Blue Dwarf had only a light oaken stick to defend himself with.

He was agile, however, and possessed, as most cripples do, immense strength.

Stepping back, therefore, he swung his stick round his head in the form of a figure 8, and brought it down with tremendous force on Francois' arm, just as the knife gleamed over his head.

"Wretch!" cried Michaut, as the knife spun away in the air, "you have broken my arm."

"Not so," said the Blue Dwarf, quietly, "it is only wrenched. However, I will now leave on you the marks of my anger."

So saying, he rushed upon Michaut and seized him by the collar.

Sapathwa's object was not to injure his antagonist, but simply to humiliate him.

Down therefore, came the blows of the stick like hail.

They were here, there, everywhere.

Francois swore — yelled — shrieked —kicked, but in vain.

Sapathwa was possessed of enormous strength, and carried him as well and as easily as if he had been a child.

At length, wearied out with his exertions, he flung him from him.

Francois lay crushed—beaten—humiliated on the green sward.

He attempted to rise, but could not.

"Curses on you you whelp—you monkey," he cried, "I will be even with you yet."

Sapathwa laughed a light scornful laugh as he replied,

"It is now afternoon. In an hour or two you will be able to move. Lie quiet until then, and come home as soon as you can, or I shall send the doctor to you."

No answer.

"I think that would hardly be prudent though," he continued, "because it would then be known all through the settlement how sound a thrashing you have had. Adieu!"

And he walked away followed by the loud and blasphemous curses of the baffled assassin.

When he arrived home, he entered the room where they were all sitting.

"You look excited," said his stepfather, "what's the matter?"

"Nothing," said he, quietly, "Francois Michaut endeavoured to take my life, and I have flogged him. That is all."

Reginald started up.

"That consummate villain," cried he, "where is he? This shall not end here."

"Yes, sir," said Sapathwa, "let me beg of you to allow it to pass off quietly. The thrashing I have administered to him he will never forget. Let that suffice for the present."

CHAPTER XL.

BLIND LOVE.

That evening Miriam retired to rest extremely early.

Her room was on the first floor.

Before the window was a broad terrace, supported by pillars.

From the casement could be seen the heaving billows of the sea, and the road leading to the town.

The night was very warm.

She threw her casement open, therefore, and undressed, as it were, in the open air.

She discarded her things one by one, perfectly unconscious that her every movement was watched.

She had finished her toilet, and was standing in her nightdress, just about to extinguish her light prior to entering her bed, when a whissing sound was heard, and a crumpled piece of paper was thrown into the room.

She opened in haste and read—

"My own dearest Miriam,—I must see you at once, I have something most important to tell you. Can I come into the house secretly, or can you come out.—Yours, FRANCOIS."

Miriam thought a moment, and then scribbled an answer, and threw it out.

Then wrapping herself up in a shawl, she locked the door, and awaited her lover.

In a few moments Francois Michaut swung himself up to the terrace, and was in her room.

"My dearest girl," he cried, clasping her in his arms, "this is, indeed, kind."

"Stay, Francois, let me extinguish the light. Otherwise people passing may see us."

She put out the lamp, and then sat down by the window.

"What is this all-important information?" asked Miriam; "but stay, before you tell me answer me one question."

"What is that, dearest?"

"Is it true that you attempted Sapathwa's life?" she asked.

"True—can you believe such a thing of me?"

This was Francois' usual evasive style of answering.

"Say, truly, did you or did you not?" asked Miriam.

"I did not. He attacked me." said Michaut, "He had a huge stick, and I threatened that I would use my knife. Thus he concocts an attempt at assassination on my part."

Miriam believed him.

She was so blindly, passionately, in love that she was ready to believe anything, provided it was in favour of her lover.

"And now, then," she said, "what is the great discovery?"

"It is, indeed, a discovery. replied Francois, in a low voice, "a vessel sails away to-morrow for Europe. Let us, then, go away in it, and thus escape persecution."

Miriam stared at him wildly.

"We are not married, Francois," she said quietly.

"No, no, dearest, I know that," said Francois, "but we can be married at the first town we touch at."

This reasoning did not please Miriam.

She saw before not only doubt and uncertainty, but the sorrow of her mother-in-law, and the deep grief of her father.

"No, no, Francois," she said, "I cannot agree to this, indeed I cannot."

"Then you love me not," said Francois.

"Oh! I love you deeply."

"No, I believe it not."

"But, indeed, I cannot consent to go. My father will curse me."

"But will you not sacrifice something for me?" asked Michaut.

"Something—oh! Heavens, Francois," exclaimed Miriam, weeping, "have I not already sacrificed my father's love for you, and now you would have me sacrifice honour—all, because you refuse to wait."

When a woman weeps half the battle is won.

Francois Michaut knew this well, and took advantage of it.

"Miriam," he said, taking her in his arms, and caressing her fondly, "Miriam, the first letter which your father and mother receive from us will contain our marriage certificate."

Miriam trembled violently.

She was beginning to relent.

"Do, my dear girl—do consent, and I will get all ready."

"When does the ship start?" said Miriam.

"At five in the morning—that is the day after to-morrow—so that we must start to-morrow night."

"Thank Heaven!" murmured the weak girl, "that I shall be able to bid adieu to my mother and father."

"Then you will fly with me?" cried Francois Michaut, in rapture.

"Oh! can I trust you?" asked Miriam, in an agony of tears.

"My dearest girl," said he, "how can I give you greater assurance than I do of my love—my devoted love for you?"

"1 believe you, dear Francois. But leave me now. It is very late, and I fear that some one may observe you."

"At ten to-morrow night, then?" asked he.

"Yes, dearest, I will be ready."

Then, with a passionate embrace, they parted.

Miriam crept into bed, and there, in the darkness of the night, wept over her great love and her weakness, over the recollection of her mother, over her father's certain anger, over the uncertainty of the future, over the speedy fulfilment of her hopes, and so, in a whirlwind of changeful feelings, she fell asleep.

Meanwhile, Francois Michaut descended stealthily from the terrace.

No one appeared in sight, so with a jaunty air he walked away from the spot where he had left his betrothed in tears.

His aspect was entirely that of a triumphant man.

Not a bit of the successful lover was in his aspect.

He was nearing the place of his residence when a hand was placed lightly upon his shoulder.

He turned round with a startled air, and saw, standing by his side, the Blue Dwarf.

"How now?" he cried, "what do you want with me, fellow?"

"Be polite, young man," said Sapathwa, "remember any time and place is the same to me, and I shall think no more of thrashing you now than I did before."

"Is this all you have to say to me?" said Francois Michaut.

"No, I have seen you for the last hour in the bedroom of Miriam Spelthorne. I watched you at the window. You remained there fortunately. had you disappeared, I should have entered and strangled you. I overheard, also, a few words. From these I gather that she has consented to fly with you. Beware! if she attempts to fly with you you are lost."

Francois turned towards him with an angry gesture, but he was gone.

CHAPTER XLI.

FAMILY COUNCILS.

REGINALD SPELTHORNE had for a long time been projecting leaving the colony.

He had, as I have before said, amassed considerable fortune, and he desired once more to tread English soil, and spend the latter days of his life in quiet.

The next morning at breakfast time he said to Sapathwa—

"John, your mother and I have at length made up our minds to go to Europe."

The Blue Dwarf started, and answered—

"Oh! indeed. A ship sails to-morrow."

Miriam turned pale as ashes.

"That is too soon, my boy," said Reginald; "another sails in the course of a fortnight—we will go by that."

"I am indeed glad to revisit England," said Ethel, smiling.

"I expect they will look upon me as an escaped ouran-outan," said Sapathwa, with a slight laugh.

"Never mind what they say at first," said Reginald, "they will soon discover your excellent qualities."

"I am sure," said Ethel, "when I am once more in England I shall feel as if I had never left it. All these strange events will seem like a bewildered dream."

"That is just as I feel," said Reginald. "We will go to Castle Ferry, and there renew our troth."

Ethel laughed happily, and then said—

"Our Miriam here is silent; she does not appear to be very glad to leave Borneo."

"I am not, indeed."

"And why?"

"Because I was born here; because all my associations are bound up in this place, and I know nothing whatever of England."

"She speaks truly," said Sapathwa, gravely, and glancing fixedly at her; "when she leaves Borneo she will be leaving all her friends to plunge herself into a vortex of people who know nothing of her and care less."

Miriam understood his meaning; but her father said—

"You are talking nonsense, my dear John; all her friends go with her."

"Yes, yes, father, all her relations, but not all her friends. The whole colony is her friend."

He turned the conversation thus delicately because he saw how painful each allusion was to the poor girl.

Oh! how he longed for supernatural power, that he might open to her his own heart, and the heart of that false one who was weaning her away from her best friends.

The day passed.

Sapathwa said not a word to his father or mother in regard to the discovery he had made.

Reginald's statement as to going to Europe had changed the current of his thoughts, and he had matured a plan for saving Miriam, even at the risk of his own earthly happiness.

The night came.

The evening closed over the settlement calm, bright, and warm.

Miriam took a more than usually affectionate leave of her father and mother.

"You seem sad to-night," said Reginald, as he kissed her and looked at her tearful eyes.

"I am not well, father," murmured the girl.

"What is the matter with you, Miriam—shall I fetch the doctor to you, my dear girl?" said he kindly. "I have not liked your looks lately at all."

"No! no, dear father," exclaimed she, vehemently. "I want no doctor, it is only a nervous headache—sleep will do me good."

And, so saying, after again kissing her father and mother and Sapathwa, she left the room.

"God bless that dear boy," she murmured to herself, as she ascended to her room, "he knows all and will not betray me."

"Miriam looks very ill, Ethel," said Reginald, when she had left the room, "I have not liked her looks of late."

"She is still pining for that fellow, Francois," answered Ethel. "My heart bleeds for her; I could give anything in this world if she had but taken a fancy to a worthy man."

"I think she has made a mistake throughout," said the Blue Dwarf. "She has imagined I fancy that you intended her for me—and me alone. Heaven knows I do not wish it so; if I could gain her love by laying down my life for it, I would. But I would not force myself upon her."

"She has no right to suppose so," said Reginald, "but what has become of Francois—I have not seen him to-day in the streets. I used to be constantly running against him."

Sapathwa knew well how he had been employing his time.

But he would not betray Miriam.

So he only answered,

"You forget, father, the thrashing he has had. Probably he is resting himself in bed after it."

Reginald laughed, and said,

"Ah, yes; that certainly may be the case. But in going to Europe, Miriam will see new faces and new scenes, and may there find some one whom she may love and marry."

A spasm passed over the face of the Blue Dwarf as he answered,

"I hope so, indeed. I am going out for a walk now, father. Good night, mother."

And so he left them.

"Poor boy," murmured Ethel, "he loves her better than his life."

CHAPTER XLII.

THE ELOPEMENT.—CROSS PURPOSES.

Half-past ten had struck by the church clock, as Francois Michaut swung himself up on the terrace opposite Miriam's room.

The poor girl was bathed in tears.

"Oh! Francois," she cried between her sobs, "I thought you were not coming, after I had screwed my courage up to leave them all; I imagined you were about to disappoint me."

These words pleased the fellow's vanity, and with a smile he answered,

"No—no, my pretty one. But we are indeed late. Are you ready?"

"Yes, dearest."

"Have you no luggage?"

"No, I forgot that."

Francois laughed heartily.

"You forgetful little thing. Never mind, we cannot stop now. You must buy other things when we arrive at Singapore."

He helped her down the ladder he had fixed against the terrace; and they were soon hurrying along the road towards the harbour.

Many a time did Miriam glance tearfully behind her as she saw her father's house receding from her view.

"Miriam, dearest," said Francois Michaut, "That infernal brother of yours knew all, and intended stopping us to night."

"I thought he did," answered Miriam, "because he made such strange remarks to me during the day."

"He has made some error in the time," continued her lover, "otherwise he would inevitably have been there to stop you. He swore he would last night."

A weight seemed indeed taken off Miriam's mind.

"Oh, I am so very glad," she said, "I should have died with shame and terror had he made his appearance."

"Yes, indeed," said Francois abstractedly.

He was inwardly chuckling at the success of his plans, and more than at anything else delighted at having overreached Sapathwa.

The lights of the harbour were now twinkling in the distance.

"We have not far to go now," said Francois. "I did not engage a palanquin for fear of being discovered."

"Oh! I am not tired," said Miriam; "I could walk with you to the end of the world."

And, indeed, at that moment she felt as if she could have done so.

Poor infatuated girl!

Just like the moth and the candle, she would insist upon flickering round her own destruction.

"I think myself indeed happy," said Francois, kissing her, "in having your love so entirely. It makes me capable of anything."

He was right.

In his fierce animal way he did madly love her—if the term love can be applied to such a passion, and nothing in this world would have stopped him.

The harbour was now reached.

The ship lay there quietly at anchor—an ugly-looking, dirty brig.

But to the mind of Miriam it presented itself as a fairy vessel which was to waft her away to realms of light and happiness.

The captain was on deck.

"Good evening, Mr. Michaut," he said.

"Good evening, Mr. Van Holstein," said Francois. "This is Mrs. Michaut. Is her cabin ready?"

"Oh, yes—there, behind—you will find my wife there. Deliver yourself over to her, my dear madam," he added, "and you will be quite safe."

"Thank you, sir," said Miriam, tremblingly.

Francois conducted her to the place specified.

"I shall not be long," he said. "I have to go on shore again; but we do not start for three hours yet."

"Don't be long, dear Francois," murmured the poor girl; "I shall be so lonely."

"No, dear. I shall be back in an hour. Kiss me. Good-bye."

"Don't say good-bye—say good night."

"Very well, then, good night."

And, kissing her, he leaped up the cabin stairs and went on shore.

*   *   *   *   *

About a quarter of an hour after Francois Michaut had left the ship a gentlemen stepped on board.

He was short and stout, and wrapped up in a huge cloak.

He demanded to see the captain.

With Meinheer Von Holstein his conversation lasted about twenty minutes or half an hour.

At the end of that time they parted. The captain went down stairs for a few moments, and then returning on deck went on shore.

A strange smile was on his face, and gold chinked in his ample pockets.

*   *   *   *   *

"Miriam!" said a voice.

"Yes, love," answered she.

"I want you; come up on deck."

"Very well, dear. I am coming."

And she ascended the cabin steps.

When she reached the top a hand seized her firmly.

"Come, unhappy girl," said the Blue Dwarf, for it was he, "say not a word. Thank Heaven! I have saved you again."

"I will not come. Oh! do not be so very cruel," she cried in an agony of tears.

"You must come. There is no help for it. I have bribed the whole ship. I would drain the sea to rescue you; you know that."

And seizing her in his arms he carried her swiftly on shore.

There a palanquin awaited them.

Into this Miriam was placed; and borne by a circuitous route back to her father's house.

*   *   *   *   *

About two hours after leaving the ship Francois Michaut returned.

Meinheer Von Holstein was sitting calmly smoking on the deck of the White Swallow, as the vessel was named.

"You are over your time," said he between his whiffs.

"Not much."

"Only two hours instead of one."

"So much?" exclaimed he in surprise, as he advanced towards the cabin.

"Stay; don't disturb her," said Von Holstein, detaining him. "She has been rather ill—excited like, and has now gone to sleep. It's rather a rough sea; so if I were you I would not wake her up, but let her get the first shock of it in her sleep."

"You're right," said Francois; "I will not disturb her."

"No, no, that's right; she hasn't been to sea before, I think," said the Dutch captain.

"No—never."

"Ah! then leave well alone."

"I will," said Francois, lighting a cigar. "It's very cold. I shall be glad when morning comes."

"It strikes me you won't," muttered the skipper.

"What did you say?"

"Nothing."

So the good ship White Swallow set sail with a fair wind at five o'clock in the morning, and in the bright clear morning Francois Michaut watched the land receding from view.

Then he went below to seek Miriam.

CHAPTER XLIII.

"SAPATHWA," sobbed Miriam, as she was borne away swiftly towards home, "you are the curse of my existence."

A pang of deep sorrow shot through Sapathwa's heart as she uttered these bitter words.

"Oh! Miriam," he said, "I have saved you from sorrow and misfortune."

"You have broken my heart."

"I have saved your honour."

"My honour was safer in his keeping than in yours."

"I will not reproach you, Miriam, for your unkind words. Some day, however, you will repent all you have done; and even then thank me."

"Never," said Miriam.

And she relapsed into silence.

In the course of half-an-hour, during which the Blue Dwarf forebore to harass her by words, they reached the garden of Reginald's abode.

"And now," said Miriam, bitterly, "I suppose I am to be led in before my family like the lost sheep found."

"Miriam," said Sapathwa quietly, "against the terrace is the ladder by which you escaped. Ascend that. You will find your window open. Enter you room, and go to bed; and as far as I am concerned no one will ever know what has happened this night."

He then moved to go away.

Miriam could not but appreciate his wonderful love and generosity, and throwing her arms round his neck, she said,

"Forgive me, dear John. If you do wrong, I see you do it because you think it is for my good."

She then hastened across the grounds, ran up the ladder, and entered her room.

Sapatha removed the ladder, dismissed the palanquin bearers; and no one in the settlement or in the house ever knew of the events of that night.

Meanwhile Francois Michaut was in great sorrow and anger.

He went down, as I have said, into the cabin to seek for Miriam.

He met Mrs. Von Holstein.

"Good morning, ma'am," he said, "it's a fine sea. How is Mrs. Michaut this morning?"

The lady glanced at him with a surprised air.

"How is she this morning?" he repeated.

"What, don't you know?" said she.

"What *do* you mean? Explain yourself," he exclaimed, impatiently.

"Mrs. Michaut, as you call her, that is Miss Miriam Spelthorne, went away last night with her brother," said Mrs. Von Holstein.

"Oh, my Heaven," cried he, "this is not true," and he tore open the cabin door.

There was no one there.

He then rushed frantically on deck.

"Von Holstein," he shouted, seizing the captain by the arm, "you have deceived and tricked me."

"Eh, eh!" exclaimed the skipper, "why, what the devil's the matter, now?"

"There, don't pretend ignorance. You connived at my wife being taken away out of your ship last night."

"Eh! what's that?" cried the skipper, holding his sides, and laughing heartily, "your wife's given you the slip!—ah! ah! ah!—that's fine."

"And you assisted in it."

"You assert what is false young man," said Von Holstein, gravely, "I was away from the ship nearly all the time you were absent."

"Then your wife has done this"

"Come with me," said the skipper, "and I will ask her."

Francois Michaut, crushed, overwhelmed, faint with anger and disappointment, followed the captain, as he walked rolling his tongue in his cheek towards the cabin.

"Eh! there, wife," shouted Von Holstein.

"Well, what is it now?'

"Why, our passenger here, Mr. Michaut, accuses you of helping to spirit away his wife."

"I have nothing to do with it," cried the good woman, coming half-way up the cabin stairs. "All I know is that last night a gentleman, who said he was the young lady's brother, came down here and said that he wanted to speak with Miss Miriam Spelthorne.

"'Don't know the name,'" says I.

"'Why, it's the lady passenger,'" says he,

"'Get out,' says I, ' she's a married lady.'"

"With this he cried out—

"'Miriam.'"

"And she went up on deck to speak with him, and did not come down again."

This plausible story Francois was compelled to believe.

The skipper and his wife both appeared innocent.

He was obliged to assume they were.

His thoughts were in a state of confusion, which we leave to the reader to imagine rather than attempt to describe them.

He had heard a mention from Miriam of her father's intention of leaving for Europe, and he knew well he could not return in time to accompany them.

He endeavoured in vain to bribe the skipper to turn back.

"No, no," said Von Holstein, "I have lost time as it is. You had better land at Singapore and go back from there.

So he was obliged to be content, and yield *Chateau en Espagne.*

CHAPTER XLIV.

CONSTANT LIVERMORE.

PREPARATIONS were now rapidly made for the departure of the Spelthornes for Europe; and on the appointed day they set sail.

Their departure from the colony was a sign for a general mourning in the colony.

Every one was eager to be first to express their regret.

To no one had either Ethel or Reginald been obnoxious.

They were loved by all, and grieved for by all.

The night prior to their setting sail Miriam and Sapathwa called upon the Michauts, to bid adieu to these old friends.

Old Monsieur and Madame Colbert had been dead some time; and the house known as "Monsieur Colbert's House" was now occupied by the Michauts.

"So you are going to leave us, after all," said Madame Michaut to Miriam.

"Yes; at last."

"I am sure there is no one in the whole settlement who will not be sorry for your departure," said M. Michaut.

"You are very kind, I am sure, to say so," replied Sapathwa; "but whither has Francois gone?"

"He was very anxious to go to Europe," said Michaut; "he therefore undertook to execute my neighbour Kloot's commission for him in Berlin."

A gleam of satisfaction crossed the face of the Blue Dwarf at these words.

"Oh! indeed," he said, quietly.

Miriam's pale lips trembled as she remarked, "I suppose that will occupy a long time."

"Yes, indeed, he expects to be absent nearly a twelvemonth," said Madame Michaut.

"His voluntary exile has ended in smoke after all," thought Sapathwa.

So the Trusty set sail from Borneo with a fair wind and a quiet sea.

There were on board of her, besides her crew, four passengers, besides the Spelthornes and Sapathwa.

These were English people.

Constant Livermore was a strange man.

He had come out to Borneo about four years previously.

What his purpose in coming out there was no one knew.

He brought with him no books, nothing of any kind except merely the common necessaries of clothing.

The other three passengers were Mrs. Ritterven, a Dutch lady, and her two daughters, lively handsome girls, to whom Miriam at once took a fancy.

Sapathwa, however, immediately recognised in Constant Livermore a congenial spirit, and it was not long before they were upon most intimate terms.

Constant Livermore never but once noticed his strange appearance.

"Mr. Blakesley," he said, in a very short time after their departure; "I am a strange man, I know I shall not offend you, therefore, by what I am about to say, because you will make allowances for my eccentricity. Although you possess a noble mind you are made differently to other men. Let me, then, have one good look at you, that I may never again require to stare at you."

The Blue Dwarf laughed heartily as he said,

"Indeed I am not offended, I am only amused. Have a good look at me."

Constant Livermore then, with a serious countenance, stood opposite to him; and for a full quarter of an hour surveyed him.

Then, with a sigh, he said,

"Young man, I hope I am not deceived. But I see in you a great and good heart, and I long to possess your friendship."

Sapathwa grasped his hand as he replied to him,

"Doubtless your longing is not greater than mine, for out of the circle of my family I have never yet had one I could call a friend."

They were walking on the deck on the evening of a hot and sultry day, when Constant Livermore suddenly stopping, said:

"Blakesley, can you tell my age?"

Sapathwa surveyed him a moment, and then said,

"Truly, Livermore, I cannot. But I should say forty."

Constant laughed.

"I thought you would say so," he replied. "I am but thirty."

"You are joking."

"No, indeed. I am prematurely old. Come, let's sit down. I'll tell you my story, and you are the first who ever heard it."

"I shall indeed be glad to hear it," said the Blue Dwarf, as he took a seat by the side of his companion.

"Mind," said Constant; "it is a secret."

"How so, when you tell it to me?" asked Sapathwa.

"I mean that I tell it to you and you alone," returned Livermore. "I do not wish you to make your friends the repository of my secrets, because it is doubtful whether they would understand them. I have long desired to find some one to whom I could confide my heart's treasure, some one who could appreciate my feelings, and who, having once heard my story, would be able to talk to me of my sorrows. Such a one I think I have found in you."

"I feel deeply honoured, indeed I do," said the Blue Dwarf.

"Aye, and I have not formed my opinion of you lightly," said Constant. "The heart I am certain sometimes finds its fellow heart, to which it is drawn by a kind of strange instinct. Such a bond unites me to you."

Constant Livermore then began his story.

CHAPTER XLV.

Down in Devonshire, in the little hamlet of Favervil, lived Anne Boston.

A plain name, i' faith, you will say.

But she was not plain.

She was the bonniest girl of the county.

No matter was it that she was only the daughter of a little farmer—no matter was it that she could rarely afford to deck herself out in fine feathers. She was nevertheless the beauty of the county, and the envy of the girls far and near.

My father, Sir Tristram Livermore, and his two sons, Canute and I, inhabited Dean's Rookery, as the place was called down there.

It was an old straggling building, overhanging, as it were, the river, and extending its grounds far along the banks.

Canute was the eldest brother.

"He was like my father, haughty, proud, disdainful, from a boy, and as cruel as ever boy in this world dare to be.

We were never friends, and at the age of nineteen (when I was seventeen) my brother hated me.

He possessed great influence over my father.

Everything he said was gospel, while all I said and did was regarded as absurd or useless.

I have often thought my father nourished a grudge against me because my mother died in giving me birth.

I soon, therefore, found it more to my taste to study the beauties of nature—to wander down by the river side—to bask in the sunlight and revel in those exquisite dreams of the future which are given to all them who possess enthusiastic temperaments.

It was in one of these rambles that I met Anne Boston.

She was dressed simply.

But nature seemed to have chosen her specially to prove how impossible it is to spoil her choice flowers.

Anything looked well on her.

But on that evening she seemed peculiarly beautiful and enchanting.

She was attired in a white muslin dress, very short, so as to show her dainty little ankle just as far as the swell of her calf.

Oh! she had a pretty foot and ankle, Blakesley, something you can scarcely imagine, unless you saw it.

Her shoulders were partially bare, and over her bosom was crossed a little lace handkerchief, just tight enough to render still more tempting her little white breasts.

On her head was an apology for a hat, beneath which flowed a profusion of golden curls.

I was reading underneath a tree by the river side when she stumbled over a root and half fell by my side.

She came upon me like a vision of virgin beauty.

I rose, and speechlessly took off my hat to her.

She blushed—and said,

"I am sorry, sir, I have disturbed your reading, but I had almost lost my way."

She had dropped from the basket in her hand the flowers and wild fruit she had been gathering, and I assisted her to pick them up, at the same time saying,

"I will show you your way home, miss, if you will allow me."

"Oh! pray, sir, do not let me take you out of your way," she said, with a sweet smile. "I see now how I missed the path. I took the left bank instead of the right. I can cross the little bridge yonder, and shall soon be home."

"You will not be so cruel as to prevent my walking with you," I said.

She said nothing, so I went.

That girl, Blakesley, was innocence itself.

I never had yet enjoyed anything so thoroughly as that walk down by the river side; and when we parted it was with a promise on her part that she would meet me again.

By the time we said adieu I knew her name was Anne Boston, that she lived at Chalk Farm, and she had learned—not much to her delight—that I was one of the people at the Rookery, as we were generally denominated in Favervil.

These walks were continued night after night.

The result, of course, was certain.

I fell deeply, passionately in love, and told her so.

It was in May—

Truly a May-day dream!

We were sitting by the river side very near the place where we had first met.

Anne Boston was in the hey-day of her health and beauty, only eighteen, just a few months older than I.

Her beauty seemed to ripen with the fruit.

Each day appeared to add fresh colour to her cheeks, fresh loveliness to her features.

"Oh! Anne," I cried, taking her round her waist, and pressing her to my heart, "I love you."

She blushed and smiled with happiness.

"Do you love me, Anne?"

"Yes, Constant."

"And will you be my wife?"

"Oh! Constant, have you well weighed this?" she said. "Can you marry me?"

"Yes, oh yes, Anne. I will marry you in spite of all." And so we plighted our troth.

From that moment our days passed like wild dreams of happiness.

But I have often blamed myself since for not thinking more of the future.

I was, however, very young, and so was she.

We used then to lie for hours together, locked in each other's arms, by the river side, thinking only of the happiness of being together, and never peering further into the future than to think we should some day be married.

A rude shock, however, awaited us.

I was called into my father's room one morning hastily.

"Constant," said Sir Tristram; "your tutor tells me you have finished your studies. I am glad to hear so good an account of you. You remember, however, that you are my younger son, and as such cannot expect so large a portion as Canute. I have, therefore, until you come of age, accepted for you a post which I am sure you will fill with fidelity—as secretary to Lord Auvonmore. He is a good, kind man; you will be very comfortable with him, and he will introduce you into society which will be useful to you in after ██."

I expressed my thanks briefly.

I am sure I endeavoured to appear pleased.

But I was not, and he suspected it.

"You do not seem to like your employment," he said kindly.

"Oh! yes, father, indeed I do," I replied; "but I naturally feel sorry at leaving the Rookery, and all I hold dear in life."

I meant more than was evident to him.

He said merely,

"Naturally you do. You leave here to-morrow."

Here, then, was a short time to take leave of my friends and of Anne Boston.

I met Anne at the usual place.

She came up to me happy, smiling, merry as usual, never dreaming of the bitterness in store for us.

"You look sad, Constant," she said, when I had given my kiss of welcome.

"Yes, dearest," I replied, as we sat down by the river, and I drew her towards me; "yes, dearest, I am indeed sad."

"Why, Constant?"

"I am going to leave you."

"Going to leave me?"

A paleness like that of death overspread her features; her lips trembled and quivered; then her bright eyes filled with tears as she flung herself on my breast, crying—

"Oh! Constant, leave me not."

"You speak as if I wished to leave you, dear Anne," I said, reproachfully. "I have no will in the matter. It is my father's will that I go away to the metropolis as secretary to a certain lord, whose interest I am told to cultivate. I am a younger son, remember Anne, and I have to carve my own fortune. I go to obtain a fortune for you and me."

"I want no fortune, only your love," she said, with smiles and tears.

So she said, and so many have said before her.

But, alas! it is very foolish.

The old proverb is, after all, a true one—"When poverty comes in at the door, love flies out of the window."

"We must have wealth of some kind, my dear Anne," I said, laughing; "we cannot live on love."

The moment at length came for parting.

I left her, like Niobe—all tears.

We exchanged vows of eternal fidelity; and if there was any difference between us, I think she was the more vehement of the two in pledging herself to undying constancy.

Whatever, then, were my sensations at leaving Favervil and Anne Boston, I went away with a comparatively light heart.

She at any rate loved me.

She would await and pray for my return home.

Whatever might be my failures and my disappointments she, at least, would be true to me.

My parting with my brother was cold and formal.

He wished me every success; and was evidently by no means regretful at the necessity which took me from the Rookery.

My father was exceedingly kind—pressed my hand warmly when I leaped into the carriage which was to take me to London, and, as we started, flung through the window, with a knowing look, a purse filled heavily with gold.

I waved my hand in earnest affection; and, overwhelmed by a terrible presentiment, gazed eagerly out of the window at my father.

I never saw him again!

We whirled along rapidly towards the metropolis.

It was a dull, stupid journey; and I was heartily glad when we arrived at the house of my patron in —— street.

My life with him I need not describe to you.

It was pleasant enough—very little work, plenty of excitement; if political hubbub can so be called.

I was introduced to many of the leading men; made a few public speeches; and, as my patron told me, was rapidly progressing towards the assumption of that position which he had promised my father I should attain.

But no success rendered me oblivious of my boyhood's home and dream.

I corresponded regularly with Anne Boston.

My letters were always full of bright hopes for the future, in which she was ever the presiding genius.

Her letters to me were, for a long time, full of warmth, and love, and hope.

But, after a while, her manner changed.

There seemed to me a strange constraint in her words.

She would commence an epistle with every outward sign of joyousness; but, after a moment, there would be a paragraph full of incoherent sentences, blotted with her tears, and evidently dictated by a heart full of agony.

I repeatedly questioned her as to her grief—implored her to open her heart to me; but she always evaded my requests—pleaded illness or sorrow at my absence.

At length her letters became short, hurried, irregular; and then ceased altogether.

I wrote to her again and again without avail.

I then communicated with a young friend whom I thought I could trust, and begged him to clear up a mystery which, had it not been the very middle of the political season, would myself have gone and discovered.

He was not long in answering me.

His letter I could not then understand.

I did not then see the hidden meaning which his affection for me would not allow him to declare more openly.

I can see it all now, and know how much he must have pitied me.

This was his letter:—

"Dear Constant,—I have made inquiries about the Bostons. The family went away from the town some three weeks ago; but why or whither I cannot tell you. I hope you are getting on well. You must come down and see us as soon as Parliament is prorogued.

"Yours ever truly,

"FABER WATSON."

"Why or whither I cannot tell you"—those were his words.

I understand now that he could not tell me because he feared to wound me.

Time went on; and, just before Parliament closed, I received a letter to say that my brother

Canute was in town, and that he wished to see me.

I went to the address named.

One of the domestics whom I had left at the Rookery opened the door.

He smiled and bowed when he saw me.

"I will go and announce you," he said.

Some strange whim seized me.

"Surely there is no need to announce me to my brother," I said; and bounded up the stairs.

I opened the door and entered without ceremony.

What a sight of shame met my eyes!

Mr. Blakesley. my blood froze and my heart

stood s ill then : it seems now to have scarcely strength to beat.

On a sofa by the window of a room luxuriously furnished sat my brother Canute.

By his side, dressed in wanton elegance, was Anne Boston.

I stood petrified. She looked at me with intense agony, and then fainted into his arms.

Oh ! how it curdled my blood to see him fondling her, and striving to bring back the life to her by kisses.

"Canute," I said, in a choked voice, "you have brought me to this house of shame purposely to insult me. If you desire to see me, there is my address."

I flung my card upon the table and left the room and the house.

He spoke not a word,

A storm of anger and frenzy was gathering on his brow, but there was no time for it to burst.

He came that evening.

Purposely I had invited friends ; while, strange to say, he brought with him a Captain Everett.

We dined in comparative quiet.

I introduced him to the company as Canute Livermore, a relation of mine, a second cousin, in fact.

He stared, and then turned pale ; but allowed it so to be.

My blood was on fire.

I had determined to chastise him ; and, when the wine was on the table, I said to young Frank Selby, who sat at the bottom of the table—

"Selby, we are all men of the world here, and have sometimes our whims and fancies about women. But, nevertheless, there are certain relationships which should not be tampered with. Do you not think so ? "

"Yes, most certainly," said Frank; "a wife, in my eyes, is sacred."

"So, also, is a girl to whom a man is betrothed."

"Perhaps, in her innocence, she is even more sacred," said Selby.

"Well, then," I continued, enjoying the astonishment of my brother, who sat in complete silence, "what is your opinion of a man who, knowing that a friend of his—perhaps a near relation—is betrothed to a young girl, takes advantage of his temporary absence, not to wean her affections away and marry her, but to seduce her—aye, gentlemen, to seduce her—and then ask his friend or relation to visit at his house to see her shame and his degradation ?"

"He is a blackguard," said Selby.

"Oh ! a contemptible knave," echoed Lord Henry Franklin.

"Unfit for the society of gentlemen," said another.

"Well, then," I said, rising from my chair, "as I consider you all gentlemen, and my most esteemed friends, I imagine it my duty to inform you that my cousin here, Canute Livermore, has treated me in the manner I have described : and in my house I refuse to sit at table with him."

All my companions followed my example.

Canute rose in a terrible fury of anger.

"You are a vile calumniator and a ruffian," he cried, furiously, "and I will force you to give me satisfaction," and, with these words, he seized a glass of wine and dashed it in my face.

"That is enough," I said, eyeing him quietly, and calmly wiping the wine off my vest and shirt. and face—"Gentlemen, there is no time like the present. Let us take a conveyance and have a ride into the country. Don't stay for your carriages. You, Lord Franklin, and Frank Selby, be my seconds, and the others wait here and finish their wine. We shall not be long. I shall return and go through the evening with you."

Captain Everett and Faber Watson volunteered themselves as Canute's seconds.

Poor Faber ! he was dreadfully alarmed.

He had come up from Favervil on the day before, and this was his first dinner with me.

He endeavoured, in every way, to dissuade me from my purpose ; but I resolved to be firm.

"Canute demanded satisfaction," said I, "and then insulted me. I must do it."

He came in the capacity of second merely because he had a faint hope of being able, at the last moment, to avert the calamity.

We started together, I and my seconds, in one conveyance ; my brother and his friends in another ; and went away for five or six miles, until we came to some lonely meadows.

Here we alighted ; and told the cabmen to wait.

Dr. Foster, my surgeon, whom we had called for, accompanied us, and begged me hard to desist and apologise.

I laughed him to scorn.

He determined to make a final effort.

"Gentlemen," he said, when the ground had been measured, "I think it my duty to inform you that these are two brothers."

My seconds regarded him with astonishment.

"Yes, gentlemen," he continued, imagining he had made an impression upon them—yes, gentlemen, they are brothers, and they should not be allowed to fight."

"Can this matter be arranged ?" said Lord Franklin, coming forward with Selby.

I felt at that moment like a demon.

"No," I cried, in a hoarse voice ; "Anne Boston's shame, and my anger, call to me for vengeance. If this is not a duel it will be a murder."

Nothing more was said.

We took our positions, and the lot fell to me to fire first.

I felt a presentiment that Canute would never live to stand and fire at me in his place.

I took deliberate aim ; and I own that I felt a kind of malignant pleasure when I saw that he visibly trembled with fear.

I fired.

He fell instantly.

His seconds rushed to him.

There was no hope ; the ball had penetrated his lungs.

I stood still on my ground ; and my brother asked to be held up.

He was dying fast, so they complied with his request.

None knew his purpose ; but had they known it they would not have dared to oppose him.

I had fired first: he had, therefore, a right to fire also.

With his dying hand, therefore, he took deliberate aim and fired.

The devil lent the ball its aid. It came straight to its destination, and penetrated my shoulder.

I dropped—fainted, and the horrid scene was over.

When I recovered my senses I was in a carriage, whirling away rapidly towards my home.

"Is he dead?" I asked faintly.

"Yes," said Frank Selby.

"That is right," I replied, and relapsed again into a dead sleep.

The affair was hushed up. My patron and my father had influence enough to set it right, and I was kept out of the way for a time.

My brother was pitied by none.

I was commiserated by all.

My father, however, refused to see me, and died within a month after Canute's death.

Mingled with the commiserations I received at these sad events, I now had congratulations.

I was now Sir Constant Livermore.

But what cared I for the title.

It was to me only a constant recollection of dread scenes and sacrifices.

When my father had been buried I resolved to take possession of the Rookery.

It suited my morbid disposition, and promised me a life of quiet.

Before going to Flavervil, however, I went to Anne Boston.

She received me in great grief.

"Anne," I said, "it is useless to repine now. What is done cannot by any human power be remedied. Are you repentant?"

She sobbed an answer, and kissed my hand.

"If you are," I continued, "I will rescue you from your position. Do you know where your father is?"

"Yes; but I dare not go to him. He will never forgive me."

She told me his address, and I went to see him.

At first he was harsh, cruel, uncompromising as she had represented him to be.

But I said,

"Remember, Mr. Boston, although Anne has done wrong, you have no right to compel her to do worse. I, who had hoped to marry her, and had framed all my hopes of happiness upon her love—how must I feel? Nevertheless I forgive, and I propose to you to receive her again into your house. I will settle upon her a sum of money which will keep her always in comfort, and enable her to bring up respectably the child which she unfortunately carries in her bosom. Do not refuse to watch over her."

Tears glistened in Mr. Boston's eyes as he took my hand and said,

"You are a noble boy. The girl was mad to have deceived you."

And so it was arranged.

I went down to Dean's Rookery, and lived in as great seclusion as a hermit.

Anne Boston and her father resided within a few miles of us.

Thus time went on, until she gave birth to a boy, whom I insisted on naming, in my queer way, Constant Livermore.

If it is his child, thought I, it is also Anne Boston's, and it shall never bear his name.

Poor girl—she did not long survive her trouble.

She died within a year after the birth of her boy, who always thinks I am his father.

Her body was embalmed, and placed in our family vault.

"But her heart is not there," said Constant, taking out a large gold locket from his breast, and showing it to Sapathwa.

It was a case like that of a watch, fronted with glass.

Inside it were a few burnt ashes, like the ashes of paper.

"Those," said Livermore, "are the ashes of her heart. There is very little but ashes left of mine."

CHAPTER XLVI.

THE SHIPWRECK.

A DEEP melancholy settled upon Sapathwa when his companion said these last words.

"I will tell you my story," he said, "if you will allow me. The drama is not complete yet, but it bids fair to end in much the same way as yours."

While the Blue Dwarf tells his tale let us glance at the weather.

It was now evening.

The wind all day had been strong—at night it blew a gale.

So it went on until midnight, when the wind gave a sudden shift, threw the ship into the trough of the sea, and started the sternpost.

An ugly leak was thus effected, and four feet of water was found in the hold.

The men went to the pumps and worked with a will, but it was all in vain.

The wind blew all in gusts.

Their work was no sooner done than it was undone.

A tremendous gust sent the vessel on her beam ends, and there she lay like a log in the water.

The masts were cut away one after another.

Everything that could possibly be thrown overboard was cast away.

But it was of no use.

The morning broke and found them still lying there—still working at a hopeless task.

The calmest of those on board were Constant Livermore, Sapathwa, and Reginald.

The first was like a rock.

His countenance never once changed.

His muscles seemed to have assumed a stable rigidty.

"You are a brave man," said Sapathwa.

"No—mistake me not," said Livermore. "I am not brave. It is custom entirely. I have faced death so often that I fear it not. How-ever, I think this will be my last turn."

"Say not so, my dear friend," cried the Blue Dwarf; "we are not in a hopeless state."

"My dear Blakesley," returned Constant, "do not deceive yourself. I say everything that is hopeful before the women, but this ship is doomed."

"Why?"

"It is settling down fast. We can never hope to save her. Our only hope is in the boats. Some of us probably may be saved. Probably one of us two may be. Will you, then, promise to do me a favor, should you survive me?"

"Willingly—most willingly."

"My brother's son is living at Arelegh, in Devonshire. He is now eight years old. I wish him to have all my property. My soli-citor, Mr. Ducan, of the Temple, has my will. Take him the news of my death."

"But my dear friend you are not dead yet," said Sapathwa.

"No; but I may die."

The Blue Dwarf now went down into the cabin, where his mother and Miriam were sitting.

"How are you, my dear mother?" he said, kissing her; "and you, Miriam!"

"I am very calm, dearest boy," replied his mother; "but I fear this will be fatal. Miriam, poor girl, she is very, very brave."

On Miriam's face there was a quiet, settled melancholy; but no fear.

She smiled, and kissed Sapathwa; but her heart was too full to speak.

"Sapathwa," said his mother, "you have those papers I gave you?"

"Yes, mother."

"Should anything happen to me," continued Ethel, "they will prove your identity, and obtain your entrance into John's family."

"Do not talk of such things, mother," said Sapathwa, in a broken voice; "we are only in danger. We must not give way to despair?"

"I do not give way to despair," said his mother. "I only wish to be prepared for the worst."

The door now opened, and Reginald appeared. He was calm and serious; but no dread was in his face.

"You must come on deck," he said, taking Ethel's hand.

"Why?" asked she.

"Come along, love; don't be inquisitive," he said. "It is pleasanter up there."

"Why is this?" whispered Sapathwa.

"The water will be in the cabin in a few minutes," answered Reginald.

Upon deck it was scarcely possible to stand.

The wind still blew fiercely, and the deck was so aslant that one had to hold on by anything that was nearest.

No attempts at navigation were made.

The men all worked in turn at the pumps, and that was all.

Every one was on deck, and few spoke above a whisper.

The other family sat weeping and trembling by themselves; while the Spelthornes and Blakesley were calm and collected.

At seven o'clock in the evening the last meal of the day was served out.

People ate their food mechanically, feeling as if every morsel would choke them.

"This is the last meal we shall take on board, I am afraid," said Captain Culliver, who sat with them.

"Do you think so?" asked Reginald, with as much calmness as he could muster.

"Indeed I do, sir," he replied. "I would order out the boats now, but the wind is very heavy, and I hope it will be calmer towards night."

"You are wise," said Livermore; "this sea is too much for a small boat."

"You are all ready to get in the instant the order is given?" said the captain.

"Yes."

"Then I will see you get places," he replied calmly.

He went below, and returned with a brace of pistols.

These he examined and approved.

"I am glad," he said to Reginald and Sapathwa, "that you also are thus prepared. You will find them of much use."

Just as he was speaking a confused noise was heard below: the ship trembled, and the men came rushing up.

"I know what this means," said the cap-tain.

"What is it, in Heaven's name?" cried Regi-nald.

"They have abandoned the pumps. Get your pistols ready, and follow me."

Culliver advanced towards the boats, and calling to his men, said—

"What's the matter, boys?"

"The pump is useless—we must have the boats," said they, surlily.

"Take them, then," said Culliver. "Lower them quickly. Let the women go first, and let them not be crowded."

The men obeyed orders well. They lowered the boats; and in half an hour had completed a large raft.

Into the first boat got Reginald and Ethel, the other family, and four sailors; and Sapathwa and Miriam were about to follow, when they pushed off, declaring they were full.

The other boat was a frail affair; and so, trusting rather to the raft, the Blue Dwarf seized Miriam in his arms, and leaped upon it.

Only just in time,—the sailors pushed off, and left on the deck all their comrades and the captain.

"'Twas twilight, and the sunless day went down
    Over the waste of waters, like a veil
Which, if withdrawn, would disclose the frown
    Of one whose hate is masked but to assail.
Thus to their hopeless eyes the night was shown,
    And grimly darkened o'er their faces pale
And the dim, desolate deep: twelve days had fear
    Been there familiar, and now death was here.

"At half-past eight o'clock, booms, hencoops, spars,
    And all things for a chance had been cast loose
That still could keep afloat the struggling tars;
    For yet they strove, although of no great use.
There was no light in Heaven but a few stars.
    The boats put off, o'ercrowded with their crews;
She gave a heel, and then a lurch to port,
    And going down head foremost—sunk, in short.

"Then rose from sea to sky the wild farewell,
  Then shrieked the timid, and stood still the brave;
Then some leaped overboard with dreadful yell,
  As eager to anticipate their grave;
And the sea yawned around her like a hell,
  And down she's sucked 'neath the whirling wave—
Like one who grapples with his enemy,
  And strives to strangle him before he die.

"And just one universal shriek there rushed,
  Louder than the loud ocean, like a crash
Of echoing thunder—and then all was hushed,
  Save the wild wind and the remorseless dash
Of billows—but at intervals there gushed,
  Accompanied with a convulsive splash,
A solitary shriek—the bubbling cry
  Of some strong swimmer in his agony."

CHAPTER XLVII.

THE RAFT.

THE morn broke over the sea calm and beautiful.

Not a sign of the storm was to be seen.

But the night had been one of terrible tempests.

The wind had been blowing fearfully, not in steady streams, but in gusts.

When, therefore, the morning broke, the raft was alone.

The two boats had disappeared.

It was almost impossible that they should have drifted so fast in the night as to have passed the raft.

It allowed of no doubt.

They both had swamped, and Miriam and the Blue Dwarf were orphans.

They scarcely dared to speak of it as a certainty, although both knew it was folly to hope.

Constant Livermore, Miriam, Sapathwa, and four of the crew constituted the company on the raft.

A good deal of foresight had been evinced in the formation of the raft.

A keg of brandy ornamented one corner of it, while on the other was a cask containing some biscuit and salt beef.

A strong pole occupied the centre, on which a sail had been rudely hoisted.

The first day on the raft, therefore, went on merrily.

The sailors had eaten nothing all the day before.

They had worked incessantly at the pumps, and drank rum, but had had no time to partake of animal food.

The had feasted heartily, improvident as sailors always are in trouble; they thought not of the morrow, but consumed more provisions than ought to have been used in three days.

When Sapathwa offered to Miriam her portion of the oft-repeated meal, she wished to decline it and save it until the next day, but Constant Livermore prevented her.

"Miss Spelthorne," he said; "it is of no use. These men *will* eat and drink, and as perhaps we may have much suffering to go through, I would advise you to take as much sustenance as possible in preparation for that time."

The first day passed, the second day, and the third, and as the fourth day dawned it dawned upon a famishing crew.

All the provisions had gone, all the brandy had been drunk, and all the fresh water, and with parched lips they sat looking vacantly at one another, and uselessly laving their mouths with the salt water.

That day they caught a turtle.

This was scrupulously divided between the seven, and served somewhat to revive them.

A fresh breeze too sprang up, swelled out the sail, and carried them along briskly through the water.

The next day nothing was eaten, the sixth, the seventh, the eighth, the ninth, passed, and still no food.

A week went by, and the men sat there with glaring eyes, each thinking of the same thing, but none daring to avow it to the other.

Miriam alone was almost unconscious.

They had hitherto tended her with most scrupulous care, caring for her every request, and giving her the most of all the provisions.

Now a horrible thought took possession of their minds.

One whispered it to the other, he passed it on until their thoughts were given out more boldly.

"I say, comrade," said one to the Blue Dwarf; "it is no use in such times as these to be particular; the lady is dead or dying, and we have no food. You understand."

Sapathwa shuddered.

"No, no, anything but that," he cried. "I will never allow it. If she dies I will die with her and sink our bodies in the sea, but she shall never be eaten."

The men grumbled something about being six to one, and advanced towards her.

Sapathwa knelt up by her side and drew his pistols.

"The first man who touches her dies," cried he, fiercely.

Strange was it indeed !

On that lone raft death stared them all in the face, yet no one dared to advance towards the pistol.

Constant Livermore put a stop to the strife.

"Comrades," he said; "be quiet a moment. I will suggest a remedy. But first of all let me ask you four some questions."

They sat around him in a circle.

"First of all, Harry Mastin," asked Constant; "have you a wife?"

"Aye, that I have, sir," replied the tar, in a hoarse voice; "and two little ones. I shall never see her again I suppose."

"And you, Chalcott?"

"I also have a young wife," said the man; "whom I love dearly.

"And you, Fletcher?"

"I have no wife," said he; "but I have an old mother wholly dependent on me. My death will be her ruin."

"And you, lastly," asked Livermore of the youngest of them all, Dick Bradley. "Have you a wife?"

"I have no wife nor parents," said the young fellow with a tear in his eye, and with a trembling voice; "but I have a sweetheart whom I was to marry when I returned to Eng-

land.   Poor Anne !   I fear me she'll never see
Dick again."

There was a magic in the name of Anne for
poor Constant.

His voice trembled as he said, turning to the
Blue Dwarf,

"I know, Blakesley, that you have something
to live for.   I now am aware that these poor fellows have also something to live for. I, comrades,"
he added, "am a lone man.   I have nothing
to live for.   My life is only a prolonged misery.
I will die for you."

The men shed tears.

It was truly a noble sacrifice : but oh ! how
terrible !

They grasped his hand, and in low whispers
thanked him for the terrible boon.

"I only ask one thing," he said. "I want
an easy death.   I will bleed to death."

It was useless to endeavour to persuade him
from his purpose.

Sapathwa saw this.

Some one must die, and he himself dared
not take the place of his friend for the sake of
Miriam.

"Constant, my dear friend," he said; "if
you are determined on this sacrifice I have
pistols."

"Thank you, God bless you, Blakesley," he
said, and took the pistol.

He then embraced them all—pressed a kiss
on Miriam's cold brow—and went away behind
the sail.

All wept—those hard stern men wept like
children.

Not many minutes elapsed.

A solemn stillness certainly there was for a
few moments, during which he said his prayers,
then a loud report, and all was over.

The horrible meal was then proceeded with.

Sapathwa could not touch it, nor dared he
to offer any of the terrible sacrifice to Miriam.

And so, glutted with human flesh, the sailors
lay and slept.

CHAPTER XLVIII.

STARVATION !

ANOTHER two days past.

The men were raving mad.

Some deliriously sang merry drinking songs.

Others mumbled incoherently about home,
fancying he had already arrived in England.

One plunged headlong into the sea and was
drowned.

At length, one evening, a clear, bright evening, a sail was seen on the horizon.

This seemed to inspire life into Sapathwa and
Miriam, and to drive away the cloud of madness which clouded the intellects of the others.

One of them climbed up the mast and waved
his shirt aloft.

Then, when it came nearer, the Blue Dwarf
fired off a pistol in the hope that some one in
the vessel might hear it.

It was truly a moment of intense anxiety.

The ship neared them.

Smiles of gladness beamed over their pale and
haggard faces.

But then, how bitter the disappointment.

The ship neared them—passed them—went
sailing away, until at length over the edge of the
horizon, they caught the last glimpse of her
masts.

Then they sat down in helpless despair and
wept.

"What are we being punished for ?" asked
Miriam, gently.

"Alas, Miriam, I cannot tell you," said
Sapathwa, "we cannot fathom the designs of
Providence.

"Yet it seems very cruel," murmured the
poor girl.

"It seems cruel, perhaps, but who knows, it
may be the opening to a brighter future.

He said "It may," but his heart belied his
words.

That night a bird fell tired on the raft.

The sailors glanced eagerly at it.

Sapathwa divined their thoughts immediately.

"No, comrades," he said, "I and my sister
here did not interfere in your repast, of which
even now you have some left. Let us, then,
partake of this little sustenance together."

He plucked the bird carefully, lit a few sticks
by firing his pistol, and roasted a leg and a wing.

Of these he made Miriam partake sparingly,
and picked the bones himself.

The sailors looked on with a hopeless, maniacal
grin, and then, going behind the sail, partook of
some more of their horrible food.

Luck now came to them.

The morning broke early, brightly, merrily
over the sea ; and around the raft were gathered
numberless tortoises asleep.

Sapathwa and his three companions gathered
them in shoals, and piled them on one side of
the raft.

Then, with tears, they committed the remains
of poor Constant Livermore to the deep.

Sapathwa and Miriam had, as I have said,
abstained from tasting human flesh.

Their heads, therefore, though burning and
racked by excruciating agony, were, nevertheless sufficiently clear to enable them to know
what was best to do.

They therefore ate sparingly, and cooked their
food.

The sailors, on the other hand, who were still
delirious with human blood, ate ferociously, and
lay gorged in the broiling sun.

Sapathwa again and again awoke them, until
it was of no use.

One after another they became torpid, and
before evening the Blue Dwarf and Miriam
were the only living beings on the raft.

Silently they committed the bodies of their
dead companions to the sea, thanked God for
His mercy in preserving their own lives, and
went to sleep.

They had now with them plenty of food.

The tortoises were alive, and therefore could
be preserved in numbers, and one of them
boiled in salt water produced tolerable soup and
excellent food.

For several days this kind of life continued.

On the evening of the fourth day some seaweed was washed against the edge of the raft. Sapathwa fell upon his knees and thanked Heaven.

"What is it, Sapathwa?" said Miriam, in astonishment.

"We are nearing land," he cried, clasping her in his arms, and kissing her.

"Oh! Heaven be praised," exclaimed she, with tears of thankfulness in her eyes.

Land-birds now swooped around the raft, and one more bold than the rest perched on the mast.

Then a low line of land was seen, in which was soon to be distinguished a bay overhung by lofty trees.

Toward this Sapathwa steered as well as he was able, and by eight o'clock was lying gently rocking in the calm waters of a little harbour.

"Oh! Heaven is kind indeed," cried Miriam. "We are saved!"

The raft floated gently on shore, and rested against the edge of the land, which sloped gradually down from a lofty hill to the very margin of the water.

As the famishing crew in the shipwreck described by Lord Byron in "Don Juan" did they feel when they came to land—

They felt the freshness of its growing green,
 That waved in forest tops and smoothed the air;
And fell upon their glazed eyes like a screen
 From glistening waves and skies so hot and bare.
Lovely seemed every object that should sweep
Away the vast salt, dread, eternal deep.

CHAPTER XLIX.

The shore looked wild, without a trace of man,
And girt by formidable waves ————
                                    BYRON.

IF they felt thankful when they saw in the distance the long low line of land, how much more intensely grateful were their hearts when their feet touched the solid earth, and they trod once more amid the green meadows?

The island, for such it appeared to be, gave no signs of human life.

They seemed, at any rate in that part of the island, to be the only beings existing.

"We have landed on an uninhabited island," cried Miriam. "Our lot is not much improved after all."

"Say not so, dearest sister," said the Blue Dwarf, "let us be thankful we are on land at all."

"Yes, Sapathwa, I am, indeed," she cried; "but how shall we be able to live?"

"Although the island is uninhabited," answered he, "there is no reason to think that there are no animals upon it. We have food for to-night. We will explore the place in the morning."

The raft had been moored to the shore, and upon it were still about twenty tortoises.

These Sapathwa brought upon shore, and placed in a hollow where there was some water.

Then, killing the largest of them, he lit a fire, and cooked the meat in the shell in fresh water from a spring which bubbled up under the trees.

This made a savoury dish, which seemed like a gift from Heaven to the poor creatures who had so long been existing upon brine.

Under the forest trees Miriam slept that night, the sail spread over her, and Sapathwa walking like a sentinel round and round her to ward off an enemy.

Then in the morning, when she awoke, he partook also of a few hours' rest, and she watched over him.

After partaking of a breakfast, consisting of the same materials as their supper, they started on their exploring expedition.

The island was of very small extent.

It was oblong.

From one side to the other it was scarcely six miles, while from end to end it was twenty.

There was not a living soul on the island.

They were truly like our first parents.

"The world was all before them where to choose
 A place of rest————"

Animals of various kinds abounded in the place, but none larger than the wild hog.

One of these latter Sapathwa shot.

Cocoanuts also were to be found, and various wild fruits.

"Truly," said Sapathwa, "we have landed upon an island of plenty."

"Yes; we will try and be happy until it pleases Heaven to take us away," said Miriam.

The raft which had brought them on shore was left untouched where it was moored. The mast, however, and the sail served to form an extempore tent until a better habitation could be built.

This Sapathwa succeeded in accomplishing in a few days, forming a kind of log hut under the shade of the forest trees.

The next thing was to erect a pole on which to display some sign of human life.

About twenty long sticks tied together formed a pole some hundred and fifty feet high, supported on either side by sticks around the base, and resting against it.

On the top of this floated a flag formed of an old shirt upon which Sapathwa wrote in letters of blood the word "HELP!"

Their life was very monotonous.

But more so to Miriam than to the Blue Dwarf.

She, although feeling deep sorrow for her father and mother's death—although also experiencing the most intense gratitude for her own safety and the undying love of Sapathwa, felt still a craving after Francois Michaut.

That worthless fellow had certainly made an impression upon her soul which could never be effaced except by his own act.

She appeared, however, to the Blue Dwarf to be comparatively happy, and to him, therefore, this life at Deliverance Bay, as they had named it, had the most sweet attractions.

Here, whatever might be his privations, he could be near her, watch over, attend to her every want, and receive a kiss of true love from her every night ere she retired to rest.

The log hut had been formed into two chambers.

The inner room, and, therefore, the one furthest from any possible danger, was occupied by Miriam—the front one by Sapathwa.

Oh! how madly, how passionately, yet how purely did he love that girl!

Many a night he would kiss her brow when she retired, and then apparently settle himself in a corner to rest.

But when she had disappeared he would creep to her chamber door, listen to her breathing to see if she were asleep, and, being assured of the fact, he would enter and gaze in rapture upon her sleeping features.

Sometimes he would stoop down and kiss her forehead, and one morning she awoke and found him sitting there.

"Is that you, Sapathwa? she said, in surprise. He started.

"Yes, dear Miriam," he said, "I felt nervous about you last night. You looked ill, so I have sat here by your side."

"You have not slept, then?"

"No, dear."

"Then you must be tired. Foolish boy, I am well enough," cried Miriam.

"I am not, indeed," said he, "and I enjoyed sitting infinitely more than I should have enjoyed being in bed. You know I like being near you."

"Poor Sapathwa!" exclaimed Miriam, rising and kissing him, "I know your love for me is true. I do not pity you because that would be an insult. I appreciate your love and respect you for it."

"Oh, I would that you could do more than that!" said Sapathwa.

"I do so, too," replied Miriam, "but it would indeed be wrong to marry you when my heart is pledged to another. I love him still, I cannot help it, Sapathwa, and yet I can see that your affection for me is greater even than his."

"Bless you, my dear girl, for these words," said he, "they give me more happiness than I have experienced for a long, long time."

"How long have we been here now?" asked Miriam as they sat down that morning to their usual breakfast of broiled pork and cocoa-nut milk, "I have never kept any account of time."

"We have been here now a month," replied he, counting the notches on the stick he used for an almanack.

"It does not appear so long as that."

"Then the time has passed pleasantly," cried the Blue Dwarf, "although you have had no other companion but me."

Miriam laughed.

"The time certainly has gone by quickly, but why, I do not know."

"It has, indeed; but then I can account for it," said he.

"Why?"

"Because time is always light and gladsome to me when you are with me."

"Dear John, I do love you for your love," she cried, incoherently, as she kissed his forehead.

These words sank deep into Sapathwa's heart. They were calm, indeed, to his wounded love.

CHAPTER L.

HOPE AT LAST.

TIME went on thus—another month passed, and still no sign of aid.

The spot where they had erected the pole was upon a hill which commanded a view of the whole island, and the sea around.

Here they generally sat in the day time, watching for a sail, and talking home and the future.

These moments were the extreme happiness of the Blue Dwarf.

Gradually, imperceptibly, not by any reasoning in her own mind, she began to shape that future as the future of both of them.

Sapathwa was always included in these dreams of coming happiness, and although not as her husband, yet it seemed to him that, in whatever position she might be, she contemplated their always being together.

"Miriam," he said one day, "I sometimes feel so happy that I scarcely regret the world."

He spoke truly, for had she consented to become his wife he would never have wished to leave the island.

She was his world.

All beyond her were excrescences.

"I also," she said, as she lay with her head on his shoulder, "I also sometimes feel a certain happiness, which I would not change for anything."

Sapathwa gazed at her fondly.

"Oh! Miriam, you give me hopes of better times," he said, playing with her tiny hands.

She blushed deeply and answered not.

"It seems, indeed, like old times, Miriam," he continued, "before anything came between us to destroy our happiness. Miriam, you have lost all your dearest friends. I ask you *not* to love me as well as you loved them; I ask you only to try and love me a little. Dearest girl, may I yet hope that you will be mine?"

Miriam trembled violently.

"Sapathwa," she answered, "I know, I always knew, your great love for me; but, believe me, I loved as strongly, and it is not easy to take from the heart the shackles of a love like mine. Francois Michaut is gone away from us; he may in Europe, forget the face of the one who loves him so deeply, so passionately. If I see him not in six months from this time I will be your wife, for I love you next to him."

Sapathwa did not burst forth into passionate cries of ecstacy.

His delight, his joy, were too great to be given vent to in violent exclamations.

He merely pressed her to his bosom, kissed her dewy lips, and said, as he gazed at her fondly,

"My Miriam! you are an angel of mercy."

They lay there on the green sward: the one in speechless joy, the other in calm happiness at the happiness of another, until the time came for their evening meal.

They then descended towards the log hut, where, upon their rude table, Miriam spread out the materials for dinner, while Sapathwa went

down towards the bay to fetch some spring water.

He came back in great haste, and with a pale and anxious face.

"What is the matter?" asked Miriam, as she saw him close the door, and fasten it carefully with the rude bolts he had been enabled to fashion.

"There are men on the island," he said.

"Well; but that is no reason to be in fear," she answered. "We are daily watching for men to take us away."

"Yes, yes," he said; "but we are watching for the advent of white men—civilised men. These are not white men."

"How do you know? You have not seen them, I suppose."

"No; but I have seen a foot-print on the sand. It is not the foot-print of a white man, because he would wear boots. It was the mark of a naked foot."

Miriam sat down to her dinner in fear.

They had longed for the advent of men.

For two months they had never seen a human being; now the idea of seeing one filled them with fear.

"They may be a friendly race," said Miriam.

"Yes, truly they may be," returned Sapathwa; "but it is as well to be careful. You had better retire to rest early, Miriam, because we do not know what they may do; and if they come here with any evil intentions we cannot say when they may take it into their heads to descend upon us."

"But you will wake me up directly there is any danger?" said Miriam.

"Oh, yes," cried the Blue Dwarf, laughing. "Don't you think I am going to allow you to be idle. You will have to assist in defending our home."

Very soon after dinner Miriam retired to rest.

Sapathwa stationed himself at the window, whence he could command a view of Flag Point as they passed the cliff upon which was erected the pole.

He had with him in the hut a rifle and two pistols.

He had, also, the powder-flask of the sailors who had perished on the raft, so that he was prepared pretty well against a siege.

Provisions they had in plenty, but water was very scarce.

He had been sitting there about half an-hour watching the flagstaff, and dreamily thinking of the hopes which Miriam had held out to him, when he heard a rustling among the trees, and a savage came cautiously forth.

Then, with a cry, he sprang up towards Flag Point.

CHAPTER LI.

LONG RANGE.

"MIRIAM," said Sapathwa, shaking her gently.

She had lain down in her clothes; so, starting up immediately, she said—

"Yes; what is the matter? Have they come?"

"Yes, dearest, come; I want you to help me to defend the flagstaff."

They returned to the front room, and found, peering in through the windows, a naked savage.

The island upon which our two lovers had been shipwrecked was the island of Tuo-namo, which, to this day, is uninhabited, but which is frequently visited by the cannibal population of a neighbouring group, for the sake of the fruits and wild hogs in which it abounds.

For it must not be supposed that a cannibal eats human flesh alone.

He simply fails to see the reason why he should *not* eat it when it falls in his way.

These men were of a race which Sapathwa had seen before.

He, therefore, knew their propensities, and was aware it was useless to temporise with them.

The little window through which the savage was peering was, of course, devoid of all glass.

When, therefore, the man peered in, Sapathwa made gestures to him to go away.

The man grinned, and put his head in through the aperture.

Sapathwa motioned him again to be gone.

The man could easily understand by his face and his movement that he was angry; but this only appeared to amuse him.

He grinned, therefore, more horribly, and pushed his shoulders through.

Sapathwa then raised his great fist, and, striking the savage between the eyes, sent him flying back upon the green sward.

He rose, after a moment, and rushed up to his twenty companions, who were now dancing round the flagstaff.

He jabbered a few words to them, and they commenced tearing away the foundations of wood upon which the pole rested.

This was too much for Sapathwa.

He shouted lustily, but no answer.

They proceeded with their work of destruction.

Raising his rifle, therefore, he took deliberate aim; and shot down a man who was engaged in endeavouring to uproot the pole.

The flash—the report—and the fall of their companion seemed to astound the savages.

They crowded round him, examined him, and finding he was really dead, took him away, and for a time disappeared.

"They are gone, thank Heaven!" said Miriam.

"Yes love, they are gone; but they will return presently and attack us. They had no weapons with them when I fired."

He was right.

In about an hour's time they returned, reinforced by about ten more.

They carried bows and arrows, long knives, and spears.

They halted about a hundred yards beyond Flag Point, thinking, no doubt, that the messenger of death could not reach so far.

Here they sat down in a circle to consult.

"Do not fire at them again," said Miriam.

"No, no, I will not fire; I wish not to shed blood unnecessarily," returned the Blue Dwarf.

They watched the savages intently.

The war council was evidently an animated one.

Many speeches were made, and much discussion ensued, if one might judge by the frequent and excited gesticulations of the various speakers.

At length, after one of their number had chaunted a kind of war song, they all sprang to their feet, and ranged themselves in a long line around the log hut.

One of their number then fired off a bow and arrow to try the distance.

The arrow struck the door, and stuck there quivering.

After this succeeded a rush of weapons from all the thirty savages.

No harm was done.

They stuck in the wood, and remained there —that was all.

Then a report—a flash—and one of their number fell dead.

They uttered a loud cry of fear, and fled.

A new line of conduct was at once decided on between them.

They would go beyond the reach of the strange missile, and sit down in a circle, and starve the strangers out.

They moved off, therefore, until there were five hundred yards between the log hut and the nearest man.

"This is well," said Sapathwa. "They are afraid, I will frighten them still more."

"What are you going to do?" asked Miriam, in alarm.

"You will see," he said, with a strange smile.

Taking up the water bucket, he added, "We shall want water before morning. I will go and fetch it."

He went out, leaving the door wide open, and descended, rifle in hand, towards the bay.

The savages sprang to their feet, and discharged a volley of arrows at him.

They all fell short by some three hundred yards.

It was madness on their part to try and hit him.

He went down and got the water.

Just as he was returning the savages noticed that he had left the door open, and one of them sprang forward to intercept him.

The rifle instantly was brought to the shoulder, and down the savage fell before he had advanced ten yards.

A cry of amazement and terror arose from the savages, and they moved further away.

"My plan is succeeding," said Sapathwa; "I am now going to Flag Point."

He ascended to the very topmost portion of the cliff, and commenced opera ious.

The savages were, as I have said, sitting round the hut in an immense circle, none now being nearer to him than six hundred yards.

Seated under the flag, Sapathwa drew forth his pipe, fashioned out of a wild root, and commenced smoking.

He had not been there many minutes before they again tried their skill by firing at him a volley of arrows, which fell far short.

He then rose up, and, making an angry gesture, raised his rifle and shot the first man in the row.

This done, he went on in succession, loading and firing as fast as he was able, until six of their number had fallen.

This utterly mystified and frightened them.

So, without waiting to take up their dead, they fled into the woods, leaving Sapathwa to go quietly home.

CHAPTER LII.

SHORT RANGE.

"WELL, I think I have got rid of these brutes for a time," said Sapathwa, entering the hut, closing the door, and throwing himself, weary, on his bed of leaves and twigs.

"Poor John," cried Miriam, kneeling by his side, and kissing his heated forehead.

"I don't half like killing away at that rate," he continued, "but it can't be helped; and I expect I shall have to shoot a few more before they're done with."

Miriam smiled.

"You forget," she said, "they might kill you."

"They might, but they won't," he replied; "but, hark! what is that noise?"

Upon rising, and looking out of the window, they at once saw how matters stood.

The savages, seeing how far the rifle would carry, had determined to rush down quickly in a body, and try if they could succeed better in a hand-to-hand fight.

They were, accordingly, rushing down upon the hut in a close body at full speed.

"Now, then," said Sapathwa to Miriam, "take these two pistols, and when they near the window fire at them, and don't miss."

Sapathwa then aimed and fired.

That shot killed two, and sent several of the rest, who stumbled over them, sprawling down the hill.

They soon, however, picked themselves up, and followed their companions, who never ceased running until they were right under the window of the hut.

When here they crowded round the window, as if eager to court death.

Sapathwa's rifle and Miriam's two pistols went off at once, and three savages fell.

Then, with a yell of fury, they fell upon the hut.

Knives, hatchets, spears, were dashed against the door.

"Miriam," said Sapathwa, "that door will last a quarter of an hour. I can load once a minute, so can you, that is two shots a minute. We can kill them all before that time has elapsed. Come, fire!"

Three more fell dead.

There were now only seventeen left.

These worked at the door, somewhat out of the way of the window.

Miriam sickened at her task.

"Miriam," cried the Blue Dwarf, "you are growing tired of this bloodshed. You load, and I will fire."

He dashed out a piece of the woodwork of the door, and then waited patiently until the three weapons were loaded.

He then fired them off in rapid succession, one after another, a savage dropping under every shot.

Fourteen remained.

The door was giving way.

"They will be in upon us now," cried the Blue Dwarf, as he hastily loaded his rifle.

This time two only fell, the third escaped with a slight wound.

This was an encouragement to the savages.

They raised a furious yell, and threw themselves bodily against the door.

It shivered and trembled.

"Into the bedroom, Miriam," cried Sapathwa, "and get the bolts ready."

She did as she was bidden, and just as they were safely in, and the door closed, the outer gate gave way, and the savages, with a shriek of joy, entered.

They uttered yells of rage at not finding their victims within, and flung themselves against the second door.

This was formed of some of the planks and beams of the raft, and was cooped together with the iron from the brandy-cask, and the barrel which had contained the salt meat.

It opposed, therefore, a formidable obstacle to their progress.

They, however, prepared to destroy this also.

They had certainly more leisure for their work, for from the bedroom no shot could be fired at them.

They, besides, anticipated reinforcements.

At the commencement of the more serious part of the fray the chief, who was now numbered with the dead, had despatched a messenger to a distant part of the island, where the remainder of the savages were encamped, telling them to send down thirty or forty men to the rescue.

It was now six hours since this had been done, and reinforcements might hourly be expected.

It was now four o'clock in the morning, and, as the morning broke, Sapathwa could see, by gazing out of the little window of the bedroom, a mass of savages moving along in the distance.

"We are lost," he thought. He only said, "Here are more of these wretches coming."

He resumed his work, which consisted in boring a hole in the wood large enough for him to fire through.

Two had been made, the third was now being finished.

When they were completed he first looked through, and then placed the pistols in position.

They were all three fired at once, and all took deadly effect.

The savages were standing and squalling about, never expecting such a dose, and those who survived rushed out of the house just in time to meet fifty of their friends.

A brief consultation took place, and then they spread themselves round the hut.

Three of them stationed themselves at the windows, and fired in poisoned arrows.

This was soon put a stop to by nailing a piece of board against the aperture, but they were left in total darkness, save where here and there a chink made for firing admitted a scanty sunbeam.

The savages worked with a will, but their hatchets were clumsy, ill-made things, and failed to make much impression on the hard wood.

The log hut, however, was anything but strong.

It must in time give way.

This Sapathwa knew; and, seeing how the savages had now hemmed them in, there was no chance of a vigorous defence.

He contrived, however, to make a hole large enough to fire through, and at length had the satisfaction to perceive that he could fire upon them, and utterly bewilder them, as they knew not whence the shots came.

Just as the fire was hottest, and when the savages were making vigorous attempts to force the door, Miriam cried out—

"Hush! Listen, Sapathwa!"

The Blue Dwarf listened.

A volley of musketry, and then a shout!

"Thank Heaven!" he cried, "we are saved. That is a British cheer!"

CHAPTER LIII.

A NATURAL MISTAKE.

THERE was great confusion now among the savages, who stood in bewildered groups, and ceased working at the door.

Sapathwa pulled down the board from the window just in time to see the survivors scampering away towards the forest, and about twenty English sailors making their way up towards the hut.

He opened the door, and was just about to rush forth and thank his deliverers when a sudden thought crossed his mind, and he stopped short.

"Go, Miriam," he said, "go and thank them."

"And you—will you not go?" asked she.

"No; they will take me for a savage."

As they spoke the men came up, and one of them entered.

Miriam rushed forward and kissed his hand. "Oh, Heaven bless you!" she cried, "you have arrived but just in time."

"Oh, that's all right, marm. Duty, marm," said the tar; "but who 'ave you got here? Another savage?"

This unpolite remark had reference to Sapathwa.

"No, no!" cried Miriam, "he is my brother."

"Oh, beg your pardon. Hope you're well, sir," said Jack; "only—"

"It's all right," said Sapathwa; "you would say I look rather blue. It's enough to make one feel so and look so too, I think, what we have suffered during the past night."

The sailor laughed at this sally, and led the way down to the boat.

As they brought nothing with them, so they took nothing away, except a few things in remembrance of their sojourn on the island.

They were soon on board, and introduced themselves to the captain.

"We have to thank you greatly, sir," said the Blue Dwarf, "for you have saved our lives."

"That is my duty," said Captain Howard; "but how long have you been on the island?"

"Two months."

"So long? Shipwrecked, of course."

"Yes; that raft there in the bay is the last of the vessel."

And he mentioned her name.

"Ah, indeed!" said Howard; "she is reported in London lost with all hands and passengers."

"How did you discover us?" asked the Blue Dwarf.

"I first of all," said the captain, "observed your signal with the word 'HELP' upon it. Then I heard firing; and, knowing that this was an uninhabited island, I immediately directed my men to go on shore and explore it. See, even now your friends there are wreaking their vengeance on your dwelling and your flagstaff."

Sapathwa looked just in time to see the flagstaff totter and fall over.

The log-hut was in flames, and the savages were dancing round it.

Miriam's eyes filled with tears as she saw it thus destroyed.

Just as they looked the vessel shook, a loud report rent the air, and a cannon-ball, whizzing in among the savages, killed several, and sent the blazing timbers of the hut flying in every direction.

"That is a parting salute," cried Captain Howard, rejoining them. "I am bound for Singapore; I will there land you, and you will soon find a vessel to take you to Europe."

They were not very long in reaching Singapore, and here, with many thanks, they left Captain Howard.

They found that a vessel started for Europe in the course of a week.

Their first care, therefore, was to rig themselves out afresh.

Two months' sojourn had scarcely improved their attire.

Of the light muslin dress which Miriam had worn when shipwrecked scarcely a vestige remained.

A handkerchief was tied around her head, and her feet were bare.

Sapathwa looked even more pitiable.

His coat certainly was good, because it was Captain Howard's, as were his trowsers, waistcoat, and boots.

But the coat trailed on the floor, the trowsers were too tight and too long; the boots pinched his feet, and made him hobble.

They were the astonishment and pity of the settlement when they landed.

Sapathwa, however, soon made himself known at his banker's, and in two days Miriam was again attired in all the glory of Singapore fashions.

The vessel in which they were to sail was called the Rip Van Winkle, and was bound for Holland.

On board, then, of this craft they once more committed themselves to the mercy of the waves.

The captain promised a fair voyage.

He was right.

The voyage was beautiful.

Scarcely an angry wind blew, and the Rip Van Winkle reached home with unexpected swiftness.

CHAPTER LIV.

HOPES AND FEARS.

AN incident occurred on board which tended materially to damp the hopes of poor Sapathwa.

Among the other passengers was a gentleman, an Englishman named Wild.

Jonathan Wild himself could not have possessed a more ferocious countenance than this person.

Henry Wild, however, seemed possessed of a sufficient degree of intellectual capacity.

Our adventurers, therefore, were nothing loath to cultivate his acquaintance, and upon being informed that the Blue Dwarf was Miriam's brother, he considered it quite within his pro-

vince to be very particular in his attentions to his fair fellow-voyager.

"I am going to Berlin," he said one day, as they were all sitting on board.

Miriam's voice trembled, as she said, with more anxiety than was pleasing to the Blue Dwarf,

"Oh! indeed. Do you know many persons there?"

"Yes," said Wild, smiling, "I am in business there, and have been so for two years and more."

"Do you know the firm of Stroutz and Co.?" asked Miriam.

"Yes, well. I travelled for them once."

Sapathwa's heart beat quickly.

Miriam's voice failed her.

It was the firm to transact business with which Francois Michaut had left Borneo.

Love is selfish.

So Miriam Spelthorne never thought of poor Sapathwa's feelings.

"Oh! I am so glad you know them," cried she to Wild; "I have a dear friend in Berlin, who has gone to Berlin to do business with that firm, and I cannot find his address."

"I shall be very happy to be of any assistance to you," said Wild. "Are you going to Berlin?"

"No, we are bound to England, but we can put Berlin in our route."

"In that case," said Wild, "I shall have no difficulty in discovering his address for you, and shall be most glad to be of service in any other way, as you will be a stranger in that city."

He spoke merely of her; he did not mention Sapathwa, who sat there, poor fellow, in silent agony.

"We can go by way of Berlin, can we not?" asked Miriam.

"You have decided it," said Sapathwa, rising, and withdrawing to another part of the deck.

Miriam soon found an excuse to leave Wild and follow him.

"Are you angry with me, dear Sapathwa?" she said.

"Angry," cried he, "no, you know I am never angry with you. I am only hurt, cruelly wounded, that is all."

"Hurt!—wounded!" exclaimed Miriam. "I understand you not."

"I do not doubt it, Miriam," he said, sadly, "that is why I could not feel sad with you. You speak thus because you are deeply in love. I feel thus because I am deeply in love."

"Do you not think it natural that I should be anxious to follow in the wake of Francois?" continued Miriam.

"I suppose so; and yet do you remember your promise?"

"Yes," said Miriam; "I remember saying that, if in the course of six months from the time when I was speaking, I did not meet Francois, I would marry you."

"And yet you seek him?" said Sapathwa, mournfully.

"I did not say I would avoid him, did I?" returned Miriam.

The Blue Dwarf sighed, and groaned inwardly. He knew his own feelings; and, comparing

Miriam's with his, he saw that they bore far too near a resemblance to true love to render his position anything but perilous.

"I suppose it must be so," he murmured.

"What, dear John?"

"I suppose I shall have to undergo all these troubles, all these hopes and fears, before I have a chance of reaching the goal."

"Do you, then, hope to reach it?" asked Miriam with tears in her eyes, and in her kindest tones.

"Oh! Miriam," he said, in broken accents, "knowing how I love you, how can you ask me if I hope when upon that hope alone I live?"

His deep, earnest accents were unmistakeable.

No one could for a moment have doubted the reality of his love.

He was a being in whom guile had no abiding-place.

Formed by nature to be outwardly a curiosity in appearance, he was, inwardly, a curiosity, also, in the goodness of his heart and the purity of his affection.

Miriam had always believed in his love.

His devotion to her in the island proved her belief to be correct; and, having regard to this knowledge, she could not find it in her heart to break up the last fragment of that hope upon which he lived.

It was this feeling that made her give vent to the following extraordinary speech:

"You know I love Francois; therefore it is natural I should wish to rejoin him. But your great love sometimes almost makes me hope I shall fail."

CHAPTER LV.

THE PIOZZI GALLERY.

BERLIN was at length reached.

The glare and excitement of a European city was utterly overwhelming to our wanderers from the East.

"Alas!" thought Sapathwa, "I shall never be happy here."

Love certainly seems to have no abiding-place in a large city.

The business, the anxieties of money-making, the racket, the hubbub, the gaieties, seem to leave no room, no time, for the exercise of the tenderer feelings.

I say "seems," because, after all, it is only seeming.

There may be more love in some little back attic in the dirtiest and smokiest corner of the metropolis than in the most splendid palace, in the most secluded nook, that Utopian affection could ever picture forth.

Naturally enough two young persons, arriving in a city in Europe for the first time, devoted themselves for a while to public amusements.

But although they went, it was not with the same feelings as others go.

They went not to amuse themselves, but because they felt it necessary to go.

Sapathwa imagined it would pass away the time.

Miriam thought that probably she would there meet with Francois Michaut.

Henry Wild had promised that, immediately upon arriving in Berlin, he would ascertain the address of Miriam's betrothed.

They met him in the Piozzi Gallery one evening, as they were listlessly promenading up and down, and listening to the strains of some Italian musicians.

"Ah! Miss Spelthorne, this is, indeed, a pleasure," cried Henry, in his affected way.

"Mr. Wild, I am very angry with you."

Miriam said this in a joking way, but in reality she meant it.

"I regret that exceedingly," he said, affecting sorrow.

"I daresay it is very distressing to you," she answered, "but you ought, at any rate, to know why you have offended me."

"No doubt," said Wild, "as you say, I ought to be aware; but, nevertheless, I am compelled to confess that I am not."

"Did you not make a promise?"

"Did I? But you remember the proverb about promises."

"In relation to Mr. Wild I ought to have remembered it. But, seriously, have you yet discovered the address of M. Francois Michaut?"

Beyond a simple bow and a "good evening," Sapathwa had not renewed his acquaintance with Henry Wild.

There was something in the man which he did not like.

He was evidently cold, heartless, worldly.

Besides, was he not in league, as it were, with Miriam against him?

Was he not—unconsciously, be it said, however—helping to cast from their foundations his dearest hopes?

Sapathwa leaned over the gilded railings of the music gallery, and spoke not.

He listened, however, intently.

Not a word of the conversation escaped him; and deep into his heart went the wound inflicted by the earnestness displayed by Miriam in asking after Francois Michaut.

"Ah! now," cried Henry Wild, "now I shall be able to retaliate. I have not forgotten you."

"You know it, then?" said Miriam, breathlessly.

Sapathwa was angered by the way in which Wild tantalised her, even though he dared not wish him to answer her directly.

"If you know his address, pray let my sister know it?" he said.

It nearly choked him to utter the words.

He was rewarded, however, doubly rewarded, by the look of intense gratitude which Miriam cast upon him.

"I would did I know it," returned Wild, with an almost imperceptible sneer. "I have endeavoured to find it but I cannot."

"What, then, can have become of him?" said Miriam, in alarm.

"I know not," replied Wild. "The person of whom I asked information told me that he had transacted all the business for which he came to Berlin, but they had reason to believe he had not quitted the city."

"So you cannot tell me where he is now?" said Miriam, with a deep-drawn sigh.

"No, indeed; but believe me at your service," said Wild. "I will do all and everything I can to aid you in your search. I know Berlin well. Allow me to constitute myself your guide?"

He knew this irritated Sapathwa.

The Blue Dwarf made no reply, but allowed Miriam to answer,

"Thank you, Mr. Wild. I am, indeed, indebted to you, for, of course, we are strangers in Berlin."

"I missed you when we first came to the city," said Wild, "or I should have felt it my duty to call upon you. But I am keeping you standing. Allow me to offer you my arm for a promenade."

This was gall and wormwood to the Blue Dwarf

Miriam knew it.

But Henry Wild's manner was such that it would have been positive rudeness to refuse.

She, therefore, accepted his arm, and walked up the gallery.

"Is that really your brother?" inquired Henry, as soon as they were out of hearing

"No, as I told you once before, I think, Mr. Wild," she said. "He is my half brother."

"He loves you dearly, though, I should imagine?" returned Wild

This was meant as a question, and was said with an inward sneer.

Miriam only regarded it as a sign of appreciation.

"He does indeed, most dearly," she said.

"Poor fellow!" exclaimed her companion, with affected pity; "poor fellow! he cannot be happy, with his extraordinary malformations."

"Oh! yes; you mistake him," cried Miriam, enthusiastically. "He is by no means a misanthrope. He loves others; and they forget his outward appearance in his greatness of soul and nobility of mind."

"Your brother ought to be flattered," said Wild. "You speak quite warmly on the subject of his good qualities."

"I speak warmly," cried Miriam, "because I feel warmly; for, next to one other, I love, and always shall love, my brother better than anything else in life."

A slight spasm passed over Henry Wild's features as she uttered these words, but he answered gaily,

"Should I not like to be the subject of such love! But see, your brother approaches. He will be jealous."

Sapathwa came up to Miriam with a sweet smile.

"Are you enjoying yourself, dearest?" he said, kindly.

"No, dear, not much. I think I will go home, if you do not wish to stay."

"Nay, do not rush away, Miss Spelthorne," said Wild; "the performances will be over in half an hour, and the end is the best, I assure you."

He said this as much from his desire to annoy the Blue Dwarf as from his wish for her to stay.

"Shall we stay?" asked Miriam.

"Mr. Wild says the end is the best part, Miriam," said he. "Do not go if you would like to hear it. I am quite willing to stay, for I am not tired."

"Very well then, dear, we will stop."

The performances came to an end at half-past eleven.

The crowd of amusement-seekers rushed out in a formidable body.

Sapathwa, Henry Wild, and Miriam stayed until the last.

Then, having escaped the crush, they went out leisurely; and, having hailed a public conveyance, entered it and drove off.

Henry Wild came a portion of their way home, and rode, therefore, with them.

"With your brother's permission I will take you to the Royal Theatre to-morrow night," said Wild to Miriam as they rolled along the stony streets.

"My sister does not go out alone with strangers," quickly returned Sapathwa.

"No, no, of course not," said Wild; "it is not considered the thing."

"Then why did you ask?"

"I, of necessity, included you," said Wild.

"Oh, indeed!" said Sapathwa, with a sarcastic smile. "Then on such occasions I may consider myself to receive a general invitation."

"Precisely."

"Very well, I will so understand it invariably."

After this speech, spoken in a firm and peculiar manner, Sapathwa relapsed into silence.

"You may reckon on my assisting you to my utmost," said Wild to Miriam, "in your endeavours to find M. Michaut."

He said this with a twofold purpose.

He knew it pleased Miriam, he knew it also angered Sapathwa, whom, instinctively, he hated, as all men of low minds and libertine habits hate those who are their superiors in knowledge and morality.

"You are extremely kind," exclaimed Miriam. "I assure you I am very grateful."

"More than her brother is," thought Wild; then he added,

"I shall do myself the honour of calling upon you, Mr. Blakesley, to-morrow evening at six, and we will go together to the Royal Theatre."

"Very well, sir," replied Sapathwa.

"And now," said Wild, "here is my destination. Good night, Miss Spelthorne; good night, Mr. Blakesley. Au revoir."

The coach stopped and he alighted.

"A conceited coxcomb," exclaimed Sapathwa.

He was going to say more, but his attention was attracted by something which was going on in the street.

The carriage had stopped opposite one of those glaring gambling houses which at that time were so frequent in the Prussian capital.

Before the door was a large crowd.

Sounds of altercation were heard, and then loud murmurs of a different nature.

"Do not look out," said Sapathwa to Miriam

drawing down the blind, "there may be a disturbance."

He himself leaned out and looked.

The crowd was so great that it stopped the coach.

Presently four men appeared at the doorway of the gambling house.

They wore the private dress of the police.

Between, with his hands in fetters, was a man.

Sapathwa strained his eyes to catch a glimpse of his face.

The lamp at the corner of the street fell full upon his countenance.

There could then be no mistake.

"Coachman," cried Sapathwa, "drive on if you can, and drive quickly."

He then closed the window and relapsed into silence.

The face of the man in fetters was that of FRANCOIS MICHAUT.

CHAPTER LVI.

A VISIT TO THE COUNTRY.

WHEN Franchois Michaut arrived in Berlin he soon completed the business which had been entrusted to him, and devoted the remainder of his time to pleasure seeking.

Soon after his arrival he made the acquaintance of Mr. Faunlieben, a wealthy banker, who invited him to spend a short time with him at his country seat.

This just suited M. Francois Michaut.

The banker was, as I have said, very wealthy; he had, moreover, two very pretty daughters.

It can easily be understood, therefore, that he should desire to make an effort when he arrived at The Twelve Arches, as the country house of Mr. Faunlieben was called.

He had plenty of money for the present.

The future was a wild, undiscovered sea, which it was useless to endeavour to cross before its time.

He, therefore, ignored it altogether; and, with great zest, set about spending the money he had, which, at the rate he wasted it, he might reckon upon lasting three months, or rather less.

At the age of twenty-two young people are still so closely verging upon childhood as to be guilty occasionally of committing silly or childish actions.

Therefore out of every hundred, perhaps ninety-nine at least might be met with who would have conducted themselves as Francois Michaut did—sillily and effeminately.

Francois packed up, therefore, his most becoming shooting costume, the handsomest of his guns, and the prettiest hunting knife and sheath to be found in Berlin.

He packed up also his collection of waistcoats, of the most marvellous patterns and materials, grey, white, black, shots of every hue, straw colour, chinas, double and single-breasted waistcoats, with collars of all shapes, lying down, standing up, buttoned to the throat, &c.

He took every variety of shirt collar and cravat then in fashion.

He took a couple of dress-coats from his best tailor, and the finest linen he possessed; he took his beautiful dressing case, with its gold fittings, a present from his mother.

He took also his numerous collections of trinkets, not forgetting a charming writing case which had been given to him by the most amiable of women—in his estimation, at least—a lady of taste, whom he called Ada, then travelling with her husband warily in England, the victim of certain suspicions, which necessarily interfered, for a time at least, with her happiness.

He added a quantity of delicately-tinted paper for the purpose of writing her a letter every fortnight; and, finally, a cargo of knick-knacks, as complete as it was possible to make it, among which, from the riding-whip which serves as the beginning of a duel, down to the pair of beautifully inlaid pistols which terminate it, were included; such articles and implements as a young idler of fashion makes use of to occupy his time and to trifle away his existence.

He came in the *coupé* of the diligence, the whole of which had been retained for his own use, for he had been unwilling to spoil a most charming travelling carriage which he had ordered for the purpose of going to meet his dear Ada, that great lady whom, &c.

Francois fully reckoned upon meeting, at least, a hundred people at Mons. Faunlieben's residence; upon being able to hunt in his forests; and, in fact, to lead then the life which is usually led in country houses.

For the purpose, therefore, of making his first appearance in a befitting manner, he had put on a travelling costume, in style the most simple and *recherché* that could be devised, perfectly *adorable*, indeed, to make use of a word which at that time had special applications to what was regarded as perfection in anything or any man.

On the way a hairdresser had curled his beautiful brown hair, and while there he had changed his linen and put on a black satin necktie with a round collar, which set off his fair, bright-looking face to the best advantage. A frock-coat, buttoned half way up, fitted closely to his figure, and displayed a Cashmere shawl waistcoat, underneath which he wore another waistcoat, but white.

His watch, carelessly thrust in his pocket, was fastened by a small gold chain to one of his button-holes.

His grey trousers were buttoned at the sides, and the seams were embroidered with black silk in an easy graceful manner; he dangled in his hand a cane, the carved gold handle of which was not calculated to soil the purity of his primrose-coloured gloves, and, lastly, his hat was in the most perfect taste.

Thus attired, he felt prepared for everything, anything, everybody, and anybody.

He went down to the Twelve Arches ready to enjoy himself to the full, and make love, though never doubting that he had only to waive his hand to make all women bow at his feet.

He had found Berlin very much pleasanter than Borneo.

There, certainly, he had been able to take advantage of a few inexperienced girls.

Here women were to be found in abundance, who admired his appearance, craved for his money, and helped him to spend it.

He soon forgot all about Miriam, or, if he did think of her, he consoled himself, and quieted his conscience by saying,

"Well, now, at length my blue brother can be happy."

CHAPTER LVII.

THE TWELVE ARCHES.

MR. FAUNLIEBEN'S residence was a little paradise upon earth.

It resembled, if it, indeed, could be likened to anything, the Petit Trianon at Versailles.

There was a mansion built in heavy solid style.

But, at the extremity of his grounds, M. Faunlieben had erected a villa of the highest and most exquisite style of architecture, just at the edge of a beautiful and extensive lake.

On one side of this lake was a miniature Swiss village, with its church, its school-house, its windmill.

The plantations were laid out in beautiful style, and cut into labyrinths.

The lake spread from the villa to the principal mansion, so that to communicate, the one with the other it was only necessary to enter one of the fairy-like boats which were for ever dancing lightly on its sparkling waters.

The Twelve Arches, from which the estate was named, consisted of twelve natural arches of rock, leading to a subterraneous grotto, which conducted you from an island in the centre of the lake into the villa.

This passage was, however, scarcely ever used, as the water oozed through the roof, and it was necessary, in one place, to pass over a chasm of unknown depth by a little bridge, which was anything but safe.

Sometimes this chasm was full of water.

At these times it could be passed by a boat.

At others it was empty, black, dark, and dismal.

Mr. Faunlieben's household consisted of himself, his wife, two daughters, and four female servants, besides the ordinary number of male "slavies."

Madam Faunlieben was a fine looking woman, of some forty-five years, preserved well because she had little to care about.

Her life had been one succession of happinesses.

Everything her husband touched seemed converted into gold.

He became, when very young, the wealthiest and most respected banker in Berlin.

Her daughters were born to wealth, and grew up beautiful and healthy.

Anna, the eldest, was a dark girl, with dark eyes and black hair.

Her figure was tall and majestic; and even at the age of nineteen, her broad lips and well-developed figure gave her the appearance of the goddess Juno.

Her waist was small, and contrasted admirably with her full bust and hips, her neck was white and round, her eyes large and languishing, her nose straight, her lips dewy red and bow-shaped.

Her sister Gertrude was the very greatest contrast to her which nature could well have conceived.

About the middle height, some three inches shorter than Anna, she had long golden curls hanging in profusion over her snowy shoulders.

Though only one year younger than her sister she appeared to have been formed in an entirely different mould.

Her figure was slight and delicate.

Her bust was like that of a girl of fifteen; but her face was purely beautiful.

Her skin was of that exquisite fairness which always accompanies golden hair.

Her eyes were large, and as blue as the heavens above us.

Her nose was straight, but not Grecian, her mouth small, and resembling more than anything else an opening rosebud.

These two ladies had to wait upon them a girl who was equally gifted with themselves.

It was a strange and unusual sight those two girls and their maid.

You might have traversed Europe and not have found in one habitation three beings of such perfect loveliness, more especially holding such relative positions.

Grace Dalton was an English girl.

Such you would, at once, have reckoned her to be, from her peculiar style of beauty.

She seemed to unite in her person the beauties of the two sisters.

She possessed Anna's dark curling locks, with Gertrude's blue eyes and bright complexion.

She was as tall as Anna, and, perhaps, even more voluptuously formed, but she had all Gertrude's grace and delicacy of manner, and moreover appeared entirely unconscious that she, if anything, surpassed both her mistresses in beauty.

She was a favourite with all the household.

Indeed, both the banker and his wife treated her more like their own daughter than a domestic.

Grace Dalton was a well-educated girl.

She was the daughter of a clergyman, who, being possessed of one of those excellent livings which the descendants of the Apostles reserve for their more obscure brethren, was unable to make any provision for his family.

Dying, therefore, he left his only daughter to battle with the world alone.

She had received a good education, knew French and German, and was therefore delighted when a chance presented itself of placing herself with a German family as lady's-maid and companion to two sisters.

She was two years older than Anna, but scarcely looked it, while Mr. Faunlieben would often remark that he did not believe she was as old as she said, because he knew that so beautiful a girl as she was would never have been allowed to remain single until the august and mature age of twenty-one.

Nevertheless, so it was.

There was, however, in her heart, more than she dared confess.

Among the guests who, from the first moment of her stay at the Twelve Arches, had been a constant visitor, was Frank Holben, a young gentleman artist, of good family, but scarcely any means.

The worthy banker never dreamt that Frank would have the audacity to raise his eyes to the level of his daughters; and, liking the young fellow and admiring his genius, he gave him a general invitation to the Twelve Arches.

Frank Holben took advantage of this invitation pretty often.

He was a student of nature.

Nature presented itself in some of its most beautiful shapes in the gardens of the Twelve Arches, and he found, also, that it presented itself in still more beautiful shapes in the forms of the three lovely girls who formed its great attraction.

He was a bright, sunny-hearted, handsome fellow, this Frank Holben, full to overflowing with animal spirits, inspired by true genius, and a rapid and pleasant conversationalist.

Without endeavouring to do so, or, perhaps,

from that very fact of not endeavouring, he soon won the hearts of his three fair companions.

Anna, in the pride of her heart, at once imagined that his attentions were directed pointedly at her.

Gertrude really thought and sincerely hoped he loved her.

Grace Dalton wept in secret over a love she felt was hopeless.

And poor Frank Holben, the cause of all this mischief, was supremely unconscious.

CHAPTER LVIII.

GRITCHEN OF THE GLEN.

DOWN in the depths of the glen, which nestled under the chateau of the Twelve Arches, was a little hut, inhabited by a solitary woman.

Who she was, or what her occupation was, no one knew.

People had an instinctive prejudice against her.

Why they disliked her they could not explain, but there was a venomous appearance about her eyes, and a croakiness in her voice, and a sting in her words which betokened that age had brought with it anything but a love for the rest of mankind.

She scarcely, if ever, emerged from the precincts of her hut, except to purchase such comestibles as she required from the market people who passed on the road to Heimberg.

This strange being, who had the reputation of being an adroit fortune-teller, sometimes, however, remained a fortnight at a time in her hut, without once making her appearance.

The market people, thinking she must be dead, and knowing how little food she had bought, would sometimes knock at her door.

"What is it ye want?" old Gritchen, as she was named, would cry in accents of anger.

"Oh, all right," the driver would say, "as long as you're alive it's all right."

"A deal you care whether I am alive or dead," was the usual grumbling answer of old Gritchen.

It was assuredly more from curiosity than interest that they made their inquiries.

And no wonder.

She was not gifted, certainly, with the power of living upon nothing.

Therefore she must have food.

She did not buy food of the market people.

Ergo, some one must bring it to her.

Thus reasoned the people of Heimberg and the surrounding hamlets; but they took no very great pains to discover her means of livelihood.

She had now lived at the hut in the glen for a year, and no one troubled her.

The hut she rented of a cowherd; she paid her rent regularly, never injured any one, and only occasionally frightened the young people of the town by her bad auguries.

One evening, about a month before the arrival of Francois Michaut at the chateau

of the Twelve Arches, the light in Gritchen's window burned longer than was usual.

The old woman was proverbially solitary; but a man, passing in a cart at twelve o'clock, averred positively that he heard voices talking in the hut.

"Pooh, pooh!" said the man to whom he related it; "it was the old dame talking to herself."

"Not a bit of it, not a bit of it!" said he; "the other was a man's voice."

The man was right.

That night Gritchen did entertain a visitor.

About nine o'clock in the evening she carefully closed and bolted the door.

Then she also closed the windows so that no one could possibly look in.

Then, after stirring the fire and making the place comfortable, she sat down and impatiently awaited some one.

At length a knock came—not at the door, but at a board beneath her feet.

Immediately she sprang up, and then, kneeling down, drew up the board, and instantly there sprang into the room a young man of some twenty-five years of age.

"Here I am, Gritchen," he exclaimed, "punctual as ever."

"And welcome as ever," she said, in a very different tone from that in which she addressed her fellow-creatures in general. "How do your works progress?"

"Our first passage is now full of water," he replied, seating himself by the table, on which Gritchen, running about with all the activity of youth, was placing comestibles of various descriptions; "but it has nearly reached the chateau. We can already sound the vaults."

"Ah! well I am sure I shall be glad when you have finished," she said, with a sigh, as she sat down, after having placed on the table a mug of foaming ale.

"What! are you getting tired of the glen?" asked her companion, laughing, as he helped himself heartily to the cheese and bread.

"Yes, indeed I am," replied she. "I have heard of prisoners pining in dungeons for years, and then going mad: a dungeon must be a palace to this place."

"Say not so; do not repine, Gritchen," said the young man, "your imprisonment will soon be over."

"I have, at least, the green fields and the bright sky," resumed Gritchen. "You may say this, but I dare scarcely go anywhere for fear of observation."

This remark was accompanied by a sidelong look at her companion, to see what effect her words produced.

He laughed lightly, and said,

"Yes, I believe you are a pretty good specimen of a recluse. But never mind, it is only for a time, as I say."

The young man who on this night was the companion of Gritchen of the Glen was, as I have said, about twenty-five years of age.

His face was dark and bronzed, his hair and moustachios black, his figure tall and agile.

He was attired in a loose blouse, of some coarse blue material, under which lurked a brace of pistols and a dagger; while his small hose were of leather, descending into capacious top boots.

His black curls were confined in a tight-fitting cap of shining leather, from which depended a tassel.

Altogether, he was a handsome, fine-looking fellow, of the brigand stamp; and yet, withal, he appeared too open and hearty-looking to be a thief.

Nevertheless, as appeared certain from the conversation which he and Gritchen carried on far into the night, he was engaged in some undertaking in which property, if not life, was endangered.

This danger, whatever it might be, was certainly directed towards the people at the Chateau; and as Gritchen, when talking, shook her fist threateningly in the direction of the Twelve Arches, it was evident that her animosity was strong in that direction.

"David," she said, at length, "it waxes late. You have eaten all my cheese, and drank all my beer. I think it is almost time for thee to go."

"Ever the same way of sending me away, Gritchen,' cried David, rising instantly. "This day week I shall be here again punctually at nine. Meanwhile, lass, as probably the exchequer is low, here is something to replenish it with."

And so saying, he flung two gold pieces on the table.

Gritchen opened the door, and looked out upon the night.

"It will be a dark night across the moor," she said.

"Aye, and a cold one. A kiss, lass—a kiss to warm me ere I go."

And so saying he snatched an embrace and departed.

A strange smile passed over Gritchen's face as she said, watching him over the moor,

"Poor fool! he has wasted a year more of his life, and, in all, one of mine, in following a shadow."

CHAPTER LIX.

HOW TO SET A SNARE.

FRANCOIS MICHAUT then came to the chateau of the Twelve Arches, in all the splendour of three waistcoats and consummate conceit.

Anna at once voted him a fop, but still a fellow who might, upon an emergency, take the place of Frank Holben, in case that young gentleman's heart were to take flight elsewhere.

Gertrude saw in him merely an ordinary individual, whom she never could, with any amount of trying, enable herself to like.

Grace Dalton hated him the moment he entered the house .

Mr. Faunlieben had, two mornings before his arrival, said to his wife at breakfast-time,

"My dear, we shall have company at the chateau the day after to-morrow."

"Oh! indeed," languidly responded his spouse. "Who is it?"

"A young gentleman."

"Is he handsome?" asked Anna.

Gertrude thought the same question.

The banker laughed.

"A true woman's question," said he. "Well, I promise you he is handsome."

"I certainly shall fall in love with him, then," exclaimed Anna, casting a slight glance at Frank Holben, who was breaking an egg.

He appeared supremely indifferent.

"You had better not," said Faunlieben, laughing; "for, although he dresses very grand, I know nothing of the amount of his exchequer."

"Who and what is he?" inquired the prudent Anna.

"He is the son of some merchant in the Indian Archipelago," said Faunlieben, "and very likely is wealthy. But I must find this out first before I allow either of my daughters to fall in love with him."

Francois Michaut, when he did arrive, seemed scarcely to notice the two daughters.

Grace Dalton was in the room when he was introduced, in all the splendour of her charms, and he was at once struck with her maturer beauty.

He seemed utterly oblivious of the fact that the two only daughters of a rich man were doing their utmost to make themselves agreeable, and was in a perfect stupor until Grace left the room.

"Who is that young lady to whom you have not introduced me?" he asked, with apparent indifference.

Anna determined to settle the question at once.

"She is a servant," she said.

"A servant!" exclaimed Michaut, in unfeigned astonishment. "She is a most beautiful girl."

"She is, indeed," said Gertrude; "and she is not exactly a servant. She is our lady's maid and companion, and we love her as a sister."

She said this because she understood her sister's purpose; and also because she well knew that Francois would understand it and despise her for it.

"It is seldom you find three graces in one house," said Francois, gallantly.

"Ah! but there is only one grace here," cried the banker, laughing.

He was unconsciously uttering a great truth.

"How can that be true when the presence of your fair daughters denies it?" said Michaut.

"My daughters are Anna and Gertrude," replied Faunlieben, who imagined he was uttering a great witticism, "she alone is named Grace."

Francois Michaut was in a brown study.

That girl's face had made a deep impression on his mind.

Her face and form were of that voluptuous beauty which entrances all men; but more especially men of Francois Michaut's character.

Some men fall in love with young girls.

Others admire women.

Anna and Gertrude were lovely.

But they were very young, and their beauty

paled before the majesty and maturer charms of Grace Dalton.

The reflections which, at that moment, crossed the brain of the young adventurer were of that stamp which hardly can be thought complimentary to any woman.

Anna and Gertrude Faunlieben were both beautiful, and both wealthy.

One, therefore, might prove a quarry worth snaring for the sake of her riches.

In another way Grace Dalton would be well worth snaring and deceiving, for the sake of her beauty.

He soon framed an excuse for leaving the room, and sought, under plea of fatigue, the chamber which had been prepared for him.

Here, until the dinner bell rang, he sat planning.

Miriam had entirely left his mind.

Grace Dalton he desired for her beauty.

Anna Faunlieben, as the eldest, and likely, therefore, to have the largest dowry, he desired for her riches.

He went down to dinner, therefore, fully resolved upon the course to take, and to his surprise found that Grace Dalton sat at table with them.

CHAPTER LX.

OUT ON THE LAKE.

"You will find our neighbourhood exceedingly pretty and picturesque," said Faunlieben.

"Yes; I saw, when coming along, that the country is most beautiful," replied Francois. "Can you tell me, by the way, what that hut is which nestles in the little glen by the roadside?"

Anna laughed.

"You have already discovered our mystery, then," she cried. "That is the hut of old Gritchen, the fortune-teller."

"A fortune-teller!" exclaimed Francois; "that is, indeed, romantic."

"She is a very accurate one, I can tell you," said Anna; "she has told many a girl's fortune in Heininberg exactly."

During this conversation Michaut observed that Grace Dalton listened intently.

"I must go and try my luck," cried he; "I will go this very night, and to-morrow I will proclaim my future."

A deadly pallor overspread the face of Grace Dalton as he uttered these words.

He noticed it, though no one else did.

In the evening he was strolling through the plantation at the rear of the villa, intending to take a row across the lake towards the mansion, when he suddenly ran against Grace Dalton.

"Good evening, Miss Dalton," he said, taking off his hat to her.

"Good evening, sir," she answered in English, as she hurried by him.

"Nay, nay," he said, walking fast, in order to keep up with her; "do not run away. At least allow me the pleasure of walking with you."

"I am in a great hurry," she replied; "I am going across the lake."

"Fortunate, indeed," cried Francois. "I am about to row across myself. I shall have much pleasure in taking you over."

This offer Grace could not, without absolute rudeness, refuse.

She was, therefore, compelled, however much against her will, to accept; and with him entered the boat.

"I must ask you, Mr. Michaut," she said, with a sweet smile, "to do your best in the way of rowing, for I am in a great hurry."

"Miss Dalton," he said, as he pushed off and settled himself to his work, "may I be allowed to ask you one question?"

"It depends upon what the question is," replied she.

"I was going to ask whether you had any particular reason for being so greatly affected at the mention of the fortune-teller this afternoon?"

The question was a rude one.

It was not one, moreover, which he would have addressed to her had she not been in the position of a domestic.

This he knew, and guessed she would perceive it.

But, if he administered poison, he knew, also, the antidote.

Grace Dalton saw in this man an enemy, and determined openly, and without reserve, to grapple with him.

"Mr. Michaut," she said, firmly, "that is a question you have no right to ask me, and I shall not answer it."

"Excuse me, Miss Dalton," he exclaimed, "I feared lest I should offend you. But I shall be able, I am sure, to dissipate all your doubts as to the sincerity of my kind wishes. You will allow me to exculpate myself, will you not?"

"Certainly, if you can."

This answer meant a great deal.

It made Francois beware of the strong enemy with which he had to grapple.

"I have, in my residence in India," he continued, "been placed in positions where I have repeatedly come in contact with similar impostors. If, therefore, this old woman has been working on your feelings in any way, let me explain away her prophecies."

"She has told me nothing," said Grace Dalton, quietly, "therefore I have nothing to have explained away. At any rate, I should not betray what she confided to me as a secret."

"That is all I wish to know," exclaimed Francois; "and," he added, making his words an excuse for seizing and pressing that warm, plump, white hand, "I trust I have not offended you by endeavouring to do you a service."

"I never allow myself to be offended by such things, sir," answered Grace, quickly disengaging her hand.

Francois bit his lips.

He resolved to try if his suspicions were correct.

"I am glad you do not," he said. Then he added, "I myself am going down to the glen to-night to try my luck."

"So you said at dinner-time," observed Grace, striving to be calm, although a deadly pallor overspread her features; "but I wonder you do so if you have so great a contempt for the race."

"That's nothing," said Francois, leaning towards her, and gazing in her face with a strange expression on his countenance; "there are many among the human race for whom we may feel nothing but contempt, but who may, nevertheless, afford to us abundance of amusement, and even pleasure for a while."

"Indeed," cried Grace, "I do not think so. I cannot understand you, for if I feel contempt for any one, be it a man or a woman, I cannot help displaying it; and never allow myself to be much in their company. You are, however, so very interested in your conversation that you do not work at the oars. Pray let me assist you, for I am in a hurry."

"Nay," exclaimed Francois, bending to the oars with a will, "it is your conversation which so distracts me. I am never so happy as when I am in the presence of beauty."

"You are only for beauty, then, and it is no matter how sordid the soul is in your opinion?"

"I love beauty for itself."

"I hate beauty in man or woman if it is only the cloak for selfishness, for cunning, for heartlessness."

This so exactly described Michaut's character that he winced under it.

"You speak warmly."

"Yes I do, for I feel warmly."

They had now neared land.

Grace Dalton stepped quickly out of the boat.

"Mr. Michaut, do me one favour," she said, in her sweetest tones.

"What is that?" exclaimed Francois, who almost guessed what was coming.

"Do not go to Gritchen's to-night."

"Why?"

"Ah! that is my secret; but I wish it."

"You wish it; and why should your wish be my law?"

"Because I know it is."

"Well, then," said Francois, laughing, "I will not go if you desire it so very much."

"Thank you; good evening, Mr. Michaut."

"You will at least shake hands with me?" said he.

Grace Dalton held out her hand, allowed him to press his lips upon it, and then darted away.

"I have conquered him," cried she, to herself.

"I have half won the battle," thought he, "but, nevertheless, though unseen, I will be there to-night."

CHAPTER LXI.

MOONLIGHT IN THE GLEN.

About ten that night Gritchen was just preparing to go to bed when a loud knock came to her door.

She started, listened, and then called out, "Who's there?—go away, it's too late."

"No, no, I must see you," cried the voice; "I will give you any money, but I must see you."

Gritchen grumbled much.

It was not her custom to admit persons into her hut at so late an hour.

How did she know that this might not be some thief, attracted by the loneliness of the situation and the reports which were afloat as to her wealth?

Taking down a pistol, which always hung over the mantlepiece, she approached the door, and opening it slightly, peered out.

She saw before her no thief, but a young, handsome-looking fellow, dressed in elegant costume.

Need we say it was Francois Michaut.

"Enter, good sir," she said. "You are very late, but still, if I can be of service, you are welcome to it."

"You can, indeed, be of service," said Francois, seating himself on one of the rude chairs. "A young lady is coming here to-night to have her fortune told. I want to be here when she comes. Can you secrete me anywhere?"

Gritchen thought a moment.

"It is against my rules," she said.

"Yes, but there is no rule without an exception," returned Francois, laughing heartily at his own joke. "This is a very peculiar case, and I will reward you well."

"Well, I will do it, on one condition."

"And that is?"

"That you tell me your reason."

Francois started.

"No, I cannot do that."

"Then I refuse your offer."

He eyed the old woman attentively for a moment.

In every line of her face was written discrimination.

"I will tell her a lie," he said to himself, "she will know no better."

"I love this girl," he added aloud, "and I wish to marry her. She unfortunately loves another. I want to learn whom."

Gritchen laughed—a low, dry laugh.

"And you think thus to deceive me," she exclaimed, standing by him and gazing intently in his eyes. "You desire the girl's beauty; you wish to ruin her; you want to know the lover's name that you may put him out of her way."

"Vile hag," he cried, "you lie!"

"Vile hag, indeed. Get thee gone this instant," she shrieked, seizing her pistol and levelling it at him, "or by the powers above us I will fire!"

At this moment a gentle tap came to the door.

"Yet, no," she murmured, "get thee in there," pointing to a cupboard, "and listen while I warn her against thee."

Francois cast upon her a glance of malignant hatred, and entered his hiding place.

The tap was repeated.

"Hoity-toity," exclaimed old Gritchen, going to the door and opening, "methinks we are in a hurry. How now, whom have we here? It is very late young lady, and I ought to be in bed."

"It is I, Grace Dalton," said the girl, "but are you alone? I thought I heard voices."

"No such thing—no such thing," said

Gritchen, "come in and warm yourself, the night is cold."

Grace entered.

Her face was pale, and she trembled in every limb.

"I have brought you some wine and cake, Gritchen," she said, as she sat down by the fire.

"Thank you; you are ever kind; always thoughtful. But what makes you come out so late to-night."

"I come on a very different errand to my usual one," she said.

"And what is that?"

"To hear my fortune."

"Ah," said Gritchen, smiling sadly, "then you believe in it at last."

"I do not know whether I believe in it or not," murmured the poor girl, "but I feel unhappy, and perhaps you can help me."

"Well, question me."

This was Gritchen's method.

She always made her visitors ask her a certain number of questions.

"How many may I ask?"

"Four."

"I am in love. Is my love returned?"

"Yes."

"Will my love involve me in trouble!"

"Yes."

"From whom am I in danger?"

"From a stranger, one whom you have but just met. A man with a bright face and a smooth tongue, who is seeking your ruin, and of whom I say beware!"

"Will he offer to marry me?"

"Yes, but do not believe him."

"Oh! answer me once more—once more," said Grace, clasping her hands.

"I cannot, indeed I cannot; yet stay—what is it?"

"Will my lover marry me?"

Gritchen pressed her hand against her brow for a moment, and then said—

"I cannot tell. My thoughts are confused. Beyond the prescribed number I can answer nothing. But I will give you some advice. Your lover, Frank Holben, loves you; but others love him; therefore you must look well to your own interests. This fellow who seeks your ruin will promise everything—anything; but believe him not. He is a cunning, selfish fellow, and is destined to be the destruction of all who trust him."

These words struck home to the heart of Francois Michaut; and he trembled violently.

"I thank you sincerely, dear Gritchen," said Grace, rising, "I must now go or I shall be missed," and, imprinting a kiss on the old woman's forehead, she glided forth.

Instantly Francois burst from his concealment.

"Vile old woman," he cried; "is it thus you betray your friends?"

"My friends! I have none; nor should I seek your friendship."

"You have, then, my hate!" cried he, as he strode forth; "and you will see what that will brew for you."

Grace Dalton had hardly proceeded a hundred yards through the forest when a hand touched her on her shoulder, and turning round, she saw, standing by her side, Francois Michaut.

"Good night, Miss Dalton," he said. "I am, indeed, lucky in this meeting. I shall be able to escort you home, for it is not safe to be alone at this hour in these wild forests."

"Until the present moment I never thought them unsafe," returned Grace, hurrying forward.

"I assure you it is not safe, though," he said, in a grave voice, as if not understanding her meaning, "allow me to offer you my arm."

"Thank you, I would rather not."

"Come, now, that is unkind."

"I do not desire your protection, Mr. Michaut; I would much rather return alone."

"Well, I will allow you to return alone on one condition."

"And that is—"

"That you will remain in the forest with me for ten minutes first."

"Oh, my God!" exclaimed Grace, turning and flying.

Francois rushed after her, and, seizing her round the waist, cried—

"Miss Dalton, you make a most fatal mistake, indeed you do. Allow me to explain. There is the trunk of a tree; sit with me there a few minutes while I tell you something, and then we will part, and go by different ways to the chateau."

Grace sat down.

Who can wonder at the interpretation she placed upon his words after the warning she had received?

The moon was shining brightly, and cast a flood of silver light over the spot where they sat.

Francois could see that she was deadly pale.

"I want to tell you, Miss Dalton," he said, in a voice full of such emotion that she listened in mute surprise—"I want to tell you, Miss Dalton, that I am very unhappy. My unhappiness only dates from this morning. I am a man of quick impulse. The instant I saw you your appearance caused my heart to vibrate in a manner it never did before. I know that this is but the beginning of a deep and earnest affection; but this itself causes me the utmost wretchedness, as I am convinced, from your manner towards me, that I am an object of aversion to you. Why it should be so I cannot conceive, but that it is so I cannot but believe. I never have, for one moment, failed in my respect towards you. I have always behaved towards you as I should behave to any other lady, and yet, in one day, you seem to have taken a rooted prejudice against me."

Grace thought during this speech that she had made a fool of herself. Assuredly he had always treated her with respect. He had never done or said anything to cause her to dislike him; there was nothing but Gritchen's warning to induce her to feel in any way unfriendly towards him.

"Indeed, Mr. Michaut, I have taken no prejudice towards you. If I have offended you there is my hand. And now, I am sure, you will think it is time to go."

He took her hand, bent over it, respectfully kissed it, and then releasing it, said—

"I thank you, Miss Dalton. I am glad we are

friends. I am sure that nothing on my part shall ever make us otherwise, though I hope some day I may claim a dearer title. You would prefer returning alone, I think, or shall I accompany you?"

"No, thank you, Mr. Michaut; I think it is better to go alone. Good night."

"I have utterly upset that old hag's warning," thought Francois.

"He seems, after all, an honest, straightforward young fellow," thought Grace.

CHAPTER LXII.

THE SECOND STEP OF THE LADDER.

IN the recesses of the densely populated regions of great cities there are often to be found nooks which, to those who inhabit them, are paradises, but which afford to others nothing but pictures of squalid misery.

In the street leading from the castle gardens of Heinenberg to the market place, which was at that time the most thickly inhabited, and therefore almost, as a necessary consequence, the poorest street in the town, lived an old couple, who kept a queer, ill-looking sort of place, similar to one of the lowest beershops of London.

Carl Hoffman and his wife were real specimens of German sottishness.

His head was, in general, as muddled as his beer, and his wife, out of pure compassion, used always to keep him company when he got drunk.

Out of the union of this strange couple, however, had sprung a being as unlike them as light is from darkness.

Carl Hoffman the younger was destined by nature to receive into his own soul all those purer feelings which seemed to be excluded from his father and mother.

From boyhood he had revelled in the beauties of the sky, the air, the foliage of early spring, the glories of summer, and the fading tints of autumn.

He was often known to walk ten miles to a neighbouring monastery and ten back to borrow from an old monk, who had befriended him, a book of ancient history or of classic lore.

He spent some of his leisure time in modelling in clay; and, in spite of the angry protestations of his brutish father, would persist in turning his bedroom into a sculptor's study.

Gradually, as he grew older, he obtained work in a modeller's; and, owing to the extreme kindness of his master, he soon excelled all other apprentices in his tasks.

At the time I introduce him to my readers he was twenty-one years of age—tall, athletic, with an eagle eye, and a proudly-carried head.

He was now foreman at Von Sorben's shop, and spent only four days in the week at the manufactory.

The other two he devoted to the study of his art.

His evenings were spent away from home, that is to say, one hour every evening, but none knew where.

Some said he had a sweetheart, others suggested things not half so reputable, others, again, said he drank.

But, as his eye was always clear, and his hand always steady, this latter assertion was simply ridiculous.

One day he was sitting by the road-side, drinking a summer drink, which, with glasses, was placed on a table in front of the beer-shop, and explaining to a friend the different beauties of a little figure of Venus which he held in his hand.

A gentleman on horseback, with a slouched hat, and a paraphernalia of artistic materials strapped upon his back, stopped to take a glass of the sour beer in which Carl Hoffman's beer-shop abounded.

He glanced at the figure; and then, dismounting from his horse, went respectfully up to Carl, and, bowing to him, said,

"May I be allowed to look at that figure?"

"Certainly."

And Carl, not without some pride, handed to him the charming portrait of Aphrodite.

"Is this your own workmanship?" asked the stranger.

"Yes, sir."

"It is very good."

"I am glad you think so."

"I do, indeed. I am an artist myself, otherwise I should not presume to make a remark upon it."

"I am sure I am proud of your good opinion," said Carl.

"Is this your profession?"

"Alas! no."

"Indeed! only an amateur?"

"Not exactly. I am engaged at a modeller's. I spend my leisure time in endeavouring to build for myself the foundation of better things."

"You are fond of art?"

"I adore it. It is my life."

"Would you like to visit Italy, and study?"

"Oh! sir, you mock me. See you not how poor I am?"

"But I am not," cried the stranger. "Come, say will you come with me? I want companionship. I will take you with me."

Tears started into Carl's eyes as, grasping the eccentric stranger's hand, he said, in a thick voice,

"Sir, you mean this? You are not jesting with me, are you?"

"Indeed, my boy, I mean all I say. Shall it be so?"

"Yes—oh! yes."

"But when can you come?"

Carl's face clouded.

"How soon do you wish to start?"

"Well," said the stranger, "I only stopped to drink. I was going straight onwards. But I will wait in Heininberg two days, if that will suit you."

"Oh! you are too kind," cried Carl. "I only want until to-morrow morning."

"Ah! that is well."

"Meanwhile, sir, allow me to introduce you to my parents."

"Yes, it would be as well," said the artist

"Perhaps they will not quite approve of my invading their home and robbing their nest in this style."

The stranger did not know the character of Carl Hoffman the elder.

When he heard the proposition his first thought was,

"One less mouth to feed."

His second,

"One less hand to help."

But the first suggestion had the most weight, and he readily approved of the proposed plan.

Carl was on thorns during the interview.

His father's coarseness made his heart ache, while it made the stranger laugh heartily.

"And pray, sir, who are you, who go about wasting your money thus on vagabonds?"

"I leave to you the use of such terms," returned the stranger, "since you understand your own mode of education better than I. But as for myself, I am an artist,—fond of novelty, a rapturous admirer of art, and my name is Heinrich Haushel, Baron of Heininberg."

"Bless my soul!" cried Carl, casting a furious look at his son. "I beg your pardon, my lord; but really these fellows are so stupid."

Baron Heinrich certainly had his own opinion as to which side the stupidity lay; but he said,

"I prefer travelling under the simple cognomen of Mr. Haushel; so, Carl, when you are with me you must call me simply Heinrich."

"Yes," said Carl, mechanically.

He was engaged in a brown study.

He had always imagined the road to fame to consist of a high ladder.

When he persevered, and became a self-taught sculptor, he ascended the first step.

He had now mounted the second.

CHAPTER LXIII.

FAREWELL.

LOVE, under different phases, is either the make-all or the mar-all of existence.

When a young man, full to overflowing with ambition, starts in life, the love of a virgin heart is an incentive to exertion.

For that one being who loves him he will sacrifice everything much more cheerfully than if the fame was only being attained for himself.

But then this arises from the fact that his passion is ungratified.

Let a poor man, who is ambitious, ever marry, and farewell to all chances of fame.

Carl Hoffman, unknown to his parents or to any of his friends, had, for nearly a twelvemonth, nourished a sincere and ardent affection for a young girl who lived a little beyond the precincts of the town, and whom regularly each evening he visited.

He had met her accidentally in the meadows, and renewed the acquaintance again and again, until at length the meetings were prolonged, and their troth was plighted.

He never dreamed of marrying for years to come.

He had full faith in her constancy, and never for one moment imagined it necessary to bind their love together by the bonds of wedlock.

He knew well what a dead weight marriage is to a young, poor, and ambitious man.

Children may be olive branches, but they sometimes are more like the ivy, and cling around, and fetter, your every limb, in the battle of life.

On the night on which Baron Haushel made his appearance at Carl Hoffman's, the elder, young Carl, having seen that all was prepared that was requisite for the stranger's comfort, set out through the meadows which led towards the glen.

He was enabled to be there before his usual time, because he had no means of communicating with her whom he hoped to meet.

He had, as I have said, met her accidentally, but he knew not, even to that time, who she was, or whence she came.

Elizabeth Horustaneru was a lovely girl.

Her queenly stature and her personal bearing might well have induced the belief that she was of noble blood.

Carl often facetiously suggested this.

But she always assured him it was not so.

She merely said it was necessary she should keep her birth and parentage concealed for a time.

He knew little, therefore, of her, except as he could see her in their nightly meetings.

Truly, her beauty was great, and yet, withal, it was a puzzle.

" It is a beauteous face, and yet it brings,
    Contending thoughts into the pondering mind;
    The soul in all this loveliness enshrined.
Hath it kept pure and free its hidden springs ?
Hath it retained its earth surmounting wings ?
Hath it rejected petty chains that bind,
And moved still free as sunshine and as wind ?"

Down by the forest, which draped its shadowy branches over the glen, Carl Hoffman met her that night, when he was to bid her farewell.

She came along the path tripping, smiling brightly, but her face suddenly fell when she saw the cloud on the brow of her lover.

At that moment, when he saw her fairy form hastening to meet him, all his golden hopes of the future were eclipsed—all his desires for advancement were swallowed up in the great agony created by the idea of leaving her.

"What is the matter, dear Carl ?" she said, as he bent down and kissed her.

Oh, that kiss! it almost made him fall from the second step of the ladder.

"Dearest, I am sad because I am going to leave you," he said, mournfully.

"Leave me—oh, say not so! Oh, no, you must not leave me."

"You say so now, Elizabeth," he exclaimed, "but when I tell you all, you will wish me to leave you."

"Wish you to leave me,—oh, never !" cried she, passionately.

Carl quickly explained how matters stood—the visit of the Baron of Heininberg, the admiration he had evinced for his work, his kindness, his intended visit to Rome, and his hopes of future advancement.

Elizabeth no longer said a word against his going.

"You do, indeed, almost make me wish you to leave me," she said, smiling, "for your ambitious views will now all be realized. Will they not, dear Carl ?"

"Bless you, yes : I hope so," he said ; "but you must not be too sanguine."

"Sanguine !—oh, no ; but no one can fail to recognise your genius."

"Every one does not see with your eyes, my own," returned Carl, laughing.

"You will never forget me, Carl," said Elizabeth, as they stood under the shadow of the dark elms.

"Forget you—oh, no ! Can you dream that I could do so ?"

"You think so now ; but remember that in Rome there will be a thousand influences at work to wean you from everything you love and dream of here."

"I shall always write to you, and thus keep you ever in remembrance," said Carl, fervently.

"You say so now," cried the young girl, tearfully, "but oh ! Carl, how long will you say so ?"

"Always—ever."

They sat down upon the trunk of an old tree, which some convulsion of nature had cast across the path under the avenue of trees through which they were proceeding.

Upon them streamed the soothing beams of the

full moon, which seemed to cast a ray of hope over their prospects.

Carl for a few moments seemed wrapped in thought; and then, straining Elizabeth passionately to his bosom, exclaimed,

" Oh ! I swear I will never, never forget you."

" I will not swear," answered she, " I will not swear that I will not forget you, because I cannot."

The dark shades of night had fallen thickly and heavily over the landscape before they parted, with many tears—aye, tears on *both* sides, and many protestations of eternal fidelity.

Carl took his way homeward with a heavy heart.

Elizabeth wended her way quickly down the forest glade, and entered a thick wooded glen which spread itself along the edge of the path.

Ten minutes after she had disappeared a figure appeared.

It was that of a female.

Eagerly and anxiously she gazed round to ascertain she was not watched, and having discovered that she was alone, she walked hastily across the open space and made for the hut in the glen.

In passing out from among the trees the full glare of the moon fell upon her face and figure.

It was Gritchen, the Fortune Teller of the Glen.

CHAPTER LXIV.

SNARES.

FRANCOIS MICHAUT being, as I have before said, possessed of a handsome face and winning manners, had become an intense favourite of the banker.

M. Faunlieben had no knowledge of character.

If he had he would, in spite of Michaut's glossy exterior, have easily seen how superficial were his attainments, and how superficial, too, was his heart.

Manners make the man—says the proverb.

That is to say all the external manifestations by which a man is known — these are what we intend to indicate by manners.

Every act of life belong to manners.

There is a way—a best way—an awkward way—and a worst way of doing every possible thing.

A careful inspection of Francois Michaut's manners might easily have enabled the observer to recognise the hollowness of his character.

That he was earnest in one thing, however, there can be no doubt.

And this was in his determination to possess himself of one of the daughters of the banker.

Faunlieben imagined that it was the beauty of his two girls which bewildered the young man, when he observed how uncertain he was between the two.

As I have said before, both Anna and Gertrude were in love in their way with the young artist, who had bestowed his heart wholly and irrecoverably upon Grace Dalton.

But yet Francois Michaut being a welleducated, handsome-looking young fellow, they neither of them were loth to receive his attentions.

One evening Michaut was walking alone along the terraced part of the chateau when in the conservatory he fancied he heard voices.

There was no light in the place.

The moon, too, had declined to rise that night, and had veiled itself from human observation behind a massive drapery of clouds.

The whole scene was dark and mysterious —full of suggestions of romance and adventure.

The dark trees, which grew opposite and right up to the very walls of the chateau, waved heavily over the Conservatory and rendered it completely dark, and prevented also the possibility of anything without being observed from within.

Francois Michaut, therefore, who never had shown himself beneath the performance of a scurvy trick, drew close to the conservatory and listened.

There were two persons inside.

This he could discover only by the voices which spoke in rapid succession, for to see anything was perfectly impossible.

They were the voices of Van Holben and Anna Faunlieben.

" Oh ! Frank," she said, in a faltering voice, " after my confession, is that all you have to say to me ?"

" You speak as if you accused me of cruelty," exclaimed he.

" Oh ! indeed, I do."

" Unjustly, though," replied the young man earnestly, " I would have spared all this anguish but you sought it."

" For that reason you should be more lenient towards me," cried Anna.

She was placing Van Holben in an awkward predicament.

He saw it.

When a young lady throws herself thus upon your mercy, what can you do ?

He determined, however, to have a trial.

" My dear Fräulein Faunlieben," he said, taking her hand, " I have never before this noticed your preference for me. You have this evening made to me a confession which, however gratifying it may be to my pride, cannot but serve to grieve me. You say you love me. I assure you I am unworthy of your love—because my heart is totally another s."

" Oh, Heavens !" exclaimed Anna, passionately, throwing herself upon a couch in an agony of tears, " then I am indeed lost."

" Lost, say not so—you would be lost if you were to have your wish, and many an one whose heart is irrevocably another's. There are many men better, handsomer, more intellectual than I, who would be glad indeed to secure so rich a treasure. Believe me, my dear Miss Faunlieben, *your* secret is mine. Not a word of this shall ever pass my lips—but I will ask you one favour."

" What is that ?"

" That you will never allow yourself again to place yourself in a man's power."

A bright flush overspread Anna's features.

"Sir," she cried indignantly, "are you insulting me?"

"For Heaven's sake, Miss Faunlieben do not allow yourself to believe such a thing. I should consider it impiety to insult such a love as yours."

The entrance of persons into the large saloon adjoining the conservatory caused the couple to separate at this juncture.

Frank Von Holben entered the house, and Anna rushed out upon the terrace.

She was about to enter a window which stood open at the further end of the balcony, when a hand was placed upon her shoulder.

She uttered a suppressed cry and turned round.

It was Francois Michaut.

"What do you here, sir?" she inquired angrily and quickly.

"I might ask you the same question, sweet Anna," replied he satirically.

Her eyes gleamed with fierce passion as she answered,

"How dare you apply such an epithet as that to me, sir? You will leave the chateau to-morrow, if I have any influence with my father."

"No, Miss Faunlieben, no," replied he. "I have heard all. Will you allow me to enter that room with you a moment?"

Anna thought a moment.

"I cannot, sir," she at length said in a thick, short tone, "it is my bed-room."

"That is of no consequence," said he, bowing sarcastically, "you may reckon on my discretion."

Anna accordingly entered her room followed by Michaut, who closed the window and drew down the blind carefully.

CHAPTER LXV.

DECIDEDLY INTERESTING TO ALL PARTIES CONCERNED, IF NOT TO THE READER.

"AND so, sir, you are an impostor?" was the first exclamation of Anna Faunlieben, as she flung herself on her luxurious couch.

Francois laughed.

"How so?" he asked.

"Because you came here in the garb of a gentleman, and you are discovered to be a villain."

"I like frankness."

"You will always find it here."

"And here—listen. I and another friend—I never do things by halves you know—were present, in so far as listening and seeing are concerned, at the very interesting moment when you popped the question to Frank Von Holben, that gentleman being in love with—"

"My sister."

"No—no, you mistake entirely. That gentleman, as I was saying, being in love with your lady's maid, Grace Dalton."

"Grace Dalton! Oh! what humiliation! To be refused for a maid servant."

"Declined the honour of your hand. This is scarcely pleasant to a young lady's feelings. I am willing, however, to preserve your secret on one condition."

"And that is—"

"The hand which, with all its jewels and its fortune, could not tempt that votary of pure love, Frank Von Holben."

At any other time this would have been exactly the thing which Anna Faunlieben would have accepted with eagerness.

After Frank, Francois!

So it had been.

But now the offer came to her in an offensive shape, and her blood boiled at the succession of humiliations.

"Sir!" she exclaimed, indignantly, "do you imagine I would accept an offer made to me in such a fashion? Never, sir! never will I wed a man who has attempted to foist himself upon me in such a manner. I trust, indeed, you will not remain in the chateau longer than you are compelled.

Francois Michaut smiled.

"Lady," he said, "you wilfully mistake me. You said just now that I was a villain. I am not, but you can make me one."

"I, sir! I shall not trouble myself to aid or harm you."

"Allow me, madam, to explain. As long as you do not endeavour to thwart me, I will preserve your secrets; but if you refuse me, I will inform your family and all Heininberg of the little scene I and my friend witnessed this evening."

Anna trembled.

For the present, at least, she was in the power of this man.

"I will consider of it," she said, resignedly, at the same time glancing at him tremulously from beneath her eyelids.

"No, madam," said Francois, not rudely, but firmly, "there is no time for consideration. I must have my answer definitively this night.'

"I cannot."

"You must. I have a certain power over you, and I intend to use it. I will use it kindly if you will allow me. If not I must command."

Anna saw how helpless she was, how utterly at his mercy.

To resist, therefore, at any rate at present, was useless.

So, after much inward questioning, she resolved to accept, even at any hazard, the future which seemed destined for her.

"Mr. Michaut," she said, "I suppose I must accept my fate. I will be your wife."

"So far so good," said he; "but there is one thing I wish to explain, and that is, that I do not wish you, by word or deed, to prevent your father from bestowing upon you all that fortune which he has intended for you."

"I will not; and, Mr. Michaut, pray leave me."

Francois Michaut took her hand, bowed, and left the room.

CHAPTER LXVI.

BLACK WOOD.

TIME went on.

Francois Michaut was the accepted suitor of Anna Faunlieben.

He represented himself as the son of a very wealthy merchant in India; and as his manners and his conversation proved him to be a gentleman, the old banker saw no objection whatever to make to it.

It was about two months after the arrival of the adventurer at the chateau that four figures might have been seen pacing hastily and impatiently up and down on the borders of the Black Wood.

Their gaze was ever and anon directed towards the Chateau of the Twelve Arches.

Evidently they expected one of the inmates.

At length, when the shades of evening had closed thickly over the forest, a fifth figure joined them.

"You are here punctually, then," cried Francois Michaut, for it was he.

"Yes, indeed," said Edgar Barklay, a young, dark-looking Englishman, who seemed placed at the head of the small company who had met that night at the desire of the young adventurer. "We have been waiting some time, and had almost given you up."

"No, no; I was detained," cried he. "I had, indeed, almost hoped to have been able to dispense with your assistance."

"What! Did she appear inclined to come to terms?"

"Well, I even hoped that, but it is of no use. We must proceed to business."

"Is she at the villa or the chateau?"

"She is at the chateau, but she sleeps this night at the villa. She must be met on the lake, and detained."

"Does she come alone?"

"Yes."

"Is she, then, in the habit of making these journeys by herself?"

"Yes; she rows herself alone across the lake. I will take on myself the responsibility of stopping her."

"That is well," said Edgar Barklay, "for I fear it will be a dangerous game."

"What! afraid?"

"Oh! no; but still I'll not deprive you of the honour."

Evening now waned into night.

The crescent moon hung like a diadem over the silent lake.

Nature had clothed herself in the most beautiful robes, which she ever decks herself with at night.

"Hang the light," said Edgar. "She will see us, and then all's up."

"I will go out alone on the lake," replied Francois, "bring her boat to the shore, and then you must assist me. But hark! here she comes."

He was right.

A figure, dressed partly in light clothes, emerged from the trees of the grounds, and approached the borders of the lake.

Unmooring a light skiff which lay by the margin, she entered it, and pushing off, began to row herself gently across the lake.

She looked extremely graceful, as she bent to the oars, and sculled the light skiff across the bright waters.

Her back was towards the point where her enemies awaited her.

She, therefore, had no chance of perceiving that a boat containing a man was approaching her in an opposite direction.

She had reached the centre of the lake, when the rustling of oars in the water attracted her attention.

She started, and turned round.

A slight scream escaped her lips, as she perceived it was Francois.

"Do not be alarmed," he cried. "Why you out so late?"

"I sleep at the villa to-night, sir," answered, gently rowing along by his side.

"But I wonder you like to be out alone in the dark night."

"Oh! the innocent have nothing to fear."

"That is to say that, if I were innocent, I I should not imagine that you would be afraid."

"Just so."

"You are very unkind."

"Pray, sir, do not renew that conversation."

"I will not yet," said Michaut as they reached the shore."

He leaped out first, and then helped her out.

Scarcely had she placed her foot upon the shore, when the assistants of Francois seized her.

Her mouth was instantly gagged, and her arms pinioned.

Then leading her along a helpless prisoner, they took her to the entrance of the subterranean passage, which led to the island on the middle of the lake.

Pushing aside a huge slab of stone, they entered together the underground corridor, closed the entrance again, and Grace Dalton found herself in utter darkness.

CHAPTER LXVII.

WAR TO THE KNIFE.

THE conversation which had taken place prior to the abduction of Grace Dalton, and to which she alluded on meeting Francois Michaut on the lake, was of a most singular character.

During the two months which he resided at the chateau of the Twelve Arches as the recognised suitor of Anna Faunlieben he had not ceased his attentions towards Grace Dalton.

She, however, resolutely spurned his advances, and threatened to inform Frank Von Holben of his persecutions if they were continued.

Unfortunately, however, Frank was suddenly summoned away to a distant portion of the country on business.

Thus she was left without a protector.

Her position at the chateau was now anything but enviable.

She knew that both Michaut and the two sisters were aware of the preference which the young artist exhibited towards her, and would lose no opportunity of doing him an injury.

When, therefore, he was summoned away, and she never heard anything of him, it may readily be imagined that her mind was kept in a constant turmoil of excitement.

She fancied all kinds of terrible occurrences.

And her suspicions too, were directed towards the right quarter.

She hated and feared Francois Michaut, and she was right.

As the recognised suitor of Anna Faunlieben, he could not, of course, pretend that he wished to marry her, and yet, with the utmost effrontery, he persisted in his attentions: and though making no definite proposition, continued to call her the thing he held dearest in life.

It was about a month after Frank Von Holben's departure that she entered the little anteroom, which adjoined the large apartment which looked out upon the terrace in front of the house.

It had no outlet except into this large room or out upon the balcony.

She sat down upon the couch and thought.

An idea had just struck her.

Could Francois Michaut have intercepted her letters?

This idea, although it tortured her, was, nevertheless a source of some comfort, inasmuch as it gave her hopes that Frank Von Holben had not forgotten her.

She was thus in meditation, when the door opened, and Francois Michaut stepped in.

"Ah! good evening, Miss Dalton," cried he.

She rose to go.

"Stay, do not go," said he, "I have much to say to you."

"Which I decline to listen to, sir," replied she. "I must beg of you to allow me to go."

"Not so. Pray sit down."

He was between her and the door, so she was compelled to submit.

"Grace," he said, striving to take her hand, "it is now some three months since I first made my appearance at the Chateau of the Twelve Arches. During the whole of that time I have carefully noticed your conduct, your manner, and your personal beauty, and I have utterly lost my heart. This heart I offer to you. It is yours, take it."

"I love another," replied Grace Dalton; "and, more than that, you also have devoted yourself to another."

"No; I swear not."

"You speak falsely, sir, you are engaged to Miss Faunlieben."

"Engaged! yes; engaged to be married. But what does that mean? Does that bind the heart? Does that do away with the fact that I love you?"

"Then why, sir, if you love me, do you insult me by offering me your love when you intend to marry another?"

"You seem to misunderstand me," replied he, impatiently. "I will marry Anna Faunlieben, but I shall not love her. My love will be yours just the same, no matter who may be the holder of my name."

"You mean, then," said Grace, "to insult me deliberately by asking me to become your mistress?"

"You use harsh terms. I ask you to share the wealth I shall obtain by my marriage with Anna Faunlieben. She will certainly be my wife in name, but you will be sole mistress of my actions and heart."

"It is of no use gilding iniquity," replied Grace, "you ask me to be your mistress, and I refuse."

"Unconditionally?"

"Yes, unconditionally."

"Will no persuasion move you?"

"Then, by Heavens, it is war to the knife. I promise you I will use force!"

"I defy you, sir."

"Defy me! Is that your word? Then let it be war to the knife. I will use force."

* * * * * *

At eleven o'clock that night Grace Dalton, as I have said, was in the underground corridor leading to the Chateau of the Twelve Arches.

CHAPTER LXVIII.

THE STORY OF EDGAR BARKLAY.

EDGAR BARKLAY was a young Englishman who had come over from England to seek his fortune by his wits.

He came out to Germany without a penny.

Born in Cornwall, of a good family, he had been educated to believe himself destined to have his fortune made for him without any exertions of his own.

His father, Sir Edgar Barklay, Baronet, of Twinley Hall, was a successful man.

He had speculated in mining schemes which had turned out golden harvests.

He had secured the ear of the county member, and could, therefore, obtain for himself the credit of local improvements.

He was, therefore, a most popular man in his neighbourhood, and the waving of hats was most numerous when he came home from his church on Sunday in a carriage and four.

Edgar was the younger son; but, like all children who see these manifestations of popular adulation, he thought himself as great a man, and quite as much entitled to consideration, as his elder brother, who was heir to the title.

Henry Barklay was a proud fellow, full of malevolence and false dignity.

He was the pride of his mother and father, and the plague of the servants.

Between him and his brother there existed anything but a cordiality of feeling.

Edgar was proud—falsely proud, as I have said; but he nevertheless possessed good qualities of which his brother was entirely devoid.

He, therefore, scarcely ever associated with Henry, reserving himself, even at the school to which they went in common, for strangers of a different class of character to his brother.

It was when Edgar was about ten years old that a change came over the household of the Barklays.

One morning he entered the study where he had concocted so many of his successful schemes.

He rang the bell.

His favourite domestic appeared.

"What is it, sir, she asked ?"

"Tell your mistress I wish to speak with her directly," said he.

In a few moments Lady Barklay appeared.

"What is the matter ?" she cried, anxiously.

It was natural she should ask, for he was deadly pale.

"I have bad news—very bad news to tell you," he said. "Take a seat here near me, and I will disclose to you something which will, I fear, break your heart as it has done mine."

Lady Barklay sat down mechanically, fearing in her own heart what was coming, but fearing also to shape it in her mind.

She loved her husband devotedly, and sat there holding his hand as fondly as does a young mistress with her first love.

"Gertrude," he said, in a low voice, "we must leave here."

"Why love ?" she inquired, her heart standing still with dread as she spoke.

"I am ruined, utterly ruined," he replied. "My mines have failed ; the man who bought my stock has sold out and become a bankrupt. I have not a penny left."

"You have the estates," replied his wife, as if to give him comfort.

"Yes, thank Providence, they are left to my son. No one can touch them, but of ready cash I have not one penny."

"If we have lost our fortune, dear husband," said Lady Barklay, "we must endeavour to do without it, we must not allow ourselves to repine."

Sir Henry Barklay paced wildly up and down the room.

"Gertrude," he said at length ; "I want to see Henry."

"Why, he is but a boy ; he will not understand the meaning of the intelligence you have to communicate."

"Nonsense—fetch him, Gertrude. He is eighteen ; surely he can understand all I have to say."

"Well, I will go, then."

Lady Barklay had reached the door when her husband called her back.

"I wish," he said, "to state one thing at once while I think of it, and that is, that if anything should happen to me I should like you to see that everything in my will is carefully carried out.

He was perfectly calm when he said this ; so calm, indeed, that he alarmed his wife.

"Henry," she said ; "I dare not leave you ; I fear, I know not what. I dread you will——"

"There, do not be silly, love," said her husband ; "come here and kiss me, and do not give way to gloomy forebodings."

Lady Barklay threw her arms passionately round his neck, and kissed him again and again.

Then, disengaging herself, she went out in search of her son.

She was for some minutes occupied in searching for him ; and at length, having discovered that he had gone out for a walk with his brother Edgar, she returned to the room.

The door was locked.

She knocked gently at first, for fear of disturbing him.

No reply.

She then knocked more violently.

No answer came.

She became frightened, and summoned the servants.

One of the men broke open the door.

A terrible sight met their gaze.

On the floor was a long dark pool of blood, and in his arm-chair, quite dead, was Sir Henry Barkly, with his throat cut.

At this moment Henry rushed in.

He saw and at once appreciated everything.

His father was certainly dead, but then was *he* not Sir Henry Barklay ?

CHAPTER LXIX.

DISASTERS.

THE entanglement in which the late Sir Henry had left his affairs was terrible.

But ultimately it was decided that his debts should be satisfied by the ready money which he left, and by the sale of the furniture, &c., and that the estate should remain in the hands of the heir.

The will of the deceased baronet was useless, except as regards two things, viz. :—That of whatever was left after the payment of his debts, his wife and younger son were to have one third divided equally between them.

As, however, it would have been inconvenient to divide the estates, the new Sir Henry persuaded Edgar and his mother to accept the value of their share in the property in money ; and, in the case of the youth, the cash was deposited at a bank to bear interest and be paid to him upon attaining the age of twenty-one.

Misfortune, however, seemed to hover like a cloud over the prospects of young Barklay.

He was about twenty years of age when his mother died.

By her will she left her share of the property to her younger son, and with this addition it might be considered that Edgar Barklay was possessed of a good competence.

Just, however, as his twenty-first year approached, and he had made arrangements for the disposition of his money, he received intelligence that the bank in which his money had been deposited had failed, and absolutely paid no dividend.

Sir Henry expressed his regret at the misfortune, but offered no assistance.

Edgar was compelled to ask his aid— course which he certainly should not have cared to adopt had not absolute necessity compelled it.

"Sir Henry," he said—he always addressed his brother by this formal name—"Sir Henry, I am obliged to ask you to assist me. As long as I have had no money of mine own you have kindly enabled me to live, but now I suppose that, having arrived at the age of maturity, you consider I have no longer any claim to your protection."

"Just so."

"But how am I to live?"

"How do others live?"

"I know not; that is precisely my misfortune.'

"You have inherited wits, use them."

"It is all very well for you to talk thus to me, Sir Henry," replied Edgar; "but remember I am your brother, and, as such, entitled to some consideration."

"You are certainly my brother, but that is no reason why I should keep you."

"I ask you not to do so; I only ask for a small loan to enable me to go abroad and try my fortune."

Sir Henry hummed and hawed, and spoke of his incumbrances, his wife, his child, his establishment, and at length of the honour of the name which it was necessary to sustain.

"Yes; that is precisely what I wish to sustain," cried Edgar, "will you not assist me?"

"Do not press me," replied Sir Henry; "I would help you in a moment, but I cannot."

It was not in Edgar's nature to press further a subject which was so evidently distasteful to Sir Henry.

He therefore said—

"As I have but ten pounds in the world, perhaps you will not object to lend me ten pounds."

"No, not at all," said Sir Henry, and forthwith drew a cheque for the amount.

Edgar thanked him, bowed, and was that evening on his road from home.

His thoughts were anything but cheering.

The past was a blank.

The future appeared as nothing but a pathless wilderness.

He knew no trade, no business; and, indeed, his absurd pride would scarcely have allowed him to imagine the possibility of it had he known a handicraft.

This pride—false pride—is the bane of society.

What is the necessary means of existence in a poor man is considered a degradation in one who is rendered poor by misfortune.

Edgar Barkley, in his journey, therefore, thought only of how he could contrive to live without any labour.

It mattered not to him how poorly he existed, so that no one would think that he lived like an honest man, on the labour of his hands.

———

CHAPTER LXX

EYES IN THE DARK.

It was evening when Edgar Barklay left his home to cast his bread upon the waters.

Not darker than his heart was the pitch darkness which overhung everything.

He determined to eke out his money as much as possible, by going to common inns, and changing his name.

The first place at which he set up was the "Fox and Grapes," where, according to the voluntary assurance of the landlord, he could obtain everything requisite for the accommodation of man and beast, for next to nothing.

It was here that he met a man whose fortunes were ultimately closely bound up in his own.

Seated at the tap-room table, when he entered, was a short, broad-built man, with a large, bull head, a short, thick neck, and a face which denoted the extreme of craft and deceitfulness.

"Good evening, sir," said Edgar Barklay, as he seated himself at the table by him.

"Good evening, sir," said the other. "Come far?"

"Yes—I am tired. Landlord, a tankard of ale and some bread and cheese. I am hungry."

"Aye, aye, sir."

"Yes," continued Edgar to his companion, as he stretched himself at full length upon the seat; "I have started for London to seek my fortune."

The man eyed him attentively for a moment, and then said—

"Young man, you say you are going to the capital to seek your fortune?"

"I am."

"And you are not accustomed to any kind of labour, if I may judge from your appearance."

"I am not."

"You want, then, to discover an honourable livelihood which will not require you to work."

"You take me exactly."

"I also am going to London," said the man; "I will accompany you, and introduce you into society where you will soon double your capital."

Edgar laughed.

"Double my capital, say you," cried he, "I have only got twenty pounds."

The man's eyes glistened.

"Twenty pounds! you may soon realise a fortune with that if you act properly. I will show you how."

Edgar was not a very great adept in the ways of the world, but even he could perceive a peculiarity in the man's manner which he did not like.

However, the fellow might be useful to him, and he therefore, while he resolved to be on the watch, determined also to accede to his proposals.

"I accept your kind offers," said he, "may I ask your name?"

"My name, sir, is Powell," replied the other; "I start to-morrow."

The evening passed, night came, and Edgar Barklay retired to his room.

He had never been accustomed to sleep in such domiciles as that he was now in, and we may, therefore, readily suppose that he did not adopt many precautions to secure himself against intrusion.

In the middle of the night he was disturbed by a loud noise in his room.

Rising up, he fancied he could see at the door two eyes twinkling brightly in the dark.

The door was open, and Edgar rushed out upon the landing.

Nothing was there.

He lit the lamp, and searched every no k and cranny, but nothing appeared.

He, therefore, was compelled to return to his couch, and wait in anxious suspense the breaking of the day.

* * * * * *

The next morning. at nine o'clock, the two newly-made acquaintances took the road to London.

Suspicion was lying deeply in the heart of Edgar Barklay.

Although he had not absolutely seen Powell in his room, he had shrewd suspicions that the midnight intruder was none but he.

On the other hand Powell could easily comprehend that his companion did not place much reliance on his word.

Therefore, their understanding can scarcely be termed cordial.

There was one link between them, however, and that was mutual suspicion.

CHAPTER LXXI.

HEATH INN.

It was towards the close of a November day that a solitary traveller stopped at a lonely inn on Hounslow Heath.

He was a red-faced, jovial fellow, about

twenty-eight years of age, and the gaiety of youth flashed in his brilliant eye.

"Hilloa, there within! some one come and take my horse," he called, as the landlord answered to the summons.

"Comin', sur," bawled the ostler, and immediately that functionary appeared in drab leather shorts, no braces, a coat, his shirt sleeves tucked up to the elbows, and a red handkerchief round his neck.

In the taproom into which the traveller entered were a few individuals smoking.

They were talking lively, and most of them appeared to be mechanics, probably from the surrounding hamlets.

Two of them, however, had the appearance of soldiers. They wore old uniforms; but, instead of the military cap, they had upon their heads the hat worn at the period.

"On furlough, I suppose?" suggested the young man, after looking at them for some little while.

"Not exactly that, altogether," said the individual addressed. "If it is a furlough, I think it is likely to be a long one."

"How so?" said the traveller.

"Why the fact is," said the man, "we were disbanded this morning, and are just going west, to see how many of our kin are in the land of the living. For my own part I have had quite enough of the army. What say you, Powell?" addressing his companion.

"What do I say, Morris?" replied his partner. "Why, if eight-and-twenty years are not enough to tire a man of business, I don't know what is."

"And what may bring you to these parts, sir?" said the landlord, placing a jug of ale before his customer.

"A little business," replied the traveller.

"I suppose so," returned the landlord. "Not that I care a straw about the matter; 'tis nought to me."

"Why, it is no great matter. I have been to town to recover some money, and I am expecting a friend to keep me company the remainder of the road home."

"Quite right," said Boniface. "An extra pair of hands is of service sometimes on a dark night like this."

"And in the day-time, too," said the young traveller, "such times as these. This heath is so open, and every track so well known to those gentlemen of the road, that if a fellow is robbed, and escapes being murdered, he cannot follow the rascals."

During this conversation between the young traveller and the landlord, the two soldiers appeared to be inattentive to the conversation; they finished what they were drinking, and, after bidding the company good night, left the inn, as they said, for the next village.

"I shall not now wait for my friend," said the young traveller, and, bidding the landlord good night, he followed the two soldiers out.

"I hope he will come to no harm," muttered the landlord, as he followed the young traveller out in the dark, and then returned and closed the door.

CHAPTER LXXII.

THE MURDER ON THE HEATH.

WHEN Morris and Powell left the inn, instead of proceeding on their journey, they directed their steps towards town, and had proceeded for some distance along the road, when Morris exclaimed,

"Hush! I think I hear him coming. You seize the horse's head, while I drag him off behind."

"Ay, ay!" said Powell, "never fear me. I'll do what's correct."

"You see by that," continued Morris, "if he carries pistols, and we are not together, it will distract his aim; for as I pull him backwards it will raise his arm, and he must fire in the air."

"I see," said Powell; "but don't let us have any blood spilt if we can help it."

"No, no," said Morris, with a sneer, "not if we can help it."

"Here he comes, then," replied Powell. "Now let us get him between us. You go forward a little."

Having said this, Powell remained where he was, while his companion went a short distance onwards.

The horseman now approached, and having passed Morris, the latter made a sudden spring, and aimed a violent blow at the rider from behind, which, falling upon the horse's crupper, caused him to start; while his master turned round in the saddle, with pistol in hand, to see from whom the blow proceeded.

He had no sooner turned than Powell seized the horse's head in front, when its master again turned to see what opposed his progress, Morris knocked him from the saddle with a violent blow from behind, and the pistol went off with a loud report.

"Stand back, ye dastardly ruffians!" said the horseman, recovering himself in an instant, and drawing a second pistol from his bosom, "or, by Heaven, your life shall pay the forfeit!"

"Come, come, young gentleman," said Morris, in a sarcastic manner, "just quietly hand over your purse, and there will be an end to the matter."

"Not while I have life to defend it," said the horseman, with a determined voice.

"Then we must make you," replied Powell, and at the same time struck him a violent blow upon the shins, which caused him to fall upon his knees; while Morris, at the same moment, aimed another at his head, which laid their victim prostrate.

During this scene the pistol which the horseman carried went off in the struggle, and the horse being without its rider, started off at full speed in the direction of the inn, and there stopped.

While the horseman was upon the ground, half stunned with the blow, he had still sufficient strength left to struggle with his enemies, which he did with considerable energy, when Morris said,

"If we do not make short work of it the

horse which has gone towards the inn will tell tales."

"Well, then, young gentleman," said Powell, "if you won't give us the swag quietly we must make you, that's all," and, sitting upon the chest of their victim, one held the legs, whilst the other drew a large clasp knife from his pocket, and, with a terrible oath, drove the blade into his skull, near the temple.

For a moment their victim gasped as if for breath, while his life's blood poured in a stream of clotted gore from the wound; there was a slight shivering of the frame, and all was over.

"It's a cursed job, but it can't be helped now," said Powell.

"Then, quick is the word for us," replied his companion, and, so saying, they commenced dragging the body along the heath, and, when they were some distance from the road, they stopped.

The wind now blew fearfully across the heath, and the dark and murky clouds, as they shot across the face of the moon (which had now risen), allowed a dim and partial light to be thrown over the surrounding objects.

The starting eyes of the corpse glared fearfully from the livid flesh, while the creaking of the chains of a distant gibbet every moment, caused the murderers to start, while they robbed the dead of the gold and the notes the pockets held.

When they had accomplished their bloody purpose they divided the booty, and each pocketed a thousand pounds. They then dragged the corpse into the centre of the mass of bushes, and departed by different routes.

Having separated, Morris made the best possible speed to London.

The next morning he changed his notes for gold, and immediately set sail for France.

Powell, on the other hand, crossed the heath, and having found a spade near a cottage door, and fearful lest the notes might betray him, went to some distance, and, having marked the spot, buried them with a portion of the gold, and then returned the spade to the place from where he had taken it, and following the example of his companion, also set sail for France.

* * * * *

In the French newspapers of the day there was, some few weeks after this occurrence, a full account of a frightful murder which took place in England, on Hounslow Heath.

Morris was reading the account in a café, and chuckling over the success of their scheme, when his eyes caught the following:—

"The deceased has been recognised as Sir Henry Barklay, Baronet, who so lately had succeeded to the title."

"Oh! my God," exclaimed the wretched Edgar, for it was he, "I have slain my brother!"

CHAPTER LXXIII.

WEAVING THE WEB.

To explain the terrible chain of circumstances h led to the horrible catastrophe ab

narrated, it will be necessary to retrace our steps for awhile, and follow the steps of Edgar Barklay and Powell on their road to London.

Constant companionship strengthened the very slight bond which existed between them.

Powell did everything which lay in his power to prove himself a true man; and by the time they arrived in the metropolis they had agreed to throw in their lots together, at any rate, for a few months.

Powell, being an old stager in the metropolis, undertook to find a residence, as well as to cater for their mutual appetites.

It is needless to say that the money which Edgar Barklay brought with him soon exhausted itself.

When this juncture arrived, and not till then, did Powell suggest the necessity of obtaining some money.

He had, previously to this, spent his time and his companion's money in going the round of all the London amusements.

He now suggested to Edgar, that, having enjoyed themselves, it would be as well if they endeavoured to raise the wind by some means or another.

Accordingly, one evening Powell entered their room with a flush, and an apparent gleam of satisfaction on his countenance.

"Barklay," he said, "it's all right; I have discovered a crib where we may make no end of money."

"Where is it?"

"Oh! not far from here."

"And what is it?"

"It is a gaming house, kept by a friend of mine," said Powell. "He knows I am hard up, and will be very likely to put something good in my way."

"All right; when are we to go?"

"To-night."

"Very well, I am ready," returned Edgar Barklay, resignedly

The sense of propriety had not quite left the mind of the young adventurer.

He had, however, as I have said before, such a disinclination to labour, and the glitter of artificial pleasures so completely carried him away, that he was scarcely anxious to discriminate too keenly between right and wrong.

When, therefore, Powell proposed to him that they should endeavour to retrieve their fortunes, and prepare for the future, by the chances of the gaming table, he merely looked upon it as a necessity to which it was incumbent upon him to succumb, and accepted it accordingly.

So, in the evening, he took his way with Powell along the busy streets of the metropolis.

Hundreds were running and bustling by them —busy labourers in the work of life—and among them, perhaps, not the least anxious were those two who were on their way to weave their fortune.

At length they reached a narrow street, at the extreme end of which, where there was no thoroughfare, was a large house, apparently wrapped in gloom.

Not a single sign of life was visible.

It looked, in fact, more like a deserted prison

than any habitation where human passions and human aspirations had their full play.

Powell, who seemed quite at home, knocked at the door three times, and then, after a moment's pause, three times again.

A few minutes more passed, and then the door was half opened, a thick chain preventing the entrance of any one into the passage.

"Who is it?" asked the man who opened the door.

"Garry Owen," replied the man.

"What is the meaning of that?" asked Barklay.

"It is an Irish name," said Powell, "it is only used as a pass-word."

The door now swung back upon its hinges, and was closed instantly after their entrance.

Their conductor led them along a long corridor, at the end of which was a large room, brilliantly illuminated.

Here men and women, the former belonging to the higher orders, the latter to a certain class, were congregated together.

Roulette, rouge-et-noir, ecarté, piquet, and other games were being proceeded with in different portions of the room.

One couple, in particular, Edgar noticed attentively.

An old man and a young girl sat together at one end of the room.

He was engaged in playing ecarté with a young fellow, and the girl was inciting them both to play for larger stakes.

The old man was at least seventy years of age.

His white hair flowed over his aged shoulders.

His face was wrinkled and whitened with time, and his hands trembled as they dealt the cards.

The young man was, perhaps, some twenty-five years old.

He had light brown hair, very curly; light blue eyes, and a countenance smooth and young looking; and altogether denoting one who was perfectly satisfied with himself.

He eyed the old man every now and then with a strange gaze, and then cast peculiar glances at the young girl.

She, herself, was most lovely.

Her figure was round and elastic; her hands small and delicate; her solid gold bracelets displaying to advantage her white and polished arms.

Her face was melancholy and pensive; her dark eyes and sweet mouth rendering her exceedingly attractive.

Her neck, which was as graceful as that of a swan, descended into a bosom as polished as ivory and as pure as snow.

Her dress, very low in front and at the back, displayed to advantage her lovely shoulders and her glistening breasts, which heaved temptingly under the influence of the scene.

Edgar sat down near the girl, and remained gazing at her for some time.

Powell at length came up to him, saying,

"Come now, Edgar, here is a chance now, enter this rouge et noir; set and win a fortune."

Edgar was disinclined to move.

Powell saw this, and at once recognised the reason.

"You are very foolish," whispered Powell. "If you want her you must win money to gain her."

Edgar rose with a sigh and entered the set.

Fortune seemed specially to smile upon him.

He won again and again.

Large bets were made upon his breaking the bank.

A circle collected round him, not least anxious among which was Lamia Folville, the young girl who had so attracted his notice.

"You are very fortunate, sir," she said, at length, as, leaning on her companion's arm, she watched him placing the bank notes and rouleaux of gold in his pocket.

"I am," he replied, looking deeply into her eyes; "I am fortunate, but not so fortunate as I should wish to be."

She coloured slightly, and then, with a peculiar tone, said,

"Oh! one so handsome and so lucky can hope for anything."

This invitation sufficed.

He felt supremely contented.

Game after game was decided in his favour, and he went home, for the time, a contented man.

In his pocket were, certainly, piles of gold, but there was also one thing which the silly fellow valued much more dearly, and that was a note from Lamia Folville, offering to meet him on the following night, at a certain place, alone.

CHAPTER LXXIV.

LAMIA FOLVILLE.

So Edgar Barklay set out on the high road to the devil.

He kept the appointment with Lamia Folville, and found, as Powell had insinuated, that now he had plenty of money, and so forth, the young girl was willing to cast in her lot with his.

She had been, up to the moment when he saw her radiant face, the mistress of an old man, Captain Terence O'Flaherty, who now, in his declining years and fortunes, found it difficult to cope with one so young, so energetic, and so handsome as Edgar Barklay.

So, at the first invitation, she left the veteran, and betook herself to the handsome apartments which Edgar had prepared for her.

Powell was extremely indignant at the course adopted by his young *protegée.*

Not that he objected to his proceedings from any moral sense, but he prophesied ruin and degradation as the consequences of all needless extravagance of the kind.

Edgar, however, was infatuated.

Lamia exercised the most perfect dominion over his thoughts and actions.

Whatever she wished him to do he did as willingly as if she had sacrificed her home and her honour for him alone.

Oh! when a woman has left her father, mother, sister, brothers, and cast her bread upon the waters with you in spite of the opinion of the world, we can understand you devoting your time, your life to her.

But when a woman only comes to you because her lover is old, or poor, it lowers you immediately in the moral scale if you descend to make yourself her slave.

Lamia, however, when she had for some time been with Edgar Barklay, began to exhibit signs of weakness which proved her to be possessed of a heart above the generality of her class.

She, in fact, in her peculiar way, began to love him.

She was ever at his side, attending to his slightest wants, with the utmost eagerness; soothing him in anger, and calming him in the height of his despair.

Powell noticed this.

Interpreting it in his coarse way, he warned Edgar against her.

"Now, my dear friend," he said, "do not let that girl succeed in her endeavours."

"What mean you?" inquired Barklay, in surprise.

"She is trying to insinuate herself into your good graces, that she may persuade you to marry her."

"Well, and what then?"

"Great Heaven! would you marry a girl who is another man's cast off mistress?"

"I would marry any woman," returned Edgar, "if she clearly proved to me that she had a kind and affectionate heart, and that she loved me."

"You are a fool."

"Probably, but still I decline to believe in your capability of judging."

"Now do not be obstinate, my dear friend," said Powell, "remember that you are living in an uncertain manner, and if you hang this millstone around your neck you will be obliged to continue in the course which we have adopted."

"Nonsense. Let's talk of something else."

"Yes, yes; that is the way you always put me off; but I will not be put off. I will stick to you until I persuade you to throw off this unhappy connection."

"It is useless, I assure you," replied Edgar, calmly, "when I have once made up my mind, nothing on earth will turn me."

"Then have you made up your mind to marry her?"

"No, I have not."

"That is right; she will ruin you."

"I certainly admire your earnestness. A week, however, will decide one way or another."

"I hope for the best."

"Amen," said Edgar.

*   *   *   *

Ten days after the conversation above narrated, Edgar Barklay led to the altar the beautiful but frail Lamia Folville.

Powell tried hard to stop the marriage, but he could assign no sufficient reason, and he was compelled to swallow his chagrin and disgust.

CHAPTER LXXV.

DESCENDING THE LADDER.

I HAVE now to speak of events which were but the natural results of the reckless course into which Edgar Barklay had plunged.

The kind fortune which had presided over his first efforts in the gambling houses gradually deserted him.

He had every chance of retrieving himself.

The blow did not come all at once.

By slow degrees his luck abandoned him.

His money flowed away into the pockets of others, leaving him not entirely ruined, but every evening less and less chance of retrieving his lost position in the world.

Both Powell and Lamia tried their best to stem the torrent.

They saw his luck failing day by day.

But nothing could stop it.

He refused to listen to reason, and at length found himself without one halfpenny of his own in the world.

Lamia was scarcely the being which Powell imagined her to be.

Misfortune did not, as he imagined, drive her away from her husband to the arms of another.

The more he suffered the more kind and attentive she endeavoured to be.

Even Powell was compelled to acknowledge, much against his will, be it said, that she had not used arts to catch him, but had only given vent to her natural feelings.

Be this, however, as it may, it was time something was done to retrieve their shattered fortunes.

Powell's gains were few.

He was a reckless player—gambling without any regard to the fact that if he chanced to lose there was no possibility of his being able to pay.

Lamia even determined to add her mite to the general fund; and in spite of the endeavours of Edgar to prevent her, she took in little fancy articles of apparel to make up for these grand ladies of fashion among whom she had once moved so proudly.

But all things must have an end.

Misfortune followed misfortune—poverty increased to hopeless penury; disgrace and humiliation accumulation accumulated until we at last find Edgar Barklay and Terence Powell flying before an avenging demon over the dark Heath of Hounslow.

CHAPTER LXXVI.

DOWN IN THE CAVERNS.

As soon as Grace Dalton had been conveyed below, Edgar and his companions left her to the tender mercy of Francois Michaut.

The chamber into which she was conducted was more like a natural excavation than an artificial cavern.

It was of an oval shape, stretching out at one end into the long passage, across which went the broad and deep chasm to which we have before alluded.

The walls were rugged, green and reeking, the ceiling daubed and hanging with stalactites, which reflected a thousand varied hues under the influence of the torches which blazed round the strange apartment.

"Why have you brought me hither?" inquired Grace Dalton.

"For safety," replied Francois Michaut significantly.

"Your apartments are truly not too elegant," she added.

"*These* are not," said he; "but I do not purpose keeping you here. Allow me to introduce you to a chamber where you will find every luxury—more elegance, in fact, than even is to be discovered in the chateau."

So saying he opened a door which was concealed in a corner of the strange cave.

A blaze of light streamed forth over the stalactites and the humid floor.

"Enter here," said Francois.

The trembling girl obeyed, as if impelled by some strange power.

It was scarcely Francois Michaut who impelled her forward, it was the impersonation of hopeless fear.

The room into which they now entered, and the door of which was instantly closed and locked by Francois, was entirely different from that they had just quitted.

It was a small elegant little apartment, quite a snuggery in its way, and admirably adapted for the vile purpose for which it was intended.

It was in the highest style of voluptuous splendour.

The carpet was so soft and downy that the feet sank into it at every step.

Ottomans and couches, and chairs of the most silky and springy materials were ranged artistically round the room, while bright glasses inserted in the walls reflected from all sides whatever passed in the apartment.

In each of the high and arched windows was hung a cage containing two love-birds, while between the casements stood a beautiful fountain for ever casting into the perfumed air the spray of a scented stream whose ripplings and gentle murmurings mingled with the trillings of the birds.

A piano on one side answered to a harp on the other, while various little tables, what-nots, and fancy ornaments stood grouped about in corners.

The rugs before the fireplace, and in the window recesses were of the same soft downy materials as the carpet.

On the table it was desecration to place books of a serious nature, and accordingly elegantly bound volumes of amorous subjects were ranged round upon the richly-brocaded cloth.

Over all this hung a magnificent chandelier, with glasses made of a thick opaque material, through which at night, the gas cast a rich mellow light over the eastern sun, which, even in the day time, never received upon it the full light of day.

Thick laced curtains hung drooping over the windows, while inside again were dark red velvet hangings which effectually kept out the glare of the sun.

To crown all, and keep the least breath of cold air from entering this abode of luxury, thick tapestry work drooped over the door.

Francois Michaut had done all in his power to render the place as attractive as possible.

Having snared the bird, he gave her a golden cage.

"This is a paradise, is it not?" said Francois Michaut triumphantly.

"It is, indeed, beautiful," exclaimed Grace Dalton involuntarily.

A smile wreathed itself over the mouth of the wily scoundrel at these words as they proceeded unwittingly from the lips of the innocent girl.

"I am glad you admire it," he said taking her hand and leading her to the couch.

"Why?"

"Because I wish this to be your home."

"My home, sir!" exclaimed she in terror, and vainly endeavouring to start to her feet. "I could never exist in this place, cut off from all communication with mankind."

"There is no reason, my dearest girl, why you should be cut off from mankind. If you consent to my terms, you can come and go just as you please."

Grace Dalton knew well the intention of Francois Michaut in conducting her to this abode of false glitter and gloom.

But still the reality was by no means less terrible because she had previously been aware of his wishes: and when he spoke those cold words and glanced at her with an amorous gaze into her very eyes, blushes mantled over her cheeks and she said in a half-choking voice—

"Sir, it is quite useless to renew such a conversation. I have said once that I will not consent to anything you propose. Therefore, why annoy me, and humiliate yourself by continuing the subject?"

Francois smiled.

"You forget, my dear Grace," said he, "that in this place you are wholly in my power."

Grace trembled.

She saw her danger: and thought it best to temporise.

"I know it; but I am sure you will not abuse your power."

This was said with a sweet smile, and a trembling voice.

"I do not understand you?" said Francois in a softened tone.

"I will consent to remain here: but in anything else, you must grant me time. It is absolutely necessary."

"'Tis well," said Michaut, "I will now leave you. Every thing is here which you can desire. In that recess you will find a bed. Refreshments of every kind are in the room. I will be with you early in the morning. Adieu!"

So saying, he imprinted a passionate kiss upon her lips, and departed.

As soon as he had gone and the key had turned in the lock, Grace Dalton prepared to retire to rest.

In the first place, however, she examined the walls carefully to endeavour to discover some means of outlet.

But she could find no means of egress, and so undressing herself, she took a moderate draught of wine, and laying down, was soon in the arms of the sleepy god.

*   *   *   *   *

Meanwhile Francois Michaut left the cave, and sculled across the lake in the direction of the chateau.

As soon as he had landed another boat emerged from behind the shadow of the dark trees, and followed the other.

Arrived at the shore its occupant leaped out, and glided along under the spreading elms until he reached the chateau.

Here he stepped up to Francois, lightly touched him on the arm, gave him a note, and disappeared.

The note ran thus :—

"*Your proceedings are watched by a friend of her whom you are endeavouring basely to betray. He will not be loath to punish you. Therefore, beware. He is one who is daunted by nothing, and resents any injury done and any insult offered to Grace Dalton.*"

"I must beware," muttered Francois Michaut, "Franz von Holben is returned. None other but he would take so deep an interest in Grace Dalton."

CHAPTER LXXVII.

THE DISCOVERY.

THE evening following the abduction of Grace Dalton, had been selected for a gala which had long been promised to the people of the neighbouring country houses.

The mysterious disappearance of the lady's maid, had created considerable excitement among the people of the chateau : but there was not sufficient time to put off the ball and the fête.

Anna had even gone so far as to consult Gritchen of the Glen as to her whereabouts, but either she would not tell or she could not.

"She is in safety," she said vaguely, "and will remain so. But where she is I know not."

"How, then, can you be aware of her safety?" asked Anna.

"I only know that she is secure from danger. I also know the danger which threatens her."

"And that is ?"

"The lust of Francois Michaut."

Anna turned pale.

"And will he be successful?" she enquired in a trembling voice.

"He will not."

Anna said no more, but crossing the fortune-teller's hand with a piece of gold departed.

So the gala at the Chateau of the Twelve Arches took place.

The people far and near flocked to behold it, for the place was well known for its rugged beauty, and its vast extent.

The Chateau of the Twelve Arches was not one of those square staring buildings which modern builders set up in our English cities for the benefit of ruralising cockneys.

It was one of the German mansions of the old style, high, massive, turreted, irregular blackened, and dried by the dirt and winds of ages.

A large park, or rather wood, of fine old trees rose behind it with dim, dark groves, sylvan dells, and wooded knolls, with here an artificial fountain, and there a natural flow of water bubbling up amid the stunted undergrowth, and winding away amid the greensward till it appeared in the distance like a thread of silver.

There was no chaining of nature in this place, no studied beds, no frail exotic plants, no clipped and pared trees.

Here the oaks and the elms intermingled with the ivy-coloured branches into a dense canopy ; here the wild flower grew up amid the shade of their mossy trunks, to form a soft and perfumed path for the walker, who seldom passed that way.

Here the birds, unmolested by the cruel hands of their senseless destroyer, lived, and sung, and died.

Small as was the place, Mr. Faunlieben wished it to to be as good a type as possible of the primæval forest, wild and grand, and natural.

Nature is always grand in its own garb.

It is only when it is checked by the over refinement of civilised man that it becomes mean and paltry, and fails to excite our admiration.

It loses its beauty in losing its simplicity.

There is something majestic in one of those giant oaks, throwing its arms wildly towards the skies, with its foliage torn and ragged, and blasted by the fire of heaven.

But what grandeur is there in the thing we see in our modern gardens, with its boughs cut down to a certain shape, with every rebellious bough cast aside.

Depend upon it that in nine cases out of ten no nature cannot be improved on—at any rate as far as appearances go.

Nor was this place so wild and rugged that there were no paths or even no pleasant walks.

There were there bowers of natural growth, where lovers might have sat and dreamed there was no world beyond—there were there paths amid plants and wild flowers, and ever-winding rills, crossed by fallen trees, such as would have inspired the dullest mind with poetry, where the delighted ear might have listened to the notes of the linnet and the nightingale, who forgot it was day amid the darkness of the branches where all was quiet and natural.

The house itself corresponded with the grounds.

Everything there was good and massive.

There were to be seen the old oak tables of ancient days, and the carved chairs and the polished floors, and the halls hung with armour.

It was only the inmates that did not harmonise with the place.

Mr. Faunlieben, it is true, loved and courted every sign of old times, but Anna and Gertrude were too fond of the New World to bestow a thought upon things past and gone.

The day waned calm and beautiful.

Not a breeze stirred the branches.

Nature seemed to have donned her sweetest and most fairy-like garb expressly for the occasion.

The sun set in golden splendour, casting up its glorious rays right over the chateau and the grounds, and gradually giving place to a cool twilight, which, in its turn, melted into night.

At ten o'clock the people began to arrive, and at once set themselves to work to enjoy themselves to the utmost.

It was truly a scene of wild gaiety.

But Francois Michaut partook little of the spirit of the scene.

His thoughts were elsewhere, although bodily he was compelled to be present.

The dancers wheeled round in merry circles—the singers warbled sweet melodies—the bands played enlivening airs; but all was lost upon him.

He was standing upon the terrace watching the merry scene.

The dancers were busy on the lawn.

Lights of various colours gleamed amid the foliage of the trees, and cast a lurid glare over the windows of the mansion and the forms of the assembled crowd.

Suddenly he was roused from his reverie by a voice near him.

"You appear abstracted, Mr. Michaut."

He started and looked around.

It was his betrothed.

"I am not so—though—I do not care for such scenes."

"You are changed. I thought you liked gaiety?"

"No, I do not."

Miss Faunlieben thought this sufficient.

She left him with a formal bow.

"Devilish glad she is gone," said he, as he walked away, "I must now go and see my beloved."

He directed his steps through the dancers towards the lake, where the bright lights of the lamps were reflected upon the dancing waters.

Putting off in the boat he soon reached the grotto, and let himself down into the chamber where Grace Dalton was confined.

He found her in wonderful spirits.

"You seem happy to-night," said he.

"More happy than you have a right to expect, certainly," replied Grace.

He sat down beside her and placed his arm round her waist.

She did not resist, and he was about to proceed to take further advantage of her good humour when a loud crash was heard at the door.

At length it burst open and three men rushed in.

In the foremost Francois immediately recognised Frank von Holben.

There was not the slightest use in attempting to drive them from the place.

The only thing to be done was to make a dash for escape.

He, therefore, rushed forward with his drawn sword, and dashing through his antagonists cleared the door, and gained the outside just in time to close it and lock it, before the others could recover themselves.

He had hardly crossed the lake, however, before he saw his enemies following him.

They had burst open the door, and were now close at his heels.

CHAPTER LXXVIII.

AT BAY.

FINDING himself thus hotly pursued Francois Michaut seemed paralysed for a moment, but seeing that his only chance of safety depended upon instant flight, he stopped to collect his scattered thoughts. A moment's reflection, and he remembered that whilst watching the Chateau of the Twelve Arches, in the vicinity of the stables, he had been nearly surprised by a mounted lackey who suddenly came upon him, and then proceeded to put up his reeking steed.

Hesitating no longer, he flew to the stables, where he found the horse covered with sweat, as if from a long journey, and still saddled.

In a moment he sprung on his back, and striking his spurs into the animal's flanks, was soon proceeding at a rapid rate along the road which led to the forest of Kiemmes, whence, trusting to his knowledge of the locality, he felt certain of leaving his enemies at fault.

A race of twenty minutes sufficed to bring him up to a brook overshadowed by drooping trees, beneath the shelter of which he now proceeded more slowly.

Across this brook was a small, rustic wooden bridge leading up a narrow pathway, scarcely wide enough to admit a man on horseback.

Leaving the noble beast which had born him thus far with safety to find its way back as best might be, Francois Michaut started into the wood, and in a few moments came in sight of a dell where oftentime before he had strolled in agreeable company on fine moonlight nights.

He sat down and congratulated himself upon his escape—not that Michaut lacked courage; but simply held with the old adage that discretion is the better part of valour.

This increased rejoicing was not, however, unmixed a feeling of disappointment, as he remembered how nearly he had drained the cup of sensuality, when it was rudely dashed from his lips.

Whether of a satisfactory, or unsatisfactory nature, however, he was not destined long to enjoy his own thoughts.

At first a slight and distant sound as of branches being moved and thrust aside caught his ear, but he heeded it not, thinking it might be the effect of the wind.

Presently, this sound becoming more distinct, he lent an attentive ear, and was then conscious of the approach of footsteps.

In an instant he was again on his feet, and darting across the dell.

This movement, however, was not executed

soon enough to save him from being perceived, and in answer to the shout of triumph raised by his pursuers as they *debouched* in the opening, he looked round as he reached the edge of a plantation, spurred by that irresistible impulse which leads us all to measure the weight of our danger rather than to fly from an enemy whose strength we ignore.

Anxious as Michaut was to escape, the appearance of Edgar Barklay, who led his pursuers, acting on his impulsive nature, had the effect of bringing him to a standstill. Rage took possession of his breast, and for a moment he thought of rushing to meet him, and bringing their enmity to an issue.

Prudence assumed the ascendant; darting at Barklay a look of defiance, he turned to enter the plantation, but his pursuers, who had turned the pause to their advantage, sprang forward with renewed energy, and, ere he had taken many steps, Edgar's party was at his heels.

We have said that Francois Michaut did not lack courage. Flight had now become impossible. He was not the man to yield passively. It seemed to him that the girl whom he had so lately endeavoured to outrage, should she hear of his capture having been effected without resistance, would despise him. Her hatred he could endure, but her contempt should not be his.

Turning sharply on his pursuers, he gave a hasty glance around him for some weapon with which to defend himself.

At a short distance from him was a bundle-stake still left planted in the ground. To reach i t was the work of an instant, and it was as instantly wrenched up.

But his glance had been detected by the foremost man of the pursuing party who, being somewhat younger and more light of limb, than his companions, was slightly in advance of them. Anticipating Michaut's intention, he rushed in the direction the latter had taken with the view of opposite opposing him.

"Back, my friend," shouted Michaut; "I have no quarrel with thee; see thou touchest me not," keeping his eye fixed on his antagonist, who hesitated, as he surveyed the athletic and well-knit frame of Michaut, he brandished his weapon over his head in a manner which denoted annihilation to the enemy, who prudently held back. "Yield to me," shouted Edgar, springing on him with such impetuosity with his drawn sword, that all he could do was to strike the blade aside, and save himself, by a leap, on to a small raised projection of gravel and sand. "There's my answer," replied Francois Michaut, aiming a terrific blow at Edgar's head. He parried it, but the thin and brittle blade was shattered like glass, and, deprived of one-half its force, he received the blow on his shoulder. He then grasped the stake by the middle, and, giving it a rapid rotatory motion, kept his enemies at bay for some moments longer. But numbers were against him, although much favoured by his lucky hit which had deprived Edgar of his only means of aggression. But the youth, whom Francois had warned off with a recommendation, was destined to be his most successful foe. Having crept down a small pit close by, he suddenly and cautiously came upon him from behind, and tripped him up.

Falling forward, he grasped the trunk of a sapling, which bent beneath his weight, and saving himself for a moment, aimed a last fearful blow at the head of one of his antagonists, which, reaching him full on the forehead, laid him senseless beneath him.

The cavalcade, consisting of six men, four of whom supported the insensible form of Francois Michaut, now took their way back towards the Chateau of the Twelve Arches.

They were on the way, when they were met by Franz Von Holben.

A grim smile passed over his face as he saw his helpless enemy, and he accompanied the bearers as they carried the body past the scene of revelry towards the villa.

They took him down into the cavern, placed him under the care of two men in the little apartment where he had concocted the vile scheme against the virtue of Grace Dalton.

Francois woke just as Franz Von Holben was quitting the room.

"Ah! ah! is it you, Franz," he cried, faintly, "that have thus betrayed me? I shall be even with you yet."

"You may. But the probabilities are against it. Good-night."

CHAPTER LXXIX.

"Sweet is revenge, especially to women,
  Pillage to soldiers, prize money to seamen."
                                    —Don Juan.

FRANZ VON HOLBEN was not of a revengeful character.

His heart always stepped in to save where his reason told him to sacrifice.

He had now, however, been attacked in a vital point.

To assail his own person, his own honour, his own life, was to excite his derision and contempt; but to assail the honour, the person, and perhaps the life of his betrothed was to excite in him the fury of a demon.

When he left his enemy bound in the cave, he had parted from him with a rage glaring in his eye which struck dismay into the cowardly heart of Francois Michaut, who had from the first anticipated a violent death, but now could look forward to nothing but a lingering death by torture.

Left alone with his own thoughts in the dark, however, it must be allowed that they reverted less to his present danger and to the disappointment of his sensual appetite than to the chance of losing for ever the hand of Anna Faunlieben, and the money which that hand brought with it.

And all this time the mild blue sky of a tropical morning was beaming down upon the quiet home of the Blue Dwarf and Miriam Spelthorne in the island of the cannibal Archipelago.

When Franz Von Holben had time to reflect upon the nature of the outrage attempted to be committed on his betrothed, it of course occurred to him that he was bound to take a deadly revenge upon his enemy.

He was, therefore, occupying himself with considering the means by which he could best effect this, when the door opened and Anna Faunlieben entered the room.

Franz started as she came in, and rising from the chair, upon which he was seated with his hand pressed to his brow, said—

"Miss Faunlieben, what is the matter? Are you ill?"

She did indeed seem so.

Her face was pale, very pale, her lips were compressed, her brow darkened, her eyes gleaming with a strange fire.

"I come to ask you a great favour," she said, in a trembling voice.

"Indeed," exclaimed Franz, in surprise, and with a fervent hope that she was not about to renew her extraordinary request of some two months before.

"I come to ask of you to spare the life of my intended husband."

"Your intended husband?"

"What, sir, do you pretend to forget the fact that Michaut is betrothed to me?" replied Anna in some disdain.

"I knew he was, but I scarcely imagined that the engagement would hold good under such circumstances."

"I can make allowances for more than you think, sir."

"You must, indeed, if you receive him again after he has so disgraced himself."

"You are avoiding the subject, sir—I came to ask you a favour which I trust you will grant."

"And that is——"

"The life of Mr. Michaut."

"It is granted; I wish not to attack his life," said Franz Von Holben, significantly.

"You may not, perhaps, attack his life, but you are still planning a revenge. Promise me to deliver him up free from injury, and I will undertake that he never again molests you or your betrothed."

Franz Von Holben paced quickly up and down the room.

His thoughts were in a terrible state of confusion.

He wished strongly for revenge; should he now give up all chance of accomplishing his wish to please the whim of a woman?

"You can surely have no reason for revenge. Do, for my sake, spare him, pleaded Anna Faunlieben."

Franz Von Holben stopped short, and taking her hand, said,

"And you really will marry him after the way you have been so shamefully served by him."

"Indeed I will—I love him—I will marry him, and he will certainly behave well for my sake, when he finds how thoroughly I have forgiven him."

"Well, if you can so forgive I will not be less forgiving. I will set him free."

"And when?"

"Before morning."

"I thank you," said Anna Faunlieben; "but there is is one request that I wish you to grant me."

"What is that?"

"That you will bring him first of all to me."

Franz smiled a strange smile; but having acquiesced, Anna left the room, while he went in search of the prisoner.

He found him sitting in the cave, looking up at the grey dawn as it struggled through the little skylight at the top of the little room.

"What have you come to me for?" said Michaut, in a savage voice.

"To set you free," replied Franz Von Holben.

"You *come* to mock me," answered the wretched prisoner.

"Not so; you are free to go, on one condition."

"And that is, of course, one which you are aware I cannot accept."

"Not so, the conditions are not mine; they are imposed upon you by Miss Anna Faunlieben."

"Well, let me know them."

"They are simply these: that on leaving this, you go away with me and see Miss Faunlieben."

A contemptuous smile passed over the face of Francois Michaut as he answered,

"Is that all? Come, then, I am ready to go as soon as ever you like."

Anna Faunlieben sat in her room waiting like a judge for a criminal coming up for sentence.

Francois Michaut entered the room alone.

He felt very much ashamed of himself, and looked so.

"So, sir, you have been disgracing me and yourself?"

Francois threw himself on a lounge, and made no reply.

"You do not reply," said Anna; "but you will have to do so, when you desire to leave here; for until you have acceded to my terms you will have to remain here."

"Then this is only an exchange of prisons," replied Francois, with a careless laugh.

"Just so."

"And pray what may your conditions be?"

"They are, that you sign this document."

Francois took the paper which she held out to him, and which ran thus:—

"*I hereby declare that it is perfectly true that I made an attempt upon the honour of Grace Dalton, and was liberated through the kindness of Franz von Holben.*"

"I will never sign any such document," exclaimed Francois Michaut, indignantly.

"That is just as you please," said Anna, quietly. "I do not wish to force you to do anything for the present. You may consider yourself quite at liberty to take your own time, only while you are coming to your determination you must remain here."

"And pray how are you going to use this document?" asked Francois.

"Merely as a means of keeping you in due subjection."

Francois Michaut thought a moment, and then said,

"Well, give it to me. I will sign."

Anna handed him the affidavit, and he signed it; then, with a curse, he flung himself from the room, his persecutress gazing after him with a smile of demoniacal satisfaction.

CHAPTER LXXX.

ORNAMENTAL WRITING.

IT was a dark night.

A chamber in the Chateau of the Twelve Arches.

A man leaning anxiously over a table, and writing by the aid of a bright lamp.

A silent house. Shadows flitting to and fro, but no sound.

Such was the scene which we now lay before our readers.

The man who sat there engaged in deep study was Francois Michaut.

He seemed perfectly engrossed in his undertaking, and kept up his labour till late in the night.

Then he lifted a small slip of paper from the table, scrutinised it narrowly, and said,

"That *is* devilish good. It will never be discovered."

What was he doing?

What was the result?

*   *   *   *   *

Some weeks after the scene above described Francois Michaut was summoned to Berlin on important business.

An affectionate farewell was taken by him of all at the Chateau of the Twelve Arches.

M. Faunlieben was extremely sorry to part from his young friend, and pressed him to return soon, when a happy bride would await him.

Francois expressed himself eager to return, and parted with them with great apparent sorrow.

Little did he know how soon he would return under compulsion and in disgrace.

*   *   *   *

Anna Faunlieben was seated in her boudoir.

Francois had been gone from the chateau some three months, during which time she had received constant communications from him, many of which, however, were far from satisfactory.

During this time great changes had occurred in and around the Twelve Arches.

Grace Dalton had married Franz von Holben, who had returned to Heininberg with considerable means.

Elizabeth Horenstein had had the pleasure of receiving back to her arms the form of the one she loved, who had returned from Rome with bright prospects, and came only to carry her with him.

As we have said, Anna Faunlieben was seated in her boudoir in the evening, three months after the departure of Francois Michaut from the chateau.

It was about nine o'clock, and the lamp was growing dim, and she herself was falling gradually into a reverie, when a light form rushed into her room through the terrace window.

Anna started to her feet in surprise.

"Who is this?" she cried. "Who dares intrude upon me in this manner?"

"It is I—do you not recognise me," said the new comer, "I am Gritchen of the Glen."

"Ah!—and why come you?"

"I come to fetch you to my hut. *He* is there—Mr. Michaut—you must come directly, it is a matter of life or death."

Anna asked no further questions, but attiring herself quickly, prepared to follow her strange companion.

Along the dark avenues of trees—by the silent river, down into the lonely dell they went, until arriving at the hut, they paused, and tapped quietly at the door.

"Who is there?" asked a man's voice—one whom Anna failed in any way to recognise.

"You have deceived me Gritchen," she cried. "That is not the voice of Francois Michaut?"

"No—it is my betrothed."

"Your betrothed!" exclaimed Anna in extreme wonderment, and gaping at the old woman with a puzzled look.

"Yes, yes, I will explain all, enter."

The door was now opened by a stranger, in whom the reader will recognise Carl Hoffman.

Behind him was Francois Michaut.

He looked pale, haggard, and terror-stricken and his clothes were covered with the dust and stains of travel.

"My God," exclaimed Anna, "what is the matter?"

"Oh, I am in great trouble Anna," he exclaimed, "there has been some fearful mistake, and I am flying from justice."

Hoffman and Gritchen (who was in truth none other but Elizabeth Horenstein), had left them alone, and there was no reason, therefore, for restraining any display of feeling on either side.

Francois, therefore, as there was little time to lose, resolved upon making the best, of what time there was.

Clasping Anna in his arms, therefore, he cried, "My dearest Anna, I must leave Heininberg to-night. I have come only to hear from your lips whether or not, you will consent to fly with me?"

"But there is no occasion."

"Yes, there is occasion—your father will never consent to your marriage with me, while I lie under these suspicions, and I must depart to-night."

"Oh! I cannot—indeed I cannot, replied Anna. I have, Heaven knows, never had much proof of your sincerity, and how am I now to be certain you are not deceiving me?"

"Deceiving you, why should I deceive you? I have no motive for doing so. I have come here in the very jaws of danger to ask you—why then, disbelieve me?"

"Because it seems so strange that your sentiments towards me should have suddenly become so strong."

"But you have never yet said that you are innocent of the charge which has been brought against you."

"Yes—yes, I say it is some dreadful mistake."

"Then, why not stay, and face it out like a man?"

"Because," stammered Francois Michaut, because—you see I am so mixed up with——"

"Hush," cried Gritchen rushing in, "you must fly for your life, Mr. Michaut; here is a body of soldiers coming down towards my hut—wait not, but fly."

"And I?" said Anna, now feeling anxious to accompany him.

"You, my lady, must remain behind. Fly, sir, fly while there is yet time."

Francois Michaut snatched a hurried embrace from Anna Faunlieben, and then ran to the door and opened it.

"What way do they come?" cried he?

"From Heininberg!"

"Farewell, then, shouted he, and plunged into the darkness in an opposite direction."

A few minutes after a body of soldiers drew up—and grounded arms before the house.

"I come to seek Francois Michaut," said their leader entering.

"He is not here," replied Anna Faunlieben, "but why do you seek him?"

"I come in the King's name to arrest him," said the officer, "*for the crimes of forgery and coining.*"

CHAPTER LXXXI.

"What's Hecuba to him or he to Hecuba
"That he should weep for her?"

Hamlet.

WHEN the Blue Dwarf saw Francois Michaut dragged from the gambling house in Berlin, he ordered the coachman to drive on, and hastily drew down the blinds.

As evidently his soi-devant friend had been captured for a criminal offence, he knew well how to find him, so that it was quite unnecessary to harm Miriam's feelings by a detailed account of a disturbance—what she looked upon as a mere street row—or to make her anxious about her lover's fate, when he might be accused innocently of a crime.

About his innocence, however, the Blue Dwarf had his own opinion.

He had seen enough of him while in the Indian Archipelago to disabuse his mind of any sentimental regard for him, and having once set him down as a scoundrel, he thought it very probable that he had carried his blackguardism with him from India to Germany.

He was perfectly right.

Francois Michaut having escaped from Heininberg made the best of his way to Berlin, and lived as best he might upon the produce of his forgery and his "aptness" at gambling, in which latter occupation he had a clever assistant in the person of Mathilde Fournet, a little French girl, whom he regarded as his *chere amie*.

Mathilde was a clever little thing, not very scrupulous, but very pretty.

She had dark blue eyes—dark brown hair, a rounded cheek, and a mouth with rich red lips and white teeth.

Her figure was of middle size, her waist being small, and her bust magnificent, her little round breasts swelling out temptingly under her tight boddice.

She was pretty and voluptuously rounded enough to tempt a saint, and artful enough to cheat the devil.

With this companion time passed pleasantly enough with Francois Michaut, and money, too, found its way quickly out of his pockets.

Mathilde was not like Lamia Folville—she had no idea of saving.

She lived and existed solely in extravagance—in luxury, in sensuality, and when want threatened to come in at the door, she never thought of warding it off by saving; but only feared its approach as that of hopeless death.

So it was not wonderful that as time went on, and monetary wants increased, Francois Michaut found it necessary to frequent many places of public resort, and the consequence was that his presence in Berlin soon became known to the authorities, and one evening, he was traced to the gambling house and taken.

The gaming room was full at the time he was taken.

Everything was going on swimmingly with Francois.

Both he and Mathilde had been winning considerably.

She was there, with her pretty form dressed lightly in a muslin dress, without stays, so that her fresh breast glistened underneath, and caused the old fellow with whom she was playing to gaze at her instead of at his game.

This was Mathilde's trump card, and she knew how to use it.

She invariably found that if she attired herself in a voluptuous style, her antagonist lost, and judging that love was so severe an enemy to good card playing, she resolutely stuck to her plan.

Suddenly a disturbance is heard.

Loud and angry voices are shouting on the stairs.

Swords clash, and a cry rings through the house.

Then a loud voice says,

"In the name of the law," and several of the German police entered.

Francois Michaut turned pale.

He knew instinctively that it was for him, and though he continued to play, his hand trembled and his face turned deadly pale.

The officers at once went up to him and carried him from the room.

Had Miriam gazed out of the carriage window she would have seen her betrothed handcuffed between six officers, and a woman in evening dress weeping behind him.

It would naturally have occurred to her to inquire why he was handcuffed, but still more naturally who that woman was, and why she wept for him.

CHAPTER LXXXII.

"Thus even-handed justice
Commends the contents of the poisoned chalice
To our lips."

Shakespeare.

FRANCOIS MICHAUT had certainly forgotten almost the existence of Miriam Spelthorne.

He had staked his fortune upon the chance of marrying Anna Faunlieben, and still hoped to see her, and having done so, his amours in the Indian Archipelago only appeared to him in the light of a boyish fancy.

He had, moreover, heard of the total loss of the ship in which she and her family were said to have embarked.

When once in prison, therefore, his only chance lay in an application to Anna.

He sent an epistle full of fervid appeals to her love and to her generosity, expatiating upon his grief at being separated from her, and entreating her to bring herself the money to enable him to bribe the man upon whose behalf he had been arrested.

But during his absence an event had occurred which completely shelved Michaut's plans.

Baron Hanshel had returned from Rome, visited M. Faunlieben's house, seen Anna, fallen in love with her money, and married her off-hand.

So the answer he received was not satisfactory.

This was it :

"*Sir,—I am instructed by the Baroness Hanshel*

(*formerly Anna Faunlieben*), *to inform you that being married she declines to receive any more such letters as the one addressed to her by you. She regrets your position, but can do nothing for you. A certain document, which you entrusted to her, she will retain, and not use if you refrain from publishing certain facts which she desires not to be made public.*

"*I am, &c.,*

"CARL HOFFMAN."

Francois Michaut sank like one devoid of strength when he read this epistle.

Anna was the only one to whom he could apply in this terrible emergency.

He knew not how near to him was one who, little as he deserved it, loved him dearly, passionately.

He was in this state of painful anxiety when when the creaking of the doors betokened the arrival of a visitor.

He looked up eagerly as his own door opened, and started back in wonder and dismay when he saw enter the Blue Dwarf, who extended to him his hand.

Michaut took the hand mechanically, not knowing exactly how to take the offered courtesy.

"You meet me in a strange place," said he, in a low voice.

"I do indeed," said Sapathwa; "but I trust that I may be able to get you out of it. Of course, there must be some mistake."

Francois coloured deeply as he answered, nervously—

"Well, yes, there *is* some mistake; but it is deuced awkward and unpleasant, and I am afraid I shall get into queer street in consequence of it."

"Well," replied the Blue Dwarf; "it is of no use attempting to disguise matters from your friends. Let me know all about it, and I will then tell you what is to be done."

Francois was silent.

"Do not be ashamed to tell me," said Sapathwa, kindly. "You will have to tell your lawyer; why not confess to me?"

Francois hesitated to take this step.

He was himself such an adept in villany that he could scarcely understand the presence of magnanimity in another, and more especially in one from whom he had no right to expect kindness.

However, whatever might have been his hatred to Sapathwa, he could not but acknowledge that his character was one of almost perfect purity.

He therefore decided to confess to him.

"Sapathwa," he said, "I am about to take a dangerous step. I am going to tell you all. You may use it to injure me—you may use it for my good."

"Be assured it will be the latter," said the Blue Dwarf; "though I will candidly acknowledge to you that all I do is not on your account, but upon that of Miriam."

"Well, then," said Francois, "I will tell you all. But first of all answer me—does Miriam know that I am here?"

"She does not; I have spared her that pain."

"Thank heaven!" exclaimed Francois; then

he continued, "I will commence by saying that the charge against me is true."

"True," cried the Blue Dwarf, in surprise and grief.

"Ay, true, but do not interrupt me. I have not much to tell, but let me say it quickly, that I may avoid the painful subject, and come to the pleasanter one of discussing how I can best manage to escape from this horrid den.

"When I first came to Berlin I had very little money.

"Neither I nor my friends knew how quickly your purse empties in these European cities.

"I soon found myself without any ready cash whatever.

"I unfortunately found myself to possess an extraordinary art of copying signatures; and an opportunity discovering itself I forged the name of Strouss and Co., the great firm for whom I came to Berlin.

"The cheque I forged was a small one, but finding it was not discovered I tried my hand again.

"I was again fortunate enough not to be found out, and should probably have proceeded in the course of iniquity, when I was invited to the Chateau of the Twelve Arches, the country house of Mr. Faunlieben, the banker.

"My expenses there were few, but still I wanted money; and when the time came that I parted with a sigh from my last sovereign, I determined to have one more try at the game for a good round sum, and then drop it.

"But it is the last feather that breaks the camel's back.

"I forged for £500, and with the cheque I started for Berlin.

"But my absence from the capital proved fatal to me.

"The forgeries committed on the firm of Strouss and Co. by me and others had become so audacious that they had, since my departure, adopted a new signature, and instead of 'Strouss and Co.,' they now always signed 'Strouss, Kemplin, and Co.'

"I sent the cheque to the bank, where it was, of course, stopped, and it was only by dint of extraordinary agility that my messenger contrived to escape, and informed me of the terrible news.

"I was dodged, pursued—hunted from place to place.

"Somehow or another—the devil himself only knows how—they hit the scent correctly, and discovered that I had done it, and though knowing all my family they seem determined to let me have no mercy. I scarcely think they would now take a compromise."

During this recital, which Francois gave with frequent breaks, the Blue Dwarf had sat silently drinking in each word, and carefully weighing probabilities.

He now slowly raised his head and said quietly—

"It is no more than I anticipated. From the moment of your arrest I thought you guilty. But, nevertheless, for Miriam's sake I will do all I can for you. If money will get you out, you shall be out to-morrow."

"Heaven bless you," said Francois, as Sapathwa extended his hand to him on leaving. "Hang me, if I ever feel ashamed of myself it is when I am talking with that fellow."

CHAPTER LXXXIII.

"By this Lord Angelo perceives he's safe,
"Methinks I see a quickening in his eye."
—*Measure for Measure.*

SAPATHWA'S precautions with regard to Miriam were, unfortunately, perfectly useless.

On arriving at home he found her bathed in tears.

"What is the matter dearest?" cried he, as he raised her in his arms and kissed her fondly, "has any one been annoying or insulting you?"

"Oh, love, no; but have you not heard this terrible news about Francois?"

"What dearest," asked Sapathwa, who clung to the hope that she had not heard the worst.

"They have arrested him and thrown him into prison on a charge of forgery," she cried frantically. "Poor fellow, can I go and see him?"

"No—no," said Sapathwa, "I trust he will be set free to-morrow, and you can then see him here; let me spare you this misery. But one thing I think it my duty to tell you, and that is, that he is not innocent."

"Not innocent?" cried Miriam, "oh! yes he is—he cannot be guilty."

"Nevertheless he is guilty, and has confessed his guilt to me."

"He may have been led into it by others—he may have done it for a good purpose," pleaded Miriam.

Oh! sophistry of the female heart!

The Blue Dwarf did not attempt to refute her reasonings, but, leaving her, he went straight to the firm of Strouss and Co.

The head clerk stared at the short, becloaked, and extraordinary individual who presented himself, and asked to see Mr. Strouss on private business.

However, Sapathwa was at length admitted, and introduced into the presence of a short, little, dumpy man, who, not knowing what business brought him there, and being well acquainted with the name of John Blakesley, was the very pink of politeness.

"Pray take a seat, my dear sir," said he. "I trust I see you well this morning."

"As well as deep sorrow will permit me to be," said Sapathwa.

"Have you met with a misfortune, then?" inquired Mr. Strouss.

"Yes, indeed. A young man in whom I feel an interest, has been charged with forgery; guilty or not guilty I desire his release."

This was said in a tone which implied, "I will rescue him at any price."

Mr. Strouss assumed a severe demeanour as he replied—

"I have placed that young man in the hands of the law, and there he must be left."

"Not so," replied Sapathwa, quietly, "you forget that no evidence has yet been given. He is merely arrested upon suspicion."

Strouss thought a moment.

"He is a bad young man—a confirmed forger. It is not as if he had only done this once; he has done it again and again, and if not punished will probably do so at a future period."

"But *I* will take care he does not," said Sapathwa.

"Are you aware of the amount of his peculations?" inquired Strouss.

"No."

"They amount to nearly a thousand pounds sterling," replied the head of the firm, "are you prepared to pay that?"

"Yes, certainly, and all law, and incidental expenses."

"And do you not think I shall be acting wrongly if I allow him to escape punishment?" said Strouss sententiously.

"I will not enter into that question," said Sapathwa. "I came only to transact a matter of business. I am willing to pay what you require—shall it be yes or no?"

"I will leave you one moment," replied Strouss, while I consult my partner."

And so saying he quitted the room.

After a few moments he returned, observing—

"I have spoken to Mr. Kemplin, and we have agreed to release the young man from prison on a payment of £1,500, interest, principal, and costs."

Sapathwa said nothing.

The charge was excessive.

But then was not the crime excessive?

"Very well," said he; "I will pay it." And sitting down at the table, he took out his cheque-book, and wrote out a cheque for the amount.

"There, sir," said he; "there is the money. Now I will thank you for his discharge."

Mr. Strouss, in amazement, immediately replied—

"Certainly sir, certainly; but I must go to the prison to do that. A moment, sir, and I will be with you."

CHAPTER LXXXIV.

BEHIND THE BARS.

FEW persons who have not vegetated for some time behind the bars of a prison can imagine the intensity of inward misery, combined with outward affectation of mirth, which is to be found there.

In the Razenburg Prison, where Francois Michaut was confined, there was a strange mixture. Between innocent and guilty the law made a little difference.

The non-condemned were allowed the freedom of a large courtyard; they could meet together in a common room where various games were always going, and a considerable amount of gambling done.

The personages awaiting in this den their various sentences were many and peculiar.

Chief among the number was an Irishman named O'Riley, who had been detected in some gross fraud, and was expecting a stiff "dose."

He was a tall, ill-made, sandy-haired fellow—very cross-grained, and always ready to bully and take advantage of the weak, and even the strong—in words.

He was, however, somebody in the ward, and had assumed, after a suppositious election, the place of leader.

Then there were Stephen Fussy, and Terence O'Rattlebrain, who prided themselves upon their chess-playing, and went mad drunk over it when they lost.

There Von der Best, the hypochondriacal German, with a little squat body and a hook nose, and a pretty wife; Thomas Odenio, a converted Italian priest; Moses Haunsh, Abraham Strauss, Isaac Isaacs, and various other Jews, all in prison for some petty fraud, having, as Jews often will, perilled their future credit for hundreds for the sake of a few paltry pounds.

Francois Michaut took up with Stephen Fussy and Terence O'Rattlebrain—the former of whom was an Englishman who, having run through his own property, began to try and run through the property of others, and was "nabbed" accordingly.

The latter, who as his name tells plainly enough, was an Irishman, had at first been consigned to the tender custody of a debtor's prison, but having, while there, insulted and goaded his creditor to desperation, he found himself, one morning, arrested for fraud, and lodged in Razenbury gaol.

He was plenty of company in himself; though whether good or bad we say not. His conversation never flagged, but went on unceasingly, morning, noon and night, upon all imaginable subjects, but chiefly upon his own prowess at chess, which in his own eyes was wonderful.

Indeed his greatest enemy in the prison was a young man, a chess player also, with whom he quarrelled, simply because he naturally refused to regard him as a demi-god.

Francois Michaut had made up his mind for a long stay, and accordingly set to work to make himself as agreeable as possible to everybody.

He never until afterwards knew the terrible disappointment which fell upon his friends.

Sapathwa and Strouss came together to the prison door and lodged the discharge with the governor, a fat, good-looking, pompous little man, who superciliously looked at the paper, and then said,

"I regret to inform you, gentlemen, that this is no use."

"Of no use, sir?" exclaimed Sapathwa, in fear.

"I have said so," replied the governor.

"Perhaps you will be kind enough to explain yourself," remarked Strouss; "because as *I* am the man who placed him in prison, the law allows me to release him."

"Yes, in so far as your affair is concerned, you speak truly, but, unfortunately for him, other large forgeries have been discovered, for which the Government considers it its duty to prosecute him."

Sapathwa turned deadly pale.

"I dreaded something of this kind," said he, "directly you objected to the discharge. But cannot this also be arranged—indeed, sir, much—life itself—depends upon your answer."

"I know that, sir," said the governor, kindly, "but unfortunately the matter rests not with me. The Government having taken the matter in hand, none but the Government can release him."

"Is it of any use applying to one of the ministers?" asked Sapathwa, in eager tones.

"I am afraid not—yet stay. Count Renenburg may be able to do you a kindness. He is a personal friend of mine. I will give you a letter of introduction to him."

Having received the missive and thanked the governor for his courtesy, Sapathwa proceeded towards the house of the minister, which was situated in the street which has received so poetical a name from the stolid Germans—"Unter Den Linden."

CHAPTER LXXXV.

UNDER THE LINDENS.

IN those days the crime forgery was punishable with death.

As in England they made no distinction between who stole a sheep, who placed another man's name to a cheque, or who took a fellow-creature's life.

So Francois Michaut, the accomplished forger, the heartless seducer—the vile traducer—the pitiless foe was awaiting his trial for a capital offence.

No wonder then was it that Sapathwa, with white lips and pale, haggard face, hastened to the house of Count Renenburg, under the Lindens.

The count, as the governor had said, was a particular friend.

But what does political friendship mean?

It means a friendship which, like all other friendships, flies at the sight of misfortune—hides its face at the aspect of sorrow, cannot stand against the breath of calumny, and cannot more especially live, if pride and sudden success steps in to attack it.

So it was with Count Renenburg, the Home Minister, and Meinherr Vander Bolden, the Governor of Razenbury gaol.

Vander Bolden had been a man of some political influence; had assisted materially in the erection of Count Renenburg's political fortunes: he asked naturally for reward, and after becoming rather irritated, and threatening to become a somewhat dangerous foe, he was given the Governorship of Razenbury gaol, to quiet him.

The Count gave Sapathwa an immediate interview.

He was standing with the letter in his hand, when the Blue Dwarf entered.

"Good morning, Mr. Blakesley," he said cordially; "I am afraid you come here on a very unpleasant errand."

"It is so, indeed, Count," said Sapathwa, "but I trust I shall be successful."

"If it were in my power to grant his immediate discharge," said Count Renenberg, "you should not wait a moment without it. But I assure you, my dear sir, it is beyond my power. I dare not do so without first of all consulting the council. It is as much as my place, my reputation, even my life, is worth."

"Are you afraid of the issue of the trial?" asked the Blue Dwarf, anxiously. He forgot that Francois Michaut, though so dearly beloved by Miriam, was not Count Renenberg's friend.

The count smiled slightly.

"You speak to me as if I knew your friend," said he; "but I assure you, that if I *were*, I should most certainly xpect a verdict of guilty.

I speak thus plainly because, in the face of such undoubted evidence, I dare not bid you hope."

"You have before you the evidence in the case," said the Blue Dwarf.

"I have, and I think it my duty to tell you that I consider the evidence incontrovertible."

"I must await the issue of the trial, then?" said Sapathwa, and after a few more words he departed.

"A troublesome customer," exclaimed the count, as soon as his visitor had departed; then he added, as he flung himself on a couch and rang the bell, "I must see what can be made of this."

What the signification of these strange words were will be explained hereafter.

They were only the expression of a certain

spirit which the name of Lord Bacon, in spite of servile apologies, will ever recall to the minds of all students of history.

A servant entered in answer to the summons.

"Hans," said the Count, "I wish you to follow the gentleman who has just left me; and see where he lives. Make the usual enquiries about him, and return immediately. This is a matter of more than ordinary importance."

CHAPTER LXXXVI.

FOR LIFE OR DEATH.

TIME wore on.

The trial was over.

Francois Michaut, white and trembling in the felon's dock, had received sentence of death.

The agony of a first meeting and a last farewell was over.

Miriam, in terrible sorrow, had taken leave of him, and in a week more he was to be executed.

Sapathwa had several interviews with Count Renenburg with no apparent success; but a conversation which they had together, four days prior to the day of execution, instilled such hopes into the mind of the Blue Dwarf that he continued, unwearyingly, his exertions.

"These things can be done," said the count; "these things can be done."

This was now the day before the execution.

Francois Michaut had been removed to Razenbury gaol, where the execution of prisoners generally took place.

There was no time to be lost, and the Blue Dwarf naturally became exasperated.

"Sir, sir!" he cried, in great excitement, "you seem to forget that the life of a fellow-creature is at stake. Tell me the terms, whatever they may be, and I will see if I cannot fulfil them."

"Well," said the count, slowly and cautiously, "supposing I were to discover a mistake in the evidence—supposing I were to see an imaginary flaw in the testimony of the various witnesses, and thus peril my position, how would it avail me?"

The Blue Dwarf looked him long and steadily in the face, and then said—

"I would give you—"

His speech was interrupted by the abrupt entrance of a page.

"May it please you, Count Renenburg," cried he, "you are requested to give an immediate audience to his Excellency the Premier."

Count Renenburg had only time to whisper to Sapathwa—

"To-morrow at six a.m., when no one will suspect you have been with me."

When the Premier entered the Blue Dwarf was compelled to retire.

"Six o'clock in the morning," thought he, "when Michaut is to be executed at eight; and the gaol of Razenbury is fifteen miles distant. He will die ere I can reach him."

The next morning tripped rosily, merrily,

over the Eastern hills, gently tinging all nature, and gilding everything with the bright rays which give us hope of happy futures.

Sapathwa, who had never closed his eyes in sleep that night, was at the minister's door at six a.m., exactly; after having left Miriam Spelthorne in an agony of tears.

The count was alone in his study when Sapathwa entered.

He was pale and very agitated, and his visitor surprised him, in the act of pacing the room, hurriedly and anxiously.

"You seem ill at ease this morning," suggested Sapathwa.

"I am, indeed, ill at ease," cried Renenburg in a low, thick voice, "I am on the verge of ruin."

"Good Heavens!" thought Sapathwa, "he will be so engrossed with his own misfortunes that he will attend to no tale of mine."

Nevertheless he said—

"Have you thought over my request—the life of my friend."

"Come, now, time is precious," said the count, "let us understand each other. Your friend is to swing this morning at eight, unless I grant him a pardon which will probably risk my position. Now, I am on the point of ruin. Somehow or another the finances of my department have been misapplied, by whom I cannot say; but they have been misapplied, and I cannot discover the miscreant or make up the deficiency. I am in want of £5,000—give me that sum, and your friend is pardoned."

The count then took out his watch.

"It is now half-past six," said he, "you have an hour and half—good riding will do it."

"Give me pen and ink," replied the Blue Dwarf, taking out his cheque book.

He quietly wrote out the cheque, and presented it to the count, who immediately pocketed it, and then took out the pardon ready made from his pocket book.

He had counted upon the success of this last move.

Sapathwa nodded his head, rushed down stairs, sprang on his horse, and, with a shout of "Life or death!" gallopped along the road to Razenbury.

CHAPTER LXXXVII.

WHAT IS IT?

A HUGE tide of human beings surged towards the spot where Francois Michaut was to breathe out his last breath under the hands of the executioner.

Round about the scaffold vast barriers had been erected, for the Government expected intense excitement upon the occasion of the execution of a foreigner.

Francois Michaut had now abandoned all hope; but, with the extraordinary tenacity characteristic of all criminals, he refused to say one word in respect of the charges brought against him.

It was now half-past seven in the morning.

The scaffold was erected in an open space beyond the gaol, and towards this, in the bright morning, the mournful profession wended its way.

Francois Michaut was placed in a cart, and subjected to the unreserved scrutiny of the huge crowd which followed in his wake and on every side.

There was, indeed, no room left now for hope, even to the most sanguine mind.

There was the crowd—there was the scaffold—there was the executioner—could the most earnest believer in a good destiny have one particle, one ray of hope in such a position?

The cart rolled on.

But time rolled on still more quickly.

When the culprit arrived at the place of execution it was a quarter to eight, and, as he ascended the scaffold, a yell of execration arose from the crowd; and a cold shiver of fear and hopeless despair ran through his frame.

Fifteen minutes more and he would meet his fate!

There was now no room for hope.

He had given himself up for lost, and was sitting carelessly watching the sea of heads that surged and waved round him, when a small speck was seen moving along the eastern road.

He started up convulsively, and pointed in the direction of the object.

Every one directed his eyes in that direction.

Nearer it came, and nearer, and yet no one could distinguish its form.

Cold perspiration stood on Francois Michaut's brow in large drops, and burst out, too, over all his body.

The fickle crowd now strained every nerve of sight to distinguish what was coming.

They had just execrated the prisoner; they were now eager to see how the messenger affected his fate; and would have been sorely disappointed if his coming had not brought advantage.

The executioner and the sheriff consulted for a moment together.

"What say you?" asked the former, "shall we wait for this horseman?"

"We wait until the clock strikes eight, not later," returned the sheriff.

"But this man may bring a pardon," suggested the headsman.

"That matters not," returned the sheriff, "our orders are to execute the prisoner at eight. We cannot stay the judgment for the sake of a chance."

"What is the time now?"

"Five minutes to eight."

The headsman silently leant upon his axe, and watched the coming of the horseman.

Nearer he came, and nearer, and now his shouts could distinctly be heard.

"A pardon! a pardon!" shouted the crowd. "Stay the execution, it is a pardon!"

Francois Michaut stood grasping the hand of the executioner, his eyes straining towards the messenger of mercy, his breath coming short and thick, his breast palpitating with intense emotion.

The horseman now was close to the spot.

In one hand he flourished a letter.

Time had failed to beat him.

As the clock was striking eight Sapathwa's trembling, panting horse drew up below the scaffold.

"What is it?" asked the sheriff as the Blue Dwarf leaped up the steps of the scaffold.

"A pardon!" cried he, thrusting the letter into the functionary's hand.

"'Tis so," said the sheriff, when he had glanced it over, "Francois Michaut, you are discharged at once from custody, by the kind intercession of his Excellency Count Renenburg."

Francois Michaut did not speak.

His heart was too full for utterance.

He simply grasped Sapathwa's arm, and, descending with him the steps of the scaffold, made his way towards the town.

When he *did* speak, he only said,

"My God, Sapathwa, how shall I ever repay you for this most wonderful kindness?"

"By doing your duty to her," replied the Blue Dwarf, solemnly."

"What!" exclaimed Francois, in rapture, "will *she* still speak to me?"

"Speak to you? You know her better than that. As usual, unfortunately for her own happiness, she is too forgiving, too trusty. She will believe nothing against you."

It was at that moment, if ever in his life, that Francois Michaut repented of his crimes.

It was not vengeance pursuing him, but Nemesis punishing and chastening him.

CHAPTER LXXXVIII.

THE FATAL MARRIAGE.

THE picture of disinterestedness, which we have here faithfully drawn, is, perhaps, somewhat extraordinary, but it is, nevertheless, another chapter in its history.

The Blue Dwarf loved Miriam Spelthorne with a love which it is seldom the lot of human beings to receive, and it was of such force that he could receive a certain degree of negative satisfaction in beholding his mistress happy even in the arms of another.

Such pure love is rarely met with, and, perhaps, it is well that it is not, because it would be certain to be misunderstood and misused.

The meeting of Francois and Miriam was an agony of joy and tears.

Tears were shed on both sides; but while those of Miriam were only the bursting forth of a fountain of pleasurable sensations, those of Sapathwa were tears of blood.

"And now, Miriam," said Francois, on the evening of the day on which he was to have been executed; "will you fulfil to me the promise you made to me in the Indian Archipelago?"

"Yes," was the murmured answer, which brought a bright glow over Francois's face, and nearly broke Sapathwa's heart.

So they were married.

After all the devotedness, the disinterestedness, the patient love of the Blue Dwarf, he received his reward in the shape of thanks from the young couple, and more especially the thanks of Miriam, who, even in the midst of her happiness, felt a fierce, inward struggle as to the cruelty of thus punishing him for his love.

Francois and his bride took up their abode in a small house outside Berlin—a little villa surrounded by beautiful gardens, and suited for the abode of two truly happy hearts.

The Blue Dwarf remained in the city, and seldom, if ever, visited Michaut Villa.

He knew they were happy—he was content that it should be so. Sometimes their happiness was more than his stoicism could bear.

Matters went on thus for some time, when the Blue Dwarf received the following letter from his agents in England:—

10, *Tokenhouse-yard.*

Sir,—I am directed to inform you that your presence in England is necessary in order to the arrangement of certain family matters which cannot be settled without you. This letter has been written to you by me under the direction of John Blakesly, who begs me to convey to you his respectful compliments.

For WHIP *and* SNAPPER,
JOHN RENCH.

Sir John Blakesly, Esq.

Sapathwa thought long and anxiously over this stiff starched epistle.

"I suppose I must go," said he; "I suppose I must go. And yet, even if it be to proclaim me heir to a fine property, I do not like leaving Miriam here alone."

"Alone," he said.

Had she not her husband with her?

Alas! in Sapathwa's eyes his presence constituted her loneliness.

The young couple were surprised that evening by the entrance of the Blue Dwarf into Michaut Villa.

The greeting which he met with was cordial in the extreme; but Sapathwa could still perceive Miriam's eyes were red with weeping.

"You are unhappy, dearest Miriam," he said when Francois left the room for a moment.

"No, indeed not: but I cannot be very cheerful, you know, when you are going away to England."

"It is of no use endeavouring to deceive me," returned Sapathwa; "you did not know that I was going away before I came this evening to tell you so; and yet I surprised you weeping."

Miriam cast down her eyes, and answered not, and the Blue Dwarf was about to add a few words when Francois entered.

"Mr. Michaut," said Blakesly, "I wish to say a few words to you before I go. I have done for you what few men in this world would have done under the circumstances. I have saved Miriam's life twice for you, and I have saved your life for her, although you well know she has been, and always will be, the idol of my heart. Now I charge you before I go—be kind to her. When I came in this evening her eyes were red with weeping."

"What!" cried Francois, interrupting him with flashing eyes, "has Miriam been complaining of me?"

"If she had complained of you," replied Blakesly, coldly, "I could well have believed her words true. She, however, is too infatuated to believe that you could do wrong."

"This is not just or fair," cried Francois.

"Well, well, perhaps not. At any rate she is your greatest champion: give her cause to be still more enthusiastic than she is. I, however, go to England to-morrow."

"Is your business very important?" inquired Miriam Michaut, anxious to divert the conversation from its unpleasant channel.

"It is. I have received news from England to the effect that I am the heir to the Blakesly baronetcy; and I have to go over in order to see my uncle, to whom, in case of my death, the fortune and title revert."

"Indeed," said Miriam, laughing, "then you are now Sir John."

"Just so."

Another hour and Sapathwa left them.

The following day saw him before wind and tide, steadily moving towards that land, which, though his proper country, he had never seen; and the soil of which was destined to be so pregnant of extraordinary adventures and perils.

CHAPTER LXXXIX.

SHADOWS OF THE PAST.

IT will be necessary for us to remind our readers of a few circumstances which occurred prior to the attempted assassination of young Edgar Blakesly.

In a by street, turning out of Andover-square, was a little six-roomed house, inhabited by an old woman and her daughter.

The dame herself was some seventy years of age: while the girl was about eighteen, fresh, rosy, and plump; just the sort of creature to form the subject of a picturesque statuette; though, if we take Byron's word for it, we are bound to say that the simile is bad; for statues are—

"A race of more imposters if all's known.
I've seen more lovely women, ripe and real,
Than all the nonsense of their stone ideal."

She was, however, a lovely girl, and one, moreover, that created considerable interest in the neighbourhood when she tripped out by herself in the peculiar dress of the period.

Say what we may about the beauties of crinoline, and the grace of modern attire, it must have been very tempting to behold the lovely girl in that light floating drapery, which displayed, in their full extent, the beauties of her form and the roundness of her limbs.

She was walking one evening wrapped in thought—an unusual thing for her—along a shady avenue of trees which skirted Andover-square.

but which now has followed its forefathers to the grave, when she observed that she was the object of some one's constant attention.

She, like a prudent girl as she was, looked neither to the right nor the left; but she could nevertheless, perceive that she was followed.

Presently a tall, elegantly dressed gentleman, with a lace embroidered coat, came up beside her, and, bowing low, said in a gentle voice—

"Good evening, Miss. Surely it is scarcely right for one so beautiful to walk alone in the streets of this gay metropolis?"

The young girl blushed crimson as she answered—

"I know how to take care of myself, sir, I trust."

The gentleman laughed gently at this rebuke, and answered—

"If you did not there are always cavaliers ready and willing to protect the innocent. I for one never take advantage of a young lady's being alone to say anything which propriety would condemn or courtesy not permit."

This polite and delicate speech so completely revolutionised the feelings of the lady in regard to the cavalier who addressed her that she looked up timidly at his face.

He was tall and slightly built—his air, his manner, and his general appearance at once proclaimed the gentleman.

His face was not absolutely handsome, for his features were anything but regular, but there was a pleasing expression about them which rendered his countenance extremely attractive, especially to a young and experienced girl like the one whom he addressed.

In that one glance was concentrated a host of emotions.

In him she at once saw personified all that was manly, generous, and beautiful, in her dreams of a companion for life.

His was a face which she would have trusted.

It spoke, apparently, of a generous heart, a sympathising mind, a kind, open disposition.

The girl looked cast down, her eyes blushed, and said,

"I did not mean to offend you, sir; but you know it is scarcely prudent for young ladies to form acquaintances in the street."

This apology considerably amused the young gentleman, who remarked, gaily,

"I trust you may place me among the exceptions to the rule."

"Perhaps."

"Will you tell me your name?"

"Why so?"

"I shall not see you again," said she, with almost a melancholy inflection of her voice.

"Why not?" returned he, noticing, with considerable inward satisfaction, the evident desire which existed in her mind to see him again. "I, for my part, trust that we shall meet often again. Pray, tell me your name."

"Marie Carabosse," murmured the young girl, timidly.

"You are French, then?" said he, in surprise. "You speak the English language perfectly."

"You flatter me, sir."

"Oh, no, not at all; but—— "

He suddenly interrupted himself, and gazed in considerable perturbation at something in the distance.

After a moment he said, hurriedly,

"To-morrow at nine here! Pray, come! One kiss before I go!"

She answered not, but permitted him to take what he asked, and then walked slowly away.

She stopped, after a moment, however, and looked round.

The cavalier had muffled his face up in his cloak, drawn his hat down over his eyes, and was walking hastily away down a bye street.

Here he was stopped by a fellow in a leathern doublet, who, seizing him rudely by the arm, arrested him in anger.

The young gentleman endeavoured to shake him off, but could not, and blows were about to be exchanged when Marie's attention was drawn off by a lady, who, seizing her by the arm, cried,

"What know you of that gentleman who has just left you?"

"Nothing," replied Marie.

"Take care, then," said the other, in great agitation, "that your knowledge extends no further. Beware of seeing him again!"

She then left her; and, when Marie again looked up the street, the man in the leathern doublet lay stretched upon the ground, and her late companion was hurrying away from the scene!

<hr>

CHAPTER XC.

THE OLD, OLD STORY.

PERTURBED, anxious, doubting, Marie Carabosse returned to her home.

Who could this gentleman be?

What could be the meaning of his abrupt departure, the attack upon him, the warning she had received?

What were his intentions towards herself?

These and other perplexing questions occupied her mind during the night, in company with one more important question.

This was—should she meet him on the following night?

This question, truly, was all-important, for on that meeting would, probably, depend her whole future.

She never closed her eyes that night, but thought on, meditated, wept on until morning; and when morning surprised her, with her eyes red with weeping, the result of her agitations was—"I will meet him this once, and tell him I will see him no more!"

The evening came, and found Marie Carabosse and her newly-found lover in the inner garden of Andover-square.

The gold and purple curtains of the west had been drawn around the couch of the retiring monarch of day, and the stony pall of night lowered silently between.

The evening shadows lay dim and wavering on the river which glittered beyond, and the roofs and spires of the city veiled themselves with a cloud of misty darkness, till presently the round, grill moon, came sailing up gloriously from behind the hills.

The couple stood in silence, with arms lovingly interlocked, and eyes fixed upon the beautiful scene spread out before them.

There is a nameless but potent and irresistible influence emanating from the full moon when she rises up so resplendently, so majestically, yet withal so silently sailing queenlike amid the far unknown waves of ether.

Light, trivial, and false words will die off from the lip while the eye is watching this majestic course.

The invisible and ethereal seem to reach out to us a palpable and living hand to lift us up from earthly mires and doubts to the calm plains of celestial truth.

It was, therefore, with a sudden start that the gentleman noticed a roll of paper which fell at his feet.

"My Heavens!" cried he, in a half-whisper, "I am watched and persecuted everywhere. Can I be quiet and unmolested nowhere?"

He opened the paper and read these words:—

"*You must be circumspect. You are again watched by certain high personages. I dare not presume to advise, or I should say, leave the place at once!*"   "H. M."

The gentleman smiled at the implied advice, and, placing the paper in his pocket, said,

"I have a misfortune which few have—I have too many friends!"

"And I have none," sighed Marie Carabosse.

"None! say not so. Am I not your friend?"

"Alas! you may be my worst enemy."

Her companion frowned at this suddenly inspired exclamation.

"Surely you have no right to say so, at anyrate, until you know one better."

"Then you admit that, when I know you better, I shall look upon you as an enemy?"

"Not so, indeed, my dearest girl; I assure you I mean nothing but what is honourable and true towards you."

"If I could but believe, sir," sighed Marie.

"What can I do to convince you?" asked he. I will tell you my name, my rank, my intention, then you will see that I am acting no part."

Oh! Luna, to what innumerable false vows are you the witness!

"My name, he continued, is Ratcliffe Somers. I am the only son of a gentleman of some wealth, who supplies me with a liberal allowance, and I am, therefore, my own master. If you can bring yourself to love me I will marry you, and place a coronet on your brow!"

Marie trembled.

His words seemed to contradict each other.

He first offered marriage, and then a coronet.

"I want not the title," she said, timidly, "I only want the love of one heart and marriage."

This was the word which seemed to stick in the gullet of the fine gentleman.

He avoided the subject as far as lay in his power, poured words of passionate love into her ear, and built for her magnificent *Chateaux en Espagne.*

When Marie Carabosse left the *parterre* the impression of a burning kiss was on her lips, and the last name she murmured ere she slept was that of Ratcliffe *Somers.*

CHAPTER XCI.

THE BANE OF LOVE.

THE result of these repeated meetings was that Marie Carabosse's life was rendered one of complete misery.

The happiness which she had was short and fitful.

There was no joy; but only the harassing, never-ending torment of secrecy.

She never told her love,

"But let concealment, like a worm i' the bud,
    Prey on her damask cheek."

Often and often her mother questioned her anxiously as to the cause of her misery.

But the only answer she received was a sigh and a tear.

Time wore on.

Marie Carabosse was about to become a mother; and her parent would no longer fail to recognise her critical position.

"My dearest girl," cried she, one day, as Maria sat in her little room with her eyes red with weeping, "pray make a confidant of me: whom will you find better than your own mother to unveil your heart to?"

"I have nothing to tell," said Marie, weeping.

"Say not so, poor child," returned Madame Carabosse. "You are about to become a mother. Who is the villain?"

"Call him not a villain," cried Marie, vehemently; "he is my heart's best treasure."

"Are you his wife?"

"I am; indeed I am, dear mother. See here," she added, going to a drawer and taking from thence a paper and a ring, "here is my certificate of marriage and a ring—these prove I have spoken nothing but the truth."

Her mother embraced her, and said, in a low voice—

"Poor child! certainly these are evidences that a marriage has taken place; but where and when was the ceremony performed?"

"It was performed by special licence," returned Marie, "in his own drawing-room. A very great lady was the witness on his side, and Flora Campbell on my side."

"And why is not the marriage made public?" asked Madame Carabosse, who was naturally incredulous.

"Because he dare not offend his friends by confessing a secret marriage. In a short time he is going to make it known, and then I shall be Lady Earlecroft."

"Poor child! you little know how long will be your trial," murmured her mother. "What is the name of the priest. Let me see the certificate again—ah! the Reverend Herbert Conway, Edesden Rectory, Edesden, Essex. I will go there at once. I will let no delay step in between me and the discovery."

Madame Carabosse was a woman of her word.

That same day saw her on her road to Edesden.

It was a pretty little hamlet, with its grey towered church, its white dotted churchyard, its straggling cottages sprinkled over green meadows, and the winding lanes.

The rectory was an old-fashioned red brick house, standing back at the end of a long garden, waved over by tall full leaved trees, and decked by innumerable light flowers in the bloom of youth and beauty.

The door was opened by a neat looking pretty country girl, who smilingly asked what Madame Carabosse wanted.

"I wish to speak with Mr. Herbert Conway."

"Mr. Conway, ma'am. There's no Herbert Conway lives here."

"What is your master's name?" asked she.

"The Reverend Francis Lorimore."

"Will you ask him to see me, if you please?"

The servant went out, and, after a moment, returned, saying—

"Please walk up into the drawing-room a moment, ma'am, and master will see you."

Madame Carabosse was shown up into a large old-fashioned room—warmly, cozily furnished, and was left awhile to her own thoughts.

What could all this mystery mean but that her child had been deceived, cajoled into a false marriage.

She looked at the certificate; it was dated nine months before.

Here, then, was a ray of hope.

He might have been superseded by Mr. Lorimore, and gone away to another place.

Mr. Lorimore now entered.

He was a tall, benevolent-looking man of about sixty years of age.

He bowed slightly as he entered and said—

"In what way can I be of service to you, my dear madam?"

"I wish to know where the Reverend Herbert Conway, the prime rector of this place, resides at present?"

"I have been rector here for ten years, madame, and I never heard of the Reverend Herbert Conway."

Madame Carabosse turned deadly pale, and could not speak.

"What ails you, my dear madame?" said the clergyman.

"Look at this, sir," she said, holding out the marriage certificate.

The clergyman gazed at the document in unfeigned astonishment.

"Where did you obtain this document?" he enquired.

"It is my daughter's marriage certificate."

"Then madame," said the old man, "I am sorry to inform you that it is a false one."

The scene which followed can be better imagined than described.

Suffice it to say that Madame Carabosse left the house soon after, and reached her home in a condition which alarmed her daughter, who anticipated from her manner nothing but misery to herself.

When, however, she did know the full extent of her unhappiness, she took a solemn vow which was, that she would never desert her child if it lived, but never again speak to its father except it were to ascertain whether the name he had assumed was his correct one.

CHAPTER XCII.

PHILIP IN SEARCH OF A FATHER.

TIME wore on; and the son to which Marie Carabosse had given birth was growing up.

From the time of its birth she had seen nothing of its father.

It was not, however, forgotten, and frequent remittances of money proved satisfactorily the fact that its father not only cared for its welfare, but was capable of providing for it well.

Philip, then, as the child was called, grew up fatherless; and, in spite of the strenuous endeavours of its mother, nothing was heard of him for two years.

At the end of that time—Marie's mother had been dead some months—a gentleman, tall and elegantly dressed, called upon her, and begged a private interview.

He was shown up-stairs, fondled the child, and was altogether guilty of several familiarities which surprised and annoyed Marie.

At length, after a conversation of some minutes, entirely about nothing, she summoned courage to enquire what his business was.

"Surely, Marie," he said, taking her hand, which she quickly withdrew, "surely, Marie, two years cannot have made so great a difference in me."

The poor girl looked at him in mute astonishment.

At length she said—

"I really do not the least understand your meaning, sir."

"What!" cried he, in great apparent surprise, "do you not remember me?"

"No, indeed, sir; I never saw you before."

A strange smile passed over the stranger's face as he answered—

"It would be strange, then, your child should be my child. I am Ratcliffe Somers."

Marie gazed at him long and anxiously.

"No; she could not be mistaken.

Those dark cold eyes, that wide simpering mouth, had never been Radcliffe's.

"Sir," she said, impetuously, "do not imagine you can so deceive me. You are an impostor."

The stranger laughed heartily.

"Well, Marie, this, to say the least of it, is not the reception I expected."

"What, then, could you expect, sir?"

"Expect?" replied the other; "why, not this manner—this coldness."

"You imagined, probably, sir," exclaimed she, indignantly, "that I should be ready to throw myself into the arms of the first stranger who dared to come forward and say he was my boy's father. But you are greatly, most immeasurably mistaken. I mourn his father as one dead; and knew not, before this, that my secret was known to any."

The stranger considered a moment.

"Well, since you do not feel inclined to fall in with my views I come to tell you that in future the boy will not be fatherless. I will adopt him for my own. Whatever you may choose to think I care not; but *I* know best whether that is my son or not; or, at any rate, if not, that I, as Ratcliffe Somers, have a right to think it mine for the sake of my honour and your virtue. However, as I said before, I care not as to your belief. I come here merely to tell you that I will adopt the boy, give him a decent education, and not molest you, as you seem to wish it so."

Marie thought a moment.

It would be madness to refuse such an offer.

"I may see the child sometimes, I trust," said she, in a low tone.

"Oh, yes, certainly; I am glad to see you are inclined to listen to reason. I will come again to-morrow."

* * * * * * *

A carriage waited round the corner of the street.

Upon its panels were the royal arms.

"Well," said a person inside to the gentlemen who had visited Marie, "well, how about the child? Have you succeeded?"

"Yes, your Royal Highness, I have succeeded," said he, as he bowed low to the personage in the chariot, "all was well. Every detail will be settled to-morrow."

The carriage door then opened, and the man stepped in.

This man was James Tyrrel Blakesley.

———

CHAPTER XCIII.

SECRET FOES.

THE Blue Dwarf arrived safely in England, and at once made his way down to the Blakesleys, whose address he found upon application to Messrs. Whip and Snapper, of Tokenhouse-yard.

William Blakesley was supposed to be upon the point of death when Sapathwa arrived; and the latter found it necessary, if he desired to come to any business arrangements, to settle all matters at once.

William Blakesley was a man about thirty-six years of age; but a tremendous course of dissipation had initiated a disease which appeared now to be hurrying him to his doom.

When, therefore, Sapathwa arrived at Blakesley Hall, he was welcomed with eagerness by his relative, who, being forewarned as to his peculiar appearance, did not express any surprise when he saw him enter.

"Well, Sir John," cried William Blakesley; "I am right glad to see you, for though you come to dispossess me of my title, yet I see in you a guardian to my child."

"Speak not of guardians, dear sir," replied Sapathwa; "he will need none but you since we do not intend allowing you to die just yet. There is one thing, moreover, which I must beg you will humour me in, and that is this, I do not wish to assume the title. I wish you to continue in its possession, that it may descend with its accompanying fortune to your little son, who even now I see is a fine, intelligent little fellow."

"You mean this?" cried William Blakesley, who caught at the idea of retaining for himself and his family the title which they had supposed to be so entirely their own.

"Yes, Sir William, I do mean it; and unless some wrong is done to you and yours I will never assume the title."

"What do you intend me to understand by that?" said William, with a perplexed air.

"I mean that, should we lose you, and any harm is intended to you and yours, I would assume my right in order to defend them; and then I could easily enough re-transfer the title to your son."

Edgar Blakesley was now six years old.

Two years had passed since the above conversation.

Sir William Blakesley—as we must continue to call him—did not die.

Strangely enough, while Sapathwa was with him, his strength revived, the hectic flush on his cheek disappeared, his eyes no longer gave out the brilliant cold flash which so alarmed the Blue Dwarf when he first beheld him.

"You seem, indeed, to be a wonderful physician," said he to Sapathwa, as they walked together in the grounds; "you appear, without giving me any medicine, to have entirely cured me."

"Have you any especial enemy?" abruptly inquired Sapathwa.

"Why do you ask that?" said William Blakesley, turning round in great surprise.

"Because it has just occurred to me that you may have been cured by ceasing to take your medicine."

Sir William was lost in thought a moment.

"No," he at length said, "I know of no one whose interest it is to poison me. I have distant relatives, but it would be scarcely worth their while to attempt such a thing, as they would have to wade through a perfect slaughterhouse to reach the title."

"Oh, there are many who would not scruple at a little bloodshed. But tell me, what is the name of your nearest relative?"

"Mr. James Tyrrel Blakesley, my cousin, whom you have seen once, is the next heir to the baronetcy failing you and my son."

"Ah! indeed!" said Sapathwa.

He spoke little but he thought much.

This James Tyrrel Blakesley was a man whom the Blue Dwarf could not, in any way, amalgamate with.

He was a hard man, evidently cunning and unscrupulous, and also as evidently attached to Lady Caroline, who was too weak and too imprudent to repel his advances.

This man Sapathwa felt was not to be trusted,

and although it would have been unjust to state such a belief publicly, he was firmly assured, in his own mind, that this James Tyrrel Blakesley's ambition was at the root of Sir William's illness.

CHAPTER XCIV.

POOR MIRIAM!

It was, as I have said, two years since Sapathwa left his friends in Berlin.

Miriam's form was ever present in his dreams!

And oh! that deadly sickness which came over him when he thought that she was fondled by other arms, pressed in the embraces of another, and that other a forger and a murderer!

Had Sapathwa believed in destiny he would certainly have been excusable, for when he saw the young, the beautiful, and the pure, uniting itself with the coarse, the brutal, and the criminal, did it not seem as if a terrible fate was impending over her and him?

One morning he received the following letter :—

"*Berlin, June 10, 18—.*

"*Dear Sapathwa,—Come over immediately; your presence is necessary. Myself and little one are well.*

"*Your ever loving sister,*
"MIRIAM.''

"Poor girl!" cried Sapathwa; "something is wrong, I see, because she endeavours to conceal something. Ah! 'myself and little one' are well. She makes no mention of Francois. I must go instantly."

Three days after he left Blakesley Hall.

He left friends in sorrow; he went to friends who, alas! were in an agony of grief.

On arriving in Berlin he went immediately to Miriam's old address.

She was not there, nor did they know where she was to be found.

He made every inquiry; he advertised for her; he set the police to work, but it was of no avail.

He could hear nothing of her whereabouts.

"Poor Miriam!" thought he; "I fear the end of all your fierce love is that you are starving with your poor child."

He was not long kept in suspense, however.

The night was cold when he met her.

It was in the fasionable street of Berlin—Unter den Linden.

There was a glare of lamps, a bustling crowd, a noise of many passers.

Suddenly, at the corner of a cross-road, rose an exquisite thrill of melody.

It was a sweet German melody.

The beauty of the voice made many stop and listen; but still more tarried to listen to the words as they rolled forth from an evidently foreign warbler.

Sapathwa pressed forward with the crowd, which every moment increased.

A strange presentiment hurried him forward to where the singer stood.

It was a young girl, with a child in her arms.

Her tattered garments scarcely covered decently her delicate limbs, her head was bare, and her long curls wantoned over her half-naked shoulders.

Her face, pale and agonised, looked strange out there in the glaring street, amid so many merry people.

Why did she intrude her misery amid their joy?

Ah, why?

Sapathwa pressed forward, looked in her face, and exclaimed—

"My God! it is Miriam," and rushed towards her.

She could not see the features of him who accosted her.

She only felt an arm take her child from her, and a kind voice say,

"Come away, my soul, come away. I am Sapathwa."

Not a word more spoken.

Her heart was too full for utterance.

Only her large, bright eyes gazed up at him in deep gratitude as he called a cabriolet and took her away with him from among the wondering, gaping crowd.

"Oh my God. Sapathwa! that you should see me thus," sobbed the poor girl, as she hugged her baby closer to the cold bosom in the coach.

"Say not that, Miriam," said the Blue Dwarf, "say rather how sad is it that you should have brought this on yourself."

Miriam sobbed.

"Oh! John, how unkind you are—is this a time for reproaches?"

"I reproach not; I merely regret that I had not the opportunity of trying to make you happy."

———

CHAPTER XCV.

AFTER MARRIAGE.

IT was again the old story.

As soon as Miriam was married she discovered how terribly she had been deceived in her husband.

Him whom she had imagined all kindness, all affection, she discovered to be a mass of selfishness and cruelty.

It was scarcely a month after his marriage that Francois began a career of dissipation, which ended in his being from home nearly every night, and sometimes even for a week at a time.

Gradually her money dwindled away.

The demon of gambling had once more possessed Francois Michaut; and health, happiness, fortune, were being driven away before it.

In the midst of mental misery, though it was too early for poverty, a child was born to them.

A bright, sunny child, was little Leila, exactly like her mother, with her dark, blue eyes, her winning smile, her gladsome expression.

This quieted Francois for a while, and for a short time he remained at home, and attended, though much against his will, to his wife's wants.

But, with her convalescence, came a renewal of his feverish desire for drink and gambling, and every night saw her again alone pining for him who never came.

The home to which Miriam took her old lover was one which was well adapted to strike terror and grief into his heart.

It was a top garret, almost entirely destitute of furniture. There was some straw in a corner, a broken chair, the former serving for a bed for the poor mother and child.

"And where is Francois?" said Sapathwa, as he stood gazing at this scene of terrible misery.

"He has left me."

"Left you?"

"Yes, left me, now that he has squandered and exhausted all my fortune."

"I will find him," said Sapathwa.

"For what?"

"What? do you not wish to see him again?"

"Oh! I am afraid," sobbed the poor girl.

"What, did he ill use you?"

"Oh! ask me not, ask me not."

"I will find him though, if it only be to punish him," said the Blue Dwarf. "Meanwhile, my poor girl, come with me, this wretched hovel is no place for you."

Without a glance behind her Miriam wrapped a shawl round her poor, shivering child, and followed him who should have been her husband.

A strange pair, indeed, they seemed when they entered together the hotel where the Blue Dwarf was staying.

People stared hard—but, then, people stare at everything—and whispered strange things; but Sapathwa pushed by the gaping waiters; had the best bedroom prepared for her; a fire lit in her room, and everything done to render her as happy and comfortable as possible.

"Make this your home, my dearest girl," said Sapathwa, kindly, "until I discover for you the husband who ought never to have deserted you."

Husband! How that word grated upon his ear.

That name which should have been applied to him alone.

"You will never find him," said Miriam; "he will elude every effort of yours."

"No, he will not elude me," replied Sapathwa, quietly; "I will find him though I spend my life in doing so, and, in proportion to the wrong he does you, so will I punish him."

"Oh! do not speak of revenge," cried Miriam, weeping. "I have forgiven him—you must forgive him also."

"I have forgiven him, Miriam, far too much already. I forgive him no more."

CHAPTER XCVI.

THE WILES OF THE LOST ONE.

IN a chamber in —— street, in Berlin, sat two persons.

The one, a young girl of about twenty, the other Francois Michaut.

The girl was very pretty, but her beauty was of a peculiar cast.

She evidently belonged to a certain class, among which, indeed, Francois seemed especially to select his friends.

Her dress was of a style designed to attract, as much as possible, the notice of the connoisseur in beauty.

Her dress was very low, displaying to advantage her magnificently moulded bust, the globes of which were only hidden by an almost transparent chemisette of open-work lace.

Her form was tall and voluptuously rounded; her whole appearance, indeed, seemed designed to excite, as far as possible, the passions of the opposite sex.

She was lying, when we introduced her to the reader, negligently, fantastically, upon a couch opposite where Francois Michaut sat buried deeply in thought.

"My dear Francois," said she, "you are very dull this evening."

"I am."

"Why be so?"

"Enough to make me so when all my money is gone, when not only has it vanished, but has gone away steadily without one turn of luck in my favour, that there appears no chance of righting myself."

"Nonsense. Do not despair in that way."

"Despair! what else is left to me?"

"Do you not remember that when the crisis is come there is always a turn. This is the crisis, good luck will come to-night."

"Then you intend that I shall go to Mark's to-night?"

"Yes, and I will go, too."

"Why so? why do you go? You can do no good."

"You forget, I can go and wheedle the old marquis."

"Yes, as you did last time, and nearly got me arrested for fraud. I've had enough of prisons I can tell you."

"Prisons! do not talk so foolishly, Francois, I will manage him well to-night."

"Very well, I will go to-night," returned Francois, sullenly, "but, if I lose to-night, this is my last venture."

"Well love, be it so," said the wily charmer, drawing his head down upon her heaving bosom, "anything to make you happy."

Oh! false one!

Oh! false heart!

Oh! wily tongue!

Are you not even preparing to leave him if he gains no money to-night to dress your charms, to feed your vanity, to buy your love?

The evening passed away, and, about eleven o'clock, Francois and Speranza Maloni, his Italian mistress, issued forth from their house, and directed their steps towards a cabriolet rank, where, hiring a vehicle, he ordered the driver to take them to Mark's Hotel, Unter den Linden.

Speranza was dressed in the blaze of Berlin's most costly fashions, and sailed into the room with the air of a queen.

Francois, too, swaggered in with a kind of false dignity.

He had been recognised long as an invetetate and determined gambler, but had never yet been known to fail in his payments.

So they were greeted lustily when they entered.

In a few minutes Francois was surrounded by a crowd of eager players, and Speranza by a mob of loathsome admirers.

I say loathsome, because a man's admiration for a woman is loathsome when all he admires is her size, her bust, her form.

The men in this den of iniquity only regarded Speranza as a beautiful animal.

That was all.

"Ah! Marquis, I am glad I have the honour of seeing you here to-night," exclaimed Speranza, with one of her most bewitching smiles.

It was true.

She was glad.

But, then, why?

Not as he thought, because he had succeeded in attaching her to himself in any way, but because she hoped to fleece him.

"*Ma belle Speranza*," exclaimed the Marquis de Cantalari, "I am most delighted to see you. A game of ecarté of course?"

"You are so gallant."

"Ah! that is right," cried the marquis, seating himself at once at a table, and placing himself in dangerous proximity to the chair which it chanced his fair antagonist to occupy, "that is right, that is right. I shall then, after all, have a pleasant evening."

"You are complimentary."

"Not so, indeed."

"Ah, but I understand flattery—you cannot deceive me."

"It is not flattery, indeed I mean all I say. I would give twenty pounds to be allowed to kiss those rosy lips but once."

"You may have your wish for much less than that," said Speranza, laughing; "you shall kiss them for nothing if you behave yourself. Now it is your play."

"May I to night?" asked the enamoured marquis, making his first false move in the game.

"Yes, indeed, now, while no one is looking," cried Speranza, trumping his cards when she could have followed suit.

The marquis leaned over her and imprinted a kiss upon her lips.

Oh, that fatal kiss!

It cost him a hundred louis.

They were playing for high stakes; and although he did not absolutely lose a hundred louis at once, still her manners and her wantonness made such an impression upon him that he found it impossible to play aright.

So, as I have said, before the Marquis de Cantalari rose from the ecarté table that evening he had lost a hundred louis.

It was sufficient, during this time, for Speranza to know that Francois could not be losing much.

Their whole capital, when they entered the room, was five louis.

Therefore, if he had lost his capital, she had multiplied it twenty fold, and he must be losing—if losing he were—on credit.

This reasoning, satisfying her that all was right, she was perfectly content to remain in the room, quietly receiving the fulsome flattery and adulation of the men who crowded round her.

Presently she stepped out upon the balcony to listen to a singer who was warbling sweetly beneath.

"A pretty girl in sooth," cried one.

"Aye, if her eyes did not glare so," said another.

"I will give her something," exclaimed Speranza, proceeding to undo her purse.

"Stay!—give her nothing, insult her not," cried a hoarse voice, and Francois Michaut pushed his way out upon the balcony.

"D—n it!" said one of his companions, "'tis no insult. She would not sing did she not want money."

And so saying, he cast a gold piece down.

Just as it fell with a ringing sound upon the pavement a dark form came up and led the girl away.

Francois Michaut uttered a cry, and dragged Speranza away.

"What is the matter?" said she in a whisper, as she saw his pale and haggard face.

"Nothing—nothing. The excitement of the evening, perhaps, has worked upon me, nothing more."

"Well, have you been successful?"

"Yes, love, I have won two hundred louis; and you—"

"One hundred."

"Ah! that is well; that will do well for a first trial. To-morrow we will begin again."

The worthy pair then left Mark's Hotel, and proceeded homewards.

Why did he turn pale?

Why did he beg Speranza not to bestow alms on the poor singer?

He had recognised, first of all, his unfortunate wife Miriam, and then Sapathwa, whom he had imagined safely caged in England.

He knew now that the day of retribution had come, and trembled.

CHAPTER XCVII.

THE BEGINNING OF THE END.

No sooner had Sapathwa left England than Sir William Blakesley's health began again to fail him.

Mr. James Tyrrel Blakesley was a constant visitor at the house, and expressed his sorrow at the determined nature of the disease which seemed destined to carry him away from the bosom of his family.

Lady Caroline also was a victim to inconsolable grief.

She saw the evil impending, and even seemed as if she was aware whence it came; but, whatever it might be, she preserved it a secret, and allowed it to prey constantly upon her mind.

Shortly after the departure of Sapathwa for Berlin, however, she made a fearful discovery—a discovery which, in other hands but her own, would have led to the inevitable frustration of deadly plans of hatred and ambitious treachery, but was useless to her, cramped as she was by fearful oaths and promises.

Wandering alone by the little glenside which skirted Blakesley Hall she came suddenly upon two persons who were standing eagerly engaged in conversation behind a thick clump of trees.

Either impelled by curiosity, or a presentiment of evil, she hastily concealed herself and listened.

Well might her face change colour, well might her heart all but stop, well might her blood curdle.

This was the conversation she heard—

"But you forget one thing," said the croaking voice of an old woman; "you should administer it in smaller quantities."

"I do now administer it in doses small enough, goodness knows!" said the man. "I only give him a quarter of a grain every morning."

"Well, and does he taste it?"

"No, it appears not; but it makes him sleepy."

"Ah, I must remedy that; I will give you another preparation. Discontinue the other for awhile."

" In order, I suppose, that he may recover his strength ?"

" Not so ; he will only have two days to rest," said the old hag with a fiendish laugh.

" Then when am I to meet, you again ?"

" The day after to-morrow."

" Here, at this same spot ?"

" Yes, here."

" And you'll then bring the new kind of medicine ?"

" Yes ; it is much simpler in its use and effect than the other. Has Sir William a cough ?"

" No, not in particular ; he is troubled with a slight consumptive cough, but he never takes anything for it."

" That is awkward," philosophised the old hag, " very awkward. We shall have to produce one. Well, *au revoir*."

So saying, the old dame hobbled off, leaving the man alone.

He stood wrapped in meditation for a moment, and then moved slowly away.

As he did so he felt a hand lightly touch his arm, and a voice saying—

" Mr. James Tyrrel Blakesley, what do you here ?"

" Great Heavens, Caroline !" exclaimed he, starting round in affright, " what do you here ?"

" You need not ask me, sir, what I do here," answered Lady Caroline Blakesley, " but I should rather ask you how you dare to plot against my husband's life on his very grounds."

" I plot against your husband's life ? Why, Lady Caroline, you are dreaming ?"

" I dream not, sir, I heard it all, and shall warn him against you."

James Tyrrel Blakesley laughed a long, mocking laugh, as he answered —

" Warn him ! you dare not. But come, this is child's play. You are entirely, absurdly mistaken. Allow me to conduct you hence," and so saying, he offered her his arm.

" Touch me not, reptile !" exclaimed the incensed lady, " but remember, since you have dared me, that, to save my husband's life, I will risk all, aye, everything, sir, honour, fortune, even life itself."

" Well played, well acted, indeed," exclaimed Blakesley, " the world little knows what a great actress is lost to it. But, seriously speaking, you must not think any more of anything you heard. It is your own morbid imagination which coins these imaginary terrors. I was obtaining from that good lady a recipe of some medicine which will cure your husband quickly, aye, much more quickly than any of your quack doctors, when you must needs come up and think we are concerting a scheme to poison him. But, madame, I give you credit for more foresight, more knowledge of the world than that. Of what avail would it be for me to slay your husband while your son lives ? And does he ever seem to pine ? Does he ever show symptoms of being poisoned, eh ? Answer me that truly ?"

This speech was exceedingly plausible ; but though it, for a moment, staggered Lady Caroline, she soon returned to her former belief.

" Be it so, then," said she. " I will take especial notice, and if, within the next two days, my husband becomes better, and then becomes visibly worse, I shall at once, and without fear of consequences, tell him all."

So saying, she left James Tyrrel Blakesley alone.

" Damn the woman !" he exclaimed, as he saw her majestic figure sail up the walk, " with all her weakness she will foil me now if I take not especial care."

CHAPTER XCVIII.

THE GOLDEN DROPS.

NEXT day Sir William Blakesley grew visibly better. The day following that again better.

On the evening of that day Lady Caroline, sought James's chamber.

" Now, remember, sir," she said, firmly, " remember what I have sworn. My husband has become better these two days—if he becomes worse to-morrow I tell all."

" Foolish woman ! I cannot control Providence !" exclaimed James Tyrrel, in affected indignation, " perhaps there may be a reaction to-morrow, who can tell ?"

" Well, then, look to it," said Lady Caroline, determinedly, " I shall be obstinate on this point. If he be worse to-morrow I discover everything to Sir William."

" Not omitting, I trust, the part you have played in the affair yourself."

" You are right. I shall not omit in my tale the part I have played in the affair myself."

" Then if I sink you will sink with me."

" That I will risk," said Lady Caroline."

The next day came.

James Tyrrel Blakesley went out early, and returned after an absence of four hours.

All that day Sir William had a violent cough, but, in other respects, was better.

" Well," said James to Lady Blakesley in the evening, " well, does this satisfy you?"

" You have saved yourself for one day," was her answer.

On the following day the baronet became worse, and his wife asked for a private interview.

" Let me warn you in time," cried James, seizing her fiercely by the arm ; " beware what you say, or by Heavens you shall rue it."

" I fear you not," said she, as she swept past him into the room.

He applied his ear to the key-hole, but could distinguish not one word of the conversation which could lead him to understand what she had said.

All he could hear was now and then a kiss, and once or twice the words—

" Oh ! Caroline, that I should hear this from you."

Then there were violent remonstances, expostulations, entreaties, but of what nature he could not tell, for all was said in a whisper.

Lady Caroline came suddenly out of the room at ten o'clock, and found James listening.

"I have heard all," he said, at a venture, and assuming a bullying voice and demeanour.

"You heard nothing," returned Lady Caroline, contemptuously, "or you would not dare to be here."

On the following morning, at eight o'clock, before James Tyrrel Blakesley had entered their room, a messenger came in all haste to the Hall, with a message for him.

He brought a note, which ran thus:—

"*Come at once, delay not. No matter what betides come. An hour may turn the tide.*

"C."

"C! What is that for? Ah! I have it, Carabosse. It concerns Philip. Well, a day does not signify. He can take a double dose to-morrow."

So, with this disjointed speech, he proceeded to dress himself, and was soon on the road to St. Peter's, the place from which the letter was dated.

Half an hour after he departed a postchaise, drawn by two horses, came up to the grand entrance of Blakesley Hall.

Into this got a gentleman, assisted by a lady, who afterwards got in with him.

Then Lady Caroline made her appearance, and, after an affectionate parting between her and the person in the coach, the vehicle drove off.

In the evening of the same day James Tyrrel Blakesley returned to the hall.

He seemed flurried and perplexed, and eagerly asked for Sir William.

"He is gone, sir," said the servant whom he addressed.

"Gone!" cried James, a pallor as of death overspreading his countenance; "gone where?"

"Ah! that's what I don't know, sir," responded the man; "he went off all of a hurry this morning, but, excepting Lady Caroline, I really do not know of any one who is aware of his destination."

"D——n!" cried James. "Tell Lady Caroline I must see her at once."

"I will ask my lady to grant you an interview," replied the man.

"Curse that infernal meddler," muttered James Tyrrel Blakesley to himself, as he paced up and down the room, "she shall pay for this well."

CHAPTER XCIX.

"I dare do all that doth become a man,
Who dares do more is none."
—SHAKESPEARE.

"So you have dared to interfere with my plans," cried James, in a voice trembling with rage, as Lady Caroline entered the room.

"Dared, sir? I dare do anything to save my husband from your clutches," replied she, bravely.

"Where has he gone?"

"Where he will be out of your reach."

"Do you intend to keep his place of abode a secret?"

"I do; nothing in the world shall wrest the knowledge from me."

"And you intend remaining here?"

"I remain here, sir, only until I receive certain information, and then I join my husband."

"And, pray, how long may that be?"

"Before a week is over our heads I shall leave this place for good."

"Yes, if I do not prevent you," muttered James Tyrrel Blakesley.

That night, when all the household had retired to rest, a light tapping noise might have been heard at Lady Caroline's window.

She opened it stealthily and looked out.

Though she expected a visitor she could not repress a shudder.

The night was so cold; so still, so dark.

Her window opened out upon a broad balcony, from which steps descended into the garden.

Hastily casting a shawl around her she extinguished her lamp, and descended into the grounds.

"Lady Caroline," said a voice in a whisper, as she reached the bottom of the steps.

"Stay, do not speak here. Wait till we reach the grotto."

The grotto was, properly speaking, a summer house, which had lately been erected at the further end of the garden.

This reached, the new comer—a young man—presented to Lady Caroline a letter, which she eagerly opened.

She read it anxiously, while an expression of joy overspread her features.

"It is all settled," she cried. "Go, Herbert, bring round the carriage to the front gate in the lane, there I will join you in ten minutes."

Lady Caroline sped back to her room.

All was quiet.

Only a few things had she to take with her.

In a few minutes she had closed her room, and rejoined the young man, who waited in the lane beyond with the carriage.

In five minutes longer the man at the turnpike gate was awakened from his heavy sleep, and came grumbling out to open the gate for the Blakesley chariot.

"I wonder what these Blakesleys are up to," mumbled the old fellow; "they've got mighty queer of late. I wonder when I shall have to turn out again to open this blessed gate for them."

Well he might wonder.

It was many years before he opened that gate again to the same persons.

James Tyrrel Blakesley came down stairs chafing with anger at the conversation of the night before.

Breakfast was laid for one.

"Where is Lady Caroline?" he asked, as the servant brought in the things.

"She went away last night, sir," replied the servant.

"Went away?—went where?" shouted James.

"I do not know," said the man.

"And are you aware for how long a time she has gone?"

"Not the least. She left word that the Hall was to be closed as soon as you had time to make preparations for going."

James Tyrrel Blakesley said no more.

In four days he left the Hall, and it was more than as many years before he again entered it as a guest.

CHAPTER C.

THE ANGEL OF RETRIBUTION.

FRANCOIS MICHAUT and his mistress were once more up in the world.

Having won three hundred louis, however, and recruited their dress and health, they thought it necessary to proceed periodically to Mark's, and every evening saw them there.

With varying luck these companions in crime proceeded in their career.

But some how or another fortune refused to smile upon them.

Everything went dead against them: and, after two months of incessant suffering and persevering debauchery, they found themselves without a farthing.

It was after three days of all but starvation, and after a scene of bitter reproach and recrimination, that one evening a female, dressed in shabby finery, knocked at the door of the Marquis of Cantalari.

"Whom do you desire to see?" inquired the domestic, glancing his eyes superciliously over her attire.

"The Marquis de Cantalari," replied Speranza, haughtily.

"I think the marquis is engaged," replied the man.

"He is never engaged to anyone when I am here," replied she.

"Oh! madam, I beg your pardon," said the man, recognising her. "If you will step into the *salon de la reception* I will inform him of your presence."

In a few moments the Marquis de la Cantalari appeared.

He smiled, and advanced across the room eagerly, when he saw, reclining on the sofa, the superb form of Speranza.

He came up to her, imprinted a warm kiss upon her white and dimpled hand, and said,

"This is, indeed, an unexpected pleasure. For what have you come?"

Speranza flushed, and then pointed to her clothes.

"Ah! money," cried the coarse-minded marquis. "All I have is yours!"

Speranza bit her lip.

"You put it in an unworthy light," she said, crimsoning all over her beautiful neck and bosom. "I love you, I come to tell you so!"

"Then will you remain here to-day?"

"Willingly: but you must first order your carriage, and drive me to your jeweller's; then I want some dresses—I want everything!"

"And you shall have them, said the marquis, eagerly, now for the first time caressing her unreservedly.

Speranza looked up fondly at him with her large, beautiful, treacherous eyes.

The marquis was delirious with delight.

"Oh! how beautiful you are," exclaimed he, leaning his head upon her breast, "and you will never leave me?"

"Never."

Poor infatuated old fool!

She had just left one in every way superior, in person, in manners, in attractions, because the demon of poverty had intruded itself between them.

So Francois Michaut was left alone in his misery.

He knew not until afterwards that she had gone.

He watched, and she never came.

So he knew that the angel of retribution was already hovering over him.

He could hear the flapping of her wings, could feel the air, as it were, around him.

So he knew he had better prepare for the worst, and prepared accordingly.

He had seen Miriam starving, and knew it was his work.

He had seen the Blue Dwarf rescue her from degradation; and, knowing how he had before acted in regard to him, he knew that in him was personated all that an avenging spirit could possess of unswerving honour and determined revenge.

CHAPTER CI.

THE MURDER IN THE HOLLY TREE-LANE.

IT was a black. unearthly night.

The sky seemed as if it were striving to hide its face from the sight of some crime, so thickly was it veiled in clouds piled in black tiers one over another.

It was a night when darkness so thickly shrouded all objects around that the trees had no shadows, and scarcely any visible form.

Their branches, and the sky above and behind them, seemed to intermingle into one black, lowering mass.

One of those nights it was when everything seems to produce apprehension, and nothing to bring cheerfulness; when a tolling bell, or chirping sparrow, or even the human voice raised in anger would be considered a welcome sound.

Dense masses of clouds passed across the heavens, but their course was so uninterrupted and unbroken that the eyes were strained in vain to see whether they moved at all.

The wind blew hard, and the shadowless trees flung abroad their arms like black phantoms.

Francois Michaut, overcome, as he was, by the thoughts of his crime, shuddered as the night wind roared amid the leaves, and trembled as the branches of the dark trees whistled behind him.

The very sound of his own footsteps on the falling leaves seemed to startle him, and he trod softly, and whistled a tune to himself to keep up his courage.

There was no light near him, and, as he advanced into the grove, the very sound of the animals, as they sprang from their hiding-places, frightened the mental criminal.

Why did he advance into this gloomy, sepulchral forest in the unearthly darkness, when his thoughts were bent upon his crime, when every sound was the signal of alarm, when every breath of wind seemed to bear with it the whispering of conscience.

Borne on by a presentiment of he knew not what, he went onwards towards Holly Tree-lane.

He had not penetrated very far into the wood when he heard the sound of carriage wheels advancing rapidly up the road.

He could discern, in the distance, the lamps of the vehicle swinging from side to side as the horses bore it along at a tremendous pace.

Just as they were approaching the spot where Francois stood the light seemed suddenly to be extinguished, and the carriage stopped.

He heard a scuffle, then the sound of men shouting angrily, then a cry.

A horrible reflection crossed his mind; he unslung his gun and rushed over brake and briar towards the high road.

Some years previously to this the parlour of the inn at the end of Holly Tree-lane had been a source of great festivity.

The working people of the place had gathered together to enjoy a friendly frolic and a little social recreation.

Such meetings as these, however plebeian they may be, are agreeable things in their way, and there are times when, in such company, you can see very useful displays of human nature.

Then were gathered there the carpenter, the shoemaker, the artizan, the sexton; all the well known members of the village, and each of them sang characteristic songs.

The festivity and fun was at its height when the door of the meeting room opened, and in walked two men dressed as farm labourers.

They seemed pretty well known among the company, but did not appear very much inclined to talk.

Money, however, was apparently of no consequence to them.

They pulled out purses well lined, as ignorant people always do, treated the company to unlimited sour beer, &c. &c.

At length one of them was asked for a toast and a song.

Being pushed into a corner, he cried, with a laugh—

"Well, then, I'll give you an extempore rhyming toast :—

"Here's a health to the bride to the altar led,
Here's a health to the husband newly made,
Here's a health to the widow alone in her bed,
Here's a health to the sexton's trade.
                              Heigho,
Here's a health to the sexton's trade.

For he merrily digs, merrily digs,
He merrily digs, heigho.
He doth merrily dig,
And sends small and big
To the deadmen down below,
                              Heigho,
To the deadmen down below."

The sexton smiled grimly at this lugubrious ditty, and the company stared.

"Gilbert's rather queer to-night," whispered the carpenter to the shoemaker, "what's up?"

"Why," returned the shoemaker, "there's a little queer business on hand, I think."

The two men did not seem at rest; they were continually consulting the clock that hung over the dingy mantle piece, and when, at length, the hour of ten struck they took a hurried leave of the company and departed.

"You are a rum cove," said Franz, the one who had not before spoken.

"I don't 'xactly see the use of going to that ere place on purpose to be found out."

"Now, every one knows we're here."

"Franz, you never had no heart," returned the self-conceited ruffian. "Why, of course, it looks more honester like to go there first, and nobody will suspect that we've had the impudence to do such a thing."

With all his conceit Gilbert went the best way to be found out.

Somehow or another thieves and murderers have a sort of dogged liking for old associates and associations, and even when they know, after the commission of a crime, that they are thus most likely to be detected, they will persist in frequenting their old haunts, and visiting their old companions.

Before the half-hour had struck they had proceeded a good distance up the dark lane.

"It is devilish dark to-night," said Gilbert; "it makes one queer coming down here for such a thing."

"You don't mean to say that you are afraid," said Franz; "I should never have thought that of you."

"No; only I shouldn't object to a little light."

The approach of the carriage now stopped all conversation.

They posted themselves in advantageous positions, and, as the horses came dashing up, a rope thrown adroitly by Bill brought them to the ground. The driver was thrown head foremost into the road, and quickly secured by Franz.

The carriage which Francois Michaut saw advancing along the road contained Baron von Stroleng, the wealthy banker.

The robbers knew well that the carriage contained a large sum of money, which he was carrying to Berlin for special purposes of Government.

The old man was no coward, and, opening the door, fired at his assailants.

Just at the moment when he had expended his ammunition, and was at the mercy of his antagonists, a shot from the wood wounded one of them severely.

Then another shot was fired.

"We are surrounded," cried the thieves, "let us fly!'

So they fled in terror; and when Francois

F. BRETT.

Michaut leaped over the hedge, and reached the carriage, no one was to be seen.

The old man had received such severe injuries that he was lying insensible in the road.

The box containing the gold was already broken open.

Bright, glittering pieces lay about.

The demon of avarice came into his soul.

What if he left him there where he was lying under the dark sky, and carry away the property?

No sooner thought of than accomplished.

Cramming into his pockets as much as they would, possibly, hold, he was about to make off with his gains when the tramp of horse soldiers was heard.

He leaped instantly out of the carriage and turned to flee.

But it was too late.

The carriage was surrounded and Francois Michaut arrived in Berlin that night, and was delivered over to justice as a murderer.

CHAPTER CII.

THE CONDEMNED CELL.

WHEN the gates of Razenburg goal had once more closed behind him, and he was seated alone in a dark cell, the thoughts which crowded into his brain so bewildered him as to leave him no room for calm reflection.

He could not realise to himself the idea that he who, a few months before, had been the possessor of wealth, a votary of pleasure, the careless, reckless man about town, whose career the burden of an awful crime was not sufficient to check—he could not realise to himself the idea that he was to spend his hours in that cell, to sit there day after day, and night after night, until the dread hour when, by a violent death, he should depart from this world to meet in another those whom he had wronged.

Death to every one is terrible, but to a man who has committed a crime, how infinitely more terrible must it be !

Did none of those men, whom this victim of bad passions had fed and pampered—did no one of these boon companions, who had almost existed on his bounty—of those who had been enabled to get out of their difficulties by his ill-placed and lavish generosity—or those who had praised, and flattered, and courted him in his palmy days—did none of these come and see him ?—did no one, come to comfort him or speak a word in his favour ?

Need we say that, as usual, the friends of prosperity were the revilers of adversity, and turned upon the hand that had fed them.

The trial came on in due time.

Need we say how it ended ?

Francois Michaut was condemned to death, and awaited the certain execution of the sentence.

This time there was no hope for him.

He had been recognised, at once, as the man who had, upon a previous occasion, been condemned to death and reprieved, and no effort would have been great enough to release him.

Sapathwa, ever on the watch, was the first to hear the fatal news.

From Miriam he contrived to conceal it entirely, but he hinted several times that he heard rumours of his death.

The evening before the execution he made his way to the goal, and entered the cell.

It was the first visit he had made to the wretched prisoner.

"My God !" exclaimed Francois, clasping his hands, "have you come to save me ?"

"I have, in one way," said the Blue Dwarf, solemnly. "Your cup of crime is full—you have chosen an inheritance of disgrace—you have enjoyed it. To-morrow you will suffer the penalty. No earthly power can save you from death, but that is no reason why that inheritance should descend to your wife and to your children. You must die, but not by the hands of the public executioner."

"I understand you not," muttered Francois, in a hoarse, thick voice.

"Here," replied Sapathwa, drawing from his pocket a small phial, "here is poison, drink it."

"I will not," cried Francois.

"Wretch !" exclaimed Sapathwa, "are you, then, determined to overwhelm your unfortunate family in your own ruin ?"

"She does not care what becomes of me, why should I care for her."

"Miserable coward ! you speak thus of her whom you have basely deserted and ill-treated."

Francois winced.

"Does she know of this ?"

"She does not, nor shall she know the extent of your baseness."

"But I am innocent of this crime. I swear to you I am innocent. Let me explain—"

"Explain nothing. I know all. I know you are innocent of the murder, but you were found committing a robbery. You deserve death—you will inevitably receive it—do not, then, drag with you into public disgrace your unhappy family."

"Will you swear to me there is no hope ?"

"I swear there is none," replied Sapathwa, solemnly.

Francois knew well the character of the Blue Dwarf, and, when he took his oath, he believed him.

"Give me the poison," he said, in an almost inaudible voice; "how long will it leave me if I take it now ?"

"An hour."

"Is it certain ?"

"Here, then, is a health to thee," cried Francois, as he applied the phial to his lips with trembling hands. "Are you now satisfied ?"

"I am," said Sapathwa, softly, while a tear stole down his cheek ; "give me your hand."

Francois, over whose face a ghastly pallor was spreading, mechanically grasped Sapathwa's hand, as he asked,

"Do you forgive me ?"

"Everything."

"Then leave me, I wish to write."

"Farewell, Francois Michaut ! may Heaven forgive you for all your sins as I do," and the Blue Dwarf turned and went.

*   *   *   *   *

So the morning rose over Berlin merrily.

Heavily, during the night, had the hammers of the carpenters resounded before the goal.

Dense was the crowd which, as the dawn broke hazily over the eastern sky, collected opposite the scaffold.

Eight o'clock came, but no criminal.

Then, at nine, the carpenters came out, and slowly removed the scaffold.

Hereupon the crowd commenced to crack jokes.

"It is an invisible execution," cried one.

"Let us hang the crawler," said another.

This was the nick-name of the executioner.

But the crawler had not made his appearance, and so they were disappointed.

In his cell, in the calm sleep of death, Francois Michaut had been found.

On the table was a note to this effect,

"*I die by my own hands, having drank poison I had previously concealed for the purpose. Therefore blame no one. I die innocent of the crime imputed to me, though, alas ! not of many others.* FRANCOIS MICHAUT."

He died with a lie upon his lips, but that lie was to save the life of another, for it was death to save a criminal from the executioner.

CHAPTER CIII.

THE REWARD OF PATIENT LOVE.

WHAT are poor women to do?

Ah, indeed! what are they to do?

I should be the last to blame a widow, left by her husband dependent on her own exertions for subsistence, and the subsistence, perhaps, also, of five or six children—I should be the last, I say, to blame a woman so circumstanced for marrying a second time. But when a young girl has once loved a man, and their paths in life have diverged, perhaps by accident, perhaps through a slight quarrel; perhaps because friends step in and prevent their union, then I *do* blame her if she marry another man merely to obtain some one to support her. If she have any means whatever of living respectable, let her live singly, and await the time of his return, for, if she have confidence in him, she will certainly expect such a return. If she have not, then she cannot love him; and, in the nature of things, she may marry whenever she may like.

Many a girl marries, or, at any rate, declares that she marries, merely because her home is not comfortable; and very often, moreover, marries a man she does not love, because the man for whom she has a real affection is not in a position to marry her. But does she suppose that, by leaving this home which is so uncomfortable, and entering the home of a man for whom her heart experiences no love whatever, she will better her condition? If such are her thoughts she is grievously mistaken, at least as I imagine, for I cannot believe in love formed after marriage.

When people, thus united, live together for some time; when children have been born to them, and they are thus bound together more strongly by these most blessed of earthly pledges of affection, a feeling of calm happiness and contentment in each other's society will very often arise.

But this is presupposing that the man loved the woman before their marriage; for, in cases where neither love before, it must, I think, be a miracle if they ever do so afterwards.

This feeling, which grows out of companionship and mutual affection for their children, may, perhaps, compensate a woman for the sacrifice of herself, but it is not love.

For love is a warm, passionate feeling, which must grow up before, not after marriage.

I do not, by this, intend to convey the idea that love cannot exist after marriage.

There are pernicious teachers who try to persuade the young never to marry, because marriage is the grave of love.

In my opinion marriage acts upon love as the sun does upon the flowers and fruits of this earth, nurturing, and fostering, and ripening it into a better and more holy feeling.

It is only after we have been married to the woman we love, and we have lived with her, and enjoyed her society, and listened to her words, and witnessed the thousand little actions and kindnesses of her daily life, that we feel our being bound up, as it were, in her's, and experience pangs of regret at parting from her for a day, or even an hour.

In truth it is then only that we arrive at an idea of the magnitude of our love for her; then only that we can become aware of the sacrifices we can make for her; it is then only that we feel that we have, by uniting ourselves to her, made ourselves happy for our lives, and encircled ourselves with a girdle of affection, and kindness, and tenderness, which will never, in all time, be broken.

On a man such as Francois Michaut the bestowal of the intense love, the soul worship of a woman like Miriam Spelthorne was utterly wasted.

He was too selfish—too utterly careless of any one's comfort but his own, so that he could not appreciate her.

Now, at length, her eyes were opened to his faults.

She understood that he was dead, and moaned him as such; but, although feeling, in some measure, sorrow that he died thus away from her, she could not but feel a certain degree of relief.

But what preyed upon her mind mostly was the knowledge of what great love she had cast away.

Time wore on.

Leila was about five years old—a sunny, bright-eyed child—when Sapathwa one evening passed his arm round the young widow's waist, and said,

"Dearest Miriam, I am going to ask you a favour, which, I am sure, you will not refuse me."

Miriam guessed what was coming, and spoke not.

A blush, however, mantled over her face and her neck.

"I am going to ask you, my first and only love, if you will be my wife. I have waited long and patiently. Surely you will not again refuse me; you know my great love. Will you say yes."

"Yes," said Miriam.

Sapathwa spoke not.

His heart was too full for utterance.

He only pressed her fondly to his heart, and kissed her again and again on those cherry lips.

So the Blue Dwarf and Miriam Michaut were married.

A strange pair, truly, they seemed, but no two were more loving and, in heart, better suited to each other.

A happy morning truly was it when Sapathwa called Miriam his own; but yet a tear glistened in his eye as he received the reward of his patient love.

CHAPTER CIV.

GONE TO THE SILENT LAND.

ABOUT ten years after the event narrated above a middle-aged man, dressed in deep mourning, arrived at the Oak Leaf Tavern, near Blakesley Hall.

He was a short, stout person, of rather peculiar appearance, but seemed perfectly well acquainted with the neighbourhood.

"Is Sir William Blakesley in the neighbourhood?" asked he of the waiter, who was smoothing down the white tablecloth before him.

"Yes, sir," replied the man; "yes, sir. Strange to say, sir, he returned but a week ago."

"Was he well when you saw him?"

"Not very, sir. Seemed so when he returned from abroad; but he became ill again directly upon his arrival. Air, sir, doesn't agree with him, I think, sir."

"Probably not, probably not," remarked the stranger, and relapsed into silence.

That night a visitor arrived at Blakesley Hall.

He was shown into the drawing room, where he found Sir William propped up in an easy chair, Lady Caroline with him, and also with them Mr. James Tyrrel Blakesley.

"Ah! my dear Sir John," cried Sir William to the Blue Dwarf (for it was he), "I am truly glad to see you. But you are mourning for some one."

"I am in mourning for my wife," said Sapathwa, gloomily.

"Oh! I beg your pardon for touching on so melancholy a subject," said Sir William. "Poor girl! I fear I shall follow her soon."

"Have you arrived here lately?" asked the Blue Dwarf abruptly of James Tyrrel Blakesley.

"A week before the arrival of Sir William I came here," replied he.

"Indeed! well you seem to bring malaria with you wherever you go," said Sapathwa. "Some years back, when I was over here, Sir William's illness began with your arrival and ended with your departure."

This was sufficiently plain, and Mr. James Tyrrel Blakesley looked excessively small.

So Sapathwa came to England a widower.

His life with Miriam had been one of uninterrupted happiness.

He found her, as a wife, all his fondest imaginations could have depicted her.

How bitterly did she regret that she had not bestowed her virgin love upon that being who loved her now so intensely, so passionately, and who had always loved her more than his own life.

Heaven gave them no children, so that Leila became the pet of both these fond hearts, who, with all their earnest love for one another, could yet spare a little for that child of misfortune.

It had not, however, from the first escaped Sapathwa's attention that poor Miriam was in very bad health.

The dreadful misfortunes, the grief, the privations, the anxiety she had undergone, had told upon her frame, and been the cause of an incurable malady.

Consumption had fixed her for its own, and, after nine years of happiness she quietly sank into the grave.

"Oh! Sapathwa," she cried, as the film of death was closing over her eyes; "oh! Sapathwa, dearest husband, I love you, and, for my love, promise me one thing. Take care of my Leila, never leave her, and oh! do not let her marry any one like *him*."

"I love her, dearest Miriam," said Sapathwa, parting her curls from off her poor forehead, "as if she were our own. Oh! my dear girl, believe me, if I wonder how I can spare any for her when all my heart is going up *there* with you."

And, so saying, the poor fellow burst into a passionate flood of tears.

So Miriam Blakesley died, as she prayed to die, in the arms of one whom she loved.

From that moment Sapathwa lived for others, and others only.

All his earthly ambitions, all his worldly aspirations, had gone with Miriam's soul up into the Silent Land.

CHAPTER CV.

HOW TO MAKE A REPUTATION.

THE Blue Dwarf particularly requested Sir William Blakesley not to allow Mr. James Tyrrel Blakesley or Lady Caroline to know who he really was.

They imagined him simply the agent of a foreign estate belonging to Sir William, and, as such, he took care to introduce himself.

Soon after his first introduction he withdrew himself from the hall, and took up his residence in a small cottage in the neighbourhood.

Here he changed his attire, and, throwing off his fashionable dress, was generally to be seen stalking about at night in the lanes and the fields under the clear moonlight.

Strange antics, fantastic tricks, accompanied by his still more fantastic appearance, soon acquired for him in the neighbourhood a considerable reputation, and he was generally known as Goldie Gordon or the Blue Dwarf.

He was regarded by all as a supernatural personage, though, withal, a beneficent spirit.

Although dressing in poor clothing, associating with gipseys, and apparently living in a poor little cottage, he seemed to have plenty of money, and, numerous were the acts of charity which he performed in the neighbourhood of the hall.

If anything of value were stolen by the gipseys it was generally through his instrumentality that it was restored; if a poor family were in need of funds Goldie Gordon was the person through whom aid came to them.

*   *   *   *   *

Goldie Gordon, having disappeared from among the acquaintances of Blakesley Hall, James Tyrrel Blakesley had the stage to himself.

Sir William Blakesley gradually declined in health.

In spite of all Lady Caroline's precautions he became worse by degrees, and at length died.

Then the Blue Dwarf, in his new character, bestirred himself.

He procured an inquest on the body of Sir William Blakesley, although that gentleman had, apparently, died of a lingering disease.

Upon his body being opened there were certain strange appearances visible, which were not to be accounted for; but no absolute evidence of foul play could be adduced.

So the affair was hushed up, and Mr. James Tyrrel Blakesley remained at Blakesley Hall as a guardian to the young Sir Edgar, who was, at the time of his father's death, fourteen years of age.

Lady Caroline wore her weeds in sore trouble.

Not that she was so absolutely inconsolable for her husband's loss.

That was scarcely the fact.

But her relative was excessively intrusive, excessively tyrannical, and apparently fond of her to an alarming degree.

Her husband had been scarcely dead a month when he pestered her to marry him.

"Do you, then, wish me to be considered a murderer as well as yourself?" replied Lady Caroline, with a weak display of indignation.

"Murderer!" exclaimed James, with a suppressed laugh, "I don't understand your compliments, they are so very peculiar. But, at any rate, as you so strongly object I will not press you at present. I only wish to be certain on the point."

"Upon what point, sir?"

"Whether you will ultimately marry me," replied James, "I have set my mind on marrying you."

"What can you see in me?" simpered Lady Caroline.

"See in you!" exclaimed James Tyrrel Blakesley with affected enthusiasm, "why, dear me, Lady Caroline, you do yourself an injustice. Believe me that, at the present moment, if I did not know your age, I should take you for five and twenty."

This was the compliment which won Lady Caroline's heart.

She allowed James Blakesley to sit close to her, to take her hand, and even to pass his arm round her waist.

Then a sense of wrong came over her.

She repulsed him.

James was surprised.

"Why do you repulse me?" asked he.

"I have done wrong," she answered, blushing. "I must not allow this now."

"But when may I hope?"

"You may not hope now, but only hope in the future."

"But you are so indefinite," urged James, who saw the future already in his grasp.

"I am obliged to be."

"No, not to me. I will confide in no one. Tell me, dear Caroline, when it shall be?"

Lady Caroline blushed violently, and, after a few moments' thought, answered,

"In a twelvemonth after my husband's death I will marry you. But, of course, that depends upon your behaviour in the meantime."

James Tyrrel Blakesley smiled.

Oh! what a "smile" was there!

"Dear Caroline," he said, in a voice apparently broken by emotion, "you have made me happy, very, very happy; believe me that, during my period of probation, you shall have no occasion to complain of me."

"During his period of probation," he said.

He was right.

But as to his conduct afterwards—what then?

CHAPTER CVI.

A MOTHER'S ANGER.

THE twelvemonth passed quickly.

The familiarity of Mr. James Tyrrel Blakesley and Lady Caroline was for a long time the subject of conversation, and prior to the end of the period of probation it was noised about everywhere that a marriage was in contemplation between them.

The wedding was fixed for the 14th of January.

On the 13th of January a light might have been seen streaming across the green lane which skirted the dell at the edge of Blakesley Park.

Angry voices were waging a wordy warfare inside the little cottage which overhung the glen, near the ruins where, a year afterwards, Sir Edgar Blakesley was attacked by his foster-brother.

"I tell you," exclaimed Madame Carabosse, for it was she, and the white-faced, cowering wretch to whom she spoke was James Tyrrell Blakesley—"I tell you, you shall not marry her. I will come into the church and proclaim to the world how you seduced my daughter by a false marriage, and then abandoned and killed her."

The woman was very old, and her voice trembled with age and anger.

"I have told you, again and again," said he, "that I am not the man. Philip is the son of the Prince Regent—he is *not* my son."

"You lie!—he is your son," cried Madame Carabosse, who had an interest in standing by her story.

"Why, then, did your daughter deny my identity when I came to assume my position as a husband?" said James, with a diabolical grin.

"Because she desired to be rid of you," answered Madame Carabosse; "but that will avail you nothing. You were the cause of my daughter's death, and you shall suffer for it."

"D——n!" cried James Tyrrel Blakesley, pacing up and down the room in great anger. "You know in your own mind that, as I am not the father of Philip Carabosse, I cannot be the cause of her death. Why, then, pursue me?"

"If it were as you say, you would still be my enemy," said the old woman. "The very fact of your being the Prince Regent's friend would make me hate you. But it is folly to talk of this—you were my daughter's husband, you are her murderer. You never shall wed Lady Caroline Blakesley."

"You may do as you please, mad woman," cried he. "I defy you."

"We will see," said his companion; "you will be in the church, so will I. But I shall come with the officers of justice."

"You forget yourself," said James Tyrrel Blakesley; "you do not remember that your daughter died a natural death."

"Natural death!" shrieked Madame Carabosse. "Call you a broken heart a natural death? She died when you abandoned, deserted, and insulted her. Aye, and her curse rings on my ear now—that terrible curse of hers on you and yours."

James Tyrrel Blakesley ground his teeth, and walked angrily up and down the room."

The old woman watched his changing countenance, and grinned horribly when she saw him turn pale.

"Ah!" she muttered between her teeth, "you fear me, I see."

"Fear you!—no; but I feel hatred and contempt for your perjuries."

"Perjuries, eh!" shrieked Madame Carabosse, "perjuries, eh! You will find that I tell the truth, and that they will believe me, too."

"They will look upon you as some mad woman, and turn you out of the church," said he, savagely.

"Turn me out!" cried she; "yes, but in order to be turned out I must be there first, and before they have time to send me away I will have said my say, and stopped the marriage."

James Tyrrel Blakesley vouchsafed no reply, but turned abruptly and left the cottage.

The old woman, muttering heavy curses, undressed herself, and was soon wrapt in sleep.

CHAPTER CVII.

TEMPTATION.

IT was a lovely night as James Tyrrel Blakesley emerged from the glen cottage, and sped along the green lane.

Strange thoughts agitated his mind.

He was upon the eve of accomplishing that which he most desired in life—marrying a woman with a large fortune, and thus securing to himself, as he imagined, a competency without performing that which he hated more than anything in the world—labouring for his daily bread like other honest men.

But the warnings of the old woman he had just left were not without their effect.

Though well knowing that he was not the father of Philip Carabosse, and that his mother had died by natural death, he could not conceal from himself the fact that an exposure of the affair would do him infinite injury.

What, then, could he do?

How could he stop her mouth?—how avoid this humiliation?

He was in this train of thought when he saw, walking slowly along the lane, a tall, slight figure.

"Ah, Philip!—he will do this," exclaimed James, and he hurried towards the new comer.

"Ah, Philip!" exclaimed he cordially, "how are you? You are out late to-night."

"No, not later than usual," drawled the precocious youth. "I generally retire about twelve."

"Well, I want to have a chat with you," said his companion; "so come up to the Hall with me, and have a weed and a glass of grog."

This was treating him like a man—just what Philip liked.

"Very well," said he, "I will come up. Anything new on?"

"No, nothing particular."

"Why, you're going to be married, old cock, to-morrow—isn't that something new?"

"Nothing very fresh about my bride, I'm thinking," said James, as they entered the Hall; "but enter softly, my boy. I have particular reasons why they should not know at what hour I came home to-night."

"Where is Sir Edgar?" asked Philip, as they sat down by the dining-room fire.

"He's gone to bed, I suppose," returned James Tyrrel Blakesley.

"Pooh!" remarked the conceited young fellow; "he's quite as old as I am, and yet he is sent to bed like a child."

"It's his own choice."

"Well, he's only a milksop; we'll dismiss him from the conversation," pursued Philip. "What have you brought me down here for?"

"Why, I'll tell you the exact truth," said James Tyrrel Blakesley, clearing his throat as if about to say something very important, the fact is, that your grandmother has anything but friendly ideas towards me, and intends to-morrow to do something disagreeable towards me in the church. Now I want her kept away if possible."

"How is that to be done?" said Philip, puffing away vigorously at his cigar.

"You can do it for me if you like," said his companion.

"I!" cried Philip, in surprise.

"Yes, you better than any one."

"Well, I'll do it, if you'll tell me how," said Philip, rather pleased than otherwise at being chosen for such a task. "Am I to shut the old woman in her room, or not?"

"No, no, that would be but clumsy work. She takes her grog to bed with her, does she not?

"Yes," answered Philip, anxiously.

"Well, I have here a sleeping potion," said James Tyrrel Blakesley, "which, if put into her grog, will keep her asleep all day to-morrow. Don't put too much in, as it might make her ill."

"I don't half like it," said Philip.

"Why, d—n it all, man—what is there to be afraid of?" cried Blakesley. "She will only sleep a little later than usual—that is all. Come, take the bottle."

Philip took the bottle mechanically.

"Very well," said he, "but I am hanged if I like it much."

"My dear fellow," cried James Tyrrel Blakesley, patting him on the shoulder, "there is no danger—there is nothing to be afraid of. If you are afraid of the old woman waking up too soon, and kicking up a dust, lock the door, and be one of the guests at my wedding."

This was exactly what Philip Carabosse desired.

"Oh! yes, I should like that very much," said he.

"Well, have another glass of grog," cried James, "and then trot off, or you will not have time."

Philip poured out a glass of raw spirits, drank it off, and, after shaking hands with James, left the house.

The spirits had their effect.

He was quite intoxicated.

Staggering and stumbling along the green lanes, and almost falling into every ditch, he at length reached the cottage.

Everything was quiet.

It was very dark, too.

And Philip, being beside himself with drink, had strange visions, and imagined that a tall phantom, with dark visage and long unearthly arms, was beckoning him to enter and perform his task.

Strange !

But, then, drunken people see strange things.

CHAPTER CVIII.

A MARRIAGE OF CONVENIENCE.

THERE are three important eras of our life—birth, marriage, and death; the intermediate one being only important if it happen but once.

Birth is, of course, an all important and necessary matter, but marriage has something in it more important and more serious still.

Prior to a man's birth there is no necessity or call for his particular existence. If he were to remain for ever unborn there would not be any loss to mankind, or to himself in his peculiar case, and therefore neither to himself nor to others is birth so solemn and important a thing as some would have us imagine.

But when a man is born, and has passed through the stages of his early years, he looks about him for a companion, with whom he may thread the intricate mazes of life—with whom he may live the easy, voluptuous life of the rich, the quiet life of the gentility, the busy life of the trading classes, or the toilsome labours of the poor.

In a very few instances, indeed, has he more than a short period allowed him to suspect the character of the one who is to be his partner in life, in some instances not more than a month or so.

However long, or however brief the duration of a "courtship," as it is vulgarly called, may be, marriage is a solemn thing.

Briefness of acquaintance will increase its importance; no length of knowledge will absolutely do away with it.

No certainty can exist in our minds that we are choosing the right person; no certainty that, when we have given up our happiness, our fortunes, our lives, in fact, to one person, we shall find in that one person the being we seek.

We may find her uncompanionable, unsociable, unkind, unmotherly, or we may find him surly, ill-tempered, undomestic, and unfatherly.

Marriages made up in ball rooms, and any public and private meetings, are scarcely ever happy, unless persons of the same temperament happen, by chance, to come together, which, under such circumstances, is very rarely the case.

Home is the place where the true aspect of a woman's heart can be discovered.

The frank, gay, good-natured flirt of the ball room may be the shrew, the tyrant, the domineering elder sister of home.

The girl who wins your heart by the kind manner in which she speaks to her aged parents, or to a younger sister, may be a perfect devil in human shape when the veil of this flimsy outside life is lifted.

And yet men and women fancy that, in an evening, they can discover one another's characters.

How, in a few evenings, can we find out all the intricate workings of the heart ?

How can we read, in so brief a space of time, the book of the affections; how are we to know that our tempers, our educations, our tastes, our habits are congenial; how can we tell that the companion of an evening will be a companion for life ?

But, on the other hand, I imagine that people are in the wrong who, like Ovid, urge the necessity of long delay in matters of this kind.

Protracted courtships are, in my opinion, as bad as short courtships.

Why, I do not pretend to say, but somehow or another people get ill-tempered and dissatisfied with each other, and those who have thus been married, and might have lived happily enough together, become sour and morbid, and when they do marry generally fail to find what they seek.

Delay, says Crabbe :—

> "Delay shall knowledge yield on either part,
> And show the value of the vanquished heart :
> The humours, passions, merits, failings prove,
> And gently raise the veil that's won by love.
> Love—that impatient guide too proud to think
> Of vulgar wants—of clothing, meat, and drink,
> Urges our amorous swains their joys to seize,
> And then at rags, to hunger, frightened flees.

This is all very well; but, were people to follow such precepts as these, how many would marry ?

Not one quarter, not one-half of those who do so now.

Numbers of persons are born into the world who have no prospect before them in life but poverty. Why not teach them to make the most of this poverty; to build for themselves as much happiness, to obtain for themselves as much pleasure, as much comfort for this poverty as they can ?

People, moreover, are always happier who marry when they are still young, provided they do not marry before they can fully appreciate the magnitude of the step they are taking.

And why ? Because the woman who has striven with you, and helped you through adversity, is just the one to make you happy in prosperity.

When no exertions are required, when no sacrifices are called for, when all is easy and ready to hand, there is not the necessity for half so much exercise of affection as there is when we have to struggle through life together in our early life, to settle down in comfort, and, perhaps, affluence, in the vale of years.

There was not much romance in the marriage which took place at Blakesley Hall.

Both the contracting parties were far from being juveniles.

James Tyrrel Blakesley was at least forty, while Lady Caroline herself was thirty-five.

A large party assembled there, and many remarks, of a very peculiar kind, were passed in regard to the wedding.

Sir Edgar Blakesley, a fine fellow of fifteen, was one of the principal guests, while his foster-brother, Philip Carabosse, was also there.

The party proceeded to the little village church near amid the acclamations of the facile neighbours.

Philip Carabosse, as well as the "happy" bridegroom, was very pale.

Something seemed to terrify him.

Ever and anon he would start and turn round and seem anxiously expecting some one, or fearing the approach of some evil.

However, the ceremony went off exceedingly well.

No one was there to interfere with the affair, and James Tyrrel and Lady Caroline Blakesley arrived at the hall as man and wife.

Madame Carabosse did not accomplish her threat.

Why?

CHAPTER CIX.

THE BLACK PHANTOM.

So the Black Phantom beckoned Philip Carabosse into the cottage.

He reeled in, closed the door behind him, and stood for a moment hesitating at the threshold.

A lamp still burned in the room where the old lady slept.

He cautiously pushed open the door, and slipped in.

She slept profoundly.

The lamp burned dimly.

A half emptied glass stood on the table.

Philip approached stealthily.

She moved uneasily in her sleep.

Philip started.

"Thus conscience doth make cowards of us all."

The Black Phantom seemed to be hovering over him, and laughing at his timidity.

He approached again ; and, after carefully surveying the countenance of the sleeping woman, he poured the contents of the phial into the glass.

He poured it all in !

Then, as if he had committed a crime, he rushed out of the room, and locked himself in his own chamber.

Sleep came to him easily.

He had drunk deeply, and, although his terror had somewhat sobered him, still his eyes were heavy.

But, though he slumbered, his dreams were such as to chill his very heart's blood.

He dreamed that, instead of administering to his grandmother a sleeping potion, he had given her poison, and that she had died in horrible convulsions, cursing him for her murder.

Then he saw himself dragged to the scaffold ; he could behold the great heaving crowd watching for his arrival; he could hear the yell of the crowd; he could feel the executioner placing the cord around his neck, and then all was dark, and he awoke with a cry.

It was morning.

"And jocund day
Stands tip-toe on the misty mountain tops."

Yet a grey, indistinct light was glimmering into his bed-room.

His dream had worked sadly upon his feelings.

He almost feared to rise and dress himself; but at length, summoning up courage, he slipt on his things and crept stealthily down into his grandmother's room.

All was as still as death.

There she lay, almost in the same position as that in which he had left her.

"Hang this," cried Philip, "I don't half like it. I think now I shall wake the old woman up."

So saying he approached the bed, and gently touched her face.

She moved not.

Philip was terrified.

A cold sweat seemed to be upon her brow ; and her face appeared contracted by some inward agony.

He shook her violently.

She made no sign.

He shook her again impatiently.

She moved not.

She was quite cold. Alas ! he could not doubt that she was dead.

Shuddering — pale and frightened — Philip Carabosse left the house and took his way towards Blakesley Hall.

He ran along the green lane and across the grounds as if some one were pursuing him ; as if, indeed, the Black Phantom was still waving his dark arms above him.

He met James Tyrrel Blakesley at the door of the hall.

"What is the matter, my boy ?" asked James.

"I gave her the medicine last night," said Philip. "But I am so frightened. She stirs not."

"How much did you give her ?" asked James.

"The whole, and she will not wake, although I shook her."

"Nor will she ever wake," said James Tyrrel Blakesley, "for you have killed her ! You gave twice the quantity I told you."

CHAPTER CX.

IN THE POWER OF THE BLACK PHANTOM.

PHILIP CARABOSSE buried his face in his hands.

A dim presentiment of evil had foreshadowed him before this.

Now it was a certainty.

"Have I, then, killed her accidentally !" he said, in a very low voice.

"Yes," replied James Tyrrel Blakesley, "you

have indeed. But be not afraid, it will not be discovered."

The boy looked up in surprise.

There was something in the tone of the man's voice which he did not like, and he knew, moreover, that there would be an investigation into the manner of her death.

"Why, of course, it will be found out," he said. "There will be a coroner's inquest on the body, and they will say she was poisoned."

"That medicine dissolves and dissipates so rapidly," replied James, "that it is never discovered in the body after death."

A dark cloud passed over the brow of Philip Carabosse.

"How do you know that?" he asked suspiciously.

"I was told so by the person who made up the prescription," returned James, hurriedly. Then he added, "As the cottage is now empty it will be scarcely pleasant for you to remain there. You had better come up to the hall to live."

Philip's eyes glistened.

"Very well," he said, "I will, and you will see I am held harmless in this affair."

"Yes, yes, I will do all that," said James, impatiently; "you are very chicken-hearted. You made a mistake; so do the best of us sometimes. There is nothing to worry yourself or others about in that."

The mysterious death of Madame Carabosse made very little stir in the neighbourhood.

Had she been a person of any consequence in

the county there would have been an inquest and a searching investigation.

As it was, the affair was slurred over.

She had died from bodily exhaustion, the doctors said.

She was an old and an ugly woman, so they did not care for the job of dissecting her. She was buried quietly on the hill-side, and nobody thought any more of the matter.

And Philip Carabosse left the cottage, and went to live at Blakesly Hall.

He and the young Sir Edgar, being about the same age, very soon became inseparable companions.

They were always together, either boating, or fishing, or shooting; and any stranger who saw them would at once have imagined that they were sworn friends.

But he would have been greatly in error.

On one side, no doubt, it was all true friendship.

Sir Edgar Blakesly was a brave, warm-hearted, frank fellow, never at a loss if any kind action was to be done, but never consenting to the smallest thing which would cause pain to another.

Philip, on other hand, was beginning to exhibit signs of a disposition exactly similar to that of James Tyrrel Blakesly.

Greedy, ungenerous, and selfish, he would be angry at the slightest symptom of favour towards the young baronet; and, finding himself encouraged in his petty spite by his reputed father, he soon began to prove himself anything but a friend to his young companion.

Then, as suddenly, his demeanour changed.

He had evidently fostered in his brain some deep plan of villany.

He begged Sir Edgar to forgive him for his moroseness; endeavoured to prove himself as great a friend as ever, and succeeded.

The young baronet had no suspicions of his honesty, and, accordingly, trusted him.

He did not know into what further abysses of iniquity and shame the Black Phantom was hurrying him.

*   *   *   *   *

"What is that?" cried Philip, in alarm.

He was seated alone by the waters of the stream which meandered along the edge of Blakesly Park.

The night was very dark.

Scarcely a star was visible; and even the rustle of a falling leaf was sufficient, in that death-like stillness, to cause a momentary feeling of alarm.

Matters were going on strangely at the hall.

James Tyrrel Blakesley was continually throwing out dark hints as to his conduct in the future; hints which he could not understand, but which were sufficient to prove to him how utterly unscrupulous was the character of the man into whose power he had fallen.

He was sitting there thinking of what decisive plan he should adopt.

His life at the hall was anything but pleasant.

He had begun to be ambitious, and the monotonous existence to which he was condemned gave little promise of a bright future

In the midst of his reverie he heard a step approaching.

"What is that?" he cried.

"It is I!" exclaimed a well-known voice. "I have come here because no one can overhear us."

The new comer now came forward, and sat down on the trunk of the tree beside him.

It was James Tyrrel Blakesly.

"Philip," said he, "I see you are discontented here; and, what is more, I know why."

"Why is it then?"

"You are envious of Sir Edgar."

The idea had never yet presented itself to Philip Carabosse exactly in this form; but it was, nevertheless, the truth.

"Well, and what if I am," returned he, surlily, "its no use envying him. I can never be in his place."

"I don't know that," said James, insidiously; "perhaps you may, by acting properly.

"How?" asked Philip, in a hoarse, thick voice.

Blakesley looked round him as if the very trees had ears, and then, leaning forward towards Philip, said, in a low tone,

"Do you remember the golden drops which you gave to your grandmother, and which threw her into such a deep sleep?"

"Aye, well."

"You are exactly like Sir Edgar in appearance, with the exception of your hair. Your features and figure are so similar that you have been mistaken for one another. Sir Edgar can drink some of these drops gradually.. They will kill him by degrees. When he is near his time you can propose an escape to sea. He can disappear by the way. You can obtain an appointment in the name of Sir Edgar, and, after awhile, return and claim the estate. Do you follow me?"

"Yes," was all that Philip could answer.

He sat there, bathed in a cold sweat; his teeth chattering; every limb in his body shivering.

"And will you do it?" asked James.

"Oh! I don't know," cried the boy, burying his face in his hands.

"This will bring you a fortune and a title," continued the tempter. "It can never be discovered; and, if any question arises, *I* can identify you."

The boy answered not.

"If you do this I will assist you," continued James; and, by our united efforts, you shall be the heir to Blakesley Hall and a baronetcy; otherwise you must remain contented in the position which I have destined for you."

"What is that?" enquired Philip, eagerly.

"Mr. Snaffles, the lawyer, has offered to take you into his copying-room next Monday at a salary of four shillings a week, to be increased when you are twenty to fifteen shillings. This is very good in these times."

"I will not go to him."

"I do not wish you to do so. But you must do one or the other."

"Well, then, I'll do—*the other*," said Philip, in a low tone.

"That's right!" cried James Tyrrel Blakesley, as heartily as if the lad had made some golden promise of good behaviour for the future. "Good night, Sir Edgar; good night."

So the tempter went away; while Philip Carabosse sat gazing in agony at the dark waters of the little stream.

Then, after a few moments' thought, he also rose and went; his whole frame trembling with violent emotion; his eyes wandering round uneasily, as if, every instant, expecting to behold the Great Black Phantom extending his threatening arms above him.

Scarcely had he disappeared when from behind the brushwood, near which those hellish conspirators had been sitting, emerged a short, thick figure, which, after standing a moment and shaking its fist at the retreating pair, struck off into the high road by the glen.

It was Goldie Gordon, the Blue Dwarf.

CHAPTER CXI.

RAISING THE WIND.

PREJUDICE is bad.

A truism, indeed, is this, but it never loses anything by repetition.

In many instances, however, it has some reason in its root; we should find that all there was not rottenness and decay.

In general people hate, oppress, and despise the Jews.

Fancy, and imagination, and high flying intellects give to them the character of a race unjustly despised and ill-used, and many imagine that, by setting themselves up as the champions of Israelites, they are displaying their magnanimity and their contempt for the ill-judging many.

But how does prejudice in the first instance originate?

Not, as most people suppose, from great public reason of religion, but from private feeling.

If there is any petty transaction going on a Jew is sure to be in it—thefts, embezzlements, frauds of all kinds, usury, incitation to crime— every imaginable degree of dishonesty, the more paltry the more sure, has certainly among its first originators a member of the Jewish persuasion.

Moses Abrahams, the Jew, a usurer, resided in ——— Street, London.

His house, being a strictly private and confidential one, was quite like the establishment of a gentleman of fashion.

All his debtors were "his friends;" and as for his creditors, they had scarcely any existence, for Moses Abrahams always paid in ready money, and took devilish good care that others did the same.

Moses Abrahams was an especial friend of James Tyrrel Blakesley, and when, therefore, he knew he was required at the hall, he was immediately in attendance.

They had often done business together, and whether the credit of his own signature, or on that of some one else's, James had always contrived to pay: and now and then, by way of keeping up the friendship, had sent him "a good dish" shot by himself in Sir William's preserves.

Moses Abrahams always represented to his friends that they were peculiarly favoured.

Each one who fingered his money was told that he alone was the one who received such benefits. He invariably requested him in the most friendly way not to mention "these little matters" to people out of doors, as he assured him he would do nothing of the kind for any one but such an old friend as he was.

"Ah! Mr. Blakesley, I am most glad to shee you," said Moses, as James swaggered into the drawing-room at the hall. "I hope it may be in my power to assist you. I must say that last bill was paid to the moment, just like a gentleman, as you always are."

"Why, yes," replied James, without noticing the soft soap, "I think you can assist me if you will. I want twice as much as I had of you before. It is absolutely necessary that I should have two thousand pounds to-morrow morning. Can you let me have them?"

James was aware that a week from that time would, in reality, be just as convenient for him.

"I wonder how long Sir Edgar might last now?"

"I am sure I do not know," said James. "Please God he will last some time."

"Mai Got!" exclaimed the Jew, "but it would be a fine thing if you had the property."

James trembled in every limb, as he answered,

"Well, I may have it in good time. What can be done meanwhile?"

"A bold hand and heart can do anything," said the Jew.

"I do not understand you," said James, who could not believe that the Jew shared his thoughts.

"Something might happen to Sir Edgar," said the Jew. Then he added, leaning over towards his victim, "it could easily be done!"

James trembled as the old man gazed fixedly at him, and firmly and slowly repeated the words of temptation.

He was a great villain, but, as I have said, the thought of murder had never, for one moment, existence in his mind.

He considered a moment.

Moses urged upon the golden opportunity, and brought out, in the most vivid colours, the advantages which would accrue to him if he would consent not to murder Sir Edgar, but to be a silent spectator of passing events.

The young man now raised his eyes off the ground, as the tempter, with one finger on his arm, hissed into his ear the diabolical scheme he had been concocting.

His thoughts travelled faster than those of the old Jew.

Dim visions of boyhood presented themselves to his mind; visions of scenes, in the innocence of which he could never again share; visions in which a mother's tender fear and a father's smile were the prominent features; visions, too, of a merry school time, and village maidens, and boyish delights and indulgences.

Then came the voice of the tempter, painting, in the brightest colours, the future, which apparently was within his grasp.

Wild scenes of gaiety, unbounded riches, scenes of revelry, in which he would receive the adulations of admiring and hypocritical parasites.

When he would be treated as a king, and be invested with "the little brief authority," which wealth always enables a man to wield.

It was not the words of Moses Abrahams so much as the aspirations his words called forth that determined him to carry out the murder of Sir Edgar, which he resolved, however, to leave in the hands of another.

"I will see about this," he said, as he showed Moses Abrahams out.

"Aye, do it at once," replied the placid Israelite; "there is nothing like the present time."

It was on the evening of this day that James Tyrrel Blakesley saw Philip on the side of the stream.

CHAPTER CXII.

SLOW MURDER.

SIR EDGAR BLAKESLEY'S health began to fail.

He had never been a delicate child, but somehow or another his cheeks began to wax pale, his eyes seemed to lose their lustre, and he became averse to the boisterous exercises in which he had been wont to engage with his companion Philip Carabosse.

Philip, on the other hand, began to be extremely morose and discontented.

There were frequent quarrels, not only between him and his father, but also between him and Sir Edgar.

Lady Caroline—poor, weak creature—had too late discovered what a villain and a wretch she had married, and saw, hopelessly, the cruelty which he daily practised towards her beloved and only child.

Sir Edgar rarely complained, but the paleness of his cheeks, the listlessness of his movements, the evident inward misery he felt, were all by her attributed to the unkindness of James, with whom she dared not expostulate upon the point.

In the commencement of our narrative we mentioned the manner in which the stepfather behaved to Sir Edgar.

He adopted towards him a course of haughty superiority, which, to the high-spirited and sensitive lad, was peculiarly offensive.

He treated him like a child; snubbed him when he spoke, and precluded him from sitting at table when company was present, while very often Philip Carabosse took his place.

It was then that Sir Edgar began to suffer in health.

Then James Tyrrel Blakesley went to town for a week, and, when he returned, the illness of the youth appeared to increase.

Then it was that these ghostly shadows on the wall might have been seen flitting about the passages of the old mansion.

But the wretch was not to have his wish.

Utterly disgusted with his home, vague terror assailing him, his mother powerless to defend him, he determined to run away to sea.

It was about a week after the conversation of Philip Carabosse with James Tyrrel Blakesley by the fish stream side that Philip's bedroom door opened, and Sir Edgar entered.

"Who's that?" cried Philip, in a trembling voice.

"Conscience doth make cowards of us all."

He knew his own evil thoughts and evil designs, and imagined that the Black Phantom was at length coming to torment him.

"Who's that?" he cried.

"It's I, Sir Edgar," said the new comer. "I have got something to tell you."

" What is it?"

"I am going to run away to sea," exclaimed the boy; "you see I can't stand this any longer. Mr. Blakesley is unbearable. I'm sick of his tyranny, and mother has not got the strength to prevent his doing just as he has done. So I'm going to cut and run. Will you come with me, Philip?"

Philip turned very pale.

Fortunately it was very dark.

Sir Edgar would have wondered at the very strange expression which first crossed his features, and then at the spasms of agony which followed.

It seemed, indeed, as if destiny were pressing him onward to the commission of the crime.

Here was Sir Edgar himself proposing what James Tyrrel Blakesley had so much wished.

He immediately answered—

"Yes, I will come. I, too, hate the place. We will go to-morrow night. Have you many things to pack up?"

"No, I only have to collect documents to prove my identity," replied Sir Edgar. "All these I can obtain to-morrow. These will enable me to enter the royal navy, and my friend, Sir Edmund Crossley, will doubtless help you too."

"That's all right, then," said Philip, or Dick, as Sir Edgar usually called him; "I will be ready. If you will provide the documents I will undertake to get the blunt and the disguises."

After a few more verbal preparations the two boys parted.

Philip never closed his eyes that night.

Here was Sir Edgar, as we have seen, proposing the exact scheme which James had so fondly desired.

Should he tell him?

No.

And why?

This boy — whose cunning had something truly infernal in it—had fathomed that man's motives, and determined to thwart his designs.

James Tyrrel Blakesley had been extremely cautious in the affair.

He had kept himself aloof from any transaction which would implicate him as an accomplice in the crime.

It was invariably Philip's hand which administered the slow poison.

It was invariably Philip who, in the dead of the night, stole into the baronet's bedroom, and changed the bottles of medicine.

In the first instance the young accomplice failed to penetrate the design which prompted these cautious proceedings.

Now he saw it all.

James Tyrrel Blakesley wished Sir Edgar to go away to sea with Philip Carabosse; he desired the latter to murder his companion and assume the title if he chose, knowing well he could disprove his identity, and, as next heir, assure himself of the fortune and title.

The young devil's whelp, therefore, determined to use James's idea; and, to make it suit his own purpose, he would keep the flight a profound secret.

CHAPTER CXIII.

THE ROBBERY.

HAVING fully decided upon the course to pursue Philip Carabosse rose and partially dressed himself.

Then, after rummaging for some time in the large cupboard in his room, he found the object of his search—a dark lantern: and, after lighting it, he stealthily opened the door.

The night was very dark, and the house looked dark, gloomy, and mysterious.

All was quiet in Blakesley Hall, not a mouse stirred.

Closing his own door, Philip crept, cat-like, along the passage, and then descended the stairs which led to the lower portion of the building.

In the kitchen he provided himself with a long, thick-headed knife, and then, as stealthily as he had descended them, he ascended the stairs.

The room in which James Tyrrel Blakesley slept *alone* was partially open; he invariably adopted this precaution for the sake of health.

It now aided the robber in his vile scheme.

He approached the room and looked in.

A lamp, almost turned down, stood by the bed-side.

On the bed—an old massive four poster—lay James Tyrrel Blakesley in an uneasy slumber, little dreaming how his own villanous plans were recoiling upon himself.

By his side, on the table, lay a pair of pistols.

He never retired to rest without these trusty friends.

Massive curtains shaded the bed and the walls.

Everything in the room was antique, costly, and sombre.

A shudder passed through Philip's frame as he saw the pistols, for he well knew what the result of a mistake would inevitably be.

A massive bureau stood on the opposite side of the large room.

This contained the family papers, and, as Philip hoped, James Blakesley's ready money.

"This is rather a dangerous game," he thought, as the sleeper turned uneasily in his slumber; "however, here goes."

So saying, he pushed open the door, and entered the room, obscuring altogether the light of the lantern he carried, and trusting only to the dim lamp which flickered on the table by the bedside.

He advanced to the bureau and tried the lock.

It was a strong one, and even, under the gradual pressure, a slight snapping noise was occasioned.

James moved uneasily in his sleep, and half-opened his eyes.

Philip trembled.

But his alarm was causeless, his father was soon again asleep.

The lock at length yielded to the pressure, and the money lay within his reach.

His disappointment, however, was great when he discovered that, instead of counting by hundreds, as he had hoped, he could not even count by tens.

Twelve pounds was all he could discover, although, in the face of discovery, he spent an hour searching the drawers and the room.

With this, then, he was forced to be content, and he sullenly returned to his room.

On the following day the unsuspecting Sir Edgar busied himself in finding the papers necessary to his own identification, and, when they retired to their room that night, everything was ready for departure.

Our readers have read how the two adventurers succeeded; how the one, yielding to a soporific, was stabbed by the other; how Philip assumed the character of the young baronet; and how Sir Edgar was saved by the Blue Dwarf.

We are now approaching the retribution.

A criminal is, in general, very cunning, and readily comprehends the motives of other criminals.

There is, apparently, a kind of freemasonry in villany, which enables scoundrels to recognise each other at first sight, and at once to see through each other's designs.

When, therefore, James Tyrrel Blakesley was accosted by Philip, on the morning following the robbery, with the words, "Father, I want you to give me ten pounds," he answered quietly, "No, I will not lend you any. The twelve pounds you took out of my drawer last night will serve you for some time I should think."

Philip did not reply.

There was nothing to answer to this; and, moreover, he feared that a discussion would lead to a discovery.

So he wisely held his tongue, and left James Tyrrel Blakesley as wise as he was before.

CHAPTER CXIV.

SIR EDGAR'S GUARDIAN ANGEL.

THE will of Sir William Blakesley contained a secret clause, which was directed especially against James Tyrrel Blakesley.

This clause ran as follows:—

"In the case of the death of my son, Edgar Francis Sackville Blakesley, I hereby declare that I, William John Stuart Blakesley, am not the heir to the baronetcy, but only hold it under permission from John Stuart Blakesley, who is the real heir to the title of the family, as being the issue of the elder branch of the Blakesleys."

On the outside of the clause was written—

"This is not to be opened except in case Edgar Francis Sackville Blakesley is deceased."

Even in secret, then, the Blue Dwarf was the guardian angel of the young baronet !

He had often, moreover, mentioned a secret vow which he had taken in regard to him.

This vow was intimately connected with the sealed clause in the will.

Sir William Blakesley was not alone when he died.

Lady Caroline never left him. And, although James Tyrrel Blakesley again and again endeavoured to force his way into the room, all his efforts were unavailing.

He was told, first of all, politely, then rudely, that his presence was not required.

Another being watched by his bedside.

This was Sapathwa, the Blue Dwarf.

"Will you swear to me one thing ?" asked the dying man.

"Anything which will bring you comfort," said Sapathwa.

"Well, then, swear to me that, should anything happen to my son—which Heaven forbid !—you will not allow James Tyrrel Blakesley to take the fortune and the title of our family, but will assume it yourself ?"

"I will."

"And will you swear one more oath," asked Sir William Blakesley, "of a character much dearer to me still. Will you swear to me to protect and preserve him —— "

"Aye, with my life."

"Until he becomes of age, and is capable of protecting himself ?"

"I will."

"Then I die happy," said Sir William.

After a moment, he added,

"Caroline !"

"Yes, love."

"Come nearer to me."

She leaned over him.

"Do not marry again."

The dying are often selfish. Sir William could no longer bask in the sunshine of his wife's beauty, therefore he wished that none other should be warmed by a ray from her loveliness.

A spasm passed over her face for a moment.

She knew by whom she would be persecuted.

"I will not," she answered, firmly.

Poor fellow.

He fathomed the meaning of that spasm, I fancy, for he added, with a smile,

"Remember, Caroline, I only ask you this under the supposition that you feel as I do. Whenever your heart really wishes to marry, then marry again."

He then relapsed again into silence, and soon after expired.

Having taken this vow Sapathwa turned his attention especially to the safety of Sir Edgar Blakesley, who afterwards, as William Lennox, proved such a tax upon his patience.

He saw, at once, that Philip Carabosse was

being initiated into the diabolical schemes of James Tyrrel Blakesley.

He noticed the frequent visits at the hall of Minto Malespina, the Italian herbalist, who enjoyed such a vile reputation in London.

His acquaintances generally lay among young wives wedded to old, rich husbands ; young men who had married women old enough to be their grandmothers ; expectant heirs whose fathers had provokingly good health ; curates whose incumbents would not die. This worthy Sapathwa had met abroad, and knew well.

His visits to Blakesley Hall could, he was well aware, have no other than one object.

When, therefore, he observed how pale Sir Edgar Blakesley was gradually becoming he understood how the golden drops were working, and adopted measures accordingly.

He bribed the servants to allow him free access to the house.

When, therefore, Sir Edgar took his medicine, he invariably took an antidote ; so that, although the constant antagonism of different physics in his stomach made him grow pale and weak, his life was not absolutely endangered.

He overheard the whispered conference between the two boys in regard to going away to sea, but then he had also been a witness to the scene between James Tyrrel Blakesley and Philip Carabosse by the side of the fish stream, and knew well that the crisis had come.

CHAPTER CXV.

CONCLUSION OF THE BLUE DWARF'S STORY.

"When, therefore," continued Sapathwa, as his unwilling hearers were ranged round him in the Great Rat-Trap ; "when, therefore, the two boys had lowered themselves down from the window, and emerged upon the lawn, I let myself out by the back gate and followed them.

"My efforts to save Sir Edgar were twice on that evening upon the point of being unavailing.

"The hour of meeting had been fixed for one in the morning, and at twelve Sir Edgar was still buried in profound slumber.

"My usual station at night was beneath the old fourpost bedstead, upon which the young baronet slept, and I fancied that upon that night at least he would be exempted from the usual nocturnal visit of his young murderer.

"I was right.

"But, nevertheless, he had a visitor.

"The escapade was suspected and provided for.

"Shadows were moving about that old rumbling house during the whole of that night.

"Shadows here along the passages—shadows entering and emerging from rooms — and, at length, shadows coming into Sir Edgar's room.

"The moon hung like a great, white star, just on the horizon, and shone full into the room where Sir Edgar lay.

"His face and body were completely enveloped in a silver glory, and the door, too, being open, a flood of brilliance poured through it into the corridor.

"A slight rustling in the passage I heard.

"Then a man's figure appeared in the door-way, standing right in the centre of the moon-beams.

"The night goddess peered right brightly in his face.

"It was James Tyrrel Blakesley.

"The coward had entrusted the work of murder to one younger than himself, but had now summoned up sufficient of the dastardly courage common to murderers to help in the labour himself.

"He stealthily approached the bed.

"I could see by the moonlight how pale he was, and how the agonies of fear and mental torture distorted his features and shook his frame.

"Upon the table, by the bed-side, stood a bottle of medicine.

"This he took up, put in his pocket, and replaced it by another.

"Then, with trembling and faltering foot-steps, he left the bed-chamber.

"I immediately took away the poison he had left, and placed there, in its stead, the colourless liquid which served as its antidote.

"I had scarcely done this when Philip's door opened, and he came stealthily along the passage.

"I passed through a door into an ante-room, and heard all.

"'Ah!' muttered the young ruffian, 'he's asleep. Good opportunity now, only these things are always found out if done in houses. Besides, that damned blue devil may be skulk-ing about somewhere, and if he discovers me my goose is cooked.'

"After this soliloquy, so complimentary and pleasant to my feelings, the excellent young man proceeded to awaken Sir Edgar.

"'Edgar! Edgar!' he cried, 'get up.'

"'Eh? eh? what's the matter,' said he, 'is it time?'

"'Yes, yes; it is one o'clock nearly, and we've got a good way to go.'

"'All right. I shant be a moment,' said Sir Edgar, as he leaped out of bed.

"They were soon ready.

"'Now,' said Philip, 'I will go down by the ladder and see if all's right.'

"'Hadn't I better come, too?'

"'No, no. I'm often prowling about the hall, but, if the gamekeeper saw you, he'd think that something was up, and stop us.'

"He opened the window.

"The moon had disappeared, and dark clouds obscured the stars.

"Low mutterings began to be heard in the distance.

"'We're going to have a storm,' said Philip, 'but I'll be back in a few moments, and, if we're caught, we can make for the old mill.'

"He then descended.

"The few moments he was absent seemed an age to Sir Edgar.

"He paced the room eagerly, anxiously.

"Presently some gravel knocked against the window.

"'Is that you, Dick?' said he.

"'All right, Sir Edgar,' cried the other, as he re-ascended.

"Then followed the conversation, already nar-rated, in regard to ways and means. Then they both descended into the grounds, and hurried across them towards the high road.

"The storm now howled loudly over the face of nature.

The sky, lately so bright and silvery, was now covered with gloomy clouds, ever and anon parted by the arrow of the lurid lightning.

"The old mill, which Philip had mentioned, stood upon the edge of a little glen, surrounded thickly by trees and brushwood.

"A ruin it was, crumbling, mossgrown, and tottering; its cracked and tottering walls seemed to warn the passers-by not to trust to its shelter.

"It will be remembered that they had agreed to take the coach at daybreak, and proceed at once to Portsmouth, where Sir Edmund Crossley was staying.

"So, through storm and rain, they proceeded, Philip cowering beneath the shadow of the dark deed he meditated, Sir Edgar rejoicing at leaving a cruel and rapacious step-father, and a home and life he detested, and casting himself upon the free and adventurous existence of a sailor.

"I followed them.

"I guessed all was not right. Philip's words and manner had convinced me all was not right.

"They walked quickly, but I followed them, keeping them constantly in sight as they silently made their way over the three miles of ground which intervened between the hall and the mill.

"Destiny seemed, however, to be working against us.

"A vivid flash of lightning, then a deafening clap of thunder, and I lost sight of them.

"I knew their destination, however, and pressed onwards.

"The roads were heavy with mud, the fields were almost impassable, and it was a long time before I cleared them and reached the highroad on the edge of which stood the ruined mill.

"As I had imagined, I was too late.

"The drug had been administered, the dagger even then was buried in the breast of the victim, and, with a cry, the murderer was rushing away into the darkness.

"With a loud yell, which made him halt and tremble with fear, I leaped over the crumbling wall, and found my nephew weltering in his blood.

"Then I turned towards the second Cain, but he had fled out into the night, and gone to seek his reward.

"I took the form of the dying boy in my arms, and sped away towards the tents of the gipsies whose encampment stood close by Blakesly Hall.

"There he recovered, under one of those magic cordials, for which the race is so cele-brated; and there, for the first time, he met with Lilian Winterton.

"The rest of the story you all know.

"You yourselves have been so intimately

bound up in all his fortunes that I need say no more.

"You have heard the story of his early wrongs; and you will see his revenge."

CHAPTER CXVI.

THE RAT-TRAP AGAIN.

THE feelings with which the occupants of Sapathwa's drawing-room listened to the extraordinary narrative, which he gave to them, night after night, can scarcely in any way be described.

Most of those present had been mixed up in the plot against William Lennox (otherwise Sir Edgar Blakesly) either as enemies or as friends; and those who had stooped to the lowest of crimes to further their designs now would have stooped to the lowest of humiliations to escape that punishment which they saw to be inevitable.

Sapathwa they knew to be just; and therefore they feared him.

Captain Winterton endeavoured to be facetious, and said—

"Really, after this long yarn of yours, Sir John, we shall require a little fresh air."

The Blue Dwarf eyed him sternly and significantly as he answered—

"Do you, then, suppose that I have been narrating this story to you for the sake of amusement?"

"No, we don't suppose that, said the Honourable John, in his usual drawling tones, "because there's no amusement in it."

"Seriously speaking," chimed in the Duchess of Castello, "what is the object of your narration?"

"You have imagined," said the Blue Dwarf, "that I have been acting to you all the part of an enemy. You have thought that, without any reason, I have persecuted you, thwarted your plans, allowed justice to follow you. You see, now, with what object I have done all this. In William Lennox you behold Sir Edgar Blakesley; in me his uncle. When, therefore," he added, turning to James Tyrrel Blakesley, "when, therefore, you laughed at me when I presented myself as the agent of Sir John Stuart Blakesley, you were insulting that gentleman in person."

"For the sake of Sir Edgar's mother," he continued, "I shall allow the spirit of retribution to pass lightly over you, for, in spite of your murder of Sir William, I will allow you to go in peace.

"The crime was not publicly proved against you.

"Therefore I say to you, go in peace, and I only hope that your future life may be a recompense to me for my leniency."

He spoke like a despot, and they feared him.

"I shall settle my accounts with you first,' said Sapathwa to John and Frederick Winterton. "Accompany me, if you please, into this room."

He led the way into a chamber adjoining.

They followed, half in dread, half in wonder. Those left in the room looked on in surprise.

What could this mean?

What could this calm summons signify?

What evil awaited them?

Loud cries were heard in the next room.

Oaths and imprecations were distinctly wafted in through the window which adjoined that of the chamber in question.

Then, again, all was still.

Then entreaties, then a struggle, then a calm voice, speaking quietly, though authoritatively.

Then, again, a prolonged, anxious silence.

Then the Blue Dwarf reappeared.

His face was calm and rigid, his brow slightly compressed, his eyes emitting a bold glitter.

"What have you done with those men?" asked the real Sir Edgar Blakesley.

Sapathwa did not answer, but took his seat on the raised chair.

CHAPTER CXVII.

THE FORCED DUEL.

THIS is what had happened.

On entering the room, into which Sapathwa introduced them, Frederick and John Winterton started back with surprise and fear.

The room was square.

At one end was a small table, on the other were two coffins on stands.

On the table were two pairs of pistols.

Four men stood by the fire-arms, near which lay a little heap of additional ammunition.

"What means this farce?" cried Captain Frederick, who, though alarmed, began to have an idea that he was being imposed upon by child's play.

"This is no farce, sir," said Sapathwa, solemnly; "John and Frederick Winterton, your lives are forfeited to your country for the many crimes which you have committed. Your murders—your forgeries—your other atrocities—are all well known to me. Therefore I have no compunction in following the course which I feel myself called upon by justice to pursue. You must die.

"What!" shouted Captain Winterton, with a loud curse; "do you mean to murder us in cold blood."

A curl of contempt passed over the lips of the Blue Dwarf.

"I do no murder," he replied; "I perform the behests of justice."

"Then why not allow us the chance of escape," cried John Winterton; "the law may regard our lives as its own: but there is no occasion to forestal its decision. Leave to us the chances of escaping from it and becoming useful members of society."

The Honourable John was contemptibly eloquent when pleading for his own life.

Sapathwa looked at him with intense scorn.

E.B.

"It is because I know that the law *will* have its way with you," said he, "that I intend to forestall its decision. I don't wish my family to be disgraced by the fact of one of its members perishing upon the scaffold. Therefore you will die, and die here!"

"You speak authoritively," cried Captain Frederic; "you forget you cannot treat us as children. We are men—desperate men if provoked."

"Your desperation, sir, will avail you nothing with me," said Sapathwa; "but of one thing I will disabuse your mind. I mean no murder. You two have robbed—murdered—committed upheard of atrocities hand in hand—by one another's hands you shall die."

"What mean you?" said Captain Frederic.

"I mean this," said Sapathwa, "that there are pistols. You shall fight a duel and die thus. It is a more honourable death than any you could ever have hoped for."

The Honourable John turned deadly pale.

Captain Frederic, in the presence of certain danger, seemed to reserve all his courage.

"If we are to die," cried he, fiercely; "we may as well die one way as the other. We will die defending ourselves."

So saying he rushed towards the table where the pistols lay.

The four men closed round it and prevented his approach.

He seized a chair, however, and, lifting it up by the leg, shouted madly—

"If I die I'll kill others also!"

Sapathwa smiled.

"Stay," he said, waving his hand; "be not too hasty."

They saw in his gesture a chance of his relenting.

They were wrong.

That wave of the hand was their death warrant.

As Captain Winterton placed the chair again on the ground, both he and the Honourable John were seized from behind and pinioned by the four men who had stood by the table.

"Then you will murder us if we do not consent to commit suicide," shrieked Captain Frederic.

"Mark me," said the Blue Dwarf, "you die this day, either as I have told you, or by the hands of an executioner. Jacques," he added to the black servant, who constituted one of the four, "bring in the rope."

The black servant departed, and, in a few moments, returned with a long, thick rope.

This he ran up by a pulley, so that it formed a double gallows.

"Choose now," cried Sapathwa, "the gallows or the duel."

His eyes glared—he spoke excitedly.

Captain Frederic spoke not.

His face became still more deadly pale, while the Honourable John trembled like an aspen-leaf.

The men proceeded with their deadly task.

The ropes were fixed—the nooses prepared.

"Now," said Sapathwa, "I give you one more chance. Recollect I have no mercy; choose the duel or the gallows."

"I choose," cried Captain Winterton, with a wild glare in his eyes, "the duel."

"You have chosen well," said Sapathwa. "As far as you have injured me I forgive you both. Farewell."

He turned to go.

Captain Winterton detained him with a gesture.

"What do you wish?" asked Sapathwa.

"Two quarts of brandy," answered Captain Frederic.

"You shall have them," replied the Blue Dwarf. "And now, once more, farewell."

CHAPTER CXVIII.

"GIVE not a thought to care or woe,
But drown them in the bowl."
SONG.

"WELL," cried Captain Frederic Winterton, "as we are to die, John, let's die game. Here's brandy; take a swig, and let's be jolly together for the last time."

The Honourable John did not seem quite to see the force of his cousin's argument.

He sat, pale and trembling, in the chair he had occupied when Sapathwa left the room, allowing himself mechanically to be unfettered, and as mechanically lifting the tumbler of raw brandy to his lips.

His teeth chattered—his tongue refused its office.

So Captain Frederic had all the talk to himself.

"How now?" cried that worthy to the black servant; "have you no manners? Let's have some cigars—some hot water—some sugar—some lemon! I'm not going to sit here, upon my last debauch, and drink fire to scald my throat. I'm not a salamander—let's have water.

"Now, then, my hearty," he shouted, slapping the Honourable John on the shoulder, "wake up. Imagine you're at the 'Hummums'—fancy we've got a couple of pretty girls by our side, and forget that we're playing tragedy instead of comedy."

The Honourable John was now a little more lively.

The brandy unloosed his tongue, and cleared his head slightly.

"It's all devilish fine your being so jolly," said he, "but I don't like it."

"What's the use of disliking it when there's no alternative," philosophically suggested Captain Frederic.

"No alternative?" cried the other; "why you never tried. He told you you were to die. and you say, 'Oh! very well; I'll die, only give me some brandy.'"

Captain Frederic laughed long and loudly.

"Well done, old stick," cried he; "why, you're getting quite facetious over it."

"But you don't answer me."

"Because I can't."

"Why, I say, you consented at once; why not try our strength with those men?" he added, in a loud tone.

"Hopeless, I fear," said the captain, glancing at the four men, who stood, as rigid as statues, with the instruments of death in their hands. "Devil take his precautions," he added, "there's not the slightest hope, so here goes."

He drank off another half tumbler of raw spirits, John did the same, and their courage began to be reanimated.

"We'll die like brave boys, as we always have been," said they, grasping each other's hands in drunken friendship.

"And now," cried the captain, "to pass away the time, I'll give you a song."

"'That's right, old boy," said the Honourable John, regarding him with a kind of awe-struck admiration; "you're a game bird. Give us a good ditty, and I'll join in chorus."

They were utterly depraved, these men.

At all times human nature was seen in them in as bad a light as she could well be.

They had, throughout their lives, dared everything.

Law and justice they regarded as mere playthings.

Honour existed not in their vocabulary.

They, in truth, though soldiers of Fortune, were the merest tag-rag and bobtail of her followers.

Now, when placed by the Blue Dwarf in their present terrible position, they had not one soul to whom they could turn for assistance.

Such men as these never make friends.

Friendship to them is a folly—a thing to be jeered and scoffed at—and so, when they needed its kind offices, it was not to be found.

They were too absolutely wicked, too depraved to seek help where alone help could be obtained.

They simply cursed the man who considered himself called upon by inexorable justice to punish them with death, and resolved to die, as they had lived, in folly and deadly sin.

The Honourable John acted thus from sheer stupidity and crushing fear.

Captain Frederic Winterton, on the contrary, performed his part in the drama because, although a bad man, he was a bold one—as courageous as a lion, reckless, daring always, and now rendered more so by sheer despair.

So, before his senses gave way under the influence of fierce, intoxicating drink, he gave vent to his devil's glee in a song which ran somewhat as follows:—

"Sing! sing! there is nothing like singing:
  The stars sing above us, the ocean below;
The trees, in delight, their old branches are swinging,
  As through them the squalling winds go.

Sing! sing! there is nothing like music,
  In weal or in woe, to shorten the day:
Are you merry or sad? are you well or are you sick?
  The plan is the same—sing away!

Sing! sing! and ne'er in the middle stick:
  Nature herself is a grand medley song:
The stream and the pebble are fiddle and fiddle-stick:
  All things to music belong.

The heart of a young girl is but a piano
  For love, with his magical fingers, to play:
Mar not the beautiful strain, naughty man, O!
  But sing, sing away, sing away.*"

"Capital, capital!" cried the Honourable John. "You're a first-rate fellow, you are. It's a pity we've got to part company so soon."

"Part company," laughed Captain Frederic, "what makes you think that? Don't make any mistake about it, my boy; sink, or swim, or die, we shall go together, be sure."

Another glass and they became maudlinly philosophical.

"After all," spluttered the Honourable John, "after—all—you—know—(hiccup)—it's what we've—(hiccup)—all got to come to."

"Just so," said Captain Frederic, half asleep.

"And it's better to die thus than run the chance of getting 'collared,' as we very nearly were in Spain," facetiously added John.

"Just so," again chimed in his more drunken companion.

"Is that all you've got to say," cried the Honourable John, indignantly.

"Just so."

"Why, you drunken fellow—(hiccup)—you nasty wretch," hiccuped John; "here its getting dark, the game's nearly up, and all you've got to say is 'just so.'"

"Just so," said Captain Frederic.

The terrible farce was now rapidly drawing to a close.

The clock struck nine.

The black servant approached.

"The time has come," he said, in a stern, yet half respectful voice.

* The above lines are from the pen of a well-known gentleman and scholar—Mr. Leitch Ritchie.

Drunk, dead drunk as they were, this summons partially sobered them.

The Honourable John cast a furtive glance of inquiry at Captain Frederic.

"Yes, my boy," cried the latter, "it's all up with us—the game is over. Give us your hand, and let us have done with it."

They both rose staggering.

Leaning against the table they extended to each other their right hands, trembling with the effects of the brandy.

"Good bye, old boy," cried the Honourable John; "good luck to you."

"Just so," said Captain Frederic; "where are the barking irons?"

"You're in a deuce of a hurry, I think," said John, who was now trembling and quivering with fear.

Captain Frederic answered not.

Drink had almost entirely obliterated his memory.

He appeared to forget that it was the game of death which he was playing, and seemed rather to imagine that he had some duty to perform that night which it was better to get rid of quickly.

A pistol was placed in each of their right hands; with their left they again shook hands.

Then, with steadier aim than might have been expected from men in such an advanced state of intoxication, they raised the weapons to a line with their heads—and fired.

They had chosen positions well.

They were too near each other to allow a chance of escape, and they fell heavily to the ground.

The black servant approached, and raised them.

They were quite dead.

So the grim tragedy was completed.

The game of death was played out, and the actors in the scene departed.

Sapathwa, in his own room, heard the sound of the fire-arms, and sighed a long sigh of relief.

CHAPTER CXIX

"It is the midnight hour:
  The house is hushed and still;
The bell of the old church tower
  Sounds loudly o'er the hill.
Yet one pale taper's light
Sheds radiance on the night."
                          M. A. BROWNE.

THE terrible retribution above described was enough for one day.

The inmates of the Great Rat-Trap were left to themselves for the rest of the few hours.

That night, however, was a terrible one.

Slimy Jones knew well what part he himself would enact in the tragedy.

He was aware that the Blue Dwarf would consider him beneath his own especial notice, and would deliver him over to be dealt with by the law.

So on this night he resolved to carry into effect a plan which he had been maturing during the whole of his sojourn in the house.

Sapathwa slept at the extreme end of the long corridor in which lay all the rooms of the prisoners.

Slimy Jones was confined in one not far from his, and for weeks past he had employed several hours each night in forcing open the lock.

He had succeeded now in loosening the fastenings so much that the slightest effort would dislodge the lock; and, as soon as the shades of night had shrouded the household, he opened the door, and crept out into the corridor.

The place was buried in profound darkness, and, as he crept along the passage, he had to feel his way.

At length he reached a room, the door of which was open.

No light was within the chamber, and the night itself was so intensely dark that nothing was visible within.

He stumbled as he entered.

The slight noise awoke the sleeper, in whom, had there been a light there, he would have recognised James Tyrrel Blakesley.

James was alarmed.

He dreaded some midnight murder.

So, when the intruder said,

"I beg your pardon, into whose room have I come?"

He answered,

"It is my room—Sapathwa's."

"Just so," said Slimy Jones. "I made a mistake."

And he glided away.

In less than ten minutes James Blakesley was again fast asleep.

Slimy Jones re-entered the room.

All was dark.

There was no fear of discovery.

He approached the bed, felt for his victim's heart, and struck.

Stab—stab—stab!

Only a sigh, scarcely a groan escaped the murdered man.

The deed was done well.

Just as he turned to go, however, the moon, suddenly peering from behind a cloud, shone full on the face of the victim.

"Great Heavens!" cried Slimy Jones, as he recognised James, "what have I done?"

Cold perspiration stood in great drops upon his brow.

A glass of brandy stood by the bedside.

"Just so," said he, as he drained it off, "this will give me courage. Eh?—damnation! what's this?"

James Tyrrel Blakesley knew little of the character of the Blue Dwarf.

Otherwise he would never have imagined that he would be selected as one of the victims of his revenge.

But so it was.

Imagining, therefore, that morning would see him in the clutches of the myrmidons of the law, he had provided well for the emergency.

It was a deadly poison which was contained in that brandy.

So deadly was it that its victim was scarcely allowed time to cry out, or to think of his fate.

Heavily, therefore, but silently, Slimy Jones fell across the bed never to rise again.

To him this fate was, perhaps, the best that could have befallen him.

He had judged rightly.

Sapathwa *would* have considered him beneath his own regard: and the morning would have seen him seized and conveyed to prison by the officers of justice.

A brief trial—the condemned cell—and the scaffold—such would have been his future.

Therefore, had he had time to reflect, he should have been grateful that, in the very commission of a crime, he found mercy.

So the Dark Phantom, which had so long hovered over the head of Philip Carabosse, now descended upon the head of him who had first tempted him to evil.

His gloomy wings flapped heavily over that house of death that dark night.

And in another chamber another scene was being enacted — almost as terrible, more pitiable.

So, when the morning broke over the household, four of the most deadly enemies of the Blue Dwarf had, by their own act, ceased to be.

It now remained for the less guilty ones to be disposed of.

CHAPTER CXX.

REPENTANCE.

LORD CHARLES LUTTERELL had been a very silent and a very attentive listener to the Blue Dwarf.

Good thoughts take a long time to enter our minds.

They seem to have some trouble to wade through the slough of evil which, as it were, encompasses our being.

But even when they do they are not fulfilled to the same extent as we could wish.

Evil thoughts, on the contrary, are very quick in coming into our minds; they do not, moreover, lie there long—the seeds burst forth, and the plant grows quickly to maturity, and finds its end.

But, for the first time in his life, Lord Charles, on that terrible evening of retribution, thought of how he could reward his brother for the patience with which he had hitherto borne his conduct.

He was influenced in this more by his own sense of growing weakness, and the remembrance of his father's parting curse, than by love for his brother Leopold.

There is something inexpressibly touching in old age.

Under whatever aspect it may appear, whether we find it in a rich mansion, or a humble cottage, or begging in the streets, there is always a kind of sadness appertaining to it.

There is a feeling in your mind which is a combination of respect, and tenderness, and pity —at least it is so with me.

I cannot help thinking that we ought to be kind and good to old people who have, in the nature of things, but very few years to live in this world; for it seems sad that they cannot, in the last moments of their existence, receive from those around them words indicative of respect and tenderness.

There is something infinitely pitiable in the sight of an aged person, with long, white hair streaming in the wind, and their poor old heads unsheltered from the "pitiless storm," standing begging in the public streets.

And there is something still more pitiable in the idea that they are compelled to look for subsistence during the last days of their life, to the alms of their fortunate and more charitable fellow creatures.

He had before him a dim vision of an aged face—a pair of straining, anxious eyes, a vacant stare.

A curse, too, rang upon his ears, long, trembling, and woeful: and, if he did not heed it then, soon it came with its full force upon him.

That night, when the Blue Dwarf's vengeance upon John and Frederic Winterton had been completed, and when Slimy Jones was wandering about the building seeking whom he should devour, he summoned Captain George and Sapathwa into his room.

They both gave an involuntary start when they saw him.

His eyes glared.

His face was haggard and wan.

His whole frame trembled.

"Leopold," he said, addressing Captain George, "I wish to make amends for the past. Before Sir John Blakesley I acknowledge (and it is unnecessary for me to acknowledge the fact before others) that you are the elder son, and, therefore, the heir to the estate. It was I who killed Arabella. Forgive me, brother, if you can."

A violent spasm crossed over the face of Captain George.

He stood for a moment irresolute.

Oh! that moment of irresolution; that interval between knowledge and forgiveness must have been one of terrible suspense!

"Yes," replied Captain George (or rather, we should term him Lord Leopold Lutterell) "I do forgive you."

"And will you allow me to go in peace?"

"Yes," replied Sapathwa, looking towards Captain George, "as far as I am concerned I am in no way interested in detaining you."

"And I," responded Lord Leopold, "can have no wish but that my brother, repenting of what evil he may have done me and others, may have time and opportunity to make that repentance good."

Lord Charles spoke not for some moments.

At length he said—

"Our poor father is dead: you are, therefore, the heir to the dukedom. All I hope is, that you may be happy in it. Now leave me."

After a few more words they left him.

Next day his place was vacant; and as Lord Charles Lutterell he was never seen again.

CHAPTER CXXI.

TWENTY YEARS AFTER.

MANY years ago there was a steady, intelligent clerk, whom people called Desmond, who ultimately became partner in the firm of Messrs. Myers, Goldschmit, and Co.

He gradually became the principal man in the house, the whole of the management of the affairs of an extensive banking establishment being entrusted to him at an early age.

The business of the house was extensive, but heavy losses had been encountered, and Desmond found himself beset with difficulties.

He was a shrewd thinker and a hard worker, and he set himself to the task of clearing the house of its liabilities, and building up its credit on a sure foundation.

Alone, night after night, he remained in his private room at the bank, assiduously examining into the affairs of the establishment.

Gradually he might probably have overcome the difficulties in which he found himself, but the sudden demand made on the house for £170,000 threw all his calculations into disorder.

He now began seriously to speculate upon what was to be done. He was himself involved in trouble, for though no gambler, in the ordinary sense of the term, he had daubled in stocks, and lost a large amount of capital.

One of two courses it was clear he must take: either the house must stop payment, or money must be raised at any cost.

At any cost!

Imagine Desmond, the educated gentleman, the man of fashion and refinement, the wealthy banker, sitting alone in his private room, the long-wicked candles flaring on the table, and casting a fantastic shadow of the banker's figure on the wall. How absorbed he is in thought; how dejected his expression as he glances round the elegantly-fitted room, and murmurs to himself, "at any cost!"

Brown and Jones have gone home, perhaps, thinking to themselves, in their family circles, how fortunate a thing it would be if they could change places with the banker—if, instead of being the poor drudges of desk and counter, their homes were like his home, and they, as well as he, were borne to their villas in dashing equipages of their own.

Who would not be Desmond the banker?

The porter down below looks round on the water buckets, and muskets of the bank, to keep its golden stores from fire and thieves, and wonders how a gentleman like Mr. Desmond can spend so much of his time over the dreary ledger: and Desmond, sitting in his room, is saying to himself, "it must be done at any cost."

All is perfectly right at the bank.

No breath of suspicion has tarnished its brilliancy as yet; but, by some means or another, that most touchy and fidgetty old lady of Threadneedle-street grows nervous of Desmond paper, and obstinately refuses to discount the bills of the house!

Well, never mind.

The age and sex of the individual must be taken into account.

Desmond will not break his bank or heart on that account.

The Bank *must* honour certain powers of attorney; they bear correct signatures, they are safe, safe as the bank. Certainly they are presented with extraordinary frequency, but what of that?

Desmond sits one morning in his private room at the bank.

He is busy with his morning correspondence.

He has certain cheques to sign, made ready for his signature.

The business of the house is just beginning.

Here are Brown and Jones, fresh from the suburbs and domestic comfort, wishing still, perhaps, that they were in as good a position as the gentleman banker who employs them.

Ah me!

How unequally fortune scatters her favours.

Brown is not a banker, and Desmond is—aye, and a wealthy one.

Why should fortune favour Desmond, and set poor Brown no better work to do than shoveling up guineas for other people?

Two gentlemen come in.

We say "gentlemen," you know, for the sake of convenience. They want to see the banker.

The clerk whom they address distinctly mentions that it cannot be done except the business be peculiarly urgent.

Yes it *is* peculiarly urgent—peculiarly urgent indeed!

Desmond will see them, certainly. They have followed quietly in the clerk's footsteps, and are in the room as soon as he.

The clerk was directed to retire, and one of the two gentlemen said—

"Mr. Desmond, I am a Bow-street officer, and arrest you on a charge of forgery!"

"Good Heavens! Can't this business be settled?"

"Pray make no disturbance. Please to finish what you are engaged upon, and we will step out with you and talk over the matter!"

Desmond's face was deadly white.

He seemed, indeed, to have grown ten years older in a second.

Mechanically he takes the pen and signs the necessary cheques; then he leans towards the man who had first spoken, and whispers—

"Ten thousand pounds are yours if you can assist me!"

"Pray be calm. Step out with me and talk over the matter."

"Be calm," said the man.

Aye, that was the moment for calmness, truly, when forgery had been committed, and death was the punishment for forgery!

So the banker passes out of the bank through the lines of wondering clerks, who are amazed at his pale face, and the stern faces of the "two gentlemen" who accompany him.

No one dreams of the reality.

They only think he has heard bad news—the failure of some firm, or something of the kind.

But to the bank he never returned.

The trial approached.

Every one looked forward to it.

Every one was anxious to see the gentleman forger. But the one great question which was on everybody's lips was "Will he be hanged?"

This was the treat to which everyone looked forward.

It is astonishing how common a feeling is morbid curiosity.

To the generality of people there is something infinitely pleasurable in gloating over the remains or the clothes of a murdered person.

They will pay any reasonable or unreasonable amount of money just for a peep at them.

They will go any distance, suffer any fatigue by walking, or fighting, or elbowing their way through a crowd, for the sake of seeing a man hanged.

For my own part I would go miles out of my way to avoid such a sight; and I think that a man who can calmly witness the struggles and expiring agonies of a fellow creature on the scaffold is not very much more advanced in his tone of mind than the murderer himself.

For this reason such exhibitions as "Madame Tussaud's Chamber of Horrors," and other sights of a similar nature which abound in London, are a disgrace to the metropolis.

It may be all very well for persons to visit a collection of waxworks in order to behold the similitudes of men who have been an honour and an ornament to their country from their genius, their patriotism, or their courage; although, by frequenting these exhibitions, they are likely to depart from them with very erroneous notions of the men whose portraits they have seen.

This may show curiosity, or it may evince a respect for the characters whose similitudes they desire to behold.

But, in visiting a "Chamber of Horrors," people merely go to satisfy the cravings of a morbid animal appetite, by gazing on scenes and faces in which, in well regulated minds, exist nothing but abhorrence and disgust.

Young ladies who would blush or be indignant at your mentioning before them an ankle or a leg, will enter this loathsome den of horror, and gaze complacently at the faces of Rush, or Tawell, or Greenacre, or at the expiring agonies of Marat in the bath; and they will ascend the steps of the guillotine, and feel the edge of the axe, and look at the pail full of sawdust which was placed ready to receive the head; and do all this with a face unmoved, or with a few expressions of disgust, such as "Dear me! how horrible! What a wicked man he must have been!" &c., and other evidences of childishness and weakness of intellect.

So, when people heard that Desmond was to be hung, they were delighted.

On the day of the execution the place was crowded.

Upon the scaffold a man was brought.

He was supported by three others, for there seemed scarcely any life left in him.

He was led up; the noose was placed around his neck, and the body in a few moments swung in the breeze.

But was this Desmond?

The crowd was satisfied.

Justice had proved herself impartial.

The gentleman forger was treated the same as the common thief.

But, again, was this Desmond?

* * * * * * *

A month after this occurrence a pale, haggard man stood upon the deck of a vessel bound for one of our colonies.

A sigh of relief escaped from him as the shores of England faded in the distance.

In that man you might have recognised Desmond the forger, whose stuffed effigy on the scaffold at Tyburn gratified the morbid desire of the English public for an execution; and in that man, too, a friend might have seen the semblance of him who was Lord Charles Lutterell!

CHAPTER CXXII.

CHAFF TO THE WIND.

IT remained now for the Blue Dwarf to exercise his justice upon the Duchess of Castella, Pauline, and Philip Carabosse.

The former, in spite of her manifold crimes, it was difficult to punish.

Having, therefore, exacted a written promise from her that she would never again visit England, or disturb the peace of those whom she had so much injured, he permitted her to depar for Spain.

This, of course, though a better fate than she might have expected, was anything but pleasing to her mind.

In England were to remain those who had injured her; and in England, therefore, she would have wished to be left.

But they would not agree to it.

They knew well that, if they permitted her presence in this country, she would act to them, and upon all their fortunes, like a blight—withering up all their best hopes—scorching up all the golden promises of the future.

So to Spain she was compelled to go; and, with bitterness and hatred at her heart, she signed her promise never to return.

Her parting from William Lennox, whom we must now call Sir Edgar Blakesley, was characteristic.

"Farewell," she said, as she extended her hand majestically towards him, "I trust your happiness will be as great as is my pity for you. I pity you, as I pity all men who are not capable of comprehending love."

What course to pursue towards Philip the Blue Dwarf scarcely knew. He was a young man, in the full vigour of health and strength.

He had time and opportunities to reform.

But, then, had he not committed crimes almost as heinous as those for which the others had suffered?

Sir Edgar suggested the course to be pursued.

"Allow me, dear uncle," he said to Sapathwa, "to have the disposal of my foster-brother. I forgive him freely whatever injury he may have done me, therefore will you not do likewise?"

"If you forgive him," said the Blue Dwarf, "how can I say otherwise? But what do you propose he shall do in the future?"

"I propose that he shall marry Pauline and proceed to the United States. What say you, Philip?"

The young man trembled like a leaf.

This communication was anything but what he had expected.

"Sir Edgar," he said, in a voice broken with emotion, "Sir Edgar, I could scarcely expect this kindness from you after all I have done to injure you. But I'll tell you this much, that if you mean to do this I'll see that you never repent it. Come, Pauline, what say you? You have wronged me cruelly, but, then, I have been a sad rogue, I forgive you. So shall we, after all, try and remain happy together."

Pauline was performing certain evolutions with her handkerchief, but she gave him her hand.

"That's enough," said he. "So then, Pauline, I will even now perform the promise I made you down on the seashore of *la belle France*."

"Edgar," said the Blue Dwarf, solemnly, "you have done exactly as you should have done. Now nothing remains to do but to see you and Lillian, and Lord Ernest and Leila, happily united. Yet stay, I must not forget one other."

"Who is that?" asked Edgar, who was half afraid of the reply."

"Poor Jessie!" replied the Blue Dwarf.

CHAPTER CXXII.

NEVER TOO LATE TO MEND.

SOME two years after the events described in the above chapter there stood, in a bright spot in the American backwoods, a little white house, surrounded by well cultivated fields, stored with the riches of nature, which smiled in the brightening rays of the sun.

The garden, which was tastefully, indeed elegantly arranged, was the scene of the virtuous play of several cleanly-dressed children.

Over the house waved the dark branches of some tall trees, which alone had been spared of the prairie that had once luxuriated on the land around.

Cattle of various kinds dotted the pastures, some engaged in drawing the rude carts of the farm, some grazing on the flowery meadows.

Inside the spacious rooms, rudely built but heavily furnished, presented so many pictures of comfort and wealth.

There was something hospitable about the house. This may appear a strange, and out-of-the-way idea, but, in my opinion, hospitality exists as much in the house as in the host and hostess.

There are some tenements so gloomy and uninviting that it appears impossible that hospitality can have the courage to enter therein.

And, if the house looks thus, it is ten to one the owner looks so too, and why?

Because it is their inhospitality that renders

the spot uninviting; although, in some instances, it is the opposite.

We enter a house and receive hospitality, and then we gaze around us, and behold the good things which Heaven has kindly granted to the owners, and we wonder they can be unkind to others.

Often it happens that, in the humblest places, and among the humblest people, we discover most philanthropy.

But Prairie Lodge was a spot where the bright goddess of hospitality reigned supreme, for Mr. and Mrs. Carabosse, who remembered the troubles they had themselves endured, were always ready to extend the hand of comfort and kindness to their less fortunate fellow creatures.

Many a trapper, and many a benighted traveller, had reason to bless the "people at the lodge," who had always a smile and a hearty welcome for the stranger.

Their escape from England had not been unaccompanied with risk, and every person who came on board, when the ship stopped at the ports to which she was bound, was a source of the most racking anxiety to the poor fellow.

Once landed on French soil, however, he was comparatively safe; and the first vessel which sailed for America saw Philip and his wife on their way to freedom.

My readers can imagine better than I can describe the feelings with which the wanderers landed on the shores of the Republic.

How Philip roused his energies the scene at the Prairie Lodge is the best proof.

And now, when the summer is coming, and the harvest is heavy, or when the cold winter's blast roars down the broad chimney, and the wolves howl hungrily round the door, Philip can hardly credit his happiness.

Our colonies are peopled by a very heterogeneous population: every one in every country who wants to make his fortune, or to retrieve a loss, or to begin life anew, flies immediately to the English colonies, or to the American Union for the purpose.

America is, perhaps, the best of any of these refuges, because it is easiest of access, possesses a good climate, and altogether resembles, more than any other country, the land the emigrant leaves behind him.

If we were to believe agents of emigration societies—if we were to credit the numerous "touting" advertisements there are every day in newspapers, we should imagine that every one of our colonies offered the same advantages.

In fact, the further the country in question lies from England the more beneficent is the goddess which presides over it, according to the assurances of those professional philanthropists, and for a very good reason.

The greater the distance, the greater the required inducements.

Peace, plenty, and happiness reign over these luxurious spots, while gold nuggets absolutely trip you up as you walk in the streets of the towns.

The best proof of this popularity among the emigrating classes of Canada and the United States is the absence of any other special "touters."

People do not require to be bounced into going to the United States; they are simply told that steamers sail on such and such days, and they go.

There are spots of strange loveliness in the back woods of America—spots where civilisation seems struggling with nature—where from amidst giant trees and primeval forests you come suddenly upon an oasis where cornfields wave their golden plenty in the bright sun—where a little hamlet lies nestling among the best and purest of the gifts of Providence—where the energy of the settler, and the abundance which surrounds him, betoken how much can be done by man when, leaving the turmoil and vicious excitement of great cities, he sets himself honestly and heartily to work to reclaim from the wilderness and chaotic confusion of uncultivated nature sufficient to enable him to live himself and support around him a large and thriving family. "I can hardly believe," Philip will often say, when he gazes with his wife at the broad acres, the pretty farm, the gardens and the sunny little faces that shed brightness over the whole, "I can hardly believe that I have ever sinned. It seems that, if I had, so much happiness could never be." "Yes, my dear," answers Pauline, "but, then, remember the motto, 'It's never too late to mend.'"

CHAPTER CXXIV.

"MAN's life's a bubble, born of empty bliss,
    Flung on the ocean of unebbing time,
To drink the hues of every sunbeam kiss,
    To take the dyes of every varying clime,
Expanding, mid the growth of every crime;
    Creation's veriest friction without name;
End, aim—a hollow toy; from out the slime
    Of over-wrought existence forth it came,
Expanded, burst, and left no trace where it had
    lain."

ANON.

THE courtship of Lillian Winterton and Sir Edgar Blakesley, as well as that of Leila Michaut and Lord Ernest Wyndham, had been one of tears as well as of smiles.

All courtships are, more or less—theirs had been essentially so.

But even this, perhaps, had had its advantages as well as its disadvantages; for the young couples had had opportunities of discovering the characters of one another, which few have the good fortune to obtain.

What a gay day it was at the Hall, the day of that wedding.

And yet it was not a racing, tearing, boisterous, gilded affair, such as some people delight in.

It was a very quiet, modest, unostentatious wedding.

Lord Leopold Lutterell and Lucy, Mrs. Winterton, and a few other friends, composed the party, which wound down the carriage-way that lovely morning, and rode down the quiet little country lane, lined with flowering hedge-rows, to the ivy-mantled church.

The children from every cottage near strewed flowers in their way, and lined the path up to the church porch.

Crowds were thronging the pews inside, and crowds thronged the door outside.

People everywhere were stirring, and quizzing, and hurrying, and shouting, and making the most boisterous displays of merriment and pleasure.

But the two couples were, for this day at least, selfish, and thought only of their past troubles and their present happiness.

The generality of people do not seem to understand this kind of feeling.

They appear to imagine that young people like to be surrounded by a pandemonium on the day of their marriage.

All the nuisances in the neighbourhood surround the house.

Every man who has a broken fiddle or an old drum feels himself called upon to rush to "the festive scene."

Every German band for miles round arrives in due course, while "Punch and Judy" perform their domestic drama, *with variations*, for the benefit of the admiring throng.

Not least amid the people present outside might have been seen the famed firm of Jottley and Co., who performed a melo-drama suited specially to the occasion.

And so, amid the yelling of children, the cheering of men, and the blessings of women, the couples dashed down the avenue of Blakesley Park, on their way to the railway station.

No one more fervently breathed a parting blessing than the Blue Dwarf, who, as he turned back into the Hall, said to himself,

"Well, one task more, and then my mission to this country is over."

What was this task?

Surely, reader, amid all the excitement and bustle of the double marriage, you have not forgotten "poor Jessie?"

Hers, indeed, was a difficult case to attend to.

Another man, constituted differently to the Blue Dwarf, would have reasoned that, as she had committed one fault, therefore she must be left to destruction.

But, to the credit of the male sex be it said, it is rarely men who crush our fallen sisters.

It is women who scout a sister when she has committed one error, and force her into the commission of a thousand others.

So, adopting the pure justice of Him who taught us all we know of love and mercy, and true morality, he preferred to say, " Go, and sin no more."

"My dear girl," he said to her, "you understand for what reasons you must not visit at Blakesley Hall ?"

Jessie knew he alluded to Sir Edgar and Lillian, and meekly answered, between her sobs,—

" Yes."

" But as it is my earnest and sincere wish that you may yet have a happy home of your own," he continued, "I have made arrangements for your residence with Mrs. Francis, a lady of my acquaintance in London, who sees some company, among which you may discover one worthy to be your husband."

Jessie Browne could not answer.

She kissed his hand, and assented joyfully.

CHAPTER CXXV.

Bright Hope's for ever gone,
And Sorrow sits in tears on her abandoned throne.

MRS. FRANCIS was a widow lady, residing in Carlton-square.

She was not what is termed a widow—indeed; for she was one of those persons who consider it better and more profitable to take care for the present and the future, than to fret and fume over the occurrences of the past—to indulge in vain regrets for actions which can never be recalled—to pine over day-dreams which can never be realised.

Her house was a scene of continual gaiety and festivity.

"Poor, dear Mr. Francis " had left her in possession of a comfortable income—sufficiently comfortable to render her an object of extreme interest to those numberless adventurers whose impecuniosity was their only recommendation.

But Mrs. Francis was proof against all the allurements of the male sex.

She was perfectly aware for what reason she was sought and courted.

Not caring, therefore, to enrich some young scapegrace, who would spend her money on reckless extravagance, she determined to remain single until some one took her own fancy—some one who did not know her position, and who would, therefore, love her for herself, and not for her guineas.

Jessie Browne came to her with her soul entirely wrapped up in the misery and sorrow of the past.

When the Blue Dwarf had dismissed her with his usual kindness, she assented joyfully to his proposition, because she was glad of a home where she would be treated well, and where, also, there would be a constant round of excitement, which would suffice to obliterate all melancholy remembrances.

When Sapathwa obtained for her this home with his friend Mrs. Francis, he explained to her the whole circumstances of her former life; and entreated her not to allow her to dwell on her errors, but rather upon the means of forgetting them.

From the first moment that Jessie saw Lillian Winterton the aspect of her life was changed.

The giddy, frolicsome girl was altered into the steady woman, and at the age of twenty she looked as staid and set as a person some six or seven years her senior.

Her beauty, however, did not fade away with the passing away of her gaiety.

The sad, thoughtful aspect of her face made her loveliness even more lovely still than the winning, sunny brightness she had worn before.

Her position, indeed, was a pitiable one.

And it was the more so because her heart, strong in its passionate love, was also strong in its constancy.

To love another man seemed impossible to her when she had taken the last farewell of Sir Edgar; to marry another man still more impossible; and so satisfied, as it were, that she had, during her life, never met with a being whom she could love, the poor girl determined to devote herself in future to the memory of her lost affection.

How even hearts will change !

In the first instance, she had experienced an eager desire to become acquainted with the creature who had so completely filled his heart that no room was left for her.

But she now was glad to be deprived of her presence as well as of his since it only served to cherish the feeling which she had endeavoured to smother, and to keep alive a grief which she desired not to indulge.

This love, once possessed and lost, was truly fearful.

How maddening was the feeling to her when she reflected upon the lot which would be Lillian's, and which she had fondly hoped would have been her own—to bask always in the sunshine of her lover's smiles—to lie upon his bosom—to be always near him, in sorrow and in happiness—to tend him in sickness, and be tended by him—to be able, in fact, to have him all to herself, with no one who possessed the power or the right to stand between her and his love.

Truly the poet is right when he exclaims—

The poet says '"tis better to have loved
And lost than never to have loved at all.'
Ah! no ; 'tis better far to pass through life
Unknown. uncherished, unbeloved, alone,
Without the sympathy of one true heart,
Than to have this, and have it but to part."*

Mrs. Francis, knowing exactly how matters stood, proceeded at once to adopt means to rouse her from her morbid recollections and regrets.

"My dear," she said to her one day when she was more than usually gloomy; "my dear, you should not indulge grief in this way. The past is a void; it has come and gone, and except once, and sincerely, to repent for any wrong you may have committed, you should cast it utterly away from you."

"Oh! I cannot."

"Why ?"

"Because I live upon it."

"That is just what I tell you is wrong," replied Mrs. Francis. "You must forget the past, and live for the future. I warrant I will, in six months, make you a new person altogether."

"How ?" said Jessie, with an incredulous smile.

"First of all, you shall fall in love."

"Never."

"Nay—but you will; and then you will marry," proceeded the widow.

"Still more impossible."

"Not at all; I will answer for it."

Jessie Browne laughed, and kissed her friend.

"It is very kind of you," she said, "very kind of you, indeed, to indulge in all these day-dreams for me; but it will never be, it cannot be, something tells me I shall never be a wife."

"Nonsense, my child!" exclaimed Mrs. Francis, rising; "come, now, and get yourself ready for Lady Goodwin's ball. I shall be angry if you are not the *belle* of the room."

CHAPTER CXXVI.

IN WHICH JESSIE FINDS THAT THERE IS SUCH A THING AS SECOND LOVE.

LADY GOODWIN'S ball was certainly a first-rate affair.

The rooms were large, and not crowded.

Flowers decorated the walls and the chandeliers, and hung in elegant festoons from the pillars which supported the vaulted ceiling of the room.

It was a fancy dress ball.

Here could be seen a Turk; here a soldier; here a Greek—there an Albanian peasant; there an Eastern maiden, with her tight boddice over her elastic figure, and elegant muslin trowsers, spotted with gold, encasing her legs, while green fringed slippers covered her dainty feet.

Here a Roman Catholic priest made desperate love to a Swiss peasant girl, with her straw hat—and her short dress showing to advantage her elegant limbs and pretty ankles.

Among the guests no couple were more elegant, both in dress and in deportment, than a French huntsman and a Greek dancing-girl, who danced almost continuously together throughout the evening.

The former was a tall, elegant young man, with dark eyes, and long, black hair.

The dress which he had chosen was admirably suited to his figure.

His companion was exceedingly beautiful.

Her turban of pure white, spangled with gold, surmounted a row of glossy, light curls, which fell in wanton profusion over her elegant shoulders.

A light boddice of black velvet was held in at the waist by a broad circlet of gold, while the trowsers were of the same material and appearance as the turban.

Those two were Jessie Browne and Henry Vincent Fortescue.

Once during the evening—and only once—an Eastern princess passed by the Greek dancing-girl, and whispered in her ear,—

"Oh! what if this was the beginning of the fulfilment of my prophecy ?"

This was Mrs. Francis.

"How foolish that woman is," thought Jessie, to herself, "she *will* insist upon it that I am to fall in love, whereas the idea is preposterous."

But, then, Vincent Fortescue *was* handsome.

"And," she said to herself, as she disrobed before her glass that night, "and I think he is something like William."

Oh, these fancied resemblances!

Take my advice, young ladies.

If ever you have had a fancy for any one with whom your connection is entirely broken, and you do not *wish* to lose your heart again, never indulge in resemblances.

So Jessie thought Fortescue like William: and, what was more fatal still, she told Mrs. Francis her thoughts.

The consequence may be easily imagined.

Henry Vincent Fortescue was among the constant visitors at Mrs. Francis's.

It was no use.

The little perverse god had taken up Mrs. Francis's cause, and had resolved upon proving her prophecy a correct one.

So, night after night, he came; and, night after night, Jessie unconsciously suffered her heart to be weaned away from her.

He was a fine, noble fellow, this Henry Fortescue.

One evening Jessie Browne, with tears in her eyes, crept into the drawing-room, and, kneeling at Mrs. Francis's feet, buried her face in her lap, and burst into a passion of weeping.

"What ails you, my dear child ?" said the widow, clasping her fondly in her arms.

"I am so unhappy."

"Why so ?"

"Because I am so wicked."

"Wicked, my child ?" cried Mrs. Francis in surprise; "what have you been doing?"

"I have acted wrongly, dear madam;" answered the poor girl—"very wrongly. I have allowed Mr. Fortescue to love me; I have given him encouragement, forgetting that I never, never can be his wife."

"Why so?—why not?"

* From a poem by Mr. Vane Ireton St. John, the author of "Undercurrents," &c. &c. &c.

"Oh! madam, do you think that, after all that has happened, I would deceive him into marrying me?"

Mrs. Francis was silent a moment.

At length she said,—

"Has he asked you to be his wife, Jessie?"

"He has."

"And you—"

"I refused him."

"Refused him?—why, my dearest girl, this is madness. He is young, rich, handsome, and possesses, what is better than all, a good and affectionate heart."

"Yes, I know that; and, therefore, I refused him."

"I do not understand you. But still—tell me—what did you say to him?"

"I told him I could not—I dare not marry him; and requested him to ask you why, and you would tell him all."

"That is right," said the widow, gladly, "you have done very right, for, rest assured that, after he has spoken to me, he will again ask you a question. When does he come?"

"He comes to-morrow, but I shall never see him again."

She said this.

But her heart told her otherwise; and, somehow or another, before she retired to rest that night the conviction had forced itself into her mind that Mrs. Francis had spoken nothing but the truth.

Next morning Henry Vincent Fortescue came.

He was received by the widow with smiles.

"I come," he said, in an agitated voice, "to learn why Miss Browne, whom I so fondly hoped to make my wife, has so unconditionally refused me. There is surely some fearful mystery or some terrible mistake."

"She would have told you could she have spoken," said Mrs. Francis, "that she had loved before, and—"

"That is nothing," exclaimed Fortescue, "so that her heart is disengaged now."

"You interrupt me, Mr. Fortescue," said Mrs. Francis, "I would have added that she loved not wisely but too well."

Fortescue started up.

A deadly pallor overspread his features, and for a few moments he paced the room in terrible agitation.

Then he came and sat down by the widow's side, and, taking her by the hand, said, in a low, crushed voice,—

"Tell me all, madam—tell me all."

And so Mrs. Francis told the tale of Jessie's sorrow.

"I could have wished it all a horrid dream," cried Henry, when she had finished her story; "but, nevertheless, tell her that I love her still—that I will marry her to-morrow if she will have me."

A month after this scene wedding cards reached Blakesley Hall.

On them were inscribed the names of Mr. Henry Vincent Fortescue, the eminent barrister, and Mrs. Henry Vincent Fortescue, neè Jessie Browne.

The Blue Dwarf's mission in England was over, but he lingered yet.

He remained long enough to see the day when Lillian presented Sir Edgar with a son.

A day of unalloyed bliss was this, as it always is.

It is at this moment only that the reality flashes across our minds; then only do we truly recognise the relation which is between us and the woman we love.

In order not to be behind hand, and in order, we suppose, to have the congratulations over at one time, Leila, a few days after, brought into the world a daughter.

The usual expressions of delight were given vent to; the usual amount of kisses bestowed; and "boy" and "girl" were voted the most extraordinary productions in animated nature.

None, however, was so delighted as the Blue Dwarf.

It had always been the desire of his life to unite Sir Edgar with his step-daughter Leila; and now, though in another generation, he was enabled to betroth their children to one another.

Lillian and Sir Edgar lived in a very retired manner—not that they abjured society, or the companionship of that world which is so necessary to our existence.

But they were unaristocratic enough not to imagine it absolutely incumbent upon them to come to London every year for "the season;" and they also exhibited their want of "good breeding" in being able to spend the greater portion of their time in one another's company.

I have often heard fast young men and fast young women expressing their wonder at the possibility of existence in a slow country place.

They cannot conceive how it is that young people can live without constant gaiety and excitement; and fancy, therefore, that London is the proper centre of attraction.

But, somehow or another, our friends' notions were different.

Not that they considered it necessary to remain in the country to seek an Arcadia, because they knew that with love the heart has its Arcadia even in a city.

They were very happy — happy in each other's affection; in the beauty of their children; and in the company of congenial friends.

The Blue Dwarf saw this; knew that the fabric of their happiness had been built, in a great measure, by his own hands, and was happy also.

Years went by.

His health failed him, and he determined to go abroad.

When, therefore, the two fair children, which had been born to his young friends, had grown old enough to climb upon his knee, he departed from the Hall.

"I go, my friends," he said, "beyond the sea. For where my heart is buried there must I also rest."

————

THE DROP SCENE.

I.

"Deeply we have quaffed together
Passion fervent, love sincere,
But the chalice is not empty,
Some hath gone, but much is here

In vain the world has brought us sorrow,
You have been my solace true;
Every wave of adverse fortune
Hath been bravely stemmed by you."—Anon.

In Arabia once there were two lakes lying side by side in verdant meadows.

They were upon a lofty piece of table-land, and, from their margin, a view could be commanded of miles of country round, and in the distance the ever rolling sea.

These lakes, nestling close to one another, gradually increased their boundaries until they joined together, and formed a large sheet of silvery, rippling water, on the lofty hill-top.

The scene was one of perfect tranquillity.

Waving palms, drooping their slender forms, gazed at themselves in the waters.

Down came the mountain goats, to slake their thirst at the fountain; and frequent was the traveller who, having climbed the steep sides of the hill, threw himself, blessing them, on their fragrant banks.

Suddenly, without any apparent cause, the waters of the lake became troubled, and they receded from one another, and the earth shot up a volcanic barrier between them.

Then there came, one night—one dark, inauspicious night—a terrible storm.

The country rocked with the roar of thunder as with the shocks of an earthquake.

Forks of violet lightning shot through the dense masses of trees which formed the forest near, while the reflection of their flashes in the waves of the troubled lakes made them appear like seas of liquid fire.

The flood of waters which descended into the lakes caused them to burst their bounds.

On one side the hill descended gently, sloping gradually, through fields of waving corn, to the sea; and the waters of one lake ran rapidly down towards the ocean, calm, and rippling, and undisturbed.

On the other there were rocks, rough, precipitous, jagged; and the lake, as it descended, formed itself into a furious torrent, destroying and uprooting everything which opposed it.

Now it was turned aside by some inequality in the land—now it overwhelmed a village—now it tore its devouring way through the harvest fields of Arabia.

But neither of them were destined to reach the ocean.

Just by the margin of the sea was a valley almost surrounded by beetling rocks, and the streams, ere they reached the fathomless billows, rushed wildly into it, once more embracing—once more commingling—until they eventually settled down into a calm and placid rest.

Such is the life of many.

And this, O, reader! is typical of the lives of William and Lillian.

II.

"Where, where is peace? How oft the breast,
Ere stilled in death's untroubled rest,
Breathes forth the words! How oft a sigh
Is all that echoes in reply,
Where, where is peace?"

E. Walker.

Ten years have rolled away.

Another generation has begun.

A horseman is riding down towards Berlin from the hills.

Down fell the black rain in torrents, and far from the mountains you might hear the rushing of the swollen streams as they poured into the bosom of the valleys.

The sullen, continual mass of cloud was broken, and the vapours hurried fast and lowering over the heavens, leaving now and then a star to glitter forth from the darkness, like a gem in the tiara of some black houri.

At the lower verge of the horizon the forked and violet lightning rent the canopy of Heaven.

The trees rocked and groaned beneath the rain and the storm, and immediately above the bowed head of the solitary horseman broke the thunder that, amidst the whirl of his own emotion, he scarcely heard.

Down by the banks of a stream near the city was a gipsy encampment.

Deep darkness was over the water; and the light of their fire shone out brightly in the night.

The children of the gipseys came forth to gaze at the traveller as he passed, and ran back, shivering and trembling, to their mothers when they saw his face.

Who was this man? and what was there in his countenance which should make others tremble?

The city gates were reached.

The keeper came forth grumbling at being called out in such a storm, into which he said no mortal man should venture.

But when he saw the face of him who summoned him he spoke not again, but, making the sign of the cross, hastily unbarred the city gate and allowed him to pass.

"Jesu! Maria!" muttered he, as he reclosed the portal, and, shiveringly, betook him back to his home, "I said no mortal man should venture into such a storm; but that was no mortal man that passed me then!"

The city of Berlin seemed deserted by all its inhabitants.

The rain, which came down so steadily, so incessantly, had driven all the wayfarers out of the streets.

The thunder still boomed terrifically, and the lightning played vividly round the spire of Berlin Cathedral, illumining its gilded dome, and casting a lurid glare over the square beneath, and the white fronts of the houses.

No one seemed to dare to trust himself to the fury of the storm.

Our solitary horseman was the only one in the streets.

Wrapped in his ample cloak, he advanced at a rapid pace until he arrived at the door of a small tenement which adjoined the sacred edifice.

Dismounting, he thought a moment, and then, taking his horse by the bridle, he retraced his steps across the square to a spot where a faint, glimmering light displayed the presence of a hostelry of moderate pretensions.

At this place he left his steed, and quickly retraced his steps.

Although, however, his pace was rapid, yet he evidently advanced with considerable effort, as, ever and anon, he would halt, as if to recover breath before plunging on at the same speed.

The small tenement reached, he knocked loudly at the door.

It was some time before any one answered the summons, for the terrific roar of heaven's artillery seemed almost to drown all else.

At length, however, the door was opened, and an old man appeared.

He started back at the sight of the strange visitant.

"What is it you require at this late hour?" he inquired, in trembling accents.

"I desire access to Vault 20," the stranger answered in a low, faint voice.

"It is late—very late for such a visit," suggested the keeper of the vaults, gazing at the new comer with something of compassion in his glance. "Will not to-morrow satisfy you; I am early at my post?"

"I have an order from Herr Klingen," said the other, with some authority in his voice; "shall I return to him and say I am refused admittance?"

"Nay, then," replied the man, as he saw how great was the anxiety depicted on the agonised features of his visitor; "nay, then, I meant not to refuse you anything. For your own good I advised you, not for mine."

Making, therefore, no further remonstrance, but closing his door, he led the way into the cathedral.

The church looked sombre enough on that dark, stormy night.

The wind, too, whistled through the corridors, and the windows, and the seats; and the owl started from the nest which it had made for itself under the arched roof.

The keeper of the vaults had oftentimes entered the sacred edifice at an equally late hour; yet, as he led the stranger through the echoing aisle, an extraordinary degree of awe came over him, and he trembled violently when he addressed him.

His voice was hollow, and each word seemed to be enunciated with pain.

When they arrived at the entrance to the vaults—

"Thank you," said the stranger; give me your light. I know my way now. I will not trouble you further."

"The lamp will not last you long," suggested the old man.

"It will last quite as long as I shall require it," said the other.

"And, when you come out again, may I ask you to be so kind as to fasten the portal after you?"

"Yes!" replied the stranger, with a strange, sad smile; "when I come out I will do so."

The keeper then tremblingly gave him the light, and the unknown descended.

"Well," thought the man, as the other disappeared, "I shouldn't much like to go down there so late, and on such a night as this; but there's no accounting for tastes—he looks quite delighted at it. Well, he's gone, and I will go too."

He *was* gone.

The door closed after him, and closed after him *for ever.*

He never returned; and not until his dying day did the old man narrate to any the story of his strange visitation.

"I should," said he, "have regarded it as a terrible dream had not the key of Vault 20 been absent, and had not the landlord of the inn opposite my house shown to me a beautiful horse which, on the same night, had been left at his hostelry by the stranger."

It was about the time of the old keeper's death that the foundation of Berlin Cathedral was found to be slowly sinking, and it was necessary for workmen to descend into the vaults.

The mystery of the strange visitant was then, at length, cleared up.

In that vault which contained the coffin of Miriam Blakesley was discovered, clasping the last relic of the inanimate form, the skeleton of him who was known in life as THE BLUE DWARF.

THE END.